VEILFALL

ADRON J. SMITLEY

First Edition: June 2020

Cover Artist: Javier Rodríguez Corpa, alias "Jr Korpa" (jr-korpa.com)

Digital ASIN: B08BRV3L55

Print ISBN: 9798656245371 / Print ASIN: B08C93M4L8

0 6 2 3 2 0 2 0

Printed in the United States of America

Burn bright . . . for there is no darkness, only an absence of light.

by Adron J. Smitley

<u>SOOTHSAYER SERIES</u>

VEILFALL

JINN

*POWERLESS (*FORTHCOMING)*

<u>NON-FICTION</u>

PUNCHING BABIES: A HOW-TO GUIDE

PEN THE SWORD: THE UNIVERSAL PLOT SKELETON OF EVERY STORY EVER TOLD

adronjsmitley.blogspot.com

CHAPTER ONE

Banzu seized the Power, a focal invocation both gift and curse.

Hazel irises flaring grey, vibrant waves of luminous twilight flooded his pulsing vision in undulating cadence to his quickening heart, filling him with bridled magical potency. The slowing world burst into keen brilliance sharp as crushed glass, magnifying his senses acute. Intense yet familiar, the flushing rush of energies flowed through every budding capillary of his relaxing body, priming mind and muscle for accelerated response, for the fever of Power enhanced, strengthened, invigorated . . . perfected his heightened senses and all they afforded him.

He listened to organs at work in thrumming tune to his steady breathing. Smelled the once-faint tangy aroma of now-pungent pine sap wafting along the cool mountain breeze prickling across the fine hairs of his face and neck and hands. He could count the individual flaps of the nearest snapbeetle's wings mid-flight if he so chose to turn his head left and squint. He could trace each tiny vein in every slow-tossing leaf decorating the moss-bearded aspens and bur oaks dappling the minty evergreens surrounding the forest-encircled clearing in which he stood . . . if not for the other swordslinger standing before him in challenge.

The initial influx of the Power would have overwhelmed otherwise normal senses to the point of sanity's abandonment if not for Banzu's particular circumstances of birth and his years of habitual training with both the Power and the sword in his strong and steady hand. Concentrating, he banished all outside distractions from his young though well-trained mind until the intimate *heartbeat-of-the-world* pulsed its soothing precedence through him, honing true focus for the dance of swordplay moments in coming.

Thump-thump.

And though the magical energies coursing through him as blood pumping through veins allowed limited manipulation over the flow of Time itself, speeding him up in relation to the entire world round him, there stood against him another man also enhanced by the same time-slowing manipulation of Power. For they two were not just mere aizakai, those born gifted in the natural abilities of magic, but Soothsayers, those above all aizakai the world feared most.

Thump-thump.

Banzu drew in a deep nostril breath, tasted the faint salty tang of his opponent's brow sweat. He squeezed his sword-hand, earning creaks of tightly wound leather pinching between cold steel hilt and the warmer flesh claiming it, accompanied by the tiny sinew *snaps* of thin muscle fibers in his flexing fingers. He exhaled overlong through pursed lips, waiting, gauging the subtle tells of his opponent's first offensive maneuver.

Thump-thump.

Jericho, the elder to the youth, lunged into his opening swordform *Scorpion Stings the Frog*. He darted forward, feinting low for Banzu's feet, then sprung up slashing before reversing his attack into a downward-thrusting stab.

Banzu spun into *Pedal Shakes the Dew*, sweeping the fast attack aside in a crash of sparks then finishing his counter-twirling swordform by delivering a smacking *thwack* on Jericho's rump with the flat of his sword as their bodies glided past one another in Power-fueled momentum, landing a playful though stinging counterstrike that would have otherwise cut a debilitating stroke across the hamstrings if he instead kept his sword unturned and lowered by inches.

Thump-thump.

The two dueling swordslingers moved unlike everything else captured within the slow-moving warp of time a Soothsayer's aizakai Power influenced upon the world outside of themselves, though the Power did not slow the world down as per their supernaturally heightened perception showed them so much as speed its invoker up. A single passing second of normal time was to a Soothsayer stretched and lengthened, a pause given them within a pause, a heartbeat extension between heartbeats. And though the two combatants contested alone of all prying eyes, to the outside observer the dancers of death would appear as if shifting through their combative actions in sight-blurring motions of deceiving speed.

Thump-thump.

Jericho grunted and stumbled two steps forward before catching balance. He rubbed at his swatted behind with his free hand then turned round, arm extended, and leveled his bastard sword out between them, aiming the three-foot length of steel in warning praise.

"Good," he said. And raised the sword, twisted it so that its thin edge split his measuring gaze, the whites of his eyes tinged with the first returning signs of familiar threatening red absent a scant moment before. "But not good enough."

Signs of the bloodlust, Banzu knew. Awakened though caged.

Thump-Thump.

Banzu reared back into the flashy defensive swordform *Willow in the Breeze*, measuring his balance as he swayed to and fro, shifting his weight from one foot to the other in brief dance, then he paused for a mocking come-hither wave.

"Come at me, old man."

Half-smiling, he drew in a deep nostril breath and tightened his inner grasp on the Power while tightening his outer grip on his sword, squeezing each for increased purchase in preparation for their next trade of blows.

Thump-thump.

Jericho cocked one bushy eyebrow. Then burst forth into a flurry of graceful swordform attacks, chaining high thrusts and low slashes together with the flowing proficiency only a veteran swordslinger of his high caliber could achieve, his ease of efforts pure locomotion. Stabbing and spinning, whirling and thrusting in spectacular targeting efficiency that would have outpaced and overwhelmed the lesser defenses of any ordinary swordsman within seconds.

But Banzu was no ordinary swordsman let alone a fool with some found steel in his hands. He too was a master swordslinger, trained by the best.

He danced backwards, blocking and dodging and parrying with equalizing measure of skill and Power-heightened speed, the rapid clangor of steel biting steel ringing successions between their joining blades.

Until experience triumphed over impetuous youth, and after fighting through Banzu's tight defenses Jericho feinted high then caught the younger's exposed middle with the flat-wise smacking of his blade.

Thump-Thump.

Banzu grunted from the burst of pain-fire clenching his belly tight and forcing him into bending over at the middle, followed in rapid succession by a stinging lash as Jericho finished the speedy twirl past him while landing a second smacking *thwack* across his upper back, striking the breath from his lungs.

Thump-THUMP.

Banzu stumbled forward sucking wind, his too-tight hold on the Power straining loose from his inner grasp while focus parted for rising anger. The Power-slowed world blink-shifted out from its slow flow of speed into the normalized passing of time for a hairsbreadth before blink-shifting back again; slow-*fast*-slow.

No emotion, he commanded mentally, the pain of his stomach and upper back fading as he straightened, teeth clenched, pride bruised. He concentrated on the mantra. *No emotion.* Words meant for calming, for regaining focus. *No emotion.* Words meant to divide the Power and the sword and the man wielding them from the rest of the world, the rest of himself. *No emotion.* Emotional men made mistakes. *No emotion.* Emotions got men killed. *No emotion—*

"Don't puke them guts out," Jericho said. "We ain't finished yet."

Banzu grumbled a curse, turned round and forced a smile. *No emotion.* But the emotional suppression proved a struggle for the older, more experienced swordslinger knew where to prod and poke.

Thump-Thump.

"Tit for tat." Smirking, Jericho cut a lazy X through the air. "This old man ain't as old as he looks."

"I'll tit your tat," Banzu said, raising his sword to guard.

Jericho chuckled. He lowered into the instigative swordform *Dancer's Dip*, sliding his left leg forward and hunching his shoulders while extending his sword out to his right side, exposing several vitals in open askance, a mocking though deadly pose meant for luring opponents in through false confidence.

"You move any slower, boy, and I'll have my afternoon nap in before I even break a sweat." He shot Banzu a playful wink. "How's it feel?"

"How's what feel?"

"Being second best."

Thump-THUMP.

Banzu answered nothing to the teasing jest but for a terse nostril sniff. He knew his swordforms well enough that he should refuse such offered bait. But he had something to prove, and not just to himself.

He hawked and spat, bared a snarl, shifted his heels, and measured his next batch of targets. Then unleashed, rushing forward in a Powered burst of eager steel.

THUMP-THUMP.

Jericho's bravado fled as he sprang backwards through fluid reflex. He swept Banzu's first thrusting strike aside, deflected the next chopping four with fanning back-and-forth parries, then ducked the overhead sixth by sinking low only to rise up spinning through a masterful riposte, reversing the seventh strike back upon its enforcer in a swift change of momentum and an answering flurry of steel.

Banzu staggered backwards two steps, steel scraping steel, then three more, steel pounding steel, his parries turned blocks weakening against the increasing barrage of Jericho's fierce strikes allowing no return.

THUMP-THUMP!

"Halt!" Banzu yelled between jarring bangs of sparking steel, his muscles burning with fatigue, his loosening inner grasp on the Power equally pushed to the edges of his straining limits. "I give!"

But his words fell upon ears deaf and uncaring to the unrelenting aggressor moving against him, and the red-threatening eyes of feral lust glaring through the whirring deluge of steel moments from tasting his blood. "I give!"

THUMP-THUMP!!

The brutal onslaught continued upon Banzu's waning defenses as Jericho turned a man possessed by the latent release of a suppressed rage boiling over. Until the blurring fury of his accelerating strikes broke through Banzu's failing defenses for the sought-after opening his red-threatening eyes craved to penetrate.

Jericho stabbed high for the face, forcing Banzu into leaning his upper half backwards or else lose an eye, then he spun into a vicious twirl, slicing sideways and with full Powered momentum fueling his chopping stroke seeking decapitation while Banzu reversed his backwards lean into forward rebalancing and presented his newly exposed neck—just like Jericho knew he would do.

THUMP-THUMP!!!

* * *

The action froze, both swordsmen standing inert mid-pose.

Jericho held his sword to within a hairsbreadth of Banzu's exposed throat, extended arms trembling from the sheer Power coursing through him, his tensed face a belligerent mask of silent lusting rage teetering upon the brink of full release. And his eyes . . . those terrible, ominous, red-threatening eyes piercing in their feral glare.

Banzu remained static, his Power-infused eyes stretched wide and his mouth agape, right foot hovering inches above the ground mid-step, sword poised high overhead mid-stroke in a double-fisted clutch, his concentration broken as his straining inner grasp on the Power dangled from the precipice of forced released. Once-caring eyes now almost void of all but the single-minded purpose of murder glared back at him, and for a panicky moment he considered the very real possibility that their contest remained unfinished.

Jericho's lips parted in a scarifying smile; he'd wanted to follow through—again—and restraining his killing stroke had not only taken everything in him but took everything in him still. His temples pulsed, the whites of his eyes rouged red from his fierce struggle against the Nameless One's curse of the bloodlust striving to escape its inner spiritual prison and posses his physical vessel.

"Give?" Jericho asked through gritted teeth, his edged voice a partial growl where lived barest restraint.

Banzu dared move only his eyes, breaking contact from that predatory glare and looking down at the sword held so close to his throat his swallow would draw blood. "I give."

Banzu eased back and away, lowering his sword while releasing his exhausted inner grasp on the Power, enduring the sensation of stiff fingers peeling free. Time sped up again, blink-shifting back into regular flow. Colors returned to his normalizing sight, replacing fading Power-greys in lackluster appeal. A total sense of relaxation flushed through him, that of allowing a long-tensed muscle to soften and rest, while the acute sensitivity of Power-heightened senses vanished for the inferior stimulus of the ordinary world.

Jericho lowered his sword and released his own inner grasp on the Power, expression pained, bright grey irises pooled in bloodshot sclera returning blue. He shook his head, attempting to loosen the sticky cling of unwanted thoughts, then stabbed his sword into the ground and bent forward, huffing, palmed his thighs and drew in a few shuddering breaths. Through it all he voiced nothing of his cruel inner battle, and he didn't have to—his eyes betrayed enough.

Banzu estimated his uncle a cautious moment, then raised his eyebrows in silent question when Jericho looked up, blinking hard, the bridled bloodlust fading white round his tortured blues.

"I'm fine," Jericho said, words a struggle.

Banzu raked one hand back through his fiery locks, silent. His uncle looked exhausted, drained from more than physical effort, and he knew the reason why. They were Soothsayers, cursed by the Nameless One with the bloodlust earned them all by the legendary savior-slayer and Soothsayer Simus Junes during the Nameless One's banishing long ago. And though Banzu had yet to kill and thus awaken that dark and primal curse within, his uncle could make no such claim.

"I'm fine," Jericho said, repeating the words as much to himself. He straightened, scrubbed the back of one forearm across his sweaty brow and blew out his cheeks. "I'm fine." He forced a smile. "See? All better now."

Banzu returned the smile leaving his eyes untouched, his heart gripped and squeezed by the doomed destiny of his future self. As much as it pained him to admit it, "It's getting worse."

Jericho's face slackened. He nodded but said nothing. He walked to a nearby stump and plopped atop it, his sword a forgotten stab in the earth. There he hunched and gazed into his upturned palms after flexing trembles from his hands. "One of these days, I'm afraid . . ." he began then trailed off, balling his hands into fists.

Afraid you'll break again and surrender to the bloodlust. Though Banzu put no voice behind those cryptic words not just a possibility but an eventuality. If Jericho turned to the bloodlust—no, *when* Jericho *re*-turned to the bloodlust—Banzu's options dwindled to kill or be killed.

The cruel irony of their shared curse demanded that once a Soothsayer turned to the bloodlust they hunted down all others until only one remained, the Power itself linking them, acting as an inner homing sense. History provided the brutal reminder of Soothsayers hunting Soothsayers, as well the countless thousands of innocent victims caught within their stalking paths, prompting fistian law to require the whereabouts of all Soothsayers reported to the Academy in Fist so that its trained aizakai enforcers could hunt them down and end the Nameless One's curse through elimination.

Hundreds of years of hunting and killing until only Banzu and Jericho remained. They lived in seclusion, hidden far from Academy assassins, their days overshadowed by the bloodlust's looming inevitability. And that awful, unspoken truth between them resurfaced yet again.

Banzu knew this, had always known this, but he refused to surrender hope for his uncle. For himself.

No Soothsayer in recorded history had ever fallen prey to the bloodlust's possession and survived as anything more than a physical vessel for its insatiable killing lusts. Yet there Jericho sat as testament to the impossible, saved from the bloodlust now a perpetual fever begging constant release inside him.

Every time he seized the Power proved a struggle to contain the bloodlust fury from eviscerating the last shreds of his defiant humanity. The Nameless One's curse a seed of corruption lying dormant until that first human kill watered it into sprouting life, once awakened, the bloodlust sought immediate and unrelenting possession of its Soothsayer host until they surrendered to its rapacious killing hunger and its indiscriminate rage consumed them mind, body, and soul.

Jericho had rescued Banzu as a boy, saving his life, then raised him father to son, their bond close and strengthened through eleven years of hiding and training. But Jericho spoke little of his troubled past, when at all.

And time, like Jericho's restraint, grew shorter by the day.

"I need to know," Banzu said. "You know I do. How'd you do it? How'd you come back from the bloodlust?"

Jericho looked up, thinned his eyes a quiet moment then shook his head. "You don't have to worry about that so long as you never kill."

"I'm not talking out there," Banzu said, sweeping his arm in broad gesture at the rest of the world beyond the clearing, the forest, the mountains of their hidden home. "I'm talking here. You and me. Sooner or later it's going to happen, and I need to know what to expect."

Jericho scrunched his face, sniffed hard. "I've trained you how to kill so you know how not to kill. Leave it at that."

"Cut the crap." Banzu stabbed his sword into the ground and crossed his arms. "You're training me so I can kill you when you turn. We both know it, even if we never say it. Well I'm saying it now because I'm tired of dancing around it."

Jericho opened his mouth—then closed it with a snap of teeth.

"Either you're going to kill me," Banzu said, "or I'm going to kill you. But it doesn't have to be that way. You came back from it once. Maybe there's something we haven't thought of, something we can use to keep it from taking you again. Or if it does . . . please, just tell me. How'd you do it?"

Grumbling, Jericho slapped his thighs into standing. "I've told you a thousand times already, there ain't no coming back. At least not on your own." He turned his back, stared away into the eastern distance in habitual practice, his mind's eye probing far beyond the trees where the frosted peaks of the Calderos Mountains lined the hidden horizon, where lived the private tortured longing of his forlorn past. "I'm only here now because I was saved by another. And it cost a lot of innocent lives to do so."

He plucked the brass necklace round his neck, whispered and kissed its silver ring, then dropped the precious reminder of his life's regrets beneath the front of his shirt. His voice soft, distant as his stare ahead. "And that was a lifetime ago."

Banzu reached out to grip his uncle's shoulder, not to turn but to console, then withdrew his hand inches before contact. "What does it feel like?"

Jericho gazed down into his upturned hands, holding something disturbing yet vital only his eyes could see. "You're not giving up, are you?" A pause, a mirthless chuckle. "You never do." A sigh, the slow shake of his head. "The bloodlust is chaos. Madness." His hands closed into fists. "Absolute power." Those fists trembled. "The Power feeds on our lifeforce, Ban, aging us faster. But the Power corrupted feeds on the lifeforce of others. Every kill makes you stronger. But only for a time. It gives you a taste then leaves you wanting more. And you'll crave more until your insides ache, believe me. Until they burn with fire."

He turned round, locked gazes with his nephew, and licked his lips in a slip of reverie, tasting the faint remains of something sweet, something precious taken, something he wanted back in terrifying return.

"It feeds on your humanity, Ban. And your sanity, until there's nothing left. It becomes you, and then it destroys you as you destroy everyone and everything around you. Not just because you can but because it makes you want to. Because nothing else matters but the killing."

Jericho glanced at his sword, flexed his hands, knuckles popping. "Only the full Power, the Source, can cleanse the bloodlust curse. And only the last Soothsayer can regain access to it. Now do you understand?"

Banzu nodded and hugged his uncle. "I'm sorry."

"Don't be." Jericho smiled and slapped him on the shoulder. He walked to his sword and yanked it free. "It hasn't gotten the best of me yet." He sliced the air and smirked. "And neither have you."

Banzu reached for his sword . . . then withdrew his empty hand and fisted the air. Every man had a breaking point, and Jericho looked to be reaching his.

* * *

"We should hold off on our training for awhile—" Banzu began.

"No," Jericho said, tone stern, eyes a defiant glare. He ran one hand down over his face and worked some semblance of calm back into his features, his voice. "You have to keep training. You need to be ready. You know that." He glanced at Banzu's sword then waggled at it with his own. "Pick it up. There's still plenty of daylight left."

"No." Banzu held the testy measure of his uncle's stare before turning away, leaving his sword in a forgotten tilt stabbing the ground behind. He inhaled deep, released a deflating sigh, and scanned the scenery of their mountainside home.

For the moment he tasted the cool air breathing through the crisp leaves and damp evergreens in a river of scents flowing over his buds and filling his lungs. In hidden places the faint crackles of spring's thawing against the imminent threat of summer under the warming sun sounded beneath the low buzzing of insects and chirping of birds, affording them a peaceful life up on the Kush Mountains of Ascadia.

Yeah, peaceful and boring. And worst of all meaningless.

He sighed, tired of hiding from the rest of the world. Everything now just felt so mundane, so claustrophobic amid the forestry trapping him within his purposeless existence.

He craned his head and appraised the blue ocean of sky brushed by scuttling drifts of white-cotton clouds, wanting to scream though holding it in despite no others for miles to hear the venting outburst of the festering yell begging for guttural release in his belly.

My life . . . is this all of it? Is this all there'll ever be? Hiding? Waiting to die? Eleven years. I can't take it anymore.

He hung his head, shoulders slouching with the full weight of melancholy, arms hanging limp at his sides, and whispered, "I don't want this anymore."

Soft words from behind: "Come on. Training's done for the day. Asides," Jericho said, "I think a storm's heading our way." He *sniff-sniff-sniffed* the air, nose crinkling. "I can smell it. Best we get back before the rain."

Only half listening, Banzu replied nothing, moved nothing. He continued staring off in contemplative silence.

"Come on," Jericho said. "Enough's enough."

A gentle squeeze upon his shoulder and Banzu turned, met his uncle's gaze.

Silence.

"What's wrong?" Jericho asked.

Banzu averted his gaze to his feet, pretending they held interest, and shrugged. "I dunno." He kicked at nothing particular on the ground. "I just—" And huffed. "I'm tired of this. I want more, you know?" He glanced at his jutting sword, then sidestepped and yanked it free of the ground, spirits perking. "I'm sick of here. I want to travel the world. Be a part of it. I want to help people."

He leapt backwards, spun round, raised his sword and fended against imaginary conjurations of enemies, stabbing and twirling, ducking while parrying the thrusts of invisible attacks. "I want adventure!"

"No!" Jericho yelled, his flaring scold of voice a cracking whip.

Banzu froze, sword leveled out, his other arm held extended behind in counterbalance.

"Ain't going to happen." Jericho paused, squinting, his tensed visage softening a touch, tone less sharp.

"What's really bothering you?"

Wilting, Banzu lowered his arms, the tip of his sword pricking the ground next to his boot, and met his uncle's scrutinizing stare though said nothing, some unspoken truths too private for sharing. "Nothing. Just . . . nothing."

Jericho sighed. "I know what you're feeling, but some urges are better left alone."

Banzu sighed right back. "I know. It's just—"

"You're lonely."

Banzu nodded.

Jericho forced a smile. "You have me."

"Yeah, but—"

"But what?"

Banzu chewed his bottom lip. "I want more." And hoped his uncle would understand. "I want to live. And—" He paused, hesitating voicing his most painful ache locked away in his guarded heart. "I want to love." *And be loved.* "It's not fair. I didn't do anything to deserve this—this life, if you can even call it that."

Jericho estimated his nephew a long and silent length. He nodded, judicious eyes betraying their sympathy.

"I know what you're feeling," he said. "That hunger inside. That yearning to do good. To seek out others and help them, to protect them. Hell, Ban, I feel it too. I've always felt it, and so will you. It's the counterbalance to the bloodlust, and it's much stronger in us because of it."

He closed the distance between them by a single step before going on, his tone softer, more heartfelt.

"And the other part. I feel the same heartache. But you have to bury it down and move on. We're not like everyone else. We don't get normal lives."

"Yeah." Banzu frowned, shrugged. "I know."

His Soothsayer fate sealed by numerous threats since birth, the world feared them, wanted them dead. And others sought to control them, to bend them to their will while enslaving them for their aizakai ability of time's manipulation.

And beyond that lived the toll they paid through the Power itself. It fed on their lifeforce with every use, and though the Power allowed them to manipulate the flow of time, to speed themselves up in relation to everyone and everything round them, stretching a single passing second into several for them and them alone, the cruel cost aged them faster than the slow-flowing world round them.

For slight moments at a time, true, but those moments stacked over the years, seconds building into minutes, hours into days, weeks into years . . . and Banzu viewed those effects staring back at him.

A man in his forties, Jericho's continued use of the Power altered him so that he looked fifty at best. Sharp gray ran streaks through his black hair, chin and cheeks peppered with silver stubble. Wrinkles bunched round the corners of his tired eyes and mouth, and deep creases lined his forehead. They had lived up on the Kush Mountains for the better part of eleven years, hiding, training swords alongside the Power's accelerated aging.

Everything possessed a cost, and time, life's most valuable commodity, tolled theirs for using the Power. The one endowment allowing Banzu to perform amazing physical feats proved the same drawback keeping him from what he desired most in life. Love.

I'm seventeen, but how old am I really? Nineteen? Twenty? Older? Friggin hell, I don't even know the real number. He raised a hand and touched at his chin and cheeks, though more so the two day's worth of stubble growth not there only a few short hours ago. *How much of my lifeforce has the Power taken from me already? All our training . . . years gone, just like that.*

"Helping others in need is admirable," Jericho said, breaking into Banzu's somber introspection. He swung an arm out in broad gesture indicative of the whole world. "But you go out there looking for trouble and you'll find it. If it doesn't find you first. You can't just go walking around using the Power all willy-nilly, not with the Academy's bounty on our heads."

Banzu opened his mouth for protest—but his uncle clipped him short with an upraised palm and a firm eye.

"And don't even try convincing me again how you won't. We've been through this a thousand times. Birds fly. Fish swim. We use the Power. Might as well try holding your breath for the rest of your life as not use it ever again, and you know it."

Banzu opened his mouth again, then closed it and expelled a nostril huff.

"I know it hurts," Jericho continued. "But you have to bury it down and bury it deep. It's all a man can do." He gave Banzu a consoling pat on the shoulder before turning. "Come on. I've worked up a powerful hunger, and my belly's going to start eating itself if I don't get something in it soon."

Jericho walked away.

Banzu stared after his uncle, estimating the man who had raised him, the master swordslinger who trained him, the eventual enemy who in the end would kill him or be killed by him. Every time Jericho used the Power rekindled the constant battle for control, for survival. And yet there remained much to admire in a man who refused surrender despite the overwhelming odds stacked against him. Such determination inspired hope.

Banzu pursued his uncle, his steps a bit lighter as had become his accepting mood.

Jericho, sword propped atop his right shoulder, spun round and walked backwards. "Last one back guts the fish?"

Banzu shook his head and pursed his lips to prevent his trickster's smirk from showing. He enjoyed gutting fish about as much as he enjoyed stubbing toes in the dark and his uncle knew it.

"Nah," he said, feigning disinterest. "I'm wore out. I'll gut 'em this time, you can gut 'em the next."

Gawking, Jericho recovered from a backwards stumble. He thinned his eyes into brief suspicious squint, then shrugged, turned round and kept walking. He struck up a whistling jaunty.

Banzu seized the Power and burst into a speedy blur, landing a stinging slap across his uncle's unprotected rump with the flat of his dull training sword in passing, the Power-fueled momentum adding bite to the playful offending *thwack!*

Startled, howling, leaping, Jericho dropped his sword and grabbed at his struck bottom while hopping round.

Banzu released his hold on the Power only long enough to twist round and shout, "Last one back guts the fish, old man!"

Laughing strong, he ignored his uncle's feisty curses and shouts of cheating as he sped home through the woods in a Power-fueled blur knifing rapid between the trees.

CHAPTER TWO

The next morning and Banzu rolled out from bed, washed and dressed, gobbled down a bowl of cold leftover fish stew. After some personal time and a quick shaving, he set to the usual chores. Swept up. Chopped wood. Yanked handfuls of weeds from the little garden behind the cabin. Skimmed the rain barrel free of collected bugs and leaves.

All in Jericho's absence. His uncle gone. No warning. No goodbye. No telling when he would return.

Banzu shelved his curious nature. His uncle often disappeared without word, and he knew why for they shared the same restless spirit. Their isolated cabin stood midway up the Kush Mountains and surrounded by miles of forest. Here, where the world moved along a separate timeline away from the rest of everything, there existed too many places one could venture for him to waste time looking.

At least not yet.

Mid-afternoon when he decided to head back inside and tend their chipped and dented swords. Training with Power and sword formed the core element of his life since he'd first stepped upon the mountainside as a boy of six, and would remain so until the day . . . *the day I kill him or he kills me.* Only then would Banzu's training be complete, survival his true test thereafter. Until then, always be on guard, ready and alert for whatever threats may come.

He paused in the doorway, turned and stared in wonder of what prompted Jericho's sneaking away. No worries yet, but a few hours more and he would hunt after his uncle. Not that nightfall presented any challenge if it came to that. The Power provided perfect vision in even the darkest of pitches. But there existed other threats roaming the mountains asides the animal dangers awoken by night.

Their remote cabin a place of seclusion, its private location nested deep in woods did not prevent occasional hikers and hunters from the lower villages wandering round by happenstance. Jericho could handle himself against animal dangers, but the outcome against human threats worried Banzu something fierce. If forced into killing, Jericho's precarious restraint on the bloodlust would shatter.

Always be on guard, ready and alert for whatever threats may come.

Banzu lingered in ponderous stare, wondering who would return—Jericho the cheery uncle, or Jericho the bloodlust killer—then shrugged the useless toil he could do nothing about aside and continued inside the rustic cabin.

He cleared a spot on the floor of the front room two parts parlor and one part kitchen, and sat with legs crisscrossed. He rested one of the dulled, dinged practice swords across his lap. There he worked an oily rag along the tarnished blade while honing its roughed edges keen through meticulous care with a small stone scraper. Shearing sounds knifed the quiet of his steady breathing as the tension of waiting out Jericho's return built within, bunching his nerves.

He finished honing the first sword's blade sharp after one hour, though it remained far from elegant steel despite his best efforts, then set it aside to begin working on the second practice sword of the pair. As he set the oily rag down to pick up the scraper and lay in to more smoothing repair, the door at his back pushed open and in walked his uncle whistling a merry tune.

Banzu flinched tensed by instinct and twisted round for better vantage, right hand gripping leather-wound hilt in a creaking squeeze, legs bunched and ready to spring him up into standing, the clenching depths of him prepared to seize the Power and fend. "What the frig. You've been gone half the day. Where've you been?"

"Out."

He fixed a steady bead on his uncle's blue eyes, cautious grip relaxing round hilt. *Thank gods.* "I was starting to get worried."

"What are you, my mother?" Jericho smiled and winked as he removed his wide-brimmed hat, black as his hair used to be, and tossed it atop the little wooden stand beside the door. "My legs were itchy. So I scratched them with a nice long walk."

Banzu caught that mischievous twinkle with a smirk. "Out playing tricks again?"

Jericho's devious smile spread, affording him the grin of a pleased cat. "Maybe."

Banzu shook his head. His uncle enjoyed amusing himself every now and then by venturing down and stealing the traps set throughout the lower woodlands by the local hunters. He detested those who used such trickery on animals, cruel devices often offering torture instead of providing a fast, clean death void of suffering. Hunting for food was one thing, but trapping an animal for its hide by means of a slow and painful death Jericho refused to abide.

And Banzu agreed.

The local trappers even developed a few legends because of Jericho's mischievous games, fables of angry animal ghosts stealing their missing traps.

"They'll learn sooner or later," Jericho said. "Either that or they'll run out of traps."

He removed his traveling cloak, folded then draped it over his hat, and moved to his rocking chair. "Ahh," he breathed while easing down, his rocker creaking in tune to several of his joints popping. "That's the good stuff right there." Relaxing back, he rested both hands atop his stomach, fingers interlaced, and smiled. "Seven more traps for the river's belly, by the by."

Banzu chuckled. He stood, sword in hand, and glanced out through the small round window beside the front door. "A bit late for training now." He raised the sword between them, turned it over this way and that, showing unfinished work. "And I'll be another hour on this one."

"Never mind that. I'll tend it. I've been out all day nibbling on twigs and berries like some darned rabbit. So how about you go snatch us a snowshoe or two for dinner, eh?" He unlocked his finger and gave his stomach a few pats. "Nice and delicious and plump. While I rest my aching bones."

"Really?"

Jericho nodded. "Really."

"Okay." Banzu handed over the sword and scraper, the oily rag. "But what about—"

"Training?" Jericho glanced at the sword in his lap with a smirk. "Catch our grub without the Power. There's your training for the day."

Banzu rolled his eyes at the jest. "Yeah. Sure. I'll get right on that."

"I'm serious. And I think you're right. Maybe we've been pushing it too hard. I need a break. We both do."

"Yeah?"

Jericho motioned at the door with a sideways jerk of his head. "Go on. Get." He sat forward, thinned his eyes into squinting slits. "But if you come back empty-handed, I swear I'll thump you good. My belly's been gnawing itself for hours, and you know how my belly fouls when it doesn't get what it wants."

He sat back, frowned down, gripped his belly with both hands. "Feed me!" he said in a mock grumbling voice while shaking his pinched bit of fat. "Feed me dinner or feed me Banzu!" He looked up, shoulders jerking out a quick shrug. "See? A mind of its own. Go on, now. Have some fun. Just don't forget our dinner."

"I'll just take this, then." Banzu scooped up the first sword from the floor and feigned innocence to the leery arch of his uncle's scrutinizing eyebrows. "What?"

"You know what."

"I'll tend it when I get back. I promise."

"Don't make promises you can't keep," Jericho said, wagging a finger, then tapped the sword in his lap. "I'll tend this one while you're out. But that one better be fine and shining come morning or you'll get a cold bucket of water kissing you awake. That *I* promise."

Banzu laughed and shook his head. He found the sword's companion belt and scabbard, fastened the worn leather round his trim waist. He sliced the air for good measure, stabbed the sword home at his left hipwing, checked the trusty belt knife hitched at his right hipwing he always carried, then turned and headed outside.

"Be careful!" Jericho called after him, his rocker creaking with his twisting motions. "And don't do anything I wouldn't—"

The closing door shut off his voice.

Body craving movement, Banzu seized the Power, burst into a blurring sprint and sped away.

* * *

"—do," Jericho finished to the shutting door, smile fading once alone.

He stared at the sword lying crosswise in his lap. And collapsed into dark reverie while tracing a fingertip along its battered surface, the rough reminder of its scars beneath his gliding touch, the hard years of training and struggle and sacrifice transferring through the marred steel.

He wondered how many more of those precious years he had left to give, if any. And not for the first time he considered thrusting the sword into his chest in Banzu's absence.

With his suicide leaving Banzu pure of killing, his nephew would become the last Soothsayer while bypassing the bloodlust curse.

One sacrificial plunge and he could change the cruel course of their condemned fates while saving Banzu's soul.

One plunge . . . salvation delivered.

Jericho withdrew his tremulous hand and flexed it closed, his soul shuddering in the condemning silence of his haunted solitude.

A silence broken by the pitiful whisper of a single word breaching his lips, trembling him with knowing: "Coward."

* * *

For an hour Banzu roamed through the mountainside woodlands with his trusty sword in hand, fighting imaginary bandits every few minutes in playful wander, the sky bruising a light purple while the sun fell along its lazy westward descent. A few more hours until nightfall reigned. And though darkness offered no hindrance to Power-enhanced vision, he preferred not having to expend any more of his lifeforce than necessary for something so minor as returning home in the dark because he lost track of time.

I'm tired of shaving three friggin times a day.

He beat back the reaching limbs from thieving trees seeking his pretend coin-filled pockets. He impaled their dastardly comrade bushes laying in wait. He sliced through breeze-floating flitters of leaves daring attack while patrolling through the forest of his makeshift domain, braving and besting imagined bandits and robbers blocking his meandering path to saving a pretty princess who would gift him a thankful kiss for her safe delivery from the evil clutches of her deviant captors.

His criminal foes fell by the dying score to the superior swordplay of the Soothsayer hero protecting these woodlands, and he refused to allow any criminal deeds to go unpunished beneath his watchful eye of justice repaid by blade. He planned on chasing down a hare or two for dinner before returning home—*Jericho'll thump me good if I forget*—but for now joy burst in his heart just to be out stretching his legs while letting his mind wander and his body play without using the Power.

Imagination running amuck.

* * *

He soon spied one of his favorite thinking spots and veered north from his easterly path, the criminal conjurations fogging away where they would lay dormant until his return trip home, seeking then to rob him of his hare bounty.

He climbed atop the high cliff overlooking an enormous depression of a natural landscape bowl miles distant, as well the frozen white world of the great Thunderhell Tundra farther north beyond, and plopped down with his legs dangling over the edge of the flat rocky perch and stared overlong. His focus, as always, drawn to the tall spire structure standing mid-center of that natural bowl, its lower half blocked from view by thick vegetation surrounding its hidden base while filling the natural bowl with strange jungle splendor.

The ancient structure of his study, one of the Builder's towers from ages long past, captivated his wonder every time he sat this place and gazed. Treasures lay hidden within the towers of Enosh the Builder god, mysterious and forbidden towers spread all across the One Land of Pangea, magical stuff of legend and lore, strange and powerful artifacts created by the mortal avatar of the Builder Enosh, the last known god to have lived among mortal man before disappearing sometime after the Thousand Years War ended over three-hundred years ago. The last mortal avatar asides Locha the many-faced trickster god of thieves, of course.

Banzu delighted in daydreaming about stealing inside the black builderstone structure of his study, always imagining though never knowing what manner of curiosities he might discover therein. But he knew those as impossible thoughts, for all the Builder's towers stood protected by way of deadly magical barriers set upon them by Enosh before the god's disappearance from the One Land. As well fistian Academy law forbade such encroachment upon penalty of death. Not that their rule extended way out here in any real manner of threat so many miles distant from the city of Fist itself. Only a greedy fool or desperate thief would dare attempt the breaching of a Builder's tower for looting, though that neither stopped Banzu from musing otherwise nor soothed his adventurous curiosity.

He toyed for a time on what he would do with any of the valuables hidden inside, which led his thoughts into a depressing direction of conclusion. *Nothing.* What could he do—sell them? To whom? *And do what with the money?*

No point in risking life and limb for wealth if you can't enjoy your riches. Besides, having little actual need for coin produced little want for it. No, his interests lay in the exciting act of the thieving itself. He never dreamed of obtaining wealth, but of living adventure. Though those dreams would remain as unfounded as the ancient treasures secured within that distant tower.

He swept his gaze aside to nowhere in particular, sighing and slouching. "I have no purpose here," he muttered, the words cutting deep reflections of pain.

He raked one hand back through his unruly hair and blew out his cheeks, disappointed at his current lot in life, withering to introspection.

Friggin hell. Trained by a master swordslinger and I can't even use the skills for anything more than playing through the woods, fighting stupid branches and bushes and dreams, accomplishing nothing that matters to no one.

He blinked at the lowering sun, the world less bright and inviting to his fouling mood.

I'm nothing here.

I'm no one.

I don't matter.

To anyone.

He closed his eyes, shrouded in loneliness.

* * *

A shrill noise arose in the distance above nature's sedative ambience. Banzu raised his head, drawn out from his solitary musings on high expecting to catch early sight of a leathery-winged screecher bird soaring overhead. The nocturnal cliff racers sometimes crept out from their daycaves to hunt while braving the fading light which burned their leathery skin. He craned his head though saw none of the predatory reptilian gliders hunting the open sky. He twisted on his bottom, attempting to ascertain the true origins of the unexpected sound.

Silence but for the soughing winds breathing past.

Carnivores, with six-inch talons and a twenty-foot wingspan, an adult screecher bird possessed enough muscled bulk and animal cunning to swoop down then carry away a full-grown man. To say nothing of its razor-sharp beak cutting through flesh and cracking bone. Rare this early, but not unheard of.

A second shrill noise, faint though undeniable, and he stood on his high rocky perch, faced east.

Was that a . . . scream?

He waited, ready to seize a flicker of the Power the moment a third disturbance sounded so as to intensify its volume and better judge its direction.

Silence.

He decided to investigate anyways, curiosity growing while he climbed down. Also rare but not unheard of for an occasional traveler to wander through these woodlands and suffer some unexpected mishap or another. A twisted ankle earned from slipping atop loose scree, or broken from a misplaced foot into a deep snakehole shielded with leaves or snow, or worse from stumbling into a hunter's forgotten snare or biting trap.

Most folks stayed their wandering to the lower paths of the mountainside—if they dared brave them at all—but sometimes travelers strayed too far for too long, be it by accident or on a hunter's purpose, and soon found every direction looking much the same. Especially so to any stranger's unfamiliar eye of the dense woodlands and their thick canopies—canopies possessing nature's cruel confusion of blocking out miles of sky.

He reached the bottom of his descent, dropped the last few feet to the ground and started east where his best guess told the strange noise originated. With light steps and ears pert, he traversed over hills and between trees and round thorny patches of itchbriars, crisp or soggy leaves crunching or squishing underfoot while excitement bloomed along with imagination.

Maybe a misguided pilgrim wandered off course up the mountainside, rousing the hungry interests of a predator, and stood in dire need of saving. Or bandits set upon a wayward traveler awaiting some brave rescuer. Maybe a foolish merchant chanced trekking over the mountains instead of round, instigating attack by a roaming band of greedy thieves.

Though as Banzu's imagination mused through fanciful wonder, he knew there stood a far better chance the foreign sound issued from a hunter who stumbled into another's hidden snare or triggered one of their own forgotten traps while wandering home drunk. Jericho came across as much many times over the years while out and about, for the haunting tales of his trap-stealing antics often instigated the need for a draught of liquid courage before the more foolhardy trappers dared wander too far from the lower villages while seeking the hides of the more dangerous and thus more profitable mountain game.

Another noise pricked Banzu's hearing, closer though still faint with distance, so that he adjusted his direction and quickened his pace, left hand squeezing the leather-wound hilt of his sword in hammer-fisted flexes of building anticipation.

Thick vegetation slowed his advance. He parted leafy branches, intent on stepping through to the clearing beyond, then startled paused before withdrawing his forward leg, gaze captured.

By someone sprinting toward him. Their face obscured by a hood. Their body's defining contours hidden beneath a wrapped and flapping cloak. Boots snapping twigs, kicking up leaves. The running stranger stole panicked glances behind to where the clearing ended and the forest began anew, stumbled into a clawing fall for regaining balance and pushed their fevered run into a sprinting . . . *escape?*

Banzu tensed. *Someone's chasing them. Someone or something. Bear? Wolf? People?*

He wrestled with the strong urge to leap out from his hidden place of spying and approach the stranger running toward him. But years of warning over never revealing himself in the guise of his uncle's stern voice suppressed that powerful desire to act.

Instead he eased back, settled down into a low crouch, allowing the parted branches to close in and reform a natural screen through which he peered. Stay hidden, at least until he could assess the situation further, showing himself and revealing himself two different conclusions though both carried the same threat of exposure.

So he waited, squirming, muscles tensing into anxious coiled springs of pent energy, his body craving movement, action the natural part of him, while his mind said run, run before it's too late.

* * *

Impatience won the best of him. He seized a flicker of the Power, a fraction only, to supernaturally heighten his vision for better viewing vantage of the faraway though approaching stranger—and flinched, struck with peculiar wonder.

Eyes flaring luminous Power-grey then dulling hazel through the span of a startled blink, details flashed vibrant and crisp while slowing then fasting again—everything but the blurred stranger sprinting toward him.

He shook his head, blinking hard, then refocused and seized another Power-flicker, this a full second stretched overlong. The slowing world brightened luminous and crisp again—except for the stranger blurring to his Power-magnified sight.

What the frig? He flinched and blinked, rubbed his lying eyes and blinked again. *Something's different. Something's wrong.*

He seized the Power and gripped it strong, crisp twilight greys flaring luminous again. Yet the spherical air round the blurring stranger, their sprinting motions slowing alongside the rest of the affected world, betrayed a translucent shimmer resembling invisible waves of heat, encasing them inside a strange giant projection of bubble moving with them at its epicenter while denying the visual enhancement of the Power.

Perturbed, releasing the Power, Banzu hung his head and rubbed his closed eyes with finger and thumb, white flares of phosphenes fading behind his massaged lids. When he looked up again, hoping his fourth try of Power played no such trickery upon his lying vision, the stranger already raced halfway across the clearing and unaware of closing in on his hidden position.

Friggin hell. Another minute and they'll run right through me.

He shifted anxious in his spying crouch, deliberating announcing advancement against rushing retreat while a confused sense of urgency flushed his prickling nerves, staying him to place. His heartbeat quickened, muscles tensing nervous and springy. Jericho's stern voice of warning spoke through his mind, telling him to stay hidden, ordering him not to reveal himself, commanding him to turn and go before—

Banzu rebuked it and stood. He parted the leafy screen of branches and stepped forth from cover, hand gripping hilt, breath captured deep in his lungs for announcing shout. But he startled mute when a big ugly brute burst mid-sprint from behind the far line of screening trees and brush across the clearing in the stranger's wake, the chaser revealed.

The newcomer slowed his pursuit once he cleared the trees behind, and removed something from the fat leather pouch at his belt. Unfurling the bola, he spun the device in a wide and whining circle overhead then threw his beefy arm forward, releasing the spinning snare.

The speeding bola sliced the air in a whirring disk. It reached its fleeing target, wrapped round the stranger's kicking legs and bound them together, coiling them tight. The taut entanglement brought them down in a violent tumble. Their hooded head rebounded the ground, and their body lay limp.

"Friggin hell!"

Banzu seized the Power in a strangler's grip, the slowing world bursting into luminous twilight greys, and stole into a blurring sprint toward the fallen stranger, giving no care to concealment against another's life in clear danger. That same visual-blurring bubble hindered his heightened sight, covering the ensnared stranger inside a shimmering dome, but he ignored it for the fierce need to help and protect, his body locomotion knifing the air, his mind closing all avenues but ahead.

Powered momentum carried him to the unconscious stranger, covering several hundred feet within seconds. But as he approached the still body, approached too that mysterious shimmering dome surrounding it, his world changed forever.

The Power tore loose from his inner grasp the moment his fevered sprint penetrated the outer expanse of the mysterious shimmering dome, and with it punched an abrupt halt of speed as momentum jolted him clumsy.

What the frig!

He stumbled, pitching forward in overbalance, while tripping over disobedient feet, then fell tumbling into a short and painful roll, clings of wet leaves thrown.

He pushed up onto hands and knees, balance sloshing, eyes a vertigo whirl, disoriented though aware enough to thank the gods he broke no bones let alone his neck in the wild tumble. He shook his head, shedding stray leaves from his whipping hair, and glanced aside. The unconscious stranger lay prone a short crawl away. He elevated his gaze when two more men rushed out across the clearing and joined the bola-throwing first.

Not one but three chasers. Friggin hell, what have I gotten myself into?

He tried seizing the Power—to no avail. *What the frig?* Panic flushing, he tried again—and again he achieved nothing. *Oh gods.* His guts clenched up something fierce. *It's gone. How? Why?* Twigs snapping underfoot drew his attentions to the three newcomers. *Doesn't matter. Later.*

"Hey." He crawled toward the crumpled stranger twined in bola. "Hey!" But no time to waste in rousing them awake let alone freeing them so that he stood and faced the chasers no longer in hasty pursuit but watching him watching them.

One remained behind, studying the scene from a safer distance, while his two companions stalked closer. The bola thrower, a big ugly brute, pointed at Banzu then gestured signals with his meaty hands. The second man, thinner by half, his beady eyes and pinched face affording him rodentine features, smiled and nodded while returning similar hand gestures, then he split open the front of his dark coat and unsheathed the shortsword from his right hipwing.

The two men split their stalking course into an advancing V, seeking to flank Banzu. Between them, maintaining good distance, stood the third with arms crossed and watching, a pleased yet curious grin on his goateed face.

"Wait," Banzu said while raising his hands palms out in the common gesture of peace between strangers, earning no amiable response but predator glares so that he lowered them seconds more and fisted grips of air, sinews flexing round popping knuckles. The two men wearing smiles leaving their eyes untouched slowed while flanking his sides, these hunters of human prey.

Muscles priming taut with bridled action, anxious heart aflutter, an unexpected thrill flushed through Banzu's nervous network of prickling nerves. He drew in deep and steadied his rapid breathing while glancing between the two men whose eyes betrayed lethal intent and the brutal need to see it finished.

This isn't training. This is real. Banzu gripped his sword's leather-wound hilt in silent warning. *And without the Power . . . friggin hell, what happened to it?* "Back off."

The two men ignored him, crept closer.

Godsdammit. He pulled the bastard sword from his left hipwing and leveled it out in a double-fisted grip to guard. He turned left, right, then backed up a space to keep both approaching men within view as best he could considering their flanking positions.

"Stop!" he yelled.

The two men stopped.

"Look," Banzu said. "I don't know what this is about, but I don't want to hurt you." He threw his flankers sideways glances. "Either of you."

The big ugly brute chuckled, and his rat-faced companion chortled.

Banzu cringed. He twisted and threw a glance behind while nudging the limp stranger with the instigative heel of one boot. *Wake up, godsdammit.* But they returned no signs of waking anytime soon. He twisted back, carving warning strokes of air first right then left, when the two men dared closer. "I said back off!"

"Wrong place, wrong time, kid," Big Ugly said, unhooking a long club from his belt the length of Banzu's arm, its bashing end banded round with a strip of spiky metal tines.

The lanky rat-faced companion laughed, more a hissing giggle, and produced a dagger from his belt to match the shortsword he carried.

Banzu stole a glance at the third man, the watcher standing far across the clearing, then ignored the spectator awaiting the brutal amusement soon employed by his determined fellows.

This is not going to end well. Wary swordslinger instincts shifting his stance, bracing for action, Banzu sought reassurance in memorized swordforms but found instead a broken chain of foggy memories hampered by his frazzled nerves, Jericho the only human opponent he'd ever faced. He swallowed hard, licked his lips, and inhaled a calming breath to steady his trembles. *Relax, godsdammit.*

"No emotion," he whispered, speaking the words helping apply a firmer grasp upon their meaning. Never before had he faced another man in true mortal combat, let alone two at once. Years of habitual training earned him many cuts and bruises, his body a testament of fine hairline scars despite the Power's accelerated healing, but neither he nor his uncle intentionally tried to kill the other during their training sessions.

"No emotion."

Jericho worked hard at pushing him to his training limits, and the major part of his training focused on control, ending precise killing strokes a hairsbreadth short of true delivery through discipline. Any man could hack away in wild abandon with a sword, but it took a master swordslinger to restrain those strokes, to harness them with efficiency and redirect them so that one could disarm and disable instead of kill.

"No emotion."

"What's he whispering?" Rat Face asked his companion.

"Praying for a quick death," Big Ugly said in jesting response.

"No emotion," Banzu whispered. And the words found purchase on his calming nerves, however tenuous their grip. In stronger voice he said, "You don't want to do this."

Both men chuckled.

Banzu turned his attentions to the taller, brawny brute approaching at his left. He opened his mouth to give Big Ugly a final warning—and caught swift movement in his right peripheral, a blur of motion. He spun on instinct, flinching while leaning back, evading Rat Face's thrown dagger speeding past his face inches from slicing off the tip of his nose but for the swift turning of his head.

Seizing distraction, Rat Face pursued his throw by lunging for the quick kill, stabbing with the shortsword before his dagger met the ground.

Petal Shakes the Dew and Banzu beat aside the lunging thrust meant for piercing his guts, reacting on subconscious level before conscious mind could finish the ordered course, his trained instrument of body requiring no need for the mind to command it before flowing into necessary response.

He lowered crouched while stroking sideways, his fanning steel slicing Rat Face across the ribs while Big Ugly's heavy club whiffed through the empty air over his ducking head, ruffling the tangles of his drifting hair. The grunting brute behind him stumbled through the force of his missed blow as Banzu spun round and flowed into *Heron Spears the Salmon.* He stabbed the man through his meaty calf, twisted steel before yanking it free, and brought Big Ugly down to one knee crunching atop a crisp patch of leaves.

Banzu danced behind the kneeling brute.

Rat Face pulled a second dagger from somewhere hidden beneath his coat and tried his throwing trick again. But Big Ugly straightened between them by chance and took the thrown dagger into his shoulder.

Banzu darted backwards two steps, flowing into *Dancing Bear* in preparatory defense against the shortsword. Rat Face advanced three steps then stopped. He shifted his focal glare upon the unconscious stranger between them and lying beside his kneeling companion. Rat Face sneered, flipped his shortsword end over end, raised it on high in a double-fisted grip for downward thrusting stab into the stranger's unprotected back.

"No!" Banzu booted Big Ugly's broad back, shoving the grunting brute sideways before he could wrench the dagger free from his bleeding shoulder, and lunged the empty space, stabbing without thought.

Rat Face gasped while jolting still, his beady eyes stretching wide. His surprised stare rolled down, gazing between his upraised arms at Banzu's extended sword pierced inches deep into his chest left of center. He released a hiss of breath, the shortsword slipping loose from his parting hands.

Dread punched Banzu's clenching guts while he locked with those startled blooms waking to the imminent truth of death. Rat Face grasped Banzu's sword with palsied hands in a futile attempt at pulling the penetrating blade free as his final defiant act in life, then his shifting gaze betrayed him when it focused past his younger executioner.

The crunch of leaves behind and Banzu yanked his sword free, spun in reaction to those traveling eyes. Big Ugly's spiked club swung down. Banzu thrust up in an awkward twist while tilting his head, intent on receiving as much of the blow meant for caving his skull against his shoulder. Instead Big Ugly's angle of attack brought his brandishing arm down onto Banzu's rising sword, impaling forearm while arresting the attack short.

Big Ugly yelled through clenched teeth, eyes blooming wide and wild, his hand somehow maintaining its strong grip upon the club despite his transfixed forearm. Instead of backing away and freeing himself, he pressed forward with the full weight of his muscled bulk.

Extended arms unhinging at the elbows, Banzu sank to one knee beneath the enormous brute's oppressive weight. He tried wrenching his sword free, but it remained trapped, pinched between thick muscle and bone at the middle of his driven blade. Cold panic flushing, his mind scrambled through avenues of escape.

Big Ugly glanced at Rat Face's dagger jutting from his bleeding left shoulder, fat lips peeling back from yellow teeth in a vicious snarl. Grunting, he raised his free arm and gripped Banzu by the throat.

Gasping, thick fingers closing round the whole of his neck in a strangler's crushing clutch, Banzu squirmed, trying to tug his sword free while shoving against the brute's wall of chest to no avail.

Big Ugly grunted and squeezed.

Rasping, Banzu sank to both knees, face flushing hot, temples pounding, mind fogging, vision tunneling, seconds away from suffering a crushed windpipe.

He raised his free hand in frantic bid, fingers groping for desperate purchase up the length of Big Ugly's extended arm, clawing sleeve, raking over tensed muscle the girth of his leg. He dared not loose his other's grip upon the impaling sword and allow what little space it kept between them to shrink in a blink.

Amid the struggle he achieved the knife's handle, grab and twisted it, prying open the heaving brute's bleeding shoulder wound. Big Ugly grunted and growled though fought through the pain.

Banzu blinked through fractured prism vision, forced a single strangled word out through the tight clutch of his throat from the depths of his burning lungs, issuing the bare whisper of a name in a desperate plea for his uncle.

Big Ugly pressed forward, forcing Banzu into a painful backwards arch threatening to snap his protesting spine while his shoulders lowered toward the ground, his legs trapped beneath him.

Lungs burning, nightmare darkness collapsing his vision, Banzu wrenched the dagger free in a last defiant surge. He stabbed blind—then gasped in precious air when the tight restriction round his throat released. He collapsed backwards, coughing and sucking wind, each sweet relief of air painful in his aching throat. But he welcomed the pain for all the glorious breath it afforded him.

Big Ugly staggered backwards, the club slipping loose from bloody fingers, his right arm weighed down at his side by the sword impalement he carried with him. He raised his good arm and touched at the dagger sticking out the left side of his bull neck, wiggling fingers testing the handle then gripping it.

He yanked the dagger free, loosing an arcing jet of arterial blood. A child's panic in his eyes, he dropped to his knees, gurgling, clutching the spurting wound. Then he tottered forward, crashed facedown to the ground and moved no more.

Banzu sat up in dizzied stare, blinking hard while massaging his aching neck, teary eyes regaining focus.

Then scrambled into standing, trapped Big Ugly's arm underfoot, yanked his sword free and faced the third man watching from across the clearing.

The goateed spectator closed his eyes, raised fingertips and touched at the dark tattoo decorating his left cheekbone, lips moving through inaudible words.

Banzu braced tensed, expecting some unknown form of magical incantation to steal across the clearing and assail him. But seconds more and the man turned round then vanished into the forest.

"Hey!" Pulse a racing fever, Banzu pursued three steps then stopped and lowered his bloodied instrument of death. He wanted to give chase, to catch the bastard and make him explain the insanity behind this unnecessary madness. But he resisted the urge, instead turning away. And there he surveyed the carnage of his battle with waking clarity.

"By the gods," his voice a bare whisper. The sword slipped loose from his opening hand and found the ground with a dull *thud* upon a wet nest of leaves. "What have I done?"

* * *

Banzu stared down at the slick blood befouling his hands remarkably steady despite his pounding pulse, the blank slate of his detached mind, and the burning urge to vomit rising at the back of his throat. He flexed them closed, amazed for the first real time at what these tools had accomplished in such a short span, the rending of two lives, their true capability revealed at last.

Warm blood darkening the hundreds of minute cracks made maps of his palms already cooling against the chill mountain air. A proud disgust overwhelmed him so that he sank to his knees and wiped his bloody hands clean upon damp snarls of grass and soggy leaves. He brushed his hands in vigorous back-and-forth motions . . . *no amount of scrubbing will* . . . then he stopped, having rubbed the grass away in his frantic chore to the bare dark dirt beneath.

He swiped his palms down the tops of his thighs, sagged back bottom atop heels, and stared across the clearing in dull wonder.

Three men came. Two men died. The third a runaway. And for what?

Somewhere something snapped.

Banzu flinched, twisted left, right, eyes darting. He gulped the air and held his breath for better listen.

To the buzzing of insects and distant chirping of birds, leaves fluttering in the breeze, branches creaking through lazy sways . . . but nothing more.

He focused inward and tried seizing the Power. And felt nothing but a void of absence where once burned the living flame of aizakai energies within the chamber of his being. A candle having been snuffed.

He raked his hands back through his hair and blew out his cheeks. He stared at the bloody sword resting beside him in brutal reminder, amazed how so crude a weapon caused such devastation. Years of training, habitual turned instinctual, the blade becoming an extension of his arms. Reaction without thought, killing without effort, his body flowing through the necessary motions as a mindless machine knowing nothing but action and reaction.

The reality of it silenced him, as well the ease of the killings—Rat Face at least—sickened and excited him at the same cruel time.

A hot and anxious flutter twisted through his guts in stark reminder of the bloodlust curse. He drew in a sharp nostril breath and held it overlong, body tensing, spirit bracing for inevitable impact.

That never came.

Confusion swept in, punctured by a brutal truth deep in rooting.

"Oh gods. I've killed. I'm a killer."

He wormed his tongue in a mouth gone dry, swallowed spit the consistency of sand. He craned his head and gazed skyward, knowing life would never be the same again.

CHAPTER THREE

One hand raised of its own accord, surreal in its mechanical lift, and fingers touched at Banzu's cheek, inviting remembrance, a voice speaking, faint yet firm, his uncle's, though younger, and a time years past replayed through vivid recall, foggy at first though clearing sharp as crushed glass, a distant memory until now forgotten, repressed . . .

"Dig," Jericho said, tossing the shovel at six-year-old Banzu's feet.

Banzu glanced down. "Why?"

Jericho held silent, expression wooden.

Banzu huffed—he wanted to play, not work some stupid chore—then bent and picked up the shovel, huffed again. "What am I digging?"

"A hole," Jericho said, the upper half of his visage hidden in the shade of his wide-brimmed floppy black hat.

Banzu scrunched his face. "We're gonna *bury* her?"

Jericho nodded.

Banzu eyed the corpse nearby, its spilt innards steaming in the cooler autumn air, thin drifts of dissipating white. His uncle killed her only a few minutes ago, but he smelled the stink from her already, that distinct aroma of blood and bowls wafting upon the winds. They'd taken a break from building their new cabin home. Assumed they were alone for miles in every direction. In the middle of eating when out from the woods behind them charged the woman, wild-eyed and shouting something about a curse and rushing straight for Banzu.

But Jericho moved quicker. He cut her down without taking so much as a scratch from those strange fanged knives of hers. A single ducking pass, his sword slicing across the middle, making of her guts poured porridge from a tilted pot. He hadn't even used the Power to do it, so efficient his blade's delivery.

Banzu had never seen anyone killed outright before, and to his surprise it less scared and more excited him. Mesmerized by the dynamic fluidity his uncle wielded the sword with such ease of proficiency despite no touch of Power involved.

"We're gonna bury her?" Banzu repeated, added, "after what she done?"

"Freedom ain't free," Jericho said. "Every man has to pay his due, and this is our part of the price. Asides, she came for us both. I killed her. You can bury her."

"But I thought you said we can't kill no one or else—"

"We can't. But it's different when it comes to their kind. You'll learn that soon enough. Now dig."

Banzu stabbed the ground with the shovel, stomped his right foot onto the shovelhead, sinking it deeper, paused and looked up. "Why'd she wanna kill us for anyhow?"

Jericho stared somewhere east, as he often did. "They all want to kill us. Best you learn that now."

"Oh." Banzu grunted as he uprooted the small chunk of earth and swung the shovel, tossing dirt, the ground proving hard with first frost, the shovel twice as long as Banzu tall. "Ain't you gonna help me?"

Jericho crossed his arms, shook his head. "Nope."

Banzu sighed, rolled his left shoulder and grimaced, the burns beneath the bandaged poultice still sore, raw with movement. He stabbed and stomped, grunted and flung more dirt. "Are we gonna go to the Hell for this?"

Silence.

He stabbed and stomped, grunted and swung, glanced at the dead woman. He stabbed again but did not stomp. He squinted up. "You don't wanna kill *me* now, do you?"

"Not yet." Jericho glanced away. He uncrossed one arm, pointed at the ground. "Now dig. The day's getting old and we've still got plenty of work ahead."

Banzu huffed, stabbed and stomped, grunted and swung. Stabbed and stomped, grunted and swung. Stabbed then paused for breath. "This ain't fair. Why do I have to do all the digging when you're the one who—*ow!*"

His head whipped forward from the sting of Jericho's smacking hand. He rubbed the back of his head and hissed, then frowned up and flinched it back into a meek squint. His uncle had turned mean-eyed again, no fooling. And again he knew that cold flush of fear at the hidden glare behind those hard blue eyes, something other than the man staring back at him, dissecting him, something dangerous and wanting out.

"Life ain't fair," Jericho said, voice gruff, his face a tense mask of forced calm. "Get used to it."

Banzu scowled though kept his voice low. "You're mean."

Jericho's features held tight, though his eyes flinched soft, regretful. "I have to be." He shifted his gaze to the shovel in silent command.

Banzu stomped, grunted and swung. Stabbed and stomped, grunted and swung. Stabbed and stomped, grunted and swung. Another pause, another glanced at the dead woman. "We have to move again, don't we?"

"Maybe. Maybe not. I don't know yet. Dig."

Banzu's bottom lip quivered, bulged. His eyes grew hot and wet. He stared at his feet. Until Jericho knelt on one knee beside him, turned him by the shoulders while careful not to grip the bandaged left too firm where lived sharp memories of fire, then raised Banzu's tucked chin with an instigative finger to better meet his pensive gaze.

"I have to be hard on you, Ban. You have to be better than me. The world hates us for what we are, and what they think we'll become. But you're going to prove them wrong one day." Jericho stood. "Until then it's survival. Hope for the best but prepare for the worst. It's all a man can really do. Always prepare for the worst." He turned and stared away into the eastern distance, from where the violet-eyed woman rushed them. "The worst always comes when you least expect it."

"Like her?"

Jericho nodded.

"But she deserved it though, right?"

"She tried killing us—"

"But you killed her back good," Banzu said, smiling up. "I ain't never seen—"

Jericho slapped him across the face, ending words quick with pain.

Banzu stumbled two steps sideways, dropping the shovel. The left side of his face stung, and tears welled up, fracturing his prism vision.

"I didn't do it because I wanted to," Jericho said, tone hard, glare cutting. "I did it because I had to. There's a difference. You got that?"

Banzu blinked through hot tears and swiped his cheeks clean. He glared up but said nothing. Nodded.

"Killing is never a good thing," Jericho said. "But sometimes we don't have a choice, even when we do."

Banzu sniffled runny snot threatening his upper lip. "I don't get it."

"You will. One of these days there'll come a time when you have a choice but you'll feel like you don't, and on that day you'll understand. Look at her."

Banzu looked at the dead woman lying prone in her own spilled gore.

"She'll never laugh again," Jericho said. "She'll never love again. She'll never feel anything ever again. I did that to her. I took away all she's ever had and all she's ever going to have, just like that." He snapped his fingers. "I didn't want to kill her, but I did. And I did it because of you. Because no one can ever know what we are or where we are. Ever. Look at me."

Banzu looked back.

Jericho slapped him across the face.

"Ow!" Banzu's head whipped sideways. He reeled on his feet, more tears welling up, but he refused to scrub them away. "What was that for?"

"That," Jericho said, pointing a stern finger in Banzu's face, "is so you'll never forget it." He turned, crossed his arms and stared off into the eastern distance. "Go on, now. Dig."

Banzu picked up the shovel, stabbed and stomped, grunted out another hard clump of dirt then swung it aside. Stabbed and stomped, grunted and swung. Stabbed and stomped, grunted and swung. Stabbed, stomped, grunted, swung . . .

Keeping Banzu pure from killing remained Jericho's greatest hope. To protect him from committing the one finalizing act that would awaken the bloodlust within. And with the success hopefully bypass the bloodlust curse from Banzu with his natural death when body surrendered to age. Jericho's greatest hope. But hope only lasted for so long as one embraced it.

For eleven years Jericho taught and trained Banzu to ensure if the time came and Jericho surrendered to the bloodlust, that Banzu possessed the necessary skills to bring him down. They trained until every last swordform ingrained into Banzu's natural rhythms, instinctive as breathing.

Action without thought.

No emotion.

Banzu could not falter when that fated time arrived. No holding back, and no clinging to the emotional ties binding them as kin or friends. If Jericho turned, a void of emotion would become an absolute necessity. Emotions made men hesitate, and hesitation got men killed.

Jericho beat that into Banzu's head for eleven hard, long years of training.

Banzu often lay awake at night pondering for hours over the conundrum of their lives. With his beloved uncle's death, he would become the last Soothsayer, and only then could the Nameless One's curse be cleansed through the full Power, the Source. But he must never kill, must never awaken the bloodlust before then, or else be corrupted before the Source's cleansing then condemned to stalk the One Land of Pangea in a murderous rampage.

Never awaken the bloodlust.

His uncle's greatest hope.

Never kill.

* * *

Banzu waited . . . and waited, the repressed memory of his youth fading quick as it came. But the bloodlust never claimed him. Or, if it had, he sensed nothing of it. No overwhelming urge inducing him into a murderous rage.

"Huh." One word heavy with the weight of many questions.

Maybe Jericho's wrong?

Or maybe it won't happen until I seize the Power again.

I have to try.

I have to know.

Best I do it here. Now.

He braced for inward-punching impact and attempted focal invocation of the Power again.

Nothing happened.

I don't understand. Where's the Power? Where the bloodlust? Was he . . . was he lying all this time?

A howling of the risen winds, the rustle of leaves on creaking branches. The coppery scent of fresh blood wafting through the air roused his focus outward.

Banzu crawled on hands and knees toward the unconscious stranger. He removed the trusty knife from his belt he never left home without, hitched at his right hipwing, and cut the bola's taut binding cord free from round those long twined legs. He tucked his hands beneath and began rolling them over for a better look though paused at the femininity of their form, firm yet soft in all the right places.

He overturned the unconscious woman onto her back, leaned forward for closer inspection, then sat bolt-upright, eyes blooming wide, breath hitching in his chest.

"By the gods," he whispered, something unfelt before gripping his startled heart.

For a time he stared, captured in the beauty of her.

He leaned forward, slid back the hood of her earthen-toned traveler's cloak, revealing long pale-blonde hair, the swell of a knotted bruise upon her forehead earned from her tumble. One of her temple braids lay draped over her chin. He plucked at it, moved it aside, the back of his hand brushing across her warm alabaster skin in so doing, the brief contact prickling the hairs on his arm through the gentle exchange. His face flushed hot and his quickening pulse skipped several fluttery beats.

Worries of the Power, the bloodlust, the broken promise to his uncle faded. He sat captivated by the dusty rose of the woman's cheeks, the generous curves of her parted lips, her exquisitely dainty nose.

He reached out to trace a gentle fingertip over those full soft lips, his body reacting before the mind, then withdrew his hand a hairsbreadth before contact and sat back, blinking hard, shaking free of his adoration. He glanced at the two dead men at his sides, regaining focus.

"What am I doing?"

He stood, scanned the forest across the clearing where the escapee had run off in lieu of trying and dying along with his two fellows. *There might be more of them out there somewhere.* Perhaps the man fled seeking reinforcements or just plain run off.

Banzu wished to leave this brutal scene behind soon as possible. *Home. I want answers. And this woman, whoever she is, needs our help. Gods, Jericho's going to kill me. But I can't just leave her, not like this. She'll freeze out here. And if that other one comes back she's as good as dead.*

He reclaimed his sword and wiped its blade clean upon the broad back of Big Ugly's cooling corpse before returning his sword to the worn leather scabbard at his left hipwing. He stared down overlong in dark reflection, the awful scene and his part in it replaying in knifing flashes so that he shut them out by closing his eyes and rubbing them.

"No," he whispered. "Don't even think about it. Just blank it. Blank it and move. Before anyone else shows up."

He squatted next to the woman, tucked his arms beneath her neck and knees then scooped her up. But his arms would tire out in a matter of minutes so that he maneuvered her limp body over his right shoulder, gave a parting glance round the clearing to ensure no followers then started away west.

* * *

Jericho'll know what to do with you, Banzu reassured for the umpteenth time while walking. *But what will he say about everything else?*

Those worries plagued his thoughts as he ventured home, navigating the meandering paths through the woods in a slow but steady pace while keeping the unconscious woman from jostling loose atop his aching shoulder.

Gods, it's like carrying a soft sack of rocks.

He worked up a good lather of sweat in minutes, with miles to go before reaching home. He considered stopping for rest, and possibly waking the woman then assaulting her with a flurry of question, though he wanted to put as much distance as possible between them and that gruesome scene.

She's lucky she didn't snap her neck in the tumble. That bump on her head's knocked her out cold. She might not wake for hours. And when she does she'll probably have addled brains. But at least she's still breathing. She better thank me for hauling her all this way. Friggin hell she's heavy.

Without breaking stride he twisted again and glanced behind, ensuring no followers pursued their trail.

Curiosity over his carried burden and her eager chasers blossomed at the forefront of his working mind, shelving worries for questions he possessed no answers.

What if she's a criminal?

Though he doubted such a pretty woman capable of any crimes requiring execution for theft or murder. Not that he possessed any experience in the wily ways of women. But she carried nothing of value. *Unless she dropped it during the chase.* And no blood stained her hands. *Unless she washed them clean. Why else would they be chasing her and willing to kill? To die?*

No. Those weren't innocent men seeking justice. They wanted her dead, and why don't matter. Murder burned in their eyes, no doubt about it.

I had no choice.

Gods, Jericho's going to snatch my face off then wipe his ass with it when I get home. Or worse. He'll probably beat me black and blue till my bones hurt.

Abolishing the grim premonitions of his uncle's surefire wrath for later dealing, he stole sidelong glances of her bottom while entertaining notions of sliding a hand up from the backs of her thighs and giving that attractive backside a healthy squeeze.

She sure is pretty. And probably has a voice like music. And a . . .

Lost in youthful musings, the woman's soft groan passed unnoticed beneath Banzu's straying attentions. Until she kicked her legs and pounded her fists upon his back, rousing awake in frantic abandon.

"Put me down, godsdammit!"

Startled, he let slip the thrashing woman from his shoulder and stumbled backwards, dropping her onto her bottom.

She met the ground with a wincing grunt. She stared up at him, violet eyes wide and mouth agape.

He froze, stammered for words, mind flashing blank.

She sprang to her feet, eyes darting while she turned about, taking in her new surroundings.

He opened his mouth, but words failed his fumbling tongue.

Satisfied they stood alone, she fixed her full attentions on him, the initial shock gone from her face and replaced by a cutting glare of thin-eyed scrutiny, her voice a cracking whip. "Who the hell are you?"

The question a slap, sudden, stinging, he fumbled through speech. "Uh, uhm, I—"

"I asked you a question." She challenged him a step closer, glare violet fire. "Answer me, boy."

He withdrew a cautious step, surprised by the strength of presence belied by her slender frame. She stood taller than him by a head, forcing him to look up to meet those intense violet eyes regarding all of him, her demeanor of natural authority tangling his response into an awkward mumble. "I, uh, uhm . . ."

She scrunched her face, nose crinkling, and huffed a terse breath at the babble of his non-answer, then turned away and started off, the bottom of her traveler's cloak swirling round her long-striding legs.

"Wait!" Banzu called after her.

He pursued by instinct. And stopped short soon as she spun round, long temple braids twirling and almost slapping him so that he flinched back by inches while they whiffed past his face.

She spread her feet and planted fists to hips, lips tight in a fine red line. Everything about her stance declared defiance. Her earthen-toned cloak belted tight round her trim middle, she possessed an athletic build, curvaceous yet firm in all the right places, small breasts atop a slender—

"If you're done groping me with your eyes," she said, "then you'd best tell me who you are or leave me the hell alone."

"Banzu," he stammered out, cursing his roaming gaze. He cleared his throat—twice. "My name's Banzu. I saved you. Those men chasing you." He threw a hitcher's thumb over his shoulder in gesture behind. "I killed them."

"You killed them," she said, tone flat. She backed up two steps and appraised the length of him, eyebrows arching. "*You?*"

He frowned and snapped, "Yeah, me." And cringed against his too-high voice so that he squared his shoulders while puffing his chest and, after rumbling his throat clear, said in deeper voice. "Yes. Me."

She glowered, tone bitter. "I suppose you want a reward, is that what this is all about?"

His smile faltered. "Uhm."

"And what do you expect in return, hmm?" She cocked one eyebrow, a cute though menacing gesture, and leaned a slight forward at the waist. "A hug? A kiss? A quick tumble in the grass for my gratitude?" She shoved a stiff finger at his face. "You have my thanks and that's all you're going to get!"

He flinched through backwards lean, eyeballs crossed over the focal point of her admonishing finger jabbing inches from his nose.

"I don't have time for this." She flipped her hood up, turned round and started away again.

"Wait." He reached out to grab her by the crook of the arm. "I'm only trying to—" *Help.* But he clipped short the instant his grasping fingertips brushed against her elbow.

She spun round in a tornado of woman, her hands a blur of motion untying her belt then, split cloak flapping, those hands vanished up behind her and reappeared whipping-quick fisting two fang-shaped daggers the length of her forearms from pommels to tips.

Banzu startled stiff, the curved tip of one dagger poking the soft underbelly of his chin, the other's pressed against his crotch.

"Don't ever touch me again." She applied threatening pressure beneath his chin, forcing his head up to better meet her smoldering gaze. "Do you understand me?"

He nodded, the motion prompted by the dagger beneath his chin. He quested inward for the Power on instinct—and met only failure, his insides twisting into confusing knots. "Uh-huh."

"Good boy." There played a dangerous half-smile curving her lips. She withdrew two steps, spun her strange fanged daggers through deft twirls of her wrists then returned them up beneath her flapping cloak quick as she'd produced them. She eyeballed him a moment overlong then turned and walked away.

"Friggin hell." He raked a hand back through his hair and blew out his cheeks, watching her go, wanting to help her though also wanting to go home and get some answers. "Fine." He lowered his hand to the hilt of his sword and squeezed in imaginary strangle of her neck. "Be that way."

She stopped twenty paces away, pulled out a folded piece of paper from beneath her cloak, unfolded it, glared at it, glared round, then threw her hands up and cursed.

A map. Banzu smirked, knowing these woodlands with his eyes shut, knowing too traveling in them proved far different than viewing their inked scratches on a map. "You lost?"

She spun round scowling, voice curt. "No." She advanced in a stomping gale and slapped the crumpled map against his chest with a feisty shove, the motion rocking him. "Here, take this." She spun and walked away.

Banzu caught the wadded map before it fell to the ground and stared after her.

She stopped five paces out, turned round facing him, planted fists to hips. "Well?"

"Well what?"

She rolled her eyes. "Well look at it, stupid."

Stupid? Why you ungrateful little—He chewed back a fiery retort and smoothed the crumpled map on his chest then glanced it over while questioning the sanity of her demand. "Yup. It's a map all right."

"Do you see it?"

He frowned. "Of course I see it. It's in my friggin hands."

"Not the map, stupid, the mark!" She backed away another five paces. "How about now?"

Oh gods, she's crazy. He cocked her an eyebrow while considering asking just how hard she'd hit her head.

She withdrew another two steps. "How about now?"

"You hit your head pretty hard. Maybe you should sit down and—"

She flared her eyes, her voice, while stomping and pointing. "Look at it!"

"Okay okay!" He huffed and rolled his eyes, then appeased her by looking at the map again. And startled at the glowing red dot thereon the paper absent a moment previous. He drew back while extending his arms, blinking hard, testing the sanity of his eyes.

"Do you see it yet?" she asked.

He nodded, held the map closer and squinted at the obvious magic at play.

"Put your finger on it," she said.

The 'it' could only mean one thing. He eased his right pointer finger forward in a cautious test, fearing the burn though detecting no presence of heat. But the glowing red dot disappeared before he could touch it. "What the frig—"

"Don't move!" she shouted while charging forward.

He poked the indicated spot of map and held his finger to place.

While she strode back to him then rounded and stood at his side. She looked to where he pointed then snatched the map away and started off west.

He lingered a hesitant moment then pursued her, interests piqued. "Why are you going there?"

"None of your business, that's why." She folded the map into a small square and tucked it beneath her cloak. She glanced behind, glaring him back, then quickened her steps. "And stop following me."

But he kept after her, the indicated spot of map clarifying in his mind and all too familiar. He sped his steps to match her hurried strides while maintaining cautious distance between in case she whirled on him again. *Gods, she's feisty.*

"Why are you going there?" he asked again, feigning only slight interest.

She answered nothing.

His focus lowered to the pleasant distraction of the enticing sway of her hips, that backside bouncing atop those long legs, his mind detaching from his mouth. "Why are you looking for him?"

She stopped, spun round.

Banzu froze mid step, cringing to his errant slip of tongue.

"Him?" She estimated Banzu a silent length, eyes a thinning scrutiny. "You know him." No question to her statement. "Take me to him." She flared her eyes, her voice. "Now."

"Uhm." *Friggin hell. Me and my big mouth.* He shifted his feet, feigning ignorance. "Him who?"

She tightened her glare. "Don't play stupid with me."

He glanced behind, considered running. *She'll only chase me. And where will I go? Home's the other way.*

"Now!" She fisted the front of his shirt and yanked him into following.

He stumbled after her. But seconds more and he pulled free of her grip and stopped. *I've had just about enough of this.* "Just hold on. I'm not taking you anywhere until you tell me what's going on."

She crossed her arms and smirked. "Is that so?"

"Yeah." He nodded. "That's so. Who are you? What do you want? And why where those men chasing you?"

Frowning, she expelled a long and hissing sigh through pursed lips. "My name's Melora. I've come a long way to find him. And that's all you need to know."

"Find who?"

"Don't play games with me, boy. You know who."

"Jerrriiicho?" he asked, as if stretching the word out would somehow mask the true identity of its namesake.

"Obviously."

Oh gods. He raked one hand back through his hair and blew out his cheeks. No denying the truth of it now. Or that mysterious glowing dot indicating the location where he and his uncle called home for the past eleven years. His mind worked through a flurry of excuses and the various practiced stories they prepared to deny themselves as anything more than simple mountain folk struggling to survive. Yet there battled the strong urge to speak the truth of it all, to spill it out and be free from the running, the hiding, the lying. The loneliness.

"Well?" Melora asked, breaking into his troubling chain of thoughts. "Are you going to take me? Or do I have to make you take me?"

He crossed his arms and grinned. "The least you can do is ask me nicely. After all, I did save your life."

She opened her mouth in a pretty O if indignation then closed it with an ivory click of teeth. She sniffed hard, face scrunching, nose crinkling cute between rosy cheeks. She forced a smile leaving her smoldering eyes untouched. "Please?" she asked through clenched teeth.

He chuckled at her twisted chore of expression. "Thank—"

She fisted the front of his shirt again and jerked him into following.

* * *

They traversed the woodlands in silence, the sky viewed through sparse open patches in the high canopy purpling with the imminent threat of nightfall. The sun had yet to set, but already winding trails ran as shadowed paths of tripping hazard to the unwary step. Angled spears of sunlight stabbed through overhead breaks of foliage here and there, throwing motes of intense color into an otherwise gloomy cavernous world. Another hour and blackest pitch would suffocate all light from the forest interior, making travel all but impossible to unaided eyes.

Trailing behind Melora a safe distance, Banzu attempted small talk when not pointing out their meandering western route at every split or bend, probing for anything more than her name. She provided nothing but a few curt words thrown over the shoulder. Apparently she'd come from "Too far, now shut up" and had been traveling "Too long, so stop asking."

"We're good friends," came his vague explanation after she strung together her longest chain of words and asked how he and Jericho knew each other, keeping their blood-ties hidden. Afraid she might turn on him demanding more under threat of those fanged daggers hidden beneath her cloak, he let conversation fall to the wayside for walking, wanting answers but reluctant to give.

Melora carried herself strong, moving in physical match to her fiery personality—brazen and bold, fierce and determined—though soon her tenacious gait slowed as fatigue set in, her shoulders slouching, strides shortening, and thrice she protested yawns with a covering hand.

"How much longer?" she asked, half-turning, and tripped over her own bumbling feet.

Banzu rushed and caught her by the arm, arresting her fall short.

She jerked her arm free, scowling, tired lids aflutter through rapid blinks while gathering herself straight. She drew in deep and mustered the energy for a proper glare.

"If you're leading me on some wild chase, I swear I'll"—a pausing yawn—"I'll gut you like a fish."

"It's not much farther," he said. "We can rest here if you want. You look like you need it."

She snorted a terse huff. "No. I'll have time to rest when I'm dead. Keep moving."

He sighed though brooked no argument, fell back into stride alongside her now in case she tripped again. They continued on in silence. Minutes more and they reached a familiar break in the woods.

"There," he said, pointing at the rustic cabin across the open field lit by the fading light of the dying sun, its little chimney puffing smoke.

"Are you sure?"

"Of course I'm sure. That's where I—" *Live.* But he clipped his betraying words short to keep his story straight. *Gods, I feel as tired as she looks.* He slapped the sword at his side and grinned. "That's where I come for training."

The cute crinkle of her nose again, and small disgust entered her tone. "He *trains* you?"

"Yup."

She thinned her eyes upon him. "Just how much do you know about him?"

Banzu shrugged, feigning ignorance. "He used to be a soldier. He got tired of fighting so he moved up here to get away from it. I come up when he needs supplies, and I suppose he gets bored being up here all by himself so he teaches me how to fight. The old man used to be pretty good with a sword. Or so he claims."

Her face pinched up with the taste of something bitter spoiling on her buds. "He's wasted all these years hiding up here teaching some mountain boy how to play with a sword. Perfect. Just perfect."

Banzu frowned.

She sped away toward the cabin, leaving him behind, though she glanced back and added, "You can go away now." And shooed him with the dismissive flick of her wrist.

"Wait!" Panic flushing, he caught up alongside her. "Wait a minute. You can't just go barging in there—"

"I go where I please, thank you very much." She dipped a hand beneath her cloak then shoved her fist into his hand, forcing something into his palm. "There's your reward. Now go buy yourself a nice pretty goat and hump it, or whatever it is you mountain boys do, and leave me the hell alone. This doesn't concern you."

He stopped and gawked at her shrinking back for a struck turn. *Hump a goat?* He considered the silver coin in his hand for all of three seconds then fisted it, strangled it, and grit his teeth. *Friggin hell!* He punched the coin into his pocket and broke into a run, passing her. He stopped and turned round, blocking her way before she reached the cabin's front door. "Wait!"

She stopped, frowning, her eyes level under drawn brows. "Get out of my way." Her upper lip twitched with the threat of a snarl. "Now."

He backed up two steps, those twin fanged daggers hidden beneath her cloak flashing through his mind. "Just give me a minute, okay? You can't just go barging in. He might be naked, or sleeping, or . . . well, uhm, asides, he knows me."

"Fine." She crossed her arms and cocked her hips, the right half of her face buried beneath shadow, the left bathed red in the setting sun's lurid light, pale blonde hair framing it all. "You've got thirty seconds."

"What?"

"One." Her left boot tapped the ground in count. "Two."

"Okay, okay."

"Three."

He frowned. "Just hold on and let me—"

"Four."

He opened his mouth.

"Five."

Then snapped it shut, stifling the curse, and spun away.

"Six."

Gods she's intolerable! He cracked the door open enough to slip through, shimmied inside, then shut it quick and pressed his back against it. He closed his eyes and drew in deep, blew out his frustrated cheeks, thankful for the spare moment to—

"Where've you been?" Jericho asked from across the foreroom. "And who were you talking to?"

Banzu opened one eye then the other. His uncle sat in his rocker by the smoldering hearth, stirring the simmering black kettle at his right with a ladle, a long wooden spoon in his other hand.

"And where's our dinner?" Jericho continued, shaking the spoon. "You've been out so long I had to reheat this godsdamned stew. Big as you are, don't think I won't bend you over my knee and tan your sorry hide." He set the spoon atop his lap and patted his belly while speaking to it. "It's okay, boy. I know you're hungry. Don't you worry. Dinner's coming. Shh, it's okay."

"Uhm." Banzu floundered for words, unsure where to begin or even how. "Uh."

Jericho squinted at him. "What's gotten into you? You look flushed. And why are you sweating?"

Banzu cleared his throat and took one step from the door. "Don't kill me, okay? But there's a—"

"Kill you?" Jericho returned his attentions to the kettle at his right, stirring the ladle. "I have half a mind to if there's no hares behind the door."

Banzu braced and blurted out, "There's a woman outside."

Jericho flinched, head snapping left. "A woman?"

Banzu swallowed, nodded.

"Is that what's got you all flustered, a woman?" Jericho abandoned the ladle and sat forward, rocker creaking. "Well now, why didn't you say so." He grinned while brushing down the front of his shirt. "I hope she's pretty."

Banzu sighed, muttered, "Pretty mean."

Jericho licked the tip of one finger and traced it over his bushy eyebrows, smoothing them handsome. "Let me guess. Some young crumpet got turned around in the woods so you brought her here for the night, eh?"

"Not exact—"

The door pushed open. "Thirty!" Hitting Banzu from behind and knocking him to the floor as Melora barged inside. "Jericho?" She stepped onto then over Banzu's fallen sprawl, locked eyes with another. "Jericho Jaicham Greenlief?"

Banzu pushed up onto hands and knees, grumbling every sore inch of the way. He stood, intent on unleashing a hot string of curses though stifled silent at his startled uncle's haunted stare.

"Those eyes," Jericho whispered in a forward-hunching lean, his face slack, body tensed, hands gripping knees. "Impossible."

Melora took a hesitant step toward him. "I'm Spellbinder Melora Callisticus. Vizer to king—" She clipped short, wincing, began again. "Vizer to the former king of Junes." She threw a wary glance at Banzu. "I was sent here by direct order of Head Mistress Gwendora Pearce of the fistian Academy. And I've come to bring you back to Fist."

Banzu cringed while floundering in the spill of information.

***

Jericho ran a hand down over his face while easing back in his creaking rocker, staring more through Melora than at her.

A Spellbinder? Of course! Those eyes . . . Banzu almost spoke the jolting epiphany aloud but for the startlement of it all. *No wonder the Power failed me. Gods, how could I be so stupid?* Then his risen spirits plunged. *Is it only a temporary? Or gone for good?* He closed the door by leaning his back against it, eyeing Melora from behind, having no idea just how a Spellbinder's aizakai powers actually worked.

"Spellbinder," Jericho said, tone a listless repeat. "Vizer to King Junes. Sent by Gwen, you say." He blew out his cheeks, tapped the eating end of the long wooden spoon against his chin while studying her. "Fist is a long way from here, young lady."

Melora threw Banzu a suspicious glance over a shoulder then advanced toward Jericho another cautious step. "Former Vizer to the now deceased king of Junes. And yes,"—she dipped a hand beneath her cloak and produced a worn envelope sealed with blue wax, held it out for the taking—"Head Mistress Pearce sent me to give you this. Here."

Jericho moved nothing.

She shook the envelope, frowning. "Well take it, godsdammit."

Jericho ran the tip of his tongue over his teeth, nostrils flaring. He rocked forward into standing—and Melora flinched backwards half a wary step though gave no protest when Jericho took her by the shoulders and guided her to the chair opposite his rocker where he forced her into sitting. He shot Banzu an accusatory glance in passing.

To which Banzu averted his guilty gaze by pretending his feet turned fascinating objects of study for several grueling seconds, his mind a deluge of questions and confessions binding his tongue.

Jericho moved to the kettle, ladled a healthy scoop of warm stew into a wooden bowl and brought it to her. "You look half starved. Here. Eat."

She held out the envelope, a crumpled stick of paper in her strangling fist. "Take it. Read it."

Jericho sighed, glanced at Banzu. He exchanged envelope for bowl. Halfway back to his rocker he paused, considered the sword lying on the floor—the twin to the one sheathed at Banzu's left hipwing—his free hand flexing, knuckles popping, but he left the weapon untouched and reclaimed his rocker.

Melora's haggard eyes darted from the bowl nestled in her lap to Jericho and back again. She licked her lips while inhaling the enticing aroma then attacked the fish stew by removing the oversized spoon in her way to make room for scooping fingers.

Jericho lay the sealed envelope in his lap and clasped his hands atop it. He watched her eat in silent study.

Banzu crossed the room and stood next to his uncle, joined in watching Melora empty the bowl's contents in starving fashion.

Silence but for Melora's gobbling chews.

"More," she said when finished, holding the bowl out. She sucked clean the fingers of her feeder hand. "Gimme more."

Jericho said, "You heard the lady."

Banzu rolled his eyes though took the bowl and refilled it then carried it back. Before he could so much as outstretch his arm, Melora leaned forward and snatched the bowl away. She ate slower this time, using the spoon.

Banzu returned to his uncle's side.

"Open it," she said between chews, watching Jericho watching her. "You need to open it now."

Jericho smoothed the crinkled envelope upon his lap then held it up. "You mean this?"

She paused the spoon halfway to her mouth, eyes thinning. "Obviously."

He returned the envelope to his lap, tapped at its blue wax seal, pointed at her. "I don't know who you are . . . Melora, was it? But I do know a thing or two about a thing or two." He extended his pointer finger, the others curled. "First of all, there hasn't been a king of Junes since Simus Junes was hunted down and slain after the Thousand Years War. Everyone from here to the Rift knows that." He extended his middle finger. "Second, Agatha dar'Shuwin stood next in line for ascension to Head Mistress, not Gwen." Ring finger extended. "And third, even if what you say is true, that I somehow have it all wrong, there's no way Gwen could know where I am."

Melora fixed him with something akin to languid disdain and mild amusement when she set the bowl aside, reached beneath her cloak—earning a flinch from Jericho and Banzu alike—and pulled out a folded piece of paper. She threw it, making of it a bladed star crossing the space between them.

The spinning paper struck Jericho against the chest and fell into his lap atop the envelope. He frowned down, then grumbled when he unfolded the thrown paper and relapsed into a silent stare, hands turning tremulous.

Banzu leaned in for a peek at the map from earlier though absent the glowing red dot.

"This can't be," Jericho said, his voice a thin whisper. He shook his head. "How did you get this? Who gave this to you?" He sat forward, rocker creaking, tone edging. "Why are you really here?"

Melora shifted on her bottom, glanced at the sword lying the floor between them, glanced at the door, glanced at the sword again, then thinned her eyes at Banzu before fixing upon Jericho. She cleared her throat and mustered straight, chin high and shoulders back. "By Head Mistress's orders. Your former Spellbinder, Agatha, gave it to her."

"Aggie," Jericho whispered. He settled back in his creaking rocker, slumping. He bowed his head and shook it while pinching the bridge of his nose, eyes closed. "Oh gods, Aggie, no . . ."

Banzu shifted his feet, guts twisting, body craving movement though nowhere to spend it, mind demanding answers to the flurry of new questions tumbling round his head. He considered his uncle, bemused and irritated by unanswered secrets, part of him wanting nothing more than to yank Jericho from his rocker and punch him square in the nose, another part wanting to grab him up by the shoulders and shake those secrets loose. *All these years and he never said a word about any of this.*

But he cooled his flaring animus with a calming breath, at last finding his tongue. "Who's Aggie?"

Jericho lowered his hand to his chest and clutched his shirt, though more so what lay behind it, and raised his head while withering through exhale. He twisted and gazed up at his nephew through eyes naked and wounded. "Aggie's . . ." A pause, an audible swallow. "Aggie's my wife."

Banzu's jaw dropped.

CHAPTER FOUR

Banzu crossed the room and claimed the nearest chair in a stupefied funk, the deluge of questions about his uncle's private past revealed—*a wife* and *a Spellbinder?*—making a tangled knot of his disobedient tongue lathered in accusations unvoiced. So he listened while Melora explained her situation to Jericho. She threw Banzu's unwanted presence occasional scrutinizing glances between pauses and despite Jericho's assurance that his 'good friend' should stay, could be trusted.

The forces of an upstart warlord named Hannibal Khan had attacked her stationed city of Junes far east in Thurandy well beyond the Calderos Mountains dividing it from Ascadia. The Khan stormed into Junes during a city-wide festival of wedding celebration, calling down lightning from the sky as would some vengeful god while his fanatical worship-followers filled the city's streets in a terrorizing flood of brutal aizakai slaughter.

Three chaotic days this lasted until the khansmen overran then overtook then overruled all of Junes and its surviving citizens. Hannibal Khan punctuated the triumph of his new reign with the public execution of the newly wedded and first king of Junes since the infamous Simus the Savior-Slayer three centuries previous, smiting the naked royal with a searing bolt of lightning in the enormous city's square and making of the man a smoldering mound of blackened char in view of the thousands of awestruck citizens gathered in witness to the ascension of their new ruler, their Lord of Storms.

Melora failed at both protecting the king and her ensuing attempt at retribution upon his Khan slayer, escaping Junes by the skin of her teeth and fleeing west to the Academy in Fist seeking help. Where began her long and arduous journey to Ascadia for the last Soothsayer after Head Mistress Gwendora Pearce, instigated by Mistress Agatha's confessed possession of the magical map spelled to Jericho's person wherever he may roam so long as he lived, sent Melora in questing bid for Jericho's return.

Through it all Jericho maintained a quiet intensity belied by a cold, detached stare, his bridled tensions announced through the intermittent creaking of wood joins while his hands flexed tensing grips upon the armrests of his still rocker.

Banzu's mental seams split to bursting with more questions, a building sense of fate earning him anxious squirms and fidgets so that he wrung his hands and popped his knuckles to spend the nervous energy in lieu of rushing his uncle and demanding answers in angry choking outburst, though he interrupted nothing throughout Melora's retelling. Jericho held deeper ties to the fistian Academy than he'd even known, though now he understood why his uncle remained so tight-lipped about his former life.

Jericho Jaicham Greenlief, captured in his youth before his first killing and forced into bondage, made a Soothsayer servitor of the fistian Academy, trained into a weapon, Paired with Spellbinder Agatha dar'Shuwin to act as his protection against the bloodlust then his executioner once he inevitably turned to the curse as all Soothsayers before him. For years they traveled the world in Academy service, hunting down and executing other Soothsayers until only Jericho remained. They became the fistian Academy's last known Pair, and he the last known Soothsayer.

The Academy sought to end the Nameless One's bloodlust curse through Soothsayer elimination then Jericho's life cut short by the hands of his Spellbinder's pledged duty. But they'd fallen in love and married in secret, a blasphemous crime against Academy law. Hours before his scheduled execution he disappeared.

Agatha betrayed her sworn oaths to the Academy by aiding Jericho's escape. Only to aid in his finding when Melora returned from Junes harboring grim news of its change in ruling power and Agatha relinquished her secret ensorcelled map. Jericho left its promise with her as the sole means of finding him if she ever left the Academy for good.

Banzu hoarded every detail Melora spilled out while waiting for his part in it all to surface and oust his true identity. To his surprise she revealed no knowledge of him. Thankfully Agatha hadn't divulged every secret in her confession, leaving Jericho's reasons of escape to the obvious though not entirely true fact of his inevitable execution.

If Melora knew Banzu's true nature then she guarded it well.

She also spoke of other things, though these words sounded in a *shshshshsh* of voice Banzu, and his uncle by the tell of Jericho's tensing then relaxing face, forgot within seconds after the subject passed over her lips, Banzu unsure if he even heard the curious strings of words at all in the aftermath of their faded delivery.

". . . and then I woke up," she finished, and gestured at Banzu with the flick of her wrist. "Carried over his shoulder, groping me."

Banzu flinched and frowned. *Groping?* "Wait a minute. I didn't grope—"

She talked over him, ignoring him, attentions fixed upon Jericho. "And now I'm here." She sat back, touched at her bruised forehead, hissed while wincing, then afforded Banzu another absent flick of her wrist and crossed her arms. "If he hadn't showed up and killed those sons of bastards—" She paused, face scrunching, violet eyes thinning into contemptuous slits. "I only wish I'd been awake to watch them die. Or have a hand in it. Godsdamned khansmen every time I turned around."

"I see." Jericho swept his pensive gaze aside at Banzu. "So he killed them then."

Melora nodded. "So he says. But I didn't see it." She uncrossed one arm, touched at the bruised swell of knot on her forehead again, then crossed it. "Something snagged around my legs. One moment I was running then tumbling, the next I know I woke up." She shot Banzu a sidelong glare for emphasis and added, "Being groped by Chester the Molester here."

Banzu ignored her false slight against him, too enfolded in the silent scrutiny of his uncle's hard stare probing the depths of him.

Jericho cocked an eyebrow.

Banzu opened his mouth then closed it. He averted his gaze to the floor between his feet. With effort he swallowed the dry lump in his throat, and nodded.

Yes.

I killed them.

I'm sorry.

But he put no voice behind it.

***

Melora untied the nape of her cloak, split it open and revealed a thin silvery metallic collar looped round her slender neck. She slipped two hooking fingers through the inch of space between and tugged, grimacing disgust. "I had to put this godsdamned thing on or else lose it when that last chase began. Two, no, three—" She huffed a terse breath. "I don't know how many days ago."

"What's that?" Banzu asked, finding his tongue.

Melora thinned her eyes upon him. "None of your business." To Jericho she said, "Undeniable proof the Enclave has returned."

Jericho leaned forward by inches to better view the collar through closer squint. "A kohatheen." He shifted his gaze to Banzu. "Made from lanthium. Wizard's metal. Indestructible once forged." Then settled back in his creaking rocker, expression an ugly twist. "An old and terrible device, that. Infused with Spellbinder blood. A slaver's collar to any aizakai unlucky enough to know its cruel embrace." He rolled one hand in gesture at Melora. "Asides yourself, of course."

"Not so old," Melora said, tap-tap-tapping the lanthium kohatheen with a fingernail *click-click-click*. "The Enclave," she continued, touching once more upon the archaic cult holding manipulative ties to the Thousand Years War as well as Hannibal Khan, their newly chosen messiah of power, "has been forging these in secret. Bleeding Spellbinders dry and enslaving every aizakai not killed outright by their fanatic worship-followers. Their methods of extraction are excruciating to say the least."

"I'm well aware of what those horrible things are for," Jericho said, nodding, expression pained. He reached up to feel at his throat though lowered his hand before making contact.

Banzu watched that hand turn tremulous so that Jericho closed it into a fist of strangled memories, his mind making disturbing connections better left unvoiced. For now. He caught Jericho's wary glance, detected the hint of fear betraying those tortured blues.

Melora frowned and pinched the nape of her cloak closed, concealing the kohatheen collar. "Good," she said, emphasizing the word with a curt nod, as if some agreement between them had just been struck. "So we can get going now."

She erupted into standing—and swayed on her feet so that she plopped back down, heavy lids fluttering. She touched the soft swell of bruise marring her skin a light purple above her left eye, the knot earned during her bola tumble.

Jericho sighed, shook his head. "You can't just show up like this and expect me to follow you back there like everything's all fine and dandy. My Academy ties severed a long time ago. Those were different times. I'm not that man anymore."

She drew back by inches. "But—" Frowned and tugged at her kohatheen, the motion evincing her want for yanking it through her neck. "But—" Then surged into standing again, scowling. "But you have to. It's your sworn duty!"

Jericho said nothing, though his gaze flickered to the sword lying the floor between them.

Banzu squirmed his chair, Melora's feathers ruffling and the gods only knew what she planned on doing with those hidden daggers of hers. He kept track of her hands, tensing ready to spring up and wrestle her to the floor if needs be.

"Haven't you been listening?" she continued, hands waving about, voice a petulant flare despite her tired eyes. "Junes is only the first. The Enclave's been planning for this since the Thousand Years War. It's aizakai genocide all over again! Don't you care?"

Jericho opened his mouth, closed it, answered nothing.

She stared at him overlong, huffed a derisive breath then sank back into the chair where she hunched forward with elbows on thighs and hung her head. She rubbed the inside corners of her closed eyes with pointer and thumb, expelling a sigh that withered her.

"You weren't there," she said in a tone less fierce. "You didn't see what they did. What their Khan can do. He captured lightning from the sky and discharged it from his hands. They killed so many. I've never seen such horrors before." She looked up, lips a bitter twist. "And now, whether fear or awe, the survivors praise him as a living god for it all."

"Lightning," Banzu said, still struck by the notion of a man capable of wielding such awesome power unheard of among aizakai. "How is that even possible?"

Melora flashed him a dismissive glare that said he shouldn't even be there let alone partaking in the conversation so shut up and don't interrupt.

"Yes," Jericho said. "How?"

"Hannibal Khan possesses the gauntlets of the Dominator's Armor," Melora said. "Stolen somehow from one of the Builder's towers. The Enclave no doubt, the snake-faced bastards. The gauntlets make him a living conductor of lightning, summoning it at will. I've seen it myself, and I—"

A yawn cut her short. She settled back in the chair and closed her eyes, rolled her head from shoulder to shoulder, wincing through kohatheen collar pinches on her skin so that she tugged at it, grimacing, then huffed and dropped her hand from the futile chore of earning the kohatheen's release from round her neck.

Jericho studied the envelope in his lap, tracing a fingertip over its cracked though unbroken blue wax seal.

Banzu raked a hand back through his hair and blew out his cheeks, watching them both, Melora left, Jericho right. So much information to digest in so little time. He wished for a private place to withdraw and think or better yet batter his uncle with questions the half of which he dared not voice in front of her without revealing his true identity.

"More will come," she said of the three khansmen assassins in the woods, earning Banzu a flaring glare from his uncle. She leaned forward, drawing Jericho's attention with the snap of her fingers then an admonishing jab of her pointer. "You know that. Just like you know the Enclave overtook Junes first for a reason. If they found a way inside a Builder's tower despite the protective wards then they surely know of that monster's crypt sealed beneath the palace."

She paused, shivered visibly.

"It's been almost two years since I left Fist. There's no telling what else the Enclave's managed since. And they gained possession of the necromaster's ring the moment their Khan seized the throne. It's only a matter of time before they resurrect that godsforsaken creature and finish what they started with the Thousand Years War. *Shshshshsh* and they must be stopped, Jericho. If they *shshshshsh* the *shshshshsh*—" She paused, frowning. "Never mind that. You forget it soon as I speak it. Look. We have to—"

Another yawn cut her short so that she blew out her cheeks and rubbed her tired eyes.

Banzu blinked a return of focus, the *shshshshsh* of her words fading from his memory. The infamous ring of the savior-slayer Simus Junes, he mused, a mythical relic though after her explanation he knew more of that ring than the purported lore allowed.

Simus Junes defeated the Nameless One's mortal avatar at the end of the Thousand Years War, wielding the Source to rend the Dominator's Armor apart while earning himself and all Soothsayers through him the bloodlust curse, a final parting gift bestowed during the Nameless One's banishment from the mortal plane.

Simus and his Soothsayer Grey Swords, strengthened by an aizakai army, also battled the Nameless One's subservient necromaster Dethkore, the unliving creature better known as the Eater of Souls, though more commonly Soultaker. But Dethkore would not die, so Simus burned his body then entombed the ashes below his homeland palace in Junes before Simus' eventual turning to the bloodlust curse, taking Dethkore's soul-imbued ring as a trophy passed down through the generations from queen to queen, for the ending of the Thousand Years War marked the beginning of the dark age of bloodlust-corrupted Soothsayers the Academy spent the next three centuries trying to abolish.

Melora said, "If they find the crypt and resurrect Dethkore, there'll be no stopping them. You know what he can do, and you know that ring is his only source of control. Hannibal Khan will be the least of our problems."

"Three-hundred years is a long time for planning," Jericho said.

"Planning only goes so far. They possess someone with foresight. A young slave girl, Sera. Little else is known beyond that. But she's an aizakai, so there's hope she's only giving them enough to keep herself alive."

Jericho sighed. "Sounds like quite a mess."

"Mess?" Melora frowned. "This isn't spilled milk in the kitchen. The Enclave already rules Junes. If their Khan isn't stopped, there's no telling how far their corruption will spread. Think, Jericho. If they conquer Fist and gain access to the Book of Towers . . ." She trailed off, shaking her head. Began again. "This world cannot survive another Thousand Years War."

"Well then." Jericho rocked into standing, stuffed the unopened envelope inside a pocket. "First thing's first—"

"Gods, finally!" Melora sprang to her feet. She swayed a bit though fought herself straight. "We've wasted enough time here already. First we need to—"

"Sit," Jericho said, voice stern, commanding.

Melora flared her eyes in feisty rebuttal.

"Now," Jericho added.

She snapped her mouth shut, huffed and sat, crossed her arms and scowled.

"You've come a long way to find me. One more night won't make any difference. Asides, you look two shakes from passing out. And that full belly of yours isn't helping any. Take some rest. You need it."

Jericho turned for the door, caught Banzu in the sweeping gesture of his eyes to follow suit.

Banzu stood.

So did Melora. "And where do you think you're going?"

"Out," Jericho said. "I need some time to think." He walked to the door and opened it, the cool mountain air blowing in through night's black curtain beyond. "We'll be back shortly."

"We?" She thinned her eyes upon them both, fists clenched, and advanced them a challenging step. "You two aren't going anywhere without—"

"Enough!" Jericho's voice a cracking whip, he shot her a warning glare. "Hush." He snapped his fingers and pointed at her then the chair behind her. "Sit your ass down before I sit you down."

Banzu tensed, expecting her to burst at them with daggers stabbing.

Jericho said to her in edged tone, "I won't tell you again. Sit. Now."

Paused mid step in halted pursuit, Melora flared then thinned her eyes. She turned and kicked the wooden bowl across the room, then grumbled curses at them both while plopping in her chair, arms crossed, her glare a burning menace.

"That's better." Jericho turned away, fetched Banzu a glance in so doing, then left outside.

Banzu paused at the open door, looked back at Melora muttering curses while tugging on the kohatheen collar locked round her neck.

Until she caught him watching and bared a snarl. "What!"

"Nothing." He tensed his lips to hide the smirk begging for release. "We just need a few minutes outside, okay? Relax. You're safe here. I promise."

"You've got five minutes," she said, where began the steady tapping of her counting right boot. "Then I'm coming out. And I swear to gods if you two even think of running off I'll . . ."

But she trailed away, grumbling threats while tugging at her kohatheen.

* * *

Banzu removed outside, pulled the door to a sliver within closing, turned round and froze dead to rights in his uncle's piercing stare.

Silence but for the soughing winds.

Above, the unobstructed moonlight cast them in its muted glow.

Banzu swallowed, unsure where to begin or even how.

"There's no taking back what you've done." Jericho glanced away, east. *You've failed me*, the gesture said.

"I know. And I'm sorry." Banzu reached out to give his uncle's shoulder a consoling squeeze while begging forgiveness.

Jericho withdrew two steps, inhaled deep, sighed, warm breath a misting plume taken upon the sharp chill.

Banzu shivered, though his uncle appeared oblivious to the cold, distanced from it, a minor distraction ignored for the new troubles plaguing him.

"If you want to make the gods laugh . . ." Jericho closed his eyes and craned his head, shook it. "Then tell them your plans."

Banzu winced. "I didn't mean for this to happen, I swear. I just wanted to help her."

"We'll talk about that later. Right now someone needs to go clean up that mess of bodies you two left out there." Jericho glanced east through the black pitch. "Maybe I can still fix things." He stared through Banzu at the cabin, more so the woman inside. "Some things, anyhow."

"I had to do it," Banzu said. "They would've killed her if I hadn't stopped them. There wasn't anything else I could've—"

"You don't have to explain yourself to me. Those days are over. What's done is done. Just go back inside. Keep her busy till I get back. I've work to do thanks to you."

Banzu hesitated. "I'm really sorry."

"Yeah. Well." Jericho looked away. "Doesn't matter now, does it?"

Banzu cringed. "No," he whispered. He turned for the door, turned back. "What about her?"

"She's right. After what she did . . . what you both did, more will come. I'll deal with her when I get back. For now you just stay put. And keep your trap shut. You've mucked things up enough as it is. Don't sink us any deeper or there'll be no clawing out."

"I won't," Banzu said.

Jericho walked away.

Something wrong and cold slithered in Banzu's gut while turning for the door. He paused, hand on handle, frowning, then, slowly, inexorably as comprehension dawned, his eyes widened, that cold slither of wrongness prickling through his guts. *No. He won't. He can't.*

"Wait!" He chased after Jericho, grabbed him by the arm, stopping and turning his uncle round. Hard eyes met his questioning own, but he dared not shy away, not now.

"What do you mean you'll deal with her?" But he already knew the answer. Should've expected no other recourse the moment he agreed to bring her there.

Jericho's hard stare answered volumes of murder.

"No." Banzu shook his head. "No." He jabbed a finger in his uncle's face. "No!"

Jericho swatted that admonishing hand and all its accusations aside. "You know how this has to go, Ban. They came for her, and they'll keep coming until they have her. She doesn't know what you are, which means they don't know about you. Yet. And I didn't spend all these years keeping you safe for nothing. The less we leave behind the better."

"No. You can't—" But he clipped short, the rest of his words stolen by the cold detached stare of a natural killer where played predatory cunning behind those calculating blues, setting Banzu on wary edge.

"You know what has to be done," Jericho said. "It's best if you make your peace with it now."

Banzu's guts plunged. "But we can help her."

Jericho shook his head.

"We can't just kill her."

Silence.

"I can't let you—" Banzu began then clipped short, nerves frazzled, pulse quickening, palms sweaty, feet shifting. "I won't let you—" He clipped again, unable to finish the worst of his fears aloud.

Jericho looked down between them, withdrew a single step, mouth a tight line, gaze a steady bead on Banzu's hand gripping the hilt of his sword still sheathed at his left hipwing. He raised his gaze, stood his ground. "You do what you have to do."

Banzu jolted at his hand having pursued the hilt by instinct. And yet . . . and yet he maintained his grip, taut muscles primed for the blade's pulling.

Silence wedged between them . . . and just like that, ties forever severed.

Without another word Jericho turned and walked away, fading into the dark gloom.

Banzu stared after him, lingering in despair. He forced the slow release of his tremulous hand, fingers peeling from leather-wound hilt. He raked that hand back through his hair and blew out his cheeks. *Gods, what a friggin mess.*

He returned inside the cabin, preparing a defense against the sure flurry of questions about Jericho's absence. Then thanked all the gods of Melora fast asleep in her chair, cocooned within her cloak, her fiery spirit no match to exhaustion.

He crept to the rocker across from her, undid his belt and eased down while wincing through its announcing creaks then rested scabbard and sword across his lap, held the hilt in a lazy grip for ease of pulling.

He watched her sleep while awaiting his uncle's return, knots of looming dread twisting his guts, the events of the day replaying through his mind punctuated by knifing flashes of his killing part in them.

Until sleep pulled at him with torpid, heavy hands.

He slid out his heels and stretched his legs, yawning.

Eyes fluttering, lids heavy.

Mind fuzzy, his tired body betrayed him.

Within moments he sat fast asleep.

* * *

Banzu stopped breathing.

He startled awake, eyes snapping open, limbs flailing, Jericho's strong hand clamped over his mouth, the other raised with a finger barring lips.

"Shhhh."

Banzu froze while breathing through his nose.

Jericho peeled his hand away, gestured with his eyes across the room at Melora still curled in deep slumber. "Outside," he whispered, then crept to the door and left.

Banzu eased out from the rocker, wincing through its betraying creaks. He belted the sword back round his waist and made his way outside, muscles stiff from the awkward position of his nap. He closed the door in soft pull, walked to where his uncle stood waiting twenty paces away. He rubbed the sand of sleep from his eyes.

The blood-red sun peeked over the eastern treetops, announcing another day.

"Morning already?" Banzu's breath misted in the morning chill. He stretched on tippy-toes, back arching, arms out at his sides, mouth gaping in a long yawn. Then he stopped mid-stretch, taking due notice of Jericho's change of clothes, the floppy black hat, the packed rucksack beside him . . . and the true sword Jericho wore sheathed at his left hipwing.

Griever, the exquisite sword of his uncle's past. Jericho kept the personal treasure locked in his private trunk, hidden away with the rest of his former life and all its unspoken pains. He only removed the superb weapon for an occasional cleaning twice per year, and sometimes Banzu enjoyed the pleasure of holding the flawless perfection of steel—though only brief and before its cleaning so as not to tarnish the immaculate blade with skin oils.

Eleven years since Griever last adorned Jericho's hip. The sight of it now stole the voice from Banzu's lungs.

"I'm going to Fist," Jericho said, as if that were that, the sky blue and water wet. He'd returned sometime during the night, sneaked inside and gathered his things while Banzu and Melora slept.

"You're leaving?" Banzu asked. "Now? But what about her?"

"Plans change."

"So we're not—" Banzu paused, tensing, glancing at the cabin. "You're not going to—"

"No. We don't have to kill her."

Banzu relaxed. *Oh thank gods.* "So what do we do about her then?"

"We?" Jericho smirked. "You are going to stay put and make sure nothing happens to her. Asides,"—he dipped one hand into a pocket and pulled out a wadded ball of purple cloth—"I'll be much faster on my own."

"On your own?" Banzu frowned. "Wait a minute. If you're going then—what is that?"

Jericho separated the purple wad, revealing two foot-shaped coverings. He bent and pulled them over his boots, first right then left, both a snug fit.

"What are those?" Banzu asked.

Jericho grinned, a playful twinkle in his eyes. "Now they're my boots of blinding speed. Watch."

He spun round, whispered some manner of incantation lost to Banzu's hearing, took a single step forward—and shifted into a blurring streak of rapid movement covering the distance of ten full paces in one singular step.

Banzu startled, blinked hard. "What the frig?"

"See?" Jericho shot him an over the shoulder smirk. He stepped backwards with the same foot—and returned to his original spot in reversing blurring streak. He whispered the incantation again before turning round, smiling.

"Uhm," Banzu said. "What just happened?" He rubbed his lying eyes. "Did you just do what I think you did?"

Jericho nodded, busy black eyebrows dancing. "Yup. And precisely why I'll get there faster alone." He picked up the rucksack and slung it over a shoulder, arm stabbing through the loop of one strap. "I've got to be careful though. One wrong step and I'll end up kissing a tree." A playful wink. "And I'm ugly enough as it is."

Banzu stared at his uncle's boots. "Where'd you get those?"

"I've had them for as long as I've had you," Jericho said. "Only you don't remember. You were too young and scared back then. Too soon after the fire and—but never mind all that anyhow. Aggie retrieved them from a Builder's tower after we found out about you." He plucked the silver ring of his brass necklace, kissed it, tucked it beneath his collar and sighed. "She sacrificed a lot to help me keep you safe."

Aggie. Banzu frowned, the truth of his uncle's 'lucky charm' a wedding ring revealed the previous night. A fire rekindled inside, bridled anger flaring.

"Yeah," he said. "About that. A wife? Were you ever going to tell me? All these years and here you've been lying the whole friggin time." He jabbed a finger in his uncle's face. "I want answers, and I want them now."

"I never lied," Jericho said, tone stern. "I only stretched the truth a bit. And left some other parts out." He swatted Banzu's hand away and replaced it with his jabbing own. "And you remember who you're talking to. There's a whole lot that needs explaining, I know, but now's not the time. I need to get to Fist and handle some business. And you"—he poked Banzu's chest for emphasis—"are staying put until I get back, you hear me?"

Banzu huffed and swatted his uncle's hand away. "So you're taking off. Without any explanation. And you're just going to leave me here. With her?" He crossed his arms and muttered, "She's as mean as a hydraviper."

Jericho chuckled, shrugged. "She's a looker though, huh?"

"Yeah," Banzu said, allowing a small smile. "She is pretty—wait, what?"

Jericho grinned though sobered it away. "I did my best to clean up that mess you two left behind. There's no tracks leading back here now despite you fools snapping every twig and printing every patch of mud from here to Green River. The Enclave is serious business, Ban. And they're not the kind to give up easy. You see anyone, you hide, understand? She doesn't know about you, and you have to keep it that way. If she finds out what you really are . . . well, she might try something stupid. And then you'll have no choice because she won't give you one."

Banzu sighed, glanced at the cabin. "Why can't I come with you? I don't understand—"

"And you don't have to. Some things are better left alone until they're finished. But believe me, this is necessary."

"Yeah. Right." A flash of remembrance. The arching of his brows. "That letter she brought. What did it say?"

Jericho frowned, shook his head. "That's my business, not yours."

"That's not good enough," Banzu said, refusing surrender. Something removed murder from his uncle's mind and he wanted to know why. "After everything that's happened, and now you're just up and leaving like this? I deserve an explanation."

Jericho worked his jaw, chewing his words before spitting them out. "It's a meeting. Nothing more."

"A meeting," Banzu said in monotone. "About what?" He thinned his eyes. "What aren't you telling me?"

Jericho sighed. "I've never lied to you, Ban. I've kept certain things from you for your own good, but I've never lied to you." A lengthy pause, more chewing of words. "Answer me something. When you came across her out there, why'd you do it?"

Banzu shrugged. "I had to. They were going to kill her."

"And you could've let them. But you didn't. Why?"

"I couldn't just let them kill her. I had to do something."

"And I have to do this," Jericho said. "Do you trust me?"

Banzu looked at his uncle funny, enduring a guilty pang upon hesitating. After last night . . . but even that did not erase the years of trust between them. "Of course I do. You know that."

"Then trust me now. You're better off not knowing until I get back. I don't want to get your hopes up if I'm wrong and it all turns out for nothing. Now seize the Power."

"What? Why?"

"Humor me."

Banzu drew in an apprehensive breath; he hadn't seized the Power since his encounter with Melora and her Enclave chasers. He closed his eyes, braced, and through focal invocation seized the Power. The quickening rush of magical potency flushed through him same as always, familiar and unchanged and untainted by the bloodlust. He released his inner grasp, the Power leaving him along with a relieving exhale, and opened his eyes.

"How's it feel?" Jericho asked.

Banzu shrugged. "The same, I guess."

"You guess or you know?"

Banzu nodded, glanced down as his uncle's hand gripping Griever's hilt. "It's the same."

Jericho smiled, relaxing. He released his grip of hilt and slapped Banzu on the shoulder. "Thank the gods. After what happened, well, I only figured otherwise after some heavy thinking."

"What do you mean?"

"She saved your life and you don't even know it. A Spellbinder's void-aura nullifies all other forms of magic within a certain distance of them. You didn't awaken the bloodlust because you were inside hers when you killed those khansmen. Otherwise you wouldn't be you anymore."

Jericho removed his floppy black hat, smoothed his hair back, replaced it, squinted at the cabin. "I ain't never met one so powerful before. I was flexing squeezes for the Power while we were talking and I didn't feel a thing. Her void-aura radiates from her far beyond the normal range. Usually it's only a foot or two at most, sometimes only inches from their skin, but hers is strong. Count yourself lucky she was there."

So she kept me from turning while I killed those khansmen. Friggin frig. He'd never taken a human life before, let alone two, and almost died in the process. He touched at his throat in absent reminder of Big Ugly's strangling choke, neck muscles still tender from that crushing squeeze, then caught Jericho with a curious squint.

"Is that how you did it?" he asked.

"Did what?"

"When you came back from the bloodlust. Did Aggie—"

"I'm not talking about that," Jericho said, curt and final.

Banzu prodded elsewhere. "So how long are you going to be away?"

Jericho shrugged. "Don't know. A few weeks, maybe more." He glanced at his boots covered in the magic purple fabrics. "I haven't used these since I brought you here, so it'll take me a limbering stretch or three to get used to them again." He turned away, gauging east. "Get back inside and mind what I've told you."

"A few weeks," Banzu muttered, then added in louder voice, "And what am I supposed to do with her? Tie her to that chair before she wakes up? She'll cut me three ways from sideways when she finds out you're gone without her."

Jericho chuckled, turned round. "I'm sure you'll think of something. Asides, she'll probably sleep the next few days after all she's been through. It's a long haul on foot from Fist, especially with khansmen chasing you the whole way. Let alone braving the Jackals of Mar festering all over the Calderos. You just sit tight. When she does wake up, tell her only what she needs to know. Play stupid." A pausing smirk. "So act natural."

Banzu frowned. "Hey."

Jericho continued. "You're just watching my things while I'm away. Other than that you don't know jack about squat. She won't have no other choice but to stay here until I get back anyways." He grinned at his boots. "What's she going to do, chase me? I'll be miles gone before you even get back inside."

"And if others do come? What then?"

All mirth fled Jericho's face, his jovial tone fading. "Then you do what you have to do. You wanted to play the hero, well now's your chance. Just stay close to her. If you're inside of her void-aura then you won't be able to use the Power which means you won't be able to give yourself away. And more importantly, if others do come, that'll keep you from turning if they leave you no choice. Gods know you've got the skills."

Banzu frowned, knowing what no choice meant: killing. Again. He shifted his stance, the sword at his side heavier than it had a right to be.

"Best I be off." Jericho started into a parting hug but stopped short and offered his hand instead.

They shook, the lean, cabled muscles of those familiar with hard, repetitive swordwork flexing strong.

"I wish I could go with you," Banzu said.

"I know. But right now your place is here. She may be a spitfire but she needs you. Promise me you'll do as I say."

Banzu nodded. "I will."

"Say it."

Banzu rolled his eyes. "I promise."

Jericho thinned his eyes, his tone. "Say it like you mean it."

Banzu sighed. "I promise I'll look after her."

"And?"

Another roll of his eyes. "And keep my trap shut."

"That's better." Jericho turned to go.

"Wait."

He turned back. "What?"

"That warlord," Banzu said, tensing, fearing the answer. "Hannibal Khan. Are you really going to kill him?"

Jericho shook his head. "The Academy's affairs ain't my affairs anymore. I'm on my own business, and when it's settled I'll be on my way whether Gwen likes it or not. However they deal with him is on them. Like I said, it's just a meeting, nothing more."

"You think it's true? That he can shoot lightning and all that?"

"I don't know. But Aggie never would've given me away unless she thought it absolutely necessary. And Gwen certainly would have never agreed to—" Jericho clipped his words short with a grimace. "Too much to explain right now. Best I be off before I start growing roots. And don't you go fiddling in my trunk, you hear? I'll see you when I see you." He turned to go.

But Banzu caught him by the arm, turning him back. And held his uncle's gaze a silent length. *Everything's changing. I can feel it.* "What if you don't come back? Or what if you do but—"

But he couldn't finish voicing Jericho returning possessed by the bloodlust, his uncle no more.

"The gods know we haven't had it easy," Jericho said. "But sometimes things change for the better, and I'm hoping this is finally one of those times. Hope for the best—"

"But prepare for the worst," Banzu finished by rote. "Yeah yeah, I know." He feigned a smile. "You'd better tell me everything when you get back. And I mean everything. Those boots, your wife, that meeting. All of it. I'm not a kid anymore, so stop treating me like one."

Jericho nodded, smiled. "No more secrets. I'll spill my beans when I get back." He glanced at Banzu's sword. "Asides, it's about time I told you everything anyhow."

"Promise?"

"Yeah."

Banzu smirked. "Say it like you mean it."

Jericho chuckled. "I promise."

"You'd better."

"Go on, now. Get. You know I hate goodbyes."

"This isn't goodbye."

"Yeah, I know but—*hey!*" Jericho startled back a step while pointing past his flinching nephew. "What's that?"

"What?" Banzu spun round, tensed, hand gripping hilt. "What's what?" He saw nothing but the trees. "I don't see any—" He turned back. "—thing."

To Jericho already speeding away in a blurring streak, each step carrying his uncle the distance of ten until Jericho slipped into the eastern trees and disappeared into the forest beyond, gone.

* * *

Banzu lingered in pensive stare, the rising sun breaking over the high treetops and giving him squints. So much more he wanted to know but now he had to play the waiting game until his uncle returned.

If he returns . . . no, best not to think that way.

"A few weeks," he muttered. "Friggin hell."

Melora possessed plenty of answers, but he had to keep his mouth shut round her lest he reveal the truth. The gods only knew what might happen then.

Sure, she slept now, but what about when she woke up? He toyed with tricking her into drinking some moonglum tea, only he had no idea if the sleeping draught would even work on someone like her.

And even if it does, then what? Somehow trick her into drinking a cup every few hours until Jericho returns? Hold her pinned and force it down her throat? Too much of the stuff and she'll sleep forever.

He sighed, jealous at the chance for leaving despite the reasons why. *If not for those friggin boots!*

He walked toward the cabin while contemplating its sleeping occupant within and what to do about her. A strange turn of events brought her into his life—*Melora, such a pretty name, Melora. I wonder if she's married?* He sighed. *Everything's changing.*

But maybe things weren't so bad after all. He'd killed, true, but he did so while saving her life and without triggering the bloodlust. That fact put a proud spring in his step. It felt more than good, felt meaningful. And he realized then what she'd given him: a purpose.

Smiling big as he approached the cabin, ready to slip back inside and wait out the day while preparing for the sure fury of her ire when she woke and found Jericho gone.

At least the Power's back.

He reached the door—just as it burst open wrongways on its protesting hinges, frame splintering, the swinging door's edge hitting him square in the face.

CHAPTER FIVE

"Friggin hell!"

Banzu stumbled backwards while clutching the flaring abuse of his struck face, vision a hot blur of tears. Bearings scattered, he sank to one knee and groaned, his face a throbbing nest of pain from the door hitting him.

Melora charged outside the cabin and stormed passed him. She stopped, scanned round, turning this way and that, cloak swirling, eyes darting, curses flowing. Then she rounded on Banzu.

He stood on shaky legs, pinching his throbbing nose, afraid he'd lost a few front teeth. A quick probing of his tongue, the salty taste of blood, and he thanked the gods he still possessed all his teeth intact. He lowered his hand, sniffed into his palm. No blood there, at least. He pinched the aching bridge of his nose, fearing it broken, and jerked his hand away, hissing. Sore but no break. And it throbbed something fierce.

He turned, wiping his palm clean on his thigh, and met the fiery glare of the culprit to his throbbing face.

Melora eyeballed him hard, a feral she-cat shifting her feet in preparatory pounce. "How could you let me fall asleep!"

"Huh?" The accusation slapped him out from one daze and in to another. He blinked hard. "What?"

"Where is he? Where's Jericho?"

"Oh." Banzu sniffed, winced. "He's gone." He wriggled his nose. "You know, you should really watch where you're going." He glanced at the cabin's front door, either shouldered or kicked open from within, its warped hinges ruined, its frame splintered. "And learn how to open a friggin door." *Now I have to fix the friggin thing and—*

"Gone?" Apparently hearing none of the rest, she closed the distance between them in three stomping strides. "He gone?" She fisted Banzu up by the nape of his shirt and jerked him closer. "What do you mean he's gone?" She thinned her eyes into a cutting glare. "If you have any part in him escaping me I swear by all the gods I'll—"

"What? No! I didn't—"

"Godsdammit." She huffed a derisive breath in his flinching face then shoved him back two stumbling steps. "Godsdammit." She turned round, scanned round. "Godsdammit." She tugged at the kohatheen collar fastened round her neck. "Godsdammit!"

"Easy," Banzu said. "He'll be back just as soon as he—hey stop that!" He backed away while slapping at her darting hands when she attempted fisting him up by the shirt again.

"Where is he? Where'd he go? Tell me. Now!"

"He left for Fist." Banzu pointed past her, east. "Just like you wanted."

She scrunched her face ugly while glaring east, then spun round and spat. "Godsdammit." Then proceeded to stomp the ground three times while rage-chanting: "Dammit! Dammit! Dammit!" Her outburst expelled, she stalked away. East.

"Wait!" Banzu called out. "You'll never catch up to him!" He watched her go, a smirk toying on his lips. Then frowned when he realized she wasn't listening, wasn't going to give up and come back because she had no idea of Jericho's magic boots. *Friggin hell.* "Wait!"

She ignored him.

Banzu caught up from behind, intent on grabbing her by the shoulder to stop her but withdrew his reaching hand inches before contact as those hidden twin fanged daggers of hers flashed cautious reminder in his mind.

"You'll never catch up to him," he said, talking to her back. "He's too far gone by now."

She fetched no look back. "I didn't come all this way just to let him slip through my fingers."

"You don't understand, you can't catch up. He's using magic for faster travel."

Melora stopped. Spun round. Struck Banzu with a flurry of rapid-fire questions rife with accusations and curses. He tried explaining as best he could, only instigating her fury. Trying to change her mind proved akin to convincing fire not to burn, and he hadn't even finished his third sentence before she charged away again.

He watched her go. "Really?" Threw his hands overhead. "Seriously?" Lowered his arms and grumbled, "Stubborn as a friggin stump."

And chased after her again, catching up from behind.

"Stop following me," she said.

He huffed and rolled his eyes at the back of her head. "You're not listening—"

"No, *you're* not listening." She glared over a shoulder, eyes violet fire, voice a lashing whip. "Go away!"

He chewed back a frustrated string of curses. "You can't just leave."

"Watch me." She sped up.

So did he, ignoring that fierce sideways glare when he caught up alongside her. "You're supposed to stay here. Why won't you listen?"

"Because."

"Because why?"

She stopped and stared him down. "I have enough problems as it is. I don't need one more following after me. What don't you understand?" A pause, an overemphasis of every word: "Leave. Me. Alone!" She walked away.

He caught up again, matching stride beside her. "You don't get it. He's long gone by now. And he said to stay here until he gets back, and—"

"Jericho can kiss my rosy red cheeks for all I care. Crack too. It's my duty to bring him back"—she tugged at her kohatheen, grimacing—"one way or another." Then jabbed a stiff pointer in Banzu's face. "And no one's going to keep me from it. Didn't you listen to anything I said last night? Hannibal Khan must be stopped. And to do that I have to return to Fist—*with Jericho.*"

She estimated him a silent length, crinkled her nose and gave a dismissive flick of her wrist. "What do you care, anyways? You're not aizakai. None of this even concerns you so go away."

Banzu opened his mouth for feisty rebuttal—then closed it without word, slowing behind her, stung in an unfamiliar way. One errant slip of his tongue and things would turn for the worse. He needed to stop her but she refused listening to reason.

Friggin hell. If she's not going to stop then I'll make her stop.

He raced past her, pulling his sword, turned round and blocked her path. "I said stop!"

She stopped. Frowned. Eyeballed him up and down. "You have to be kidding me."

"I promised to look after you while he's away and I aim to keep it," he said, raising the sword between them in threat of skewering her. In his best commanding tone he added, "So turn around." He waggled the sword. "Now."

An amused smirk toyed across her lips beneath thinning eyes. She glanced at the sword leveled between them as if it proved no more threatening than a child's stick. She met his gaze with challenge and took a deliberate step forward, one eyebrow cocked. "And if I don't?"

"Uhm." He took an immediate step back, eyes darting from her to sword and back again. "Then I'll, uhm, I swear I'll, uh, I'll . . ."

But his tongue turned a fumble, thoughts hitting a mental wall. *What can I do, stab her? Friggin hell, she knows I'm bluffing. She'll probably impale herself just do her stupid duty. Friggin hell!*

She advanced another challenging step, bringing her chest to within inches of the sword's tip. "You'll what?"

He chewed back a frustrated curse. "I'll, uhm, stop you?" And winced, the words betraying more meek question than bold statement. He rumbled his throat clear, added in firmer tone, "I'll stop you."

She slid her right foot back, hips twisting cocked, hands withdrawing inside and up behind her flapping cloak, what little patience she possessed killed by her challenging glare and dangerous smile. "You can try."

He wavered, feet nervous shifts, and stared into those rancorous violets dissecting every piece of him. Until the absurdity of it all struck him for the fool she thought of him.

Haven't I done enough by saving her life? By the gods, I killed two men already and all she's given me is a disgruntled thanks and a stupid coin! Who am I to stop her if she wants to take off on some impossible chase? Let her wear herself out. She'll come crawling back.

"Fine," he said, and lowered his sword. "You win." He stepped aside and waved her on by. "You want to go? Then go. Just don't blame me when you get yourself killed."

She scrunched her face in bitter twist, furious at the attack on her competence. Then shoved past him despite the space allowed. "I can take care of myself, thank you very much."

Turning, watching her go, Banzu stabbed his sword into the worn leather scabbard at his left hipwing with more force than necessary. "Fine," he grumbled. He crossed his arms and huffed a terse breath. In a louder voice he added, "Fine." Then uncrossed his arms and threw them overhead, yelled at her shrinking back, "See if I care!"

***

Banzu entered the cabin all grumbling curses. He tried slamming the door to punctuate his foul mood but it mocked his efforts by swinging loose on busted hinges.

Godsdamn that crazy woman!

He paced the foreroom in careless strides, throwing curses while kicking things out from his way. When he plopped down into the nearest chair he jolted to his feet, yelping and cursing, his sword having caught and pinched his skin.

Godsdammit!

He fought the belt undone from round his waist and threw it across the room before plopping back down unimpeded.

And there he tried focusing on anything other than Melora. But flaring frustrations afforded a short attention span. She might as well be standing there slapping him upside the head while he tried not thinking of her.

He drew in a deep breath, exhaled overlong through pursed lips. "Relax," he muttered through clenched teeth. "Just relax. Everything will be fine once Jericho gets back."

Godsdamn you, Jericho, leaving me like this.

Another deep inhale, another tense exhale. He gripped the chair's armrests and strangled the wooden necks, taut forearms trembling so that he forced release of his hands and sighed.

Godsdamn her.

Whether he liked it or not, a bond existed between them now.

She saved me from the bloodlust, but I saved her life in turn. An even trade as far as I'm concerned, not that she knows anything of it.

So why do I feel so guilty?

More will come, that's friggin why.

He glanced at the half-open door hanging crooked on busted hinges while wondering how long before she realized her chase a fool's endeavor and came back. But that much crushed to dust beneath the gravity of her reality.

Abrasive, stubborn, a sharp-tongued fool who—

He drew in a calming breath.

She's a strong woman. No, a violet-eyed viper. Possessed by duty and a one track mind to see it done. Gods, talking to her is like beating my friggin head against a friggin wall. Might as well expect the sun not to rise as expect her to come back and admit how right I am.

She deserves what she gets. Probably lost already. Won't know her bung from a hole in the ground in those woods.

And more will come.

"Shut up," he muttered. "Just shut the hell up already."

But the internal voice persisted, impossible to ignore . . . *more will come.*

He sat stewing, grumbling in resentful deliberation for one-half turn of an hour, making the same conclusion no matter how he turned or twisted the situation.

She needs my help whether she wants it or not. My fault if she gets killed. I can't—-I won't let that happen. Friggin hell. I didn't save her just to let her die.

Her and her stupid duty.

He sat forward, sat back, wrestling hesitation. Something new had awakened inside him with their chance encounter, something vital, and soothing to the festering ache he carried in the guarded depths of his heart. No, not just an ache soothed but a hunger fed. A powerful hunger craving more.

Protecting Melora evoked a necessary function of his worth as a swordslinger, but more so as a man.

And he promised Jericho to look after her.

He bared a wicked grin. "I'll show her duty."

He smacked the chair's armrests then his thighs while erupting into standing. He spent a few minutes gathering necessaries for his journey ahead, stuffing a rucksack and reclaiming his thrown sword.

He strode outside, seized the Power and sped away in a determined blur of Power-fueled momentum knifing east.

* * *

Covering multiple miles within scant minutes, Banzu sped between the Power-grey trees stealing past his heightened peripherals though released his inner grasp on the Power at first sight of that disturbing blur of magic-nullifying void-aura bubble shimmering the air round Melora walking far ahead, that void-aura shimmer of air disappearing upon the Power's release. He slowed into a steady stroll without fetching her notice, careful not to crunch any leaves or snap any twigs underfoot in his devious stalking.

He admired her swaying backside while approaching from behind, the form-hugging cloak cinched tight round her slim waist and gripping her hips, its split bottom hanging loose round her long-striding legs. He closed distance to within a few paces and broke into a whistling jaunty.

Melora stopped, stiffened, spun round, violet eyes flashing wide with surprise then thinning into suspicious slits.

Banzu stopped, smiled and waved. "Hello again."

"How did you—" she began only to clip short while leaning aside, gazing past him on down the long and empty trail cutting through the forest behind. "When did you—" She scrunched her face, upset he'd snuck up on her without notice. "Where did you come from?"

He grinned and did the best he could feigning an indifferent shrug considering the rucksack strapped to his back. "I'm a fast runner."

She frowned, unamused. "I told you to stop following me. You're not a part of this, and I don't need you slowing me down."

He laughed. "*Me* slow *you* down?"

"Go away." She turned round and walked away.

Banzu raked one hand back through his hair and blew out his cheeks. *Okay, if this is how she wants to play it.* He jumped into step, caught up alongside her. "Nice day out for a stroll."

Silence, and faster walking.

He sped up. "So, are you from around these parts?"

Silence, scowling.

"I'm headed to Fist. How about yourself?"

Silence punctuated by a contemptuous sidelong glare.

"I hear tell you have a map you can't read on your own," he said, poking at fire—and it felt good.

She opened her mouth—then snapped it shut with an ivory click of bared teeth.

Enough funning. "Look. You said it yourself. More of those khansmen will come. I promised Jericho I'd look after you. And whether you like it or not you need my help. Asides,"—he patted the sword at his hip for show and grinned—"I can protect you."

She stopped. Glared him down. "Protect me?" She planted fists to hips. "What do you think this is, some kind of game? We're talking life and death here. I don't know what you uncivilized, uneducated, ignorant mountainboys do out here with your time, but you can just go back to doing it because I don't want your help. I made it here on my own and I can make it back—*on my own*." She jabbed a finger in his face and yelled, "Go away!" Then continued on her way.

Banzu watched her go, face flushing hot, pride bruised. He clenched his hands into tight fists at his sides and grit his teeth to refrain from lunging after her and choking her pretty little head off her shoulders. He drew in a deep nostril breath and yelled out his frustrations at the top of his lungs: "Stop!"

And to his surprise she actually stopped.

Anger flaring, he strode right up to then rounded on her, met those violet eyes in stern challenge, stuck *his* finger in *her* face. "You didn't make it all the way here on your own. And you're forgetting those khansmen I killed to keep you alive. Do you have any idea what that felt like? What it still feels like? I've never killed anyone before! So the way I see it you owe me for that. Asides, you think you're the only one with something to lose? Jericho's my—"

Uncle. But he clipped short just in the nick before his tongue betrayed him.

"Jericho's my friend. My best friend. And now he's run off to deal with the gods only know what because of you. You're so friggin determined to do your duty, well I have a duty too and that's protecting you. I already told you there's no catching up with him. But you won't listen past the roots in your ears. So I'm coming with you."

She opened her mouth for feisty rebuttal.

And he talked right over her.

"I didn't save your life just so you could go and get yourself killed. So we can stand here arguing about this all day long if that's what it takes, but I'm coming with you whether you like it or not. And that's that!"

She stared back mute, eyebrows cocked, rage boiling beneath the surface of her twitching visage. She looked poised and ready to explode into him tooth and nail. Until an eerie calm settled over her while played a curious notion of cunning behind those violet eyes assessing all of him.

She held his gaze an extra measure before shoving past him. "Fine."

Surprise replaced anger in the span of a coinflip. "Fine?"

"Fine!" she shouted, fetching no look back.

"Fine," he repeated, slack-jawed and watching her stalk away. *Well, that was . . . easy?*

* * *

Catching up proved the easy part, keeping up the hard.

Banzu spent the last eleven years hiking these familiar mountainside woodlands, though now even his healthy stamina waned while matching stride with Melora's dogged pace. *But if she thinks she'll exhaust me away then she's in for a rude awakening.*

He wondered how long she expected to maintain such brisk walking, and wanted to warn her to slow before she collapsed from exhaustion, but he feared another tongue lashing so that he decided on a more subtle approach. He slowed his pace, hoping she would slow with him.

And nope.

So he trailed behind, refusing to catch up. And once more the pleasant allure of her swaying backside seduced the full attentions of his lingering stare. The surrounding woodlands diminished for a time, and all thoughts fled save for those of the beautiful woman walking ahead under the brunt of his groping gaze, the steady rhythm of her shifting hips drawing him in, the form-hugging cloak cinched tight round her slender middle accentuating hidden curves.

She moved with the natural flow of a dancer's fluid grace, as if her body forgot how to be clumsy in even the most minor of ways. For a long while he followed, enticed by that disarming snake-charmer's swaying gait, a big grin at play on his face, carnal lusts aroused by the hidden depths of those concealed mysteries.

"You intend on staring at my backside the whole time?" she asked without looking back.

He startled, and almost tripped over his own bumbling feet when he caught up alongside her, face flushing hot. He rumbled his throat clear for a quick change of subject. "You need to slow down. Fist is a long ways from here. No sense in exhausting ourselves before we get there."

"We." She scoffed the word, her face a bitter twist. "I don't have time for a casual stroll. You let Jericho get away, and on top of that I have duties in Tyr before I return to the Academy. Duties he was supposed to help me with. And now—" She clipped short, flicking her dismissive wrist at him in the manner of swatting away her annoying Banzu gnat.

"I didn't let anybody do anything," he said. "Jericho's his own man, and he never would've left if not for you anyhow."

"You think I wanted this? I was perfectly fine until that godsdamned Khan showed up and ruined everything. And if Jericho hadn't run off years ago I wouldn't even be here." She glowered, muttered, "That godsdamned fool."

Banzu smirked. "That fool is the smartest person I know."

She thinned her eyes upon him. "And how do you know him again?"

He averted his gaze, deciding on a change of subject before another accidental slip of the tongue. "What's in Tyr?"

"Oh, I forgot. You're probably too busy humping goats to keep up with the rest of the world." She huffed and muttered something under her breath.

Ignoring her goat-humping slight, he waited for the answer, but she spared none. "Well? What's in Tyr?"

"None of your business, that's what."

"Really? Sounds important. None of my business. I always wanted one of those. How much do they sell for these days? I figure—"

She yelled, "Oh my gods do you ever stop talking!"

"Yes." He held a pause comprising all of two seconds. "So what's in Tyr?"

She grimaced. "If I tell you will you shut up?"

He considered her a short space, shrugged. "Maybe."

She sighed, rolling her eyes. "You're intolerable, you know that?"

He grinned. "I try my best."

She huffed then said, "King Garnihan closed Caldera Pass the moment he seized the Iron Crown of Tyr fifteen years ago. Which broke Tyr's allegiance to Fist after his rebellion, cutting all trading ties with Bloom along with the rest of Thurandy. The Pass has remained closed ever since. It's the only viable route through the Calderos Mountains into and out from Thurandy, and Garnihan closed it up like a puckered butthole. That's what took me so godsdamned long. Hiking over those godsdamned mountains takes a hell of a lot longer than going through." She gauged him with a sideways look, shook her head. "Why am I even telling you any of this?"

Banzu shrugged, smiled. "Because I'm a good conversationalist?"

Another sigh, another roll of her eyes.

Soon a familiar tree all twisted branches and gnarled roots caught Banzu's wandering gaze, its dark bark marked with an X in distinctive display Jericho carved thereon some few years ago, prompting Banzu's mind into working along another course.

"There's fresh water up that way." He pointed north. "A clean source from mountain runoff. I brought a few waterskins. Best we fill them now. There isn't another one around for miles."

"That way doesn't take me to Fist," she said without even looking, too adamant ahead.

"We need to fetch for water."

"So fetch."

"I'm not going without you."

"And I'm not stopping."

"We'll need the water."

"I'm not thirsty."

"You *will* be."

"*You* will be."

"What? What's that even mean? Of course I'll—"

"Shut up."

He chewed back a fiery retort, but it refused the full swallow. "Fine. Die from thirst. See if I care." *Why does she have to be so friggin difficult? Sooner or later she'll tire out, and it'll serve her right if I let her collapse just so she'll have to crawl the rest of the way.* "How you even made it here on your own is beyond me. All beauty and no brains, that's what you are."

He walked ahead five strides before realizing she stopped. He turned facing her. She stood silent, features unreadable. He feared prodding her one time too many and tensed, staying out from clawing reach. "What now?"

But she ignored him, turned her head while *sniff-sniff-sniffing* the air, nose twitching. She looked left and sniffed, right and sniffed, down and sniffed. She scrunched her face.

Banzu's eyes darted among the trees. "What's wrong? Did you hear something? See someone?" He gripped his sword's hilt in preemptive pull. "What?"

"I've changed my mind."

"About what?"

"The water. Where is it?"

"Oh." He pointed north. "That way."

Without another word she walked north.

* * *

Banzu parted the bushy screen of branches and stepped forth into the small glade Melora entered ahead of him. She squatted at the lip of the large source of fresh water pooled beneath a tall cliff of frosted jagged rocks, drinking from her cupped hands, hood pulled back, the tips of her long pale-blonde hair dangling atop her thighs. He approached next to her, set his rucksack down between them and worked a few minor kinks from his upper back and neck by rolling his shoulders and stretching his arms out.

"A bit cold, but it'll do." She stood, a thin trickle of water dribbling from her parting hands. She untied her belt from round her waist and let her cloak slide free of her arms after shrugging it off, dropping round her feet. She slipped off one boot then the other, then her socks, began undoing the buckled straps of the leather harness hugging round her trim torso, the handles of her fanged daggers sheathed angled down for easy reach from up behind though held in place by straps thumbed unbuttoned before the pull. She paused and peered over her left shoulder. "Turn around."

Banzu stared back mute. *What in friggin hell is she doing?*

"Gods I stink." She pulled her outer shirt up over her head and dropped it. "I haven't bathed in ages." Fingers fiddling with the front buttons of her white undershirt. Another pause, another left-shouldered peek, the thinning measure of her eyes. "I said turn around, you creep."

Oh my gods, is she . . . "What? Here? Now?"

She half-turned, cocked one eyebrow, her undershirt partially unbuttoned with the middle curves of her small breasts exposed.

He stared at that luscious V of bare flesh, raised his gaze and jolted caught dead to rights the instant he made eye contact with those violet spurs. Face flushing with heat, he spun round and presented her his back.

Soft laughter from behind. "And see that you keep it that way." The whispery sound of clothes sliding free of skin. "And don't even think about touching my dachras."

Sounds of splashing.

He glanced by his feet at her crumpled pile of dirty clothes, at the bunched leather straps of her strange weapon harness, the two sheathed dachras of her twin fanged daggers. *So that's what they're called, not daggers but dachras. Huh.* Then slowly, inch by twitching inch, he turned his head until he stole sight of Melora's bathing play within his peripheral from over his shoulder. New heat flushed elsewhere than his face.

She stood nude, facing the frosted cliffs, the kohatheen collar locked round her thin neck her only adornment, the water forming round her a shimmering skirt leaving the top half of hips and firm bottom exposed. She lowered herself, dipping beneath the cool pool's rippling surface, the top of her head disappearing for a few bubbling seconds then popping up. She flung her head back, long pale-blonde hair whipping out a rainbow mane of shimmering droplets through the air, some of which dappled Banzu's back and hair.

He spied numerous pink scars flawing her alabaster skin in haphazard trails of chicken scratch—across slender shoulders and down curved back, rounding hips and farther down atop glistening buttock arch while hinting at more upon long legs hidden beneath the water's reflective surface—and to his surprise the tableau of scars did not mar but added to the allure of her willowy beauty hardened in all the right places by strong muscles earned through rigorous training.

Dazed in lusty fascination, he turned evermore, stood all smiles and captured within the enticement of her bathing play. He drew in a breath, held it in an attempt to absorb the moment for all its worth. Her soft skin glistening under the bright afternoon sun shining down over the exposed glade through a break in the high canopy overhead. Cool mountain winds lapsing into a gentle breeze soughing through the trees and kissing over her lovely contours where danced athletic twitches of muscle. The way time seemed to slow while her slender arms guided working hands over supple curves and hidden parts, lapping water here, lapping water there.

Gods . . . she really is beautiful.

She caught him staring over a shoulder.

He startled flinched, eyes popping wide then snapping shut. He turned away, breathing hot and heavy, short and rapid, heart a quickened race. More splashing behind, but he dared not peek again. Then Melora's bare, glistening arm shot out beside him from behind, nudging him.

"It's cold." She waggled her fingers. "Give me something to dry off with."

"Uhm." He squatted and scrambled open his rucksack then rummaged through its content with fumbling hands. *What am I looking for again?* He found an extra shirt, held it up, eyes averted, then fell to task of digging out the forgotten waterskins.

"One for each." He set the two waterskins aside, then pretended more rummaging while she dried off behind him. Long legs stepped into his left peripheral, bare thighs inviting the turn of his head while she dressed, flapping out dust and dirt from each article of clothing in turn before pulling them on.

He made a conscious effort to keep his gaze everywhere but the one place it hungered to visit. He stood with two handfuls of various clutter he had no reason for holding.

"You're very beautiful," he said, cringing soon as the words escaped his errant tongue. He risked a sideways glance while trying to fight the stupid grin from his stupid face, but his stupid mouth refused obedience. He squeezed his hands, balling up wads of clothes in clenching fists, and wanted to bury his head in the ground to smother his burning cheeks.

He flinched when she turned him by the shoulder and shoved the damp wad of his shirt-turned-towel against his chest, forcing him to abandon everything in his hands lest it fall.

"I don't need your approval." She struck him with a glare that included him and every other man in the world. "I know what I look like. And I earned every one of them."

"Uhm." *Them. Not the beauty but the scars.* He shrank beneath the scrutiny of her chastising stare. But he did not look away. Instead he held the burning measure of her gaze, for in the moment he swore he detected a flicker of inner pain peeking from behind the high guarded wall of her defenses. The glimpse of something private and wounded, distinct from something so simple as physical scars.

Her stare wavered, shifted to the waterfall tinkling soft splashes over rocks.

"I'm sorry," he said. "I didn't mean—" He stopped, swallowed, began again. "I wasn't making fun. I meant you're pretty even with them." *Gods, that didn't come out right. What, she'd be prettier without them?* "The scars, I mean." *Just shut up, Ban.* "Sorry." *Stop talking!* "Uhm."

"Most of them were a parting gift from the Khan," she said, crossing her arms and staring ahead. "After I—" A wincing pause. "After I failed killing him, I barely escaped. I ran and hid but not well enough. He found me, called down more lightning. The blast threw me and the wall between us into the river across the street. If not for the waters carrying me away I'd be dead." She tugged at her kohatheen, wincing. "Or worse."

"Oh." He rubbed at his left shoulder by instinct, his own scars beneath. Then revealed them a peek by tugging his shirt aside.

She looked at the tortured tracks of his skin pinker than the rest of him, eyebrows curious arches, but said nothing, though the glare shied from her eyes.

Banzu focused on the damp wad of shirt in his hands, wrung it through a few awkward twists, squeezing out droplets of water speckling the toes of his boots, then did the only thing his brain allowed while affording no audible explanation: he smiled up at her.

Those piercing violets softened as her defensive countenance relaxed. "Silly boy." The tiniest hint of a smile crooked up one corner of her mouth, there then gone. "Just fill the godsdamned waterskins."

She walked away.

Banzu watched her leave. Looked down at the scatter of clothes round his feet and smiled. He shoved his rucksack full, filled the waterskins from the freshwater pool after fetching a satisfying drink, then hurried after her.

***

They traveled the rest of the day in silence, Melora glancing behind and Banzu following while pointing out every next necessary fork or bend in the trails snaking through the woodlands. She slowed her dogged pace, though not by much, the reality of never catching up to Jericho sinking in.

Farther down the mountainside, weaving round fat spruces and prickly pines damp with melted frost, towering oaks and aspens shivering loose light dustings of snowfall upon lifting breezes, at last leaving behind the sparse patches of snow which lay hidden away in some of the deeper pockets of stone untouched by the sun's rays for warmer climate below.

Though the brisk winds still carried the sharp bite of the great northern Thunderhell Tundra's southern-sweeping chill, the fresh smells of spring's thawing blew antagonist up from the lower regions, hinting at the warmer weather waiting to greet them once they descended the Kush Mountains and struck flatter terrain in the next several days.

The sky bruised purple. But before Banzu could survey a spot for making camp, Melora broke from their easterly path and chose one for them.

"We need a fire." She bent and gathered rocks to fashion a ring. Without looking up she added, "Get some wood."

Banzu unburdened his rucksack to the ground, contemplated telling her to ask instead of expect, then thought the better of engaging in a losing battle over her established chain of command.

He started off to task, a curious notion popping into his mind two steps away, giving him pause. He seized the Power—or tried to, but felt nothing of it while within the magic-nullifying range of her Spellbinder void-aura. So he held his seizing attempt as he walked away . . . *three, four, five* . . . counting out paces . . . *seven, eight, nine* . . . until the Power flared into flowing potency within, startling him stopped. *Ten.* He released it just as quick.

Melora peered up from the beginnings of her little circle of rocks at him just standing there. "Something wrong?"

"Ten paces," he whispered, relieved at the knowing. *Or there roundabouts.* Not that he'd taken an exact measurement.

She straightened, a rock in each hand, looked at him queer. "What?"

"Huh? Oh. Nothing." He smiled. "I'll be back."

She frowned and bent back to task.

He strode off into the woods, good to be alone with his thoughts after keeping such a tight-lipped rein on them. Then he cursed himself while ducking round a tree, realizing he could have given himself away with that little test of the Power out of sheer ignorance. He possessed no idea how a Spellbinder's aizakai power worked, only that it nullified magic round them once it intruded their void-aura. Hers ten paces by his rough estimate.

As he labored over the next hour fetching firewood, he couldn't shake the nagging suspicion she would be gone each time he returned with another armload of sticks. Though she remained every time instead of escaping during his absence. Finishing the rock circle. Then sitting and watching him while tugging on her kohatheen. Then hunched and cursing while trying to spark a fire to light with her scraping dachras but without the necessary dry kindling beneath her piled sticks. Then sitting cross-legged and glowering at the sticks as if to ignite them with her burning glare.

Upon his fifth return, Banzu surrendered to sympathy and, squatting beside her, arranged the sticks into a little teepee while explaining the shaving of thin kindling into its hollow.

"Despite the breath of poets," he said, "it takes more than a few sparks to ignite a fire. Once it smokes, start blowing. Not hard but steady. Or else you'll just blow it out. Here, do you want me to—"

She shoved then waved him away. "I got it, I got it." She shaved thin kindling strips from a stick with one of her dachras.

Nightfall descended.

He returned with his sixth armload of sticks to a smiling Melora sitting hunched before a lit fire and warming her hands, shadows dancing across her hooded facescape. She straightened, shoulders back, chin up, smiling proud.

"See?" she said. "Not so hard."

He returned her a smile, a nod. "I knew you could do it."

He dropped his armload of sticks atop the rest and sat facing her opposite the crackling fire between them. And wondered how she made it this far from Fist with no sure skills in wilderness survival, then chalked it up to that fiery spirit and tenacious drive. Still, how she hadn't froze let alone starved to death proved a tangled mystery better left unraveled for now.

Frowning, she muttered something, snapped the twig she'd been toying with in the dirt and tossed it into the dancing flames.

"What?" Banzu asked.

"Nothing." But her frown deepened, eyebrows twitching in irritation when she tugged upon the kohatheen. She uncrossed her legs only to crisscross them the other way, agitated at more than suffering the cold winds and the hard ground.

"What's wrong?" he asked. *Too many sticks up your butt?*

She glanced over the fire and huffed. "I was just wondering where Jericho is." She snatched up another stick, snapped it, tossed the two bits into the fire. "While I'm stuck here with you."

Banzu ignored the slight, thoughts reflexing inward. The Power connected them as it once had all Soothsayers, though he dared not explain that aloud. He could seize the Power, close his eyes and spin, and still point out the exact direction of his uncle's whereabouts if he focused hard enough. Though the actual distance between them remained a mystery, the direction itself never failed. Not that he would reproduce the trick for her.

Jericho knew more about Spellbinders than he ever let on, and since Banzu traveled with one he wanted to learn as much as possible. But he needed to broach the subject through subtle persuasion.

"Are there a lot of aizakai like you in your family?" he asked.

"Like me?" She frowned, eyes thinning. "What's that supposed to mean?"

He sighed. *Why does every answer have to be a bite with her?* "Nothing. I'm just making conversation is all."

"Yes," she said, tone flat. "We're all Spellbinders. Even my dear old father."

"But I thought—" He began then paused. Everyone knew all Soothsayers were male, same as all Spellbinders female. *No, she's mocking me. Again.* He plucked a pebble from the dirt, ignored the impulse of throwing it at her and flicked it into the fire, eliciting sparks. "You're really hard to get along with, you know that?"

"I'm also hungry." She crossed her arms, frown deepening. "But I'm undecided as to which delicious banquet before me to sample first, the rocks or the sticks. Because my *genius protector*," she overemphasized the words while scorning him with her eyes, "forgot to bring any food."

He sighed and rolled his eyes in surrender, catching her drift. "Fine." He stood. "I'll be back."

"Where are you going?"

Away from you. "To find some food." He unfurled an arm while gesturing her a mocking bow and a sarcastic, "M'lady."

She scowled. "I'm Spellbinder. It's Mistress, not m'lady."

"Oh, well then, excuuuuse me." Another mocking bow punctuated by a sarcastic, "Mistress."

"But you can't see anything."

That's what you think. He straightened. "Do you want to eat or not?"

"Yes," she said.

A little too curt for Banzu's liking so that he began sitting. "Because I can just—"

"No!"

He paused halfway down. "I didn't hear please."

Face scrunching, she bared her teeth in what past for a smile. "Please? I'm hungry."

That's better. Sort of. He straightened into standing. "Then I'll be back." He offered another bow. "Mistress Melora." And stalked off into the woods.

* * *

The black pitch of night beneath a moonless sky pinpricked by twinkling stars offered no hindrance to the Power illuminating the gloom into a vivid grey twilight, its luminous details sharp as crushed glass. All while leaching Banzu's lifeforce in cruel trade, though amplifying his senses ultra keen and slowing the world round him. His body craved rapid movement, but his hunt required slower focus.

The *heartbeat-of-the-world* thrumming in tune to his quickening own, he prowled through the woods guided by the faint though magnified *thump-thumping* patters of animal hearts distinct to his heightened hearing above nature's cacophony of buzzing and chirping insects. He stalked round bushes, eased branches aside, his creeping tread light and careful.

A particular Power-slowed motion caught his hunter's peripheral so that he burst after it, legs uncoiling springs, body fluid locomotion, recognizing his favorite boyhood chase.

Planting his next step atop a fallen trunk, he leaped, the Power-momentum propelling him up from the gnarled trunk, his launching boot scraping free bits of bark into lazy float. He sailed through the air over twenty feet with the ease of a normal man jumping a puddle, landed kicking up leaves, startling the hidden prey into slow-flowing response to bolt away but for that he snatched the frightened hare by its hind legs just as it sprang into a Power-slowed leap of escape.

Releasing the Power, he held the jostling catch out with a smile, allowing it to tire, then whispered a thanks to the creature before ending its life with the quick snapping of its neck.

Flickers of the Power sped him back to camp in mini-bursts, though he stumbled and groped the last stretch unaided so as not to give himself away. He approached holding the dead hare up for show, smiling. "You said you were hungry?"

Melora stared up from the fire, eyes wide. "That was fast."

"Uhm." He eyed the dangling hare, shrugged. *I should've waited a bit before coming back. Stupid!* "I, uh, was lucky. I found it caught in a snare. Trappers leave out so many they forget where they set half of them. This one was close by."

"Oh." She studied his furry catch, nose crinkling. "Well I'm not eating that if it was dead already. Who knows how long it's been out there."

"Not long, I promise."

He sat with legs crossed and lay the carcass on the ground in front of his V'd knees. "Can't be more than a day or so dead," he lied. "Or else another animal would've gotten to it first. Asides, the cold preserves the meat and—*hey!*"

That's when he noticed it. Melora, having gone through his rucksack during his hunting absence, sitting on his bedroll.

She smirked, said nothing. She patted the soft bedroll beneath her, then twisted on her bottom and lay down onto her side, propped her head up with an elbow and continued watching him. Satisfaction never looked so bold.

"Funny," he said, tone flat, eyes narrowed slits. "Reeeeal funny."

"What?" She feigned a hurt look, false pouting lips. "You don't expect me to sleep on the cold, hard ground do you?"

He sighed and rolled his eyes. "Of course not."

"Good." A smug smile before rolling onto her back, hands forming a finger-woven pillow beneath her head. She released a satisfied "Ahhhh*"* while making a show of stretching out her legs on his confiscated bedroll, the only one he thought to bring in his haste for leaving after her. "At lest one of us should sleep good tonight."

Banzu edged his teeth together, jaw tensing. He glared at the dead hare, drew in a calming breath through flaring nostrils. Entertained getting up and yanking the bedroll right out from under her. Rolling it up and beating her over the head with it. Or emptying the waterskins over her face the second she fell asleep. Or—

"Pouting isn't cooking that rabbit any faster," she said without looking.

"It's a hare," he said. "Not a rabbit. There's a difference."

"Whatever."

"I said I'd protect you, not serve you."

She rolled her head sideways, offered a feline grin. "I was being subtle."

He expelled a mirthless chuckle, muttered, "You're about as subtle as a punch in the face."

She sat up, eyebrows arched. "What was that?"

"Nothing." He removed his belt knife from his right hipwing to begin the necessary skinning and gutting.

"Eww." She scrunched her face in disgust. "You're not going to do that here are you?"

He ground his teeth, wanting to stab his knife into the hare and shake its guts out all over the place. Maybe cut open its belly and dump the bloody innards over her head. Maybe even scoop out a handful of entrails and squash them right in her pretty face!

Instead he stood, the hare dangling from his fisted grip, fingers squeezing round its hind legs as if instead wrapped round her throat, and flexed the grinding of bones.

"Of course not," he said through clenched teeth. He turned before she could say anything more and walked away. Just as he reached the outer rim of firelight he flinched paused at Melora's voice: "And don't forget more wood!"

He stumbled through the black pitch for several irritated minutes, kicking through bushes and swatting aside annoying slaps of branches while concluding she intended on annoying him to death so that he stopped and unleashed his frustrations in a shouted flurry of curses.

Then cringed at Melora's voice calling out to him through the black pitch: "I heard that!"

"Good!" He kicked something hard and unseen that went rolling through the dark, earning stubbed toes. "Ow!"

"I heard that too!"

Friggin hell!

CHAPTER SIX

The Lord of Storms' Receiving Room within the Divine Palace hung heavy with the pungent fragrance of burning incense, bubbling oils, and smoldering coals of exotic sweetrocks, the aromatic vapors drifting about the silent figure in white seated on his ivory throne padded with silvery-buttoned cushions of crimson silk threaded with golden weaves.

Tiny colored birds fluttered and chirped in brass cages nearby, their songs accompanied by the soothing notes of a beautiful harpist plucking her soft melody akin to water tinkling over chimes. The young woman maintained her smile despite the length of chain locking her ankle to the large instrument she played, and though her vacant stare hid nothing as to her fate if she so much as plucked a single note in error, its focus held to the center of the room where stood a little girl of nine whom continued the latest of her foretellings before the attentive warlord listener.

". . . a Soothsayer," Sera finished. She opened her brown eyes, blinking loose from the wispy visions of her aizakai foresight clearing from her mind's eye, and shuddered. She risked a glance up from the palace floor and succumbed regret the instant her hesitant gaze received the piercing stare of the man watching her from upon his great ivory throne, the circular rise of dais beneath it.

Hannibal Khan, the Lord of Storms, the warlord turned divine god-king reborn and made flesh, looked on with the same veiled fascination as would a pitsnake considering its next meal, and frowned. His handsome visage framed with blond curls depending to his broad shoulders tensed annoyance piqued by the low-throated *Hmmmm* of a growl, the rumbled purr of his thunder deep and low inside his muscled slab of chest.

The Khan did not accept failure in any form. Failure revealed weakness, and weakness earned no place within the dominating plans of the Lord of Storms.

Sera had foreseen the latest Enclave Trio's failure even before the surviving Third reported their disappointing results over retrieving the runaway Spellbinder through his aizakai farsight. But the Khan preferred thoroughness in his plans, especially when unexpected complications arose such as those Sera just revealed. That man, the Third, would now lead the next Trio of Enclave hunters as their First, earning swift death by his two companions for punishment of another failure.

Sera cringed, though she hid it well, for even the slightest change in the Khan's expression insinuated death—or worse. Her aizakai foresight proved too valuable a tool for him to command her execution, but the stripes of scars across her back attested to the torturous punishments inflicted upon his most favored slave despite her contribution to his divine cleansing of heathen aizakai and impending conquest over the One Land of Pangea.

Plans of domination required tools, and though her foresight proved her only saving grace from the aizakai execution pits, to the Khan she remained just another utilized tool, a loathsome means to the greater end of his genocidal cause. He squeezed opportunity from her aizakai foresight as one sought blood from a stone, and once he bled her stone dry he would continue squeezing until he crushed her to dust within his power-lusting fist.

I hate you. A familiar, nagging guilt roused within as Sera lowered her gaze to the spot of patterned stonework between her bare feet, eyes lingering over the Khan's godsforged lanthium gauntlets of power in their slow descent. *I hate you so much.* Those terrible tools provided him frightening control over lightning, making of his muscled body a living conductor channeling smiting death from the sky and through him redirect its destructive power. *And it's all my fault.*

The Khan put her valuable aizakai foresight to sinister use the moment his worship-followers tore her from the fighting arms of her screaming parents two years prior. Their deaths the quick slitting of throats, unlike Sera's long and torturous captivity as the Khan's favorite slave and dependable tool, to toy with as he pleased by right of force, her foresight carving his path of conquest, each vision preempting marches of progress by the Lord of Storms' fanatical worship-followers and his growing army of Bloodcloaks.

How much longer before she outlived her usefulness . . . that time would come eventually. The Khan used and abused then cast his depleted tools aside for her to believe otherwise.

Now though, after her latest vision, fear gripped her by the heart.

Each night she prayed for escape to unlistening gods, every morning she cursed the bane of her aizakai ability to foresee the forking future possibilities of others' lives though never herself, the truth to the branching paths of fated puzzlement only revealed to her mind's eye once the person acted upon some significant decision within their own lifeline. The moment they set into motion the life-altering decision, a variety of future possibilities sprouted while the previous potentials of unchosen branches withered, adding more intricate pieces to the already elaborate puzzle of fate.

But at least her foresight saved her from sexual servitude in the Khan's royal harem of Spellbinders. Khansmen torturers bled dry the older women for the forging of kohatheens, while the younger girls of an age with Sera and ripe with the innocence of influence were reeducated, molded then folded in among his personal pleasure stock. She knew little of what that meant, though she suspected enough not to envy a place among them with their frequent sore bottoms and funny walking.

"A Soothsayer." The Khan spoke slowly, the baritone words drifting from his mouth in deliberate taste. A muscled arm lifted from the armrest of the high-backed throne and raised gauntleted hand to his face, extended pointer finger tracing down the thin pink scar running his left cheek from brow to chin, caressing the only mar on his otherwise handsome visage. "So she still lives."

Sera nodded, eyes downcast, tensed lips restraining the bridled pleasure of the Spellbinder's tenacious capacity for surviving yet another Trio of hunters, she his malevolent fixation since his invasion of Junes, that facial scar her parting gift before her harrowing escape. The Lord of Storms set generous bounty for the former king's Spellbinder Vizer Melora Callisticus the moment his victorious banners flapped high atop poles throughout the renamed Holy City of Khan, though tracking such elusive prey immune to magic proved difficult despite the devious methods the Khan's fanatical worship-followers possessed.

Melora's ever-present void-aura distorted Sera's foresight into a disorientating chain of broken and foggy glimpses, hazy and vague at best. Scrying the Spellbinder's whereabouts proved a painful education taught to Sera by admonishing whip, though eventually she learned not to focus on the woman herself but to hone her concentration instead upon the details outside of Melora's impeding void-aura. Similar to spying out fish, Sera perceived the swimming shapes though the murky surface itself obscured the details beneath.

"I want her found!" The Khan slammed his fist upon armrest, his booming shout an echoing thunder. Hairline fissures raced down the thick ivory beneath his pounding fist, loosening miniscule bits of powdered white grit sprinkling atop his boot and floor in a dusting cloud puffing beneath his notice.

Sera bobbed her head, chewed her bottom lip while fighting down a startled squeal. The hundred Bloodcloaks aligning the four walls of the Receiving Room shifted on their feet, bits of polished red-gold armor scraping and clanging, their brooding Khan's agitation bleeding into their nervous regards. Two palace servants backed away from the elevated dais while maintaining their sweeping duties, gazes downcast to prevent the accidental drawing of the Khan's infamous wrath.

"Look at me," the Khan said.

Sera peeked up. "Yes, my Khan?"

He leaned forward by inches, propping one elbow atop his muscled thigh, and settled his strong chin atop thick lanthium knuckles. And there studied her a long and silent length. "Well?"

"Yes, my Khan." She bowed her head, closed her eyes, flexed her mind's eye into further future viewing. Darkness faded for buffeting swirls of colors forming shapes, an audible collage of noises . . . and she traveled again, projecting focus, covering the long span of miles within short astral seconds. Flashes of images became flutters of shapes became moving pictures of events . . . though obscurities remained, complicating her viewing task.

Several sweating, twitching minutes passed. Sera withdrew from the mental struggle, willing astral ejection from within the mishmash of vague visions. Numerous branching possibilities had forked and split since the last Trio's failure, and yet . . . and yet.

She shivered.

A strange new anomaly existed asides the Spellbinder's obscuring void-aura, asides her new protector. Troubling, yet offering Sera the tiniest glimmer of something more, something fragile, something unfelt since her enslavement to the Khan. An odd sensation she assumed dead along with her parents: hope.

And there she prickled, unsure of the irrevocable fate of her doomed existence. A potential savior revealed, though she dared not speak such blasphemy aloud.

Instead she said: "The Soothsayer protects her." She shook her head, eyes shut tight, face tensed in visible strain to her internal working. "Her void-aura is so strong, it . . . it clouds too much. I'm sorry. I can see no more."

Body slumping while she regained present focus, the wispy strands of her visions faded. She swallowed the lumpy sensation of betrayal at her words, that sickening stab-in-the-gut feeling always accompanying her scrying for the Khan over his Spellbinder fixation turned obsession, then bowed her head in shame.

"Forgive my failure, my Khan."

And tensed for the doling of her punishment.

But to her surprise the Khan did not rise, did not rush forth and beat her to the floor, nor did he order his loyal subordinate Horace, the Bloodcloak brute standing at his left, to deal with her failure through pain. Instead he sat back in silent contemplation, pensive eyes transfixed ahead, staring more through Sera than at her.

His lips peeled back, revealing a snarl, his baritone voice a low-throated growl. "Soothsayer."

Lanthium-gauntleted hands tightened into fists while he relapsed into brooding silence.

* * *

Another finally came forth from his place of lingered listening, though Hannibal Khan's umbrage remained checked toward the sole being even he yielded to.

Purple robes whispering over the patterned stonework and presenting the illusion of gliding across the floor, the talons on his hidden clawfeet *click-click-clicking*, every of his subtle movements speaking hidden purpose, the one named Nergal stepped onto the dais and approached the throne's ruminating occupant. He stood tall beside the Khan with clawhands clasped behind his proud back, scaly lips and flat nose peeking out from beneath his shadowed hood.

The Khan gazed up at the serpent-priest, acknowledged the most high acolyte of the Enclave in silent askance. Nergal bent forward at the hips, whispered something into the Khan's ear which produced a budding smile. Then the Khan's upper lip twitched, curling that smile vicious.

Nergal straightened, turned and swept his gaze.

Sera peeked up in the lingering silence, a brutal regret the instant she met Nergal's horrible gaze upon her, calculating eyes tearing at her, dissecting her on a level far beyond the physical. She had watched the Khan call forth lightning from the sky and raze destruction, had witnessed his cruel domination over countless screaming victims while in the brutal throes of his conquering ecstasy. But the fear she retained for the Lord of Storms paled to the panic penetrating her most private depths earned from Nergal's inhuman serpentine stare.

Soulless yellow eyes divided by black vertical slits gazed from a blank mask of scaly green flesh. There lived a deep dark hatred in that terrorizing stare so profound in its rending hypnotic power. Nothing human approached that look, the intelligence behind it awful and alien, unfeeling and unreasoning, infinitely terrible, speaking volumes of control.

Nergal held the highest station above the Enclave's other acolytes positioned within the Khan's inner circle, representing their old and secret order directly to the Khan. No, not just to but above. When Nergal spoke, the Khan listened. And when he commanded, even the Khan obeyed. By choice or by force.

Nergal descended the dais in a whisper of robes and stood before Sera in towering loom. He leaned forward at the hips, cupped her chin betwixt his long, thin, scaly fingers each tipped by sharp black talons. He said nothing, only stared while squeezing until her chin slipped loose from his pinching grasp.

She winced, her head snapping back. She made every effort at clenching her insides to prevent wetting herself. Every taut inch of her screamed to turn and run, to abandon all sanity and surrender to the fleeing impulse. But Nergal's penetrating gaze captured her within its festering depths, trapping her immobile, his hypnotic stare compelling her paralyzed, the weaker tethers of her will severed from her physical self as warm urine trickled down her trembling thighs.

Nergal lowered his deconstructing gaze to the puddle forming round Sera's bare feet and his scaly lips peeled away from pointed teeth, revealing a brief smile. A hissing chuckle as he withdrew two steps, returned his clawhands behind his back, then turned and faced the Khan.

"The Spellbinder is of little consequence," Nergal said.

The Khan sat forward, frowning. "But the Soothsayer—"

"Will not be a problem. There will be no repeat of Simus Junes. Master's curse is assurance of that." Nergal turned and paced, purple robes whispering, the black talons on his hidden clawfeet *click-click-clicking* the floor. "The bloodlust will consume him along with the woman. Leave them to the irony of their condemned fates and forget your personal vendetta. You are no longer the petty warlord who summoned me. You're a Khan now. Act like it."

The Khan sat back grunting.

Nergal stopped, faced him. "The Book of Towers is what matters most. You will continue building your army as planned, until we are ready to move upon that heathen's den in Fist. Everything else is trivial."

"Trivial?" The Khan ruined his handsome face with a proper scowl. "I will not—"

"You will do as you're told!" Nergal shouted.

He approached the Khan in three swift strides. Bent forward and met the Khan glare for glare. When next he spoke, his S's issued stretched in the threatening lisp of a serpent's warning hiss.

"The power you wield isss because of our doing. The empire rising around you isss because of our influence. You are worshipped as a living god because we allow it. We've provided you the necessary toolsss, but they can be stripped away from you as easily as the flesh from your bonesss."

He raised his right clawhand, extended one finger and traced down the thin pink scar running the Khan's cheek, his short black talon scraping over softer skin with the dark whisper of a demon's breath.

"We will not allow three-hundred yearsss of planning to come unraveled because of your wounded pride. We made you, warlord, and we can unmake you." He tapped the Khan's strong chin with the tip of ebony talon. "Do not ever forget that."

He lowered his clawhand, tapped the silvery lanthium ring dangling from the golden necklace strung round the Khan's bull-thick neck. "Or do you wish to suffer the same fate as the last one who failed us, yesss?"

Sera shivered at mention of the creature they'd resurrected from the crypt beneath the palace a few weeks previous, the necromaster Dethkore, the infamous Eater of Souls. She shut her eyes, but the horrid memories assailed her regardless.

That dark and musty crypt sealed deep within the catacombs beneath the palace. The screams of sacrificial children as Nergal ordered them fed alive to the abomination unearthed. The unliving creature returning to life then feeding on flesh and drinking of blood, its pale substance rejuvenating with renewed vitality from blooded ashes sealed long ago by the infamous savior-slayer and last Soothsayer king Simus Junes before his own undoing.

The lanthium ring in the Khan's possession housed Dethkore's undying soul. Another tool of power provided him by the Enclave, the necromaster's soulring vitus existed as the only method of control over the unliving creature whom almost destroyed the world during the Thousand Years War. And yet, with the soulring clutched within the Khan's manipulative grasp, he enslaved the necromaster as another utilized tool, not very much unlike Sera herself. A powerful tool currently carrying out the Khan's orders in southern Thurandy, advancing his growing army of Bloodcloaks in further conquest against all dissidents by raising the dead into battle under the warring sigil of a silver fist clutching a single golden bolt of lightning upon a crimson banner, killing in the name of the reigning Lord of Storms, achieving fealty through surrender or death.

Nergal straightened tall, his temper retreating by tell of the stretched S's of his serpentine tongue reverting to that of a more human pattern of speech when he next spoke.

"Return our Master to this world and you will earn your immortality, human. Fail him, and you will regret the day you dared bargain our services."

The Khan averted his gaze ahead. "I know well what I've given to get," he said, tone low, gauntleted hands flexing strangles of the air.

"As do we," Nergal said. "For now, I must return. Master awaits, and he is anxious."

He turned his back to the Khan, pausing in display of his authority over the Lord of Storms. He stepped down from the dais and walked toward the large circular depression in the floor, those he passed darting from his path while avoiding the measure of his wicked gaze.

But Nergal refused to be so easily forgotten. Stopping halfway across the room, he caught the wandering eyes of a palace servant before the young woman could shift her gaze to the broom in her trembling hands. She flinched at turning away from him, but something compelled her still and staring up at the towering serpent-priest in sanity's abandonment.

Nergal peeled back his hood, exposing his scaly hairless head, revealing the full brunt of his hypnotic gaze. The woman's eyes grew wide with new haunt, her face pinching then slackening. Entranced. The broom slipped loose from her hands and clattered to the floor forgotten.

"Knife," Nergal said without breaking eye contact. Within seconds a knife skittered across the floor to a stop nearby the woman's feet courtesy of Horace. "Remove your tongue."

The woman bent and picked up the knife. She raised the six-inch blade to her opening mouth, stuck out her tongue and pinched its end. She winced and whimpered though faltered nothing in the cutting of her tongue. Ribbons of blood streamed from her mouth while tears ran her cheeks. And when she finished, she held the self-mutilation out in offering upon her upturned palm, presenting him her gift.

Nergal refused her. "Swallow it."

She popped the severed tongue into her mouth and swallowed.

"Smile and sweep."

The knife clattered the floor next to her feet. She recovered her broom, presented Nergal a gory smile, then returned to sweeping task, eyes a blank stare, blood running her front, the broom's stiff whiskers smearing red gore across the floor.

Nergal considered the Khan at silent length. Said nothing but for his amused smile. He turned away and finished across the room to where the floor's depression awaited him. The traveling pool, formed of concentric ringed steps, led down to a reservoir of sacrificial aizakai blood therein its depressed eye.

He paused at its brim, slipped nude from his robes and tossed them to the floor, revealing a rangy hybrid body the cruel mixture of human and serpent, more man than reptile though equally demonic. Wiry muscle and bony contours wrapped compact in scaly flesh, with a little nub of a tail protruding by inches above flat buttocks. Four digits per clawhand, three thicker each clawfoot, all decorated with short black talons. Of human ears he had none but for two small holes.

He descended into the traveling pool, its crimson surface churning reactive upon contact, rippling round his lowering intrusion into bubbling agitation while the carven symbols marking the traveling pool's outermost ring flared aglow with pulsing throbs of violet witchlight.

Bubbling blood arose past his knees, hips, shoulders then head, then Nergal gone. The traveling pool's frothing disturbance abated within seconds, the archaic symbols snuffing their luminous witchglow.

Silence but for the sounds of sweeping.

* * *

Hannibal Khan closed his eyes, drew in a deep nostril breath, blond curls licking his broad shoulders rising, then he raised one gauntleted hand up before his face and clenched his fist. Bright blue sparks crackled and danced thereon the silvery lanthium while thunder rumbled outside the Divine Palace. He considered the arcing sparks at play with the fixed stare of bridled psychosis, a silent storm of power and the fevered need to spend it brewing therein the loosening restraint of his narrowed eyes.

Sera cringed in trembles, though a small part of her pleaded for the Khan to indulge his spiking ire, to summon lightning through the palace roof in a fit of rage and end both her torturous captivity and her miserable life in a violent blast of crushing rubble. That same part of her envied the tongueless sweeper in a way, the entranced woman moments from bleeding out and oblivious to her self-inflicted injury while under the lingering hypnotic effects of Nergal's demonic compulsion.

"I will have my vengeance," the Khan said, glaring at some private space of viewing through his spark-crackling fist, speaking to the power it contained. Gauntlets of the Dominator's Armor. Pieces to the whole he sought to gather through the Book of Towers. He glanced at the traveling pool, scowling, voice rising into a booming shout. "I will have it all!"

The Lord of Storms hammered his fist atop the thick ivory armrest in tune to a synchronous eruption of thunder rumbling outside. Sera flung her arms up, cowering, shielding her face against the explosion of ivory debris, wincing as jagged chips stabbed and cut her forearms and legs.

A strong wind kicked up within the Receiving Room, flapping tapestries loose from walls, knocking over flaming stands and scattering their glowing contents across the floor while making of their lambent coals strewn sparkling rubies. The beautiful young harpist screamed and yanked on the length of chain linking her to her heavy instrument while golden cages crashed, releasing fluttering birds taken upon the risen winds.

Servants scrambled in fright, giving no care to the hot scatter of coals crunched underfoot as they fled for safer chambers into any of the four corridors removing them from the Receiving Room. Others froze, swaddled in paralyzing fear, their clothes whipping beats in the violent gusts.

And through it all the bleeding sweeper remained autonomous, docile with her broomwork. She continued her duties unabated, smearing the floor with streaks of her dripping gore. She swept and bled, swept and bled, long black hair whipping round her head.

The fierce winds died away.

Sera lowered her defenses, tingling arms and legs bleeding from countless tiny nicks and cuts.

The Khan stood glaring down at the ivory debris round his white boots loosened from his pounding fist.

"Every day she lives is a black mark carved upon my throne." He bent and picked up a fist-sized chunk of ivory, raised it in brief study. "I want that Spellbinder bitch brought back alive." He squeezed, crushing to powder the chunk in his mighty grip, and continued squeezing, his spark-crackling fist all trembling fury. "I will not have my vengeance taken from me." The clench of his strong jaw, neck veins bulging. "Not by anyone!"

He glared at Nergal's traveling pool, grimaced and spat at it. He stomped on a nearby bird fluttering the floor with a broken wing and ground his boot, then fixed upon Sera, and there flashed a wicked grin. He approached her in five bounding strides and seized her by the throat.

She gasped, stiffening by reflex, then resistance fled as her body melted limp. She lifted from the floor with the rising pull of the Khan's strong grasp, feet dangling, a dark and distant part of her begging for the sweet release of death while his powerful squeeze denied her breath.

"A name," he demanded. And shook her by the neck. "I want the Soothsayer's name!"

She stared back mute, hot face purpling, eyes bulging, tunneling vision a fractured prism of tears. Seconds only and he released her, dropping her to the floor in a crumpled heap.

Coughing and gasping for precious air, she clutched at her aching throat, consciousness swimming through a twinkling darkness receding from the edges of her vision. She blinked through tears, struggled onto hands and knees, limbs trembling, heart a racing patter. Something warm and wet on the floor. The acrid stink of urine beneath her. Groaning, she struggled into standing.

While the Khan returned to his fractured throne. He sat with his arms crossed, head tilted to one side, waiting for her answer.

Across the room sounded the clatter of wood punctuated by the smacking *thud* of flesh slapping floor. The bleeding sweeper had collapsed, lay facedown, limp, blood pooling round her broken face.

"His name," the Khan said, adamant stare unbroken.

Sera coughed and cleared her aching throat, wincing, the task akin to swallowing broken glass. The name came out in a hoarse, low-throated whisper she repeated twice, earning the Khan's approval, rectifying her earlier failure however little difference it would make in the end. Before her latest visions, she would have thrown herself at his feet and begged for death.

But now, after what she'd gleaned of two Soothsayers, she hid her smile well.

The Khan requested a name, so she gave him one.

One.

Satisfied, the Khan issued command. A fist of five Bloodcloaks strode forth from the walls and knelt before their beckoning Lord of Storms with helmed heads bowed.

"Dispatch more Trios," the Khan said. "Have them drop coin into the greedy palms of every cutthroat and warrior they cross. I don't care what it takes. Find the Soothsayer and kill him. And have the Spellbinder brought back to me alive." The pleasured twisting of his lips, a cursory glance at Nergal's traveling pool. "I want her begging for death while I bleed her dry myself."

"Yes, my Khan."

The fist of Bloodcloaks stood in unison, pounded gauntleted fists over breast-plated hearts in salute, then strode from the Receiving Room in jounces of red-gold armor to relay his orders to the zealous worship-followers of the Enclave's vast webwork of contacts awaiting communication through speed of magical methods.

Sera cringed when the Khan's penetrating gaze captured her again. There betrayed a disturbing madness within those eyes projecting the conviction that the capability to do something excused justification enough for doing it. The permanent touch of too much power building within one man while poisoning its host. A clear psychosis slow in growing since the moment he first donned those nefarious godsforged lanthium gauntlets of power and begun his destructive campaign of Pangean conquest.

She tensed and held her breath, the balance of her life dangling upon the precipice of his next words.

"Take her away," he said, punctuating the dismissive command with the metallic clap of his gauntleted hands.

Horace, Sera's big brute of a watchdog, strode down from the dais, his ugly face twisting in silent pleasure while he removed the kohatheen collar from his belt and locked it closed round her neck. He grabbed her by the wrist, his strong grip threatening the crush of her bones, and yanked her along behind him to leave away.

A defiant part of her wanted to smile, though she stowed that private pleasure for later when alone. Having satisfied the Khan's desires for a time, she almost thanked him for the mercy of not having her stripped and beaten, but she knew better than to provoke once his attentions shifted elsewhere. Better to be taken away now than to stay and—

"Oh, and Horace?" the Khan said.

Horace stopped.

Sera cringed, risked a peek back.

The Khan smiled. "Take her to the Overseer."

Horace bared yellow, broken teeth in a cruel smile. "Yeth, my Khan," he said over a clipped tongue earned from the same Spellbinder of the Khan's scarred obsession.

"No." Sera whimpered and strained for release from Horace's refusing grip. "No!" To throw herself prostrate into begging at the Lord of Storms' feet. "Please, no!"

Horace laughed and dragged her by the arm, the pain flaring in her tortured shoulder turning furthers pleas for mercy into sobs of regret.

CHAPTER SEVEN

Banzu roused awake to sounds of movement from behind; the shifting *swish* of leaves and the crunching *snaps* of twigs underfoot punctuated by grumbled curses dwindling. He'd fallen asleep with his back to the fire while watching the woods, leery of creeping predators both animal and man.

Tensing, hand gripping his sword's hilt by instinct, he threw his blanket aside and sprang to his feet in one quick motion.

Startling Melora cringing paused twenty paces away and attempting to leave him behind, his confiscated bedroll tucked beneath her arm in a tight bundle.

"Godsdammit." Frowning, caught, she dropped his bedroll and walked away at a brisk pace, giving no more care to her noisy tread.

"Hey!" He glared at her shrinking back in the soft morning light. "Wait a minute!" Watched her go. "Friggin hell."

He gathered his blanket and bedroll in a grumbling scramble, stuffed them into his rucksack. After a quick pee on the hissing nest of embers, killing their dying fire into white chuffs of smoke, he chased after her, rushing to catch up, his value as her human compass diminishing considering Fist awaited her in more or less a steady straight course east.

Her void-aura prevented her from spying out the magical dot evincing Jericho's present location upon her ensorcelled map, though it hindered nothing of the inked landscape itself. And once out from the immense density of the woodlands, wherein direction could turn the unfamiliar traveler round and round with its twisting series of winding paths, Banzu suspected she intended leaving him behind for good.

They spent the rest of the morning in silent descent through the mountainside woodlands, Melora enforcing her natural authority as leader while Banzu pointed the quicker routes at every splitting bend in the labyrinthine trails.

Along the way he snagged a handful of yellow-veined britchleaves, minty and fibrous. He popped two into his mouth and offered Melora the other two upon his upturned palm.

"What for?" she asked.

"They clean your teeth."

"Yeah? So?"

"So you chew them."

She considered the leaves in thin-eyed scrutiny.

He sighed and rolled his eyes. "They're not poisonous." He bared his teeth and the clinging bits of green mush thereon. "Obviously."

She snatched the leaves from his hand and stuffed them into her mouth.

"Chew but don't swallow," he said after a time.

"Why not?"

He shrugged and spat minty saliva. "Explosive diarrhea."

She stopped and burned him with a shrewd glare.

"What?" he asked.

She spat her fibrous mush out and stalked away.

"What?" he asked her back, laughing.

She bothered no look behind, shouting, "You know what!"

Their only conversation.

Hours passed.

Banzu prodded and poked at questions unvoiced tumbling round his head, fearing the errant slip of his tongue. Melora's dogged chase after Jericho abandoned, her sole focus now aimed at returning to Fist fast as possible. *And probably slapping his face off soon as she sees him again for abandoning her with me.*

He toyed with more complicated issues too. A Spellbinder to protect, and he knew next to nothing about those hunting her. As to how he would explain himself once they arrived in Fist, well . . . *I'll just have to figure that out before we get there. Got plenty of time. But I'd better make it good or else Jericho'll have me for breakfast.*

He glanced up through a rare break in the high canopy at the sun striving for zenith. They'd covered fifteen miles by his rough estimate, which meant another mile or so ahead awaited Green River.

He took the lead down the next hilly descent, foliage giving way to the formidable river, its flowing blockade greeting them when they reached the western bank.

"We'll have to cross here," he said, stopping shy of the short wooden dock its eastern counterpart far across the rushing expanse, the two docks built where the ample river's banks thinned to less than one mile apart.

She gazed across, eyes tight and searching. "Why here?"

He shrugged. "We can always make a go for one of the bridges, but it's two day's travel on foot that way,"—he pointed north—"and double that to the south." Not that she didn't already know considering she crossed the river on her way in, impossible otherwise. "Of course, if you're in no hurry—"

"Whatever." She crossed her arms and frowned, gaze hunting the river's opposite side, the thick forestry beyond. "Just get me across."

A small bone horn hung from a nearby tree, strung by a rope and hooked on the short stub of a cut branch. Banzu brought the horn's blowhole to his lips, drew in deep and blew hard.

"Ha-rooooom!"

Branches above them shivered and shook with birds startled into flight at the loud peal. He hitched the horn away and stared out over the glossy river reflecting the unobstructed sun and sky.

"I haven't been across these waters since I was a boy."

"Then go home."

He suppressed a sigh. "I told you I can't do that."

"And I told you this isn't a game. The last thing I need is your death on my hands on top of everything else. You've brought me this far. Good for you. How gallant. I can make it the rest of the way just fine on my own. I don't need you—"

"Ha-rooooom!" An answering peal sounded from across the mighty river expanse, cutting her short.

Banzu smiled. "Won't be long now."

She scrunched her face in that angry-cute way of hers, said nothing more.

He picked up several flat rocks dappling the muddy bank, chucked them out in skipping abandon while the ferryman far across the way readied his raft for transport. Above their heads hung a long, thick rope strung across the river, its ends secured high round trunks from bank to bank. The tether line served as a means for aiding the raft across in lieu of the strong currents sweeping it down river, the guide rope running through metallic loops on two large poles bolted to the long flat raft.

Minutes passed with the faint songs of cicadas. The brawny ferryman labored at pulling his raft to the halfway point in practiced ease, thick arms and beefy hands tugging the guide rope overhead.

Melora leaned forward at the waist, squinting. "Is that a . . . a cyclops?"

"Uhm, yeah?" Banzu eyeballed her funny—*maybe she crossed one of the bridges on her way in?*—then pointed at the vibrating rope twanging the air above their heads. "He swam it across. Tied off one end then carried the other over in his mouth. At night. With rocks on his back." He chuckled, shrugged. "At least that's the way the story goes."

She frowned, unamused. "I'm sure he did."

Banzu knew the Green River ferryman by reputation alone, and that mostly from his uncle. On rare occasions he accompanied Jericho to one of the bridges where congregated villagers and trappers and farmers in bustles of local commerce, trading pelts for supplies and sometimes catching chatter about the Green River ferryman.

Cody lived on the banks earning sparse coin by ferrying occasional travelers and hunters and pilgrims across, though his reputation varied among the peoples of the nearest villages.

The largest river in Ascadia, the lands west of the Calderos Mountains—the extensive range of mountains separating western Ascadia from eastern Thurandy in a long spine running from the northern Thunderhell Tundra clear to the southern Presh Desert—Green River spanned several miles wide at its most distanced parts. Which brought sinister allure to brash youths fond of testing their teenage bravery by sneaking away to the river and attempting to swim across while battling the strong currents before fear or fatigue or both forced them into struggling return. Or worse, drowning in Green River's frigid depths.

Some tales told of Cody swimming out and saving potential drowners, while other stories said he cheated travelers out from their monies before tossing them overboard.

Banzu pondered the truth. As notorious for their love of coin and barley spirits as for their extraordinary strength and sudden outbursts of anger, stories of Cyclops ran the gamut from bravery to savagery.

Jericho welcomed all stories that helped deter others from wandering too near their isolated cabin, and so decided years ago to leave alone any investigation into the ferryman and his possible criminal doings.

Banzu turned to Melora, struck with a curious notion. "Cody's real strong, but since you're a Spellbinder . . . will he be able to pull us across?"

Their supernatural strength the stuff of legend, the pure bloodlines of the cyclopean race died out over three centuries previous during the wide-spread chaos of the Thousand Years War. Quarter-breeds like Cody still possessed the awesome strength of several normal human men, though not so much as their rarer half-breed cousins.

Melora looked at him as if he'd grown another head. "Cyclops is a race, dummy. They're not aizakai and neither is their strength." She flicked a dismissive wrist at Cody and his raft. "Besides, it's not as hard as it looks." With that she flipped her hood up, concealing her face while shielding her ears from any more of his ignorant questions.

Dummy? Banzu turned away frowning, toying with the entertaining notion of sneaking behind her then shoving her into the river. Maybe even kick some mud in her face while she screamed bloody murder . . . *as the strong currents carry her away? No. Bad idea, that.*

He skipped more flat rocks out over the river while watching Cody muscle the raft closer, then abandoned the idle play when a warning voice crept into his thoughts.

More will come.

He scanned the forestry screening the opposite riverbank for any signs of others hiding and watching, laying in wait. That third chaser, the one who fled instead of engaging. *Gods, I'd almost forgotten him.* But the dense woods prevented Banzu's visual scouting with any certainty, and without the senses-heightening aid of the Power he could make nothing out beyond the green and brown screen of trees and bushes and high grasses across the glistening river's mighty expanse.

He glanced at Melora, said nothing. He twisted for a look behind where evinced no passing signs of their potential assassin. He faced the river, gave his sword's hilt a reassuring squeeze that passed beneath Melora's preoccupied stare at Cody towing his raft closer ashore.

* * *

Cody pulled his raft into butting against the dock's end and tied the flat craft secure to the anchor pole jutting from the muddy bank, the only signs of his tugging labors a few shiny beads of sweat on his bald pate. The brawny cyclopean presented an impressive specimen of muscled bulk, his hairy forearms resembling thick timbers patched with black moss, upper arms twice as muscle-plump as Banzu's thighs, and he stood two heads taller than Melora despite his natural stoop.

But the hybrid mix of cyclops and human blood left him deformed in odd ways, cursing him with a permanent bulbous hunchback—though that hunch resembled more a pack of muscle than some hindering deformity—and the natural eye-catching draw of the ferryman's physical malformations did not end there. Cody's upper torso looked as if having sucked into it most of the muscle of his lower body in cruel trade, doubling the size of what sat atop a normal man's hips and legs. The contrasting effect made him appear that a strong wind would topple him over, though his flat feet, each spanning twice the width of Banzu's own, provided plenty of natural stability against the illusion.

Cody dipped his beefy thick-fingered hand into the chunky leather pouch tied to the front of his belt, produced a crew of walnuts akin to small pebbles in his massive hamhand and squeezed, cracking the hard shells to bits with an ease leaving his face untouched. He single-eyeballed his two potential customers, giving Banzu's sword a scrutinizing pause while the thick black caterpillar of his bushy eyebrow bunched.

"Two?" Cody asked, voice deep and heavy.

Banzu nodded. "Yup."

Cody flicked through the broken walnut shells atop his upturned palm, plucked a few nutty bits and popped them into his mouth.

"You two lucky," he said, bovine-like tongue rolling thick while he chew-talked. "Some thief in the night bastard stole me raft." He paused a measured beat, the folds of leathery skin round the single eye dominating his face creasing, then he stomped—*thump!*—rocking the raft beneath him. "I had to swim over and fetch it back." He glanced over their heads, an easy task achieved given his towering height, in a quick scan of the woods behind them. "Any others?"

Banzu shook his head. "Just us." He gave Melora a sidelong smirk. "The both of us."

"Three coppers to cross," Cody said. "Each." His lone eye narrowed, wide tongue licking fat lips. "No change."

Banzu opened his mouth—then closed it, realizing himself for the blundering fool. Asides food, he'd forgotten money. Jericho kept a few stacks stowed away in his trunk for emergencies, earned from their years of selling pelts, but little in their lives the Power could not provide required coin so that Banzu never carried any.

Hooded head bowed, Melora fished round beneath her cloak, produced a silver piece upon her upturned palm.

Banzu blew out his cheeks in relief, their payment across the river settled.

Cody grinned all blocky yellow teeth while dipping at the knees to better steal a peek at her face. He snatched the silver piece away and stepped aside, waved her by. "Right this way, purdy lady."

Silent, hooded head bowed, Melora passed him onto the raft.

Banzu started after her.

Until Cody stopped him by way of stiff-arming a meaty palm against his chest.

"Purdy lady paid," Cody said. "Tiny man didn't."

Banzu frowned up at the one-eyed wall. "But that's enough for both of us and then some."

"But nuttin," Cody said. "Living not free. No coin, no crossing river."

Banzu huffed a terse breath. He leaned aside, looking past the immense ferryman for anything in the way of help.

Melora offered a smug smile beneath the shade of her hood before turning her back.

Friggin hell. Scowling, Banzu shoved his hands into his pockets, balling them into tight fists—then jolting, smiling when the touch of something forgotten pinched into his right palm.

"Here you go," he said, producing a matching coin to Melora's silver piece.

Cody frowned down at the offered coin.

"Well?" Banzu asked. "Are you gong take it or what?"

Cody fetched a glance at Melora's turned back, then his blocky-toothed grin returned in full. He snatched the coin and pocketed it with the first before stepping aside. "On you go then."

Banzu joined beside her at the raft's edge, looking out across the river. "I never did thank you for paying me." He prodder her with a teasing smirk. "Thanks."

Melora's eyes flashed daggers beneath the drape of her hood.

* * *

Cody untied the raft from the anchor pole. With a jostling heave he tugged on the thick guide rope in strong pulls, urging the raft and its three occupants from the dock out onto the rushing waters. He grunted in tandem to his pulls while muscling the flat craft across at a lazy though steady pace.

Both Banzu and Melora kept a balancing hand upon the vertical length of pole between them, its metal loop of eye feeding the guide rope, while the raft pitched and swayed beneath them. Her hopes of leaving him behind squashed, and in no mood for idle conversation, Melora glared at the eastern riverbank while Banzu's mind reflexed inward and toying at musings of his uncle.

The Power's catalyzing momentum of increased velocity provided the leaping of great distances far beyond the capacity of any normal man. Banzu often tested his leaping limits when wandering through the woodlands, bursting into Powered leaps propelling him into false flight with the speed of a shot arrow, his best attempt achieving him two-hundred feet over the deadly swallows of deep chasms. But Power-leaping the full expanse of Green River from bank to bank, even here at its thinnest span, he suspected an impossible feat on his best day.

He considered turning round and questioning Cody about Jericho's possible crossing. Then remembered those peculiar magic boot coverings his uncle revealed before departure and decided they provided too many options for figuring out. He intended a nice long talk when they reunited in Fist. So many unanswered questions, and so many miles before they reached that far city of wonders in Thurandy well beyond the Calderos Mountains.

Banzu suppressed a sigh. *He'll be furious when I show up. No getting around that. Not like she gave me any choice. Still—*

The raft jostled stopped.

Balancing hand slipping loose from the vertical pole at his left, Banzu stumbled two steps and almost pitched off the raft but for catching his balance just in the nick. He caught Melora by the crook of her elbow to prevent her from falling into the river. She thanked him by jerking her arm free while baring teeth in a snarl.

"You're welcome," he muttered, then turned to the ferryman. "Is something wrong?"

Cody shook his head, thick fingers fiddling with the guide rope and the metal loop atop the guide pole next to him. "Kink in line. Nuttin serious. Only take minute. Enjoy view."

Banzu turned back, stared out across the river's glistening expanse reflecting ripples of unobstructed sky.

Beside him Melora shifted her feet in anxious tell of diving in and swimming the rest of the long way across just to be done with it.

"Don't even think about it," he said. "These waters are runoffs from the Thunderhell Tundra. They're not as cold down here but they'll still steal the breath from your lungs and lock you up tight. Unless you like hypothermia. If you don't drown first."

She replied a hooded scowl. After some idle time, she crossed her arms and huffed an irritated sigh through pursed lips while tapping an impatient foot in silent count.

"Relax," he said. "The bank's not going anywhere. What's gotten in to you anyways? You've been acting funny ever since we got here."

She rounded on him, fists on hips, eyes thinning menace, voice a petulant flare. "Don't you tell me to—" But she clipped her words short, head turning right.

As the raft swayed beneath the clomping rush of heavy feet charging toward them.

Banzu turned his head left—or began to.

"Look out!" Melora yelled, and shoved him by the chest.

Banzu's world spun. He tumbled backwards, rolled over the southern edge of the raft, legs splashing into the cold water though he caught the last plank's inside lip with the sliding tips of his clawing fingers in a twist of bitter luck preventing his full plunge. He hissed through clenched teeth, the frigid waters chilling his everything below the waist. He mustered total focus into maintaining his straining grip against the river's formidable current attempting to pry him loose and carry him away.

He kicked and clawed, trying to work his forearms farther onto the raft. While Cody grappled Melora chest-to-belly, squeezing her in a crushing hug, her arms pinned useless to her sides.

"Let her go!" Banzu yelled, his struggles divided between fighting the relentless current seeking to tear him free and the growing weight of his rucksack strapped to his back soaking heavy with the river's water.

Cody arched his back, lifting Melora off her kicking feet, and shook her in a violent head-whipping frenzy while attempting to crush the rest of her in his trapping arms.

"No!" Banzu clawed forward by struggling inches onto the rocking raft—only to slip gained purchase while jerking his hands away when Cody issued blind stomps for his working hands.

One hand maintaining a precarious hold on the jostling raft's edge, Banzu reached his other in frantic bid for his belted knife, somehow fumbled it out from sheath without losing it to the river. He strangled its handle, threw his arm up and over while pulling with his other, stabbed down through the top of Cody's nearest foot, hammer-fisting six inches of steel through flesh and bone and pinning the foot to the wood beneath.

Cody roared in pain, but he refused release of his grappled captive even as he failed at yanking his stabbed foot free from the raft.

Melora, hugged squeezed against the ferryman's front, seized distraction. She craned her head, opened her mouth then sank her teeth into the ferryman's face over his bulbous nose.

Cody unleashed a scream muffled behind her clamping mouth, then again when his stabbed foot pulled free from the raft, taking Banzu's knife with it. He stagger-limped backwards while keeping hugging hold of Melora, blood running red ribbons between their bite-locked faces. He tried jostling her teeth loose with another violent shake, but her clamped jaw refused in mighty protest.

Frigid river water splashed over the rocking raft, swishing and swirling Cody's blood.

Banzu clawed and kicked while pulling himself onto the slippery raft inch by frantic inch. He wanted to relieve the heavy burden of his rucksack, but that meant abandoning everything within it to the river's depths. The sword at his left hipwing begged for release, but the attempt would only slip him loose into the river. He ached in desperation for seizing just one single flicker of the Power, an impossible endeavor with the entire raft encompassed within the magic-nullifying bounds of Melora's void-aura.

Cody limped and staggered, jostling the raft with his stomping lurches, Banzu's knife jutting from the top of his bleeding right foot an annoyance forgotten when he reached up, gripped the sides of Melora's head, tore free her prying mouth and threw her backwards by the head then clutched at his bleeding face.

Melora crashed and tumbled toward the eastern edge of the raft for the water beyond. But in a fit of feline grace she twisted, caught a clawing grip upon the vertical guide pole just as her boots splashed water.

Banzu kicked and clawed for all his worth, struggling to climb free from the pulling current in a surge of grunting strength. But his hands slid loose on slippery planks so that he caught the edge, half submerged again. A losing battle fighting the slick surface of the raft, the river's strong current, and his heavy rucksack together.

Cody lowered his hamhands from his bleeding face and bellowed all in one word: "Immagunnasquashyew!" And charged, his stomping bulk tottering the raft.

Crawling toward Banzu on hands and knees, seeking to pull him onto the raft, Melora caught the ferryman's raging bulk out from her right peripheral, began twisting while reaching for her dachras beneath her cloak. But too late. Cody punted her in the stomach, lifting her from the raft. She spun round twice in the air, arms flailing, and crashed facedown in a groaning heap.

"No!" Banzu scrambled for more desperate purchase onto the raft, but found it an impossible task.

The cyclopean's rage contorting his bleeding face, Cody stomped toward Melora, grabbed her by the back of the neck and one leg and lifted her overhead. Her arms swung in wild abandon. A flash of steel glinting the sun. And fanged dachra blade sliced through the thick guide rope by awful chance at the height of her ascent.

Cody reversed his efforts and slammed her down onto the raft into a crumpled heap of stillness. He limped back, blocky teeth clenched, blood running his face, lone eye blinking smears of red.

The guide rope severed, the raft spun out of control and downriver under the chaotic will of the river's unruly currents.

Banzu cursed and clawed, his efforts shifting to clinging to the uncontrolled raft, its edge pressing against his stomach while the frigid waters worked at sucking him under by the legs.

Cody yanked the knife from his foot with a grunt and threw it to the river. He limped over Melora's still crumple toward Banzu, his fat lips curling into a bloody snarl, his eye a menacing glare. "Double the kill, double the pay."

Panic flushing, Banzu stared up at that looming one-eyed face of impending death, arms clamped tight on the careening raft, his frantic mind grasping hold of waning hope. Letting go and braving the waters meant abandoning Melora to her doom, and holding on he was good as dead.

"Mushbrains," Cody said, closing in. He raised his injured foot for a skull-smashing stomp atop Banzu's head.

Shink-shink.

Cody froze, grunting, jolting tensed. His eye startled wide, rolled forward into looking down at the two fanged metal tips sticking out from his chest. He expelled a wheezing gasp, face turning slack.

Behind him stood Melora, her face a mask of honed rage. She yanked her dachras free from the cyclopean's back and administered a savage frenzy of bladework, flowing with the fluidity of a dancer's grace despite the rocking raft, slicing and slashing Cody's backside from neck to hamstrings in fantastic sprays of blood earned by the snaking weaves of her butchering dachra fangs.

Cody dropped to his knees, screaming. Melora booted him from behind, sent him tumbling headfirst over a ducking Banzu and the edge of the raft both, his screams turned gurgles as the river swallowed him under.

Holy gods . . . Locked in mute stare, Banzu strained at keeping hold his clutched position on the raft while the eerie calm of nature's quietude returned.

Melora spun her dachras through the deft twirls of her hands, flinging glistening rubies of Cody's blood from the fanged blades, then sheathed them up beneath her flapping cloak, wincing through the quick motion. She hugged at her sore ribs, her eyes a feral glare.

Banzu risked another reach to board the raft then slapped his pawing hand for purchase lest the current pull him loose. "Are you going to help me up or what?"

The murderous gleam in those piercing violets answered No. She looked ready to kick him in the teeth and be done with him.

"Please," Banzu said. "I can barely feel my legs."

She grabbed him by the shoulders and pulled him up onto the raft while unleashing a string of curses under her breath.

* * *

Banzu rolled over, soaked and shivering, spun on his bottom, stood into a half-squat to steady his sloshing balance on the careening raft, legs numb with trembling chills, teeth chattering. And stared at the river, Cody drowned, the knife Jericho had gifted him as a boy lost to the waters.

"Godsdammit!" Melora yelled. "I told you to go home! I didn't want you involved in this! Why can't you listen!" She glared at the eastern riverbank gliding by, turning while the raft spun. "I need to get across, godsdammit."

"How?" Banzu did the best he could with a shrug beneath the burden of his sodden rucksack. The river's current pulled the raft closer toward the eastern bank, but that could change in the span of a coinflip given the chaotic will of the rushing waters. And with no guide rope to lead them across they floated at the mercy of the river's vagaries.

"Thanks for saving me." He hunched and rubbed some feeling into his shivering thighs. "Gods, I can't believe he tried to kill us. I don't understand. Why in friggin hell would he—"

Melora dove into the river.

Banzu shouted after her, but too late. He held his breath for a few heart-pounding seconds then released it when Melora's head popped up and, despite the strong waters fighting against her, she swam across, each stroke taking her closer toward the eastern bank while the current pulled her farther south.

"Friggin hell."

The raft jostled, shifted course, floated toward the western bank.

"Friggin hell!"

You're not losing me that easily.

He removed his rucksack, gripped it by the straps and backed up, waited for a space, hoping she wouldn't look back, then seized the Power and broke into sprint, finished the length of the raft and jumped, Powered momentum carrying him across the water fifty feet before he plunged into the frigid river's depths behind her.

Chill gripped him by the throat. He broke the surface and swam his way across in one-armed strokes while tugging the deadweight of his heavy rucksack fighting to pull him under.

Several struggling, head-bobbing minutes later and his kicking feet touched mud as he gained the eastern side of Green River. Panting, he crawled onto the grassy bank, exhausted limbs numb shivers, the sword at his side pinching into his skin with every shift of his hips. He shoved the sopping rucksack aside, collapsed onto his back and stared at the blue ocean of sky while sucking wind through chattering teeth. He rolled his head right, at Melora lying the grassy bank fifteen or so paces away, gasping and shivering.

"What . . . in all . . . the hells . . . was that about?" he asked through panting breaths.

She rolled her head left. "Those khansmen chasing me . . . must've gotten to him . . . there's a bounty . . . on my head . . . stupid."

Regaining her breath, she sat up and shot him a glare. "And that includes anyone with me. I told you not to come." She stood, smacked away clinging bits of mud from her wet clothes, muttering curses with every angry swipe.

Banzu groaned into sitting up, in no mood to argue. He gazed over the river. "I can't believe he tried to kill us."

"Believe it." She threw him an accusatory point. "This is your fault! If you hadn't let him escape then this never would've happened. He probably paid the idiot off on his way through."

Banzu gawked at her—*my fault?* He twisted onto hands and knees, preparing to burst up and charge, to argue with her at a proper closer distance. But he stayed on all fours. Her three chasers. He'd killed the first two, but the third had run off.

"The Enclave's influence knows no bounds," she continued, squeezing water from her hair then parts of her cloak. "Their agents are everywhere. And those that don't work for them do so without even realizing it. The Khan put a bounty on my head before I even stepped foot out from Junes." She gave over the futile chore of drying herself, cast her glare over the river. "They've amassed enough gold to bribe kings. A simple ferryman is of little consequence to them. They would've slit his throat before the gold even touched his greedy hands, the godsdamned fool. Serves him right. All we did was save them the trouble."

She hawked then spat, returned her glare to Banzu and spat again. Pointed at him, yelling, "*Shshshshsh!*" Then expelled a frustrated huff and stormed away without another word.

The *shshshshsh* of her words fading then forgotten as if never spoken, Banzu sat back bottom atop heels, watched her leave into the forest slapping branches aside and kicking through the tall grass. He rolled his shoulders, lifting then shrugging off the tension.

Some protector I am.

Twice she'd saved his life. He promised to protect her, but did she even need it? After witnessing her butchery of Cody, he wondered just who protected who.

He drew in deep, blew out overlong, the exhale withering him.

Maybe she's right. Maybe she doesn't need me. Maybe . . .

He glanced across the river.

I could still go home. Take one of the bridges over. Wait like I said I would.

He shook his head, fisting then tearing up handfuls of grass, ashamed at considering abandoning her.

No!

I can't.

I can do this.

I need this.

And she needs me.

He stood, slung the sopping rucksack over his shoulder, and trudged after her, his soggy boots *squish-squishing* every determined step of the way.

CHAPTER EIGHT

Toward midday towering banks of clouds sweeping down from the north in a long line, gray as smoke beneath and white as new-bleached wool above, rolled high overhead as seen through the larger frequent breaks in the canopy now that the forest thinned. The churning mass swelled and billowed, mocking Banzu's festering desire for stopping and drying out.

Melora returned to her dogged pace in part to warm herself, ignoring him trailing far behind. She reminded him of a boulder rolling downhill: unstoppable once set into motion and willing to crash through anything in its way just to get to the bottom where it planned on aggressive domination, mindless in its linear path of destruction.

Thunder whispered on the risen winds blowing stronger through the lower mountain woodlands, shivering the trees while lifting fallen patches of leaves spinning random paths across their trail, the wind biting despite the warming sun. The frigid chill of the Thunderhell Tundra rode upon those northern-born winds, its gliding frosty touch a nipping reminder of the frozen wastelands which lay many miles to the north, a vast desert of ice.

The misery of the cyclopean ferryman's attack, and the quick death Cody earned via Melora's dachras, weighed heavy on Banzu's mind in grim reminder of the untold dangers they faced ahead. Though over the hours of their journey since, his squishy boots and soggy socks gave way to cranky feet, turning dreary reverie into painful longing for finding a spot to rest while drying out. Travelers lived and died by their feet, and they still had weeks to go before reaching Fist.

A clap of thunder rolled, its booming rupture a mocking rumble. Banzu peered through the high canopy and groaned when the first fat drops of rain plunked onto the leafy branches above, plopped onto the trail where they raised tiny puffs of dust. His hopes of drying out dashed for the time, he suppressed another miserable groan.

They achieved steady progress while suffering through the downpour, its chill sharpened by the sweeping northern winds, inviting bone-deep shivers. Moments only before the rain quit and the clouds parted before the sun, just enough to keep them soaked.

But their respite lasted minutes, for the angle of the sun told the day's travels had eaten away more time than either suspected.

Melora broke from their path without comment and chose a dry spot beneath a tall aspen, its branches forming a natural roof. She stripped from her wet clothes while grumbling tugs on the irritating kohatheen fastened round her neck, her bare back turned to Banzu. "We need a fire."

He answered the command with a sour grunt. He shrugged out from his sopping rucksack then stretched small relief into his achy shoulders and back before walking away in random direction, his wrinkly-sore feet affording him boot-squishing fits.

Away in the woods he cut branches for firewood, the wet cling of his irritating clothes sucking and rubbing his skin raw in parts. On his third return with another armload of wood he jolted from his miserable funk. Melora had built a fire in his absence using the teepee method he taught her.

He smiled at that, brief and wan.

She also sat nude with her hunched back to him, the fire, shadows and firelight dancing the glistening sheen of her back and the tableau of scars thereon. Round her jutted sticks, each stabbed and leaning toward the fire where hung her wet clothes from their angled tips, the rest of her attire strewn round the circle pit of rocks or dangling from the low-hanging branches of her sheltering tree.

Banzu stared overlong, arousal flushing despite his miserable mood, the load of wood bunched in his arms forgotten for the bare curves of her slender shoulders partly hidden behind long damp strands of pale-blonde hair kissing trails down her back, their hooked ends curled over the numerous little scars. And farther down where slim waist widened to curvy hips above pert buttocks and—

She twisted and shot a sharp glance over one shoulder, jolting him from admiring stupor. His gaze snapped up. Their eyes met. He dropped the wood and spun away, face flushing hot, and blew out his cheeks as weariness settled in.

He stripped nude and sat opposite her with his back to the fire, the contents of his rucksack strewn upon the ground for drying, his clothes hoisted nearby the fire upon their own driven sticks, the warmth of flames crackling between them in the stillness of night.

Too quiet.

She'd spoken four words to him since the debacle of crossing Green River.

He closed his eyes, palmed his lids.

I'm sorry. I'll do better next time, I promise.

He glanced at his sheathed sword strung by the belt on a nearby branch and sighed, hung his head between slouching shoulders, the cautious whims of voicing the apology staying his tongue. Energies sapped, his body craved rest, his mind no argument.

But relaxation eluded him while wrestling with the monster of his wounded pride, darkening his brooding.

"Your family must be worried," Melora said, breaking the silence. "They're probably wondering where you are."

He sighed. *This again?* "I'm not going back."

"I didn't say that."

You didn't have to. He closed his eyes, rubbed them with pointer and thumb while invisible knuckles kneaded inside his head. *She's goading me. Probably wants to argue just for the sake of it. Not that I blame her after what happened on the river with Cody.*

And . . . *she's trying to protect me, to turn me away before I get myself killed. Just a bumbling bumpkin in her way.* The truth cut, almost as deep as his earlier failure at protecting her.

He drew in deep, exhaled in a withered hunch. Considering what happened on the river he couldn't blame her. She had—and despite how much he hated admitting it, no other word seemed appropriate—*allowed* him to come along as her protector. So far he bungled it up. How long before another mishap? Or worse, another attack in which he accidentally got her killed? The way she tore through Cody, so immediate and exact, shivered him.

Thank gods she didn't do the same to me when I tried stopping her from leaving.

And yet . . . and yet, impossible to deny the arousing flush of her lethal abilities revealed.

He peeked over a shoulder, considered confessing his true identity. *So much easier if I could just be myself instead of pretending otherwise. I'm a master swordslinger, godsdammit.*

Melora huffed a terse breath. She snapped a stick in half then threw it at the dark. "Will you please just go home?"

He winced, returned his gaze forward. He raked one hand back through his damp tangles and blew out his cheeks, in no mood for exchanging barbs. "No."

She sighed, long and deliberate. "Your family—"

"I don't have any family," he said in partial lie. "My parents are dead. No siblings."

Silence.

"Oh," she said. "I'm sorry."

Me too.

In softer voice she asked, "What happened?"

He slid his heels in and hugged his knees to his chest, forming a nude huddle, hesitant to answer, unsure how to frame it while maintaining his guise as Jericho's friend, his mind reflexing back upon the haunt of his childhood in Sutta Village when life still burst with endless possibilities.

Having just turned five years old, little Banzu and his eager friends—too young to enter the competitive footrace moments from starting during some festival he couldn't recall the name of—formed a line of their own on down Runner's Field for a race apart though alongside the real race of older boys, young men in truth. The signal horn blew, and the teenage runners broke into sprint. So too did Banzu and his friends.

He wanted to beat not only his friends but the older boys competing in the real race for their chance to earn a kiss from the Mayor's pretty daughter awaiting the winner far across Runner's Field. He cared nothing for the kissing prize and everything for the bragging victory. His friends always jibed him about being the slowest among them, so he spent the entire summer practicing alone after his chores just to prove them wrong.

He burst into sprint before the signal horn finished its loud peal, straining with speed, pumping his little arms and legs for all their worth, hands flat and cutting the air at his sides because all little boys knew knifing hands made for faster running. The older runners raced ahead in lengthier strides, but he didn't care for he'd achieved the lead amongst his slower friends throwing startled curses at his back. He closed his eyes, thinking it would help him run faster, pretending himself a charging horse wearing blinders.

And then *it* happened.

The first eruptive surge of alien Power blooming inside him, stark and flushing.

Too young to understand, his ignorant mind too concentrated on running, he noticed nothing of the risen winds blowing past, the expanded leaps of his feet, the oversensitive sensation of the springy grass underfoot, the heightened taste of the storm that had swept over Sutta Village several hours earlier scenting the air fresh with worms and mud, all of it paling to the exhilarating aliveness waking inside his body pure locomotion but for the determination to beat even the older boys carrying him across Runner's Field in a rapid streaking blur.

His first seizing of the Power lasted seconds only, but seconds proved enough.

The unfamiliar Power escaped his weak, untrained inner grasp as he stopped and opened his eyes. He'd achieved across the whole one mile of Runner's Field, stood well past the real racers' finish line.

Confused, the silence struck him a startling blow. All sounds of the festivities—the music, the laughing, the dancing and cheering—all of it swallowed mute.

He turned round, faced the runners far away, having stopped, staring at him. So too the pretty girl in frilly green dress he'd sprinted past, her face pale as candle wax framed in dark curls, terror in her wide eyes, her bouquet of flowers dropped at her feet. She backed away, turned and ran. Toward the hundreds of stunned spectators, unvoiced horror betraying their unblinking stares.

Banzu's parents rushed to him, Mother crying and hugging, Father hesitant at touching his son while saying nothing of the fear in his troubled eyes. They rushed him home while angry shouts arose at their backs.

After that, those who didn't avoid Banzu threw rocks or animal dung along with spiteful curses of Soothsayer accusations at him when he ventured outside, even his friends, so that his parents kept him inside.

Two miserable week passed.

The villagers formed an angry mob armed with torches and farming tools. They surrounded Banzu's home, demanded him and his parents leave the village that very night, and they made no bones about seeing it through by any means necessary.

Arguing became shouts of murderous threats, and when Banzu's father shut and braced the door, the unruly mob set their torches to the house and busted the windows with rocks.

Then memory grew fuzzy from a little boy's overwhelming terror. He remembered coughing and choking, eyes and lungs burning from the harsh billows of smoke. Mother's screams and Father's shouts. The blazing waves of heat while the air shimmered and cooked.

Then, amid the flaming chaos, a stranger showed up and rescued Banzu away.

Only Banzu.

While the fire claimed his parents inside the collapsing wreckage of their burning house.

He withdrew from the awful reverie, blinking back tears and the pain of his parents' faces faded with time into blurred obscurity. "They died in a fire when I was a boy. That's how I got this."

He stuck out his left arm, the gnarled flesh thereon pink scarring from the elbow up and wrapping over his shoulder where it spread in wicked fingers across his upper chest and back.

His uncle tried convincing him to get his scars healed through restorative magic by way of a Lady's Chapel, and though he'd often considered it, erasing his only reminder of the last time he'd seen his parents alive provoked a shame too unbearable to accept.

If not for me they'd still be alive. If not for me . . . Jericho's all I've got left.

"Got what?" Melora shifted behind, twisting for a better look at his outstretched arm, the scars thereon his shoulder. "Oh. Right."

A moment more and he cradled his arm back round his gathered knees. "I'd be dead too if not for Jericho. He pulled me out of the fire. I owe him my life." *No, more.*

"That's awful," she said. "I'm sorry."

"Don't be." He twisted on his bottom to better face her over the wicked reminder of his dead parents' killer burning between them. "It's not your fault." *It's mine. All mine.*

Their gazes met in the silent exchange of a truth unspoken. Burdens were born from the loss of innocence. Naïveté. While the innocent yearned to lose their innocence, those who already did so in turn envied the innocent, and knew grief in what they lost.

"Scars," she said in almost-whisper, her knowing smile a generous touch of empathy. "I guess we have that much in common."

He smiled, nodded. "Yeah. I guess so."

***

Cool winds sweeping in low through the trees, howling round trunks and up through swishing branches, dancing leaves in the dark while adding a shimmer effect to the shadows beyond the agitated light of their little fire.

Banzu shivered, the chilly breeze rolling over his drying skin, nipping at damp nooks and crannies. He scooted backwards closer to the fire in an attempt to draw more warmth, settled into silent musings.

He stirred both outside and in. Behind him sat a veritable source of untapped knowledge if only he could keep his tongue from slipping loose secrets. Not trusting himself to speak, and not knowing what he might say if he did, he remained silent while chewing on thoughts until the words tasted right.

After a time he decided on some gentle probing.

"So what about you?" he asked. "Isn't your, uhm, husband worried you've been gone for so long?" *Please don't have one, please don't have one, please don't—*

"Spellbinders never marry."

Yes!

She added, "The Academy forbids it."

But . . . "Jericho married one." And he swore he heard the rolling of her eyes signaling the relapsing of her eased mood.

"That's different," she said. "They married in secret."

He peeked over his scarred shoulder. "Who's Aggie?"

"Spellbinder Agatha dar'Shuwin," she said, correcting with emphasis of the proper title. "Mistress Agatha to you."

"Oh. Okay. Well, how long have they been married?"

Silence.

"Why didn't she come instead of you?"

No answer.

He huffed and crossed his arms. "Fine. Don't talk. Just sit there like a friggin stump. See if I care."

She twisted round—and so did he, meeting her glare for glare. Shadows danced their faces.

"Why are you so godsdamned insistent on pestering me?" The angry-cute scrunching of her face, the petulant thinning of her scrutinizing stare. "What are you getting out of this?"

He opened his mouth—closed it, said nothing, held the brunt of her violet ire. *A reward beyond price. A reason for being. Some small measure of meaning to my existence beyond hiding away on these isolated mountains.* Instead, honest and open, he said, "A chance to make a difference."

The fire died in her eyes, her features slackening. She held her study of him a silent length then turned away.

"Mistress Agatha is his Spellbinder—*was* his Spellbinder," she said. "They were the last official Pair in the Academy, before Jericho disappeared. She was next in line for ascension to Head Mistress. But that changed when she confessed her hand in his escape." She paused, laughed, soft and short.

Banzu smiled at the delicate sound of her turning mood. "What's so funny?"

"Nothing."

"No, tell me. What?"

She huffed a terse breath.

And he huffed one right back. "It's not like we're going anywhere."

She sighed. "Since I was a child, stories of Jericho the rogue Soothsayer crossed the lips of every aizakai in training. We were told he'd already been killed years ago. But every Spellbinder boasted about bringing him back one day anyways. None of us really believed it. Then Junes happened, and I learned the truth."

She drew in deep, exhaled through pursed lips. "Took me two years but I found him. Then I let him slip right through my fingers. When I get my hands on him I swear to gods I'm going to wring his scrawny neck until his godsdamned head pops off!"

Banzu chuckled, no need for turning to confirm she sat choking the air.

Darker thoughts intruded then. He twisted, looked at her ensorcelled map spread on the ground beneath a scatter of rocks weighting it from blowing away while it dried.

"Mind if I have a look?" he asked.

An absent shrug, the dismissive flick of her wrist.

He slid the rocks free, wondering where that glowing red mark would reveal his uncle's present location. As if on cue to his musings, a strong gust of wind blew in through the trees, catching beneath the map and sending it flapping. He tried snatching it from the air though it slapped against the side of his bare thigh. He peeled the rumpled paper from his leg and set it down with a fist-sized rock on top, realizing only then he sat too close within Melora's void-aura and so made a mental note to check his uncle's whereabouts later in private viewing.

He stared over the map, enduring belly squirms. Even if he knew where Jericho was, he had no way of telling what dangers his uncle might be in.

Jericho's voice recalled: *'A meeting, nothing more.'*

But Banzu knew there *was* more—a lot more. Jericho changed his mind from murder then left for reasons unexplained.

Something to do with the letter Melora delivered him, I know it. Not that she'll ever tell me, if she even knows. Jericho concealed something before leaving, but what? And why?

Banzu mulled on the mystery of it all: the Enclave . . . khansmen assassins . . . Hannibal Khan conjuring lightning . . . the unliving creature sealed beneath the palace in Junes.

A shiver ran through him while turning over that last.

"That . . . that thing," he said, knowing no other proper word. "The one you mentioned before. The creature the Khan is looking for in Junes—"

"The necromaster," Melora said. "Dethkore. What of it?"

"So it's really true then?"

"I wouldn't be here if it wasn't."

He suppressed another shiver. Some legends from the Thousand Years War were that—legends. Exaggerated tales of fancy wound round slivers of truth slipped loose from the eager tongues of bards entertaining drunken audiences while earning coin. But others . . . history interwoven by nightmares all too real.

The twisted tales of Dethkore, the Nameless One's servitor during the Thousand Years War, poisoned undying legends almost as much as the sinister stories of the infamous savior-slayer Simus Junes. Leading an army of aizakai against the Nameless One's defiling hordes, Simus harnessed all the Power of his Soothsayer Grey Swords by seizing the Source, endured recurring losing battles by skipping back through Time until finally rending the Nameless One's essence from the Dominator's Armor and banishing him from the mortal plane while earning all Soothsayers through Simus the bloodlust curse.

And for it the world's aizakai population decimated by the Thousand Years War, their numbers diminished to paltry survivors. But the Nameless One had not chosen just *a* necro-*mancer* as his servitor but *thee* necro-*master*.

Simus and the surviving aizakai defeated Dethkore and his unliving hordes, burned the necromaster alive and entombed the ashes then claimed the necromaster's soulring vitus as prize of his victory. A lanthium ring bound with Dethkore's soul by dark arts unknown, the indestructible relic passed down through the Junes bloodline from queen to queen.

And thus began the dark age of Soothsayers, centuries of slaughter prompting the fistian Academy to hunt them down in an attempt to end the Nameless One's curse through Soothsayer extermination.

From the moment of Simus' turning to the bloodlust, only queens ruled Junes. Until, and according to Melora, the most recent queen broke tradition and married. Her husband then murdered by Hannibal Khan, her ring taken along with her life, their Spellbinder Vizer fleeing for Fist.

"The evil locked inside that crypt is forever," Melora continued. "It can't be killed, only controlled, and that but barely. Which is why the Enclave chose Junes. If Hannibal Khan resurrects Dethkore, his army of Bloodcloaks will become unstoppable. You cannot kill what is already dead."

She paused, muttered a curse. "Why Simus didn't scatter those godsdamned ashes to the wind and throw that godsdamned ring into some bottomless pit I'll never know. With it, the Enclave seeks aizakai holocaust to prevent another army from stopping them from ushering in another Thousand Years War."

"He saved the world though," Banzu said, unable to deny the sympathy of support between Soothsayers. "Simus did."

A mirthless chuckle. "Yeah, and then he almost destroyed it. Again. This world would've been better off if Soothsayers died with the war. Every last godsdamned one of them."

Banzu cringed. He twisted round. "You don't really believe that, do you?"

She twisted facing him, held his eyes for a silent measure, then turned away. "Enough talking. The fire's getting low."

"Oh. Right."

* * *

Banzu leaned aside, reaching at the pile of sticks close by. And froze to the whispering unease prickling the fine hairs on the back of his neck when he caught sight of two tiny bluish twinkles hovering within the shrouding gloom beyond the firelight. He squinted, the parallel twinkles expanding by a minute fraction. And tensed as more twinkling sets revealed into view at random places round the two fire dwellers. Two sets . . . three sets . . . more sets.

What the frig . . .

Behind, Melora's voice, tight and rising. "Uhm, Banzu?"

He dared not look away. "Yeah?"

"Are you seeing what I'm seeing?"

An elevating chorus of low growls arose in the dark pitch.

"Yeah." He withdrew his reaching hand from the piled wood, gaze darting to his sword dangling by the belt from a branch—over ten paces away. He swallowed a curse. On either side of that tree trunk stared back two sets of hungry blue . . . *eyes, that's what they are. Friggin eyes.* "And I don't think it's anything good."

Shadows swept aside from five furry heads set upon shaggy shoulders the height of an average man's waist entering into the outer wan light of their campfire. Creeping forward, rising growls rolling forth from fanged and gaping maws the lower jaws of which twitched in guttural vibration.

"I think we've got a problem," Melora said.

"I think you're right." He pulled his legs in beneath him, stood into a hunched squat, palming the ground. "I can't get to my sword. What about you?"

Melora spat curses while joining up onto her feet in a low naked crouch.

He risked a glance behind at the same mistake she'd made after stripping bare, for her twin fanged dachras hung sheathed by their leather torso harness straps from a branch well out of reaching distance.

One of the two looming furred faces flanking the tree brushed beneath his dangling sword in a mocking pet of its massive head as the slavering, saw-toothed wolves stalked closer into the revealing dome of firelight. Of a different breed than any mountain wolf Banzu had ever encountered, the blue-tinged fur of their raised hackles glittered as with frost matching the savage cerulean gleam of their eager gazes, muscles rippling through forward-creeping twitches of paws the size of Banzu's feet.

His insides clenched. *Oh gods. Dires? From the Thunderbell Tundra. But why are they this far south?* No matter that now. "Backs together," he said in harsh whisper.

She backed up in a low crouch, rounding the fire, while he did the same, putting his naked back to hers and keeping in a low squat.

"I think I can get to my dachras."

"What? Are you crazy? Those things'll tear you apart! Just stay close to the fire. Maybe it'll scare them back."

The pack of five dire wolves circled round their trapped prey in growling fascination, cutting off all avenues of escape. Two facing Banzu to the three emerging upon Melora.

One of the three wolves near her crept closer, stopped and sniffed the air, ears twitching. It withdrew by inches, finding her scent distasteful. And as if by way of some mental exchange a second wolf near her did the same. The third between them stayed its position while the two at its sides split into a slow stalk round the perimeter, each in a wide semicircle, joining their two other companions on the far side in some inner bestial sense that told them Banzu should be dealt with first.

He snatch a grab for one of the sticks from the piled wood nearby to wield as a makeshift club, prompting the closest wolf less than ten human strides away to snap its jaws in warning bite while loosing hot gobs of saliva reflecting glints of the firelight. He slid the stick the size of his forearm behind, next to Melora's foot, then risked another snatching grab for a makeshift club of his own. Earning another snapping growl when the wolf rose up on its haunches then slapped the ground with its forepaws in stamping threat.

Behind, Melora pounded the ground with her club in an attempt at scaring back her lone wolf sentinel. But the effort did little more than irritate the predator into snapping at her, its hot breath misting in the cold air.

"What in the hell do we do now?" she asked, her voice a thin strain.

"I don't know."

"Not what I wanted to hear."

His dangling sword mocked him beyond the two wolves barring his way, their two joiners flanking his sides. With the Power he could weave between the creatures in a rapid burst and gain his weapon while suffering little more than a few scratches at worst. But Powerless while inside her void-aura, the wolves would rend him to pieces in a matter of seconds. *Even if I can somehow run past them, that means leaving her exposed.* And the moment he ran back inside the magic-nullifying bounds of her void-aura to fend the wolves away, the Power would slip from his inner grasp regardless.

He raised the knotted baton in pathetic replacement of his sword, mind racing for possible routes of escape though finding none. Tenacious creatures known for chasing prey into exhaustion when necessary, wolves possessed the stalwart patience of trapping their prey up a tree then waiting for days until it tired and fell so that they moved in for the easy kill.

No, fighting through them and running away is out of the question. And they'll bide their time until we collapse from exhaustion—if they don't tear us to shreds first. If not the both of us, then it's her or me.

"They're concentrating on you for some reason," she said, punctuating the obvious separation of the wolves. "If I can get past the one on me, I can get to my dachras. But . . . Banzu?"

He stole a glance behind. Met her eyes in silent exchange. Saw for the first time real fear in those strong violets stripped of their brazen pride into pleading pools of askance for anything in the way of help.

Men she could deal with through proficient riposte of a lashing tongue or fanged dachras. But these animals . . . fighting ferocious wolves of a mindset not just to kill but to feed proved another matter. Men sought murder from wounded pride or greed for wealth and power or even out of simple necessity born from misfortune. But where men possessed the ability to reason, these primal beasts possessed the savage necessity to hunt.

Taut muscles twitched through anxious flexes, his mind straining for focus. If only he could reach his sword. If only he could use the Power. If only . . .

He drew in deep, set his jaw, concentrated on the four wolves closing in at him by slow-pawing inches. And there arrived to conviction. "I said I'd protect you. And godsdammit I mean to. On my mark get ready to move."

"What?" She glanced behind. "Where?"

"Your dachras."

"What are you doing?"

"Protecting you—*go!*"

* * *

Banzu snatched the fist-sized rock from atop the map, spun while springing up from his crouch. He took quick aim and threw the missile over Melora's head at the lone wolf sentry blocking her path to her dachras, startling the wolf into the beginnings of a lunge. He spun back, facing the four others with his brandished club.

Behind him the rock struck Melora's lunging wolf against the side of its head, producing a yelp while sending it crashing sideways off lunging course into brief thrashing roll.

A second yelp as Melora leaped over the recovering wolf while pounding its rising skull with her club. She landed and rolled through the new opening provided by Banzu's distracting throw, sprang up twisting, threw her club at the turning wolf, then spun and ran. She reached her hanging leather harness in five bounding strides, tore it loose from the branch and yanked her dachras free.

The injured wolf turned, blood matting fur on the top and left side of its struck head, faced her though stayed its place on wobbly legs, shook its head, left ear dangling limp beneath the bleeding split in its skull. Another of the wolves noticed its companion's injury, for it shifted predatory intent from Banzu to Melora, rejoining beside its injured brother while splitting their human prey. Both wolves pawed forward then stopped, sniffed the air then settled into growling stares.

Twin fanged dachras in hand, Melora danced forward to press an attack, then darted backwards against the tree from the blocking wolves' snapping, slathering jaws keeping her at bay.

The three remaining wolves on Banzu's side lunged forth as one, seizing the opportunity of their prey's separation. He ducked while dodging to his left, avoiding the first wolf's high daring leap and snapping jaws meant for rending his face as it sailed overhead, landed in the fire where it yowled while kicking up a flurry of twinkling firefly embers, scrambled out from the glowing nest of hot coals in a thrash of burnt fur while knocking aside sticks and clothes.

Banzu rose and spun, clubbing the second charger against its open muzzle with a sideways swing of his club, beating the wolf aside in a spray of broken teeth and bloody saliva twinkling amid the caught firelight.

The third wolf lunged just as Banzu reversed his swing in counter stroke. Its strong snapping jaws chomped his left forearm in a spasm of agony.

Godsawful pain jagged through the crush of his arm—then released when he finished his clubbing swing, struck the wolf between the eyes and by chance one pointy nub protruding by inches from his stick punctured the wolf's left eye. The beast released its clamping bite and backed away howling.

Heart a racing thunder behind the cage of his ribs, Banzu spun, hugging his bleeding arm against his middle, the rage of adrenaline a coursing hot fury through his veins. He confronted the two wolves facing him, the fire-leaper limping on blackened forepaws, the other salivating dark gore from its struck jaw.

One-Eye withdrew to the outskirts of the firelight, the weeping mess of its punctured socket running its face, content for the moment with allowing the others to finish off their intended meal.

And beyond her two wolves stood Melora trapped with her back to the tree, her animal captors keeping her at bay by snapping bites of the air every time she darted forth while slicing. Strangely, the wolves stayed their positions instead of moving in for the Spellbinder kill.

Banzu stole glances behind while creeping backwards toward the tree where dangled his sword. He gave struck pause when something odd happened.

Four of the wolves but for the initial first turned as one collective mind, set their full attentions on him, while the non-participant maintained its growling focus on Melora, preventing her interference. Three wolves stalked round the fire. Even One-Eye relapsed from the shadows.

"Lower your dachras!" he shouted on impulse.

Melora glared past her wolven sentinel, denied him with the shake of her head, wet blonde tangles swishing.

"Lower your dachras!"

"Are you crazy?"

"Just do it!"

She eased up from her half crouch. Oh-so-slowly lowered her dachras. And flinched surprise when her lone wolf sat upon its haunches, its warning growl lowering into a warding rumble. She raised one dachra in testing bid—and the wolf stood, its growl elevating. She lowered her dachra and the wolf sat again.

He cringed at the strange flushing mix of relieving dread, his suspicions confirmed. Melora squatted and set her dachras on the ground then stood. The wolf before her losing interest, it stood and backed away, turned and swept its gaze at Banzu.

Her void-aura. "They don't want you," he said, grim realization coiling his guts. "They want me."

The wolves stalked round the fire, closing in.

"Come and get me!" he yelled, then threw his club and spun, abandoned his dangling sword and ran past the tree, sprinting away into the darkness, naked, injured arm hugged round his middle, a slathering pack of wolves loping chase.

* * *

Melora finished dressing when Banzu broke through the darkness and returned to their camp in a running huff, startling her. She abandoned the boot in her hands, sank into a preparatory crouch with hands behind her back gripping dachra hilts for pulling, froze tensed.

He bent at the waist, sucking rapid gasps while palming his bare thighs. The fire blazed, all the wood he'd collected fed into it during his absence and making of it a beacon to ward the returning wolves before she stole away. He sidestepped closer to the inviting warmth, shivering, lathered in sweat, skin a glistening sheen.

"They're gone," he said between panting breaths.

Locked in stare, Melora straightened. She opened her mouth, closed it. Took two steps, arms spreading in the beginnings of an embrace, then stopped short, gathered herself. "You're alive?"

Catching his breath, he straightened. Smiled. Realized his nakedness and covered his crotch, wincing not from embarrassment but at the painful strain of his injured left forearm all throbbing ache. And hoping she wouldn't slap his face off for running away.

"Gods," she said. "I thought you dead for sure." A cautious glance past him. "But how did you know?"

He shrugged, glanced behind, lowered his gaze to her feet. "Gut feeling, I guess." And tensed, preparing for that angry slap regardless. *She must think me a coward.*

Another wary glance past him. "But how?"

He'd led the wolves away through a Powered chase, seizing intermittent bursts so as not to lose them, covering distant miles before he doubled back while leaving them far behind.

"Guess I'm faster than I thought."

"Apparently." She shook her head, thinned her eyes at the darkness, hunting for any activity beyond the firelight.

"Don't worry, they're gone. But we need to get moving. Now." He held her appraising gaze, his tongue a fumble. "I'm sorry. I wasn't abandoning you, I promise. I just—"

"I know why you ran. Though at first . . ." She closed the distance between them. "Guess they don't like the smell of Spellbinders." She took gentle hold of his injured arm, easing it closer for inspection. "Or the taste." She looked up and smiled, her eyes soft violet pools, her words a whisper. "Thank you."

He smiled and grimaced at once.

"Are you okay?" She traced her fingertips over the torn skin of his bleeding forearm. "Gods, it looks nasty. You're lucky they didn't tear it off."

"I'll be okay. It feels a little better now anyhow." And strangely it did. Until he withdrew his arm and, wincing, grunting, flexed his hand in brief test. *Not broken. And no muscle damage. Thank gods for that much at least.* "At least you're okay. That's what matters most."

The soft touch of her hand sliding up his arm, feeling over the rough scars he'd suffered as a boy, then fingers cupping round the back of his neck.

Their eyes locked and held.

Everything else fell away as Banzu lost himself in those violet pools assessing him.

She pulled him closer—and kissed him.

He startled flinched. "Why'd you do that?"

A smirk toyed at her lips. She withdrew her hand, fingers tracing down the length of his arm then gone when she stepped back. "Because you wanted me to."

He licked his lips, tasting the sweet memory of her lips. And leaned forward, closing in for another kiss.

But she stopped him short by palming his chest. "Easy, now. One is all you get."

"Uhm." He fumbled for words. "Thanks?"

To which she laughed. Though short lived. Her brow furrowed while she regarded his injury, frowning. "It looks bad."

"I'll be fine."

"It could get infected. Maybe you should—"

"No," he said, more curt than he meant. He hugged his injured arm against his stomach. "I'll be fine. It won't slow me down."

She considered him a moment. "I hope not." She turned away, gathered her boots and pulled them on.

Cold nudity and the possibility of determined wolves soon returning overtook further need for talking. Banzu scrambled round, gathering his damp clothes strewn about the grounds in disarray. He cleaned his injury courtesy of the waterskin Melora handed him, then cut strips from an extra shirt and wound his left forearm tight in the makeshift bandage, his mind already ticking off particular healing herbs to keep an eye out for along their way. He stuffed the rest of his belongs into his rucksack and belted his sword back round his waist in relieving comfort.

Melora cursed the loss of her ensorcelled map having blown away somewhere into the darkness they wasted no time searching in lieu of the returning wolves.

Dawn remained several hours away.

A distant howl arose in the west.

Neither looked back while they groped their way east through the black pitch.

CHAPTER NINE

They traveled through the dark woods in blind gropes of trunks and cautious stumbles, progress slow though steady. Two chilly hours passed before the first warming rays of sunrise pierced through the trees ahead, its golden lancing bars offering guiding light while pulling smoky mists from the chilled ground which blanketed the cooler earth in wispy patches. Spots of frost crunched beneath their dew-speckled boots kicking up swirling zephyrs through the dawn-honeyed mists, churning the wakes of their treading into ghostly trails.

The low-hovering veils of morning's thaw thinned moment by moment. Birds perched in the trees here and there, little dun sparrows twittering and chirping songs announcing the rising sun. All traces of the wolves left behind, the hungry pack chose another prey to track and kill, leaving Banzu and Melora to their long journey for Fist at a steady pace through the thinning woods.

They finished through the final scatter of trees an hour later where the meandering trails funneled together, converging into a dirt road beneath the open sky.

"Thank gods," Melora said, sighing audible relief. "Finally. If I never see a tree again it'll be too soon."

Banzu smiled though said nothing, a slight disquiet at their new exposure.

A few miles ahead stood a village with people outside already hard at work chopping wood or fetching buckets from wells, pushing wheelbarrows or feeding penned animals.

Hesitant, Banzu teetered on the verge of suggesting they go round instead of through, but Melora preempted him with her own cautious tongue.

"Best not to draw any attention," she said, making a V of her pointer and middle fingers and gesturing at her Spellbinder violets. "Just in case."

They diverted south from the road, bypassing the small community by crossing an empty field then a quick fetch through a scatter of maples and birches before rejoining the road, the village shrinking with distance.

Warm morning bloomed into warmer afternoon. They reached a babbling brook.

"I'll catch up," Banzu said, stopping.

"You do that." While Melora continued ahead, headstrong to a fault, her pace brisk and course sure after achieving flatter, open ground.

He spent a few restive minutes alone cleaning his wounded arm, the tender injury throbbing with a peculiar coldness sending prickling shivers up to his shoulder.

He sat next to the stream, wincing while poking round the sensitive tissue of his wolf bite. Strange faint blue jags resembling dark veins had spread beneath his skin round the canine punctures and ran up his arm to the elbow. He'd suffered animal bites before—impossible not to given his upbringing—but he'd never seen such infectious signs before. Of course, in all his years living on the Kush Mountains he'd never encountered dire wolves before either.

He raised his injured limb to beneath his nose, seized a flicker of the Power, wincing as he did so for his arm flared with lancing ache, and sniffed through heightened smell, scrunched his face at the pungent coppery tang of blood accentuated by the sour confirmation of infection.

He sighed, muttered, "Great. Friggin great."

He settled the irritating arm atop his lap, thoughts straying, his right hand drifting up, fingertips touching his lips in idle reflection.

She kissed me.

He smiled at the pleasing reverie, though it fled a moment more when another shivering throb jagged through his arm.

He frowned down. *Needs some stitching, but I don't have any hook and gut. And there'll be scars regardless, but at least it's not broken.* He flexed his left hand in testing bid, grimacing. *Gods, at least I still* have *my arm. Could've been a lot worse.*

He leaned forward and submerged his injured limb into the cleansing cold of the flowing stream for a full minute, enjoying the sun's baking warmth on his skin while the wind breathed gentle caresses across his face and neck. He dunked the bandages next, squeezed them out then rewrapped his left forearm taut, wincing through the task. A quick filling of their waterskins and he started off.

He approached Melora from behind, earning a glance though no pause in her unyielding stride, only to fall back just shy of her void-aura when a thought struck him, so natural the habit it only occurred to him now.

Duh! I'm so stupid. Why didn't I think of it before?

Trailing, he seized the Power through brief, intermittent flickers, the dull ache of his injury flaring into cold jagging throbs with each testing seize. The Power fed upon his lifeforce, aging him faster while also healing him faster, inducing rapidity into the natural functions of his body. A fact he would use to his advantage.

Minutes this lasted until he surrendered the meager trials at speeding his recovery along and caught up beside her, each Power-seizing effort too brief for the trade of flaring pain involved. Later, though, he intended on excusing himself alone and spending longer time in accelerated healing.

Hidden beneath his sleeve and his makeshift bandages, the spreading infection troubled him two-fold. The last he wanted was for her to wield the injury against him as good excuse for berating him into turning back while she continued to Fist without him.

And yet . . . and yet. He flexed his hand in testing bid, earning no jolting jag through his tender arm, its ache a distant and dull throb.

Hmm. That's odd. Feeling better already. And—

She kissed me.

He smiled at the delightful intrusion resurfacing.

"What are you smiling at?" she asked, fetching him a sidelong study.

"Huh? Oh. Nothing. Just happy to be alive."

He glanced at her hand between them, considered feeding the hunger for risking a hold of it but decided against it.

They continued on.

He kept an eye out for some Mother's Kiss, the sweet herbs good at easing pain while staving infection, but found none. Though he plucked a handful of numbweed in passing by the yellow-berried bush flourishing in a ditch, ignoring the poisonous berries while discarding the leaves commonly dried then smoked for their euphoric sedative properties, and chewed the bitter sprigs which numbed his mouth while fogging his mind, not so much dulling any pain as distancing it.

His luck turned an hour later when he spotted some Mother's Kiss, a single patch of it by glancing chance, bright orange veins on the underside of its droopy, broad leaves flipping in the lifting breeze. He paused and plucked several handfuls, spat the bitter numbweed mush out and replaced it with a few leaves while pocketing the rest.

Minutes more and he stopped while Melora walked ahead. He made a quick poultice for his wound, aching again, grinding some Mother's Kiss between two rocks while feeding drops of water thereon then packing his wolven bite marks full to covering. The herbal balm stung when first applied, though the cold throbbing flares of pain softened in seconds.

He rewrapped the bandages taut then caught up alongside her again. And to his relief her ever-present void-aura did not abate the poultice's medicinal affect. *So I could've drugged her into staying with moonglum after all.*

"You're pretty good at that," she said. "Ever think of becoming an herbalist?"

"Nah." He shrugged. "I'm a mountain boy. Knowing herbs is just a part of life." A pausing smirk. "When we're not busy humping goats."

She chuckled.

Though her demeanor took a sour turn minutes later when, frowning, she tugged on the kohatheen collar locked round her slender neck and, scowling, grumbled a hot string of curses over her lost map.

"We don't need it," he said of the irretrievable map. "Another week and we'll reach the King's Highway."

The long stretch of road feeding eastbound travelers to Tyr, he knew the route only by stories from his uncle, the King's Highway connecting Ascadia to Thurandy through Caldera Pass. But his reassurance only provoked her darkened mood.

"I'm not an idiot." She gave another grimacing tug on the kohatheen before abandoning the futile chore of removing the locked metal loop through her neck. "I know where the sun rises and sets. That map was my key to Jericho's location. I don't need it to keep track of me, I need it to keep track of him."

She punctuated this with a glare Banzu interpreted for the underlying truth: useless to her alone for tracking Jericho because of her void-aura, with the ensorcelled map lost she saw little need in having Banzu around.

She fetched his injured arm a deliberate stare, abrasive silence thickening between them and remaining so for the next few miles.

The dull ache of his injury flared into rhythmic throbbing jolts of cold in tune to his heart and lancing pulsing chills up his arm when he stopped to clean then redress his wound with a fresh poultice while Melora continued ahead. Though the pain abated when he caught up alongside her again.

At one point he stopped and dug up a handful of edible tubers after catching sight of their tall, red-speckled stalks, the flowers thereon still closed green buds awaiting summer's bloom. After washing the tubers clean, they munched on the raw sweetness of the fibrous white roots while they walked, relieving him from the burden of hunting down dinner. Nose runny, sinuses stuffy, his body craved rest and plenty of it.

He'd also taken to carrying a stick plucked from the side of the road along the way, squeezing it every now and again in his left hand, tensing, relaxing, flexing wincing strain through injured forearm muscles, ensuring their proper function while the Mother's Kiss poultice continued its slow healing.

Nightfall.

They made camp a mile north from the road, setting a small fire behind a convenient cluster of tall rocks next to a lone tree so as to draw the least amount of attention from any passersby and other potential threats stalking through the surrounding gloom.

"I'll take first watch," Melora said, standing opposite the fire. "You look like you need the rest."

Banzu, sitting on his spread blanket, nodded. "Okay. Sounds good." *More than good.* He lay down, relaxing on his better side, enjoying the stretch of his legs and—

But she didn't turn away, just stood there staring at him, though more particular at his left arm, frowning, orange firelight skating across her glum face and making reflective pools of her eyes.

"What?" He sat up. "What's wrong?"

She crossed her arms. Sighed. "Nothing." And walked away twenty paces to the tree, rounded past it and sat with her back against it facing east.

He stared at the obstructing trunk between them. Winced as cold pain flared anew in his arm so that he flexed his hand, grimacing, but the pain remained, gone one moment then there the next, its frigid teeth gnawing at his bones for the marrow.

She sees me as a liability now more than ever. If something bad happens, I've got one good arm. And the infection's spreading despite the poultices.

No need to unwind the bandages for another look. Those underlying jags of blue veining just beneath his skin inched their way up past his elbow in slow climb toward his shoulder. And his hand possessed a bizarre coldness to it, deep and rooted, fingers stiff, knuckles crunching more than popping every time he flexed it.

The soggy wool of his mind making deeper thoughts harder to pick apart, he lay down on his right side with his left arm draped over his chest, and fell asleep watching the fire dance.

Only to startle awake and alert by a prodding boot nudging the top of his head. He sat bolt upright, gazed up at Melora in standing loom.

"Wake me at dawn," she said while turning away a little too quick. She fed sticks into the glowing nest of coals while blowing it into flaming life, then retired opposite the fire to his bedroll now hers and fell fast asleep, swaddled inside her wrapping cloak.

He sat watching her through the firelight dancing agitated flickers across her sleeping face. Noticed a puffy redness round her closed eyes more prominent than the natural rosacea of her cheeks. And again the following two nights when she startled him awake in the same like manner. But he said nothing of it.

And he didn't have to.

Crying in her private watches while he slept. And growing more distant since their escape from the wolves. One word answers when she spoke at all. Miles of silence. Curt glances.

The fierce need to hold her, to comfort her, to tell her everything was going to be okay edged Banzu's tongue yet never produced into anything more than guilty musings while he watched her sleep.

A silent, dividing wedge driven between them.

She needn't speak it.

On top of her unvoiced burdens as Spellbinder, he slowed her down.

And yet . . . and yet.

So why hasn't she run off?

* * *

The next day and Banzu found he disliked stealing horses despite knowing the animals provided them a faster means of travel. But after Melora spotted the farm's stable across the field south of the road, she refused surrender to what she declared a necessary thieving.

So they waited until nightfall and sneaked into the stable, filching the two chestnut mares and the necessary tack from the dilapidated farmstead. She left behind three silver pieces atop a wooden post, stifling Banzu's threat of shouting the poor farmers awake.

"We have to leave them something," he'd said, words a harsh whisper in the dark. "Or I'll yell. I swear I will."

"You make one godsdamned peep and I'll slit your godsdamned throat," she hissed back, her teeth a savage gleam. Though a moment more she cursed. "Fine." And produced the three silvers from her hidden money pouch, slapped them down atop the post. "Happy?"

Neither the argument nor the payment of ten fold what the two horses turned out to be worth further endeared him in her eyes.

Too dark for riding without risking injury to themselves or their stolen horses, they led the saddled mares along the road until afforded better light than the thin slice of moon offered.

Soon as the sunrise peeked over the eastern horizon, Melora mounted her horse and rode it fast as it would carry her. Which, and to Banzu's inexperience with horses, proved not very fast at all considering the feeble state of the old mares.

Despite the leisure trot, every jostling shift in the unfamiliar saddle elicited in Banzu startling dread of pitching sideways and breaking his neck. Made all the more irritating by Melora who sat atop her horse as if born with it between her legs. He trailed far behind her for much of the day, though also learned as he rode, his methods aided by the faint traces of the skills of other riders—other Soothsayers—transferred into his subconscious mind over the years through the Power.

The Power connected all Soothsayers, absorbing traces of their skills and memories while it flowed through them, and mixing fragments of their personalities back into the *Well of Power* to be seized by another. Sometimes Banzu knew things unlearned because of that connection, though he had no choice as to which particulars he knew or for how long.

He remembered the morning he awoke speaking fluent Trussian, seven years old and well before he possessed firm control of the Power, not even realizing doing so for the foreign jargon sounded right in his head. Jericho explained the how and the why of it to his ignorant nephew, though as the day wore on Banzu's fluency faded, making fumbles of his tongue until the last rolling R'd Trussian syllable escaped his normalizing speech.

Another time, after Jericho gifted him the present of his knife now lost to Green River, Banzu sat for hours whittling a cherry knot of wood into an immaculate flute with the proficient ease of a master carver only to realize he no longer possessed the ability to play the instrument when he raised it to his lips. Yet the entire time he'd hummed through intricate melodies another had learned through years of practice, the musical expertise escaping Banzu's confused mental grasp as if he'd never possessed it—which *he* hadn't.

The riding experience of other Soothsayers bled into his aptitude while he rode, helping him adapt to the animal. Tensed hand relaxing on leather reins, pinching thighs easing their grip of saddle, feet more sure in stirrups, body less rigid and more fluid instead of fighting against the bouncing sways. Soon he closed distance behind Melora though she still rode half a mile ahead of him, urging her horse fast as she could manage.

The first night after their successful robbery, he voiced concern about running the horses lame from her determined pace. She agreed to a slower pressing of the animals, though over the next two days he noted little difference in the way she rode her tiring mare other than the encouraging curses she berated it with.

Two days later and they lost her horse to a broken foreleg. Its hoof caught in a deep rut while crossing a field covered in snarls of high grass, throwing Melora out from the saddle while the horse tumbled with a startling cry and a sickening snap of its twisted leg.

Panic flushing, Banzu scrambled down and rushed to Melora's side, fearing her injured or worse dead from a broken neck. He rolled her over—and she fought off his helping hands with angry slaps then sprang up spitting curses at the world and every horse in it. After dusting off, she slit the injured horse's throat with a dachra.

He watched the logical butcher's coldness without comment, no argument for leaving the animal alive and defenseless against any predators.

Later that night he popped the last bit of cooked horse meat into his mouth, sucked his greasy fingertips clean. The meat tasted sweeter than beef. "Not too bad."

Melora, sitting cross-legged opposite the fire and finishing her own meal, looked up and swept her gaze past him to the remaining horse she'd earlier unsaddled and tied off to the tree behind him.

"Runner," he said, glancing back. "That's what I named her."

She frowned. Stabbed a chunk of horse meat with her dachra and teethed it into her mouth from the fanged tip, chewed and swallowed, waggled her dachra at him. "You shouldn't name what you intend to eat."

He frowned right back. Threw another glance at Runner. Said nothing.

"Two of us." She stabbed then teethed another chunk of meat, talked through generous chews. "Only one horse."

He thinned his eyes. Assumed they'd be taking turns in saddle from here on out. "What's that supposed to mean?"

She licked her glistening lips, smiled and shrugged, answered nothing. A deviant twinkle in her eye.

The following morning proved the matter settled. Soon as Banzu finished tying off his rucksack behind the saddle, Melora claimed Runner's back and rode off. He pursued them afoot, catching up through intermittent jogs then slowing behind while fetching his breath, his injured arm an aching throb.

Hours later he trailed within shouting distance, his left arm aching something fierce, each beat of his heart catalyzing cold lancing pain through his arm and earning him shivers despite the day's heat and his profuse lather of sweat. He grit his teeth and powered through it, flexing his hand round his new walking stick, determined to keep Melora in sight.

And reaped the opportunity afforded him by seizing intermittent Power-flickers to accelerate his healing. Though every seize shocked jags of pain through his arm so that he surrendered after five grimacing tries, then he surrendered to the routine of walking while flexing his hand and gritting his teeth, walking and flexing and gritting, a painful pattern of boredom.

Lathered in sweat yet shivering, he slipped the nape of his shirt aside with his good hand for a quick check. The blue-veined infection of his wolf bite spread to his throbbing shoulder despite the medicinal poultices of Mother's Kiss.

To his relief the throbbing pain subsided when he approached Melora who had stopped to make camp for the night. Tired and sore, his body craved rest by the fire already burning. He trudged to it and plopped down with a grunt.

"You know," he said, abandoning his walking stick to warm his hands in hunching lean, "if I didn't know any better I'd swear you're trying to run me lame."

She feigned a hurt look, replied an exaggerated, "Me? Noooo."

"Yeah you." He glanced at Runner munching grass nearby, huffed a derisive breath. He removed his boots and watched Melora eat the last of their horse meat while he thumbed his aching arches.

She sucked her greasy fingers clean while keeping steady eye contact with him over the fire, then licked her lips and shot him a smug smile. "Ahhhh. That really hit the spot." She stood, unbelted her cloak so that it hung loose about her full belly which she patted with both approving hands. "You look beat. I'll take first watch."

You always take first watch. And I am beat, no thanks to you hogging the saddle all godsdamned day. "Fine."

She walked to the eastern edge of the wan firelight where she rounded past a small boulder and sat.

He muttered a few choice curses under his breath about his foot and where she could put it. He pulled his boots back on, removed the blanket from his rucksack—and the bedroll. "*My* bedroll," he grumbled after spreading it out then slapping it flat. He lay down and rolled his back to the fire. Where he locked stares with Runner.

His empty stomach growled.

"What are you looking at?" He plucked a pebble and flicked it at the horse. *Godsdamned sack of glue is probably in league with her.*

Runner tossed her head, whinnied, eyeballed Banzu sideways, her bold eye reflecting firelight.

He rolled onto his back, glared up at the twinkling stars, sighed, closed heavy lids and relaxed, left arm nestled across his chest cradled by his right.

***

Sleep brought nightmares of fire and ice. Banzu lay coiled in a sweaty, shivering bundle, tossing and turning through warring elemental tides waxing chaotic in their relentless assault.

A breath of fire swept over his face while claws of ice raked through his insides. Heartbeat racing. Breathing a chore.

He thrashed, a helpless victim caught within the raging turmoil of illusions inviting panic overwhelming.

He startled from slumber, sitting upright, gasping, shivering, trembling, wincing in pain. His injured arm throbbed with icy ache, his sweaty hair a mat of damp tangles, his breathing short and rapid. An impossible fire of ice stole through him so that he threw his blanket aside only to reclaim it close in clinging hug. Confusion running rampant.

Still dark.

Too dark.

He rubbed the remnants of sleep from his eyes and seized the Power, craving the touch of something familiar to calm his frazzled nerves. Lancing pain shot through his left arm from fingertips to neck. Time slowed while crisp Power-greys claimed the world, illuminating his heightened vision, the black pitch of night surrendering to the radiant flush of twilight possessing a surreal quality akin to the master hand of some mad artist lifting every detail into something more profound.

And there he jolted tensed at his ability to seize the Power unrestricted. He released it, grey eyes returning hazel, luminous twilight vanishing, the world speeding up again.

He twisted on his bottom, eyes darting.

The fire beside him a glowing nest of dying embers.

Melora gone.

Runner too.

"Friggin hell!"

Anger flaring, he threw the blanket aside and sprang up in a cursing burst, kicking and flailing in wild abandon—then hunching while hissing through clenched teeth, a rampant spasm of agony torturing his left arm.

Then worry gripped him by the heart. The buzzing hum and whine of insects terminated with his outburst, he listened through the haunt of his solitude for any betraying sounds of others.

Silence.

Godsdamn her.

A violent chill jagged through him he ignored for kicking up a spray of dirt at the mocking embers betraying Melora's hours-long absence.

Godsdamn her!

She'd stolen away with Runner. *But she can't be far. Not in this dark.*

His mind a burning fury, he gathered his blanket and bedroll in a mad scramble and stuffed them into his rucksack, punching them deep. He slung it to his back and strode in the only possible direction she stole away: east.

That lying, no-good, underhanded, scheming, headstrong . . .

* * *

Banzu walked a steady pace broken by short bursts of the Power to cover faster ground while the luminous Power-grey twilight brightened his pursuit of Melora through the black pitch.

Walking . . . a Power-burst . . . more walking . . . another Power-burst, in repeating cycle.

He battled lethargy born from the infectious wolf bite sapping his energy so that he continued unaided by the Power for a time, afraid of tiring before he could find Melora. *And choke her godsdamned head off!*

She had ample time for putting miles between them despite the hindering dark, especially if she mounted Runner and risked a faster pace before sunrise.

He traveled for hours, mind a soupy fog, body protesting through painful shivers its cold lather of profuse sweat turning every shift and twist of his damp clothes into irritating pinches against his skin.

With every flat stretch of land he broke into Powered bursts while enduring agonizing stabs of cold in his throbbing arm. But he powered through the torture seeking to slow him from his dogged chase, refusing surrender.

Even if it kills me.

He entered a patch of woods, passed another grueling hour navigating the winding road through it and out.

Miles of open ground lay ahead, punctuated by the blood-red top of the rising sun peeking over the far horizon. He stopped and cursed, knowing the moment she reached this spot she would have mounted Runner and sped away if she hadn't already done so.

And still no sign of her.

He glanced behind, considered his futile endeavor.

No. I can't give up yet. Just a little farther. Another hill. Or two. Or . . . I swear to gods I'm going to kill her. Her and *that stupid horse!*

He harried on, relentless, unyielding. Imagining all the wonderful ways one could carve the choicest cuts of meat from a horse.

He ascended the gradual incline, descended the next slope. Minutes passed. He blew out his cheeks and raked his good hand through damp tangles, took a firm grip of hair in frustration and squeezed out glistening beads of sweat, flung them from his flicking hand. Ahead more open road aligned by empty meadows.

And still no sign of her.

Friggin hell! Okay, okay. One more hill, and then I swear to gods . . .

Cresting atop the next hill, he stopped and stared, tensing, his voice a whisper. "Oh gods, no."

Half a mile ahead, Runner lay in the shin-high weeds alongside the road, arrows jutting from her neck and ribs and rump, with three bodies strewn round the dead horse.

Banzu seized the Power, cold agony flaring through his left arm, and turned a sprinting blur speeding down the hill toward the bloody scene, a long cloud of dust churning up in his wake. He released the Power, ground his heels to skidding halt next to the dead horse, glanced round and breathed relief.

She's not here.

Two bodies lay supine, dead eyes staring at the sky, their shredded clothes dark with blood, their face and chests, their arms and legs a plethora of savage cuts. The third man lay prone, his entire backside shredded into dark scarlet ribbons, evincing the brutal handiwork of Melora's butchering dachras.

Banzu rolled the third body over with a pushing foot against its twisted hips. He withdrew a step, breath hitching in his chest. Here lay the khansman who'd run off after Banzu dispatched his two companions, Big Ugly and Rat Face, in the woods back home while protecting Melora.

Well I'll be godsdamned.

He inspected the tiny, dark tattoo imprinted upon the khansman's left cheek high on the bone. A single jagged bolt of lightning clutched in a fist. Another hunting Trio courtesy of Hannibal Khan and the Enclave he served.

Banzu read the struggle plain enough from the all the blood, the many shifts and prints in the dirt road, the matted patches of bloodstained grass, the arrows peppering Runner's hide. *An ambush gone wrong.*

He blew out his cheeks, breathing a little easier. Then followed a short course over several tracks of footprints, stepping onto and through them in what he estimated their motions to be, replaying the fight in his mind, at last returning to the road where a lone set of prints led east.

He smiled. *She sliced and diced her way through these khansmen before taking her leave alive.* A strong flush of arousal stole through him as his spirits perked.

He followed the road at a faster pace, concern growing over the dark droplets of blood in the dirt making a dotting trail.

Oh gods. She's bleeding. She's hurt.

He ascended another hill, pausing, a proud little quake in his nervous heart upon sight of the distant solitary figure walking far ahead. He seized a flicker of the Power, enhancing his vision, confirming Melora by the shimmering blur of void-aura bubble round her. He fought down the urge to maintain his hold on the Power and speed down after her.

He walked on, closing the distance between them by half, shouted, "Hey!"

The tautening posture of Melora's tall form stopped. She spun round in a swirl of cloak, left arm whipping up behind her back while she sank into a half-squat, eyes a feral gleam. She straightened upon recognizing who hailed her, her mouth a bitter scar in her face. Her right arm hung limp, the feathered tail of an arrow sticking out her right shoulder.

Banzu approached her in a Powerless rush, wanting to berate and hug her at the same time. But he stopped short, not trusting himself to do either or both, his face the cruel mix of a glaring smile, their eyes transfixed in the silence tossed between them.

He took a calming breath, let it out, took another, let it out, took a third and let it out, taming anger. With each one he recovered a little saner, a little more himself, a little less rabid that she'd done this to herself. He pointed at the obvious arrow.

"Are you okay?" A part of him begged to yank the arrow out then beat her over the head with it. "What happened?"

"What does it look like?" Her voice a scornful note, a scowl grew beneath those piercing violets. She afforded the arrow jutting from her shoulder a dismissive glance only. "Another godsdamned ambush from another godsdamned Trio of that godsdamned Khan!" A breeding darkness settled over her features, bleeding distance into her murderous glare. "They thought they had me this time. They thought wrong."

She spun on her heels and walked away.

"What? Wait!"

He rushed and grabbed her by the good arm, stopping her. She spun round, jerking her arm free—or tried to, but Banzu's iron grip proved inescapable.

Violet eyes flaring, she opened her mouth—

"No," he said, curt and commanding.

—then shut it just as quick, balking at his scolding whip of tone.

"I've had enough of this," he said, days of frustrations all bunched up and spilling loose. "Now you listen to me and you listen good." He gave her arm a good hard squeeze before releasing it, earning from her a wince. "I never would've thought someone like you could be so friggin stupid. What the hell were you thinking leaving me like that? You're lucky you're not dead, you know that? You still don't get it, do you? We're in this together, and there's nothing you can do about it."

"You're not—" she began.

"I'm not finished." He paused, held her eyes. "And I'm not stupid, so you can cut the crap. I know why you left me behind. Now look at us, we're both hurt."

She tried speaking again—and he talked right over her.

"Did it even occur to you while you were sneaking off that you could've gotten us both killed? You're so godsdamned worried about me being some godsdamned casualty. What if they'd killed you? What then? They would've come for me next. Is that what you want, both of us dead?"

"No, I—"

"Taking off like that was the stupidest thing you could've done. How do you expect to make it to Fist if you're dead, huh? Is that your master plan *oh wise Spellbinder*? Charging blind into the gods only know what? Stupid!"

"I'm—"

"Gods!" He flung his hands overhead in angry gestures then cringed, hissing, pain flaring in his left arm so that he hugged it against his middle. "I can't believe you."

"I'm—"

"I'm not the fool you think I am, Melora. I've been worried sick, and you don't even care."

"I'm—"

"What!"

"I'm trying to apologize you idiot!"

He startled flinched. "Uhm . . . what?"

In lower tone, almost fragile, she said, "I'm sorry. You're right. I never should've left you like that. I guess . . . I was hoping you'd just go home when you found me gone. Enough people have been killed already and it's only going to get worse before all of this is through. A lot worse. I just . . . I don't want to add your name to the growing list of casualties because of me." She lowered her gaze to the ground between her feet, whispered, "I'm sorry."

"It was never your decision to make," he said, confession surmounting. "And . . ." A pausing sigh. "And protecting you was never mine. I see that now."

Something compelled him into action. He tucked his right hand beneath her chin and raised it to better meet her eyes, and somewhere in the back of his mind the act surprised him. But he no longer cared about hiding his feelings for her.

"I promised to protect you, but I was wrong. You don't need that." Years of solitude and loneliness strangled brief hesitation in his throat while he held the measure of her stare. "You're a strong woman, Melora. And I really admire that in you. But you don't have to do this alone."

He smiled, lost in those beautiful violet eyes, the softness of her warm skin resting atop his. Heat flared in his cheeks while the moment lingered into an awkward stretch of him just standing there with his hand tucked beneath her upraised chin so that he lowered his hand, withdrew a single step and cleared his throat.

"I've never had any friends other than Jericho. But I know a friend should be there when you need them. Well,"—he spread his hands in indicative gesture of himself—"I'm here. For you. And I'm not going anywhere. Unless you ask me to leave. Right now. I'll go if that's what you really want. Or I can stay. And we can go to Fist together. But I need you to know you can trust me or else none of this even matters."

She appraised him a quiet length, turned away and stared off at the eastern distance.

"Trust," she said, repeating the unsavory word, tasting the bitter feel of it on her tongue, and with a touch of real asperity in her tone she placed a wealth of comment in the word. "My mother trusted the Lady's Chapel priests when the bleeding began during my birth and their healing arts wouldn't take because of what I am. I trusted my father who blamed me for her death before he abandoned me in the middle of the wilds because he couldn't suffer killing me himself. My former king trusted me as his Vizer to protect him when the Khan's fanatics stormed into Junes."

A pause, the slow shake of her head.

"No, trust isn't something the gods ever saw fit to bless me with. I've given my entire life to my duties, to the Academy. It's not just what I do, but who I am. And Hannibal Khan took all of that away from me in one fell swoop. If I fail . . ."

She faced him, determined violets shimmering with the teary-eyed depths of a profound sadness endured. "This is all I am, Banzu. I have nothing else. I *am* nothing else."

A wrenching seize gripped his heart and squeezed while he gazed into those self-disparaging eyes. And in the moment something passed between them, the truth delivered as to why she cried when she presumed him asleep and unaware. Duty to her was everything and all that she knew, and with each passing day away from Fist she castigated herself as more of a failure.

"You're wrong," he said. "You're more than that. Any fool can see what kind of woman you really are. Asides, you have me. I wouldn't still be here if you didn't. If you fail, then, well, let's fail together."

A small smile budding one corner of her mouth bloomed across her lips. She nodded, slow but sure. "Okay." She sniffled, glanced away and swiped at her cheeks. Rumbled her throat clear. Cocked an eyebrow. "You know, Banzu—"

"Ban," he said. "Call me Ban."

"Ban. You're a lot older than you look."

At that he couldn't help himself—he laughed.

CHAPTER TEN

Two days later . . . and Banzu stumbled—again.

His sore nose wouldn't stop dripping snot—every harsh swipe of his torturous sleeve raked his tender nostrils and upper lip with the scraping fury of wet sand—the soupy slosh of his foggy mind turned chaining thoughts into an incoherent chore, and violent shivers wracked him every few minutes. His cold left arm dangled numb and possessed the distant detachment of an amputee's phantom limb, his stiff fingers making of his hand a rigid claw.

He trudged alongside Melora in silent misery, every lethargic inch of him protesting aches unvoiced, clinging clothes damp with profuse sweat rubbing patches of his irritated skin raw in grinding nooks and crannies. He craved another layer of clothes despite the high sun beaming overhead. By the gods but he wanted to bundle inside a swaddling blanket next to a roaring fire for all the cold gnawing at his bones.

He concentrated on counting steps, his only viable focus, slogging one foot in front of the other then the next, matching Melora's slowed pace though she said nothing for it. And he maintained firm grip on his walking stick with his good hand, now more an aid than he would admit.

He tended his injured arm alone, excusing Melora ahead behind a false smile while he rested for a bit before catching up. The exchange of herbal poultices provided temporary relief to the throbbing agony of his wolf bite, slowing though not staunching the spreading infection.

Gods, it's creeping into my neck, reaching for my spine. The sensation of tiny icicle spiders marching their wicked course beneath his skin shivered him.

He considered the nasty option of cutting open parts of his arm along those dark blue forking tracks in desperate bid at bleeding out the infection. His extra shirts provided plenty of fresh bandages, though no hook and gut for the necessary stitching afterwards, his supply of Mother's Kiss gone unless they happened across another patch, and the real trick existed in hiding the gruesome doctoring from Melora.

She said nothing while he soldiered on beside her, though her eyes betrayed volumes of suspicion with every glance. But she possessed her own worries considering her wounded shoulder, her right arm cradled in a makeshift sling fashioned from Banzu's dwindling supply of shirt-torn bandages, the wound healing beneath the poultice of his last handful of Mother's Kiss. She confessed to favoring her right hand despite the ambidextrous nature of her twin fanged dachras, punctuating trepidation over encountering another khansmen Trio.

They skirted wide cautious berths past villages where farmers toiled at breaking ground for planting crops when not corralling bleating flocks of woolen sheep or bellowing herds of horned brahmadin, then towns with increased populace bustling the streets. They diverted from the road while avoiding trundling wagons and travelers alike. Two eventless days afoot and still several weeks away from Fist.

Banzu fetched her another sidelong glance, hoping she would stop soon to redress her injured shoulder while he stole more rest. But she walked strong, chin up and shoulders back, defiant to her injury, challenging it, rebuking it, evincing no signs of slowing but for the setting sun in a few hours. A darker part of him wished the arrow took her leg instead.

Least then I wouldn't have to struggle so godsdamned much just to keep up. Friggin hell, she's tireless!

He stared ahead, concentrating on putting one foot in front of the other, gaze fixed on the graveled road while his mind strayed backwards, reflecting on the fierce determination Melora showed after the second Trio's attack.

He'd heated a sharpened stick as instructed while she snapped off the arrow's fletched end protruding from her shoulder, though he pulled the other half of shaft free from her back because she couldn't reach it. Locha's Luck the arrowhead protruded out the other side by inches, otherwise he would've had to shove it through for removal. He poked the heated end of his stick turned surgical spear into her wounded back first, searing it shut, then administered the same gruesome doctoring to the front wound.

Impossible to forget the spasms of agony on her face, her screams muffled behind a bunched mouthful of shirt, or his guilt of imposing such necessary torture on her. The smell of her burnt flesh. Catching her in his arms when her quivering legs unhinged at the knees and she collapsed, him lowering with her, her breath hitching, trembling and sweating, clinging to him while she clung to consciousness.

So much of her true character revealed in such a short span. And she felt so good in his arms, and—

"You look like crap," Melora said, urging him out from his reflective musings.

He frowned at the scrutiny of her studious gaze crawling his sweaty face. "I'm fine," he lied, forcing a smile leaving his eyes untouched. "It's just a—" He clipped short in another stumble of bumbling feet, cursed and glared at the road seeking to undo him. "Godsdamn ruts." Another lie. He sniffled runny snot, raked his right sleeve beneath his sore red nose, wincing, then hugged his left arm tight against his middle and suppressed another shiver. "It's just a stupid cold. It'll pass."

"You need a Lady's Chapel and a few days rest. You can always catch up after you—"

"I'm fine!" he snapped. And regretted it immediately. "Sorry. I'll be fine. Really."

She frowned. "You're sick, Ban. And it's getting worse. Too worse."

He ignored her by staring ahead. Eyes sunken, pale skin clammy, lids heavy, he ran the tip of his tongue across his cold lips in warming attempt. "I'll walk it off."

She shook her head, sighing. "Sure you will. Look at you, you're dragging your feet as it is. That stick and your pride are the only things keeping you up."

He glowered, said nothing.

"You need medical attention."

"I'll be fine."

She thinned her eyes upon him. "Oh really." Her darting left hand a snaking bite, she grabbed his left forearm and squeeze—hard.

"Ow!" Startled by the flaring pain, he jumped back while jerking free, grimacing against the agonizing burst of cold jagging through his arm, lancing down into his hand and up through his shoulder, excruciating pain jolting the left side of his tensing neck. "Friggin hell! What'd you do that for?"

She drew up to her full challenging height and glared him down, left fist planted on hip. "To prove a point. You're not fine." She closed distance, features softening along with her tone when she reached for his arm again, slower this time. "Here. Let me see it."

He hesitated, cringing by inches, then surrendered against his better judgment. *Well, it's out in the open now.*

She rolled up his sleeve to the elbow with an ease of tenderness, unwound his soiled bandage for a closer inspection. And gasped.

He cringed, averting his gaze.

"Holy gods," she whispered. She probed his wound, jerked her hand away, then brushed gentle fingertips across his forearm, tracing the dark underlying blue jags forking and veining the length of his exposed arm to up beneath his higher sleeve, the bite marks having mended closed days ago, leaving irritated red puncture scars plump with puss.

His gaze strayed back to her.

She met his eyes with confused concern. "I don't understand it. You're freezing cold."

He withdrew his arm, rewound the bandage taut, wincing as he did so, then rolled down his shielding sleeve and turned away, stared on down the road. "It'll pass."

She studied him in the lingering pause broken by words unfinished. "Ban . . ."

"I'll be fine." He flexed his numb hand open and closed, knuckles crunching more than popping, trying though failing at hiding the flinching pain from his tensing face. His hand possessed full movement, not that he felt anything more than the blood crystallizing. "We should get moving."

Neither moved.

She reached out again.

And he withdrew by inches, fearing another punishing clamp on his arm.

Instead she placed her hand on his shoulder, turning him to better meet her eyes. "You're sick." A hesitant pause. "Maybe—" She paused again, longer, brow knitting, and glanced west, the way they'd come. "Maybe you've done enough."

He shook his head, words edging at the back of his throat.

She stalled them by shifting her hand to palming the side of his face so that he closed his eyes and leaned in against the gentle warmth.

"You're shivering," she said.

The warmth of her hand slid from his face. He opened his eyes, aching for the return of her comforting touch, lowered his gaze from the pity in her eyes.

"The next town," he said. "If there's a Lady's Chapel then I'll have it looked at."

"And if not?"

He said nothing. Lady's Chapels offered the magical healing services of their virgin priestesses upon payment of gracious donations, their grounds considered holy blessed and sacred in the name of The Lady, Ahzra'il, the goddess of love and mercy. They turned none away regardless their criminal past. And if destitute, the Chapel required an exchange of labor befitting the extent of their healing services.

The only coin to his name already given to Cody, Banzu wanted the healing though not the exchange of labor required, days spent mucking stalls or scrubbing floors or collecting alms while Melora continued to Fist without him. Though . . .

"How much money do you have left?" he asked.

She shrugged her left shoulder only. "Some." And fished beneath her cloak, produced a muffled jungle, removed her empty hand and frowned. "Less than I thought." A deliberate pause. "One day, Ban. That's as long as I can wait. I'm sorry, but if you're not healed by then—"

"That's all I'll need." He forced a smile, perking up a bit, while trying to work her into the situation. "And you can get your shoulder looked at too."

She winced. "I'm a Spellbinder, remember? Their healing magic won't work on me."

His face slumped—*oh gods, I'm so stupid*—as realization dawned. *For her to even go near a Lady's Chapel after what happened to her mother* . . . "I'm sorry. I forgot. I didn't mean to—"

"Doesn't matter. Come on. We're wasting precious time just standing here. Sun's getting low."

They turned though stayed put.

Two miles east, on down the road, approached a figure having crested over the far hill during their brief respite. They watched, waiting for two possible others to appear. But the traveler walked alone. Not another khansmen Trio then.

"Come on," she said, flipping her hood up, then turning to divert from the road and out from the traveler's path by habit. "No sense in taking any chances."

Banzu caught her short by the crook of her good arm, stopping her. "No. You're right. I need this bite looked at. Asides, they've already seen us." He squinted at the approaching figure. "Maybe they can tell us how close we are to the next town and if there's a Chapel there."

"Or maybe they intend on slitting our throats before emptying our pockets," she said.

"Yeah, well, they try that and they'll get more than they bargained for. Asides," he gave the hilt of his sword a reassuring squeeze, hoping the sight of it alone provided deterrent enough against possible robbery, "I'll ask real nice."

She smirked, mischief dancing in her eyes.

"What?"

"Someone's finally gotten a burr up their butt. I kinda like it."

* * *

More prowling than walking, the lone traveler approached, revealing himself a tall and muscled hulk of a man. Long hair a flowing raven mane. The hilt of a sword peeking from behind the right boulder of a shoulder and slanted for quick ease of pulling. Honey-tan torso bare to the waist but for the crisscrossing leather straps binding the weapon to his broad back in an X stretched to capacity from the muscled bulk it contained. Dark leather breeches hugging round trunk-thick legs. Calf-high boots ringed with tufts of gray fur. Purpose lurked therein his unbroken strides. Stalking intent.

Banzu blinked at what he assumed a mirage from unsure eyes. "Gods, he might as well be a Trio. Look at the size of him. He looks like he ate the other two for dinner."

Beside him a mirthless chuckle. Melora's feet shifted gravel, her gaze captured by the enormous traveler.

Banzu squinted for better assessment of the walking column of muscle's face, hunting hints of response at seeing two people standing there watching. Stone emotion stared back at him.

"I don't like this," she said. "He could be a paid man of the Khan. Come on, let's go before—"

"No," Banzu said. "I'm sick of hiding anyhow."

Minutes passed.

The hulking stranger stopped to within ten paces, yielding them attention as if only then did he notice the two standing in his path. Then more, a strangeness to his abrupt halt, impassive face tensing, icy blue eyes hunting. And more still. Speckles of blood on the chiseled slabs of his chest. Glistening trails of it on his meaty forearms. Fresh blood.

The behemoth of a man put even the cyclopean ferryman's incredible size to shame by comparison, though he looked plenty human enough. He stood three heads taller than Banzu, not a single strip of fat marring the carven musculature which gave his bronzed skin a taut look, the plump muscle beneath living on the constant verge of bursting through with every corded flex and twitch. Arms bulging without effort, broad shoulders twice the width of Banzu's waist.

Banzu swallowed, nodded in gesture, fingers fanning round his sword's hilt sheathed at his left hipwing in warding display. "How goes it, stranger?"

The man repaid no signs of common greeting. He stared mute through piercing blue eyes cold as frosted peaks, mysterious eyes housing the same icy brilliance as those of the wolves they encountered many days past. Yet those eyes burned with a smoldering hunger belied by an impassive visage.

"By the gods," Melora whispered, though only that.

The man raised his right arm, wrapped his meaty hand round the hilt jutting from behind his shoulder, claiming it, engulfing it, and held this position.

No misinterpreting the gesture, Banzu stepped in front of Melora by instinct, making a shield of himself, and relayed his hilt an answering squeeze, knuckles flashing white, swordsman assessing swordsman. He drew in a steadying breath, forcing focus through the fog of his mind while distancing from the nagging ache gnawing in his injured arm. Pulse quickening, a shiver stole through him.

Those icy blues appraised Banzu's motions with approval, earning the hint of a smile toying across the stranger's lips accompanied by the *thud* of his massive left fist pounding against his muscled slab of chest.

"Ma'Kurgen al'Kor," the massive-thewed stranger said in a baritone voice possessing its own weight and thickened with foreign accent sharpening the R's. Stare unbroken, his right hand did not stray from hilt while his left removed one of the two small leather pouches tied off at his belt, one to each hip. He tossed the clinking pouch to the ground at Banzu's feet where spilled forth an incalculable wealth of gold coins. He pointed at Banzu. "I challenge."

"What did he say?" Melora asked from behind. "Is that . . ."

Banzu ignored her, cursing himself for not taking leave when they'd had the chance. He glanced at the strewn gold coins catching glints from the sun, wanting to kick them back though fearing doing so would only anger the stranger. "We don't want your money. And we don't want any trouble. We just—"

"I challenge." Ma'Kurgen slid free the weapon from his back.

Banzu's eyes widened upon reveal of the largest sword he had ever seen, it twice the width and length of his puny own, a broadsword in the truest sense, its surface mottled with blood.

Ma'Kurgen leveled the weapon out between them in a double-fisted grip, muscles twitching through ripples of bridled power, the extended blade looking that it would take everything a normal man possessed just to lift it from the ground let alone carry it. Yet this man, this Ma'Kurgen al'Kor, brandished the broadsword with an ease of casual strength.

Friggin hell. Banzu blew out his cheeks, suppressed a dizzying shiver, released his instigating grip of hilt and removed the cold sweat dappling his brow before it stung into his eyes with the quick stroke of the back of his good forearm. He raised his hand palm-out in quelling gesture.

"Easy now, big fella." Backing up a step. "I don't know what this is about, but we don't want any part of it." Backing up another. "We'll just be on our way and you can be on yours." Bumping into Melora behind. "No one gets hurt, and everybody's happy."

"No." Ma'Kurgen's voice curt and commanding. "I challenge." He gestured at the leather pouch and its golden spill of coins with the stab of his broadsword. "You win, you keep. I win, you die like the rest."

Melora said something behind, her voice a quaver, words lost to Banzu's focus locked onto that of Ma'Kurgen's stone mask fracturing into waking trembles of emotion through a terrible process revealed.

Abrupt change, swift as hot breath misting a cold pane of glass, madness waking through a cascade of expressions. Ma'Kurgen's twitching lips peeling into a beastly snarl beneath flaring nostrils. Eyes blooming wider in snorting pace to his increasing huffs. Massive upper back and shoulders jerking in tandem to quickening heaves. A thick froth of spittle formed at the corners of his mouth, becoming dripping ropes of glistening saliva. Seething anger boiling to the surface in the count of five heartbeats. He spoke in words nothing more than a guttural growl no human ear could understand but through fear.

Melora gasped, whispered, "Oh gods. Oh dear gods no. A tundarian berserker."

Banzu's guts coiled then cramped. *A what?*

Ma'Kurgen roared while surging forth, raising his broadsword, boots kicking up gravel in his raging charge.

Friggin hell! "Run!" Banzu yelled.

But he allowed her no such time to obey. He turned and shoved her away, spun back, hands frantic fumbles for pulling his sword but too late. He dove into the opposite direction of Melora's stumbling fall as

Ma'Kurgen rushed them with surprising speed, split the air between them with the chopping stroke of his broadsword biting the road while spitting gravel.

Banzu tucked and rolled. Fought off the burden of his rucksack. Sprang to his feet ripping the sword from his left hipwing. Startled at Melora beyond the berserker on hands and knees, an easy target. "No!"

Banzu ran forward, intent on impaling Ma'Kurgen's turned back in protective impulse—then stopped short when the hulking man spun and faced him, ignoring Melora behind as nothing more than an inconsequential hump in the grass.

She straightened, kneeling, cradling her slinged right arm tight against her front, her face a contorted twist of anger and pain warring for dominance. She began standing, left arm dipping beneath her cloak for dachra.

"No!" Banzu yelled to her. "Stay back!" Then at Ma'Kurgen: "Hey!" when his adversary glanced behind, so as to draw the big man's attention. "You want a fight, you crazy bastard? I'm right here!"

Ma'Kurgen roared and charged with a pantherine grace, broadsword flashing glints of sunlight as he raised it overhead for another chopping stroke.

Instinct gripped Banzu by the balls and squeezed while tugging him into the natural rhythm of his reactive body. He flowed into *Willow Shakes the Breeze* and raised his sword—*clang!*—deflecting aside Ma'Kurgen's falling stroke seeking to cleave him in half from skull to crotch, but barely.

Teeth clenched, the delivery of Ma'Kurgen's mighty hammerblow spent bone-jarring shockwaves through Banzu's arms and rattled his spine while forcing him backwards in a stumbling tremble of vibrating muscles, Ma'Kurgen's brute strength and larger broadsword proving a disconcerting combination throwing off Banzu's defensive swordform game.

Ma'Kurgen spun in a sideways sweep of extended blade that would have split Banzu at the middle if not for his leaping backwards while hunching and sucking in his gut, the broadsword whirring through the air while cleaving wind in a fanning *whoosh!* The big man followed this by lunging into a graceful thrust, unrelenting in his self-imposed rage and his fierce need to spend it in full brutal payment.

Clang!

Banzu twisted while beating the skewering thrust aside at the last, the snaking broadsword stabbing the air just shy of his turning ribs. And in the moment he recognized this tundarian hulk, though overcome by berserker fury, possessed the fluid tells of mastered swordforms foretelling of one who spent a lifetime in training.

Violent shivers shocked increasing frigid jolts through Banzu's system in tune to his thundering heart as their blades crossed thrice more, each blocked or parried hammerblow making quakes of his fending sword, its sweat-lathered hilt threatening to escape his precarious grip, every riposting countermove a protest of grinding joints and taut muscles restricted from their natural flow by his sickness subdued only by the hot pumping fury of adrenaline. His left arm flared with lances of agony while he worked it through counterbalancing motions to his right compensating for the hindrance of his one-armed defense. He strained for focus in the thickening fog of his mind, achieving little but for that training under a master swordslinger provided recognition of shared skill in this enraged brute, however unrecognizable the foreign swordforms.

Melora stood by, anxious and watching the dance of death while shifting her nervous feet, right arm cradled in its sling, the fingers of her left hand wiggling for the eager pull of a dachra, captured gaze hunting Ma'Kurgen's flowing weaves of broadsword cunning for a possible opening of her own at his turned back.

Banzu stole a scolding glance at her between clanging parries of steel biting steel. *Run, godsdammit!* While he had their attacker distracted. He beat aside Ma'Kurgen's quick series of bone-rattling hammerblows through rapid back and forth fannings of his protesting blade groaning against the broadsword's pounding thunder, the attack forcing him backwards, ever backwards on quivering legs straining to maintain challenging balance against Ma'Kurgen's relentless press.

No end to the tireless berserker's onslaught. Banzu needed an out, and he needed one quick. And if not then he needed to secure Melora's safety before his brutal demise.

"Run, godsdammit!" he yelled at her between desperate deflecting crashes of hammerblows wrenching his spine through savage twists of his hips. "Run!"

Options dwindling, he put his frigid, rigid claw of left hand into active use with his right, gripping his bastard's hilt in a double-fisted clutch while dancing back, allowing the broadsword to pass instead of fending it aside.

Ma'Kurgen swung wide, continued through the twirling momentum of his spin, brought his cleaving broadsword up and over then down.

Banzu raised his sword to the felling stroke, bracing, hoping his inferior blade issued no surrender to the joining of their biting steel, arresting instead of snapping. He blocked in crosswise fashion Ma'Kurgen's mighty chopping downstroke unhinging both Banzu's straining elbows by inches, the jarring impact crunching him into a grimacing half-squat.

His gaze flickered past the dominating tower of tundarian muscle, at Melora staring overlong. *I can't do this much longer. Run, godsdammit. While you still can!*

Swords pressed together at the cross-guards, Banzu pushed against the hulking loom using his legs, twisted right while turning Ma'Kurgen aside, blades scraping loose, then he dove into rolling left. He sprang up twisting round while extending his sword in a sideways-sweeping cut at the full extension of his arm, the tip of which sliced across the turning tundarian's rippling flesh of exposed chest by thinnest margin, scoring a fine red line from right collarbone to left nipple then past.

Ma'Kurgen paused. Smiled. Burst forth in savage swinging grace, crazed eyes wide and wild, his roar a guttural release.

Banzu ducked by barest inch the sideways sweep of broadsword intent on lopping off his head, the whiffing pass tearing out trailing strands of his floating hair. He dodged left in another diving roll, stumbled when he came to his bumbling feet, tripped forward then rolled onto his bottom, the thickened grease in his disobedient joints congealed by frigid sickness and hampering mobility. Locha's Luck he yanked in his outstretched legs a fraction before Ma'Kurgen's chopping cleave divided them at the knees and instead bit into the ground, buried inches deep.

Ma'Kurgen tore his broadsword free in a spray of dirt. He twisted and chopped again—ground only, for Banzu rolled backwards just in the nick.

Banzu stood in a wobbly crouch, drenched in sweat, damp clothes sucking at every moving part of him. He raised the abused steel of his battered sword while backing away, panting short and rapid gasps of precious air sucked through clenched teeth, racing heartbeat a thunder in his throbbing temples, lethargic muscles burning with fatigue, bones heavy leaden.

Dizziness stole over his vision. He blinked hard and shook his head, wet hair flinging glistening beads of sweat. He gazed past the tundarian eyeing vital targets, locked eyes with Melora, mind issuing screaming pleas for her run but for his fevered lungs too active with sucking wind to voice the words.

What are you waiting for? Run!

But Melora stayed her place, watching it all with a queer little smile toying her lips and a dazzle of lust at play in her captured stare.

The moment fled, hewn away by Ma'Kurgen blocking her from Banzu's view through sideways shift, his muscled bulk eclipsing.

Cerulean eyes wide and wild, white teeth bared in a savage rictus grin, glistening ropes of saliva seesawing his mouth, the broad shelf of his shoulders rising and falling through seething heaves, the bellows of his strong lungs stoking the blast furnace of berserker fury therein his swelling chest, Ma'Kurgen charged, foregoing skill for sheer brute strength, swinging recurring blows through back and forth chops, his contorted face a rabid mask of distorted rage behind the frenzied blurs of his broadsword.

Banzu floundered in a maelstrom of panic, back-stepping while swinging desperate blocks side to side to side, the sparking clangor of their joining swords producing a reverberating thunder jolting his tiring limbs, shoulders burning with exhaustion, arms numb from fending the rapid succession of crashing hammerblows, each beating parry and the next threatening to send him toppling sideways.

Desperate to the last, skill dwindling from his waning defenses, he tried seizing the Power while fending against Ma'Kurgen's zealous onslaught, no longer caring if he revealed himself the Soothsayer in lieu of dying. And earned no flush of the Power's vital energies, for their battle had moved him once more into the magic-nullifying expanse of Melora's void-aura.

I need to finish this before my body gives out. She can't survive this madman alone. Only the furious turning of Banzu's thought-wheels kept his mind distanced from the frigid agony jagging rampant course through his chilled swell of veins. *If I die, she dies.*

No! You're a master swordslinger, godsdammit. Act like one. Fight like one!

Mustering the last reserves of his fading skill, he blocked another chopping swing then spun into the momentum of the reversing blow—ducking it, avoiding beneath it while stepping past Ma'Kurgen and earning space, the hulking tundarian stumbling as his following stroke cleaved only air and carried him forward.

Yes!

And now the battle-fever resurged in Banzu where the Power went unfounded, the welling of cold strength that entered into every man at the imminent prospect of death. The specter of his death hovered, cackling at his shoulder.

He rebuked it with a savage grin and the defiant protest of his inner voice.

I'm alive. I'm still here. I can do this! For her.

Ma'Kurgen spun round, huffing and puffing, his own fatigue at last breaking through the berserker fury rife in his piercing blues where lived strange approval at the madness of their duel. He paused in brief respite, smiling, gathering breath in hissing sucks of air while measuring the length of Banzu in predatory cunning.

"This has . . . to end," Banzu said between huffing breaths, violent shivers racking through him. He threw a glance behind at Melora watching them, stealing purpose from her presence, absorbing it, shaping it, molding it, packing it round his spine.

He focused ahead.

Their gazed locked and held, melding.

Banzu circled left while backing away, lowering his sword with the aching ease of his tired arms in tempting lure of his vitals. He slipped his grip and flexed his cold, numb left hand, priming it for the quick repurchase of hilt.

Ma'Kurgen moved with him, circling while inching forward.

So cold . . .

Banzu continued circling left while inching backwards, baiting the tundarian into mirrored motions away from Melora.

Vision blurring, palsied legs shaky, left arm a cold numb throb, his right a hot burn of exhaustion, a plethora of mastered swordforms replayed through Banzu's head, both two-handed and one, skill his true equalizer against Ma'Kurgen's unmatched strength.

So cold . . .

Circling, backing, baiting. Sweat stung into his eyes, fracturing his focal stare, forcing the brief removal of one hand to swipe away the burning blur. He grimaced through the exchange of the sword's full weight pulling in his exhausted right hand alone while wincing through the flaring pain earned from the quick motion of his left arm. Both hands reclaimed sweaty purchase of his bastard's hilt, lungs laboring, temples pounding, teeth clenched.

So friggin cold . . .

It ends here. Now. Before his body betrayed him through collapsing surrender and his mind folded inward into dark oblivion. Strain became a word with newfound meaning. Physical limits reached, his infection rampant, his mind and body exhausted. One more exchange then he could fight no further.

This madman, this tundarian berserker, his test . . . he must pass it. As much for himself as for Melora's safety. *Do it or die trying.*

A desperate plan rooted therein Banzu's defiant hope. He stopped his circling and backed away.

Ma'Kurgen, his broad back to Melora, pursued him.

Banzu smiled inward, drawing the madman farther away from her in backwards-creeping lure, risking much, not wanting to kill his enemy of unexplainable circumstances. Inside he sought a constant draw on the Power, felt nothing, felt—

Intense blue eyes flaring, Ma'Kurgen released a guttural yell and rushed forth with violent suddenness.

Banzu answered immediate mental reaction, though his lethargic body responded slower to the screaming hulk charging in bladed fury. He raised his sword in barring defense—and Ma'Kurgen beat it aside with a powerful crash of broadsword then followed through, spinning round, swung high, steel whirring.

Banzu ducked the broadsword slicing the air a hairsbreadth above his trailing hair. He jumped when Ma'Kurgen reversed his swing through a masterful twist of motion into a low sweeping cut, avoiding losing his feet but barely. He leapt backwards, boot heels digging purchase, intent on lunging riposte while thrusting low for thigh.

But he tripped over his own sick-drunken feet and stumbled though managed to turn round while toppling and, stabbing the ground in an awkward twist, the pommel of his sword punched into his concaving gut.

Ma'Kurgen rushed forward, seizing the opportunity of Banzu's presented backside, broadsword raised on high in double-fisted clutch.

While Banzu tumbled up and over his sword acting as a lever tilting with him, his stomach the fulcrum. He maintained his grip as his back met ground, and used the momentum to rock into a standing squat.

He spun round—gasping, the Power's blooming burst of energies a startling flush avalanching through him, the world slowing, its colors gone, its details magnified crisp and luminous by twilight Power-greys flashing in his eyes, Banzu's inadvertent roll having achieved him just outside the magic-nullifying expanse of Melora's void-aura, earning him the precious stretching of seconds.

In which he gazed up at the descending broadsword seeking to cleave him in half from head through crotch, all of Ma'Kurgen's berserker fury weighing behind the defining stroke that would break through unPowered steel then crunch through flesh and bone in brutal finale to their contest.

Reacting quick, his precarious inner grasp on the Power akin to fingers pinching a wet wedge of glass given the amount of exhaustion already suffered, Banzu raised his battered twist of sword with increased velocity against that slow-stroking broadsword, their swords joining in resounding *clang* a fraction before the life-saving surge of the Power escaped him.

But it proved enough.

Banzu twisted, steel scraping steel, while Ma'Kurgen stumbled past, his hammerblow deflected, though he recovered, began turning.

While Banzu continued through his twisting momentum by spinning round in speedy twirl, his extended sword sideways-slicing death. *Oh gods, the bloodlust!* But he turned his whirring blade at the last, changing its killing stroke into a flat-wise smacking blow delivered to the side of the tundarian's turning head.

Thwack!

Ma'Kurgen's head bent sideways on his bull-thick neck. He twisted, fell sprawling, the broadsword slipping loose from his disobedient hands and pitching away. He lay on his stomach, limp though groaning, blood wetting the upturned side of his head, skin split from the force of Banzu's clubbing smack, the thick muscular cushion his only savior in preventing a broken neck.

Banzu staggered back a space, panting, staring over the felled tundarian, his heart a hammering thunder straining against the press of his heaving ribs, the chill of his leaden bones making noodles of his exhausted muscles. Surprised Ma'Kurgen remained conscious from such a stout blow to the head. *So close . . . I almost killed him.*

"By the gods!" Melora's voice from behind. "By the godsdamned gods!"

Banzu paid her outburst small mind, too focused on still living. *I actually did it.* Victory tasted sweet, an exaltation burning away self-doubt. *I won!* Smiling, he turned to Melora gaping at him in wide-eyed, open-mouthed shock.

"I . . . did . . . it," he huffed out between panting heaves so labored the effort of speech hunched him over at the waist. Though he straightened seconds more at the explosion of triumph in his chest. "I . . . won."

Groaning, Ma'Kurgen pushed up onto hands and knees. He shook his head in the manner of some lethargic beast rousing from unwanted slumber. He wobbled from side to side on trembling limbs regaining stiffness. Touched at the blood trickling down the right side of his wounded head.

"It's over." Banzu stepped back, drew in a few deep breaths through flaring nostrils. He lowered his sword to his side, an easy task considering how heavy it pulled in his tortured grip. Only to raise the battered blade with grunting effort when the tundarian twisted round on knees and faced him. "It's over, godsdammit!" He aimed his sword out between them, the effort of keeping it from sinking to the ground trembling his arm. "It's over."

Ma'Kurgen stared back through glazed eyes, their gazes on equal level with the giant tundarian's kneeling, his crazed mask of berserker fury gone, wild rage replaced by a strange and breeding sadness slackening his features.

"The killing wind," Ma'Kurgen said, a note of surprise in his voice, icy blue eyes big as saucers. "Finally." He smiled. "A worthy opponent." He hunched forward, palming the ground, presented his head on outstretched neck in offering. "You have earned my execution."

"What?" Banzu stared on, dumbfounded. "*What?*" He withdrew a step, lowered his sword, glanced at Melora. "No." Shook his head in denial. "Gods, no."

Ma'Kurgen raised his head, met Banzu's gaze in disturbing appeal. "Kill me," he said, eyes sullen pools of askance, tone pleading. "Kill me now."

"You're friggin crazy."

Banzu withdrew another step, then another. He looked at Melora, but she offered no help but for standing there gawking at him, her lips twitching as though containing a wild grin seconds from breaking loose.

"Kill me!" Ma'Kurgen roared. "Give me my honor back!" He craned his head, whipping long black hair in a rainbow mane, sullen expression replaced by a twisted mask of growing outrage. "Kill me!" He pounded the ground with his fists. "Kill me!" Then beat at his chest. "Kill me!"

Gods, he wants *to die.* Banzu spun away from the tundarian's rekindling madness while sheathing his battered twist of sword at his left hipwing, having to force the abused blade therein the protesting leather. He tried telling Melora to run before the berserker's fury returned in full reckoning, but his lungs too racked with pain provided no more depth to his words than a harsh whisper.

So he rushed to her, grabbed her by the closest hand and, jerking her out from muted stupor, broke into a frantic run, allowing her no choice but to follow or be dragged behind.

And run they did.

Away from the kneeling madman begging for death in tortured screams.

CHAPTER ELEVEN

Melora gasped the moment Banzu clamped his frigid grip round her right hand and yanked, startling her out from staring stupor. She bit back a scream behind teeth snapping shut, her arm jerked from its cradling sling into full extension, the wrenching of her injured shoulder a painful torque of protesting socket.

They ran away from the kneeling tundarian berserker pounding the ground while yelling for his death in shouts so brutal and raw she tasted its crazed fire in her own throat.

Abandoning the eastbound road, they raced across the northern field, kicking through high grass then dense brush and bush in reckless abandon, achieving the face of a hill. Halfway up the incline Banzu stumbled, fell, pulled her down with a jolting jerk. She bit off another scream.

Before she could voice her want for stopping, for regaining her scattered bearings, he scrambled onward, pulling her along while he kicked and clawed up the remainder of the hill, his strong frigid grip refusing release. The agony flaring in her abused socket and the brutal cold entrapping her hand proved a wicked combination burning tears in her eyes. She struggled at keeping pace lest he drag her.

Fear Banzu's relentless whipping master—of that she gleaned in his eyes with every panicked glance behind, not at her but past her—he looked more afraid for her safety than his own. Her mind roiled in such a tizzy that speech surrendered to running.

After cresting the hill, they fought through lashing branches while dodging and weaving between trees. And still the tundarian's raging bellows sounded from the road in mad pursuit of diminishing echoes riding the winds.

Banzu's stumbles increased, as did the wrenching flares of pain in her abused shoulder. Her mind divided from the efforts of her working body, splitting confusion and shock into some semblance of truth slow in dawning, while questions accumulated in heaps and stacks over distance gained.

His eyes . . . so brief, and the way he moved . . . so fast . . . did I really just see what I think I saw? How is this possible? Why didn't the Head Mistress tell me about—

Another yanking stumble tore her loose from those chaining thoughts. She captured glimpse of Banzu's hazel-eyed glance betraying no hint of the luminous Soothsayer grey she swore she'd seen seconds before he ended his contest against the crazed tundarian berserker, his motions during that impossible glimpse stealing into rapid blur, there then gone, a fraction of reveal.

Grunting, wincing, she clenched her teeth and stifled another protesting scream while he pulled her round a cluster of trees. They reached another hill, the base of which ran thick with wicked hookbrush, its nest of sickle thorns raking and clawing at clothes and skin. They scrambled up in another fitful climb.

She yearned for the mercy of stopping, of catching her breath while assessing their new situation, of allowing the torment in her shoulder a moment's reprieve. But every time she slowed she stumbled, every time she opened her mouth there jolted another painful yank on her arm snapping her teeth shut. His vise-like grip chilled her clamped hand numb by transfer, inviting the prickling of gooseflesh up to her elbow. Yet through it all she knew a flourishing excitement over newfound possibilities. She wanted to know—needed to know—but Banzu's frantic towing provided no space for anything but running.

They reached the crest of the hill and broke into another struggling sprint. She ducked just in the nick, avoiding a broken nose via the low overhanging branch swooping past that pulled loose errant floating strands of her trailing hair, the tree of which Banzu bounced off of by accident before ducking past while pulling her along.

Another field. More running. Grueling minutes passed.

Lungs burning. Heart pounding. At last her hand slipped loose from Banzu's weakened grasp, his energies spent for he turned stumble-drunk and collapsed mid-run. He tumbled to the ground in forward-pitching momentum, rolled onto his back, lay splayed, chest rising and falling through gasping heaves, heart pounding with such fury its rapid beats pulsed visibly beneath the sweaty fabric of his shirt.

Melora's tired legs unhinged at the knees. She plopped onto her bottom beside him, huffing, staring south while flexing warmth and feeling into her right hand, grimacing against the throbbing aches screaming in her injured shoulder. She listened to the distant yells of the tundarian madman's faint beckoning for death, her attentions divided between Ma'Kurgen's possible pursuit and the boy—*no*, her mind corrected, *not a boy but a man; the boy in him disappeared days ago*—the man lying beside her wheezing through labored struggles of breaths, Banzu's sickly pallor disturbing beneath a glistening sheen of profuse sweat.

The fight then flight had sapped all his remaining vigor, and whatever the sickness ailing him he teetered on the verge of surrendering his life.

She regained her breath through decreasing huffs while working jumbled thoughts into some semblance of understandability, the mind often playing tricks when enduring times of great stress. And yet . . . and yet, *I know what I saw.*

Banzu's chattering teeth snapped together with a defining *click*. Shivering, he sucked in a long hiss, then trembling, he broke into a coughing spasm heightened by thrashing limbs.

Oh gods! She palmed his cold and hitching chest, rubbing and shushing while trying to ease him still, afraid of giving away their position. Rasping wheezes, he trembled beneath her touch, relaxed into shivers. The faraway stare of his eyes, more through her than at her, betrayed shrinking hope as to how much longer he could endure clinging to life by its fraying thread.

Stupid! A deeper part of her wanted to apologize for the terrible way she treated him, insulting him, berating him, trying to instigate him away at every turn, to confess she'd only been trying to avoid what lay before her now. But the rest of her burned in furious want for leaning over and grabbing the sides of his face, for sinking in fingernails while glaring into those glassy eyes and screaming how right he'd proven her after all.

"Ban?" She gave his chest a rousing shake. "Banzu?" She slapped at his cheek. "Ban!"

His only response the slight rolling of his head, that glossy-eyed stare not at her but through her.

He's dying. Oh gods, he's dying!

She bent forward, palmed the side of his face, jerked her hand away with a hiss. *So cold.* Despite their long, exhaustive run. The profuse sweat added a grave sheen of depth to his growing cyanosis. She brushed aside damp tangles of hair from his eyes. *I don't understand, he's fevered and yet . . . and yet he's freezing to death.* The reality of it baffled her. *I should bundle him up*—but for they'd abandoned his rucksack and his blanket therein to the road in their hasty escape.

She palmed the sides of his face between the warming nest of her hands, ignoring the shocking transfer of cold flushing her palms, wincing against the throbbing ache of her shoulder. His lips tinged the same blue round his sunken eyes. *I'm losing him.*

"Ban?" She rubbed her thumbs in little circles, massaging his cheeks. "Ban, please come back to me. Ban!"

Blue lids fluttering, he blinked momentary recognition into watery eyes where shined the tortured depths of a profound sadness revealed. In a wheezy struggle of voice so faint it dared not call itself a whisper he said, "I'm sorry."

"What?" A sensitivity too honest to be other than genuine gripped her by the heart and squeezed. "No." She rubbed his cheeks, trying to restore warmth through imposed circulation. "Don't be sorry. Don't—"

He reached up then, palsied hand rising to her face. She flinched at the chill of his delicate touch though did not draw away as his finger brushed her cheek upon the hot trail that was all that was left of the unknown tear he wiped away.

"I'm sorry . . . I failed you," he said with effort.

His hand fell between them when his face twisted tensed, eyes staring out as if witness to a shattered faith, a terrible revelation at the moment of impending death. His blue lids fluttered, closed. Tension fled his neck. His head rolled limp in her hands. Gone from the conscious world.

"No." Panic seized her by the throat. "No, godsdammit." She shook his head to no rousing avail. "No!"

Chaos blew her thoughts apart, scattered her logical mind into swirling motes. She fisted his damp shirt, tried shaking him awake and alert. But her efforts achieved nothing as to lifting him out from death's slow enfolding embrace.

***

The daylight hours grew longer at this time of year, a reminder of the last of winter's thawing into life-blooming spring. A transparency, a frailty to the light in the sky suggested sundown soon.

Melora sat huddled next to Banzu. He lay unconscious, shivering yet sweating that strange cold sweat, his labored breathing short and low and raspy, faint with wheezing. Still alive, but for how much longer . . .

She'd dragged him arms-beneath-the-pits a good distance north from where he collapsed, through a field of tall grass to a small clearing therein shielded by a thicket of waist-high weeds. There she stopped for rest, wanting a better hiding place to wait out the night though the sunset refused her, and the incessant nagging jags and jolts of pain in her injured shoulder combined with the efforts of dragging Banzu's dead weight exhausted her.

So she sat ticking off numbers in her head in distracting count while keeping a watchful eye on the southern part of their little weedy perimeter. If the tundarian berserker pursued them here she intended first responsive pounce with lunging dachra fangs. Banzu indisposed, she sought every advantage, especially so considering her injured shoulder the mobility of which limited her. Not that she could best the hulking tundarian in mortal contest, not after what she witnessed of his capabilities with that giant sword. But if it came to that she would try, by the gods she would try.

The setting sun dipped below the west, providing the cover of night. No signs as yet of Ma'Kurgen seeking them out.

Locha's Luck he's moved on in his madness, seeking other victims to challenge in his strange game of suicide through combat.

She shuddered upon thinking how many victims the tundarian already killed before they chanced across his warpath, and again on how many more would die considering Banzu failed at doing the world a favor by killing the lunatic when he had his chance.

Did he even realize how many lives he could have saved if only he'd killed Ma'Kurgen instead of leaving him alive? Though, now she knew the truth of him, and understood why he balked instead of delivering the killing stroke.

She gazed at him where he lay shivering beneath her monitoring palm atop his chest beneath which beat the weakened patter of his heart proving he still clung to life by barest fraying thread.

"Two," she whispered, still astonished, still amazed. And feeling so stupid, so blind, so ignorant of it all. *This whole time and I never knew.* His killing of the khansmen, not that she witnessed it but he must have done so while inside her void-aura. *Otherwise . . .*

Godsdammit but she wanted to slap him awake to curse him and kiss him at the same time. Instead she brushed aside a damp stray tangle of hair from his frigid, sweaty brow then returned her hand to his chest to continue monitoring his labored wheezes, the sluggish beat of his heart, the cruel fading of his lifespark as he slowly froze to death.

Her mind reflexed backwards in constant replay of that subtle change in his motions during the fight. He moved so fast, hazel eyes flashing luminous grey, brief as a blink, the rapid blur of his riposte to the tundarian's chopping downswing. She'd never seen anyone move so fast before, Jericho her first Soothsayer encountered. She assumed it for the trick of her lying eyes at first.

So mesmerized by the sight of two master swordslingers locked in combat, the fleeting glimpse of Banzu's swift change, his true unveiling there then gone, almost slipped beneath her notice. Almost.

Jericho Jaicham Greenlief, the world's last known Soothsayer. *He found another. And he trained him!* The notion passed over her with the vivid unreality of a dream, and once more she entangled in the webwork of recent memories.

Two weeks chasing after Jericho, all while oblivious to the Soothsayer traveling right under her ignorant nose. Thank the gods Banzu refused her efforts at leaving her alone. Though now those same cruel gods saw fit to leave him dying beneath her hand. If only she could—

Something snapped in the dark.

Melora tensed, swiveled her head round, held her breath overlong, ears pert, listening, waiting.

Silence.

But for Banzu's low wheezes and the calming of her quickened heart.

She frowned over him. "Don't you die on me now," she whispered. "Don't you dare."

The distant forlorn howl of a solitary wolf brought her head round again, eyes darting. Flashes of dire wolves bursting in at them through the high grass knifed through her mind, producing inborn shivers. A cool light wind soughed through the swaying grasses, rousing motions in the black pitch in everywhere abundance. She scanned their weedy perimeter, hunter's gaze unaided by firelight, earned nothing but swishing black pitch mocking her hindered senses while the winds softened then died.

Anger simmered with no outlet for spending it but to herself. Alone. Afraid. No idea of what to do next. She needed help but refused to move on without him. She might as well kill him herself as leave him now. Yet staying accomplished nothing. A frustrated scream buried deep in her lungs ached for tearing loose to ride the winds.

He won't survive the night. Not like this. And I can't drag him for gods know how many miles to the next town. I . . . I don't know what to do. She glared over him, fisting his shirt, wanting to yank him awake though denying the impulse to see it through. *Why didn't you say something days ago? We could've stopped. We could've seen you healed. We could've . . . godsdamn you, Ban, we could've done something!*

Too focused on moving, on returning to Fist so she could beat Jericho every which way but loose for leaving her behind, she paid no attention when Banzu stopped and gathered herbs she knew nothing about but leaves for making poultices. *I'm no herbalist, I'm a godsdamned Spellbinder!*

At least she knew the cause of his sickness, for all the good that did her now. Infectious animal bites could kill if left untreated, but one which caused a slow death through internal freezing? She'd never heard its like before. Years spent studying at the fistian Academy when not training the fangs, she only sampled its massive library of books when Head Mistress Pearce scolded her into boring study.

A weighty decision to make, and little time for making it. *Godsdamn you, Ban. Why didn't you just tell me?*

But she knew why.

The kohatheen locked round her neck existed as proof of that truth.

Spellbinders knew pride—the invisible bone that kept the neck stiff—and held their sworn duty in highest regard, vows sacred, never allowing petty emotions to obstruct their performance no matter the cost.

But you care for him. That's why you can't abandon him and you know it.

The sickness . . . freezing away his life while sapping that curious innocence in him surviving the rough and tumble of their travels together and despite her best efforts at thwarting him away.

She suspected the mysterious infection not just lupine in origin but of magical substance as well. Unexplainable otherwise. Several species of venomous animals, though none she recalled by name given her limited studies, bit their escaping prey then pursued while their magical poisons took to task, so why not tundra dire wolves?

Under normal circumstances she would prick a fingertip and squeeze a few drops of blood remedy into his mouth, staving the magical affliction from within. Ingested, Spellbinder blood provided a magical curative to non-aizakai, but a poisonous paralyzing agent to aizakai. In Banzu's weakened state, even a few drops of her blood would slow his organs, inviting quicker death.

She considered this. *At least I could ease his suffering*—"No."

She drew in deep, exhaled overlong. Stuck, mired in despair, and yet some small measure of hope remained.

Despite it all—the Enclave's assassins, Jericho taking leave to Fist without her, her ignorance of trying to leave Banzu behind, the greedy and treacherous cyclopean ferryman, the vicious wolves, another bloody encounter with the Khan's Trio, the tundarian madman attacker, and now the brunt of Banzu's sickness—she knew a resurgence of inspiration flaring within, an internal phoenix fire of hope.

He's a Soothsayer. And a master swordslinger at that. The internal mechanisms of her duty shifted and clicked, locking into their new proper order of alignment. *I have to get him to Fist so he can join in the fight against the Enclave. We'll Pair, of course. I found him. He's mine by right. And if the gods be good we'll kill Hannibal Khan and end another Thousand Years War before it restarts. Two Soothsayers.* She smiled, brief and wan, sharpened by cunning. *The Enclave won't stand a chance.*

Then she sighed, deep and long, the effort withering her. *I'm getting too far ahead of myself. None of that can happen if I don't keep him alive.*

* * *

The moon arose as a thin sliver, a horned thing of silver offering little light.

Patience dwindling, doing nothing never a part of her, Melora reworked through plans, thought-wheels turning, frustrations mounting.

Another hour and she would sneak south to the road under cover of night to retrieve Banzu's abandoned rucksack, the waterskins and blanket and bedroll and other such things therein.

I'll bundle him up nice and warm. If it's still there. If that madman hasn't taken it with him or stolen through it.

Still no sign of the tundarian berserker pursuing them.

He must've moved on, if not then I'll just have to cut my way through him, bundle Banzu up then head east for help. Bring someone back with a wagon too for transport. Locha's Luck there'll be a Lady's Chapel.

If only she'd paid more attention on her way through, not that escaping Trio after Trio of khansmen afforded her any chance to take in the scenery. Avoiding as many others as she could. Hiding in stables or up trees while stealing a few hours of sleep. Thieving food, and horses she ran lame. Paying occasional stupefied strangers to point out the glowing spot on her ensorcelled map for her in case it moved, hoping when she left them they betrayed nothing of her passing to the stalking Trios never far behind.

Considering the far influencing reach of the Enclave—the organization's recent resurgence unknown to her until the Khan chaos in Junes sent her running to the Head Mistress where she learned the secretive inner fold of the Academy's true purpose—her violet eyes betrayed her to everyone she met.

No, she paid little attention to the scenery in her long and arduous journey west, most of which she spent climbing over the Calderos Mountains while braving the dangerous Jackals of Mar living thereon because of closed Caldera Pass, forgetting towns soon as she passed them by, committing none of them to memory and certainly no Lady's Chapels. But she had to try for Banzu's sake. What choice otherwise? More than his life depended on healing him now.

She craned her head at the twinkling stars, sighing, preparing for the southern sneak, the cool air thick with foreboding, heavy with a sense of the destiny of the coming moments.

Alone, vulnerable, exposed, Banzu after she left him for help. Yet who could she trust?

The common remedies of chewing on porkroot to abate a sore tooth, of snuffing bauchleaf powder to reopen stuffy sinuses, or sipping moonglum tea for easing headaches while inducing sleep offered no help, and her limited knowledge of herbs ended there.

A fighter and nothing but, she dedicated all her years of Academy training to mastering the martial forms of Dancing the Fangs, unequaled by all but her rival Rasputina, while some of their Spellbinder Sisters less proficient in the physical arts spent their years—after the Academy's minimum requirement of three years of dachra training—afield in arduous study of every natural medicinal possible.

Cruel irony lived in that bitter truth. And as such those Spellbinder Sisters acquired a vast array of herbal remedies at their disposal Melora possessed nothing of. The Academy sold the protective services of its Spellbinders to nobles and royals, to kings and queens, and the more they knew of poison antidotes the higher the annual price paid. Especially so the more scrupulous nobles living in constant fear for their lives, their Spellbinder Vizers tasting each meal for poisons while watching every slip of shadow for lurking assassins.

Born of a different ilk, Melora proved a natural warrior ill-suited to the intellectual pursuits of her Sisters. Her dachras existed as the natural extension of her hands, the martial weaves and flows of Dancing the Fangs an instinctual pursuit of her athletic body, her fierce spirit driven by a deep-seeded, soul-twisting anger her softer Sisters did not possess, fueled by an indomitable fury none but an abandoned child who had inadvertently caused her mother's death simply by being born could never understand. Her body a tool, she forged it into a living instrument of bladed death unparalleled amongst her Sisters. Though little good that did her now.

Reflecting back, she almost wished it otherwise. Almost. But the Head Mistress chose her for a good reason, and not because of Hannibal Khan's attack on her stationed city of Junes. Strong, hard, cast-iron born then tempered-steel made, Melora Callisticus never quit, never surrendered, never broke, her void-aura the strongest expanse the Academy knew in centuries. Only Rasputina's void-aura rivaled hers in scope, and that by half. But above all Melora would die to see her duty through.

Banzu produced a shuddering moan, breaking into her chain of thoughts. Shivers turned whole-body trembles turned convulsions as his shallow breathing hitched into gasping strangles of labored wheezes. Closed blue lids fluttered, snapped open. He jerked taut, sunken eyes rolling back, their yellow sclera blue-veined round dilated pupils.

Oh gods no. She slid her right arm out from its sling, leaned over and pressed her palms atop his chest in an attempt at holding him still. She clenched her teeth against the stabbing pain in her injured shoulder while he thrashed and twisted beneath her.

"Oh gods," she whispered. "Please don't die."

His seizure lasted several minutes. Arms flailing, legs kicking, thick mucus rattling in his heaving chest. Sticky bits of spittle blew forth from blue lips, dotting cold pinpricks onto parts of her over-leaning face. His mouth stretched wide in voiceless scream. She feared he might swallow his tongue so that she scanned round for any preventive stick she could snatch up and place between his teeth but found none on hand. Her mind screamed, *Enough! Move! Run! Get help now!* But before her body obeyed, his violent seizure subsided into trembling shivers.

She sat back while easing pressure on his chest, breathing tortured relief. She closed her eyes, swiped cold spittle from her speckled cheeks, then palmed her hands together and whispered a desperate prayer.

A sharp snap in the dark behind pricked her ears up. She straightened, tensing, twisted round and froze, listening, eyes darting, breath held. Another snap, closer, the swishing of parting grass, then another snap, closer still. She stood in a low crouch, faced the elevating sounds, hands questing up beneath her open cloak, gripping the welcomed handles of her fangs in preparation for pulling. She stared into the black pitch, gaze hunting, slicing the gloom's tangible shroud.

The high blocking grass before her rustled and swayed with the winds, mocking her senses. Beyond it she spied two obscure, close-set little orbs of blue glistening in the faint moonlight, capturing it, reflecting it. Naked fear flushed through her of those wolves having somehow returned. But no, those piercing blues hovered too high in the dark.

She squinted at the walking silhouette hidden amongst the shadows. The high grass parted while the figure pressed forward. She tensed into coiled readiness, preparing to pounce, intent on killing.

"I have not come to kill you," said the silhouette-turned-tundarian stepping forth through the grass wall, his sharp blue eyes penetrating the dark depths. He stopped just inside the clearing, his impassive mask half hidden in shadows, half lighted in faint moonlight, and set down the dark lump he carried in his left hand.

Melora's gaze darted from him to the lump and back again. *Banzu's rucksack?*

"My honor—" he began, taking another step closer.

"Stay back!"

Silence.

Somewhere in her mind returned the tundarian berserker's name.

Ma'Kurgen raised his beefy arms, held his hands out in quelling gesture. He advanced another step. "But my honor—"

"I said stay back!" She pulled her dachras in a rapid flow of her arms, the pain in her shoulder distanced, the keen fanged blades reflecting glints of moonlight. "Or I swear by all the fallen gods of Hell I'll gut you open."

He lowered his arms. Said nothing. Stood a massive shadowed pillar of muscle staring back at her in the dark.

* * *

Crouched in a heated glare, heart a quickened patter, muscles bunched and primed for lunging, Melora considered Ma'Kurgen and all his vital targets. She knew little of tundarians but for a solitary people residing on the remote northern wastelands of the frozen Thunderhell Tundra, a desolate place she had never been. Rumors alone. Though she witnessed first hand the infamous rages earning their warriors the feared title of berserker. The tundarian hulk standing before her roused an undeniable fear, for despite her threats he need only set those powerful hands against her to quite literally tear her limb from limb.

Her bared fangs posed little more than a veiled threat considering the proficient skill he possessed with the broadsword strapped to his broad back. Let alone the berserker rage his kind willed forth on command, a self-induced possession of fury making pain an absence. Locha's Luck she could pierce an organ or two before he took her down then ripped her to pieces.

Ma'Kurgen's piercing gaze shifted past her, to Banzu behind, and a pained expression stole over his face. "The killing wind." His tone a soft rumble. "Is my honor . . . dead?"

He took another forward step then flinched back at Melora's snarling hiss when she slashed the air between them. She shifted her feet on coiled legs, ready to spring forth slicing and dicing. But something held her at bay. Something which eased the tension from her preparatory lunge. Despair on that shadowed mask paused her. And those eyes betraying sorrow, regret.

"What in all the hells do you want from us?" she asked, cutting to the quick of it.

He pointed past her crouching defense at Banzu. "My honor." He frowned, shifted the brunt of his smoldering focus back on her, hands large enough to engulf a man's skull forming fists at his sides, his tone taking edge. "What have you done to him, she-witch?"

She-witch? Tension returned in a flood, her mind hunting targets. *Gods he's big!* She needed to end this before it escalated beyond her control and he killed them both. But she stayed her place, bemused by his change of character.

"What have *I* done? He's sick you stupid oaf! He's sick and you tried killing him. Now he'll die unless—*stay back!*"

She darted forward, slicing the air in feral warning when Ma'Kurgen stepped forward, reaching, then withdrew, grimacing.

"You do not understand—" he began.

"No! It's you who doesn't understand. If you take one more step—"

"My honor cannot die." He moved one slow, easing step forward, holding his empty palms out in passive gesture. "Please listen."

She flinched at his cautious advance, though focused on his eyes sympathetic pools pleading back at her. He reached over his boulder shoulder, slowly, slid free the massive broadsword sheathed to his broad back and, to her surprise, upturned it then stabbed it into the ground next to Banzu's rucksack and withdrew a space.

"I must help him."

"What?" She shot him a queer look while questioning her sanity. *What?* "First you want to kill him, and now you want to help him? You really are crazy."

Ma'Kurgen said nothing, staring through her at Banzu. He took a cautious step closer, then another.

And for the life of her she stayed her fangs from tasting his blood. She twitched at his every move, body craving to burst forth and deliver dachra death. Yet she made no move against him.

As if the tundarian sensed the hesitation holding her at bay, he moved round then past her in a wary semicircle, lowered to one knee opposite her next to Banzu's pale and shivering form. He reached out.

Stop! Wait! What are you doing? But she put no voice behind it. Instead she watched Ma'Kurgen deliver gentle probing touches to Banzu's face.

"I know this sickness," he said. He probed round, pausing when he found the soiled bandage beneath Banzu's left sleeve. He unwound the injured limb with a gentle ease belying his strong thick-fingered hands, leaned and smelled it then shook his head and grimaced.

"What are you doing?" she asked.

His elevating gaze scolded back at her, bleeding into his voice. "You should be doing something for him, she-witch. This is no good. The chillfever has my honor in its grips."

She replied an owlish blink. *Chillfever?* She opened her mouth for words that never came, thoughts swirling in a tizzy of desperate confusion. Everything in her urged her to lunge while plunging her dachras into his chest, to kill this man before he could—

He stood, a rising tower, and stared her down, his gaze smoldering blue fire beset in a pained expression. "There is little time. We need to warm him. I will build a fire. Take off your clothes."

Take off my— "What?" She gawked at him. *I'm losing my mind. That must be it.*

Ma'Kurgen turned, walked away.

"Wait!" she said, her words erupting before the logical thought behind them. "Where are you going?" *And why do I care so long as it's away?*

Ma'Kurgen paused before breaching the high grass wall swaying in the gloom. He offered no look back when he said, "I know what you are, she-witch. If my honor dies—"

And there she realized his 'honor' meant Banzu.

"—I will tear you apart with my bare hands. That I swear."

He walked away, disappearing into the black gloom.

She stared after him, phobic of his return in a charging fit of berserker rage, some strange game of madness played. And yet he left his sword behind, a giant metal cross stabbing the ground. Not that he required it to crush her skull to pulp in those beefy hands.

Minutes passed in silence but for the rustling grasses.

Gods, what am I doing? Has it really come to this?

She settled down next to Banzu, kept a watchful bead in the direction of Ma'Kurgen's wake, ready to spring up and fend if he charged at her through the dark. She waited, her left palm monitoring the slow, labored rise and fall of Banzu's chest, her right hand clutching dachra in a sure grip atop her lap. The throbbing jags of pain in her injured shoulder nagged something fierce, but she refrained from returning her arm into the sling in case, in case . . .

She craned her head, stared at the open sky and its vast ocean of twinkling stars indifferent to the world of human suffering beneath. She drew in deep, expelled through pursed lips a heavy sigh that withered her shoulders hunched. Frustrations left her lips in hot cursive whispers over the awful irony of a Soothsayer killed by sickness—*what did he call it, chillfever?*—out in the middle of nowhere, while the gods watched on and did nothing.

She condemned them through the scorn of her eyes.

Thousands dead already, and millions more to come if the Enclave has their way. Do you not care? You pitiless bastards.

The righteous begged and called it prayer, the pious lied and named it faith. Never one for approbation, yet desperation brought her to the point of bargaining.

"Please don't let him die. I swear I'll . . ."

But the rest of her vain plea trailed away unfinished. She hung her head, unsure what else she possessed left to give in trade. Desperate to the point of waiting, of trusting in the obscure motives of a tundarian madman.

She stared at Banzu while memories stirred with emotion, thick as honey, the last of her personal barriers crumbling apart. He had fallen for her—that glimmer of attraction brightening his eyes in every one of his silly glances an impossible ambience to dispel—and she admitted an equal attraction to his boyish charms.

She preferred her men tall and brawny whereas Banzu stood short and lean, all wiry muscle. And worst of all stubborn, refusing to listen no matter how right she always was. His inability to comprehend just how dangerous her duty irritated her to no end, but he possessed a sweetness of loyalty, an innocence of hope.

And you never gave up on me, did you?

No matter how lashing her barbed tongue, how mean her glares, how hurtful her words, he stayed by her side because he wanted to protect her. Asking nothing in return but her company. Even at the cost of his life.

In her experience men only pretended selflessness until they tried taking what they really wanted from her.

But not you.

She smiled, seeing his raw character for what it was. And it pleased her in an unexpected way unfelt before. His genuine caring. Caring for another even at the detriment of his own safety. A goodness she assumed lost to the world long ago.

If he survives.

A painful squeeze gripped round her guarded heart. She leaned over and kissed his cold, trembling lips. Sat back and listened to the world's slow turn while the risen winds dried new tears from her cheeks.

"Don't you die on me," she whispered. "Don't you dare leave me now."

Somewhere in the dark echoed the noises of Ma'Kurgen moving about his strange business, faint sounds lost to Melora's ears beneath the wrenching grind of her dying hopes.

* * *

Floundering within a dark and frigid abyss, Banzu clung to the sharp precipice of his expiring life by the barest of grips. There existed nothing but cold, the world a gulf of suffocating darkness.

So cold.

No sounds but for the distant mewling torture of his inner monologue, his fingers slipped loose from the precipice. And he fell, plunging into catching despair. Hollow. Empty. Devouring.

Useless.

Raw pain. A cavernous guilt of shame, of regret, of sorrow swallowing him whole.

So cold.

Dying . . . he had failed.

Dying . . . a failure.

Dying . . . alone.

I'm sorry, Melora.

I tried . . . I tried.

CHAPTER TWELVE

Sera lay lost in the faint remains of an agony long in leaving.

Though her physical torture ended days ago, the mental anguish lingered in incessant memories, clawing and raw, knifing through her mind . . . of glowing hot iron pokers jabbing the bottoms of her tender feet, of wet cactus-cloth choking taut over her nose and mouth, of crushed-glass-dusted sticky-stones rolling sharp pricks over her naked body, of tight leather cords trapping her wrists and ankles to the torturer's spine-stretching rack strangling all feeling from her hands and feet though not before pinching pliers broke her fingers and toes, nor before the heated needles pushed beneath her fingernails and toenails.

The Overseer of her punishment ordered her healed throughout the ordeal of course, though this by intermittent fractions ensuring her fading lifespark never snuffed between his defiling acts of torment ravaging her bleeding canvas. She'd gone unfed while strapped to the rack though allowed occasional life-sustaining sips of spiced water burning down her throat her mind refused but her parched mouth accepted with shameful abandon against her broken will's wishes of dying.

The sweet mercy of death elusive, truth dragged her into a maddening level of existence beyond the physical tortures inflicted. Hannibal Khan's favorite tool denied the peaceful surrender of death's freedom until he squeezed her dry of usefulness in his obsessive crusade for immortal glory and total domination.

Time slowed to her suffering perspective when the Overseer first put his tools to gruesome work, a maddening illusion wrought from the torture while he worked his deft skills through his proud collection of wicked instruments. Sera surmised her rack-bound torment lasted a week or so before Horace dragged her by the arm, semiconscious and limp, to her room where he doused her with a bucket of water then left her naked and trembling on the cold stone floor—laughing as he did so in his tongueless, grunting fashion, and laughing as he left—the torture having carved something vital from her shriveled spirit forever.

She no longer clutched the hope of outside deliverance from her imprisonment, the ignorant dream abused from her within the first horrendous hours upon the rack when she still possessed the energy for screaming. Now, lying abed, partially healed then fed then left alone for aching days, her only movements slinking across the floor to squat over the chamber pot then slinking back to bed, she considered inviting death if only she possessed the strength of will to remove the knife she'd stolen from her last food tray then hid it beneath her pillow so she could plunge it into her breast and punctuate the misery of her life.

Without the guiding aid of her aizakai foresight, the Khan's and Nergal's plans would halt to standstill. Without her, the Enclave's conquering schemes would flounder.

And yet . . . and yet.

Something new and unfamiliar roused within. Cold, accepting, yet defiant to those suicidal wants. Her ravaged innocence a festering void where naïveté no longer bred false hopes, she embraced the emptiness despite the confusion it brought.

And gloried in her present solitude, victorious in the small portion of her that remained her own despite the Overseer's ruthless aggressions that she never revealed her little secret. Oh how she wanted to cry out in pleading wails while the fires of defiance smothered in soul-wrenching agony. But fate proved a tricky, masterless entity even her aizakai foresight could not predict let alone control.

The old and guilty fires of despair and regret smothered and replaced by another fire—no, a blast furnace—of pure scorn no longer for herself or her insufferable plight or even for those she blamed by proxy but for the one who destroyed what she once called life by condemning her to this miserable existence.

In the brutal throes of her tortured lesson escape became a forgotten thing as total obedience to the Khan returned in full. If not for her inability to speak through the cactus-cloth restricting her voice in that defining turning point where the taut umbilicus of hope severed, she would have screamed her little secret in a desperate attempt at earning an end to the unbearable tribulation.

She knew not if her confession of a second Soothsayer would please the Khan or instigate his wrath for withholding such substantial information, though in the moment of her breaking she cared for nothing but an end to the abuse. But when the Overseer, ignorant of her secret and so asking nothing of it, peeled the sticky cactus-cloth away, only woeful moans and incoherent ramblings escaped her bleeding lips, bare and ragged whispers these, her exhausted mind and ravaged body wracked.

Beaten and broken, ushered by pain to the brink of her mortality over and again, stripped of everything she once was, the punishing process imparted a greater wisdom during her manipulation by forces she could do nothing about, an epiphany delivered only after her removal from the rack and returned to her room in solitary confinement.

The Overseer sought to break her, and break her he did. But from the shattered remnants forged a new instrument harder than steel, crueler than poison, keener than any assassin's blade knifing through the dark.

The good gods answered nothing to her desperate prayers, and even the fallen gods ignored her bargaining pleas for merciful escape. But the Overseer of her torture removed her kohatheen before the brutal lesson, his error freeing foresight visions crashing waves of revelations round the island of her soul while her body lay bound in painful heaves and throes.

Hatred grew into a being of its own, a cruel and cunning entity of higher purpose revealed. Hannibal Khan must pay for his ruination of her, and now she determined to collect that debt in full no matter the cost.

Somehow . . . someway. Escape abandoned for retribution, her life she no longer valued the toll for savory betrayal. She served a new master now, one contemptuous and resolute, more powerful in its persuasion over her than Hannibal Khan or even the Enclave serpent-priest Nergal. That darker master's name Vengeance in all its vowing glory.

Surviving and enduring no longer enough. Waiting and obeying while hoping for outside rescue no longer enough. Torture christened her with new and cunning purpose.

Though how to exact her betrayal she knew not—yet. And she must keep that calculating part of her hidden away, preserve the umbilicus between *Seras* as it were, exist as two separate persons all the while pretending her obedient best to please the Khan. Until she devised the perfect scheme for doing him irrevocable harm.

She possessed that power now, bestowed her by the Khan through his Overseer's accidental gift.

Vengeance's devious voice whispered through her working mind while she lay toying with the Khan's potential demise, a small smile budding across her lips. For him she wanted more than simple pain, he deserved no less, and for that she would play her role while planning for—

The door to Sera's room swung open on squealing hinges and banged the wall, startling her out from dark musings.

Horace the horse-faced brute stalked inside with a purpose of his own.

* * *

Sera sat up, flinching tensed, considered reaching beneath her pillow for the knife if only to clutch its meager comfort against her chest in pathetic shield. But Horace closed distance in five bounding strides and, snagging a crushing grip on her wrist, jerked her from the bed then yanked her into following behind. Hot tears stung her eyes from the flares of pain in her abused shoulder, her sore padding feet. She blinked them away, wincing through achy steps keeping pace with the silent brute lest he drag her.

Her panicked mind sampled through worries unvoiced. Another punishing visit to the Overseer? Maybe Horace intended taking her to a private place to beat and defile and ravage her as he sometimes did with servants. Or perhaps the Khan ordered her return to the aizakai execution pits?

But no, she banished those thoughts. Whatever torments awaited her, the Khan refused the kindness of killing her until he squeezed out every last useful drop of her aizakai foresight.

Be strong, Vengeance whispered. *Control your fear. Face it. Challenge it. Wield it! I am coming.*

Spine stiffening, cold resolve distancing the pain of Sera's aching feet, she matched pace alongside Horace's lengthier strides, bold and brazen, for death, however sweet its release, would rob her of precious vengeance.

Horace, glowering at the unexpected display of her pretense, squeezed her wrist in his massive hand, dull sloe eyes seeking the satisfaction of her wincing countenance.

Pain no stranger, Sera smiled up at him while swallowing down the whimper edging at the back of her throat.

That's it . . . good.

They navigated through the Divine Palace, passing sentinel Bloodcloaks nodding helmed heads or pounding fists to chests in salute and wary servants clearing immediate space from their path, on through long corridors and up several sets of stairs until they reached the carven doors to the Khan's private bathing chambers.

Inside, Horace flung Sera to the smooth white-tiled floor then stepped back from the steaming, circular bathing pool at the room's center where he set his broad back against one of the many thick stone columns joining floor to ceiling and waited.

". . . and then they'll all see my true power," said Hannibal Khan, continuing the conversation with himself despite the others in his bathing pool, a bizarre habit increased the longer the power-suffusing madness of his godsforged lanthium gauntlets coursed through him, warping twists of his mortal sanity.

Sera pushed up onto hands and knees, squinted through the suspended haze of steam at the back of the Khan's bare shoulders and head visible above the bathing pool's rim, his blond curls damp corkscrews. He sat in the hot water while three young Spellbinder harem girls continued their gentle scrubbing over his muscled chest and arms and neck with handfuls of velvety flower petals a fourth girl sprinkled from a basket atop the water from her perch at the bathing pool's far edge, all of them naked. A fifth girl sat beside the fourth, pouring scented oils containing hints of cinnamon from the small collection of colored glass vials decorating the silver tray beside her, drip-drip-dripping the oils into the water.

While the reclining Lord of Storms relaxed therein, nude but for his lanthium gauntlets of power, permanent attachments to his physical self since the first moment of their donning. The gold necklace which bore the enslaved necromaster's soulring vitus the Khan both treasured and despised for its power of control over the unliving creature whom he regarded as a challenge to his own rising power removed so as not to taint the cleansing of his bating ritual, as always.

The Khan sought the glory of becoming a living god—envisioned himself as one already—and despite possessing soulring control over the necromaster currently away and resurrecting slain enemy troops while Bloodcloaks swarmed and warred, the reality of Dethkore's resurrected existence irritated his fragile ego almost as much as his obsession over the Spellbinder who gifted him that dachra kiss scarring his left cheek from brow to chin.

Sera pushed from all fours into standing, glanced at the nearest stone column where Dethkore's lanthium soulring vitus dangled from a little metal hook by its thin golden necklace. And battled the urge for reaching out, for snatching the soulring from its hook and . . . and do what with it, run? Horace would grab her before she could steal past him for the door, the brazen defiance earning her another agonizing stretch upon the Overseer's torture rack if not execution from the Khan.

And yet . . . and yet. Her gaze lingered on the silvery soulring strung so near while she entertained catalyzing that sure course of death. In one impulse she could take the ring and die for it. She turned facing it, flexing hands eager for grabbing, anxious feet shifting to move her forward those few necessary steps and—

No! Vengeance flared, reining her to place. *Patience. Death will come, but from our choosing. We have that power now. And he must pay before it frees us. Suicide achieves nothing.*

She tore her gaze from the soulring's teasing invite, returned it to the back of the Khan's upper half visible through the haze of steam, and waited.

Sullen violet eyes reflecting unvoiced stories of misery and abuse caught Sera's gaze when the farthest harem girl glanced up from her sprinkling petalwork, pausing while presenting the faraway stare all the girls of the Khan's Spellbinder harem possessed, beggar's eyes pleading volumes of regrets.

The Khan took notice, neck stiffening. He twisted for a look behind over one shoulder at Sera and Horace. He opened his mouth—then closed it with a snap of teeth, intentions stifled by the angry tensing of his handsome features punctuated by a sharp hiss earned by the errant scratch of misplaced fingernail from one of his scrubbing attendees paying more attention to the new guests than her washing duties.

He sat up twisting, lunging forward, whirling steamy zephyrs while splashing water across the floor with his quick motions. He seized the harem girl by the throat, forced her up from the water to her bare privates. The caught girl's violet eyes popped wide, her hands releasing wads of petals in feathery clouds. She pawed at the Khan's strangling clutch engulfing her slender neck.

Fingernails produced frantic *click-click-clicks* against the lanthium gauntlet, though no sparking arcs of power produced thereon in tandem to his spiking anger despite its infusion of divine magic trumping aizakai magic, even that of a Spellbinder's void-aura, for the Khan needed no supernatural power to aid him in this, his awesome strength alone proving enough. The girl's twisted visage purpled.

"Scratch me again," he said, "and I will have your skin removed!"

He shoved the girl away, throwing her backwards in fanning waves of water, her gasping efforts to breathe again choking short when she plunged beneath the bathing pool's surface. She popped up coughing water, collected herself and glided forward between his legs, stammering apologies while collecting more petals in her trembling hands. The fright in her eyes diminished, that faraway stare returning, and she scrubbed gentle strokes over his chest while kissing parts of him.

"That's better." He relaxed back, outstretching both arms atop the bathing pool's edge curving at his sides, the brutal flare of his voice softened serene when next he spoke without looking behind. "I see you've forgotten to collar her, Horace. Again."

Horace glared at Sera. Grunted. Reached to undo the kohatheen tied off at his belt while starting toward—then stopping at the Khan's behest.

"No," he said. "Leave it off. I require another vision."

Horace grunted, withdrew, and crossed his arms.

"Come here, my pet," the Khan said. "Now."

Sera approached at his left, the bathing pool's smooth upper lip stopping just shy of her chest, the top of the Khan's head level with her own. "Yes, my Khan?"

He bothered no look at her. "Tell me, what do you foresee of my conquering of Fist? I tire of waiting. When will we be ready to move?"

"However I can please you, my Khan."

She bowed her head, hair damp from the profuse steam and loosing a few glistening beads to the floor. She withdrew three steps from the bathing pool, ensuring she stood well outside the magic-nullifying proximity of the Khan's attending Spellbinders, then closed her eyes and drew in a deep and concentrative breath.

The inner flexing of her aizakai will and visions bloomed to luminous life therein the darkness behind the black canvases of her shielding lids, painting future scenes while she concentrated on the Lord of Storms and all the possibilities his focal point afforded her scrying. Time slipped forward in coalescing swirls of multi-colors forming shapes before her roving mind's eye while she sought . . . then found.

And gasped, tensing, shuddering. Lambent red eyes transfixed her pierced and paralyzed with an executioner's avarice beholding a lusting intensity so hateful the terror trembled her. Her startled heart a quickened flutter, she staggered backwards, eyes snapping open, and for the moment breathing turned a chore.

Panicked eyes darting, jolted heart a thunder behind her cage of ribs, she glanced behind at the door, everything in her screaming to run. But fear arrested her to place while the initial shock settled.

Horace glared at her, though the Khan took no notice of her momentary indiscretion unseen. She breathed deep, recapturing her breath, closed her eyes and braced while the deluge of visions assailed her in a torrent of dread . . . revealing a maelstrom of severed limbs, decapitations and disemboweling slashes of sword that sent her reeling. She strained for focus through the cacophonous sea of screaming faces, the piles of bodies and parts of bodies dividing flowing rivers of blood, the violence rushing her from all sides while the inescapable horror of those lambent red eyes penetrated her behind fanning blurs of rending steel . . . the brutality of it overwhelming so that she withdrew from the swallows of visions before they collapsed her to the floor.

Panting, she shuddered against the terrible images burned as searing brands into her brain. *No savior coming,* Vengeance whispered, *only the deliverer of death, his appetite voracious. This is good.*

"Well?" the Khan asked, staring ahead and seeing none of her struggles. He turned his head by inches for a better listen behind. "Out with it. Or I'll return you to the Overseer. What do you foresee of my victory?"

"I—" she began then paused. *Use it,* Vengeance commanded. *Embrace it. Twist it. Wield it now! This is it. This is how the end begins. Deny me and I will leave you. Provide me and you will reap.* She rumbled her throat clear, and in stronger voice tempered by cold resolve she said, "The Soothsayer is coming, my Khan."

"What?" The Khan's neck stiffened. "Has he turned to the bloodlust?"

Not yet. Not until . . . "He will."

The slow nod of the Khan's head. "How long?"

Careful, Vengeance whispered, *these planting of seeds. Gentle. Do not push too hard, too fast, too deep for sprouting.* "A few days, my Khan."

Silence.

Broken by the Khan's soft laughter.

"Finally," he said, relaxing anew. "So he's coming to kill me after all. And so soon! I was afraid—" He paused for thought, tone evincing a touch of disappointment. "A shame, that. I wanted to be the one to kill them both. I suppose Nergal was right. That Spellbinder bitch proved her own undoing after all." A heavy sigh expelled. "At least she's finally dead and—"

"No," Sera said, cutting the Khan short by impulse in a dangerous ploy of his ego.

"No?" He sat forward, shoving the three harem washers away, then he twisted round, struck Sera with filaments of cruel suggestions in his thinning gaze. "What do you mean no?"

She flinched at his scrutinizing glare, downcast her gaze to between her feet. She wormed her tongue in her mouth while wrestling hesitation.

This is it, Vengeance whispered. *We're stepping off the cliff. Wield your liar's tongue and take the plunge. Or rue my leaving.*

Sera drew in deep while nodding, decision made. She elevated her gaze to enjoy the look on his stupid face while she delivered the rest.

"The Soothsayer is not coming to kill you, my Khan. He's coming to join you."

Vengeance whispered, *Yes!*

* * *

Disbelief a startling slap, Hannibal Khan's eyes bloomed wide, his mouth opening where no words sounded. The wading washers of his harem flowed away from him lest they be knocked back when he erupted into standing, splashing water in fanning waves, the haze of steam round him wispy agitated swirls. He faced Sera in full glistening nudity, his visage a battlefield of warring emotions both delighted and disturbed.

A wicked smile captured his lips while he considered Sera in silent study. Then he turned away, sank nipple-deep into the bathing pool, craned his head and laughed. He threw both gauntleted hands overhead, gripping the air, flinging glistening beads and broken ropes of water across the white-tiled floor, and shouted, "I am Khan!" He dropped his arms, slapping more splashes of water, then threw them overhead again, tossing more streaming beads. "Even the last Soothsayer will bow before me!"

Horace, grunting, clapped approval.

Though the Khan's joyous boasting ended a moment more. For a time he stared ahead at some private space of viewing, lost in concentrated thought, the five harem girls round him quiet, paralyzed in their fear of provoking him out from pleased musings. At last he raised his right hand before his steady gaze, closed it into a fist. He sighed, broad shoulders rising and falling, only then struck by the notion of something precious stolen from his covetous grasp moments before its closing squeeze.

"It would have been such a glorious battle." His voice low, almost apologetic. He lowered his fist into the water with a splashing *plop.*

The silence of a spoiled child told their first No persisted while the Khan's turning mood traveled the dangerous terrain of somber brooding, the rising madness seeping out from him a permeable psychosis akin to a Spellbinder's void-aura.

Recognizing this, Sera withdrew two steps from the bathing pool.

"That demon has given me power along with a leash," the Khan said in darkening soliloquy, gripping his bare throat as if about to choke himself, then he slid his hand free, closed it into a fist at which he glared. "I am no one's pet. I will have my glory. I will not be undone." He paused, fist trembling, strangling the air. "By Nergal or any other."

Sera inched away.

"You." The Khan reached forward in splashing fervor, snatching the closest Spellbinder by the hair. He pulled her with him while relaxing back. "Please me." He plunged the girl's head beneath the water between his spread legs while gesturing a shooing motion with his free hand without glancing behind. "Take her away, Horace. I'm done with her for now. Ahhhh, yes."

Horace strode forth in grunting obedience. He enclosed the whole of Sera's neck within his strong sausage fingers before she could so much as begin turning round to face the ugly brute and led her by ease of force out from the bathing room.

She stole a passing glance at the dangling soulring vitus in their leaving, and despite the pain clamped round her neck she breathed a little easier now that she had pleased the Khan. Or so he thought.

The bubbling gurgles of the submerged harem girl's splashing struggles accompanied by the Khan's cruel laughter faded as Horace removed Sera from the bathing chamber, returned her to her room where he threw her inside then shut and locked the door.

Alone, in a crumpled heap. She pressed up from the floor. Limped to her bed and sat. Rubbed at her sore neck . . . and jolted that Horace the stupid horse-face forgot to collar her before taking his leave.

She stared at the door.

Then closed her eyes and, flexing her will, opened her mind's eye once more, breathing deep while visions swirled in colorful zephyrs, making bends and angles of forming shapes while time skipped ahead though only just.

She honed her focus, mind-shifting elsewhere than before, concentrating on the second Soothsayer, the one the Khan presumed she envisioned for him only moments previous and not her little secretive other. The younger of the two, the fire-haired swordslinger once believed to come saving her as he had the Spellbinder of the Khan's fixation turned obsession.

She shivered cringed at the new reveal, the dread malaise of death's frigid embrace closing its damning squeeze round his waning lifespark.

He's dying. Though it mattered little now. *He's—*

The door burst open and in stormed Horace, startling Sera out from her visions with a jolting squeal. He strode to her, ugly horse-face twisted in anger. Sera sank from the bed to the floor, muscles jellied, the knife tucked hidden beneath her pillow forgotten, terror that the Khan had somehow seen through her lying ruse locking the breath in her chest.

But instead of beating her and dragging her back to the brutal agony of the Overseer's torture rack, Horace yanked her up by the hair and snapped the kohatheen collar round her neck. He threw her to the floor, kicked her in the stomach. Turned and strode away, slamming then locking the door behind him.

Sera lay curled in a groaning fetal ball of hurt, the kohatheen fastened round her neck a cold and unforgiving touch against her warm skin. Minutes passed. She crawled to the bed, climbed atop and lay staring at the high ceiling.

A smile blossomed across her lips. And though alone, she covered her face with her hands. It did little to muffle the mad laughter pouring forth. She set the Khan upon his path of ruination at last with one little lie.

So much power in such a simple thing it astounded her still. The cunning seeds of Vengeance planted, all she need do is wait. Wait for the reckoning sure in coming.

CHAPTER THIRTEEN

Days later, within the Receiving Room of the Divine Palace in the Holy City of Khan.

Sera stood next to the Lord of Storms while trying her best to ignore the sucking sounds emanating from between Hannibal Khan's spread thighs where bobbed the raven-haired head of a kneeling harem girl servicing his sexual pleasure. He sat relaxed upon a newly carven throne sculpted from the massive ivory horn of a colossal borewhale, the males of their species known for beaching themselves upon the eastern shores during the spring mating season. This new throne possessed a faint rosy hue evincing the borewhale's blood absorbed therein.

Five Spellbinders of the Khan's imperial harem, all less than bleeding age—their only saving grace from the ill fate of their captured elders bled to forge kohatheens—occupied positions round the seated ruler, one and two massaging scented oils into the glistening skin of his thick neck and broad shoulders from behind while three and four knelt at either side of the sucking fifth and washing the Khan's feet in rosewater bowls.

Horace the horse-faced brute stood close at Sera's left, ensuring she stayed her place in silent regard of the Khan. Not that she could make her leave otherwise, no, for over the course of the previous days she returned to her expected subservient role of attending the Khan in whatever duties he required of her aizakai foresight, the last of which they waited to pass, that of Nergal's return.

She stared across the Receiving Room at an insignificant spot on the far southern wall between helmed heads where stood armored Bloodcloaks aligning the square chamber in silent guard, hoping the focus of her concentrative efforts would stay her wandering attentions from the disgusting labors of the young harem girl appeasing the Khan's sexual desires, and for the time she reflected inward.

The Khan celebrated her news of the Soothsayer's unexpected joining, pleasing news to Nergal when the serpent-priest returned via his traveling pool to command initial movement of the Lord of Storms' vast army of Bloodcloaks against Fist for the Head Mistress's Book of Towers necessary to piece together the rest of the Dominator's Armor and make of the Khan a living god, the precious book of Academy secrets containing the precise locations of the Armor's scattered pieces hidden away in the plethora of Builder's Towers. Upon learning Sera's revelation changing the Enclave's plans, the ecstatic serpent-priest raced to his traveling pool, saying nothing more than that there were duties he needed to deal with until the Soothsayer's arrival.

The Khan viewed Melora's presumed death as a personal loss, though Nergal offered the reassurance that once they marched against Fist, now with not only the Forsaken One in Dethkore resurrecting their troops in battle but with the bloodlust-corrupted Soothsayer in their conquering midst, the Khan would enjoy a bounty of other Spellbinders to add to his harem collection once they sundered the fistian Academy and enslaved what remained of its heathen aizakai not dead beneath the rubble smoldering round his victorious feet.

Sera stayed locked in her room undisturbed for two days after her revelation of the Soothsayer's imminent arrival while the Khan relished in his impending victory that would begin, according to her, in the shortening course of days. Until he'd summoned her to attend him again, commanded her to foresee how long before Dethkore returned from campaigning in the Khan's name in the southern regions of Thurandy.

"Today," her reply, pleasing the Khan.

And so she stood a silent spectator, biding time while playing her subservient role, her kohatheen collar hanging from Horace's belt instead of locked round her neck in case the Khan required further foresight viewing.

Hours passed, his amiable mood souring, his short patience wearing brittle thin, his rising ire verging despite the harem girl attempting to calm him through sexual gratification.

The southern doors so near Sera's chosen spot of focus opened, issuing inside the knot of five Bloodcloaks returning from their order of satisfying another of the Khan's many insatiable indulgences, drawing Sera's attention back to the cruel reality round her.

The Bloodcloaks led forth two emaciated men, both stripped to the buff but for the kohatheens locked round their necks—an indication of the heathen aizakai blood coursing through their tainted veins—and both showing desperate hope in their darting eyes as to why they had been rescued from the aizakai execution pits and brought before the reigning Lord of Storms.

Sera needed no foresight visions to show her what awaited them. The Khan enjoyed playing the game of allowing condemned aizakai to believe their pending executions stayed almost as much as he enjoyed watching their change of expression when he severed that desperate thread of false mercy to which they clung.

The Bloodcloaks led the two aizakai men in front of the elevated dais then kicked out the backs of their legs, forcing them kneeled, and removed their kohatheens. A flick of the Khan's wrist and the obedient soldiers returned to the ranks of their Bloodcloak fellows aligning the walls. The two kneelers bowed before the merciful Khan, each attempting to outdo the other through fawning praises while swearing their lives to serve the true King of Kings through whatever capacity he desired for sparing their worthless lives from the pits.

The Khan listened with a muted smile, allowing false hopes to linger for pure amusement.

"Fight," he said, his voice a command. "To the death. And I will spare the victor."

The two aizakai stiffened, considered each other, their disbelief as always requiring a few struck turns before truth registered. Wide eyes thinned, snarls bared. Seconds only and the two men twisted on their knees then dove together, limbs flailing, bodies twisting for alpha position while they crashed to the floor, locked naked in feral combat.

Minutes passed as the two men wrestled, grunting and twisting, rolling the floor in wild abandon, vying for the dominance of top position. Then, as the brutal acceptance that one of them must die won over in that savage moment of clarity the Khan desired most, all aspects of humanity fled for the primal instinct to kill or be killed.

They're already dead. Sera turned her head away in a brief lapse of disgust—only to have it turned back for her when the massive paw of Horace gripped the back of her neck and squeezed, forcing her into watching the brutal entertainment. His a delighted smile, the big ugly horse-faced brute's dull sloe eyes gleamed with excitement.

Wet slaps of skin. Guttural grunting and punching became clawing and gouging became biting and tearing. A slather of sweat and blood greased the two combatants, each struggling for domination over the other, slick bodies thrashing in a primal chorus of screams echoing through the Receiving Room atop the thudding sounds of flesh pounding flesh in an arrhythmic melody.

At the height of the contest, when the combatant dominating the top position seized full control and pounded his bloody fists into the mashed face of the loser straddled beneath him, the smiling, wide-eyed Khan released a delighted gasp. He closed his eyes while applying holding pressure to the top of harem girl's head no longer bobbing but choking between his legs. Ecstasy bloomed across his slackening features while the squirming girl attending him gagged on his ejaculate. He opened his eyes and leveled his heavy-lidded gaze upon the bloody scene also reaching its climax.

The straddled loser lay splayed on the floor, energies spent, his swollen pulp of a broken face smashed beyond human recognition. His chest rose and fell in rapid, struggling wheezes while he gagged and choked on the blood draining into his throat and filling his laboring lungs, showing signs of life still remained, however faint and fleeting.

The aizakai victor straightened, his glistening chest panting heaves, head hung low, pieces of torn skin dangling loose from parts of his shoulders and arms where riddled bite marks. He upheld his bloodied, swollen fists and stared at their grisly dripping gore through eyes wide and wild, and jolted, only then recognizing the brutality they achieved upon the dying canvas of the man betwixt his straddling legs, the detachment of killing his fellow captive a slow-dawning realization now that the adrenaline surge of primal instinct fled.

Fists trembling, he spread them apart, fingers unfurling, and gazed between at the dying man beneath him, his face a withering mask of guilty disgust. He stood on shaky legs, turned and faced the Khan, silent in the brutal shock of his humanity returned.

Having achieved his will of the harem girl servicing him, the Khan removed her by the hair from between his legs and threw her aside before concealing his flaccid member by doing up the front of his pants. The girl toppled against the young foot-washer at her right, sending them both crashing to the floor while spilling the rosewater bowl. Both girls scrambled to their hands and knees and cleaned their mess by lapping the water from the floor in lieu of any towels lest they anger the Lord of Storms by distracting him from his present enjoyment.

The Khan raised one gauntleted fist in signal. Horace stepped forth, removed a dagger from the collection of weapons at his jangling belt, tossed it skittered across the floor then withdrew position beside Sera while affording her a delighted wink in the process. He knew the next moment.

But so did she, and for that she almost smiled back—almost.

Soon, Vengeance whispered.

The aizakai victor glanced to the dagger at his feet beyond the twisted curls of his broken toes. He raised a look of silent plea to the Khan punctuated by the slow shake of his head.

The Khan said, "Finish him and earn your freedom."

"Please," the aizakai began, his raspy voice a quaver. "No more—"

"Finish him!" The Khan's voice a booming shout commanded silence throughout the room but for the struggling wheezes from the dying man upon the floor.

The flinching victor stood all trembles. He nodded, bent and picked up the dagger, fisted its handle, strangling it, drips of blood squeezing out between his fingers. "No," he whispered. Then he straightened, unleashing a wild scream. "No!" As he broke into snarling charge toward the dais in a raging attempt upon the Khan's life, hammer-fisted dagger poised on high for stabbing. "No!"

So unexpected the man's rushing attack that the Bloodcloaks aligning the walls advanced but inches from their positions while the wild-eyed attacker closed the distance to his target by half, the visible muscle damage of clawed cuts and bites earned during his fight providing little hindrance upon his ability to run.

Sera's heart skip a fluttering beat, but only that, for she knew the outcome of this man's defiant charge before Horace's dagger graced his hand. *You're not the Khan's slayer, I'm sorry, not you.*

"You dare—" began the Khan, rocking forward, gauntleted hands gripping the thick ivory armrests of his throne in the beginnings of standing, muscles rippling tensed, eyes widening, teeth bared in a snarl. While the attending harem girls abandoned their tasks and scrambled away.

Sera cringed, wanting to look away, unable to remove her captured gaze.

Beside her Horace shifted, hands taking hold of several choice weapons dangling from his belt.

The suicidal aizakai rushed the throne's rising occupant. But soon as his forward foot achieved atop the dais's lip, the dagger poised overhead in preparation for a hammer-fisting stab into the Khan's broad chest—*thuhchunk*—his body twisted aside, wrenched by the thrown spear taking him in the ribs courtesy of a Bloodcloak.

The force of the driven spear's penetrating impact spun him from the dais and the half-risen Khan, the dagger flying out from his loosening hand while the heavy barbed spear's momentum carried him twisting through the air and away from the Khan. He struck the floor, his gore-slickened body sliding several feet before stopping. Where he lay in a groaning, crumpled heap, blood a spreading puddle beneath, the delivered spear sprouted from his ribs on tilted lean.

To the audible disbelief of those watching, the injured man pushed up onto hands and knees and tried pulling the barbed spear free to no avail. Horace shoved Sera aside and stalked forward, gave the aizakai a helping hand in removing the hindering projectile by setting one booted foot against the shoulder then yanking the weapon free, tearing loose bits of organs and muscle containing juts and bits of shattered ribs. The man gasped and collapsed, dead, shreds of his torn innards dangling from the arrowed spearhead's wicked barbs.

Hannibal Khan, standing, viewed the scene through a condemning squint. He turned. Approached Sera. Backhanded her across the face. Sent her sprawling off the dais and rolling to the floor.

Her mind tumbled through semi-conscious spins of vertigo. She twisted on the floor, sat up blinking twinkling stars from the fractured prism of her teary *wob-wobbing* vision while holding the struck side of her throbbing face, tasting blood, unsure of a broken jaw.

"Where was your warning!" the Khan demanded.

She winced through stammers, eyes darting, achy jaw throbbing with every painful twitch of her working mouth, frantic mind grasping logical excuse for her lie. "I, unh. The Spellbinders, unh. My Khan, they, unh, block my visions—"

A second punishing backhand spun her round to greet the floor again. She clung to consciousness by fraying thread, bright pops of stars fading to tunneling vision. She pushed up onto hands and knees, swaying, balance sloshing, limbs palsied tremors, every inch a struggle. She looked over her shoulder, and through the watery sting of her eyes a lanthium-gauntleted hand reached at her from the blurry backdrop of the Khan's furious expression shutting out all else behind it.

***

The Khan's reaching bid stopped inches shy of gripping Sera's throat. He withdrew, turned at the elevating sounds of hissing and bubbling behind. Within the Receiving Room's concentrically ringed depression where resided the aizakai blood of Nergal's traveling pool there toiled a bubbling froth accompanied by the low hum of soft purple witchlights sparking into waking life from the surrounding glow of carven arcane symbols thereon the floor. Every gaze fixed upon the traveling pool.

The naked, sinuous figure of Nergal arose from within the boiling portal, each ascending step revealing lower inches of his rangy human-serpentine hybrid body. The tall Enclave serpent-priest ascended up and out from the traveling pool, most of the blood running the length of his scaly skin disappearing through absorption when not dripping the floor round his clawfeet. He paused beside the wooden post where hung his purple robes and donned them in a whisper of fabric.

Silence while Nergal's inhumane stare hunted round the room, attention lingering on the gore of the corpse Horace stood over before settling on the Khan across the way.

"What isss all thisss?" Nergal flipped his hood up. "And where isss the Forsaken One?" Yellow eyes divided by black vertical slits flickered beyond the Khan at Sera, stabbed her with penetrating focus. "Soultaker should be here by now."

The Khan half-turned, glared at Sera, then shifted his gaze to the five Spellbinders clustered in a frightened huddle behind his throne. "I'll deal with you later. Go!"

The whipping gesture of the Khan's arm, the brief crackle of his lanthium gauntlets announcing his flaring ire, and the Spellbinders fled the Receiving Room in a whimpering gaggle, taking their leave through the eastern doors opposite Nergal, a knot of Bloodcloaks following them out.

The Khan faced the serpent-priest, his sour expression a brazen twist foretelling he viewed Nergal's arrival more an intrusion on his celebratory games than a necessary presence. He crossed his muscled arms and spread his feet in silent challenge. "I'm enjoying myself while I wait. What else am I expected to do?"

Nergal thinned his serpentine glare. "You're expected to do as you're told." He eyeballed the corpse on the floor no more than a few feet away from where he stood, surveyed Horace and the dripping spear, considered the other body which lay at the center of the room clinging to life through rasping wheezes, and frowned. "And you're wasting valuable resources better used elsewhere. These pitiful wretches should earn their deaths fighting in the coming battle for Fist, not dying for your entertainment."

The Khan huffed a dismissive breath. He returned to his throne, stared down into his upturned palms, fingers curling, grasping invisible thoughts.

"I wield this godly power," he said, tone edged, "and yet you condemn me to sitting here, waiting, always waiting for orders when I should be out conquering nations." Gauntleted hands closed into fists. "While men quiver at my feet begging for their lives." Those fists trembled. "And your creature." He looked up then, eyes glaring menace, peeling lips revealing clenched teeth. "It sickens me enough that I must sit here while that *thing* disobeys me at every turn. I want what was promised me, demon. I want the rest of my Armor."

"Oh?" Nergal hissed derisive laughter. "Or what?" He flicked his clawhand in dismissive gesture at Horace, and the big brute withdrew. "The Forsaken One is a necessary tool in taking Fist. He will make of your Bloodcloaks an undying legion." He approached the dais in a slow though purposeful illusion of gliding, robes whispering, clawhands clasped behind his proud back, faint footprints of drying blood trailing his wake, the hidden talons of his clawfeet *click-click-clicking* the floor. "Everything is according to plan"—his gaze flickered at Sera—"despite the recent changes."

Sera cringed at Nergal's glance, then winced when Horace's strong grip clamped round her arm. He yanked her to her feet and jerked her back to place upon the dais beside the throne.

"Patience," Nergal said, stepping onto the opposite side of the dais, admonishing gaze locked with the Khan's bold stare. "All of Thurandy will soon be yours, as Master promised. But we must move in accordance with his plans or—"

"I'm growing bored with his plans," the Khan said, then added in lower tone, "And with you."

Nergal flared then thinned his eyes. "With the Forsaken One's return, and soon the Soothsayer at our disposal, nothing will stop us from taking Fist and crushing that heathen's den. You will have your war and your glory, and once we procure the Book of Towers you will have the rest of the Dominator's Armor as promised." He flicked a clawhand in gesture at Sera. "The child had foreseen it."

"She has foreseen many things." The Khan broke eye contact, glared ahead, drew in deep and expelled a terse huff, strong square jaw flexing through the grinding of teeth. "Fist should be in smoldering ruins by now. And the Soothsayer . . ." He glanced at Sera on his left, scowled. "I've changed my mind. I want his head on a pike, not sharing the power you promised me." He raised one gauntleted hand and touched at the thin pink scar running his left cheek from brow to chin, grimaced, closed his hand into a crushing fist. "He took what was rightfully mine. And for it I'm going to tear his heart out." He locked gazes with Nergal. "A god does not share power, demon."

"Pawns," Nergal said, bending forward at the waist to better meet the Khan's eyes. "You are the chosen Khan, and they are nothing more than pawns at your disposal. We will use them, and when we are done we will destroy them."

Just like he's using you. Sera deviated her stare to the floor while schooling her smile from showing. *Just like I'm now using you both.*

"Not all of your pawns have been as willing as you say." The Khan's lips twisted into a sarcastic curve. "Your creature is proof enough of that."

Scowling, Nergal straightened to his full towering height.

Field reports returned during Sera's torturous lesson with the Overseer recounting the disturbances from the south where the Khan's imperial army of Bloodcloaks secured full surrender and control over the marshlands of Grey Raven's Keep and its surviving resisters, leaving only Fist and Bloom to the west before all of Thurandy conceded to his expanding rule. But despite the great success, unforeseen difficulties arose.

Intended to raise the enemy's dead alongside the Khan's fallen soldiery, thus serving his true resurrected purpose, control over the necromaster proved loose at best, especially so considering the source of Dethkore's only real obedience resided in the lanthium soulring vitus strung round the Khan's neck long miles to the north during his conquering army's southern campaigning.

According to the reports, the necromaster ceased working his dark arts of reanimation mid-battle, refusing further orders. Beating him provoked no response, and torture proved a useless endeavor despite his handlers possessing the burning bane of silver instruments scoring his unliving flesh where steel failed to produce anything more than resealing wounds.

And so they caged him, ushered him back for punishment, should have arrived already according to Sera's foresight.

"Your impatience," said Nergal, rounding the throne to standing in front of its glowering occupant, "has long since passed annoying. Speak against Master's plans again and it shall be the last time you speak a word that does not consist of begging for the torture to end. Which it will not. You've bargained you're mortal soul for power, and your lusts for glory and immortality will be fed. But if you disrupt his plans, I promise your immortal life will be nothing short of everlasting agony."

Sparking blue arcs of bridled energies crackled to life thereon the Khan's lanthium gauntlets in tune to the thunderous rumble sounding outside the Divine Palace. Seething rage built behind those malicious eyes and bled their corners upon his tensing face twisting into a darkening thunderhead of brewing madness. He glared up at the serpent-priest, gauntleted hands closing into spark-crackling fists then pounding atop the thick ivory armrests, furious visage rife with contempt threatening volumes of rage, his mouth opening, his body a defiant rise from the throne.

"No!" Nergal arrested the half-risen Hannibal short by slamming both grasping clawhands down atop the Khan's thick wrists, pinning gauntlets to armrests, his scaly skin sizzling atop the spark-crackling lanthium trapped beneath his clutching grips, his hooded face twitching through agitated strains against the burning while he leaned to within inches of the Khan's glaring visage. "You will obey." Nergal's scorning voice a command, his serpentine eyes swirled lambent with hypnotic demonic compulsion. "Obey!"

Sera cringed while holding her breath through the tense exchange where played across the Khan's twisting visage a visible battle of resistance, his defiant will struggling defiance against Nergal's demonic compulsion. Seconds more and the Khan's face slackened, tensed body loosening. He wilted into the throne, the sparking crackles of his gauntlets quelling.

"I will . . . obey," he said, his monotone voice a mechanical statement repeated.

"Yesss." Nergal released his clawed grips and straightened, allowing everyone clear view of his power and control over their reigning Lord of Storms. At his sides he flexed his burned clawhands emitting wispy curls of dissipating smoke then swiped them upon his robes, bits of charred scales rusting in fluttery flakes crisped black. "You reach too far too fast. And—"

A struck *bong* of gong rang outside the Receiving Room, sounding beyond the open doors of the southern corridor, to which Nergal turned, his thin lips spreading in the beginnings of a wicked grin. "And I have not returned for you."

***

Nergal stared across the Receiving Room, clawhands clasped behind his back, erecting into that of his tall vulture's stoop. "Watch what happens to those who refuse to obey."

The Khan issued no reply but for his blank stare ahead through clouded eyes.

Attentions of the room shifted to the southern corridor where sounded a second announcing *bong* of gong followed by the approaching rustle of movement, shifting bits of red-gold armor and padding feet punctuated by the elevating wail of a high-pitched groan.

The Khan's slackened features tightened while recognition of the present returned his maddened faculties through a series of hard blinks. He shot Nergal a sidelong glare though held his tongue despite hands balling into fists where tiny arcs of crackling blue sparks danced over lanthium gauntlets then died in a fading whisper of power bridled.

"My Lord of Storms," said the acolyte who rushed inside from the southern corridor and stopped before the dais. He knelt and bowed his forehead to the floor, hands thrust out with palms upturned. "The Forsaken One is returned."

"Excellent," Nergal said, preempting the Khan's response.

The Khan's jaw tightened, eyes thinning, but he added nothing. Instead he raised one hand to his chest and fingered the silvery lanthium soulring vitus thereon his golden necklace while a nefarious grin played across his mischievous lips. He glanced at Nergal—then engulfed the ring in his spark-crackling fist, strangling it in fathoms of transferred power.

A tortured scream erupted from within the long southern corridor. A man's scream, mad with soul-wrenching agony.

Sera flinched, struck stunned by the fleeting glimpse of an unexpected vision knifing through her mind's eye, an abrupt flash there then gone. She stifled her startled gasp behind a bitten lip.

The Khan chuckled, released his shocking grip on the soulring vitus, ending the painful connection. He ignored Nergal's glancing glare and flicked his wrist before settling his arm upon the throne. The acolyte peeking from the floor stood at once, bowed then backed away, allowing space for the team of Bloodcloaks wheeling forth a large iron-barred cage into the Receiving Room, its metal wheels protesting through high-pitched squeals while crunching bits of floor grit as they rolled their captive forth, he a nest of pale and black huddled atop a pile of soiled straw.

"It seems the Forsaken One has regrown a conscience," Nergal said after the squealing pitch of the wheels stilled, the cage and its lone occupant positioned before the dais. "A pity, that."

The quick flick of Nergal's wrist, and a Bloodcloak rushed to heed. He unlock the iron-barred door to the cage designed so its tight confines crunched its hunching sitter with no spare room for moving, swung the heavy door open on squealing hinges, and stepped aside, rejoining his Bloodcloak fellows surrounding the cage, their faces slacken or ashen or both, who prodded and stabbed their silver-tipped spears between the iron bars, rousing through pain the huddled occupant therein.

Out crept the necromaster Dethkore in all-black attire, his clothes literal swaddles of shadows writhing and hissing against the instigative silver prods and pokes, his motions loosing clinging bits of straw to the floor. He straightened to his full towering height thrice that of the wheeled prison behind him, the thrusting bites and prodding jabs of Bloodcloak spears piercing his pale flesh and wetting their tips with hissing glistens of black ichor the substance of his unliving blood, though his sullen tombstone visage betrayed no signs of strain nor the existence of any pain suffered but for the permanent melancholy of his unblinking stare.

An eager, younger Bloodcloak dared too close to the necromaster in his prodding bid to urge Dethkore forward and please the Khan. In so doing the spear slipped from his hands turning palsied, clattered to the floor while he withdrew a staggering space, face paling, cheeks bulging, one hand gripping his stomach as the other rose to cover his opening mouth but too late. He spewed vomit onto the Bloodcloak beside him, sudden nausea induced by the sickening miasma radiating from the necromaster akin to a Spellbinder's void-aura.

Two soldiers grabbed the vomiting younger by the arms and dragged him from the Receiving Room while their others continued their work mindless of the vomit squishing beneath their boots, prodding the necromaster forward from behind. The twisted expressions of the older soldiers attempting to keep safer distance by gripping the butts of their long jabbing spears evinced their previous sharing of the unpleasant experience.

"Fools," Nergal whispered, then raised his curt voice. "Stop! And withdraw your miasma at once."

Dethkore stopped five paces short from achieving the dais, the throned Khan thereon.

Sera gazed upon that pale and angular face framing soulless devil's eyes locked in blank stare, white stabs of pupils within black sclera, the sullen expression betraying no indication that a being of any human feeling existed therein. And though she stood outside the shrinking expanse of his miasmic death-aura, her churning stomach swam through queasy fits regardless, and hot beads of sweat dappled her brow while fever licked hot tongues through her crawling skin.

The Khan began rising.

"Sit," Nergal said without looking. "I'm here do deal with this matter myself."

Hannibal Khan hesitated before settling down, frowning.

Nergal moved down from the dais, unseeing of the Khan's piercing glare at his back, and approached the necromaster in slow, gliding strides. He peeled back his purple hood and locked stares with the infamous Eater of Souls known to children's nightmares as Soultaker. Nergal's serpentine glare swirled through brief hypnotic flare, though this born from rising animus for their compelling effect proved useless on the unflinching necromaster with his soul removed to his lanthium soulring vitus.

"You ungrateful wretch! You above all others know the importance of what we seek. The new Khan is chosen, and you will obey without question." Nergal took a challenging step forward, closing distance between them to within inches, and glared up to meet Dethkore's higher face. "Or you will never be returned to your slumber."

Unresponsive, Dethkore stared more through Nergal than at him.

Nergal hawked, neck muscles bulging, the serpentine glands of his hybrid species activated therein the back of his throat, then spat in Dethkore face, his acidic spittle hissing skin where burned cruel little craters into pale flesh. Tiny black licks of shadows flickered from expanding pores, and those crater burns healed seconds more, shadow tongues receding while leaving dissipating wisps of smoke trailing away from resealing skin. Through this, Dethkore stood a perfect statue of blank emotion.

Nergal stiffened, yellow eyes flaring contemptuous at the necromaster's open defiance.

The Khan chuckled then sighed while stirring upon his ivory throne. "Allow me to kill this miserable creature and be done with it already."

"You cannot kill what is already dead." Nergal struck Dethkore across the face with a strong backhand that sent the necromaster twisting to one side. Dethkore straightened—and took another punishing backhanded across the other turning cheek before Nergal withdrew two agitated steps. "But there are still ways of making it suffer. Bring me the box!"

He clasped his clawhands behind his back and smiled at Dethkore while servants rushed away obeying his command. "Maybe a few days of penance will remind you of whom you serve." He fixed piercing scorn upon

Sera. "And you! You'll beg for the execution pits if your visions fail me again."

Sera averted her gaze to the floor between her feet before those cruel yellow eyes gripped her by the will and squeezed. Her foresight scrying refused to work on Dethkore for reasons unknown, but Nergal only heard excuses of failure. Dethkore's recent disobedience had lengthened her torturous visit to the Overseer, the reports delivered during her prolonged time upon the rack. She provided Nergal a tool for utilizing and nothing more, and he expected his tool to perform when needed and without question.

She startled then, looking up, at the rousing of an unexpected voice the sound of dried leaves crunching underfoot.

"Do not hurt the girl," Dethkore said. He glanced at Sera, returned his stare to Nergal, though said no more.

"What?" Nergal flinched, stiffened. "*What?*" He shot Sera a cutting glare then drew up taller in an attempt at staring the necromaster down, serpentine eyes flaring, swirling hypnotic though to no proven effect upon the immune being before him. "What did you just say?"

Silence but for the Khan's low chuckle.

Nergal strode forward, clawhand clenching into a fist in preparation for delivering another admonishing backhand—then he stopped, his tensed expression relaxing for a sinister smile revealed. "You've grown weak. It sickens me. And you showed such potential once as the first Khan."

He turned away, approached Hannibal Khan, held out one clawhand, scaly palm upturned. "Ring. Now."

The Khan drew in deep, exhaled overlong through pursed lips. He removed the golden necklace and its silvery soulring from round his neck.

Nergal snatched it away. He strode toward the nearest flaming stand and upheld the necklace so that its fire licked inches beneath the dangling soulring vitus. "Now you're nothing more than a disappointing example!" He lowered the soulring into the burning heart of the flames.

Dethkore collapsed to the floor, screaming in thrashing spasms, the swaddling shadows of his clothes whipping and hissing, burning away from the pale rest of him.

Struck an internal blow, Sera reeled on her feet. She shut her eyes tight against the deluge of unwelcome visions flooding into her mind's eye but to no avail. Rapid flashes of ancient memories knifed through her mind heightened by crashing waves of emotions, of scream-stretched faces, of darks arts learned through a love destroyed, the soul-crushing devastation of a humanity forsaken through a sinister bargain made in vain. Betrayal beyond the twisting of knives. A desolate aloneness thereafter. A cataclysm of guilt plunging into a maelstrom of shame buried beneath a crushing, suffocating avalanche of sorrow and regret.

Excruciating torment triggered via the heated soulring vitus burned wicked course through Sera's and Dethkore's intertwining spirits in boiling jets of fireblood reversing her foresight. Never before . . . but now she knew . . . oh gods not just viewing but sharing the tribulations of his tortured past in a millennia of pain replayed over the cruel course of seconds while centuries stole past in the span of blinks.

Their essences melded together in a correlating twist of interweaving lifethreads, Dethkore's . . . no, not Dethkore but his true name, his human name before the binding of his soul by the Nameless One Malach'Ra, Metrapheous Theaucard . . . his memories imprinting searing brands upon her scarred soul.

Only once before, in the crypt beneath the palace unearthed and the necromaster resurrected in sacrificial slaughter, had she experienced the first subtle tells of the disturbing connection assailing her now. Though at the time it proved little more than a brief chaotic flash she attributed to the overwhelming fear gripping her more than any visions earned from her aizakai foresight.

Nergal wielded the soulring then in same fashion as inarguable proof to Dethkore of who had awakened him from his ancient slumber and who now controlled and commanded him through pain in the name of the Enclave's chosen Khan with promises of return to his slumber after he submitted to their bidding.

They sent him afield, aiding the Khan's conquering armies by raising the enemy's dead while turning the tides of battle in favor of the Lord of Storms' Bloodcloak legions. And so Sera and Dethkore lived tortured lives separated by physical distance, though now she knew that separation proved the only reason why the connection between them remained dormant, inactive.

Until now.

The truth of his sinister corruption by the Nameless One tore her mind apart while shredding her grieving heart.

A millennia of memories whipped past in the space of blinks. Of a devoted husband to a beautiful wife, Maria. Of a loving father to a cherished daughter, Marisha. Of a grief–stricken man whose honest prayers went unanswered by all but the darkest of the fallen gods, Malach'Ra. A desperate vow sworn, a sacrifice made, a wife murdered in cruel trade, a daughter resurrected in wrong and terrible ways . . . then the burning yearning to rend the world apart through retaliation against the cruel gods. And then—*oh gods and then!*

The Thousand Years War.

The torture of Dethkore's voracious haunts ripped through Sera's defenseless senses without mercy. At the heart of his existence beat a profound anguish squeezing every last sheddable tear from her withering core in grieving empathy. And in the moment, despair proved too weak a word for the regret and torment festering inside the hollow pit of his existence endured over a thousand agonizing years of guilt.

"Maria!" Dethkore screamed while thrashing on the floor. "Marisha! No!"

Acrid smoke arose round the writhing necromaster, steaming from his pores, the black haze of it permeating the air with the musky perfume of roasting flesh, the sulfur stink of burning hair and blackening nails. Seconds more and his charring patches of skin burst ablaze. Twinkling red firefly embers spun and danced through swirling zephyrs round his flailing limbs engulfed in flames their heat source internal.

Sera hunched into a standing fetal curl, hands clamped over her ears, fingernails digging scalp, in a futile attempt at shutting out the horrible screams both within and without. Her legs quivering threats of collapse, her heating skin flushed red beneath a profuse lather of sweat dripping round her trembling huddle.

"Stop!" she screamed, unable to contain the pain any longer, her temples pounding beneath her pressing palms and aching to split in bleeding seams. "Stop! Oh gods stop!"

Tottering and dizzy, enduring increasing flushes of inborn heat, she sank to her knees, erect only by raw agony clenching her muscles taut and staying her from the full collapse, her voice a ragged whisper. "Stop, please . . . oh gods just stop."

Spiritually exhausted, sick with grief, balance sloshing, her blood a hot sluice of fever, she pitched forward onto hands and knees, molten spine a pliable bend now that the deluge of nightmare visions removed from her mind's eye. Panting, quivering, shuddering from the trauma, she opened her eyes in vertigo whirls. She shifted her palms and knees in sticky peels upon the floor to stay her from total collapse. Copious amounts of her hot sweat stippled the floor. She flexed jellied muscles round leaden bones, her sloshing balance seeking to right itself through rapid blinks while the spinning world slowed.

Silence.

She craned her head, met Nergal's captivated stare beyond the flaming stand, his mouth agape, his arms hanging limp with Dethkore's soulring vitus dangling safe and withdrawn from the punishing fire.

All eyes upon her, but she transferred her gaze across the way to where lay the nude display of the necromaster's blackened body upon a thin bed of ash, charred parts of him twitching though his thrashing struggles ended. A soft, raspy moan escaped the parting of his blistered lips, putting to faint song the reminder of an agony so brutal it brought tears to her eyes where before she harbored none left to give.

Nergal approached her in five gliding strides. He stood looming with bitter calculation in his downcast glare, the Khan's necklace dangling from his left clawhand.

Energies spent, Sera possessed no strength for cringing. "Please." Her soft words a struggle. "Please stop hurting him."

"What did you see?" Nergal asked.

She swallowed, the effort raw and scraping, then shook her head and spoke through ragged breaths. "Nothing, I—" Another hard swallow. "He cannot be read."

"What did you see!" Nergal shouted while stamping a clawfoot, purple robes rippling.

Wincing, she shut her eyes and made a smaller ball of herself against the floor. She shook her head in silent denial, her mop of brown hair a hot wet nest flinging beads of sweat. She risked a look up into those inhumane eyes attempting to dismantle all of her, whispered, "I can only foresee the living. Please, no more."

Nergal thinned his scrutinizing glare upon her, expression twisting bitter. "You . . . *pity* him?" He spat the word out, disgusted by the foul taste of it, and threw a glance behind at the groaning sufferer stirring upon the floor. He hissed laughter. "Foolish child. You misplace your pity in one who is void of all humanity. Even you have no idea what the Forsaken One is truly capable of. But you will." A scarifying smile. "You all will."

She hung her head on a limp neck, the effort of speech beyond her. *Wrong. I do know—now. And more than I ever thought possible. Of him. Of myself. When a person hurts enough inside, all they can do is hurt back. A human trait you will soon understand, demon.*

***

Nergal stooped, grabbed a clawhandful of Sera's sweaty hair and yanked, forcing the side of her tensing face close to his mouth. His voice took on a slithering drawl when next he spoke in the almost-whisper of a delighted conspirator, scaly lips scraping against her tear-moistened cheek.

"After we obtain the Book of Towersss in Fissst, I'm going to enjoy peeling the ssskin from your bonesss before I bathe in your blood."

His hot breath puffing Sera's eyelids closed, Nergal licked her face from chin to cheek with the slow stroke of his tongue then spat aside. She winced and whimpered against the painful lick of his acidic tongue sizzling her skin in a brushstroke of hot grease.

"But if you are wrong about the Sssoothsayer," he continued, "I will not wait until Fissst before doing exactly that. Make no missstake, aizakai, there isss no essscaping Masssster's reach. Even death itssself crawlsss like a worm beneath hisss damning touch. Look!"

He straightened while yanking Sera up by the hair onto her tippy-toes and forced her by controlling grip into watching across the Receiving Room as he waved his free arm out in flourishing gesture at the necromaster's blackened body flipping over from back to belly where began a slow crawl by way of slapping palms and clawing fingers toward the forgotten loser of the Khan's earlier contest who still lay clinging to life by the barest of threads. The loser's faint laboring wheezes heightened the quiet of the room while everyone held their breaths, looking on in growing horror.

"Watch," Nergal said, "and witness what he truly is."

Sera could not look away. She wanted nothing more than to close her eyes, though doing so would earn her the sure wrath of Nergal's claws removing her eyelids.

Dethkore pawed across the floor in a slithering belly-crawl toward the dying man whose struggling breaths wheezed from a broken jaw twitching on busted hinges. He closed distance, pausing while craning his head, issuing a wailing moan, then his eager fingers dug into the feast of flesh before him, tearing skin while his teeth ripped larger chunks from face and throat, his victim's wheezing moans turning sickening gurgles.

As Dethkore fed, his motions grew stronger while the crisped parts of his burned and blackened flesh regenerated anew, charred patches of skin flaking away, revealing rejuvenated pale skin beneath. He fed not just upon living manflesh but devoured the lifeforce therein his twitching victim offering no resistance but for agonized squirms, the gruesome process restoring the necromaster's stolen vitality and physical abuse.

Nergal applied a wrenching pull on Sera's hair, forcing her attentions from the gory spectacle. "Where is your pity now?" He laughed in her face, a rasping hiss, then threw her aside.

She tumbled in a crumpled heap. Pushed up onto hands and knees. Locked eyes with the unliving creature staring up from its grisly feeding chews. And froze.

Crimson gore besmeared the necromaster's face, his hands and arms and chest. He stared at her with growing recognition, what little humanity remaining therein the soulless chamber of his physical vessel rebelling against the atrocity of the defiling act of his feeding so that his working jaw slowed, blood and bits of meat dripping forth, while those dark devil's eyes displayed the blooming pull of intolerable sorrow escaping the depths of him in a wailing moan.

"Enough!" Nergal threw a look at the man who had entered sometime during the gory spectacle now standing beside the open cage with a small perforated metal box upheld upon his gloved hands. The man's mouth hung open, eyes wide with frozen terror, having returned in time to witness the brunt of the necromaster's horrific feeding.

Nergal gestured through the flick of his dismissive wrist. "Take him away!"

Two Bloodcloaks standing round the cage broke the chains of their horrified stares and rushed forth. They removed iron hooks from their belts, pierced their sharp instruments into Dethkore's tendons via the ankles and dragged him out from the Receiving Room while smearing a long and bloody streak across the floor from the partially eaten corpse to the southern corridor. Dethkore offered no resistance to the sallow-faced soldiers pulling him away, his arms limp dangles trailing over his head. One of the takers vomited at the necromaster's foul proximity though he did not otherwise slow in dragging task, while the other wretched dry heaves.

The remaining team of Bloodcloaks surrounding the iron-barred cage tossed their spears within it, slammed its door shut, then pulled the cage away on squealing wheels via ropes at its back, following behind the unlucky duo dragging the necromaster out from whence they had come.

The sweeping gesture of Nergal's arm, and the new arrival rushed forth to present the metal box he carried. Nergal raised its lid, allowing the hot nest of glowing coals therein more air, then upheld the golden necklace and smiled at the dangling soulring vitus.

"Everyone has their place," he said, and shot the Khan a caustic glance. "Everyone must obey." He dropped the necklace and soulring atop the ember's rich red-velvet glow, prodded the ring deeper into the hot nest with a pushing black talon, and snapped the lid shut.

A tortured scream echoed through the southern corridor, fading with distance.

Cringing tensed, Sera steeled against more visions assaulting her senses. But to her relief she suffered only a few minor flashes, faint and fleeting, the physical distance between her and Dethkore providing just a tiny sample of their connection.

Nergal clasped his clawhands behind his proud back and smiled. "Begone." Then spun round facing the enthroned Khan while the gloved servant removed away carrying the box and its imprisoned soulring to store it elsewhere.

"Leave the box undisturbed until my return," Nergal said. "The Forsaken One must relearn his obedient place. As to the rest . . ." A glance at Sera, but he added nothing.

"You're leaving?" The Khan sat forward, frowning. "Now?"

"I will return shortly." Nergal paused at the western lip of the dais. "Smile, warlord. Your annoying impatience is at an end. Once the Soothsayer has proven subservient to Master's curse, we will march against Fist and you shall have all the bloodshed you desire. And when we crush that heathen's den and procure the book, you will be gifted the rest of the Dominator's Armor as promised. Along with the immortality you bargained for." A pause, a malicious grin. "With the Forsaken One and soon the Soothsayer at our disposal, none will oppose us."

The Khan settled back, eyebrows arching. "And if he resists?"

"Then I will enjoy breaking him," Nergal said, pleased. He gave the Khan an idle flick of his wrist, sleeve flapping, before returning it behind the small of his back with the other. "And you will enjoy killing him. But no matter that. There is no resisting the corruption of Master's bloodlust curse. All have failed before him."

The Khan produced a dismissive grunt above the creaking of his gauntleted hands closing into tight fists. "I would rather just kill him and be done with it."

Nergal thinned his eyes into a cutting glare. "Stow your foolish pride. We stand upon the precipice of another Thousand Years War. Your warlord lusts will be satisfied soon enough. Fist will fall, and then Master's true plans will begin through you. Do not misstep now that we're so close."

He turned away—turned back at the sound of another of the Khan's irritated grunts, serpentine eyes flaring.

"You will obey or you will suffer!" Nergal yelled. "This is the last time I warn you, then it will be your screams filling these halls. Do I make myself clear?"

The Khan answered with a curt nod only.

"Excellent. Now, I have one minor task to attend before begins your true ascension to godhood. Relax, and enjoy what little remains of your mortal life. Soon you will breathe the breath of gods."

Hissing laughter, Nergal strode toward the traveling pool where he disrobed then descended, submerging into the bubbling crimson portal, then gone.

* * *

Sera watched the violet witchlights of carven symbols wink out from round the traveling pool while the bubbling froth of aizakai blood therein returned placid. She breathed slight relief, stood from on scraped and bleeding palms and knees, every trembling inch an ache. At the Khan's gesture Horace strode forth, grabbed her by the arm and returned her to her place between himself and the brooding Lord of Storms upon the dais.

A heavy reticence filled the Receiving Room for long minutes as everyone awaited Hannibal Khans's next words while he awaited Nergal's imminent return. He sat his throne staring transfixed beyond the gore of two corpses lying the floor at the traveling pool in stewing silence.

As if by silent command, a flurry of servants rushed forth and scrubbed the blood from the floor while several of their fellows adopted the task of dragging the two aizakai corpses across the room to deposit the bodies into the crimson depths of Nergal's traveling pool.

The Khan drew in breath, held deep and overlong, released an audible hiss through clenched teeth. There played a brief crackling surge of arcing sparks over his godsforged gauntlets which gripped the blocky ends of armrests. Irritability gnawed on his handsome features, twisting them ugly. He swept the room with waxing psychosis dancing within a gaze hunting to appease his waning patience through the entertainment of yet another victim while he waited out Nergal's return.

He smiled at Sera. "You."

She flinched, caught within that piercing stare.

"Tell me," the Khan said. "How long must I endure that demon's advisory before I am free?" A glancing glare at the traveling pool, his gauntleted hands flexing into fists. "Before the privilege of killing him?"

She shifted her feet though dared not look away, unsure after her ordeal if she possessed enough strength for more visions. She opened her mouth.

An eruption akin to thunder sounded outside the Divine Palace somewhere close by in the Holy City of Khan, though muffled by the thick stone walls. There sounded another. And another.

Sera closed her mouth, tensing. *Were those screams?*

Servants paused in their cleaning work, eyes darting for the origins of the mysterious noises, for the Lord of Storms' godsforged gauntlets remained undisturbed of their spark-crackling power, having induced no such outside tremors.

The Khan frowned.

The metallic shifting of red-gold armor, and the hundred Bloodcloaks aligning the walls shifted, stepped forth, swords and spears brandished aloft. Until the Khan stilled them back to their guarding positions with an upraised fist and a stern command.

A tense moment passed.

More recurring booms and screams, closer than those previous.

The Khan scowled.

The western set of doors pushed open from without, and in rushed a Bloodcloak yelling, "Seal the doors!" while behind him the doors closed. "Seal the doors, godsdammit!" He waved his arms in wild gesture while running toward the Khan in such a rush that when he fell to his knees he slid and banged them against the dais's lips, pitching him into a fast bow that loosed his helm from head in a rolling clatter past the throne.

"Forgive the intrusion, my Khan." The Bloodcloak touched forehead to floor. But he did not keep it there, instead looking up and presenting wide eyes of panic. "Fires erupting throughout the city, my Khan. They're random, but they're everywhere!"

A distraction, Vengeance whispered. Sera enjoyed the warming ease of a relaxation unknown in two years of brutal captivity flushing through her. *Soon has finally arrived.*

The Khan sat forward, grimacing at the trembling Bloodcloak kneeling before him. He opened his mouth—

But there arose a clamor beyond the western doors punctuated by muffled screams in the corridor beyond.

Sera straightened, spine a stiffening iron rod of resolve and acceptance. She looked at Horace. *He's here.* Met the Khan's contemptuous glare in brazen defiance, embracing the freedom of peace moments in coming, with a bold smile.

Face contorting with rage, the Khan erupted into standing, pounding gauntleted fists upon fracturing ivory armrests, glaring at the western doors and the noises beyond. "Who dares!"

"You wanted him," Sera said, soft but sure, firm and knowing. "And now you have him." But her pleasured answer fell lost to the attentions gripped by the elevating sounds of the approaching disturbance.

The muffled cacophony outside the western doors turned mute for a reticent length. Then sounded the loud *bang* of some outside force slamming against the doors, hinges loosening while sprinkling grit, the noise amplified by the tense silence within the Receiving Room.

Another bang—and again!

A small lapse of quiet.

The crisscrossing flash of a steel blade cutting an X through barred timber. Then those thick wooden doors imploded inwards, blasting apart, erupting in an explosive spray of wood and metal and stone striking nearest Bloodcloaks from their feet who skittered across the floor, armor scraping, where they lay in shifting groans of agony, those not killed outright from the burst of deadly shrapnel.

A roiling cloud of dust and debris filled the gaping maw of the western corridor. The obscuring haze swirled and swarm round the lone figure standing therein where pierced through the settling cloud a pair of lambent red eyes beset in a shadowed mask of lusting death. Strewn corpses and parts of corpses littered the full length of the corridor behind the newcomer, crimson gore having sprayed unto darkening the walls and floor and even dripping from the high ceiling in his fighting bid through the Divine Palace to reach the Receiving Room, those staring therein.

The bloodlust-corrupted Soothsayer stalked inside, blood, none of it his own, soaking his clothes dark and dripping from every inch of his prowling movements and the wetted sword he carried angled forward in his sure grip. His savage rictus grin beheld not just the Khan but them all.

What remained of the hundred Bloodcloaks broke free from their stunned bewilderment. In hive mind they rushed forth, attacking the red-eyed invader.

But it was not enough.

Hannibal Khan roared in challenge, raising his right hand overhead while outreaching his other toward the grim figure glaring defiance from across the room, his godsforged lanthium gauntlets of power coruscating into waking life as his fingers outstretched in the beginnings of calling down his lightning, to channel then command it forth in an awesome display of his godly smiting power.

And still it was not enough.

Seething with Power, enveloped in a permeable and pulsing throb of rage, Jericho shifted into blurring murder, his sword rapid fannings of quicksilver promise, his body fluid locomotion, and advanced upon them all within seconds.

Thunderous rumbles shook the palace walls, loosening puffs of grinding mortar grit between stone joins, as powerful winds swept and swirled within the room, coalescing then funneling into a whipping tornado enclosing the conjurer of those gale-force breaths while blowing away the few Bloodcloaks rushing their Khan in failed attempts to surrounding their Lord of Storms in bodily defense.

The blood-curdling screams of the Khan's dying loyals felled by the score filled the room in a dire singsong in tune to the dread melody of the Soothsayer's mad laughter as a mass killing ensued, streaks of his bloodletting wetting the buffeting winds with a red rain.

The high stone ceiling blasted open as the searing white-hot fury of the Khan's smiting lightning jagged down from the splitting heavens, making of him a human conduit of charged scintillating brilliance while sending charred rubble falling in a battering shower of smoking stony hail.

A hissing scream pierced the cacophony of violence as the crimson contents of the traveling pool gurgled, the carven circle of arcane symbols lining its outer rim burning bright with violet witchlight flickering in the tumultuous winds—then winking out when falling debris from the blasted ceiling crashed upon the rising head of a returning Nergal, crushing the bewildered serpent-priest down into the crimson portal before he ascended more than shoulder-high from the bubbling froth, the smashing pummel of rocks splashing fountaining waves of arcing blood across the floor while debris filled the traveling pool.

Through it all played the delighted melody of a little girl's crazed laughter—cut short beneath a crushing stone squashing Sera to the floor.

Chaos ensued in a storm of screams and slaughter and lightning.

CHAPTER FOURTEEN

Slow . . . in . . . rousing . . . awake . . . Banzu's lids fluttered open, vision blurry, dry tongue scraping round the hot sticky peel of his parched mouth, foggy mind clearing in burning mists of lethargic awareness groping at diaphanous feathered mysteries of memories too vague for grasping firmer hold.

How am I . . . where am I . . . the last I remember . . . so cold.

He lay supine and viewing up at the bruised sky, unsure whether dawn or dusk, though the time of day meaningless.

I'm alive? I'm alive. How?

Motionless but for the ease of sure breathing, he wormed his tongue in futile effort at producing moistening saliva into the dry cave of his mouth while reflecting upon the chilling abyss of his wolf bite's infection conquering him mid-run, memories of the event recalled through skipping flashes separated by blank black spaces refusing connection.

Yes, running then falling then nothing but cold and darkness and surrender.

The muscle-clenching, joint-locking, bone-gnawing chill jagging through every tortured inch of his failing body . . . gone, replaced by a surprising though comfortable warmth.

He lay sweating—a lot. Lay bundled up somehow.

In his right peripheral, pale blonde hair rested close to his face. Melora lay half on top of him with an arm and leg draped over his chest and lower parts respectively, the left side of her face resting upon his pillowing right shoulder and upper chest.

Swaddled together.

He startled flinched, breath hitching, pulse quickening, awareness expanding, body tensing beneath the resting pressure of her sleeping against him, the how and why of it all too much a strain on his mind in need of nourishing repair to process so that he surrendered relaxed.

If I'm dead or dreaming then I don't ever want to wake.

He closed his eyes and bathed in the sheltering comfort of her warm embrace with neither question nor care. He listened to the steady rhythm of her breathing, her exhales soft and silky whispers brushing his skin. Let the world have its worries while he lay cocooned and oblivious. Nothing else mattered but the moment.

He basked in the soothing nurture of her tender snuggle—then jolted, fearing its end, when she showed signs of rousing from her slumber by exhaling a soft moan while readjusting her draping limbs into a tighter hug against him, her bare and sweaty skin sliding over his.

We're naked?

He tensed.

We're naked.

He held his breath until her motions stilled, afraid of shattering the beautiful illusion by waking her. Yet he squirmed parts of himself in inching shifts, testing what must be nothing more than the vivid unreality of a hallucination.

No, this is real. He relaxed, smiling, nestled in the embracing bliss of her sleeping cling. *And it's wonderful.*

She squirmed again, readjusting by hugging him tighter, and exhaled another soft moan this tickling the fine hairs of his closest ear so near her parted lips. The heat from her unguarded sex breathed warm against his bare thigh, her soft breasts pressing, sliding against his right arm and chest nestled between them. The rousing flush of her sleeping fidgets proved too much for his youthful, reactive body to ignore.

Oh gods. He swallowed hard with effort, tried forcing mental distance from her physical embrace. A useless endeavor, his body betraying him through the sure arousal of his manhood. Draped over him, her right leg impeded his sex from rising so that it pressed stiff against her warm, slick inner thigh in throbbing attention.

He flushed with nervous heat, heartbeat a thrumming panic. If she awoke and found him in such a state, how would he ever explain himself?

She stirred evermore, pulling, hugging, every embracing inch of her instigating more arousal from his stimulated body.

Oh gods! Cold dread flushed so that he closed his eyes, feigning sleep. But his pounding heartbeat betrayed an obvious tell while Melora stretched, rousing from sleep.

He rolled his head right to better meet her waking face.

Her lids fluttered, opened. She raised her head from his chest, withdrew by inches, eyes expanding, mouth forming a silent O of surprise.

He smiled.

* * *

Melora stared at him a silent length, disbelief expanding in the black centers of her violet eyes while a budding smile provoked subtle curves to her closing lips. She sat up, their blanket sliding from her bare shoulders, her alabaster skin a glistening sheen of sweat. She made no move to cover her breasts while Banzu viewed them in all their glory.

"You're awake." She leaned closer, brightening eyes appraising him, and palmed the side of his face, testing temperature through gentle feel. "And your chillfever's finally broken, thank the gods."

He closed his eyes in brief enjoyment of her soft touch until her hand slid free of his cheek. His voice rusty with disuse, he rasped more than asked, "What's a chilly fever?"

She laughed the sound of music. Without answering she flapped away the blanket from over their lower halves and slid her draping leg away.

Oh no. He jolted into sitting up, hands frantic fumbles grabbing for the blanket at the same time her leg slid free. He tried telling her to *Wait!* but the order stalled short at the back of his parched throat, turning the word into a harsh cough, the effort dizzying him so that he lay back, blanketless hands covering the embarrassing arousal of his exposed member at full attention. Cringing, he shut his eyes tight and rolled his head left, face flushing with heat, wishing the ground to open and swallow him whole.

Smirking, she twisted away, twisted back. She set a plump waterskin atop his bare chest between the valley of his upper arms and patted it. "Drink, you silly boy," she said, then stood.

He opened one eye then the other. Tucked his chin and eyed the waterskin's precious bounty bestowed upon his ravenous thirst. He sat up and managed enough restraint to at least pull a handful of shielding blanket over his crotch before thumbing the stopper popped then craning his head while attempting to drain the waterskin empty in one swallowing draw. But the water so soothing in his dry mouth went down jagged and wrong in his aching throat so that he sputtered it out in a half-choking, half-coughing fit fracturing the world into wet prisms.

"Slowly," Melora said, facing away and dressing. "Small sips, or else you'll just sick it back up." She paused and peeked over a shoulder. "It's been awhile since you drank anything on your own."

He rumbled his throat and sniffed his sinuses clear, wanting to ask how long the 'awhile'—along with a hundred other questions—but the precious water demanded all his attentions. He nursed the waterskin while scanning round the new surroundings.

Trees and forest scrub everywhere, blocking the outside world in every direction but above where the unobstructed sky brightened by the minute. *Dawn, then. Not dusk. A new day.* He squeezed another satisfying pull on the half-empty waterskin then paused, allowing the churning queasiness of his otherwise empty belly to settle.

"What happened? Where are we? How did I—" But there he clipped short, looking down at his wolf bite wound wrapped in clean bandages, the infectious blue jags of sickness once spreading the full length of his left arm gone. Perplexed, he flexed his left hand. No pain. No cold. "How am I still alive?"

"You were sick with the chillfever," Melora said, the firm cheeks of her backside giving a pleasant little jiggle when she pulled up the tight waistline of her pants then began doing up the front laces. "Those wolves that attacked us? They wandered south from the Thunderhell Tundra."

She bent at the waist, snatched up her shirt, the sweat on her silvery kohatheen collar catching soft glints from the growing light of the rising sun stabbing through leafy breaks between the eastern trees.

"Frostwolves." She fiddled with the front buttons of her shirt from the bottom up. "They carry a miasma of magic in their saliva that infects escaping prey, freezing them from the inside."

She closed the top button of her shirt, turned round smiling, bright eyes estimating him.

"My void-aura slowed the infection. Made it dormant when you were near me. But it had time to build up in your system every time you weren't. Until . . ." She trailed away. Took two steps closer then stopped, smile vanishing. "I thought you were dead. I thought—" She bit her bottom lip, eyes glistening.

He grinned up at her. "So did I." Then cocked an eyebrow. "Wait a minute. How do you know all of that?"

She crossed her arms, appraised him with a smirk. "A lot's happened in the two weeks you've been out."

"Two weeks?" He jolted stiff, the news a long spike of cold steel pounded through the length of his spine with one hammering blow. He glanced round at answers unfound. "*Two weeks?*"

She nodded, smile returning with the slow shake of her head. "I still can't believe it. All this time and I never even saw what was right there in front of me." She thinned her eyes and beheld him in silent regard.

"What?" He shifted on his bottom. "Why are you looking at me like that?"

"You know why." She planted fists to hips, arms akimbo, eyes flaring along with her voice. "Why didn't you tell me you're a godsdamned Soothsayer!"

He flinched at her slap of words, guts bunching, eyes darting everywhere but her. "Uhm." He raised the waterskin to his lips, squeezed and swallowed, buying time against the accusation, unable to refute it. "Uhm." He raked his free hand back through his sweaty tangles, blew out his cheeks and gazed up at her. "Uh. I guess I have some explaining to do?"

"You're godsdamned right you do—" she began then cut off short, turning at the sounds of approaching footsteps rustling through grass and snapping twigs underfoot from somewhere unseen beyond the eastern line of trees. A screening patch of leafy branches shook then spread, parting round the hulking figure walking through, a collection of sticks tucked under the crook of one massive arm.

The tundarian berserker stopped and met Banzu's widening stare. A flicker of surprise flittered over his otherwise impassive features. The collection of sticks clunked to the ground when he freed them and reached up, gripped the sword hilt jutting from behind his right boulder shoulder, dark hope glimmering in his cold and smoldering blue eyes.

"My Honor is awake at last," Ma'Kurgen said.

Blood-quickening panic flushed through Banzu, locking his body taut. He gaped at the hulking tundarian pulling free the massive broadsword strapped to his broad back. Melora said something, but her words fell lost to Banzu's ears pounding muffled with the thunder of his racing pulse. She stepped aside, and the tundarian walked past her, closing distance, broadsword brandished.

Paralyzed but for his darting eyes, Banzu stole a panicked glance past the approaching giant at his own sword sheathed and lying on the ground well out from reach. At Melora just standing there watching them both, her arms crossed and hips cocked, wearing that infuriating smile. Banzu stammered for speech, mind racing through avenues of escape yet finding none, and words died away when Ma'Kurgen knelt before him and lay the broadsword at his feet then bowed, head low.

"Will my Honor deliver me the Righteous Death?" Ma'Kurgen asked.

"What?" Banzu dug in his heels, kicking up dirt and leaves while scooting backwards by inches. "What?" he asked the top of Ma'Kurgen's bowed head, then looked at Melora. "*What?*"

"Relax." An amused smirk toyed at her lips. "He's asking you to kill him."

"Kill him?" Banzu stared at the top of Ma'Kurgen's bowed and nodding head, the presented length of broadsword between them. He considered kicking the big man away yet feared a broken foot against all that muscle—or worse, instigating Ma'Kurgen into another murderous fit of berserker rage. "What in all the hells for?"

She shrugged. "He's been wandering in exile from his tribe on a death-quest to cleanse his shame, though he won't say why. It took me a week just to figure that much out from as little as he talks. Those frostwolves followed him down from the tundra, feeding off his battle scraps until he killed their mother and chased her pups away."

"Frostwolves?" Stupefied, Banzu gaped from her to Ma'Kurgen's bowed head and back again. "Pups?"

She nodded. "Pups, yes. And apparently they were only toying with us. If they'd been full grown dires—"

"He's crazy!" Banzu shouted.

"He's proud," she said. "Tundarians are warriors who consider suicide the worst desecration of their souls. He seeks a warrior's death. But you refused him. Now he considers himself bound to you until you kill him. He helped me keep you alive. He told me about the chillfever."

Gods! What mad world have I woken up in? "You're crazy," he said to Ma'Kurgen, then to Melora, "The both of you."

She laughed. "Twice since you passed out he's saved us from attacks by Enclave agents. He cut them down before I knew they were even there." She shot the big tundarian an approving glance. "He may be crazy, but he's also proven useful. And he's waiting for your answer."

Ma'Kurgen raised his head, locked eyes with Banzu, long black hair framing his face. "Will my Honor deliver me the Righteous Death?"

"Apparently you're his Honor now," Melora said, smirking. "After besting him in battle."

Banzu did the only thing his mind could frame in applicable response: he took the waterskin from his lap and threw it. "No!"

The waterskin struck Ma'Kurgen's unflinching face and dropped. The smoldering depths of his blue-eyed stare turned glare deepened with bridled fury. He emitted a throated growl while baring his teeth in a savage gleam, then stood, returned the broadsword to his back. He glared over Banzu in silent loom. With no more words he turned and walked away, disappearing through the trees from whence he'd come.

Banzu drew in deep and held it, watching the branches reform their shielding wall round Ma'Kurgen's leaving, then blew out his cheeks. "So . . . is that it? Is he gone?"

Melora chuckled, shook her head. "If only it were that easy."

* * *

Weakened by two weeks of malnutrition, Banzu spent the remainder of the day chewing roots and sipping water when not drifting through short bouts of sleep, dozing off then startling awake in panicked sweats of Ma'Kurgen returning through the bush in a berserker charge.

Dusk bruising the sky, Banzu sat a nude hunch in his nest of blanket while battling confusion over the strange change of his rescued life.

Ma'Kurgen returned carrying the bloody haunch of hunted stag over his left shoulder, refilled waterskins tied off at his belt, and more wood bunched under his right arm for the fire he then built, silent in his labors, saying nothing while he fell to task skinning the haunch.

Melora sat cross-legged facing Banzu and without asking washed the sweaty grime clean from his bare torso with a wad of rags cut from one of his rucksack shirts, dipping them moist in the puddle of the makeshift bowl of concave rock beside her, her right shoulder bandaged though her arm free of sling.

Ma'Kurgen spitted the skinned haunch over the fire then withdrew from Banzu and Melora a good distance and sat with his back to a tree, his sun-bronzed torso bare but for the crisscrossing leather straps of his sword harness, oblivious to everything round him but for his current task. Silvery moonlight danced with shadows across his muscular twitches while he worked an oiled cloth in meticulous rubs and sweeps across the glinting length of his broadsword between sliding scraps of a whetstone, the impressive steel resting flat-wise atop his timber-thick thighs and capturing all his focus.

Melora scrubbed Banzu's arms with gentle strokes while he stared past her at Ma'Kurgen, unable to relax despite the pleasure of her work. She winced every now and again while pausing and rolling her injured right shoulder, the activity helping to loosen the kinks binding round her healing joint.

"Hey," he said, catching her gaze then gesturing with the tilt of his head, keeping his voice low. "What's his deal, anyways?"

She glanced Ma'Kurgen an over the shoulder peek, shrugged her good shoulder. "He's immune to the cold. A common aizakai trait among tundarians. And he doesn't particularly like being near me because of it." A pausing smirk. "He thinks I'm a witch, that I'm doing it on purpose whenever he gets within my void-aura."

"Huh." Banzu gazed in wonder, finding it strange Ma'Kurgen provided such tender care to his weapon considering the death he sought. *Gods he's big. No, bigger than big. Huge!* A great swell of pride straightened his spine. *And I bested him. Barely, but I did it.*

Though his swordforms foreign, Ma'Kurgen's proficient skills proved an even match for Banzu's during their swordslinger contest. Reflecting upon their fight brought him an exciting thrill. Despite the chillfever wracking him, he proved his worth. Though the saving grace of the Power providing him unfair advantage tarnished his victory.

"Are they all that friggin big?" he asked. "Tundarians?"

She chuckled, nodded. "Yes. Up." She lifted his right arm by the wrist, washing over his dirty ribs.

He flinched a tickle. "I can wash myself, you know." But even he heard the lack of conviction in his words.

She smiled. "I know."

He smiled back. *She looks at me different now.* His gaze traveled left, fell upon his sword lying close by for easy reach. His smile withered into a depressing frown. The bent and battered piece of steel lay ruined beyond repair, evincing the punishing hammerblows of Ma'Kurgen's broadsword. A twisted, miserable excuse for a sword no longer. Abused proof of Ma'Kurgen's incredible strength and berserker fury.

If not for the Power, that final chopping stroke would have cleaved through my sword and cut me down the middle. He glanced at the silent tundarian giant. "I wish he'd just go away," he muttered.

"Wish in one hand and spit in the other and you'll see which one fills up faster." She lowered his arm for washing his chest. "Or just give him what he wants and be done with it."

He scowled, withdrew by inches. "I'm not killing him."

"Then you'll have plenty of opportunities to tell him."

He thinned his eyes upon her. "What do you mean?"

She threw a glance behind at Ma'Kurgen tending his broadsword and oblivious of their words. "You met his challenge and bested him. He expected you to kill him but you didn't. He's not going away until you do."

Banzu huffed and stared past her, toiling over what terrible acts a man could do to possess him into seeking his own death as penance, then surrendered a sigh and hung his head. "I can't believe it. I just can't friggin believe it."

She tucked a hand beneath his chin and lifted it to better meet his eyes. "Believe it." She pulled him closer by the shoulders and continued washing his chest. "He'll kill everyone who intends you harm until you do kill him. There's that at least."

Banzu shook his head. "He has no idea what he asks of me."

She paused her washing. "He wants to die, Ban. And he wants you to kill him. You accepted his challenge and now he sees you as the only one worthy of redeeming whatever it was that sent him into exile."

He stiffened, voice raised. "I never accepted—" But there he stopped, sighed, the point beyond arguing. In a lower voice he asked, "Why?"

She shrugged, returned to washing task. "Don't know. I asked him once. But after the look he gave me I'll not ask again."

He stared past her, drew in deep through flaring nostrils, a cold strength entering him, and expelled a deflating huff. "He has no idea. With the Power I could kill him as easily as breathing."

"Then do it," she said in the nonchalant manner of claiming the sky blue and water wet.

He glowered at her. "You know I can't. And now you know why."

She paused her washing and met the challenge of his stern stare. "You can within my void-aura. You did it once already. And that's the point of a Pair."

"I—" He paused. *She's right. I've done as much before.* Then shook his head. "No. I don't want to kill him. I don't want to kill anyone. I just want to see you to Fist."

She smiled, fleeting, there then gone. "And after that?"

I don't know. But I do know Jericho'll tan my hide soon as he sees me. Gods, I almost forgot. But he put no voice behind it.

"He's not giving you much of a choice," she continued. "Sooner or later . . ." She trailed off into her washing work after wincing through another roll of her bandaged shoulder.

Banzu blew out his cheeks in a deflating huff. It felt good to talk openly about it all now that she knew the truth of him. Yet still he hesitated, words sticky in his throat, habitual years of holding them back.

He said, "All these years and Jericho never told me how he survived the bloodlust. He never wanted to talk about it, even when I pressed him." A glance at Ma'Kurgen. "Now I wish I'd made him tell me." He plucked a blade of grass and flicked it. "Before he ran off without me."

"Wait." Melora straightened, brow furrowing in curious pinch. "You don't know?"

Banzu endured gooseflesh prickles. "You do?"

"Of course I do. There's not a Spellbinder in Fist who doesn't know the story of what happened when he—" She paused, face scrunching. "He really never told you?"

The slow shake of his head.

"Oh gods." She shifted on her bottom. "I know more now than most because of what I learned after returning from Junes, but—" She paused, chewing her bottom lip. "No, I shouldn't. I can't. You should wait and hear it from him."

"No, please. Tell me."

"Are you sure?"

He nodded.

She hesitated, holding the measure of his pleading gaze.

"Please?" he asked, taking her by the hand and giving it an instigating squeeze. "I need to know."

She nodded. "Okay." She nested her hands in her lap. "He and Mistress Agatha were sent out to hunt down a rumored Soothsayer in some remote part of southern Thurandy. In Grey Raven's Keep or somewhere past it, I don't know, this was years before my time. Only there was no Soothsayer, just a small army waiting for them. One of those greedy fools had the bright idea of sending a false report about a rogue Soothsayer to the Academy in a stupid attempt at making some coin. But it was a lure. They planned on killing Agatha and capturing Jericho then returning him to the Academy for a hefty reward. But—"

She stopped there, looked down at the rags in her fiddling hands beholding false interest.

After a time Banzu asked, "But what?"

Melora drew in deep, raised her gaze. "Jericho killed them. All three-hundred of them. And in the maddening throes of his waking bloodlust he turned on Agatha."

Oh gods. "Oh."

"There's only one rule when it comes to a turned Soothsayer. Kill. Period. But they'd been a Pair for years, married in secret, and Agatha loved him. They fought, and she tried to subdue him, to bring him back. But he was too far gone by then. He'd already killed so many. So she threw herself upon his sword and her blood leaked into his cuts. That brought him down in seconds."

She gave an indicative tug on the kohatheen locked round her neck and grimaced. "That's why these godsdamned things work so godsdamned well. Our blood is a poisonous paralyzing agent to all aizakai. The presence of it staves magic. Locks up the limbs and slows organs if ingested. More is fatal. If Head Mistress Finch hadn't acted on her suspicions and sent Mistress Gwendora to follow after them, Agatha would have died. And Jericho . . . Gwendora could've killed him. It would've been hours before he recovered from paralysis. But Agatha pleaded as she lay bleeding with his sword punched through her guts to collar him instead.

"Gwendora did. Then she carried Agatha to the closest Lady's Chapel where the priests sewed her up. Somehow by the grace of gods Jericho's sword missed her vitals, though the wound turned her barren. They kept what happened a secret, twisted the events to hide the truth. But they couldn't hide Jericho's turning for long, so he and Agatha planned his escape behind Head Mistress Finch's and Mistress Gwendora's backs. Mistress Gwendora was raised to Head Mistress in Agatha's stead because of it, shortly after Head Mistress Finch fell ill and died from waterlung. I only learned the end of it when Head Mistress and Agatha filled me in before I left out from Fist. Before that I assumed the same as everyone else, that Jericho turned on Agatha then fled, leaving her for dead."

"Gods," Banzu said in a low whisper. "No wonder he never wanted to talk about it." He paused, unease creeping in. "But . . . what are they planning on doing with him?" He shifted on his bottom, nervous of the answer. "Why did Gwen send for him after all these years? There has to be more to it than just killing Hannibal Khan. That envelope you brought him, what did it say?"

Melora shrugged, shook her head. "I don't know. She only told me to find him and deliver it then bring him back." She scrunched her face, wrung the rags in her lap in irritated strangle, her tone gaining edge. "Just like she never told me about you, godsdamn her."

Banzu frowned. "What if he turns again?" He looked at Ma'Kurgen, his words a whisper. "What if I turn?"

She palmed the side of his face, returning his gaze. "You don't have to worry about that now." She slipped her hand back to her lap. "And once we're Paired in Fist you won't have to worry about that ever again."

He jolted stiff. "Paired in Fist?"

A soft laugh, a sly smirk. "You don't really think I'm going to let another Soothsayer slip through my fingers do you? Mistress Gwendora sent me to bring back the last Soothsayer, and that's exactly what I'm going to do." Her smirk spread into a feline smile. "You're mine, now. All mine."

"Wait a minute—" he began.

She leaned in and kissed him full on the lips.

Whatever else he planned on saying vanished as he closed his eyes and kissed her back, deep and long, their joined mouths a natural fit, enjoying the stifling peace in those soft lips and caressing tongue. He wanted nothing more than for the moment to last so that he continued kissing air after she withdrew. Until a light, playful slap against his cheek brought him alert.

She laughed. "Silly boy."

He smiled. Said nothing. And he didn't have to. Their eyes conversed on a level beyond words while the euphoric awakening of a new and wonderful appreciation for the world and everything in it bloomed alive in the flourishing depths of him as for the first true time in his life he felt necessary in all the right ways.

* * *

"You can finish from here." Melora dropped the wadded rags into Banzu's upturned hand and stood, winced while rolling her right shoulder. "I have some washing of my own to do." She turned away though peeked him the reveal of a playful smile over her good shoulder. "And no, you're not returning the favor." She walked away.

"Wait!" He rocked into standing then plopped back down while pulling the fallen blanket round his bare bits. He shot Ma'Kurgen an obvious glance. "You're just going to leave me here? With him?"

She paused at the outskirt of the firelight, considered the silent giant who sat with head bowed in concentrative focus while tending his broadsword. "If he wanted you dead then you'd already be dead. He's had plenty of opportunities to kill us both. I won't be far. There's a stream nearby. You boys behave while I'm gone."

Banzu watched her leave away into the gloom of night. He sighed, shoulders slouching, then flipped the blanket from over his lower half and washed his legs and such. Minutes more and he froze when Ma'Kurgen stood and returned the glinting moonstruck broadsword to his back. Ma'Kurgen picked up a shadowed pile nearby, carried then dropped Banzu's boots and washed clothes between them. He stood in silent staring loom, smoldering blue eyes twin stabs in the dark. Then he turned round and moved to the fire where he squatted and, after prodding the glowing nest of coals with a stick, rotated the roasting spit of haunch, his broad hunch a boulder of muscle shadowed in the dark.

Banzu dressed while keeping steady watch on Ma'Kurgen's turned wall of back, stiff muscles groaning through the slow motions. He stood, every sore inch aching protest, and worked on his boots. *I don't want to kill you.* But grim certainty assured no hesitation if it meant protecting Melora.

So easy to take those few necessary steps and with a quick seize of the Power snap that bull-thick neck from behind in one Power-fueled wrenching twist, though he balked at committing such a cowardly act. Even on this man who almost killed him.

He's probably killed dozens already, wandering around and challenging people in suicidal combat. What in friggin hell's his problem anyways?

Banzu flexed his hands while envisioning the reaching grab, sinews snapping, knuckles popping. *I'd be doing the world a favor if I—*

"No," he whispered, speaking the word helping abstain from indulging in outright murder, let alone triggering the bloodlust in the absence of Melora's void-aura. He scrubbed sweaty palms dry on his thighs, balled his hands into tight fists, swallowed hard, glanced at where Melora walked away. He took a hesitant step toward Ma'Kurgen. "Can't you just go away?"

Silence but for the crackling fire, the hissing of juices dripping on glowing coals beneath the roasting haunch.

Another hesitant step closer. "You're wasting your time, you know. I'm not going to kill you, so you might as well leave us alone and find someone else." *You crazy—*

"I know what you are." Ma'Kurgen voice, deep and rolling. He did not move, did not turn his gaze from the fire as he spoke. "They said you were the Killing Wind."

"They?" Banzu asked. "They who?"

"The three who paid me to stray from my death-quest and find you."

Ma'Kurgen stood, a rising column of muscle, but he did not turn round, instead he beheld the fire past his feet as if it contained some private fascination only his eyes could perceive.

"My people have many stories of your kind," he said. "Old tales of destruction and bloodshed. But you are different from the stories our elders speak of the others. You are weak where they were strong. You hesitate where they did not. You fear death where they embraced it. You stay your hand instead of delivering the savagery of your kind." He expelled a derisive huff and shook his head, long raven hair swishing across his broad back. "I am glad now I killed those men. I only wish I had pulled out their lying tongues."

The three who paid . . . those men . . . another Trio? "Does she know?" Banzu asked.

"The she-witch knows nothing."

A wary glance at the dark. "You don't understand," Banzu said. "I can't kill you—"

"You will."

Ma'Kurgen turned round, presented the icy calm fury smoldering therein the blue-eyed depths of his serrated glare. The muscles along his square jaw twitched. His meaty fists trembled tight, strangling invisible necks. His right hand moved to his left hip, gripped the leather pouch and yanked it free from his belt. He tossed it to the ground between them with a jangle then spat at it.

"You keep," he said. "I have no use for their coin or their Khan. And I do not care what the she-witch has planned for you. Eat. Rest. Tomorrow you will abolish my shame with the Righteous Death." He clenched teeth bared in a savage gleam. "Or I will tear your woman apart with my bare hands, piece by screaming piece."

Anger a hot burst in his clenching guts, eyes brutal flares, Banzu bared a snarl. He took one challenging step forward, stomping, and threw an accusatory point. "You touch her you big son of a bitch and I swear to gods I'll—"

But there he clipped short, for Ma'Kurgen turned away, walked away. He disappeared into the gloom in the opposite direction of Melora's leaving.

Glaring at darkness, animus seething, the profound surge of bridled rage within him turned the breath of ice held deep and overlong until its searing touch burned with ache in his chest. Everything in him screamed for seizing the Power, for stalking after the tundarian and tearing out the berserker's still-beating heart then squeezing it crushed while Ma'Kurgen lay watching in dying stare.

And smiling up at me for giving him what he wants most, godsdammit.

He dared not risk the killing without the safety of Melora's void-aura protecting him from waking the bloodlust. *I'd kill him then I'd turn on her. Just like . . . gods, just like Jericho did Aggie. Friggin hell! If it's not one thing it's another. Always another.*

He glared at the battered length of his useless sword then stomped the leather pouch beside it. Out spilled gold coins.

He plopped down, plucked a coin from the ground and inspected by firelight the stamp of a fist clutching a bolt of lightning, then clenched the coin inside his squeezing fist.

"Godsdammit." *Just like she'd said after Cody almost killed us. The Enclave's reach knows no bounds.*

He stared at the charring haunch spitted over the low fire. Leaned forward and gathered the scattered coins into the leather pouch. Pulled its drawstrings tight then stuffed it away, hidden at the bottom of his rucksack, unsure how he would explain a Trio's failed attempt at paying for the tundarian's killing services to Melora if at all.

No. Not failed. Not yet. And me without a sword.

"Oh gods." He raked a hand back through his hair and blew out his cheeks. *First khansmen, and now this. What've I gotten myself into?*

* * *

Banzu licked his greasy lips clean of the remnant juices from the delicious meat of the stag's roasted haunch. He watched Melora, sitting at his right and sucking clean the glistening tips of her fingers, until she caught his steady gaze and paused, a finger in her mouth.

She slid her finger free from puckered lips. "What?"

He glanced at the black space of Ma'Kurgen's earlier leaving. The tundarian had yet to return, and she knew nothing of their shared words, and more so Ma'Kurgen's threats, during her absence. "What's he doing out there anyways?"

"Same thing he does every night." She bit off another mouthful from her cut hunk of meat and spoke through chews. "Stalking the perimeter."

He gave the fine red fuzz of his cheeks and chin a pinching rub. She'd shaved him a few days ago using one of her dachras after she suffered enough of his itchy beard grown during his unconscious battle against the chillfever, providing her annoying scratches as she lay nestled up with him while her void-aura accomplished its slow remedy against the magical infection.

He dropped his hand to his lap. "We should leave while he's gone."

She popped the last of her meal into her mouth and shrugged. "He'll just follow us." Chewed and swallowed. "Follow you."

He looked at his battered sword and frowned while flicking his wrist in irritated gesture at the ruined twist of steel. "I might as well throw it away for all the good it'll do me now."

"The sword doesn't make the man, Ban. The man makes the sword. You proved that much when you bested him."

"I was sick," he muttered, his souring mood allowing no enjoyment of her compliment. "And I got lucky. If not for the Power—"

"No, Ban, you were better. You're a master swordslinger and a Soothsayer. That's what you are, but it's not who you are. Stop being so ugly. It's unbecoming."

She picked up the waterskin between them and guzzled down a few long pulls before handing it over.

But he waved her off. "I want to leave." He threw another glance at the dark. "Now. Let's just go. Please? It'll probably be hours before he even knows we're gone. By then who knows? Maybe he'll give up and find someone else to murder him."

"Or maybe he'll hunt us down while killing everyone in his way to finding you." She stared him over a silent length. Leaned in and took him by the hands. "There's a lot of cruel men in this world, Ban. Believe me, I know. And for a long time I thought you all the same. But I was wrong. You showed me that. Because you're not one of them. That's why you didn't kill him when you could have. But you can't run from this." She gave his hands a gentle squeeze. "It's not murder. It's what he wants."

He slipped his hands from hers and scowled. "For all you know he's waiting for us to fall asleep so he can slip back in and kill us. You saw how crazy he is." He blew out a frustrated huff, lowered his voice. "Why are you arguing? I thought you wanted to get to Fist?"

"I do. But . . . I don't know how many he's already killed, but I do know he'll keep killing until someone gives him what he wants. Do you really want that on your conscience?"

He frowned down into his lap, said nothing. If only she knew of Ma'Kurgen's threat against her. The confession edged his lips, but he chewed it back.

She raised him by the chin to better meet her eyes. "You won't turn, Ban. I won't let that happen. It's why Pairs were made in the first place. I'm your protection against the bloodlust." She smiled, stroked his face. "Sometimes killing is a good thing. Sometimes you have to take a life to save a life. You did it before. I wouldn't be here if not for you."

She twisted on her bottom, lay back and stretched out on the bedroll, intertwined her fingers and nested her hands behind her head, closed her eyes. "Whatever you decide, I'll be right here with you."

He stared at her while wrestling the urge to crawl atop her and smother her with kisses and then some. He wanted her with a desperate depth of feeling burning a fever in his heart, and elsewhere. But he stayed his place, afraid indulging in such pleasures would be too far a leap too soon.

He watched her doze while wondering how on earth he was supposed to fall asleep considering the tundarian berserker prowling round them in the dark.

Minutes more and he lay down beside her, careful not to rouse her awake, lids heavy the moment he settled his head for his enervated body still craved copious amounts of rest. He kept one hand on his sword despite the useless weapon beaten into nothing more than a bent and twisted metal club.

After a jaw-stretching yawn, he rolled his head sideways, smelled her hair, her neck, while the meal in his full belly turned his thoughts drunk with sleep.

I wish Jericho was here . . . he'd know what to do.

Come morning he had a tundarian to kill.

CHAPTER FIFTEEN

"*Banzu . . .*" sounded a soft, melodious chime of voice rousing him from slumber, a distanced herald calling through the foggy depths of a tired mind and body disturbed from too-little sleep. "*Yoohoo, Baanzuu.*"

The dream world . . . fading. His eyelids twitched into fluttering.

"Ban!"

His eyes snapped open where he lay on his back. Still deep in night. Groggy, unsure how long he'd been asleep, might still be nestled within a cozy dream. He rolled his head right—Melora, gone—where glowed the unfed fire, its nest of coals offering a dim orange dome of incandescence in the suppressing dark pitch.

"Wakie wakie," said the voice, its mocking scorn possessing familiar notes unheard in weeks, "eggs and bakie."

Banzu blinked the heavy cling of sleep from his eyes, squinted through the faint light at the shadowed figure sitting hunched and watching him opposite the soft orange glow just beyond its illuminating reach. Motion in the dark as the other threw something round and possessing long pale tendrils whipping the air while it sailed over the glowing nest of coals. It struck the ground, rolled stopped.

Banzu startled at Melora's face staring back at him on tilted lean.

The figure hissed a curse, shook their hand as if attempting to soothe cool a burn. "You should've killed me when you had the chance."

Cold panic flushing, eyes blooming wide, Banzu battled shock through a rapid series of blinks, unbelieving, and yet . . . and yet.

Oh gods. It's really her. And this is real. Oh gods, no.

Melora ended her tenure of the world with her pretty face distorted by the ugly stretch of terror, those dead violet eyes piercing in their haunting stare through him, containing fathoms of accusations.

He broke inside in a burst of mourning, the crucial parts of him shattering to the hammerblow of a terrible truth revealed.

I was supposed to protect you, to keep you safe, to keep you alive.

She'd captured his heart.

And now she's . . . gone.

Murdered while he slept.

The wrenching grind of his grieving heart stole the breath from his lungs, Melora's stare carving something vital from his spirit forever.

He raised his gaze, stared with jolted eyes at the lone figure shrouded in darkness watching him. At those lambent red eyes blazing with concentrated hate cutting through the dark, the claustrophobic effect of the hearth between them making towers of the trees pressing ever closer in on them.

Oh gods.

Paralyzing fear gripped him by the throat and locked his muscles tight, pinning him to the ground, unable to speak, while cold prickles of terror crept through every taut inch of him.

Motion in the dark, and the figure tossed a log into the coals. Its crunching impact kicked up a swirling flurry of twinkling firefly embers popping and snapping while feeding new life into rising light pushing back the darkness, scaring the black depths of shadows from the other's grinning visage, giving way to stark revelation at last.

Oh gods no.

Jericho's bloodlust-corrupted eyes betrayed fathoms of terrible and tenacious vitality reflecting flickering glints of firelight on a face inexplicably rejuvenated with youth and framed by silky black hair the length of his shoulders. Physically younger, more robust, the last twenty years of his life returned. Yet the deep lines torturing round avid eyes spoke of a man who enjoyed several lifetimes of hard murder and hungered for more of the same.

More motion in the dark as Jericho threw another *something* from across the fire followed by the flap of his hand punctuated by a hissing curse.

Banzu followed its brief flight while it captured reflections of firelight then *clinked* to the ground next to Melora's decapitated head.

Circular. Metal. Silvery lanthium smeared dark with blood.

The kohatheen once locked round her neck. Still closed. Removed unopened.

"She was supposed to put that on me," Jericho said, his tone the serrated calm of bridled fury moments from bursting loose. "If I didn't agree to go then she was supposed to make me go. *Hah!*" He spat aside, licked clinging bits of spittle from his lips. "I knew that the second she walked through the door and I saw those godsdamned eyes. Conniving bitch!" A pause. The lowering of his voice. "But if you want to make the gods laugh—"

He rocked on his bottom, mad laughter echoing in affront to the silence. He slapped his thighs then rubbed his hands, leaned forward into hunching leer.

"I gave her the courtesy she didn't give me. Made sure she saw me coming." Jericho bared his teeth in a feral white gleam. "She never looked prettier, I'd say. *Hah!*"

Banzu stared into that godsawful gaze of predatory lust reflecting the craze of psychosis. He swallowed the hot bile rising at the back of his throat, rolled right, pushed up on trembling arms threatening collapse, his mind a toil of reasons unfound. He sat up, breath hitching, stomach clenching, endured sickening waves of vertigo sloshing his senses. He hung his head and waited for the spinning world to settle straight, fingers clawing into dirt, his mouth a tepid cavern of pooling saliva. He swallowed, battling the urge for sicking up. Words breached his lips in a broken whisper.

"This . . . can't be . . . happening."

Jericho chuckled. "Oh it's happening." He slapped at his boots, stomped one foot then the other, shifting on his perch of rock. "Godspeed. Was I right or was I right?"

The risen winds shivered through the trees, rustling branches, rippling the firelight in a fluttering ebb of shadows, there then gone in brief reveal of a misshapen clump of two bodies piled at the base of a far tree drawing Banzu's gaze.

Jericho's too. "*Hmm?* Oh. The big one fought like he wanted to die. I'm surprised we didn't wake you. Sure woke her though."

"What have you done?" Banzu's words a fragile whisper. "You . . . you killed them."

Jericho straightened, puffed his proud chest and nodded. "I sure did. I killed 'em good." He leaned forward, forearms sliding atop thighs, hands clapping, smile dwindling beneath thinning eyes, tone descending into guttural scorn. "And now I'm going to kill you."

* * *

Petrified, the battered twist of his useless sword a forgotten thing beside him, Banzu's mind roiled through empty avenues of appeal. He met Melora's dead stare and cringed, shriveling round the remnants of his withering soul, then stared at his uncle in abstract plea.

Those eyes, so full of hate. No need to ask what happened in . . . "Fist."

Banzu flinched, realized he'd spoken only after the word escaped him.

"Oh, that?" Jericho's question a mocking chime followed by a chuckle.

Motion in the dark. A crumpled ball of paper hit the ground rolling. Stopped inches from the kohatheen.

"Gwen's pardon," Jericho said. "All a ruse, of course. Just another one of the Academy's lies. She wanted me to kill the Khan. A suicide mission. Said my life would be forfeit in trade for your freedom. *Hah!*"

He shook his head, *tsk-tsk-tsking*, his next words a sarcastic singsong parody accompanied by the side to side tilting of his head.

"Kill the Khan and end the curse. Two birds with one stone." Jericho erupted into standing, pointing at nothing, yelling at phantoms. "And that's when the gods laughed at her fucking plans!"

Panting, eyes wide and wild, he scrubbed the back of a forearm across his mouth, wiping away bits of blown spittle. He paced while grumbling harsh curses between incoherent babbles, then he stopped, drew in deep, returned to his rocky perch and sat. Stood again as if sitting by mistake, then sat again. He huffed, lids half-closed, face going slack. The false visage of forced calm while he stared into the fire.

"Sending the Spellbinder was her first mistake," Jericho said, frowning then smiling then frowning again. "Expecting me to die along with the Khan was her second mistake. Thinking I wouldn't return to kill them all when I was done." The slow shake of his head. "No no no." He licked his lips and smiled. "That was her last mistake, oh yes."

He hunched forward scowling, face tensing. "What?" He flinched, crazed eyes darting. "What!" He straightened, throwing sideways glances at imaginary haunts only his eyes could see, then shot Banzu a pained look slow in blooming. "Ban?" His voice a desperate whisper. "Aggie." He ran a tremulous hand down over his face, trying to swipe clean unwanted memories. "Oh gods . . . Aggie. What have I done?" He clenched his hands into fists strangling the air. "Godsdamn you, Gwen!"

Oh my gods. He's breaking apart. Right in front of me. Years of madness all bunched up and bursting. Though Banzu put no voice behind it.

Jericho erupted into standing, took one step closer toward the firelight skating across his twisting features. Teeth clenched, nostrils flaring, he picked up a sizable stick and threw it into the dark, branches swishing, and yelled after it, "You forgot who you were dealing with!"

Banzu flinched despite the good space between them, unable to look away, the reality of it all still registering. *There's no coming back from this. Any of this. The bloodlust has him now.*

Jericho paced again opposite the fire, hands raking through hair, tugging handfuls of it while he muttered and cursed. He stopped, pointed accusation at Banzu, face contorting in seething rage. "You! It's all because of you." He beat at his chest. "My life. My right!" He pointed accusation again. "Your fault." He paused, blinking brief recognition, tensed face softening with a glean of pain, voice a fragile whisper. "Ban?" But the sane lapse vanished, the scolding hate of his lambent red eyes returning to fevered jewels reflecting captures of firelight and promises of murder. "Your fault!"

"Why?" Banzu asked, the word expelled in a breathless whisper. Then with more voice, "Why?"

"Why?" Jericho repeated in mocking jest while feigning a hurt look bordering false tears. "Why? Why? Why!" He craned his face to the sky and laughed, then shot Banzu a fixed glare. "Because I can, that's why."

Jericho raised his hands before his face and stared into his palms then clenched them into tight fists, knuckles popping, and licked his lips, tasting the faint remains of something sweet.

"You have no idea how this feels," he said. "I never should've let her to take it from me." He paused, no spiking rage on his part this time; his face and his tone darkened gradually instead, a summer sky surrendering before the encroaching thunderstorm. "Every kill rejuvenates me, makes me stronger. Oh gods how I've missed this." He lowered his fists by inches, locking eyes with Banzu over knuckles. "But as long as you're alive it will never be more than a fleeting taste. And I want it all. I deserve no less."

Banzu stared back mute.

Jericho crossed his arms and smiled. "I've wanted to kill you for so godsdamn long. And now—" He drew in a sharp breath, released a shuddering exhale, threw an accusatory point. "You knew this was coming. I told you it was only a matter of time." His right hand lowered unto gripping Griever's hilt at his left hipwing, eager fingers fanning sure purchase round the leather-wound hilt. "I'm going to carve you up into little pieces and take what's rightfully mine. Mine! All mine!"

Banzu shook through trembles, body craving movement, to get up and run, run away. Instead he looked down at the frozen horror of Melora's face. He sniffled, vision blurring from the hot sting of welling tears as sobs hitched in his chest.

Jericho drew back in squinting disgust. "Are you . . . are you crying?" He laughed and crossed his arms again. "Go ahead. Grieve for the Spellbinder whore who wanted to collar me like a dog. Come on, give us a show. I'll wait."

Tears running his cheeks, Banzu leaned forward and reached to touch at Melora's face but withdrew his trembling hand inches before caressing contact. He clenched a fist and pounded the ground, shook his head, teeth clenched, anger flaring through the grief.

He glared up, accepting death, his voice gaining raw edge clawing through his throat. "Do it. Kill me. What are you waiting for?" He pounded the ground with both fists, yelling, "Kill me!" He grabbed two handfuls of grass and dirt and threw them across the fire. "Kill me you coward!"

"Coward?" Jericho snarled at the slap of words. "Coward!" Molten red eyes flaring, he half-pulled Griever's blade while rushing round the fire.

Banzu braced tensed.

But Jericho stopped short. He glared at Melora's decapitated head between them then withdrew while shoving Griever's half-drawn blade to home at his left hipwing. He denied the brazen killing request with a stern shake of his head and a taunting wag of his finger.

"No no no," Jericho said. "Not like this. Look at you, you're pathetic. I've wasted too many years keeping your sorry ass alive. But I have my life back now. And I want to enjoy killing you."

Banzu slumped, stared at Melora's cold dead face through eyes naked and wounded and fractured by tears. "You're not you anymore," he whispered to the thing of his uncle. "You're not you." He stared overlong, aching to reach forth, to draw Melora's head into his lap and cradle it.

"Look at me, godsdammit!" Jericho kicked up an arc of dirt, then squatted to better meet Banzu's shifting gaze from across the fire, and smiled. "You're going to die a nobody out in the middle of nowhere. How's that grab you by the balls, hero?" A deliberate pause. "Or you can finally show some godsdamned guts for once in your miserable life and end this now."

He pulled Griever in full reveal and stabbed its tip inches deep into the ground then danced backwards to the edge of the firelight, presented his turned back with arms outstretched.

And waited.

Banzu stared at Griever's bared steel glinting captured flickers of firelight, its hilt a beckoning plea for his hand. He began standing, then plopped back down. "Fuck you."

"Fuck me?" Jericho peeked over a shoulder. "Fuck me?" He slapped his backside, bent over while gripping it, then snapped straight, hair whipping, and spun round pointing, yelling, "Fuck you!"

He marched to his sword and yanked it free, raised it while advancing a step then stopped, considered Griever's exposure overlong through crazed stare. "No no no," he whispered to while smiling at the immaculate blade, caressing it with his free hand. "Not like this. Pain before pleasure." He sheathed the sword to his left hipwing and fixed focal upon Banzu. "And you call me a coward." He hawked then spat, missing Banzu's face by inches. "You never did have it in you."

He turned away, held considerable pause, then threw a peeking smirk over a shoulder. "I passed a tasty village on my way in. I think I'll go have me a snack before the main course." A playful wink that flared contemptuous. "You've got till tomorrow to find your spine, boy. Then we'll see who's coward after I rip your yellow guts out and claim my Source."

Whistling a jaunty tune, Jericho strode away into the darkness closing round him, absorbing him. Gone, just like that.

Banzu stared at the gloom of Jericho's leaving, endured the haunting melody of mocking laughter fading with distance.

He looked at the frozen horror of Melora's face, at the bloody kohatheen beside her decapitated head.

Mourning sobs wracked him.

* * *

Banzu sat the night staring in broken misery at Melora's head and the kohatheen beside it, the unfed fire having snuffed hours ago. Fearing to touch either testament of Melora's death, fearing the realness of it all, denial lingering.

But she's dead.

Because I failed her.

He hunch into forward-reaching lean, intent on picking up Melora's head to cradle it in his arms while awaiting Jericho's imminent return. But his hands moved of their own accord, sought the kohatheen instead.

He raised the lanthium collar and stared it over, unsure why he even picked it up. He reared his arm back while twisting, preparing to throw it into the dark. Instead he lowered the kohatheen to his lap and traced his fingertips over its cold metal surface. He wanted to snap it in half and chuck the ruins but for that it was lanthium, unbreakable, impossible to destroy.

Just like Melora's resolve.

He stroked his fingers over her dried blood crusting its silvery surface, gliding them along the circular path . . . until they reached its locking mechanism and paused.

He exhaled a morose chuckle upon realizing the irony of how easily the kohatheen could be opened if one looked directly at the puzzler's lock instead of fumbling blind to unlock it while wearing it. Intentional in its cruel design.

A constant irritation, Melora locked the kohatheen round her neck to prevent losing it during her long chased journey from Fist, unable to remove it herself. The cursing ghost of her annoyed grumbles whispered in grim reverie while reflections of her tugging on the kohatheen in futile fits flittered through Banzu's mind.

Her proof of the Enclave's renewed activities. Her last resort in taking Jericho back to Fist. If only she'd been able to remove it and lock it round Jericho's neck before his sneaked leaving then she'd still be alive. If only . . .

His fingers fiddled about the lock, toying with its puzzler's design in abysmal reflection . . . *click*.

The kohatheen swung open in his hands, two separating halves of a circle connected by some invisible swivel hinge.

And sudden clarity washed over him.

* * *

The first red rays of dawn brightened the eastern sky while Banzu finished his gruesome business then washed up thereafter.

Escape futile, running a pointless endeavor, he'd spent his whole life running and hiding.

That part of him died with Melora.

Giving birth to hope flourishing in his sundered heart.

* * *

Banzu rolled his shoulders while adjusting the crisscrossing leather straps of Melora's dachra harness gripping snug round his larger torso for ease of breathing.

A tight fit, but it'll do.

It has to.

I've nothing left.

He spent the next hour performing quickening pulls of the dachra fangs sheathed at his back, clumsy and slow at first while learning though faster and familiarizing himself to the foreign kinetics of Melora's fangs, thumbing their button straps then snaking out rapid stabs of practice then returning the twin fanged daggers to their upside-down sheaths only to execute the maneuver over and again through repeat successions, tuning his instrument body until the motions ingrained to his muscle memory, his mind blank of all but the ritualistic chore and the tenuous hope it afforded him.

After which he gathered the rest of his necessities, tied off the kohatheen to his belt at the small of his back, then the two filled waterskins each to a hipwing.

He walked away.

East. The direction of Jericho's leaving.

Hours passed.

While he continued intermittent pulls of dachras, losing count after several hundred expressions of stabbing intent until his arms ached so that he surrendered the repetitive exercise while allowing its imprint to integrate into the fluid response of his receptive sinews possessing the eager aptitude cultivated from eleven years of habitual training.

He entered a village though did not slow. Bodies and parts of bodies lay strewn everywhere. The streets. Porches. Corpses hung limp through busted windows. Others decorated floors beyond kicked-in doors in tilted lean on busted hinges. Men cut to bloody shreds. Women and children . . . none were spared the rapacious wrath of Jericho's bloodlust thirst. Black and buzzing swarms of flies hovered round the spilt guts of horses and hounds killed for sheer pleasure.

All a macabre little sample of what would come if Jericho killed Banzu, became the last Soothsayer and achieved access to the full Power, the Source, while in the corruptive throes of the bloodlust.

Silence but for the crunching of his booted tread, a few clucking chickens pecking at festering wounds and oozing eyes, these scrambling from his path only to regather behind while he walked on.

Hours more.

He strode the road while the sunset struck his back. Until something gave him pause mid-step, the prickling unease of being watched so that he turned round.

Jericho stood a silhouette framed against the blazing orange backdrop of dusk.

Banzu waited. *No emotion.* A task easily achieved considering he had little left to feel.

Jericho approached in a leisure stroll, smiling, whistling, his purple boots of blinding speed inactive upon his swagger. He closed distance to twenty paces between them and stopped. "I expected you to run."

"I'm through running."

Jericho smirked, red eyes shifting, smile fading. "Where's your sword?"

"Don't need it." Banzu untied the waterskins from his hips, upheld one in each hand. "Because I'm not going to fight you."

Jericho scowled. He clamped his right hand round Griever's hilt and stormed forward—then stopped with a jolt ten paces short, glare a thinning scrutiny. "You think I'm stupid, boy? I can smell that bitch's blood from a mile away."

Banzu undid the stoppers with his thumbs, raised both waterskins over his shoulders and squeezed. Melora's blood poured forth, soaking into his shirt front and back, running down the length of him and dripping the ground round his feet in makeshift creation of a void-aura.

Jericho bared his teeth in full display of his umbrage.

Banzu tossed the empty bloodskins aside. "If you want to kill me then you'll have to do it without the Power." He sank to his knees. "What's the matter? You afraid of a little blood? Here"—he put both hands behind his back—"I'll make it easy for you."

"Bastard!" Luminous red eyes fevered and flaring jewels, Jericho's face a contortion of seething rage, he strode forward undeterred. "You won't take this away from me! It's mine!"

Catalyzing a flush of heat rising from the blood wetting Banzu's clothes. But he ignored it while maintaining his dispassionate stare ahead, as if mortal lives could be reduced in meaning, reduced to surgical judgment: obstacle or ally. Nothing else mattered. He understood the comfort of seeing the world in that manner now, a colder and crueler world without her, the ease of its simplicity.

Halfway there and Jericho's charge faltered. He staggered and rambled through a furious string of curses, grimacing. He stopped to within a single step, stood in glaring loom over his kneeling nephew, his face a bitter twist of strain, his lambent red eyes all feral gleam. Sweating. Shaking through little trembles. The bloodlust raging through him locked in heated battle against Melora's blood fighting to void the air of magic on some ethereal plane of equal existence.

Jericho's tensed visage, dappled with glistening beads, gave way to twitching strains while he struggled and failed to seize hold of the Power-corrupted, fevered eyes burning bright with unbridled fury.

Wisps of smoke arose from Banzu's warming clothes, the bloodlust burning away the nullifying bane of Spellbinder blood through their warring ethereal battle. He clenched his jaw against the baking heat and stared into those predatory eyes, raised his chin and offered the sure lure of his throat.

Jericho pulled Griever free from his left hipwing, his voice a strain through clenched teeth. "You're pathetic." He reared his arm back and set one foot forward in preparation for swinging. "You make me sick!" He licked his lips, his measuring gaze growing wide and wild. "It's mine!"

Banzu's right hand shot out from behind his back whipping-quick while he rocked forward on his knees in an obvious attempt at stabbing Jericho's front leg with the bloody dachra in his grip.

But Jericho twisted and kicked the stabbing attempt away—just as Banzu intended.

The dachra slipped loose from Banzu's distracting right hand at the same time his left arm whipped forth. He stabbed the second bloody dachra into Jericho's kicking leg.

Eyes flaring, Jericho yelled and staggered backwards. He strode forward while twisting at the hips though could not complete his intended death-stroke for his injured leg buckled. He sank to one knee, hissing through clenched teeth, Griever's hilt slipping loose from his disobedient fumble of hand. His other leg trembled, then his foot slid backwards bringing that knee down to the ground into joining the first.

Their eyes met on the kneeling level.

Jericho threw his hands round Banzu's throat in strangling bid—that weakened in seconds. Palsied hands slid free, hung at his sides. He sputtered for words, taut face twitching through spasms, raging red eyes fighting through fluttering blinks. His body shook in increasing trembles while he struggled for speech against the constricting paralysis locking up his throat. Chest hitching once . . . twice . . . three times, mouth moving though no words produced but for the strangled garble of cut syllables.

The hot blood of Banzu's clothes smoked up the air between them while that ethereal battle between void-aura and bloodlust raged to a head. He grit his teeth, skin raw and peeling, but he distanced the pain for that which lived in his broken heart.

"You were right," he said. "I should've killed you when I had the chance. Only I didn't know it then."

Banzu reached behind, untied the kohatheen from his belt at the small of his back and brandished it between them.

Body taut, Jericho's eyes rolled down, his lips twitching in an attempt at producing words that never came but for the strangled groan loosing from his paralyzed throat.

"I'm sorry." Banzu's only words as he raised the opened kohatheen then snapped it closed round Jericho's neck.

Jericho sucked in a strangled gasp cut short by teeth clicking together. His fevered eyes rolling up, back arching, hands rigid claws at his sides strangling grips of air, he swayed on his knees seconds from collapsing into a violent seizure.

Banzu embraced his uncle in a powerful hug unreturned, squeezing while keeping Jericho from toppling over. Hot tears of scared fury wet the sides of their touching faces. And there expired the last of Banzu's childhood as rising heat stole his breath away.

His clothes burst into flames. The stink of burning hair. Skin blistering. But he did not pull free, instead he held tighter.

"Forgive me," he whispered into Jericho's ear with what remained of his breath. He squeezed harder, his uncle's strangled scream torturing hot and merciless against his ear.

Banzu endured the pain, embracing it while embracing his uncle in a tighter pull against him. Until the fire died out and their burned clothes fell away from blackened and blistered torsos. He let loose, leaned back. And Jericho collapsed aside, sucking wind through clenched teeth in strangled wheezes. He lay twitching, hairless, red skin the same scarred marring of Banzu's own while the last of Melora's blood burned away to ashes taken upon the risen winds.

Banzu sagged back bottom atop heels, drew in ragged breath, every inch of him blazing in pain. He glanced aside at the emptied bloodskins burned into nothing more than two small piles of ash dusting away on the breeze. And he thought of her.

Even dead you protect me.

But his true work remained unfinished. What came next mattered most. What happened now determined the course of everything.

He'd defeated the vessel, but not the source.

The Source.

He stood with grunting effort, every tender inch of his burned skin protesting blazes of pain. He gazed over Jericho who lay twitching in limb-locked spasms, clawed hands reaching in futile bid for the kohatheen lock round his neck, its Spellbinder blood as indestructible as the lanthium containing it.

Cutting him off from the Power.

Leaving only Banzu.

With limited space in which to act. He needed his uncle alive for his plan to succeed. If Jericho died, the connection of Power between Present and Past would severe before Banzu cleansed the bloodlust. *Oh gods I hope this works.*

Banzu turned and walked away in final parting. Away from his uncle. Away from this world he no longer wanted any more part of. Away from this cruel reality he intended to erase.

Simus Junes had been the first. Now Banzu Greenlief was determined to be the last. Even as it killed him.

Time to make the gods laugh.

He walked in no particular direction. Closed his eyes. Drew in a ragged breath. Opened himself up to the Power.

And for the first time in Banzu's life the Power seized him.

* * *

The world shattered round him as energies engulfed his spirit in avalanching flushes and swells, ripping his essence from the physical rest of him. Floating . . . then falling through fragments of a broken reality tumbling away in a million glittering scatters, each reflecting parts of a whole.

Then everything: darkness.

Falling . . . tumbling . . . plummeting through the Power.

The blackness closed in, formed a cylindrical tunnel pulling him through Time and Space. A vortex of colors burst round him in rapid-fire streaks stretching the spinning walls. Colors became shapes became moving pictures. Daunting in their realness. Familiar.

Memories.

Motion everywhere. Vivid scenes playing out in their own pockets of space.

My memories.

Falling through the infinite tunnel of Time. No, finite. Comprised of his own lifeline.

The Source taking him back, farther and further at once. Guiding him. Projecting him. Erasing him.

No . . .

A jostling shift. He gazed down beyond—no *through* his insubstantial feet. At darkness's end gleamed a pinprick of cruelest red glare blinking into existence. Expanding through inevitable approach. An eye, staring, watching his closing fall. Red and lambent round a black slit of pupil. Inhuman. Demonic.

No, something far worse.

The eye's lids twisted into hideous lips peeling away from black and jagged teeth opening round the pupil slit now a cavernous throat.

Inhaling Banzu in.

Moments from consumption.

No.

The jostling shift of his falling essence above ravenous snaps of red jaws awaiting to devour all that he was, all that he'd ever been, all he would ever become.

No!

YESSS!

Laughter blasted past his falling essence, tearing loose parts of him in flaking shreds of sanity.

Who am I?

A thousand voices erupted from the throat in a cacophony of hate.

Where am I?

Music of the wailing dead, of the corrupted essences of all Soothsayers before him claimed by the bloodlust screaming in welcome.

Why am I?

He closed his eyes.

Melora.

And remembered her.

NOOOO!

Yes.

Banzu spread his arms as wings—and soared. Away from the snapping jaws of that gaping red expanse intent on devouring him. Rising upon the buffeting winds of a thousand tortured screams. And flew into the expanse of his memories with guiding purpose, viewing pockets of his past while seeking their promises of hope . . . seeking . . .

* * *

. . . Banzu *re*-seized the Power—*thuuummmp-Thump!*—and the existence-jarring disorientation of his soul-jolting arrival backwards through Time shattered comprehension.

He startled aware mid-movement, bearings scattered, viewing the world anew through another's eyes. His eyes, and yet the eyes of his former self. The *heartbeat-of-the-world* pulsed through him while the jostling shift of fusion between future and past selves melded together, finalizing, materializing into—

Jericho lunged into his opening swordform *Scorpion Stings the Frog*, darting forward and feinting low for body-vessel-Banzu's feet then sprung up slashing before reversing his attack into a downward-thrusting stab.

Banzu-not-yet-*Banzu* spun into *Pedal Shakes the Dew*, sweeping the fast attack aside in a crash of sparks then finishing his counter-twirling swordform by delivering a smacking *thwack* on Jericho's rump with the flat of his sword as their bodies glided past one another in Power-fueled momentum.

Thump-thump.

Jericho grunted and stumbled two steps forward before catching balance. He rubbed at his swatted behind with his free hand then turned round, arm extended, and leveled his bastard sword out between them, aiming the three-foot length of steel at Banzu-not-yet-*Banzu* in warning praise.

"Good," he said. And raised the sword, twisted it so that its thin edge split his measuring gaze, the whites of his eyes tinged with the first returning signs of familiar threatening red absent a scant moment before. "But not good enough."

Thump-Thump.

Body-Banzu frowned, though he knew not why. He reared back into the flashy defensive swordform *Willow in the Breeze*, measuring his balance as he swayed to and fro, shifting his weight from one foot to the other in brief dance. And for an awkward moment felt somewhat off-kilter, as if the balance of his feet belonged to another.

He shirked the strange feeling aside, drew in a deep nostril breath and tightened his inner grasp on the Power while tightening his outer grip on his sword, squeezing each for increased purchase in preparation for their next trade of blows.

"Come at me, old man." But the words released mirthless and void of playful challenge.

Thump-thump.

Jericho cocked one bushy eyebrow. Then burst forth into a flurry of graceful swordform attacks, chaining high thrusts and low slashes together with the flowing proficiency only a veteran swordslinger of his high caliber could achieve, his ease of efforts pure locomotion. Stabbing and spinning, whirling and thrusting in spectacular targeting efficiency.

While Banzu danced backwards, blocking and dodging and parrying with equalizing measure of skill and Power-heightened speed, the rapid clangor of steel biting steel ringing successions between their joining blades.

Until Banzu paused in hitching step while flashes knifed through his mind—of a pale-haired beauty, as well inexplicable gleanings of their contest here and now yet seconds in coming—jolting him out from dance, his tight defenses failing so that Jericho's flat-wise smacking strike caught him against the middle before he could react to the strange preemptive awareness of seeing that stroke before its punishing delivery.

Banzu grunted from the burst of pain-fire clenching his belly tight and forcing him into bending over at the middle, followed in rapid succession by a stinging lash as Jericho finished the speedy twirl past him while landing a second smacking *thwack* across his upper back, striking the breath from his lungs . . . just like Banzu somehow knew he would do.

Thump-THUMP.

Banzu stumbled forward sucking wind, his too-tight hold on the Power straining loose from his inner grasp while focus parted for rising anger . . . a smoldering anger unknown to him before, cold and calculating yet disturbing in its familiarity.

The Power-slowed world blink-shifted out from its slow flow of speed into the normalized passing of time for a hairsbreadth before blink-shifting back again; slow-*fast*-slow.

No emotion, he commanded mentally, the pain of his stomach and upper back fading as he straightened, teeth clenched, pride bruised. *It's easy when you're dead inside.* And gave pause at the detached sound of his inner voice.

He blinked hard and shook his head, focus straining while a bizarre sense of replay stole through him, growing in intensity with each onrushing pulse of clarity.

Thump-Thump.

"Don't puke them guts out," Jericho said. "We ain't finished yet."

Banzu turned round, eyed his uncle. *Something doesn't feel right.*

"Tit for tat." Smirking, Jericho cut a lazy X through the air. "This old man ain't as old as he looks."

"I'll tit . . . your tat." Banzu said, pausing before raising his sword to guard.

Jericho chuckled, then lowered into the instigative swordform *Dancer's Dip*, sliding his left leg forward and hunching his shoulders while extending his sword out to his right side, exposing several vitals in open askance, a mocking though deadly pose meant for luring opponents in through false confidence.

And here words stole through Banzu's mind in a whisper of soliloquy so that he mouthed them unvoiced: *You move any slower, boy . . .*

"You move any slower, boy," Jericho said, "and I'll have my afternoon nap in before I even break a sweat." He shot Banzu a playful wink—that turned into a curious arch of his brows. "You all right? You look dazed."

"I'm . . ." Blinking hard, Banzu shook his head, readjusted his grip of hilt and nodded. "I'm fine. Let's do this."

He wrestled control over his wavering concentration while Jericho waited, baiting him in. He blinked again—and jolted stiff as the crashing tide of newfound awareness flooded in, washing over his awakening soul, future essence reclaiming past body in a snap of blending minds.

Banzu-now-*Banzu* paused only briefly before rearing his sword back. *Gods forgive me.* He rushed forth, same as *before*, in a Powered burst of determined steel and contrite heart.

THUMP-THUMP.

Jericho's bravado fled as he sprang backwards through fluid reflex. He swept Banzu's first thrusting strike aside, deflected the next chopping four with fanning back-and-forth parries, then ducked the overhead sixth by sinking low only to rise up spinning through a masterful riposte, reversing the seventh strike back upon its enforcer in a swift change of momentum and an answering flurry of steel.

Banzu staggered backwards two steps, steel scraping steel, then three more, steel pounding steel, his parries turned blocks maneuvering in tandem to the increasing barrage of Jericho's fierce strikes allowing no return.

THUMP-THUMP!

Banzu issued no call for halt between jarring bangs of sparking steel, his muscles burning with fatigue, his loosening inner grasp on the Power equally pushed to the edges of his straining limits while grim hesitation over his betraying act stole through him. He concentrated on those red-threatening eyes of feral lust glaring through the whirring deluge of steel moments from tasting his blood.

THUMP-THUMP!!

The brutal onslaught continued upon Banzu's waning defenses as Jericho turned a man possessed by the latent release of a suppressed rage boiling over. Until the blurring fury of his accelerating strikes broke through Banzu's failing defenses for the sought-after opening his red-threatening eyes craved to penetrate.

Jericho stabbed high for the face, forcing Banzu into leaning his upper half backwards or else lose an eye, though this time he caught his balance upon his back foot in prescient reflex, while Jericho spun into a vicious twirl, slicing sideways and with full Powered momentum fueling his chopping stroke seeking decapitation—same as Banzu remembered.

THUMP-THUMP!!!

Banzu ducked and spun.

Jericho's sword sliced through empty air.

While Banzu continued his rising twirl, momentum fueling his sideways-slicing blade aimed true.

THUMP—Jericho's head turned opposite that of his body-twisting missed attack, and in that breathless span tortured eyes met tortured eyes a final time—*THUMP.*

***

Banzu's sword sliced clean through Jericho's exposed stretch of neck, cutting through spine then throat and severing head from body in one fateful stroke.

Spinning momentum twisted him away from the fountain of blood that followed, the spray of which speckled his turning cheek. Tears welled behind closing eyes while he released the sure grip on his sword and the weapon slipped free from hands loosened by remorse.

The sensory-piercing scream of the bloodlust's raging death-rattle erupted in Banzu's mind, tortured loose from future-Jericho's throat in a guttural release of agony as Time's umbilical connection of Source linking Past and Future severed and separated, the Past resolving into Present while the Future dissolved.

The profound sense of loss and relief sank Banzu to his crashing caps where he crumpled forward palming the ground on unsteady limbs threatening collapse.

Panting, muscles taut with trembling, he sagged back bottom atop heels, drew in deep, held his breath overlong with reflection. But it did nothing to appease the guilt in killing the man who had saved then raised and trained him, and in the end betrayed him.

He relaxed through purging exhale, breathing all that mattered now—and gasped as the shocking surge of Power released him at last, the Future no more than memory, his and his alone.

He collapsed, wholly spent.

And lay curled and quivering for long minutes until the tremors subsided. He stretched his limbs, pushed up into standing, and took gruesome account of the scene before him with a melancholy joy.

It's over.

It's finally over.

He breathed with new ease in his sundered heart.

The deed done. The sacrifice made. The bloodlust cleansed. The Nameless One's curse earned by the first Soothsayer afflicted in Simus Junes then outdone by the defiant last in Banzu Greenlief.

His uncle's headless body lay close by, squelching spurts of blood from its severed stump of neck. The head rested a few feet away, its frozen expression staring silent accusations back at him from its tilted position on the bloodied grass of their training grounds.

"I'm sorry," Banzu whispered, then added in stronger voice, "Thank you."

He craned his head skyward, closed his eyes and drew in a deep, rejuvenating breath as hot tears ran his cheeks. He gazed down into his upturned palms, closed them into fists. He needed to know, needed to be sure his uncle's sacrifice had not been in vain.

He closed his eyes tight and, bracing, seized the Power through focal invocation. Budding energies bloomed from within, filling the chamber of his being with soothing pulses of tingling warmth, as the slowing world burst ultra keen with luminous twilight greys flaring his eyes. Yet he flexed in strain, strove for more.

Barriers shattering as he drained the Power's deep reservoir of Well, drawing in every last drop of potent energy until he achieved the full capacity of the Source in a soul-shuddering gasp of newfound inner awareness.

Though outward, oblivious to his body ejecting an effluent burst of dazzling multi-colors projecting a radiant beam that pierced the sky and there spread outward in racing appeal.

He was *one*. He was *the* one. He was now the *only* one.

The last Soothsayer.

Seconds only—memories of lives unlived knifing through his mind in rapid flashes, hitching his breath, quickening his pulse, while a thousand voices called at him in a screaming cacophony linked to his drawing seize by the shared collective essences of all Soothsayers—before fear and the strain of enduring it catalyzed into terror so that he released the Source and pitched forward palming the ground in panting heaves, the world a slowing vertigo whirl to his readjusting eyes.

So much power . . . so much influence.

Older of spirit.

Younger in body.

He trembled with knowing.

Shuddered to truth.

And there he wept mourning tears of solace.

CHAPTER SIXTEEN

IT began as a whisper surging in overhead from the west on a distant rolling tide of sound at first muted by the deafening clangs and clangor of clashing metal and voices erupting in pain and dying. Thousands locked in brutal rampage of bloodied steel, be they Bloodcloak loyalist or Grey Raven defender, men and women killing beneath the soft cry of new spring's rain falling in tickling kisses over the raging battlefield, its glistening drops plinking off dented bits of armor, joining the blood and sweat and tears and more blood in a churning of war.

Numbness seeped into one particular man's unliving extremities and his angular face, though he knew not the origin of that which caused his sudden lapse into stillness—yet. He jolted stiff, struck by some thunderbolt of wonder from within. He lowered his arms, cutting short the manipulations of his dark magic conjurations, and drew in an unnecessary breath tasting of regret and shame and of the coppery flows of mortal blood perfuming the air that produced both.

As a strange touch of the familiar pervaded his thoughts. *I . . . yes, I have been here before.*

Momentarily confused, he watched his testing exhale curl in a white stream breaching pale lips before sucking it inward to the darkest of darknesses therein the chamber of his being. The winds cold despite the afternoon sun burning away the clouds and driving spears of heat into the mucky churn of earth until the air steamed round those contending below its radiant shine while affording eerie life to the misty bogs upon which devout soldiers slogged for their lives and their rulers' challenged or challenging reign. Standing amid two colliding oceans of warriors fighting in mad hornet swarms of flashing and crashing steel, this particular man realized he stood as the first taking peculiar notice of the happening moments from overwhelming them all.

IT grew into a rumble, vibrating the earth beneath his feet, turning the marshlands into swampy fields of writhing worms contesting with renewed life beneath stomping boots and those who lay dying. The unnatural thunder rolled across the battlefield outside the defending kingdom of Grey Raven's Keep, far to the south of Junes in Thurandy, where men and women fought and screamed and died by the thousands. Motionless within the chaotic mix of blood and sweat and laboring steel stood the towering pale figure of the once-man Metrapheous Theaucard, an unliving being feared over the centuries as the necromaster Dethkore, a reviled and infamous creature reborn and renamed the Eater of Souls who, garbed in all black, wore his clothes more shadows than fabrics wrapped round his slender frame.

Dethkore held struck pause upon the thunder's heralding passage, an awakening *twang* of epiphany resounding within the miniscule sliver of his festering soul—that tiny fleck of uncorrupted humanity he long ago snatched back from the Nameless One despite the rest of his fractured soul still housed within his lanthium-bound soulring vitus remaining his one true master—and for it he severed the soul-bonding ties to his unliving manipulates, hungars these reanimated corpses, his vibrating core the dusty bell struck and for the first time in centuries by the hammering smash of some invisible yet inevitable force, drawing his attentions elsewhere.

Round him the hungars he'd detached from death's embrace through reanimation into obedient killing creatures knowing no purpose but for satisfying their newborn insatiable appetites for living flesh and fighting against their still-living Grey Raven defenders collapsed into the boggy marshlands, string-cut puppets these hundreds of dead men and women returning to their swampy graves, for he no longer cared to control them nor even leave their twisted minds to the primeval sways of rapacious hunger by tying off their captured spiritual soul-binds unto themselves for wreaking the single-minded havoc all hungars sought once reanimated into horrific rejections of death.

He craned his head and gazed at the beautiful blue ocean of sky, then closed his eyes, allowing the spring sunshine to glaze the permanence of his sullen tombstone visage through the light curtains of rain while memories both recent and ancient stirred behind pale lids basking. And he waded through an oblivion of regrets to remember what IT was that struck him paused while the man in him toiled at recapturing what it would be like if only he could truly feel the sun's warmth again through the shielding pallor of his cold dead husk of skin.

He jolted from an arrow piercing into the left side of his neck, inches below angular jawbone, not so much rocking the towering necromaster on his feet as did jerk his responsive head a touch to the right. In calm manner he raised his left hand, gripped the offending arrow's shaft and yanked the protuberance free, pale skin ripping though void of pain, and he returned focus to the raging battle now so mundane, so insignificant, so meaningless, so beneath his distracted attention.

In no hurry he gazed through the soft spring shower sparkling captured glints of sunlight as would trillions of trickling diamonds poured from the purses of gods, and scanned his gruesome surroundings with a new discerning eye dazed in unexpected wonder. Thousands of soldiers screaming while the sea of bloodshed ebbed and flowed, not an unfamiliar sight to one so long-lived though ever rife with scorn for man's petty game of thrones. Yet he stood the sole participant afield taking notice of the inevitable . . . *something* mere moments from overtaking them all.

He glanced left at the western horizon where a vast grainy cloud expanded while sweeping not just eastward but also north and south, spreading, bursting outward from some distant westward point of origin, glittering with a hundred-thousand pale reflections akin to the wind flipping the underside of birch leaves at the edge of a colossal forest made of shifting light. The unnatural thunder continued ITs rolling bid eastward, the keening wail of ITs inevitable approach elevating in pronouncing volume and whiny pitch, closer and closing fast.

Dethkore relaxed his grip and let slip the offending arrow from wet fingers, hearing at first then listening, truly listening, while realizing through slow awakening this place of war his enslaver and current ring-bearer Hannibal Khan had sent him to conquer and bolster the power-hungry warlord's ever-expanding army held no more significance but to the Khan and his loyal Bloodcloaks and worship-followers striving for dominance beneath his flapping banners.

"Soultaker!"

But the title and the shout for Dethkore's distracted attentions fell lost upon the preoccupied Enclave servitor. The airy expanse of his miasmic death-aura, radiating from his withered core ten feet in all directions while keeping his immediate area clear of all but the dead and those who sought a quick though excruciating death by feeding their sapped lifeforces into his capturing own, pulsed and throbbed in shimmering yellows and greens of visible plague.

Another yell, closer now, the same man's raspy voice. "Forsaken One!"

Dethkore turned his head and fixed his unblinking stare upon the familiar Bloodcloak of high rank shouting address while standing but a few wary steps outside the miasmic bounds of his death-aura, the bulky soldier's face wrenched in anger's strain and his right arm drawn back mid-unfurling of the bullwhip lash in his hand, its cattail ends decorated with the thorny burning bane of silver barbs.

The Bloodcloak shouted, "Back to work, godsdamn you!"

Something roused within the necromaster then, something familiar though undisturbed for centuries, and with its recognition of renewed life, alertness bloomed into a stern disobedience not possessed since the Khan and Nergal had awakened him from the ancient slumber of his crypt buried deep below the palace of Junes.

"No," Dethkore said in an almost-whisper. And yet the single word contained the same bold defiance sparking to light within his rebuking stare, eyes black sclera pinpricked by white pupils—his deadeyes. He settled the full brunt of that testy gaze upon the Bloodcloak whipmaster, and the man's glistening face flashed recognition through surprise then fear then a return to anger beneath his gleaming half-helm in the span of a coinflip.

I remember . . . I remember fades of Nergal . . . fire and pain . . . a girl . . . a box . . . but the elusive memories slipped his mental grasp in dissipating wisps of vanishing recall.

Dethkore turned and gestured acknowledgment with the slight upward tilt of his head and the thinning of his focal stare accompanied by the awful surge of his dark magics, the nefarious effluence of unholy sorcery unleashing from the deadman's flexing core while he closed a single lengthy stride toward the whipmaster on half-again-longer legs, white pupils flaring silver.

"It screams," he said while planting his forward foot in the sucking mud, the death-rattle words creeping loose from his mouth containing fathoms of command and manipulation.

Before the Bloodcloak whipmaster could so much as outstretch his whip to score pale flesh in punishment, two necrotic, bloated hands shot up from the thick muck round the squat khansman's ankles, gripped his meaty calves within their clawing grasps and sought to pull him down into the shallow depths of the swampy bog. Eyes startling wide with blooming terror, he released a guttural scream when bony fingers, their jagged tips broken sharp, pierced through leather boots and punctured deep into tender muscles therein with the ease of sticks probing wet sand, his punisher's silver-barbed bullwhip forgotten to the pain lancing up his legs.

His straining efforts did little to keep him upright. One leg collapsed followed by the other. More reaching pairs of unliving hands attached to the plethora of nameless fallen erupted from the bog's stinky waters in surrounding bursts and latched onto the kneeling whipmaster's arms at his sides and shoulders from behind, pale hands tearing free dented bits of red-gold Bloodcloak armor from snapping leather straps, clawing and ripping at flesh while pulling their screaming captive backwards and down.

The thrashing man's last act in life the failed attempt at clutching the dying hope of the flashing sky as dark waters pooled round his sinking head then covered his face while drowning his rasping gasps into a bubbling gurgle of surrender. And Grey Raven's marshes claimed yet another victim to be tolled alongside the hundreds already fed into the swampy grasslands since the first crack of dawn's burning light.

Dethkore closed his eyes while enjoying the suckling feed of the newly riven lifeforce into and through the absorbent miasma of his death-aura, its delicious energies feeding his not lifeforce but deathforce while nurturing the endless hunger of the Blackhole Abyss housed within the chamber of his being.

Sounds of splashing behind the necromaster alerted him, but too late. He turned—even as a massive broadsword, silver-dipped and holy-blessed, fanned down and crunched through his left shoulder, tearing a path that snapped ribs, sliced through sternum and spine. The blow dragged the tall necromaster down and kneeling to one side, burning along its tortured cut. And in aching reflex Dethkore pulsed his miasmic death-aura into flaring expansion even as the scream locked up his throat with scorching pain.

The paling Bloodcloak offender reeled through the effluent blast of sickness flooding against him in a gothic tide of pox. He stumbled backwards vomiting bile down his front, blistering sores swelling then popping open on the exposed skin of his face and neck and hands though he managed enough grit to maintain his grip and pull his broadsword free, dragging it along with his forced withdraw, the great length of blade trailing ribbons of Dethkore's black ichor gore which steamed and smoked and hissed and crackled upon the silver tongue burning away the substance one would call blood from the unliving's banesword.

The Bloodcloak retook a double-fisted grip with puss-oozing hands tremulous more from sickness than fear and targeted another charging swing, bloodshot eyes their sclera yellow thinning with malice while knowing the next stroke might very well undo him along with the betraying necromaster.

But he was Bloodcloak, a sworn man of the Khan, and his duty to the Lord of Storms took precedence even over his life, a duty foretold to usher his brave spirit to the otherworldly Heaven promised him by the Khan for his proven fealty through sacrifice.

Already other nearby Bloodcloaks turned their attentions upon the disobedient necromaster now that his felled whipmaster Keeper lay disposed. But fear or combat or both held them at bay.

The stricken soldier had a decision to make, an example to give. With sacrificial vigor and a warrior's arrogance to break before bending in front of his watching fellows, he uplifted his silver-coated broadsword and charged while shouting.

Dethkore gestured at the brawny attacker, his hand a tight fist clenching wicked energies imperceptible by all but his unliving deadsight wherein throbbed orangy heats of life and living upon the dull backdrop of the cooler world, then he flexed his fingers splayed, issuing forth waves rippling the rainy air, arresting the brazen Bloodcloak charger three splashing steps into his chopping swing.

The broadswordsman's grimy mask of wild frenzy twisted into a new state of panic then pain when tendrils of shadows erupted round him, long and lashing then spreading and connecting in creation of an enormous translucent black bud encapsulating him.

Dethkore fisted his outstretched hand.

And the black bud of shadows crunched smaller, the Bloodcloak captive therein contracting in on himself, groaning bits of armor denting beneath tautening serpentine twists of sentient darkness, his shoulders drawing inward, hands abandoning hilt, legs bending backwards then snapping at the knees, his contorting body rife with juts of bones puncturing through flesh compacting evermore into a smaller and smaller ball of bleeding wreckage, his agonized screams becoming muffled grunts within seconds.

Dethkore opened his hand, fingers splayed, and the density of shadows unfurled, separating, returning to long sinuous tendrils wherein each sounded the faint rattle of hellsteel chains evincing their conjured spines.

The squishy human ball of Bloodcloak spiked with white ruptures of broken bones splashed down to the muck atop receding shadows alongside the dropped broadsword, silent and still but for the deep groan of compacted muscle and bone accompanied by the audible gasps of the nearest horrified soldiers representing both warring sides of battle.

Dethkore inhaled deep and overlong, chest swelling, not just his lungs but his deathforce essence drawing in the musky decay of the marshlands while he inhaled then absorbed then assimilated the riven lifeforce, consuming its energies into the reservoir of his parasitic deathforce. A rejuvenating potency filled his being where begun supernatural healing from the scoring broadsword's wounding rent resealing closed while he regained his feet into standing, bones fusing, pale flesh mending, bits and licks of sentient shadow knitting his torn cloths, his dread miasmic death-aura rupturing the immediate air round him in effluent pulses of nausea and shimmers of sickness.

He staggered while memories of pain rippled through his long limbs before familiar whole-body numbness returned to plague his forsaken soul in stark reminder of the vile creature desperation and a dark pact sworn had wrought from the man he once was a millennia past. A glance at the broadsword followed by a grimace then the commanding flex of his will, and the foul silver-dipped bane sank into the swirling mud and muck swallowing it in obedience, murky black waters hissing and bubbling then stilling but for the rippling drops of rain plinking thereon.

The dispossession of his lanthium soulring vitus rendered his powers to one-hundredth of their full capacity. Yet even such limitations inflicted upon him by his current ring-bearer many far miles to the north could not deter the necromaster from snuffing life as specks of dust motes scattering beneath a swatting godhand.

"You cannot kill what is already dead," he said with a grin containing nothing of humor when he turned and surveyed the growing inward-facing ring of surrounding Bloodcloaks and khansmen worship-followers many of whom tossed their useless steel aside for the silver-dipped swords and maces and poleaxes and even daggers dolled out in prevention against the necromaster's possible turning against them.

Over fifty khansmen moved inward in shrinking cordon.

Then IT overwhelmed them all, as the world . . . *shivered.*

Recognition punched into Dethkore then, while the world rumbled and quaked then settled in profound silence.

"The Veilfall."

The words rolled forth from Dethkore's lips in a foreboding whisper risen above the hushed masses of Bloodcloaks and Grey Raven soldiers alike stilled in their fighting bids, war a forgotten struggle, thousands stunned mute and staring up, appraising the changing above in waking awe as the whole dome of sky turned awash with cascades of yellows and lancing greens, streaks of oranges and bursts of blues, blushes of reds and particles of purples fanning outward from a darker point high overhead, its western-born origin far beyond the limits of human sight seeking past the jagged horizon of the distant Calderos Mountains and its spiny miles of frosted peaks.

The vibrant array of multi-colors shone overhead in broad and blazing rays humming the air while racing the sky, the brightness intensifying while darkening into deep shades of violet encroaching the entire ceiling of sky. The mesmerizing show resembled peering into the heart of a flower of glorious light whose multicolored petals rippled in a breeze unfelt—a breath from beyond this planet—the event evincing the visual sundering of a god's protective magics.

Memories long hidden delivered sweeping return into the waking minds of the stunned populous as the Veilfall prevailed after over three-hundred years of inactive slumber.

Jolted with recall, Dethkore reeled while the closed buds of memories unfurled, anamnesis blooming in epiphanies of awareness locked away by some godly force opening in this the moment of the Veilfall's reckoning.

The profound inhale of silence passed over to carry forth its awakening across the rest of the world along with the dazzling lightshow racing the sky while the stunned hush reigned over all the onlookers below as the sky returned a pale blue, the Veilfall's keening wail rushing beyond the eastern horizon, and the light patter of spring rain became the only sound plinking off bits of battered and bloodied armor adorning the upward-gazing thousands.

Somewhere a horse whinnied.

A lone horn wailed its mournful note. And as if a harbinger's signal, the moans of mortal misery sang in solemn chorus issued from those who lay dying in rising reminder of the battle paused before the Veilfall's reawakening of ancient latent memories.

For the length of a dozen heartbeats Dethkore studied the bewildered faces of the weary soldiers weighing the intent of the bloodied weapons in their hands as they glanced at those nearest them, friend or foe, in stunned challenge, the webwork of renewed memories ushered by the Veilfall fluctuating into vigorous synapse response behind their questioning stares regaining focus. But these warriors were soldiers bred for war and hungry with the greed for killing, and the pause lingered little before battle lust reclaimed their mortal hearts and the frenzy resumed.

Horns blew. Voices shouted. Ranks crashed together with renewed vigor. Blood poured. Screams knifed the silence away amid growing clangors of steel biting steel.

Most of those forming the cordon of Bloodcloaks surrounding Dethkore did not balk from sworn duty despite several of their fellows turning and running away through the chaotic mix, these shoving while shouting praises or condemnations about the risen Veil or the fallen Godstone or both, the more determined killing themselves a successful route through their surprised fellows while others, attempting to hack an exit path and flee the battlefield for their newly realized and remembered purpose of hunting the Godstone for its limitless all-power, were swiftly cut down by more Khan-loyal soldiers or trampled beneath the stomping hooves of their stalwart superior officers mounted atop armored warhorses knowing nothing of retreat.

The frivolous plights of mortals overshadowed by the spiteful dissolution of a deity awakened.

Eyes swirling with the unfathomable black depths of Purgatory's brimstone shadows, Dethkore inhaled rending promise into his unliving lungs, capturing transmogrifying energies deep and overlong, then released the surmounting pressure by screaming a blasting cloud of bloodflies out from his gaping maw, as would a creature exhaling an atmosphere of buzzing primordial dread, while pulsing the miasmic sorcery of his death-aura into a strong outward expansion of pestilent influence.

The cordon of surrounding Bloodcloaks screamed in unison, over half their numbers tossing weapons aside for frantic swats and slaps at the stinging and gnawing swarm of bloodflies burrowing into the uncovered parts of their skin when not boring into ear holes or through clamped eyelids or flying up nostrils or into open mouths. Others of their fellows clawed or stabbed or sliced at their arms or chests or faces, tearing skin for the feeding insects beneath, while bursts of writhing maggots poured from their eye sockets or mouths or both. Soldiers burst open at their middles from within, their sides, and even their rears as the maggots found other ways of expulsion from the soft nests of flesh.

The sound a keening chorus of voices, it chilled the air, this wail of souls twisted past torture, transforming pain into a macabre ambience of music.

The silver-baned cordon of Bloodcloaks dispatched, Dethkore turned to the north, ignoring the chaotic tides of battle *crash-crash-crashing* together while soldiers awakened by the Veilfall returned to their blood-shedding purpose in the name of their godking Hannibal Khan. He walked with a renewed purpose of his own, his miasmic death-aura surrounding him in a sorcerous bubble of retching sickness and humanity's decay ripping screams from throats while rotting flesh from crumbling bone. It took hold of all it touched, pushing outward in febrile-inducing terror while sucking inward the rending of life, clearing the necromaster a northbound path for the reclamation he sought.

It has begun, he mused with forlorn trepidation. And not for the first time, not since the Thousand Years War, his ancient patience turned from a contest of indifference into a hunter's calculating designs.

With all the grace of wicked poetry lengthening Dethkore's calm yet determined strides, the sea of soldiers parted before his ominous tread in human fractures of ice, their bodies bursting in spills of maggots, their scintillating lifeforce energies swirling round his feeding essence in ghostly moaning wails of agony, the arrogant disregard of his wake a corpse-laden path of decrepit receipt.

He flicked an open hand in passing gesture at the empty, iron-barred cage of his transport. Black shadow tendrils erupted and enclosed round the protesting metal groaning then, Dethkore's hand clenching, the iron cage crunched, shadow tendrils compacting while making of it a shrinking ball of twisted iron that would cage him no more.

The twitch of his hand and the bunched shadows formed a giant black mimicry of his own, lifting the iron ball. A flick of his wrist and that shadowhand threw the iron projectile on high. The shake of his hand and the shadowhand burst apart into whipping tendrils sucking into the marshy ground. While the iron ball arced then plummeted then crushed and rolled atop scores of bodies.

Dethkore walked as if gathering suffering unto himself, mindful of that which awaited him ahead, vengeful for that which had been taken from him by the Enclave's newly chosen Khan, the ire of his ancient contempt awakened by the Veilfall knowing no bounds.

CHAPTER SEVENTEEN

The next day and Banzu, after gathering his necessaries for the journey awaiting him, placed his uncle's bundled body and head, both wrapped tight in Jericho's favorite blanket, inside their solitary cabin home upon the Kush Mountains then, leaving his belt knife atop his uncle's body while whispering a parting promise, he set their cabin ablaze in funerary pyre.

All cried out, he stood back watching the licking flames, the rising churns of black smoke announcing the burning purge of his former life and all its scarring forfeits.

His uncle's sacrificial death dissolved the terrible Future while resetting the Past, leaving Banzu's trampled fabric of life wide open with newfound possibilities. Those future memory scars would never fully heal, for he had lived them and relived them still every time he closed his eyes, those scars his burden alone to carry forth.

After a time, the cabin no more than smoldering char and cinders, he turned away east. He slung his packed rucksack to his back, weaving his arms through the straps while careful not to twist a pinch from the new sword belted round his trim waist and sheathed at his left hipwing in fine black leather scabbard. He plucked his uncle's silver ring on the brass necklace he wore, kissed it then tucked it beneath the nape of his shirt. He smiled down at his new boots of blinding speed, unable to activate the magic of the purple coverings though wearing them for their comfort of memory, then stared at the eastern line of trees, not viewing so much at them as through them.

He walked away with purpose in his stride and a fierce need in his heart to see it through.

* * *

Banzu pulled Griever—his uncle's former sword now his—loose from his left hipwing while stepping out of his hiding spot from behind the screening of trees and bushes after watching the cloaked woman run past in her frantic bid for escape.

Her three pursuers—khansmen assassins of the Enclave, Banzu knew for he had been here before, the Trio of hunters dispatched to kill her if unable to retrieve her for their tyrannical ruler—who rushed out after her into the clearing from the dense woods startled at the armed stranger stalling their chase in brazen reveal of himself.

Banzu seized the Power-cleansed.

Hazel irises flaring grey, vibrant waves of luminous twilight overtook his pulsing vision in undulating cadence to his quickening heart, filling him with bridled magical potency. The slowing world burst into keen brilliance sharp as crushed glass, magnifying his senses acute. The flushing rush of energies flowed through every budding capillary of his relaxing body while the Power enhanced, strengthened, invigorated . . .

perfected his heightened senses and all they afforded him, priming mind and muscle with accelerated response for the cold butchery seconds from commencing.

These three khansmen sought murder, and they found it in the last living Soothsayer who burst into action, his body a rapid blur of locomotion, Griever's bared immaculate steel carving whispers of promise through the air at his side. He raced across the clearing, achieving hundreds of feet in seconds, crisp patches of leaves swirling aflutter in his speedy wake, and there he flowed into blur-shifting swordform after blur-shifting swordform, Griever's thirsting tongue whistling through fanning strokes slicing seams of flesh while loosing glistening ruby beads and broken ropes of khansmen blood arcing lazy jets through the Power-slowed stasis of air.

As he moved through his executioner's dance, delivering Griever's promises of cleaving strokes, guilt tempered anger, though not a hot guilt over extinguishing the lives of these khansmen but a cold and dissatisfying emptiness in knowing these dying three harbored no responsibility for his uncle's sacrificial murder. That blame lay elsewhere in Hannibal Khan.

But they had been sent *by* the Khan, and for that they deserved no less than death.

And the target of their chase . . . for her he delivered them pain first, however brief.

He plunged Griever to the hilt into the third khansman's chest left of center, impaling the tattoo-cheeked bastard's cruel heart, locking eyes with the khansman's blooming revelation of startled face, enjoying the snuffing of the lifespark winking out in those surprised eyes, delighting in the hitching gasp of a final breath inhaled. While the first two khansmen, Big Ugly and Rat Face, dead before they met the ground, continued their sluggish collapses, their scream-stretched faces, their arms and legs, their chests and backs gruesome tableaus of cuts evincing Griever's keen handiwork, their clothes wet shreds.

Banzu yanked Griever free from punctured heart and turned away from the corpse sinking to its knees behind him, while round him the suspended sprays of khansmen blood blink-shifted into faster gushes and spurts when he released his strong inner grasp on the Power and Time's decelerated flow snapped into faster prominence.

Thump—thump—thump behind and at Banzu's sides, and the khansmen corpses struck to ground, the tortured echoes of their dying screams strangled short in their throats, their death-locked faces forever twisted into bloody masks of sculpted frozen horror.

Banzu faced the stunned woman who had turned round, stood gawking at him with wide violet eyes and mouth agape, the tangles of her pale-blonde hair what stuck out from her hooded cloak hanging about her face in framing disarray. And the sight of her trembled his aching heart, for the last time he'd lain eyes upon her . . . decapitated. By Jericho.

But now, so beautiful, so alive, and restored through the Source delivering Banzu back to the past while erasing the terrible tribulations of the future in all but his mind.

Melora closed the distance between them to within five paces then stopped. "Who . . ." She took another hesitant step then stopped, pulled back her hood. "Who are you?"

Banzu knelt and wiped clean the blood from Griever's blade upon the grass in a long stroke—*flip*—stroke, then stood and sheathed his sword. Between them swirled a collection of leaves blown about the ground upon risen winds in a little serenade to their silent exchange. He closed his eyes, drew in a calming breath to quell the blood-quickening rush and alleviate what remained of the battle-lust adrenaline priming his muscles to remove the hard edge from his voice if he spoke too soon.

"You know who I am," he said at last. And smiled at the glorious sight of her, at the spark of life in her marvelous violet eyes appraising him in return. In him a storm of feelings and memories fought for the forefront of his mind, threatening to pour from his mouth on eager tongue so that he wrestled them back, taming them through nervous hands flexing at his sides to keep from reaching at her, from drawing her close and hugging her, feeling and smelling her, kissing her, loving her, instead content with watching her, basking in her all.

A flurry of unvoiced emotions flitted across her face. She scrunched it up in that angry-cute way of hers, nose crinkling. "I do?"

"I'm the one you're looking for." He advanced a single step and offered his hand out between them. "I'm the last Soothsayer."

Her gaze widened then thinned, her natural suspicion reining wonder. "How did you know—" she began, then said no more.

The suffering in her eyes flickered brief relief at his words while betraying a quick discerning for the truth nestled inside them. Apprehensive warred with the hope that had brought her here while she considered him in silence.

His smile turned brittle while trepidation of the unknown folded over him, adding a heaviness to his outstretched hand still empty in offering. His anxious heart skipped several flutters.

Though seconds more and his smile returned in full bloom when she closed the space between them, accepted him by the hand and smiled. He'd lost an uncle though regained this angel in killing trade.

And although neither of them knew it, this was the first true day of the rest of their lives. Together.

* * *

"You can trust me," Banzu said, falling lost within those strong violet eyes regarding him. He gave Melora's cold hand a warm and reassuring squeeze, enjoying the softness of it nestled in his welcoming own as someone fevered enjoys the cool hand lain upon their hot brow. He breathed relief, relaxing, the final assemblage of his rebalancing world righting itself at last, she the missing piece reclaimed.

He withdrew a half step, his roving gaze considering every inch of her, she some rare and delicate vase that might be shattered in a moment, a vaporous figment of his conjured imagination threatening to vanish away if he but squeezed her hand too hard or breathed too much at once.

Glorious to see this beautiful woman of his captured heart's desire alive and standing before him again after suffering the soul-wrenching heartache of losing her, of having traveled back through Time via the Source unto yesterday's point of re-beginning with the purpose of returning her into existence by killing his uncle while cleansing the bloodlust curse.

He stood absorbed and transfixed by the reality of her, not just seeing but by the gods touching her again. And for the life of him he would surrender anything for the moment to last forever and frozen in time.

"Trust you?" The words escaped her in a soft whisper, testing while tasting them on her tongue as they rolled forth from rose-budding lips. Her smile turned vicious in the span of a coinflip, eyes flaring along with her voice. "I don't even know you!"

Banzu startled flinched, the illusion of his joyous reverie shattering while tension squeezed his hand and crimped his fingers. He cringed against the wrenching twist she applied to his bending wrist, the stroke of pain lancing through his arm forcing him to his knees before her swift feral change, the fingers of his caught hand curling into rigid digits from the unexpected torque imposed upon his manipulated wrist-joint.

"What are you doing?" Another wrenching twist of wrist, Banzu's back arching. "Ow!"

"I saw what you did, Soothsayer." Her voice a lashing whip of admonishing scorn, she glanced past him at the three mangled corpses of her Enclave hunters courtesy of Banzu's intervention. In a flash of movement her free hand untied the belt binding her traveler's cloak at the waist, disappeared up beneath flapping fabric then reappeared fisting a dachra. She pressed the keen curved edge of the fanged blade perpendicular against his exposed throat. "I saw the killing."

Banzu tensed in awkward kneeling pose, wanting to speak though knowing a simple swallow would draw blood. He held her measuring glare with his pleading own, silent and grimacing, his longing for her overwhelmed by the threat of a slit throat.

Until she eased the pressure of her dachra just enough to allow him safe speech.

"Explain yourself," she commanded, she who had faced down kings. "Now! Or I'll bleed you out like a stuck pig." Though she allowed no space for answering, for she pummeled him with a flurry of questions. "Who are you? Why are you here? How do you think you know me? Why did you kill those men? How are you not—" A pause punctuated by the flaring scorch of her condemning eyes. "If the bloodlust has you, Soothsayer, I will end you here and now."

He shook his head, denying the accusation, the gesture slight given the dachra held against his throat and seconds from the slicing stroke. Mind racing, juggling through information, trying to make sense of it all again. Coming back to her existed all well in the planning, but the reality of it proved infinitely more complex. So he spoke, each word a careful effort to prevent a bleeding cut.

"My name's Banzu. I'm the last Soothsayer—*ow!*"

She cut him short with another wrenching twist of his wrist applied via her pressing thumb. "Wrong answer. I would know if there was another." More thumbing pressure, wincing pain. "Where's Jericho?"

Banzu swallowed hard, the rolling bump of his throat scraping behind the dachra's curved edge. "He's dead."

"What?" Melora startled flinched, eyes blooming, face slackening. "Dead?" The word left her in harsh whisper issuing challenge to all that brought her here. Her firm grip relaxing, she released Banzu's trapped wrist and withdrew a dazed step, then another, shaking her head as if the physical act could abolish the truth of his words. "No. He can't be dead."

Banzu swayed on his knees, hunching and hissing while rubbing over his sore wrist. Then he straightened, jolting tensed with epiphany. *Oh gods, I'm so stupid. Stupid! How could I forget? She doesn't remember anything because to her, this her, it never happened. We never happened.*

He stared up at her, unsure where or even how to begin, so engrossed with seeing her alive and again his words turned a jumbled mess in his head so that he chose the simplest few.

"I killed him." Profound guilt from voicing the confession withered him into a kneeling hunch. In a low voice he added, "I had to." *Not just for me but—* "For you."

She stared more through him than at him, mute, his words a mystery to her bewildered trance. Though seconds more and emotion regained her slumped face while awareness fed the riling flames in her vindictive gaze. The pink tip of her tongue darted out, wetting lips trembling with the breath of words which never came. Legs unhinging at the knees, she shifted her shoulders back and forth in the slow, unconscious motion of a cat before it pounces, eyes thinning into a serrated glare, teeth bared in a feral snarl, turning boots seeking firmer purchase of the ground while her right hand imposed a strangler's squeeze on dachra hilt, its knuckles flashing white, her empty left hand stealing through eager flexes of the air.

"No!" Banzu shouted, sensing that pounce before the leap. "Wait!" He raised his hands palms-out between them. "You don't understand—"

"Liar!" She pulled her second dachra out into joining the first while crouching low upon coiling legs. Then she pounced forward all feral she-cat, eyes wide and wild, intent on killing the messenger of her failed journey.

On instinct Banzu flexed inward for seizing the Power at the same time he erupted into standing—but of course felt nothing of the Power's blooming energies while within the magic-nullifying expanse of her void-aura—and stumbled backwards while thanking all the gods he possessed the quick reflexes for pulling Griever and brandishing the bastard sword in a rising bar of steel-turned-shield.

A clanging spray of sparks burst between their faces as Melora's lunging attack drove him farther backwards, her dachras targeting for his face instead scraping and biting Griever's blocking edge while Banzu twisted the blade through fanning guard first to one side then the other and back again in quick defensive bid. He regained his balance after three backing steps—and the furious blitz of her pursued him, her arms whipping, her dachra fangs relentless stabs and slashes hunting bites of his flesh from both sides, forcing him back while he deflected her driving stabs and snaking thrusts in ricocheting clangs of steel.

"Stop!" he yelled, and again, "Stop!"

But his words fell upon ears deaf to all but the ringing repeat clangor of their joining blades, her only reply spat curses while she flowed ever-forward through dachraform after dachraform, a slicing tornado of whipping arms and steely fangs, her long temple braids twirling about her head, her open cloak aflutter round graceful legs skating through fluid dances.

Then a brief reprieve where she paused her assault and backed away two steps, seconds only, Banzu catching his breath then that breath hitching in his chest when Melora surged forth and leaped into a fantastic cartwheel up and over him, attempting to achieve his back while her dachras stabbed and thrust for his head through her acrobatic flight.

What the frig! He ducked and twisted while raising Griever overhead, fending the jabs and slices of her passing peppering fangs by thinnest margin.

She landed and, no pause in her onslaught, commenced her forward aggression in another flurry of dachras.

Banzu backpedaled, Griever fanning blocks, a terrible ache building within while fending against her unremitting efforts imposing a damning squeeze on his tortured heart over this woman he loved so intent on killing the man she held responsible for ending her long and arduous journey short with failure.

She doesn't know the whole truth, and friggin hell she's allowing me no quarter to explain it. I killed him for you, godsdammit! Stop and let me explain! Please stop!

But Melora pressed ever-forward, stabbing and twirling, cloak whirling, her long hair spinning in fannings of pale-blonde sunshine, feet knowing no retreat, providing Banzu no choice but for moving backwards while fending against her relentless barrage through side to side parries.

I don't want to hurt you! But the words died at the back of his throat behind straining grunts.

She hopped back, digging in heels.

Banzu opened his mouth to issue a shout for stopping.

Melora lunged into another attack, this a rising, jumping twirl of fangs and cloak, her body spinning round thrice in the air. Her dachras bit steely chimes up Banzu's shielding blade while he continued backing away, she pursuing forward, aggression claiming every stolen inch of his forced withdraw.

The muscles of his well-trained body ached to spend into any of the numerous riposting swordforms flashing through his mind, perfected maneuvers he struggled at holding back in lieu of injuring her while punctuating a cruel end to this unnecessary madness.

Though he considered that aspect of himself with much scrutiny when she paused again, huffing through clenched teeth, and revealed she had so far only been testing him, at first fueled by a deep and possessive rage born from a long-building frustration she harnessed in moments, regaining control of it through sheer strength of iron will in this her moment of refocusing.

Her predatory glare turned calculating, cunning, and thus infinitely more dangerous.

Within this brief pause, Banzu, panting with effort, lowered his sword and tried again for halting appeal. But he clipped his words short and braced while raising Griever just in the nick when Melora lunged in at him, this time with a more concentrated focus of aggression, the clang and clangor of steel resounding between them.

A great swell of panic absorbed him. A master swordslinger, he possessed no training in dachra defense, and the unfamiliar angles of her attacks let alone the twice-times burden of fending against two separate bladed hands threw off his defensive game.

A dividing part of his trained stem brain worked on the subconscious level, separating itself from conscious toil, studying the changes of angles and subtle turns of her graceful maneuvers, for the instinctual part of his swordslinger's subconscious awareness refused to do otherwise when faced with an adversary, any adversary, even her.

Melora lowered into a crouch, muscles bunching, eyes calculating darts, then she sprang forth, straightening to the full length of herself with dachras arcing in overhead hammerfists poised for plunging.

I could end her now. Her middle's exposed. I could—no!

Another clanging spray of sparks as Banzu betrayed the instinctual response of his body and instead upturned Griever sideways. He caught that sinking snakebite of dachras lengthwise across his arresting rise of blade then twisted, scraping fangs sliding Griever's length from hilt to tip, wrenching her aside.

She stumbled then spun through twirling momentum, skidding heels kicking up dirt and leaves.

And there, so brief the span as their gazes locked, ignited a touch of carnal thrill in her eyes while Banzu shared the same arousing stimulus to their contest in his reactive loins.

They licked their lips in tandem, exchanging a fighter's fevered kiss between them beyond the simple act of touching lips.

Gods I missed that look. Banzu opened his mouth to rebuke another advance.

But Melora outpaced his voice by flipping her dachras through spins and snatching them from the air then lunging again.

Banzu surged forth and met her lunge for lunge, steel chiming steel, blocking high then low in quick succession before twisting round and passing her. He spun, hoping to boot her away by the rump into a stumble while earning space enough for expelling another attempt at halting appeal after sucking some precious wind into his laboring lungs.

But she turned too quick, low and spinning, her left leg extended so that Banzu jumped it lest she knock his feet out and sink him. Soon as his boots regained the ground, Melora burst forward, her arms extended at her sides then stabbing inwards in a hug meant for piercing both sides of his ribs. He hopped backwards while hunching forward and sucking in his stomach. Her dachras slashed the air a hairsbreadth from opening his guts as they crossed then slashed in reversing strokes.

Friggin hell that was close! But he put no voice behind it, lungs too strained with breathing, body twisting fanning bars of Griever's steel beating aside her continuous snaking stabs at his arms and legs, the back and forth torquing of his spine a wrenching protest to her merciless lead in this their deadly dance. *Why won't you listen!*

So he decided to exhaust her, see if that worked.

She can't keep this up forever.

But neither can I.

I have to do something before my body gives out.

As he fought aside another slicing twirl of dachras, he spied another opening through which his body ached to maneuver. But he hesitated, refraining from delivering the impaling riposte, instead held steady in his defensive-only dancing, refusing the opportunity of injuring her while ending the combat with one debilitating thrust of his sword.

Within that brief moment of hesitation, Melora forged an opening of her own by way of a high feinting stab for his face which lured both his arms up and to one side, instigating Griever into blocking the false phantom strike. At the same time she slashed low with her other steely fang, forcing him into jumping back his lower half lest she open his forward leg across the thigh so that his upper half leaned forward in compensation.

Melora shot up in a calculated dachra-fisted uppercut, intent on driving her fanged blade into the soft underbelly of Banzu's exposed chin.

But he reversed his forward lean just in the nick, and her rising thrust stabbed only air yet passed so close to his face that her knuckles grazed the tip of his nose.

Banzu flinched, stumbled backwards, arms pinwheeling at his sides, balance sloshing.

And in her fluid trickery Melora leaped in upon his opening guard. Her attacking pounce slammed her against his exposed chest with her knees doubled up in her scant flight for stronger impact.

In fraction reaction Banzu rejoined his hands together and squeezed Griever's hilt to keep it from spilling loose while his tensing body braced in the beginnings of falling backwards, his sword upheld between them in awkward position. Melora's crisscrossed dachras sheared down Griever's front blocking edge spitting sparks inches between their closing faces before she forced the sword aside, relieving it from his hands mid-fall.

She landed atop him, her full weight crushing the breath from his lungs when he slammed to the ground grunting, her falling weight crunching him beneath, the back of his head rebounding against the earthen pillow possessing no soft give.

Dizzied, bright pops of stars overtaking the vertigo whirl of his eyes, Banzu struggled for breath through gasping coughs and strangled wheezes while his vision tunneled black. Melora divided her legs while shimmying lower atop him, relieving the pressure on his chest, and straddled him with her knees tucked to his armpits and her bottom resting atop his stomach. His thoughts scattered to the wind, he flexed empty hands round a sword no longer there, lay blinking through stinging tears while a dull ache throbbed the back of his struck head.

He gazed up through fractured prism vision at Melora looming with her arms crossed at the wrists and her dachras pressed to the sides of his neck, pincers these. He sucked in enough precious air to extinguish the fire from his burning lungs while the murderous brunt of Melora's glare pinned him stilled beneath her.

"You lying sack of wine!" she yelled, accompanied by hot bits of spittle speckling Banzu's flinching face. She lowered her twisted visage to within inches of his, near nose to nose, and for a silent measure stared into his eyes, probing their depths, hunting their truth for secrets hidden beneath.

Out from his right peripheral lay Griever so near and within reach if only he dared the condemning task. But he paid the lost sword no mind, instead focusing his stare into those discerning violet pools judging over him. Within her testing gaze existed a lingering species of frustrated disgust, a bitter indignation not only for his murderous claim but for him holding back in their fight and she knew it. That he hadn't given their contest his full ability proved an attack on her character no offending steel could equal.

He relaxed beneath her sitting weight, surrendered to the truth in his heart begging for release upon his lips if only she would listen and know and believe. "I won't fight you."

"Why?" she demanded. "Why!"

He swallowed, a dangerous chore with his neck trapped between her dachras pincers, his need for her swelling and roiling, yearning to spill loose in desperate plea for her to understand if only she could remember anything of him at all.

"Why!" she yelled again.

"Because—" But there he clipped short, choking on raw emotion. Staring back at him through the anger lived the aloneness, the fear of trusting him, the fear of not trusting him. The moment called for something more to stay her fangs from opening his throat. And if these would be his last words then he wanted them meaningful.

"Why?" she asked in softer voice.

"Because—" A heaviness gathered in the center of his chest. He'd never actually told her before of his deep feelings for her so that he shuddered at the thought of speaking them now in the hopes of sparing his life, the act somehow demeaning the words in trade. And yet . . . and yet. His chance stolen by Jericho, he refused to die without voicing the only sure thing in his life. "Because I love you."

CHAPTER EIGHTEEN

Tensed feral aggression retreating by slow increments on Melora's slumping face, she opened her mouth then closed it, open it again, her eyes betraying little blooms of startlement at Banzu's confession of loving her in the silence of her stolen voice. She withdrew her looming face from his beneath it by inches, then retreated inches more, requiring space to comprehend the unforeseen counter to her demand for his reasons. The pressure of her dachra pincers easing from his trapped neck, though only slight, her mouth framed voiceless words of stunned wonder.

"Melora . . ." he began, then said no more, uncertain what else to attach. He lay beneath her, watching the gradual connection of his answer taking hold behind active violets seeking new balance in the turbulence of her changing world.

Her voice a brittle whisper when next she spoke. "My name. How do you know . . ." She leaned forward again and stared at length, probing his hazel depths. "Who are you?"

"Banzu." His tone soft, eyes pleading. "I'm the last Soothsayer. Melora, please. If you'd just let me explain—"

"Shut up." She thinned her eyes upon him, hunting outward while inward she searched for clues through the dustier corners of her mind. And found nothing but lost whispers in the dark leading her nowhere. "You've got three seconds," she said, tone edged, forearms tensing, hands squeezing round dachra hilts, "and then I'm going to cut your godsdamn head off."

He considered attempting bucking her off to one side while rolling away to the other—*and for it she'll slit my throat, no.* Instead he remained still, his next confession paining him. "You don't remember me. But you know me—*knew* me, I mean."

"One," she said.

Tensing, panic flushing, his mind scrambled for answers and the proper order of unpracticed words. *Stupid. I should've prepared for this. So stupid!* "You came here before. You were looking for Jericho then too. I mean you are looking for—"

"Two." She raised her elbows to better leverage her hands for scissoring her dachras across his throat.

He cringed beneath her, pulse quickening, mind scrambling for facts to attach. "Hannibal Khan. Head Mistress, uhm . . ." *What's her name? Oh gods, what's her friggin name? Think, stupid. Think—Gwen! That's it.* "Head Mistress Gwendora Pearce sent you after Jericho to stop the Enclave and their Khan from resurrecting Dethkore and starting another Thousand Years War."

"Not good enough," she said, stiffening, the pressure of her dachra pincers tightening against the sides of his neck, their keen curved edges a hairsbreadth from breaking skin. "Any khansmen could know that by now. Three—"

"Your mother died giving birth to you!" he said, the flurry of memories from their time together in the future now dissolved in all but Banzu's head spilling forth in a heated rush of words. "She bled out. The Chapel priests couldn't heal her because of what you are. And your father—" He paused through a hard swallow, fearing the sting from his next words though knowing the need for their brutal honesty. "He blamed you then abandoned you because he couldn't bring himself to kill you for it."

Melora flinched, her eyes blooming pulls of disbelief, unable to rebuke the truth she carried alone in her guarded heart, while Banzu's words penetrated deep, impossible to ignore.

"How . . ." she whispered unfinished. She sat back, relaxing the pressure of her dachras from his throat, and held them as forgotten tools in her loosening grips. "How do you know that?"

"Because you told me." He gazed up into those troubled violets attempting to make sense of the world. "But you don't remember me because you can't. No one does. But I did it. I cleansed the bloodlust. Melora, please, I know it sounds crazy but you have to believe me."

The blank stare of a feathered mystery, the slow shake of her head. She studied him as if viewing him for the first real time, the zealous fervor of her challenge against him quelled. A chilly gust of spring winds blew over them, edged with memories of winter, swishing creaking branches in the pervading silence, swirling leaves at their sides, lifting stray tangles of her pale-blonde hair which streamed across her face then fell away.

"I . . . do." Her words sounding more question than statement, she scrunched her face in that angry-cute way of hers, nose crinkling. "Godsdamn you, but I do."

Banzu drew in deep, expelled an inner shudder of relief, while she rose then fell atop him by inches. *Oh thank gods.*

* * *

He lay watching up at her, transfixed by the inner working parts behind her contemplative gaze struggling to make the right of him and all he'd said. She could end him still if she but chose to do the cutting. But there swam a despair in those discerning violets wading among the confusion, a sense of loss no longer private wrenching Banzu's grieving heart and his unvoiced yearning to soothe their shared aches together.

He remembered that same look in someone else's eyes when the haunting response of memory of his uncle's bloodlust-corrupted ghost flittered through his mind, provoking a dark shudder over the living boon straddled atop him regained in killing trade.

The anguish of that hurtful exchange so brief before the decapitating stroke of his sword, of sacrificing one love to save another, gripped him by the guts and squeezed, she his constant brutal reminder of an uncle killed. But he buried the pain deep lest he blame her for anything more than existing—*Jericho died by my hands, not hers, no matter the reason*—and stared up at her in the silence, his eyes a trace suggestion of those poignant thoughts better left unsaid.

Melora slid her dachras from his throat and rested them atop his upper chest, two idle tools held loose in her hands refusing full removal. She straightened, cocked her head to one side, brow furrowing.

"The Veilfall," she whispered, nodding. "Of course." Then in stronger voice, "You can let go of my ass now."

Banzu flinched. "Uhm. What?"

"My ass? Let go."

"Uhm." He flexed his hands, realizing only then they had slipped down past her V'd legs and secured grips of her backside in a preparatory buck of his hips, a last resort of throwing her off in case his words failed to stay her dachras from cutting his throat. "Uhm." He released his grips, cringing. "Sorry."

She stood into a wide-legged stance over him, her spread feet shifting beside his ribs, and spun her dachras through deft twirls then caught their handles in hammer-fisted grips.

Banzu sat up—

"Don't," she said, her voice a cracking whip.

—then lay back down, afraid of instigating another pouncing round of antagonizing questions while under the threat of those steely fangs.

She considered him overlong, then withdrew to a few paces past his feet where she sheathed her dachras away up behind and beneath her flapping cloak in a flash of motion. She crossed her arms and regarded him through a discerning gaze questing for answers.

"Uhm." He tucked his chin to chest, watching up at her. "Can I get up now?"

"I don't know, can you?" Frowning, she unfurled one arm and gestured at him with the flick of her wrist then tucked her hand away just as quick. "Slowly."

He sat up smiling, basking in the sight of her.

"And wipe that stupid grin off your face," she said. "It's creepy."

He tensed his mouth, fighting back his smile only growing with the reminder of her fiery spirit rekindling memories of their first chance meeting in these same woods several weeks ago to him though only a few minutes ago to her. He raked a hand back through his hair and blew out his cheeks.

"Gods," he said. "I completely forgot. You don't remember anything that's happened." He paused, smile fading. "That you don't remember me."

Her frown deepened into a scowl. "You're touched with madness for all I know. You could've killed Jericho then turned to the bloodlust." A terse sniff through flaring nostrils. "If not for your eyes."

My eyes? Of course. The Power turned them a shining grey, the bloodlust a lambent red. He glanced at Griever nearby, gestured in askance with the sideways tilt of his head.

Her thinning gaze followed that suggestive tilt, to which she shook her head. "I don't think so."

"Ooookay." He rocked into standing.

And she took an immediate step back, every inch of her tensing taller, arms uncrossing, hands open at the ready for pulling her dachras and baring her fangs again at a moment's notice.

"It's okay," he said, thrusting his arms with palms out. "I won't hurt you." He threw a deliberate glance left at the three dead khansmen lying no more than a few bounding strides away. "I think that's obvious."

Her gaze flickered to the bodies while thinning at the suggestion that she would ever be afraid of him or anyone else. Eyebrows arching, she cleared her throat with a rumble that said she expected a convincing explanation or her dachras came back out.

"Uhm." Unsure where to continue or even how after confessing his love, he wanted nothing more than to reconnect with her and nurture their severed bond. He sighed, his tongue a fumble spilling parts of words.

"First off," she said, cutting him short while raising a stiff finger and jabbing at him while she talked, "you're going to tell me just who in the hell you really are. Then you're going to tell me why I shouldn't kill you and be on my way. And third, if you don't stop staring at me like that I'm going to slap that stupid smile right off your stupid face." She planted fists to hips and added a fierce, "Go."

He did the best he could with dismissing the offending smile and risked a cautious step closer, inches only—almost reluctant to admit any hope back into his heart after what just transpired between them—and she stood her ground, her stance all challenge.

"Jericho is—*was* my uncle. I killed him when I cleansed the bloodlust. I had no other choice. It's a long story. You might want to sit down and—"

"I'll stand. And I would've been told if there was another Soothsayer. Go on."

"Gwen sent you to find him, but—"

But there he stopped, unsure how best to frame it all. *So much to tell, impossible to summarize without sounding crazy.*

And his mind . . . parts of it still jumbled from the jolting transition of his re-beginning. Replacing himself in the Past now Present through the Source and cleansing the bloodlust curse left pieces of his brain scrambled in unexpected ways compounded by his brief testing seize of the Source thereafter Jericho's death, the effort inviting a daunting deluge of memories born from a thousand Soothsayers, the Power connecting them all, their shared collective a screaming maelstrom of imprints burning into the neural patterns of his brain.

So much power and influence riding the tide of a thousand raucous voices. The potency of the Source too overwhelming to endure for more than a few sparse seconds before his release. To invoke it again might break his mind, leaving only shards of madness behind in the wake of his shattered sanity. How Simus Junes survived the Source while invoking it against the Nameless One in repeat battles left Banzu clueless.

Extraneous to explain all that to Melora so that he did his best at keeping things simple, he hoped, with facts of her duty and the events of its undoing that brought her here.

"The Head Mistress sent you as Spellbinder Vizer to Junes. Then Hannibal Khan—" He paused, grimacing, latent ire spiking after the name rolled from his mouth in bitter release. He flexed his hands into strangles of air at his sides while a black and beating rage descended over him, clouding behind the eyes, a profound anger born from the killing of his uncle, an animosity nestled in focal blame festering without hope of release but for the swift death of Hannibal Khan himself, the true catalyst of Jericho's return to the bloodlust.

A knifing flash of memory replayed through Banzu's mind in stark reminder of his uncle's bloodlust relapse, of the night he awoke and found Melora dead.

"Wakie wakie, eggs and bakie," teased the voice soughing inside his head while memories flexed and flared and Banzu remembered . . . oh gods how he remembered rousing awake, feeling caught within a dream, blinking the heavy cling of sleep from his eyes, squinting through the darkness at the shadowed figure sitting hunched opposite the soft orange glow of firelight just beyond its illuminating reach.

Then motion in the dark when the other threw something round and possessing long pale tendrils whipping the air. It sailed over the glowing nest of coals, struck the ground, rolled stopped.

Melora's face staring on tilted lean.

"You should've killed me when you had the chance," that shadowed figure said, Jericho's lambent red eyes so full of hate piercing the night's gloom and—

Banzu blinked hard while banishing the nightmare. He drew in deep through clenched teeth, seeking calm from that brutal subject before going on, the promise of reconnecting with Melora a torturing comfort rife with guilt.

A life for a life. It's not her fault. Don't you blame her. Don't you dare.

He considered this version of her at silent length, she the same yet not the same. Nothing much had changed, except everything. But the difference of her experience with him, erased through the dissolved Future, made her face no less dear to him. In fact, he craved her now more than ever. Something precious lost then found, he yearned for embracing her and never letting go.

And yet . . . *a life for a life.*

He averted his gaze while collecting himself, began again after quelling the inner rage for Hannibal Khan edging his tone.

"You escaped to Fist after the Enclave's attack on Junes. You fled to the Academy, then Gwen and Aggie—" He paused at Melora's scrunching disapproval and corrected himself. "Then Head Mistress Gwendora and Mistress Agatha sent you here to find the last Soothsayer so you could bring him back and kill the Khan. But that's me now. Because Jericho is dead. Because I killed him. Yesterday."

"Yesterday," she said, rolling the word over, sampling it, tasting it, sounding it while trying to decipher deeper meaning than mere date. "Go on."

"You're Melora Callisticus. A Spellbinder. I know you, and you know me. Or you did." A wincing pause. "Look, I know this all sounds crazy, but . . . I'm from the future."

He braced at the ridiculousness of his words, half expecting her to pounce upon him in another bladed outburst of dachra fury.

But she stayed her place, moving nothing save for her arching eyebrows which said *Go on* where words did not.

So he did. "You came here once before and I saved you then too." He pointed down. "Right here. In this exact same clearing from this exact same Trio." Then pointed at the khansmen corpses. "That's how I knew to be here again, only Jericho wasn't dead then. I took you to him, to our cabin. And when you told him you came to take him back to Fist, well, he left without you. You were exhausted. He slipped away while you were sleeping. So we followed after him, but he used magic to get there a lot faster. He made a deal with Gwen to kill the Khan, just like you wanted. But in doing so he returned to the bloodlust and—"

He clipped paused, deciding it best to skip over the gruesome details of her murder. "Then he came hunting for me. He killed you. And then I killed him."

She lowered one eyebrow, leaving the other cocked in queer amusement. "So I'm dead then." She smirked, her monotone a flat mockery. "That's news to me."

"Yes." He rolled his yes, shook his head. "I mean no. I mean you *were* dead, but now you're not." He threw his hands up and huffed a curse. "I don't know how to explain it any better."

"Try." Her one word response possessed a gravity leaving no questionable doubt she expected better—or else.

He raked both hands back through his hair, gripping frustrated tufts before letting go, and blew out his cheeks. Words spilled forth while he described everything from their first true meeting and his saving her life. From them chasing after Jericho to crossing Green River, to facing down frostwolves then battling a crazed suicidal berserker from the Thunderhell Tundra. Banzu almost dying because of his wolf bite infecting him with chillfever, to her saving his life with her Spellbinder void-aura. Then a bloodlust-turned Jericho returning and killing her and the tundarian Ma'Kurgen. Banzu traveling back through his own timeline using the Source and killing Past Jericho while Future Jericho, kohatheen collared and cut off from the Power, allowed Banzu access to the Source, to cleansing the bloodlust while undoing everything that had happened from that defining moment forward.

Several weeks of his life expelled in a flurry of words, yet to her those weeks existed within the shortened span of only yesterday.

". . . and now I'm here," Banzu finished. "With you. Again."

He crossed his arms and waited, all the while trying to present his best winning smile.

She assessed him through half-closed lids, the hint of a smirk toying at one corner of her mouth. "So you traveled back in time and killed the last Soothsayer to become the last Soothsayer," she said, surmising his long-winded explanation into one concise sentence dripping mockery. "And all of it yesterday."

He nodded. "Yesterday to me. But weeks ago to you. I mean the other you. To this you it was yesterday." He sighed, his explanation confusing him almost as much as her and he'd lived through it.

"Yesterday," she said in self-whisper, her focus decoupling more through him than at him. "Yesterday the Veilfall happened."

Veilfall? That foreign word again. He assumed the converging of timelines restored everything back to the familiar. But that word, she spoke it with prominence, and he remembered nothing of it from before his re-beginning . . . but for faint recollections of whispers in *shshshshsh*'ing hushes though clearing inside some hidden recess at the back of his mind. "What's a Veilfall?"

"The Veilfall," she said, firmer, as if that were that, the sky blue and water wet. She struck him with a vexing look when he shrugged as if playing ignorant on purpose.

"I don't know what that is," he said. "Why, am I supposed to?"

She scrunched her face pinched. "What do you mean you don't know? Everyone can remember now that the Veil's been lifted and the Godstone's fallen."

Veilfall? Godstone? He shook his head in mute reply, belly squirming with new unease, feet shifting. *I don't like where this is going.*

Scowling, she uncrossed her arms, planted fists to hips and worked her eyes into scolding flares. "Yesterday when the entire godsdamned world shook and the whole godsdamned sky lit up!"

"It did?" He scanned round the clearing for any signs of the supposed calamity then jerked her another clueless shrug. "Yesterday?"

"Yesterday!" A diminishing roll of her eyes. "Yesterday afternoo*oooh*." Those eyes widened as slow-dawning realization bloomed therein and bled from her violet pools across her face. "Yesterday when you cleansed the bloodlust," she said in a lower voice to herself again. "Of course." Pacing, she threw her arms overhead in shouting epiphany, "Of course!"

He watched her talking to herself for the span of ten heartbeats while her claim took logical root, his mind skipping back while snatching for reasons excusing his obliviousness. *It must've happened while I seized the Source.* The entire universe could have blown apart then reformed itself without his notice in those astonishing seconds where sang the deafening screams of a thousand dead Soothsayers.

He tried explaining as much, but she ignored him in her pacing mutters.

Then, and sounding as if reciting a passage out from some ancient prophetic text, she said, "'The Veil will lift and the Godstone will fall for the savior-slayer reborn.'" She stopped her pacing, struck him with a cocked eyebrow, then relapsed into more deliberate self-whispers punctuated by her natural conclusion. "I can't believe it's finally happened. I feel so stupid for not—"

But there she clipped short. She stared him over in silent study, eyes expanding, thinning, expanding again. In a tone so low it dared not call itself a whisper she said, "You *are* him."

* * *

Banzu shifted his feet against the assessing brunt of Melora's weighty stare. He flinched tensed when a hot and feathery whisper tickled through his mind. *Fist.* Flexing hands craving Griever's hilt, he averted his gaze to the sword lying nearby. *Hannibal Khan.* Anger rousing in a prickling flush of heat tingling through his warming skin, the threads of his waning patience frayed while the cold and calculating reminder of what he was about now that he had her back in his life returned in full sweeping charge of his conscious mind riding dark tides of darker purpose. *You have a Khan to kill, an uncle to avenge. And it's not getting done just standing here.*

"So," he said, after taming the guttural growl in his throat, "can we go now?"

"Your eyes," Melora said, quick and short, ignoring his question. She closed distance in three strides, fisted the front of his shirt and pulled his face to within inches of hers. She said nothing, just stared at his upturned face for a lengthy measure before releasing her grips while stepping back, apparently satisfied with her little inspection. She turned staring west, the way he'd come, contemplating the remaining stretch of her long and arduous journey stalled short, her lips pressing into a fine red line of silent debate.

He suppressed a heavy sigh into his lungs, the bloodlust cleansed through the proof of his eyes, his killing of the Trio then not killing her. *What more does she want from me?*

He chewed the question back, in no mood for instigating another argument. But she never accepted anything on faith of words alone, a trait he admired. Headstrong to a fault, as hard on herself as she was on others. He watched her mumbling self-debate, knowing she believed him yet striving through every available excuse not to.

She evinced the slow dawning of someone who had been searching vehemently for something, and now that they had it, now that it was actually a reality, the skeptical part of them refused to believe. No surrender until she exhausted every possible excuse.

Friggin hell. An idea struck him then. *Her map.* Ensorcelled and magically keyed to Jericho. *But not anymore.* Jericho's death dispelled the magical marker while rendering her map nothing more than ink and paper.

Grimacing, Melora raised her hands and gave the lanthium collar locked round her slender neck an irritated tug between whispered musings so that Banzu snapped his fingers and pointed at it, drawing her out from soliloquy.

"You put that kohatheen on when this last Trio started chasing you," he said, rehashing her words from their time together before his re-beginning, the memories of her bursting charge into their cabin and the long conversation afterwards flooding back. "You were afraid of losing it. You brought it here as proof of the Khan and the Enclave and—"

He clipped short, the grim remembrance of his uncle's words a black echo knifing through his mind in haunting appeal. *"She was supposed to put that on me,"* Jericho's words recalled. *"If I didn't agree to go then she was supposed to make me go."*

Pulse quickening, hands clenching strangles of the air at his sides, Banzu grit his teeth and glowered. He rumbled his throat clear of stinging accusations better left unsaid, his mood fouling while the reminder of his promised vengeance flourished into an overwhelming presence possessing its own sentience and commanding his full attentions elsewhere so that he turned facing east and glared through the forest beyond the clearing.

Jericho . . . Hannibal Khan.

The pain of knowing there existed no more he could do about the first and everything he could do about the second pulled at him. His body craved action, yearning to run, to snatch up Griever then seize the Power and speed away in a blurring fury knowing no calm but for the satisfying delivery of death repaid.

But a perfunctory glance at Melora and he resisted the burning sense of urgency by thinnest margin, the terrible knowledge that Hannibal Khan still lived and breathed because of his re-beginning a source only of agony. *I didn't restore just her life. And I'm just standing here, doing nothing.* He scourged himself for that. If not for her—

He tore away from the east and all it represented, and faced her again. He forced a smile leaving his eyes untouched, every taut inch of him begging to run away hunting in a bursting blur of Power, to deliver his promised vengeance upon the Khan and put an end to the raw torment earned in cruel trade for the life of the woman he loved and—

No! It's not her fault. Don't you dare blame her. And yet . . . and yet, every time he looked at her, a life for a life.

Sickening regret swelled his guts, she his only reason for staying put and wasting precious time instead of on the move.

I've explained enough. She'll just have to make due with figuring the rest of this out along the way.

"Your duty is to bring the last Soothsayer to Fist." Banzu spread his arms in presenting gesture of self. "Well, here I am. Willing and waiting. For you."

Melora squared her shoulders, planted fists on hips, opened her mouth in apparent rebuttal then closed it and shrugged. She glanced at the dead Trio, threw another west, then looked at him. "I guess so."

"Good." He strode to Griever without asking, scooped up the sword and drove it home at his left hipwing. Removing outside the magic-nullifying expanse of her void-aura, he seized the Power and sped return to where he'd abandoned his rucksack by the shielding stand of pines. He slung it over his left shoulder then sped back to her, stopping just shy of her void-aura while releasing the Power. Zephyrs of agitated leaves rose then fell upon the diminishing winds in his wake. He smiled at her mute gape. "Then let's get going. Again."

Without another word he walked away east.

CHAPTER NINETEEN

"Wait!" Melora shouted from behind.

Banzu ignored her and kept walking, his need for achieving Fist soon as possible pulling at the vital parts of him, the glamour of seeing her alive and well again burning away before the scorching firewall of his vengeance and the fierce need to spend it through Khan slaughter waxing strong while his mind played the dangerous game of reliving unforgettable pains.

Some pain you could distance yourself from, while other pain continued dusting over your cobwebs for years after it's taken in, rooting deep and nestled in scars, no matter how hard you tried shaking it loose. Jericho's death proved one of those other pains, life-altering and lifelong no matter how recent the nefarious deed.

Drudging up the raw freshness of that grievous event, a darker part of Banzu stroked the sore sting swollen with kinslaying venom while nurturing the vehement hatred he harbored for Hannibal Khan. And for the Head Mistress who manipulated Jericho into his relapse of bloodlust.

Though for her, Gwendora Pearce, Banzu festered a cold disdain instead of the hot animosity smoldering for the true culprit of his uncle's demise.

He reflected on the night of Jericho's return, mental floodgates releasing a deluge of torment in a mash of bitter memories replaying behind the eyes.

"Gwen's pardon," Jericho's voice a haunt of wealth touching upon the contents of the envelope Melora delivered him. *"All a ruse, of course. Just another one of the Academy's lies. She wanted me to kill the Khan. A suicide mission. Said my life would be forfeit in trade for your freedom. Hah! Kill the Khan and end the curse. Two birds with one stone."*

Banzu blinked hard, wincing, banishing the memory away before tears betrayed his cheeks. *She manipulated him, yes, but she did it in the best interests of the potential victims Hannibal Khan has yet to brutalize. I need to remember that when I meet her in Fist. Or else . . . or else I might do something I'll regret.*

"Wait, godsdammit!" Melora's elevating shout from behind while she chased after him. "I said wait!"

He ignored her. Glanced down in consideration of the purple boot coverings he wore, magical weaves of ensorcelled cloth Jericho called his boots of blinding speed for they increased the distance of the wearer's steps, making ten from one through magic Banzu knew nothing of how to activate.

Jericho never shared those special words of invocation, same as he never shared he even possessed the magical boot coverings until just before rushing off for Fist while leaving a confused Banzu and a sleeping Melora behind.

Even if I knew the words I couldn't use them anyhow, not without leaving her behind. And her void-aura makes carrying her impossible.

Knowing Melora alive and well again flipped an internal switch of focus, diverting his concentration down the dark avenue of revenge and nothing but. Revenge so simple in that way, with only three parts to it, really. One, you needed someone to kill. Two, you killed them. And Three, you either got away with it or you didn't. After that . . . well, you had to care about the after for there to be an after that, and he planned no further ahead than killing the Khan.

Distracted in his silent musings, he took no notice of Melora catching up until she yanked on the crook of his left arm in a failed attempt at stopping him.

"Where do you think you're going?" she asked, walking alongside him.

"Fist," he said, sparing her no more than a cursory glance. "Where else?"

"We need to talk."

"So talk."

"I've only just found you." Frowning, she huffed a terse breath, as if walking and talking at once proved too much a single irritating chore. "And now that the Veilfall—"

She clipped her words short at his blatant disregard, spat a string of hot curses, then grabbed him by the crook of his elbow and yanked him stopped. "Godsdammit, will you stop and listen to me?"

"What!" he yelled in a misplaced flare of spiking ire while rounding on her, earning from her a backing flinch. He cringed apologetic, lowered his gaze, and in so doing caught a glimpse through the open nape of her cloak of the silvery kohatheen, a sight inducing the fuller haunting memory culled from before his re-beginning.

"She was supposed to put that on me," Jericho's voice recalled in whispering scorn. *"If I didn't agree to go then she was supposed to make me go. I knew that the second she walked through the door and I saw those godsdamned eyes. Conniving bitch!"*

Banzu blinked hard, banishing the painful memory and all it afforded him while rousing focus back to the present and the angry beauty in front of him, tall and taut, her lips a pressed cut, her eyes fiery reservoirs reflecting fathoms of incense bleeding into her tone when next she spoke.

"You yell at me again," she said, "and I'll cut your tongue out then wipe my ass with it before sewing it back in."

"I'm sorry," he said in softer voice still lingering with edge. "I didn't mean—" He paused, breathing. "It's just—look. There's plenty of time for talking on our way there. What is it anyways, a hundred miles or so to Fist?" His mood brooding a shade darker over such a delay as distance, he gripped Griever's leather-wound hilt in open display and administered a flexing squeeze, knuckles flashing white where twitched sinews beneath his skin. "I have a Khan to kill. And it's not getting done with us standing here flapping our gums."

The toiling demon of his promise made to Jericho's memory in the moments before setting their cabin afire ghosted through his mind, though in there festered more than just personal revenge driving him east. Hannibal Khan had caused tremendous grief and loss in more lives than his, including hers. Her pain now his pain, and he sought to remedy that pain through the cold steel of vengeance via Griever's blade thirsting for Khan's blood and Enclave slaughter. Nothing else mattered.

"That bastard has no idea what he's done," he continued, staring more through her than at her. "But he will." He tensed his jaw, lips pressing into a fine red line until the raging guttural scream begging for release withered back down into the pit of his stomach and continued its cancerous festering. Now was not the time to unleash his rage blindly and without appropriate target—that would come later, and with the alleviation of full release. "I swear by all the gods both righteous and fallen he will."

"You're . . . trembling," she said.

With fury, yes. It was then he noticed her cautious withdraw from him two wary steps, her feet shifting into preparatory stance of defense, hands flexing at the ready for pulling dachras, her gaze a steady bead on his sword. He released his strangler's grip from Griever's hilt, fanning fingers peeling free, and closed it in a tight fist at his side. He said nothing. He turned and walked away.

A curse from behind, then she caught up beside him again and snagged him into stopping with another arresting yank on his arm.

He jerked his arm free and spun to her.

She met him glare for glare, budging nothing.

"I want Hannibal Khan dead just as much as you do," she said, then added a stern "Shut up!" when he opened his mouth for interruption. "But things have changed. Things you obviously aren't aware of. The Builder's Veil has lifted and the Godstone has fallen. And with the Veilfall, all the memories from the past once hidden by the Veil have been returned to everyone." She paused, frowning, and flicked her wrist in gesture at him. "Everyone except for you, apparently. We need to get to Fist as soon as possible and—"

"That's what I'm trying to do!" he yelled. And winced, regretting the outburst the moment it betrayed his lips. In softer words a stammer he added, "I'm—I'm sorry. I didn't mean to—it's not your fault."

He turned away, embarrassed, ashamed, and drew in a deep and calming breath that did little to stifle the anger trembling the depths of him. *Gods, what's wrong with me?* He felt able to grip a tree and tear it lose by the roots while screaming at the world and everyone in it. No, not just anger, not just fury, but rage, awakened by Jericho's death, so prominent, so anxious and immediate to flare and spend regardless the target. *I've never felt like this before. Something's different. Something's changed. Something's . . . wrong. In me.*

He turned back to continue his apology—into her punching fist. Pain struck his left cheek as his head swiveled aside while bright pops of stars twinkled through the whirl of his eyes. He staggered a step, hunching, gripping his jaw while working his mouth open and closed, ensuring no broken hinge. He straightened, blinking his vision clear.

I deserved that. He faced her though studied the ground between his feet before meeting the violet contempt of her glare above a satisfied smirk, her arms crossed.

"You finished yelling at me yet?" She unfurled one arm and shook her raised fist. "Or do I have to knock a few more teeth loose?"

"No, no. I'm sorry. I really am." He raked a hand back through his hair and presented a smile that didn't keep. "It's just . . . friggin hell, the last time we did this you were so determined to get back to Fist that I could barely keep up with you. And now——" He threw his hands up between them and expelled a frustrated huff. "Why are you trying to stop me? I thought this was what you wanted."

"Because of the Veilfall, stupid!" she yelled. "Haven't you been listening? Everything has changed!" She paused, huffing wind, regaining calm. "And I need proof of—"

"You'll have your proof when I hand you the Khan's head." He issued Griever's hilt a perfunctory squeeze. "And the rest of his body. In pieces."

She shook her head. "That's not what I mean. I was sent here for Jericho but instead I've got you. If you really killed him then show me his body. The Head Mistress will want confirmation, and—"

But there she clipped short at Banzu's scarifying mask glaring in a silence so black it stunned her quiet, his face tensing murder-hard. Plenty of times before when she had upset him, even angered him to the point of wanting to choke her head off. But her suggestion now drew a fine line between them better left uncrossed—even for her.

"We're not going back there so you can go digging through the ashes for his bones," he said, grinding the words out through clenched teeth, his tone raw with serrated edge. "I've let you push the line between us many times, Melora, but I will not allow you this."

She thinned her eyes, glanced down, withdrew two cautious steps. And raised her hands up beneath her dividing cloak in reach for her dachra fangs.

While Banzu realized with a sickening plunge of spirit his right hand, having moved of its own accord, gripped Griever's hilt in reactive threat for pulling so that he removed his hand albeit slowly.

She considered him overlong while hunting for subtle tells of possible sudden action against her, the hardened man standing before her no longer the same naïve youth she remembered nothing of, his face marked by experience, much of it pain, his soul scarred by loss and regret. All this betrayed in her eyes, and the truth of it imposed a wrenching grind on his aching heart.

He imagined nothing worse than hurting this formidable yet vulnerable woman he had gone to terrifying lengths to restore into his life, and yet he'd just crossed that shameful divide of threatening her, truly threatening her, by his own condemning hand born from a seething rage existing outside the precarious limits of his restraint. He drew in a ragged breath, seeking emotional control beyond the disgust of himself.

She lowered her empty hands from beneath her cloak and straightened tall while resettling. "I'm sorry. You're right. That was unkind of me."

Banzu flinched at the unexpected apology. *You're sorry?* "No. Don't be sorry." *I have every right to be, not you.* He cleared the gruffness from his throat. "Just don't ask that again, okay? Please." A pausing twinge of pain, and in a lower voice he added, "You have no idea what I've been through already." He reached up, curled a thumb under the thin brass necklace strung round his neck and pulled his uncle's silvery wedding ring out from the nape of his shirt. "Besides, I wouldn't have this otherwise."

Her eyes widened. "Is that—" Then thinned. "That's my proof." She tried snatching the necklace away in her abducting cat's paw of a swipe.

But he withdrew by leaning backwards while tucking the necklace and ring away beneath his shirt. "No. His ring stays with me."

Frowning, her gaze lingered on his chest for a space until she elevated it and conceded him a nod. "Fine. Then listen. The Veilfall has changed everything . . . Banzu, is it? It's important now more than ever that I get you to Fist as soon as possible before—"

He interrupted with a mirthless chuckle. "What do you think I'm trying to do?" Whatever this Veilfall business, it wasn't getting him any closer to Fist or any closer to killing the Khan. "And we'll get there a lot faster if you stop arguing and start walking."

He shot her a cocked eyebrow punctuating his point before walking away.

Melora blistered the air with a short string of curses. But he spared her no glance behind, expecting her to follow his obvious lead.

She caught up alongside him, open mouth on the verge of releasing another feisty protest. Until she snapped her teeth shut with an ivory *click* and matched his stride, glowering.

"You should be happy," he said. "Not slowing me down. Besides, this is what you want isn't it? Justice?"

"There's a big difference between justice and revenge," she said.

"Not anymore." He gnashed his teeth, jaws bunching taut. "You weren't there, Melora. I had to put Jericho down like a rabid dog because of the Khan. And you weren't there because you were dead."

"You're right. I wasn't there. But I know killing the Khan won't bring Jericho back. Just like I know there's more important . . ."

She went on.

But Banzu heard only parts and partials now that his blood flushed up again, hot and savage and pulsing through his ears in muffling beats, his stare ahead focal and tunneled. *So what if killing the Khan won't bring Jericho back?*

". . . because of the Veilfall, and he doesn't matter anymore," she continued. "Godsdammit, Banzu, are you even listening?"

It'll sure as hell make me feel a whole lot better.

She punched him in the shoulder. "Did you hear anything I just said?"

No. He sped up, replying nothing.

"Hey!"

And left Melora trailing in his wake.

* * *

Until her furious shout from behind penetrated his shielding rumination: "Hannibal Khan doesn't matter anymore you idiot!"

Banzu jolted stopped. *What?* He turned round. "What?" His face, unknown to him, growing severe. "How can you say that? After everything he's done, everything he's going to do, how can you possibly say that?"

She closed distance in two bounding strides, drew in a sharp nostril breath and mustered up taller in an attempt at admonishing him glare for glare. "You're not listening—"

"No," he interrupted, and corrected her with, "*you're* not listening." He stood gripping Griever's hilt again, strangling it in effigy of Hannibal Khan's neck, uncaring of her wary glances the gesture afforded his hand, though in truth the action helped stay the trembles from showing, fevered trembles bleeding into his voice while threatening the release of tears. "I have to kill him." *With you or without you*, though he dared no voice behind the ultimatum. "He took everything away from me. And he's going to pay for it in blood." He released his grip of hilt, raised his hand and pointed at her. "So don't you tell me he doesn't matter. Don't you dare. He . . ." But he trailed away while turning away, sniffled and swiped a stray tear from his cheek. *Friggin hell, I'm crying? And right in front of her? Get a hold of yourself!*

She tugged at his arm, instigating him facing her again, her tone softening. "I know it hurts. I've lost people too. But your anger is blinding you. And we need to—"

"I don't care." He walked away.

She flared then thinned her eyes at his turned back, then craned her head and screamed at the sky, at the world, at every stubborn man in it. No words. Just fury. Frustrated outburst expelled, she rushed up alongside him again.

"Things have changed, Banzu. You can't just leave like this now that—are you even listening?"

"No." He sped up.

So did she. "You're going the wrong way, godsdammit!"

Silence. No sparing glance.

She slowed her steps, grumbling curses. Then broke into a furious rush, brushing against him while pulling out her dachras in passing sprint to gain the lead. Where she spun round, open cloak twirling, and blocked his path while holding her bared fangs at her sides in hammer-fisting grips. "Stop!"

He stopped. Frowned. Eyeballed her up and down. "What."

For a testy length they challenged each other glare for glare, unvoiced tensions rising between them in the silence but for the cool mountain breeze blowing sharper chills in from the north, stirring up a rustle of leaves swirling round her spread feet planted to stance, soughing winds shivering through the swaying treetops with false whispers.

She raised her dachras flipping-quick, threatening to pierce his lungs if he dared farther against her. "If you won't listen then I'll make you listen. Turn around." She waggled her twin fanged daggers for emphasis.

"Now, godsdammit."

Despite himself, Banzu's tight expression loosened into an amused little smirk at the cruel irony of her stopping him in opposite replay of their time before, after she'd awoke and found Jericho gone and he chased after her. He glanced at the stabbing threat of her dachras, met her stern gaze with his unyielding own and took a deliberate step forward, closing space so that keen fanged tips poked his chest a hairsbreadth.

"And if I don't?" he asked.

But in this the reverse of their erased past she answered no withdraw as he had her challenging advance. Nor did she fumble for reply. Stare unwavering, she increased the pressing pressure of her dachras, eliciting from him a grunting grimace when their sharp tips pricked his flesh through shirt.

"Then you're in for a painful day," she said.

He budged nothing, a darker part of him wanting to instigate her threat by hopping back while pulling his sword. Instead he held the measure of her unrelenting stare, no trace of fear therein but for her duty and the determination to see it through no matter the cost. All Spellbinder again, she had a job to do and the gods and Banzu and everyone else be damned.

So he drew another weapon at his disposal, one keener than Griever's steel calling from his hip, and brandished it with a knowing smirk. "You didn't come all this way just to kill me."

She opened her mouth, closed it, shifted her feet, eyes darting from his brazen stare to dachras and back. She worked her jaw through silent chews. She withdrew her dachras, each fanged tip dark with hints of his blood, and lowered them to her sides. And there she huffed, shoulders slouching, eyes pleading pools of askance. "Will you please just listen to me?"

He rubbed his pricked chest then crossed his arms and blew out his cheeks, quelling the urge for charging past her—friggin hell, for charging through her. *Anyone else and you'd be dead by now.* He nodded. "Fine. I'm listening."

"Thank gods." She returned her dachras away to their sheaths strapped to her back up beneath her flapping cloak and cinched her belt tight. "Like I've been trying to tell you, there are bigger things at play now than Hannibal Khan. For starters, those gauntlets of his are far more important than the man himself. They're only a piece to the whole of the Dominator's Armor the Enclave seeks to reform—"

"I already know about—"

"Shut up. But now that the Veilfall has happened, even the Dominator's Armor pales in comparison to the Godstone." She tapped at her right temple for emphasis. "Perspective, Banzu—"

"Ban."

"What?"

"Call me Ban."

She rolled her eyes, huffing. "Fine. Whatever. Ban. Look. This isn't about you." She poked the center of his chest with a stiff finger, jabbing sternum. "And it isn't about me. We have a responsibility to protect those who can't protect themselves. And to do that we have to set our personal grievances aside. I want Hannibal Khan just as dead as you do. But rushing out blindly and killing him won't take care of the Godstone, and that's out priority now. Understand?"

He chewed his bottom lip, saying nothing. He didn't know what a Godstone was and didn't care to hear it. Same with the Veilfall, neither got him any closer to the Khan.

In a turning slip of mood he said, "Yeah, well, you can take your perspective and your responsibility and your Godstone and—" *And shove them up your sassy ass!* But he clipped the words short a hairsbreadth before the rest slipped loose form his errant tongue.

She leaned forward by inches, eyebrows arching. "*Aaaannd?*"

"And nothing," he grumbled, while averting his glare to the space of false interest between his shifting feet.

"That's what I thought," she said.

He uncrossed his arms, left hand reverse-gripping Griever's hilt in pulsing squeezes, right flexing fists at his side, his body craving action. He drew in through flaring nostrils, the unspent rage within him the breath of fire captured deep and overlong until its searing touch burned in his chest. He sought calm and control over the scalding animus sundering parts of him from the man he no longer was while his mind's heart fished for excuses to deter her from his path. But she didn't know, not truly, because she remembered none of the pain he carried alone.

Jericho, dead. And this restored version of her . . . everything once built between them, gone. He'd told her the gist of it all, but she received the information without any of the passion of direct involvement.

Not this her. The other her. The murdered her. The one I fell in love with. Gods, still falling despite every look at this her reminding me of what I lost in trade—stop it! It's not her fault. The Khan did this to us. He . . . you ruined everything.

Everything! You're going to pay for what you did. I hate you! I'm going to carve your godsdamned heart out and show it to you before I—

"You're trembling again," she said. "Stop it."

The vague recognition of her voice pierced the red veil of his inner brooding so that he hissed in a sharp breath through clenched teeth while seeking calm, attempting to tame the bridled depths of tempestuous resentment, his hate a sentient lust, moments from splitting him at the seams in a burst of indiscriminate rage, pleading for release, begging for his surrender to the promise of its chaos and—

No! Not at her. Never her.

And yet . . . and yet. The Veilfall and the Godstone, neither mattered, both could wait. Nothing compared to the Khan. Nothing. No one.

There's only vengeance in my heart now. Gods forgive me, but until it's sated there's room for nothing else.

"I don't want to hurt you," he whispered through gritted teeth, and in such a low voice he almost heard none of it. "Please just move."

"What?"

The battle of his burning want of the Khan and his yearning need for her climaxed inside him. He raised his gaze, swallowed the hot lump of guilt clogging his throat, and in as level a tone as he could manage said, "Get out of my way, Melora." He shrugged the rucksack from his back to the ground while removing his left hand from Griever's hilt, leaving it exposed for the other's swift taking. "I won't ask you again." He flexed his right hand, knuckles popping, sinews snapping, fingers fanning. "And I won't hold back this time."

She flinched at his threat. Withdrew by inches. Her voice a forlorn whisper. "You would kill me to kill him?"

The critical stab of regret in the hollow of his chest stole his breath. *Oh gods.* Rage leached out of him as would poison drawn from a snakebite. *What am I doing?* He wanted to speak but feared the words. *What have I done?*

Silence but for the soughing wind rising, falling, breathing agitated floats and tumbles of leaves round them, between them.

Contempt tensed her features a bitter twist. She shook her head, disgusted at his lack of answer which in turn provided his answer. She removed from him a step, then another, her eyes drawing tight and framing the shame entering full bloom in her condemning stare—shame for him.

"You were supposed to be better than this." Her scorn of words brittle yet cutting. "You were supposed to save lives." She untied the belt from round her waist and divided her cloak. "The last Soothsayer." She spat the words out while raising her hands up behind her, questing for dachras. "How disappointing."

Boots grinding the ground for surer purchase, she lowered into the beginnings of a fighter's crouch in preparatory pounce, lithe body shifting through minute adjustments, the violet stabs of her eyes hunting vital targets.

"Wait!" He withdrew two steps and threw his hands up between them, palms out. *What in friggin hell am I doing?* "Please, just . . . wait."

She maintained her coiled position, hands still hidden up behind her cloak at the ready for pulling those dachra fangs. She said nothing.

Banzu lowered his hands, expelled a withering breath. "I don't want to do this. Again. And I don't want to hurt you. Ever. I just . . . gods!" He raked both hands through his hair, grabbing frustrated tufts of it before releasing his arms into limp dangles. "I'm just trying to do what's right. I thought that's what you wanted."

"What I want is for you to listen." She straightened, arms lowering, hands empty, voice not curt but firm. "You're the last Soothsayer, Ban. You have a duty to uphold whether you like it or not. And revenge is not the way, no matter how right it feels. All revenge does is get people killed while blinding you to everything else that's happening around you."

He looked at her through eyes naked and wounded. "He took Jericho from me. Took you." He paused, the memory of his lips tasting hers a knifing reflection of pleasure nestled in the pain of knowing to her it never happened. "You don't remember us, but I can't forget it. And I can't forget the Khan."

She smiled, brief and wan. "Well I'm here now aren't I?" She spread her hands in gesture of her obvious self. "And I'm not asking you to forget the Khan, just to ignore him for the time being. There's a difference, Ban. Trust me, I promise we'll deal with him later. But for now our focus must be on dealing with the Godstone. Head Mistress knows exactly what to do, and she can explain it better than I can, but our time is limited because of the Veilfall."

He closed his eyes, craned his head and sighed. "I don't even know what that is."

Her touch on his shoulder so that he opened his eyes.

"You trust me and I'll trust you," she said. "That's how this works." A hesitant pause while she considered him a silent length. "You said you love me. Prove it now and listen to me. Don't just hear, listen."

He stared at her in the silence of his breaking heart, while some terrible part of him, down at the core, raised its face to the world with a red grin, welcoming the chance, the excuse, for the coming moments of purity in which his revenge sailed upon the roaring tide of Khan's blood. The rage would sweep away everything else, including the harbored sorrow of his uncle's murder. Including her. And he could no longer fathom his existence without her.

Without her, nothing else matters. Not even the Khan.

He drew in deep then blew out his cheeks and nodded, not so much quelling as shelving the rage for later. "Okay," he said. "Forget the Khan. So what do we do now?"

Her response came warm and immediate, in the form of a satisfied smile.

CHAPTER TWENTY

"So you really want to get to Fist as soon as possible?" Melora asked, and seriously, as though they hadn't just finished arguing over that very subject for the last turn of the hour, told by the sun's westward drift as seen through the scattered breaks in high canopy of treetops overshadowing the clearing below.

Banzu bunched a groan into a mirthless little chuckle. "That's rhetorical, right?"

The slow roll of her eyes. "Obviously."

Chin up and shoulders square, the iron spine of Spellbinder authority back in rigid support of her fiery spirit, she held his gaze a silent beat, daring another interruption before going on, though now the pause betrayed more a frisky tease than any real challenge against him, the arguing behind them, amends fresh between them.

"I wasn't sent here just to find Jericho," she said. "There's something else I need to get before we can leave."

Her gaze followed Banzu's hand drifting up to cover over the ring beneath his shirt, but she shook her head and waved a dismissive hand at his fending gesture.

"Not that. Something else. And I don't have a choice. Which means you don't have a choice. Because I'm not giving you one." Another daring pause accompanied by the softening of her eyes, her voice. "You said you love me—" She paused again, this time her face betraying the slight wince of an uncomfortable unease chasing those words. "But do you trust me?"

He eyeballed her at length in this her moment of his testing, wary of the unexpected changes in his life, suspicious of her wily womanly charms she had and would continue wielding against him, her beauty an unconscious lever upon the conscious fulcrum of her cunning, these tools a natural part of her formidable influence upon men she captured in her clever web of disarming beauty.

You know I do. At least, you did. Before. "Yes."

A triumphant twist of her lips. "Good. Then listen. And don't interrupt. I need to get you to Fist, but the Veilfall has changed things. Now that I've found you I have to get to the nearest Builder's tower before we can—"

"What does a Builder's tower have to do with anything?" he interrupted anyways. And for it earned a scolding frown. He gazed north by habit, unable to view through the dense forest skirting round the clearing though knowing where the closest Builder's tower stood from their current position. Knowing well enough to imagine the structure in his mind's eye of memory so that a precise picture formed.

Academy law forbade anyone entry into the plethora of Builder's towers scattered across the One Land of Pangea, not that the Head Mistress need station any guards to enforce the centuries-old decree considering the deadly magical wards of protection the towers possessed which dispensed unspeakable nasties upon any thieving intruders foolish enough to attempt breaching the protective wards while seeking plunder of any valuables.

Melora continued talking.

But Banzu, locked in stare, captured only faint wisps of words through the distracting flush of curious zeal piquing his interests at the prospect of actually entering a Builder's tower after a lifetime of only staring at one from afar in unfed wonder. So long as he stayed inside her void-aura they could walk through the tower's protective magics without earning so much as a scratch. Enthusiastic wheels of fantastical speculation spun round in his head, conjuring images of jewel-encrusted weapons atop golden spills of treasure between scattered stacks of arcane spell books and—

Snap! and he flinched alert at her fingers snapping inches from his nose, demanding his attentions back.

"Huh? What?"

She lowered her hand. "I said—" But she paused, sighed, shook her head. "Never mind. I'm not repeating all that. Are you always this abstracted?"

His brow furrowed. "What's abstracted?"

"Distrait."

He shrugged. *Uhm.* "What's distrait?"

"Inattentive."

Oh. "No."

"Absentminded," she continued. "Scatterbrained. Oblivious."

He frowned. "I'm not—"

"Waddlefooted. Stumpheaded. Mudfaced. Woolbrained."

He scowled. "Now you're just making words—"

"Wouldn't know your bung from a hole in the ground because your head's so far up your own—"

"Okay okay! I get it. Pay attention." He glanced north. "So what's in there and why do we need it?"

"Maybe if you'd listened."

Another glance north. "I'm listening now."

"Too late."

He overemphasized a frown. "Come on."

She smirked. "Spellbinder business, that's what. For me to know and you to find out. And until we're Paired in Fist, you're on a need-to-know basis. Now look, I don't remember a single thing about anything you've claimed has happened—"

He opened his mouth to interject while she talked right over him.

"*—buuut* I'm willing to believe your whole 'I'm from the future' business if you're willing to trust me and do what I say when I say it."

"Oh, is that how Pairs work? You say jump and I jump?"

She feigned surprise. "See? Paying attention's not so hard after all."

He frowned, mumbled, "I've got your attention right—"

"What's that?" She cupped an ear, pretending for a better listen. "You'll have to speak up." Then removed her hand into a fist between them. "I can't hear you over me thinking so loudly about punching you in the mouth again."

He huffed a very terse and very low breath. "Nothing."

"That's right." She touched at her chest, indicating herself and all Spellbinders in general. "We've been guardians of the memories and knowledge hidden by the Builder's Veil for over three-hundred years while the rest of the world forgot and carried on. Before the Veilfall, if I'd said anything to you about it or the Godstone you would've forgotten it seconds after I spoke of it."

He nodded while reflecting back through memories not so much forgotten as hanging on the cusp of recollection, that strange *shshshshsh*'ing recall of her voice from before his re-beginning, before the supposed Veilfall, her words vanishing soon as she spoke them to Jericho while Banzu listened to her longwinded tale of finding him.

She must've been talking about the Veilfall or the Godstone or both, then. At least now they're sticking. Proof, I guess, that this Veilfall thing is real.

"But that's over with," she continued. "The Veil's gone now. Lifted yesterday. Though I still don't know why you can't remember." She gestured her hand between them, shooing the subject away for another. "Regardless, knowledge is power. True power. And Spellbinders were the only ones exempt from the world-wide memory-wipe of the Veil's effects. That's why with Pairs it's a Spellbinder's duty to lead and her Soothsayer's duty"—she pointed at him as her lips curled round the word for emphasis—"to *follow* her lead."

"We're not Paired yet," he said in defensive response, wincing at the words cutting deeper than expected though more so at the memories those words elicited, knifing and raw, fresh with ache.

Before his re-beginning, after she rescued him from the chillfever's frigid brink of death, she expected to Pair with him soon as they reached Fist. She even kissed him again and yet for the first real time, no brief joining of their lips but the long melding of their mouths exchanging equal flares of passion and promise, the shields of her guarded heart lowered, Banzu's own bursting with the profound joy of budding love. Until his world plummeted into a downward spiral of loss and regret and pain thereafter.

Pain.

So resonate, so tender, he almost spoke the word aloud.

Nothing good ever came without pain in his life. Dead parents. A life spent hiding. Hard years of swordslinger training. Suspecting everyone, trusting no one but his uncle, and even Jericho only so far while his possible return to the bloodlust existed as a festering boil between them begging for lancing, threatening to burst at Banzu's turned back so that he lived in a constant state of unease knowing no true relax, always sleeping with his bedroom door locked and one of their practice swords lying beside him hand on hilt. Pain had a way of making you appreciate its absence all the more, same as its cruel way of not letting you forget how you'd earned it and why.

"I'd hoped," he said then paused, rumbled his throat clear. "I'd hoped when I came back that everything would be the same between us. But—"

But there he clipped short, averting his gaze down at his feet—then at Melora's booted toes stepping into view when she closed distance between them.

"Banzu." She tucked a hand beneath his chin and lifted it to better meet his troubled eyes. Her probing gaze waded through the sullen depths of his moon-eyed stare while she held him there with a kind smile in the fantastic capturing of spider and fly. "Ban."

He returned a wan smile leaving his eyes untouched, afraid of initiating the full reveal of it in display of his anxious heart. *It can be again*, those stark violets shining with sweet invitation implied. Only he suspected the conception of those words born from his mind playing tricks through false hope to the response he craved for hearing if only she would speak it aloud and prove him wrong.

Gods, if only she could remember. His lips formed budding words unvoiced, thoughts scattering of all motives but his strong desire for the tall beauty standing within grabbing distance so that he flexed his hands with appetite while enduring the tremendous ache of wanting to pull her closer by the hips, to kiss her long and sure same as before yet now for the first time again.

He trembled with compulsive need. He reached up without word and took hopeful hold of her hand tucked beneath his chin, claimed it inside his gentle grasp, raised it, intent on kissing it and—

"No." Melora slide her hand loose from his as she withdrew from him a space, apprehensive, uncomfortable, shielded in reluctance and refusal. "I . . . we . . ." But she trailed away unfinished.

Silence.

He lowered his empty hand, suffering the withering pang of expecting too much from her too soon so that he condemned his errant slip of open affection. *Stupid. If I pull too hard too quick I'll only push her away. Friggin hell! Why is this so godsdamned complicated?*

And yet . . . and yet. *But she's alive again. There's that much at least. A second chance to reconnect those Source-severed ties between us anew. Stronger, even. Now that I don't have to hide who I really am from her anymore. And no worries of triggering my bloodlust either, thank gods.*

Though the Khan's hunting Trios . . . *more will come for her. And let them. She has me now. No one will ever hurt you again, Melora, I swear. And I swear to gods I'll kill everyone who tries.*

Though with their journey diverted to the Builder's tower, at least some of the threats they encountered before they could bypass now. However painful the erasure, having lived the future once already provided him certain unique advantages.

"I'm sorry," he said. "I shouldn't have—"

"Forget it." A wan smile toyed at one corner of her mouth while the uncomfortable air cleared between them, the moment there then gone. In teasing tone she added, "Silly boy."

He smirked. Drew in deep, collecting himself while shrugging an invisible burden from his shoulders. *At least she didn't slap me. Baby steps. Little by slowly.*

"Well," he said, "I'm yours for the asking. So if you say tower then tower it is."

She smiled, jubilant, as though she just won something.

***

Banzu picked up his rucksack, slung it to his back and walked north. The sooner to the Builder's tower, the sooner to Fist.

Five steps away, a glance behind, and he stopped, turned round. "You coming?"

Melora answered nothing, too intent with unfolding her map.

"It's okay," he said. "We don't need it."

She peeked over the half-unfolded map, eyebrows pinching together. "Why not?"

"I've lived on these mountains practically my whole life." He hitched his right thumb over his shoulder. "The closest Builder's tower is that way. I could close my eyes and still find it."

"Oh." She lowered the map to her thighs. "Right." Then folded it into a tiny square and tucked it away beneath her cloak. "I guess we go that way then."

She strode past him—and staggered mid step, stumbling for balance, legs unhinging at the knees.

"Whoa." He caught her by the arm, preventing her full collapse. "Careful."

She swooned on her feet.

"Are you okay?" he asked. "Maybe you should sit."

"No." She straightened, eyes aflutter. "I'm okay. I'm just a little lightheaded. It'll pass."

He cursed himself for not thinking well enough ahead. "I forgot you haven't eaten anything in days." Two days? Three? Since that last Trio began chasing her, and they only the latest in a long line of Trios pursuing her from Fist for almost two exhaustive years. "The last time, you were so tired you passed out in our chair while—never mind. Doesn't matter. The day's half past already. And it's a long hike to the tower. We'll camp here. You can rest while I hunt us up something to eat."

"No." Voice sharp and curt, she mustered up taller, rebuking his words in challenge while feigning reserves of energies unspent behind a false smile. "We've wasted enough time as it is. And the Veilfall's only shortened it. I'll be fine. Come on. The tower's waiting."

With that she strode away north, determined to close as much distance as possible between them and the tower before nightfall without asking how far the long hike.

He watched her go. *Headstrong to a fault. Stubborn as ever. I try stopping her and she'll just drag me there by the shorthairs.* So he followed after her, hoping that fiery spirit didn't burn her out on her feet. *It's good to have her back.*

***

Trekking through forest, Banzu guided them upon the surest routes along the meandering branches of northbound trails weaving through the woodlands while Melora extrapolated intermittent pieces about the Veilfall, though otherwise little conversation played between them for the physical hike up or down or round steep hills studded with dense thickets of aspens, stands of towering oaks, and scatters of bushy evergreens their needles dripping glistening melts of frost damping patches of ground muddy. Though there remained plenty of crisped leaves crunching underfoot atop loose bits of scree threatening twisted ankles so that Banzu's experienced eye roved cautious and he pointed these out before Melora turned a foot thereon by accident, spraining an ankle or worse breaking her leg.

A protective magical barrier the Builder god Enosh wove into existence at the end of the Thousand Years War, the Veil not so much erased as blocked the world's populace from remembering specific aspects of the war, knowledge of the Godstone especially.

Unable to eliminate the entire past from everyone's memories or else the Veil's magic would fail from being stretched too thin, Enosh instead *poked holes* in it—Melora's term—while leaving the rest as historical common knowledge. And for some reason she said only the Head Mistress could explain, Banzu was bound to it all, had triggered the Veilfall the moment he killed Jericho and became the last Soothsayer. At that, though, her knowledge ended short.

He contemplated all this while speaking none of it, unsure what disturbed him more: living his entire life ignorant of the Veil's existence, or that the previous version of her could have already explained as much to him before only he forgot it soon as she spoke it.

But why can't I *remember?* With the Veil's lifting, she assured him everyone remembered those repressed memories, thus the Veilfall's purpose. Yet he possessed no inkling of the Veilfall or the Godstone. *Why me alone?*

He strained for remembrance though earned nothing for it, and put no voice behind the grim conclusion. *Maybe I'm not supposed to remember?*

He shirked the enigma aside for later dealing, easier to just go along instead of concentrating to the point of headache. *The Head Mistress will know. And Aggie . . . Jericho would want her to have his ring.*

Besides, enough to consider in front of him already given the changes after his re-beginning. Not that Melora answered his questions about what awaited them inside the Builder's tower but for Spellbinder business punctuated with a sly smirk and a half-lidded glance so he stopped prodding the guarded subject.

Miles of hiking in silence strayed his attentions to more relaxing play of focus on the pleasant sways of her glides and shifts while he trailed behind her dogged pace a few steps in fondling gaze, content with watching her, enjoying her, appraising all of her.

At one point she stepped through a golden bar of sunlight beaming down through a small break in the high canopy, it making magic of her pale-blonde hair for precious seconds. He walked in envy of that patch of sunlight sliding over her, moving unopposed the length of her tall and supple figure, accentuating the subtle curves of her shoulders and swaying hips and . . . and there alluring memories from their time together before his re-beginning drifted in to haze over all other activity occupying his tiring thinker, wonderful memories of them lying bundled up naked and together while her void-aura burned the chillfever's infection from his shivering body, gradually edging him back from the precipice of freezing to death just by existing next to him.

Only one moment in an unmarked hundred shared between them, a single atom of event from a future erased, but the beautiful reflection of memory forever nestled in his heart stole his breath again same as the reality of waking naked to her lying in sleeping cling against him had then.

Waking to the mild *thump-thumping* of her heartbeat's soft patter, their bodies slick with shared sweat, the swaddle of blanket wound round them in a peaceful cocoon. The slow pattern of her breathing while she slept curled against him in embracing clutch. The hot tickle of her breath first upon his neck then against his ear when she shifted in her sleep and her closed lips brushed ever so gently against his skin, parting.

He closed his eyes, smiling, drifting back, clutching at memory, squeezing it, returning life into it, blooming it vivid and sure in his mind's eye, afraid not remembering would fade it.

A particular bead of sweat among the rest when at last she awoke then untangled herself from him into standing, the slow roll of it tracing down her slender neck, trailing between her small breasts, trickling farther over her smooth stomach then lower still where it caught as glistening dew upon the curly shorthairs of her honey-colored thatch above creamy bare thighs.

He cringed, eyes snapping open, frowning that it never really happened, that precious peace shared between them, not to this version of her. The icy clutch of bitter truth gripped him by the heart and squeezed, cold and unforgiving.

I've lost so much. Too much. Those times are gone now, erased by my re-beginning in all but my memory. And only that until time fades them like all forgotten things. He fetched a deflating sigh. *But we can make new memories now. Together.*

Before his re-beginning he possessed a strong though unfocused urge to prove himself and the desire to do right. She strengthened and harnessed that urge beyond what he ever believed possible before knowing her. But his cleansing of the bloodlust and the killing of his uncle tempered his soul in a white-hot crucible, and ever since he felt more someone else. Same but different. Changed. Altered. Reshaped. Corners sanded sharper. Edges more defined.

And he feared his brief testing seize of the Source in the moments after killing Jericho planted the seeds of madness delivered from a thousand dead Soothsayers screaming in his head, the full raging Power of the Source untouched since Simus Junes' recurrent battles against the Nameless One crashing through him in daunting waves, avalanches of memories unlived dizzying him, shattering the fragile depths of him, while knifing through his mind in rapid and raucous vertigo flashes so that he only assumed himself still sane.

No. I would know. Crazy people put their own sanity on trial against the supposed insanity of the rest of the world while never realizing they were the real crazy one. But no, crazy people possessed no notion of their broken mind, a fact making their madness all the more real. *Wouldn't I?*

Not that he could ask Melora anyhow. *Am I crazy?* The question itself would elicit its own unwanted response.

His left hand gripped Griever's hilt in a reassuring hammer-fist of pulsing squeezes while hot whispers unraveled through his mind, teasing upon the fringe of his questioned sanity. And, to his shock, prompting response.

'Why are you wasting precious time traipsing through these woods? You have a Khan to kill! She's slowing you down, you fool. Just be rid of her already and be on your way to—'

Banzu jolted tensed, tripping stopped. He shuddered and shook the voice loose through a series of rapid blinks. *Who in friggin hell . . .*

"You coming?"

"Huh?" He looked up at Melora watching him from halfway up the next hill. "Oh. Yeah. I'm coming."

No. Not just maybe. I am different.

* * *

Hours later and they stopped to make camp in the lee of a large pinewood while daylight faded into velvet night, the gliding chill of the dying winter's reminder sweeping in upon the rising winds shivering through the trees with added bite this close north to the Thunderhell Tundra.

Melora plopped down for a rest, every inch of her slumping. Then transferred herself with a Thanks and a smile to Banzu's bedroll after he rummaged through his rucksack and—removing his purple boot coverings from his boots and tucking them away, seeing no good point in wearing them—laid the softer pallet beside her, unrolling it in two flapping shakes accompanied by a smile and the inviting wave of his hand.

"What are those anyways?" she asked of the purple coverings he'd stowed away.

He smirked. "Remember how I told you Jericho slipped away after you fell asleep in our chair? Well—" He paused, then just spilled it all out. "He said Aggie stole them from a Builder's tower. That's part of how he escaped the Academy. They're magic. And they make every one of your steps ten."

Melora thinned her tired eyes into suspicious slits upon his rucksack. "Really."

"I don't know the words to activate them though," he said. "Jericho never told me. I can't use them, but—"

"But we'll return them to the Head Mistress," she finished for him, her firmer tone brooking no argument. She added in self-whisper, "So that's how he did it. Son of a . . ."

Banzu bit back a chuckle. Stood and went about quick business.

Melora sat hugging her knees to her chest and watching him, eyes wondrous blooms too slow in darting while he sped round outside her void-aura in blurring shifts of Power-flickers while gathering several armloads of sticks, one man accomplishing the work of several in seconds. After which, and still outside the magic-nullifying expanse of her void-aura, he rubbed two sticks together into burning life, his hands a vigorous blur of Powered motion, then he carried them aflame to the piled kindling and, squatting down, set their fire for the night.

"Impressive," she said, tired eyes agleam with active wonder.

"Thanks." He suppressed a cocky grin while feeding sticks into the growing hearth, its flickering light turning every woodsy shadow surrounding them into a watching face. "The Power has its advantages."

"Is that what you call it? The Power?"

He shrugged an ease of freedom at talking so openly about it. "That's what Jericho always called it, so yeah. It feeds off my lifeforce though, so I don't like using it unless I have to. But it's cold, so I figured I'd hurry the fire along."

She smirked, then covered her mouth to stifle a yawn, and grimaced at the rumble of her empty belly. "I don't suppose . . ."

"I'm hungry too." He smiled and stood. "I'll go hunt us up something to eat. You rest. You need it." He turned and started away. "I'll be back."

"Wait. In the dark?"

He turned round, walking backwards. "The Power takes care of that too."

Another yawn stifled her reply. She stretched out her legs while inching forward on her bottom and spread her feet beside the fire.

He spun away—and stopped, taking notice of the light white dusting falling, tiny crystals these, the kind so perfect they almost chimed against the ground.

We're higher, farther north. She'll be cold.

He returned to his rucksack, dug out his only blanket. When he turned round he paused, spellbound by the sight of her sitting there with her head craned, eyes closed and mouth open, waiting for a snowflake to chance drifting into the warm cave of her accepting mouth, the soft flexing fireglow dancing over her pretty features just so, making of her a thing of pure beauty.

"Last snow of the year," he said, smiling at the sight of her, the soft sound of her music when she captured a snowflake and laughed, the wad of blanket forgotten bunched in his hands. "It won't last long."

And it didn't. Only minutes. But it made her look an angel while he stood watching her licking at stray snowflakes, wishing the moment could last forever. If he could stop time, this would be one of those special moments in his life for doing so.

But the moment passed with him just standing watch.

She shivered and scrunched her face, nose crinkling in that angry-cute way of hers, while administering her kohatheen an annoyed and wincing tug, her mood turning foul. "Godsdamned thing's soaking up the cold."

"Here." He rounded the fire. "Let me help you with that."

She followed him with her drowsy gaze flinching alert. She twisted on her bottom while he moved then squatted behind her and set the blanket aside to free his hands.

"What do you think you're doing?" She straightened tensed from some reserve store of energy he assumed walked out of her miles ago when he took her by the shoulders and squared her facing straight and away.

"Easy." He gave her resisting shoulders a gentle squeeze. "I'm not going to hurt you. Just relax."

But she huffed and twisted round, back stiff, eyes suspicious slits over her shoulder. "What are you doing?"

"I trust you and you trust me, remember? Now it's your turn."

Scowling, she eyeballed him a silent length. Then squared her shoulders straight. "Fine. But if your hands get gropy they're coming off."

"Tilt your head forward."

She hesitated. "Why?"

He sighed. "So I can take the kohatheen off."

"You're wasting your time. You don't even know how to—"

He shushed her quiet.

She turned then tilted her head forward. "I'm watching you."

"I'm sure you are." He parted her long hair then tugged down the back of her cloak and shirt the few necessary inches for the kohatheen collar locked round her neck. A gentle spin of it and he turned its locking mechanism into exposed position for his working fingers.

"She was supposed to put that on me," whispered Jericho's ghost of voice in his head, giving his fingers brief pause and his stomach a queasy punched-in-the-guts clench. *"If I didn't agree to go—"*

But Banzu banished the haunting reminder from his mind with a quick shake of his head and worked the tiny tumblers into their proper placements of alignment with the precise manipulations of his nimble fingertips, the task at first a chore for he only ever unlocked a kohatheen once before, though the puzzle of little tumblers proved easy enough with direct attention, their purpose impossible for the wearer themselves to unlock. A minute passed before he achieved the satisfying *click*.

Melora flinched as if pricked.

He swung the unlocked kohatheen open from round her neck, revealing a red ring of rubbing on her alabaster skin that burned in him the strong desire for leaning forward and kissing it well. It took everything in him not to make that affectionate mistake—*no, too much too soon, don't push it*—and instead leaned back while providing her sore neck that kissing comfort only in his mind.

"Oh my gods." She rubbed round the redness of her bothered neck. "You did it?" She rolled her head from shoulder to shoulder, moaning low pleasure. "You did it. *Ahhhh*, that's *soooo* much better."

He stood, all smiles, the cold kohatheen in his hands forgotten for the joy of having eased her pain, basking in the comfort of having repaired one of the numerous broken links in the proverbial chain of their erased relationship mending little by slowly.

She twisted and caught him with a smile over her shoulder. Their gazes held, the moment brief before she turned away, but he swore he spied the barest twinkle of their shared history's reflection in her eyes, imaginary or not, the possible lingering trace of him from before his re-beginning existing somewhere therein the housing of her mind, buried deep.

No. Impossible. She can't remember . . . can she?

He looked down at the kohatheen and frowned, black memories sweeping in, those of closing this same kohatheen round Jericho's neck so that he blinked hard, banishing the cruel reminder. He considered turning round and throwing the foul tool of aizakai enslavement away into the darkness where it could stay forever for all he cared. Instead he rounded past Melora and, snapping the kohatheen back together wholly O, held it out in a playful half-bow.

"Your necklace, Mistress."

"Necklace my foot." She snatched the thin lanthium hoop from his hands and scowled at it. "Wait a minute." Scowled up at him. "Where'd you learn how to do that?"

That's not the first time I've unlocked it. A sly smirk pursed his lips. He said nothing.

She considered his silence overlong then mumbled her thanks and set the kohatheen aside.

"What was that?" He cupped a hand to his ear in exaggerated lean and listen. "Did you just say something?"

Her eyes flared then thinned. She opened her mouth for feisty rebuttal, then softened her voice. "Thank you."

"You're welcome." He turned away to the fire, squatted and fed in a few more sticks. "So . . . what's in the tower?" he asked in his best casual voice, hoping to catch her off guard in a distracted slip of her tongue.

"Nice try." She lay down and shimmied on the bedroll, making herself a comfortable nest before drawing the blanket over her. "Wake me when there's something to eat."

Friggin hell. Banzu lingered, focusing on the crackling fire.

CHAPTER TWENTY-ONE

Forearms resting on knees in a hunched squat, hands dangling between spread thighs, flickering firelight skating across his face, Banzu blew out his cheeks, venting a weary sigh, while staring at the fire, his not-so-subtle plan of filching information from Melora about what awaited them inside the Builder's tower failing as expected.

Though in truth he applied their destination no more deliberation beyond getting there and taking whatever she required so they could continue to Fist posthaste. All mental avenues led to killing Hannibal Khan regardless the direction he diverted his inquisitive sights, his conscious feeder streams of resolve flowing into their mother river gushing red with Khan's blood.

Lingering, he poked at the fire with a stick, shifting orange glows of coals while disturbing a few crackling pops and twinkles of firefly embers dancing the chill breeze in lazy floats. Procrastination finished, he pushed on his thighs and stood, intent on hunting down some food before sleep, though he paused while staring overlong into the fire at his feet. "I hope it all works out this time."

Behind him a yawn and sounds of bedroll shifting. "It will," Melora said. "And if it doesn't then you can just do your little time travel thingy and go back again." A longer yawn. "Or whatever it is you claim you did."

Claim. The word pricked him while dispute flourished then withered at the back of his throat. He raised his gaze to the black pitch, vision readjusting, and swore to the faint soughing of Jericho's distant voice haunting back at him from somewhere unseen.

"It doesn't work like that," he said. "I can't go back again." In lower voice he added, "If I could—" *If I could I'd figure out some way of keeping Jericho alive too.* But he clipped short, thoughts flexing backwards.

I've cleansed the Power of the bloodlust curse, but the Source . . . he suspected it still rife with the threat of bloodlust madness. *All those screams, all those memories, the shared collective of a thousand dead Soothsayers seeking to crush me in an avalanche of our combined Power's promise.* So new and raw, he understood none of the why of it all and so refused tapping into the Source again by restricting himself to only using the Power. At least until he figured out the . . . the wrongness of it pervading his cautious bones.

Behind him she voiced an "Oh" stretched overlong through another yawn. Losing to exhaustion, only half-listening in her waxing drowse, hearing him more than listening.

He snapped off an inches-long piece from his stick then tossed the short bit into the fire and watched it burn while reflecting inward for a quiet time. So confident everything would be the same upon his return, and yet so many things had changed—were changing still.

She's in my life again. I've got what I wanted most. But the Veilfall, triggered with my re-beginning, why? I just want her. But with her restored so is Hannibal Khan. I brought him back, godsdammit. And how much of that is different too? What if I've made it worse somehow? What if—

He swallowed the hot rise of ire flushing for release inside, taming it from edging his voice when he asked, "Do you think he's still in Junes?"

"What?" An agitated little grumble from behind. "Who?"

You know who. "Hannibal Khan."

A groaning sigh. "We've been over this already. I'm tired. And hungry. And you're annoying. Stop thinking and start doing. Food. Bye."

He turned round, gripping the stick in both hands, bending it pliable through agitated back-and-forth flexes while he gazed down over her. *Two years since she fled Junes, too long away to know the true answer.* But he craved the reassurance if only for the comfort of her lie. "He has to still be there, right? I mean, where else would he be?" He paused—no answer—then prodded her with another, "Right?"

A low-throated growl. She opened her eyes and glared up at him, voice curt. "Let it go, Ban."

He snapped the stick in half—*crack!*

"Feel better?" she asked, frowning. "Good. Then wake me when you've fetched some grub." She rolled left, facing away, and drew up the blanket into a fetal curl, her voice a grumbling mumble. "Already said . . . Head Mistress . . . Fist . . . sleep . . . go away."

Jaws bunching taut, teeth gnashing, he spun to the fire and glared into its glowing heart while images flashed behind his eyes, hot and savage and satisfying, of thrusting Griever's thirsting steel into the Khan's chest, of watching the lifespark snuff therein those eyes startling to Griever's wrenching twist punctuated by Banzu delivering Jericho's name as the last words Hannibal Khan would ever hear.

Then stop wasting time and do it!

He shuddered through a flush of anger stealing into his voice while his mind diverted down a different set of tracks. "I don't know why you can't just tell me what's in the friggin tower."

"Shut up, Ban."

"You act like it's some precious godsdamned secret. Like I'm not going to find out when we get there anyways."

"Shut *up*, Ban."

"I swear to gods if I'm wasting my time—"

"Oh my gods!" she yelled at his turned back. "You don't stop, do you?"

He chucked his two bits of broken stick into the fire, one ill-aimed and bouncing out so that he kicked it back in then stomped on it while stirring up a flurry of embers round his crunching boot.

"I just"—*stomp, stomp*—"want some"—*stomp, stomp*—"friggin answers!"

More frustrated stomping while he grumbled out a string of curses, uncaring of his smoking boot or its wafting stink of burned leather. He cursed again at having stamped out the fire to nothing more than glowing coals so that he squatted and fed more sticks while blowing fire to life.

"You want answers?" She rolled over, glaring at his hunched back, then erupted into sitting up. "Fine! Then listen up because I'm only going to say this once."

He twisted on his heels and regarded her sideways.

She said, "The Khan and the Enclave invaded Junes for Dethkore's soulring so they can resurrect him and—"

"I already know—" he began.

"Shut up! So they can resurrect him and through him control an army of the unliving to attack Fist for the Head Mistress's Book of Towers. In it are secrets passed down from Head Mistress to Head Mistress that date back to before the Academy's founding, most important to the Enclave the locations of the rest of the scattered pieces to the Dominator's Armor. Hannibal Khan already has the gauntlets. Now he wants the rest to become a living god."

She held seething pause, bared teeth a white glean, her eyes a feral glare daring another interruption.

"That was their plan," she continued. "But this isn't about the Khan anymore. They remember the Godstone now along with every godsdamned greedy outlaw from Junes to the Rift because of the Veilfall. And unless we find it first and destroy it, the Enclave will start another Thousand Years War just like they did the first time the Godstone released. Only now there's no Simus Junes or Grey Swords or aizakai army to stop them."

Her voice raised an octave while she pointed accusation at him in the form of a stiff finger, shaking it with venomous emphasis.

"*You're* the last Soothsayer. *You* caused the Veilfall. So it's *your* duty to make things right." She slapped at her chest. "And *I'm* here to make sure of it." She pounded the ground with her fist. "Can I get some godsdamned sleep now?"

Not waiting for reply, she slapped her hand atop the kohatheen beside her, gripped it, raised it between them so that her piercing glare stabbed him through the lanthium hoop's hollow.

"Or do I have to wrestle this on you to shut you up?" She slapped the kohatheen back to ground and raised him another admonishing point of her jabbing finger. "And don't think I won't. Or can't. Because I—" A hard yawn cut her short, prompting her all the angrier. "Because I will if you don't stop pestering me and let me get some godsdamned sleep!"

Stunned mute for a pause, Banzu narrowed his eyes at her threat and the added sting of her Veilfall accusations tossing his mood fouler so that he stood, ounces of him bunching taut, fists strangling grips of air.

"That doesn't tell me why we're wasting time here," he said through clenched teeth. "So maybe I'll just be on my way and you can catch up after you're done with your stupid tower."

She flared then thinned her eyes, her mouth opening then closing in a snap of teeth. She whipped the blanket aside and drew her feet in, seconds from bursting up and pouncing at him tooth and nail so that he took a half-step back from her regardless the challenge of his stance.

"You want to start walking your happy ass back to Fist?" she asked, legs compacted coils beneath her hunching crouch. "Then you're more than welcome to try." Threat tightened her eyes, warning her voice. "But you won't make it very far, I can promise you that."

Silence but for the grinding of his teeth, anger and lust all mingled hot together so that he wanted to punch her and kiss her at the same time. Instead he raised his gaze past her, east in vehement stare, then back to her.

"No," he said. "I lost you once. I'm not losing you again."

She huffed, scowling. "Get this through your thick skull." Voice flaring. "I'm not yours to lose!"

He flinched at her cold slap of words squashing his anger into the depths of him where it compacted into a dense ball of hurt. He opened his mouth, closed it. Averted his gaze.

"Banzu—" She paused, huffed another terse breath. "This world cannot survive another Thousand Years War," she continued in a tone less heated. "We don't have the numbers anymore. Millions were killed, Ban. Not hundreds. Not thousands. Not hundreds of thousands. Millions. Dethkore is an evil far worse than

Hannibal Khan. The Khan is a power-hungry tyrant, but Dethkore—"

She paused through betraying shiver. "There's good reason why he's called the Eater of Souls, Ban. And as much as you want the Khan dead, he's nothing compared to that godsforsaken necromaster the Enclave is trying to raise. Or they already have by now for all I know. And if they get their grubby hands on the Godstone there'll be no stopping them this time. If you go walking in there all ate up with hate and hunting for death then that's exactly what you'll find. You can't kill what is already dead. But there's ways of stopping it. Do you understand now? Is any of this sinking in yet?"

She sank back onto her bottom, relaxing from her preparatory crouch. "Our only hope is if the Enclave does resurrect him then he and the Khan will turn on each other. Buy us time while we find the Godstone before anyone else and destroy it. The Veilfall's given us no other choice."

He stared at her while chewing on his bottom lip, staying regrets from loosing forth. *It all comes back to the Veilfall. Back to me. My fault.*

He turned away, rounded the fire and sat opposite her in brooding hunch, hands trembling furies flexing squeezes of air, sinews snapping, knuckles popping. He hungered for someone to strangle—anyone—and appease the tensions.

She watched him for a time then asked, "Were you like this before?"

"Like what?"

"Angry," she said, her face an unpretty twist. "Mean." A pause, the softening of her melancholic voice. "So full of hate."

He flinched. *Hate?* "No, I . . ." He flipped his palms inward, stared at them overlong, then looked up, wincing and wounded by her scrutinizing gaze assessing him, dissecting him, weighing and measuring the disassembled parts of him for the core of their binding whole. His anger—no, his rage, burned a molten course through his veins, pulsing savage beats of askance with every furious throb of his unrequited heart.

"I'm sorry. It's just—" He rumbled his throat clear of edge and began again in kinder tone, needing to voice the fierce pull on his heart. She deserved no less than honesty. "I don't care about the tower. I don't care about the Veilfall. I don't care about the Godstone. I don't care about Dethkore. What I care about is you. But—"

"So you weren't listening," she said, frowning. "Figures. You stumpheaded—"

"I wasn't finished."

She considered him a pregnant pause. "Finish."

"But you need to know this. Whatever happens in Fist, whatever you and your Head Mistress have planned for me, none of it trumps killing Hannibal Khan. I made a promise, and I won't break it. No matter what. Hannibal Khan is going to die by my hands for what he did to Jericho if it's the last thing I do."

"Oh my gods you're exhausting." She closed her eyes and rubbed at their inside corners with pointer and thumb. She hung her head, shook it then raised it. Sighed and snapped her eyes open. "Don't make me say it, Ban."

He cocked an eyebrow. "Say what?"

She considered him overlong, chewing on her words before the spit. "Hannibal Khan didn't kill Jericho. You did. And the sooner you accept it the better off you'll be."

Guts clenching, face scrunching, body tensing, indignant anger flaring up his throat from the guttural depths of him, he yelled, "I did it for you!"

His booming shout blared through the darkness where routed animals unseen. He erupted into standing, seething, blood clubbing pounds behind his accusing glare, his hand squeezing Griever's hilt in a strangler's grip eager for pulling while a red haze misted over his vision in throbbing cadence to his quickening pulse coursing hot through his swell of veins in torturous sluices of molten grief.

Startled by his outburst, Melora rocked forward into preparatory crouch, cautious and guarded, one hand beneath her open cloak and up behind her back, the other gripping the kohatheen beside her. Not angry—she moved past that now—but calculating of the moment teetering on the verge of another fight.

Outburst expelled, rage clearing to the touch of fear betraying her wary stare against him, Banzu removed his hand from Griever's leather-wound hilt, fingers peeling free in slow release, his voice a brittle whisper when next he spoke. "I did it for you." He plopped down, raked trembling hands back through his hair, stared at the ground between his V'd knees, afraid of meeting those twin violet stabs. "I'd never hurt you." *What in friggin hell is wrong with me? It's like someone else . . . keeps taking control.* "Never."

Silence but for the risen winds soughing through the trees and delivering new chill so that he glanced up, gave an absent flick of his wrist in gesture at the paltry fire between them. "Pull your blanket up. I don't want you getting sick."

Her gaze shrewd and searching then softening, she scrunched her face and smirked.

"What?" An uncomfortable shift on his bottom, the fiddling of fingers, the rise of his eyes. "*What?*"

"You're a living headache, you know that?" She lowered her arm from behind her and flicked her wrist in shooing gesture. "Now go fetch me something to eat before I starve to death." She eased from her crouch and lay down, pulling the blanket up, and rolled facing away—then rolled right back in warning glare. "And don't you even think of slipping in here beside me, you got that? You keep those hands to yourself or you'll lose them."

He swallowed down a chuckle tickling up the back of his throat, the taut tensions between them easing. "Don't flatter yourself."

She thinned her eyes into teasing violet slits then rolled facing away where she mumbled something about the unlikely joining of her foot and his rear if he disturbed her again without food.

* * *

Banzu fed more sticks into the fire before taking leave, ensuring her warmth in his absence, though he paused at the edge of the firelight and watched her for a quiet length.

She vexed him at times, challenged him at every turn, and somehow left him always wanting more. *She sets a fire in me then enjoys watching it burn.*

Their back-and-forth part of the excitement, part of the allure, part of what made tangling with her so frustrating yet enticing. Arousing, even. Both of them natural fighters, and fighters enjoyed conflict, yearned for that tantalizing heat of in-the-moment tension when the air thickened with anticipation for the unforeseen strike while hoping to riposte it then sally your best.

He lingered in reflection, afraid if he took that first step away there'd be no turning back. While thoughts folded over into dark envisaging of Hannibal Khan, the scab he couldn't stop picking, the sore tooth he couldn't quit running his tongue over, the loose thread he couldn't keep from tugging.

He tried cooling the returning swell of anger, hot and foul and leaving no good aftertaste, with a deep nostril inhale and a deliberate swallow. But the burning urge to be off, to kill, proved slow in ebbing. And there came the kicker—he'd never even laid eyes upon the man, possessed no real idea of what the Khan looked like. And yet—

Body tensing taut and rigid, nerves at full stretch, heartbeat a quickening thunder behind his cage of ribs, the rush and roar of blood in his ears . . . Banzu shut his eyes where flashed stolen glimpses catalyzed by the faint whispers of another's fevered ramblings soughing through his mind.

Flickering stutters of memories knifing, of himself but not himself carving a bloody swath with Griever through the shouting rush of Bloodcloaks in a Powered bloodlust maelstrom of severed limbs, a frenzied tumult of decapitations and disemboweling slashes sending bodies and parts of bodies tumbling away while Banzu not Banzu but Jericho strove across the Receiving Room amid his slaughter for Hannibal Khan through buffeting winds making rain of his bloodletting, each life he took and the next absorbed through the bloodlust's nutrient feed of lifeforces invigorating him while priming him with stolen youth and vigor.

His-not-his lambent red eyes pierced the depths of the conjured storm enveloping the Khan in a crackling tornado of obscuring winds, fixing upon that smudge of face hidden therein, seeking to discern any scrap of detail—but for the commencing crash of lightning punching through the exploding roof in a blinding white flash stealing all sight.

Banzu gasped while jolting loose from the assault of his uncle's memories bleeding into him of their own volition in reaping reminder of the future erased. He adjusted back to present through a series of hard blinks. Nothing but dark and trees and Melora lying swaddled in blanket beyond the fire. Panting, sweating, trembling, Banzu flinched at holding Griever out in a double-fisted clutch with no memory of the involuntary pull.

"Gods," he whispered, unsure of himself.

He swallowed with effort while groping for reclamation of sanity's brief abandonment of his faculties, and sheathed Griever to his left hipwing before Melora rolled and caught then assumed Griever's bared steel as some slip of betrayal against her. He drew in deep, raked a hand back through his damp tangles and blew out his cheeks, seeking calm and control while assessing his precarious grasp of both. He'd structured his life round that necessity. Control of emotions. Control of the sword. Control of the Power. Control slipping loose since cleansing the bloodlust and tapping the Source.

His gaze darted while faint laughter haunted through the dark. *No, not out there but in here.* He closed his eyes, willing the laughter gone, unsure if it had ever been there at all. In self-whisper he asked, "Gods, what's happening to me?"

"What?" Melora rolled over, squinting at him over the fire through heavy lids. "You're still here?"

"Nothing." He forced a smile. "Go back to sleep. I'll wake you when the food's ready."

She rolled away muttering words trailing off into sleepy mumbles.

He lingered at the outskirts of the firelight, shadows cloaking his back warring against the orange flickers dancing his front, for the first time not trusting himself around her. He considered leaving her behind if only for her own safety. It would be so easy . . . and so painful, that separation.

Pain. He scorned the word. *Nothing good ever comes into my life without pain. Not even her. A life for a life.* Then embraced it. *But she's worth all the pain in the world.*

He walked away, shrouded in the dark, harboring gloom.

* * *

Banzu's hunting removed him several miles farther north, and not by chance that he chose the same route they would travel come tomorrow. Scouting ahead as well as seeking food, both tasks fell by the wayside to curious musings of what awaited him in Fist once they finished their tower business here upon the Kush Mountains.

Questions abound. And the Head Mistress held the answers. Melora assured him of that much through his pester of questions. Though how much truth Gwendora Pearce would deliver remained uncertain at best.

Two birds with one stone, whispered an inner voice of recollection.

He sighed, ignoring it, afraid entertaining it would somehow inject realness to the haunting soliloquy. The bloodlust, the Veilfall, the Godstone . . . gods, everywhere he turned there materialized another malfunction twisting the sure course of his life to crooked bend.

The voice pervaded. *My life in exchange for your freedom—*

"Shut up."

Laughter before the voice vanished.

I'm not crazy, I'm grieving. That's all this is. Friggin hell, it's only been a day since I killed—no, murdered the most important person in my life. Eleven years gone with the stroke of my sword. I never even got to tell him sorry. No wonder I'm hearing things. Whispers of guilt, that's what. Get a grip, Ban. That part of you's over. Taken by the Khan. Melora's what matters now. Little by slowly.

He seized the Power again through focal invocation and burst into blurring sprint, packing his festering mourning and all the harbored woes it afforded him into the recess of his stricken heart by concentrating on the here and now, blanking his mind to all but action. He ran for miles through the luminous twilight greys of the woods speeding past, knifing between trees and leaping over patches of briars, his body pure locomotion, enjoying the active stretch of his limbs, the rush of brisk winds breathing across his skin and waking him to the focal thrill of the hunt. Mindless of all but the distracting task at hand.

Searching through the cacophony of insect life an elevated pronouncement chorus of chirps and buzzes, the familiar smell of damp fur a guiding twinge on his ultra keen senses, the throttle of a startled heartbeat captured his attentions.

He sped through a shivering screen of bushes and, dipping low, snatched up the plump white-and-brown spotted mountain hare by the hind legs mid escaping leap. The captured animal thrashed and squirmed while squeaking then surrendered still in his grip. He snapped its neck with a Power-flicker twist of his wrist, then decided on chasing down another hare before returning to camp when his empty stomach protested hungry grumbles.

She hasn't eaten a proper meal in days. Maybe even weeks considering how long her grueling chase. And I haven't eaten in . . . gods, not since the night Jericho killed her. No. That's the other me. The future me. Gone, now. This body ate . . . friggin hell, I can't even remember when. Two days ago? Doesn't matter. I'm hungry and so is she.

But as he moved through the forest by speeding ease of Power-flickers bolting him through rapid stretches, each brief seizing enacting a leaching feed upon his nutrient lifeforce in cruel trade of accelerated aging, he traveled farther than intended, stopped at achieving the upper brim to the giant landscape bowl surrounding the Builder's tower of their destination. He stared down therein, gaze captured by the distant flickering pinpricks of light glowing in the black pitch through deep foliage breaks.

I've never stood this close before. His toes edged the precipice of entry into forbidden territory. Even with Power-enhanced eyesight he perceived little through the thick canopy mesh from his good distance. And many miles to foot before reaching the tower itself standing silent sentinel at the lower natural bowl's center, a tall black builderstone column only the very top of which peeked above the dense foliage surrounding it in a nest of jungle, the strange growth an anomaly to these colder parts of the world.

Within the dark expanse glowed several throbbing spots of light bunched close, these he presumed possible tricks on his eyes wrought from the tower's protective wards of magic. A touch of the Power keening his senses and he sniff-sniff-sniffed the warmer updrafts rising from the natural bowl, swore the faint hint of smoke and burning wood.

He took a step then stopped. Glanced behind. Battled back the urgency for slipping down within for a closer inspection before returning to camp. But such a trek would not be brief, even with the Power affording him supernatural speed, for the strange jungle lush filling the massive landscape bowl thrived in a tangled garden of thick confusion. An odd, hot contrast to the cold mountain upon which it grew. He suspected it the result of the magics radiating from the Builder's tower.

He lingered for minutes while grasping intermittent seizes of the Power, listening to a whole universe of life twittering and buzzing within that jungle bowl, watching diminutive secrets of motion and flitters of shadows disturb the vibrant screen of vegetation filling the colossal crater.

Heightened senses a seduction, he hungered for questing down inside. Instead he stayed his place and breathed deep while gripping the Power, inhaling the tang of the smaller world within the larger whole from afar, tasting the scents of the raw crack of cold rock behind him mixing with the sweet perfume of the warmer mud in front. Despite the cost of accelerated aging, the Power offered something better, an exotic taste of life sampled beyond the sensitive buds of his tongue. In much the same way Melora spiced his palate of life.

He released his inner grasp on the Power with a melancholy sigh. Night's black shroud returned while luminous twilight greys snuffed and his senses normalized, the world and everything in it returning so . . . ordinary again.

Everything but her.

He smiled while smoothing some few wrinkles upon his trampled fabric of life.

It's so good to have her back, even if she remembers nothing of me. Little by slowly. We'll make new memories. Better ones, even.

He turned to leave away, eager for return, yearning to watch those beautiful violet eyes brighten awake and enjoy the smile she afforded him when he presented his catch and she licked her lips in savory presumption of taste.

But he hesitated, turned back and faced the bowl when a flush of curious dread swept through him born from the forbidden tower's alluring cling tugging upon his curious nature.

If only I'd paid attention when she explained it. Too . . . what'd she call it? Abstracted. If I knew what she's after I could go there now and fetch it for her, surprise her with it, then we could be on our way to—no. Stupid. Don't even think it. Without her void-aura I've no safe way inside the tower myself. I try it alone and I'll die for it. No telling what the tower's protective magics will do to me without her. Besides, even with the Power it'll take hours to hack through all that jungle.

Another voice intruded into his inner monologue, faint though harsh and reprimanding, a scolding whisper. *Stop wasting time. We don't need her. We should kill—*

"Shut up," Banzu said, frowning, curt and commanding though holding disturbed pause. *We?*

Silence.

He dismissed the intrusion and turned from the landscape bowl, the dead hare dangling in his fisted grip and still warm. Through focal invocation he seized the Power and, the slowing world bursting to luminous twilight greys flaring his eyes, he sped away south.

* * *

Banzu returned to camp within an hour of his leaving. Melora lay curled and swaddled and sound asleep, her back to the low fire.

He approach in slow creep so as not to disturb her awake, two dead snowshoe hares dangling by their long ears in his fisted grips. After feeding more wood into the fire, he skinned and gutted then spitted the hares. After which he disposed of the entrails, burying them out of camp so as not to draw any unwanted predators. He washed blood from his hands with a waterskin then sat and watched her sleep while turning the spit.

Sweating juices dripped sizzling hisses upon the glowing nest of coals breathing shimmers of heat beneath the roasting meat. Minutes only and Melora roused awake to the delicious smells permeating the air. She sat up sniffing—then startled tensed and twisted sharp while flapping her blanket away, legs drawing beneath her in preparatory crouch for springing from the bedroll.

"It's okay," he said. "It's only me."

"Oh." She relaxed, violet eyes twinkling captured fractures of firelight, her approving smile at the cooking meat between them prompting his in response.

They ate in silence save for her devouring grunts while she tore into her meal with ravenous hunger, the dark trees towering round them watchful giants closing off the rest of the world but for the buzzing whines of insects and occasional distant caws of leathery-winged screecher birds hunting the night's sky afar.

Banzu finished first, affording her the larger of the two hares, tossed his cleaned skeletal pickings into the fire then sat watching her tear through what remained of hers while she gnawed every last speck of meat and gristle from bone.

"Snap the bones and suck the marrow out," he said. "You need the extra nutrients."

She paused mid-nibble, crinkled her nose at the bone held betwixt both pointers and thumbs. "Really?"

He nodded. Fixed his stare into the flickering flames between them where bones blackened and cracked to the backdrop of Melora's lip-smacking chews and approving little moans, the snapping of bones and her suckling of marrow. For a time content . . . until the restlessness to be off for the Khan returned despite the settling meal adding weight to his heavy lids.

I should try pulling more answers from her before she falls back asleep.

But there the blackness of his past folded in again, blurring questions so that he stared deeper into the fire while unwanted memories knifed through his mind . . . of awaking to Melora's tossed head . . . of Jericho's lambent red eyes piercing the dark . . . of the kohatheen she brought to force Jericho back to Fist if he refused her, the same collar resting beside her now.

Banzu relapsed into brooding over what awaited him in Fist, he in exchange for Jericho prompting the Head Mistress's shifting intentions. So consumed with seeing Melora again he afforded the matter little thought beyond getting there. He considered the kohatheen beside her in contemplative stare, one hand an involuntary conscious touch at his neck in phantom strangle of the kohatheen he wanted no part of.

I should've carried it away the moment I unlocked it and buried it somewhere no one would ever find it. For all the good that would do me anyhow. Gwen probably has a hundred kohatheens. No, a thousand. Stores of them. She's the Head Mistress of an Academy full of aizakai. She probably collars every one as punishment who even looks at her wrong.

No. Melora wouldn't let her do that to me . . . would she?

He toyed with the brass necklace of his uncle's silver wedding ring tucked beneath the nape of his shirt, then lowered the agitated fiddling of his hand into his lap.

Maybe I should ask her. Gwen did send her to collar Jericho if he refused. Like a godsdamned dog. If not for Gwen he'd still be alive. Though if not for her I'd of never met Melora.

A life for a life.

He intended a few choice words for Gwendora Pearce when he met her face to face in Fist.

But I have to keep my cool, otherwise my hands'll slip and do some Head Mistress strangling. Then I'll be in a whole heap of trouble. Will Gwen even care Jericho is dead? They were friends once. Good enough that she didn't kill him when she had the chance. And Aggie . . . Locha's Luck I can trust her at least. Maybe. Though who knows how she'll react when I explain what happened and why it's me there instead of Jericho.

Sorry I murdered your husband, Aggie, oh and please don't kill me for it.

Gods, she'll probably skin me alive before I even finish the confession. Maybe I should . . . no, she deserves to know the truth. If not for her intervention I'd already be dead or jailed in the Academy with a kohatheen locked round my neck.

Still, Gwen played her part in all this mess. She's almost as much to blame as the Khan. And whatever she wants of me, she'd better have some friggin answers for the price I've paid. Good ones. Or I swear to gods I'll—I'll—

Glaring at the fire, he spent his irritated energy by popping each of his finger joints.

"Stop that," Melora said. "It's annoying."

He glanced up at those violet stabs of color in her pale-ivory face half-hidden in oranges and shadow, her hood up against the elevated chill and making a cave framing her grimace. "Sorry."

"You glare any harder and your eyeballs'll pop."

He averted his gaze to the fire. "I'm just thinking is all."

"Planning murder more like." She tossed another bone into the fire after sucking out marrow. "You look two shades from killing."

"Maybe I am," he grumbled. *And maybe I'll choke your stupid Head Mistress's stupid head off her stupid shoulders when I see her.* He picked up a pebble and threw it at the fire—and flinched at a thrown bone hitting his chest, its splintered end pricking skin through shirt. "Hey!"

"Hey nothing." She sucked the glistening tip of her finger clean and pointed it at him. "We're not going over this again. Godsdammit Ban, I thought we already settled this. Tower now, Khan later. You can kill him as much as you want after we deal with the Godstone."

"That's not what I was—" But he clipped short with a terse huff of breath, instead voicing truer concerns. "You won't—" He paused, tensing, bracing, fearing the impact of her answer though needing to hear it for true. "You won't let her collar me, will you? Your Head Mistress? When we get to Fist?"

She glanced at the kohatheen resting beside her in close ease of reach. "Things have changed."

He frowned. "That's not a No."

She shrugged. "She's my Head Mistress."

His frowned deepened. "Still not a No." He plucked another pebble from the ground, tossed it away, then fiddled with the thrown bone in his lap. "I know what's in that letter she gave you. Jericho told me after he killed you. Go ahead. Open it up. Read it for yourself."

"Can't. I already burned it."

He flinched. "What? Why?" Then assessed her in forward-leaning squint over the fire. "When?"

"When you weren't looking. Obviously. Not that it matters now anyways. And I didn't read it. What was in it was for Jericho alone. Now that he's gone—" She clipped short and glanced at the kohatheen beside her, nearest hand reaching then stalling short by closing into a fist she drew back to her lap. "She's not going to collar you, Ban, okay?"

"Says you," he mumbled.

"Yes," she said in stronger voice, spine stiffening her taller by inches. "Says me. I found you. That makes you mine."

He opened his mouth, closed it. *I'm not a stray dog.* But he put no voice behind it while enjoying a little bloom of pleasure in the depths of him at her wording. Though it vanished in seconds, anger returning in an agitated flush so that he plucked another pebble from the ground and threw it at the fire.

She scrunched her face, eyes thinning. "What's gotten into you?"

"Nothing." He crossed his arms and hunched. "I'm just fine and dandy."

She leaned forward, studying him. "I've got eyes, Ban. And your face is an open book of angry."

"Then don't read it." He plucked the splintered bone from his lap and tossed it into the fire, resisting by thinnest margin throwing it at her. "What do you know anyhow? You didn't have to kill him. You don't understand."

"I don't understand?" She stiffened up, flung another bone his way that whiffed inches past his flinching face. "I don't understand?" An abrupt charge of raw emotion tensing her face, she leaned forward and cut him with a thinning glare. "I don't care what you think you know. Don't you ever tell me I don't understand, you got that?"

He opened his mouth—then closed it with a click of teeth. He crossed his arms and stared at the fire while shifting on his bottom, every inch of him antsy for getting up and moving. "Fine. Whatever."

"Ban."

"What?"

"You weren't there," she said, her voice losing bite. She settled back, face falling slack as a shine entered her eyes, wet memories surfacing. She picked at her blanketed lap. For a time said nothing.

"Where?" he asked.

"In Junes," she continued in softer voice. "You weren't there, Ban. You didn't see what that monster did. I do understand because he destroyed my life."

She looked up through wounded eyes glistening reflections of firelight. "Do you know what lightning does to a person? Their eyes burst from their sockets. Their screams turn to strangled gurgles while they choke on their boiled blood. Their skin bubbles and splits and flakes away like black bits of rust."

She paused and shook her head, attempting to deny the emotional haunt of bridled pains betraying her eyes and bleeding into her voice, her shoulders bouncing little trembles while her breath slipped hitches between words.

"The godsawful smell of burnt flesh. Children screaming. Bodies everywhere. Junes was chaos. And the king—" She sniffled, swallowed, hands balling into blanket-bunching fists nested in her lap. "I was his Vizer. I was supposed to protect him. And I failed him just like I failed everyone else there."

Banzu shifted, craving to move to her and console those terrible memories away in holding embrace. Instead he watched the toil of her phasing despair play out while she continued torturing herself over failures beyond her control.

She stared down into her opening hands, fingers curled and grasping torment in her lap.

"His blackened flesh . . . so hot," she said while flexing her hands round the memories she spoke into them. "It peeled right off in my hands, like warm jelly from a stick." A pause, an audible swallow. "I tried, I got so close, but in the end I couldn't do a godsdamned thing about it but run." She balled her hands into trembling fists, stared off into the gloom of night, away from Banzu, away from any judgment he might lay upon her confession. "Like the godsdamned coward I am."

He flinched, her confession crushing him. "Coward?"

She sniffled and swiped a stray tear betraying her cheek.

"Hey," he said.

Staring away, she ignored him.

"Hey," he repeated in firmer tone. "Look at me."

She looked at him then, eyes glistening fragile pools.

"Don't you say that. Don't you dare. You're anything but a coward. Believe me, I know, I've seen it. You don't remember, but I do. I watched you take down a cyclops single-handedly while saving my life. You cut him up from head to heel then kicked him into the river while I clung helpless to the raft. And the other Trio—"

"What other Trio?" she asked, sharp and quick, tensing.

"Not here," he said. "Not now. Not for awhile yet. If we even come across them at all considering our changed course from before. Before my re-beginning, I mean."

"Re-beginning?"

He shrugged. "My return to here from the future. Don't know what else to call it."

She smirked. "Oh. Right. That."

"The first time I saved you," he continued, while watching her eyes, inner parts of him pleading for any spark of recognition igniting therein while he relayed their shared history, "I was so surprised at your void-aura taking my Power away that I only killed the first two while the third khansmen escaped. He showed up later leading another Trio. But by then I was sick from the chillfever. One of the frostwolves that attacked us bit my arm and infected me. Only I didn't know what it was at the time. You snuck off while I slept, hoping I'd just go home. But I chased you down, madder than spit. I found you walking away from a dead Trio. They ambushed you, but you killed them. And," he tapped at his right shoulder while indicating hers, "you took an arrow in your shoulder for it. Then that tundarian berserker showed up and almost killed me."

"Frostwolves," she said. "Chillfever. Arrow in my shoulder. And a tundarian berserker."

He nodded at her summation. "Uh-huh. And don't forget Cody."

"Cody who?"

"The cyclops who almost killed me when we crossed Green River. That raft you stole across to get here is his. Though we won't have to hire him to ferry us across this time. It's closer crossing a bridge this far north. Though I'm half tempted to hike it down his way anyways just to punch him in the face, knowing what I know now. Stupid cyclops anyhow."

"That's . . . a lot to take in," she said.

He plucked the thin sliver of hope splintered in his heart and asked, "Does any of that help you remember anything?"

She considered him a moment. Shook her head. "No. Sorry. Nothing."

He cringed inward.

"But maybe if you—" she began then clipped short, her gaze shifting from his face to over his shoulder behind him, thinning into a scrutinizing squint.

"What?" he asked. "What's wrong?" A sharp *snap* behind flinched him tensed. He twisted on his bottom, stared at the darkness beyond the firelight. No, not just darkness but motion. Branches moving, pushing aside. "What the frig?"

"Sooth . . . say . . . er," spoke an uncanny voice drifting forth from the gloom.

He squinted at the approaching black motion. Stood and faced it.

Behind him Melora said, "Ban."

But he answered no look back, instead concentrating on the shifting darkness in front of him, the creeping whiteness slow in taking shape from the gloom between parting branches.

"Sooth . . . say . . . er."

That's when he saw it, the shambling horror of some malformed manlike creature stalking forth from the shadows, breaching the outskirts of the firelight in slow reveal of lacerated skin and bloodied shreds of clothes, pale visage familiar.

"By the gods—" The breath hitched in his chest. His hand fell to gripping Griever's hilt. But his arm, along with the rest of him, froze static in cold flushing dread. "Impossible."

"*Sooth . . . say . . . er,*" the pale lurching creature drawled in the unnerving tongue of its deadspeak, calling out to Banzu in a garbled voice the nightmare rasp of a man speaking with a slit throat, its full black eyes glossy reflections of firelight. "*Sooth . . . say . . . er.*"

It staggered forward into better light with a creeping limp, the coils of its guts hanging loose from its opened stomach so that they slung down over its shifting legs, the unliving creature one of the three khansmen from the Trio earlier killed during Banzu's saving of Melora.

Eyes locked with the glistening black gaze of the shambling horror, Banzu jolted free from paralysis and tore Griever from his left hipwing. The blade wavered in his trembling hands as the unliving thing lurched ever-forward, its arms outstretched, its pale dead fingers wiggling in eager reach.

Banzu yelled a mash of words and curses. He lunged and stabbed the shambling horror in the chest where he presumed its black heart resided. It continued forward uninterrupted but for that jolting stab, sinking Griever's penetration deeper without perceivable effect, moaning while clawing for tearing the flesh from Banzu's panicked face.

He tried yanking Griever free but earned no space for pulling his driven blade from the creature's punctured cavity as it closed distance with new fervor now that its intended target stood so close at hand. The dead man's gaping maw snapped hungry bites of air round a swollen black tongue, emitting a putrid stink wafting from the horrible cave of its salivating mouth.

"Sooth . . . say . . . er!"

Banzu twisted and shoved. But the unliving creature's cold dead fingers pried grips of his hair, arresting his escape, clutching the sides of his head, pulling his face closer to its hungry mouth leaking black ichor fluids in glistening strings of saliva slime so that he stumbled backwards while thin wisps of smoke arose from the advancing creature's pale skin burning to some manner of internal heat.

"*Sooth . . . say . . . er,*" sounded another garbled voice of deadspeak from somewhere behind him. Punctuated by a third from somewhere unseen among the concealing shadows. "*Sooth . . . say . . . er.*" The other two khansmen of the dead Trio arriving and joining the first.

Melora shouted a hot string of damning curses.

Banzu spared her no glance behind, too intent with contended against the unliving horror seeking to eat his face off, its dangling coils of guts wetting the front of his clothes, its cold dead hands straining at pulling him closer toward its biting mouth with surprising strength.

Another shout from Melora—and cold panic fled for hot flaring anger. Banzu grit his teeth and thrashed, earning enough space between the putrid creature and himself to bring up one foot and set it against the thing's hip. The grunting shove of his extending leg stumbled it backwards while removing Griever's blade sliding free from its punctured chest where poured glistening black ribbons of ichor. He measured then lunged and swung, decapitating the abomination in sideways-slicing stroke.

He spun away as the creature's headless body collapsed. Two more pale and shambling shapes crept forth from the darkness toward Melora who squatted crouched and facing them, her dachras hammer-fisted at her sides. Though the two stalking horrors stared not at her but past her at Banzu.

He started round the fire—surprise stopping him ten bounding strides short of engagement.

Pale, outstretched hands clutching eager grabs of air burst afire.

Long and tortured moans escaping their throats, thickening wisps of smoke trailing from their charring skin and beneath blood-damp shreds of clothes, the two lurching khansmen collapsed through jouncing increments, their legs giving way beneath them first at the ankles then the knees then the hips while their pale flesh bubbled and blistered, cracked and fissured, releasing putrid oozes of black ichor gore hissing while snuffing random flares of flames, their muscles . . . *gooifying* round protrusions and juts of bones, their arms outstretched, their smoking hands clawing forward purchase of the ground, then the rest of them liquefying, stilling.

Silence.

Melora straightened in mute stare at the two stinking heaps of corpses fouling the air less than ten paces out from her. She flinched when Banzu joined beside her in shocked study.

One full minute passed before he glanced behind at the decapitated body of the first still clawing at the ground, its separated head nearby rolling this way and that as its active jaw continued biting at nothing in particular. He drew in deep to blow out his cheeks, and for it almost wretched from the rancid malodor drawn into his lungs.

He hawked and spat then asked, "What in friggin hell was that?"

"Death magic." Melora shook her head, crinkled her nose and spat her distaste. "Godsdammit." She spun her unblemished fangs through deft twirls then sheathed them to her back up behind her flapping cloak. "Godsdammit!"

She turned facing him, opened her mouth to extrapolate—then scowled while continuing her turn toward the headless corpse still pawing the ground in futile bid for Banzu. She snarled and strode past the fire. The struggling body as well its separate head burst into flames upon her advance. She kicked the detached head away into the darkness, a rolling ball of fire snuffing, while its burning body beside her continued clawing the ground for a space then stilled but for the hissing of its pale flesh liquefying round bones into a putrid, smoky puddle.

"Thank gods for my void-aura," she said.

"But—" Banzu began then stopped. He regained composure through a series of blinks. He squatted, swiped the fetid black ichor from Griever's steel upon the grass, then stood and returned the sword sheathed at his left hipwing while hoping no curse somehow fouled the depths of Griever's tainted steel. "But I killed them. How in friggin hell . . ."

"Doesn't matter now." She spun facing him, face slumping along with the rest of her. "They've done it." She gathered her cloak about her while hugging herself, attempting to tame the newborn chill rising in her bones, flames of awareness igniting in her distant stare. "They've godsdamned done it." She whispered a curse. "Dethkore lives again."

"Oh gods." Banzu flexed his hand to stay its trembles then raked it back through his hair and blew out his cheeks while surveying the grounds. "Can it get any worse?"

Her voice a bare whisper, "It just did."

CHAPTER TWENTY-TWO

An hour before dawn, in the black throat of night, Banzu slipped away from their pinewood lee, making no more sounds than whispering silk, seeking privacy on a high shelf of frosted rock peppered with sparse blue-green scrub sprouting through various cracks though clear of woods.

Dealing with the putrid remains of the unliving Trio proved a sickening chore still ripe in his disgusted mind hours later. Unable to drag the gooey partial corpses away for proper disposal, he decapitated the other two for reasons of safety then chopped all three bodies of Big Ugly and Rat Face and Tattoo Cheek—well, what remained of their bodies—into reassuring pieces then kicked dirt over the fetid puddles of their melted flesh and buried the remaining solid parts mostly bones with soggy clings of burned flesh. Heads and arms and legs and other chunks that quivered and twitched with unholy life once removed from Melora's void-aura. Her natural Spellbinder protection made a repugnant mess of the dead khansmen.

A quick washing in a nearby creek then Banzu changed his shirt and tossed the soiled garment into the fire while Melora slipped back to sleep with the ease of unfed exhaustion.

Though not before she attributed the attack to the Veilfall's worldwide awakening of latent memories in Enclave minds and, her only logical excuse, prompting the last Soothsayer's removal from their renewed quest of finding the Godstone that had fallen . . . fallen somewhere in the One land of Pangea only the gods knew where. The rest she said only the Head Mistress could explain then killed the subject by lying down and fetching some shuteye, swaddled in blanket and nestled in the comfort of her void-aura.

One thing for certain: after three-hundred years of buried slumber, the unliving Trio proved the Enclave achieved the Academy's worst fears of Dethkore's resurrection from the depths of his Junes tomb in soulring servitude to Hannibal Khan.

"We're really in the thick of it now," a bleary-eyed Melora said while snuggling up beneath her blanket. "If they find the Godstone before us, there'll be no stopping the aizakai genocide. It won't be a war but a slaughter and . . ." But she trailed away into groggy mumbles about her Head Mistress.

Banzu watched her sleep for a time, guarding her, his gaze darting at every slip of shadow beyond the warming firelight, his body tensed at the ready for springing into action, his hand a constant loose grip on Griever's hilt imposing intermittent squeezes. Until agitating whispers arose in his head containing harsh and teasing notes of Jericho's voice, instigating uncomfortable shifts and squirms so that Banzu upped and slipped away before he awoke her by talking at himself to banish the incessant whispers.

His ensuing Powered sprint and its accompanying adrenaline flush alleviated the whispers . . . for a time.

He stood atop his high shelf of rock, staring out while reflecting inward.

The gibbous moon rode westward at his back in the star-brilliant sky while far east the faint crimson blush of waking dawn glowed behind the distant jagged peaks of the Calderos Mountains, frosted peaks shrouded in their own country of clouds capturing Banzu's pensive stare for what lay beyond them. *Fist.* And who. *Hannibal Khan.*

"Godsdamn you."

The curse escaped in a visible plume of breath dispersed by the chill winds blowing against his face, eager for shouting it out with the full force of his lungs though managing restraint over his festering acrimony. He'd come seeking calm respite from the mental wrestling keeping him awake.

Peaceful is what Jericho used to call this brief space of time when nocturnal life surrendered to sleep while diurnal creatures still slumbered in their own hidden retreats. The serene silence of the in-between. A brittle silence fractured by the elevating reminder of a dead man's voice soughing for murder in Banzu's head.

Not just a murder but Melora's. And not just any voice but Jericho's.

Kill, it whispered. *Kill.* Over and again. *Kill.* Quiet and haunting. *Kill.* Almost shy in its begging plea. *Kill.*

Harsh as a guilty secret. *Kill.* Pausing though never ceasing. *Kill.* Fevered, relentless. *Kill.*

"Godsdamn you."

No question to it now. Some aspect of his slain uncle's essence had bled in to him through the shared collective of the Source, a poisoned splinter driven deep in his brain impossible to pluck free.

He closed his eyes, drew in a deep nostril inhale while capturing flavors riding the sharper wind into his lungs, grasping for a little soothing slice of calm when the breath smoked from his pursed lips in slow exhale. For the moment that strong spring smell in the crisp air enacted a freshening tonic of pine resin and new grass and eager sprouts of flowers attempting peeks through the dying thaw, of a clean sharpness through which winter's fading chill departed from the lowlands and replaced by promises of something new and fresh and good.

Up here on the Kush Mountains winter died slow and refusing, though fresh bracken already curled up in gothic green shoots coloring the brown drying carpets of shedding evergreen needles and scattered litters of leaves, and the first primroses would be out soon to unfold their yellow petals in little bursts of tiny suns having sprung from the thawing muds amid the drab dry patches of loose mountain scree.

Peaceful . . . and for the time Banzu's calmer mind did wander.

He drew in deep again, the sensory-heightening rush of the Power unnecessary for tasting the keen scents of birthing spring sweeping up from warmer parts below. Deep in the midst of the range the snow remained inviolate all year round, and even among the lesser Kush peaks the drifts lived deep and cold. The rare frozen corpses of hunters and trappers and wayward pilgrims rested upon the flanks of these mountains, though one need search high and deep to find them before the carnivorous reptilian screecher gliders who made their caved nests in the highest mountain cliffs sought them out and picked their bones clean unto matching them white with the covering snow.

Kill.

Again the guilty reminder.

"Godsdammit."

He raked a hand back through his hair, gripping tufts of it while he drew in another deep breath then released it in a frustrated huff of cheeks. Reasons for staying with Melora battled excuses for leaving without her, each warring for dominant control of his roiling mind. Nothing going as planned, he knew an ironic symmetry about it all, as though these burdens lain upon his trampled fabric of life benefited the amusement of some mad and scheming god.

And there lurked darker reason for his meditative withdrawal, an inexorable ache in his chest its bruise a dull throb while he gazed in fixed stare at the Calderos Mountains mocking him with distance, dawn's slow glow brightening behind them and making of the incredible range jagged teeth mouthing a foreboding red yawn seeking to swallow him whole.

The world as he knew it, over.

"I could've left," he whispered. "I should've left. I could still leave before . . ."

He trailed off, cringing against the shame for even considering abandoning her despite the incessant whispers urging him otherwise in haunting reminder if not for her he'd already be on the move for Fist. For Hannibal Khan.

He considered the voice perhaps not Jericho's but instead a dark echo reflection of his own guilty conscience while he stood in the midst of losing his sanity to the slow onset of madness catalyzed by his re-beginning and his tapping of the Source. But for the voice's familiar tone impossible to misinterpret, even among the thousand others of the shared collective soughing their own fevered whispers beneath Jericho's prominence.

I wanted him back, and now his ghost is more a part of me than ever.

Fear of releasing more of his dead uncle's influence, or any of the other thousand dead Soothsayers, within himself restricted him from seizing the Source again for only the Power.

At least the Power's not contaminated. I have that much.

He viewed the Source as a poisonous contagion. Swallow a few drops or the whole phial and you're still dead, the only real difference being the length of agony you suffered before it ended you.

I can't risk tapping the Source again. I won't. If I do there's no telling what will happen to me. To her. If I lose control. If another takes it away from me.

He sighed, long and withering, breath a misting plume trailing from the corners of his mouth in fading wisps.

I don't understand. I cleansed the bloodlust. So why do I hear it clawing out their throats every time they scream at me? Can I trust myself around her? No, don't think it. Just asking as much provides the answer. You can. You have to.

Kill.

He cringed and said through clenched teeth, "Shut up."

He considered his crossroad, stay or leave, options dwindling by the rising sun.

In staying with Melora he hoped to reclaim something precious of her again. While leaving her, if only for her own safe sake, would shatter their rehabilitating relationship into disrepair. *She'll never forgive me if I—*

Kill.

"Shut up!"

Realizing he stood clutching Griever's leather-wound hilt in a white-knuckled stranglehold, he forced the release of anxious tension from his hand by removing his fingers in a fanning peel, watching blood return color over his knuckles, his anger a palpable thing, his control loosening while imposing sudden mood swings.

He rumbled his throat while trying to clear his thoughts for better focus. Flashes of the past stole through moving pictures behind his stare so that he pushed his palms into the hollows of his eyes and rubbed them while rubbing raw memories away. He'd come to this spot seeking peace through deliberation, but the peace he sought would never come until the Khan lay dead at his feet. Only vengeance would sate the rapacious hunger of his starving soul. Only death would usher an end to that haunting voice, that driving need, that powerful urgency to—

Kill.

"No."

Yes!

Banzu startled flinched at the impossibility of that undeniable response from the voice he hoped nothing more than the inborn illusion of his grieving conscience.

He tested it through mental speak. *Jericho?*

And waited, bracing, in a neurotic hold of breath.

Silence.

He blew out his cheeks. *Gods, I'm talking to myself as if I'm two separate people. I really am losing it.*

The shared collective contained aspects of all Soothsayers, binding their spirits through the Source and bleeding into the invoker through the Power. Maybe, if he closed his eyes and imagined Jericho there, he could will his beloved uncle into some sort of ethereal existence if only in his mind's eye.

Questioning his sanity, he closed his eyes and . . . and instead thought of Melora, imagined every vivid detail of her warm and naked body lying curled against his while he sweated out the chillfever.

And there it is . . . she's my peace.

He enjoyed the music serenading his reverie of her, not loud but strong, the hum one feels when receiving a silent though knowing smile from a loved one, soft yet powerful in its unmistakable exchange, a shared secret lost upon the rest of the world and thus making it all the more special.

We had that once, the bloom of it anyways.

Gods, I want it again.

I won't accept anything less.

The Khan is nothing compared to her.

And she's waiting for me, sleeping, while I'm out here like an inconsiderate fool debating abandoning her.

The notion sickened him so that he stole a last look at the far eastern range of the Calderos Mountains then, shirking them and all they afforded him aside, he sped away in a burst of Power, back to camp, the dawning promise of a new day together brightening his eager mood for more of her.

* * *

Banzu returned to camp in the same whisper-quiet fashion he slipped out. He stood smiling over the sleeping beauty lying swaddled in a fetal curl on his bedroll, and for some few minutes just watched her sleep, enjoying every peaceful moment of her while conscious of the revenging fire inside subsiding to his musing passion replacing one burning yearning for another.

He could have stood there for hours basking in the soothing calm she provided his restless spirit but for that the morning tolled and the tower awaited them.

"Melora." He nudged her butt with the toe of his boot. No response. Another nudging toe. "Hey, Melora."

"Ungh . . ." A soft groan while she hugged the blanket in a tighter wrapping cling. "Go away."

He chuckled and nudged her again, harder on the rump. "Time to get up and get going."

"Wha . . ." She rolled over, coming-to, lids fluttering, then eyes snapping open when she jolted tensed and alert at the sight of someone standing over her so that he jumped backwards to keep from being knocked over while she bunched then sprang to her feet in a fighter's crouch, threw the blanket aside and pulled her dachras in a speedy flash of hands, eyes darting everywhere, hunting for lurking threats both living and unliving.

"Whoa whoa!" Banzu held his hands up between them, palms out. "Relax. It's just me."

She blinked through recognition of him, straightened tall and thinned her eyes into a cutting glare above a scorning scowl. "What kind of idiot kicks someone awake!" she yelled, then huffed, relaxing by increments. She sheathed her dachras away up beneath her open flapping cloak, her face a bitter twist. "I could've killed you, you know. Gods, after last night—"

"I'm sorry. I didn't mean to startle you."

The fire died in her eyes and voice, her scowl diminishing into a lingering frown. "Yeah. Well."

She bent over and touched her toes, then straightened and lifted her arms in an arching stretch of her back that transformed her breasts into small round globes tautening the fabric of her shirt. She glanced up for a quick sense of time. Ran her hands through the tangled nest of her long pale-blonde hair, then jerked her open cloak closed and belted it tight round her trim waist. Without another word she turned and walked away.

"Where are you going?" Banzu asked.

"Lady business," she said without bothering a look behind. She scooped up the kohatheen in passing and tied it off at her belt. "Have everything ready when I get back. We're not taking all day just to . . ." Her voice faded while she disappeared into the woods.

Banzu released a light chuckle overruled by a heavy jaw-stretching yawn punctuated with a sigh. *I'm going to pay for staying up all night. Not that I could've slept a wink after those . . . those things came after me. Best get moving and keep moving. I stay in one place too long and my eyes'll betray me.*

He flapped loose clinging bits of leaves and dirt from his bedroll and blanket then folded them up and stuffed them away into his rucksack, flourishing excitement over venturing inside a Builder's tower in a few hours granting energy in place of missed sleep.

He busied himself with kicking dirt over the cooling hearth of coals then washing his face and neck and pits and hands via a waterskin then toweling dry with an extra shirt he replace in his rucksack.

Melora returned by then, shoving and slapping and kicking more than moving aside branches and bushes out from her impatient way. "Let's go."

He nodded while fighting down a yawn with the back of one hand, then slung his rucksack to his back, turned north and gestured with the lazy sweep of his right arm, waving her along. "Ladies fir—" Another yawn clipped him short.

Melora considered him in silent scrutiny.

"Uhm." He shifted his feet. "What?"

She crossed her arms and frowned. "Did you even sleep?"

No. "Of course I—" Another yawn betrayed him. "I got enough."

She thinned her eyes upon him. "You're lying."

He feigned offense. "Am not."

She cocked a stern eyebrow while making a questioning stretch of his name. "Baaan?"

"What?" He glanced away at the sudden interest of trees. "I slept. A little."

She planted fists to hips, frowning, said nothing.

"What?" He kicked at nothing on the ground. "*What?*"

"You're no good to me asleep on your feet. And we're not stopping until we get there. Not after last night. You were supposed to wake me for a watch. Why didn't you?"

He bounced out a shrug. "You needed the rest. Besides, how in the frig was I supposed to sleep when dead people are trying to eat me? Gods!" He huffed and looked away. "I've too much on my mind for sleep anyhow. Every time I close my eyes—"

He closed his eyes then, and rubbed at his lids with finger and thumb, producing flares then fades of phosphenes. Gentle persuasion on his arm lowered his hand from his opening eyes regaining focus. "What? I said I'm—"

"A lot is going to be expected of you in Fist, Ban. You've lost a lot already, I know. Be strong."

In unexpected gesture she palmed the side of his face, weighing his unvoiced concerns.

And he leaned into the soothing touch of her warm hand cradling his cool cheek so that he closed his eyes again and smiled, enjoying the moment of her and him and no one else. Until she delivered him a soft though rousing slap.

"Come on," she said, turning, walking away. "Time's wasting."

He fought down another yawn and pursued her.

***

A few hours of walking the northbound trails, and Banzu led Melora out through a break in the woods near the same spot he'd stood gazing between hunting hares the previous night. As they approached the massive landscape bowl's brim allowing a high overview of its jungle interior, there rippled a shimmering lift of heat sweeping up from the jungle down within. But the heat contained no magic, and Melora proved as much when she stepped up beside him and the shimmering effect continued making little waves of the air round her.

For a small stretch of time both stood silent and gazing at the drastic change of scenery awaiting them, the top of the black builderstone tower peeking out above the thick jungle lush though the rest of it remained hidden behind the dense green mesh of tangled growth miles deep and across. The vegetation wall started a quarter of a mile beyond the brim, its sweeping heat warming their faces in stark contrast to the cold mountain gusts chilling their backs.

There lived a tropical strangeness to what grew within the jungle expanse, everything therein appearing larger by far, the fanning species of deep green leaves vast in spread, some even large enough to wrap a person whole. Moss-bearded trees strung with depending ropes of flowered vines stood hundreds of feet tall, their mahogany trunks thick and gnarled, their high joined tops making smaller jungles above. Signs of life everywhere Banzu scanned—leaves shaking, branches swishing, vines swinging—though not the actual life itself.

This jungle crater forbidden him most his life, adventurous excitement of the unknown flourished nervous butterflies through his anxious belly. The sensation quelled a moment more to the physical labor their entry required. His muscles burned with preemptive ached from all the necessary hacking and cutting through the dense foliage obstructing their passage inside.

Gods, miles of the stuff before we're through it to the tower. Nothing's ever easy, so why should this be?

"Well," Melora said, "let's be at it then." She started down.

Banzu arrested her short with a barring arm. "Allow me." He gripped Griever's hilt, bared its immaculate blade by inches in gracious gesture. "No need for both of us killing ourselves cutting inside all that. Asides, this is man's work. I'll start us a path while you keep an eye out. Here." He shrugged out from his rucksack and dropped it to the ground next to her feet, rolled his shoulders. "You can carry this awhile."

"Man's work?" She cocked an impish eyebrow, glanced at the rucksack, at the jungle, met his gaze. She added no dispute to the order given but for crossing her arms and smirking. "Man's work. Okay then. Have it your way, Mr. Man."

He walked down the decline into the bowl, unsure if he'd just tripped some invisible snare though ready to break a sweat. The decline lessening flat, he stopped before the towering jungle wall where balmy heat emitted thick. He rolled up his sleeves to the elbows and pulled Griever free from his left hipwing, wishing for a machete instead. *Or a farmer's scythe. Gods, it's friggin thick.* He threw a glance at Melora watching him, still smirking her private smile, then he started his way inside, hacking and slashing while attempting to forge them a path through the dense jungle growth.

Seconds only and beads of sweat dewed his forehead and neck. Minutes more and his pits and back ran slick. For what seemed an hour though no more than a few laborious minutes he cut and slashed while advancing a step, cut and slashed and advanced, cut and slashed and advanced, inching deeper through his makeshift tunnel and concentrating on the task before him while keeping his route directed straight toward the middle of the landscape bowl for the Builder's tower within.

Exhausting minutes more and he paused, huffing and puffing, shoulders and forearms burning, sweat a profuse lather dampening his clothes. He scrubbed his wet brow with the back of one forearm then looked behind and cursed. Despite all of his hard work at cutting a tunnel, the efforts so far earned little more than a few strides inside the thick growth.

Melora, having ventured down with his rucksack, stood twenty paces behind him, arms crossed and still smirking, a devious twinkle in her steady bead on him. She danced her eyebrows though said nothing.

"Friggin hell." *It's going to be a long day.* He faced round to continue advancing his makeshift tunnel—and startled flinched at the area he'd just cut open having closed up. "What the frig?" *No, my eyes are playing tricks. Must be the heat.*

Melora's laughter from behind so that he spun and met her amused smirk with a frown.

"What's so funny?" he asked.

"Nothing." But her lying smile answered otherwise. She unfurled an arm and flicked her wrist, gesturing past him. "Well? What are you waiting for? Go ahead, Mr. Man. Don't stop your man's work on my account."

He thinned his eyes upon her. *I just had to say it, didn't I?* Then returned to hacking and slashing task while grumbling curses, annoyed, swinging harder, faster, yet somehow advancing less than before.

After several grueling minutes he stopped again, panting, and swiped profuse sweat from his face. He squinted, swearing movement, then seeing it for true. The whispering swish of leaves curling, the low creaking of branches shifting, the jungle tunnel in front of him closing round while filling in so that he withdrew a wary step, blinking hard, then rubbing his lying eyes with pointer and thumb and blinked again. Before him a thick screen evincing no hacking slashes but for the parts of leaves lying atop thick snarls of grass. "What in friggin hell?"

Behind him mocking laughter.

He spun round scowling, jabbing the air between them with Griever. "You want to give this a try? It's a lot harder than it looks, you know." He shook his head, damp tangles loosing beads of sweat. He turned from her, glared at the jungle screen, turned back, shrugged his aching shoulders. "I don't get it. It's like it's growing back almost as fast as I can cut it—*whoa!*"

Motion stole in his peripheral so that he darted sideways while slashing at an ambushing snake bursting uncoiled from the camouflaging vegetation at shoulder height and snapping for his face in a blur of movement and color. Griever cut through its stretched length, severing head from body, and bright green juices spurted from the stump as it fell slapping atop his right boot then withdrew into the foliage in whipping recoil.

Banzu blinked down at the snakehead not a snakehead but a red-petal flower snapping bites of the air with thorny brown teeth then stilling seconds more. No snake then but some manner of living vine. "What in friggin hell is that?"

Melora craned her head and belly-laughed. "That's because it is growing back, you dummy! This jungle feeds off the protective magics of the Builder's tower inside it. How else do you think all of this grows clear up here in the cold? Man's work, I swear. You'd need a whole crew of slash-and-burners to get inside before it grows back and swallows you whole. Which we don't have." She flicked her wrist in dismissive gesture at him and Griever both. "Now put that boy's toy away and watch how a woman gets things done. It's called proper."

"Uhm." He considered his sword, considered rushing in and fighting through the jungle while shouting curses just to refuse her. Instead he stabbed Griever sheathed at his left hipwing and rolled his achy shoulders. "You could've said something, you know. Before I soaked myself."

"And miss seeing your face? I don't think so, Mr. Man." She closed distance in a leisure stroll, his rucksack slung over one shoulder, the kohatheen tied off at her belt slapping against the side of her right thigh. She dropped the rucksack at his feet and offered him a cunning smile.

He shifted his gaze ahead and there gaped in open-mouthed, stupefied awe at the wondrous display of her void-aura revealing itself in a strange new way. The thick jungle growth shrank away at her approach in swishes of leaves retreating in furling shivers, branches creaking while angling away, the thick turf of springy grasses wilting limp, as if the vegetation possessed a sentient presence and she some mental command over the jungle not just alive but aware.

"Planimals," she said, as if that was that, the sky blue and water wet. She reached out in passing stride, traced the tip of her pointer finger down the side of Banzu's sweaty face to underneath his hung jaw and shut it for him by tucking up his chin. "A lot of towers have them. How else do you explain a jungle on top of a mountain?"

She laughed again, light and musical, and while she strolled ahead with an unnecessary regal lift to her chin so did the dense jungle round her continue expanding open while shrinking away in every direction from her but for the ground itself in far too easy the creation of a tunnel.

Banzu stared mute at her back as she walk on through the recoiling foliage unimpeded, a Spellbinder queen before the parting planimal crowd. Until pressure at his back and sides from head to heels alerted him so that he spun round to the jungle lush reforming closed behind the removing expanse of her void-aura.

Seconds from being tangled and swallowed within the active vegetation if he didn't catch up inside the safety of her void-aura, he snatched up his rucksack—or tried to. But several snaking vines had slithered out from the thickening jungle, tangling round his rucksack's other shoulder strap while biting thorny purchase with their strange flowered mouths. He tried yanking his rucksack free—and yelped at a thorny sting on his left forearm from a darting bite of planimal vine so that he jerked his opening hand away from strap.

Five animate snakevines arose into the air over the rucksack in protection of their others winding round their newfound bounty, claiming it. Banzu jumped backwards, avoiding a snapping bite of red-petal jaws lined with thorny brown teeth attempting the juicy taste of his thigh. He glanced at his forearm, at the tiny dots of blood welling up evincing his initial bite, and cursed.

While the jungle planimals thickened closer round him.

He snatched a grip on Griever's hilt, intent on hacking the pesky snakevines into piece while freeing his rucksack, though stayed the full pull of his blade when the snakevines drooped and withered, those hovering in the air falling limp to the ground, then all of them withdrawing back into the recoiling foliage while leaving his rucksack behind.

"Having fun?" Melora asked, having ventured back during his little battle.

"Oh yeah. Loads." He raised his bitten arm for a closer inspection of the two opposing crescent rows of tiny red dots. Scratches, really. Maybe. "Hey, those things aren't poisonous are they?"

She glanced at his little wound and shrugged. "How should I know?" She turned and walked away.

"Wait a minute. What do you mean—*hey!*"

Banzu snatched up his rucksack before more pestering snakevines crept out for another fight and followed after her while the jungle enclosed behind him in the removal of her void-aura.

***

For the next turn of the hour Banzu walked alongside Melora in a fading daze of wonder, the planimal jungle opening ten paces in front of them while enclosing ten paces behind, her invisible radiance of void-aura making of their immediate area safer space for travel.

"So this is what it's like being you," he said, carrying the unease of being watched while his gaze roved the enchanting flux of planimal shifts and shivers in everywhere abundance, his peripherals glimpsing recoiling darts of reds and greens here, feathery patches of yellows and oranges there, purple and blue blotches appearing among greens and browns then disappearing just as quick. "Huh."

He wondered on the smell and the taste of it all if he seized the Power—Melora's magic-nullifying Spellbinder company excluded, of course—while surrounded by this dynamic community of sensory stimulation, suspecting an overload of his amplified senses inducing a headache.

He listened too, trying to discern particular sounds from the eclectic collection of hidden noises above their treading footfalls, but the teeming discord of it all proved too thick and he feared slow reaction if some prowling beast leaped out at them with claws or fangs . . . or dead prying hands.

"I don't have any control over it." She frowned while waving her hands round in indicative gesture of self. "It just, well, is." Her brow furrowed. "I've always wondered what magic actually feels like, but—" She paused, wincing, added in lower voice, "But I'd trade it all away if . . ." But she trailed away unfinished.

The constant magic-nullifying void-aura of her Banzu already knew though never seen it put to such obvious effect before. He prodded her away from the sore subject of her dead mother, in the different direction of their destination.

"So what exactly are we looking for in the tower anyways?" he asked. "I can't help you find it if I don't know what it is. And it better not be big. Or heavy. Because I'm not lugging it all the way to Fist if it is."

She eyeballed him sidelong, an inviting feline mischief thinning her eye while the closer corner of her mouth perked up a devious crook. She answered nothing, instead returned her focus forward to the opening tunnel.

He huffed a terse breath at her non-answer, liking none of that look and wondering how any man ever figured out the enigma of women.

Soon they achieved their exodus from the jungle, reaching the interior ringing wall of the steamy wilderness which peeled away at their approach, revealing a circular clearing surrounding the tall black spire of the Builder's tower standing at the clearing's center with half a mile radius of flat ground round its base. And more.

Melora stopped short at sight of the other people ahead, Banzu alongside her, both startled. Without word she crept backwards while snagging him by the closer arm and pulling him with her cautious withdraw until the reforming vegetation concealed them but for leaving small space ten paces ahead through which they spied out.

At several groups of men moving about their makeshift camp, having pitched a cluster of tents, cook fires churning white puffs of smoke, while a team of more men labored at digging some manner of trench.

Cursing Locha's Luck, Melora crouched, pulling Banzu down into a squat beside her.

"What are they doing here?" he asked, squinting through the small opening ahead obstructed by leaves and vines, wishing she had control over her void-aura so that she could expand or contract it at will, if such were even possible. Spying through the tiny window while ten paces away limited their view. "How?"

His best guess put the others' numbers somewhere round fifty, most of them workers whose heads and shoulders bobbed above the top line of the trench while digging, flashes of their working shovels and pickaxes rising and falling between flung heaps of dark soil adding to the line already unearthed in a long, low pile parallel to their trench.

One of the men standing watch over the trench of diggers stuck out like a sore thumb—quite literally looked like a human-sized sore thumb by the rotund shape of him and the pink flush of his alabaster skin. Not a lick of dirt on his expensive clothes, a tailored white suit and a black-banded hat rimmed wide. He possessed the soft fatness of a man used to ordering others through the work he deemed beneath him though the thickness of a youth spent laboring before striking a richer avenue in older life. He clutched a white wad in his plump right hand and dabbed at his glistening face and bullfrog neck sweating to the jungle's pervading humidity. And surrounding him a lazy guard of ten stout roughs, most of them armed with swords or hatchets.

A bearded older fellow dug at his fingernails with the tip of his knife in bored chore. Another sat cross-legged and testing his yew bow by stringing then unstringing it in idle distraction. Between them a strapping youth stood stripped to the waist and swiping sweat from his bared chest and arms while stealing smirking glances at the only female among them, a short and short-haired woman sitting not far atop a crate licking her approving lips while rubbing the insides of her spread thighs with her dress hiked up to her knees in playful response.

Banzu studied them all, and the laborers in the trench aimed for the base of the Builder's tower though still a hundred feet from reaching it. *Those lights I saw while hunting hares. Must've been their fires.*

"Godsdamned thieves," Melora said in hissing whisper, keeping her voice low. "They're breaking Academy law just being here."

"But how?" Banzu asked of the obvious planimal jungle.

"They slashed and burned their way in." She pointed across the way to where, though now closed, evinced an obvious change of color in the growth where new and brighter greens stood out against the older and darker greens framing it, the immediate grounds in front of it patched with blackened grass. "Look." She shifted her aim to the group of men near the far edge where clearing met jungle, five men sitting in a circle atop boxes and barrels and playing at cards, drinking and laughing. Machetes, axes, and farmer's scythes lay scattered by their feet or resting on tilted leans against boxes or barrels. "They've come to plunder the tower because of the Veilfall."

"Well that was fast."

"Greed doesn't take long." She swept her pointer arm sideways-right, air-tracing down the length of the trench then past it to the tower, at the twenty or so bodies strewn on the ground on the long space between trench and tower yet to be unearthed. Corpses, these, with limbs bent in wrong ways, their faces locked in frozen screams, their eyes empty crusted sockets. "At least the tower's magical wards killed some of them."

"You'd think they'd pack up and leave after all that."

Though he could only speculate on how the tower's protective magics rendered those victims dead, especially so considering not a single one of their fellows bothered retrieving any of the bodies. Or maybe they had but succumbed to the same ill fate, adding to the numbers of the dead.

Banzu's apprehensive guts twisted up at the sight of those dead men. After contending with the unliving Trio the previous night . . . but no, these dead men lay still. *For now at least.*

"They've got the numbers," she said, estimating their new turn of situation with a discerning stare.

And weapons. He tallied a quick note of the swords and bows and others such carried by the men standing round the fat man in a loose group, some of them watching the diggers while others stood idle in conversation. "Maybe they'll leave when they can't get inside?"

"They're thieves, Ban. They live and die by the coin. Some of them already." She pointed at the corpses littering the grounds near the tower's base, punctuating the reminder. "They probably think the tower's easier game now because of the Veilfall. Fools. Trying to dig their way under, like the Builder's protective wards don't go below ground as well."

"Uhm, does it?"

She didn't answer, too focused ahead.

"So what, we just sit here and wait?"

"I don't think so." Melora erupted into standing from her spying crouch, shoulders back, chin up, her eyes afire, her grin savage, every inch of her defiance. In raised voice that brooked no argument she added, "Not while I'm here."

"Wait a minute—" But before he could finish, she yanked him into standing him then pulled him alongside as she stormed out through the spreading foliage into the clearing beyond.

***

Seconds only before a tall, lean man with a bow strung over his right shoulder, standing half-turned to the fat man in white and half-turned to where Banzu and Melora stepped forth from their dense jungle shielding then stopped, detected their entrance into the clearing and pointed while alerting his fellows to the presence of the two newcomers.

The bulbous boss—for he shouted orders and the loose group of armed men clustered round him obeyed without argument, swarming into sloppy formation at his sides then following—walked toward them. The fat leader's black eyepatch over his left eye contained a single tiny sparkling jewel sewn into its center, the false pupil catching twinkling fractures of light from the unobstructed sun high overhead.

Eyepatch waddled more than walked, one plump hand gripping the flap of his white vest nipple-high while the other dabbed glistening sweat from round his shiny face despite the shade of his wide-brimmed hat. The plumb-shaped thumb of a man revealed curly corkscrews of black hair when, as he and his attending ruffians closed distance to Banzu and Melora by half, the heavyset boss tucked his wad of cloth into the upper left pocket of his vest then removed his black-banded hat and fanned himself. He possessed a greasy look, and wore a too-big smile in his bold approach.

Behind him and his little posse, the hunched laborers digging the trench stalled their efforts and straightened for peeks over the shoulder-high berm. Until a bearded man standing watch nearby with a leather bullwhip removed the aforementioned man-handler from his hip and put it to use, cracking the air above the workers' heads and motivating them back to digging task.

Banzu studied Eyepatch and his eager gaggle of followers through thin-eyed scrutiny, assessing numbers. *Friggin hell, it's always something.* He glanced at the Builder's tower, wanting only to slip in then out then gone for Fist. *Figures. Nothing's ever easy, is it?*

"I have a faster way of handling this—" he began while gripping Griever's hilt for pulling in open display of his intentions.

"No!" Melora's voice curt and commanding, she slapped her right hand overtop his hilt-gripping own, staying Griever's pull while meeting his eyes. "No. Murder is not the Academy way. Just because we can doesn't mean we should." She held his gaze an extra measure, then removed her hand after a little squeeze on his wrist. "They can't bypass the tower's protective wards anyways, so they can stay out here digging till their pricks rot off for all I care. All we need is a way inside."

She cleared her throat, raised her chin and set her shoulders back, mustering tall and all Spellbinder Melora Callisticus again. "I'll handle this"—yet the word pained her even as she spoke it with emphasis, "*diplomatically*."

Diplo— "But the punishment for breaking Academy law into a Builder's tower is execution on sight." Not that he intended on killing them, but the threat of it might scare them off. Though off to where, considering the planimal jungle, he knew not. *They slashed and burned inside, so they can slash and burn their way out.*

"It is." She pointed at the bodies strewn round the tower's base. "The wards ensure it."

"Oh." He removed his hand from Griever's hilt. "Okay." He shrugged from his rucksack then kicked it away a space and waited. "If you're sure."

"I'm sure." She gestured her left hand palm-out in signal at the approaching group and said in raised voice, "Palavar?" In a lower voice said out from the right corner of her mouth, "Don't do anything stupid unless I say so."

Stupid?

"And keep your mouth shut," she added, "unless I say so."

He grit his teeth though relented a nod.

Eyepatch halted short, smile faltering, and stared a silent length. His too-big grin returned when he raised his right hand overhead in return signal. "Palavar," he said back, nodding his round head, a glint of fractured sunlight catching twinkles of his little eyepatch jewel. He ordered his men behind and continued forward alone, fanning his sweaty face with his hat while waddling closer with the careless ease of someone seeking only pleasant conversation.

"Palavar?" Banzu looked at Melora sideways. "What's that?"

"Tongue for two leaders of their respective groups to meet and discuss peacefully. Something the Head Mistress demands while forcing everyone she talks to into drinking her disgusting tea." She made an unpleasant twist of her face indicative of what she thought of said tea, then held a ten second pause before adding out from the corner of her mouth, "Grab your sword, but don't pull it. And tell him to halt . . . *now*."

Banzu nodded and gripped Griever's hilt. In his best commanding tone he said, "Halt. That's far enough."

Frowning, Eyepatch stopped ten paces away and studied them both. He began replacing his hat atop his head when his good right eye popped wide then squinted tight. He lowered his hat and wrung its brim in his fiddling hands while offering an apologetic smile that augured well for his place as a thief with his filching hands caught deep in another's cookie jar: bemused on the surface, sly beneath.

"Why, a good day to the both of you," Eyepatch said, greeting them in a merry baritone. Hat in hand, he made a sweeping gesture of his arm while leaning forward in partial bow. "Bartholomew J. Eddings, at you service."

"You and your trespassers are in violation of Academy law," Melora said, smooth yet firm.

Bartholomew straightened, feigning offense, plump hands fidgeting with the hat in front of his bulbous belly. "Please forgive our undisclosed intrusion, Spellbinder. But my honorable business associates and I are merely here to provide your esteemed Academy and all its noble and may I say beautiful Mistresses with the necessary assistance required given the spacious divide between here and Fist. Why, I took it upon myself to procure a reputable team of guardsmen, I did, the instant the Veilfall sparked up the sky."

He replaced his hat atop his wooly head and tucked his plump thumbs into the pits of his vest. "One never knows what manner of scoundrel will come seeking plunder. And I'm sure the Academy will offer a fine compensation to those of us willing to protect their towers in these trying times, of course."

"Of course," Melora said, tone flat.

"And the trench?" Banzu asked.

Earning Melora's admonishing glare. She worked her face back to a blank slate of diplomacy. "And the trench?" she repeated.

"Oh, that?" Too much surprise blossomed on Bartholomew's fat face. He glanced over his left shoulder at the trench and the team of diggers within it then returned Melora a look that said he never really even noticed the trench in mention until just then. "Why that's just a latrine, good Spellbinder."

Smiling strong, Bartholomew pulled the bottom left of his lower vest away, revealing the hilt of a shortsword, in case its polished brass scabbard slapping against his fat thigh during his approach slipped beneath their notice. "And for burial purposes as well, of course. Any potential thieves encroach here and they'll stay here. That is a promise." He closed his vest and tucked his thumb back into his left armpit and there flapped his arms in imitation of a rotund chicken. "I'm happy to see the Academy has acted so fast in sending you here, Mistress . . . ?"

He paused for Melora's name, but she gave him nothing in response but for the thinning of her eyes.

"Well," he continued, "as your eyes can attest, there's been several thieves who have tried their unlucky hands at stealing inside already. But we have everything well in hand, good Spellbinder, and I assure you that—"

"Of course." Melora's face pinched up the slightest fraction, and her upper lip twitched, threatening a snarl. But she smoothed her features calm in the span of a sneeze, all Spellbinder Melora Callisticus again. "I thank you for your services, Mr. Eddings, but they are no longer required. I'm relieving you and your men at once. Thank you for your hospitality. You may return to your homes now with the grace and favor of the Academy's blessings. Good day."

Bartholomew lapsed a brief scowl he worked into another too-big grin. "And who might you be, Mistress . . . ?" Again the question and the pause, and again she answered nothing so that he went on. "So that I can request payment from the Academy for my gracious services already rendered, of course."

Melora opened her mouth—but Banzu interrupted with the quick raise of his left hand in firm, silencing gesture while drawing the rotund liar's lone-eyed gaze.

"Spellbinder Melora Callisticus." Banzu crossed his arms over his puffed chest. "And I'm her Soothsayer." He slid his right hand down from the inner crook of his left elbow and gripped Griever's exposed hilt in obvious show while eyeballing Bartholomew hard. "You got a problem with that?"

Bartholomew opened his mouth, closed it. His gaze shifted between them. "A Soothsayer?" He gripped his ample belly and laughed, the softer parts of him bouncing. He turned round, faced his watching crew, shouted, "A Soothsayer, he says!" And turned back laughing while laughter arose behind him.

Banzu frowned, eyeballing him extra hard.

Laughter fading, Bartholomew pulled his damp kerchief and dabbed at his sweaty face and neck then tucked it away. "That's a good one, lad. A right chuckle. You even almost look the part."

Melora issued the deliberate clearing of her throat. She looked at Banzu, looked at Bartholomew, and smiled.

A serious calm slayed the lingering mirth from Bartholomew's tensing face then. "A Sooth—" He clipped short in a cracking voice, high and sharp. He rumbled his throat clear. "A Soothsayer?" His right eye stretched wide, darting from Banzu to Melora and back again. He withdrew a wary step and raised his hands between them, palms out.

"Oh no," Bartholomew said. "I've got no problem a'tall, good sir." He squinted at Banzu. "Soothsayer, eh? I thought your kind was long gone. Hunted down and killed off by them fistian bitches—*ahem!*" He rumbled his throat, beady eye nervous darts looking everywhere but Melora. "I thought all you Soothsayers had been dispatched by the proper authorities of Fist, beg your pardon. Please, forgive me. Now that you are here, Mistress Melora, my humble associates and I shall happily be on our way."

He withdrew another cautious step backwards, hands waving.

"And please," he continued, "no compensation is necessary. Let it never be said that Bartholomew J. Eddings was ever lack for helping the esteemed Academy in any way. I've no doubt you'll mention my kindness to the good Head Mistress upon your return, praises be upon her beautiful head. That is more than enough payment for me, I assure you. And for my associates."

Bartholomew blew out his jowls, removed the white wad of cloth from his vest pocket and swiped his glistening face and neck folds. "No compensation necessary," he repeated, round head bobbing rapid and reassuring nods. Through lips more gritted teeth than smile he added, "Spellbinder."

Backing away to a safer distance, Bartholomew's too-big smile returned to his greasy fat face. He spun round, leaving no breadth for response, and waddled away to inform the watching others of their early departure.

Banzu chuckled and shrugged while watching Bartholomew waddle away in a comical rush, every bounding stride making the fat man look about to topple sideways. "That was easy."

"Too easy." Melora frowned, made a V of her pointer and middle fingers and indicated her eyes. "He knew me for a Spellbinder before we exchanged a word. His eye? The split tip of his nose? The missing pinkie on his right hand? This isn't the first time he's been caught thieving, only the first of a tower. Even a green thief knows trying to steal from a tower is a death sentence. No, they'll pack up their things and go then bide their time and come back after they think us gone and . . ."

She continued on, but Banzu only half-listened, too perturbed that those obvious marks of thievery on the fat man had slipped his notice. Too preoccupied in getting past these men so they could be in and out then gone. He half-turned from her, then advanced two steps and watched the men gathering round Bartholomew while the fat man returned to them in bobbing waddle. An exchange of words, then Bartholomew turned back grinning. He stepped aside and out from the way of the man holding a drawn bow with an arrow notched and aimed at—

"Look out!" Banzu yelled just as the twanging bowstring released its arrow into flight. Impossible to outpace the missile by shoving her away, he twisted sideways while ripping Griever free from his left hipwing in an upward-drawing motion.

Rising steel brushed through the tail-end fletching of the arrow as it sped past his face, knocking the projectile a hairsbreadth off course toward Melora's surprise-blooming face so that it flew past just shy of her right cheek and puffed through her hair then gone, disappearing somewhere into the jungle behind her.

Banzu's quickened heart skipping several beats, he lowered his sword and stared at her, at the fine red line appearing across her cheek below her right eye. It turned minutely thicker, smiled for an instant then released a single drop of blood which ran the right side of her face in a dark tear, her spooked eyes narrowing into violet smolders. She raised her hand and wiped away the little ruby trail from her cheek with the tips of her swiping fingers. Half an inch to the left and she would be missing an eye—and dead.

"Son of a—" she began while untying her belt to open her cloak for pulling her dachras as she started forward.

"Stop." Banzu's harsh voice a command. Cold, immediate, exact.

She stopped, startled by his order. She flared her eyes and opened her mouth.

"Shut up," he said, his voice a guttural growl.

She snapped her teeth shut.

He challenged her glare for glare—and won. "Stay." He turned and stalked away.

She said something to his back.

He heard nothing but the private voice in his head urging him forward with the focused stillness of instant violence, the cold plunge of fear at almost losing her again surrendering to the hot swell of rage boiling in his guts in a rapacious battle-fire lust hazing all thought but for the stark butchery playing behind his seething stare ahead at men no longer men but targets.

CHAPTER TWENTY-THREE

Banzu's collective anger—at Hannibal Khan for instigating Jericho's death, at the changing world he could do nothing about, at himself for causing the Veilfall, at Melora for not remembering him, at the fat eye-patched bastard's lies of the tower, at the thieving roughs standing round Bartholomew risking mocking smirks, at the bowman in their midst for daring to take Melora away from him—imposed a pantherine quality of relaxation loosening his fluid jointless strides forward, tunneling his focal stare with sure purpose while shutting out the qualms of the rest of the world for the potential violence awaiting him ahead and his fierce need to indulge in its bloody feast while sating the hunger of his ravenous heart.

In his predator's stalking calm he sheathed Griever to his left hipwing mid stride while a single word reverberated in his skull between echoes of mad laughter.

Kill . . . it whispered, this tantalizing voice pleading in tender yet eager askance, so much the lover's hot seductive breath tickling across the roused stimulus of the fine hairs of Banzu's inner ear then punctuating the request with its probing tongue licking across responsive skin, inviting, enticing . . . *Kill.*

Melora's voice diminishing with distance at his back, Banzu strode across the clearing in a smooth gait toward the loose cluster of thugs huddled round fat Bartholomew at their center, assessing their numbers while gauging them all though fixing his focal point upon the tall bowman standing within the motley midst of cocksure men taking lazy claim of the weapons hitched at their belts.

Several laughed at Banzu's lone approach, while others smirked or sneered as they brandished what they assumed for intimidating clubs or swords or hatchets or daggers or other paraphernalia of arms. Though a scant few among their haughty fellows recognized the intent closing in before them and judged the supposed Soothsayer's approach through cautious eyes thinning while ignoring the arrogant boasts and jests of the ignorant disbelievers beside them.

Melora, heeding Banzu's order to stay back, watched his advance with a clipped tongue, her cut cheek crying another tiny ruby tear she swiped away while smearing it in a false blush of her alabaster skin.

The toiling diggers in the trench paused their labors and straightened for a watch over the shoulder-high berm, while their distracted whipmaster punished them nothing for the delay of work, he too intent on watching as well. The only woman among their fold hopped from her perch of box into standing, smiling, licking her lips, tasting the new aroma of violence riding the humid air. Behind her the crew of card players ended their game short for placing bets as to who and how quick Bartholomew's guards would kill the red-haired swordslinger claiming the impossibility of Soothsayer blood.

All eyes upon him, Banzu ignored the others for forward, only forward now. There existed no direction but ahead.

He could have seized the Power the moment he removed outside the magic-nullifying influence of Melora's void-aura. Instead he carried the promise of its reassuring flame within the chamber of his being, untouched though ready for flaring. Not slow but no rush in his steps, hands open and empty, a cold smile pursing his lips beneath smoldering eyes sighting targets.

Many of Bartholomew's men laughed and threw crude gestures at the false Soothsayer, spitting while issuing mocking curses at the foolish youth pretending the infamous aizakai role the world believed exterminated years ago, the last known Soothsayer executed through the fistain Academy's relentless efforts at ending the Nameless One's curse and thus rumors of their aizakai kind existing on the cusp of myth.

Amid these voices arose Bartholomew's boisterous orders of taking Melora—alive or dead, he cared neither way—to use her Spellbinder blood for bypassing the tower's protective magics so they could procure the bounty of treasures awaiting them within. And his words instilled new and eager confidence into the greedy hearts of his crew of roughs.

Banzu continued ahead, priming his hands by flexing squeezes of air at his sides while rapid flashes of violence played and replayed behind his eyes. *Let them believe me a lie. All the more easy.*

The lanky bowman who scored Melora's cut cheek notched a second arrow at Bartholomew's order, drew aim and let fly—*twang!*

And now it begins. Banzu seized a flicker of the Power, restraining himself against the full release not from fear but for satisfaction of the effect. The world jolted fast-slow-fast in a luminous pulse of twilight greys, there then gone, though within that prolonged stretch of heartbeat pause his right hand blurred to his left hipwing with the sure ease of quickness. He tore Griever loose and enacted a fanning sweep of blade through which he cut the shot arrow speeding for his face from the air then replaced his immaculate sword to his hip all in one smooth Power-blurring motion. The two bits of arrow separated while passing by inches his unflinching face.

Unsure startlement flinched across the gaggle of faces watching back at him, the deflection too quick for eyes to catch the full of it and believe it for true.

Banzu buried his smile behind clenched teeth while Jericho's approving whisper stole through his mind. *And there it is, that fragile shatter in their eyes, the breaking of their confidence.*

The bowman froze in all but his blinking stare and opening mouth, the flutter of his lids attempting to deny the lie of his eyes and the miss of his arrow. Those beside him shifted their feet while gawking stunned, many switching their weapons between hands seeking reassuring purchase of hilts and handles while awakening to the truth of the real threat approaching them.

By impulse of another watching out behind his eyes Banzu flexed that strong inner muscle hardened by years of habitual training and through focal invocation seized another Power-flicker while inhaling sharp and deep through flaring nostrils, his amplified senses tasting the delicious salty tang of their growing fear an intoxicating perfume seeping from their pores and riding the winds between them.

Bartholomew regained control over his startled pie-face and slapped the bowman at his left on the chest with the back of his fat hand then fisted the two-head's taller archer's shirt and yanked him hunched while pointing at Banzu and ordering more arrows and truer aim against that failed shot surely nothing more than a misdirected trick of the eyes. The bowman shoved free and straightened, grimacing, hard eyes a thinning scrutiny of his target. He raised his yew bow, notched another arrow and drew aim then let fly—*twang!*

Banzu pulled Griever in another Power-flicker and cut the whispering missile from the air then sheathed his fanning blur of steel all in one fluid stroke while earning no pause in his forward stride. Again two bits of arrow sped past his unflinching face.

"Another!" Bartholomew yelled at the disbelieving bowman mid pause of pulling another arrow from the quiver strapped to his back, then Bartholomew broke into cursing shouts when several of his smarter crewmen abandoned their weapons in hasty tosses while turning scattered into runs away from the rest of their group who betrayed nervous shifts of staying put, not that they had anywhere to escape considering the planimal jungle enclosing them all inside the clearing.

Trapped, whispered Jericho's enticing lilt of voice. *We have them fish in a barrel. We—*

Shut up, Banzu commanded through mental speak, the 'we' insinuation unnerving him while earning a slight hitch in his step. *There's no we. Just shut up!*

Cussing out frustrations that his previous two shots failed at hitting their mark, the lanky bowman notched another arrow at the behest of his one-eyed employer barking orders to earn his monies. He spent a few deliberate seconds measuring steady while aiming true before releasing his next shot.

The snapping *twang* of bowstring sang again.

Closer now, refusing the pull of his sword, Banzu seized another Power-flicker and, his rising arm a fanning blur, snatched the Power-slowed arrow to halt inches short from piercing him between the eyes.

A hush stole over the clearing . . . broken by the brittle whisper then the repeated shout of it. "Holy gods!"

The brawny youth stripped bare to the waist and standing beside the bowman's left gaped at Banzu's undeniable catching of arrow then he considered his club through jolted eyes. He looked left, looked right. The club slipped loose from his opening hand. He spun on his heels and, shoving others out from his path, ran away opposite Banzu's closing approach.

A second man, squat and bearded, pointed with his hatchet at Banzu and shouted in quavering voice, "He's a godsdamned Soothsayer!"

A third man dropped his spiked mace onto the foot of the staring fellow beside him and pointed accusation at his one-eyed employer while the other abandoned his sword for hopping round and holding his painful foot. "The tower's cursed us! You've doomed us you fat bastard!" His head whipped side to side, darting eyes seeking possible avenues of escape, then he ran away in the brawny youth's wake—a youth who now stood across the way and facing the dense wall of planimal jungle obstructing his escape, waving his arms while darting forward then jumping back from the planimal snakevines snapping for bites of him, eager for latching then twining then pulling him inside in carnivorous feed.

While elsewhere unseen behind the thick jungle screen pierced several tortured screams, two overlong and one strangled short, evincing the grim fates of those having risked reentry.

Heads turned and eyes darted, attempting to fix upon the origins of those fading screams. Bartholomew's clustered crew twisted in panicky consideration of braving through the planimal jungle rather than facing the solitary Soothsayer swordslinger moments from closing space, but these men betrayed only twitches of movement, otherwise paralyzed in the middle of some contradictory debate their distressed minds proved incapable of deciphering.

As Banzu closed in upon them, stopping brazen in the middle of their crescent-shaped group. The courage of trapped prey and knowing it produced false intimidating stares upon him. Several raised their weapons while fighting hard at staying their trembles from showing. Others looked everywhere but him, the killing tools in their hands abandoned or forgotten. The stink of one man soiling his pants wafted strong, mixing with the urine fumes of another wetting his trousers. Beyond them, every digger in the long trench stood watching over the shoulder-high berm, so too their whipmaster with his uncoiled tongue of punishment hanging limp in his hand.

"Excuse me," Banzu said through gritted teeth, staring the taller bowman in the eye. He raised between them the unbroken arrow he snatched from the air, point up and fletching down, its thin shaft strangled in his tight grip of fist. "Is this yours?"

The bowman's gaze lowered to the arrow, elevated back to Banzu's molten stare. He opened his mouth, hung jaw vibrating, though produced no words.

Pressurized anger burst into focal rage flaring from the guttural depths of Banzu. He seized a Power-flicker and closed the bowman's mouth by shoving the arrow up through the soft underbelly of the unresponsive man's chin, snapping teeth shut and breaking while forcing with Powered velocity the arrow's steel tip into sprouting out the archer's blooming bridge of nose in a spray of blood and bone that pinned the man's jaws together.

A second Power-flicker and Banzu stepped back while cocking his hips then kicked forward, Power-booting the bowman in the center of his chest while producing a sickening *crack* of the man's breaking sternum. The transferred momentum of Power lifted the bowman up off his feet. His head and arms and legs whipped forward round his concaving middle while the rest of him shot backwards.

Broken ropes of blood loosening from his punctured face, the human missile of bowman bowled through those behind him and continued through the air twenty feet where he impacted a smaller cluster of Bartholomew's unlucky crewmen, crashing into their startled mix, his ragdoll body knocking them to ground in twisted heaps, though the bowman continued through and past them a short distance before meeting the ground in a flailing roll that ended just shy of the watching diggers peeking over the berm of the trench at the twisted ruins of a dead man lying so near.

Fear made men do stupid things, and those remaining at Bartholomew's sides proved no different. Weapons already in hand, the obvious threat standing so close in front of them, they attacked with the desperate fervor of prey gnawing its captured foot free from the tripped snare.

Or tried to. But against Banzu's incredible speed fueled by brief and boosting flickers of the Power, his retaliation proved impossible to counter by these slower playthings it made of normal men and their paltry bids against him.

What ensued next turned a chaotic flurry of memories, each action supplanting the next as he engaged them with brutal ease, seizing Power-flickers kinetically charging every bone-crunching blow he struck, his hands and feet blurring locomotion strengthened by velocity and hardened by force.

His blood up and thundering hot in his ears, the adrenal charge of Power mixed with the roaring rage driving his fierce need to hurt, to maim, to *kill!* Churning his mindscape into a savage frenzy of roiling violence sequestering the maddening insolence that they sought to take Melora away from him. *She's mine!*

Griever became a forgotten thing sheathed at his side, for he wanted to feel every ounce of pain inflicted through the abusive touch of his own bare hands. He possessed no formal training in empty hand-to-hand combat, and he needed none for the Power's added force provided the unyielding strength of punching fissures in solid rock without suffering more than knuckle scratches on his Power-hardened skin. His fists became swung hammers, his feet anchors of solid steel.

As Time dissolved into a rampage of destruction.

Motion in his right peripheral. A Power-flicker and Banzu grabbed a downward-stroking arm at the wrist, arresting the dagger short inches from stabbing into the top of his head. The wrenching twist of his strong trapping hand and bones snapped. The stabber loosed a terrible scream Banzu stifled by uppercutting the man's jaw, head whipping back, the transferred momentum lifting the man off his feet and backwards.

Motion in his left peripheral. A Power-flicker and Banzu slapped the slowed thrust of sword aside and shoved his foot down the front of another man's leg, grinding the outside edge of his boot so that the man's pants and skin beneath ripped down the front of his backwards-breaking leg to the splitting shin bone in a hanging, bleeding flap. Another scream pierced the air in music.

The slow flow of time ripple-snapped into faster passing for a brief space between Power-flickers. The two dispatched men tumbled backwards and away from Banzu's sides in screaming agony. He smiled, unfinished, and eyed new batches of targets.

"Ban . . ." Someone called to him, the female voice a lengthened stretch of his name his primal mind recognized though shelved aside to the outskirts of his awareness, for in this moment he knew only the doling of pain.

Power-flicker-twisting and Banzu swiveled his hips while throwing an elbow. The impact crunched the struck man's face, tilting him backwards, head whiplashing sideways on breaking neck, his broken nose releasing a beautiful arcing spray of blood to the air.

"Ban . . ." His name again, but he ignored it, buried it, drowned it, swallowed it beneath the effluent rage flaring inside him and heightened orgasmic through pent release.

"She's mine!" he yelled, raw and guttural, a defiance to the world and everyone in it, his emPowered voice ripping the air.

He spun away and delivered a rapid series of five Power-blurred punches in the stretched breadth of a single second, each struck blow landing to muscle-rippling effect upon the jolting man's stomach and chest punctuated by the dark jet of blood escaping the man's mouth from his pulverized innards punctured by the splinters of his cracked sternum and ribs.

"Ban . . ."

Banzu turned facing the inception of an elevating shout erupting at his left. Through Power-flicker he slipped past the felling stroke of machete and shouldered away the charging brute of muscle, sending the man tumbling backwards. Through another seize of the Power, this one longer by seconds, he twisted and thrust his palm out, striking another man dead center of chest while lifting him off his feet, the crunch of sternum bone a stretched breaking *snaaaap* of a noise heightened by the Power's exhilarating sensory rush. The impacted man's head and limbs threw forward while the rest of him collapsed backwards in a spine-arching human C.

"Ban . . ."

"Mine!" Banzu spun away, lowering, seizing the Power in increments of seconds now. He hooked his right arm out and caught behind the taller man's left leg by the crook of the knee. He continued his twisting spin while rising, tearing the man off his feet and spinning him lengthwise in the air. Banzu raised both fists overhead while the slow-flowing man's lazy suspension turned horizontally flush with the ground. Banzu brought both hammering fists pounding down atop the air-lying man's chest and stomach and jackknifed the body mid-air then crushed it down to the unforgiving ground. "Mine!"

Vomit and blood and mashed parts of organs erupted from the man's gaping mouth in a revolting fountain of smashed innards.

Banzu spun away from the gory spray, fevered eyes hunting more targets to destroy.

"Ban . . ."

By now Bartholomew turned to run.

Banzu seized a Power-flicker, blurred forward while reaching out. He knocked off the fat man's hat while catching him from behind by a handful of curly black hair, forcing the rotund man into the beginnings of bending over backwards. Banzu brought up one knee, planting it into bracing against Bartholomew's arching back while careful not to shatter what little spine the rotund man possessed, stopping the fat man from falling over. He yanked hard, scalping the one-eyed bastard in a skin-tearing jerk of wooly hair producing the satisfying sounds of ripping leather.

Released, Bartholomew rebounded up, his forward-whipping head throwing ropes and beads of blood through the air. He stumbled two steps forward and dropped to his knees in screaming agony, his trembling hands reaching for though not touching the bleeding wound of his missing scalp, too afraid of confirming his torn top as real through feel.

Banzu considered booting the fat man in his back and shoving him facedown to the ground while digging in his heel through the layers of fat on into spine just above the lower back to paralyze the wailing, blubbering mess, then decided to let the rotund man enjoy the agony given him.

Let the fat bastard sing for awhile.

"Banzu . . ."

The voice behind him again, closer now though still a faint sound lost within the raging presence of his mental fog.

He caught movement out from his right peripheral and spun through Power-flicker, stuffed the bloody scalp of greasy black hair into the open mouth of another man mid-yell and mid-swing of a steel-banded club. The stalled man's eyes bulged from his sockets in startlement. In one quick motion Banzu caught the attacker's club-swinging wrist while V'ing the pointer and middle fingers of his other hand. A stabbing thrust and those bulging eyes popped round Banzu's impaling fingers, oozing yellow-red goo.

He did not stop there. Instead and through another Power-flicker he drove his stabbing fingers forward, breaking through nose bridge into brain, and wiggled his invading fingers in the pulpy mush they made of brain matter before removing his offending hand and flicking it free of the gore.

"Banzu . . ."

The face-crushed man fell backwards, dead before he hit the ground.

Sailing the roaring red tides of rampage crashing through his hot swell of veins in a deluge quickening his heart with exhilarating thunder, Banzu spun facing his remaining targets, for to recognize them as true opponents elevated them beyond the lower station he deemed these pathetic excuses of men beneath him, his face a savage rictus grin, his wide and wild eyes afire. He cocked his fists to unleash another bone-crunching flurry of fatal strike as he seized the Power—or tried to but startled at feeling no purchase of Power contained within his eager inner grasp but for fading whispers of promise akin to a hand clutching smoke.

Melora's sharp shout from behind, "Banzu!"

"What!" Voice the raw fever of a guttural growl squeezed through clenched teeth, panting less from physical exertion and more from the animalistic rage burning through him and begging only for more release, he spun round, his clenched fists raised between them, and recognized through the enraged fog clearing behind his predator's glare Melora standing five cautious steps away though close enough to ensure her void-aura contained him within its magic-nullifying expanse, her stance a fighter's crouch, a dachra fisted in each of her hands, her face a terrible mask of dread astonishment.

The fear betraying through the condemnation of her scrutinizing glare struck him with the startling slap of a god's blow. But there lived something more in that uneasy look, an undeniable touch of awe delivered through silent exchange from a natural warrior appraising the work of another.

The red haze of his roiling mind cleared at the sight of her, while round him sang the agonized groans of his victims still alive and clinging to the pain he made of their brutalized bodies.

Banzu lowered his fists, knuckles throbbing sore, his hot roar of battle-fire extinguished, and there between them a quiet moment reigned but for the breaking of his heart while she assessed the possibility of his turning against her.

"By the gods," she whispered, straightening taller while regaining control of her consternation. "I can't believe . . . what have you done?"

Banzu opened his mouth, closed it, said nothing, his tongue a fumble.

Her gaze assessed a quick sweep of the carnage of felled men among the dead. She considered her dachras, considered Banzu, weighing both with equal measure, her cut right cheek from the bowman's initial arrow a thin scarlet smear of blood. Her face pinched up tensed, and violet fire sparked alight in her tightening gaze, her voice a scolding flare.

"What in the hell is wrong with you!" She advanced one commanding step toward him, but only that, gaze scanning the scatter of dead and injured, the few of Bartholomew's crew still standing shivering in paralyzed fright.

Banzu winced through a withering shudder earned by her accusation thrown against him. He gazed down at his upturned hands, stared at the cooling spots of blood thereon, flexed them closed and lowered them, wishing them clean. He half-turned from her, scanned over the ruins he'd made of these men in the span of a few deep breaths. Turned back, fixated on the smear of blood staining her cheek from the offending arrow's passing cut, and bridled fury pulsed with the threat of giving new rise to another blazing torrent he quelled a moment more through an audible swallow.

"I'm sorry." He looked once more at his bloodied hands in stupid wonder while the violence inflicted flashed rampant through his mind from an outsider's perspective, almost as if delivered by another's condemning hands and he the spectator. While fading echoes of laughter chimed through his mind. "I don't know what came over me."

But he did know, and he'd possessed barest control over it.

"Look at me," she said.

He responded nothing, stared overlong at the cruel tools of his hands.

"Look at me," she repeated in stronger voice.

Diminishing laughter soughing in his head, he flexed his hands, staring at the drying spots of blood thereon, his voice a whisper. "I've never done anything like that before."

"Look at me, godsdammit!" she yelled.

"What?" He elevated his gaze to her discerning glare.

She studied him overlong by leaning forward at the hips and squinting, peering into the depths of his soul through his eyes.

Banzu cringed. *She's checking for signs of the bloodlust. And I don't blame her after what I've done.*

Satisfied, she leaned back while lowering her dachras from between them, straightening tall. She drew in deep and huffed a terse breath, then put her bared fangs away—slowly, not breaking eye contact while she did so, caution lingering.

"It's okay," he said, voice a low tremor.

Behind him the sounds of diminishing footfalls evincing several of Bartholomew's crew breaking from their paralysis and running away. But he bothered no look back, did not care, too afraid of what she might assume of him after witnessing such unbridled fury.

"I won't hurt you." *Not you. Never you. Can't you see? I did this* for *you.* He dared a step closer while reaching out to her. "I would never—" And halted cringed at her immediate removing a wary half-step back from him so that he withdrew his offending touch. "I just—" A pause, a steadying breath. "I just lost control." *Gods, I almost had no control at all.* "It's okay now."

"It's not okay." Her voice a disapproving scorn, she threw her arms out in sweeping gesture at the strewn mix of maimed men and brutalized corpses lying the ground. "By the gods, Ban, look at what you've done."

For you. But he dared no voice behind it, too captured by the judgment of her glare, unable to persuade his gaze away. A powerful sense of urgency punched an ache in his chest for closing distance and reaching forth to soothe her cut cheek with the tender caress of his thumb, to draw her near and kiss her hurt away despite knowing her Spellbinder blood could lock him paralyzed if he licked it from his consoling lips and swallowed it. A tactic he'd wielded well against his bloodlust-corrupted uncle moments before his re-beginning. Instead he asked, "Are you okay?"

"Am *I* okay?" A lengthy pause. A dry chuckle. She crossed her arms and stared him down . . . for all of about five considerable seconds before the barest hint of a smile betrayed across her lips. "More than what they deserve." She gave another quick scan of the felled men and shook her head, whispered the word, "Incredible."

***

"Ooooh gods it hurts." Bartholomew's wailing moans elevated above the scattered others groaning over their own miserable abuses while squirming and twitching on the ground. "Ooooh gods the pain!"

Banzu turned, considered with no amount of pity the rotund man rolling round from side to side on his back, feet kicking beats of the ground, fat hands clutching at his missing scalp where ribbons of blood flowed generous between his plump fingers, his round pie-face a glistening crimson mask, his black eyepatch removed sometime during the tussle so that the hollow of its socket contained a tiny well of blood.

Unsure of what to say, not that Banzu even considered apologizing after what provoked the altercation let alone Bartholomew's voiced intentions of using Melora's blood to gain entry into the Builder's tower dead or alive, Banzu said nothing to the fat man wallowing in misery. Bartholomew suffered no injury beyond the profuse bleeding of his torn scalp. He would live to regret his mistake, if he did not bleed out over the next few hours in the clearing where he'd come seeking untold tower treasures the stuff of legend yet found only consequence.

"Why?" Banzu asked in the clarity of the aftermath. He glanced at the tower. "Why would they do such a stupid thing?"

Melora brushed against him while walking past, their gazes locking in briefest exchange—a silence of carnal heat flaring between them, felt more than seen—then she stood looming over Bartholomew, fists planted to hips. She surveyed the dismantled crew and smiled, shook her head, scoffed a curse then kicked the fat man in his ribs, producing a wheezing squeal from the rotund boss of thieves curling smaller into a bleeding ball of hurt.

"They were busying themselves with the trench," she said to Banzu, "hoping to luck a way inside the tower, all the while knowing someone might chance inside here because of the Veilfall." She made an admonishing *tsk-tsk-tsk* sound then kicked Bartholomew in the side of his head. "Isn't that right, little piggy?"

Bartholomew answered nothing but for moans and groans while he tottered through sideways rolls on his back in the grass.

"My fault, really," she continued. "I should've known they were prepared to spring an ambush at a moment's notice. Guess I was too focused on getting inside."

"That's one friggin hell of a coincidence if you ask me," Banzu said. "How would they even know we were coming? The Veilfall happened only two days ago."

"Not us in particular," she said without looking behind. "But someone, eventually. Every thief from the Rift to Junes knows the protective magics of the Builder's towers are failing now because of the Veilfall. Soon all of the towers will be left unprotected and ripe for plundering. All they had to do was wait, but their greed got the better of them." She jerked out a little shrug. "And then we happened along. Go figure the timing."

"The magic of the towers is failing?" Banzu asked.

Melora gave a last kick to Bartholomew's bleeding head then turned away, met Banzu's eyes. And for the life of him she did something so unexpected he was unsure he'd even seen it—she winked.

"Remind me never to make you angry," she said, smirking, then her visage tensed hard and warning edge bled into her voice when she raised her hand and waggled a stern finger at him, jabbing the air between them with emphasis. "And don't even think of speaking a single word of this to the Head Mistress, you got that? She'll twist my tits in a sling for what you did here." She lowered her admonishing hand and slapped at the kohatheen tied to her belt dangling at her right hip. "And not collaring you for it."

He nodded, said nothing.

She strode past him toward the tower. "Come on. You can't get through the tower's protective wards without me, so keep up."

He watched her walk away while working his hung jaw for some manner of response that never came. After a moment of just standing there, he turned from her shrinking back and scanned round, taking in the full spectrum of the gory mess he made of these greedy fools.

The diggers peeking over the berm of their trench ducked down, a long line of heads disappearing beneath the swept of Banzu's gaze. Most of the other thieves had taken flight during the one-sided brawl, scattering in panicked runs ending them short of the planimal jungle perimeter caging them in. They stood at various edges of the clearing, several with machetes in hand and debating braving an escape through the jungle in lieu of risking hope that the crazed Soothsayer spared them from the same brutal means inflicted upon their companions. The remaining few of Bartholomew's dismantled cluster of hired guards left untouched via Melora's stalling of Banzu's punishment stood with eyes wide on tensed faces, the fortunes promised them stolen in one quick and savage frenzy, the hot resentment of anger mixed with a greed denied replacing fear.

Faint cries sounded from the jungle, evincing the carnivorous planimals therein hard at work upon several escapees risking the outside world to no avail. While the remaining thieves collected together, safety in numbers flocking them, these scrambling about the grounds and fetching to hand the tossed weapons of their runaway fellows and those lying scattered between them.

Banzu swept the gatherers eyeballing him and Melora's turned back with a harsh gaze then turned and, through emPowered run, he surged into blurring sprint across the clearing to where lay his rucksack. Releasing the Power, he squatted and swiped remnants of blood from his hands upon the dewy grass then scooped up his rucksack and slung it to his back by weaving his arms through the straps.

He rushed in another Powered burst of speed into catching up with Melora from behind, the Power torn from his inner grasp the moment he entered the nullifying bounds of her void-aura so that he stumbled before catching balance, ensuring he walked within her protective void-aura before she closed distance to the Builder's tower awaiting them and breached its lethal magical wards.

He fetched an anxious glance behind.

At the bandits, those physically able, regrouping while re-arming. Several shouted curses while shaking reclaimed weapons aloft in threat. One of the men at their little group's front, his shirt damp with blood running from his broken nose, raised the dead archer's procured bow while notching an arrow the shorter man beside him cradling a broken arm handed off with his remaining good arm.

"Come on," Melora said, glancing over one shoulder, either not noticing or uncaring about the doings of the thieves regrouped behind them, the Builder's tower her only focus. "Play time's over, Ban."

But he slowed his steps regardless, trailing behind while she continued ahead. He said nothing while turning round and walking backwards, slowing, a fire rekindling inside and eager for burning through more victims. Just as the tail-end of her void-aura expanse removed from him there sounded the springy *twang* of bowstring so that he stopped and seized the Power while the bowman bandit let fly his notched missile in misguided retribution.

The loosed arrow speeding for the back of Melora's head slow-flowed mid-flight while the world brightened through luminous Power-greys flaring Banzu's senses ultra keen and his reaction into quicksilver promise. The air vibrated with a low whistling pitch of the arrow continuing its Power-prolonged flight. Until Banzu snatched it from the air while turning just as it began passing his face to pierce the target of Melora's head farther past. He snapped the captured arrow into two useless bits and flung them aside, while the bowman's expression elicited blooms of surprise hardened by resentful failure.

Kill them all. They deserve no less.

Still grasping the Power, Banzu grit his teeth, his right hand a fanning blur gripping Griever's hilt in a strangler's clutch. For a considerable moment he toyed with the notion of surrendering to the raging inferno requesting another release, of running into the fight and this time—*tear them all limb from limb. Spill their guts. Carve out their hearts!*

No!

He drew in a deep nostril breath and regained some semblance of control by squashing the emotional flare into a hot and savage ball he buried deep in his cooling depths.

He turned away while administering a reluctant release of the Power, and ran up to Melora from behind then, not stopping, he grabbed her by the hand and yanked her into following while rushing for the tower's open archway entrance ahead. "Come on!"

She clipped her protest short, body tensing resistance for the space of a blink then relaxing loose the next as she broke into run alongside him, given no other choice.

They closed in on the tower, and to Banzu's amazement the first shimmering protective wards of its invisible magics visualized before them in a shroud of rippling air surrounding the entire tower glimmering with faint touches of rainbow hues throughout. These perceivable energies divided round the surrounding bubble of Melora's dispelling void-aura in multicolored waves and crackling splashes bending split course, opening in front of them while closing in again behind them. He drew in a cautious breath and held it overlong, bracing for any magical impact despite knowing so long as he stayed within her protective void-aura he should be safe. He hoped.

He stole another glance behind at others joining the regrouping cluster of thieves beyond the lethal perimeter of the tower's magical wards staying them from pursuit, several raising their collected bows and notching more arrows. At his look Melora threw a glance behind and produced an "Oh!" of indignant surprise.

Breaching farther inward through the outer magical barrier of the tower, the air round their protective void-aura bubble popped and crackled and hummed alive with conflicting energies, the sounds of which muffled the belligerent shouts and curses issued from the bandits and their multiple snapping twangs of bowstrings releasing a slew of arrows.

On their way through the tower's high open archway entrance, and Banzu yanked Melora over to his side of the archway, spinning her on her feet while encircling her in his arms and spinning himself to press her back up against the inner wall a hairsbreadth before the pursuing flight of missiles shot through her absent space. The arrows *thwip-thwip-thwipped* past them by inches and *tink-tink-tinked* against the massive black builderstone column rooted up through the middle of the tower's otherwise hollow interior, wood shafts snapping against unrelenting builderstone, broken arrows falling to the floor.

Face to face now. Melora glanced over Banzu's shoulder at the broken scatter of arrows on the floor. "Oh," she said, only then realizing he had saved her just in the nick from becoming a human pincushion. She scrunched her face in that angry-cute way of her, nose crinkling. "Oh."

Her body tensed within his encircling fold of arms, craving action. She tried moving against him, tried freeing herself from his wrapping cling to venture outside yelling curses so that he released his grips and palmed the wall behind her while making restrictive bars of his arms at her sides.

"No," he said. Strange, some small part of him not beguiled with standing so close to her mused, how their situation turned the reverse in the span of a coinflip, he now keeping her a bay. "Just . . . no."

He lingered against her, arresting her to place while enjoying her prettifying features so close to his face, their lips inches apart, their locked gazes melding . . . and everything else vanished to the burning yearning for the taste of her mouth compelling him into leaning forward those few precious inches and kiss her.

But her left hand had come up unbeknownst to him and gripped him by the hair at the back of his head, stalling his pursuing lips a hairsbreadth short from touching hers where between their mouths joined breaths mingled.

An eager hunger gleamed in her approving eyes. The pink tip of her tongue darted out, gliding across her parting lips before disappearing back within the moist cave of her inviting mouth. But she put no voice to the strong carnal magnetism between them when she said, "Let's keep our eyes on the prize for now, okay?"

She gestured an indicative glance to her left beyond his barring right arm, past the open archway at the metal staircase spiraling up the circular wall through the incredible heights of the tower.

He ignored it, and tried for another kiss.

But she issued a little tug on his hair, depriving him short again, before letting go, and with her other hand she delivered a soft rabbit-punch to his stomach, producing from him a little grunt while pushing him back by inches.

Three more arrows *thwip-thwip-thwipped* through the archway and *tink-tink-tinked* against the builderstone column, a bare distraction in the background of their moment.

"Uhm." Banzu cleared his throat, hesitating withdraw, knowing he could steal a kiss with her hand free from his hair. But he wanted it returned. He tried concentrating on something other than her moist lips—at least the razor-thin cut high on her right cheek had crusted over into a fine line of dried blood—but the forced distraction proved too brittle to endure for more than a few longing breaths, there then gone in a hot flash of arousal's return. The strong gravity of her probing gaze drew him leaning in again, his eager lips parting with ache.

But she intercepted her hands up between them, palming resistance against his chest, stopping him just shy of connecting their mouths, the only sounds their commingled breathing, a breathy exchange between lips almost touching . . . until she eased him away a few torturous inches, then one full and agonizing step back from her, a hand pressing against the longing thunder of his heart beneath it, their eyes locked in sultry embrace.

"No," she breathed more than said. Though another pink darting of the glistening tip of her tongue gliding across her upper lip invited otherwise. She cleared her throat, and in an almost-whisper so faint Banzu barely captured it she said, "Not yet."

He made to question her implied promise—then hissed against the sharp curling of her fingers at his chest, her nails digging into skin through his shirt, arms tensing, eyes betraying the bridled intent of pulling him forward and kissing him regardless.

But just as quick she released her grips then dipped at the knees and ducked beneath his barring arms, slipping away.

CHAPTER TWENTY-FOUR

"Not yet?"

Banzu's sexual appetite lingering strong though the hungriest parts of him unfed by Melora's removal from between his barring arms, he repeated her whispered words in low voice to the empty space of wall in front of him, making of them a palpable promise tasted on his tongue while unsure if he'd heard them at all yet refusing them as imaginary.

Not yet.

He blinked refocus through the breaking of her sensuous spell their intimate proximity had cast over him, slipped his planted palms from the black builderstone wall and straightened, turned, watched her walk away.

Not yet?

Warm flushes of carnal heat slow in cooling, he considered every luscious contour of her gliding body from pale-blonde hair tumbling down over her narrow shoulders to her swaying backside shifting atop long toned legs adding suggestive little tilts to her cloaked hips with each swaying step, his lascivious stare fondling every feminine inch of her lithe frame, his deprived hands eager squeezes of air craving the substance of her soft flesh and the hard flexes of muscle beneath.

Not yet.

He blinked at her turned back. His hand rose of its own accord and fingertips touched at his lips, kindling the memory of their first kiss before his re-beginning, short and quick and thankful, then evoking that of their second kiss, deep and long and meaningful.

Neither of which this version of her remembered.

Her cloak belted tight round her slender middle accentuated her athletic physique in teasing ways only concealed curves afforded the prying eyes of one's aroused mind undressing the hidden figure beneath, eliciting hot whispers in the dark of his mind despite the screen of cloak depending below her waist hanging in a loose skirt split round her high-booted feet.

The moment fading, Banzu lowered his hand from lips to palming his chest atop the spot where she'd dug her fingernails into his skin while fisting bunches of his shirt before slipping away from him. He rubbed at her marking scratches beneath the shift of his uncle's necklaced ring, drew in a deep breath, sighed overlong through unfulfilled urges settling deep and festering, while toying with the dying hope that she might turn round at any moment and rush return into the fervent fold of his welcoming arms and yield to his exploratory hands and lips.

But alas, having achieved inside the Builder's tower, she became all Spellbinder Melora Callisticus again, a duty to perform and the focus to see it through.

"You coming?" she asked while glancing at him from over a dipping shoulder, the peering lure of her smoky violets offering trace suggestion of their tease from only a short moment before.

"Yeah." He nodded. "I'm coming."

They navigated round the massive builderstone column, which stood through the middle of the otherwise hollow interior of the immense Builder's tower as a wide black cylinder, moving opposite the open archway entrance while keeping the thick column between to avoid the bite from any more pesky arrows the resentful marauders clustered outside might shoot inside at next sight of them. The tower's protective magical wards prevented Bartholomew's bandits from entering the tower themselves.

But for how long?

Banzu stole a leftward glance at the high open archway before it disappeared from view when he pursued Melora into the safety behind the thick black column obstructing them from outside view.

She said the protective magics of the Builder's towers are failing now, fading since the moment I triggered the Veilfall.

He considered the hostiles awaiting them outside and how best to deal with them once she finished here and they continued for Fist.

The longer we're inside, the longer they have to devise some manner of trap.

But seconds more and the worry fled for little kid wonder fluttering curious butterflies in his stomach.

Gods, I'm actually inside a Builder's tower!

Though the bareness of it soured his waning excitement, the disappointing truth of its empty interior diminishing his years of imagining golden and silver spills of treasure pimpled with sparkling jewels between ancient magical artifacts lying atop or resting beside piles of arcane spellbooks and ensorcelled weapons the stuff of legend. The protective wards restricted all but Spellbinder entry, though they prevented nothing of the wind or rain from blowing in through the large open archway facing western Ascadia one could drive a loaded wagon through without so much as touching its wide sides or high top.

Something crunched beneath his next footstep so that he paused, earning a mute glance from Melora. He lifted his boot from the crushed bones of a small animal he did not recognize but could have fit into the upturned palms of both his hands together. *So, not all living creatures are barred entry then, only humans.*

As if to punctuate this actuality, a fine cloud of gnats so thin they bordered on invisible passed by his face in a low-buzzing swarm of breath. He blew at the annoying insects, shooing them in a scatter, then he drew in the musty, fungal air and swore to taste the passing of hundreds of years upon his tongue while he glanced round and up, wondering how long since a previous Spellbinder interloper encroached this tower if ever.

Enough room here to place a small house inside if one removed the builderstone column at its center—a thing he assumed acted as some manner of support, for the otherwise hollow tower possessed incredible height yet no bracers or crossbeams or any other such architectural support. Even Melora's expansive void-aura bubble—stronger by far said Jericho than any Spellbinder known, not that Banzu possessed any experience through which to compare it—shimmered the air round them its space of ten paces out from her in all directions where beyond lived agitated whorls of fluorescent energies and yet left the black builderstone walls untouched with plenty of space between.

Banzu reprimanded his roving attentions and closed more distance behind her, nervous of an accidental slip outside her protective void-aura and catalyzing the tower's lethal wards rendering him dead as the bandit corpses strewn round the grounds outside evincing an excruciating death. He imagined the gruesome torment of his ears bleeding and his eyes popping runny in his sockets while his tongue swelled in his throat and his skull collapsed. His agonized screams filling the tower with resounding echoes then cutting short from vomiting up his bubbling guts, his lungs afire to the poisonous air a vaporous acid—until he shoved aside those dire thoughts he could do nothing about other than stay within the protective scope of Melora's void-aura.

His avid gaze roamed the expanse of the tower's interior while he followed behind her, the only natural light by which to see in these shadowed windowless depths reflecting off the glossy blackness of the builderstone walls and floor provided by what little angled inside through the high open entrance offered from the sun seeking eventual dusk. Though supernatural displays of multicolored dazzles and sparkles broke their invisible glamours in the air in luminous splashes of glowing liquids bursting alive—in bright yellows and angry reds and twinkling whites and glittering purples and more—against the outmost bounds of Melora's void-aura bubble housing them as they moved together behind the wide column.

The Builder's magical safeguards hummed and thrummed and crackled and fizzed in elevating agitations of energies attempting to pierce the defiant void-aura bubble for the two trespassers protected therein. Sinuous throbs of luminous streams swirled and snaked through the air with a sentient presence of mind, shaping into aggressive serpentine bands of magic attracted to the life moving within their disturbed tower nest. These attempted snapping bites of the human morsels though upon void-aura contact each burst into sparkling explosions of glistening dewdrops which did not fall away so much as disperse into lazy floats through the air defying gravity's pull then coalescing moments more.

Others such hissed while darting in at them though bounced away into reversing their stabbing trajectories as if Melora's void-aura swatted them back. Others still, blinking their soft pinks or electric blues or glowing greens, drifted inward and there hovered to within inches of her void-aura perimeter, daring no contact with its spherical edge, content with watching and perhaps cognizant enough to understand the self-destruction of its baneful touch.

Glowing snowflakes of flickering white-gold magics trickled down from the impenetrable darkness high above in flittering floats round them that fizzled into nonexistence upon void-aura contact so that Banzu entertained the urge of reaching out and capturing a stray drift of flake despite knowing the effort would earn him intense pain the moment his testing hand breached through Melora's void-aura and trespassed into the world of magical activity beyond. Or worse, the deliberate try might remove his hand altogether before he could recoil it to safety. Unsure of the true affect, and he wished no risk of learning the answer.

Flitters of their long trek through the planimal jungle stole through his mind, but the vegetation tunnel opening round them paled when compared to this.

So this is what it's really *like for her.*

He opened his mouth to voice the thought aloud then tamed it quiet in his throat. Immune to magic in a world full of it, Melora had never and would never feel its direct influence because of her circumstances of birth. Not just a Spellbinder but the most powerful Spellbinder alive. And her aizakai void-aura enclosed her, wrapped her, trapped her inside its magicless world she carried with her always.

Banzu realized then the true unhappiness a Spellbinder's void-aura imposed upon them along with the good of its constant protection.

They can never feel magic, and worse they can see its taunting play forever beyond their incapable reach. Gods, I never realized its . . . its torture.

Melora's void-aura had prevented the attending Lady's Chapel priests and priestesses from staunching her dying mother's profuse bleeding with healing magic during her bloody childbirth. As well it cost her the father who blamed her for the death of his beloved wife, then earned her abandonment to the wilds as a helpless child.

Banzu swallowed down the sympathetic pang welling in his throat while restraining the urge for closing in on her from behind and taking her in his arms and just holding her. Instead he gazed through the protective window of her void-aura with a wiser eye, a little less fascinated though still enticed by the hypnotizing swirls and whorls of magics at play round them. Amazing their riot of colorful splendors now and inside, so vibrant and alive, where before and outside they appeared as nothing more than faint translucent shimmers of air.

"Are all the towers like this?" he asked.

Melora shrugged, fetching no look behind. "I don't know. This is the first tower I've even been in."

"Uhm." He jolted stopped, a cold nervous hitch flushing through his clenching guts. "What?"

But she said no more as she finished past the thick column toward the bottom of the spiral stairs waiting to facilitate them all the way up to the tower's dark top.

* * *

They reached the bottom of the spiral flight of stairs—these wrought from a thin dark metal Banzu did not recognize though it appeared sturdy enough despite its narrow width denying them side-by-side climbing—which snaked its winding track up the rounding interior walls of the tower and disappeared into the inky blackness high above.

Melora started up first, Banzu following.

The strange corrugated steps chimed soft metallic echoes of their footfalls, and the luminous magical marvels pursued them while lighting their climb. Banzu, three steps behind and thus eyelevel with Melora's backside, dismissed the lightshow for the seductive sway of her hips, enjoying every jounce of her ascending steps and all they afforded her butt jiggling beneath her tight cloak. His blood flushed hot and eager again so that he fantasized leaning forward and partaking a frisky bite accompanied by two handfuls of juicy squeezes—then shook himself free of the crazy notion that would earn him a fierce slap and a backwards tumble down the stairs while delivering him outside her void-aura to a sure death.

He averted his gaze to everywhere but ahead, yet thoughts of her retaliating slap aroused him even more. He forced repulsive images of the unliving Trio into his mind as deterrent to the lusting itch begging for the satisfying scratch.

Three dead khansmen with coils of guts hanging loose from their split bellies, salivating maws gnawing bites of the air in hungry want of chomping Banzu's flesh, full black eyes voids of humanity reflecting captured glints of firelight, their bloodied shreds of clothes and pale skin lacerated from Griever's earlier handiwork, then bursting afire and collapsing into putrid piles and melting flesh upon entering Melora's burning void-aura, then the gruesome work thereafter of clearing their camp.

Banzu shuddered through the thought, arousal abandoned.

They continued up the spiral stairs, Melora's fingertips gliding atop the waist-high metal railing to their right in gentle tracing as that of a lover's long leg for the choice goodies above and—

"Friggin hell," Banzu muttered under his breath. Try as he might, there existed no escape from the invasive thoughts of her touch after their little intimate encounter below. He bit his bottom lip, tasted blood through the flash of pain.

"What?" Melora paused, half-turned and looked at him. "You say something?"

"No," he said—or tried to, but it came out an obscure sound with his bottom lip pinched tight between his clamping teeth.

She shrugged and returned to her steady though unhurried climb.

He took the railing in a loose grip to better occupy his mind, unsure if the thin length of safety metal might snap if he leaned against it and so edged closer to the rounding wall on his left while following up behind her, averting his gaze to everywhere but ahead as they ascended into the heights of the darkness above shying away into magical soft-glow with every step.

He paused at one point and leaned sideways for a peek over the railing, and in a dizzying moment of vertigo he swayed to the downward spiral evincing hundreds of feet already climbed. He closed his eyes for a stretch of imbalance then blinked refocus. And yelped, jolting, when something hot and sharp stung his backside so that he rushed the stairs and caught up behind with Melora.

"Best keep up or lose a buttcheek," she said. She laughed, and the music of her voice carried through the depths of the tower in playful echoes. But a moment more and her tone returned serious. "Or worse. Don't straggle. Now's not the time for mistakes when we're so close."

"So close to what?" he asked while rubbing the sting from his prickling right buttocks that had slipped just outside her moving void-aura during his pause. But she answered nothing so that he held his tongue a few climbing minutes more before trying again. "So, what is it we're looking for again?"

Silence but for the soft metallic echoes of their ascending footfalls, though she punctuated her mute glance with an arching tease of her brows.

He sighed, pursuing. *At least we're here. Can't be much longer.* And glanced up. *How high up do these friggin steps go anyhow? My calves are burning. No matter. We'll get what she's after, whatever the frig it is, then be on our way to Fist. And if it's heavy she can carry it. Still have those stupid bandits to deal with though, and . . .*

* * *

Their long and spiraling climb lasted a quarter turn of an hour by Banzu's rough estimation. Beads of sweat dappled both their brows by the time they finished atop where ended the metal stairs butting against a short run of builderstone platform leading to another open archway, this second one an exact match in size and upside-down U shape to the one making the bottom entrance, neither possessing doors. Beyond it awaited a large domed room, a rotunda capping the tower.

"Thank gods," Banzu whispered while scrubbing sweat from his brow with the back of a forearm.

Melora started forward.

"Wait." He snagged her back and aside. "Might be traps inside."

"My void-aura—" she began.

"Not the magic kind."

He shrugged from his rucksack then tossed it through the archway into the room in underhanded pitch, where is slid a space while rousing up puffs of dust, attempting to spring any possible physical traps therein.

Nothing happened.

She made a face and started forward again.

But he barred her path past him with his extended left arm then proceeded ahead of her, his right hand testing Griever's hilt in anxious little squeezes and his swordslinger instincts at the ready in case some unforeseen danger lurked therein. Her void-aura prevented any magical attacks, but he wanted the familiar reassurance of tangible steel in his masterful grip regardless.

They entered the rotunda exposed by tall thin slits running along the walls from floor to ceiling, inches-wide slits with several feet of thick builderstone wall between each slice three hand spans wide, allowing in strong bars of sunlight at this time of day along with a gentle airflow which breathed more than blew. Though the new light proved unnecessary compared to the sparkling brilliance of conflicting energies losing constant dazzling battles against the nullifying periphery of Melora's void-aura which chased away all remaining spots of shadow not already burned clean by the checker of golden sunbars piercing into the domed room.

The rotunda appeared more a dusty storeroom half-full of all manner of mysterious prizes and strange junk. Fragments of chainmail here, many of the links rusted into an orange mass. Broken saber-blades there. Moldering uniforms of exotic weaves and unrecognizable sigils elsewhere. Several wooden tables large and small rested with clutter atop, a variety of mysterious trinkets and unnamable tools scattered thereon.

The top of the thick cylindrical column running up through the tower's middle jutted waist-high from the floor's epicenter and ended there, well short of the high dome ceiling.

The place betrayed some manner of workshop, a Tinker's playroom wrought from a child's active imagination, with lathes and mallets and chisels and other such tools hanging on little metal hooks suspended on the curving walls where not scattered atop the assorted tables and parts of the floor. Some tools Banzu recognized, though most he did not.

He stepped over his rucksack, approached the closest table, and studied the collection of bizarre gadgets crusted in dust, poking first then picking one up and turning it about while inspecting it.

"Stay inside my void-aura," Melora cautioned, following after then passing by him.

Too fascinated by the curious baubles for bothering a look up, he nodded.

"The Builder actually made these?" He turned while holding up one of the peculiar little devices so she could better see it, a deceptively heavy thing with a bent handle attached to the end of a length of hollow metal tube which made a kind of curved L shape. He fumbled it round in his hands until it came into a way that felt a perfect position for holding it—an L turned rightways.

Melora, who dismissed the tables and their collections of dusty trinkets and papers with a passing glance only and had walked straight for the rotunda's center to the stony column's top, glanced him an indifferent shrug. She set her palms upon the stone edge of the column's top and leaned forward.

He frowned at her indifference then thumbed the little piece of metal that resembled a tiny hammer sticking out of the top bend on the L-shaped thing in his hand, applied some pressure and watched as the little barrel side of it turned then *clicked* into place as if specifically designed to do just that. He poked his right pointer finger inside the little loop beneath that rotating barrel then curled it round the thin curved sliver of metal sticking down within in much the same manner as a crossbow's trigger.

"Hey, look." He raised the small though heavy gadget out so that its length of pipe pointed at her. "What do you think this does?"

She faced him from the waist-high top of the column, squinted at the peculiar doodad in his hands and shrugged. *It is what it is*, that shrug said, disinterested. "You might want to put that down. My void-aura only protects you against the magics here, not these mechanical gadgets." She gave the device in his hands a dismissive flick of her wrist. "Whatever they are and whatever they do."

Both arms extended in the curious way of a natural feel, and still aiming the L-shaped device at her, Banzu began squeezing his pointer finger against the thin sliver curvature of metal trigger, which possessed some springy give, watching while its little cocked hammer vibrated with snapping intent . . . then he eased the squeezing tension from his finger and returned the mystery to the table, deciding it best not to test the odd device. Just in case. *The thing probably doesn't even work anyways, whatever the frig it is.*

A light stir of dust puffed round the alien contraption that shown the unfamiliar words ***Roland .45*** stamped into the side of its metal tube in tiny print. He waved his hand through the cloud—a gesture only serving to waft it up into his face—and coughed. He flicked and poked through a few more of the strange devices lying about the table then walked to Melora, his curiosities shifting anew.

"Whatcha looking at?" he asked, looking down at what held her studious gaze.

The top of the column proved not solid but hollow, evincing some kind of well. A deep and empty well, its straight throat black and long. He palmed the builderstone edge beside her and leaned forward for a better view down in the hollow column. "Looks like it runs the whole way down through the tower. Maybe even farther. But why?"

Melora stepped away, leaving him there to ponder the mystery in solo regard.

"What the frig is this for?" He leaned forward more, peering down into the deep black hole into which he hawked and spat then watched the tiny white dot of his spittle disappear down into the black abyss.

"That," she said from behind, "is a Traveling Well. All of the Builder's towers have them, and all are linked to the fistian Academy for when the last Soothsayer is found." A hesitant pause, the clearing of her throat, her gaze darting away then back. "It's what will take you to Fist."

Paying her limited attention, he leaned forward ever more, staring down into the black pitch of the seemingly bottomless tunnel of the purported Traveling Well. "How does it—" he began then clipped his words short.

You, she'd said, his mind awakening to the slow dawning of a new and painful understanding. Not *us*, but *you*.

Jaws bunching, he chewed back a curse. His fingers tensed into rigid claws atop the Traveling Well's waist-high edge.

Friggin hell. I'm so stupid. She's been baiting me here this whole time. I nibbled the carrot, and here's the stick.

"You tricked me," he said, not turning from the well, fingernails scraping upon the stonework edge while his hands curled into tight fists. Whatever the magic at play here in this tower, it would deliver him and him alone to Fist. He raised his fists then slammed their clenched meat down against the unforgiving stone lip. Sharp pain shot through his forearms to the elbows. But he ignored it. "You lied to me."

"I did what I had to do," she said from behind, her tone low but unashamed, soft though unapologetic. "And now we're here. Right where we need to be."

"I believed you," he said through clenched teeth. "I trusted you."

She approached closer behind him. "And I'm trusting you to do what must be done."

Godsdammit. He closed his eyes, drew in a deep nostril breath. *Godsdammit!* But the anger scalding his guts refused surrender to anything but release. He turned round to unleash his fury in a cursing flare of voice and—

—and she was there, pressing close against him, smiling, her intense violet gaze capturing his, the heat of her breath a tickling presence brushing across his lips.

He wanted to lash out at her for tricking him here all the while knowing it meant leaving her behind. But his desire for her burned away all other thoughts and . . . wasn't he supposed to be mad about something? He made to speak—and she hushed him quiet with the risen tip of her barring finger.

"Sages claim the eyes are the windows to the soul," she said, their gazes locked, her tone a low and seductive purr. "That's how I really knew you weren't lying. And that's also how I knew you'd refuse to go without me. I don't remember anything of what you say was there between us before." She brought her other hand up, touched her left temple. "But there's a feeling of memory here, like an itch at the middle of my back I can't reach but can't ignore. I felt . . . something between us when you were there, stepping out from nowhere to save me. But I wasn't sure what. Because I've never felt it before."

"Why didn't you say anything—" he began.

But she cut him short by sliding her barring pointer finger down into his mouth where she hooked him by the bottom teeth and pulled him those necessary inches closer so that the tips of their noses touched. She slid her finger out from his mouth, raked her fingernails back through his hair where she gripped a handful of it and gave the back of his head a playfully serious little tug, her mesmerizing violets never once leaving his captured gaze.

"Saying and doing are two different things." She teased herself forward into brushing the pink tip of her licking tongue across his bottom lip before easing back and starting her words anew, an exchange of hot breath between their open mouths so close. "Promise me you'll forget the Khan and focus on the Godstone." A pause while she glided the glistening tip of her tongue across her lips, wetting them. "Or you'll never have me again."

"Again?" Held tantalized by her, he tried leaning forward and closing that painful distance between their mouths. But her hand restrained his head back by the hair, denying him satisfaction. "I thought you said you weren't mine to—"

"I lied." She kissed him full and deep while pressing up against him in urgency for his pressing return.

And his need for her took precedence above all else. He moved against her in mouth and in body, taking her in his arms while forcing her backwards a step, then another. And she pushed against him, two lovers fighting for surrendered control over the other so that his bottom pressed return against the Traveling Well's edge.

She withdrew a step, and he pursued forward. But she shoved him backwards into place against the well and shook her head.

"Stay." She untied her belt, opening it with slender competent fingers, shrugged out from her cloak and flung it away into a forgotten swirl. Those hands moved down to the front of her pants, began undoing them open.

Banzu watched her, mouth hung, his quickened heart an anxious flutter hammering in his cage of ribs, his breaths short and rapid, his mind aflame with desire burning through the stupefying fog denying the moment. *Is this really happening? Here? Now?* He made to speak.

The front of her pants undone, she strode forward and slapped him across the face.

Wincing, startled and loving it, the sting of his cheek stoked the carnal fires inside, flaring them, as his head whipped aside. He looked at her—and her striking hand was there again, caressing gentle strokes to the rosy abuse of his left cheek, her pets the soft gliding touch of crushed velvet.

"Promise me." Her voice a silken hiss.

"I promise. But—"

"Hush!" A hungry smile. "No more words."

Her hands quested down between them, first yanking up the tucked-in front of his shirt, then undoing the front of his pants for his aroused member bulging beneath.

The reality of her working hands strangled him mute. Then raw, carnal instinct gripped him in its fevered clutch and made of him all animal desire for her delectable flesh when she squatted while jerking down his pants and underwear, bunching them round his ankles, then straightened tall all in one quick motion.

He shifted through little back and forth stamps, not so much freeing a leg as reversing the length of pant still trapped round it. While Melora stepped back a space and removed her pants and panties, baring herself nude below the waist.

The warm wet heat of her sex licked against his throbbing member when she glided forward and pressed against him, their mouths tangling briefly before she leaned back and propped her right foot up behind him atop the well's edge pressing against his bottom. She reached down and gripped him at the same time she leaned forward and caught his bottom lip between her pinching teeth. She gave his throbbing member an assertive squeeze, rose up on tippy-toes then slowly, in gasping increments, settled herself atop him, accepting him inside her, as she released his caught lip, their eyes carnally locked, him inhaling her satisfied exhale during that first welcoming thrust joining them together as one . . .

* * *

. . . at last and after spilling his seed inside her, Banzu settled his bottom atop the Traveling Well's edge and resigned into soothing relief after Melora withdrew from off him and backed away, her face and neck flushed, the delectable flesh of her milky thighs glistening, his hands sliding free of her bare hips as his arms lowered down from round her, both of them panting as the sedative relaxation of true gratification spread through them.

Their gazes held in a silent exchange of spent passion, and for a time silence reigned between them.

"I'm sorry," she said at last, taking one full step back from him, her tone a crushed whisper of a thing.

And for the life of him he smirked and chuckled, wanting nothing but more of her. "Don't be sorry—"

"For this." She surged forward, both hands shoving against his chest, pitching him tumbling backwards over and into the deep dark depths of the Traveling Well's gaping maw swallowing him from behind, his spread legs rushing up at her sides then over her head in a quick-tilting V and whipping of his pants.

The world rolling, his arms pinwheeling at his sides, he tumbled backwards over the well's edge and fell down into the darkness of its abysmal black throat. A panicked scream locked in his hitching chest, he flailed and twisted in the air to no rebalancing avail, the smooth circular builderstone walls flashing upwards in peripheral blurs, the darkness deepened by the whooshing air rushing past while flapping his clothes in fluttering beats.

Griever's sheathed tip banged, and knuckles scraped against the flowing stony walls as he fell so that he hissed against the barks of pain while recoiling his flailing arms inward, his tumbling sense of imbalanced direction lost save for the strong pull of gravity yanking him deeper and down. His startled heart pounded cold thunder, and in his tumbling plunge he caught glimpses of a shrinking pinprick of light through which she'd shoved him inside.

Oh my gods I'm gonna die I'm gonna die I'm gonna die! His only repeating thought in this mad spiral plunge of panic, stark realization of the well's bottom rising up to deliver its stopping splat the crush of bones. *I'm gonna die I'm gonna die I'm gonna die oh my gods!*

Desperation took instinctive control.

Banzu captured a deep breath, bracing for impact, and seized the Power.

The darkness exploded through fantastic blooms of luminous twilight greys bursting alive with swirling rainbow waves of bright vibrational magic engulfing him in his falling frenzy while at the same time transmogrifying the air into some thickening agent of abstruse viscous liquid substance.

The growing physical pressure slowed him in a strange sensation of submerged gooey fluid so that he feared drowning in the multicolored spasms of magic their effervescent blooms and shifts shaping then snaking while twining round him. Falling became floating became a torrent of pulling, still down, the activated magics of the Traveling Well guiding him . . . ushering him away . . . taking him away from her.

* * *

Melora gasped while startling back several steps from the coruscating eruption of energies shooting up from the mouth of the humming Traveling Well seconds after Banzu's backwards tumble inside it, the fierce luminosity blasting up then splashing outward across the rotunda's domed ceiling while the entire Builder's tower trembled and shook with vibrational resonance.

She closed her gaping mouth into a frightened smile, shivering orgasmic through the virgin rush of terrifying exhilaration flushing through her prickling network of nerves at the Traveling Well's magical effluence penetrating her void-aura in recurring waves of tingling warmth, each more potent than the previous, leaving her in awed wonder. A smile burrowed into her savage beauty, and her breathing quickened short and rapid as a deep sensual pleasure coursed through her, the sensational radiance of its influence upon her stimulated senses marvelous beyond the limited scope of paltry words.

She craned her head in mute wonderment to the ceiling where rippled an expanding ocean of rainbow splendor—that seconds more coalesced, shrinking, withdrawing, when the magical dazzle of heated lights inhaled return down within the Traveling Well's deep dark abyss, seconds only, vanishing in a vacuum swallow, the Builder's tower stilling its vibrational resonance, leaving behind a stunning silence of inactivity.

For a long and confounding moment she stared in dazed reverie at the Traveling Well while wrestling with the myth made real, Academy lore unknown since the Thousand Years War, the Divine Magic of the gods, the only magic capable of trumping the nullifying influence of a Spellbinder's void-aura.

And I felt it. By the gods I actually felt it!

She pulled her panties and pants back on while her recovering mind circled round the purpose for her coming here and of the lusty minutes shared before that necessary push where reason had melted into intense passion between her and Banzu. He had thrilled her from the very beginning, not that she allowed more than a hint of her approval from slipping loose, though in the end her attraction to him overpowered her sense of duty.

But I did it. He's in the Head Mistress's capable hands now, and gods bless her because she'll have her hands full.

She did up the front of her pants while looking to her right, gaze hunting for her discarded traveler's cloak while her mind sought to reorient itself, already devising ways of slipping through Bartholomew's bandits awaiting her return outside, already begrudging her long lone walk back to Fist afoot.

An odd sense of presence across the room, that of someone watching her, prickled her innate sense of guard. She tensed, gaze shifting, sought its origin and squinted for better focus upon the shimmering crimson swirl of energy disc hovering vertical mid-air past the Traveling Well, its soft whisper crackles distinct in the quiet aftermath of siphoned magics. She fixed upon the little round vortex window of a thing floating beyond the shimmer-thin translucent membrane bounds of her void-aura.

"What the . . ."

She approached it, as well the impossible visage of the one watching back at her through it, while questioning the sanity of her lying eyes.

CHAPTER TWENTY-FIVE

The spacious Receiving Room within the Divine Palace of the reigning Lord of Storms hung heavy with the brooding silence emanating from the muscled figure seated upon his great ivory throne. Its ruminate occupant, stripped bare to the waist, presented a disquieting statue of dark contemplation.

Splatters and speckles of blood stained Hannibal Khan's bleached leather breeches and boots while smears of it painted across his proud swell of sweaty chest, his wide-muscled shelf of shoulders and broad back, some of it dry and flaking, more of it wet and warm and dripping, none of it his own.

A seething indignation thundered within the Khan, demanding silence lest any of those present earn the smiting brunt of his infamous wrath, a maelstrom of rage contained by thinnest margin though brewing since yesterday's world-wide awakening wrought by the Veilfall.

Thus far he displayed precarious control over his rage, having beaten to death through the vicious pummeling of his gauntleted fists a fair sum of no less than fifty aizakai scapegoats extracted from the execution pits beneath the palace, their pulverized corpses dragged then tossed by attending serviles into the absent Enclave serpent-priest Nergal's traveling pool before returning to his throne, the voracious appetite of his killing lusts fed though still unsated.

The gory spectacle of his barbarous brutality delivered a savage show to the wide-eyed spectators within the Receiving Room, his hundred attending Bloodcloaks aligning the walls in red-gold armor at first cheering on the wild ferocity of their Lord of Storms while serviles gasped and stared though dared not turn away lest they become part of their acrimonious godking's gruesome entertainment.

Though over the course of long hours—with intermittent pauses between savage beatings, the Khan sitting his throne and resting while sipping spiced wine or nibbling smoked meats and cheeses before ordering in his next victim, and one restful snooze upon his ivory perch lasting but three hours before he awoke eager for more—even the most desensitized loyals of the Khan's veteran Bloodcloaks cringed silent as the frenzied beatings took the dark turning from quick punishment into lengthy sadistic pleasures of torture.

He ripped limbs from sockets through the incredible ease of his muscled bulk and with the laughing glee of a deviant child plucking wings from insects, after snapping femurs or stomping tibias shattered. He tore entrails from stomachs for means of strangling when not yanking organs out through splintered cages of ribs and squeezing them into crushed pulps he stuffed down choking throats. All while cursing the Veilfall and the Godstone and the absent Nergal.

His brutal rampage started yesterday afternoon with the beautiful harpist whose discombobulated fingers plucked sour notes announcing the Veilfall's flush of memories affecting her waking mind. Riled by the heated exchange of Nergal's hasty leaving moments after the Veil's lifting, the Khan crushed the huge harp into a groaning twist of brass mass then proceeded to beat the screaming harpist to death—with her own leg he tore from her hip, its foot still chained to the destroyed instrument.

Tantrum unfinished, and bellowing about the Godstone, he yanked golden cages from their suspensions of chains or kicked them over from their tall stands and stomped them flat while crushing the squawking birds therein.

He returned to his throne for a space while terrified servants rushed the room and cleared away the bloody wreckage.

Dissatisfied, the Lord of Storms' blood up and boiling behind his piercing stare where lived depths of murder and the fierce need to appease it, he ordered more victims with a viper's smile.

The condemned heathen aizakai—most of these men though including several women and children, for the Khan proved generous in his doling wrath and did not discriminate even among his lowliest subjects—told by the Pitmaster who dragged them forth in chains then again by the tyrant warlord to kill him earned their freedom, he pulverized to death or nearly so in what amounted to little more than a long file-line of human chattel filling the southern hallway outside the Receiving Room with emaciated casualties-to-be shuffling along to their eminent slaughter at the gauntleted hands of the mad godking.

Of course, the Khan's generosity knew no bounds so that he allowed the nearly-so's the grace of choking on their blood while he returned to his throne for a temporary reprieve of panting and sipping and nibbling. Tremulous servants rushed the dais and dabbed away glistening sweat and splotches of blood from his heaving swells of muscles with soft white linen towels while he watched with a forgiving smile beneath ecstasy-glazed eyes over the heathen aizakai fouling his floor with their teeth and bits of teeth and blood and evacuations of bowels and bladders where they lay gasping strangled wheezes into their crushed lungs, their hitching struggles of breath music to his almighty ears.

Eyes upon him now, from those that dared look, and the labor of his breathing settled calm in his muscled slab of chest while the storm within roiled and swelled behind the basilisk stare of his pensive gaze forward. Every now and again he raised one gauntleted hand before his handsome face and engaged with musing glee as bluish arcing sparks of tiny lightning tongues shocked in crackling magical dance over its silvery lanthium surface where burned away the bloody spatters and clings of skin from his pummeled victims only to will its power bridled a tense moment later and return his hand to the thick ivory armrest dappled with blood and thin streams of blood, where fingers closed into joining its other as a clenched fist of stern arrogance.

And the thin pink scar running down his left cheek from brow to chin, that Spellbinder's dachra kiss the only observable mar on his otherwise handsome features topped with golden curls . . . he considered touching it at times between godsforged gauntleted seizings by raising a finger to it then settling the hand into the makings of a fist a hairsbreadth before contact.

His ongoing plans for hunting down the woman who gifted him that facial scar, the former slain king's Spellbinder Vizer Melora Callisticus, she who dared mark him so before escaping his smiting wrath, those plans abandoned after two years of persistent chase by his otherwise proven Trios of assassins.

His adamant hunt for the woman of his fixation turned obsession a failure replaced by another dreadful fascination—though he demanded a final piece to that irritating puzzle in capturing Melora through the foresight visions of his favorite aizakai pet Sera.

The latest Trio failed him, dashing his fading hopes of exacting savory revenge upon the elusive Spellbinder bitch evading every attempt at retrieving or killing her.

Now more significant matters lay in hand, heavy with weight and demanding immediate attention. Hannibal Khan contemplated a different warring front, this of his earlier obligation to a greater importance than vengeance, an obligation unchanged though impacted regardless by the Builder's wretched Veilfall. His attentions returned to procuring the rest of the Dominator's Armor, its pieces scattered, its reassembly the sole purpose of his soul he bargained to the Enclave.

The Dominator's Armor, a godly relic of immeasurable power from the Thousand Years War and suffused with divine magic. He wore the godsforged lanthium lightning-calling gauntlets of its dismantled suit though only just. Such a terrible craving to procure the other components promised him by the Enclave who gifted him its gauntlets prior to crushing Junes under his dominant fists, for once he reassembled the entirety of the Armor's pieces the whole of it would transcend him above the lesser mortals plaguing this world and instill the immortal godhood he desired—no, deserved.

Or so the demonic serpent-priest Nergal promised.

The complete Dominator's Armor would imbue Hannibal Khan with immortality while bestowing such frightening power as to make even the gods tremble in abject terror. Just as had their mortal avatars during the Thousand Years War when the Nameless One—the First of the Fallen, the Ebony Prince, the Breaker, his true name Malach'Ra—wore the unholy suit and stalked the One Land of Pangea to devastating consequence of all inferiors both god and man crushed beneath his destructive tread.

Until Simus Junes, backed by his Soothsayer Grey Swords and an army of aizakai, dismantled the Armor while banishing Malach'Ra from the mortal plane thus ending the Thousand Years War, separating its pieces to only the Head Mistress's precious Book of Towers knew where.

Hannibal Khan cared nothing as to how the wicked-tongued devil-eyed serpent-priests of the Enclave came to possess his gauntlets without the Book of Tower's special knowledge. Nergal assured him possession of the remaining pieces once he tore the book from the Head Mistress's cold dead grasp—after crushing the aizakai heathen's den of the Academy in Fist, the second glorious step of his spreading rule after conquering Junes.

Until the Veilfall happened.

Cruel impatience swelled while Hannibal Khan waited for his demonic link to the Enclave to return.

Yesterday's Veilfall changed everything in Nergal's mind yet altered nothing in the brooding Khan's. The expanse of his empire continued regardless the Godstone's fall.

A heated altercation tempered only by Nergal's demonic compulsion took place before the serpent-priest slipped away into his traveling pool, the argument disturbing the current course of the Khan's dominating plans which until yesterday saw his vast army of loyal Bloodcloaks and fanatical worship-followers advancing from the Holy City of Khan with the drilled remorselessness of some terrible machine spreading their godking's rule throughout all of Thurandy. To the west only Fist and farther Bloom remained absent his imminent rule, while southern Grey Raven's Keep presently fell beneath the crushing tread of his divided forces. An army that, once gathered, would flood over Fist then Bloom in a deluge of blood and screams then pour out through Caldera Pass upon the rest of the world in rolling tides of slaughter, the birthing pangs of his empire rippling from Thurandy to the Rift then beyond those savage lands clear to the western coast of Pangea.

Only the full scope of the world would satisfy his conquering lusts.

Though most witnesses to the Khan's brutal outbursts spent through fits of blind rage against the Veilfall's awakening held their tongues in silent guard lest they join the pulverized aizakai victims of his wrath, some shared private whispers of the Builder's lifting Veil sucking the momentum dry from the unstoppable juggernaut of his conquering plans while dousing the fires of conquest. The Lord of Storms brooded, inactive, upon his bloodstained ivory throne, awaiting Nergal's return, a scolded dog ruminating its absent master, while opportunistic others, awakened by the Veilfall's flushing return of memories, had and continued sneaking away, abandoning their sworn oaths and their homes, their families, their duties, forsaking all for the purpose of seeking the fallen Godstone's deifying all-power for themselves.

The latent memory of the Godstone's existence restored through the lifted Veil, the precious relic of legend waited somewhere beyond the palace walls in the wide unknown for anyone to claim its apotheosis, be they pauper or prince, aizakai or no, the almighty all-power of the Godstone undiscriminating in its empowering gift.

And for that fact alone Hannibal Khan hated it.

* * *

The brooding Lord of Storms gazed ahead with deliberate focus, the clear psychosis of his piercing stare transfixed upon the center of the Receiving Room where stood a barefoot little girl of nine in the tattered rags of a threadbare dress who continued the latest of her new though scrambled foretellings before her watchful master as commanded.

". . . has cleansed the bloodlust," Sera finished in a quavering voice while shaking her head in frightened denial over this her most recent and bitter failure of viewing the possible futures fated for the Khan. She opened her eyes once the torrent of wispy visions catalyzed by her aizakai ability of foresight cleared from her mind's eye, and there endured a terrible shudder. She risked a glance up from the bloodstained palace floor and succumbed regret, flinching, the instant her wary browns met the condemnation of the Khan's disapproving stare.

He scrutinized her with the same veiled fascination as would a pitsnake considering its next meal, and frowned. His handsome visage framed with blond curls depending to his broad shoulders tensed annoyance piqued by the low-throated *Hmmmm* of a growl, the rumbled purr of his thunder deep and low inside his muscled slab of chest.

The Khan did not accept failure in any form. Failure revealed weakness, and weakness earned no place within the dominating plans of the Lord of Storms . . . plans disrupted by the unexpected though more important to him unforeseen Veilfall.

Sera cringed, for even the slightest change in the Khan's expression insinuated death—or worse. Her aizakai foresight proved too valuable a tool for him to command her execution, but the stripes of scars across her back attested to the torturous punishments inflicted upon his most favored slave despite her contribution to his divine cleansing of heathen aizakai and impending conquest over the One Land of Pangea.

Plans of domination required dependable tools, and though her foresight proved her only saving grace from the aizakai execution pits, to the Khan she remained just another utilized tool, a loathsome means to the greater end of his genocidal cause. He squeezed opportunity from her aizakai foresight as one sought blood from a stone, and once he bled her stone dry he would continue squeezing until he crushed her to dust within his power-lusting fist.

But after the Veilfall's ruination of the accuracy of her foresight, muddying while twisting it into a scrambled mess of too many scenes at play at once, she feared the end of her usefulness to the one man whom held her life in his condemning hands.

Especially so after today's events, the aftermath of his aizakai victims coloring the tiled floor in smears of blood, memories of torture, and lingering echoes of screams. She clutched at the stolen glimpse captured from her hindered visions and clung to hope that it satisfied him short of issuing another beating. And failing that, earning her a quick death instead of days or weeks of torture upon his Overseer's unforgiving rack. She'd never seen hands crush skulls or rip spines from backs before this day.

Relaying him no forewarning of the Veilfall, she hoped the information about the last Soothsayer proved enough while knowing it a lost cause explaining the Veilfall's breaking of her mind upon ears deaf to merciful pleas.

"Cleansed." The Khan repeated the most pertinent of her words, tasting while speaking it through a bitter twist of lips. He raised one gauntleted hand to his face where extended his pointer finger and traced down the thin pink scar while touching the reminder of his own unspoken failure. "So she still lives. And the Soothsayer has outlived the curse."

Sera swallowed and nodded, returned her eyes downcast, the lingering headache instigated from groping through the viscous muddied waters of her visions clouding her thoughts while knotting her tongue. The Spellbinder's void-aura made it impossible to scry her outright, forcing Sera to foresee of those round the Khan's fading obsession instead.

And therein her strained scrying lived insurmountable obstacles, the new interference of a thousand separate lives inexplicably tangled, projections of scattered remnants born from the Spellbinder's Soothsayer savior's future possibilities unraveled along with the Veilfall's returning deluge of Godstone memories plucked from the chaos of the Thousand Years War, turning her foresight convoluted at best, making of it a disorienting chain of flashes and glimpses, these rapid shatters of partial pictures speeding past her mind's eye and leaving her no clue how to reform them whole into any semblance of their true image.

As well the haunting echoes of Sera's own dying screams—or were these mad laughter?—chilled her to her depths where lived queer suspicion that she had lived through this moment before, or perhaps a different version of it, or just as perhaps the Veilfall's toll shattered her sanity alongside her logical sense of questionable reality.

"I want my Armor," the Khan said, his tone a whispered grumble elevating into a thunderous shout. "And I want it now!"

He slammed his gauntleted fist upon the armrest, his booming voice an eruption of thunder racing outward through the four corridors beyond the Receiving Room in diminishing echoes. Cracks forked and veined down through the thick ivory beneath his pounding fist where loosened bits of powdered grit sprinkling atop his booted foot and floor in a light white dusting cloud which puffed beneath his notice.

Sera bobbed her head, bit her bottom lip to stay its trembling. Nearby servants edged away from the dais while continuing their duties of sopping and mopping up blood, their wary faces downcast to prevent drawing the Khan's ire upon them and suffering a brutal end, for locking eyes with the viper invited its uncoiling kiss.

"Look at me," the Khan said. And waited, a mock semblance of calm overtaking his tensed visage.

Head bowed, Sera rolled her eyes up.

He leaned forward in a hunch of muscle, his golden necklace and the necromaster's silvery lanthium soulring vitus strung thereon dangling out from his bare chest by inches in slowing metronome swishes. He propped one elbow on his thigh and settled his square chin atop his thick row of knuckles. He studied her a long and silent stretch, gaze gnawing through the pervading pause. At last, and with no small amount of disgust for the turning subject displaying his face, he straightened back, glanced aside at Nergal's traveling pool across the way, then said, "And the deadman? How fares the demon's pet?" He left the rest unsaid in all but his eyes and tone: *what else has the Veilfall changed?*

Hesitation wrapped an implacable grip round Sera's spine, its icy fingers squeezing the invite of a terrible shiver at mention of the necromaster Dethkore. Unable to scry the ancient being himself, same as the elusive Spellbinder though in a different sort of way, she must focus instead on those in his proximity.

She swallowed and nodded, her voice a meek squeak. "Yes, my Khan. As you wish."

She drew in a steadying breath through pursed lips, achieving no relief to the anxious flutters in her nervous stomach. She closed her eyes and opened her mind's eye while praying to every available god that her visions did not fail her again.

And through muddies waters churning in chaotic tumbles and tumultuous roils of shards and shatters of images she tossed about and floundered round, straining to stay afloat while flailing in the mad sea of scenes its currents sloshing and slapping. But she groped and strove while snatching fragments here and slivers there, gathering them, piecing them together from the multitude of puzzles, composing their pictures while taming but barely the panic thundering in her heart . . . and there saw . . . there saw a scintillating flash of blinding white light its heat an effluent burst burning flesh from bone, the palace walls crumbling to dust while the Receiving Room shattered against crashing waves of not just darkness but a sentient whipping substance of blackest pitch lashing angry beats upon explosions of stone.

She groped astral passage with a fearful sort of determination, swimming through the murky turmoil of too many possible futures and a magnitude of memories wrought by the Veilfall's awakening, honing her concentrative focus through sheer strength of will—until something, an alien presence, gripped her by the spiritual throat and yanked her inside a swallowing gulf of black.

Her strangled screams echoed through the chambers of her mind. Then the darkness blinding her mind's eye shied away, replaced by the buffeting swirls of future colors forming snaking blurs of shapes as she strove once more the astral plane in her questing bid seeking elsewhere . . . miles south . . . Grey Raven's Keep . . . where one-tenth of the Khan's army fought alongside the enemy's risen dead in toiling conquest to lay claim over yet another falling kingdom in the name of the Lord of Storms.

Or so she thought.

But a skirling hum arose from the collage of noise above the screams of those who lay dying and the terrified men refusing acceptance of the unliving soldiers feasting on their felled fellows. Obscure flashes of images became flutters of shapes became moving pictures of events knifing through her mindscape, earning from her outward trembling winces stealing across her face, while inward a distant thunder rolled in a baying recklessness of baffled hurt and fury.

She projected past the scenes of slaughter and ecstasies of boundless murder, her mind screaming to the agony of it, her spirit writhing in impotent struggles for release from the mindgrasp holding her to place. Until and at last she wrestled free, defiant, and moved away where she found—a voice the breath of nightmares, its tone the sound of bones crunching underfoot.

"I see you, child."

No . . . impossible. Sera gasped. Cringing. Recoiling. Turning away. Screaming for escape. She tried banishing the visions, tried opening her eyes. All to no avail. Her body a vessel miles distant, the alien presence captured her sojourn spirit again. A godhand. Squeezing her. Pulling her closer . . . closer.

Oh gods no!

The unliving creature of the Khan's sought desires seized her panicked mind in Its cold dead fist.

Sera's very soul shivered . . . then relaxed, capitulating to capture, surrendering to the ancient will gripping her essence while making of her spirit a limp reed before the rush of winds.

And there she endured a torrential flood of nightmares impaling her mind's eye and penetrating into her stem brain.

Dethkore's trade, Its vocation, was the killing of Its . . . no, *his* once-fellow man. And he was good at it. But he enjoyed it no longer, found no pleasure in the rending of life since his betrayal against the Nameless One.

"It's okay, child." His voice again, an everywhere presence of sound, followed by the soothing hush of a father's reassurance born from cold dead lips implying the frightened child's safety.

Eliciting in Sera an astonishing flush of relief sweeping its warmth into her as seconds more Dethkore's essence unfurled not in front of but inside her mind's eye in stark blooms of revelations.

He possessed a deep self-loathing in the tiny sliver of humanity torn from the rest of his fractured corruption of soul existing inside his lanthium soulring vitus strung round the Khan's neck. A defiant desire for redemption surprising and amazing Sera's gleaning spirit. And in this epiphany blazed realization that though the Veilfall had shattered her aizakai foresight into disrepair, it also enacted a change upon her foresight, a rebirth of sorts, an evolution, for to shape something old into something new it must first be broken.

Broken by the Veilfall.

Though she perceived the future possibilities of others' lifelines by viewing the prophetic branches sprouting from a godtree, there kindled a familiarity to her scrying now, confirming her suspicions that she lived this same tortured life for the second time.

"Yes, child. Because you have. And now you truly see."

And this ancient creature, this resurrected necromaster, this unliving servitor of the Enclave, this rejecter of death . . . this *man*, invited her past the obstruction of her scying, allowing her the gift of not just viewing but feeling, sharing the agony of his tortured existence in a relived millennia of suffering stealing through her viewing awareness.

Centuries sped by in seconds, delivering haunts of pain.

Sera wept in the depths of her grieving soul. *But no . . . there's more.*

"Yes."

Dethkore . . . no longer submissive to the Khan's commands. Awakened by the Veilfall. And now he was . . . he was . . . oh gods not just resisting control but seeking reclamation of it once more.

"Speak not of what I've shown you, child, for I am coming."

But the Khan will—

"Death is not an end but a beginning for those I choose. And I'm coming for . . ."

But there his voice and his presence of voice faded to silence.

Coming for what?

Darkness swirled, enveloping Sera's probing mind's eye in blinding blackness.

You're coming for what?

Shutting her out. Insurmountable as a wall.

No! Wait!

She strained to maintain her viewing. But a cold godhand released her and shoved her away, slamming her home in a jolting recoil of spirit.

* * *

Sera startled out from scrying, trembling, eyes snapping open, a gasp locked in her hitching chest, her tethered spirit returned to the vessel of her body by another's irresistible force of will shoving her away in a jolting crash.

Readjustment took time while the visions faded, leaving a new anomaly, a parting gift she clung to, a tiny glimmer shining dim within the darkness of her life, a twinkling mote of dust named Hope.

Her hope a fragile thing, though it burned within her a defenseless babyflame she must shield with precious care lest it snuff to the slightest offending breaths.

And there, meeting the Khan's scrutinizing stare, she toyed with the choice of her next words for she no longer feared death itself, only the pain involved.

"What did you see, my pet?" he asked, leaning forward by inches.

She held considerable pause, still unsure of her experience, fearing it nothing more than a terrible delusion wrought from the Veilfall's breaking of her foresight, while the nercomaster's voice recalled through her mind. *Death is not an end but a beginning.*

His viper's eyes thinned upon her. "Answer me. Now."

"The Veilfall has changed so many things," she said, her words expelled on panting breath, her body slow in recovering from the venture of her scrying and all it afforded her. She shook her head against the memory of Dethkore's voice replayed. *Speak not of what I've shown you, child, for I am coming.* And condemned herself by withholding the truth. "My visions are too clouded, too muddied by the Veilfall. I'm sorry, my Khan, but I can see no more." She swallowed down a silent prayer spoken to the memory of the new god awakened and bowed her head in display of her shame of failing the Khan. "I beg you to forgive my failure, my Khan. The Veilfall—"

"Shut up." Frowning, he settled back in silent contemplation, his pensive stare transfixed ahead, more through Sera than at her, where he sank once more into dark brooding.

Minutes passed.

A Bloodcloak captured a sneeze into his hand, failing to stifle it while earning the condemning dart of the Khan's shifting glare that returned to Sera in seconds.

She moved nothing, watching the Khan, watching Horace beside him, possible torments of punishment at her failure tumbling through her mind in repeat scenes of agony upon her, each worse than the previous.

The Khan swept his gaze to Nergal's traveling pool across the Receiving Room and glared overlong. He drew in a deep breath then exhaled impatience through flaring nostrils, a snorting beast challenging untoward thoughts, his lips tightening into a fine line. The placid contents of the traveling pool betrayed no signs of the serpent-priest's return regardless the Veilfall and despite the numerous aizakai offerings delivered into feeding the gory brew in sacrificial summoning.

Sera stared at the spot of floor between her feet, contemplating the fate of her lie, the possible delusion of Dethkore's influence upon her scrying and the tangled meaning of his words containing hints of promise. Until sounds of movement stole her eyes up and she flinched tensed, compacting in on herself, bracing before the Khan erupting from his throne then stalking toward her.

He stopped and stood in hulking loom, a handsome tower of muscle smiling while the dark unbalance of bridled psychosis played therein his scrutinizing glare. He bent at the hips to better meet her eyes, one gauntleted hand darting forth in a blur of motion. Cold lanthium fingers grasped Sera's trembling little jaw, their pinching pressure pursing her lips into a budding rose. Madness warred with contempt on his disapproving visage, though he spoke in a silky smooth baritone.

"Your insignificant life dangles by a thread," he said. "Do you understand?"

She nodded, though only from his pinching fingers working her head into obedient little nods for her.

"You're still alive only because I allow it. Do you understand?"

Again the forced nod.

"But your failure is unacceptable. I have no use for dulled tools." He paused, weighing and measuring. "Though perhaps . . . yes, perhaps yours just needs sharpening. Pain is a reliable whetstone. Do you understand what you've brought me to?"

Welling tears stung her eyes up while panic flushed her loosening bladder. She tried shaking her head, but the simple gesture failed against the strength of his pinching grasp tensing, enacting a painful squeeze of her caught jaw while keeping her head immobile. No and Please died in mute whimpers at the back of her throat.

The Khan glanced down between them then removed two steps from the warm urine trickling the insides of her quivering legs where formed a puddle round her bare feet, her head snapping back with the release of his pinching grasp sliding free, her face flushed red save for the white imprints of the Khan's fingers slow in tracing away, his smiling image a fractured prism through the hot sting of tears clouding her eyes. Her mind demanded her body's collapse, to throw herself prostrate in pleading subjugation. But terror gripped her by the spine, refusing its pliable bend.

"Oh I'm not going to kill you," he said, then held unforgiving pause. "Yet. But you'll beg for death on the Overseer's rack if your visions fail you again. You are useless otherwise."

Assessing her now, that brutal stare, contemplating her punishment through which he would take great pleasure in seeing enforced. He glanced at the big ugly Bloodcloak standing upon the dais left of the throne, and a soft, demented chuckle escaped his throat in cruel implication.

Horace the horse-faced brute's fat lips peeled back in an approving smile, revealing yellow gap-ridden teeth below eyes dark as sloes and casting the dull gleam of near-animal unintelligence. Assigned the task of watchdogging Sera since her removal from the aizakai execution pits, he loathed the chore almost as much as he hated all aizakai in general. He moved one meaty hand past Sera's kohatheen tied at his belt to his crotch and gripped its bulge with squeezing interest.

Sera's mind froze, the Khan's proposal closing her throat on a scream.

"Or perhaps," he continued, sweeping his gaze across the room to Nergal's traveling pool, "I'll allow you the mercy of bleeding you dry into the demon's portal. Maybe your blood contains the proper ingredient to summon—"

But there he clipped short, for as if by command of his words there arose into flickering luminescence the eerie violet witchlights of archaic carvings upon the stone floor encircling the traveling pool while down within their circular depression gurgled the portal pool, announcing at last Nergal's long-awaited return.

* * *

"Finally," said the Khan, an irritated rumble.

He returned to his throne and there sat watching the active traveling pool bubble and froth in growing agitation, the attentions of all others about the Receiving Room locked in stare to the serpent-priest and high acolyte of the Enclave rising from within the demonic portal after almost two days of inactivity.

The bare top of Nergal's scaly green head arose from within the bubbling blood, then his face and neck and chest and clawhands and more as he ascended the concentric ring of steps in casual climb, the sacrificial aizakai blood dripping from his half-reptilian, half-human hybrid mix of a rangy body while also absorbing into his scaly skin covered in glistening red ribbons.

He stopped beside the tall though by comparison of his towering height much shorter wooden post jutting from the floor and donned the awaiting robes depending thereon in a purple swirl of fabric. He scanned the Receiving Room with the slow sweeping of his measuring gaze, causing all whom that yellow-eyed stare crawled over into cringing away.

All but Hannibal Khan whose hardened mask held tight the brewing storm of psychosis behind his piercing glare, eyes that shifted away from Nergal seconds more, dismissing the serpent-priest's arrival as an insignificant annoyance no longer deserving his attention.

Nergal ignored the Khan's open slight, sweeping his gaze elsewhere, hunting, seeking, at last settling upon—

Sera peeked up in the lingering silence making roars of whispers, a brutal regret the instant she met Nergal's horrible gaze transfixed upon her, his calculating eyes tearing at her, dissecting her on a level far beyond the physical, that inhuman serpentine stare penetrating her most private depths. Soulless yellow eyes divided by black vertical slits. There lived a deep dark hatred in that terrorizing stare so profound in its rending hypnotic power. Nothing human approached that look, the intelligence behind it awful and alien, unfeeling and unreasoning, infinitely terrible, speaking volumes of control.

Reflections of her lie to the Khan of her failed visions tensed her taut and guarded. *Would he know? Does he know already? Oh gods, what have I done?* And yet . . . and yet. *I've lived through this before. I know that now. I don't understand it. But I know it. That has to mean something.*

She breathed a little easier when Nergal disengaged his stare and flipped his hood up, covering the small black holes that served as his ears, then strode toward the dais upon which the Khan sat enthroned, the serpent-priest's long purple robes whispering across the floor and providing him the illusion of gliding while the trailing of bloody footprints painted the floor in his wake, these growing fainter with each gliding step taken, the talons of his hidden clawfeet *click-click-clicking* the floor, every of his subtle movements speaking hidden purpose.

Nergal achieved the dais, loomed towering beside the Khan's right, his clawhands clasped behind his proud back and his troubled face peeking out from the shadowed depths of his hood. He bothered no bow, for as much power as the Khan commanded Nergal served a far more powerful master in Malach'Ra.

"Massster's plansss are coming undone," Nergal said through stretched S's of his serpentine tongue he wrangled quick into a more human pattern of speech. "The Veil has been lifted, and the Godstone has fallen and—"

"I know," the Khan said, his interrupting tone a deep and dismissive rumble. He stared ahead, refusing Nergal a look up. "I know," he repeated in stronger voice. His hanging fingers tightened their grips, clenching the blocky ends of the throne's ivory armrests. His muscled arms tautened through bulging flexes, and thick roots of veins stood out along the sides of his neck. "We've already been over this, demon."

Nergal's thin scaly lips bared the snarl of pointy teeth at the Khan's blatant refusal to acknowledge his presence directly. But instead of lashing out, he tamed his lips into a wicked smile. "We have much to talk about, you and I. Much to consider. The least of which is what happens now that everything has changed."

Hannibal Khan broke his brooding stare ahead and gazed up at the looming serpent-priest, engaging the full brunt of his glare to battle with Nergal's measuring stare. Through clenched teeth he asked, "What took you so long?"

Nergal flared his eyes, his voice, in feral warning. "Do not question me! There are good reasons for my absence, *human*,"—he spat the word in derogatory slur—"and none of them require explanation to you."

The Khan frowned, adamant stare unyielding. "But the Soothsayer—"

"Cleansssed the bloodlussst, I know," Nergal said, his voice relapsing into its natural serpentine hiss, his S's stretched again in a withering lisp. "Massster's plansss have changed since the Veilfall, yesss."

He moved before the throne, bent in forward lean and met the Khan eyes while he tapped upon the necromaster's lanthium soulring vitus strung round the Khan's thick neck on a thin golden necklace with the needle-sharp point of one black talon—*tink-tink-tink*.

"And," Nergal continued, "the Forsaken One has slipped your control as well because of the Veilfall, yesss?"

Eyes expanding then thinning in the space of a breath, the Khan leaned aside and glared contempt at Sera. Until Nergal gripped him by the chin and forced his return into the brunt of his stooped scrutiny.

"It matters not," Nergal said, straightening. "Whatever disobedience the Veilfall has awakened in him, the Forsaken One will return. And he will submit as always to his precious vitus. His is of a much more . . . particular role, now." A pause, a hissing draw of breath. "We are abandoning our efforts against the heathen's den in Fist. The Book of Towers is secondary now. Recall your Bloodcloaks at once. We are moving all of your forces to hunt for the Godstone. Everything else is trivial."

"Trivial?" The Khan ruined his handsome face with a proper scowl. "I will not—"

"You will do as you're told!" boomed Nergal's raspy shout in the Khan's unflinching face. "The power you wield isss because of our doing. The empire rising around you isss because of our influence. You are worshipped as a living god because we allow it. We provided you the necessary toolsss, but they can be stripped away from you as easily as the flesh from your bonesss." He raised his right clawhand and traced down the thin pink scar running the Khan's cheek, his short black talon scraping over softer skin with the dark whisper of a demon's breath. "We made you, Hannibal Khan, and we can unmake you." He tapped the Khan's chin. "Never forget that."

Nergal straightened once more, clasped clawhands behind his back. "I assumed this would please you. Soon you will have the battle you crave, warlord. Rejoice. We stand upon the precipice of another Thousand Years War, only this time we have the numbers to see it finished."

The Khan said nothing, though his frown deepened beneath eyes brightening twin flares of bridled ire.

"The Veilfall has unraveled three-hundred years of planning," Nergal continued, his tone firmer, his serpentine hiss less pronounced into a more human pattern of speech. "Everything has changed, and we must act now. Master's plans—" He paused, tensing, and stole a glance at his traveling pool. "His plans have failed. Even now this city empties. People whom once flocked to swear you their undying fealty are leaving to seek the Godstone for themselves." A pause, the licking of his lips. "But my plans, yesss . . ." He trailed off, smiling malice.

Hannibal Khan stared ahead, his face the tensed tell of surfacing emotion stealing through little twitches. He raised a hand and turned it about, fingers extended, tracing his godsforged lanthium gauntlet of power over with a meticulous gaze.

"I care nothing for the Godstone," he said, and curled his fingers into a fist. "Our bargain was for the Armor, demon. My Armor—"

"Silence you fool!"

The Khan issued neither vocal protest against Nergal's command nor the slamming of his gauntleted fist upon the ivory armrest. Instead he stared ahead in obedient silence. No, not just staring but contemplating, while an eerie calm enveloped him, shrouded him, betraying a presence at work behind his pensive gaze.

"Gathering the Dominator's Armor is secondary to the Godstone." Nergal gestured with the absent flick of his clawhand at the Khan's lanthium gauntlets, insinuating them as insignificant tools having lost their shine. "You have the gauntlets, be satisfied with that. In time you may possess the rest. If I allow it. But that will only come after the Godstone is found. Master's plans are—"

"Broken," finished the Khan.

"Yesss."

Sera endured a foreboding shiver when bubbling disturbance arose within Nergal's traveling pool, its agitated contents frothing and hissing, as if the Nameless One were listening and angered by the discussion.

Nergal glanced at the bubbling disturbance. "Yesss," he said to the Khan in a pleasured hiss, nodding. "His plans are broken. But mine have only just begun." The bubbling agitation intensified into boiling so that he gave the traveling pool another, sharper glance before continuing. "Gather your Bloodcloaks. We march for the Godstone as soon as the Forsaken One returns. And he will return, I assure you, for now he remembers, yesss. But we must—"

There he paused, thin lips pinching tight. "But we must make haste. The Soothsayer will seek the Godstone, and he will either destroy it or use it against us. That is inevitable. Now, assemble the legions. We must find the Godstone before the Soothsayer can—"

"My Armor," the Khan said, glaring up at the towering serpent-priest. "I want what was promised me—"

"Silence!" Nergal struck the Khan across the face with an admonishing backhand delivering a resounding *smack* of flesh, forcing his head whipping aside.

Startled gasps stole throughout the Receiving Room. One-hundred Bloodcloaks stirred their positions aligning the four walls though dared no forward step. Serviles raised their hands and covered gaping mouths beneath expanding stares. Horace advanced a step though stopped, his hands gripping at though not removing the weapons at his belt.

Sera cringed in mute stare.

"The Godstone is what matters now!" Here Nergal's scaly lips spread into a malicious grin beneath hungry, expectant eyes. "And with it I will become the new master, yesss."

Across the room the boiling contents filling the traveling pool hissed and spat while thin jets of the sacrificial aizakai blood therein erupted into the air in splashing red geysers, the low skirling hum of its violet witchlights elevating into throbbing beats of erratic pulses and luminous flares. Nergal shot the traveling pool a contemptuous glance before returning his attentions upon the Khan.

The red imprint marking the left side of the Khan's turned cheek out-colored the thin pink scar marring that side of his face. He turned his head straight, veins throbbing roots on his bull-thick neck. He looked up at Nergal, and though no emotion displayed on his face, there brewed a terrible storm behind his eyes. His gauntleted hands flexed round ivory armrests, and his wide shelf of shoulders twitched in indication that he might give rise. But nothing came of it as he remained seated, silent and stewing.

Nergal cackled, amused. "Do you think to strike me back, warlord? Hmm? Do you really think you have any power over me? *Me*? I was ancient before your whore mother even conceived you."

The Khan's brow turned thunderous, eyes murderous, lips tremulous. Yet still he said nothing, moved naught but through flexing twitches of muscle.

Nergal released a slithering chuckle, cocked his head aside in contemplative stare. "Do you know what is truly sad about your misbegotten kind? You live under the delusion that physicality trumps intelligence. You humans and your insignificant lifespans—" He hawked then spat, the little acidic gob of which shot past the Khan's tensed visage by inches and sizzled upon the floor somewhere behind the throne. "You assume your short lifecycles apply to everything and everyone around you, but you have no conceivable idea how incorrect you really are. The fact is, most of your lives are as insignificant as the dust motes in the air you breathe. Less than one per cent of your pathetic species will even be remembered in the annals of your history."

Nergal leaned forward and poked the Khan's bare wide slab of chest with a talon while emphasizing choice words. "Your mortal lives are *meaningless*. Humans are a *virus* feeding upon this ball of energy that sustains you. And when it is drained then so too will all of your kind be *slaughtered* like the chattel you are."

Hannibal Khan lowered his insolent stare at the talon prodding his chest, the lanthium surface of his gauntleted fists spark-crackling into terrible life for the space of a breath then gone.

"You knew as much when you summoned me and bargained for immortal life," Nergal continued, prodding harder with emphasis, ignoring the Khan's twitching visage. "And it was that fact alone why you were chosen as the new Khan. Do *not* presume you have somehow risen above the *insignificance* of your *lowly* place!" His last emphasizing poke pierced skin, drawing a single drop of welling blood from the Khan's chest that seconds more cried a ruby tear down to his stomach.

And then it happened.

The Khan's right gauntleted hand raised in blinking speed, grasped round Nergal's prodding own and squeezed, producing an audible crunch of bones and a gasping yelp from Nergal who cringed against the crushing pain imposed upon his ruined clawhand yet rallied against the Khan's brazen audacity.

"How dare—*ACK!*" Nergal, wide eyes swirling with the hypnotic compulsion of his serpentine species, cut short as Hannibal Khan released his crushed clawhand and gripped the serpent-priest by the throat. The enraged Lord of Storms stood from his ivory throne in an eruption of muscle.

Servants gasped, several screaming as they abandoned their mopping duties and fled from the Receiving Room. Bloodcloaks stepped forward from the walls, weapons brandished, then held position, unsure what to do and whom to serve—their reigning Khan or his Enclave superior he clutched by the throat.

Startled by the scene playing out in front of her, Sera's mind screamed to run though her body stood paralyzed with shock arresting her feet from play.

Horace shifted his feet, anxious, nervous, confused, watching, the unintelligence in his sloe eyes gleaming with the threat of violence moments in coming so that he licked his fat lips and flexed anticipatory grabs of air at his sides.

"Do you know what is sad about your kind?" asked Hannibal Khan in a rumble of voice, all that had been building in him since the Veilfall pouring forth from the savage gleam of his bold stare, the full spectrum of his wrath enveloping him in an aura of harnessed rage. "You assumed this entire time you were in control, when it was I who was controlling you."

"How . . . dare . . . you—" Nergal rasped loose in a broken chain of strangled words ending short when the Khan raised his mighty arm and in a tremendous display of strength lifted him from the floor by the stretching neck, Nergal's dangling clawfeet kicking swims of air, the tips of talons scraping the floor beneath—*clickity-click-click.*

"I will have what was promised me!" The Khan's surge of rage stilled the air on all sides, the psychosis of his unyielding gaze promising horror. His godsforged lanthium gauntlets of power spark-crackled with potent life inviting hundreds of tiny arching tongues of bluish lightning into flicker-licking over their gleaming surface while burning Nergal's scaly skin trapped therein. "I don't need you to crush Fist beneath my stomping boot, demon. And I don't need your pathetic creature. A god does not share power! I will claim the Dominator's Armor. And I will ascend to godhood as is my birthright!"

Yellow eyes bulging, Nergal raised his clawhands in a futile attempt at prying loose the Khan's stronger grip from round his captured throat. Seconds more and he clawed at the Khan's face, raking black talons ripping flesh and drawing blood. But the enraged Khan stood unfazed by the pain, though he straightened his arm to full extension while leaning backwards a space, thus removing Nergal's frantic clawhands by inches from scoring more flesh.

"I am the only master here!" the Khan yelled while shaking Nergal.

In sequence to his words there boomed a deep and rolling thunder outside the Divine Palace, shaking its walls, vibrating bits of mortar dust and grit loose from between stones fittings. In through the four corridors blew powerful winds bearing screams from without riding along the buffeting torrents.

Sera shrank to the floor in a protective huddle, throwing her arms over her face as shields to the flapping tapestries torn loose from their walls, the flaming stands knocked over and spilling their glowing nests of coals across the floor in strewn scatters, other mundane objects with sharp corners or edges flying in the increasing roils of gusts, sliding or rolling by her she avoided by inching shifts.

Though she peeked through the thin slice of space between her covering forearms at the two sinister powers before her locked in turning contest. Nergal's swirling hypnotic gaze fought to regain any semblance of compulsive control over the furious Khan. But his efforts proved a miserable failure, his demonic compulsion unable to penetrate the raging psychosis of the Khan's malevolent glare.

The air round them crackled and hissed with suffusing charges of electrical energies wrought by the Khan's godsforged gauntlets teeming with potent crackles and fueled by his maddening rage. Nergal's purple robes smoked as scintillating arcs of lightning jumped and danced in transfer, then his flapping fabrics burst afire. Mangled screams passed through the Khan's tight clutch round Nergal's charring throat, long limbs flailing, flames burning away the flapping robes from his rangy body, making of green scales black snowflakes scattering upon the gale-force winds sweeping in.

Sera inched backwards, her statically risen hair flowing about her head while the buffeting gales blew throughout the Receiving Room in tidal waves and crashes of air rattling Bloodcloak armor and stealing weapons from their hands in skittering clatters upon the floor. She almost wet herself again when she backed into the blocking legs of Horace who had moved unseen behind her sometime during the chaos. But he spared her no glance, his attention captured by what all remaining eyes of the room watched in abject terror.

The bulging swirls of Nergal's distended yellow eyes popped into a runny mess of puss streaming down his blackened cheeks, bits of the gooey spatter speckling the Khan's crazed face.

The raging tempest reached its climax when the Khan threw Nergal away to where the blind and burned serpent-priest's charred and smoking body struck the floor rolling, limbs flailing, blackened scales flaking away in swept flurries. Nergal slid stopped, lay nude and writhing, moaning, blisters rising, splitting and popping with ooze, his scorched and scaly reptile-human hybrid body a pathetic gangly nakedness of sprawled and squirming pain on full display, his robes nothing more than black ash flittering in calming winds as the tempest settled.

"Be . . . tray . . . er," Nergal hissed in a raspy wheeze.

The Lord of Storms strode forth, glared down over Nergal in standing loom, his face a bitter twist.

"You have failed me, demon." The Khan spat a white gob onto the blackened char of Nergal's upturned face. He drew in a deep nostril breath, and the last of the risen winds died away as if collected into his lungs. "For the last time."

He gripped Dethkore's soulring vitus strung round his neck on golden necklace, gave it a long transference of gauntleted shocking via his spark-crackling fist, then tore the necklace free and held the captured soulring outward dangling from his fist. He appraised the lanthium band with deepest loathing then threw the soulring aside as some useless trinket no longer worthy of his attention.

The shifting of his gaze, a snarling glare at Sera. "And you."

She flinched, cowering lower against the floor, the Khan's piercing stare impaling what little remained of her raw courage. She wanted to stand, to turn, to run—but for the big ugly wall of Horace standing behind her.

"You failed to warn me of the Soothsayer," the Khan said in a tone so calm nightmares could flower. "You failed to warn me of the Veilfall. And you failed to warn me of this pathetic creature's treachery!" A smile that left his stormy eyes untouched. "You have worn out your use." His basilisk gaze traveled above her head to the brute behind her, and that smile turned scarifying. "Horace, you have my permission to kill her now."

Horace's meaty hands gripped the sides of Sera's head from behind. He pulled her up from the floor, stretching her neck until her dangling feet kicked frantic swims of air. He turned her one way then jerked her head with a sharp twist the other and snapped her neck.

Sera's world turned the black oblivion of nothingness, her last memory of life Hannibal Khan's approving smile and the perfume stench of Nergal's charred flesh.

* * *

Hannibal Khan did not fear death, he feared failure. And though he feared it in himself as he once feared the brutal fists of his drunken father, he loathed it in others. Failure disgusted him. And yet it surrounded him at every godsforsaken turn of his head.

Surrounded by lies. Surrounded by weakness. Surrounded by pathetic beings unfit to feel even the crush of his boots—as had his father's skull.

He contemplated this while sweeping the Receiving Room with a meticulous gaze. The contents of the traveling pool had spilled over onto the floor in puddles of drying blood, though the pool itself placid once more.

He spared the heathen girl's life from the execution pits, and what did she given him in return? The ungrateful aizakai bitch failed to forewarn him of the Veilfall. He made a dark pact over his soul with the Enclave through Nergal, and the serpent-priest failed to deliver the rest of the Dominator's Armor as promised. And the Soothsayer . . . cleansing the bloodlust curse instead of succumbing to it. In that, even the Nameless One failed him.

Failure at every turn. The wretched stench of it thicken the air as he drew in a deep lungful through flaring nostrils, threw his hands on high and released a booming shout. "I am Khan!"

His godsforged lanthium gauntlets of power spark-crackled with hundreds of dancing arcs of lightning, while outside and overhead the roiling churn of darkened sky rumbled deep with thunder which shook the walls of the Divine Palace. The hundred Bloodcloaks aligning those vibrating walls stirred on their feet, though none dared speak or move from position until beckoned.

The Khan turned from the two bodies decorating the floor and ordered forth a knot of Bloodcloaks who rushed forward to stand then kneel as one unit before him.

"Empty my harem at once," he commanded in the sepulchral silence. "Take the Spellbinders to the Pitmaster. All of them."

"What for, my Khan?" asked the Bloodcloak at their gathered front.

"Slaughter," he said, adding a savory lick of his lips. "I will need their baneblood for the battle to come. Aizakai heathens abound in Fist. And ransack this city bare of all supplies. Draft everyone, kill any who refuse. Leave nothing of use behind. We move at once. I have lingered long enough. I am finished here. Today, my Bloodcloaks, we march for Fist." An emphatic smile. "Today my glorious ascension to true godhood begins. Go!"

"Yes, my Khan. It shall be done at once."

Hannibal Khan turned and gazed upon his blood-speckled ivory throne while the knot of Bloodcloaks arose to his turned back, pounded their mailed fists over their loyal hearts in strong salute, then rushed away to carry out his orders by all means necessary, their others breaking from the walls and filing out from the room in marching ranks behind them, flooding the four corridors.

The Khan gazed westward then, staring, as if the febrile measure of his condemning glare proved enough to view the city of Fist through stone walls, a heathen beacon blazing strong behind a gauzy veil. He smiled, intent on answering the day's unexpected turn of events with a vengeance no less terrible.

Behind, Horace stepped onto and over Sera's limp little corpse, approached the Khan and stood awaiting his next orders.

Hannibal Khan snapped his head left where sounded a withering hiss from Nergal's sprawled char of body in a pitiful whisper almost unheard. But there lived no time to wonder, for his ascension demanded all his attentions now. He would achieve godhood by reassembling the rest of his Dominator's Armor as intended then find and destroy the Godstone to ensure he alone stood a god—the only god—among men, and for that he required the treasured Book of Towers hidden in Fist.

The curse of knowledge, the power to act on it, the will to commit. It consumed him, made of him a pawn to his unwavering ambitions regardless the Veilfall's interference.

He spat disgust on the smoky ruins of his former Enclave contact, ignoring the merciful impulse to stomp Nergal's blackened skull into a pulpy mash and end the twitching spasms of pain.

Rectified, resolute, the Lord of Storms turned away and strode from the Receiving Room on the march for war.

CHAPTER TWENTY-SIX

Banzu twisted and turned, curled and spun, tumbled round and round, churning inside the tidal currents of the Traveling Well's swaddling flux of viscous fluid energies pulling him deeper and down through its tunneling vortex.

Though direction proved no relevant indication for there existed zero sense of 'down' or 'up' but for his own constant shift of perspective, only moving in his mad tumble.

Eyes shut tight, fearing the energies sweeping him away from the Builder's tower, and away from Melora, might melt his eyeballs from their sockets, he wrangled his panic and surrendered them open to the greater fear of losing his sword belted in the crumple of his pants wrapped bunched round his left boot.

A mayhem burst of rainbow colors dazzled his vision.

He tried drawing his knees up while hunching and failed the groping reach for Griever's hilt, the resisting currents of the mysterious fluid acting against his efforts while lengthening his body taut.

Every tachyon of his being vibrated in tune to the engulfing hum of energies elevating to deafening pitch bleeding into his hearing, and the riotous swirls of multicolors coalesced while brightening into a blinding white flash—leaving only darkness.

Black silence pervaded in this his tumultuous womb.

For the moment he considered the possibility of his sudden splat at the Traveling Well's deep and empty bottom, excusing the magical plunge as nothing more than some lunatic manifestation wrought from his fading lifespark clinging to precious fractions of existence before death drew him inside its cold embrace, the tether of his spirit detaching while his body lay a broken twist.

But he shirked the crazed notion away a moment more. *No. I'm still thinking. I'm still alive. For now.*

His inner grasp on the Power released seconds after the focal invocation of it triggered the Traveling Well, he clutched the waxing fever of holding his breath in lieu of drowning while he collapsed inward, reflecting on Melora's cruel trickery played against him moments after their carnal coupling. But the loose projection of thought turned scrambled, too preoccupied with holding his waning breath, his lungs a burning ache begging for precious gulps of delicious air so that he focused every ounce of disintegrating willpower into keeping his throat locked tight and his lips pressed together.

Hope arrived in the form of a tiny pinprick of white light piercing the darkness and blooming into existence far ahead, providing truth through the black illusion that the vortex tunnel possessed some form of exit. The physical sense of shifting, an increase in flowing speed, and the torrential black currents towed him toward the distant source of light, the bright white hope expanding to his approach the breadth of miles.

Painful hot spasms hitched in his chest. He clenched his jaw, refusing his mouth open for the crucial gasp his betraying lungs craved with fierce need.

Until necessity to breathe overpowered his straining efforts, and in the breaking of his willpower his mouth opened in an agonized inhale of fluid flooding into his lungs, cold and clawing. At the same time the distant source of light expanded through an effluent burst, speeding past the edges of his peripherals to infinity while whiting out the darkness with blinding brilliance.

He vomited up and out from another Traveling Well's mouth in a mad and spinning tumble, spewed forth in a geyser of wet energies so that he rose then floated then fell. He captured the well's rounded wall of lip in a flailing of arms and clung to the black builderstone, the initial impact punching into his stomach and expelling the fluid from his lungs, his upper half dangling over the outside while his lower half dangled inside the well's throat, making of his limp body a perched V.

Coughing and gasping the return of precious air, the world a sickening vertigo whirl, he tottered atop the stone lip for a groaning space, dizzied, then endured the startling flush of panic when he slipped back down within so that slapping hands sought slippery purchase upon the smooth black builderstone gliding beneath his frantic palms. He gripped the inner lip, jolting his shoulders while arresting his fall, and there hung by his fingertips, arms at full extension. He stole a frightening glance down at the deep dark throat of empty well awaiting another swallow.

Oh gods oh gods oh gods!

Adrenaline proved his savior. He pulled himself up, legs swimming kicks of air, Griever's sheathed blade tangled in the bunch of his pants round his staying left boot swinging and banging against the well's interior. Through grunting strain he managed his chest up then over the lip, tottered upon his bent middle, then his balance sloshed forward and he rocked free, his bare thighs and tender bits between sliding across the glassy-smooth surface.

He met the floor in a rolling tumble, the bundle of his bunched pants producing a wet *slap* punctuated by Griever's muted *thunk* smacking the hard cold floor.

He lay splayed on his back and panting for several shuddering minutes, uncaring of his nude lower half or his new surroundings, too amazed with survival.

"By . . . the . . . gods." Hot breath misted in dissipating plumes from his mouth.

He rolled his head from side to side on rubbery neck. He tried sitting up but succeeded only in raising his head and shoulders a few meager inches before collapsing flat again. *So cold.* He tried raising a hand to feel at his face, craving the surety of physical touch, but muscles tensed through shivers prevented his tremulous arm from bending so that he darted his gaze through the surrounding black pitch while listening to the odd sound of clicking insects. Until he realized it for his chattering teeth producing *chit-chit-chitting* echoes in the dark of his new environment.

Summoning dwindled reserves of strength, he flopped over onto his stomach. There he attempted pressing up from the tiled floor though achieved only inches before collapse. He spent a restive moment reorienting his recovering senses, then pressed up onto hands and knees, limbs trembling though pliable, frigid shivers quelled through the spreading warmth of forced movement, his head hung between shoulders, the crimson tangles of his hair dangling in damp strands.

Soaked to the bone, and yet the translucent fluid that had delivered him to this place evaporated while it dripped from him, becoming vaporous wisps vanishing soon as they dotted the floor.

He stared at the wispy dapples evaporating between his palming hands, his clothes as well the rest of him drying through increasing blooms of heat. *Huh.*

Ungh. Then his guts clenched against the sickening urge to vomit while new fever gripped and shook him by the spine. His balance sloshed and swayed, and his dark surroundings spun. Blackness tunneled his *wob-wobbing* vision. He dry heaved, hot strings of saliva seesawing his mouth. Limbs tremulous, his hands and knees slid away beneath him. He collapsed, wincing, grunting when his turning face struck the floor.

In a fading bid of energy he flopped onto his back, arms pathetic flails, seconds before blacking out.

* * *

Eyes snapping open, Banzu startled awake on the smooth tiled floor to ambient heat and soft white light.

I'm . . . still alive?

And warm. And dry. His shivers gone.

I'm still alive.

He sat up groaning, endured a moment of imbalance while his eyes adjusted to the new light, and gazed down the length of himself.

And I'm half naked.

He gathered his ankle-tangled pants, punctured his free boot through the stray right leg, and pulled them up to his knees, then rocked into standing and yanked them to his waist, buckled his belt, adjusted Griever at his left hipwing then gave the leather-wound hilt a comforting squeeze. *Thank gods I didn't lose you.*

He gazed round while turning round.

Wide windows containing no muntins formed the four walls and high ceiling of the square room housing him, the room itself empty save for the waist-high Traveling Well's rounded mouth jutting from the floor's center. And beyond the window-walls an endless gray desert beneath a vast black ocean of sky, the barren terrain evincing no detectable signs of life, neither animal nor plant, the alien landscape flat but for its plethora of craters.

Where in friggin hell am I?

He gave Griever's hilt a reassuring squeeze as he turned to the Traveling Well and considered the folly of his venture through it here imposed by Melora's apologizing shove. He approached it, gazed down inside its empty black throat.

This is not Fist. He pounded the waist-high lip with both fists. "Godsdammit."

He turned from the Traveling Well, strode across the room, his footfalls hollow echoes upon the smooth white tile floor, and approached the window-wall where he stared out across the desolate gray expanse while trying to make logical sense of it all. *No structures. No people. No animals or plants.* Melora said the Traveling Wells connected themselves in a magical circuit to the Academy.

Definitely not the Academy. Unless some apocalypse happened I'm not aware of.

He hammer-fisted Griever's hilt in his left hand and pulled the blade free from sheath. He raised the sword and tapped its pommel against the window-wall—*tink-tink-tink*—testing its thickness while considering his only option of busting through it and—

"Quarthunian plaztik," spoke a voice from behind.

Banzu jolted tensed.

"From the Andromeda galaxy," the other continued. "An ingenious cohesive polymer of nanosands scooped from the burning dunes of the Exclese Cyb Zones and mixed with the bleeding resins scored from the weeping trees of Tar Mak Uun. And a bit of carbon fiber weaving, to be precise."

Banzu spun round—at the same twisting time removing his left hand from Griever's hilt, leaving the upside-down sword hovering mid-air for the slightest of breaths before snatching it into his right hand while flipping the immaculate length of steel over and up rightwise, all in one quick motion—and froze.

"The crossing did not kill you," said the short little man with golden skin standing on the opposite side of the Traveling Well's waist-high mouth, though its round lip came up to the short stranger's chest while blocking the rest of him below. He nodded and smiled, agreeing with himself. "That is a good thing."

Banzu withdrew backwards—or tried to but for that he bumped against the forgotten window-wall behind—then flinched forward one rebounding step. Griever slipped loose from his fumbling grip, and for the moment he played hot-potato catch with the sword before reestablishing his grip. Anxiety and embarrassment getting the better of him, he tried compensating by taking an intimidating step toward the stranger while angling Griever out in warning threat.

"Who are you?" he asked, voicing the first of his many questions.

"I am Enosh," said the short golden-skinned man. "I am the Builder."

Banzu's eyes bloomed wide. He opened his mouth then closed it. Fearing Griever would slip his grip again he sheathed it to his left hipwing, his tongue a fumble. "Uhm. What?"

Smiling perfect white teeth, Enosh rounded past the Traveling Well in casual little strides. He unclasped his hands from behind his back and presented sweeping gesture of himself and of the room through spreading arms, smile growing, the long sleeves of his loose red robes flapping whispers of silk despite no breeze within the closed room.

"And you are the last Soothsayer," Enosh said, "otherwise you would not be here." He clasped his hands behind his back, a perceptive gleam twinkling in his piercing black eyes jeweled with little silver pupils ringed in gold. "Welcome to the Nexus. I've been waiting a long time for your arrival. Three-hundred sixty-seven years to be precise." A slight pause, an even slighter twitch of his golden brow. "One-hundred thirty-three-thousand nine-hundred fifty-six of your Earth days to be even more precise."

Impossible . . . but Banzu put no voice behind it. He gripped Griever's hilt though stayed its pull while eyeballing the lying stranger. "Who are you?" he repeated in stronger voice. "Where the frig am I?" Impatience winning over, he pulled Griever the threat of a few baring inches. "I want answers, and I want them now."

"Patience." Enosh's voice calm and smooth, his smile faltered nothing when he pointed past Banzu out the window-wall behind him. "It's a simple matter of deduction. You were there, and now you are here."

"There?" Banzu glanced behind at the window-wall, then turned fully, gaze captured by the blue orb nestled in scattered swaths and churns of white the substance of clouds hovering in the black sky he'd paid no mind to through the shock of it all. One full minute of staring passed before his hand removed from Griever's hilt and raised to cover his mouth befitting the dying dubiety of his working mind. "Is that . . ." he began then trailed off, unable to finish the impossible admission aloud, his mind struggling through dismantles of suspicious logic.

"Earth, yes," Enosh said. "That is where you were. This is Luna, which is where you are now. This place, this construct, is called the Nexus. *A* Nexus, really, for there exists countless others upon the vast array of satellites in the infinite number of galaxies as well. All throughout the expanding macrocosm of the universe to be precise."

Logic a forgotten thing, Banzu leaned forward until his nose pressed upon the window-wall. "That . . . is Earth?" The plunge of his guts. "But it's so . . . small." He swallowed. "And far."

"And humbling," Enosh said, chuckling, approaching Banzu's right. "I know."

Somewhere in Banzu's mind he flinched at Enosh having sidled alongside him, but the reaction died to the awing truth in front of him. He straightened back, the tip of his nose leaving a tiny smudge of oils on the window-wall. And squinted while watching the smudge clean itself through micro activity at play therein the alien glass.

The irrational part of him wanted to grab the little man by the shoulders and shake him in tangible test of this daunting unreality. Instead he stared overlong, locked immobile, gaze transfixed, mind awed to the overwhelming plunge of insignificance flushing through him. "So I'm on the moon?"

"Correct."

He shifted his stare round and beyond the blue ball of Earth at the endless black ocean of space, his rational mind seeking avenues of excuses and escape. "But . . . but where are all the stars?"

"The limited scope of the human eye cannot perceive sources of light in space," Enosh said. "Only the celestial objects said source of light reflects upon, such as the earthshine you see now. You can view stars from Earth only because Sol's light refracts through Earth's atmosphere."

"Sol?" Banzu asked in a squeak of voice.

"What you call the sun," Enosh said. "But here on Luna there is no longer atmosphere." He flicked a wrist in gesture at the self-explaining spacescape. "If I were to remove these protective walls and you looked at Sol, you would only see blackness though its unfiltered spectrum of light would blind you regardless. Not that you would survive long thereafter. Minutes, perhaps. The absence of heat would freeze you while the vacuum boils the oxygen from your blood."

Banzu tore his gaze away from the black depths of space.

Enosh smiled up at him, a knowing gleam twinkling therein the black pools of his sagacious silver-jeweled eyes containing their own depths of galaxies.

"And you're Enosh," Banzu said in monotone voice, as if speaking the words added palpable substance for which to grip them and ensure their realness. "The Builder God."

Despite Enosh's shock of silver hair depending to his slender shoulders, not a single line of age marred the little man's golden skin, a man smiling up at him with the joy of enjoying just another beautiful day in some private garden, the skin of his upturned face and neck and hands emitting a soft glow of golden radiance that hummed the immediate air round him.

For a dulling moment Banzu questioned whether he should fall to his knees in prostrate veneration, but for the niggling suspicion this man, this being, this professed deity was not the true form of Its existence and—

"And you would be correct in that hypothesis," Enosh said, nodding, his smile spreading.

Banzu flinched at having his thoughts read as one would emotion from another's face. Disturbed by the invasion, he tensed and scowled at the violation while attempting to will the closing of his mind though he possessed no idea how to accomplish such a sorcerer's practiced task. But he flexed his will regardless—

"Concentrate," Enosh said, his tone instructive. "Visualize it."

—and imagined some form of shielding presence constructing into place. He built upon it, thickening it, doming it round his brain while Enosh's smile wavered and his golden brow furrow, as Banzu's mental blockade secured his thoughts to him and him alone.

"Excellent," Enosh said. "Your will is strong. That is unsurprising. And of necessary importance. But have no fear, Soothsayer, you are safe here."

He stepped forward then stopped, frowning when Banzu withdrew with a hop while pulling his sword and leveling it out between them.

Enosh sighed, frowned. "Please put that barbaric instrument away." He waved a hand at Griever in the same cursory gesture of one swatting away an annoying biteme fly. "You were not brought here simply to kill me."

"Kill you?" Banzu expelled a mirthless chuckle at the absurdity of pulling simple steel in false threat upon a living god. He lowered Griever to his side. "But you're a god, right?"

Enosh shook his head, smile returning. "I am the mortal avatar of a god, yes. I am *a* god but not *thee* God. This body provides a physical vessel to my spiritual essence. Think of it as ageless, though still quite susceptible to lethal means." His silver-jeweled pupils ringed in gold shifted in deliberate gesture at Griever. "Now please put your primitive utensil away. We have much to discuss before you decide to . . ."

Only half listening now, Banzu turned away and faced the window-wall while switching his grip upside-down upon Griever's hilt. He raised then banged its steel pommel against the window-wall again, harder than before—*thunk-thunk-thunk*.

"Please stop that," Enosh said, a touch of irritation bleeding edge into his otherwise smooth tone. "The vacuum of space is an inhospitable environment to humans as well this mortal cavity housing my essence. Though you will find it quite impossible to long scratch the plaztik's surface before its nanosands heal the markings, attempting to test its durability is a futile endeavor on your part and more precisely a waste of our valuable and limited time."

The vacuum of space? Banzu hesitated, a dark speck of his questionable sanity yearning to test Enosh's words and the window-wall by slamming Griever's hilt against it or thrusting its blade through it. Instead he sheathed Griever to his left hipwing, giving the hilt a comforting squeeze before release. "What is this place?"

He scanned the room, earning nothing but more questions, and frowned as a strong sense of memory kicked him in the rump of his mind. *Godsdamn you, Melora.*

"This Nexus is a place of temporary stasis," Enosh said, reclaiming Banzu's straying attentions. "A place where all the known realms converge. This Fantasy Realm of ours, and other realms as well, each existing in overlapping though distinct dimensions separated by their individual vibrational resonances."

Banzu scrunched his face. "What the frig does that mean?"

Enosh spread his hands between them, palms upturned, in the manner of opening an invisible book. "All of my towers on your Earth connect to the Academy as their central hub. Think spokes on a wheel. When I created the Veil, I linked my towers so their Traveling Wells would bring you here first. A necessary precaution, for I had no way of knowing if you would arrive consumed or cleansed, be you Soothsavior or Soothslayer. You are, after all, the savior-slayer reborn, and could be either one. Are, in fact, both."

"Uhm. I'm the *what?*"

"I may be a god," Enosh continued, ignoring Banzu's question, "but even I possess limitations." He frowned, and in a lower tone added, "Especially after my weaving of the Veil drained my essence so profusely."

Banzu opened his mouth to pose his question again, only with more words and more force. But Enosh spun away and faced the room's center, his thin golden fingers wiggling.

The soft white light of the room brightened, filling it while removing all lingering traces of shadows, though the origin of the light itself remained unseen. Perhaps it occurred in the air itself.

Enosh spun back facing Banzu, smiling, his red robes whispers of silk. "My Veil has lifted, releasing the Godstone again. Thus the Great Game has restarted, and now it is time for you to play it." He paused, smile wavering. "Or rather it is time for you to finish it."

The Great Game? Banzu possessed no logical idea what to make of that. Too many questions perhaps the problem.

He walked his thoughts backwards, questing for answers unfound, ending with Melora. Their carnal sexing. Her apologizing shove. His venture through the Traveling Well. Arriving on the moon instead of in the fistian Academy. None of it made any sense. All of it overshadowed their intimacy. *She tricked me here.* And he wanted her back if only to choke her head off. *But she's so far away now. Gods, I'm on the friggin moon!*

His blood flushed up, hot and angry swells of it. He eyeballed Enosh's mortal avatar through suspicious squint, jaws bunching, teeth clenched, hands flexing grabs of air. "Why am I here?"

"All will be revealed. That is your current purpose." Enosh turned, clasped his hands behind his back, and walked away. "Come. We have much to discuss and little time in which to do it before you finish the Game."

"Wait!" Banzu pursued two steps forward then stopped. "Game? What game? What in friggin hell are you talking about?"

Enosh slowed nothing, bothered no look back. "Patience, Soothsayer. Please, come with me and—"

"No!" Banzu claimed Griever's hilt in preparatory pull. "I'm not supposed to be here. And I'm not following you anywhere until you tell me what the frig is going on." He glanced at the Traveling Well, unenvious of another daunting plunge. "Send me back. I want to go back. Now!"

Enosh stopped, turned round, estimated Banzu a long and silent moment. "Forgive my impatience. I have waited centuries for your potential arrival. Now that you are here we have much to discuss. You have questions, and I have answers. But I prefer to provide them in a more comfortable setting, one which should help stabilize your elevated stress levels while allowing you to better assimilate the necessary information required before your departure, yes?"

Banzu bared Griever's steel by inches, eager for the full pull, anxious for rushing forth and thrusting Griever to the hilt in Enosh's chest. "What the frig does all that even mean?"

"In layman's terms, relax."

"Relax?"

Enosh nodded.

"We're on the godsdamned moon!"

"Yes, we are. Astute observation. Now come."

Enosh turned away. He walked across the room, seconds from bumping into the window-wall until he waved a hand in a rainbow arc and a seamless rectangle segment of the window-wall in front of him shifted from translucent glass into a mirror's reflective surface that slid open from floor to ceiling—

shhhoooOOOooom—revealing itself a doorway and a lit hallway beyond.

He paused within the doorway, shooting Banzu a prompting gesture of his head to follow his obvious lead, and waited.

Banzu stabbed Griever to sheath, glaring, considering, debating, questioning the irritating god watching back at him and this strange place along with his own sanity. He glanced at Earth hovering in the endless blackness of space, and endured a powerful sense of urgency for Melora so far away. Then flared the burning yearning for killing Hannibal Khan just as far. He gave Griever's hilt a strangling squeeze, earning an admonishing frown from Enosh in so doing, then nodded.

"Fine," Banzu said, voice curt and gruff. "But if you're lying to me, or if you try anything stupid—" He paused, and gave Griever's hilt a deliberate warning squeeze through the fanning close of his fingers. "God or not, I'll cut your friggin head off and find my own way home."

Enosh grimaced, though his eyes projected the soft sadness of human melancholy. He shook his head and in a quiet voice said, "So angry. One would think you failed to cleanse your bloodlust." He turned away. "But of course you would not be here if . . ." His words trailed off as he disappeared into the hallway.

Banzu glared in Enosh's wake, then he gazed out at the sprawling gray desolation of cratered terra through the window-wall, focusing on the blue ball of Earth mocking him with the incredible distance of some big cosmic joke. *First the Veilfall . . . and now this?*

He spun away and glared at the Traveling Well. Considered jumping back inside and hoping for a return to . . . *where? Melora? Fist? Somewhere else? Or worse, kill me this time?*

He sighed, achieving no clear answers there.

Friggin hell.

He raked his hands back through his hair, gripping frustrated tufts of it before release, and blew out his cheeks. He followed after Enosh, hoping for answers, fearing their truths.

***

On through the long hallway lit by soft white luminescence permeating the air, at Banzu's sides beyond the translucent window-walls the vast cratered landscape of the moon sprawling away beneath the black ocean of space.

He stopped one step shy of entering the room at hallway's end where recognition struck him paused to abrupt degree. *This can't be real.* He blinked. *I'm losing it.* He rubbed the inside corners of his eyes with pointer and thumb, and blinked again. *I've already lost it.* But the haunt before him remained.

He gazed overlong at the arresting sight of his and Jericho's cabin, or rather the foreroom interior of it, as if he stood within the cabin's front door.

Enosh walked across the duplicated room, approached Jericho's familiar rocker resting next to the hearth and eased down into the perfect replica of chair with all the calmness of an old man taking rest. He smiled while rocking in little back-and-forth pushes of his legs, the easy efforts producing those same irritating little squeaks and squeals Banzu remembered so fondly of his uncle. *Reet-err, reet-err, reet-err.*

Banzu shook his head while blinking, denying the delusion, the logical parts of him rejecting it though unable to dispel the impossible simulation of his past, the disturbing scene ripped from his mind and made tangible.

"I still possess a little fade of magic left in these tired bones," Enosh said, smirking. He interlaced his fingers over his small belly paunch and gestured at the empty chair opposite him—the same chair Banzu recalled in a flitter of memory wherein Melora had sat and explained her plight at length upon her first meeting with Jericho before Banzu's re-beginning—with the deliberate flicker of his black eyes bejeweled by silver pupils ringed in a gold so thin it bordered on invisible until the light caught them just so to sparkling. "Come," Enosh said. "Sit."

"This can't be . . ." The words escaped Banzu in bare whisper. "I burned . . ."

But there he trailed away unfinished. He closed his eyes and inhaled deep, tasting the musky odors of animals pelts, the woodsy hominess of shaven logs and the earthy perfume of mud packed between their joins, the faint though persistent aroma of evergreens, while tickles of memories flushed through his mind in sweeping reflections.

After which he broke from his paralysis and moved to the indicated chair under the spelled motions of a fading daze, passing the same little wooden stand his uncle always threw his floppy black hat atop after returning from some outside venture before claiming the rocker.

Banzu eased down upon the familiar chair in testing feel of its realness—then surged into standing while enduring the strange assault of reverie, unable to relax, surrender to the confusing illusion impossible.

He said nothing while scanning the false foreroom, hazel-eyed gaze questioning everything it touched in discerning sweep in case he missed something during his walk to the chair. Then he eased down again, gaze locked with Enosh's, for they sat opposite each other, Banzu's silence a brittle dam withholding a flood of questions surmounting behind his lips.

He opened his mouth then closed it, having no true idea where to even begin.

"Please be still and listen," Enosh said before Banzu could frame a proper question. "And do not interrupt, or we will never see this all through in time for—"

"In time for what?" Banzu interrupted regardless, unable to help himself, the peculiar mingling of curious dread and blooming excitement butterflying round in his stomach, his nerves tingling anxious energy his body craved for spending through movement so that he shifted on his bottom to keep from standing.

Enosh said, "You stand upon a precipice, Banzu Greenlief. One step in either direction will determine your irrevocable course because you are the last Soothsayer, and thus the savior-slayer reborn. You are the cause of my Veil's destruction, same as Simus Junes was the cause for its construction. Because of you the Godstone is released once more upon your world. As such, it is your duty and your destiny to find it and—"

"Wait a minute." Banzu waved Enosh short, unable to suppress the delivery of Enosh's words sounding more accusations than statements. "Just wait a minute." He chose a particular avenue fished to the surface from his mind's new reservoir of mysteries. "Why the Veilfall? Why take everyone's memories away just to give them back?"

Enosh frowned, at the question as well the answer it elicited. "The Thousand Years War was a terrible event. War and slaughter and bloodshed on an unfathomable scale. Millions killed. The aizakai population decimated. If I could have removed only the necessary memories from the necessary persons then I would have stopped it there. But healing is a complicated process, and human minds no less perplexing. I had to ensure the world forgot the chaos of the past, at least until the last Soothsayer emerged.

"History is written by the winners, Banzu, and memory is all we truly are. Moments and feelings bound in snarled mass, captured in amber, strung on filaments of reason and inked to page after page of history books. Take a man's memories away and you take all of him. Chip away a memory at a time and you destroy him as surely as if you hammered nail after nail through his skull. So I had to be careful. Delicate. Gentle in my extraction."

Enosh paused, betraying an uncomfortable wince of his golden visage there then gone. "So I took, but only some. Bits and pieces of memory plucked here and there. Human minds are equal parts fragile and of complex design. For my Veil to work properly I had to allow parts of the past to be remembered and carried on through the generations so it concealed the existence of the Godstone along with the more intertwined parts of the past connected to the Thousand Years War surrounding its existence.

"Hiding everything lay beyond my capabilities, nor could I hide it from everyone, which is why I chose Spellbinders to form the first Academy. They are the keepers of that past knowledge while protecting all remaining aizakai. While the rest of the world forgot and endured, Spellbinders remembered. They needed to be prepared for when the savior-slayer was reborn through the last Soothsayer, but they also needed to ensure the bloodlust-corrupted Soothsayers did not destroy the world before then.

"My Veil erased any mention of certain particular events from the Thousand Years War connected to the Godstone. Moments after a Spellbinder spoke of them, to anyone else their words dissipated as if never voiced. Though those memories lingered on a subconscious level, repressed, festering untouched because they needed to in order for my Veil to work while imposing its influence upon everyone else, for it's a Spellbinder's duty to remember the faults of the past while ensuring they are not repeated."

Again Enosh paused, frowning. "My transgression, however, cost me dearly in trade. I was locked inside this mortal avatar vessel as punishment for my interference in the Great Game. So I've been here, waiting." Another pause, followed by a smile. "Waiting for you."

Banzu stared at silent length but for the steady *reet-err, reet-err, reet-err* of Enosh's rocker performing its work. He sat forward, sat back, sat forward again while shuffling through the blaming flood of information.

"So the Veilfalll," Banzu said, "it's because of me. I did it. I caused it." *Melora was right.* His mouth turned tinder dry. He swallowed hard and sat back, sinking deeper into the chair. "It really is all my fault then."

"Fault is not the appropriate word," Enosh said. "Whether you or another, the Veilfall was bound to the last Soothsayer."

"Which is me."

"Correct."

"Why?" That single word cut to the heart of almost every one of his questions at once. "Why me?"

"Only the last Soothsayer who resisted the bloodlust curse can therefore resist the temptation of the Godstone's apotheosis long enough to destroy it."

Banzu sat forward again, gripping his thighs, shifting on his bottom, wanting to be on with it all while at the same time wanting to hear every last word of it, his unfinished purposes back on Earth with Melora and against the Khan two constant itches far removed from his scratching reach.

"Just what in friggin hell is the Godstone anyways?" he asked. "What's its purpose? And why do I have to deal with the friggin thing?"

Enosh said, "The Godstone's apotheosis bestows several enhancements to its wielder because it saps nutrient energies from the fabric of existence, staving age, imbuing physical regeneration, providing immunity to disease and hunger and thirst, even breathing."

"Immortality," Banzu said.

"So long as it is touched," Enosh said. "Yes. As well its all-power provides a limitless source of magical potency to any aizakai whom holds it while enhancing the measure of their particular talent a hundred fold. The greed of it caused the first Thousand Years War, and it will cause another if it is not destroyed. Your world only survived the first tribulation because of my intervention, but it cannot survive another. Too many aizakai were killed, their bloodlines extinguished or nearly so, and there are too few now to unite as they did before. Simus Junes and his Grey Swords are gone in all but name. I do not possess enough magic left in me to create another Veil and protect your world from that happening again, which is why I bound the Veilfall to the last Soothsayer. Only you can finish the Great Game. It is your destiny to be here just as it is your duty to—"

"Game?" Banzu asked, scoffing the irritating word. "Is that what you call the slaughter of millions?"

Enosh frowned, said nothing.

Banzu sat back and crossed his arms, frowning while seeking calm. "And I don't believe in destiny. A man makes his own."

To which Enosh smirked. "Some things do not require your belief in order for them to exist."

"Whatever." Banzu shook his head and huffed a terse breath. "And what if I'd failed? What if Jericho killed me instead? Or if I'd turned to the bloodlust before killing him? Or while killing him? Or—"

"Then all hope would be lost and your world condemned to the corruption of the Godstone," Enosh said, a flitter of sadness softening his golden features. "That is the purpose of its design, after all. Both blessing and bane. It is a test of humanity's worthiness to exist, and the source of humanity's undoing if it fails that test." He raised a hand to stifle the forthcoming interruption from Banzu's opening mouth. "A test nearly failed by the previous savior-slayer Simus Junes until my intervention. I was unable to stop the Great Game, but my Veil did postpone it. When I saw . . ."

Enosh talked on.

But Banzu's saucy attentions shifted elsewhere. He glanced at the hallway through the front doorway of the mock cabin in consideration of what he'd left behind, his worry for Melora's safety and his want for killing the Khan creeping into the forefront of his mind, taking precedence over even a conversation with a living god.

I've tried it her way, not that she gave me any choice in the matter. And look where I am now? On the friggin moon! I need to get back and do things my way. And if she doesn't like it then I'll drag her to Fist by the hair kicking and screaming if that's what it takes.

"I've heard enough," Banzu said, interrupting Enosh short while snapping back to attention. He uncrossed his arms and slapped his thighs while rocking forward into standing. "I want to go back—"

"Sit down!" Enosh shouted in a commanding flare of voice, his face scrunched into a shatter of fine golden wrinkles, his eyes fevered galaxy jewels. He'd sat forward in stalled surge from the rocker, his hands flexing grabs of air, his arms extended in partial reach as if to force Banzu back to chair. In lower, calmer voice he said, "You will listen." He settled back in the rocker—*reeeeet*—and schooled the disapproval of his face into golden smoothness. "Please, listen."

Banzu said nothing as he mimed the action by settling back into his own chair. He raised a hand and pinched his chin between rubbing forefinger and thumb while watching Enosh through a discerning stare and with a disturbing notion occupying the center of his brain. *Is this a mad god? Driven insane through centuries of captivity here?*

"Forgive my outburst." Enosh closed his eyes and rubbed at his golden temples in little massaging circles. He nested his hands into the red-robed folds of his lap before going on, an impish twinkle playing therein his eyes once he opened them again.

"I'm listening," Banzu said.

"Thank you." Enosh drew in a breath and released it overlong through pursed lips, suffering through humanizing impatience. "There are forces at work your ignorant human mind does not comprehend. At least not yet."

Banzu frowned. "Ignorant?"

"An innocuous term, I assure you." Enosh snaps his fingers—a shimmering vortex, a hovering swirl of wormhole portal containing time and space the width of a splayed hand appears—and he side-nods in indicative gesture *Your* way. "Like them, for example."

"Them?" Banzu's eyebrows pull together in a wrinkle of confusion. "Them who?"

Slowly Enosh leans forward—*reet-errrrr*. Turns his head to the side, looks and points at You.

Hesitantly Banzu leans forward, turns his head in the indicated direction, and looks Your way through the shimmering wormhole portal of time and space hovering between You and them. But at first he does not perceive Your face peering back at them beyond the portal pages in Your hands, and so he leans forward a bit more, squinting now . . . hazel eyes thinning then expanding in waking surprise. He stiffens, withdraws by inches, gaze unyielding. "Who is that?"

Me, You think, though You answer nothing for Your voice lives beyond their Fantasy Realm.

"That," Enosh says, "is Reader. They are the reason we continue to exist after Writer creates us in his simulation matrix we call the Simulatrix. They exist in the Reality Realm and thus are the only beings truly capable of uninfluential observation over all the known realms, this Fantasy Realm of ours included. They are the Turners of the Pages, making them the keepers of the continuance of all the realms' existences. Only Reader is immune to the allure of the Godstone's tantalizing all-power, because they observe the Great Game while unable to play it. The governing laws of Writer forbid their direct influence, though indirectly they keep our existence flowing by Turning the Pages of Time held within their hands even as I speak these words. Otherwise . . ."

Enosh trails away, flicking a hand in idle gesture at You viewing back at them through the wormhole portal pages between.

Banzu glances at Enosh, back to You. "Who's Rider?"

"Wri-*ter*," Enosh corrects. "He is the creator of everything you know, of everything you've known, and everything you will come to know. His written commands form our destinies. It is said he's made of twisted steel and sex appeal. But I digress—"

Enosh snaps his fingers in the air between them—the shimmering swirl of wormhole portal fades away—and garners Banzu's full attention once more.

Banzu regained composure through a rapid series of mute blinks, his impression of You retreating through fades of loose comprehension.

While You continue Your necessary observation, separate from the struggle though more important in it than You realize.

But You will.

Because Your power lies in the caring of consequences and the Turning of life's Pages, each influential revelation of Your godhand an advancement of plight and lives.

Be gentle with them.

For I will not.

CHAPTER TWENTY-SEVEN

"Triggering the Veilfall has prohibited you from remembering the past," Enosh continued, rocking again—*reet-err, reet-err, reet-err*. "A necessary precaution in case you failed against the bloodlust. I will attempt to keep my summation as simple and concise as possible so as not to confuse you any more than you already are."

A vocal pause, the silent trial of the mortal avatar god's measuring gaze.

In which Banzu nodded while sitting back and listening with keener ear, the gleaning fog of You fading from his conscious mind, its precious knowledge repressing nestled into a subconscious recess chambered in swaddles of sleeping memory.

"We"—and here Enosh inverted his hands while pointing, indicating not only himself but his godly brethren—"spread life throughout the cosmos. Such has it always been. Once you evolve into a higher stasis, you become painfully aware the true purpose of life is continual procreation. Everything else is only the suffering of temporary amusement.

"We evolved beyond procreation sexually to procreation genetically. If your species proves worthy, in time you too will become"—and here Enosh performed fingered air quotes round the word—"*gods* like us. Replacements. Ascendants of humanity. You will travel to distant worlds, and you will spread life the same as we have done, seeding planets just as our"—implied air quotes again—"*gods* did for eons before us. Such is the great cosmic cycle.

"Our underlying purpose has always been the search for intelligent life. We finally found it in you humans on your Earth, though your primitive species required a little . . . push in the appropriate direction. We engaged in other experimentations as well, though mainly we spliced slivers of our genetic codes into the DNA of your ancestors then observed while mankind evolved superior among the rest of Earth's lifeforms while we lived as gods among your kind through our mortal avatars, teaching your developing intellects knowledge you would not otherwise possess. Art and science and mathematics and such.

"Eventually there arose the need to test humanity, to prove itself worthy as the dominant Earthen species. A trial of judgment. After considerable deliberation we proposed the Great Game. So the Godstone was wrought into existence then released upon your populous in contest with there being only one rule among us: no interference in the Great Game but for humanity itself after the chosen two were named."

Banzu began interruption, to blurt out a flurry of questions at this new rush of information—but Enosh waved him quiet while talking over him.

"The all-power of the Godstone provides a limitless source-pool of energy to anyone whom holds it for as long as they hold it. To non-aizakai it grants immortally perfect health and vigor, while to aizakai it provides those same benefits as well an inexhaustible reserve for fueling whatever magical attributes they genetically possess. Its all-power is limitless by design, and therein lives its deceiving temptation. Absolute power corrupts absolutely, though power can only truly do so by the free will of its wielder.

"As I've said, we agreed no interference in this testing of humanity. But deceivers toiled among us in the form of the Enclave, those dedicated to worshiping Malach'Ra's earthly form as The Nameless One and—"

Banzu startled bolt-upright, gripping the armrests of his chair, at such casual mention of the Nameless One's true and forbidden name. He seized Griever's hilt in preparatory grip, gaze darting to every slice of shadow, for all knew even the mere mention of the Nameless One's true name could invoke nightmare influence upon the speaker as well those round them.

"The Ebony Prince cannot touch you here," Enosh said, waving a dismissive hand before going on. "We may be gods to you, but even our capabilities allow us only one mortal avatar upon each of your realms. Once it is destroyed, our influence shifts from direct to indirect, disintegrating contact into persuasive whispers through prayers. And then we move on seeking intelligent life elsewhere." He expelled a loose sigh, the kind marking the unbinding of long-held tensions. "Or did. But this last time proved different. And Malach'Ra—"

Banzu yipped interruption, unable to keep from reacting to the impending sense of dread after a lifetime spent avoiding speaking the self-imposed curse of the Nameless One's true and forbidden name aloud so that Enosh cleared his throat, nodding acquiescence before going on.

"You humans are prone to worshiping those you perceive as greater than you, and . . . the Nameless One, as you know him, developed a dangerous lust for power after indulging in the enjoyment of worship for tens of thousand of years on your Earth. He refused to move on with the rest of us once his mortal avatar was extinguished, so he conceived a way to maintain direct influence upon this Fantasy Realm even after Simus Junes destroyed his mortal avatar.

"His Enclave servitors gathered raw lanthium and, using the blood of sacrificial aizakai and strands of their master's divine genetic code, they forged the Dominator's Armor in secret to the Great Game. Once this came to light, the rest of us had no choice but to involve ourselves. He stalked the world in mad slaughter, killing our mortal avatars to ensure his rule over all of Pangea as the sole remaining god. The purpose of his Dominator's Armor was two-fold: first to protect his mortal avatar, and second to imbue his Armor with his spiritual essence if ever it failed him. And he sought the Godstone to sustain his power and secure his immortal dominance over those whom survived the Thousand Years War."

"Why?" Banzu asked, almost spitting the all-purpose word out. "Why in friggin hell would you create such an evil thing as the Godstone?" He leaned forward, gaze narrowed. "Why?"

"Even gods die, Banzu. And others must replace us to carry on in our absence. Such has it always been. Though . . ." A hesitant pause. "We grew arrogant through worship and attempted to choose our successors instead of planting the seeds then moving on as all those before us. And honestly, after suffering millennia of the same repetitious process, we were bored."

"Bored," Banzu repeated in monotone, frowning.

Enosh nodded. "Like all creators we questioned our creation. Division ensued among us. Half of us believed mankind would prove a worthy successor, while the other half argued you were only good for war and destruction and deserved extermination before you evolved into a real threat to the rest of life in the cosmos. Man has, for the most part, coveted power above all else."

Enosh held up the pointer and middle fingers of his right hand in a V.

"We deliberated then chose two humans to represent both arguable sides of our contest. One an aizakai, the other nonaizakai. We imbued them and them alone with an inner homing sense for the Godstone's location to ensure a decided outcome to the Great Game. They could sense its presence no matter where on Earth the Godstone fell, which was a random falling to establish a fair trial. The first was the Soothsayer Simus Junes, the second the necromaster Metrapheous Theaucard.

"But the Nameless One obtained possession of the Godstone first and ravaged your world in a plague of destruction you know as the Thousand Years War. The Enclave sought aizakai genocide and almost achieved it through tides of bloodshed. Until Simus Junes and his Soothsayer Grey Swords accomplished the impossible by rending the Dominator's Armor apart while aizakai survivors banished the Nameless One from the mortal plane."

There Enosh held pause, allowing the information to stir and settle behind Banzu's contemplative stare.

"Metrapheous Theaucard," Banzu repeated in self-whisper. "Dethkore." Almost an afterthought voiced in a childlike fear, he spoke the infamous title wrought from nightmare myths. "The Eater of Souls."

Enosh nodded. "Soultaker has accrued many names, yes. And he's earned every vile one of them a hundred fold."

Banzu nodded, said nothing while reflection upon the unliving Trio of the Khan's assassins, only then daunting, truly yielding, to the cruel reality of Melora's reasons for choosing destroying the Godstone over killing Hannibal Khan. With the necromaster in his pocket the world stood no chance against the Khan's army, for an army that could not die could not be conquered. And if the Enclave obtained the Godstone, it would make of them unstoppable. No Simus Junes this time. No Soothsayer Grey Swords. No aizakai army. No second Thousand Years War because with numbers on their side the Enclave would achieve swiftest victory through unopposable slaughter.

Banzu leaned forward by inches, irritable with interest of his and the necromaster's ties to each other. "Tell me more of Dethkore."

Enosh's rocking stopped. "Soultaker is not your reason here," he said, frowning. "The Godstone—"

"I want to know," Banzu said. "I need to know. Tell me."

Enosh fetched a breathy sigh. "Very well." He shifted through nervous fidgets. "If the Nameless One fulfills your human concept of evil, then Dethkore is something far worse. Not because of intent but because of design."

Enosh paused, shivered visibly, at play on his face a conflicted inner struggle to continue though its tortured story of ancient pains resolved seconds more, the stress of untoward memories recalled bleeding into his voice.

"Metrapheous Theaucard," he continued, "was a kind and pious man once, long ago. A carpenter, a devoted husband and loving father. A devout worshipper of Ahzra'il. No touch of aizakai in his blood, though he wrought masterpieces through the shaping of wood. Before the Great Game commenced, and unbeknownst to the rest of us, the Nameless One took precautions through his Enclave to ensure his coming victory while they forged his Dominator's Armor. He sent one of his more powerful minions forth, the demon Nergal, who instigated the death of Metrapheous' daughter Marisha then entice the grieving man with the means of resurrecting her through the sacrificial murder of his wife Maria alongside the promise that she too would be restored, but only after he bargained his soul. A trick, of course. Deception and temptation have always been the Nameless One's most favored tools. He does not lie, but he is a master of untruths.

"In Metrapheous' broken despair he agreed. Obsessed, he devoted his life to mastering darkest sorceries. But his daughter and wife returned to him in wrong and twisted ways, both soulless and possessed with unliving hunger for living flesh. So he caged and sustained them through murder while searching for a way to restore them as Nergal promised. Years passed before he realized he'd been deceived by the greatest of deceivers."

Enosh paused, a tiny smile betraying his lips there then gone.

"But man," he continued, "is not a creature so easily undone. And power bestowed often takes on a life of its own. Metrapheous discovered a way to achieve the impossible by traversing the realms, slipping between this Fantasy Realm into the Horror Realm where he claimed unfathomable power. Because of it his physical vessel resides on the mortal plane while his spiritual essence resides in Purgatory. This coexistence is why he is undying. Killing him here does not kill him there. Instead he can only slumber. Not even the Nameless One could achieve such drawing of power himself. But through another, and as a tool—"

Enosh upturned his hands in his lap in mild gesture. "If one cannot become the sword then one learns to wield the sword. And that is precisely what the Nameless One did with Metrapheous, breaking then reshaping him into the weapon he himself could never become.

"In his mad obsession, Metrapheous transferred his soul into a vitus, the lanthium soulring now in Hannibal Khan's possession, leaving only a fleck of his humanity behind while replacing the rest of it with a blackhole he plucked from the stars within the Horror Realm, hoping its power would provide him the means of restoring his wife and daughter without the Nameless One's corruptive touch. But Malach'Ra"—here Enosh spoke the forbidden name again, curt and harsh and with frowning spite, almost in challenge—"proved far more cunning than Metrapheous believed. It was all just a part of Malach'Ra's devious plans and preparations for the Great Game to come. He wanted his new Khan under his complete control, and he achieved it through the soulring vitus."

"Khan?" Banzu asked, brow furrowing.

Enosh nodded. "Khan is a title. And Hannibal is not the first." He ended there.

Prompting Banzu to ask, "So what happened?"

"Metrapheous," Enosh began then paused, shook his head. "No, Metrapheous no longer. Dethkore destroyed the unliving abominations of his wife and daughter in raging despair, then he tried killing himself a thousand different ways and learned death impossible because of his soulring. Exactly as Malach'Ra intended, all of it through calculating design. Malach'Ra seized full control of Dethkore's will through compulsion, and through his new Khan control of the endless hunger of the Blackhole Abyss and its insatiable void the rending of gods. The rest of us did not learn this until after the fact, but by then it proved too late. Though we acted, having no other choice."

A pause, the slow shake of Enosh's head. "The Enclave slaughtered millions. The Dominator's Armor provided Malach'Ra a nearly indestructible means of protection and power. He killed our mortal avatars in his hunt for the Godstone. And thus began the tribulation of the Thousand Years War as the Great Game commenced. The rest you know as history."

***

Banzu blinked through the tension pressing behind his eyes while rolling the stiffness from his neck. Trying to evaluate so much information at once bottlenecked the flood of knowledge attempting to access his brain in a deluge. He opened his mouth then closed it without word, unsure where or how to continue his line of questions, new ones piling atop the old.

"We exist in stasis here on Luna," Enosh said, "but time grows shorter there on Earth. You must make a decision that will define your destiny as triumph or tragedy."

Banzu sighed, frowning. "I already told you I don't believe in destiny." He sat forward, sat back, sat forward again, body craving movement. "And I'm getting tired of just sitting here."

"I don't care," Enosh said. "And we've sidetracked enough. I am unfinished as to why you are here before Fist. What you learn next is paramount to your path ahead."

Banzu huffed a terse breath while sitting back. He made an impatient twirling gesture with the pointer and middle fingers of his left hand as if to say: *Go on then, I'm listening.*

Enosh frowned, golden brow pinching, galaxy eyes thinning disapproval at the irritating gesture. "At the end of the Thousand Years War, Simus Junes used the Source to temporarily absorb the essences of all his Grey Swords during his battle with Malach'Ra"—he spoke the Nameless One's true and forbidden name openly now—"bending time backwards on itself in loops connecting Past and Present, something even us gods could never achieve, while fighting recurring losing battles, learning from each failure while escaping them moments before his death, until he finally defeated Malach'Ra, weakening him enough for the aizakai survivors to separate the Dominator's Armor, quite literally tearing it apart while destroying Malach'Ra's avatar and banishing his spiritual essence from the mortal plane. But Malach'Ra planned for this and infused its riven pieces with his essence so that if they are ever reassembled he would return to the mortal plane inside a new mortal vessel."

"Hannibal Khan," Banzu said.

Enosh nodded. "While Simus contained the shared collective Power of all his Grey Swords, Malach'Ra struck a parting blow, corrupting Simus and thus every Soothsayer through him with the bloodlust curse. If I had not intervened during the distraction by stealing away with the Godstone before Simus could—"

"Wait." Banzu raised a hand palm-out, arresting Enosh mid sentence. "Just wait. Give me a minute. You're telling me too much at once."

Enosh pressed a sigh through pursed lips and surrendered a nod.

Banzu considered this new information piled atop the old as one tied-up and lying in a hole considered the dirt shoveled atop them: with as much deliberation as possible given the circumstances. So much about this Godstone business he did not understand, yet flashes of images catalyzed by Enosh's words flittered behind his eyes so that he clung to the familiar of the shared collective.

At times he knew things never learned—abilities, skills, languages, mannerisms, memories—then forgot them hours or minutes or even seconds later, these stolen gifts sporadic and elusive though wrought from the Power connecting all Soothsayers. The shared collective acted in much the same way as the memory-altering effects of Enosh's Veil, though in a reverse kind of imposition.

Memories that spoke to Banzu. Voices of the dead whispering of their own volition, elevated during his use of the Power, faded without it in lingering traces of dead men soughing perpetual tales of agony and murderous regret. Chief among them—*Jericho . . . are you there?*

Enosh arched an impatient eyebrow.

Where are you? No answer. *Jericho, are you—*

Enosh rumbled the deliberate clearing of his throat.

Banzu lowered his stalling hand to his lap. "Sorry. Go ahead."

Enosh said, "Malach'Ra's rending inadvertently released Dethkore from his soulring servitude, not to the vitus itself but to its defeated controller. Dethkore attempted to recover his soulring and continue the war unrestrained, but Simus slew him and—"

"Burned him alive then sealed his ashes beneath the palace of Junes," Banzu interrupted, images pulled from the past as seen through the eyes of another knifing flashes behind his eyes while the words spilled loose. He paused, rubbed the inside corners of his eyes with pointer and thumb, massaging the images away in flares of phosphenes he blinked faded. "How do I even remember that? That's something I know I knew from before. Before I came back, I mean. So did my uncle. Why didn't the Veil wipe that from our minds?"

"Bits and pieces," Enosh said. "May I continue?"

Banzu nodded.

"Malach'Ra's curse took precedence thereafter. Soothsayers turned to the bloodlust, and in a fleeting moment of victory they carved a slaughtering frenzy through the survivors of Malach'Ra's hordes. Then his curse's true affects emerged. They killed everyone around them then turned upon each other in their insatiable thirst to be the last and thus the most powerful, each seeking to regain access to the Source.

"I, along with what remained of the decimated aizakai, created the fistian Academy to deal with the ramifications of the bloodlust curse. I scattered the pieces of the Dominator's Armor in my towers then sealed them behind protective wards. Along with the First Mistress, Spellbinder Llewellyn Rular, we created the Book of Towers and made a pact to hunt down all Soothsayers to their last in the hopes that he, now you, would eventually cleanse the bloodlust curse then destroy the Godstone. As I said, my Veil provided only a temporary solution. The war tired me, and sealing my towers exhausted me. Weaving the Veil almost depleted me, leaving only barest traces of magic. I intertwined the Veil with Malach'Ra's curse and bound it to the last Soothsayer because I had no other choice."

Enosh rocked forward—*reet-err*—and palmed his thighs, fisted handfuls of red robe in the manner of one drying sweat from their palms. "You are the last Soothsayer, Banzu. Only you can destroy the Godstone. Only you can—"

Enosh clipped short, face scrunching. He closed his eyes and pinched the crinkled bridge of his nose, evincing a private battle against a growing headache betraying his golden visage through taut nests of wrinkles bunching round his eyes and mouth and across his brow.

Banzu watched him overlong, questioning not only Enosh's sanity but his own for having entertained the god this far in to Enosh's longwinded speech. *None of this is getting me back to Melora or any closer to Hannibal Khan.*

"Forgive me," Enosh said, massaging the corners of his closed eyes. "The realms have been slowly bleeding together since the Veilfall, and I am influenced far sooner than you. It is . . . confusing to say the least." Blinking hard, he nested his hands in his lap, cleared his throat and continued. "Where was I? Oh, yes. Only you can finish the Great Game. If you fail, well, there are no others."

* * *

Banzu raked both hands back through his hair, gripping tufts of it before release, then blew out his cheeks while settling back in his chair, enduring the flood of information soaking into his brain and finding none of it good.

"A game," he said, repeating the sickening word in a low and partial growl. "It's all some godsdamned game."

"Essentially," Enosh said. "Yes."

A game. Of my life. Of Melora's. Of Jericho's. For the amusement of bored gods.

Sitting one moment then standing the next, Banzu remembered none of the action between. "So the Godstone is a test," he said through gritted teeth, "and it's all because of some stupid bet."

No question in his summation, and a godsdamned disheartening one at that. His fists at his sides so clenched his fingernails dug into the taut meat of his palms, his mental blockade crumbled as his concentration shattered in a focal flare of scalding animus. He no longer cared if Enosh could read his thoughts or sense his emotions.

Kill . . . spoke a voice from the outskirts of his mind . . . *kill.*

"Not a wager, precisely," Enosh said. "More of a—"

"Friggin hell." Banzu turned this way and that, hands flexing grabs of air, gaze hunting for anything to pick up and smash.

"Calm yourself," Enosh said, his voice an admonishing though wavering pitch. "Please, sit. It is essential that you . . ."

His voice faded to the steaming fumes of Banzu's volcanic rage tunneling his vision into crimson focal clarity ahead. He fixed Enosh with a piercing glare. "Friggin hell!"

Kill . . .

Haven't I been through enough? Born with a curse I've done nothing to earn. Killing my uncle. I almost died cleansing the curse to bring Melora back only for her to forget every friggin thing about us. And now . . . now this? All some godsdamned game?

Kill . . .

Enosh's lips moved, but Banzu heard none of the words drowned beneath the roar of rage roiling inside his head but for a prominent inner voice.

This changes nothing. The Gods have sudden need of you so they pluck you from the gutter, peer at the disappointed little life they pinch twisting between their fingers, then set it down on their great gaming board where it can be put to use and toyed with. Kill him, Ban. Kill him now!

Vision a throbbing red haze, skin hot and tingling, Banzu surrendered to urge and surged forward three bounding strides. He grabbed Enosh by the throat, shoving the startled avatar god so that the rocking chair and its frightened, bug-eyed sitter almost tumbled over backwards but for Banzu's strangling grip holding him angled away at the full extension of his arm.

"If you're a god then prove it now!" Banzu yelled, his snapping snarl loosing hot white bits of spittle.

Choking out raspy clips of broken words, Enosh slapped and pawed at Banzu's strong grasp round his captured throat, trying and failing at prying fingers loose.

Banzu squeezed all the harder, pleased at seeing this pathetic excuse for a god required breath, could feel physical pain and torment, possessed the human fear of torture betraying in his eyes. Banzu's blood running hot, he yelled curses in Enosh's straining face while taking predatory delight as golden skin shaded over a deeper red through oxygen deprivation.

Kill!

"Is my life nothing but a joke to you?" Panting more from outrage than physical effort, Banzu squeezed harder, the tips of his middle finger and thumb closing in together against the opposing pressure of resisting golden flesh and larynx seconds from splintering crushed. "Melora's life? Jericho's!"

Kill!!

Cruel images of Jericho's face, of Melora's, flashed through his roiling mindscape across the fiery-red backdrop of his wounded life's scarred and calloused tapestry while a wailing dirge of Soothsayer screams sang loud and long. He jerked Enosh closer, near nose to nose, his wide and wild hazels piercing the terrified depths of those bulging galaxy eyes, his seething rage reaching that defining zenith beyond sanity's control where humanity relented for the primal reign of psychosis, teetering upon the precipice of furious madness where lived the savage frenzy dividing man from beast.

A whole-body flush of cold justice delivered a killer's calm to his rising fury, an eye within the storm. His tone steadied into a deceptive tranquility carrying the threat of the inevitable in his unblinking stare. "I should carve your godsdamned heart out and stuff it down your godsdamned throat."

Enosh's face purple with strain, his eyes bulging from their sockets, he slapped and pawed again in futile attempt at prying loose Banzu's viselike grip on his throat as he rasped out a few desperate syllables.

Banzu ignored the pleas for mercy choking through his strangler's grip. Until a particular name pierced the crimson veil of his blinding rage.

"Muh-lor-uh," Enosh rasped in a garbled wheeze, his final bid for release while his eyes rolled up behind fluttering lids.

"Don't you ever speak her name!" Banzu yelled in a raging flare of voice while shaking Enosh by the neck and seconds from enacting the savage ripping of his throat.

But her name induced the epiphany that he still needed this pathetic excuse for a god if only to return to her. Disgusted at this miserable truth, unable to refuse it, he released his grip by shoving Enosh backwards into the rocker, flipping it and the avatar god over to go tumbling sprawling to the floor where Enosh lay on his back clutching his throat and gasping for the precious return of breath.

No! Kill him! Don't—

"Shut up!" Banzu hawked then spat, feeling no more awe for this paltry god than he would some slimy worm crushed beneath his boot. "I'm not playing your stupid game. And neither is she."

He raked the back of one forearm across his mouth, removing hot clings of foamy spittle from his chin, flung them free through the whip of his hand then turned Enosh his back and gripped Griever's hilt in pulsing squeezes of intent.

Kill—

"I said shut up," Banzu said through gritted teeth, his voice a guttural growl. And the voices in his head dissipated through fading traces of mad and mocking laughter. Rage less bridled than bottled, he stood all tensed trembles. He gripped Griever's hilt in flexing pulses while refocusing, attempting to slow the thunder of his heart, trying to tame the murder at play behind his eyes, knowing if he turned too quick there'd be no turning back, no reversing the irresistible kill.

I can't kill him . . . yet. I do and I might never get out of here.

Behind him, Enosh spent one full minute gasping and coughing before collecting himself enough into sitting up from the floor. Another full minute before he could speak, his voice a ragged rasp.

"You're trying to—" Enosh began then clipped short through the rough clearing of his tenderized throat. "You're trying to find rational reasons to explain irrational feelings." He coughed and cleared his throat again. "I know. You're suffering the uncontrolled emotions of a thousand cursed men through the fractured Source because you're the last Soothsayer. But you must not—"

Enosh clipped silent when Banzu drew Griever's naked steel from the hip in a slow pull.

"I don't care about your game," Banzu said, still facing away. "And I don't care about your Godstone." He made no mention of Melora or the Khan, though both names blazed at the forefront of his mind. "Now,"—and he spun round with Griever slicing sideways through the air between them at the full extension of his arm so that Enosh fell backwards flat, avoiding Griever's tip from slicing open his flinching face by thinnest margin—"I have only one question." He kicked the overturned rocker aside and strode forward, straddled his feet wide at Enosh's sides. He glared down the angled length of Griever's steel at Enosh who wriggled while attempting to sink flatter against the floor. "Will that Traveling Well take me back to her or not?"

"But you cannot refuse," Enosh said, words a stammer. "It's your destiny to—"

"Screw destiny." Banzu loomed forward. "Will it take me back to her or not?" He urged Griever closer by inches so that its point depressed the golden skin in the small hollow of Enosh's throat. "I won't ask you again."

"And you'll let all of humanity destroy itself?" Enosh asked, his sprawled X body pinned flat.

Banzu held grim pause. He eased Griever back a hair, not releasing the pressure of its pressing tip so much as exerting more control over not shoving it forward and just getting done with it all.

"I've lost too much already," he said through clenched teeth. "And you still expect my help after telling me this is all some game?" He tightened his eyes into a god-piercing glare. "I won't have her taken from me again. Not by you, not by anyone."

"Returning to her," Enosh said, while careful not to strain his throat too much and earn Griever's puncture, "is the same as killing her yourself."

The strength cooled from Banzu's burning fury. He grimaced through the wrenching grind on his heart imposed by those honest words delivered, wondered if it might explode in his chest the way stones sometimes exploded in a hot fire. Melora had saved him from death, which did not matter, because she had saved him from loneliness and a meaningless life, and that did. To have her taken from him again, and by his own condemning hands, proved too much to bear.

He withdrew two steps and for a time stood silent, the length of Griever's steel weighing heavier than it ought to feel in his lowering hand.

Enosh raised his head from the floor and looked at him with an expression not quite forgiving.

And the candid understanding in that percipient gaze drove an icicle into Banzu's heart. In a strained voice near pleading he asked that all-purpose question again. "Why?"

"Because—" Enosh began.

Unfinished, Banzu continued in stronger voice. "Why not just have a Spellbinder find the Godstone and destroy it and leave me the hell out of it? They're immune to magic, so why ruin my life? Friggin hell, I can go back and get Melora and we can find it together. Then she can—"

But he clipped his words short at Enosh's furrowing brow and the negative shake of the avatar god's head issuing pure denial.

"A Spellbinder's void-aura *is* magic." Enosh dared his shoulders up from the floor a few risen inches and rumbled his throat clear of the gruff with evident strain at play on his scrunching face. "Theirs is not an immunity *to* magic but the absorption *of* magic. There is a difference. Magic exists in tiers." He raised his left hand flat, parallel to his chest. "No magic." Then raised his flat right hand above his left. "Witchery and sorcery and wizardry." He raised his left above his right. "Aizakai." Raise right above left. "Spellbinder." Raised left above right. "Divine magic." Then lowered both hands to the floor at his sides. "Spellbinders cannot resist the all-power of the Godstone because its divine magic trumps their void-aura."

He slid his elbows back, propping more upright to better meet Banzu's stare.

"The Godstone was wrought from the combined magic of the gods. Forged not just from one but from many. That mistake is why I could not destroy it myself. Spellbinders can be corrupted by its alluring apotheosis the same as everyone else. It would empower and expand their void-aura a hundred fold, just as it would the powers of any aizakai whom touches it for as long as they touch it. Immunity is not the correct term, though I understand it must seem that way to those who do not know the truth. But now you do."

Banzu frowned, said nothing. He envisioned picking up the overturned rocker and smashing it over Enosh's head then tamed the notion before he played it through another venting outburst.

Enosh sat up through slow and cautious increments, testing the safeness of the limited space between them. "You are linked to the Godstone in more ways than one. Only its all-power can cleanse the Source, and only then will you be capable of destroying it. Until that time the shared collective of the Source remains fractured because of Malach'Ra's malignant curse, which is why its use to you is unstable at best. And why you must mend it whole."

Banzu made to speak.

But Enosh palmed the air and talked over him.

"I know you feel it inside you because I'm looking at it now. I can see it warring in your eyes, begging for release. The madness of the fractured Source is slowly bleeding in to you through the Power, charging all your emotions by magnifying everything you feel. Your love is as unrelenting as your hate is indomitable. Soon you won't be able to control yourself because every use of the Power fractures more of your sanity, and eventually your mind will shatter into disrepair. The precipice you stand upon, this is it. One step in the wrong direction is ruin, not just of yourself but of the world."

Banzu opened his mouth, closed it, face slumping, spirits plunging, disheartened, his hope of returning to Melora and letting someone else handle this Godstone mess vanishing.

"Get up." He stabbed Griever sheathed to his left hipwing, returned to the chair and waited.

* * *

"The Godstone's all-power is, by design, irresistible," Enosh said, having returned to his mockery of Jericho's rocker, enduring the brunt of Banzu's scrutinizing glare. "Even I almost succumbed to its corruptive temptation when I stole away with it. Thankfully I did not need to physically touch it to remove it."

He paused, frowning, hands upturned in his lap flexing grabs of memories while the tip of his tongue skated across his lips, tasting the faint remains of something precious, something sweet, something once sampled nestled in the craving lust for more of it, followed by an audible swallow.

"Its apotheosis is a succubus of incredible seduction. But you . . . you resisted the temptation of the bloodlust, an equal seductress, proving your willpower is stronger, which is why I bound the Veilfall to the last Soothsayer. Only you can mend the fractured Source then destroy the Godstone. But to do that you must retrieve the Essence of the First and heal the fractured Source, otherwise you will condemn yourself to madness and possession the moment you touch the Godstone."

Banzu blew out his cheeks, tired of juggling so many frustrations at once. "Retrieve the *what?*"

"The Essence of the First," Enosh repeated. "The cause of the fracture in the Source. Simus Junes was not the first Soothsayer, but he was the first to earn the bloodlust curse in his recurring battles with Malach'Ra and so he became known as the First, just as you are the Last. You are not whole because the Source remains fractured. The essence of Simus Junes was removed from the shared collective connecting all Soothsayers after Malach'Ra's banishing. This is why you cannot touch the Source without suffering the madness of the tainted shared collective. That is also why you were able to cleanse *your* bloodlust, but not *their* bloodlust."

Banzu's eyes widened as the slow dawning of realization spread over him. At last the answer for why he could not seize and hold the Source as freely as he could the Power. The Power existed individual to each Soothsayer, the Source a combined whole of those Powers gathered. *The shared collective . . . of course.* The answer invited chills alongside the comfort of revelation.

The evil you know is better than the evil you don't. At least then you know what you're dealing with.

And now he knew.

"The bloodlust of the shared collective that is made up of the essences of all Soothsayers," Enosh went on, the words an eerie reflection of Banzu's thoughts so that he suspected another probing violation of his unguarded mind. "You've cleansed the Power, *your* Power, but now you must cleanse the fractured Source. And to accomplish that you need the all-power of the Godstone. But first you require the missing piece of the shared collective that is the spiritual essence of Simus Junes."

Banzu huffed. "Okay. So where the frig is that?"

"The Essence of the First was removed from the shared collective and sealed away. Without the missing Essence, the fractured Source remains corrupted. But with it the Source can be restored whole again. Only then can it be cleansed. Only then can you achieve your true potential. And only then will you know how to destroy the Godstone."

"Fine," Banzu said. "So how am I supposed to do that?"

"The Head Mistress of the fistian Academy," Enosh said. "Her duty above all else is to guide the last Soothsayer to retrieve the Essence of the First so he can seek out the Godstone and destroy it. She has been waiting for you since before the Veilfall signaled the savior-slayer's return. Go to her, Banzu. I implore you. Retrieve the Essence of the First, then find the Godstone and destroy it before the Enclave uses it to start another Thousand Years War."

"Let's say I agree." Banzu sat forward with a renewed surge of energy, palming his thighs. "How do I destroy it?"

"That," Enosh began then paused, eyebrows drawing inward. He chewed through words before speaking them. "That I do not know. Not even Spellbinders know how to destroy it. But you will. Once you retrieve the Essence and find the Godstone, you'll just . . . *know*. Through the cleansed shared collective. I do not know how better to explain it than that."

Banzu sighed and rolled his eyes, reflecting on Melora in the tower and the bandits awaiting her outside. "You're a god and even you don't know how to destroy it, but you expect me to *just know* how to do it. If I can even find it."

Enosh nodded. "Once the fractured Source is mended whole, the same homing sense for the Godstone's location that once beat within Simus will transfer into you."

"Great." Banzu sighed. "This just keeps getting better and better."

"Knowledge is power," Enosh said, "but wisdom is capability. That is why you are here before the Academy. As to finding the Godstone, once you retrieve the Essence of the First you'll be drawn to it like iron filings to a lodestone. But understand, the moment you retrieve the Essence you will reawaken within Dethkore the same homing sense for the Godstone that transfers into you from Simus. I had hoped he would remain in slumber and out of play, but alas the Enclave undermines everything I've planned."

"I know," Banzu said, reflecting upon the unliving Trio. "Believe me, I already know."

Enosh scrunched his face. "Soultaker has already made contact?"

"Contact?" Banzu expelled a mirthless chuckle. "More than contact. Three dead khansmen tried to eat my face off."

Enosh sighed, nodded. "They control the necromaster. For now. But his undying lust for the Godstone reawakened with the Veilfall. He knows not where it has fallen, though he knows that it has fallen. But there's still time for you to get to it first, however short, for he cannot sense the Godstone's presence until you retrieve the Essence of the First. Above all else, even above the all-power of the Godstone, Dethkore craves repossession of his soulring vitus. It is his only source of control, and it provides him access to his full powers. Without it his capabilities are diminished. With it he is—" Enosh paused, grimacing, a touch of fear betraying his eyes. "Almighty is the only appropriate term for such a being. And combined with the Godstone he'll achieve omnipotence."

"But if I don't retrieve the Essence," Banzu said, walking the logical pathway leading him out from this forced duty, "then Dethkore won't be a problem, right?"

Enosh frowned. "Wrong. Now that he remembers, he will seek reclamation of his soulring vitus then seek possession of the Godstone regardless of if you retrieve the Essence or not. Removing him from the equation does not remove the need to destroy it. Power does not sit idle for long before someone comes along to abuse it. Such is the defining nature of man. And . . . there is also the matter of the keyrings."

Banzu huffed a terse breath while lifting then dropping his hands atop armrests in frustrated gesture. "Friggin hell, there's more?"

Enosh nodded. "The keyrings will allow you to unlock the Essence of the First. It's sealed away deep beneath the Academy grounds behind a barrier of magic impassable by all but for the bearer of the keyrings. A safeguard against the Soothslayer. Fortunately I already gave the keyrings to First Mistress Rular when we established the fistian Academy. Like the Book of Towers, they too have been passed down from Head Mistress to Head Mistress while awaiting the Veilfall and the savior-slayer reborn."

Fist. Banzu almost spat the word aloud. Everything led him to Fist. Everything but—

"And Melora?" he asked. "What about her? I'm just supposed to leave her there with those godsdamned thieves? She's a capable woman, but if she tries leaving the tower they'll kill her. Especially after what I did. There's too many of them for her to deal with alone." He glanced at the hallway, at the Traveling Well beyond his sight, eyes tightening, hands gripping armrests. *Bastards. I should've killed them all.* "I can't let that happen. I won't. None of this matters if she dies."

"The Godstone is far more important than your Spellbinder," Enosh said while flicking a dismissive gesture.

Banzu scowled at the blatant rejection.

"Besides," Enosh added, "returning to her will condemn her along with the rest of the world. I've already made that perfectly clear. You and Metrapheous are the only two beings capable of resisting the Godstone's all-power, and he made his choice in the matter long ago. If you return to her now, your stalled arrival in Fist will prove too late. I used nearly all of my magics to banish the Godstone and create the Veil, and most of the rest of it to secure my towers and power the Traveling Wells to ensure your arrival. It permeates these bones, but what little reserves I have access to are fading, and much faster now after the trigger of your arrival here. There was only enough left for two travels. The first to bring you here, and the second to take you out. Once you choose, there's no turning back."

"Doesn't sound like much of a choice," Banzu said, frowning.

"The triumph or tragedy I spoke of earlier," Enosh said. "Your destiny." He sat forward, locking gazes. "Are you finally beginning to understand? Power corrupts. Absolute power corrupts absolutely. And unlimited power, well . . ." He spread his hands as if presenting some tangible point between them. "The Godstone must be destroyed. The Head Mistress will provide you with the keyrings to retrieve the Essence of the First and mend the fractured Source whole again. But I warn you that you must subdue the Essence of the First until you find the Godstone, or else—"

But there Enosh stopped short. He sat back and averted his gaze, apprehension twisting his golden features into a grim visage of silent contempt.

"Or else what?" Banzu asked. But Enosh did not answer, only stared down into his hands so that Banzu sat forward and repeated the question in stronger voice. "Or else what?"

Enosh drew in deep, expelled overlong, the effort deflating him. "Or else the bloodlust-corrupted Essence of Simus Junes will stalk the One Land again, through you." He raised his gaze and feigned false confidence with a too-big smile while swatting the air with a dismissive flick of his wrist. "But let us not dwell on your possible failure. What remains is for you to accept your duty and fulfill your destiny."

Banzu thinned his eyes into suspicious squints. "What are you getting out of all this?"

Enosh captured silence a considerable pause while returning his stare down into his upturned hands, his fingers curling grasps of something invisible only his eyes could perceive.

"Well?" Banzu asked.

Enosh clenched his fists. "Relief," he said without looking up, his voice low and tremulous, bordering on weak. "Relief from the burden of guilt in knowing that I am the cause of it all. I am the Builder. I—" A hesitant pause. "I am the one who forged the Godstone into existence. And I am the one who first proposed the Great Game." He raised his gaze, presenting eyes of fragile stare possessing depths of sadness shimmering therein the galaxies of his silver-jeweled eyes. "Even a god can make mistakes."

"Wait just a godsdamned minute," Banzu said, tensing forward, seconds from erupting into standing. "You created the Godstone but you don't know how to destroy it?"

Enosh shook his head. "That knowledge was taken from me and placed within the chosen two as part of the Great Game. I took magic from all us gods to create the all-power of the Godstone, and in turn they took from me the knowledge to destroy it. A game must be fair, you see. A game must have rules and boundaries. And all games must have players." He interlaced his fingers out before him then settled his intertwined hands atop his belly paunch and presented a smile leaving his eyes untouched. "You see? Destiny. The force you do not believe in."

Banzu eyeballed the avatar god, resisting the urge to pounce forth and choke him again by thinnest margin. He settled back and considered his fate. So much to fathom in one terrible sitting. A whole host of impulses came roaring at him only to be beaten back.

For her. I'll do it for her.

And for the Khan, a darker part of him added in malicious whisper. *Go to Fist . . . go for the Khan . . . go for the kill.*

Banzu sighed through gritted teeth as the hunt within won over him, all roads leading to Fist. "Fine. Then I guess I'm going to Fist."

* * *

"One last thing before you leave," Enosh said to Banzu's back where they stood facing the Traveling Well. "The magic of this particular Traveling Well functions by way of willpower. You have to want it to take you to Fist. And . . ."

Banzu stayed his concentrated gaze upon the dark depths awaiting his plunge. "And?"

"And you must forget the Spellbinder, or else it will return you to her instead."

Banzu stiffened tense. Did not turn, did not speak.

"That must not happen," Enosh continued, his sharper tone turning his words more threat than request. "Once you leave here, there is no coming back. Forget her. She has finished her crucial part in the Great Game, but yours has only just begun. Besides, her time is limited considering the fading magic of my towers. The moment you are expelled they will wither then die. Leave her to her fate. She does not matter anymore—"

Banzu spun round while snatching a quick pull on Griever's hilt. He tore the blade loose, allowing Enosh no time for finishing, extending both arm and sword in his spasm twirl.

Griever sliced inches deep through the front half of the avatar god's throat in one clean sweep, spilling a slash of golden droplets into the air trailing its death stroke.

Enosh stiffened, eyes startling wide. Gurgling, his tremulous hands raised to touch at the golden fan of blood pouring from the new lower smile Banzu bestowed upon his slit throat. Wiggling fingers bumped beneath his chin. His head tilted backwards upon the uncut back of his neck working as some grisly hinge. Spurts of golden blood squirting out from round his spine.

"She matters to me." Banzu turned away to the Traveling Well. He flicked golden beads of godsblood from Griever's keen tongue then stabbed it sheathed at his left hipwing.

Behind sounded the fleshy *thud* of Enosh's limp collapse to the floor.

She matters to me. Banzu palmed the Traveling Well's waist-high lip, captured a deep breath into his lungs, and leaped over down inside. Falling, falling, falling . . . he seized the Power, triggering an effluent burst of rainbow energies thickening the rushing air while slowing his plummet in a viscous engulfing vibration of fluid.

Past him, up through the Traveling Well, erupted then inhaled luminous crackles of magic, leaving silence broken by the choking gurgles of a dying god in his wake.

CHAPTER TWENTY-EIGHT

Banzu flowed through the viscous torrent of fluid sweeping him away from the Luna Nexus, holding his breath while forcing his body relaxed and hoping the limp calmness helped smooth his second transition through no alarming repeat of the frightening first.

For the moment his thoughts turned peaceful while he abandoned tension and focused on the sole task of reaching Fist for the Head Mistress awaiting him in the Academy, smiling, his mind adrift in the cozy predator afterglow of slaying a god who deserved no less for such instigative claims of abandonment and destiny.

I fed you what you wanted, you hungry little bastard. An end to your terrible wait. How did it taste?

A satisfied voice arose in pursuant whisper to his thoughts.

Godslayer, yes. Kinslayer. And soon, Khanslayer.

Followed by echoes of Jericho's diminishing laughter.

Banzu blanked his mind and floated with the ease of a long-tensed muscle relaxed, surrendering trust to the Traveling Well's guiding whims, tumbling and tossing though earning no resistive whips of his limbs while the effervescent whorls and rainbow flares and luminous bursts of multicolors died to blackest pitch swallowing him.

A faraway pinprick of white light sparked aglow and akin to a candle's tiny flame miles distant, evincing an end to the black throat carrying him, sweeping him, pulling him along . . . though at a lazier pace than his initial venture.

He fixed upon the white light expanding outward, that lotus of hope and destination slow in blooming.

For a fleeting moment he reflected upon Melora in the tower and yearned for her, craved the scent of her pale-blonde hair, the salty tang of her sexual sweat upon his tongue and lips, the slick warmth of her moist cleft sliding carnal grips round his throbbing thrusts while their hips danced in animal tandem, the strength of her fingernails-digging clings and the moaning grunts of her voice hot against his tickled ear . . . to yell at her for tricking him before taking her in his arms and loving her again.

And more. To explain he'd actually been to the Moon, that he met the mortal avatar of Enosh the Builder god and learned the truth of her Spellbinder magic as well the necromaster Dethkore and the Veilfall and the Godstone and his own fractured Source. That the cruel gods played some petty game with their lives, and for it he'd slain the arrogant messenger requesting her abandonment—on second thought maybe he'd leave out that last murderous bit.

His thoughts returned lusty and longing, reminiscent of their carnal union before her apologetic shove, Banzu's first experience of sex replaying through eager thrusts of passion and desire throbbing inside her slickly-sweet cleft accepting him, claiming him, demanding him and—

A jostling shift of sensory confusion startled him back to present. The direction of flow changing, rerouting his destination through his mistaken shift of focus from Fist to Melora, Enosh's parting warning rebuked so that Banzu banished distracting thoughts of her and the tower and concentrated through chants of Fist in mental mantra, earning an abrupt jostle of correction to the sense of his directional flow.

Fist . . . Fist . . . Fist.

The anxious moment of deviation passed, and his greater concern became holding the breath dying in his heating lungs, this second journey taking longer than the first, sluggish and slower, the translucent fluid thicker, the active magics of Enosh's Traveling Well growing lethargic while dying round him, losing strength, its energies spending with effort.

Friggin hell.

He almost opened his mouth to issue the curse while inviting the fluid into his lungs as cold panic prickled in, hoping to reach the lotus's expanding white light exit before his mouth and his thirst for precious air betrayed him so that he pressed his lips while locking his throat tight.

He fixated on the white light far ahead, a hot agony blooming in his chest, seconds feeling the painful stretch of minutes.

It's taking too long. I won't make it. I can't die here. Alone.

He broke into the frantic motions of swimming, hands groping for hope as much for faster progress toward the destination of expanding white light ahead. But his physical efforts achieved no influence upon the speed of his magical transport. And worse they burned away his dwindling reserves of oxygen while strengthening his savage urgency for breathing.

Fist . . . friggin Fist . . . Fist godsdammit! Oh gods, I can't die here. Not like this. Just a little farther. Fist!

The white light's mocking exit continued through slow and slowing expansion of accepting his coming to birth—for that was what his brain imagined of the traveling, awareness of expulsion through birthing pangs. He abandoned his futile struggles and tensed while surrendering into a fetal drift, teeth clenched and jaws bunched against the craving fever of his aching lungs.

He thrashed and shook, defiant to his body's stronger needs winning over—and sucked in a desperate, irresistible gasp of fluid.

Profound chill sank into the roots of his teeth while flooding down his throat and punching into his expanding lungs where it bloomed throughout the rest of him, frigid canines gnawing at the warm marrow in his trembling bones. His mind divided from body in hysterias of terror. His consciousness watched from behind in tethered float the frantic struggle of his physical self reaching out, clawing desperate rakes at the expanding source of white light's escape.

Though somewhere in the morbid calm of his mind, a detached place of peace free from the drowning pain, he accepted his impending demise while his body refused surrender through desperate swims.

The beauty of her face. The warmth of her skin. The music of her voice. I'll never enjoy her again. Touch her. Smell her. Taste her . . . no! I can't. I won't. I must—

His body convulsed in violent spasms beyond his dying control, turning him limp in shocked stasis.

He floated in blackness while more of it tunneled his shrinking peripherals as debilitating regrets of words unsaid and efforts unfinished cradled him. Melora's beautiful angel face resolved to his unblinking stare, a swimmer striding to the surface of his fading consciousness in a last vestige reflection of his life's most crucial triumph in offering of that tranquil dier's song all men hope to know at their life's end.

No, Fist!

In final act he seized the Power, gripped it, strangled it—and jolted in a mad tumble toward the white light lotus expanding to blinding infinity and beyond, his body a whiplash of limbs.

Fist! Fist! Fist!

He vomited up and out from the Traveling Well's expelling mouth in a flailing tumble, arcing on high through no sure sense of height then falling angled and away, ejected in a violent spray of fluid energies erupting then inhaling as he crashed upon the hard stone floor front-first with a wet smacking slap of pain, the resuscitating impact of which punched the fluid from his lungs.

He lay coughing and gasping the heaviness from his chest, convulsions wrenching his stomach muscles raw, hot tears of painful joy stinging his eyes blurry while he sucked cooler air into his thankful lungs.

I'm alive . . . still alive.

The blazing pain in his chest subsiding through the last evacuation of fluid from his lungs, he lay trembling for a time, then tried pushing up onto hands and knees while his sloshing sense of the world rebalanced. Limbs feeble quivers, his hands and knees slipped out beneath him and he collapsed flat, rolled onto his right side where he curled, body craving warmth against the pervading cold.

A crazed smile crossed his lips at the cruel irony of the trip almost killing him when weighed against its purpose of bringing him here. But no laughter escaped through the paralyzing shivers keeping him curled upon the floor, shrouded in darkness.

* * *

Several minutes passed. Banzu lay curled and battling through shivering aches while clinging to consciousness, his muscles locked tight and squeezing every ounce of warmth afforded between taut fibers, his arms pulled inflexible against his chest, his hands rigid claws, his chattering teeth producing echoing *click-click-clicks* in the dark pitch.

He clutched victorious relief at avoiding death by thinnest margin, escaping the condemnation of floating aimless and adrift within the Traveling Well's otherworldly plane of existence, that static sea of forever wrought from spent magics.

He huffed misting plumes of warming breath on his palsied hands while flexing them through resistive flares of icy ache. Achieving their full movement, he grunted through more flares of cold pain while forcing his body unfurled from shivering fetal curl, embracing the gradual blooms and spreads of heat through cramped and protesting extremities.

He looked round, eyes darting, vision adjusting to the surrounding black pitch, the darkness total in its dominance of his new environment though he knew he lay within a colossal chamber of sorts by the carry of his raspy voice when he tested it.

"Hello?"

He listened.

No answer.

And no true perception of the far walls or high ceiling though he sensed their presence through breadth of emptiness.

The cynical part of his brain formed a prison of the darkness where menacing nightmares lurked within the foreboding black pitch awaiting to devour him.

A whisper stole through his mind, harsh and sharp though hushed, containing fathoms of suspicions, the paranoid warrant of a cruel man having done cruel things and expecting crueler retribution. Unsure to whom the voice belonged, his own mindspeak, his dead uncle's, or one of the thousand other dead Soothsayers lurking in the deep recesses of his subconscious mind making up the shared collective of the fractured Source, he shirked it aside.

Though not the flush of hot anger it elicited, pumping more invigoration through him. He craned his head from the floor against stiff neck muscles, cautious eyes darting for any slip of shadow, trembling hand lowering for the reassuring grip of Griever's leather-wound hilt.

At least this time I'm not half naked with my pecker hanging out.

Move. The other's voice again, hot and savage, curt and commanding. *Get up and move.*

Banzu shifted on the floor, stretching through warming flexes, wiggling fingers and toes, making pliable bends of his arms and legs through lingering cramps. He rolled to his stomach and pushed up to hands and knees, the dark world sloshing through a moment of imbalance while waning chills left him.

Blind feel of the rough floor beneath him. *Not tiled smooth like in the Luna Nexus but stone.* He straightened onto knees then sank back bottom atop heels and tested the projection of his voice again.

"Hello?"

And waited.

Listening.

No answer.

He fondled over his damp shirt and pants, then twisted for a look behind. The black builderstone mouth of the Traveling Well presented an outline of presence to eyes hindered by the impenetrable darkness.

That inner voice again, *They aren't gods at all but manipulators. And now we're in the den of—*

"Shut up," Banzu said, frowning, voice carrying away in the dark. "Not now."

He palmed the floor to aid his shaky legs for standing and—"Ow!"—jerked his right hand away with a winching hiss, having pressed upon some unseen sharp bit of grit slicing open the ball of his thumb in accidental press. He muttered a curse while flicking his hand, flinging a few droplets of blood, then stuck his cut thumb in his mouth and sucked the coppery pain away.

Seconds more and the darkness behind him shied away so that he twisted for a look at the soft azure glow emitting from the Traveling Well's mouth in a slender flame tall as a man. He welcomed the unexpected source of light in this dark and desolate place, used it to his viewing vantage while scanning round.

The blue flame cast strange and wavering shadows about the enormous room so tall and wide he could not place its ceiling or walls beyond the black depths outlying the flame's limited flourish of light. The air tasted stale, unbreathed in centuries. In his mind a single prominent word rang out: *tomb.* Punctuated by: *Academy.*

But where the frig is everyone?

The famous fistian Academy. A residence of aizakai housing for over three centuries. A safe haven for all aizakai to live and learn and train while developing their magical abilities under the experienced tutelage of veteran aizakai masters and the watchful eyes of Spellbinders. An institution of learning as well one of political power and military might, led by the current Head Mistress Gwendora Pearce and dominating all of Thurandy . . . until the return of the Enclave and the rise of Hannibal Khan.

Banzu sighed at the disappointing hollowness and the truth of this place. *Well, not* all *aizakai are welcome.* They might accept him now, as the last Soothsayer, but for the past three centuries the Academy hunted Soothsayers while attempting to end the Nameless One's bloodlust curse through elimination. He cringed through the deliberation of his possible mistake in coming here alone instead of returning to Melora so they could arrive together.

No, she'd probably just shove me right back inside the well again after slapping my face off for returning.

A dull pain arose deep in his chest so that he removed his bleeding thumb from his sucking mouth and coughed up a final bit of viscous fluid from his lungs. He spat the gob out, and it vanished to a smoky vapor mid-air before reaching the outskirts of wan blue light.

No point in just sitting here. Get up, seize the Power so I can friggin see and find an exit then find the Head Mistress.

He stood, vaporous wisps lifting from his drying clothes and hair—and froze, tensing at the sound of a rising hum of noise piercing the silence though muffled from somewhere beyond the hidden walls while soft vibrations stole through the floor. He listened to the disturbance, at first low and deep though elevating in volume and pitch into an ear-piercing shriek puncturing through the walls while filling the chamber with a kind of physical resonance.

Wincing, he palmed over his ears while hunching forward, eyed closed tight, teeth clenched, wailing pain stabbing his eardrums, knifing into his brain where its harpy blades of sound twisted and screwed despite his shielding hands. Grimacing, he sank to his knees, collapsed sideways, clenched teeth grinding, temples pounding, and cringed into a fetal ball while the deafening skirling assaulted his senses with the fury of a siren.

Painful seconds stretched to grueling minutes.

The ear-piercing shriek cut off, receding from the room, sucked in through the walls where it continued low and thriving beyond the muffling stone.

Banzu opened his eyes and sat up, peering through the dark pitch for the unknown source of noise.

An inhaling *whoosh!* behind as the Traveling Well's azure flame flared then disappeared down inside the mouth of the well, extinguishing through the last of its magics while snuffing all light.

Followed by a second *whoosh!* proclaiming the spark of unnatural fire above head-height igniting upon the far wall, a red spot of flame bursting alive and dancing atop the torch there fastened to stone. Another *whoosh!* followed by another then another still—*whoosh!-whoosh!-whoosh!* Through mysterious means more torches flared into flaming life in a long horizontal line all along the walls in consecutive saffron bursts, one after the other in rapid-fire succession while illuminating the room as the torches lit themselves round the vast chamber unto completion of their surrounding circuit.

"What the frig . . ."

He gained his feet and turned round in a curious daze, the outside humming a faint song of distraction to the revelation of his cavern environment. He gripped Griever's hilt in pulsing flexes while scanning the massive room through the better light offered him . . . but by whom? Or what? And why?

The tall stone walls formed a massive square of a room hundreds of feet wide and across and high, with the Traveling Well and himself beside it at the room's center. A surrounding row of statues carved in human effigy aligning the four walls captured his roving gaze, each of these standing beneath the mysterious self-lighting torches above their bowed heads.

He studied the stone figures from afar, unsure what to make of them. Carved in similar human model yet each possessed distinct features of face and clothes and body representing a variety of individuals. Men, all of them. Soldiers, perhaps, though obviously swordslingers by tell of the stone swords held before them in upside-down fashion with tips stabbing the floor between their stone feet, stone hands resting one over the other atop stone hilts. Their eyes closed, implying the impression of petrified men asleep on their feet.

Banzu turned about, hunting further details. He stopped at the relieving sight of the large set of closed double doors far across the way which broke the circuit of torches and stonemen aligning the walls, evincing no other entry or exit but for the Traveling Well.

He walked toward the tall doors in cautious strides while listening for any sounds above his own hushed breathing and padding footsteps. Whether he could push or pull the enormous doors open or carve an exit through them then so be it.

Sounds of crunching and he stopped mid-step. He scanned round, eyes darting, breath held. The strange crunching sounds elevated, all around him now, crunching at him from the walls.

What the frig . . .

The statues opened their stony eyes as one hive mind, revealing blazing crimson gazes burning within glaring earthen sockets as the statues-not-statues of swordslingers awoke from petrified stasis into horrifying life and movement. The raw snapping cracks of stone breaking from stone as they shook loose from their set places against the walls, stepping forth while tearing free, rubble and grit and chunks of stone tumbling and littering the floor round their forward-shifting feet.

As one active unit connected through shared sentience the animated statues turned inward and set their blazing red gazes upon Banzu standing at their epicenter. They raised their stony swords in double-fisted unison performance of ceremonial ritual, then held their poses while returning still.

Silence but for the muffled hum singing beyond the chamber walls and the rapid patter of Banzu's heartbeat thundering behind his cage of ribs. He stood frozen in all but his eyes, panic fluttering through his quickening pulse.

I'm surrounded. By living statues?

For he had seen that same lambent red gaze before in another's bloodlust-corrupted eyes, only here it blazed from too many sets of eyes for counting. Twenty, perhaps. No, thirty? No . . . more.

Oh gods, what is this place?

Through his mind echoed cruel and mocking laughter, the owner of some private joke.

He scanned the room in a slow turn, flexing cautious squeezes on Griever's hilt, waiting for further signs of movement.

A minute passed without interruption.

He relaxed and walked toward the double doors under the silent watch of the saluting swordslinger statues, all the while preparing words for when he met the Head Mistress.

And Aggie. I can't forget her. I have to return Jericho's wedding ring. He would want her to have it back. Gods, but I don't even know what she looks like. Hopefully she won't kill me after I explain how I have it and—

He stopped ten strides out, rumination crumbling to the rumble of stone feet stomping with leaden plants of boots when the living statues broke from their saluting poses as a whole and moved in upon him while closing their cordon together before the double doors, the hive mind of stonemen marching forth in slow bid, their motions strangely fluid and human-like despite their earthen bodies of living rock.

Banzu backpedaled until he butted up against the Traveling Well, jolting at almost tumbling backwards down inside it. No escape there. He turned this way and that while stony feet pounded and rumbled the floor as the living statues stole into forward charge, increasing speed while making of themselves a shrinking circle of attack, their combined tromps an elevating thunder.

He threw a panicked glance at the closed double doors far across the room, mocking him with distance, the route blocked by the encroaching stonemen.

Flight no option, fight or die instincts gripped him by the spine, catalyzing that anticipatory purity of impending violence and its desperate struggle to pull life from death which surpasses any philosopher's sere quest for truth.

Fine. If this is how you want it then so be it.

* * *

Banzu seized the Power while pulling Griever to natural guard from his left hipwing, his vision bursting bright while colors vanished to luminous twilight greys, his ultra keen senses flaring sensitive while the slowing world rumbled through the rolling growl of the encroaching stonemen's foreboding thunderous stomps.

He drew in a sharp nostril inhale, tasting the aged flavor of the stale air and the fresh raw crack of stone scenting it, the flaming torches lining the four walls brightened to saffron suns emitting sooty aroma, the surrounding stonemen's lambent red glares magnified into molten projections of hateful fire nestled in the lust for spending it upon their sole human target, his own predator's gaze restless with unease making of his eyes crisp and vivid portals absorbing the bounty of stimulation at play round him.

Details sharp as crushed glass, he considered the ancientness of this mausoleum to these animate statues stomping toward him with the combined heavy tread of many tons, these stonemen active after what must be centuries of stillness, each kicking up swirling zephyrs of sparkling dust motes Power-caught in lazy dances of agitated air making a whole of a churning galaxy confined within the imprisoning walls.

Up his legs trembled slowed pulsing beats vibrating through boots and flesh and bone the floor pounded beneath the spread tonnage of over thirty charging statues punishing the anvil canvas in repetitious stomps of their eager inward tread, each slow hammerblow of foot a striking thunderclap. Powdered eddies of rippling dust parted from the paths of the stonemen's strident legs while they advanced with stone blades brandished, the muffled skirling hum beyond the walls singing in louder peal to Banzu's enhanced hearing though ignored for the immediate threat shrinking in at him from all sides.

Concentrating on the now, he drew in a steadying breath while seeking the familiar *heartbeat-of-the-world* in honing focus of the visual pulsing waves of internal rhythm for the dance of swordplay about to begin. But though these statues stole through supernatural life, they possessed no living substance of flesh and blood and bone but stone, and therein beat not a single heart for which to gather and feel along the tracer lines of spirit upon the Power's spiderweb of sense.

Good, he mused over the absence of true life in these inhuman beings. He tightened his inner grasp on the Power while tightening his outer grip on Griever's leather-wound hilt, squeezing each for increased purchase, as there spread a viper's grin upon his approving lips. *Real good. No holding back, then.*

The enlightening conversation with Enosh left him in a black mood shaded all the darker with Melora so far removed. The seething rage for the Khan, building within since his re-beginning, flared into an aching promise of wrath begging for the sweet deliverance of incautious release. He'd sampled the delicious taste of that unbridled satisfaction when dealing with Bartholomew's bandits outside the tower, and now he could unleash his pent swell of aggressions upon these stone men-not-men with no consequence of murderous guilt.

He released his strong hold on the Power, and time within the chamber blink-shifted return into its normal speed of flow. Fluttering torches painting orange ripples across the advancing stonemen through darkness and light and shadows in all their flavors, Banzu stood loose and ready, waiting and baiting, allowing his attackers to close in while making of himself an easy target.

But as much as he wanted to surge forth in bladed fury, the rational part of him reprimanded he should carve a pathway to the double doors through the stony aggressors using controlled Power-flickers while employing as little of his lifeforce as fuel for the Power in cruel trade.

This is not the true battle. None of these are Hannibal Khan.

But the stronger, savage part of him countered with enjoyment of this contest, taking delight in the release of his festering animus while making a killer's game of these stonemen same as the gods had made a game of his life.

He considered the closed double doors no more, concentrating on the now.

They want us to play? Then let's play!

* * *

The thrilling rush of surrounding stonemen aggressors closed distance in an elevation of stomping thunder as Banzu sank into a half crouch on legs of coiled springs, muscles priming through anxious flexing twitches, his predatory gaze measuring round in slow hunt, targeting motions, seeking that first crucial opening when confronted by superior numbers—*there!*

Bursting forth in a Power-flicker Banzu lunged, covering the space of five bounding strides in one propelling push of his back foot, sinking low while gliding beneath the sideways-swiping stoneblade whirring through empty air inches above his ducking head then, in another Power-flicker burst, he twisted round in sideways slicing return, cleaving through the stoneman's solid middle back-to-front above its stony hips, the velocity of his stroking sword strengthened by Power-momentum providing enhancing transferred force into Griever's steely bite so that his humming blade cut through stone as if no more than a soft column of butter providing least resistance against his sure stroke.

Twisting in follow-through of Griever's sweeping arc while the divided stoneman's parts separated into toppling over, Banzu sprang up targeting angled precision through the next oncoming stoneman's downward-slicing stroke meant for splitting his skull to the chin. He cut through the descending stonesword mid-length, reversed the stroke of his blade while turning its keen edge with the shift of his double-fisted wrists just so and removed stony head from stony shoulders with another sideways-sweeping slice applied straight as a sculptor's delicate scalpel cut. The wicked crimson flare of those lambent eyes snuffed dull same as the extinguished set of the first stoneman's seconds previous.

He spun away while sidestepping out from the falling path of the decapitated stoneman as it joined the riven first in pieces tumbling to the floor. He faced their others closing in too fast round him for proper dancing space. Seizing a Power-flicker with which he took two bounding steps, he launched high into the air while vaulting up and over the mouth of the Traveling Well.

Thank gods for lofty ceilings!

Griever raised overhead in a double-fisted clutch at the apex of his leap, Banzu measured the landing aim of his descending flight path while drawing knees to chest, forming a ball of himself, then seized another Power-flicker and drove home in kicking extension of his legs while slamming down feet-first atop the crunching shoulders of a third stoneman glaring crimson blaze up between his spread feet, the punching landing of his impact crumbling the inhumane victim to the floor and making of it an outward-blasting spray of chunky gravel and powdery grit, while at the same time he chopped through a fourth stoneman behind the destroyed third from stony head through rocky crotch, separating its blazing red eyes as he divided the rock body.

The fissured figure split longways, fell apart into two separating halves, revealing not soft internal guts and organs but solid filling within its stony body, while the lambent blaze of its separated eyes winked out.

Banzu rose into a hunch, a billowing cloud of swirling dust breathing round his legs. The shrapnel of his landing had blasted three other stonemen into a scatter of broken pieces on the floor. He drew in deep, surveying the results of his work thus far, and smiled.

Kill . . . soughed the predator's voice of his mind, a touch disappointed with no cost of life exchanged in this endeavor yet relishing the stone butchery all the same . . . *kill.*

Banzu straightened, blew out a disdainful snort through flaring nostrils. *Oh gods what a rush!* He held pause, allowing his aggressors the courtesy of moving in upon his changed location across the room while he scanned their enclosing numbers with a raptor's sweeping gaze, and by quick count put the remaining stonemen at twenty-five, give or take. The tip of his darting tongue licked away dust sticking to moist lips spreading in a welcoming grin, a darker part of him wishing for more stonemen targets while taking offence at such a meager offering.

He turned his head and spat, surveyed the enemy with an arrogant stiffening of his spine, the rumbling floor beneath his boots from the charging stonemen's relentless advance a match to the rapid patter of his invigorated heart. He snarled as he sought out his next closing target. He dodged round then past a stabbing stonesword meant for piercing his guts and lunged into lowering beneath another's sweep that cut only air. He seized a Power-flicker and shot up driving Griever's fisted hilt beneath the square jaw of the next stoneman attacker.

Its head exploded in a fantastic spray of rubble the impact of which sent painful vibrations shooting into Banzu's uppercutting swordhand through the length of his arm to his shoulder. The added force of the impulsive Power-strike softened the otherwise self-debilitating blow though did not prevent the earned pain from reminding him that as much as the Power enhanced and strengthened his fleshy body, bones could still be broken if he turned careless and reckless in aggressive surrender.

But he mustered the rush of pain into a wave of fuel thrown upon the battle-fire ignited within his flaring blaze of heart, stoking the blast furnace of his Khan-born animus. He grit his teeth and turned, surrounded by stonemen seeking his demise through their hive-mind tactics of closing unison. A combined frenzy of stoneblades arcing, sweeping, stabbing from all directions.

Banzu spun in a Power-twisting tornado of bladed destruction with Griever held at length, whirring steel shattering the assault of offending stoneblades seeking flesh into a rubble cloud while cutting a circular swath through arms and chests of the innermost ring of attackers as they pursued forward in swarming fashion, mindless in all but *attack-attack-attack!*

The inner ring of dismembered stonemen collapsed in cascades of tumbling chunks round Banzu's spinning finish. Yet more stonemen rushed forward through the scattered destruction of the first wave in an imperfect circle, kicking aside rocky remains when not crunching the broken parts of their felled fellows beneath stomping feet knowing no retreat.

Banzu dispatched two more stonemen into hewn divides of upper and lower torsos sliding free through a swift sideways sweep of Griever's immaculate Power-hardened blade cutting a long stroke through both middles in cleaving succession. He parted three more stonemen in a dancing flurry of twirling slices, his instinctive swordslinger swordforms at natural fluid work, chopping arms and legs then separating heads from shoulders in a tumble of rubble. Another two stonemen divided, the first horizontally, the second vertically, both their blazing gazes snuffing dull before their dismembered parts crashed the floor.

Muscles greased through the hot fluid groove of swordform sliding into swordform after swordform in a perfect flow of swordslinger harmony, Banzu spun round to defend his backside, seizing a Power-flicker in eager bid for scoring more debilitating strokes through Griever's offending steel. And took startled pause through frightening recognition when he came face to face with the stony visage of his uncle Jericho perfectly detailed in every shocking way.

Jolted stunned, Banzu's hold on the Power released of its own accord, a wet wedge of glass slipping loose from pinching fingers. Luminous Power-greys fled his twilight vision, and the slow-flow of time blink-shifted return into its normalized pace.

Statue-Jericho showed no kin recognition of his startled nephew but for aiming to remove Banzu's head through the decapitating swing of his stonesword.

Hesitation gets men killed . . . Banzu shook loose from the paralyzing surprise just in the nick, ducking the sideways swing of stonesword slicing the air inches above his lowering head, the whirring sweep of it catching and tearing trailing tangles of his floating hair in whiffing pass. He stumbled backwards in clumsy withdrawal and raised Griever in barring defense while Statue-Jericho advanced in reversing stroke and beat Griever aside. Banzu spun through the momentum of his turned sword, staggered backwards while earning space as the other stonemen closed round their little duel.

Banzu locked gazes with the twin red blazes of his uncle's stone effigy piercing the fragile depths of him in stunning glare.

Those eyes . . . so much the same as that night. The night everything changed. The night Melora died. The night he murdered her. The night he took everything away from me in one fell swoop.

His peripherals darkened in focal stare while innermost feelings flared through heaps and swells of tapped emotions, parts of him stripping away through the scarred layers of pain for the visceral suffering beneath. Time dissolved into a meaningless agony as those haunting lambent orbs hooked deep and clawing into the guilt and remorse of his soul while trapping him to place in a sweeping wave of arresting distortion as Statue-Jericho advanced, stonesword arcing down for splitting Banzu's face in defiant slowness.

A frightened boy paralyzed before the punishing father.

Banzu regained control of his stolen willpower and parried the death stroke aside at the last. He dove into rolling aside. Behind him sounded a *thump* and a *thunk* evincing two stoneswords from the aggressors charging his turned back biting into floor instead of his absent flesh.

The fluster of panic fled to scolding mental curses, emotions boiling up from the scalding pit of anger churning in his guts though followed quick by the cool flush of logic instilled through years of habitual training.

No emotion. Banzu voiced the swordslinger mantra through admonishing mindspeak while attempting regaining focus, a lesson taught him by the same man of this stone effigy trying to kill him now. *Emotions cause mistakes. Emotions get men killed.*

But the emotional suppression proved a useless endeavor as nightmare flashes of the cruel night when he awoke and found Melora dead and his bloodlust-corrupted uncle pleased with the brutal work knifed through his mind in rapid repeats, each more vivid than the last.

Anger bloomed into vengeful rage flaring from the hot and snarled mass of emotions tangled round his injured soul. Logic fled in a mad surge of primal fury released in a guttural yell when Banzu sprang to his feet in screaming rebellion against the terrible scorn of those bitter memories and all the misery they afforded his grieving heart.

He snarled defiant outrage at these unworthy stonemen daring to attack him, at the cruel gods for forcing his involvement in their sadistic Great Game he called life, at Melora's abandonment, at the world itself for cursing him from the moment of his birth. Eyes wide and wild, glistening strings of saliva depending from his gaping maw, a primal battle-lust and the fierce need to see it fed bloomed therein his seething core, pumping adrenaline's fury through his throbbing swells of veins its liquid fire seeking to burst his skin and burn him alive along with everything else in the blissful surrender to unadulterated rage.

Yes!

The bitter inner voice in his skull laughed now, and Banzu laughed with it, orgasmic to be alive, free of control, enveloped in chaos's immunity of destruction, to unleash without care of consequence.

Elimination sang through his mind in the chanting appeal of a thousand raucous voices as Statue-Jericho charged forward swinging.

Through consecutive Power-flickers Banzu swatted the stonesword aside, making of it an eruptive cloud of debris, then cleaved first through legs then stomach then neck of the effigy of his uncle, Griever a fanning blur of strokes. The lambent light in those crimson eyes snuffed, a grieving part of Banzu cringing through returning pangs of guilt at having sundered the mock stone effigy of his uncle. He stepped aside, allowing the momentum of the cut pieces tumbling past where they skittered upon the floor.

He glanced at the double doors awaiting his departure far across the room—with a Powered run he could cross that distance in seconds—then turned away, faced the remaining numbers of the inhumane prey set against him and licked his lips in predatory delight.

No. I am unfinished here.

CHAPTER TWENTY-NINE

The remaining charge of animate stonemen forming their shrinking circle stomped leaden kicks through the scattered chunks and strewn rubble of their eradicated fellows littering the floor while they rushed forward in continued bid to bring Banzu down.

But his surmounting rage burned in energetic fever priming his strong, agile body through instinctual swordform after pirouetting swordform in brutal display of swordslinger ballet. Griever's fanning blurs worked carved art through his hands while he twirled and twisted, dodged and danced, hacked and sliced, chopped and cleaved through oncoming stoneman after stoneman, a savage Power-flickering dancer of bladed fury answering only destruction, each sundering cut separating stony limbs while sending arcs of debris spraying in the wakes of his fluid movements and Griever's scoring strokes.

Far across the room the colossal double doors pushed open from without in a groaning yawn of heavy wood upon ancient iron hinges. The outside skirling yelled past those parting lips, enveloping the chamber in a storm of noise. The riot of sound escalated into a roaring screech which reached a raucous climax of discord and persisted as the steady siren wail filling the room vibrated the air in a wicked blare of—

Alarm! Banzu recognized through the battle-frenzied haze of his swordwork disrupted by the ear-piercing shriek stabbing its banshee song into his Power-elevated hearing. Faltering mid-step and mid-swing, he gnashed his teeth in a tensed grimace against the jolting shock of sensory overload. He released his hold on the Power, and the spasm of brainpain subsided while the debilitating noise lowered to his normalizing senses from an ear-splitting screech into an arduous though sufferable roar of noise. *It's a godsdamned alarm!*

It was then, as he recovered while dodging un-Powered just in the nick to thwart the stabbing stoneblade from piercing his heart though instead slicing open his left shoulder in a flash of pain, that realization struck him two-fold cold: he was, in fact and to everyone here, an intruder. And now everyone in the Academy knew of his intrusion.

What slipped beneath his notice during his preoccupation of surviving the attacking stonemen oblivious to all but his demise was the human figure who rushed in through the opened double doors, dark green robes flapping with their frantic sprint at the head of a trailing pride of mages following into the room, drawn by the blaring alarm, in a flowing nest of multicolored robes and wary faces. Within the mix of the fistian flock flooding in through the doorway flashed a pair of dachras glinting amongst the shifting metals of swords and shields reflecting the hallway's passing torchlights as the runners sped by them with a cluster of armored soldiers bring up the charging group's rear.

The lead newcomer—a lanky woman with her head wound tight in a bright orange turban, her expression one of startled joy—skittered stopped just inside the doorway and raised her hands overhead while spreading her feet, forming a deliberate X of her willowy frame, rooting her stance and waving her hands to the untouchably high ceiling.

Shimmering violet magelight flared into radiant life round her undulating waist in a pulsing, rotating halo which rose up the length of her to overhead where it contracted in on itself between her hands into a fat and hovering orb of crackling energy thrice the size of her turbaned head. The witching woman lowered the compacted orb out before her at chest height between her spread hands. She closed her kohl-dusted eyes while reciting charms drowned inaudible beneath the alarm then threw her hands forward, releasing the crackling orb of conjured energies which burst forth into a spreading horizontal crescent of shimmering violet wave rolling outward upon the air while expanding its inevitable spread lengthwise to the walls within the span of a few rapid breaths.

Meanwhile Banzu spun away from slicing through the legs of another attention-occupying stoneman above its knees while gritting his teeth against the spiking sensory pains seizing even the briefest of Power-flickers erupted into his head. He planted hands to floor and mule-kicked behind through Power-flicker, toppling the hobbled stoneman's upper half backwards. He surged up only to duck then dodge aside the high sweep of another stonesword by rolling beneath the whiffing stoneblade to safer space.

The pervasive skirling knifed painful spasms in his skull with every sensory-heightening Power-flicker seized. He cursed the alarm while out from the corner of his busy eye caught sight of that violet hurl of magic rush-rolling toward him in a billowing wave at too impossible a speed to avoid, too encompassing a breadth to escape.

He turned away hunching while seizing another pain-flaring muscle-tensing Power-flicker, bracing for impact as the vibrant violet tide stole across the room. And he gasped through a profound chill punching into him, expecting the magic to cleave through him if not strike him off his feet but instead it rolled over and round and past him intangible as fog, though also through him while prickling his network of nerves.

Eyes pinching tight, his flexing jaw brought teeth together with a hard ivory *click* as the amplified sensation of a thousand twisting daggers knifed into his skull. The skirling elevated in his head into a debilitating scream dispersing his thoughts but for the true reason of the alarm not meant only for alerting but also for incapacitating his use of the Power through pain.

He battled against throwing Griever away to palm over his ears while collapsing to the floor in a fetal cringe. Instead he released his jolted grasp on the Power before his body betrayed him into dropping to his knees in helpless agony where the stonemen would chop him into pieces without resistance, and the godsawful brainpain withdrew from his throbbing skull.

No wonder the magic had moved through the unaffected stonemen—*it's keyed specifically to me. They've had hundreds of years for planning this.* The acute susceptibility of his own aizakai magic had been amplified and turned against him, and would be so every time he seized the Power while trapped within this ensorcelled chamber.

A guttural rage swelled his guts as he turned through the fading pain and faced the human newcomers—*Kill.* He glared assessment at their growing numbers between the remaining cordon of stonemen—*Kill.* Therein his roiling mindscape toiled the predatory cunning of compelling pressure in the depths of his thoughts at sight of the new human enemy set against him—*Kill.* He grimaced in resistance, forcing away the onset of a murderous rampage begging for release as his mind divided into two separate halves of bestial and human, each warring against the other while both struggled for dominance over the whole of him.

If he surrendered to the murderous urgency—*Kill!* Gave in to the barbarous frenzy seeking control—*Kill!* He would kill them all—*Kill!*

"No!" he yelled.

He turned away from the newcomers, seeking calm to the raging storm of his thoughts. He shook his head, blinking hard through the intense pressure thundering behind his eyes in a raucous surf of voices, and sought reclamation of any vestige of inner peace through the turmoil.

Melora will never forgive me if I kill these people. She'll despise me for it, even hate me. I can't. I won't! I must hold back, for her.

He faced the human joiners.

His eyes widened and his breath hitched in his throat. He tensed, bracing against another magical attack, this of a razor-thin, room-wide, chest-high orange scythe-wave of crackling energies rushing at him from across the way with the speed of an arrow's shot, cutting in a sideways god's blade of magic that glided harmlessly through stonemen and continue toward him unobstructed. The orangey scythe-wave of magic did not cut through him as expected but instead slammed into his chest with the force of a giant's swung hammer, ripping his feet from the floor while striking him breathless.

On instinct he'd seized the barest flicker of the Power, accepting the knifing brainpain in trade for the hardening of his body a fraction before impact. He flew backwards through the disrupted air, gasping, limbs flailing, yet somehow maintaining a tight grip on Griever's hilt.

Seconds of awkward flight.

He slammed into and through a stoneman behind in an explosion of rubble, the collision punching flares of pain through his wracked body and vibrating his bones.

His weakened grasp on the preserving Power-flicker loosened then released of its own accord. His consciousness swam to foreign places while he crashed to his back and slid across the floor a space, suffering sharp bits of broken stone cutting and scraping his skin through bleeding rips of clothes.

He lay limp and groaning, vision ebbing in and out of focus in tune with the throbbing bloom of agony swaddling him. Seconds only until the stark fury of his battle-blood flushed up, renewed by primal flaring rage as brain dominance shifted. He sat up growling, the ache in his chest from the struck blow fading, the throbbing abuse in his entire backside banished to a dim corner of his feral mind for later appraisal—if he survived.

Kill! commanded the presiding voice in his head. *Kill them all!*

But he held strong to the shrinking twist of his humanity, the thought of facing Melora while having to explain his murderous actions his only saving grace against the animosity threatening to overtake him to that savage place of no return. He ignored the voice but barely as he stood in achy protest, lips disappearing in a bony grimace.

These people . . . he needed to explain his intrusion. He shouted for palavar—or tried to, but the blaring alarm out-sang his futile attempt at earning a peaceful resolve.

Friggin hell! They can't hear me. Not this far away and not above that godsdamn alarm. Even if I use the Power to project my voice. If they'll even listen. If they even care. Gods, they've hunted my kind for the last three centuries, trying to end the bloodlust curse through elimination. Is this their snapping trap?

No. Enosh said they need me for the Godstone. I'm supposed to be here. The Head Mistress is expecting me. And Melora wouldn't send me here just to die . . . would she?

He surrendered the futile notion of Power-enhanced yelling and concentrated instead on the immediate task at hand: survival, until he could think of a better plan.

He grit his teeth. *I should've known this wouldn't be easy. Nothing ever is. I should've expected more than just walking in and announcing myself.* And hoped this wouldn't turn into a slaughter. His or theirs.

Yes! urged Jericho's voice in his head. *Slaughter, yes!* Hot and nasty, rife with influence, fierce with sanity's abandon. *Do it. Kill them all!*

"No!" Banzu yelled. *Godsdammit, no. I cannot lose myself. Not now.*

He scanned about. *Surrounded.* Under attack from the strange golem statues of dead men—*no, dead Soothsayers in stone effigy, ensorcelled statue mocks of those whom once served the Academy by hunting down our own as Spellbinder servitors*—and what remained of their dwindled numbers continued advancing in relentless pursuit. *Gods I'm tired. And my shoulder hurts like a cranky bastard.* He considered options. *I need to deal with the stonemen first, then the rest. Careful and cautious. Controlled. Melora will never forgive me for slaughter here, let alone the Head Mistress if I kill a bunch of her aizakai.*

Melora . . . his only remaining peace. He drew in deep and reflected upon their intimacy together before her unexpected push. Angry panic receded while his mind worked with a more tempered and logical stroke of persuasion.

Without the Power I'm still a master swordslinger. The Power invites pain here, and gods it hurts something fierce, but I can suffer through it in brief trials. Power-flickers only when necessary, to strengthen Griever's blade from breaking against stone.

Pain . . . nothing good ever comes in my life without pain. Why should this be any different?

He forced away the onset of a preemptive snarl, knowing nothing good would come from murdering the whole lot of these people only defending their Academy abode from what they perceived as an attack. He would try everything in his power not to kill them. But if they refused to listen, if they gave him no other choice—

He banished the dark thought away unfinished, raised Griever and prepared for more onslaught.

* * *

Banzu flowed into a more controlled rhythm of action, dodging backwards from a sideways-slicing stonesword its tip sweeping inches shy of opening his sucked-in stomach. He seized another painful Power-flicker and jumped the lower reversing stroke meant for cleaving through his knees—enduring the immediate stab of ear-piercing, teeth-clenching brainpain knifing through enhanced senses while luminous twilight greys burst alive and all surrounding action slow-flowed.

Grimacing, he landed upon the slow-gliding stoneblade with a brief feather's touch then ran up the extended length of the slow-swinging stoneman's arms where he Power-boosted from upon stony shoulder high into the air. And released the Power the instant his propelling foot left the stoneman platform bearing the blunt trauma of his launching impact as it crunched to the floor in a breaking spill of rubble. The skull-twisting shriek of sensory overload lowered into the blaring alarm existing outside his oversensitive mind.

The necessary trade in pain for the burst of leaping Power-momentum carried him through the air far where he descended behind the gathered stonemen who turned round beneath his overhead flight as one collective. He landed, heels skidding, and spun through painful Power-flicker, slashing Griever in an upward angle from stony left hip through stony torso to stony right shoulder, then a quick figure-eight stroke above and he slashed down from stony left shoulder to stony right hip, making a precise cut of an X into the nearest stoneman all in one fluid blur of rending motion. He endured the jaw-clenching brainpain a fraction further, stepping backwards then forward into kicking the carven stoneman against its chest before releasing the Power-flicker in gasping relief.

The crimson glow of the stoneman's glare winked out a hairsbreadth before the violent separation of its stone body exploded backwards in a fantastic spray of parts, creating a hail of stony missiles which battered into and struck off of its others behind. The pelted stonemen stumbled and staggered against the shrapnel spray, suffering broken-off noses or fingers, chipped appendages or broken swordtips. He had slowed them . . . for a short time.

He turned away from the marred stonemen during the settling blast and faced the open doors at the human mix of soldiers and aizakai mages spilled into the room yet daring no farther. Colored robes flapped round arms waving communicative gestures, mouths toiled through shouts of alarm-muffled speech attempting the spread of orders amongst their others for dealing with the intruder. And though the armed soldiers filed behind the aizakai made of themselves an armored blockade across the front of the open doorway, some of the aizakai turned from the room's ongoing conflict and wove gestures at the doorway in a group conjuring.

Glowing red-gold energies sparkled and slithered round the huge square frame of the doorway, filling the empty space within while sealing the exit by way of a growing spiderweb barrier of constructing mystic weaves. In the hallway beyond, more others rushed to enter the room in the sprinting hopes of joining inside the chamber before the magical spiderweb sealant closed shut and blocked them out.

Banzu huffed a terse curse. Stonemen behind him. Aizakai and soldiers in front. His only avenue of escape sealing shut, and that godsdamned alarm blaring out any attempt at shouting for palavar with these people to explain himself.

Naught else to do but shrug the momentary defeat aside and shift focus onto the several aizakai not tending sealing the doorway shut. Three of the conjurers turned from their working comrades and ran at him with hands upraised and fingers wiggle-working in strange conjuring weaves of crackling air.

Banzu's mind divided with frantic indecision. He glanced behind at the remaining stonemen charging his rear, looked back—and flinched tensed at the dazzling emerald magelight bursting across the way from where surged another fanning scythe-wave attack rushing toward him in a cutting horizontal sweep of the room.

In his mind he *tsk-tsk-tsked* the reuse of same tactics. Instincts chose him forward. He sprinted toward the emerald scythe-wave attack racing to him at waist level then, seconds before impact, dropped to his knees while arching his back and flattened shoulders to floor while sliding beneath the fanning scythe-wave passing inches above the tip of his nose, Griever scraping a sparking trail across the floor at his side.

He sat up grunting with effort before his knee-slide ended and rocked with momentum into standing. He glanced behind and cursed, his hopes of the scythe-wave dispatching the stonemen for him dashed; it passed through them without injurious effect same as the previous two.

Closer now, at least. He made to seize the Power, to attempt another Power-elevated shout for palavar. But froze upon notice of the immediate space round him turning aglow in fiery reds. No, not just glowing but shimmering in increasing swells of palpable heat thickening while encasing him on all sides, stealing his breath away and pulling sweat from his warming skin.

He lowered into a squat for Power-leaping free from the magical entanglement at play but cringed stiff when twisting daggers of brainpain knifed into his skull again. But he had not seized the Power yet, and these proved a different intensity of torture rife with scalding stabs so that the pain delivered him down to one knee and he almost bit off the end of his tongue when his jaw snapped shut in a click of teeth.

He strained at raising his head against neck muscles taut as bundled iron rods. Across the room, through blurry eyes stung with welling tears and sweat, a raven-haired hawk-faced man in black robes ran toward him, hands outstretched and palms glowing the same fiery red as what fluttered round those working fingers weaving flaming clouds of active butterflies wrought from sparkling magefire, the new charger projecting a containment field of sorts through the mysterious trappings of his conjurations.

The elevating thunder of approaching stomps from behind.

Banzu rolled to one side—the hawk-faced conjurer's fiery magics rolling with him—just as the charging stoneman attempted chopping down through his hunched spine though missed and bit into the floor. Banzu scooped up an apple-sized chunk of rock in the dodging roll as behind him sounded the *thunk* of stone against stone. He seized a brainpain-elevating Power-flicker for transferred momentum then threw.

Half-blinded by pain and guided by desperate hope, the searing invasion of invisible daggers twisting in his skull rising and falling through brief seizing of the Power in torturous trade for his heaving throw, the rocky missile flew across the room with tremendous velocity and struck a glancing blow upon the hawk-faced witcher's left shoulder that spun the mage round twice in a jolting twist which ended with his collapse to the floor where he hunched while clutching the limp dangle of his left arm below his broken shoulder.

The scalding brainpain of mageknives twisting in Banzu's skull vanished alongside the sweltering presence of shimmering fiery reds once encasing him in a pod of baking heat. He glared at the struck huddle he'd made of the mage, resisting but barely the urge for closing distance in a Power-fueled sprint and carving the injured aizakai to bloody shreds.

No! I cannot kill these people. I must not! For her. But I'm caught between a rock and a hard place. Nowhere to run. The space between shrinking fast.

He needed a way to expand his area of safety, wanted to end this needless conflict without surrendering to the rapacious desire to kill them all and just be done with it already. *I'm not your enemy, godsdammit!* He considered seizing the volatile potency of the fractured Source then decided against the folly of testing the true measure of his sanity amid the process of survival while surrounded by enemies.

I have to take out the stonemen then deal with the others. Divide and conquer. My only chance. If only that godsdamned alarm would stop blaring!

Darker musings resurfaced, blatant and bitter. What if Melora tricked him here into this Soothsayer deathtrap same as with the tower and its Traveling Well? Same as she planned locking her kohatheen round Jericho's throat. And Enosh, he seemed real enough at the time. Though perhaps their meeting in the Luna Nexus existed as nothing more than some delusional trick wrought from the Traveling Well's magics combined with the fractured Source.

No, I refuse to accept I imagined it all. I haven't lost that much of my mind. What did Enosh say, Soothsavior or Soothslayer? But even if I dispatch the remaining stonemen will these people listen to reason?

Kill.

Shut up.

Kill!

"Shut up!"

Laughter echoed.

I have to try. For her.

Banzu banished the questioning of his sanity while his hunter's mind treaded upon a linear path. *The stonemen are closer. Divide and conquer. I have to survive this. I have to trust Melora wouldn't betray me.*

He sank into a preparatory squat and, bracing for the unavoidable pain, seized a strong grasp on the Power through focal invocation while embracing the skull-twisting brainpain as one holding their breath before the deep plunge in frigid waters. Luminous Power-greys flared in his eyes while the world slowed round him. Grimacing, he drew upon the Power until it filled him just shy of touching the fractured Source. The skirling shriek of alarm elevated into a keening wail of sensory overload, its brainpain intrusion teetering upon unbearable strain so that he feared a few more seizing trades would render him deaf. But he braved through the necessary exchange with little other choice.

He sank deeper still upon bended haunches coiling into taut and priming springs of muscles, inviting the fissuring crunch of stone round his depressing boots as the floor indented beneath his leather soles by inches. He Power-jumped up into the air, erupting straight, temples pounding, teeth grinding through the struggle, legs propelling extensions of spent energy. He released his inner grasp of Power while the initial burst delivered him up two-hundred feet, and for a brief span he enjoyed the absence of pain replaced by the freeing sensation of flying.

Until he gazed up and feared a broken neck in the ascending seconds to come so that he tucked his chin to chest while hunching at the apex of his leap and avoided bashing his head upon the high ceiling by such thin margin the reversing float of his hair tickled its stone. Then began his plunging fall into which he elongated his body for streamlining effect.

He arched his lower back, raised Griever in a double-fisted grip overhead halfway through the increasing plummet, calculating and measuring while watching the stonemen gather round his launching dent of space below in preparation for his landing return.

Oh gods this is going to hurt.

He re-seized the Power twenty feet above the floor, hardening his body to avoid the life-ending splat, the teeth-clenching brainpain renewed and dizzying his thoughts, and the momentum of his fall magnified by the Power turned him into a human missile.

He slam-landed down—*thoom!*—in front of while chopping through a stoneman from head through crotch then farther still as his feet hammered and Griever cut into the indenting stone floor by inches while sending out zigzagging fissures and rupturing cracks through the floor in every direction of his pounding sunderstrike. The extreme landing created a tremendous rumbling shockwave of concussive air exploding outwards, blasting away every surrounding stoneman into backwards tumbles across the floor crimpling through diminishing ripples of undulating stone groaning and grinding their dust-puffing joins.

Consciousness-jarring, bone-rattling agony vibrated up through Banzu's entire shuddering being, surpassing pain into a new level of whole-body numbness when he released the Power in a taut hunch. His wracked frame trembled with the dizzying ache of the sinews-quivering aftershock from his thunderous impact punching a shallow crater into the floor, and though his Power-strengthened bones remained unbroken, they creaked with tremendous strain the precipice of hairline fractures.

He straightened on trembling legs, his tingling spine groaning protest, and assessed the measure of his landing damage. His vision pulsed in ebbing throbs of focus in tune with the muffling pound of his ears. Two thin trails of blood trickled from his nose, hot and dripping over lips and chin, his teeth a gnashing rattle in his flexed jaw.

He released a withering exhalation through pursed lips, blowing a swirling churn in the cloudy haze of settling debris smoking the air round him in lazy floats of uprooted dust. He gazed round with desperate hope, and though he had knocked the stonemen away, those outside the immediate vicinity of his concussive shockwave not blasted into pieces from their tumbling throws worked quick at regaining their feet in relentless bid to continue attack.

But these remaining stonemen displayed vicious cracks forked and veined throughout chipped faces and notched chests and upon scored limbs, and several broke apart in their attempts at standing, crumbling while their lambent red gazes snuffed dull.

Far across the room the attacking aizakai mages stood paused in gaping stares. Several removed away to safer grounds near the glowing doorway or hid behind the blockade of soldiers, though others recovered their shock and renewed their magical weavings through active hands working glowing traceries of air in preparation for another attack though they maintained a cautious distance while allowing the remaining stonemen to continue their work.

Banzu huffed a terse breath and eyeballed them. *That's right.* Then reined his attentions elsewhere. He mustered his dwindling reserves of vigor through sharp nostril-flaring inhale and surveyed the remaining ten stonemen charging in at him with sustained commitment. He seized a Power-flicker, enduring the trade of brainpain, and hawked out a glob of coppery snot at the next attacker.

The shooting glob struck the stoneman's face with enough transferred momentum so that tiny flecks of stone chips flew off its impacted forehead as its head snapped craned while its body continued forward on running feet. Balance stolen, the stoneman's upper half tilted away as its lower half stumbled forward, then it began circling its arms to regain upright.

Banzu sped forth in a blur of movement, lunging in another grimacing Power-flicker. He sliced through and past the stumbling stoneman's legs above the knees, delivering a carving swath of Griever, then surged in amongst its swarming fellows and flowed into the destructive locomotion of swordform promises while seizing painful, sensory-torturing Power-flickers in a rabid bid of hasty elimination.

Twisting and twirling and spinning in a blurring flurry of Power-hardened steel, he endured explosive flares of alarm-elevated brainpain in welcomed trade while distributing cuts and cleaves both proficient and savage through stoneman after stoneman until there remained only—

Something slammed into him from behind, hard and jarring and hitting him below the base of his neck a fraction after he pulled Griever's fanning blade out through the low stroking cut of the fifth of his dwindling stony aggressors. The whiplashing impact forced him forward and smashing front-first into and through the dispatched stoneman already splitting apart before him.

His eyes shut tight in reflexive defense while darkness and the pain of running face-first into a shattering wall of stone smothered all else. A thousand invisible fists pummeled him at once. He tumbled across the floor for a flashing space before ending in a crumpled semiconscious heap.

The coppery taste of blood poisoned his mouth. His mind a dark cave of private surrender. His body a throbbing twist of agony. His hands flexed round only air and the memory of Griever's sweat-slick hilt having slipped his grip, the sword skittering across the floor to he knew not where. He lay groaning, bruised and beaten.

This is it. They've won. I'm too spent. I can do no more while holding back.

I die here and none of it matters. Melora . . . the Godstone . . . Hannibal Khan.

Kill. The word a stern command, its savage flare of voice burned through the dispersing fog of his mind in fevered request. *Kill.*

I'll never see her again.

Kill.

That's what they're really taking from me.

Kill.

I'll never kill the Khan.

Kill.

Jericho deserves no less.

Kill.

I've come so far and lost so much already.

In the moment he craved sweet surrender to the seething animus boiling inside, scalding his guts raw, begging for release. So easy that submission of control. Give in and let it take care of the rest while he watched behind the eyes as a spectator.

Kill.

A defiant geyser erupted within the chamber of his being, scolding physical pain away to the farther regions of his accepting mind submitting to the torrential rage of bridled fury taking dominance in a renewing surge of aggressive vigor.

Kill.

I can't let this happen.

Kill!

I won't.

Kill!!

I've had enough of holding back.

And he no longer valued the insignificant human lives of these ignorant aizakai or the soldiers they brought against him.

Kill!!!

Until a cooling wave of reluctance washed over his burning desires for murderous appeal.

"*Promise me . . .*"

Melora's words recalled in a voice soothing tameness through the toil of his soul, a delicate whisper there then gone.

Kill—

"No." The word left him in terse rebuke, a final preventive fleck of his rational humanity delaying his surrender into savage slaughter. "No," he repeated in stronger voice.

One last try. For her. And if it fails . . . then gods have mercy because I won't.

* * *

Banzu pushed up from the floor onto hands and knees, wiped at his bleeding face and scanned round.

Three stonemen left. Charging in at him at once and closing fast.

He caught sight of Griever lying afar and amid a scatter of rubble, its leather-wound hilt capturing his focal stare and requesting the reclamation of his hand. He stood, groaning and wincing through the agony of movement, and seized a necessary burst of the Power. He charged while yelling against the knifing brainpain between two of the three remaining stonemen, their slow-flowing stoneswords slicing the air through his blurring fade after he stole past them in screaming abandon.

He covered the fifty feet of distance in a Power-lengthened stretch of two outside seconds and scooped up Griever's hilt into the fold of his welcoming clutch. He released the Power and skittered into a dizzying stumble, a cruel reminder of his battered body and what little left it could endure.

Far across the room more aizakai broke away from their assemblage and braved charges toward him, while behind these rushing few their others continued the conjuring work of sealing the shrinking space of doorway through the red-gold spider-webbing magic closing over it until and at last that hollow center of space closed with grim finality in a vibrant red-gold pulsating barrier of webbing the weavers then sustained lest it reopen.

Banzu faced the three remaining stonemen, feral faculties making of them no more than moving targets. Patience thinning brittle, he raised Griever in preparatory strike.

But motion and light in his left peripheral stole his attentions so that he faced the aizakai rushers though more so the great dragon's breath of flames erupting from the outstretched right hand of the running hawk-faced man in black robes whose left arm hung limp and flopping at his side from a broken shoulder.

Running beside him a smirking woman with short spiky blonde hair, her skinny frame wound tight in a sky-blue tunic and leather breeches, who clapped her frosting hands together then pulled them apart where formed between their dividing spread a long and jagged icespike of a spear she gripped for throwing while earning no slow in her hasty strides.

And at their sides raced more aizakai attackers conjuring their own mystical weavings of magic into colorful life through dazzles of mystery Banzu knew not.

He glanced right at the three charging stonemen, glanced left at the line of sprinting aizakai. His recovering bid of Griever placed him between the two groups of closing enemies, hammer to anvil. He intended on dispatching the stonemen first, but magics outraced them.

Banzu leaped aside, dodging into a roll that delivered him out from the roaring jet of flames burning through his absent space. He shot up rising, twisting round, and stumbled backwards, then dropped to his knees and sank back to floor in a painful bending of legs pinched beneath him, avoiding the thrown javelin icespike sailing inches past his upturned face.

Grunting, knees flaring aches, he flopped over onto his stomach and pushed up from the floor while cursing the incessant blaring alarm. "Godsdammit, don't make me kill you!" he shouted in guttural growl at the mages. But his words drowned unheard beneath the stronger siren wail.

The air shimmered and thickened in front of him, behind him, at his sides. Five steps left and he bumped into physical resistance, four steps right and another stopping bump. He spun round, boxed inside some manner of translucent magical walls shrinking in, seeking to crush him.

He seized a Power-flicker and, braving more knifing brainpain, jumped straight up while hoping no invisible top broke his neck.

He leaped up and over the magical trapping device a hairsbreadth before its walls slammed together, the pinching tops of which just missed crushing his escaping feet into pulpy dangles. He flowed through the air over another blast of aizakai fire that burned a flaming spume beneath his kicking feet, and knew without question these aizakai no longer sought his capture.

Anger flared in a hot adrenaline surge—*If death is what they want then I'll give it to them in spades!*—followed by vivid flashes of Melora's face, so close and kissing, her voice a whispering tease, violet eyes appraising the right of him.

He willed aside the primal urge for killing in a struggle unsure he would win again.

He landed and twisted at the hips as a second javelin icespike shot so close past his face the sharpness of its jagged length sliced across his turning left cheek and split open his earlobe in passing. He seized another painful Power-flicker, ran two bounding steps and leaped over a third icespike javelin that shattered the floor in a sparkling scatter, propelling himself forward high into the air.

Nothing good ever came in his life without pain. So be it.

It's time I showed them what pain really is.

He sheathed Griever mid-flight to free his hands, forgetting the three stonemen behind for the slew of aizakai ahead, while beneath him a molten ball of flame and another icespike javelin crashing together in a bursting cloud.

He landed in the middle of the startled aizakai forefront where action blurred time into a meaningless frenzy.

He spun for momentum while seizing a brain-stabbing Power-flicker and shoved out his palm, striking the chest of the nearest conjuring foe and sending the concaving mage flying backwards over thirty feet of space to where they hit the floor rolling, limbs a wild flail, then stopped just shy of crashing into the thick shieldwall of fistian soldiers blocking the webbed doorway.

He lowered while twisting, made a hook with his arm and caught another's leg in a skull-knifing Power-flicker then sent them flip-spinning up into the air. He continued his twisting rise while raising his fist overhead then hammered down his Power-hardened blow not onto face as intended but instead upon some manner of thick iceshield conjured to place in protection of the spun other's upturned grimace.

The iceshield shattered in a sharp spray of glittering shards slicing clothes and skin as Banzu turned facing another hovering iceshield between himself and the grinning pale woman who conjured it. He cocked his fist in another painful Power-flicker then drove it through the jagged sheet of protective ice blasting its sharp spray round his thrusting arm, but he released the Power a fraction before his punch struck the surprised spiky-haired blonde in the face, knocking her stumbling backwards while taking careful pains not to hit her Power-hard lest he snap her whipping neck if not at least shatter her face as he had her iceshields.

But his restraint proved a critical mistake, for the frost-weaver conjured a mask of spiky ice over her face a hairsbreadth before impact which limited her taken damage while stubbing Banzu's punching un-Powered fist into bloody numbness so that he withdrew his hand, unsure if he'd broken bones.

While more aizakai swarmed in to surround him in aid of their struggling others. A brief stretch where Banzu danced and dodged within their midst, avoiding blazing bolts of magical energies shooting at him from every which way he turned and twisted, all the while fighting the knifing brainpain each Power-flicker invited in trade for his ballet of survival.

His mind grew dizzy, his battered body tired, and worse his waning willpower teetered upon the precipice of surrender to the murderous rage begging for release.

Twice between dodges he shouted for palavar, but the blaring alarm overrode his voice even this close inside the aizakai frenzy. So he struggled on, seizing painful Power-flickers while dodging and striking in a collage of battle, punching or kicking, earning brief space that closed with more swarmers seconds after opening.

Bones snapped.

Blood sprayed.

Aizakai screamed.

Bodies tumbled away.

While others swarmed in between the breaking spaces of bodies.

Banzu's broken hand ached. He denied Griever's pull and continued seizing Power-flickers while dodging through the relentless assault of bright magics popping and bursting the air, instead striking the relentless aizakai away with hands and feet only, his plan of debilitating them all then explaining himself afterwards dwindling to the overwhelming closure of their superior numbers.

A bright white flash erupted from a thrust hand, blinding Banzu. He seized another painful Power-flicker and spun round yelling, arms extended, fists swung hammers catching faces while whipping heads aside and forcing bodies back, earning pausing space.

Dizzied, he blinked away the fading flash from his dazzled eyes.

Twenty felled aizakai lay groaning in twisted crumples amid the strewn rubble of broken stonemen, the mages robed heaps writhing or unconscious.

No intervention from the soldiers remaining steadfast to their lines in armed and armored blockade before the doorway and in protective guard of the remaining aizakai preoccupied behind them with keeping the doorway's red-gold webbing sealed closed.

The four that remained of Banzu's nearest human attackers still on their feet withdrew from him. An emerald-eyed fellow wove his hands through the air, smiling. Banzu shouted for palavar, his issue unheard beneath the siren wail of alarm, while hands gripped his feet and groped up his calves.

He looked down at not hands but brown twists of roots sprouting from cracks in the floor and twining round his legs while trapping his feet to place. He looked up and caught the focal gesture of emerald eyes shifting behind him so that he ducked just in the nick beneath a sideways-slicing stoneblade whiffing inches over his head. He seized the Power and straightened, jumping, erupting from the floor while the entanglement of roots tore down his legs, shredding his pants while clawing skin, his bare feet ripping loose from his captured boots.

He embraced the pain of his broken hand while twisting round mid air and pulling Griever free, surrendering to the animus of survival through slaughter. *This is it. I have no other choice. You made me do this!* He transferred Griever's hilt into his other—hands fumbling, almost losing purchase when the Power inexplicably tore from his inner grasp.

He landed, stunned, sharp bits of grit cutting into his bare soles. He tried seizing the Power again to no avail, and startled with new panic, facing the three remaining stonemen distracters while catching out from the corner of his peripheral a brawny brown-haired woman lunging in low at his turned back, her confident violet glare mocking his failed efforts at seizing the Power.

She stabbed one dachra into his right thigh while slicing the other fanged dagger across his lower back inches below his floating ribs, then withdrew.

Banzu reared and screamed. He tried seizing the Power through the pain. Again nothing. The floor trembled. An unseen hammerblow of force slammed into his arching back. The jolting impact whiplashed his head and limbs backwards while punching the rest of him forward and spinning through the air.

Behind him the conjured column of snaking terra returned to the floor in an arcing splash of stone.

He strained for another desperate seize of the Power—but he possessed no concentration for the effort in his rolling world of suffering.

Griever slipped loose from his hand as he tumbled through the air, limbs flailing, head tossing on rubbery neck. Three cold stabs of ice—*shunk-shunk-shunk*—pierced his thigh and arm and shoulder, these frigid blades conjured then thrown from the mage turning beneath his sail over her head, the jagged sickles adding to the crescendo of pain.

Mid-flight a great breath of heat engulfed him in an inferno fashioned into the fiery form of a giant's clutching hand gripping him whole while jolting the momentum from his tumbling flight. Intense heat sucked his breath away while the strong fire-hand squeezed and shook, burning away hair and shortbeard and his bloodied tatters of clothes. Then came a jarring pitch when the fiery hand slammed him front-first against the floor in the manner of one squashing a caught bug.

Semiconscious, bathed in hot pain, Banzu gasped for precious breath unfound, for the fiery godhand smashed him against the floor while consuming the air, creating an area of vacuum encapsulating and suffocating him.

The physical presence of magician's oppressive heat pinned his battered naked body while blistering his reddened skin in everywhere abundance beneath its molten crush. Until seconds more it snuffed away.

Charred skin a blazing throb of inescapable ache, Banzu attempted a final desperate seizing of the Power. He grasped it inside his fragile inner clutch—for two pathetic seconds before it ripped away again.

No more fight left to give, full surrender claimed him.

He hoped they killed him quick.

* * *

Limp and groaning, parts of his charred skin crisp black patches, other parts covered in blisters split and oozing, Banzu offered no more resistance than a beaten cripple to the hands turning him over onto his tenderized back, each pressing finger inviting blazes of pain upon his oversensitive skin.

Through milky vision a pair of lambent crimson eyes hovered into view as the cracked, emotionless face of a statue stoneman loomed in upside-down fashion. It raised its stony sword on high in a double-fisted grip, intent on chopping Banzu's face splayed where he lay clinging to life by wheezing draws. He failed at raising a tremulous hand in futile shield as the stonesword began its downward stroke for opening his face.

"Stop!"

A woman's command sounded strong above the skirling siren wail of alarm. The stoneblade stopped inches above the swollen tip of Banzu's broken nose, raised then backed away.

A change of faces.

A woman's chubby visage loomed into replacing view, her hard mask a bitter twist framed by stray tangles of brown hair worked free from her tight ponytail, her smoldering violet glare contemptuous.

Banzu tried speaking, but his wracked body produced only mumbled wheezes upon smoky fades of breath tasting of soot. Staring up, his left hand flexed at his side in desperate little twitches for Griever's lost hilt, his other hand a numb throb of broken bones.

"It's really him!"

Another's voice struggling to overcome the blaring alarm, this from a woman out from Banzu's blurred view, she among the many others gathering closer.

"The Soothsayer!" A male's baritone voice.

"Soothslayer!" Another still, correcting. "Look at what he's done!"

The woman with smoldering eyes paid the others little mind. She stared over Banzu with a triumphant smile twisting her pursed lips, the violet fire in her glare questing over his nude and battered body in a butcher's way of assessing which prime cuts to carve away first. She scowled before disappearing from looming view, then returned seconds later where spread that smile into a malicious grin as she upheld something thin and circular through which she pierced her wicked gaze.

The background turned rampant with argued exchanges amongst the gathered others, yet the brawny woman's condemning glare remained hovering over their captured trophy while she knelt down over him.

"No . . ." Banzu tried rolling his head from side to side, tried raising his hands in a pathetic attempt at stopping her. But heavy feet from above his shoulders stomped down hard atop his arms, pinning them to the floor, mashing flesh between stone. And a painful groan escaped him.

"You cursed bastard." The woman's thick fingers worked quick and nimble, her unflinching gaze holding his rheumy-eyed stare while she opened the kohatheen collar then fastened it shut round his neck with a satisfying *click*.

Banzu shuddered an exhale, relaxed in complete surrender. Giving up never felt so easy. They had him now. At their total mercy to command or kill.

More faces waded into looming view, pairs of wide eyes, sets of moving lips. Those faces scattered when a stout man's angry visage came into prominent cast while shoving others aside for room. The bull-necked man said nothing, only bared a resentful, gap-toothed snarl. He hunched over and punched Banzu in the face. Then again. Then a third time.

Stars burst behind Banzu's eyes while the back of his head rebounded the floor. He coughed up blood while more of it ran ribbons down his face.

The world pitched and spun in unbalanced madness when strong hands gripped him, pulled him up and held him on dangling legs too limp for standing but for the larger man behind keeping him upright by hooked pits.

A palming grasp atop Banzu's hairless pate raised his hung head. A stinging slap across his face startled him more alert from his stupor of pain. Through fluttering lids he stole veiled glimpses of the others surrounding him, twenty at least, their mouths working though he made no sense of speech above the blaring alarm. Some pointed round at the scatter of debilitated victims lying the floor, while others exchanged gestures of handspeak through quick wiggles of fingers.

The pony-tailed Spellbinder holding his head up spit in his face and slapped him again, then struck again with an immediate backhanded blow while releasing her grasping palm so that his head whipped aside then lolled in a limp-necked dangle. The world spun through more dizzying waves of pain too distant to feel yet too real to deny. He tried forming words and nothing but bloody spittle released in dripping strings over blistered lips. The man behind and holding him up by the pits wove a hand beneath Banzu's chin and raised his head for him.

The brunette Spellbinder withdrew two steps, a muscled wall of squat woman looking more a boulder with arms and legs and a head. She glared aside, shouted, "Someone shut that godsdamned alarm off!"

Banzu suffered through another dizzy spell wrenching his guts queasy as silence filled the room. The squat Spellbinder closed distance and stared into his eyes for a considerable length. She raised her meaty right hand, gripped his bloody chin and turned his head from side to side in scrutinizing appraisal. She scrunched her face, said nothing.

"Where . . . am . . . I?" Banzu's words released in broken syllables, weak and raspy. He swallowed a moan, chest hitching, worked his aching jaw as best he could with it trapped pinched within the Spellbinder's strong grasp. "Who . . . are . . . you?"

"Madness." She hawked and spat aside, released his jaw by pinching her fingers tighter until his slick chin slid from between her squeezing pointer and thumb. She stepped back and crossed her beefy arms, thinned her eyes and considered all of him. "You've come invading the fistian Academy, Soothslayer." A wicked smile as she unfurled an arm and pointed at him. "And you've failed miserably."

The surrounding crowd of aizakai burst into a short cheer the Spellbinder did not join but for stepping forward and slapping him again. His head swiveled then hung on rubbery neck. He tried for more words but produced only stringy dribbles of bloody saliva trailing down over swollen lips.

A jostling shift as the man behind him removed one arm from beneath his right armpit and wrapped it round his neck above the kohatheen, enclosing Banzu's throat in a noose of corded muscle.

"Lemme kill him, Shandra." The taller man's voice a deep rumble over Banzu's head. "She doesn't know he's still alive." A tighter squeeze of his arm. "Lemme pop his godsdamned head off and be done with it."

"The Veil's been lifted." This from the spiky-haired blonde standing at Banzu's left, the iceshield conjurer he'd punched in the face at the cost of a broken hand. "She doesn't need him anymore." Her eyes raccooned with darkening bruises, she smiled through swollen lips, displaying a missing upper front tooth. She raised a hand into which she huffed a glittering breath. And with tinkling blue magelight produced a small spike of sharp ice sprouting from her upturned palm in a rising blade. She gripped the glistening sickle, her smile spreading vicious beneath the stabs of her bright blue eyes. "Just one little shove, Shandy. Right through his heart. If the bastard even has one."

"No." Shandra reached out, closed her larger hand round the blonde's smaller hand, and in so doing the conjured iceknife melted into watery dribbles. "Not just yet."

The spiky-haired blonde frowned and yanked her hand free. She crossed her skinny arms but said no more.

A tighter squeeze round his neck and Banzu's eyes bulged, his withered lungs burning from lack of oxygen. But no one cared that the big man holding him up also choked him, for they broke into brief argument that ended seconds more with the authoritative shout from another who strode in through the double doors, the red-gold spiderweb weavings falling loose into fizzling dissipation round her entry while in front of her the shieldwall of fistian soldiers parted, turning inward in respectful bows of helmed heads.

Banzu tried for a look-see at the newcomer through those gathered round him turning away, but his wavering vision offered only fades of motion out from his shrinking peripheral, for the thick arm wrapped round his throat choked darkness into his eyes expanding round the edges.

The world jostled and spun and blanked. The next he knew he lay on the floor, gasping for air and with no concept of just how much or how little time had passed. Pain bloomed from a kick against his ribs, then his back. He balled up, groaning.

"Melora." The name left him in a wheezing whisper. "Oh gods . . . Melora."

The crowded aizakai spread apart, feet shuffling, heads bowing, voices clipping short, while making space for the regal newcomer wearing a blue dress trimmed with silver.

Banzu stared at blue-slippered feet closing distance to his face. He moaned when the painful shifting of gripping hands flopped him over onto his back, and groaned when more hands pinned his wrists and ankles to the floor, trapping him to place.

A tall woman with bushy black hair stared over him, her skin dark brown as unsweetened chocolate, her bold violet eyes piercing, yet the fine lines at the corners of her frown foretold of a sadness unvoiced.

Then arose a flurry of voices.

"He's consumed by the bloodlust."

"Nonsense. Look at his eyes!"

"Look at what he's done!"

"He tried to kill us!"

"He came to—"

"Silence!" The dark-skinned woman's eruptive voice issued hushing command the breadth of thunder.

And there ruled silence—save for the pitiful wheezing moans of Banzu's ragged breathing while he stared up at who could only be Head Mistress Gwendora Pearce.

"Jericho?" Another's voice split the silence. Aizakai parted while a woman pushed through their fold to stand beside the Head Mistress, short and olive-skinned with almond-shaped eyes framed by broad cheeks, her shoulder-length hair black as raven feathers, her stare not nearly as piercing though just as violet. She flinched mute at sight of Banzu.

"We have to kill him before its too late, Head Mistress." Someone out from view, a male voice. "Before he can—"

The Head Mistress cut the voice short with a scything glance. She held the room in a long pause, judging Banzu with the considerable sweep of her discerning gaze.

The raven-haired woman in a tight red dress split up the sides to her petite hips broke from her mute stare and sank beside Banzu in a little squat, fiddled at his neck, removing his only remaining adornment, then stood holding the brass necklace and the silver ring interlaced upon it.

"Jericho," she breathed more than said in a tremulous whisper of voice, while a tortured story played behind her melancholy stare captured by the ring. Then in a stronger voice while her gaze shifted down. "Banzu?" She gazed up at the taller Head Mistress on her right. "It's him, Gwen. It's really him." And dared the barest of smiles. "She did it." An unmistakable sadness bled from her eyes and stole over her face. Stray tears ran her broad cheeks she scrubbed away with the back of her swiping forearm. "Melora actually did it."

No such similar emotion betrayed the stern mask of the regal-spined Head Mistress, or in her voice when next she spoke. "You have a lot of explaining to do, young man. The least of which is why you are here and Jericho is not."

Banzu fixed his stare not upon the tall Head Mistress but the short woman beside her, and released an agonizing plea nestled into a single word. "Aggie?"

But the almond-eyed woman responded nothing. She stood all trembles, eyes shifting out of focus, so intent her focus on the ring dangling from her fisted grip of necklace. "Jericho." The name a brittle whisper, she blinked watery eyes, and more tears ran her cheeks. She backed away two steps while giving little shakes of denial with her head, black hair swishing round her thin neck, her quavering tone rolling over into shaky despair. "Oh gods, Jericho . . ."

Head Mistress Gwendora Pearce offered Aggie a wan smile and sympathetic hand upon the grieving woman's shoulder. "I'm sorry, Agatha. But please, compose yourself." She slipped her consoling hand away and returned the brunt of her attentions to Banzu, her visage tensing, violet fire returning in her admonishing glare, her voice a stern crack of whip. "You're in a lot of trouble." She bent forward at the hips in leaning loom to better meet his eyes. "What happened to Jericho?"

"But the Veilfall—" someone began then stopped short at the Head Mistress's glancing glare.

"I want to hear it from him," she said.

"Dead," Banzu said, the single word a grievous effort. "I . . . killed him." He rolled his eyes and peered up at Jericho's dear Aggie, enduring stabs of guilt rupturing through him. An apology drifted across the swollen blister of his lips in motion only.

Agatha winced, half-turned away while hugging the necklace and ring against her chest in a double-fisted clutch.

"You've done more than that," the Head Mistress said, frowning. She drew in deep, expelled a heavy sigh. She glanced round at the strewn ruins of the room. "By the gods but you've done much more than that." She scowled while straightening to her full towering height, tallest of them all, and stared him over with a probing scrutiny that tested every battered inch of him. "What you've done here—" she began then stopped, set her jaw firm and began again. "I'm only going to ask you this once. How you answer will decide your fate. Why are you here?"

Banzu stared up at her, stupefied of all logical thought. Godsawful pain clawed through his body in increasing blooms and flares now that the struggle ended and he lay in suffering surrender. The words *Melora* and *Veilfall* drifted into and out from his wavering mind, graced across his trembling lips in barest whispers of response touching no ears but his. Another moan escaped him while pain enveloped him in throbbing abundance.

He lay at their mercy, yet saw none of it staring back through expectant eyes waiting for his answer. He relapsed into the failure of his promise to his dead uncle and reflections of Melora so far away in the Builder's tower.

"Khan," he said, his voice weak and raspy yet full of fire. "Kill . . . Khan."

The Head Mistress frowned, disappointment bleeding across her face. "Wrong answer." She gestured the flick of her wrist.

A large and looming presence approached Banzu's left, covering him in shadow. He rolled his head aside and caught the flashing glimpse of a kicking boot—

Darkness.

CHAPTER THIRTY

What felt as an eternity blew over Sera's buoyant soul on caressing winds borne upon wings of pure silence. Though she possessed no perceivable measure of time's true passage, the concept of it a glassy pane shattered to bits and those shards scattered to the farthest corners of everywhere and nowhere of her newfound awareness, leaving her estimation of what constituted hours and minutes, even days and weeks and years, skewed and twisted akin to a thin sheet of metal heated until all bent and malformed frames of its reference proved inconsequential.

Luminous light and warmth engulfed her in a tingling ecstasy of blissful surrender, bathing her, swaddling her, suffusing her while carrying her along its smooth and soothing current, the joyous song of it ebbing and flowing round her, the beautiful secret of its loving promise flushing over and through her while cleansing the terrible troubles of her tortured soul.

The indescribable comfort all fetuses know—yet later can only remember within dreams or times of great stress when aloneness becomes too frightening even for nightmares—of being swaddled and secured within the unconditional safety of the womb enveloped her. *Was* and *To Be* did not exist, for there only *Is* within the self-contained cosmos of that protective womb, that true home of homes all persons are ejected from only to return upon death.

Warmth and light intermingled as one.

Sera enjoyed the soul-feathery sensation of floating, and though here, in this otherworldly plane of existence, she possessed no physical body to feel or eyes through which to see, she knew in this her ethereal form she nestled within the Maker's awaiting embrace of Heaven and all its glorious splendor.

"BEHOLD," spoke a magnificent voice from within the guiding light's basking praise—No, the *Light*—the sound of which more vibration than speech. *"BEHOLD AND BE LOVED."*

The responsive sensation of crying—if tears lived here in more than mystery—over something so beautiful that to name it would tarnish its perfect existence overwhelmed her. She reached out with her mind through phantom arms in extension of her spiritual consciousness, encouraging her sailing toward the loving sounds and be welcomed into and accepted by and embraced within the loving Light in this her emerging return to womb.

Basking . . . basking . . . basking . . .

Until another's faint drift of voice sounded from behind in a shattering of peace, raspy and unclean, tainted and foul, pursuing her.

". . . sssera . . ."

And the Light wavered through undulating ripples of disturbance riding outward.

Fear flushed cold and cruel, unfeeling and unloving, the tangible corruption of the other's wicked desires licking up from beneath the essence of Sera's traveling spirit with forked tongues of scorn flickering through the wispy smoke of her materializing feet.

And here she realized her ethereal form turning tangible through contact, for now she possessed eyes through which she could see, a head she craned into looking up, gazing into the tantalizing sparkle of Light in front of her, aiming toward it while swimming in its brilliant white-gold beams pouring forth in a river of warmth streaming through an endless desert of the purest darkness so black it had no name given to it but Mystery. The protective unknowing of her womb broke through violation, and the horror of remembering who she was, who she had been, who she would become assaulted her.

"... sssera ..." came the other's voice again, stronger, closer.

And the angelic sprens of Light shimmered.

Awful chills glided in teasing brushstrokes across her tangible cheeks—the boney knuckles of a fleshless, skeletal hand stroking her skin in mock tenderness—cooling through the brown tangles of her whipping hair as the other's presence of voice drew closer, approaching from behind, for now there existed such reference as behind.

"... sssera ..."

And the Light rumbled in agitation.

The phantom-limbed sensation of her developing body reforming whole thickened with presence as the other's violation of voice drew closer still, no longer haunting but chasing. Hunting. Stalking.

"Sssera ..."

The Light trembled and shook, a luminous gong struck.

Terror gripped her, returning her, reverting to the physical, the other's voice commanding the change against her straining will with each condemning syllable spoken.

"Sssera ..."

Her drifting slowed in denial of Light.

Nooooo! her mind screamed. And now she possessed the complete physical presence to voice it aloud. "Nooooo!"

The other's voice elevated in volume, mocking her desperate plea. "Sssera!"

There flared the wicked pain of something so cold it first burned hot, of something greasy yet sticky latching its wrapping barbs onto and into her reformed physical body from just beneath her palpable essence while reversing her drift. She tried swim-kicking her legs-once-more, but the other's scaly grip proved too strong and wrenching, refusing release.

More hot-cold pain.

Stabs of agony.

She writhed and grimaced, dared look down at the black talons digging into the reformed flesh of her captured right ankle, the other's powerful clawhand crunching her bones therein its fevered clutch while pulling her down and away from the precious love of Light. Beyond that gripping serpent's clawhand hovered the furious burning hunger of twin yellow serpentine eyes divided by black vertical slits glaring at her, so profound in its terrorizing stare, the intelligence behind it awful and alien, hateful and unreasoning, infinitely terrible and all too familiar.

The cruel abyss of Nergal's dissecting eyes.

Sera's soul trembled and shook. "Nooooo!"

"Yesss ..."

She receded from the Light, Nergal pulling her down, taking her back, removing her, dragging her away from the blissful shrinking radiance of Light welcoming her if only she could break free from his defiling clutch and reach that joyous splendor of Heaven shrinking away. Darkness crept up round her legs in lashing, corruptive tentacles, latching while twining and climbing her, sucking and feeding upon her presence while pulling her down farther and further at once into something far worse than cold: an absence of heat.

Soul-wrenching, bone-gnawing frostfire enveloped her from below while the warmth fled from above as the angelic sprens of Light shrank at her withdraw into a pinprick that snuffed in a suffocation of black despair while Sera's soul sucked down, ensnared in Nergal's overpowering confines caging her grieving essence within his wrapping demonic embrace of violation.

"Yesss ..."

"Nooooo!" she yelled, thrashing and squirming though earning no release. "Nooooo!"

"Yesss!"

Struggle. And pain. Inescapable admission. Sera's tortured screams earned her nothing but agony while the demon Nergal pulled her down into the terrible corruptive abyss of the mad desires he planned for her still.

* * *

The struggling of two souls intertwining in an absence of Light . . . until the stronger demonic spirit of

Nergal's invading inhuman essence enveloped Sera's fragile existence, wrapping round it while destroying her reformed physical self in a flash of disintegration the crushing of her frenzied soul into a tiny compact ball of inescapable pain and despair.

Caging it. Trapping it. Confining it within his compelling influence as a piercing silver light surrounded them both and tore them—now together, melded, now as one—out from the dark abyss of death's oblivion.

***

The heavy human lids of Nergal's new eyes fluttered open, while in the back of his new mind echoed the tortured screams of a little girl's captured spirit caged by his commanding force of demonic will.

Blurry vision clearing . . . and he found he lay prostrate on a floor, the high ceiling a recognizable sight through active eyes blinking away the burning fade of brightness shying to a pale and angular face staring down over him, everything about it cold and sharp and white, though the thick confusion of fog enfolding him proved slow in dissipating so that recognition existed as a thing far removed from his recovering reach.

Her, he realized of his physical self, wiggling first his new fingers then new toes while attempting to strain his new neck into looking up—which caused the world to roll-shift into a sideways-lying view of the Divine Palace's Receiving Room floor without an ounce of control afforded him.

"Broken neck," said the other's voice, a familiar tone expanding into recognition, once flat and void of emotion now holding the serrated edge of some deep longing, a burning yearning rekindled inside.

Dread fright shot nightmare spikes throughout Nergal's new body, scaring his nervous system alive and awake with raw and charged emotions unfelt before, human emotions turning his demonic pride queasy with loathing and disgust. Abject terror screamed at him to get up and run, but he accomplished nothing more than lying immobile as would a lifeless corpse . . . which, ironically, was not very far from the truth of his new existence.

Soft songs of moaning agony arose nearby, several voices singing requests for a mercy life never gave them though death promised once it delivered them from the tortures of living. But these sounded as distant notes of dying despair to Nergal's hearing, his mind preoccupied with the strange labors of his adjusting body trying to breathe yet possessing no reason for the unnecessary function.

His world's view roll-shifted once more when the pale-faced other cradled the back of his broken neck within a cold dead hand, readjusting his head. Then came the honey-sweet taste of warm liquid wetting his lips, moistening his tongue, soothing down his parched throat in pure ecstasy. His mouth worked of its own accord as the precious relief of warm blood trickled then flowed down his aching throat and into his ravenous belly where spread rejuvenation throughout the rest of him in veining blooms of vitality.

He drank from the proffered source of blood, his mind blanking of all cares but for swallowing and absorbing the coppery-sweet reviving sustenance providing liquid vigor. The sounds of crunching and grinding at the base of his skull. The other worked their cradling fingers upon his once-broken neck mending through the fusion of fractured bones and torn twists of nerves while his resurrected body enjoyed the slow process of healing itself where he lay feeble and helpless though recovering.

The nutrient swallows of blood returned enough strength into his new body so that he sat up with the other's guiding cradle of help while still drinking—only to choke startled at sight of Soultaker, the Forsaken One, the Eater of Souls, the necromaster Dethkore kneeling over him and holding a brass cup to his eager lips. Until the deadman garbed in black swaddles of sentient shadow pulled the cup away, allowing Sera-body's wide brown eyes to take him in.

Noooooo! sounded her scream at the back of Nergal's caging mind. He shut it out, banished it into the dim recesses of their shared consciousnesses as one would strike the iron bars of a caged animal, sending it cowering into a far corner in forced obedience.

Her, his mind said once more. And again sounded Sera's bitter screams calling out for spiritual release, to regain mental control of their shared mindscape. But Nergal's ancient essence combined with his demonic compulsion proved insurmountable so that he willed her pleading presence of voice to the back of their blended awareness. *His* mind, now.

Having latched upon Sera's soul with the intent of undoing her through slow feeding, he intended bestowing upon her a punishment undelivered in life for her lies perpetuating his mortal demise. But plans changed when the necromaster removed Sera from the eternal brink, taking her—unknowingly taking them both—out from the ethereal abyss of oblivion through resurrection . . . but for what? And why? What did this creature even Death itself held no dominion over need with such a—

An alarming blast of human terror shot through him—*Run! Before he consumes your soul!*—the systemic charge of which provided small movements of waxing control, progressing from wiggling to flexing his fingers and toes, his little hands and feet moving in tandem twitches as dynamism spread along with the fear. Perhaps the Forsaken One knew Nergal existed there within the girl's body and returned them to enact his revenge upon his former enslaver.

"Where is my soul?" Dethkore asked, holding the brass chalice of blood aside, his voice the sound of desiccated cornhusks crackling against a cold and lonesome wind.

"More." The word escaped Nergal-through-Sera's trembling lips in aching plea, the beggar's humanness request sickening him. He tried reaching for the cup, wanting to snatch it to his mouth and drink it empty of the precious lifeblood rejuvenation, but his little girl arms afforded him no more than feeble twitches on the ground beside him.

A deep and bitter sadness stole across the necromaster's angular features, accompanied by a single word which crept out over pale lips in a shred of pain, a sheen of melancholy grief glazing over his black soulless devil's eyes pierced by white pupils while he pet Sera's/Nergal's cradled head. "Marisha."

Epiphany bloomed in this Nergal's defining moment of unholy revival. No reanimation for punishment. No revival by random choice from among the litter of dead just to answer the necromaster's question. But distinct resurrection for the grim remembrance of this forsaken creature's lost daughter born from a tortured life a millennia past and stemming from an undying ache of loss too grievous for even Malach'Ra to wield his control over.

For Sera resembled Marisha—sharing her pinch of nose, her high cheek bones and pointy chin, her brown mop of hair and round eyes, the frame of her body—the necromaster's daughter.

And the sliver of humanity remaining within Metrapheous Theaucard, that unyielding splinter of a grieving father's memory rooted too deep for pulling, invited further connections of derangement to the little girl's body housing Nergal's dominant spirit.

While at the back of their fissured mind the body's original holder remained trapped and screaming, thrashing and begging for spiritual release. And Nergal in Sera's body realized through memory imprint that he should and could and must and would use this revelation to the absolute advantage of his manipulative nature.

I am the scorpion and she the frog.

Possessing Sera's body provided Nergal access to her brain patterns in a shared neural-connected webwork of memories, and contained therein he discovered a new tool to utilize, a weapon to wield, a power to leverage against Dethkore so profound he would have burst in mad laughter if only his body possessed the physical strength to elicit the response.

He cursed himself for not piecing it together sooner, though forgetfulness—and not uncommonly delusion—vexed the bane of every ancient memory. His reasons for choosing Sera from the aizakai execution pits originated from a two-fold blessing. *Yesss.* Her aizakai foresight as well her uncanny resemblance to the Forsaken One's dead daughter. *That's right.*

"Please," Nergal pushed out on ragged breath, straining to prevent the stretch of his S's while thankful he sounded one and the same to Sera's vocal tone. But her voice provided only one tool among the many at his disposal, and he must employ them fast before the necromaster broke free from his pensive delusional state and realized what he had reawakened was not the same girl let alone the lost daughter his broken mind projected before him.

Nergal, in Sera's body. He . . . she . . . *they* reborn as Sergal.

Yesss.

* * *

"Please," Sergal said, his pleading voice a little girl's raspy whisper. Lowering his ancient pride unto begging to entertain the disgrace of issuing such a foul human word elicited fathoms of disgust, debasing himself through necessity. "Please . . . more."

He worked his eyes into beseeching pools of merciful askance—and endured a panicked flush of dread when his latent serpentine eyes made a strong play at showing through body-Sera's own. With that first draught of nutrient blood swallowed, Nergal's recovering spirit received enough vitality for readjusting into the tighter contours of Sera's unfamiliar body, much the same manner of tugging an already tight glove while flexing one's hand inside it. Dissatisfied with adopting the little girl husk as his own vessel of a tool, he wanted to confiscate the full of it in his irrepressible nature of total control. The eyes, after all, existed as the windows to one's soul. But he could not—no, he dared not allow his true self revealed, otherwise all would be lost.

He flexed his will and labored through great pains, restraining his true eyes from showing and thus betraying him . . . yet, the task requiring every sliver of his returning strength of command over their shared body. For one alarming moment he feared the black vertical slits of his yellow serpentine eyes bloomed through Sera's frightened browns, but the reveal proved no more than a fleeting shadow dancing across a pane of glass, there then gone. During which Dethkore glanced away through Sergal's askance for more, distracted, the necromaster's gaze on a silent hunt for something, and the slippage of Sergal's hidden character passed unnoticed.

"Please?" Sergal pleaded again, allowing the pitiful human innocence of Sera to bleed through in tone while making careful strains upon their shared voice, the begging coming easier now that it proved a necessity to employ.

Dethkore stared down over her for a silent length, his black soulless devil's eyes weighing and measuring the little girl before him. His thin lips parted though he did not speak. Instead he lowered Sergal's head to the floor, stood and turned, a dagger carried in his left hand, the brass chalice of blood in his right.

Unable to achieve little more than twitches while his body vessel healed its broken parts, Sergal lay listening to the unseen sounds of the necromaster's movements across the Receiving Room: the whispers of his shadow clothes and the crunch of his purposeful tread upon scatters of grit. Long seconds passed. There sounded the sharp *skritch* of keen metal sliding across flesh punctuated by a gargled scream. Longer seconds passed. Dethkore returned, knelt with the bloody chalice refilled in one hand, the dagger he used for letting its filling carried in his pale other.

Tantalized by the waft of fresh blood tingling his senses with a powerful thirst for more, Sergal battled the overwhelming urge to sit up and throw himself forward in ravenous bid. Not just for snatching away the reviving sustenance and upend the chalice to his craving lips himself, forgetting all else except swallowing the coppery nectar, but also for snatching away the dagger he knew through feel of presence contained his and Sera's blended souls, the vitus bound to him through the necromaster's ignorant resurrection of the girl.

Its spiritual tether anchoring his restored essence to this mortal plane pulled at him, Sera's soul and thus his latching parasitic own transferred into the simple blade same as the necromaster's soul existed confined inside his own lanthium soulring vitus. Invisible internal tugs issued from the dagger through necrotic weaves of spiritual threads sewn upon Nergal's and Sera's intertwined souls, producing the rhythmic cadence of a slow-throbbing heartbeat outside the vessel. Sergal's unliving body trembled with despair's waking shudder of nightmares at the dread realization of his vitus condemning him a slave to whomsoever held his souldagger.

"Drink," Dethkore said, again cupping the back of Sergal's head, lifting it while tipping the chalice to eager lips.

Sergal's vicious ambition for filching possession of his souldagger vitus vanished in a fierce flush of need as he drew in the inviting coppery aroma and his lusting thirst of it claimed all desires. He drank the proffered blood in greedy swallows then sat up with renewed vigor and coughed from some of the precious blood having leaked into his lungs between quick gulps. Though choking now existed an impossible feat considering his unliving vessel, its only labor of lungs for producing breath for speech.

He continued drinking from the proffered chalice, slower so as not to spill the precious revitalizing fluid, the necessity of breathing gone alongside any further requirement for food beyond the eating of living flesh. Strength returning, he grabbed the chalice away into his palsied hands and craned his head while upending the cup, emptying it in savage abandon and a devouring drive before he lowered it to his lap and licked his bloodied lips.

Full presence of mind achieved, Sergal's inhumane gaze willfully hidden behind the disguise of Sera's brown eyes fixed upon the souldagger in Dethkore's fisted grip. The powerful urge to take it—*take it now!*—lashed him in whipping scolds. But he flexed his stronger demonic will and restrained the condemning act lest he reveal his true nature.

"Ahhhh," Sergal breathed more than said, exhaling satisfaction on unnecessary breath. He wrestled the urge for throwing the chalice aside and commanding the Forsaken One to—*but no. I cannot give myself away. Control of deceit is my only saving grace now. One errant slip and my eyes will show. I have a part to play, and I am unfinished here. Far from finished.*

He gazed round the tableau of carnage, an aftermath of destruction. *Much has changed, yesss. How long have I been gone?* Bodies lay strewn about the floor. Black scorches marked the walls here and there round punctures of eruptions both inward and out. Broken bits of furniture lay scattered about and between scatters of rocks where jutted parts of bodies, bits of dented red-gold armor and dusted shreds of crimson cloaks. A white pile of rubble evinced the Khan's—*no, the Betrayer's*—ivory throne destroyed upon the blackened dais, a scorched hole punched through the ceiling high above it.

Sergal drew in the ruins of the Receiving Room, his cunning mind active, piecing the parts together while reforming the whole of the picture painted during his spiritual absence.

Apparently Soultaker returned to the Divine Palace with a terrible vengeance, obliterating his way through all obstacles in his questing bid to reclaim his precious soulring. Or perhaps the Betrayer Khan himself had razed the palace grounds before taking his leave in one of his infamous fits of rage. Unsure which truth, possibly a combination or succession of both, lay behind the real cause of the destruction, Sergal cared neither way.

Though the delightful sight brought an approving smile to his lips, a pleased twist of his cold dead flesh he schooled away while his insidious gaze roamed the aftermath of the room. Across the littered floor lay the burnt remains of scaly flesh, his former physical vessel, the charred and decrepit husk of its corpse sticking out from beneath tumbles of stone. Beyond it his traveling pool buried beneath more scorched tumbles, the floor round it painted in dried splashes of blood. His lips trembled so that he pursed them tight as the furious notion of Hannibal Khan's betrayal flashed through bursting fades of memories from both Nergal's and Sera's perspectives in a back-and-forth frenzy of melded retrospection, two separate though equal points of view concurring the moments before their shared deaths.

This is not over, Betrayer. My vengeance has only just begun. I will—

"Where is my soulring?" Dethkore asked, his voice intruding into Sergal's dark reverie. He stood to his full towering height while living shadows bled from the corners of his eyes, the darkness of it dancing across the pale landscape of his sullen tombstone visage. His features hardened along with his voice, his unblinking eyes a focal stare. "Where is Hannibal Khan?"

"Hannibal Khan." Sergal repeated the Betrayer's name in a low grumble. He swept his gaze away from the charred corpse of his former body-vessel and looked up at the towering necromaster, failing to restrain the anger from tightening the cold dead muscles of his grimacing face.

"You were his favorite aizakai pet," Dethkore said. A hungry urgency entered his voice while unnatural shadows danced and swam his face. "Where is he? Where is my soulring?"

Pet. Sergal's mind spat the repulsive title out. A vivid flash from Sera's perspective, the final moments of her living world before Horace snapped her neck. He resisted turning his head for a look across the room and so betray his thoughts to where he remembered through the answering touch of Sera's reflecting perspective the Betrayer tearing the necklace free then throwing its lanthium soulring vitus aside in defiant disgust.

"You will answer me," Dethkore said, his voice a commandment, his tone the sound of dried leaves crunched underfoot. He upheld Sergal's souldagger vitus in gesture, pale fingers squeezing more than mere metal. "Where is Hannibal Khan? Now."

Catalyzed by outside forces of presence compelling him into action against his weaker will, Sergal answered Dethkore's request with no hint of hesitation involved. "Fist." He shrank in on himself, feigning trembles as one assumed a frightened little girl would do, for as the second time in his long existence Sergal knew the dread compulsion of another's overpowering will working through him unopposed. First his old master Malach'Ra, and now his new master the Forsaken One.

The exchange of masters sickened him, but he possessed new tools to utilize now. Inside he smiled, gloating over the secret knowledge, while outward he projected himself as the frightened little girl.

"Please don't let him hurt me any more," Sergal begged through Sera's pleading mask of ravaged innocence. "Please . . . *Father*." He emphasized the human term in a meek squeak of voice. "Don't let the bad man hurt me any more."

To cap off his fine performance, Sergal hugged his legs to his chest and buried his face between his knees while trying to produce tears that would not come—*cry, godsdamn you!*—until he enforced his lashing will upon Sera's caged grieving and hot tears raced his cold cheeks—*victory, yesss!*—so that he craned his head and presented his feigned tortured state of innocent despair.

"I—" Dethkore paused, betrayals of sorrow tugging the pale skin round his black soulless devil's eyes and the corners of his perpetual frown while an inner war waged therein.

"Father, please," Sergal said in a mock quaver of voice. "Don't let the bad man hurt me."

Dethkore flinched, pricked by words. He opened his mouth then closed it, lines of uncertainty etching his furrowing brow framed by black hair parted down the middle its tips depending to his shoulders. He averted his apprehensive gaze, blinking hard, his low voice a struggle when next he spoke. "No. You are . . . not my . . . daughter."

Sergal cringed at the objection of Dethkore's hesitant almost-question, but he hid it well behind more false tears and real trembles while staying his tongue lest he prod the grieving father too hard too quick and shatter the fragile illusion.

The delusional necromaster reached forth to touch at Sergal's upturned face in the manner of stroking a tender hand across glistening cheek, but withdrew his reach before contact as the twitching flitter of an ancient sadness stole across his sullen tombstone visage, crinkling his pale landscape with fine lines of mourning torment.

He shook his head, wincing at some inner tremor unvoiced, closed his eyes and flinched while mumbling, fighting away thoughts threatening to override the unkempt remains of his questionable sanity fractured through a millennia of remorse.

"No," he said in brittle whisper. "Marisha, I . . ."

Sergal let slip another instigative prick of words in a meek and pleading voice, careful and precise, sharpened through demonic cunning. "Daddy, please."

The tortured story of Dethkore's eyes snapped open, revealing fathoms of harbored woes jostled in a grieving sea of delusion. Words unvoiced trembled his parting lips. The corners of his mouth twitched into the beginnings of a smile killed through a tensing grimace. "No. You are not—" He paused, regaining composure through a rapid series of blinks. "I will not hurt you. My child." A longer pause, a wincing flinch, and a desperate certainty entered his tone. "I told you I would come. I seek only my soulring, and the return to my slumber. And for that I need your help."

At that Sergal made big naïve mooneyes and feigned a smile up at the ancient being who had ritually sacrificed his wife for the return of their murdered daughter. A daughter, unbeknownst to the grieving father at the time, Nergal murdered through the savage tools of a pedophilic neighbor's child-lusting hands.

Humans are so easily manipulated. A cut here, a promise there, and they mold like warm clay in a master sculptor's hands.

He had planned on utilizing Sera in other ways when the appropriate time arrived for such devious measures. Until the Veilfall wreaked its havoc on his plans then his new plans sundered by Hannibal Khan's blatant betrayal.

Sergal remembered, swimming upstream through time's great river of ancient memories, oh how he remembered this distraught man summoning him over a millennia ago, tears streaming from his puffy eyes while he begged for Malach'Ra's dark blessing of resurrecting his brutalized daughter after the other gods turned deaf ears to his grievous pleas. Nergal delighted in explaining the necessary ritual, all of it preplanned by Malach'Ra, then savored in watching as too much drink forged a devoted husband's hands into cruel tools of murderous abuse upon his ignorant wife. 'She cannot know,' Nergal warned beforehand, 'or else you'll spoil the ritual.'

Ahh yesss, the woman Maria's wonderful screams sounded a pleasure of echoes hours in dying. Then the dead returning to life . . . in wrong and twisted ways, of course—Nergal ensured it through deceitful wordplay. Their dark bargain struck and sealed in sacrificial bid, Metrapheous condemned his soul while forfeiting his will—though not all of it, for the everlasting grief wrought from murdering his beloved wife, then having to dismember and burn the unliving abominations of his wife and daughter thereafter, kindled a defiant fire of obstinate rebellion even Malach'Ra proved unable to smother under his suffocating influence.

For the human psyche, however malleable once broken, retained strange pockets of resistance in the most surprising of places amongst the scattered shards when one sought to piece them back together into a different manner of puzzle than was before. But psyche and spirit, though interwoven, lived as two separate beasts needing tamed. And despite Sergal's loathsome disgust for it, the tenacity of the human spirit still amazed him even after all his many years. It sickened him, but it amazed him too.

And it also pleased him, for however impossible the human spirit proved to enslave by force—all demons knew the easiest way to enslave a human was to allow them to believe they were free, this more demonic instinct instilled from Hell's spawning pits than any lesson learned through mortal dealings—it could be coerced if allowed the proper amount of time and the suitable set of instigative tools.

Manipulation—especially of love, of greed, or power—provided the human spirit's bane, and Nergal-now-Sergal had not risen on high amongst his demonic brethren without becoming a master manipulator of supreme stature. Nor would he have been able to break free from Malach'Ra's control, finally and at long last, through Sera's tethering spirit if it were otherwise.

I should be pronounced the King Demon of Patience for as long as that last task took me. If not for the Veilfall I'd still be—

"Noooooo," sounded Sera's pitiful moan, wailing and weeping and full of woe, she an involuntary witness to his dark reverie.

Shut up! he commanded mentally. *Shut up you annoying little bitch.* And the irritating cries of Sera's grieving in their bundled mind—bundled because shared existed as too inappropriate a word considering Nergal's stronger force of will and growing influence—cowered within its caged area of dim recess.

I'll deal with you later. His tool in life, his intended meal in death, his physical vessel in this their rebirth, he carried Sera's consciousness nestled inside his own with the cunning intent of using her still. No disobedience here, for he *was* her now. In part, at least. The irony of their spiritual entanglement almost made him chuckle aloud.

Plans took shape behind his feigning plead of eyes, threads of potentials bridging in spun spiderwebs of promise, all of them weaving out from round the Veilfall center.

The Soothsayer will journey to the Head Mistress, yesss, as is the Great Game's fated design. And they will hunt then destroy the Godstone—if either can even resist its alluring all-power. I have to stop them before I can claim it myself. I've risked too much to fail again. Betraying Malach'Ra so openly . . . he'll send others of the Enclave against me, I know it. Perhaps Belial, that walking plague of constant schemes. Or maybe even the saichan serpent-priestess Pwicca. She always hated me most. Jealous bitch would beg for a chance at me. And she'll take delight in peeling my scales while chewing on the strips as I squirm beneath her claws.

Or worse, banished to Purgatory, passed from father to son and the ghostwalker would—no! No sense in dwelling. Doesn't matter. Let them come. There's no turning back now. Only ahead and what I can make of it.

Kill the Head Mistress and capture the Soothsayer then use him to find the Godstone. No more use to me beyond that if he survives retrieving the Essence of the First. There's hope in that too. Though if he fails there'll be no stopping what he'll become.

So many paths to tread, and all of them leading to Fist. Where Hannibal Khan, his Betrayer, surely marched for the Book of Towers to secure the rest of the promised Dominator's Armor, the only device in this world, once pieced together, which rivaled the Godstone's awesome all-power.

I cannot allow that. If Malach'Ra returns into his reassembled Armor through Hannibal Khan he'll punish me in ways I dare not think.

Unless I possess the Godstone first.

Sergal licked his lips, tasting potentials of revenge inflicted upon his Betrayer and the rest of the world thereafter. Or perhaps . . . perhaps.

"Yesss," he whispered through errant slip of his demonic tongue. He maintained his moon-eyed gaze up at the necromaster while delicious notions played out in his active mind, his giddy insides tickling with delight through foreign swells of human emotions, pieces snapping into proper place for him again in this his new and re-beginning.

Yesss. Perhaps he could manipulate his enemies into destroying each other, the Soothsayer and the Betrayer. *Two birds with one stone, yesss.* With the Godstone in his rightful possession, its limitless all-power would make of him the new master above all same as he'd planned before the Betrayer's treachery. *Yesss!*

But for his musing splendors he needed his souldagger in his own protective hands, for his physical tether to this world, his vitus, if destroyed, was now the only device that could undo him along with all of his forming plans and—

"Stand," Dethkore said.

Jolted out from reverie, Sergal endured the commanding squeeze of Dethkore's cold dead grip upon the souldagger vitus of his mental designs. His body obeyed into standing.

A fearful disgust bloomed therein. He struggled through the futile attempt at fighting the blatant manipulation of his demonic will submitting to another master by flexing his demon-born power of compulsion as he had countless times before. And though there pulsed the innate magical presence of familiar demonic potency circulating throughout his human vessel, projecting outward from his controlling spirit within, the energies of his compulsion proved restricted and diminished.

No. Compulsion did not radiate from him as was before when in his serpentine body-now-gone, instead it flowed through him, contained, its potency ebbing and flowing just beneath the tingling surface of his skin. *No!*

Sera's laughter mocking his failed efforts sounded at the back of their bundled mind so that he focused inward, intending to lash out at her.

"Come," Dethkore said, applying another commanding squeeze upon the souldagger as he turned away.

No physical hesitation involved, Sergal walked alongside his necromaster controller, his body moving for him while his mind sought to achieve paths of resistance and avenues of escape. Which led him nowhere but obedience, physical defiance beyond his limited scope of control with his souldagger vitus held within Dethkore's fisted grip. He needed a way to achieve freedom and of gaining control over the Forsaken One again before it proved too late and Nergal within Sera was discovered for what they truly were then destroyed.

He could not—*No!* He would not be returned to his former master. His blatant betrayal against Malach'Ra for the Godstone earned an eternity of unfathomable suffering in the blackest depths of the deepest of Hells. The only punishment worse would be for the Eater of Souls to consume him through the endless hunger of the Blackhole Abyss—a condemnation of annihilation even Malach'Ra feared—and for that last Sergal suffered a terrible shudder in the depths of his insolent soul.

He followed in compliant body, his mind a defiant drift. And awareness struck him, the epiphany that could set him free earned through Sera's stream of consciousness flowing through their bundled collective mindscape.

This he always knew: the Forsaken One could not detect the presence of his soulring unless worn by another, a subservient bane placed upon the vitus by Malach'Ra during its forging.

This he now knew: through Sera's reflections he recalled where the ignorant Betrayer threw the precious tool of control away moments before Horace snapped her neck.

"Yesss," Sergal whispered in a withering hiss of foreseen triumph. *Obtain the soulring then reclaim control, yesss. My only viable means of freedom now. Yesss!*

* * *

They walked across the residual wreckage of the absent Lord of Storms' former Receiving Room, and the tortured moans of others clinging to life amongst the corpses littering the floor sang an eerie death chorus serenade as Dethkore and Sergal made their way in the opposite direction from which Sergal wanted.

Angry and frightened, and at his unhallowed core disgusted that he should feel these sickening human emotions to such extremes, Sergal flexed the limited compulsion of his demonic willpower over and again in futile strain against the necromaster's coercion working him through the exploitive strings upon a marionette. And so he followed alongside his new master in complete physical obedience.

Sera's mocking laughter at his failure to wrestle even an ounce of self-control away from Dethkore proved an incessant tease so that he turned his compulsion flexes into scornful lashing strokes upon her caged spirit, flailing her derisive laughter into screams of agony that softened into a mewling of despair.

Sergal returned his attentions to the pale strider beside his faster-padding little feet, refusing surrender to such degrading puppetry imposed upon him so that he mustered his ancient will into flexing strong through another bid of concentrative resistance . . . which achieved nothing.

He relented for a short period of rest then tried again, flaring his demonic will—and his body-vessel stumbled, fell, the struck sensation of his hands and knees stubbing the hard floor as bits of sharp grit cutting into cold dead flesh produced a strange numbness jarring through unliving limbs in place of pain.

Dethkore stopped.

Yesss. Sergal drew in the necessary breath for speech into his unliving lungs and achieved the masquerade of their voice once more. "Please," he pleaded. "So weak. I need . . . more."

Dethkore turned and gazed. Considered Sergal's weary presentation at silent length through the piercing white pupils of his black devil's eyes.

Sergal cringed, though he hid it well, beneath the gauging weight of that probing stare testing him. Until Dethkore's dismantling gaze elevated, and the necromaster turned, scanning the room in a measuring sweep.

"There," Dethkore said, while imposing another damning squeeze of the souldagger's handle in his fisted grip.

Sergal stood, followed his necromaster controller across the room on veering path, walking over and round and between the strewn rubble of blasted stone, to where lay a khansman in shredded soldier's garb, bloody hands clutching the purple tangles of his bulging innards in pathetic attempt at keeping the contents of his lacerated belly from spilling forth while he bled out, his legs pulp crushed beneath a tumble of fallen wall.

The lifespark in the man's eyes faded though still twinkled bright within the dying regrets of his glistening blue pools staring up at the high ceiling, wide eyes rejecting their dying host's morality even as he clutched its bleeding proof in his hands.

Sustenance, yesss. Sergal licked his lips, a ravenous hunger flushing in a bursting surge of craving.

"Feed," Dethkore said.

Sergal dropped to his knees next to the dying khansman in a weakened crash, struck famished by the subjugating command. The soulring, the Betrayer, the Godstone . . . forgotten as he pried loose those clutching hands for his plunging own.

The dying man elicited anguished whimpers though offered no resistance to Sergal's digging hands defiling his personal contents spilling free in slides and slips of blood-greased intestines. Sergal raised the delicious coils pulsing heartbeats to his slavering mouth and bit and chewed and swallowed while moaning in orgasmic pleasure, the ecstasy of the gasping other's lifeforce sustenance sliding down his throat as the warm coppery pudding his gnashing teeth made of flesh.

He fed for several minutes, the khansman's heartbeat a slowing fade.

Until an abrupt yank upon the back of Sergal's short brown hair at the same time his meal gave over its final dying gasp removed him from the stilled corpse before him.

And though breathing proved an unnecessary function, Sergal panted from the sheer exhilaration of the feeding, his face smeared with the delicious gore and his arms covered in blood up to his elbows.

"More!" he said in hissing scorn, control over his voice abandoned for the fever of feeding. He scrambled forward to delve again into the delectable feast despite knowing only still-living blood would nurture him physically while dead blood would sustain him though poison his mind with madness and his body with necrosis, making of him an unliving hungar driven only by its fierce need to feed. But desire overwhelmed all self-control.

A second, firmer yank upon his hair jerked him away before he could plunge his reaching hands into the delicious banquet again, pulling him into a backwards sprawl.

"No," Dethkore said, the single word an irresistible command. He made to say more—but his head jolted a fraction when out from his right cheek blossomed the tip of an arrow piercing through the left side of his hung jaw. Yet the blank expression on his pale visage changed not a flinch but for one fine line of slight irritation creasing his pale forehead, as if the protruding arrow provided only some insignificant thing of minor annoyance almost too beneath him to acknowledge.

Sergal sat up, slick hands smearing the floor at his sides as he twisted for a better look inside the necromaster's open mouth. The invading shaft of the penetrating arrow placed a thin bar stabbing into left cheek crossing over tongue and teeth and poking out the right cheek.

Dethkore flexed his angular jaw shut, snapping the protruding arrow betwixt his biting teeth, then yanked its broken shafts free of his cheeks and tossed the two bits aside while spitting out the leftover splinters.

Facial wounds healing closed in a swarm of shadows leaking from his pores, the necromaster turned away, presenting Sergal his back, and faced the daring man across the Receiving Room who stood defiant to his injuries in a shouldered lean against one of the dozen fluted stone pillars running floor to ceiling. The only arrow at the man's disposal spent to target, he lowered his yew bow while brightening fear stretched the grimy features tight upon his battered face.

And once more the tenacity of the human spirit amazed Sergal, for even in clear forfeiture of hope this man condemned himself to death through brutal pain moments in coming. The man stood in no condition to walk an escape let alone run it, barely of the condition to have made his shot in the first place, and yet . . . and yet.

The foolhardy man realized new terror, the truth of his arrow not killing the necromaster striking him only after the defiant twang of his bowstring rang out with the finality of his sealed fate, for he threw the bow aside and pushed off from the stone pillar into lumbering away, hobbling atop the bleeding stump of his missing right foot.

Dethkore raised his empty left hand and aimed outstretched fingers at the impaired escapee, upturned his palm. Strewn rubble jostled and slid and rolled across the floor as the entire Receiving Room dimmed, giving way to five long black tendrils made of physical shadows rising from between cracks in the floor then forming into thicker whipping tentacles surrounding the crippled runaway, capturing and trapping him to place, an annoying insect caught within the hungry petals of some wicked black carnivorous flower.

Dethkore clenched his outstretched fingers into a tight fist, and by this simple gesture the black tentacles enclosed upon the man—who had by now fallen onto his hands and knees, turning this way and that while seeking any means of escape—in the same speedy mimicry of the necromaster's commanding fingers, shadows snapping shut and forming a large black bud. Muffled screams pierced through the undulating bud of shadows at length, the necromaster's expression unreadable as a weathered tombstone.

Dethkore opened his commanding fist—and the latching shadow tentacles unfurled in the same like fashion of his spreading fingers, tearing away stuck patches of the man's skin, peeling him alive. His screams elevated into a nightmare pitch filling the Receiving Room with a raucous song of agony and regret while his flesh ripped away in strips, exposing red muscle and white bone beneath. Heavy flows of blood poured in glistening ribbons, drenching the writhing victim while forming a spreading crimson pool upon the floor at the center of the necromaster's wicked flower of shadowy death where rattled chimes of chains hidden therein the obedient tendrils.

Sergal sat mesmerized by the torturing sight playing out before him while memories of the Thousand Years War replayed behind his focal stare.

He had seen scorpions that stung the Forsaken One die of the corruption they touched, witnessed robust humans wither into decrepit aged husks within the full bloom of radiating influence that was the deadman's miasmic death-aura, watched in fascinated terror as the Eater of Souls drained the lifeforce from his victims while shredding their existence through erasure via the endless hunger of the Blackhole Abyss inhabiting the chamber of his unliving being.

But all that before, at his full power and capacity. This example provided no more than a sample of

Dethkore's true power diminished without his soulring . . . and Sergal yearned for its control denied him when in demonic form.

Now though, in this human vessel . . . Sergal regained composure through a series of blinks, breaking free from the captivation of the great diversion playing out before his calculating gaze so that he stood and lunged, seizing the opportunity afforded him. He snatched away his precious souldagger from the distracted necromaster's closer pale clutch.

He fumbled and fought against the slippery blood slicking his skin for better gripping purchase as he spun away, the secret knowledge obtained through the last of Sera's imprinted memories turning a specific desired spot across the Receiving Room a blazing beacon of purpose beckoning him for what he ached to gain possession of before the preoccupied necromaster could turn upon his blatant treachery.

Dethkore looked down at his emptied right hand. He swept his inquisitive gaze over a shoulder behind. His pale visage broke with a disapproving grimace showing through fine lines round the corners of his mouth and in the admonishing tilt of his head. He turned from the screaming bowman in a slow twist, swept his active left hand out toward the little girl scrambling through the wreckage in her frantic bid to race across the room, a withering glower on his face.

Risking no glance behind in his scrambling rush, Sergal focused only on moving forward. Until there erupted a black tendril from the floor in front of him. Which latched round his kicking ankle in a licking whip of tangible shadow when he attempted jumping over it to reach what he sought so close at hand.

He gasped at the pain penetrating through the numbness of his unliving body-vessel, a cold and biting agony shocking through his caught appendage from toe to hip as the barbed tendril void of all heat yanked upon his leg mid-air, arresting him short of landing from his little jump.

He crashed the floor, stubbing knees and chest and hands and chin. Black fright stole through him when his souldagger slipped loose from his blood-greasy grip and skittered across the floor far out from reach.

But he refused surrender and so threw his arms forward, fingers clawing at the covering rubble for what Sera's memories revealed lay buried hidden beneath this particular spot, despite the squeezing tendril holding him to place as an inescapable tether of pain squeezing round his ankle while behind him Dethkore forgot the screaming other and beset his full intentions upon his defiant little servitor having slipped his control.

But Sergal had achieved to within reaching inches of where he needed, his hands a desperate frenzy picking through the litter on the floor. He shoved and threw charred bits of stone aside without care of the cutting damage earned upon his working hands. And closed them both into two handfuls gripping the floorstuff precious seconds before the shadowed tendril lifted him by the leg then flipped him into the air with a whipping snap of his undulating body.

He crashed onto his back in a senses-jarring flop, limp and blinking hard through momentary confusion. As the dawning shadow of Dethkore's approach grew over him, the towering deadman in standing loom.

Debris tumbled and slid away as two more black shadow tendrils erupted from the floor into joining the ankle-latching first. One looped tight round Sergal's middle while the other enacted a hooping choke round his neck, both securing him tight against the floor, their barbed and clinging wraps a burning frost evincing the necromaster's displeasure.

"You are not her," Dethkore said, his nightmare voice the disquieting sound of charred bones snapping underfoot. His soulless devil's eyes blackened to piercing voids through ebony swirls, a malevolent glare of scrutinizing destruction, their midnight pitch leaking out in inching crawls across his angular visage from beneath pale lids as some sentient presence seeking the dark release of nothing but soul-consuming finality.

While the endless hunger of the Blackhole Abyss roused awake therein the Eater of Souls, begging for sweet release through the unlocking of the soulring its gatekeeper.

Sergal thrashed and squirmed, lay facing a potential end so horrendous it would tear his spirit apart while deconstructing it into the dread, gods-rending, tachyon-shredding nonexistence of erasure only the restored Eater of Souls could bestow.

Already the frigid parasitic leaching of Sergal's trembling body-vessel earned through the necromaster's constricting shadow tendrils blackened patches of his pale skin through spreading frostbite while draining the reserve of its returned vitality. He raised his fisted grips before him as two trembling little shields—and through shattered hope revealed the thin golden chain of the Betrayer's broken necklace dangling from Sergal's right hand amid the trapped rocks and dust and grit and floorstuff scooped in two desperate handfuls.

Though too did Dethkore recognize with widening eyes the Khan's former necklace so that his pale mask took on the blooming pull of the anticipated end to some long-suffering grief realized at last. Enraptured, the necromaster leaned in forward-reaching bid, seeking reclamation of his most potent desire.

Sergal emptied his hands of all but the precious lanthium soulring vitus captured therein. Frantic hands yanked the golden strand of necklace out from the hollow of the necromaster's found soulring as two more shadowed tendrils erupted from the floor and whipped at his sides in an attempt to seek out his wrists for dividing them apart and pinning his arms to the floor.

But Sergal proved quicker in stabbing his finger two knuckles deep through the lanthium band, a victorious orgasmic shudder rupturing through him in so doing, as the necromaster's suffering reach closed within inches from stealing the ring.

Panic and pain bloomed therein those black devil's eyes swirling with fathoms of malice and surprise.

Frigid shadow tendrils twined round Sergal's wrists, dividing his hands then drawing his arms out to the floor—but too late.

The frantic flexing of Sergal's demonic compulsion, and by precious physical contact through the soulring vitus he commanded the necromaster back and away. Stark relief flushed through Sergal then, while Dethkore's pale mask slacken blank as smooth slate and its agitated veil of shadows bleeding from his eyes receded behind pale lids. The constricting shadow tendrils loosened from round Sergal's wrists and neck and chest then removed in licking whips disappearing into the floor, the scales of control shifting into Sergal's favor as the necromaster's new ring-bearer.

"Yesss!"

Hugging both hands to his chest, feet kicking, Sergal craned his head and elicited mad and hissing laughter, pleased at the turn of events. He did not wait for the frostbite blackening spots of his unliving skin to fade before standing up, brittle parts of his frigid sinews crunching through the motions.

Dethkore stood before him, still and waiting.

Across the room drifted the low moans from a bleeding huddle of a man stripped of skin and slow in dying.

Profound joy bursting his unliving heart, Sergal moved in a quick hunt for reclamation of his souldagger. He found it lying atop a sharp jut of rock, scooped it up, and stared it over while balancing it atop his upturned little palm.

A simple steel dagger before the necromaster re-forged it through dark arts into conjuring Sergal's vitus, now it soaked up the nearby light into a metal wrought blackened. Until Sergal wiped it clean of the dark grime upon his soiled tatter of dress, revealing shining silver. No, not silver, but silver-*y*. He knew better than that, for silver provided a burning bane to unliving flesh, and this did not burn within his eager though delicate touch, this dagger of hellsteel six inches long.

The small pommel possessed a wrought pentagram within a perfect circle, the blade itself covered in unholy runes of which Sergal recognized some though a select few eluded his ancient demonic memory, these known to the deadman alone. Within the pentagram the likeness of a beast's face, the ears filling two horns of the star, the long muzzle in the center. The dirt rubbed into the crevices in its features added an extra dimension of unholy presence.

Sergal chuckled at the deadman's defiant mockery of Malach'Ra through the design of the souldagger. He raised his precious vitus to his lips and kissed its silvery pommel before making to tuck it away some place safe. Only to realize he had no place for tucking.

Close. Safe. Of course.

Where better to stow it away than not on but in his own personage? He stabbed it angularly into his waist above his right hip—and cried out a hissing misery at the burning sting so that he yanked the souldagger free from flesh then threw it aside as frostfire pain throbbed round his fresh wound.

He glared at the bleeding trickle of black ichor blood leaking from the small slit puncture throbbing just above his right hip. With disturbing comprehension he knew that though his unliving body-vessel proved immune to normal pain and mortal death but for fire and silver, same as the necromaster's soulring could transfer pain into the deadman so too could the souldagger's wicked edge render such pain into its linked recipient.

Lesson learned, yesss.

He drew in an inflating breath and shouted a string of curses at all the gods both holy and fallen. He retrieved the tossed souldagger and, moving to a nearby corpse, cut a long strip of red fabric from wilted cloak which he tied round his waist as a makeshift belt, knotting it tight. Careful so as not to earn another fouling prick he tucked the souldagger into the snug waistband at his left hip, its handle tilted forward for easy pulling.

He turned round and faced his silent servitor, their relationship restored to proper order.

My necromancer Pet. Obedient as a whipped dog, his leash the soulring. What a wondrous turn of events, yesss.

Sergal bared a malicious smile, relaxing while allowing the transition of Sera's brown human eyes into the full reveal of his true serpentine own, abandoning the masquerade. He raised his fist and kissed the soulring vitus then flexed his demonic compulsion and said, "Come, my Pet. We have a Khan to kill, and a world to conquer."

***

A contradicting pair of figures—one a pale little girl with gleaming yellow serpentine eyes possessing a calculating cunningness far beyond her apparent years, the other a towering man swaddled in black fabric shadows and sharing the same sickly pallor as the girl he followed, though both of them deceptively robust as the day was bright—strode out through the strewn wreckage and stale gore of the Divine Palace.

They stood within the wide stone archway mouthing the western corridor leading out from the former Khan's Receiving Room, its thick double doors torn free from their mighty steel hinges and cast aside sometime during the necromaster's destructive return, riven chunks of missing stone from the walls of the archway providing it the look of a sideways-gaping maw displaying broken jags of stony teeth.

Beyond them, in the substantial, unkempt but otherwise sober courtyard, what remained of the distraught citizens not littering the streets as bloated or partial corpses milled about in scattered groups, hundreds of survivors picking and digging through the multitudes of rubble in pathetic attempts at recovering what they could of their destroyed livelihoods from the remains of what their former Lord of Storms and his vast Bloodcloak army left behind as the Holy City of Khan.

Ruins, mostly. The ruins of a once-great city, and the ruins of its once-proud people.

Evinced by the tableau spread out before Sergal's roving gaze where he stood surveying the quiet aftermath of a city undone, the Betrayer had ordered his vast army together then thundered and smote and ravaged the city bare of all supplies before beginning their marching bid for Fist. A thin haze of suspended dust still floated in the air even this many days after the Betrayer's leaving. Not even the destructive chaos of Junes' invasion two years previous compared to the wreckage here.

Sergal smiled, holding gleeful pause within the saw-toothed maw of the archway framing him, allowing the terrorized survivors' desperate, hopeless gazes to turn upon him and his necromancer Pet watching them all as fright stole over their sullen faces so that they scurried away over and round mounds of rubble while throwing out curses at the cruel gods for damning them so. They scrambling away, mice before the pawing cat, to any hiding place they could slink into out from sight of the girl known as the Khan's favorite aizakai pet, though more so from the godsforsaken Eater of Souls behind her, his towering height making her appear much shorter by contrast, a blade of grass standing before a tall oak tree.

Sergal laughed, his little girl's voice carrying strong throughout the courtyard, enjoying the delightful show of a broken people fleeing in terror, surprised his betrayer left any survivors behind.

He took his first steps down the wide front stairs of the Divine Palace while flexing his demonic compulsion in silent command through the soulring, more transfer of feeling than any mental speak of orders, so that his obedient Pet followed in stalking shadow. His demonic compulsion diminished after the transfer of his spirit into Sera's body, a smaller flame of it remained therein however dampened its potency.

I'm restricted to touch now. Where once his willpower of compulsion could radiate from him bodily much the same as a Spellbinder's void-aura, same as his Pet's miasmic death-aura, now it existed reduced to physical contact. *But no matter that. I have new tools at my disposal.*

Though he wished control over Sera's aizakai foresight, a most useful tool, but the tapping of that power lay beyond his spiritual reach despite their bundled connection, and so he allocated the possibility of harnessing it to the back of their fractured mind for a later time, for perhaps when he gained access to the Book of Towers. Maybe the book, in all its secret knowledge and spells, would provide him access to her foresight then.

Walking, Sergal drew in a deep nostril breath, tasting the lingering presence of death's hovering miasma permeating the air here and there in shimmering hums turned vibrant to his new unliving senses heightened via the soulring connection to his necromancer Pet. Time had turned death's presence into a faint glow of fading energies over so many days gone by, but there lingered pockets rife with the essence of death emitted from strewn corpses which Sergal absorbed through suckling feeds, drawing those energies inward while passing as he and his Pet wended their way through the ruins of the city, striding by bodies whose broken limbs stuck out from piled rubble while the echoes of unseen scramblers dodging from their path disturbed the solemn ruins of Junes in soft tumbles of rock or the diminishing footfalls of retreat.

The unliving duo set out westward by easy lead, for the path of destruction evincing the wake of the Betrayer's marching army ran as a mile-wide scar cutting through the city straight toward Fist, the battered and burned-out buildings aligning its sides making of it some terrible canyon where every few minutes another scream echoed through the eerie silence of a city torn asunder by the wrath of an enraged godking questing for war.

I'm coming for you, Sergal mused of the Betrayer and the Godstone both as he walked on, his necromancer Pet trailing obedient to his mental whims. *Oh yesss, I am coming.*

CHAPTER THIRTY-ONE

Every army had its stragglers, those whom lingered behind to enjoy one last bit of rampage before catching up or giving over and leaving with their filched pickings, and the relentless westward-marching army of Hannibal Khan proved no exception.

It moved en mass, a slow and churning beast comprising thousands upon thousands of loyal Bloodcloaks and fanatical worship-followers, while gathering ambitious mercenaries and peasants alike seeking their glories and spoils—all the while covertly hoping to procure the illustrious Godstone's apotheosis for themselves—through killing and plunder with the barbarous mindset that their swords and spears and maces and axes and other such steely reserves determined true law save for the commands of their almighty lightning-wielding godking leading the charge.

The great beast of sheer force carved a massive swath of ruination across the One Land of Pangea while it pressed ever forward in its unbroken advance for Fist and the heathen aizakai whom dwelt therein the fistian Academy, leaving destruction of land and lives in its long and terrible wake.

'The Path of the Dragon' some called it—those lucky few astute enough amid their daily toils to turn and flee at first disheartening sight of the colossal cavalcade rolling tidal over the eastern horizon in a mile-wide plague of determined men and women and thus survive its demolishing passage to spread its foreboding tale—the miles-long aftermath of carnage left in the razing army's traumatizing track, for only such a terribly beautiful creature as the fire-breathing adamantine-scaled wyvern of lore unseen since the Thousand Years War rivaled the demolition earned by the marching forces of Hannibal Khan.

A ground-trembling thunder foreshadowed the advancing army by several quaking miles in grim warning of the approaching deluge of soldiers eager for killing all that moved before their foreboding tread. Word of mouth of its terrible procession preceded its impending arrival absorbing joiners into the swelling ranks of the legion beast or killing refusers on sight, its victims paying the price all men brave to slake their dread curiosity.

Bystanders unwilling to join the marching campaign suffered the cruel fancies of bored and bloodthirsty troopers hungry for war in temporary appeasement to their violent lusts. Farmers and merchants and simple towns- and village-folk, their homes plundered then burned and goods confiscated, were either forced into the swelling assemblage or killed outright where they stood while daring their blasphemous contemplations of accepting such a gracious offer as the godking bestowed in joining the march to satiate his conquest for immortal glory. Cunning mercenaries and whores threw their greedy lots into the chaotic juggernaut's salivating maw, becoming another pair of active hands or spread legs while enjoying the bountiful spoils of its relentless rampage toward Fist awaiting it in the west.

Bloodcloaks and worship-followers rooted out aizakai from every nook and cranny of every appropriated village and town. Man, woman, child—no discrimination of sex or age involved while expunging heathen blood, these brutalized captives collared in kohatheens and made slaves forced to work while tending the Khan's soldiery needs and the greedy trains of its hundreds of supply wagons. Until their spent bodies surrendered to exhaustion and they collapsed upon the Path of the Dragon, their broken twists crushed into pulpy mash beneath the multitude of tramping boots and trudging hooves and turning wheels churning dirt and blood into mud and memories of screams.

Many aizakai slaves suffered beatings for the amusement of Bloodcloaks when not tied to saddles by ankles or wrists—or both, then torn apart between opposite charging horses—then dragged while laughing spectators placed bets over how many particular miles before the unrelenting ground pounded the towed bodies lifeless.

Other aizakai became sport of the Khan himself, beaten and stripped naked then ordered to run for their freedom with false promises of escape. The Lord of Storms pulled scintillating jags of lightning from the storm-tossed sky and struck the runners down, smiting them in eruptive blasts of rending to the cheering amusement of his approving legion watching and clapping in awed delight.

And so came and went the relentless army of Hannibal Khan, an ever-growing, steel-toothed, lightning-tongued leviathan swelling in numbers while the miles tolled, pursuing aizakai genocide while purging the lands of life on its remorseless course for Fist, carnage and slaughter its long and terrible wake.

***

Sergal and his necromancer Pet passed half a dozen hamlets during their first day in following after the rampaging Betrayer's immense force advancing west. Blackened skeletal frames of houses stood amid ash and bones, their fields ravaged bare of crops then burned. Punished lands deserted but for the few decaying corpses strewn about so maimed by steely abuse and scavenging animals and abrupt changes in unnatural weather that telling their sex, that they were once human at all, proved impossible.

Sergal afforded the satisfying destruction of human life an approving smile despite the revenging lusts he harbored for the Betrayer still so many miles ahead even the tail of the treacherous Khan's incredible legion beast remained hidden beyond the western horizon but for the dark churn of sky above it flashing intermittent crackles of lightning amid deep rolls of endless thunder. Tremors of progress and passage lingered within the trampled ground, the mashed grasses and packed dirt absorbing abuse and displaying its bruising through murmuring vibrations whispering secrets of the horrors so recently borne upon it.

Sergal scolded the distance and the invisible Khan with the loathsome scorn of thin-eyed scrutiny. *It should be me there. I designed this, not you. You're just a pawn. Hundreds of years of planning stolen moments before fruition. This is all because of me!*

Hours spent by.

Sergal and his necromancer Pet walked on across trampled pastures of animal butchery, through ravaged towns their tumbles of buildings rife with the aftermath of a human flood, and burned meadows decorated with strewn parts of bodies evincing only suffering and slaughter.

Among the litter of corpses decorating the destruction lay several still alive, khansmen these and stranded behind by broken legs or hips or both and pierced guts earned in drunken fights amongst their rowdy fellows or ill turns of luck while ransacking homesteads of spoils and life. They whispered desperate prayers to unlistening gods in their dying throes, then reached out tremulous hands of askance at Sergal while begging mercies they refused their victims. He paused and listened before passing on, a little girl ignoring their pleas through a pitiless smile beneath terrible yellow eyes knowing nothing of sympathy, her face and hands and lips painted with dried blood their last look on life before death rattled its sough from their deflating lungs hours or minutes after her passage.

The essence of death lingered everywhere along the Path of the Dragon, aforenamed to Sergal by the strangled whispers of abandoned khansmen along the way. Though he could not absorb the unholy potency of energies himself, its osmosis bled into his necromancer Pet through their soulring bond, and he perceived the eddies of energies through his deadsight as silvery wisps and of a black fog so thin as to be almost insubstantial. Dethkore soaked in the unholy vigor, absorbing it through simple passing, the energies iron filings and he the lodestone. He grew stronger, storing reserves of power, and through him so too Sergal.

They traveled on, physical exhaustion nonexistent to their unliving bodies, pursuing the Betrayer and his westward advance, his legion an unstoppable machine striving slow though relentless toward the sprawling bluegrass prairies of the Azure Plains separating Junes and Fist in miles of open country, absorbing every strong and able-bodied man into its swelling fold of ranks, killing aizakai in sport or enslaving them in kohatheens to relieve good khansmen from the menial manual labors required by such a moving force of arms.

Terrorized husbands and fathers delivered weeping wives and daughters to Bloodcloaks in exchange for their lives and their sworn fealty. Forced into the dread machine's turning gears of brutality, the women became sexual pleasure stock, used and abused then thrown away, their ravaged corpses gathering black clouds of flies round the outskirts of the army's path when not trampled under hoof and foot into unrecognizable juts and splinters of bones in the dried mud.

Sergal mused on all this while projecting himself there in thought within the legions stolen from him, sampling unshared pleasures if only he walked amongst them instead of trailing far behind in miserable rumination.

They're mine by right. I should be there, leading them. You're stealing my glory, Betrayer.

Though as much as he hated Hannibal Khan, and planned sure retribution upon the one his former master chose to lead the Enclave into a new sinistry of darken rule through another Thousand Years War, he also admired the splendor of chaos his Betrayer delivered upon the world in a vicious scar of slaughter.

Vengeance smoldered beneath burning revulsion so that he plucked and tugged at threads of possibilities as to how he could achieve retribution considering his new state of unliving existence and his necromancer Pet his only dependable tool against the Betrayer's copious legion.

He possessed no hunger or thirst beyond the cravings of living flesh and blood. He suffered no physical pain but for the cutting edge of his souldagger vitus—which he'd found a proper leather sheath for along the way, taken from the smashed hips of a trampled corpse he belted round his waist. He required breathing only for producing speech, and no sleep, and though he traveled limited by the small frame of a nine year old human girl his body surrendered nothing to nonexistent physical exhaustion.

Days of lead though slowed by sheer numbers, whereas I never tire. I'm coming, Betrayer.

Every now and again Sera's caged essence rattled mental bars in reminder of her spiritual defiance, but Sergal rebuked her pathetic efforts at regaining control as one swatting an annoying biteme fly. Though she persisted, her presence an irritating itch in their bundled mind he could not reach for scratching, at times her wailing moans proving an intrusive nuisance breaking the chain of his thoughts.

Scolding her quiet only served to instigate annoying weeps and moans, so he ignored her as best he could while focusing on the task ahead. An army to catch up to and possibly infiltrate, and a Khan to kill.

But for that I need more than my Pet, yesss.

He considered the Soothsayer for a time, though no sensation as yet of the Godstone's homing presence awakened in Dethkore. *Only a matter of time for that whether he survives retrieving the Essence of the First or not.* Sergal clutched that hope in a tight fist. *And after I find the Godstone I'll kill you too, Soothsayer.*

Dusk bruised then blackened the sky, though night imposed no restrictions upon their travels or Sergal's deadsight piercing the pitch same as day. Orange throbs of animal life pulsed with ambient heat, and impressions of their tracks lingered in trails of fading afterglows depressing the cooler grounds. He continued pursuit unimpeded, all the while formulating plans, weaving threads of potentials together, tying knots of possibilities while dissecting various patterns and plucking at strands of options, analyzing methods here, connecting modes there, weighing successes against premonitions of failure.

Silent and towering, Dethkore followed in stalking shadow, the tether of his soulring vitus an invisible leash.

Sergal spoke through rumination in self-whispers, the audible process helping him think, while hammer-fisting his souldagger's handle in eager though also frustrated pulsing flexes, for the knit of every one of his beautiful plans unraveled at every logical tug.

"So many factors to consider. I can't just walk in and kill him. Too many against me. And I want him to suffer. He deserves no less for his treachery. I made you, Betrayer, and you have the gauntlets, yesss, but you know nothing of my return. There's that at least. I have my Pet. But if someone robs me of his vitus, or worse mine, I'm finished. All for nothing. I need more resources. The Betrayer, the Godstone, the Soothsayer . . . so many high hills to climb I don't know where to set my footing first. No, the Soothsayer I can do nothing about. His time will come later. And the Godstone is out from my reach wherever it has fallen. But the Betrayer . . . yesss, I must deal with him foremost. If he obtains the Book of Towers and reassembles the Dominator's Armor, Malach'Ra will return through him. I cannot allow that, not when I'm so close."

Sergal turned round into walking backwards while assessing his Pet. *Even now I can feel him resisting, trying to slip my control. Impossible, yesss, but he keeps trying regardless. Stop begging for his help, girl. He hears you but he cannot act.* Sergal frowned, and flexed his demonic compulsion in reining flare through the soulring.

A tensing flitter stole across Dethkore's pale tombstone visage, there then gone, though rebellious notions betrayed therein his piercing stare full of hate.

He knows me now. And he'll destroy me the second the opportunity presents itself. He knew who I was the moment I slipped his vitus on and secured the bond. I took his wife and daughter away. So much hate in those eyes. I can feel its heat through the ring.

Sergal smiled, spun away, and continued deliberation of his plans.

They walked throughout the night, Sergal considering the leverage of the soulring vitus and all it afforded him against the Betrayer's legion—though more so what it refused him. Its return granted Dethkore access to his Blackhole Abyss and its gods-rending power of erasure, but the means of tapping into that reservoir of void energies lay beyond Sergal's demonic compulsion of control.

I can feel it inches from my reach, elusive and guarded. If only I could access it I could carve an unopposable swath through the Betrayer's legion, swallow his lightning then consume him and usurp command.

He frowned as he walked across a patch of moonlit road.

With my compulsion diminished, removing the soulring removes all my control. I cannot risk returning him the vitus to release the Blackhole Abyss. He'll consume me the moment it slides my finger to his, completing the necessary connection. There has to be some way of wielding it through him while I maintain the soulring. Bah! All his power and yet the greatest of it remains beyond me, mocking me.

They walked on, Sergal shelving the Blackhole Abyss for later appraisal and toiling through other, safer choices affording better rewards. And he smiled at their splendor.

Once I finish with the Betrayer and claim the Godstone, its limitless all-power will empower my compulsion and grant me unrestricted access to the Blackhole Abyss. And then, yesss, and then I will torture this world through another Thousand Years

War. Only this time I will stand its victor.

***

A blood-red dawn arose at their backs. They soon passed by more isolated farmsteads, these sparser this far west from the abandoned Holy City of Khan in their encroaching bid toward the Azure Plains, the fields of crops stripped of their resources, the homes and stables ransacked then burned by the Betrayer's colossal legion.

Sergal and his necromancer Pet came across a lonely church spared the flames and pillage lain against the rest of the sundered town, a belled sentinel standing among the blackened scorch of earth its whitewashed walls evincing absorbed patches of smoke from the tumbled ashes of buildings round it though the church itself showing not a kiss of true burns. Sergal surveyed the odd scene upon approach, realizing why the building stood defiant amid the destruction as he closed distance.

A church raised in the Khan's name after his conquering of Junes, the peasants hoping to earn his grace and favor while avoiding the wrath of his Bloodcloaks whom sought out and destroyed all blasphemous temples to every lesser god.

Sergal paused before it, studying it and the scene between.

This place of worship for the Lord of Storms displayed a brutal shrine of his passing wrath. The charred remains of over thirty people strung bound to stakes in the churchyard, the blackened stumps of their legs ending in small mounds of dead embers and ash, their corpses sagging upon the thick timbers, arms outstretched and hands pinned to wood with iron spikes hammered through their wrists and a third hammered through their crossed feet. Though one among the punished still drew breath in pitiful wheezes inflating soot-smeared ribs, a crucified woman left untouched by the flames dealt to her neighbors, her withered body nude, her head hung on limp neck, her dark tangles of hair concealing the tortured story of her face.

Curious as to why she still lived, Sergal approached the cross-racked woman while humming to the low moans escaping her. Head lolling on rubbery neck, she raised it upon hearing Sergal's pleasant humming and the crunching tread of his bare feet drawing near, presenting eyes plucked from blood-crusted sockets curtained by sagging lids and framed by soot-smeared torment.

"Please," the woman begged in a raspy exhale, her sun-blistered lips trembling with effort, "kill . . . me."

Again the tenacity of the human spirit and its desperation for clinging to life amazed Sergal. And more, he delighted in the pleasure of this living proof confirming his slow but sure progress of catching up to the Betrayer.

"A gift," he said in a pleasured hiss. He closed distance in front of her, his feet kicking up puffs of ashes, reached up on tippy toes, cupped the woman's still-intact left breast—her other sliced off then tossed or perhaps taken as a trophy or a plaything—and smiled.

The cross-wracked woman gasped and tensed and trembled at his promising touch, her fingers wiggling on hands pinned to thick timers via the iron spikes hammered into her wrists. "Kill me . . . please," she said in stronger voice, mustering fading reserves of vigor. "Oh . . . gods I . . . beg you."

Sergal flattened his feet, withdrawing his cupping hand, while the world round his focal stare throbbed and tunneled. He licked his eager lips, glistening them, with the spiking ache of hunger roused rapacious by the delicious banquet of her flesh on full display, the feast of her coursing blood imposing a new fever of thirst fierce with need, blanking all else from his mind. Bridled though building, too preoccupied with chasing after the Betrayer while devising ways to undo him, he had not fed his unliving vessel since leaving out from Junes, creating a pit of thirst inside demanding filling. His voice a desirous quaver when next he spoke, "With pleasure."

He flexed his ferocious whims through his demonic compulsion, no audible commands necessary, and his Pet obeyed.

"Hurry!" Sergal said regardless, trembling, hands flexing grabs of air, the fever of feeding consuming all rational logic with the desperation of only to see it satisfied.

Dethkore walked up behind him and picked him up by the hips, lifting him to a more appropriate height. A quick flip of souldagger, hands eager fumbles, and Sergal slashed open the woman's throat then returned the six-inch, double-edged hellsteel blade into the leather sheath at his left hip while almost stabbing himself in the hurried process. He cupped both hands together up beneath the woman's throat, catching blood into his makeshift fleshbowl, and drank through hasty slurps while the dying woman gurgled and sputtered and trembled upon her crucifix.

Sera's tortured scream arose in shameful disgust against the atrocious act as Sergal drank, the excess bloodflow running and dripping warm ribbons down their forearms and the sides of their neck.

Sergal ignored her, shuddering to the delicious swallows flowing down his throat and spreading warm tingling blooms through his cold unliving body in reactive orgasmic tickles.

Stopping proved a chore, for the hunger turned an insatiable animal battling his demonic will to discontinue. By thinnest margin he leveraged control and arrested his feeding the moment the woman's death-rattle rasped loose from her sagged body stilling upon the cross and her blood turned dead and thus poisonous. For living blood nourished, while dead blood would twist his guts with slow rot and make of him a mindless hungar.

"Ahhhh, yesss. That's the good stuff." Sergal licked his lips and sucked his fingers then flexed his demonic compulsion.

Dethkore lowered him to the ground.

Sergal smiled up at his necromancer Pet who had not reanimated him into a mindless unliving hungar driven only by the rapacious consumption for human flesh but instead resurrected him to procure the necessary knowledge for repossessing the soulring. There existed a defining difference between the two—reanimation versus resurrection—the proof of it sheathed in the form of a cold hellsteel dagger vitus at Sergal's hip.

Demonic cunning and logic flooded return while his hunger lessened in festering want for more, always more. *Hungars, yess. Of course! No access to his Blackhole Abyss, but his dark arts provide me other tools. Why didn't I think of it before? And more, oh yesss. Hungars are not the only species my Pet can create.*

Sera's voice arose in a mournful note.

Shut up! Frowning, Sergal lashed her mental cage then, scowling, reflected upon their bundled mind and body. *Two souls are not meant to share one body, not for the long term. I am unliving but diseased by our cancerous ill-pairing. The hunger grows. Soon it will claim all of me.*

A dread epiphany struck him with grim pause.

How much longer do I have left before hunger turns to hungar?

He raised his right fist and appraised the lanthium soulring too big a fit for such little hands and thus loose round his slender finger, while his left hand fell to gripping the handle of his souldagger vitus shared by opposing soul-forces.

I must find a way to remove her before she rots me from the inside out . . . but how? He considered the Book of Towers guarded in the heathen's den in Fist. *It must contain some sorcerous method of ridding the girl's poison from me. A ritual of spiritual transfer perhaps, unbinding our souls while freeing mine into another body-vessel. No other reliable way. Compelling my Pet would relinquish my control during the process. I cannot risk such tipping of scales. But I cannot remain inside this diseased vessel much longer.*

Bah! Sergal threw frustrated hands up in a waving away of worries. *I'm getting too far ahead of myself. One step at a time. The Betrayer first, then—*

Others, intruded Dethkore's mindspeech into Sergal's chain of thoughts, its withering tone that of a thousand spiders octocreeping over crumbling bones. *Coming.*

Sergal fixed his stare upon the dark bristle of movement approaching from the north-east, a fat hedgehog of motion in the distance. Men, all of them afoot, a group of thirty or so moving half in shadow and half in sunlight as the scudding clouds came and went before the wind.

Sergal tightened his eyes upon metallic glints catching fractures of the half-hidden sun reflecting off weapons and pieces of armor.

"Interesting," he said with a one-cheek smile.

***

Sergal removed from the churchyard toward the dirt road wending through the ruins of the once-town with his Pet in silent tow, the crucified corpse of the dead woman at their backs a forgotten sag for the approaching others.

The motley crew of newcomers, not soldiers but survivors having picked through the remains of the dead and abandoned to arm and armor themselves, these farmers and tradesmiths, slowed at first sight of the little girl with fresh blood staining down the front of her soiled dress and the towering man swaddled in all black beside her standing roadside and watching their approach in this otherwise desolate place. They stopped when Sergal moved into the road's middle to better face them, Dethkore behind him in towering loom.

Men, the whole lot of their rabble. Armed with forks for pitching hay, bent and battered swords, though more popular and affordable among them makeshift clubs fashioned from broken table legs with nails hammered through their knobbed ends, others still brandishing long sticks-turned-spears with their blackened ends whittled into points then hardened by fire. The lucky few who fled before the carnage of the Betrayer's passing army swept over their livelihoods then regrouped to follow in false safety of their paltry numbers.

Cowards, Sergal thought with no amount of disgust. These men who kept their lives intact by running and hiding while khansmen raided their shops and burned their homes, their wives and children abused and killed, all the while the husbands and fathers watched from a safer distance. *Cowards are always among the ones who survived the longest. Always so brave after the threat has passed them over.*

"It seems we have some unexpected company," Sergal said, glancing up at his Pet who returned nothing but a blank stare.

A solitary horseman appeared riding up behind from whence the others had come. He rode at full, reckless gallop, yanking up his mount's head when it charged round the motley band only to stumble on some loose rock in passing, and bent low in the saddle to extract every ounce of speed out of the animal. A few moments more and he reined halt a short distance in front of the shifting mob, his horse spraying foam from its mouth, nostrils flared and pink, sides heaving. The rider stared down Sergal and his looming shadow Pet, then turned his horse about, leapt off and threw his arms up in waving gesture to begin arguing with the others.

Sergal watched on, listening. He gave the handle of his souldagger a measuring squeeze, then removed his hand and spun the soulring round his finger in idle play, the unmindful action helping him think.

The rider shouted cursing argument for his fellows to turn back before their little group of justice seekers proved their own demise. But his pleas instigated cursing threats. A burly man at their front, the one with the lopsided-muscled look of a left-handed blacksmith, strode and stabbed the shouting other through the belly with his battered sword then stepped back while yanking his blade free from punctured guts. Jeering hollers erupted as the arguer hunched over clutching his bleeding stomach. He collapsed and curled into a groaning fetal ball of hurt on the dirt road.

"Yesss," Sergal said in a pleasured hiss. "Very interesting indeed. Come."

He approached the riled mob, necromancer Pet in stalking tow. They stopped a few paces out from the dying rider's horse.

The burly stabber's black-bearded mouth opened to issue words, then his face pinched at the other's bleeding groans so that he stepped forth and thrust his sword through the curled man's ribs and silenced the distraction, the twisted look on his grimy face more annoyed at the interruption than disgusted at his method of stifling it.

Sergal smiled, for he felt through his necromancer Pet the preemptive absorption of spiritual energies stealing loose from the killed man as they arose from the body, appearing as silvery swirls of twinkling eddies wreathed in burning reds to Sergal's deadsight. The lifeforce energies twirled and snaked in wavy currents drawn in by Dethkore's absorbing presence, curious moths lured to the consuming flame.

Sergal closed his eyes and inhaled deep by impulse through the exhilarating rush of the lifeforce energy absorption. And there stirred within his Pet a rising thrum of death magic so that Sergal licked his lips in spiritual aftertaste of the energies added to the negative pool of potency shared between their soulring bond.

These men desperate to the point of uncaring, they stared as one collective at the odd sight of the little girl and the towering man in black standing in the road and blocking their way.

"Move or die," ordered the burly man at their front, the lefty blacksmith. He waggled his bloodied sword in punctuation to his threat, no touch of fear betraying his molten glare or baritone voice, the mob shifting behind him.

Sergal chuckled, the tone of it releasing from Sera's body in a treble giggle. He could end the tortured lives of these men with one willful flex of his compulsion and a simple flick of his wrist—but he was curious. And though he wished not to spend his Pet's energies without good reason, not here and not upon these paltry few, he admitted potential here, and not just the potential for pleasure but purpose.

To combat the Betrayer's legion required reserves of his own.

"And where do you think you're going in such a hurry?" Sergal asked, smirking. "Hmm?"

The blacksmith said nothing, only grimaced, while behind him angry murmurs arose amongst the mob on a suicidal hunt for taking as many khansmen with them in revenge as they died. And now they faced the annoyance of a little girl and a pale man barring their path to sure death.

Cowards no longer, yesss. Pawns. Tools. There's potential here, but I must shape it.

"You crave revenge for your loved ones," Sergal said, more statement than question, toying with the soulring through idle spins round his finger while he spoke the baiting words, a wonderful idea sparking to flame. "Serve me, and I shall deliver you an abundance of revenge. Enough to overfill your blackened hearts, yesss."

The blacksmith's eyes flared contemptuous at what he took for a blatant assault of mockery upon their bitter woes, and that from no less than a little girl, while behind him others shouted curses and shook their weapons overhead in taunting threats. He charged forth to skewer the felled rider's horse aside then cut through the two mockers in their way.

Until Sergal made his point, while entertaining himself in the process, by providing a convincing sample in warning example of his true power delivered upon the animal between them.

Sergal raised his hands and flicked his wrists, accompanied by the willful flexing of his demonic compulsion flaring through the soulring bond—and Dethkore raised his hands in obedient mimicry, enacting delicate gestures of his fingers tracing invisible sorcerous weaves through the crackling air.

In trade the horse snorted a whinny of pain. It danced about, bucking, as black shadow tendrils sprouted from the ground beneath its clomping hooves, surrounding it, denying escape, whipping at and lashing upon the startled animal's rippling hide, black shadow barbs ripping brown flesh from its protesting body in bloody strips producing the sounds of torn wet leather beneath shrill equine screams.

The blacksmith halted mid step, jaw hung, eyes blooming wide. Behind him voices muted short through shocked gasps, the mob overcome with paralyzing fright and gawking at the whipping flurry of shadow tendrils peeling horseflesh from the tortured animal, its thrashing body throwing glistening ruby beads in everywhere abundance while making of the immediate air round it a red mist.

Sergal craned his head and released the laughter bubbling up his throat while the decorticated beast, stripped of its flesh, charged through a break between whipping shadow tendrils and raced away, toward then through the splitting mod, the bodies of those too slow in moving aside tumbling away, its jolting body leaking streaming ribbons of blood to the air in jouncing rhythm to its pounding rush of hooves.

The charging horse crashed the ground a quarter-mile down the dirt road where it thrashed and rolled and kicked while painting the roadside grass. A moment more and the ghastly music of its tortured whinnies died out as the red mound of horse surrendered a few twitching kicks of its stiffening legs then stilled.

The stunned mob stared at the dead horse, then turned round while huddling closer and gaped at the laughing little girl and her tall companion.

Sergal flexed his demonic will—and through Dethkore's gestures the whipping shadow tendrils sucked down into the ground, vanishing, leaving bloody strips of horseflesh.

"You want revenge?" Sergal asked. And to the mob's credit only a few at their group's rear turned and ran away. He allowed the weaklings to flee unmolested, point made and wishing no further spend of energies. "I can reward you all the revenge you desire."

"You—" The blacksmith's gruff voice clipped short. His black-bearded mouth trembled, as did the bloodied sword in his meaty hands so that he shifted his hold to maintain firm purchase of the weapon lest it slip his nervous grip. His wide eyes thinned, gaze shifting to the wet strips of horseflesh and back. His stare danced between Sergal and Dethkore, back and forth, the blaze behind those deep pools of pitiless remorse burning bright with fear though more so the fiery passion for vengeance. "What in all the hells are you?"

"I am your Master now," Sergal said with utmost confidence. "Forsake your pathetic gods who have abandoned you and follow me, and I promise you—"

There Sergal cut short when the burly blacksmith summoned the courage into lunging forward, stepping onto then over the slain rider, stabbing Sergal in the chest left of center through the heart, driving deep the battered length of steel so that Sergal jolted a half step back from the hard thrust.

He gasped in reflex despite no pain involved but for the numb pressure of penetration, the impaling sword's tip sprouting out his back the half measure of its driven blade. He did not flinch, did not scream, did not bleed . . . and did not die as intended. Instead he frowned down at the sword jutting from his chest, more annoyed than angry.

"What the—" Wide-eyed, the blacksmith's grip slipped free from hilt as he staggered backwards two disbelieving steps and tripped over the slain rider's curl of corpse though caught his imbalance through the pinwheeling of his beefy arms.

Sergal sighed. He gripped the steely protuberance and pulled it free by the blade, an awkward effort given its length and weight. The removed blade glistened with black ichor blood, the grim spectacle instigating more frightened gasps and whispered prayers from the stunned mob, several men sinking to their knees in mumbling trembles.

"You cannot kill what is already dead, you stupid human." Sergal tossed the heavy sword aside with a small grunt of effort while cursing the physical weakness of his little girl body. He met the blacksmith's gaze, drew in an unnecessary breath and hissed an irritated sigh. "Don't do that again, or I'll strip the flesh from your bones. It annoys me."

He flexed his demonic will, tapping into his Pet's reserves of energies, and through flushing cold the gaping wounds in his chest and back and the punctured organs between mended closed through accelerated supernatural healing.

"I too seek retribution," Sergal said in louder voice. He spread his bloodied hands, palms up, in a gesture of offering, presenting his perversion of the world on a platter. "Serve me, and I will bestow upon you all the power to revenge yourselves against those who destroyed your pathetic human lives. Swear to me, and I shall deliver you Hannibal Khan." A lie. He wanted the Betrayer for himself. But they needn't know that. "Accept my mark, swear me your souls, and in return I promise you vengeance."

Voices arose from the frantic mob.

"Look at her eyes!"

"She's Wiccan!"

"No, she's a demon!"

"The gods have forsaken us again!"

"That's the Eater of—"

"Silence!" Sergal yelled in a flare of voice, hushing them all. He smiled. And waited. Scanning from haggard face to face then fixing his dissecting stare upon the burly blacksmith's tortured gaze, the haunt of the broken man's eyes evaluating scales betraying burdens of loss and guilt weighed against fathoms of regret and shame.

Tears spilled from welling eyes down cheeks. Silent and trembling, the blacksmith's thick legs buckled in the breaking of his scales. He crashed to his knees, eyes dark pools of misery, his face a forlorn twist of despair. And slowly, so slowly, he their leader nodded acceptance unto serving the one before him.

Behind him the others of the frightened mob proceeded the same submissive gesture, setting down or tossing aside their makeshift weapons while joining the blacksmith in kneeling mass upon the dirt road. All of them forsaking their gods through audible oaths and curses for the ruination those same cruel gods had beset upon them and their dead loved ones.

"Yesss." Sergal appraised his new collection of pawns with a spreading grin as he approached the kneeling blacksmith and drew his souldagger. He flexed a compulsive grip of command upon dark magic reserves while tapping into arcane knowledge bestowed through his necromancer Pet. "Your name, blacksmith."

"Valdemar."

"Excellent." Sergal swiped the blacksmith's cheek of tears with his thumb then sucked the salty tang. Smiling, he raised the souldagger between them. "I am Sergal. I am Master. And you shall be the first of many."

Valdemar nodded, the motion slight, his baritone voice a quaver. "Yes, Master."

Valdemar grimaced and trembled though offered no resistance as Sergal cut a deep and bleeding pentagram encircled by tiny hieroglyphs of ancient sovereignty into the man's forehead while reciting unholy vows gleaned from his Pet's arcane knowledge of dark arts, and Valdemar's eyes rolled back beneath fluttering lids as his burly body quivered with spasms.

"Yesss," Sergal said in a pleasured hiss. He sucked the tasty wet tip of his souldagger clean as he withdrew to admire the first of his handiwork while flexing his demonic compulsion through the soulring in thrumming beat to the necromancer's mystic soulbindings at throbbing work.

Tendrils of shadows sprouted the ground and arose round the kneeling blacksmith, ebony stretches of fingers groping up the length of him in inching crawls, striving higher, then pouring their darkness into his mouth and ears and eyes and nostrils, disconnecting from the ground while slithering inside the body.

Valdemar collapsed aside, darkness misting from every pore while he writhed and thrashed, convulsing, his undulating skin paling over muscles shifting round bones breaking and reshaping, his beard and hair and body hair burning away. Purple curls of smoke arose from his carven forehead, the sizzling lines of which achieved a molten red glow. His meaty hands flexed into rigid claws. His arms and legs twitched and jerked through the spiritual seizure of change overtaking him. Bloody froth foamed from his every orifice while the spectators of his fellows watched and waited their turns of christening change.

"Yesss." Sergal smiled, well pleased. He would bind their spirits, change their bodies, and reshape their wills. "Yesss!"

* * *

Hours passed. The day failed into night.

Sergal continued the ritual baptisms of his sworn sinistry of darken rule upon the dusty road of an unknown town.

There is no darkness, he mused while carving archaic claim upon forehead after forehead of his new servitors, his demonic compulsion infusing their obedience with each gothic engraving achieved, *only the absence of light.*

He shuddered with awakening to the potency of magic and its potential for dominance and destruction at his fingertips delivered through Dethkore's control. *And I've not even begun to tap into the deathpool of magic within my Pet!*

Not unlike breathing he inhaled the transfer of death magic working in constant absorption, his Pet's miasmic death-aura a vacuum of energies, the Eater of Souls' absence of light Sergal's true weapon against the Betrayer before he claimed the Godstone and became the master of all through another Thousand Years War. *Yesss!*

For now, a divided part of his calculating mind mused over his impending victory—*no, my ascension to godhood*—while he continued his ritual work upon his kneeling servitors through cold hellsteel carving warm manflesh as dark magics flowed through the soulring bond to subjugate the offered spirits. He needed a structured plan for when he confronted the Betrayer, and the Soothsayer.

Failing to plan is planning to fail.

I will not fail in this.

My pawns are coming, and I will have my vengeance upon you, Betrayer.

Then the world.

Yesss!

CHAPTER THIRTY-TWO

Timeless black terrors ripped through the forlorn exhaustion of Banzu's foggy mindscape where emotions loped as unchained beasts howling in rampaging hunt, Guilt and Rage chief among their snarling charge. He sprinted at the forefront—no, ran from the wild pack nipping at his heels. Blurs of shadowed faces to the thousand screaming voices flashed by his peripherals as would trees in a forested sprint. No escape from the endless chase.

Locomotive limbs pumped him forward, hot breath misting in fevered pants, heart a panicked thunder behind his heaving cage of ribs. A glance behind into hunter's eyes, cold and steady and measuring above snapping jaws slinging glistening ropes of saliva.

A stumble, a fall, a twist upon his back in pathetic defense. Guts exploding in a constellation of pain while pearly sets of teeth punctured and ravaged him, his entrails torn loose through frenzied feeding and—the jolting suddenness of cold splashing him awake.

He startled alert into dark confusion, gasping—or trying to gasp, but something wet and thick covered his mouth, restricting his breathing. Covered his entire head. He tried raising his hands to claw free the dark covering, but tightness bit round his trapped wrists, denying hands movement but for their terrified grips of stiff wood running beneath his forearms.

Hooded, he realized, while the rest of him struggled for precious breath through the sodden cloth turning every sucking inhale into false gasps of drowning. Panic ran rampant, but he reined it in and forced himself calm before he passed out again.

I'm still alive . . . and sitting?

His erratic breathing slowed so that the front of the wet hood blew away and sucked against his lips while allowing better space for breath . . . as he realized waking up bound and hooded presented only the beginning of his problems.

The kohatheen's metallic duress locked round his neck denied his attempt at seizing the Power with a defiant hot flash of lanthium cooling quick after heating, while also imposing a bizarre sense of lethargy into his body, providing it a false sense of heaviness rooted in his leaden bones twined in watery muscles twitching more than flexing. He jerked his head round, the motion sluggish, but the loose wet hood offered only darkness.

Until someone yanked it free, replacing darkness with too-bright light in the flash of a blink.

He shut his eyes tight and grimaced against the sharp light stabbing into ill-adjusted pupils, then blinked through the burning fades of light shining bright round the silhouetted figure standing in front of him, they a dark mountain before the cresting sunrise. He breathed deep while his blurry sight acclimated to the light as hazy shapes sharpened into clearer detail, crisping the visual fuzz. He sat naked, bound to the chair by his wrists and ankles.

A dizzy spell struck him. The room tilted and sloshed through blurs of trailing shapes striving to catch up to their points of origin while queasiness gripped his guts and squeezed. He turned his head aside for retching up but only dry-heaved as the queasiness passed, the cold prickles of his warm skin alleviating while balance righted the world straight again.

His abused body ached in everywhere abundance. His brain pulsed with the dull throb of headache kneading its knuckles inside his skull. Inside he protested his captivity while outside he remained still, resisting testing the coarse ropes wrapped taut round his wrists and ankles binding them to the arms and legs of his chair. No point in physical struggle here, and no magical intervention either for the kohatheen assured as much, let alone his wracked body which, to his surprise, betrayed no broken bones or even scars despite he last memories awake and abused by angry aizakai.

Reminiscent flashes of fire and pain and faces flittered through his mind.

He sniffed, detecting the aroma of menthol scents, then his attentions fell upon the brawny bull of a woman standing before him, the empty tin bucket used to douse him awake resting idle on the floor beside her, the black hood a dripping wad gripped in her meaty hand.

She appeared taller than he knew her to be from his sitting position, with a plump though muscular frame possessing more mannish bulk than womanly curves. The flow of chestnut-brown hair pulled tight into a long and golden-banded ponytail added prominence to the square chin on her otherwise round face, her thick neck and wide shoulders. She possessed a Spellbinder's discerning violet eyes though marred by tiny black flecks of pure meanness buried deep within akin to glassy splinters of chipped obsidian, cold and surgical in their sharpness. And when she leaned forward at the hips into presenting him with a closer view of the smile leaving her condemning eyes untouched, the memory of her face bloomed recognition within Banzu's assembling mind born from the last moments he remembered before that kick to his turning face and the blackness it delivered.

The Spellbinder among his aizakai attackers who brought an end to their battle through dachras and pain then locked the kohatheen round his neck. And she enjoyed every second of it, same as she enjoyed his captivity now.

"What in friggin hell—" he began, his rusty voice possessing the strange raspy linger of days unused.

But the woman stifled him by shoving the wet wad of hood into his mouth, making of it a soggy black gag stuffing his cheeks with strong hands. He tried spitting the makeshift gag out, even tried chewing on it to make of it a smaller hindrance. But it bunched up behind his teeth, denying his distended jaw the releasing stretch. So he glared at her while issuing muffled curses which only amused her further, each nasal breath flaring his nostrils.

"Look who's awake." Her smile turned chiding as she straightened, squared her wide shoulders, crossed her beefy arms beneath her considerable breasts and presented a triumphant grin. "Good. I was hoping for some time alone before the Head Mistress comes to deliver your fate."

The flash of her right arm unfurling from the other, moving down and away then up behind her broad back. Banzu tensed, eyes blooming wide at the familiar motion. He produced a muffled scream while flexing through restricted shifts—and spread his legs at the knees as best he could while following the whip of her hand with a terrified gaze to where she stabbed her dachra down into the wooden seat a hairsbreadth in front of his unprotected naughty bits—*thunk!*

Panic returned, tempered with anger by the woman's amused chuckle. He chewed on the wadded gag, shrank it by sucking out as much moisture as he could swallow down. After nearly one full minute he wormed his tongue round the smaller wad so that he spat the obstruction to the floor then worked brief relief into his sore jaw.

The buxom Spellbinder watched all this with more than a touch of perverse enjoyment on her chubby-cheeked face. She glanced at the spat wad of hood but refrained from picking it up and stuffing it all the way down his throat for good measure, which he knew she could achieve with those strong hamhands of hers. She did not move, just stood there with arms crossed and watching him, the scrutiny of her gaze measuring every wet and naked inch of him.

"Who are you?" he asked.

"Spellbinder Shandra at your service," she said, proud and precise words lacking any hint of warmth. She unfolded her right arm, it flowing out between them in the manner of an uncurling pachyderm's trunk, while stepping one leg backwards into giving a mock half-curtsy. "A pleasure to meet you." She straightened, raised her hands between them in stopping gesture, palms out. "No, please, don't get up."

Fiery pressure swelling at the back of his skull, Banzu thinned his eyes and ground his teeth at her blatant jest. But it had nowhere to go and nothing to burn. He resisted the urge to try and shake loose from his bonds if only to deny her the satisfaction of the futile gesture. Rocking the chair over to the floor would earn him nothing but pain and humiliation.

"Why am I tied up?"

A mirthless chuckle, low and deep, then Shandra's eyes expanded in honest surprise as she withdrew by inches. "Oh, you're serious." She thinned her scrutiny into fine violet slits. "You attacked us." She leaned forward to better meet his gaze while gripping the dachra's bone handle between his V'd knees. "Not a good introduction of yourself." She yanked the dachra free from chair, its release spitting splinters against the bare spread of his inner thighs, and twirled it with stubby yet deft fingers while eyeballing his groin for a few considerable seconds before sheathing the fanged dagger away up behind her back. "Soothslayer." She spat the word out, a scorn of bitter poison fouling her tongue, turned her head the slightest increment while maintaining eye contact then hawked and spat so that bits of her wet gob dappled Banzu's cheek as it shot past his face. "And now you'll face judgment for your crimes."

"Crimes? What crimes? Wait a minute!"

He failed seizing the Power again by instinct, the restrictive kohatheen flashing hot round his neck, while he tested his bonds through squirming shifts, grimacing, rocking back and forth, side to side, the chair's legs a wooden clattering upon the stone floor. But the struggle gained him not the slightest bit of space between the tight cords pinching into his sore flesh so that he yielded limp in seconds, surrender made all the easier by the cooling kohatheen's imposed lassitude.

Shandra laughed, amused by the agitated mouse trapped between her batting cat's paws.

"I didn't attack anyone, godsdammit." He huffed through clenched teeth, tried keeping calm. *Gods, I feel on the constant verge of a yawn. And arguing won't get me anywhere. I'm at her full mercy.* Yet still his tongue rebelled with the fierce need to explain himself. "I was attacked." Keeping his tone level proved a chore. "I was defending myself." He thinned his eyes upon her, and a bitter edge serrated his voice. "And I was holding back." A lie, though not a full one. *I could have killed you all, but I don't want to kill anyone except the Khan. If not for that godsdamned alarm—* "What else was I supposed to . . ." He trailed off, wilting.

She stopped listening anyways, for her features softened while she studied him in silence, a strange smile pursing her lips. She leaned forward and palmed the left side of his face, a gentle display of touch, eerily entranced by his eyes, the sharpness of her cutting gaze dulled for fondling appraisal.

He tried recoiling from her touching assessment, but the high back of the chair stopped his head. So he turned his face into her nesting palm and tried for a snapping bite. But she withdrew her hand too quick for teethy purchase and he tasted only air.

"We've been waiting a long time for you," she said in the almost-purr of a whispering lover. She settled back on her heels, and there spread a new kind of smile adding the unexpected hint of prettiness to her brutish features while she pushed out on husky breath, "My whole life, actually." The change fled when she bared her teeth in a snarl and smacked him across the face with the back of her meaty left hand.

A blurring panorama of the room prickled by twinkling pops of stars behind the lids as Banzu's head swiveled aside on rubbery neck. He stiffened seconds more and ground his teeth against the sting needling the left side of his face those thick knuckles imparted. He grunted and glared at her, received cold bitterness in return.

Anger flaring, the kohatheen's bizarre lethargy dulling through the space of his emotional spike, he shouted, "I'm supposed to be here, godsdammit! I'm the last Soothsayer, and I've come to see—"

"You're a killer." The silencing accusation in her risen tone matched the cold conviction in her adamant stare. She returned a queer look, another mocking expression, then her eyes tightened into a frosty violet glare bleeding into her voice. "The last of a cursed bloodline of killers who have always had an aptitude for it, just as others can sculpt statues or make music." This she said with all the disillusion of one blaming a tiger for being a tiger. "Murder's in your blood."

He resigned any excuses for his release through a deflating sigh. *She won't untie me no matter what I say.* A strange sense of dread relaxation flushed through him, finalizing the surrender to his impending doom. "So it's torture then death. That's what this is, isn't it?"

She answered nothing, only smiled while stepping back and fixing him in stare.

He huffed a terse breath and did his best at ignoring her silent scrutiny while gazing round, scanning a lay of his execution chamber. Braziers decorated each of the four corners of the square room that formed a cell wrought from stone walls instead of iron bars, emitting a comfortable warmth under better circumstances, the charcoal within their filigreed sides bright red. A bed by the far wall, a small table next to it with two wooden chairs slotted beneath, a third chair resting empty in a corner. No windows. The only door blocked behind Shandra's Spellbinder wall of girth.

He tested the measure of his bindings again by flexing and shifting his forearms, hoping to stretch the taut ropes looser. But the more he squirmed the more they pinched and grinded round his tender wrists, chaffing skin raw. He supposed they'd tied him up for good reason considering what happened after his arrival. *But if they wanted me dead then I'd already be dead.*

"Why am I tied up?" he asked again. "Why am I still alive?"

Shandra laughed, a deep bellow, as if the obvious answer tickled her up the ribs.

Banzu frowned. "I'm not turned," he said, grinding the words out through clenched teeth. "I've cleansed the bloodlust."

He refrained from mentioning the rest, of the necessary cleansing of the still-tainted Source Enosh spoken of, let alone his killing of the god's mortal avatar afterwards. Neither confession would endear him any further in her eyes. *Eyes!*

"You can see as much in my friggin eyes. Look!" He stretched his neck forward by inches while bugging his hazels wide for emphasis and hoping the anger behind them betrayed nothing of his want for surging from the chair and choking her head off. "Do they look red to you? Huh? Do they?"

"You're wearing a kohatheen," Shandra said and shrugged, as if opining about the weather. "Besides, I don't know how it works. You're the first Soothsayer I've met. For all I know it's a trick to come and murder the Head Mistress along with the rest of us."

"Really?" He drew in deep and hissed a heavy sigh while rolling his eyes. "Seriously?" He tensed in another futile testing of his chaffing bonds, parts of his chair creaking to his brief strains, then he surrendered relaxed and wilting. "I didn't come here to kill anyone," he said in a tone edged with pleading. He glanced away when a hot flush of anger stole through him so that he flexed his hands into fists, added in a low grumble, "Except for the Khan."

"We'll see about your lies when the Head Mistress arrives." Shandra bared her teeth in a wicked grin. "Soothslayer." Her hands quested up behind her broad back through the motions of pulling her dachra fangs. "One way or another you'll spill your guts." A malicious twinkle entered her thinning violet stabs. Her beefy arms tensed, evincing the hidden grips of her dachra handles. "Or maybe I'll just do everyone the favor of killing you now, before—"

But there she clipped short, frowning, at the muffled jingle of keys and the clicking tumblers of the door behind her unlocked from without.

* * *

Spellbinder Shandra turned, hands lowering empty to her sides, as behind her the door pushed open and two women walked into the room, followed by an older soldier garbed in the fistian military colors of blue trimmed with black who stopped just inside and blocked the doorway with his thin though wiry-muscled frame. The man's left hand moved in little preparatory flexes round the hilt of the sword at his right hipwing, a tight-lipped slit of a perpetual frown on his stern veteran's face.

A southpaw, Banzu's well-trained mind noted of the soldier on some deeper level of instinctual measuring of threat. A master swordslinger assessing another swordsman without the least bit of conscious control. Of course, even a child could kill with a sword. All one really had to do was thrust in the right place when it came down to it. But this man wore the hard mask of many killings dwelling behind dark eyes beholding him in a dispassionate stare, though Banzu detected no clear enjoyment of that fact lurking therein.

The first who had entered stood a short, almond-eyed woman with olive skin, her petite frame bound tight in a glossy red dress, black hair cut short so that it formed a dark triangular skirt round her head to just below her earlobes which accentuated her thin neck while adding more point to her chin, longer in front than back.

Through blurry flashes of recall Banzu remembered her from before and grieving at sight of Jericho's ring. *Aggie.*

The second a dark-skinned woman taller than the first by nearly three heads and possessing a more regal set to her straight shoulders and upraised chin, her long kinky black hair worked up into a bushy bun tied at the back of her head with two thin stabs of silver keeping it in dutiful place, her deep purple dress a perfect match for the strong violets of her stern eyes. She wore the natural countenance of one used to staring down others through both height and status. Thin leather straps wound round the torsos of both these women as a match for Shandra's own, indicating the leather harnesses holding the twin fanged dachras strapped to their backs.

Spellbinders. Three of them.

Oh gods.

Banzu swallowed hard, the kohatheen locked round his neck imparting the false illusion of tightening.

Shandra stepped while turning aside. "Welcome, Head Mistress," she said to the taller bun-haired woman while bowing her head so that her chin touched her impressive bosom. Then to the other, "Mistress Agatha." She bowed her head again, the motion slighter, a clear display of the difference in rank between the two women.

A waft of chatter from the hallway beyond swept into the room from behind the fistian officer who maintained his unyielding gaze on the chair-bound Soothsayer, dark eyes glittering over a hawk nose and an iron-gray goatee which looked as though filed to point. The bustling sounds outside earned the Head Mistress's dark brow furrowed with slight irritation on her otherwise cool mask.

"Jacob." Her tone level though nonetheless commanding, she cracked her natural stern whip of voice without effort, though she bothered no glance behind at the noise or the soldier named, her gaze unbroken upon Banzu before her.

Jacob thinned dark scrutiny at Banzu between the two women for a lingering moment, left hand toying at the pommel of the sword sheathed at his right hipwing, considering its pull over obeying the Head Mistress's command. Then he turned and walked out from the room without word while shutting the door behind him, silencing the chatter of those gathered outside in the hallway beyond.

The Head Mistress walked to standing in front Banzu, a natural poise in her long and confident strides. She glanced from his eyes to his groin and back then raised her chin and issued the deliberate clearing of her throat.

Shandra moved into action, picking up the black wet hood from the floor then spreading it over Banzu's lap. She applied it a playful little pat, smirking, before removing back.

The Head Mistress frowned down over him, scolding violets holding his upturned gaze. The dark turning of her lips and, without looking away, she ordered, "Chairs."

Shandra removed the two chairs slotted beneath the table, dragged them across the room and set them side by side a few safe spans out in front of Banzu, facing him. She repositioned behind them, filling the middle space, while Head Mistress Gwendora Pearce and Mistress Agatha dar'Shuwin sat facing him, both interlacing their fingers while nestling their interwoven hands upon their laps as if some practiced synchronized ritual.

Agatha, sitting left of the Head Mistress, regarded him with wide violet eyes of sad wonder. But the Head Mistress . . . her discerning eyes thinned into suspicious slits on a hard though otherwise unreadable slate of face.

Unsure where to begin or even how, Banzu started with their names, proving recognition as told through Jericho. "Gwen," he said, more curt than he'd meant, then shifted his gaze to the prettier and less intimidating woman by comparison while enduring a touch of guilty sadness gripping his heart. In a much softer tone that stole across his face he said, "Aggie." A wan smile creased his lips at seeing for the first time his uncle's secret wife.

"You will address the Head Mistress by her proper title, Soothslayer," Shandra said, scowling, admonishing eyes afire. She began stepping between her two seated superiors, the bulk of her advance dominating every inch of space, her beefy hands shooting up behind her back in threat of pulling her dachra fangs into punishing abuse.

But the Head Mistress presented her left arm out in barring gesture, bent at the elbow with hand upraised, arresting the bull woman's forward bid.

"It's okay," she said, without breaking eye contact from Banzu. "I'll allow him that considering the stubborn, troublesome, rebellious fool who raised him."

She lowered her barring arm into the nest of her lap and waited in what passed for her a comfortable silence while Shandra withdrew to her guarding position, quiet save for the cracking of her big knuckles which invited twitches of Aggie's brow though left Gwendora's schooled mask unmoved.

"You are lucky you didn't wake chained to the wall with the lash scoring your back." Gwendora paused, considering all of him at silent length, while beside her Agatha shifted in her chair chaffing with impatience. "You are the last Soothsayer," Gwendora continued. "Otherwise the Builder's Veil would not have lifted, so say the scriptures. Though it remains to be seen if you have been cleansed of the Nameless One's curse or consumed by it."

Banzu rolled his eyes and sighed. *This again*? "Do I look turned to you?"

Gwendora exhaled through unchanging expression. "No. But you do look angry enough to—"

"I was attacked!" Straining through kohatheen lethargy, he tested his taut rope bonds again by attempting to erupt into standing so that his chair rocked in place, rattling the floor. "Now I'm tied to this godsdamned chair and—" He clipped his words short, closed his eyes and drew in a deep nostril inhale while seeking calm. When he opened his eyes, he began again in a softer tone—with effort. "I was attacked." He gestured with the flick of his eyes between the two women at Shandra who shifted her feet while glaring at him, an angry boulder wanting only to roll forth and crush. "Just like I told her."

"Safeguards," Gwendora said. "The scriptures say the last Soothsayer will cause the Veilfall, but they do not indicate whether he will be cleansed or consumed. That"—and here she sighed, contending with the weight of an old burden still—"is the problem with prophecies. They are forked as lightning, and many branching paths can be chosen over their course, though there are primary channels that define their main route. Prophecies work in Ifs and Whens."

She threw a disapproving glance left at Aggie, who shifted forward by inches and opened her mouth to speak, and the gesture proved enough to stifle any words from the diminutive woman settling back in her chair.

"*If* you had come here consumed," Gwendora continued, "and *if* you had slaughtered us all, and *if* you retrieved the necessary Essence, and *if* you used it to find then use the Godstone—" She paused, raised her hands in a flourish of clearing the air between them of some foul stench. "That's a lot of Ifs, and though before you arrived here all of them were possible, now that you're here we must decipher which branches have closed and which have not. And which new ones have opened. You haven't slaughtered us all. Yet. So let's have a closer look about your having turned to the bloodlust or not."

"He didn't know about the safeguards," Aggie said, speaking up at last while shedding the first skin of the subordinate nature swaddling her petite frame. "We didn't even know he was here until it was too late."

Frowning, Gwendora opened her mouth then closed it, nodded.

Aggie leaned forward again and by inches, chair creaking, and locked sorrowful eyes with Banzu. "Jericho." She breathed the name out in a low voice wavered with strain. "What happened to Jericho?" She leaned closer still, and there glistened a knowing pain in her pleading eyes. "Please . . ."

Banzu gazed at the sad visage of his dead uncle's wife a silent length, wondering how best to explain it all. He considered telling her the gruesome details of Jericho's turning to the bloodlust then death so they knew every word of it for true. But within her staring despair shimmered an undying gleam of hope, and he recognized that pain of loss just as he knew she deserved an answer, just not the grisly details about the man she once and clearly still loved.

Jericho had saved him, raised and trained him, and Aggie played a vital part in Jericho's escape as a Soothsayer servitor from the Academy's wants for hunting down and killing all Soothsayers to the last in their centuries-long bid for ending the Nameless One's bloodlust curse through elimination. She'd stolen the magic boots of blinding speed from one of the Builder's towers for Jericho who used them to steal Banzu away before his capture, and for it she paid her toll through title and station stripped away to the humbled woman sitting before him.

She's lost almost as much I have. No, more. Gods, where do I even begin?

"Yes," Gwendora said, her tone cold by comparison, "what happened to Jericho?"

Banzu drew in deep, swallowed hard—guilt took a toll on every man's throat—then explained his tale in a spill of words, realizing halfway through how ridiculous it sounded of him returning from a future undone through his Source-fueled re-beginning and Jericho's death so that none of them remembered anything about that future's erasure. But he spilled the information out regardless, all but the lusty bits shared with Melora before her pushing trickery, though he did touch upon his affections for her and her once-affections for him he hoped to restore.

". . . and then I *chose* to come here to retrieve the Essence of the First Enosh said I needed to find the Godstone," he finished, emphasizing the word 'chose' by over-rounding his mouth as he spoke it perhaps a bit too harsh. But he wanted to get his point across without argument. "Where I was *attacked*." He also emphasize 'attacked' for good measure, and with all the harshness he could muster, wanting to punctuate that important point clear if nothing else.

"Safeguards," Gwendora said, correcting him, her only emphasis an arching of her dark eyebrows.

"A deathtrap is more like it," he grumbled.

A dismissive flick of her wrist. "Call it what you will."

"So he is dead." This a trembling whisper from Aggie who slumped in her chair, staring down while fidgeting with the silvery ring she wore round her left ringfinger, twisting it back and forth as though it might unlock some mystery if only she turned it the appropriate amount and clicked those forgotten tumblers into proper place.

"None of that can be proven," Gwendora said, glancing at Aggie who spared no look up from the entrancement of her twisting ring.

"Then how do you explain me?" Banzu looked at Gwendora with no whit of softness in his eyes. "Or the Veilfall? Or—"

"That's not what I meant." Gwendora said, her voice a scolding interruption, her dark mask turning darker still. "For all we know you murdered him in cold blood."

"What?" He grit his teeth and strained against the coarse rope bonds, the imposed lassitude of his kohatheen dulling to his spiking ire, wanting nothing more than to lunge forth and choke her godsdamned head off for the blatant accusation. "Then how would I know you planned on trading his life for mine? That you wanted him to kill the Khan in trade for my freedom?" Leaning forward only so much as the rope bonds allowed, he tested them further while locking his challenging glare with Gwendora's unwavering stare. "How you used me as bait to trick him into coming back here so he could deal with Hannibal Khan for you while getting himself killed in the process?" He sat back and huffed out a terse breath, disgusted to the last. "Your letter of pardon. Two birds with one stone. Kill the Khan while ending the curse. You remember that? Huh? Do you?"

Melora burned the letter meant for Jericho during Banzu's absence out gathering firewood. But he remembered too well his uncle's revelation of it from their time before his re-beginning, the words and the memory of Jericho's bloodlust return branded into his brain.

"I—" Gwendora paused and pursed her lips. A hint of surprise flittered over her features, there then gone. "True."

"Untie me." A flat command.

Silence.

He looked from Gwendora to Aggie to Gwendora. "Please?" he asked in softer voice. "I'm not here to hurt anyone. Except for the Khan."

Gwendora sighed and shook her head.

Aggie continued staring down while fiddling with her ring.

Behind and between them Shandra glared while chewing rocks, her beefy arms crossed.

Banzu rolled his eyes at the Head Mistress. "You have a kohatheen locked around my godsdamned neck anyways. What do you need me tied to a chair for?" Not waiting for response, he squirmed his bonds again, pain biting into his wrists and ankles, while yelling, "Untie me, godsdammit!"

Frowning, Gwendora waited his outburst finished. "Are you done yet?"

Banzu mean-mugged her. "No."

She stared at him overlong.

He huffed, relaxing in all but his eyes. "Yes."

"Good. And it's rather simple." She leaned forward and met the heat in his focal glare by unflinching inches. "The scriptures are explicit on two things about my duty as Head Mistress. Guide the Soothsavior if he's cleansed the bloodlust, or kill the Soothslayer if he's consumed by it. You are the last, which means eliminating you eliminates the curse."

He tensed, panic flushing. He glanced at Aggie, a plea edging his throat—but she offered nothing, locked in stare with her ring, shrouded in silent mourning.

Gwendora continued. "My task at hand is to figure out which of those has come invading my Academy. Either is able to retrieve the Essence and—"

"Not without the keyrings," Banzu said, touching upon another of Enosh's words. "They're needed to unlock the Essence, and Enosh said only you have them."

Gwendora sat back, chair creaking, and answered him a reluctant nod. "True."

He frowned. *She's testing me. That's what this is. I've been on trial since she came in. Judge, jury, and executioner all rolled into one.* So he gave blatant honesty a try. "Look. I don't care about the Godstone. And I certainly don't care about using it to kill anyone. I'm here to kill the Khan. Isn't that what you want?"

"Yes." Gwendora held pause. "And no."

She stood, her sheer height making of her a tower, turned and paced the room through slow strides, the bottom of her dress stealing whispers across the floor.

All the while Aggie, breaking from her introspection and looking up, stared at Banzu in silent regard, lips pressed tight and holding back a flood of words dammed behind her mouth.

"There are bigger things at play now, Banzu," Gwendora continued, "and your personal vendetta is not among them. When you killed Jericho and cleaned the bloodlust, you set into motion the possibility of another Thousand Years War by triggering the Veilfall. No. Not just the possibility but the inevitability of it."

"So you believe me then," he said, watching her pace.

"Of course I do," she said in such a snapping tone it suggested believing otherwise expected water dry and clouds made of dirt. "Think. You would be dead already if it were otherwise."

"Then untie me." He exhaled a frustrated sigh, glanced at Aggie. "Please?"

Head Mistress Gwendora Pearce continued as if uninterrupted.

"The world has already fallen into the beginnings of chaos since the Veilfall. Husbands leaving their wives, mothers their children. Soldiers abandoning their stations. Aizakai forsaking their oaths and fleeing the Academy. Turmoil, Banzu. A great many people are leaving behind their lives to seek out the Godstone and gain access to its apotheosis now that they can remember its existence again. A lot of innocent people will be killed, battles fought, wars waged, and all of it culminating into another Thousand Years War before it is done. The Godstone must be found before its foul corruption destroys this world as it almost did before. If it hasn't been found already."

There, across the room, she stopped in both pacing and speech, her turned back arching in regal presentation of herself to the audience of wall in front of her.

"I am Head Mistress. It is my sworn duty above all else to guide the savior-slayer reborn into finding the Godstone to destroy it before it can destroy the world. As the last Soothsayer, you are bound to your destined duty to abide my commands. So say the scriptures—"

"I don't care about your friggin scriptures," Banzu said through gritted teeth, his blood flushing hot and angry at the prospect of forced Academy servitude, the kohatheen he wore proof of that enslavement already, same as done to his uncle. He'd promised Melora to submit to the Head Mistress, and learned much of the requirement from Enosh in the Luna Nexus, but now that he was here and so close to Hannibal Khan . . . "And I don't care about your stupid Godstone. All I want to do is kill the Khan!"

Gwendora spun round, her face a stern mask of coolness. "And therein lies the problem. Hannibal Khan is secondary now. Perhaps even less so, considering the unholy abomination raised by the Enclave. Melora should have explained that to you already. Whatever cruel designs the Khan held on procuring the Book of Towers to retrieve the rest of the Dominator's Armor has fallen by the wayside for the Godstone, most assuredly. Already his followers are breaking away to seek out the Godstone for themselves. The greed of men knows no bounds. And neither does their lust for power." She tightened her eyes, her voice. "Or revenge."

Banzu grimaced against the rubbing chafes twisting his wrists and ankles imposed on his skin, testing his bonds again, and stopped the futile struggle. "So you're just going to leave him be?"

Gwendora nodded. "The Book of Towers contains the secrets of all the Builder's towers along with valuable knowledge of the past. Among other things. Hannibal Khan already procured the gauntlets through the Enclave, and the book contains the locations of the rest of the Dominator's Armor. It also contains pertinent information on the Veilfall and the Godstone. The Veil may have wiped the world of most of the memories of the Thousand Years War, but it was all written within the Book of Towers by First Mistress Llewellyn Rular. And only I have possession of the book. It is my sacred duty as Head Mistress to protect it. And you will either submit to your duty and help me, or you will be"—a pause, a search for the proper term—"*removed* from the situation." A glance at Shandra who smiled. "Permanently."

"Murder," he said, his dark mood fouling blacker.

"Caution," Gwendora said. "And no. I am far from done with you."

He blew out his cheeks, relaxing as best he could while tied naked to a chair. "Then what do you want with me?"

Gwendora's stern eyes twinkled with a glint of hope while her voice softened. "I want you to be as the gods intended, Banzu. You reacted . . . poorly to the safeguards, but that can be overlooked given the circumstances. What I need from you is to understand why you are really here. You are destined to be here. And it's no longer for the Khan."

She approached him in gliding strides, dress swishing round her long legs, and stood before him in towering loom though bent at the hips to better meet his eyes. "Please, Banzu. I cannot force you, so I'm asking you. Help me save the world. Help me prevent another Thousand Years War. Help us all."

He stared up at her a silent length while tumblers clicked into place, and smiled. "You need me."

Gwendora's lips twisted into a reluctant frown. She straightened stiff. "Yes. But more importantly the world needs you."

"So you won't kill me," he said, "but you won't let me go either."

"I'm sorry, but I have no other choice. And neither do you."

He flared then thinned his eyes. "We all have a choice." Then snapped his gaze forward and stewed in silence, gnawing on her proposal of no choice at all, the voice of his dead uncle as well the thousand others in his head quiet so that he considered their absence an effect of the kohatheen. Reflections of Melora and her apologizing shove into the well flittered through his mind. *I'm tasting the carrot again.* He locked eyes with the Head Mistress and braced for feeling the stick. "And Hannibal Khan?"

"The Godstone takes precedence above all else," she said, leaving no room for further argument. "Even him." A pause, the tensing disgust of her scrunching face. "Even the necromaster he raised in Junes matters little to the Godstone. Though Dethkore does provide us a sense of urgency considering his own ties to the Godstone." Another pause, followed by a disparaging wrench on her lowered tone. "Hannibal is not the only Khan the Enclave has imposed its influence upon. He is but the first of many."

But Banzu only half heard her, fading lost within the turmoil of his thoughts. Bitter contempt at sharing the same Academy servitor fate as his uncle writhed his guts. He tipped a sideways-leaning glance past the Head Mistress at Aggie, but she offered him nothing more than a blank stare, her almond-shaped violets glistening wounds over the confirmation of her dead husband sitting right in front of her. And then there was Melora, here in spirit if not in body. At least in his mind he could still see her, and remember her last words spoken before the push. He wanted to rejoin her something fierce.

"Fine," he said, looking up at Gwendora. "I'll do it." *For her. Not that they're giving me any friggin choice.* "But I want two things. Melora, and the Khan's head." He leaned aside again, chair creaking, gazing beyond the Head Mistress and met Aggie's stare. "That bastard's going to pay for what he did." *For what he made me do.* "I promise."

Aggie replied nothing, but there played a silent exchange between them, the sad sheen of her eyes brightening with a touch of heat, the corners of her mouth twitching through hints of a bridled smile. Until she averted her gaze while schooling the promise of her approving smile away.

"You're in no position to make demands," Gwendora said.

"Oh yeah?" He struck her with a cocksure smirk. "Then kill me."

Gwendora opened her mouth then closed it with a click of teeth. She measured him up and down through molten violet glare, stretching the silence in reticent negotiation, calculating eyes thinning into cunning estimation.

"I cannot promise you the second," she said. "At least not immediately. Hannibal Khan must be taken alive to secure the gauntlets and provide us a link to the Enclave's plans. As to the first . . . Melora will return in due time. I will send out scouts for her return."

"No." *She wants the Khan alive?* "No!" He clenched his teeth and strained against his bonds while struggling through his kohatheen's irritating lassitude turning his motions sluggish with false exhaustion. Until a darker, more deceptive part of his mind folded over his flaring animus, cooling its flushing heat into a cold reservoir of hate. *Killing the Khan will come later, when the opportunity presents itself. For now I have to play their manipulative game.*

"I already know all about Caldera Pass," he said in smoother tone.

In their time before his re-beginning, Melora explained part of her duties in delivering Jericho was to negotiate reopening Caldera Pass connecting western Ascadia to eastern Thurandy, the only viable trade route through the Calderos Mountains closed for fifteen years. Though negotiate proved a soft term for Jericho's more probable killing of King-General Garnihan if the gladiator usurper of the Iron Crown and Throne of Tyr refused to relent on the infamous bloodfeud between Tyr and Bloom and reopen Caldera Pass.

"No one you send will make it through to her, and she can't come through it herself." *Godsdamn her. Why'd she have to go and shove me into the well? Now were on opposite sides of the godsdamned Calderos Mountains!*

"Part of her duties in returning with Jericho"—Gwendora paused, corrected herself—"with the savior-slayer reborn was to convince Garnihan to—"

"I already know," he interrupted while chastising himself for succumbing so easily to Melora's womanly charms in the tower. "And now that she's alone it will be all the harder for her to get back here. Forget the Khan. I want her back. We were going to be Paired, and now she's all alone." Again he chastised himself, this for leaving her alone within the tower surrounded by angry bandits awaiting her outside—if she hadn't already tried fighting her way out or they swarmed inside after the tower's magical wards faded. "She's what matters most anyhow. I need to know she's safe or no deal."

At that Shandra rumbled a deliberate clearing of her throat, drawing Gwendora's turning attentions. "Head Mistress, you should tell him about *our* Pairing." She emphasized the word while shooting Banzu a heated glare punctuated by a wry smile. "He's obviously fixated on the wrong Spellbinder."

Banzu flinched at Shandra's slap of words and the possessive glean in her eyes. *Oh no.* "Uhm." His guts clenched, face slumping. *Gods, no. She can't possibly mean . . .* "What?"

CHAPTER THIRTY-THREE

Confused, Banzu's apprehensive gaze darted from Shandra to Head Mistress to Aggie to Head Mistress. "What?" he asked again, hoping to gods he'd misheard Shandra's insinuation while fearing it for true. "*What?*"

Head Mistress Gwendora Pearce nodded affirmation. "Shandra is your new Spellbinder," she said in authoritative tone brooking no argument. "You will be Paired with her."

Banzu's guts plunged. "Wait. What? No!" Startled into a forward lean, testing the strength of his coarse rope bonds tying his wrists to armrests by wiggling in his creaking chair, he scanned their faces but saw no honest jest to the cruel joke played upon him. He settled back, surrendering limp to his kohatheen's lethargic imposition weighing false heaviness through his body, and considered for all of about three seconds, then replied a defiant shake of his head. "No. Then kill me now. Because I won't be Paired with anyone but Melora."

"She doesn't even remember you!" Shandra's shout the booming rumble of a rockslide, her face twisted ugly, chubby cheeks flushing red with bridled strain. "You said as much yourself, Soothslayer. Head Mistress—"

"Hush!" Gwendora whip-cracked her voice.

And Shandra clipped silent at once, her outrage at Banzu's blatant refusal flushing her wide forehead and thick neck a deep shade of red in match to her cheeks, the dark wine of her infuriated blood pooling just beneath the surface of her creamy skin.

Gwendora spared her a cursory glance before continuing. "Melora's duty was to retrieve the last Soothsayer, Banzu, not be Paired with him. That position belongs to Spellbinder Shandra. She has spent her entire life training in preparation for your arrival."

"No," he said, cold, exact, resolute. "I'll give over on the Khan." A slight pause, a mental note: *For now.* "I'll even help you deal with that godsdamned Godstone. But I won't budge on this. It's Melora and no one else." Without her, the world could crumble to dust for all he cared. He shifted his unyielding gaze to Shandra who worked her square jaw in grumbling chews, at Aggie who stared at him overlong while her fiddling hands continued idle twists of her ring, then back to the Head Mistress. "She's the only reason why I'm even here. I made her a promise and I intend on keeping it."

Promises . . . of those I've made several I've yet to keep. Thoughts folded inward on Melora then, she alone and surrounded by Bartholomew's marauders while inside a Builder's tower its protective magical wards dispelled. *If only I'd killed them all.*

"Bastards," he muttered. He'd come this far. For her. And these women had no idea how far he'd *not* gone, also because of her, holding back from slaughter during his battle against the aizakai and Soothsayer stonemen effigies. He noticed then the Head Mistress had taken a cautious step backwards despite his tied restriction to the chair and kohatheen locked round his neck, and realized how challenging his burning glare upon her. He leveled it past her at Shandra.

"The only reason you're even still alive is because of Melora," he said. "You and all your stupid mages who attacked me. I could've killed you all." He gripped wooden armrests and squeezed them in lieu of Shandra's fat neck, his tone descending into a guttural growl pushed through clenched teeth. "Maybe I should've."

Gwendora removed another step.

"Banzu, no," Aggie said while shifting tensed in her chair, a touch of fear and concern betraying her eyes, her voice.

Fuming, Shandra's meaty fists strangling the air at her sides, her red face atremble with bridled fury, she renewed her ranting protest by throwing her hands up behind her broad back while blistering the air with curses. She charged forward in the beginnings of a dachra-pulling rush between the two chairs.

But stopped short by the Head Mistress turning on the brawny woman and staring her down, hands fisting hips in challenge, unmoving as an ancient rooted oak. The two women bickered back and forth for the span of a dozen heartbeats.

While Aggie leaned forward with scolding fire in her eyes. She snapped her fingers, capturing Banzu's glare, then pointed an admonishing finger at him and mouthed the word *No.* And there stared into his relenting gaze, probing his unvoiced depths where lived deeper emotions.

Gwendora cooled Shandra's flared temper by reminding her with whom she dared argue punctuated by a long list of punishments.

Shandra bowed her head in acquiescent apology, then mean-mugged Banzu when she withdrew to standing farther back beside the door where she crossed her arms beneath her ample breasts and glared at the world and everyone in it.

Gwendora spun round and fixed Banzu a piercing glare bleeding irritation across her face. And suffered another interruption soon as her lips parted for the chastising lecture behind them.

"He loves her," Aggie said without breaking her forward assessment, her words soft yet powerful, and knowing. "Don't you?"

Banzu flinched. "I—" *I do, yes.*

But he hesitated, unsure of revealing the true nature of his deeper feelings for Melora to these manipulative women despite Aggie's personal ties to Jericho and through him to Banzu. He'd explained much of their future time together though spared the intimate details of their budding relationship before his re-beginning erased its blooming glory from his heart, let alone their sexing before her pushing trickery. His love for her leveraged his willingness to guard it as a precious secret that if shared might make of it a tainted tool used against him.

And yet . . . and yet: *Aggie knows. I never spoke it, but she knows as if she pulled it right from my heart.*

"She said we'd be Paired." He spoke in an almost-whisper meant more for himself but which spilled forth loud enough for all to hear.

"Oh yeah," Shandra said in sarcastic grumble. "In the future no one but you can remember."

But Banzu only half heard the scorned woman's jeer, and the Head Mistress commanding her hushed again, his gaze ensnared by the probing scrutiny of Aggie's closer face looming less than two handspans from his own. He wanted to turn away but could not break his gaze from those discerning violet pools assessing him on a private level while making of them the only two in the room, drawing him deeper into the measure of her focal assessment by the tugging threads of bare honesty in one who held true understanding for life's most precious gift gazing at him through years of wondering pain only compounded by having so recently learned her own love stolen from her.

Banzu winced to the wrenching grind of his aching heart. He'd only just gotten Melora back into his life before losing her again, but at least she still lived and there existed the possibility of seeing her again.

But Aggie . . . *poor Aggie. She'll never see Jericho again. She'll never hear his voice or hold him or kiss him or love him again. I did that to her. I stole the option from her forever. Why she hasn't tried killing me yet I don't know. I if were her and Jericho Melora I'd of slit my throat soon as I came in.*

"Yes," he whispered, voicing his heart's confession, Aggie's pensive stare pulling the words from his throat. He drew in a nostril breath and in a firmer voice with chest puffed proud he added, "I love her."

Shandra scoffed a mirthless chuckle.

"Oh gods." Gwendora's voice quiet, she bowed her head, shaking it while groaning and palming her face. "Oh dear gods."

Unfinished with her probing revelations, Aggie leaned forward by inches, palming her thighs, her profound gaze viewing more into him than at him, wading through his mysteries, tugging upon their threads while scrutinizing their unraveling secrets, her voice a confident recital when next she spoke.

"You returned for her, didn't you? That's what this is really all about. Cleansing the bloodlust was only a side effect to bringing Melora back." Aggie paused, nodded, whispered, "Of course."

"How do you know . . ." he began though trailed away unfinished. She'd glimpsed into the private depths of his soul, piecing together parts of him along with his tale the others had not, and she worked the puzzle of him still.

Gwendora fetched a long sigh. "Nothing is ever easy, is it?" She lowered her palming hand from face and raised her head, studied him in silence while calculations danced behind her cunning stare.

Shandra grunted and grumbled while trying her best at glaring murder past the Head Mistress in a sideways lean, staying her spot though shifting her feet, a boulder teetering upon the verge of crashing downhill from the slightest nudge.

The barest of smiles stole across Aggie's lips, there then gone, while she settled back in her chair and watched him.

"Melora's the only reason why I'm even here," Banzu said. He gazed up at Gwendora. "If not for her—"

"Does she love you?" Gwendora asked.

"What?"

"Does *she* love *you*?" she repeated, curt and sharp while over-mouthing the words for emphasis, dark brow furrowing.

"Uhm, well, I . . ." Banzu trailed away, frowning, unsure if he was more upset that he didn't immediately answer or that he didn't immediately know. His re-beginning reset everything except Jericho's death, and that included Melora's memories of and feelings for him from the future timeline erased in all but his own private reflection. *We had sex, but . . . but was it just another part of her plan to trick me here without her? Part and parcel of fulfilling her duty?*

He glanced away scowling, hating himself for even considering such a tactic from her, and hating the Head Mistress more for putting the treacherous thought into his head as a real possibility.

"I know she does," he said, the hope he clung to in his fractured heart answering for him. *She has to. After us together in the tower how could she not?*

But Gwendora proved a relentless inquisitor. "How?"

Banzu's head snapped forward. "What?"

She fisted her hips in challenging pose. "How?"

He frowned up at her. "I just know, okay? I just needed to . . . make her remember."

Gwendora frowned. "You cannot make someone love you."

He flinched at the slap of words, anger flaring, body tensing. He winced while squirming his arms and legs against his taut rope bonds chafing his skin raw. "That's not what I meant and you know it. I'm not trying to make her do anything—"

But there he stopped, for the Head Mistress, after a terse huff and the blatant roll of her eyes, turned him her back.

"He's infatuated with her," she said to Aggie with no small amount of disappointment bleeding into her tone. "Like some rutting stag." She sighed, the depths of which lifted then dropped her shoulders by inches, and shook her head. "She's too pretty. I knew we should've sent—" But there she clipped short while glancing at Shandra who tightened her smoldering glare into a tempered line of violet heat though said nothing.

"We didn't know it would be him returning, Gwen," Aggie said, sitting straighter, her voice gaining authoritative strength on par with Gwendora's as she spoke, her demure airs evaporating so that Banzu questioned whether it existed at all. "Melora's void-aura is ten times that of any Spellbinder here, and Shandra has never even stepped foot outside of Fist." She waved a hand between them in dismissive gesture. "We made the right choice. He's here now. If he wants to be Paired with Melora then I say let them."

She stole a glance at Banzu, then shifted a lean toward Gwendora who bent forward at the hips, just two dear old friends talking amongst themselves, after Aggie waved her closer.

"Look at him, Gwen. That's not just infatuation. You've heard what he's said. How he speaks of her." Aggie leaned aside and fetched Banzu a smile. "He's just like my Jericho, all heart on his sleeve."

But her smile fled and her face slumped, a part of her wounded spirit escaping through Jericho's naming, leaving her incomplete. She settled back in her chair, petite shoulders hunched, and stared down at her ring she twisted round her finger in contemplative study as she lapsed into sullen silence.

Gwendora expelled a nasal huff, straightened and turned round, tightened her eyes and mouth into sharp cuts of scrutiny. She said nothing, though she shook her head while shaving away the prospects of Banzu being Paired with anyone but Shandra with a mental razor of disapproval.

He locked gazes with Gwendora, his mood turning fouler, brazen and threatening despite his kohatheen's incessant lassitude attempting to tame it. *I may be tied up at their mercy, but I won't budge on this, no way no how. Melora's mine and I'm hers and that's that. You can take my Pairing with Shandra and shove it up your bung!* But he put no voice behind the declaration no matter how strong it edged his lips.

Instead he said, "Melora's the only reason why any of you are still alive. You have no idea what I've been through. And no idea what I'll go through to get her back." He shifted his unyielding pierce of gaze between Gwendora and Aggie at Shandra's perpetual scowl. "No, she doesn't remember me. But I remember her. And I'm not about to abandon her. Not for anything or anyone." Back to Gwendora, but he hesitated, pushing against some inner emotional wall of resistance . . . that crumbled round his instigative shove. "Even the Khan."

Aggie looked up from the thoughtful toying of her ring and flashed him a satisfied smile lasting all of three seconds before she schooled it away and shifted her brighter eyes to Gwendora. "We can untie him now. There's no danger here, just a young man in love." She appraised him in a daze of low-toned reverie. "My Jericho used to give me that same look. He won't budge, Gwen. Not on this. You know I'm right."

Behind her Shandra's arms swooped down where pounded the meat of her fists upon the wall behind her.

Gwendora half turned and shot Shandra an admonishing glare. "No," she said to Aggie, her rebuttal stern. "He remains tied until matters are settled."

Aggie nodded at the clear repositioning of the Head Mistress's authority over her. But she stood up regardless and pulled Gwendora aside by the crook of an elbow for a more private conversation halfway across the room near the bed, their backs turned. Though their voices carried given the limited space of the room.

"You've heard the things he's done," Aggie said, "and what he's been through already. We both know what he could've done here but didn't. There's goodness in him, Gwen. He wouldn't be here otherwise." A pausing peek at Banzu over her shoulder. "Melora's collared him without a kohatheen."

Gwendora huffed a terse breath and shook her head. "She tricked him here is all. He seems sane enough, but he could be hiding a broken mind." She threw Banzu a suspicious glance. "And all that nonsense about returning from the future . . . my gods, Agatha. They can slow time but they can't reverse it. That hasn't happened since—"

"Since Simus Junes," Aggie finished for her.

Gwendora stiffened straight. "Yes."

Aggie threw Banzu another over the shoulder glance. "Does it really matter? All these years and he's finally here. And he's willing to help if we relent on this one minor issue." She gripped the Head Mistress by the arm and squeezed. "This is what we've been waiting for. He's the savior-slayer reborn. Or he will be once he survives the—"

"He's supposed to be Paired with me!" Shandra shoved off the wall and moved toward her Spellbinder superiors in an attempt at intruding into their little huddle of conversation. But she stopped short at the turning brunt of both women's admonishing glares. Shandra opened her mouth for feisty protest—then closed it in a snapping huff of teeth at the disapproving arch of her Head Mistress's challenging stare accompanied by Aggie's jabbing pointer warding her back to place. Shandra withdrew to her spot of wall beside the door, crossed her beefy arms and smoldered Banzu with her burning glare while her square jaw worked through chews of unvoiced curses.

"We must prevent another Thousand Years War," Aggie continued, tipping the scales of command in her favor. "And the only sure way of it is sitting right there. We've tried ending the curse without him and look what it got us. He's not what we expected, but he's here and he's willing."

"And he's caused nothing but trouble since he arrived," Gwendora said in risen tone. "You've seen the infirmary."

"He could've done worse," Aggie said. "Much worse. You know that. We both do."

Banzu sighed while rolling his eyes. "I can hear you, you know."

Both women glanced in turn then returned to conversation, ignoring him.

"Once he passes the testing," Aggie said, "we can find the Godstone and finally put an end to it all."

"*If*," Gwendora said, correcting her while emphasizing the word. "*If* he passes the testing."

"Testing?" Banzu shifted. "What testing?"

But they ignored him.

Shandra smirked at the privy of some private joke, but Banzu refused to ask that brute of a woman anything. Instead he listened while swallowing the annoyance at being the subject of a conversation they disallowed him any part of.

"There's still so much to consider," Gwendora said.

"And little time for doing it," Aggie said. "The longer we wait, the better the chances of others finding it." She raised a hand between them and ticked off her fingers. "Everyone remembers now, and we don't even know where it has fallen yet. The Enclave has resurrected the necromaster despite our best efforts. All communications from our contacts in Junes have been silenced since the Veilfall. And the Enclave will hunt for the Godstone as surely as they seek to reassemble the Dominator's Armor."

"The Enclave will forego the Armor now that the Godstone has fallen," Gwendora said, crossing her arms. "We have that at least."

To which Aggie shook her head. "Do you really think their Khan is fool enough to trade one power for another when he already possesses the gauntlets? A bird in the hand, Gwen."

"You know how the Enclave operates, Agatha. The moment he disputes their plans they'll just kill him then replace him with another power-hungry vessel. Anyone can wear the Armor."

"Just as anyone can wield the Godstone. Regardless, time is now our greatest enemy. Stop being so stubborn."

Frowning, Gwendora raised a hand between them and pointed emphasizing jabs at Aggie. "Don't call me stubborn."

Aggie smirked and swatted the Head Mistress's hand away from her face. "You know I'm right on this."

The Head Mistress fisted her hips and held contemplative pause, long and silent and which filled the room in billowing thicks of tension. She straightened taller than Aggie by almost three heads, set her shoulders back with head high and chin up, and nodded. She strode past a turning Aggie and stood in front of Banzu, her towering figure imposing, her crisp violet eyes sharp with authority, her voice commanding when next she spoke.

"You will remain here, *in this room*," she said, her eyes flaring with emphasis. "That is nonnegotiable. Tomorrow we will begin, after you've had more time to recover."

Banzu made to speak—but she talked right over him.

"We will try to find Melora while hunting for the Godstone. And no more dispute about Hannibal Khan. Our focus now is the Godstone. After which we will deal with the Khans."

"Khans?" Banzu asked, the plural of the title striking him odd.

She extrapolated nothing but for the scrutiny of a lingering pause she ended with the stern wag of one long admonishing finger jabbing at his face. "But I'm warning you, Banzu. If you step a single toe out of line or worse attempt an escape, so help me gods I will order every last aizakai and soldier in my Academy to hunt you down and kill you." The pausing flare of her scolding eyes. "Not capture you. *Kill you.* What takes place here is of the utmost importance. If you try to run like your uncle"—she curled her pointing finger into making a tight fist and shook it while strangling every ounce of punctuation from her threat—"you won't make it far. And you won't live to regret it."

Banzu nodded, having no plans for any escape. Not yet at least. "What testing?"

"Later," she said, dismissing his query with the flick of her wrist. "For now you must agree to my terms. Swear it." She crossed her arms, face tensing round shrewd eyes thinning sharp. "Swear it on your life."

"And Melora?" he asked.

Gwendora huffed while rolling her eyes. "We will travel to Bloom and I will negotiate the reopening of Caldera Pass into Tyr myself. *If* you agree to my terms. *And* while we hunt for the Godstone. *And if* Melora accepts"—a grumbling grunt from Shandra behind her—"then I'll allow the two of you Paired. But the Godstone takes precedence above all else. Now swear it." A pause so brief it might not have occurred, the tightening of her full lips so that her mouth became nothing more than a sharp cut. "Or so help me gods I'll have you strung up by your balls and—"

"Gwen!" Aggie said, cutting the Head Mistress short. "That's enough."

Gwendora glanced her a silent scowl though said no more while she fixed her focal stare on Banzu and waited.

He considered his options in silent debate, gaze wandering the room. Shandra's face flashed such an intense red that her head looked an overripe melon about to burst from her shoulders, but she said nothing, just stood there glaring at him and the Head Mistress both through smoldering violet scorn.

"Please, Banzu," Aggie said, approaching beside Gwendora. The top of her head ended inches above the Head Mistress's right elbow, yet the athletic tautness of her petite frame impressed upon her a taller stature of authority. The bright life in her appraising gaze shined stronger now, more resolute. "Don't let Jericho's death be in vain. You were meant for more than killing Hannibal Khan, and this is it." A pausing smile. "If Melora didn't believe in you then you wouldn't be here."

"Yes," Gwendora said. "Because she would've killed you already."

He estimated the two women standing before him, gaze shifting between them in slow consideration while Aggie's last words settled deep. They knew Melora's importance to him, that when it came down to it he would choose her life over Hannibal Khan's death, but they wanted more of a commitment than his professed love of the Spellbinder they'd sent to return Jericho.

I'll do anything to have her back and they know it, even if it means forgetting the Khan for their stupid Godstone. Gods, Aggie practically pulled the words from my throat and spoke them herself.

Hesitation swelled while he held lengthy pause, his guts squirming through unpleasant shifts to the confusing discontent of knowing if Melora and the Khan stood in front of him now he might still choose killing the Khan over kissing her, not because he wanted to but because he couldn't restrain himself.

He put no voice behind the disheartening thought as another intruded. *She tricked me here, yes, but I refuse to believe our sex as only a part of her duty.* His feelings for her had grown into a fiery passion encompassing all of him, and he rued the bitter heartbreak of never knowing her intimate mysteries again if he misspoke now.

He opened his mouth to comply—but arrested mute to the strain of compelling pressure thrashing in the secret depths of his thoughts, some contradicting longing trying to break free though held at bay by his kohatheen collar, pressurized through suppression.

Gwendora fisted her hips, her voice cold and snapping. "Well? I expect an answer."

At last, just wanting to be freed already, and in as honest a tone as he could manage he said, "I swear on my life. The Godstone comes first." He squirmed his wrists and ankles, wincing while evincing his irritation at still being tied to the chair after such a long debate over the true value of his life and his intentions. "Can you untie me now?"

Gwendora crossed her arms and drew out the silence. She glanced at Aggie, considering the request and all it contained, then struck Banzu with a smug smirk. "Now on her life."

"What?" he asked. "Who's?"

"Swear it on Melora's life."

"Gwen," Aggie began, stepping closer.

But the Head Mistress unfolded one arm and waved her off without a sparing glance. "If he truly loves her," Gwendora said, "and he truly means it, then it shouldn't be a problem." She cocked him an eyebrow. "Should it?"

"I—" A hesitant pause as reluctance flushed and stole his voice. He thinned his gaze upon the Head Mistress, upset at the attack on his feelings. The suspicion of one seconds from stepping into a trap pervaded. *But it's not like the oath is binding, except to my honor. Though who knows what cruelty she'll inflict against Melora in trade if I break it.* He swallowed back a threat and said, "I swear on Melora's life the Godstone comes first."

Gwendora eyeballed him a considerable term. Nodded without reply. Her right hand stole up behind her back in a flash of movement. She removed one fanged dachra, the curved length of which ran as long from pommel to tip as her arm from elbow to wrist. She spun the steely fang in a deft twirl that fooled the eyes into making of the dagger a quick disk then caught it stopped and pointed it at Banzu, the debate in her hard stare over her next action betraying her eyes.

She glanced at Aggie, who nodded her approval, then approached and leaned forward at the hips where she began cutting loose the coarse rope restraints tying Banzu's sore wrists to the arms of the chair, the testing measure of her gaze never leaving his while she worked. Soon as she cut his wrists free she paused, held the dachra between their faces, its fanged tip angled between his eyes and a hairsbreadth from tapping a cut into his forehead if she flicked her wrist.

"Don't make me regret this." Gwendora held his gaze at length, then squatted down and cut loose the tight bindings round his ankles, pausing between cuts to eyeball up at him a final time, then she stood and backed away.

Banzu breathed a little easier in his freedom. Forgetting his nudity, he stood slow from the chair in a sluggish protest of twitching muscles and wincing aches while using the armrests for support. He strained through the imposed lassitude of his kohatheen adding false heaviness to his bones, then plopped back down when a dizzy spell struck him unbalanced in painful reminder of his recent battle with stonemen and aizakai throbbing through his bruised and battered body.

The damp hood once covering his exposed groin had fallen to the floor in his attempted stand. He placed a covering hand over his exposed crotch while leaning forward and picked up the black cloth he then draped over his naughty bits in small comfort.

His mind turned active where his body refused. The Power provided accelerated healing at the cost of expending his lifeforce in cruel trade, but the kohatheen locked round his neck extinguished the option. He pointed at but did not touch the thin metal collar, his nudity a lesser worry to his stronger desire for the collar's immediate release. "And this?"

"Oh, that?" Gwendora chuckled while waving her dachra in mocking gesture at his kohatheen. "That stays on."

He frowned, suppressing the urge to reach up and try ripping the godsdamned thing off through his neck. His experience of unlocking one before, twice now, proved the effort an impossible feat to achieve unless he possessed visible access to the small locking mechanism and its puzzler tumblers. He intended asking how long she expected him to wear it but Gwendora spoke first.

"Another safeguard." She removed her dachra to up behind her back in another flash of motion, tucking the fanged blade home in its upside-down leather sheath with long-practiced precision. She frowned, dark brow creasing. "Not all of us are blessed with Melora's expansive void-aura. The kohatheen stays on until I say otherwise. You'll get used to it's . . . sluggishness." A hint of smirk betrayed one corner of her mouth, there then gone. "Part of its design to keep you from running."

Banzu chewed back a grumbling curse. He wanted to ask for his sword, but they would never allow him the courtesy of Griever's return however precious the blade containing memories of his uncle.

"I'll have some food and clothes and a wash basin brought in along with other necessities," Gwendora said. "I suggest you rest. Tomorrow we begin."

With that said, Head Mistress Gwendora Pearce turned and strode for the door. Shandra threw Banzu a burning glare before turning to follow her superior out. Aggie made to follow their leaving but stopped halfway to the door where she lingered, watching the two Spellbinders seconds from leaving while spinning her dead husband's wedding ring round her finger in private ponder.

Banzu regarded the three women in silence, afraid of saying anything more lest he invite the Head Mistress into more tiresome conversation. Exhausted despite the kohatheen's imposed lassitude, sore from head to heel, his body craved rest. And his mind toiled through a flurry of questions, but he shelved them for later.

Gwendora gripped the scuffed brass doorknob, turned it with a *click* in the quiet, then paused and shot a glance over her shoulder at Aggie she then shifted to Banzu with stabbing effect.

"Welcome to the Conclave," she said.

She opened the door—in rushed a stream of chatter from outside in the hallway beyond—and walked out with Shandra in angry tow.

"Conclave?" Banzu scrunched his face. "What's a conclave?"

The closing door muting the outside chatter answered nothing.

***

Unsure if he'd heard the departing Head Mistress correctly, Banzu repeated his question to Aggie's turned back. "What's a conclave?"

But she stood in mute stare at the ring she spun round her left ringfinger, lost in introspection. Head bowed, she turned from the door and exhaled a long breath relaxing her petite frame released from beneath the carried tension of a burden the Head Mistress removed with her leaving.

He sat watching her in the quietude, rubbing the sore red cuffs of his wrists, unknowing what to say or how to say it now that they were alone, and feeling more naked by the passing second. His memories, his sword, and that ring of Aggie's spinning fiddle the only earthly possessions remaining of Jericho.

And the magical boots of blinding speed.

Though those he'd left behind tucked away in his rucksack occupying the floor of the rotunda topping the tower. Not that he knew the words for activating the strange purple boot coverings into magical use.

But Aggie does. She stole them for Jericho's escape. Not that that matters now anyhow.

He searched for worthy words but found none deserving his voice.

A simple Sorry won't cut it for killing her husband.

He shifted on his bottom, body craving movement if only for the sake of testing the stretch of sore muscles and the kohatheen's bizarre lassitude. He stood, slow and wincing, every inch groaning protest, left hand holding the damp black hood over his crotch while his right used the armrest for pushing support.

Aggie craned her head.

He stared at her staring back while toying spins of her ring, her lips mouthing unvoiced words to the killer of her husband.

Silence.

Banzu broke first, averting his gaze down the glistening nude length of himself, his skin a touch redder than natural though unmarred by the magefire that engulfed him in its giant's conjured clutch and burned away his hair from head to toe while making of his skin a screaming hide of blisters now gone but for the boyhood scarring of his left shoulder. No explanation there. Or of how long he lay unconscious between the kick and Shandra's splashing alarm startling him awake and hooded.

He considered sitting down before his shaky legs buckled, his adrenaline spent through his meeting with the Head Mistress, a queer tiredness of gravity pulling deep in his bones. Physically exhausted, mentally depleted, spiritually drained, closing his eyes would deliver him into a deep slumber. But guilt injected iron into his spine, keeping him on his feet, the remorseful convict facing the gallows of Aggie's stare more through him than at him into some private space of viewing.

He opened his mouth, closed it. *Gods, why won't she say something? Why can't I?*

He drew in deep and broke the silence with the only words he could fathom. "Aggie I'm . . . I'm so sorry."

She flinched while blinking back to present, and stiffened straight, adding inches to her compact frame. She transferred her doe-eyed stare from the ring while busy fingers toiled spinning it round her finger in mindless activity, her broad-cheeked face a slumped mask of pained reverie. The tilt of her head as if studying him, then her almond-shaped eyes flared with life. She strode forth while closing space in five bounding strides, her right arm whipping behind her in a blur of movement.

Oh gods she's going to kill me! Cold panic flushing, Banzu cringed into the smallest target possible while raising his crossed forearms in front of his face as a pitiful shield, defensive instinct reaching inwards for a seize of the Power though achieving nothing but diaphanous memories of energies impossible to grasp, a hand swatting false grabs through insubstantial wisps of elusive smoke while his kohatheen flashed with restrictive heat.

Aggie pulled her dachra fang and quick-flipped it spinning then caught its handle hammer-fisted, the curved blade pointed tip to floor, and brandished it as a makeshift club while reaching him. She reared her arm back and swung a solid haymaker to clout him upside the head with her dachra's fisted handle.

But Banzu backpedaled from her advance, and the backs of his knees bent against the chair's pressing edge behind so that he plopped down, avoiding the blow whiffing inches past his flinching face.

"Wait!" He coiled his legs knees-to-chest into preparation for kicking her away. "Don't kill me!"

"I should box your godsdamned ears off!" Aggie considered him, her dachra, drew her fist back for another haymaker though paused, crinkled her nose and frowned. She sheathed the fanged blade up behind her back then planted fists to hips with an admonishing scold of her eyes, the passive woman seconds previous replaced by a formidable and intimidating aggressor belied by her diminutive size. "Oh stop that. I'm not going to kill you after everything I went through just to keep you alive."

Banzu peeked at her between his crossed forearms. "You're not?"

"Of course not." She did a considerable job of glaring down at him given her short height standing her one head above his sitting eye level. "Jericho—" She began then clipped short, wincing. She withdrew two steps, drew in a calming breath and schooled her features into prettier delicacy as warm concern returned to her voice. "I can't believe you're finally here." The slow shake of her head. "I saw you once. Before he took you away. But you're so grown now. So much the man from the boy I remember."

Banzu eased his feet to the floor while lowering his hands over his crotch, relaxing as best he could considering the circumstances. He glanced at the hood dropped during Aggie's rush, though his nudity proved a menial worry, turning almost clinical. The flare of her appraising gaze possessed a mother's tender anger, and some boyish part of him broke apart at the kindness watching back at him. He barely remembered his real mother, having lived most of his life without her, the memory of her face faded over the years to nothing more than a screaming blur half-hidden behind a veil of flames.

The gnarl of burn scars running from left elbow to over his shoulder pulsed with phantom throbs at the terrible reflection of that boyhood nightmare consuming his innocence along with his parents so that he shirked it aside for the enormity of years Aggie must have been planning for Jericho's return since his escape from Academy servitude. Each passing day scoring a deeper cut as those years of absence drifted by, leaving her waiting and unfulfilled.

What can I possibly say that would ever alleviate that amount of hurt inside her?

"You look like him." Aggie inched closer, the violet fire dying in her eyes while a wan smile pursed her lips. "Around the eyes. Your chin." She leaned forward reaching to feel at his face yet withdrew her hand inches before contact. She closed it into a fist, eyes glistening threats of tears. She backed away, stare unbroken, and sat in the chair behind her. She nested her hands in her lap, fingers fiddling with her ring, spinning it in a smaller worry all its own. She stole a glance behind at the closed door, then the despair rife in her eyes bled into her voice when she next spoke. "Tell me how he really died. Tell me everything. Please?"

Banzu drew in deep, swallowed and nodded. He'd spared the gruesome details for Aggie's sake as well his own reluctance to relive the horrible event.

She's asking for closure, needs it, and I'm the only one who can give it. His killer. Two decades contemplating the mystery of Jericho's eventual return only to have her long wait terminated by my arrival proving him dead.

And so he told her, the honest words spilling forth easier in their privacy. He explained every agonizing detail in his confession, from the moment a bloodlust-corrupted Jericho roused him away that terrible night to his Source-fueled return to the past where he killed his uncle in cruel trade for the Power's cleansing though more so for Melora's return to life.

Aggie suffered through it with a brave face, blinking back tears while he filled in the gruesome gaps unmentioned to the Head Mistress, at times edging forward in her chair as if to interrupt him with a question then settling back and motioning for him to continue.

"It was the hardest thing I've ever had to do," Banzu finished. "Killing him like that. Even after what he did." No judgment betrayed those glistening violets staring back at him, but he gazed away regardless, shame flushing his face hot. "I had no other choice."

"It's okay." Aggie sniffled, sat forward, palmed the left side of his face and turned it back to meet her steady gaze. She smiled, the shine of tears adding sparkling depths to her maternal eyes so full of promises and pain. She blinked, and tears ran her prominent cheeks. But she ignored them, smile spreading as if proud of them. "Don't you blame yourself, Banzu. What you did was a good thing. A necessary thing. You two were the last of a cursed bloodline. It was either him or you, and he wanted it to be you. That's why he stole you away. Why he trained you."

Banzu enclosed her palming hand and applied it a gentle squeeze before pulling it from his face. "Thank you."

Aggie slid her hand from his and worked her eyebrows into curious black arches. "For what?"

"For helping save me. He told me. Not everything but enough. I know what you did. What you gave up. I wouldn't be alive if it wasn't for you. Thank you, Aggie."

The withering sheen of regret entered the haunt of her eyes as her wan smile fled. She withdrew, sitting back while stiffening straight. She gazed away, hands rejoining in her lap, fingers fiddling with Jericho's ring in twisty little spins.

"I prayed for his return so many nights I cannot even begin to place their number." Staring at the far wall, she spoke her own confession. "Even though I knew that meant your death. For years I wished you'd turn to the bloodlust so he'd have to kill you and he'd just come back to me." She paused and cleared the hitch from her throat. "There hasn't been a day gone by that I didn't think of him. Or you. And now—"

But she couldn't finish, couldn't even look at him. Instead she stood, her chair sliding the floor backwards from the force of her straightening legs. She turned away and walked toward the door but stopped three steps out, kept her back to him, silent, unmoving.

Banzu stood on stronger legs, wanting to go to her, to embrace her in a hug he hoped would comfort them both. Then, remembering his nudity, he bent and snatched the wet black hood from the floor and covered his crotch a hairsbreadth before Aggie turned round and flinched tense.

An exchange of stares . . . broken by her laugh at the obtuse awkwardness of their situation. And to Banzu's surprise he laughed too.

"I'm sorry," he said. "I really am."

She smiled. "I know you are. But don't be. You gave him a peace he never knew in life. For that I thank you." She glance behind at the door then tightened her eyes, her voice. "I want Hannibal Khan dead as much as you do. But revenge is just a confession of pain, not a path in life. And certainly not your path. You have to let it go, Banzu. I can—"

"Ban," he said. "Please, call me Ban."

She nodded. "I can see the pain and anger smoldering in your eyes, Ban. Like embers waiting to flare and burn everyone and everything around you into ash at the next opportune wind. Don't." She shook her head for emphasis, short black hair swishing round her neck. "Don't give in to it. Giving in to things becomes a habit. You must do as Gwen says. It's her duty to guide you, and yours to listen. That's why you're here. You were meant for this, Ban. Make Jericho proud." She glanced at the bed. "Now get some rest. Tomorrow will be a busy day for all of us because of you."

He plopped his chair, drew in deep and sighed, every inch of him sore and stiff. "Tomorrow." He upturned his hands and gazed at them, flexed them, knuckles popping. "I don't know how much use I'll be considering how beat up I am."

He spread his hands and gaze between at his thigh and the memory of Shandra's deep and wrenching dachra stab now nothing more than a thin pink scar. He traced it with the barest touch of a fingertip, afraid applying pressure would remove the illusion of its healing over such a short span of time.

"You'll be fine," Aggie said. "Shandra already rubbed you down with a concentration of healing balm while you were out."

His gaze snapped up. "She *what?*" He stiffened, and not in a good way, aware again of the faint menthol aroma permeating the room his preoccupied mind had abandoned, a minty scent he realized wafted from his oiled skin. Flashes of Shandra's strong hamhands massaging the healing balm into every nude part of him while he lay unconscious cringed him. "Oh gods, she didn't."

Aggie chuckled, soft and low. "She did. Oh! I almost forgot." She dipped a hand into an inner fold of her red dress, pulled out a skinny leather pouch the size of her palm and set it on the left of the two empty chairs between them. "From Master Normando. Tarkroot, gumblossom, wombwort, and moonglum. Fine cut." She flicked a wrist in gesture at his kohatheen. "And a few other natural herbs. Stop chewing when it starts burning. And swallow the juices only, not the cud, or it'll put you out and we'll have to beat you awake tomorrow. I'll send Shandra along in a few hours to rub you down again with more balm. And again before you sleep."

"What?" He endured another flinching cringe of those hamhands molesting him. "No she won't. I can do it my—"

"If you're not better by tomorrow," Aggie said, talking over his protest in louder voice, "then we'll have you healed through other means. We are in the Academy, after all. There's aizakai abound here." She paused, thinned her eyes with underlying warning, added, "Thousands."

Banzu sighed and transferred the pouch of herbs atop the black hood covering his lap. "What's a conclave?"

"Oh, that." She stole a glance at the door then smirked. "It's our secret little inner circle of knowing and trust. The Conclave was established with the founding of the Academy to combat the Enclave. Only those within it are privy to its secrets. The Head Mistress, of course. Myself. Her First Sword Jacob, and a few select others. You, too. Or you will be once you pass the testing. And so will Melora once she returns, though she doesn't know it yet. She's passed her initiation now that you're here."

Banzu made to speak but she waved him quiet.

"Rest. There's plenty we'll talk about tomorrow."

He sighed and nodded, said nothing.

Aggie turned to go but paused. "And don't leave this room. If you need anything, knock. Jacob is standing guard outside. You stick a toe out and he'll beat it right back in. Just try not to bother him. He's testy enough as it is knowing you're here." She laughed, a pretty little sound the scatter of butterflies. "Everyone's been on edge since the Veilfall, so just stay put and don't scare anyone into killing you."

She strode to the door, almost too quickly.

"I'm only here because of Melora," he said, the prospect of dealing with Shandra fouling his mood and sharpening the slip of his errant tongue.

Aggie froze her reaching hand to within inches of grasping the doorknob. She'd broached a tender subject before trying to make her leave, and the fire in his belly over Melora so far away would only extinguish when next he saw her face to face, alive and safe. Besides, he had something to say and Aggie needed to hear it. He owed her that much. He owed her the truth as well as his life.

"This is what Melora wants," he continued, his tone edged with warning. "It's why she tricked me here. But—" He drew in deep, expelled overlong through pursed lips. "But I want you to understand something. After this Godstone business is done, I will kill Hannibal Khan. If any of you get in my way—" A hesitant pause. "Even you, Aggie, I swear to gods I'll—" But he clipped his threat short, wincing at a flaring pang in his guts while his kohatheen flashed hot.

Aggie remained facing the door. "You'll what?"

"Just . . . please, don't get in my way, okay? I'm telling you this now so you won't make that mistake when the time comes."

"Then let us hope it does not come to that."

She gripped the doorknob though did not turn it, her voice the serrated edge of threat when next she spoke.

"The Godstone is what matters now." She delivered him a slow half-peek over her right shoulder presenting intense brutal violets assessing him, her empty hand flexing into a fist at her side, the other clutching the doorknob so that tautening sinews twitched beneath her skin. "If you screw this up after everything that's happened, I'll kill you myself." Her shoulder dipped lower, revealing the noticeable flexing of her jaw, the tensing of shoulder blades beneath her red dress. And in a repeat of his threat she added, "I'm telling you this now so you won't make that mistake when the time comes. Do *you* understand *me*?"

Banzu returned a mute nod, startled by the fierce challenge of her contemptuous glare matching him threat for threat. He recognized in her the fiery passion that tamed Jericho's unruly spirit so many years ago. *That look, those eyes, so much like Melora.* He rumbled his throat clear and in a barer voice than he wanted said, "Yes."

She cocked an eyebrow. "Yes what?"

"Uhm." He squirmed. *Oh!* "Yes, Mistress?"

She smirked. "That's right." A moment more and she relaxed. "You're naked, unarmed and collared. In the fistian Academy surrounded by thousands of aizakai and soldiers who will kill you at the snap of Gwen's fingers. And yet you still make threats." An amused little titter. "As bold as Jericho ever was."

She appraised him with a feline smile then opened the door and strode outside, shutting it behind her.

Outside sounded the jingling of keys and the clicking lock secured.

Banzu sat staring at the door for a lengthy measure while pondering his new lot in life. He gave his kohatheen a futile tug and sighed, then opened the little leather pouch in his lap for the collective mix of healing herbs within.

Great. So this is what my life has become. Naked and collared and locked in a room. Oh, and surrounded by aizakai who want to kill me. Just great. Can't wait till Shandra gets here too. That'll be fun. Friggin great.

* * *

Minutes more there sounded the muffled jangling of keys followed by the door opening for a young woman garbed in a wool dress with no underclothes, her head shaved bare and leaving only the newest short crop of blonde turf seeking to recover her scalp, parts of her skin chafed an irritated red from woolen scratches. She carried a few necessaries inside while Jacob stood within the doorframe watching Banzu in silent regard, his left hand resting on the hilt of the sword sheathed at his right hipwing while the other stroked the fine point of his goatee.

The girl who could be no more than twelve kept her shaven head bowed under the scrutiny of Jacob's stern watch, daring no eye contact with Banzu when she hurried in, set the carried items down beside the door then hurried out, scrunching past the veteran soldier before he could turn to provide her better space for leaving, and there she stole Banzu a curious glance before her hasty exit.

Jacob lingered in the relaxed though ready pose of one contemplating the pull of his sword, eyeballing Banzu for unblinking seconds before nodding with that subtle hint of respect only an experienced swordsman could muster forth with such a slight motion before making his leave, closing then locking the door behind him.

Banzu spent the next half turn of the hour washing from the pitcher of lukewarm water using the small porcelain bowl and dark blue towel provided by the girl, all the while chewing on a thumb-sized chaw of the lemon-peppery mix of healing herbs Aggie provided him puffing his cheek. His movements slow and mechanical, his mind eased into a blank state of existence that shunned all current anxieties but for the simple task of washing.

Until he swayed on his feet mid scrub, the potent medicinal effects of the herbs combined with his empty stomach pulsing increasing prickles through his sloshing sense of drunken balance.

Too strong a dose. I have to lie down before I collapse.

The wet towel stole from his tingling hands to the floor. He spat the wad of herbal cud into the bowl, staggered round and lurched to the bed where he fell onto it facedown, bouncing, then flopped onto his back with the aid of numb-tingling limbs only half obeying his sluggish mental commands which sounded more watery echoes than thought. The air throbbed and shimmered to the vertigo whirl of his vision ebbing in and out of focus in time with the slowing patter of his heartbeat as tickling warmth spread throughout his limp body, producing from him a dopy grin.

Heavy lids fluttering, closing, as he drifted . . . drifted away into a deep, deep slumber.

* * *

Banzu lay sleeping and unaware of not Shandra but Agatha returning to his room one hour later. She who carefully rubbed more menthol-scented healing balm onto his battered body then, righting him supine on the bed, covered him with a blanket. She who sat bedside watching him sleep. She who softly wept into her covering hands over the murdered husband she would never see again while his killer slept beside her. She who determined to do everything possible to ensure Banzu became what Jericho never had the chance to achieve.

And if he did not, if worse turned to worst, she who determined to kill him herself.

CHAPTER THIRTY-FOUR

Locked in erotic thrall with Melora's long alabaster leg wound round his undulating waist and her other in standing perch while she rode Banzu's eager thrusts . . . her fingernails fevered claws scoring red lines across his back when not raking through his hair and yanking tufts of it . . . their hips rhythmically jouncing in tandem while he tasted her tasting him round tongues worming through hot exchanges of mingled breaths and lip-nipping bites.

The carnal copulation of Banzu's sensuous dreamscape vanished, shattered to the startling rush of wet cold splashing him awake into the cruel reality of his prisoner's room in the fistian Academy.

He sat bolt upright in the sodden bed, gasping, sputtering curses while blinking through the gauzy prism of drowsy eyes alerted to the waking world in expanding fright. The room wobbled and throbbed before righting itself into readjusting focus through the trace lingering effects of the potent healing herbs combined with his kohatheen's perpetual lassitude providing his deep sleep. Though once the flush of adrenaline surged through his waking system, he jolted revitalized and aware of the brawny Spellbinder Shandra greeting him at the foot of his bed, an empty bucket in her beefy hands and a smug smile on her rosy round face.

"Good morning, sunshine." She dropped the tin bucket to the floor with a *clang* and struck him with a satisfied grin that spoke only of amused contempt. "Looks like someone pissed the bed. Get dressed. The Head Mistress wanted to see you an hour ago. You're late."

"Friggin hell!" he yelled. "What is it with you and buckets of water?" He scowled through the cold drips running his face. Then flinched, her words kicking his brain. "An hour ago? What time is it? How long was I out?"

But Shandra turned away without reply. She walked out from the room, leaving the door open in her wake.

He chewed down a hot string of fiery curses, fetched a heavy sigh as he raked one hand back through—no, slid his hand while grimacing over the slick feel of his bald pate, feeling only the barest patch of stubble growth. Hair no longer there, burned away through magefire. *Friggin hell.*

He flicked his wrist, releasing a thin fan of water droplets to the air. He threw the wet blanket aside, swung his bare feet to the cold stone floor and stood, groaning while stretching out the minor kinks, surprised despite the rude awakening at how well the healing herbs and menthol balm restored such serious injuries that would have otherwise left the rest of his skin resembling the scar tissue of his left shoulder.

Thank gods for that much.

He cringed at the disturbing thought of Shandra stealing into his room and her mannish hamhands massaging the menthol balm into his unconscious body. *And probably punching parts of me while I was out, knowing the bruises would heal before I woke.*

He banished the intrusion away with a shudder and blew out his cheeks while tugging on the kohatheen locked round his neck leaving only an inch of space between lanthium and skin.

Nope, it's still on. And still tiring me a bit, though not so much as before at least. Like the distant cling of sleep, but my body's adjusting. I'll manage. I have to.

He considered shutting the door and spending a few secret minutes attempting to unlock the device through blind feel then stowed the thought away.

No point there. Even if I can get the friggin thing off, the Head Mistress'll just snap another one round my neck the moment she sees it gone. Nothing I can do about it but deal . . . for now.

Naked and uncaring, he strode to the open doorway, not so sluggish as the previous day though with an underlying heaviness rooted deep in his bones, and grumbling every step of the way. He stuck his head out in forward lean for a quick peek up and down the hallway to catch his first real glimpse of—

"Hurry up." Shandra, standing outside to the right of the door with her back against the wall and arms crossed beneath her sizable bosom fixed him with a sideways glare. "The Head Mistress is waiting."

Startled for the second time in as many minutes, Banzu thinned his eyes, testing the Spellbinder brute glare for glare, then relented the futile contest by ducking back inside and slamming the door.

Just for that I'm taking my godsdamned time!

But he put no voice behind it, afraid of instigating Shandra into charging inside the room and roughing him up for the spite of it then dragging him through the Academy naked and by the shorthairs to the Head Mistress.

Not that I have any shorthairs left to grab. She's lying about my lateness just to toy with me, I know it. It's not like I have a specific appointment or anything.

But he refused to peek outside and confirm his suspicions by asking her, attributing Locha's Luck that she didn't yank him out of bed and drag him away.

Fresh clothes and boots, fistian blacks and blues, lay in a loose pile on the floor Shandra must have brought in before dousing him awake, the clean attire resting beside a small tray of smoked meats and cheeses. Hunger ravenous, he gobbled the delicious food down in eager handfuls then, stomach gurgling, used the chamber pot, all the while eyeballing the door against another intrusion. Afterwards, he toweled dry using his blanket then dressed and intended on needling his Spellbinder bully with his best mocking grin. But soon as he opened the door and stepped into the hallway, his mocker's smile wilted to Shandra's condescending grin and piercing glare.

"Come," she said, sharp and barking, after straightening from her lean against the wall. "Now." She walked away with obvious expectations for him to follow her lead, an obedient dog its master.

He frowned and followed after her though trailed the safer space of several paces behind while chewing on an irritated grumble of curses at her broad back and imagining choking that thick bull's neck till her round head popped off.

She resents me for refusing our Pairing. Yeah, well, I don't care so get over it. I'd cut my own head off before trading you for Melora.

Those thoughts wandered along with his gaze.

***

The sheer immensity of the fistian Academy's interior proved an overwhelming sight to Banzu's roving attentions. He gawked while following down the vacant hallway, his kohatheen's imposed lethargy an incessant cling distanced to his active musings.

And he wondered, *Where the frig is everyone?* Though he put no voice behind it, supposing such absence of his current hallway an order from the Head Mistress warning all her students against their captive Soothsayer.

Shandra sped up her pounding tread—just to spite him, he was sure of it—but no matter that. Not like she'd leave him behind. Asides, he busied his attentions in staring awe at the high ceiling covered in a flowing dynamic mosaic of mythical battles evincing legends torn from the Thousand Years War.

Within the streaming tesserae lived painted scenes speckled with fiery rubies depicting spumes of magefire, gleaming emeralds making rolling fields of battle beneath sparkling sapphires of magical blasts amid which tumbled caught figures of little iron-framed warriors fighting malformed creatures fashioned from glistening black opals catching flickering hints from the glowing magelight braziers aligning the walls, the plethora of starry diamonds in false night skies twinkling fractures, several of the shoulder-high braziers dimming then brightening again to Shandra's closer passing void-aura showing it permeated the air no more than a few feet beyond her skin.

The splendor of wealth proved incalculable. Forget the Builder's towers and their purported treasures, how every eager thief and bandit in the One Land hadn't rallied together to ransack the Academy lived beyond Banzu's rational scope of logic. Though considering the abundance of aizakai living here—*thousands, Aggie said*—the obvious answer laid claim to his musings.

His fascination with the flowing mosaics died along with his lowering gaze when they reached the double doors at hallway's end and Shandra pushed them open, revealing the true daunting size of the Academy proper and all its bustling inhabitants by way of the first of many colossal rooms awaiting their lengthy route to the Head Mistress.

Shandra continued on while Banzu stopped and stared.

People of all shapes and races filled the massive chamber, light- and dark-skinned Thurandians milling round the scatter of tables stacked with piles of books and plates or bowls of foodstuffs, a few jaw-tusked blue-skinned Dreshians carrying armloads of rolled scrolls, even fewer red-skinned Jighanese engaged in animated conversations as told by their active flourishes of hands while people of various ages young and old hustled in bunches into or out from the lively room through one of the ten or so passageways mouthing the towering walls.

Soldiers in fistian blacks and blues stood lazy guard, watching the students at play or study while ensuring the peace. One reprimanded a laughing group throwing buttered rolls. Another oversaw a knot of five gloomy teenagers, all of them with shaven heads and wearing wool robes chafing their skin, on hands and knees and scrubbing the floor with tiny brushes, those passing them laughing and pointing while earning sneers from the punished scrubbers.

Several cyclopes walked heads taller through the bustle and flurry, carrying bundles of wrapped weapons or armor, or rattling pots and pans, or leather-wound stacks of books tied to their hunched backs, though not slaves but happy servants as told by their bright lone eyes and blocky-toothed grins despite their lashed burdens weighing enough to crush an average man to the floor.

Banzu thought he glimpsed a single tundarian among the populace, though unsure of the rare sight, for the muscled brute of a woman appeared then disappeared behind an opening then closing space of chattering teenagers led by a raptor-eyed Spellbinder flooding past her.

He blinked and gaped in swelling anxiety. *Aizakai . . . all of them.*

He had never seen so many people in all his secluded life, let alone such a variety gathered in one colossal place made cramped by sheer numbers. He endured a nervous cringe at the enormity of it all and his smaller place inside it, the tableau before him a fraction taste of the true Academy.

A groan escaped him when he noticed Shandra already a quarter of the way across the immense chamber and showing no signs of slowing.

He lingered in the doorway as the first of many uncomfortable hushes to come stole over the sea of turning faces greeting his presence through wide-eyed stares and whispered exchanges while motions halted and voices cut short throughout the room.

Somewhere a dropped book slapped the floor, the sound magnified by the reigning silence.

All eyes upon him, Banzu swallowed hard and audible, his kohatheen an imaginary strangle.

The allure of the Academy fled as the grim reminder of his Soothsayer status took precedence over his sight-seeing wonder. A lone bloodwasp trespassing the hive of honeybees.

Those nearest him withdrew through cautious backpedals, their faces unpleasant twists, several of their wary fold hugging books to their chests in false shields, others dropping whatever they carried to free their hands in preemptive flexes at their sides. The sea of leery gazes measured the sight of him so that he considered turning round and running back to his room in escape from the anxious panic tightening the breath in his lungs while coiling his squirming guts into nervous knots.

Instead he stood there, immobile and all too aware of himself the study of everyone present, his black boots rooted to the floor by the curling toes.

His palms sweaty, mouth dry as tinder, pulse quickened and skipping anxious flutters, he surveyed the room with a swordslinger's cautious assessment of potential threats, hands flexing grabs of air at his sides and craving the reassurance of Griever's hilt.

Gods, I feel so . . . trapped.

He battled back the urge to sprint for any window and break free from this claustrophobic prison, to run and keep running and never look back. *Not that I'll get very far with this friggin kohatheen locked round my friggin neck let alone a thousand friggin aizakai chasing after me.* His sense of time slowed to an inching crawl while his eyes decoupled and his vision drifted out of focus. He blinked hard, glanced left, glanced right, feet shifting, guts aflutter, panic gripping his reins and snapping tensions through him.

Everyone's staring at me. Stop it! The walls are closing in. I can feel them shrinking. Oh gods, why am I here? I need to get out. I need to—

A gruff grunt sounded from behind.

Banzu flinched and spun round, skittish, jolting, then hopping back a step, his right hand stealing across his front and flexing airy grip at his empty left hipwing for the anxious pull of a sword no longer there.

Jacob stood before him with left hand gripping the hilt of his sword at his right hipwing and a firm set to his goateed jaw.

"Where in friggin hell did you come from?" Banzu asked, making an accusation of the question. He leaned to one side, glanced past the older soldier on down the long and empty hallway beyond. No, not empty, for well past the door to his room stood a lone Spellbinder watching them from afar amid shadows from the dimmed braziers beside her, tall and dark of hair, hips cocked to one side, picking at her fingernails with the tip of a brandished dachra, her smile leaving her discriminating cut of eyes untouched.

Banzu gulped, shifted his uneasy gaze away from the lurker.

Silent as a shadow, Jacob's dark eyes held a fierce, determined gleam. He answered nothing but for the slightest gesturing nod indicating forward accompanied by another sour grunt, his gripping fingers unwinding then curling back round his sword's hilt in a suggestive little wave from pinkie to pointer. *Move*, those eyes said, *or I'll move you. The Head Mistress is waiting.*

That's when Banzu noticed the other sword Jacob carried, its familiar hilt jutting from the veteran soldier's left hip.

"Is that—" But Banzu clipped short in a squeak of voice. He pointed at Griever then his hand turned a tremulous claw reaching forth of its own accord for Griever's precious return.

Jacob thinned his eyes and withdrew a step while baring his steel by inches. He shook his head in slow denial, his unyielding stare a command to stay that reaching hand or lose it.

Holding the cold measure of Jacob's stare where lived a lifetime of killing in Academy service, Banzu's anger flushed and flared then settled to simmering. He wrestled down the suicidal urge to lunge and snatch for Griever by thinnest margin, turned round, drew in a deep nostril inhale and blew out his cheeks.

Relax. He rumbled his dry throat clear in the pervading silence and swallowed, his laryngeal prominence bobbing against his kohatheen collar. *If they wanted me dead I'd already be dead.* He drew in another steadying breath and released it through pursed lips. *Quit staring at me.* He swiped his sweaty palms dry at his sides then fisted his hands. *I'm not a friggin animal.*

He walked off the cliff of his first step and followed after Shandra who bothered no look back while widening their gap to that of half the room. The ache of Griever's absence shifted his hips off-kilter a bit while he walked now, the sensation imposed by the knowledge of his treasured sword behind him and worn by another.

The awkward quiet persisted but for Banzu's echoing tread and Jacob's in pursuing tow. Hundreds of stares followed them, Academy students turning, watching, awed or glaring at Banzu's passing, exchanging whispers in his wake.

***

They three traveled at length through the labyrinthine aizakai school, Spellbinder Shandra leading the way while Banzu trailed behind with First Sword Jacob his stalking shadow, little communication shared between them but for Jacob's occasional grunts spurring Banzu to keep moving and Shandra's shouldered glares warning him not to dawdle too far behind.

They wended through long and winding mazelike corridors—these decorated with plush hung tapestries stretching from floor to ceiling and featuring a variety of violent magical scenes woven from a rainbow of bright colored threads—when not coursing through expansive rooms filled with diverse groups of students talking or studying or gossiping round tables bestrewn with all manner of leather-bound texts and foodstuffs. Wall-crawling bookcases stretched these rooms corner to corner and raced to the lofty ceilings, their shelves packed full of books Banzu presumed the uppermost of which an impossible reach until he noticed the hung metal ladders extending down from circular holes above the tops of the bookshelves from the floor of the upper level, several of these occupied by clinging students reaching in searching bid through the collected works.

They traversed sets of stairs, Shandra always choosing those leading up and never down, and every last person they passed stared overlong at Banzu, several onlookers stopping mid-task while dropping whatever forgotten items they carried to outright gawk at him wide-eyed and open-mouthed while removing far from his path.

The awkward fondling of the students' inquisitive stares crawled his skin. Some braved open glares of suspicious contempt while others cringed or turned away the moment his roving gaze met theirs.

Groups of aizakai, neophytes and teachers alike, turned into themselves and shared whispers at passing sight of him, while others—mostly young men too ignorant to know any better—puffed up bold and brazen and shot him arrogant challenging glares while throwing obscene hand gestures at the last Soothsayer finally returned to the fistian Academy after centuries of hunting chase.

I get it now, why Jericho was so adamant about never revealing myself to anyone. Gods, they hate and fear me and they don't even know me. After the fight with the aizakai and the stonemen, and that friggin alarm announcing me to everyone, rumors obviously spread in a wildfire and none of them good.

He endured the condemning looks by focusing ahead at Shandra's back while his mind raced through avenues of excuses for why he never should have come here in the first place.

It helped steel his worries over Melora's safety he could do nothing about this far away.

* * *

Decorative columns with flowery capitals and fluted shafts stood spaced with precision along the walls of every new corridor, and between them frescos and tapestries blazed in bold thread with heroic deeds woven from the sagas, adding spicy life to the beige stone and red granite while drawing even the familiar passerby's eye to the rich displays of histories.

But Banzu's wandering attentions soon lost interest outward and shifted inward upon his meeting with the Head Mistress while he followed his brawny Spellbinder chaperone with Jacob in silent stalking tow. Every now and again he tugged at his kohatheen while edging an irritating yawn never loosing from his mouth, instead buried deep in his chest. Several times he tested the Power through focal invocation, and felt nothing of it while his kohatheen flashed with heat then cooled in seconds.

More circuitous corridors and calf-burning stairs linked populated rooms hushing to Banzu's entry with accusing stares then filling with elevating whispers at his passing, until he followed Sandra into an inner sanctum lit bright by reflector lamps hung at high intervals between the low-burning braziers running along the cove joints where floor and walls met. He jolted paused after finishing up another flight of steps and turning the winding corner into the outer hallway of the meeting chambers.

One-hundred fistian soldiers stood in two inward-facing rows, split fifty to a side down the long hallway and presenting yet another corridor, this last lined with guards providing enough passing breadth of space between their middle to the set of gilded double doors at hallway's end for two persons to walk abreast without bumping shoulders upon proud armored chests.

Jacob grunted while prompting Banzu into motion from behind with a firm push on his back.

A unison stomp of right feet pronouncing the flurry of one-hundred hands stealing to hilts accompanied by the slight metallic grate of swords loosened in sheaths as the fistian soldiers aligning the walls tensed at Banzu's presence, their resolute stares following him every tense inch of the way behind the barred eye-slits of their hawk-shaped helms while he strode between their stern ranks toward the double doors awaiting his entry.

Shandra gave a perfunctory glance over one shoulder before pounding thrice upon the closed doorface with the meat of one hammering fist then without waiting she pushed those heavy double doors open and stepped on through.

Banzu followed after the squat Spellbinder, though halfway to the doors he glanced behind at more sounds of metallic shifting, the guarding soldiers bowing their heads while planting right gauntleted fists over their armored hearts in saluting respect to Jacob as the veteran soldier passed through their lined ranks.

Banzu gained a new and healthy respect for the man then, though it stole to the back of his mind when he reached the open doors and anticipation for what awaited him beyond flushed his nervous guts. He breathed slight relief at the contrasting lack of others therein once he strode inside.

Only Head Mistress Gwendora Pearce and Spellbinder Agatha dar'Shuwin awaited his arrival, the room three times his height and twice that sum long and wide, though tiny by comparison to the gigantic chambers negotiated along their route up through the Academy hive. And 'hive' was how he thought of this enormous aizakai sanctuary, it abuzz with bustling activity at every turn and in every place he passed through.

He hesitated his approach. With the kohatheen locked round his neck and Griever missing from his hip, he stood at a great disadvantage if something unforeseen turned against him here.

Shandra closed the doors behind Jacob's entry with the thudding finality of a shutting coffin lid. Her long and banded ponytail swung an anxious tail when she whisking across the room with the lithe grace of a woman half her muscled bulk, joining Gwendora and Aggie by the table.

Banzu glanced at the closed doors announcing the potential sealing of his doom. By instinct he reached for the comforting reassurance of Griever's hilt at his left hipwing and winced, grabbing only air, while catching Jacob's disapproving look earned from the telling motion.

Banzu walked across the room toward the three Spellbinders awaiting him. He swallowed down the nervous knot balling in his throat while giving a quick hook-fingered tug on his kohatheen, not that the possibility of loosening it existed.

Two high-back chairs faced the long side of a white-clothed table, the only furniture in the room. Gwendora and Aggie occupied the space between the pair of chairs and table, both women with hands clasped behind their backs though each presenting a dissimilar visage made all the more noticeable by the divergent woman beside her.

A cool expression on the tall Head Mistress's solemn face, her shoulders back and proud chin high, she stood fashioned in a form-hugging dress of deep blue trimmed with glossy silver adding inches to her curvaceous height while accentuating long slopes of athletic muscle beneath foretelling she not only ordered rigorous physical training but also took part in it. The sides of her dress split from its low hem concealing her feet up to her prominent hips, buttoned for the quick ease of freeing kicking or running restriction if action required the motion. Her long taut sleeves ended just past her wrists in saw-toothed jags of silver contrasting her darker skin. She wore three alternating metal bands—gold-silver-gold—round her neck, thin collars providing her chocolate isthmus the illusion of elongation while protecting her vulnerable throat, her overall posture more regal than stiff.

At Gwendora's left stood Aggie, more informal than her heads taller superior but with an underlying anxious tension floating just beneath the surface of her relaxed posture, her shoulders loose and a casual tilt to her dainty hips. She wore a loose-fitting red dress trimmed with black arguing at its shoulder-short sleeves, collar and knee-high hem. A long golden dragon twined round her compact frame from front to back and hip to shoulder, the creature of lore depicted mid flight within the golden weaves upon a crimson burst of sky. She stared ahead into some private somber space of viewing, more through Banzu than at him, though at his approach she blinked refocus of the present while her lips twitched into the beginnings of a tiny smile beneath almond-eyes still creased with her previous night's grieving of her dead husband.

Both women shared piercing Spellbinder violets as well the leather torso harnesses containing pairs of dachra fangs strapped to their backs in upside-down fashion for ease of pulling.

Banzu slowed his approach past Shandra, his gaze fixed on Aggie and her fragile smile while noting the redness sullying the whites of her puffy eyes regaining focus on him. *She's been crying, and probably all night because of me.*

He swallowed back another apology—*say it too much and it loses all meaning*—and averted his gaze to the Head Mistress as he stopped behind the two chairs, gave another hook-fingered tug on his kohatheen while grimacing, then huffed out an annoyed breath. To either woman he asked, "Can you take this godsdamned thing off of me now?"

Aggie's lips parted while her eyes betrayed a touch of sympathy.

"Language," Gwendora said, sharp and quick, frowning, her stern resolve unchanged from the previous day.

Aggie closed her mouth, added nothing.

"What?" Banzu asked.

"Profanity is the language of the ignorant," Gwendora said. "I forgave your flippant tongue yesterday considering the circumstances. But that was yesterday. And you will address me by title. Ask again. Properly."

Banzu suppressed a sigh with budding hope. "Will you please remove my kohatheen, Head Mistress?"

Gwendora smiled. "That's better." Her smile vanished. "And no. It stays on until I decide otherwise." She rolled her right hand out in fanning gesture, pointing at the right of the two chairs in front of her on Banzu's left. "Now sit."

He scowled at the command. "What?"

And the Head Mistress scowled right back. She jabbed at the indicated chair and in firmer tone said, "Sit. Now."

Banzu crossed his arms in challenge, unmoving. "I'm not a dog."

Gwendora thinned the scolds of her eyes evincing no sympathy for his collared plight. "Careful, Banzu. You are standing in the heart of *my* Academy—"

"And having seconds thoughts on it already," he said. "And thirds. And fourths." He held the moment overlong with a hard stare, until Aggie motioned with her eyes for him to take the chair as bidden because he possessed no win to this situation. He uncrossed his arms and huffed a submissive breath. "Fine."

"Fine what?" Gwendora asked.

"Fine, Head Mistress." He began rounding the chair to sit.

"Good boy," Gwendora said, wry amusement quirking one corner of her mouth.

Banzu stopped halfway between the chairs and glared at her. He opened his mouth for feisty rebuttal then turned away when a knock sounded upon the doors.

The double doors split open from without, and in walked the same shaven-headed girl on the cusp of her teenage years who delivered an armload of items into Banzu's room the previous day now carrying a silver tray supporting an array of items, the most noticeable of which a little black kettle leaking puffs of steam from its fluted spout amid cups and others such thereon.

"Ahh," Gwendora said, a small smile breaking across her pressed lips. She clapped her hands and rubbed them. "Precisely on time."

"Head Mistress." Grimacing, the serving girl dipped into a little curtsy and bowed her shaven head, all the while balancing the tray and its assortment of items atop her upraised palms with imperfect grace. She gave Banzu a cautious berth when she approached the table, the ragged knee-high bottom of her drab wool dress scraping and scoring her bare legs as she did so. Her wandering gaze caught him in passing, blooming wide in awe then stark blue pupils darting everywhere but him in nervous evasion after their gazes met. She reached the side of the Head Mistress and, still grimacing, dipped into another bowing curtsey.

Banzu caught a flash through the armhole of the newcomer's wool dress, her soft white skin showing raw red patches of irritation beneath and round her neckline, and her arms and legs where the scratchy wool ended. Punished for some reason or another, the scratchy wool dress provided rough reminder of whatever mistakes undertaken to earn its torment with every discomforting shift and twitch.

He'd seen its like worn by a handful of others while following Shandra up through the Academy, every wearer washing walls or scrubbing floors or performing other laborious chores while passing students joked at their backs. Banzu remembered one of the punished complaining about the coarse wool playing havoc on his bleeding nipples while he scrubbed the floor beneath a tending guard's admonishing watch.

"Now we can begin through a proper palavar," Gwendora said, paying the wearisome young neophyte awaiting her less mind than the objects the girl upheld upon her balanced tray.

The Head Mistress rounded behind the table while issuing clucking noises with her tongue. And the neophyte tray-bearer followed after her, bare feet padding the floor. Gwendora transferred the presented items from tray to tabletop—the steaming kettle and three white marble cups, black marble mortar and pestle, a scatter of colored vials, a small white wad of cloth, several long thin metal implements for cutting and stirring, and other such utensils—then gestured the young attendant away with the dismissive flick of her wrist. After which she shifted the white marble cups into a tight cluster then dug into a pocket and pulled out a fat brown pouch which brought a twinkle to her eye while the pink tip of her tongue glided across her full lips.

The young neophyte dipped another grimacing curtsey, turned to remove herself but stopped and dared an inquiring look up at her towering superior without inclining her head.

Gwendora caught the subtlety of the neophyte's eyes-only askance and, upraising her chin to better look down at the shaven-headed girl garbed in itchy wool, she raised her brows.

"Head Mistress," the younger said, soft voice atremble with irritation. "It'll be a month tomorrow since you put me in the woolies for my—" She paused and cleared her throat. "For my minor lapse in judgment. For the love of gods can I please take this godsdamned—" But there she clipped short, wincing at her slip of tongue, and cleared her throat again into a more supplicating tone. "May it please the Head Mistress that I be removed from the woolies to continue my studies?"

"A minor lapse in judgment?" Gwendora fisted one hip while considering the girl overlong. "That's stating it rather mildly." She glanced sidelong across the table at Aggie, who betrayed an amused little smirk, then set the brown pouch on the table next to the cups and interlaced her fingers before her. "As I recall, you poured a strong batch of lythenol into"—another glance at Aggie—"who was it?"

"Senior Alchemist Normando," Aggie said, her jaw tensing to restrain a full grin from showing.

"Yes, yes," Gwendora continued, nodding. "Senior Alchemist Normando. I wouldn't call pouring lythenol into Master Normando's morning tea a minor lapse in judgment. The man still smells like a . . . like a . . ." She undid her hands and flicked her wrist in gesture at Aggie for the proper words.

"Like a bogskunk's butt?" Aggie pursed her lips, fighting back the threatening spread of a grin.

Gwendora snapped her fingers. "Exactly. Like a bogskunk's, well, bottom. No, Lodessa. You're request is denied. At least until Master Normando stops emitting an odor so foul that he can conduct his classes again without the students having to plug their noses shut."

The young neophyte Lodessa blew out a deflating huff that withered her by inches. "Yes, Head Mistress." She hung her shaved head, pale cheeks flushing. "Of course not, Head Mistress. I beg your pardon."

Lodessa stayed her place, her imploring gaze shifting in silent askance for Aggie to speak up on behalf of her plight in all its insufferable misery. But Aggie, though grinning now, crushed Lodessa's hopes with the firm shake of her head. Defeated, turning to make leave with her empty tray, Lodessa huffed another sigh and muttered something beneath her breath.

"What was that?" Gwendora asked, eyebrows pinching together over a scolding glare. "Speak up. Because it sounded to me that you just requested another month in—"

Lodessa spun round, panic blooming her eyes, hands fumbling to maintain hold of her tray to stay it clattering to floor. "Oh no!" she said, shaking her bobbing head with vigor while inching backwards. "Of course not, Head Mistress. I only remarked on how beautiful you look today. Exquisite. Radiant. Immaculate—"

"That's enough," Gwendora said, face pinching. "Button it."

"Yes, Head Mistress. Sorry, Head Mistress." Lodessa spun away and hurried round the table, removing with the empty tray, bare feet slapping the floor with haste as she scurried past a smirking Shandra toward the doors where stood Jacob.

"I did not give you permission to leave," Gwendora said.

Lodessa froze, cringing mid step.

"Stay," Gwendora said, pointing at the far wall. "There."

Lodessa groaned and huffed into a hunch. "Yes, Head Mistress."

She shuffled in a slouch to stand with her back against the far wall, glowering at the floor between her feet while awaiting the Head Mistress to beckon her further assistance. She held the tray across her lap while behind it she scratched at hidden itches.

"Now squat for twenty, stand for ten," Gwendora said.

Lodessa pouted up at her.

"Gwen," Aggie said, "really? She's already—"

"Yes," Gwendora said in a tone brooking no argument, "really. Twenty and ten, Lodessa. While holding the tray."

Lodessa blew out her cheeks. "Yes, Head Mistress." Her back to the wall, she walked her feet out and sank into a quarter squat while resting the tray atop her lap.

"Deeper," Gwendora said.

Grimacing, Lodessa sank deeper into a half squat putting her thighs parallel to the floor, and there began mouthing through a silent count of twenty seconds before standing for ten in repeat fashion of her burning thighs while battling her itchy woolies.

Banzu stared at the punished girl, his pity for her swelling, while questioning his judgment of trusting the sadistic Head Mistress. *What have I gotten myself into?*

"Now that that's settled." Gwendora opened the fat leather pouch on the table and, humming to herself in the pleased manner of a cook working alone in her kitchen on a lazy day, she plucked out a hearty pinch of black herbs veined with green then separated them into equal portions dropped into the three white marble cups. She ground the herbs within the cups using the black marble pestle, giving birth to a spicy aroma scenting the air with the perfume of damp forest moss and licorice.

Banzu questioned the activity with a look. But Aggie answered him with a bare shrug only, and Gwendora paid him no mind at all while she hummed through her grinding work producing powder from herbs—*scrtich-scrtich-scritch.*

After a time he made the deliberate clearing of his throat. Then again, louder.

"Hmm?" Gwendora looked up from her pestle chore. "Oh." She set the pestle beside the cluster of cups, her smile easy and open. "I do love my sweetnettle tea." Smile tightening, she locked Banzu's gaze and cocked her right eyebrow as if cocking an elbow for striking. "I thought I told you to sit."

Banzu chewed back a retort and sat in the left chair. Shandra walked up to standing behind him and gripped the top backs of the two chairs in her hamhands with such squeezing strength their wooden joints squeaked, earning a disapproving glance from the Head Mistress so that Shandra removed her hands to her hips and stood with beefy arms akimbo.

"What's lythenol?" Banzu asked over Shandra's grumbling mumbles behind him.

Gwendora glanced past him and the looming Shandra at Lodessa. "Lythenol is a potent derivative of the chemical secretion from the anal glands of the tarweasel."

Banzu scrunched his face. *Anal glands?* "Eww." He twisted a leaning glance past Shandra at Lodessa, who finished another standing count of ten then sank again into another half squat of twenty, and chuckled. "And someone drank it?"

Gwendora nodded. "Master Normando has a notoriously weak sense of smell earned from an unfortunate accident he suffered many years ago. His alchemical pursuits don't always go according to plan."

"He's also an infamous curmudgeon among the students," Aggie said while rounding the table opposite the Head Mistress. She sat in the chair at Banzu's right, crossed one leg over the other and cupped her top knee with interlaced hands all in the same graceful motion. "Eighty years of suffering pranks tends to make one . . . bitter."

"He's not the most well-liked of teachers," Gwendora said. "I'll give you that. But he comes from a long line of alchemists and has earnestly served the Academy his entire life. Just as his father before him and his grandfather before that, and so on. He deserves the proper amount of respect due him." She shot a hot glance at Lodessa. "Regardless of what certain insubordinate students may otherwise presume." Then tightened her gaze on Banzu. "As do we all."

She picked up the kettle and poured steaming water into the cups, filling them three-quarters full so that their contents performed tiny whirlpools of inky black that seconds more lightened into golden yellow swirls slowing in little white marble wells. She set the kettle aside then closed her eyes, leaned forward over the steaming waft and drew in a deep nostril inhale, smiling open and easy again. She slid two cups across the table and raised the third. "Drink."

Banzu rolled his eyes at the offered cups. "No thanks. I'm not thirsty."

Gwendora tightened her eyes, her voice. "It wasn't a suggestion." She raised her cup, peered at him over the brim through fine violet slits. "Drink."

He opened his mouth to fire back a retort—but Aggie jabbed him in the ribs with her elbow, producing a grunt. "Fine," he said, making a cuss of the word. He sat forward, picked up the two offered cups, handed one to Aggie then sipped his while intending on swallowing the herbal brew down fast as the hot temperature would allow so they could just be on with it.

But the moment the first sip of sweetnettle tea flowed over his taste buds he drew the cup away, surprised how sweet the taste despite its pungent earthy scent. The steam smelled of rain and worms and moss, but the tea itself—

"It tastes like honey," he said, then swallowed another, fuller sip. "*Mmm*, it's good."

Gwendora smiled, pleased, while exchanging a quick look with Aggie through the flick of her gaze. "Liquid sunshine is what folks back home call it." She drew in a long and airy quaff, more inelegant slurp than refined sip, for savoring effect of taste, then sloshed it round her mouth before the satisfying swallow and the exhale thereafter. "Though reminiscence of home is not the only reason why I carry some with me wherever I go." She took another sip, this more delicate and with refined pinkie extended, while watching him over the steaming brim of her cup. "It helps invigorate the body while relaxing the mind, which leads to more tranquil discussions all around. I've developed the habit of drinking it before every important discussion, and certainly every palavar." A pause, the flick of her gaze to Aggie and back. "No exceptions. The effects . . . help set a particular mood." Another eyeing sip at Banzu. "We've a saying back home. 'A little shot of liquid sunshine will do you just fine.'"

Banzu sipped more of the sweetnettle tea while noting the secret wink Gwendora shot Aggie over their risen cups as they watched him. Already his mind relaxed from the pleasant brew warming down his throat and into his belly blooming through increasing tingles. Alert yet relaxed at the same strange time, and the next he knew he'd emptied his cup, several minutes of agreeable silence having passed.

He set his cup atop the table, thoughts treading calmer waters. He accepted Aggie's empty cup and set it beside his. And smiled while settling back in his chair, Shandra's looming menace behind him forgotten.

Not so bad really, being here. Gwen seems pleasant enough, after relaxing her guard and allowing the softer woman to bleed through the hard Head Mistress exterior. Melora made the tea out as some kind of disgusting poison. Tasted great to me.

Melora.

Alone.

In the tower.

Surrounded by bandits.

And nothing I can do for her here.

His smile wavered, the calming effects wrought from the tea waning to resurfacing anger.

Friggin hell, where has my mind gone?

He looked at Aggie looking at him. He gave Gwendora a suspicious squint though said nothing while he straightened and crossed his arms. The Head Mistress kept her features blank, unreadable, though fine lines of cunning creased round her calculating stare.

He shifted on his bottom, antsy with the urge to get up and move.

She's baiting me into friendlier airs, that's what this is. That's all this is.

Priorities shifted to the forefront of his mind.

I have an Essence to retrieve, a Godstone to find, a Khan to kill, and Melora to return to. And none of that gets done sitting here drinking her stupid tea.

I've tasted her carrot.

"Well?" he asked, bracing for the stick. "What now?"

CHAPTER THIRTY-FIVE

"Now?" Head Mistress Gwendora Pearce sliced through the air in front of her with her rigid left hand, dividing one subject finished before moving into the next. "Now we get down to business. There's a lot to do and little time to do it."

"Good," Banzu said, shifting in his chair, anxious at what that business entailed of him. "Great. Then lay it on me. The sooner we finish the sooner we can go get Melora."

Gwendora pursed her lips tight. "Yes. Well. Agatha?" She extended her left hand out over the table between them, palm up. "If you would, please."

"Of course." Aggie stood, removed the silver ring from the widower's digit of her right ringfinger, and placed it upon the Head Mistress's upturned palm, then sat at Banzu's right in a tenser posture than before. She shifted from cheek to cheek, flashed Banzu a little smile that disappeared while her eyes twitched at the Head Mistress in gesture for him to pay attention. *This is it*, those eyes said. *We are doing this thing, and now it's begun.*

Banzu nodded, his swordslinger's eyes ripe with focus for picking up subliminal hints of body language unnoticed by ignorant others, a trick earned from years of habitual training against a deceptive swordslinger teacher. Nervous twitches, subtle tells, slight shifts in posture, dipping or tensing shoulders, or a recurring tick just before a repeat action. Swordplay was psychological as much as physical.

Added to that Jericho learned the notice of a few choice conversational body signals from his years spent as a Soothsayer servitor to the Academy which he'd taught his nephew.

Most people scratched their neck or touched their nose or rubbed an eye only a few times in an entire day, so to commit the act several times during a single conversation betrayed a likely lie. The trick there lay in detecting the particular subject which set them to scratching that false itch, then exploit it.

Though other tells proved slighter, like a brief tugging on one's earlobe while averting eye contact, or maintaining strong eye contact overlong to punctuate a repeated lie as truth, and often with palms upturned in subconscious request. Jericho relayed that women often touched the nape of their neck or fiddled with jewelry while broaching uncomfortable information whereas men tended to cross their arms or over-gesticulate with their hands.

The list tallied on, not that Banzu possessed much experience in applying this latter knowledge to others than his uncle and Melora considering his life of solitude. But he would listen. And he would watch. For the Head Mistress had proven herself a cunning woman who believed in telling others only what she thought they needed to know while guarding the rest for leverage against them.

Gwendora dipped her right hand into a side pocket of her blue dress veined with silver trim and produced a matching silver ring, this one Banzu knew as Jericho's wedding band for the brass necklace still lay strung through the ring's hollow, broken by the hand that yanked it from round Banzu's neck after his dealings with the aizakai and stonemen. She pulled the thin length of chain free of the ring with all the delicacy of one removing a long golden strand of hair from their soup and set it aside atop the table amid the clutter, then she set both rings together in clear view between the black marble pestle and mortar.

"Two rings," she said. "A perfect pair of perfect circles. Identical in every way. And yet—"

"What's all this other stuff for, anyways?" Banzu uncrossed his arms and sat forward, his mind peeking down curious avenues while he waved a hand in fanning gesture at the spread utensil clutter thereon the tabletop. What with all the colored vials and powders and utensils and the rest Lodessa carried to the table, too many materials for the simple brewing of tea. He pointed at the two rings with V'd fingers, the center of Gwendora's attentions, and cut to the heart of the matter while watching her face for any signs of twitching at the corners of her mouth or eyes, her hands for any unconscious scratching of false itches, her stance for any awkward shifting. "And what's so special about their wedding rings?"

Frowning at the interruption, Gwendora leaned forward and slapped Banzu's pointing hand away before he could achieve plucking one or both of the rings up.

"These are the keyrings," she said. "The scriptures say they unlock the Essence of the First so that the savior-slayer reborn can detect the presence of the Godstone no matter where it has fallen and no matter the distance. Only then will he truly become the savior-slayer reborn. *If*"—and her eyes flared with emphasis—"the last Soothsayer came to us cleansed of the bloodlust, that is. The Veilfall gave no indication of your"—she wrapped her lips round the word as she spoke it—"*condition* upon your arrival, since it would have been triggered by the last Soothsayer regardless whether he was cleansed of the curse or corrupted by it."

The word 'keyrings' struck a familiar chord at the back of Banzu's mind, though faint behind his preoccupation with the Head Mistress.

"I think you know my"—and he overemphasized his mouth in mocking fashion round the word while making his eyebrows dance—"*condition* by now."

He hoped she didn't press the issue by arguing over the semantics of the still-tainted shared collective of the fractured Source. He'd kept the matter relayed to him by Enosh private while explaining his ventures leading up to his arrival in Fist, fearing the confession of his inevitable insanity might instigate his execution. Neither she nor Aggie betrayed any knowledge of the fractured Source thus far. *And if they don't know then I'm not about to tell them. It's my problem to deal with anyways. They can stay out of it.*

Warm tingles of sweetnettle tea flushed through his system, calming his irritation for standing though his thoughts skated on thinning patience.

I don't care about all this pomp and fluff. Melora's waiting. Let's just get this over with. No lecture needed.

But he tempered his tongue and added, "I think I've proven that already by not trying to kill you or anyone else in this room. I'm a master swordslinger, after all. Trained by the best."

He flashed Aggie a proud smile in passing glance while he twisted round on his seat, hung his right elbow up over the back of his chair after 'accidentally' stubbing it into Shandra's belly behind him, and shot past the squat Spellbinder a cocky sideways look over the shoulder at Jacob standing guard next to the doors. Though more so Banzu stared at Griever's hilt jutting from Jacob's left hipwing and pleading for him to snatch it back. Restraint took everything in him not to shoot up and charge the veteran while demanding his sword returned or reclaim it by force.

I could take him. Even without the Power.

"You really think I couldn't have taken my sword back by now?" Banzu announced to the room, though more so to Jacob who thinned the measure of his stern eyes into passive challenge to try just that. Banzu flexed his eager hand open and closed in obvious show, and Jacob mimicked the same flexing gesture at his right hipwing round hilt.

Aggie elbowed Banzu in the ribs. "Hush, Ban."

He grunted and shifted, though his frown proved no match against her admonishing scowl telling him to shut it or else. He shot Jacob a smirking wink regardless before twisting round and facing the Head Mistress.

Gwendora's stern crosshair violets hardened their condemnation upon him. She made a superfluous sniff of the air, nostrils flaring, then spared a glance at Aggie and said, "Yes. Well. We had to be sure. What happened during your arrival would be nothing compared to what you would have done if you instead arrived corrupted by the bloodlust curse."

"They attacked *me,"* Banzu said. He shifted his seat, wanting to spring up and grab her by the ears and scream it in her face. *And they're godsdamned lucky I held back.*

But he swallowed the rest of his feisty response while relaying a mental survey of his situation. A kohatheen locked round his neck, no sword at his side, and three armed and very capable Spellbinders standing well within stabbing distance.

One-hundred fistian soldiers outside the doors. Thousands of aizakai filling the Academy. Jacob armed with two blades and the sure skill for wielding them. And Lodessa . . . Banzu possessed no idea what threat she provided him beyond spiking his tea—*her eyes are blue, not Spellbinder violet*—though he assumed her aizakai given she lived here.

Through his instinctive evaluation of targets he took reflexive notice of the uncontrolled emotional flush aroused within—and realized he stood though remembered none of the quick motion involved.

"Ban," Aggie said in soothing voice, a hand gripping his nearest arm. "Relax."

He blinked at her. *When did I stand?* "What?"

She tugged his arm while imposing a gentle squeeze, eyes darting an indicative glance left at Shandra behind them who hammer-fisted her bared dachra fangs, and past her at Jacob who closed distance to that of half the room with his sword pulled by inches. She glanced right at the Head Mistress now removed a step from the table, Gwendora's face tensed, her hands hidden up behind her back for the pulling of her dachras. All of this catalyzed by Banzu's surge from his chair he remembered no part of.

"Please," Aggie said while applying his arm a firmer tug, "sit." *Before you do something stupid*, her eyes finished for her.

"Oh." He cringed a little before sitting. "Sorry." In lower voice he added, "I don't know what came over me."

Gwendora lowered her empty hands, then flicked a wrist at Shandra who spun her dachra fangs in ambidextrous twirls then sheathed them to her back. Another flick of Gwendora's wrist and Jacob removed to standing beside the doors again, eyeballing Banzu, his cautious hand remaining on hilt.

Lodessa stood watching—until Gwendora snapped her fingers and pointed, and Lodessa returned to her punishing chore of squatting for twenty and standing for ten in repeat fashion of silent count.

"Sweetnettle tea calms the mind," Aggie said in sideways lean. "Though sometimes it heightens one's emotions before it loosens their tongue for truths they wouldn't otherwise speak." A glance at Gwendora. "She neglected to mention the latter is all. It'll pass."

"What?" Banzu jolted tensed. "You drugged me?"

"Not drugged," Gwendora said, her mouth betraying a cunning smile. "Not exactly. The tea helps ensure an exchange of truths during palavar from both parties involved."

He glared at her, and began standing again, a hot string of curses burning up his throat—but Aggie yanked him down with surprising strength.

Shandra closed at his back and gripped his shoulders to stay him from rising again, though she removed back a step, but not before imparting a strong squeeze of her mannish hands, at Aggie's behest.

"All three of us drank it," Aggie said. "We're just more used to it. It will pass. Calm yourself and focus on the task at hand."

He leaned closer, spoke in lower voice. "Why didn't you tell me?"

She rolled her eyes. "Would you have drank it if I did?"

"No."

"Exactly. Relax, Ban. What's done is done. You have no enemies here."

Gwendora issued the deliberate clearing of her throat and fixed Banzu in her piercing crosshairs. "May we continue? Or should I have Shandra tie you to your chair?"

Shandra smiled and cracked her knuckles.

Banzu glared at her then twisted facing straight while huffing a terse breath. He gave a hook-fingered tug on his kohatheen, baring his teeth against the irritating pull of it on his neck, then dropped his hand to his lap and stared at the two rings thereon the table. And jolted to another broken trust punching his guts, his mind making connections.

"Wait a minute," he said. "You mean Jericho had one of the keyrings on him this whole time?"

"Yes," Gwendora said, nodding, the motion slight.

Banzu asked, "Did he know?"

"Yes," Aggie said. "We both did. Part of our duty was to guard them while we awaited the last Soothsayer. Their activation proves no other Soothsayers exist."

Banzu shook his head. "He knew and he never said one godsdamned word about it."

"Language," Gwendora said, curt and firm, an eyebrow cocked.

He ignored her and glanced at Aggie, who disclosed a sly smile. He loosed a dry chuckle while sitting back and crossing his arms. "Friggin hell."

Gwendora smacked the table, scowling. "Language!"

Aggie nudged his ribs with a prodding elbow.

"Sorry. Head Mistress." He eyeballed her over the two rings on the table between them. "He's lucky he never lost it. Or me, neither."

"Destiny," Aggie said.

To which Gwendora nodded agreement.

Destiny? Banzu rolled his eyes and grumbled, "Whatever." He wasn't about to go through this argument again, not with these women and not with his tongue so loose from the sweetnettle tea. He might let slip he'd killed Enosh's mortal avatar before departing the Luna Nexus, and who knew how they would take that news. *Probably as proof I can't be trusted.*

Instead he leaned forward in reaching bid to pluck one of the two silver rings from the table for closer inspection. "So what exactly are they for then?" he asked, his pinching fingers inches from the rings and closing.

Quick as a pawing cat Gwendora snatched up the marble pestle and banged it atop his reaching hand—*thwack!*

"Ow!" Banzu recoiled his hand, hissing and grimacing while shaking the throb from his cracked knuckle. Behind him Shandra laughed. Beside him Aggie loosed an amused little titter. Even Jacob chimed in with a low chuckle. Banzu glared at the Head Mistress. "That friggin hurt."

"Good." Gwendora smiled and waggled the pestle at him. "Patience, Banzu. You must learn obedience. It's my duty to guide you along the path of the Soothsavior. That is why you are here. And the keyrings being brought back together despite the odds only proves as much. Their rejoining saves us much time, and thank gods because we have little enough of it as is."

"What are they for?" he asked again, this time without daring a reach and risking another admonishing pestle crack.

"What are they for, *Head Mistress*," Gwendora corrected him.

He huffed a terse breath.

"Say it," she said.

He thinned his eyes upon her, replied nothing.

And she thinned hers right back. "Say it."

"Gwen, please," Aggie said. "Now is not the time for subjugation. He's not a student, and he's not a child. And with everything that's happened—" She paused, leaned forward and tapped the tabletop with V'd fingers inches shy from, though indicative of, the keyrings. "He's here and so are these."

Gwendora frowned, a subtle fierceness entering her unyielding stare. She pointed the pestle in admonishing gesture at Aggie then shook it at Banzu with emphasis. "There won't be another insubordinate Soothsayer running about here. Not while I'm Head Mistress. And not with everything that's at stake. Jericho caused enough trouble when he was alive. I'll not abide those same antics in another unruly, impulsive, stubborn—"

But there she clipped her elevating chiding short as her stern glare broke into softer violet pools and her tight jaw opened into a surprised O of silent regret.

Aggie turned her head aside and swiped the threat of tears from her prominent cheeks before they betrayed her momentary lapse of weakness. The bitter loss of her husband, and at the hands of the man sitting beside her no less, tore her apart inside no matter how far down she buried the hurt.

"Forgive me, Agatha." Gwendora flashed a self-conscious smile. "I didn't mean to—"

Aggie waved her quiet. "It's okay." She cleared her throat while straightening in her chair, spine rigid, shoulders back and chin high. All Spellbinder Agatha dar'Shuwin again, dutiful and down to business. "There's no point in forcing anything on him. You can lead a horse to water but you can't make it drink. So let's give him a reason to trust us, then let him drink his fill. What we talked about last night, remember?"

Gwendora sighed, nodded, and contemplated this for a deliberate stretch while considering Banzu overlong.

"What?" he asked, but received no answer. He shifted on his chair and gazed round in the stillness, all eyes upon him. "What?" He squirmed, nerves bunching. "*What?*"

Gwendora's eyes thinned into cold calculation. "Fine," she said, shattering the uncomfortable silence. She gestured the flick of her pestle. "Do it. Before I change my mind."

"Do what?" Banzu asked.

Aggie nodded and stood.

Banzu tensed when she gripped him by the shoulders and turned him facing away. He resisted, turning back. "What are you—"

She smacked him on the head.

"Ow!"

Then pinched higher and harder on his trapezius and turned him facing away again. "Relax," she said, then leaned closer and whispered in his ear, "I'm trusting you, Ban. Don't you dare screw this up."

He turned his head. "Screw what up?"

She sighed and gripped the sides of his head, forced it forward, then tilted his head and spun his kohatheen round so she could work her experienced fingers upon its puzzle-tumbler lock.

She's taking it off? He relaxed a bit. *Oh gods, she's taking it off!*

He fought back a giddy smile at the unexpected boon bestowed him. Seconds lingered into one full minute before Aggie finished working the tiny tumblers into proper alignment and triggered the kohatheen's lock open with a triumphant, resounding *click*.

Profound joy burst through Banzu's guts when the phantom strangle of his kohatheen collar swung open round his neck upon its invisible hinge connecting its two lanthium crescents. Though he tamed it down, eager parts of him yearned for erupting from his chair and bolting for the doors once the lassitude faded to flourishing reserves of energy surfacing.

"Ahhhhhh." He rolled his head while rubbing at his freed neck. He twisted round smiling, faced Aggie and Gwendora with forgiving eyes. "Thank you."

Gwendora returned him a fraction nod, her hands open at her sides for reaching up behind her back for the pull of her dachras.

Aggie smiled in full bloom, though as she made to snap the kohatheen shut and set it aside atop the table, Gwendora stopped her with the curt clearing of her throat and the stern shake of her head. The Head Mistress returned in full authoritative demeanor, she snapped her fingers at Shandra then pointed at the kohatheen.

Shandra's arm snaked in between the two chairs where she snatch the kohatheen from Aggie's hands.

"Caged or not," Gwendora said, her wary gaze shifting from Aggie and fixing on Banzu, "a tiger's still a tiger."

He frowned though said nothing for it, just happy to have the kohatheen off and not digging into his skin with every twist or turn of his head. Famished instincts screamed to seize the Power in testing bid of its return while taut muscles corded along his bunched jaw bridling the fierce need to see it through.

But he refrained, unmoving in all but his roving eyes while well aware of the thickened tensions choking the room quiet. Jacob eyeballed him extra hard, as did Shandra behind him. *I'm surrounded by Spellbinders.* And however inadequate the expanse of their void-auras compared to Melora's, the hundred armed and armored soldiers outside could flood the room in seconds.

For the moment he wondered how far the true measure of Gwendora's and Aggie's and Shandra's void-auras when weighed against Melora's. *Not much*, he decided by the tell of their wary stares upon him and their guarded postures, even Aggie's despite her smile.

The Head Mistress chose to send Melora because of her expansive void-aura, for she stood the greatest chance of them all at surviving the Enclave's Trio of hunters while eluding any possible magical tracking methods or attacks upon her. To convince Jericho's return or, if words failed, to collar and force him back to Fist. Or worse still, if she arrived too late, she stood the best chance of killing him if he already turned to the bloodlust.

Banzu shifted more comfortably in his chair. *At least the kohatheen's off.*

For now, a returning presence whispered in afterthought, a familiar tone unvoiced since his kohatheen capture. *It's off for now.*

Banzu shuddered, though he hid it well.

* * *

"Now," Gwendora said in firmer voice, and slapped the table while commanding attention. She schooled her face into a resolute mask and leveled her serious gaze upon Banzu, the pupil of her returning focus. "These keyrings have been passed down through the generations since the Academy's founding. From First Mistress Rular to Head Mistress and so forth, awaiting the Veilfall and the return of the savoir-slayer. As the last Pair, Agatha and Jericho were given them to safeguard until we were sure Jericho was the last Soothsayer." She paused, her lips tensing thin with old irritation resurfacing while her gaze shifted to Aggie then back to Banzu. "Until Jericho stole away with his keyring after he found out about you and fled the Academy."

Aggie sat and crossed one leg over the other then set her interlaced hands atop her dominate knee and used the action as her excuse to look away from the Head Mistress's solemn judgment and the underlying accusations beneath insinuating her hand in Jericho's escape, her back stiff, chin up and face proud.

Gwendora held the silence for a lengthy measure before returning her weighty expression to Banzu. Her eyebrows rose into curious little arches, daring him to jolt up and attempt replaying an escape in honor of his runaway uncle.

He smiled, resisting the urge to flinch into standing for a pretend run toward the doors just to chide her, unmoving in all but his thoughts reflecting upon the revelations of Jericho's escape though as well his uncle's first turning to the bloodlust as told Banzu through Melora.

Falsified reports of a Soothsayer luring Jericho and Aggie out in an ambush intended to murder Aggie while capturing Jericho so the ambushers could return him to the Academy for a hefty reward. But for that Jericho killed them while turning to the bloodlust, and he almost killed Aggie, impaling her with Griever, though her Spellbinder blood mixed into his cuts during their fight and paralyzed him.

Gwendora found them, and would have killed Jericho then and there if not for Aggie's desperate pleas to collar him instead. And Gwendora helped cover the debacle up from the current Head Mistress then—

Gwendora smacked the table, snapping Banzu's wandering attentions back to present.

"Are you listening?" she asked, curt and sharp.

"Huh?" He stiffened up and nodded despite not having heard anything she'd said for the past minute. "Of course I'm listening." He squirmed his chair. "But . . . maybe you should go over it again. For Aggie's sake."

Lodessa giggled then slapped a covering hand over her mouth.

Aggie frowned and leaned closer. "Pay attention, Ban. Or she'll put the kohatheen back on."

Gwendora's nostrils flared beneath the violet scold of her eyes.

He straightened, nodded. "Yes, Head Mistress. I'm listening."

"As I was saying," Gwendora continued, "Jericho was supposed to use the keyrings once he became the last." She paused, the bridge of her nose crinkling in dark little furrows while she thinned her gaze upon a memory overtaking her in a frown she abolished seconds more. "But plans have a way of changing whenever you Soothsayers are involved." A rolling of her hand in gesture over the two rings. "So now they are yours. Watch."

He opened his mouth.

"And stop interrupting."

She plucked up the white wad from the collection of items on the table and unfolded it, revealing a gauzy mask with thin string ties. She set the mask over her mouth and nose, tied its strings back into a little bow behind her head. She picked up one of the small colored glass vials, pulled its cork stopper—*pop*—and emptied out white powder into the black marble mortar by tapping the vial's side with a fingernail—*click-click-click*.

After which she chose a second vial from among the multicolored assortment and poured a thin stream of orange liquid over the tiny mound of fine white powder. She held a third vial over the mixture and shook it, peppering a glitter of silver flakes into the mortar. Exchanging the third vial for a set of long, thin metal tongs, she waited while staring over the concoction within the black marble mortar.

Pop! Hiss! Fizzle!

Banzu leaned forward palming both knees to better see the curious alchemical play within the mortar. The orange liquid bubbled and frothed while dissolving the white powder and silver glitter into some manner of fizzing red fluid that—

"Sit back," Gwendora barked while shooing him to obey with the long tongs in her waving hand. She looked ready to stab an eye out if necessary.

But before she finished waving him away, a plume of thick, acrid yellow smoke puffed up from the mortar in a little explosive mushrooming cloud that rocked the mortar upon the table while causing the collection of glass vials to shake and rattle.

Banzu rocked backwards in startled flinch, avoiding the brunt of the mushrooming plume's flaring heat from burning his face by fractions though not its strong caustic stink from wrinkling his nose. He cringed away, eyes stinging up with tears as he inhaled enough of the foul substance to induce a coughing fit that approached the point of gagging.

"Gods that stinks!" He waved a hand in front of his face while blinking his prism vision clear.

Gwendora plucked up one of the keyrings within her long pinching tongs. She maneuvered it over the mortar bowl into the cloud of yellow smoke and dropped it down within, earning an audible *clink*, then did the same with the other keyring before stabbing the tongs into the smoky mortar and stirring its active contents.

When she removed the tongs from the smoky bowl, their shorter tips shown melted off as if dipped into some sort of acidic solvent. She set them aside, uncaring of their burning hisses scoring the table through the white linen cloth, and focused her attentions upon the mortar and the keyrings and the busy concoction laboring therein.

More bubbling and hissing and popping and crackling while yellow smoke arose most foul in the air. There issued another puffing mushroom spume of smoke, this a deep purple, jetting up from the marble bowl and dispersing the yellow cloud above it. Gwendora fanned her hand over the mortar, waving clear the smoky air, then removed her mask and set it aside.

"Now you can look," she said.

And Banzu did just that. Leaning forward, he found the mortar empty of all contents save for the two rings nestled atop a little nest of fine black powder. Though some manner of change had taken place therein and now they appeared different, possessing a truer silver than before but with faint golden hints. And tiny writing engraved round their outer surfaces in unrecognized arcane script.

"Is that—" he began.

"Lanthium," Gwendora finished for him. "Yes." She plucked one of the rings out from the black mortar bowl betwixt finger and thumb with no fear of burns now that the caustic agents had spent into a fine black powder, and upheld it, blew on it, inspecting it while turning it about. Smiling, she set the keyring down then performed the same with the other.

Lanthium? Banzu leaned forward evermore. *Wizard's metal. Indestructible once forged. Godsdamn you* and *your secrets, Jericho.*

He reached for the two lanthium rings then withdrew his empty hand at sight of Gwendora reaching for the nearby pestle in preparation for another banging swat of his hand. "What was all that about?"

"Silver-coated lanthium," Gwendora said. "A concealment, and a safeguard. I had to concoct the acidic bath to remove the silver coating. Master Normando would have done it himself, though"—an admonishing glance at a sweating Lodessa mid squat across the room—"his instructions are far less pungent than his odorous presence."

"Why hide them like that?" Banzu asked.

Aggie answered without looking at him, her chair creaking with her forward leaning while she appraised the keyrings in closer inspection. "The silver coating was put on after their forging to keep"—and here her face twisted up foul as she sat back—"Dethkore from ever using them in any way if he was ever resurrected and gained possession of either of them. Silver is a burning bane to the unliving."

"Dethkore can use them?" Enosh told Banzu of his ties to the necromaster, but not of this. "But he's not a Soothsayer."

"No," Gwendora said. "But he could attempt to prevent you from—"

An interrupting pound upon the doors cut her short.

* * *

Gwendora and Aggie exchanged tensing glances.

Banzu twisted halfway round on his seat for a look behind at Shandra walking toward the doors and the knocker beyond.

Jacob turned to Shandra's passing though stayed his place, his focus on Banzu despite the interrupting knock and his closer proximity to the double doors, though his fingers fanned a grip round the hilt of good fistian steel at his right hipwing while the other hovered close over Griever's at his left in preparation for a double pulling.

Banzu studied the veteran soldier's suggestive posture by instinct, knowing from the experience bled into him courtesy of the shared collective that a double pulling of swords proved no good but for cutting your arms in the awkward process or getting yourself killed because the flourishing maneuver left you exposed. This knowledge a feather of dead men's memories left drifting round in his head from years ago, considering he never tried the flashy maneuver himself and yet he had many times through different bodies.

I'd lunge in and puncture vitals before he even drew them by half. The crossed pull protects the stomach but leaves the throat unguarded, let alone the imbalance of his arms and—

Gods, I'm doing it again. Estimating Jacob as if we're about to cross blades.

He blinked the scrutiny away and wondered just who Jacob intended for the necessary hand-off considering the lack of another swordsman present besides Griever's true owner. Then he wondered why all the sudden tension from the interruption considering the hundred soldiers outside.

He need not wonder long.

The double doors pushed open from without, splitting partways, just as Shandra reached for one of the handles then stepped back a space. A black-mustached soldier of middle years and garbed in fistian blacks and blues strode inside through the line of divided space between the parted doors, his tan face a blank slate but for the obvious years of hard soldiering told through the scars stitched upon his prominent cheeks and high forehead and square chin. He carried more than a hint of mystery into the room indicated by the roll of paper pinched at the middle in his left fist, for his right hand looked so gnarled that his fingers resembled a taut tangle of twisted roots incapable of accomplishing anything more than thumping a fleshy club.

Shandra tucked the opened half-moon kohatheen into her belt while blocking the soldier's approach. She held out one meaty hand in askance for the rolled parchment he carried.

But the soldier denied her with a reluctant shake of his head. "I've an urgent message for the Head Mistress," he said, "and the Head Mistress only."

Which earned an irritated grunt from Shandra who puffed up on her feet while balling her fists, seconds from clouting the man upside his head.

The resolute soldier noticed Jacob and saluted him with a quick head bow while pounding his gnarled hand to his chest, then he leaned aside and gazed past Shandra.

"Excuse me," Gwendora said. She walked round the table, waving Aggie down in passing, and strode across the room with gliding urgency, the silver-trimmed bottom of her blue dress whispering round her soft-padding feet.

Irritated by the interruption, Banzu glanced at the lanthium rings on the tabletop, wanting to be on with this whole keyring business so he could find the stupid Godstone then get on with the important business of killing the Khan, this annoying delay fracturing his thin patience.

Aggie stood again and clasped her hands in front of her though did not pursue the Head Mistress across the room. She watched with a twitching urgency of wanting to join them but for that her lowered position within the Academy ranks stayed her to place. Protocol between the Head Mistress and her Spellbinder subordinates overruled her and Gwendora's long years of friendship, even for Aggie who once stood in line to ascend to Head Mistress ahead of Gwendora before she confessed her indiscretion of helping Jericho escape.

Gwendora accepted the scroll from the mustachioed soldier then dismissed him with a succinct nod and the rolling wave of her hand at the doors. She unrolled the parchment for a read—or, at least, she started unrolling the scroll but stopped with it halfway open upon noticing the soldier staying his spot.

"Yes?" She addressed the younger soldier from over the top of the half-opened parchment, staring down over him from her prominent height. "And you linger . . . because?"

The soldier cleared his throat, glanced down and shifted his feet beneath the Head Mistress's scrutinizing gaze in a bizarre display of discomfort considering the hardened battle scars marking his life's rank upon his face. "Because you will have orders for me to relay, Head Mistress. After you read it."

"Is that so." Gwendora unrolled the parchment to full reveal and raised it for reading. Seconds only and she produced an audible gasp. The spread sheet quivered in her hands. She drew it closer and read its contents a second time. Then a third, punctuated by the slow shake of her head.

"Gwen?" Shirking protocol, Aggie rounded her chair, took a step forward then stopped. She glanced at Banzu. "What is it, Gwen?" She took another hesitant step—then broke free of invisible restraints and strode across the room to the Head Mistress's side, protocols be damned.

Gwendora greeted Aggie with a troubled look. She handed her the parchment without word and stole a wary glance at Banzu.

As Aggie read, her right hand let loose from the curling bottom of the scroll and covered her gaping mouth, trapping words she dared not voice. She glanced at Banzu, at Gwendora, at the scroll, at Gwendora again.

"What is it?" Banzu stood. "What's going on?"

Silence.

The soldier's gaze shift past the three Spellbinders between them, and his eyes bloomed wide with recognition. He shot Jacob a questioning look while pointing at Banzu with his one good hand, and Jacob returned a firm nod. The soldier's pointing hand dropped along with his jaw as he returned a stupefied stare at Banzu, his crippled hand settling atop the sword's hilt sheathed at his hip, checking to ensure his weapon still there.

Still unused to such frightened challenges of reactions, Banzu rolled his eyes at the soldier eyeballing him with all the intimidation of a startled rabbit, then returned his watchful gaze to the trio of Spellbinders.

"Get out," the Head Mistress said in a low growl, drawing the soldier's wary gaze. He looked from her to Jacob and back. Until Gwendora pointed past him at the doors and stamped a foot, her voice a snapping whip. "I said out!"

Lodessa, sweating from her punishing efforts, her back pressed against the wall, straightened from her half squat and produced a little squeal at the Head Mistress's flare of voice. She fanned her silver tray from down over her lap to up over her face and held it there. A tiny sidestep to her right, then another and another as she inched her way toward the double doors, hoping to sneak her way into an escape from the room and away from the Head Mistress's spike of agitation.

"Yes, Mistress!" The soldier snapped stiff, bowed his head while pounding his gimp hand to his chest over his heart in gesture. He spun on his heels and strode away, pulling the double doors shut behind him.

Not far from those closing doors, Lodessa stopped her sideways slinking and lowered the silver tray from over her face, revealing big blue eyes above lips pressed tight. Her escape route sealed shut by the soldier, she slumped against the wall, grimacing.

Silence . . . at last broken by the crinkling of parchment paper rolled up followed by Aggie's edged voice.

"Tell him, Gwen." Aggie's face almost as grim as the Head Mistress's ashen pallor, she looked at Banzu. "Or I will. He has a right to know."

Gwendora said nothing. She shook her head in slow denial while staring through Aggie into some private space of viewing.

What the frig was that all about? "Tell me what?" Banzu asked.

Aggie said, "Reports came in late last night confirming those of a few days ago, but—" She stopped, glanced at Gwendora and waited, hoping to provoke the Head Mistress into speech.

Gwendora crossed her arms and chewed her bottom lip, staring ahead though she set her right foot to *tap-tap-tapping.*

And for the first time since meeting her, Banzu noted the iron in the Head Mistress's spine melting.

"Tell me what?" His heartbeat skipped its pace when no one answered him. "*What?*"

Gwendora blinked hard and swept her refocusing stare to him, but she said nothing despite the contemplative shifting of her deliberating gaze. Beside her Aggie mouthed unvoiced words while awaiting the Head Mistress to precede her. Shandra caught the anxious fever ailing the other two Spellbinders through sheer nearness and rocked on her feet while her hands twitched through priming flexes at her sides in want for grabbing on to something more tangible than air and squeezing it crushed.

The Head Mistress regained her regal composure by taking the rolled parchment from Aggie then handing the scroll away to Shandra who strangled it in a double-fisted grip. Gwendora inclined her chin while straightening stiff, sniffed hard and cleared her throat while pulling her shoulders back in reclaiming show of her authority. Though bristling agitation pulled the fine lines of worry taut across her face, and elevated strain betrayed her voice when next she spoke.

"Hannibal Khan's army has been sighted across the Azure Plains." Another clearing of her throat, a desperate attempt at delaying voicing the inevitable. "He's preparing to march against Fist as we speak."

* * *

Scriiitch! and there tore in half the rolled parchment strangled within Shandra's hamhands who scowled at the Head Mistress's dread reveal of Hannibal Khan's advancing army, Shandra's scowl tightening round a smoldering gaze possessing depths of hunger for the imminent battle. She released the torn parchment and gripped the handles of her dachra fangs though stayed their pull.

Clang! as the silver tray slipped loose from Lodessa's hands, the girl squeaking. She threw anxious glances of longing at the double doors a mere three wide steps on her right . . . if only she could achieve slipping leave beneath the Head Mistress's notice.

Aggie appeared the most composed, saying nothing, shifting little, posture taut, her vigilant stare focal on Banzu across the room. Beside her Gwendora engaged again her private space of worry while mouthing words unvoiced. Beyond them Jacob's tightening grip creaked round the leather-wound hilt at his right hipwing in the thickening quiet.

Banzu saw all and yet none of this.

For revelation triggered the taut snare of his bridled animus while pressurized flashes stole behind his eyes, these hot skips and flitters of action spliced with brief spaces of cold black: of grabbing Aggie's chair, of swinging it overhead then smashing it to bits on the floor, a roar ripping from his throat while fury sluiced in a burst of rage beyond any dream of resistance.

A buzzing drive filled every crack in his fractured soul, packing its fissures with the seething pain of an unfulfilled promise. The melting edge of explosion trembled the orgasmic verge of savagery where man submitted to the primal side of their latent nature too rooted in genes for true burial inside the weaker humanity housing it.

An irresistible smile crossed his teeth, stretching, lips peeling, baring fevered exhales drawn through flaring nostrils. A catatonia of thought consumed his logic while a thousand inner voices sang in a rising surf of noise, prominent among them Jericho's requesting blind purpose of sole pursuit.

Kill.

Banzu's skin flushed hot and tingling.

Kill.

The edges of his vision misted crimson.

Kill.

His taut muscles soaked the adrenaline rush, priming with the fierce need for more, only more, gods more.

Kill!

He stood atremble, his rage a fever, his body craving action, his soul lusting vengeance.

The naked murder edging across his face reflected in the five pairs of startled eyes watching back him from across the room. He captured a sliver of self-control by closing his hands into tight fists at his sides, strangling the air.

"Banzu—" Gwendora began in a quivering tone so that she cleared her throat and began again in a stronger, more deliberate voice. "Banzu. Calm down. We've been over this. You're not here for the Khan. He doesn't matter now that—"

"Doesn't matter?" His voice a guttural growl, eyes hot blazes of grief, regression to revenge his only purpose stole through him in a hot breath waking the fevered parts of him. "Tell that to my uncle," he said through clenched teeth. "Oh wait. You can't. Because he's dead."

"Our soldiers will deal with the Khan," Gwendora said. "I've an entire army at my disposal." She raised her hands palms out and advanced a single step. "Please, remember your promise." She dared another step. "We have more important issues to—"

"Screw you." He turned, snatched the keyrings from the table and held them in his clenched left fist. "We already have the friggin keyrings." He shook his fist, the rings trapped therein, and squeezed so hard as to crush them into dust if such a thing were only possible. "The Khan's out there"—he threw his other arm out, pointing past her—"just waiting for me to kill him." He paused and licked his lips, tasting delicious premonitions of Khan's blood. "I could end him right here, right now."

Gwendora opened her mouth for more—then flinched backwards a step when Banzu advanced a challenging step toward her, toward them all. Aggie said something but he ignored her. He drew in deep, nostrils flaring beneath frenzied eyes of murderous promise locked upon the Head Mistress.

"You attacked me," he said. "You abused me, you tied me up, and I still agreed to your bullshit. Because I made a promise. No more!" He swiped his rigid right hand through the air. "Not on this. Not when the Khan's this godsdamned close." The shift of his murderous glare, though his tone no less feral. "I'm sorry, Aggie. But I warned you." The keen thinning of his raptor's gaze returning to the Head Mistress. "If you don't get the hell out of my way, right now, all of you, I *will* go through you." He didn't know how and he didn't care, for in the moment he only knew he would die trying. "I promise you that."

Shandra pulled her dachras.

Jacob pulled his sword.

Lodessa slid down the wall and shrank into the smallest ball of herself she could manage while burying her head beneath her crossed arms.

Aggie opened her mouth—then closed it, hands flexing at her sides.

"And if you fail?" Gwendora asked, eyebrows cocking crossbows. She drew up taller, dared another forward step, a strength returning to her voice belied by the touch of fear betraying her eyes. "What then? Or what if you lose the keyrings and—"

"Keyrings?" Banzu shook his fist at her as if able to punch her in the face from across the room. "Hannibal Khan is out there and you're still worried about these godsdamned rings?" Hot spittle webbed the corners of his mouth. "Fine!"

He spread the fingers of his right hand and slid one of the keyrings down over his ringfinger, a perfect fit. "I'm not going to tell you again," he said, and transferred the other ring into his right hand then spread his left hand open to do the same.

"Banzu, no!" Aggie yelled, finding her voice while starting toward him in the beginnings of a rush. "Wait! Don't do that!"

While Gwendora's mouth framed an admonishing shout.

"Get the hell out of my way," Banzu said as he slid the other keyring down onto his left ringfinger, "or I swear to gods I'll—"

Beneath his notice the tiny arcane script carved thereon the keyrings flared a molten orange as frigid energies punched through him, vibrating his bones while clipping his speech.

He vanished in a brilliant flash of blinding white light.

CHAPTER THIRTY-SIX

The frigid flare of all-consuming white light jolted Banzu into a darkness so sudden and silent the swallowing burst of black rattled his displaced spirit. A wave of distortion swept over him, tidal and crashing, through the jarring transition of his delivery from the Academy there one moment and gone the next, his abrupt denial of breath mid sentence startling him.

Breathing turned a precious task of worship for a terrifying juncture stretching breathless fractions into choking forevers while his awareness of self drifted outside his body floating somewhere at the other end of time where lived only stillness.

The sure tether of mind and body remained, though the distance between action and thought became a long and arduous journey unto itself. His mind sobered quick from the intoxicating rage that had enveloped him upon the Head Mistress's reluctant admission of Hannibal Khan, doused by the quickening cold flush of suffocation. But his physical self reacted sluggish and slow to the echo chamber commands of his racing thoughts.

His eyes bulged.

The whipping master of frantic panic lashed and scored his unruly spirit, yet some emotionless aspect of his cognizant mind not preoccupied with restoring breath ran through avenues of questions as to the how and the where and why of it all. Via the same accidental magic actuated through the mysterious keyrings transporting him to this otherworldly vacuum of blackness, he surmised in the blink of an eye moment of epiphany. He had triggered the keyrings with the same ignorance catalyzing the Veilfall, and now he stood somewhere void of air and light and life and explanation.

Stood.

The word rang through his thoughts, a struck bell of reason and presence toiling for any scrap of logic. His consciousness shifted back and forth through the spiritual tether existing between body and mind, seeking reclamation of both yet grasping purchase of neither. Words born upon his inner voice turned diminishing echoes racing down a tunnel inhaling all sound. He floated in specter outside his physical self, viewing the suffocation from afar yet suffering the burning strains of its aching lungs. His mind existed on a plane of time flowing faster than his choking body, thoughts recurring rapid while physical reaction occurred through strange slowness.

He groped at his throat with phantom hands in phantom struggle while his mind replayed through the seconds before his vanishing displacement here. Of Shandra and Jacob brandishing their weapons against his threats. Of Gwendora's mouth opening in preemptive shout. Of Aggie rushing toward him and yelling at him to stop but too late. Of himself slipping on the keyrings in his naïve bid to shut Gwendora up about them then transporting him elsewhere in the span of a blink.

Standing.

He perceived the notion as some distant projection of self while raking at his hitching chest with panicked hands slow to obedience though on the precipice of clawing through shirt and flesh, as if ripping a hole into his locked lungs would provide them precious air.

Until the breathless struggle of his impending demise surrendered to the last of his physical phasing through magical teleportation completing, and his separated mind and body snapped back together, rejoined through their taut spiritual tether yanking them inward, remerging them into one whole being again with such jolting force he rocked on his feet through queasy imbalance as he drew in the first of many precious gulps of vital air in a resounding gasp knifing the gulf of silence, the quick sharp suck of it amplified in echoes.

I'm standing.

He breathed deep while darting eyes hunted through the black pitch for features and forms, his frenzied mind fumbling for clues of himself and his environment. Both keyrings burned his hot flush of skin with frosty intensity, but the cold sensation existed distanced to his stem brain assessing more critical issues first.

I'm . . . who am I?

He sifted through discombobulated thoughts swirling chaotic, groping inward with drunken hands snatching out greased singles of too many memories at play from the whirling tornado of identity leaves shaping a thousand lives lived.

I'm . . .

A laughing father enjoying his children . . . a blood-lusting madman killing those children.

No!

He snagged handfuls of the scattered pieces of his life fluttering amid the confusing shared collective flurry of dead Soothsayers and clutched these precious shards of Banzu Greenlief closer while mashing them together and trying to reform the whole of himself out from the many.

I'm . . . Banzu?

Self-recognition bloomed though tainted by the collected fragments of others so that he tore the foreign memories out and cast them aside while replacing the gaping rents with memories he always knew, packing them tight, piecing himself together.

I'm Banzu.

Whole again, reflections ran rampant behind his eyes.

Arguing in the Academy one moment, slipping the keyrings on, then here the next.

Where's here?

In this place of no places, baffled and alone, everywhere blackest pitch. The magic of the keyrings enacted a transport of sorts, but the knowledge provided no appeasement to the delirium earned from his abrupt transfer between planes. He likened the experience to some invisible godhand gripping his spine then ripping out his entire skeleton only to shove it back inside his body before the boneless collapse.

Equilibrium shaken not stirred, he performed a wobbly step, the direction meaningless, and steadied his questionable balance upon the sure feel of black flooring. With no visual focal point to grasp, the dark ocean world sloshed his senses with vertigo.

He staggered left, right, backwards, all faculties disoriented, hands blind gropes of air seeking tangible purchase of anything solid, his balance agitated by the darkness mocking his pathetic attempt at staying upright. He stumbled in every direction he turned or swayed on stupid feet, the perplexing combination of his missing sense of direction and distance inducing nauseating vertigo churns.

Something unseen caught up against his stepping left boot so that he tripped, arms pinwheeling in futile bid for counterbalance, and fell forward through the aimless black pitch with no sense of where it ended but down.

Bracing tensed for impact achieved little to soften the hard ground punching against his stubbing palms while kissing his chin and snapping his teeth together with a violent *click*. The crashing impact produced white bursts of stars popping behind the whirl of his eyes while banging pain into his crashing knees and planting palms where bits of rough grit dug and cut into his pressing flesh. He hissed through clenched teeth, rolled onto his side and lay staring at the darkness of the nothingness surrounding him.

Where the frig am I?

His mind reflexed inward, nowhere else to hunt, while he squinted, hoping to pierce the impenetrable dark. Muscles corded taut the length of him, his body lifting upon the floor, as thought surrendered to instinct.

He clenched his bleeding hands into fists, squeezing warm trails of blood between the cracks. He yearned for shouting against the fear of moving keeping him still. He denied the scared little boy impulse for hugging his knees to his chest and hiding his face behind them in a fetal curl while waiting for someone to come rescue him. If something unseen rushed him through the dark then so be it, if only for the relief of anything more palpable than nightmares to grab hold of.

Immobile in all but his prowling thoughts, he knew a puzzle here. His civil mind sensed it, a tantalizing tug, the lure to explore all the facts, to turn them this way and that, to find the common thread explaining them all. But the primal part of his nature rebelled with the sense of urgency to get up and move, to go . . . but where?

He drew in deep while seeking calm, his breath a noise in the vacuum of silence. But the surge of his thoughts increased rather than subsided. He scowled at the rush of suspicions, the despairing part of him toying with the possibility that he'd been tricked after all, that the longstanding plans of the Academy and the presiding Head Mistress finally accomplished their scheming goal to rid the world of the last Soothsayer through elimination by sending him here to this place of . . . of . . . he had no idea where.

Purgatory? Elsewhere? Some inescapable hellcave hidden deep within the bowels of the world? Or worse, somewhere existing between the worlds of the living and the dead, condemned to blind groping in the dark in eternal damnation he must suffer alone.

His heart ached for seeing Melora again, but he banished thoughts of her away lest he taint them with new misery.

"No."

His voice a harsh whisper knifing the quiet.

I'll find a way out, if only to see her again.

But . . . why am I here?

The solace of knowing he lay upon firm ground calmed his frazzled nerves while his mind reflexed backwards for possible answers of his Academy departure wrought by the keyrings.

The news of Hannibal Khan's arrival across the Azure Plains wound every fiber of him taut to within a frog's fine hair of snapping. Bridled rage smoldered in his depths for the Head Mistress and for Aggie over their neglect of mentioning anything about the Khan's march for Fist before the unknown soldier delivered the truth.

I trusted them.

They knew this whole time and neither said a word about it.

Why am I not surprised?

Everyone I ever trusted has betrayed or deceived me at some point or another. Jericho with the bloodlust. Melora with the Traveling Well. Gwen and Aggie with the Khan.

Regret gnawed him, trust proving a more painful weapon than edged steel.

Armies don't just appear from thin air. Gwen knew. And worse Aggie knew. This whole godsdamned time. Their eyes showed as much despite how surprised their faces.

Omitting the truth is the same as lying. They welcomed me in to their little circle of secrecy, their Conclave, and still they kept me in the dark, a blind outsider told only what they wanted me to know while guarding the rest as leverage against me.

No wonder they were in such a hurry to enfold me into their Godstone plans. They knew the Khan was coming. And they knew I'd abandon everything the moment I found out.

I almost did. Gods, I wanted to kill right through them. And they would've killed me in turn if I'd tried.

Viewing back on it all with a more logical approach, he realized his inadvertent activation of the keyrings spared his life.

If only I'd known, I could've slipped away the moment Aggie removed my kohatheen and—and what? Hunted through the Academy by thousands of aizakai, that's what, and killed before I reached outside let alone across the plains to Hannibal Khan. By myself. Against an entire army of Bloodcloaks. Standing no chance at all.

He grit his teeth and pounded the floor with his hammering fist, hindsight an unforgiving bitch. And hissed through the pain of sharp grip cutting into his driven flesh.

Pain . . . nothing good ever comes in my life without pain.

He grinded his fist against the rough floor in bloody frustration, embracing the pain while emphasizing that cruel factor of his life, then clutched his bleeding fist to his chest in stupid regret while rolling supine.

A heavy sigh escaped him though extinguished nothing of his seething anger. He loosed a long and blistering string of curses at everyone keeping him from killing Hannibal Khan, the world set against his plight to soothe his grieving woes.

Until the cooling image of Melora's face resolved before his tortured eyes, accompanied by the soughing of her voice in vivid recall before her apologetic shove. *Promise me.*

He reached out to caress the cheek of her image fading round his hand touching only air while his demons surged from their hiding places, searing his heart and heating him to the tips of fingers and toes. He battled the outrage by closing his eyes and reciting her name while tasting its sweetness upon his lips. The task calmed him, relaxed him so that he shifted focus to the immediate matter at hand.

Find out where in friggin hell I am then get the frig out, or I'll never see her again.

Think, Banzu. Think! He drew in deep, expelled overlong. *Okay. The keyrings brought me here to retrieve the Essence of the First. That must be it. No foul play, no trickery, no baited trap or set snare. Just . . .* he sighed, hating the word . . . *just destiny. I put them on. I did this to myself. No one else to blame. And no one else to get me out of here but—*

He tensed as somewhere something roared. An impressive echo of sound. Proud. Majestic. Redolent with the howling vitality and violence of the wilderness. Then, as if to mock its efforts, a maddened cackle sang out from . . . somewhere else, somewhere much closer though just as hidden. The shadows? His mind? The shadows *of* his mind? He lay unsure from which particular direction the roar originated if at all, though he claimed a firm idea as to where escaped that demented laughter soughing in his mind from the fractured depths of his sanity.

But he refused to admit that last aloud, even alone. He shoved aside the impulse of instigating it into crazed conversation he wanted no part of as he learned to do after that particular voice he refused to acknowledge by name first plagued his mind with requests of killing Melora along with everyone else. Indulgence might bring surrender. And to it nothing mattered but vengeance.

He suppressed the introspective urge for hunting the voice and confronting it, and instead concentrated on the here and now and what he could do about it.

***

The residual chill of the keyrings ebbed round his warming fingers. He pushed the irritation to the outskirts of his awareness while creating space at the forefront for focus on the important—returning to the Academy and more so Hannibal Khan.

The latter truth a foolish notion but an honest one, deep as bones, but he didn't care. Not anymore. No point in lying to himself. There stood no others here judging his reasons or condemning his driving hate to fulfill them.

Hannibal Khan . . . so close then snatched away by his own ignorant hand, a leaf upon the upturned palm stolen by risen winds before the closing fingers fisted only air.

"Soon." The promise escaped him in a savage whisper. Time enough for vengeance paid once he escaped this elsewhere place. Until then he would shelve the hot drive of retribution, let it fester and grow in a tumor of hate. No other choice.

He rolled over while groaning curses for banged knees and cut palms. He pushed up into kneeling erect, noting the queer sensation of sucking upon his bleeding palms when he removed them from the sticky ground. A wet spot on his shirt stuck fabric to his chest from where his cut chin had bled driblets. He wiped the small gash on his stubbed chin with the back of one hand then licked it, tasted the blood of his dripping wound and liked it.

Soon.

He drew in a breath and seized the Power through focal invocation for heightened vision, gasping, jolting to the exhilarating rush of Power's potency punching into him, flaring his eyes with luminous twilight greys, while pitching him forward so that his hands drew back to the ground, pulled by some irresistible increase in gravity. His bloodied palms stubbed the rough floor, and there he strained, pushing against being pulled flat chest to floor. He grit his teeth and hissed at the grinding pain biting into his contending hands and knees, his trembling elbows locked hinges, spine arching, while there played out a strange battle against the stronger gravity seeking to flatten him.

Until he released the Power, and the strong gravity pull upon him abated, as well the luminous twilight enhancement of his vision swallowed once more into blackest pitch.

What in friggin hell was that about?

He peeled his hands free of the ground and gazed round not in total darkness now for something changed. A wan hint of soft crimson glow arose in a sigh of illumination carpeting the spot of floor where he'd planted his resistive hands. Along with the eerie red light there arose a strange humming, some dreadful melody playing out just beneath hearing so that it lived more in presence than sound.

A bitter part of him mused on the cruel repeat here of his arrival in the Academy followed by that godsawful alarm so that he grimaced at the twisted notion of another possible attack. But no perceivable stonemen aligned the walls of this elsewhere place, if walls there were, as evinced through the twilight glimpse afforded in his brief seizing of the Power piercing the dark pitch. He shuddered at the prospect of confronting more stonemen here, unarmed in all but the Power . . . and the fractured Source he dared not seize lest given no other choice.

I won't hold back this time. I can't. Not here. Wherever here is.

He held his breath in a testy moment of listening while peering round, tensed and waiting for surrounding pairs of lament red eyes to spark the dark and set their blazing gazes upon him.

The quiet moment passed undisturbed.

Alone, then. As I've always felt. Until Melora.

He hunkered down and squinted at the patch of soft crimson glow lain out before him, assessing the visible space of floor.

Not just rough rock but rough rock covered in veined throbs of lichen, glowing and pulsing, alive in more ways than lichen ought to be. Hmm . . .

Curious presumptions struck him while he stared not just at the backs of his hands but down between them, the wheels of his working mind turning. He lowered his bloody palms toward the floor again, and there sounded whispers of movements, the lichen roused and straining to reach up at him reaching down.

With contact returned the queer sucking sensation upon his palms as suspected. *The lichen's suckling my blood.*

He watched the lichen throb and writhe, mesmerized, while its soft crimson glow elevated into scarlet brightness spreading outward by slow-crawling inches, forking and veining in every direction from round his planted hands where fed the parasitic planimal. New light quested in lightning jags across the floor, darkness shying away from the encroaching luminescence. Same as the Power fed upon his lifeforce, so too the planimal lichen fed upon his nutrient blood.

Its pulsing throbs quickened stronger, more active, waking, rejuvenated by his aizakai lifeblood restoring the lichen's resuscitated heartbeat while pumping stolen vitality through the incredible webwork of its vast planimal body. As the red lambency spread outward with the sound of a thousand chewing insects, so too did Banzu's expanding view that the planimal not only covered the entire floor but also carpeted the tall walls and high ceiling blooming brighter to his widening gaze.

Cold prickles danced up his hunched back, but he did not remove the bleeding sustenance of his hands just yet. No pain there, only the peculiar tingling numbness akin to that of his hands having fallen asleep. Throbbing scarlet veins and pulsing crimson fissures stretched and crawled in greedy creeps throughout the relieving blackness of the unveiling world, while a low hum persisted, until there bloomed full reveal of his true environment.

He knelt in some manner of a cave. Across from him gaped the inviting mouth of a tunnel, his only perceivable exit, its long and winding throat swallowing down the luminous lichen.

Heat swelled round him though he shivered. No stonemen here to break away from their ancient stations against the walls and challenge him. No aizakai rushing in while throwing frozen bolts or conjured flames or snaking terra pillars of magic.

He winced and gasped when sharp pinches bit deeper into his offered palms, pain bypassing numbness with gnawing chews upon his flesh. An increase in the lichen's suckling feed upon his bleeding sustenance.

He tried pulling his hands free, but the lichen's sunken punctures of teeth refused release. The planimal acknowledged his attempt by increasing its feeding resistance so that the heavier gravity returned and draped its heavy cling upon him despite no provoking seize of Power as before.

He strained at staying upright on all fours, elbows locked, his heartbeat hammering behind its cage of ribs, the lichen's scarlet carpet pulses increasing in rhythms matching the quickening rush of his veins beat for rapid beat. Cold sweat dripped from his furrowed brow as another realization struck him, grim and exact. The vampiric lichen would continue sucking the lifeblood out from him until it made of him a hollow husk.

He wondered how much sentience the planimal possessed. Even entertained yelling at it while demanding his release. He dug his fingers into the worming carpet as claws set to ripping out tufts of hair. Another hissing gasp escaped him as the painful feeding increased its gnawing suckle round the security of his foolish grips. His arms trembled, threatening to unhinge. Seconds only before his collapse where the lichen would drain him of life.

"No!" He grit his teeth, seized the Power and, with tremendous effort and no small amount of agony, rocked back and forth while gaining momentum for pulling free. He yelled while yanking his captured palms loose from the parasitic planimal, pain flaring in his hands. He released the Power while straightening erect, the strange gravity pulling on him abating, and shook his throbbing hands, flexing them, then sagged back bottom atop heels and swayed, lightheaded from loss of blood.

Shivering. Panting. Blinking hard.

Gods that hurt.

He drew in a deep breath through the dizzying sway, catching balance in lieu of tottering over to the floor.

He gazed round the illuminated caveplace, the only darkness remaining tiny coves of shadow hiding in angled nooks and crannies fleeing to farther crevices when his roving eye caught them just so. He listened to the lichen's thriving hum, his senses absorbing scents and sounds as he stared into the beckoning depths of the descending tunnel across from him. No puzzle to that gaping maw, only entrance and perhaps death somewhere therein.

"Friggin hell."

He raised his hands upturned for inspection in the rosy glow. Hundreds of tiny thorny bites covered his fingers and palms from wrists to tips, the bleeding staunched. He flexed his hands closed and open, no pain involved to his surprise, his hands lathered in some manner of sticky residue peeling through his testing flexes of wounded skin.

He considered the lichen in grim wonder—some insects released a chemical coagulant after removing their feeder stinger so that the host only itched on the spot after the feeding took place while their bleeding stopped; a dead host provided no good host at all to any parasitic form of life which fed upon living blood—then shook his head, uncaring of the answer.

My hands are free and I can see.

He stood with animal grace and scanned the scarlet luminous caveplace lit by the fuel of his blood, hoping to score another recourse other than the tunnel awaiting him. He turned round then faced the gaping maw, his only perceivable escape, and huffed a terse breath. He scrubbed his hands up and down the front of his pants, noting the keyrings' faded chill, the two lanthium bands warm as the flesh they wrapped round.

Nowhere to go but the tunnel. He shrugged. "Screw it."

Two steps toward it and he stopped.

Is it really destiny if given no alternatives? What if I fail? What if I can't return? What if I die here? I'll never see Melora again. I'll never kill the Khan.

He stared at the tunnel overlong.

What the frig, I might as well try. If they brought me here then they should take me out, right?

He pinched the keyring on his left hand betwixt his right pointer and thumb and, bracing for the suffocating jolt of magical transportation, he slid the ring off his finger.

And waited.

Nothing happened, nothing changed. No hint of active magic roused within the lanthium band.

He relaxed, though puzzled, then tensed again while removing his right-handed ring—and waited.

Nothing.

"Godsdammit."

Anger flaring, he clenching the keyrings in his fist, cocked his arm back and made to throw the accursed things into the throat of the tunnel. But he stopped short of opening his pitching hand. *No, I better keep them, just in case. Maybe I can reactivate them somehow.*

He shoved the keyrings into a pants pocket and glared into the glowing, lichen-veined throat of tunnel waiting to swallow his entry.

* * *

Banzu ventured into the tunnel's winding throat, the guiding scarlet glow following his cautious tread in a looming presence of brighter light than the softer fluorescence ahead and behind him.

It's moving with me. Stalking me.

His footfalls produced muted crunches atop the springy lichen carpet while he walked the steady decline. A drop in temperature soon overtook him so that he paused, drew in a breath and, stoking it with belly heat, huffed a misty plume burnished with red reflections. A strange thing, that, considering he strove deeper and down into bowels where wise sages claimed resided an ocean of molten magma feeding all of Pangea's volcanoes with their hot lifeblood. Though in truth the decreasing heat proved less a temperature change and more a spiritual chill.

Gods, I might not even be on Earth anymore.

And the pervasive humming, its dreadful background melody once singing just beneath his hearing, arose with his descending advance, vibrating the archaic air with a beating thrum, the slow but continuous gothic rhythm unnoticed until he made a point of listening. It sang its soft pall of presence round him while delivering a constant glance-behind feeling of someone creeping in the short wake of his footfalls.

He continued on, flexing his hands every now and again, on occasion gripping through the ghost of Griever's hilt at his left hipwing while cursing the keyrings both for delivering him here and absent his precious sword.

Deeper and down through the scarlet swallow of throat, he tested safety round every angled bend with his advancing gaze while ensuring no long contact upon the walls and the throbbing sprawls of glowing lichen thereon with anything more than grazing fingertips. Its sticky surface licked at his skimming touches in desirous kisses requesting more of his nutrient blood, patches of the vampiric planimal writhing active in his peripherals, beats and throbs of it emitting chewing sounds active beneath the pervasive hum.

All the while the ceiling encroached lower, and the walls shrank inwards, pinching his pathway tighter by increments the farther he quested, deeper and down, colder, the tunnel's endurance irritating, his tolerance for the end thinning brittle.

He stopped and shouted, his voice a dividing echo racing away at his sides, then he grimaced at the foolish declaration while reflecting upon that hidden roar sounding moments after his delivery.

Stupid. If something's waiting for me, it knows I'm coming now.

He held his breath and listened to the diminishing echoes of his fading voice evincing he still had a long ways to go.

He drew in deep, blew out his cheeks, and walked on.

* * *

Growing up on the rugged Kush Mountains in Ascadia with bountiful room for running and climbing to his playful heart's content, Banzu shouldered plenty of experience with walking long and arduous distances both uphill and down. Still, the perpetual decline of the tunnel wore on his well-muscled calves and thighs despite their sure endurance and delivered smarting knots so that he stopped for a short rest and massaged the burning kinks loose before continuing.

He concentrated on the soft padding crunch of his boots and the growing labor of his breathing while the noticeable absence of heat within the tunnel increased to the point of giving him shivers, each hot breath escaping in smoky ribbons trailing from the corners of his mouth.

At one frustrated point he considered turning round and hiking back but for that nothing awaited him there. Fear of the luminescent lichen snuffing black lest he provide it more resuscitating lifeblood motivated him forward. He tried activating the keyrings again, slipping them on and off, one at a time then both at once, but earned nothing for it and so shoved them back into his pocket with a few grumbled curses.

The tunnel leveled straight after he walked round more a sharp corner than a curving bend, the tight orifice through which he passed offering bare inches of space a slight more than the breadth of his turned body, to where the walls and ceiling expanded into a long and empty square-cut tunnel resembling a hallway.

He paused at the brush of new winds soughing against his face, warm as breath. When he strode forward, the persistent humming accompanying his cavernous journey escalated in volume and pitch along with a multitude of voices speaking at him in a torrent of whispers playing behind his own verbal stream of consciousness, these voices hisses across silk, increasing in strength the farther he walked.

**Come . . .*
*. . . *Die . . .**
*. . . *Soothsavior.**
**Go . . .*
*. . . *Kill . . .**
*. . . *Soothslayer.**

He stiffened at the compelling pressure of those voices worming influence into the depths of his thoughts, a writhing nest of maggots attempting to consume the carcass of their birth. The sudden willingness to abandon all caution and sprint ahead in eager hunt of wounded prey assailed him. His muscles corded taut, eyes narrowing in concentration, the echo of some internal litany twitched on his lips in reminder that he was more man than animal however much the rising urgency to hunt told otherwise.

He turned round, gaze prowling, muscles not so much tensing as firming into a loose priming for action, hands flexing at his sides, breaths tasting the archaic air. A thousand voices spoke at him from everywhere now, each harsh whisper carrying the edge of threat, warning him away yet beckoning him forward in teasing dares rife with the unlogic of madness.

He continued forward, ignoring the ghostspeak as one did the scattered voices of a milling crowd.

Blackness filled the long hallway's end. He approach it and the open archway waiting to eat his passage whole. An entrance into some black cavern of despair, strange though also familiar symbols ran the face in a large horseshoe pattern decorating its stone borders, the symbols' meanings existing at the fringe of his awareness where melded touches of other lives lived. He peered into the depths beyond, drawn, compelled, an umbilical tether urging him forward.

I know there's a price hidden in there somewhere.

Five strides closer and the carven symbols round the archway flashed alight into fiery promise, molten and throbbing upon cold black rock. He startled mid step though walked on through. And stopped as darkness ahead died to the expanding red twilight rushing in past him from behind on all sides, its wall-crawling luminescence skittering in millions of angry red spiders seeking morsels of shadows while leaving throbbing lightning trails in their speedy wake not just on the rough stone walls but in them.

Seconds only and the vermillion veining illumination provided visual birth to a massive cavern.

He surveyed the revelation beyond the humming archway, welcoming the change to the tunnel traversed for far too long. Tensed, the strong beat of his pulse a wardrum pounding to the surf of voices rising in his skull, a shouting throng begging for murder, pleading for death, a thousand screamers spitting their ruinous taunts of condemnation at him in scalding gobs of venom.

He balked as one voice in particular pierced the raucous noise and called at him, screaming with hurt, yelling with the full measure of betrayal. Jericho's voice, hot and awful, maddened by the corruption of the bloodlust, demanding Banzu's suicide for the unfulfilled promise of killing Hannibal Khan between requests of deaths of those who sidetracked that revenging quest.

Staggering, Banzu closed his eyes. He had condensed the burning yearning for the Khan's death into a smoldering coal of bridled rage out of necessity. But here, now, it flared into a wildfire, stoked by Jericho's raging bellows, flushing Banzu's skin hot while threatening to consume him in a flaming gust of fanatical passion quickening his fevered blood in his swelling network of veins.

Reeling, he panted through clenched teeth.

Jericho's incessant shouts, absorbed into the collective agony of compelling noise, became sharp shards of suffering driven into Banzu's brain in pounded rods of fire.

Wincing, he sank to one knee, hands covering ears.

"Shut up!" But the voices continued their relentless chatter. Laughed at his feeble attempt to quell their mocking bids. Joining the dire singsong of Jericho's cackling demands for his suicide.

Grimacing, he sank his other knee to floor and hunched over.

A pandemonium of voices a thousand strong rushed and roared in screaming cacophony.

Cringing, he yelled, "Shut up! Shut up! SHUT UP!"

The raucous assault of voices fled in a vacuum of sound swallowed away.

Silence reined but for the rapid patter of Banzu's heart.

He opened one eye, the other. He straightened while lowering his shielding hands from over his ears. And waited, tensed and listening.

The silence pervaded.

He stood. Drew in a deep nostril breath, hawked and spat aside, his brittle sheet of patience webbed with fractures. Tired of playing games, he wanted done with this, wanted out—now.

Gaze hunting through the scarlet glow of cavern . . . *there.* Far across the enormous chamber rested a thick stone block atop a low dais. Two tall braziers stood unlit at either of the elongated block's ends, both of which sputtered into flaming life the moment he strode forward, as if lit by his intent.

Welcoming him or daring him, he could not say, did not care, for his intolerant mind continued snapping together the remaining pieces of the puzzle to this mystery while he approach across the chamber, cautious gaze darting for any signs of movement, his right hand twitching in pulsing squeezes over empty air for gripping the reassurance of Griever's hilt but finding none.

He advanced upon the low dais, stood before the waist-high block. An archaic sarcophagus, he traced his probing gaze over the carven effigy emblazoned deep thereon the dust-crusted surface of the inches-thick granite slab settled atop which depicted a closed-eyed man lying supine and with a sword positioned lengthwise beneath his chest-crossed hands, the fine tortured lines of the carven figure's expression hinting of a man condemned unto a fitful rest of disquiet agony, killed then buried away to suffer in silent regard of all things timeless, all things locked outside this deep . . . *tomb*, the only appropriate word Banzu's mind could ascribe.

A humbling flush of melancholy spread through him for the depiction, and he thought the talented artist who incised it must have done so through long hours of remorse. He leaned forward while sucking a deep breath then blew hard through pursed lips. And straightened away coughing while swatting through the uprising cloud of ancient dust seeking to invade his eyes and nose and throat.

He blinked the grit from his watering eyes as the cloud of dust floated round in a lazy haze. He leaned forward again and swiped his left hand out in a wide rainbow arc across the lid, revealing some unknown form of chiseled script which looked nothing more than many pairs of mating spiders dancing through crooked lines.

No . . . a tickle within his brain, and deep-rooted memories born from other lives of the strange spidersex letters swirled their mental images into hints of recognition upon the chalkboard of his thoughts. But the hazy memories proved much too old and long unused even for his imprinted brain to decipher the obscure markings into anything more than vague forms of clipped comprehension.

Until the voices returned, softer now, hushed as if huddled and afraid though willing to translate the archaic writing through meek whispers of dread warning blown out from the hidden protection of some shadowed corner deep within the cave of his mind.

Savior . . . Slayer, spoke the voices in shared collective, pronounced then gone as though absorbed by the stale air of this ancient tomb.

Banzu tensed with epiphany as the final piece of puzzle snapped into place. He swallowed the dry knot at the back of his throat. He retreated one step from the sarcophagus, then another, then another still.

There, he paused. And there he trembled with fear and fury at that which lay before him.

No, whom.

CHAPTER THIRTY-SEVEN

"The Essence of the First."

The words escaped Banzu in a breathy whisper. Uneasiness crept up his stiffened spine, chill despite the heat of his quickening blood. He stood panting, eyes eager, hands sweaty, mouth dry, body ready to pounce yet mind unable to will the action toward the sarcophagus of: "Simus Junes." Harshly spoken, more in curse than a naming. No, not a curse but a challenge. "The savior-slayer."

He licked the dust from his lips and swallowed, tasting the dried age of undisturbed centuries. Inside he edged forward, viewing himself shoving off the covering slab for what lay hidden beneath. Outside his feet rooted to the ground, paralyzed by apprehension.

He knew the reality of his hesitation. True fear existed here, despite the infamous Soothsayer King resting before him only in bones and rotted flesh, three centuries old and sealed away from the rest of the world by magical methods beyond Banzu's ignorant capacity to understand.

I'm a swordslinger, not some aizakai wizard. I deal in steel over magic.

By instinct he gripped the air at his naked left hipwing.

"Relax," he whispered, the word ghosting over his lips.

Separated by but a few feet of space and mere inches of solid granite, he eyeballed the sarcophagus while picturing its hidden contents and considering the true value of his place herein this mystic chamber, this tomb of Simus Junes, this imprisonment housing the remains of the Essence of the First.

This is it, their godsdamned destiny. I'm supposed to be here. The keyrings . . . gods, I can literally feel purpose vibrating in my bones.

His mind reflexed backwards in a flash of foreboding: news of Hannibal Khan, slipping on the keyrings in a fit of rage, the suffocating swallow of blinding white light transporting him here, and now . . . now, purpose surmounted, thick and pulling.

His soul turned a hotbed of warring emotions. Agitated butterflies borne from apprehension's dread and anticipation's reward fluttered round through chaotic little battles inside his clenching stomach trying to pen them in. He licked his lips, mouth moistening with expectations, and his mind flexed forward with determination as he released a triumphant laugh while plans played out through premonitions as though already accomplished in all but the doing.

Retrieve the Essence, destroy the Godstone, kill the Khan, rescue Melora. It leads back to her, this first step in cleansing the fractured Source. Take it and be gone.

"You're mine," he whispered to the chambered Essence of Simus Junes, pretending the one in charge though his voice gave him away, thin and tight.

The primordial patience of the hunting animal glistened behind his eyes nonetheless. A thrilled smile graced his lips when he approached the archaic sarcophagus, appraising it with probing gaze then hands finding purchase against the lengthwise side of the thick granite slab atop.

He dug in his heels and pushed, but disturbed nothing more than dust motes with his ineffectual shove. He tried again, grunting with strain to the same null effect. A third failure against the heavy slab evinced no budge.

What the frig.

He stepped back, huffing through clenched teeth in an unfocused effort at managing his molten temper. He kicked the sarcophagus but scored only a sore foot.

"Godsdammit!"

He hopped round in a little cursing circle while holding his bruised foot, then approached the sarcophagus for another inspection. He leaned forward to read again the ancient spidersex writings. Only then did he notice the closed granite eyes of the carven caricature atop the lid outlined with thin slits, two round fissures. Two perfect little circular fittings.

Something clicked inside his brain, patterns weaving together and snapping pieces meant for joining. He dug into his pocket, removed the keyrings, and set first one down into the left eye circlet valley then the right, both resting into their perfect fits.

The striking reverberation of thunder without sound filled the great chamber, billowing out in all directions from the sarcophagus its origin. A fiery blood-red glow blazed alive within the two hollows of the placed keyrings where closed granite eyes snapped open, molten, startling awake after three centuries of rest.

Banzu staggered backwards from the disrupted sarcophagus, pushed away through a measure of invisible violence by the soundless rolling thunder. He stumbled down over the low lip of the dais, turning aside while raising his arms to shield his face at the same time the granite slab blasted upwards into the tremendous heights of the chamber. The thick lid exploded in a raining haze of stony hail.

It was then, while peering through the diffusing cloud settling round the open sarcophagus, that he realized he might have just made the final mistake of his life.

* * *

Banzu waited, his heartbeat a thunder, for the last of the destructed lid's debris to settle into a thinning haze for better viewing, all the while hoping the portent horrors borne by unknowing fears playing out through his mind did not come to pass before him.

Thrilling to his own plot, he approached the open sarcophagus through the suspended haze shifting and coiling round his limbs, the rest of it asides its high-blown and blasted slab still intact and unscathed from the magical eruption of destruction wrought from the keyrings' placements. He returned upon the dais in two cautious strides, crept toward the exposed concrete coffin.

Closing distance to the unsealed contents, a longing filled the eager cracks of him.

His avid stare traveled up the undamaged side then, closer, down over its lip to within the sarcophagus revealing nothing inside. No decrepit corpse lying therein, no time-bleached bones, not even a fine pile of once-flesh decomposed over three centuries into fragile dust awaiting him to scatter its ancient contents with a defiling breath.

The sarcophagus rested empty, the bored insanity of the gods' cruel joke of their Great Game stomping upon his trampled fabric of life, exacting another tormenting turn while given no punch-line but for the ruination of his present cause, the ancient remains of Simus Junes expected therein offered only in rumor and shadow and with no retrievable Essence to be found . . . if it ever existed at all.

"Friggin hell."

A vile moment played its ruthless mindgame, shifting traitorous thoughts of lies and deception away from Enosh and his immortal brethren to where Banzu reconsidered his previous suspicions of the Head Mistress's plotted trickery in sending him here to be rid of the last Soothsayer through the least resistance possible his only viable explanation remaining. Irony never tasted so bitter.

Not just a tomb then but a prison.

His frenzied mind sought a target, raced for placing blame. He thought of Aggie, and for a brief relapse knew only guilty sorrow. Thoughts returned to Gwendora and all her manipulations thrown upon him. Anger flared, hot and raw and savage.

Through clenched teeth he said, "Son of a—"

A whisper of presence from behind and Banzu clipped his curse short, spun round, jolted still as a chill had its way with him.

There, scaring away the cavern's shadows, stood a scintillating figure of brilliance, the scarlet ethereal specter of Simus Junes regarding him in a silent stare of unquestionable unmercy piercing through lambent red rage-poisoned eyes, their substance bridled molten fury, twin suns blazing behind tossing leaves wrought from purpose.

With quavering resolve Banzu met that voracious glare. He delved into its penetrating depths to the cancer of the corrupted Source where thrived the bloodlust poisoning the shared collective from apart. The missing piece to the fractured Source puzzle. Therein that nightmarescape of unadulterated hatred toiled and twisted leagues and fathoms of animosity for all things living, profound in its rapacious lust.

Banzu stood in the scream-locked throat of panic and seconds from swallowed. And yet . . . and yet. He stared at an idol of absolute hate, but within himself lived an equal hatred challenging back, hot and mingled, righteous fury for the forced murder of his uncle, savage vengeance for the Khan who set that murder into motion, scorning blame for the effigy of bloodlust standing before him that had been and was still behind it all.

You. Worse yet and deeper still, the cruel recollection hot splinters driven beneath his fingernails, Jericho's murder of Melora, the atrocious act undone with his re-beginning and yet it scarred his soul with permanence. *You did this to me.* He'd earned her, lost her, then regained her only to lose her again. Another cruel joke of the gods, that mocking cycle he sought to break. That, and the Khan's neck. *You.*

The silence pervaded between them.

Banzu answered the apparition's lambent stare with the swelling hatred of his thinning glare casting all the blames of his harbored woes. Too much taken from him already, and before him stood another price to pay. His lips vibrated with the beginnings of a word. *Destiny.* An inevitable force consumed with insatiable hunger. But pride silenced him. And it did not matter. Words contained no importance now.

Or so he thought.

The scarlet throbs of lichen light sprawling the cavern: gone. Darkness everywhere but for the glowing scarlet specter Essence of Simus Junes having gathered all light unto himself. Thoughts prowled behind those blazing eyes, fast and furious and violent, but otherwise Simus stood immobile, silent, betraying no twitch of active intent. *You're going to die*, those eyes said, *and I'm going to kill you.* His stance loose and strong and easy, crisp and calm and sure.

Tensions thickened into a palpable thing shared between them.

At last movement prompted Banzu into removing backwards one full step as Simus' left hand flashed across to his right hipwing where swirled into existence the ghostly red hilt of a sword, a perfect mockery to the second ghosthilt the infamous Soothsayer swordslinger wore at his other, truer swordslinger's hip.

At Banzu's cautious withdraw Simus smiled a fraction quirk of his lips, then pulled the sword free from its invisible scabbard to the ringing tune of steel sliding against steel atop the accompanying background melody of an agonized moaning comprised of a thousand dying men, its keen length of glowing red blade producing from the empty space of nowhere while he removed the transforming sword free of himself.

Simus flipped the flickering ghostsword over in his master swordslinger's sure grip with the quick motion of pure expertise then tossed the scarlet phantom weapon out to where it landed with a dull *clang* inches in front of Banzu's booted toes.

To Banzu's credit he flinched nothing. He gazed down at the offering, watched it flash back and forth from insubstantial to corporeal, over and again, from a ghostly blazing red into a solid dull gray, through a rapid blinking confusion of visual trickery.

He raised his gaze from the transmuting sword and met those blazing scarlets so filled with hate they criticized the world from beyond the frenzied veil of animosity where reigned the eerie calm of bloodlust madness. He said nothing of the challenge lain against him, that proverbial line in the sands of his life drawn, for he knew the ghostblade lying inches from his feet would stay transitioned into tangible realness the moment he touched its flickering hilt.

No, not just tangible, but substantial . . . consequential.

All words became as meaningless as the hope that would die if he failed here.

Banzu bent and picked up the tossed sword, its hilt solidifying inside his closing hand.

As Simus drew his.

* * *

The winking-into-tangible steel sword shivered within Banzu's testing grip, heavier than it had a right to be considering its spectral origin. The hilt cold against his skin, he raised the length of spiritblade—for that was how he perceived the weapon despite its present solid state: wrought from spirit—while flexing through tiny adjusting squeezes of fingers for increased purchase, and a dark pulse of joy rang through his tingling arm so that he allowed the faintest of smiles to curve over his lips, born from the sureness of solid steel in his hand.

Akin to the hydraviper's preemptive coiling just before its whip-snapping multi-strike, Banzu seized the Power in preparation for the springing lunge—or tried to but felt nothing. The surprise of his failure betrayed his face for the space of a flinch before glower returned in kind. A yell strangled in his throat, but animal pride silenced him again.

Specter Simus smirked a nefarious response.

"I *am* the Power," he said with knowing, his bold tone cold, exact, oozing a confidence pushing past authoritative into condescending, his voice reverberating not just throughout the blackness of the chamber but as well within the cavern of Banzu's mind.

"I am the harbinger of death, the reaper of mercy, the harvester of sorrow." Another flashing smirk, there then gone, followed by the darting lick of Simus' glimmering scarlet lips, his tongue black as the surrounding pitch. "And you are nothing more than the vessel of my freedom."

Simus raised his sword and pointed, glared down the length of it at his only target, blazing red eyes flaring brighter, death eyes with the strength of the inevitable, then lowered his phantom blade.

"You are the last," Simus said. "You are my curse. And now I shall finally claim you."

Banzu swallowed hard to steady his voice, bridled eagerness to surge and kill—if killing such a phantom was even possible—swelling his muscles plump with adrenaline, the escalating energy of their standoff reaching a crescendo and seconds from splitting him at the seams.

"No," Banzu said in the almost-hiss of harsh correction. "You're *my* curse."

Or what remains of it, at least . . . an afterthought nipping at the heels of his words. And for the life of him he questioned those words from himself or if issued by another within his head. A thousand possibilities lived therein the shared collective of the fractured Source, though minus the missing fragment in front of him.

Sweltering lifeblood flushed through his veins, quickening pace while priming his taut muscles looser for action. There existed no question to it, no other course but the here and now, this issue between them settled only with death.

Banzu tightened a double-fisted grip round the bastard hilt—leather-wound now from the birth of his transforming focus—clutched within his anxious hands. Jaw flexed, teeth clenched, every fiber of his being begging for the sweet release of action, his next words escaped him with ease.

"I've come to claim you." *Or die trying.* Again the mistrust as to the origin of his verbal stream of consciousness. But he shucked the germination of doubt and threw it aside—same as infection, doubt got men killed if given half the chance.

Simus returned nothing—no reply, no reaction, no motion of advance—but for the focal impalement of his contemptuous lambent glare piercing into Banzu's tortured soul. Even his sword remained held angled down at his right side within the red flickering inactivity of his scarlet specter's hand.

A long moment passed between them, tension escalating through the silence of their shared stares.

Something stole to Banzu's notice. He squinted while leaning his upper half forward a hairsbreadth. Within Simus' blazing gaze hovered thinnest black circles, two little opposite eclipses. The keyrings, taunting Banzu through a second pair of eyes in the flames of Simus's molten regard.

You did this, Banzu reminded himself. *Your re-beginning caused the Veilfall. You put those godsdamned rings on then put them in that lid. And now you've got a sword in your hands—use it!*

He drew in deep, nostrils flaring, shook loose and blanked his mind of all but that which stood before him in challenge of his life and the precious things in it. A chore considering the stakes of the battle seconds from playing out: his mind, body and soul.

I lose here and I lose all of myself.

His swordslinger's instincts strong and sure, yet he hesitated, for before him stood not just another bladesman but the infamous legend who defeated the Nameless One through recurring battles using the unfractured Source until Malach'Ra's defeat. Simus Junes, the first Soothsayer to wield the Power in such a way by gathering the shared collective while tapping the Source, and through him cursing all Soothsayers thereafter.

Banzu drew in another full breath while averting the shudder that knowledge imposed against him. He tilted his head from side to side through minute *pops* of his spine round the base of his skull, then leveled his sword at and focus upon the scarlet specter Essence of Simus Junes in a one-handed extension of his swordarm.

I may not be much when compared to the stuff of his legends, but I'm still hell with a sword.

"You have an unnatural appetite for death." Banzu forced a smile leaving his eyes untouched yet bared the tortured depths of his soul to the bloodlusted demon before him. "Unfortunately for you I'm hungrier."

Simus chuckled, low with ricocheting echoes, stones tossed down an empty well one after the other: *CLINK-Clink-clink.*

"I *am* the unnatural appetite of death, you fool. What in hells do you think the bloodlust is?" There Simus paused, thin scarlet lips outlined in tiny ebony fissures tightening into a sharp cut. "But it's fractured, and you are its missing piece." Another pause, a dark smile. "You're a rat nibbling poisoned cheese."

Banzu flinched at the new revelation of information. Apparently the bloodlust to Simus existed as the Source to himself: fractured. Each of them the other's missing piece. But the irony, or perhaps the destiny, of it fled from him, shrugged off the shoulders of his thoughts for the moment at hand.

Slow in turning his center line, he two-handed his sword again then dipped a bit at the knees, preparing to swing from the hip. He anticipated having to parry an opening into the first expected assault from Simus . . . which never came as the moment stretched on, Simus unmoving in all but the pulsing red throbs of his glowing spirit form stealing in all light from the black cavern.

The tension crackled between them.

Come at me, you bastard. Banzu thinned the measure of his eyes. *Come at me now!*

Minutes passed through glaring torment.

What little remained of Banzu's brittle patience, that straining membrane plane stretched so thin as to border on invisible, cracked as would frosted glass catching its first hot rays from the rising sun breaking over distant peaks.

Hesitation burned away to the thousand rabid voices screaming for the kill in his skull. He sank his haunches in preparation for launching forward, Powerless, at the spiritual Essence of the man who had once condemned the world and sought to do so again through another mortal vessel in Banzu. He shoved the voices to the back of his crowded mind, into the place of forgotten things, as an urgency of singular purpose overtook him.

Kill, hard and fast.

The longer I spend here, *fighting Simus, the less I spend* there, *killing Hannibal Khan.* The fact instigated the fury of his dynamic muscles into locomotive violence.

Screaming in inarticulate rage, Banzu uncoiled with ripping movement, his body weight pulling his sword rather than striking with it.

Simus flinch nothing.

Banzu shrank the space between them in five bounding strides of loping animal grace and whirring steel.

With blurring quickness Simus swept Banzu's cleaving stroke aside, the scintillating scarlet brilliance of his ethereal form flashing brighter in the brief moment their swords clashed before he redirected Banzu past him while moving only his swordarm and the fanning specterblace gripped therein. Diversion with the ease of an adult nonchalantly knocking aside the onrush of some foolish child brandishing a silly little stick.

Banzu's intended chain of blows broken at the first, he stumbled past Simus through the patronizing parry into catching his balance. He spun round while whipping his sword out in a sideways sweeping arc to ensure safe space remained between them.

Simus faced him in a simple act of turning, the flickering scarlet of his specter presence throbbing, his sword angled down at his side as if never raised to parry, a wry smile twisting one corner of his mouth.

Gods he's fast, and he knows it. And he's mocking me.

Banzu sucked deep through clenched teeth in a scornful hiss, lips peeling back in a feral snarl, projections of the Khan awaiting him flashing behind his eyes chased by the possibility of never seeing Melora's beautiful face again if he failed here, of never again hearing the lovely melody of her voice cursing his follies and praising his gains, of never more enjoying the warm velvety touch of her alabaster skin or the caressing grace of her kisses or—

No! Something vital in him ruptured, its strong crisp snapping a splintering break. *My love is fractured, and she's my missing piece.* "I won't lose her again," he said through clenched teeth. "Not to you. Not to anyone!"

Simus quirked an amused eyebrow.

A barbaric furor descended over Banzu in a tidal hunger of primal rage washing away all trepidation but for the hazing fury of necessary action and the fierce need to see it through. He thinned his eyes into remorseless hazel slits while feeding the undaunted beast greedy for the clash of survival, domination, its raw nature bound inside a man, the most deadly predator of all. A guttural growl escaped him, vibrating from his throat.

The slightest tilt of Simus' head, as if trying to catch the underlying meaning of some whispered secret lost upon him. Tiny black flecks swarmed throughout the bloody drowning pools of his lambent red eyes, their darkness seething with possibilities and none of them good. Yet he did not otherwise move.

Banzu raised his sword, sighting targets—then erupted into a barrage of attacks, his unrelenting offense pouring forth in an intricate frenzy of bladed motion as Chaos, mother of pain, consumed him.

* * *

Time turned a lost concept through Banzu's grueling efforts at striking down scarlet specter Simus for the precious Essence housed therein, a pulsing blackheart of promise, Banzu's mind clouded with a raging fog thickened with every failed attempt.

Again and again he charged the scarlet Soothsayer swordslinger—and every time Simus beat away Banzu's offensives with shrewd proficiency and parried the intended blows aside with minimal effort while earning no foul through their unequal trades of blows though bestowing plenty of his own in quick, mocking little jabs and burning cuts of inconsequence.

But pain became forgotten along with time . . . though ignorance and awareness proved two sides of the same coin of reality.

Banzu's complex salvos tired into barbarous barrages of grunting brutality, all proving to the same ill effect. Yet he continued relentless, the building frustration of his failed assaults acting as fuel feeding the blazing inferno within while helping his working body to slow the growing fatigue burning his muscles loose and heavy.

He attacked.

And attacked.

Again and again.

Again.

And again.

* * *

Their contest proved no contest at all, really. Banzu's toiling mind closed off all avenues of reason but for the single method of attack-attack-*attack!* More of a struggle, really—Banzu's struggle.

Simus stood his ground—if 'stood' and 'ground' could be applied to the tangible specter Essence and the mystical cavern, though he interacted physically well enough—watchful and waiting, never attacking yet always reacting with perfect precision to the slowing blitzes earning Banzu nothing more than wounded failure and compounding fatigue, each of Simus' expertly negotiated ripostes stinging their fleshy targets in hot kisses licking across Banzu's glistening skin. Parts of his clothes clung damp with blood or hung in wet shreds, his profuse sweating making stinging blazes of his numerous cuts.

Simus outmaneuver Banzu's attacks at every scarlet-sparking crash of their blades. Seventeen times now by Banzu's loose count, though the true number vague considering he stopped tallying his failures three or five futile assaults ago.

Riddled with generous razor-thin cuts up and down his arms and back, across his legs and chest, he stood well back from the shimmering scarlet swordslinger in glaring pause, hunched and panting, covered in sticky layers of sweat and innumerable trickles of blood, and tired as all the hells bunched up into one big Hell. But he refused surrender, each failed assault feeding his anger instead of snuffing it, though for how much longer until his body betrayed him he knew not other than soon.

"You . . . bastard," Banzu huffed out between rapid pants of breath, the tensity of his visage adding weary testament to his labored breathing.

He's winning this without even trying. Gods, I'm beating myself.

He raised his abused sword in preparation for another assault, the battered length of steel resisting with the heaviness of twice its weight within his tired hands. His burning forearms and sore shoulders ached for dropping the burden while the rest of him collapsed, but he refused to relent. Not now. Not after giving so much of himself to the effort.

He broke into another charging attack, this one clumsiest of them all. He said something, a garble of words leaving him in more a pitiful shout than the intimidating yell he tried to make of them. His sword whiffed through empty air as this time Simus bothered no raise of his spiritblade into another masterful parry but instead sidestepped while half-turning, avoiding Banzu's passing stumble, Banzu carried by the sluggish momentum of his swung sword, the act more a clubbing swing than any real endeavor of skill.

Panting, trembling, exhausted beyond feeble, Banzu mustered strength enough for turning round. When he did, his body betrayed him despite his weary mind's protesting screams.

He sank to his knees first right then left, almost toppled forward but for dropping his sword and palming the ground, catching his sloshing balance while steadying the vertigo whirl in his eyes. Tremulous arms threatening to unhinge at the elbows, he straightened then sagged back atop heels which spread and nestled his bottom between sore feet.

There lived plenty of fight left in him but no more energy in which to spend it. His head lolled on rubbery neck. He craned it with iron resolve, determined to look up into the eyes of the enemy who struck him down.

"Surrender is your destiny," Simus said.

Destiny. The atrocious word a pebble dropped into the pond of Banzu's life, producing ripples of events turning incidents of chance into elements of purpose drawn to him, or him to them, by his aizakai gift and his curse of birth, the events coincidental . . . until he dug deeper as was now.

"You can . . . kill me," Banzu said on huffing breath, fearing death less than the parasitic possession Enosh warned him about, "but you'll . . . never break me."

"Kill you?" Simus craned his head and laughed, then lowered his crimson mask and smiled. "You forget, only together are we whole. It is the *shared* collective, after all. I know all of your secrets, your desires, your pains. They lied to you, Banzu. They all lied to you. Only I speak the truth—"

"Shut up."

"How many knives do you carry in your back? Jericho. Gwendora. Agatha. The same gods who betrayed me." A purposeful pause. "Melora."

"Shut up!"

"Let her go. She is far from here. She tricked you. Betrayed you. Abandoned—"

"Never!" Banzu roared.

"I am not your enemy. We are meant for each other. First and Last to complete the whole again. Together we can have your revenge. And so much more. You resist, and yet I feel your willingness to join me—"

"No," Banzu said, hanging his head and shaking it. "I can't. I won't."

"You will." Simus' smile spread beneath molten eyes of malice. "There is more than one way you can serve."

"No."

"Yes."

Pain. Banzu raised his head, glared up at specter Simus closing triumphant before him. He spat at the enemy—or tried to, but instead produced such little force the gob of hot saliva caught upon his lips where it clung hanging down as a glistening little length of rope, foamy and white. *Nothing good ever comes in my life without pain.*

"Join me," Simus said, "and the world will tremble beneath our feet. Surrender, and I promise you Hannibal Khan. Yes?"

Banzu made to speak, to rebuke the irresistible truth of that wicked proposal . . . and was surprised he had nothing to say in the shame of his honest acknowledgement. He shook his head, attempting to toss away thoughts that did not belong . . . until his will evaporated, dust losing its shape, a shadow of its former self decomposing into vanishing eddies and swirls of surrender punctuated by one last rally of defiance.

"I hate you!" Banzu yelled, his voice a hissing scorn.

"Hate is good," Simus said. "Hate is promise and power."

Banzu shook his head, denying the impulse to agree. *He'll give me the Khan . . . oh gods . . . no, I can do no more.*

"Embrace the hate," Simus said, "and join me, yes?"

No. A single word crept forth, betraying Banzu's lips in the brutal awakening of regret. "Yes."

Simus smiled orgasmic.

In Banzu's mind he raised his hands in a desperate attempt to ward off the blow. But outside, eyes wide with the image of oncoming death, his body refused him, accepting it. Embracing it.

As Simus thrust forward, stabbing Banzu in the chest, left of center, piercing into and through the grieving blaze of his exhausted heart, the driven tip of sword blooming out his back beside his tensing arch of spine.

A molten avalanche of energies transferred through the impaling sword, crashing into him, suffusing through him.

Banzu threw his head back, arms whipping out at his sides, body seizing. Screaming in soul-burning agony as fire burst his lungs and he felt himself lifted up, balanced on a sword's hilt while its sliding stream of molten spiritblade plunged deeper.

Pain shocked through his system while wrenching free a gasp. Searing scarlet brilliance veined throughout his rigid body in spreading fissures, making of him a human lantern. Crimson light beams shot out from the orifices of his eyes and ears, nose and mouth, from beneath the nails of his outstretched fingers attempting to claw themselves into some manner of protesting fists, even the toes of his boots glowing bright.

There arose a pulsing throb pounding inside his head, his chest, beating throughout his whole being, some manner of thrumming vibration birthing to life inside and bubbling beneath the surface of his spasming agony of surrender.

Deafening, blinding, and all at once crippling, Banzu's entire red world crumbled apart, his fevered soul crushed to dust then smeared through screaming echoes across the fractured mindscape of his impaled existence where ruled only pain.

Power's overwhelming potency crackled through him, contorting his limbs, ripping loose a raw shriek from his throat. He blazed for unknown seconds, writhing in an extremity of torment. He rose in the air and the chamber grew bright to the excess energies pouring out from him in a discharging effulgence of a captured sun bursting.

Until darkness shrank in, swallowing him in an absence of light and silence.

* * *

Banzu's lids fluttered, opened.

He lay supine on the cold rough floor, the stillness of the cavern a deafening quietude but for the heavy pounding thrum issuing from inside him, slowing in softening cadence, not vanishing but receding, a second heartbeat retreating to exist somewhere deep and discrete within some secret place of privacy at his core.

He sat up, alert and refreshed. Rejuvenated. Strong. No, stronger. A quick patting check of his arms and legs proved neither cuts nor battle scars marred or marked him. But for the open sarcophagus across the way he would have presumed the fight with specter Simus taken place within his own head. And perhaps . . . he considered that astounding possibility for a moment then shunned it aside.

Alone, sitting bathed in soft scarlet glow radiating from the lichen-sprawled walls, the only sound his slow breathing and his still-beating heart. No specter Essence of Simus Junes. Where last Simus stood lay the two keyrings resting on the rocky floor, two innocent little lanthium bands.

He stared at them overlong while questioning his sanity and the delusion of dropping the keyrings while imagining the rest.

No. He palmed at his chest, touching over the second heartbeat therein. *It was real. I can feel the Essence inside me. The fractured Source is whole again, uncleansed but whole. I need to get back. I need to—*

Hannibal Khan. A fire flared within, stoked by the reminder of that name spoken at the edge of his mind, fierce with need and promise. *Kill Hannibal Khan.*

Banzu stood with new energy and calm purpose, amazed at how springy and fluid he moved after suffering such a punishing undertaking, his muscles loose though primed with prescient reflexes, his skin hot and taut. His decisive mind secured sharper focus through the whispers urging him to act. He bent and picked up the keyrings, feeling the right of them now through imparted knowledge.

He slipped one ring down over his right ringfinger, then braced himself while intending to slip the other ring down over his left. But he paused with the tip of that finger a hairsbreadth from penetrating the second keyring's hollow, surveyed a last look at the empty sarcophagus, and smiled.

"Were," he said to the specter Essence of Simus Junes' memory, the battle won though no celebration within him, only rage. It surged and thundered, that wrath of unspent vengeance. Unfed blood hunger. Work unfinished. A dark purpose needing fulfilled. A Khan to kill. All else paled. "You *were* the Power."

He held his breath with knowing, stabbed his finger through the second keyring's hollow and slid the lanthium band down over the length of his extended finger—

***

A blinding light flashed engulfment as the elsewhere caveplace snuffed from existence in a swallow of white then replaced by the same room within the fistian Academy citadel the moment Banzu first slipped both keyrings on. Standing, in fact, on the same spot of his vanishing delivery.

"By the gods!" shouted a startled tawny-haired woman of middle years in a yellow dress patterned with brown flowers chained with branching green ivy, kneeling in front of him one moment then, after popping into standing, she jumped away from his surprising appearance the next while abandoning the colored candlesticks and chalk in her fumbling hands to the floor for gripping her white apron dusted and smeared with hours or perhaps days of sweaty swiping. Gawking mute, she backed away and sideways until she bumped into the wall then, without breaking her spooked stare, she palmed it as if pushing on it would produce for her an escaping door.

The cluster of five fistian soldiers nearest them mimicked the same stunned backpedaling, the closest of whom jumped backwards with arms whipping out while sending the shocked fellows at his sides sprawling to the floor in a flailing clatter of banging armor while another behind them stumbled sideways into crashing against the nearest wall he slid halfway down until he caught himself by digging his fingers into a deep horizontal crack in the stone.

A stew of ten more soldiers, standing by the open double doors across the way, enough men to fill that particular third of the room, shifted facing Banzu's startling materialization. They pressed forward into making fifteen out from five and ten, helping their fallen fellows to their feet.

Banzu acknowledged them with sweeping scrutiny, then glanced down at the rough white chalk outline round his feet scrawled in a crude circle marking his spot, a blackened scorch mark thereon the floor beneath his boots. Outside the outline lay cooled pools of varicolored wax and stubs of melted candles, half their wicks aflame the other half snuffed and emitting little trails of agitated smoke, between them inscribed chalk symbols evincing the woman's failed attempts at conjuring Banzu's reappearance through sorcerous methods of work during his absence.

A shocked stillness filled the room when he returned his gaze up, presenting red eyes of lidded death, and surveyed the stunned faces staring.

Silence but for the gasping of breaths, the shuffling of feet, the shifting of armored bodies spreading apart, hands moving to hilts though staying the pull of blades. The group opened up from behind, parting for their commander in Jacob who shoved to the forefront of the assemblage of dividing soldiers, his shocked expression fading into anger with every step, his veteran eyes having witnessed too much in a single lifetime to stay startled for long.

"It's been a godsdamned week, Soothsayer! Where in gods have you—" But there Jacob stopped not just in words but in approach, a touch of fear blooming his paling face when their gazes locked. "Holy gods, your eyes . . ."

Banzu blinked, as if he did not understand and did not care. Instead he found words reforming into a fermented hiss. "Hannibal Khan."

The name escaped him hard and burning, neither a question nor a statement of fact but a mission of purpose. He glared more through Jacob than at him, scanning the pack of wary soldiers forming tighter rank while taming their fear by brandishing their weapons behind their superior, making of themselves a human blockade to the only exit from the room.

"The Khan is attacking," Jacob said, his voice strong despite the trepidation in each word. He looked the twisted bunch of tired and relieved and furious all bundled up. "Has been so for seven days straight. News of the Godstone's fallen location came in less than two days ago. The Head Mistress has been prepared to leave but was waiting for—" A pause, a grimace. "We must notify her of your return immediately and make our leave before—"

But there Jacob stopped, flinching to the sure motion of Banzu's rising right hand pointing at Griever's hilt jutting from the veteran soldier's left hipwing. Jacob withdrew a cautious step, his left hand gripping his own sword hilt at his right hipwing in preparation for pulling, fingers fanning careful purchase round the leather-wound hilt.

"Soothsayer?" he asked, one word heavy with several questions.

Gaze captured by Griever's taunting hilt, Banzu's mouth watered, and his hands ached with reclamation so that he licked his lips while flexing greedy grips of air.

He sniffed through keener senses, inhaling the candles' smoky drifts wafting up the taut length of him while tasting the metallic tang of armor and the nervous salt of sweat beneath. And though muffled by the thick stone walls of the Academy citadel, the faint sounds of movement and battle outside called to him, a whispering succubus its hot breath tingling into his ear requesting action. Urgency to obey tugged upon his tethered soul. And strangely, a second inner tugging of another tether pulled at him in the opposite direction. But he ignored the Godstone second for the Khan first.

"Give me my sword," he said.

"Where is the Essence?" Jacob asked, implying it existed as some physical thing Banzu should be carrying in his hands.

"I am the Essence now." Banzu tightened his eyes, staring at Jacob dead to rights while the veteran withered in a brief slip of countenance beneath his purposeful gaze. No trepidation, no apprehension, Banzu knew only the darkening of his mood, the quickening rush of his blood, the pumping of adrenaline flushing his muscles hot and eager as he held his right hand out, palm upturned and fingers extended. "My sword." He flexed his hand closed then open, taut sinew fibers snapping in the silence of the room. "Now."

Jacob stood irresolute for lengthy seconds, his goateed mouth opening and closing, lips moving in silent oaths, the nervous soldiers gathered behind him shifting on their feet, questioning the weapons in their hands and the doors at their backs, bits of armor clinking.

Banzu's stare turned glare thinned evermore as the distant rumblings of battle outside tickled through his mindscape where scores of new possibilities danced and played, all of them dark and bloody, his mind set for only one defining purpose. Kill. Period.

An apprehensive nod, then Jacob finished his lone approach. With no small amount of grumbling he unbuckled the second leather belt and scabbard from round his waist, reversed the sheathed sword and set hilt into Banzu's welcoming hand.

"Hannibal Khan," Banzu said, making a declaration of the name while his fingers enfolded round Griever's hilt. And the sheer ecstasy of that forbidden lover's touch invited a shivering pulse, doubly so when he belted Griever home at his left hipwing. A purring sigh escaped him while his eyes turned heavy-lidded, drugged with premonitions of reckless euphoria . . . and why should he hide anything now? He felt the size of a tree. No, a mountain. Indomitable.

"No," Jacob said, frowning. "You can't. We have to—" But there he clipped his protest short at the stark murder glaring at him to which he shrank back by shifting inches.

"Stand aside," Banzu said through gritted teeth, a warning edge in his serrated tone not just to Jacob but to everyone present.

Behind Banzu, the tawny-haired woman shimmied the wall refusing her an escaping door and shrank herself into a far corner past the table, turning away, cringing smaller, hiding her face behind trembling hands.

Fifteen soldiers shifted, fifteen pairs of eyes staring at the Soothsayer standing before them uncollared and armed.

Jacob swallowed, an audible gulp, though stood resolute.

Banzu endured the urgency for pulling loose his sword, to let Griever taste and bathe in blood and be done with these lesser men daring to oppose his inevitable reaping. *A farmer threshing wheat,* a familiar voice whispered though no one spoke aloud. With Griever returned as the bladed extension of his seething fury—

No. They are not my purpose. Their deaths are meaningless, unsatisfying.

He restrained the murderous impulse with a last effort of pressing his point across through words before he thrust the point home with merciless steel.

"I did what she asked," he said to Jacob through jaws drawn tight, his tone a fevered seething. "And now I'm doing what I came here to do in the first place."

Jacob opened his mouth.

"Shut up," Banzu said.

He paused and licked his lips, teetering upon the precarious precipice of enacting slaughter. His body demanded release. His blood cried out for it. Yet he issued a final mercy he would not offer twice.

"Don't try to stop me. Don't say another word. Just get the hell out of my way. Or I swear to gods I'll kill every last one of you."

And they did.

Every last one of them.

* * *

Outside the room where Banzu expected a hundred fistian soldiers awaiting him instead he found no one. Just a long and empty hallway he started down—until there sounded a rush of footfalls then a strong hand gripping his shoulder from behind.

He spun round, tensed and ready to attack whomever proved foolish enough to try and stop him.

To Jacob's credit the veteran soldier flinched little, though he slipped his hand away while removing a step before offering his open hand out between them.

Their gazes locked, Banzu noted the offered hand out from his lower peripheral only.

Jacob opened his mouth, closed it, chewed on his words before releasing them.

"I can't stop you," he said. "No one can. Gods, I—" A pause, the tightening of his dark eyes. "So good luck, Soothsayer." He nodded a swordsman's respect tinged by the fear betraying his eyes he held in check by thinnest margin. "I'll deal with Gwendora. You kill that son of a bitch."

Banzu considered the older soldier in predatory silence. He said not a word when he grasped Jacob's offered hand and shook firm, then broke away and, unseeing of Jacob's cunning smile behind, continued well on his path to khansmen slaughter.

CHAPTER THIRTY-EIGHT

Meeting no resistance from the severe lack of military presence, stalking his way down through the towering Academy citadel while hunting exit, cloaked in purpose and concentration, his brazen gait splitting pockets and pools of hectic aizakai students who scrambled from his path while he navigated through their distraught midst though paid their startled gasps and paling faces no more heed than peripheral glances, Banzu snagged a passing soldier by the closer arm, reversing the older man's trot with a firm grip, a hard eye, and a commanding tone when he said, "Walk with me."

The elder soldier—a lanky fellow who resembled more a dried prune than a person, with shock-white hair fluffing out at the sides of his bandaged head, the unclean wrappings of which wound lower over the left side of his bruised and grimy face to just beneath the blood-crusted patch of his missing eye—grunted and nodded, his battered bits of armor and tattered blue-and-black fistian battledress fatigues evincing his escape from the thick of the battle raging outside survived by the skin of his teeth.

The wise man brooked no argument to the order. Inferno blazed in Banzu's red eyes and bled across his face, demanding compliance, and he sought to quench it with Khan's blood. But before then he wanted information of the war upon the battlefield of the Azure Plains.

Before his abrupt vanishing via the lanthium keyrings he still wore into that otherworldly place where resided the Essence of the First in the spectral spirit form of Simus Junes he confronted and . . . well, the rest remained a hazy blank of mystery, skips and flashes of disconnected memories, for he'd endured recurring losses against the spectral Essence then—blackness here—then he awoke alone and the apparent victor. A personal mindgap he sought answers to later.

He slowed through predator calm and listened while the elder soldier relayed his story and all it entailed.

Hannibal Khan and his legion advanced upon the far eastern edges of the Azure Plains then waited while its forces gathered and swelled. This a week ago, to Banzu's surprise, seven full days according to Jacob and concurred by the elder soldier, before Banzu's return from that time-skipping place where hours there ate through days here.

Now the battle roared in full appeal beyond the city's encircled protection of walls, and Banzu sought answers to that missing gap of time between. Nothing would deter him from joining the battlefield and wetting Griever's thirsty tongue with Khan's blood in the name of his murdered uncle, though the tactical part of his swordslinger's mind claimed dominance over his fierce need for vengeance to the opportune reconnaissance presented him.

"Stop," Banzu said, interrupting the speaking elder who proved the penchant for skimming over details in his flurry of words. "Start over. Tell me everything. From the Khan's arrival up to now. I don't care if it's a butterfly's fart, leave nothing out."

And as they strode down through the Academy citadel, level by level, Banzu slowed by the elder's limping cadence and every set of stairs at which he guided the soldier down with the ease of a firm hand, the noise of battle escalating with each descending tier, the nameless soldier obeyed with impressive detail considering his head injury, his words spilling forth on eager tongue.

* * *

During Banzu's absence, the vast rolling bluegrass fields of the Azure Plains turned a chaotic canvas of bloodshed unseen since the dark days of the Thousand Years War over three-hundred years past. The preemptive forces of Fist advanced the field ten miles east out from the city, making of themselves a stubborn north-south shieldwall blockade several thousand long and twenty columns deep of courageous infantry awaiting the first ranks of Hannibal Khan's westward-marching army of zealous Bloodcloaks and crazed worship-followers, while the Lord of Storms himself stayed content with remaining out of sight and out of battle well behind his ample supply of troops.

No sooner did the dedicated ranks of Fist finish marshalling into thick defense than rushed the deluge of Hannibal Khan's shock troops pouring forth from over the eastern rise, the raucous clamor of their yowling war cries in the name of their godking preceding them in a tangible terror riding upon the rising winds.

The fistian front lines hunkered down for bracing impact, stabbing the speared bottoms of their kite shields to ground and shouldering into them for extra support while leveling out over the shieldtops their lengthy spears for stabbing effect. They stood absorbent to the crash of the Khan's raving frontrunners in a tidal collision of screaming and dying warriors even the awed observers watching safe through magnifying scopes from fistian city towers ten miles behind and housed within the protection of the Academy citadel swore they felt that first armor-crunching collision of bodies breaching through the city's high defensive walls.

The Head Mistress's preparations proved a careful calculation within the short amount of time allotted her, for the Khan's vast legion relied on the grueling patience of slow but steady progress while it churned ever forward en masse to confront the enemy it sought to destroy. She took every foreseeable precautionary measure considering the limited space provided her for planning and preparing before the initial onslaught from the Lord of Storms' swarm of warriors charged forth.

But it was not enough.

At first the formidable forces of Fist believed themselves outnumbered three-to-one. During the first wave of battle, and despite the disadvantage of their lesser numbers, the better-trained and well-organized fistian soldiers cut swift response through the chaos of the Khan's onrushing warriors who charged more in a flood of screaming savages than military might retaining any semblance of order and planning. But the attacking Bloodcloaks and worship-followers possessed numbers on their side, and numbers provided an army confidence, though confidence only drove a man so far when pitted against superior skill despite the better odds.

Mutilated bodies, some alive, most dead, lay strewn about the bloody plains in broken lines and reeking piles of twisted and sickening heaps as far as one's eye could sweep, the count of the dead twice-times that of the living a few hours after the Khan's tide of warriors crashed into the long fistian shieldwall and their answering drives of spears. The defeat obvious, the fight ended, and with neither a single glimpse of the warlord tyrant himself or his terrible command and control over lightning nor the infamous unliving necromaster the Lord of Storms controlled through some manner of dark sorcery.

It came then, as an eerie silence of uneasy peace settled over the bloody wreckage of the Azure Plains, that Hannibal Khan's true army and truer plans surfaced. Those first few gory hours proved no more than some small taunting test of Fist's military defenses. Quite possibly even a small display of gruesome entertainment for the watching Khan.

A mass hush overtook the thousands of fistian soldiers standing victorious amongst the scattered dead of both sides when their false victory bloomed in slow-dawning awe. Cheers surrendered and upraised weapons lowered from overhead celebratory salute in stunned disbelief at the humbling sight their distraught gazes beheld next.

An ominous rumble of distant thunder rolled over the condemning silence as there on high formed a dark and swirling mass churning gloom and misery into the once-clear afternoon sky. An incredible line arose in the distance, one stretching across the entire eastern horizon while presenting its first real sight of the true numbers making up the Khan's colossal legion.

Three-to-one existed a grievous error beyond measure, for now ten-to-one stood waiting to charge forth and dispense bloody carnage across the battle plains in the name of their conquering godking.

Fistian soldiers scrambled to orders for regaining their positions and reforming their defensive lines as the real struggle ensued.

Not tens of thousands but hundreds of thousands of devout khansmen advanced the field in marching red-gold splendor to the pealing horns of their war-horsed commanders. But this time the armored Bloodcloak vanguards poured forth with greater organization and order amongst their swelled ranks than the sacrificial savagery of their felled fellows before them. The second wave of warriors flooded toward the frantic reformation of fistian lines, one tidal and tsunamic and irrepressible.

Marching feet and stomping hooves sung together in pounding rhythm, something both felt and heard, producing a low-rising thunder foreboding their dreadful approach. But this time the formidable fistians reforming the long blockade of speared and shielded battle lines far across the corpse-littered plains did not wait for the closing enemy.

While reinforcements poured forth from the eastern gates of the city, medics and rangers, archers and spearmen, alchemical bombers and cavalry and more arriving back to front, swelling the fistian ranks afield as they marched forth to meet the enemy while behind them more lengthy shieldwalls formed in preparation for the gory fall of those whom strode before them.

As battle died to war.

A light and misty rain dampened the air, pulled forth from the darkening churn of sky, wet kisses riding stray gusts breathing over the plains with promises of the storm dominating the entire eastern horizon.

Fistian warrior aizakai took the field soon after the second catastrophic collision then breaking apart of both front lines churning into a chaotic frenzy where reigned slaughter, the eager runs of adamant battle mages weaving through the turmoil of blood and screams on currents of sorcery when not charging on horseback while turning small tidal pockets of action with violent blasts and destructive bursts of magics. Supernatural abilities the Khan's army sorely lacked took ruinous charge over the dismay, devastating the khansmen caught within the magical tortures.

Khansmen died screaming, their meaty bodies bursting into flames which jetted and licked out from between joins of armor as conjured combustions cooked them alive inside. The flesh of their fellows sizzled and bubbled and popped from acidic incantations as noxious billows of acrid choking smoke rolled over them in undulating gusts, a good number of the victims puking out ribbons of bile or streams of blood or the sick mixture of both after inhaling the poisonous vapors while the flesh peeled and dripped from their flailing limbs and screaming faces.

Others suffered eyes burned blind from pulses of exploding magelight bursting suns of brightness before their stunned faces seconds before a timely killing blow felled them out from saddle to the churned slosh of bloody mud underfoot by way of the fistian soldiers charging ahead of the aizakai conjurers who worked their wicked witchery from behind the rushing clusters of their assaulting protectors.

Amongst the sea of thousands fighting and dying, the far fewer fistian aizakai blazed and blasted, conjured and crushed on through the night into the following day. And though the battle mages turned the tides of war despite the Khan's overwhelming numbers, the aizakai efforts provided only temporary succor, for the warlord tyrant whom had yet to take the field or even present himself amongst his dying loyals demonstrated sure preparations for assault against such devastating supernatural methods of attack.

Mass volleys of arrows flew in slewing answer to the fistian aizakai forces, over and again—*twang-twang-twang!* Each inky barrage shaping black clouds looming high in the sky for long stretches of sun-dimming seconds before arcing downward in stabbing showers of death.

Soldiers of both sides felled by the score beneath the brunt of the indiscriminate volleys. Struck aizakai discovered the driven tips dipped with the noxious blood of Spellbinders, and wounds otherwise nonfatal instead burned with the paralyzing poison pumping a furious toll through their veins, snuffing their magics and locking limbs immobile while making easy prey of the fallen aizakai victims, some of whom unable even to scream through their constricted throats while receiving a cleaving axe to their chest or stabbing blade to throat or bashing mace to skull, their assaults staunched.

By next day's end the fistian aizakai numbers lived ravaged to half, then halved again by fourth's dawn. Two days thereafter and the aizakai numbers dwindled to but a handful afield while their reserves shielded behind the city's walls prepared for a final attack.

In the terrible span of a week it became obvious the Khan's colossal legion would not be pushed back, could not be beaten, should not have been discounted as some chaotic swarming horde of barbaric savages compared to fistian military might.

All of which occurred before the Soothsayer's arrival.

***

Now . . . and Banzu strode outside from the Academy main, having left the wounded older soldier behind—who fell into helping fortify the Academy innerworks against the inevitable invasion of the Khan's conquering forces into the Academy itself, working alongside hectic servants and students and teachers and tradesmen of varying ilk scrambling throughout the labyrinthine corridors burdened by armloads of supplies or belongings or both—once Banzu heard enough and dismissed the injured man with a thanks and the release of his strong grip.

A chaos of frightened fistians bumped and bustled round and past him, yet every one heeded his approach as word spread of his presence among them and moments more the shouting crowds filling the streets parted before his purposeful tread while the dread red impalement of his eyes hushed all whom dared meet their focused glare betraying fathoms of murderous intent.

Mothers and fathers dragging their crying children by the arms huddled or scrambled at sight of him. Looters abandoned their stolen wares and rushed into alleys or cringed behind overturned carts at his passing. Ruffians fighting over precious weapons to fend against the coming khansmen invasion broke their inconsequential battles and raced away. Scatters of lawmen paused in their work of commanding peaceful regulation amid the panic, brandishing weapons to wary guard while turning and watching though never engaging the Soothsayer wolf walking among the unnerved fawns.

Banzu ignored the turmoil while knifing through it, bold and brazen and daring any foolish hand to delay his stalker's course.

For a moment he attempted gathering wayward thoughts of his misplaced time dealing with the specter Essence of Simus Junes, but these scattered to the rising throb of hot blood rushing in his ears and pulsing at his temples with every strong beat of his heart when he finished past the distressed ebbs and flows of citizens and entered the shifting mix of soldiers thousands strong and scrambling to secure the city's final defenses before prepping to join or rejoin in the war raging over what looked to Banzu's perspective once he passed through the eastern gates as the incredible entirety of the Azure Plains. A roiling ocean of bodies tossed about by countless smaller storms of fighting and dying while delivering their convergence of distant screams racing the miles between.

Soldiers paused and watched Banzu stalk with purpose through their choked ranks, their eyes twinkling bright in due recognition, for denying the crimson-eyed Soothsayer proved an impossible mistake now that he walked among their thickening numbers here, his predatory presence of air an aura of intent shrouding him near visible.

Someone issued his name above the surf of voices, prompting more turning of heads then more shouts of his name from onlookers taking notice while spreading out from his unerring eastward path, many of those he passed drawing their weapons in cautionary pulls turned salutes while bowing their heads and pounding their fists to chests as he strode by, assuming his brazen freedom bestowed by the Head Mistress as told by no kohatheen worn round his neck or manacles impeding his wrists and the absence of any Spellbinder guard.

There even arose a momentary cheer for the arriving Soothsayer, but it soon died for the strong quiet of accepting nods, reverential yet intimidated, lying beneath the understanding of proven soldiers, when those cheering others caught sight of the silencing black mask of murder darkening the hard-set features of Banzu's intense expression. Determination chiseled in marble, he walked as unchallenged alpha amongst the pack.

He broke his focal stare ahead and glimpsed from face to passing face, reading expressions.

These men and women had given everything of themselves into defending their beloved homeland, protecting their cherished city and their frightened loved ones huddled therein. They lost the battle, were losing the war, and they expected to die soon so that they communicated the impression of missing something vital and torn from their spirits shown through the tortured stories of their eyes. The forlorn lot of them having already accepted their impending deaths as a foregone conclusion. Not so much cattle led to slaughter as waiting for its inevitable denouement.

Banzu caught notice of that missing *something* shared in so many of those dejected stares upon him: Faith. A raw word containing more burden than promise. Their faith seized by overwhelming odds, sapped over the torturous course of cruel days, stolen through fathers and mothers, brothers and sisters, sons and daughters drowned in a merciless tide of khansmen.

The relinquishment of faith, the only true weapon a person possessed once stripped of everything else of lesser value, riled disapproval in his proud fighter's heart knowing no surrender, though he understood it considering the surmounting odds.

I can't leave them like this. And I can't get through the press of khansmen on my own. They need a swift kick in the ass, and I need an example.

The prowling sweep of his predatory gaze through the droves and swells of bodies . . . *there.* Within a battered and bandaged huddle of fistian soldiers too injured for combat yet not so injured that they could not continue their own private battle behind the fighting lines, stood a solitary captive removed from the field for extracting precious information.

Banzu approached the shuffling backs half-hiding the restrained Bloodcloak, the khansman stripped of all arms and armor down to his soiled smallclothes. He ordered the surrounding fistians exacting punishing interrogation upon their bruised and bloodied detainee to cut loose the rope restraints binding their captive's wrists and ankles then to step aside. He used his 'quiet' voice, the one recommending they listen—and the soldiers obeyed without question under the blazing red scrutiny of his warning gaze.

"No one interferes," Banzu said of the beaten captive. He eyeballed the khansman while licking his lips, then snatched a knife from an interrogator's hand and threw it at the khansman's feet where it stabbed the ground inches deep. He announced in a potent tone to all the spectators gathering closer round them, "If this man of the Khan kills me then he earns his freedom!"

The captive Bloodcloak, squat with muscle and marked by fierce black tattoos on his once-fair face, across his broad chest, and down his timber legs in jags of black, stared at his apparent savior with widening eyes through a dirty curtain made of long strands of greasy blond hair, parts of it dreaded with dried blood. He thinned his lids into suspicious slits, gaze darting through the crowd of resentful fistian faces, his hung mouth closing so that he licked his split and bleeding lips then smacked them, tasting the opportunity presented him with a crazed grin.

Banzu turned round, strode five steps for space, then spun back while pulling Griever. He leveled his sword out pointing so that he stared the larger khansman down the length of his blade through focus-tunneling vision, his voice a declaration of intent.

"My name is Banzu Greenlief. I am the last Soothsayer. And I've come to kill your Khan."

A distant maddened cackle tickled at the back of Banzu's mind, but he ignored it same as he ignored the brief rise and fall of fistian cheers round him, burning the mental intrusion away with one quick and fiery thought: *Kill.* He gave Griever a little flicker through his twitching wrist before adding, "Unless you kill me first. What say you to that?"

Without waiting for answer, Banzu returned Griever to his left hipwing, proffered the stupefied Bloodcloak a glass-cutting smile in so doing, then turned his back and waited.

A profound silence suffocated the immediate area of noise while eager spectators awaited the results of the proposed contest moments from playing out before their watchful eyes.

Behind Banzu, the khansman bent and picked up the offered knife. He gazed round through the bruised swells of his beaten face, mistrustful of the opportunity given him, knowing his escape impossible regardless the outcome, an animal backed to corner with no other recourse. Eyes wide and wild, he surged into a snarling charge, knife raised overhead in a hammer-fisting grip for plunging six inches of steel into the offered target of his liberator's turned back.

Banzu closed his eyes, listening while distancing noise from the elevating footfalls behind him for the space of held breath.

Refusing the Power's touch for instinctual swordslinger grace, he drew his sword once more, propelling it several feet into the air by hooking his hand loose about its hilt while throwing it upwards. With perfect fluid timing and a quick turn of his reactive body he snatched Griever's leather-wound hilt at the apex of the throw and as the sword fell he turned momentum into twisting action upon his charging stabber.

He weighed and measured the khansman's entire life then ended it with his advancing thrust, arresting the plunging knife seeking depths of his face by catching it short at the wrist with his free hand while jolting the khansman's desperate charge to halt with Griever's piercing drive, its tip sprouting out the gasping khansman's back.

He locked with those startling eyes and beheld their blooming dismay a moment overlong, the adder's smile pursing his cruel twist of lips leaving the seething fury of his red eyes untouched, the knife in the khansman's palsied hand slipping loose.

"You are only the first of many," the feral part of Banzu whispered in guttural growl, low though overheard in the quiet.

He delivered a satisfying bone-wrenching twist of Griever's hilt, instigating a shuddering gasp and the snuffing of lifespark, before releasing his strong grip of captured wrist and stepping back while yanking Griever's blade from the other's chest, the keen length of steel grating loose from punctured spine and sternum. He spun round and presented a grin which wove fine lines at the corners of his unyielding stare.

Behind him a *thump* sounded in the swallow of silence, punctuating the vacuum of voices demanding fill.

He stretched the moment by surveying the hushed crowd before returning his blood-slick sword home to his left hipwing. No need for wiping it clean, he would wet it again soon enough. He addressed the depleted fistians watching him with appraising gazes and approving smiles, a sanguine gleam returning to their once-dull eyes in slow rekindles of faith.

"They are nothing more than men!" he announced, rounding about as he spoke, taking those faces in turn. "And they die just like the rest of us." Sparing no downward glance, he stepped onto then over the bleeding crumple of khansman corpse, an insignificant bump in the road. "You know of me but you don't know me. You fear me. Some of you even hate me." He paused, skipping his roving glare from eye to eye. "I don't care! And I offer you no false promises." He whipped his arm out, pointing east. "I'm headed straight for their Khan. Any of you who wish to die with me, ride with me now."

He strode away . . . through a growing elevation of cheers, fetching no look behind at the fistians rallying then pursuing in his determined wake, their numbers accumulating tens to hundreds as word spread in a wildfire of inspiration.

***

Banzu commandeered a stout and armored warhorse from a veteran soldier of high rank who sat in saddle watching out at the ensuing war and all it afforded his distant stare.

"Down," Banzu said, gripping the soldier's nearest leg for attention. "Now."

"What?" The fistian captain twisted in saddle, scowling and about to kick the nuisance away. "Get off—" But he clipped his protest short, balking to the fierce challenge of Banzu's red-eyed stare as recognition bloomed so that he drew back by inches while gripping the saddle horn to stay from toppling. "Holy gods," he said, his voice a croak. "Soothsayer?"

Banzu nodded, the motion slight. "I have a Khan to kill and I need your horse to get me to it." He increased the squeeze of his hand on thigh, seconds from yanking the man down. "Either give it or I'll take it."

"The Khan?" The captain glanced away at the ocean of war, then past Banzu at the swell of fistians behind him hundreds strong. "But that's suicide."

Maybe. Probably. "Down," Banzu said, imposing an iron grip on thigh meat, earning the captain's wince. "Now."

The blustered captain dismounted and spent an unsure moment regaining composure.

"Go to your family," Banzu said, an offhand comment while beginning his climb into saddle.

"I don't have any family left," the captain said.

Banzu paused his climb. He removed his foot from stirrup and turned. "Then come with me and avenge them."

The captain opened his mouth, closed it. The fear of death died in his eyes then, replaced by active flares of military cunning. Straightening taller by inches, he nodded. "You'll never get through that thick on your own, son. Wait here."

"I'm through waiting." Banzu turned away, began another climb into saddle.

"Godsdammit." The captain snagged a grab of Banzu's shirt and yanked him down. "I said wait!"

Banzu spun round glaring.

The scowling captain flinched back a step though mustered his rank a moment more by stepping forward, hard years of soldiering stiffening his iron spine, thinning his scrutinizing stare, and sharpening his admonishing tongue.

"I don't care who you are." He jabbed a bold finger, prodding Banzu's chest. "And you can lose that thousand-yard stare, you red-eyed bastard." Then with same hand he pointed past Banzu. "Out there's war, and wars aren't won alone." He flattened his left hand upturned while slicing atop it with his rigid right hand. "You'll need a wedge to punch you through that hot mess and hammer for the Khan." A pause, the tightening of his eyes where glimmered hope, another stiff prod of his finger. "This'll kill a lot of my men. You'd better be all they say you are."

Banzu opened his mouth, closed it, nodded.

The captain turned away, flailing his arms while shouting and cursing orders for every available horse not already commandeered by Banzu's hundreds of followers brought through the growing swell of hundreds more volunteers committing to following the Soothsayer into sure slaughter.

Minutes passed as the captain shouted himself hoarse while obedient soldiers rushed forth armored mounts in their hundreds.

Banzu surveyed his new suicidal cavalry then turned to his own mount.

Promise me . . . spoke a feminine sough of voice stealing through his head when he climbed to saddle. He glanced west, at and through the city of Fist, beyond it, seeking the origin of that wayward whisper fading to the stronger flush of determination twisting him east again.

He rode forth, paying small notice to the hundreds and hundreds more of mounted joiners accruing behind him. His focal gaze blazed before the pandemonium playing out far across the busy plains, the battle shadowed beneath the raging storm attacking the eastern sky while transforming it into an angry ocean of booming thunder and crackling lightning amid the churning swirls of gray and black.

Hannibal Khan. He scanned through the chaotic melee ahead in preemptive hunt. *Where are you?*

Untold thousands littered the battlefield already, with thousands more pitiful maimed wrecks of humanity swearing and screaming while trying to drag themselves out of the holocaust. A murderous cauldron of insane violence where men fought and killed without thought of self-preservation or hope of rescue. Challenging miles between him and his true target.

Doesn't matter. I'm the butcher here. I'll cleave through you all if that's what it takes.

Promise me . . . spoke the woman's voice, a pleading wisp of words dancing upon the fringe of his awareness, rising, falling, forgotten.

He reined to halt, pulled Griever, and paused in a moment of inner reflection while he beheld the naked steel of another promise in his hand. He harbored no illusions about the slimness of the thread from which his survival hung. Even if victorious, there lived little hope for his return from the slaughter dominating the plains.

So be it. This is more than me now. My life for the Khan's. A worthy sacrifice.

Promise me . . . Melora's voice issued true through the trenches of his mind, a desperate plea upon his waning humanity, but her voice turned a burning fade to his stronger resolve for vengeance repaid.

Regaining interest in the world round him once more by inhaling deep, the coppery tang of blood wet his breath while filling his sinuses with savage delight.

He gazed overlong upon Griever's immaculate blade, musing how unfitting its name so out of place here where lived only vengeance.

When a sword trades hands, the new owner renames it befitting its purpose.

"Venger," he whispered, the appellation leaving him pleased. And he smiled, approving the name and the purpose bestowed. "Venger," he said in stronger voice, then thrust his reborn sword skyward and shouted, "Death to the Khan!"

Venger flashed fractures of captured sunlight above his head at the same time distant thunder rolled deep and long across the killing fields awaiting his entry.

He heeled his spotted warhorse into motion, from trot through canter to gallop, the animal's steel flanchard and shaffron and peytral plating cinched tight over ripples of equine muscle, whilst behind him the fistian cavalry one-thousand strong pursued, their forming attraction of armored ranks shaping together in locomotive charge.

The ground shook to the thunder of four-thousand hooves punishing the earth, and the battle-paean of the fistian collective forming the driving spearhead round Banzu leading its tip issued from a thousand throats beside and behind him: "Soothsayer!"

* * *

Banzu charged into the fray of war, assaulting across the Azure Plains and into the enemy ranks with the answering fury of an avenging angel—or more perhaps a revenging demon—screaming his battle cry the wordless reiteration of his dead uncle's name.

Khansmen Bloodcloaks and worship-followers quailed before the naked murder on his face, and always in the rending thrust of his juggernaut cavalry's charging spearhead he rode the foremost, dispensing death in fanning strokes, forgetting strategy and tactics and responsibility save for his one desire of reaching Hannibal Khan through the fighting masses for the precious kill.

Possessed of battle lust, he wove through the chaos while cutting down the enemy from horseback, a scytheman harvesting corn, seizing Power-flickers hardening Venger's singing steel biting through armor as easily as the tender flesh and bone beneath. Bodies and parts of bodies tumbled away at his sides in screaming blurs and gory smears of felled khansmen. He tasted their blood in his mouth and, in rushes of pleasure, swallowed it down, the splendor a coppery honey coating his throat.

Round and behind him the one-thousand fistian braves dwindled in numbers, casualties torn from saddle while their armored spearhead opened a murdering path through the enemy ranks only for that path to close in behind them. Banzu bothered no look back to the dying soldiers earning their glory, his wild lusts focal and tunneled for the Hannibal Khan prize miles ahead yet still unseen.

Kill . . . whispered a harsh voice of instigation driving him ever forward, commanding with urgency, demanding obedience.

For hard-charging miles their armored cavalry spearhead punctured a long and bloody swath through the enemy pockets, plowing into and through the Bloodcloak mobs and worship-follower throngs, a vermillion thunderbolt of riders awash in rival blood. Dozens of lighter enemy horses hurled end over end by the impacts, their stunned riders tumbles of flailing limbs making of them inadvertent weapons of flesh and armor crashing into their fellows.

The peripheral flashes of thrashing Bloodcloaks lifting high into the air on the ends of stabbing lances upraising then flinging away their impaled prizes. Fleeting glimpses of screaming faces taut with challenge one instant then torn asunder by bashing maces or swung swords or driving halberds the next. Battle cries splitting into howls of pain and dying. The enemy melted against their charging spearhead annihilating hundreds of khansmen in the space of pounding heartbeats and stomping hooves. More khansmen ran about on foot, screaming, and the juggernaut spearhead spread them as they ran or trampled them down.

Yet still the enemy advanced with the drilled remorselessness of some terrible machine. But Banzu rode undaunted to the pressurized burst of merciless butchery blazing in his fevered heart, his face frozen open in a savage grinning rictus, each brief seize of the Power and the next flashing lambent crimson menace in his brightening eyes as Venger cleaved and tore while slinging ropes of gore. All along the front of the charging fistian spearhead, horses tumbled screaming to their sides, crushing their panicked riders, or rearing up with their bowels exposed for puncturing, or backing away from the blitzkrieg and crashing into their fellow khansmen behind them where more fistians afoot swarmed in and dispensed quick death.

The numbers of their charging spearhead shrank with every mile gained, hundreds lost yet still they smashed and slashed at full career while cutting grisly course through the enemy wailing and screaming and moaning beneath the cavalry's shouts of ecstatic bloodletting.

Kill . . . sang that prominent inner voice filling Banzu's blood-drunk mind with orgasmic urgency, an arousing mantra possessing the heated strokes of sex and gaining climaxing edge with every rabid lusting repeat requesting only more. **Kill . . . kill . . . kill!**

* * *

Time's true passage diminished inside Banzu's rapacious slaughter of khansmen, minutes and hours meaningless to the here-and-now impenetrable veil of fever, the toll of bodies an impossible number tallied, his cavalry's penetration miles deep and questing deeper. Night or day no longer mattered, for he viewed the anarchic battleworld through a sepia haze of blind ambition and inhumane execution making no distinction but between himself and all those who stood in his way.

The darkening sky overhead rumbled in furious match to the thundering hooves of the galloping battering ram of warhorse working fierce beneath him and those of his stampeding spearhead of cavalry. They penetrated through the outer lines of khansmen surrounding the massive eye of Khan-born storm, a miles-thick hysteria of death and dying dominating the entire middle stretch of Azure Plains evincing Hannibal Khan's current domain of destruction therein.

Banzu caught clips of khansmen referring to the armored beasts of his cavalry as tanks in tardy yells of protest to their fellows whose faces washed away in screaming smears when he rode them down or cut them aside with Venger's rending sweeps in passing charge.

Lighter rainfall increased to spitting sprays pelting them from all sides and angles as the cold rains rode the roiling squalls and tumbling gusts of windblasts growing more turbulent the closer their unit strove inward toward the great storm's core. Closing space between the target Banzu captured through still-distant squints smiting his shadow-splitting flashes of conjured lightning therein the turmoil.

The volatile wrath of Khan-wrought weather tortured the thousands of battle-crazed warriors within destructive elements of its unnatural designs imitating nature's fury in a derecho of death pronouncing the Lord of Storms' awesome power and the honesty of his title.

Here, within the outer boundary of the true storm raging its slow though obstinate westward course across the Azure Plains, the fighting lived a chaotic mix of both sides, the turbulent patterns of weather infused by the remaining fistian aizakai dealing destructive blasts and conjured weaves of magic against the relentless enemy unto their last suicidal breaths.

Ethermage-formed tornados cut rending swaths through whole Bloodcloak battalions, ripping victims by the tens of handfuls off their kicking feet or charging mount and tossing them tumbling and twirling hundreds of feet into the air then reversing the motions through empowered gales and throwing khansmen down in armored ragdolls, making missiles of bodies smashing into their fellows beneath.

Terramancers erupted pillars of mud in spewing geysers, flipping flailing tumbles of khansmen skyward, when not shooting the terra up in rocky spikes of jagged torture piercing their Khan-sworn enemies and making of them bleeding scarecrow jokes of impalement.

Gouts of flames jetted from the flinging hands of Pyrodancers wreathed in snaking weaves of fire, their conjured bursts of dragon's breath burning tender flesh beneath steely bits of charred armor, scorching galloping horses into tumbling mounds of toasted meat while cooking their riders alive within heated red glows of armor hissing steam in the pelting rains as their dying screams added to the musical raucous of battle.

Elder aizakai experienced from a lifetime of rigorous Academy training exercised greater creative control over massive tusked mammoths similar in size and demonstrable demolition to the enemy's living beasts farther afield, these simulacrums forged in elemental mimicry from rocks and dirt and mud and brandishing ramming or piercing tusks of thick, split timbers wrought from the wreckage of siege engines blasted apart or abandoned by their teams of kohatheen-collared thralls to the muddy chaos. The conjurers of these elemental beasts tromping through the enemy, crushing bodies atop bodies underfoot, stood surrounded by shrinking rings of protective fistian soldiers fighting to shield them from the constant onrush of attacks as they worked their magical mammoths through trampling destruction until greater numbers overwhelmed the ringing fistian guardsmen for the aizakai controllers within and delivered unto them savage deaths in swarming brutality.

The conjured mammoths winked out from continuation upon the snuffing of their aizakai master's lifespark not by collapsing into spills of their bodies but through tremendous explosions of earth that bashed and battered and broke their unlucky khansmen butchers.

Huge battlecats fashioned from magefire prowled the plains, leaping and dancing, pouncing and pawing, their molten feline bodies thrice the size of the largest warhorse afield hissing against the pelting rains and flung gobs of mud while rending Bloodcloak armor and worship-follower flesh with savage swipes of their fiery claws when not implementing flaming saberfangs into ripping victims apart.

Fistian volleys of arrows rose then fell, the slews of missiles aizakai-worked into flame-hissing death seconds before piercing into the skulls or chests or unguarded limbs of their flailing khansmen targets, others unlit through flight yet bursting into fine clouds of needling splinters inhaled into laboring lungs filling with blood as screams tore loose from inflicted throats.

The rain thickened farther ahead, Banzu noted through the red haze of his charging raze, the dark churn of sky shadowing the plains in false night for miles in every direction. There ahead no such magically wrought creatures forged from magefire stalked the battlegrounds, though some few hydromancers worked patches of the rain pouring down in sheets, transforming pockets of water into jagged lances of ice which tore through flesh though splintered against denting armor.

But the fistian aizakai diminished to sheer numbers, reduced to less than one-tenth of their original tally despite reserves. And though their magics allowed them to deal with multiple targets at once, the Khan's overwhelming numbers of battle-crazed Bloodcloaks and fanatical worship-followers continued driving in upon the fistian forces in relentless swells. Here and there conjured fires winked out moments after flaring into life as steel found flesh and extinguished the aizakai lifeforces empowering the flaming conjurations into brief existence.

The carnage of war glided past Banzu's peripherals in a slideshow of action slowed by intermittent fractions with each Power flicker seized, Venger's Power-hardened tongue blurring swings of murder at his sides while he rode down enemy after enemy in relentless charge for the true eye of battle maelstrom raging ahead.

Though still a distant shape from Banzu's current vantage, the tiny figure of the false godking himself stood atop a mighty structure constructed from a forest of timbers, a slow-moving tower of sorts with mammoth beasts of burden pulling it along at its wheeled base. Arrows bounced off the tethered beasts' thick and wooly hides, their long and muscled trunks slapping fighters aside while they labored pulling the immense tower and the Khan atop it across the plains. Several carried bodies dangling impaled from their elongated tusks if not pieces of limbs disjoined from bodies flung loose from those pink-stained spears of curled bone.

The imposing Lord of Storms stood poised high atop the mobile structure hundreds of feet tall, one arm raised above his head and the other outstretched before him as lightning jagged down from the roiling mass of sky in brilliant flashes, electrify into him a terrible brilliance, making of him a living conductor then shooting forth from his outstretched gauntleted godhand in smiting jags of searing white death blasting up flailing twists of bodies into the air while beneath the tumbles of victims the ruptured grounds spewed volcanoes of hot mud.

Venger whirred slashing at Banzu's sides in vibratory pleasure for the lives it tasted, hot exhaustion lathering his burning muscles one moment then flushing revitalized through his brief cooling seize of Power and the cruel accelerated aging exchange of his lifeforce the next, the flashes of energies winking hot-cool-hot, his heart a thrumming pound in his heaving cage of ribs while he plowed through enemy upon enemy at full career, and trod them into the ground, crushing them when not knocking them flying from his punching charge. The rush and ebb of blood in his throat empowered his shouts of the Khan's name, while beside and behind him joined resounding shouts from the remaining troopers of his suicidal fistian cavalry their numbers hundreds more diminished.

Khansmen died screaming under their thundering hooves in a road of bodies. Coppery saliva wet the yawning cave of Banzu's mouth. He swallowed between shouts, tasting the tangy sweetness of impending victory.

He charged through another line of defiant khansmen, squashing their trampled bodies when not battering them aside by plated horse and swiping sword, into where the spaces between groups of fighters stood spread farther apart here than without. Surprised at earning such spacious respite, he slowed his mount while twisting in saddle for a look elsewhere to ensure he hadn't somehow gotten turned round amid the chaos—

Blood sprayed his vision over, and his horse whinnied a scream as it reared up kicking and twisting, tossing him out from saddle. The world spun while he tumbled a space, then struck the ground hard on his left shoulder and side yet maintained sure grip on Venger's hilt. He rolled his back and made to surge his feet, but startled at over a thousand pounds of horse, a spear lanced through its whipping neck between thick armor sheets, falling down to crush him.

No, it can't end like this . . . his only fleeting thought.

He tensed, unable to roll away in time by normal means. By preservation of instinct he made to seize the Power.

But there shot overhead a great moving shadow, that of a leaping horse slamming into the falling other and knocking it away from crashing course. Above him played out his fistian defender thrown from saddle as the two horses collided. But the soldier-savior's foot caught in stirrup so that his flung body swung round, trapped then battered between the tangle of beasts as they struck the muddy ground ahead from Banzu's safe position.

The decimated rest of the fistian cavalry spearhead spread apart, slowing to surround their fallen Soothsayer leader, many of the riders and more of their wounded horses dappled with jutting arrows, what remained of their frothing beasts' speed and strength pressed from the animals to this their place of final service.

Banzu stood up flinging mud. He scanned round, checking direction. A flickering bloom of lightning silhouetted the turned figure of Hannibal Khan atop his mobile tower, so much closer now and yet still so far away.

Fistian shouts of warning pierced the din of fighting and dying. Banzu glanced skyward at the spray of arrows seconds from raining down upon his fixed position. A fistian mounted at his left tumbled from saddle by way of a whirling mace crushing the woman's hip then twisting her along its swung course.

Banzu turned to lunge in upon the attacking Bloodcloak—but pitched forward sprawling when someone leaped upon his back and pinned him against the muddy canvas. He began twisting to wrestle the attacker free, then paused when the man covering him stiffened while grunting, his body a pincushion corpse accepting the arrows raining past his sides and peppering the ground.

For a humbling length of terrible seconds Banzu lay splayed and protected beneath his pincushioned savior, seeking logical coherence from the fevered pitch of control dominating his raging spirit since his entry to war. He rolled the shielding fistian corpse away and, spitting gobs of mud, achieved his feet, Venger anxious in his flexing hands reclaiming sure purchase of bastard hilt while his keen gaze swept in panoramic hunt of his grounded surroundings for more victims to feed his rapacious fury.

It was then, on a new level of understanding amid the deafening clangor of clashing metal, of voices erupting in pain and dying, of faces stretched in agony and animosity, of bodies felled by the thousands, hundreds by his own condemning hands, that the true brutality of the joined war struck him with grim and honest pause, so much the unproud squeeze round his dejected heart.

Fighting from on horseback turned the killing so distant and easy. But now, here, standing within the undeniable thick of it all, a closer part of it and a part of its cause—

Gods, so many lives . . . destroyed.

And there, as he scanned the grisly tableau of war, his hatred for the Khan deepened with hurt, achieving in him a sadness so profound he could only stare, mute with grief, as one prominent thought left him stunned and wounded of spirit.

So this is what human slaughter looks like.

A glance at Venger, slick with gore.

Feels like.

* * *

A young though non-particular soldier of Fist catching the barest notice of Banzu's sweeping gaze yards ahead jerked back with an arrow jutting from his stomach. By slightest chance he looked Banzu's way upon the Soothsayer's rising, their eyes meeting for the thinnest of measures through the sheeting rainfall before—

Two more arrows joined the first—*thunk-thunk!* And now that young pair of eyes lost their hopeful gleam of ever growing old, turning stark denial into waking regret as if finally understanding one of the truest pains in life was knowing most men never got to choose how they died no matter what they planned or how well they planned it. The wet mace slipped out from the unknown soldier's loosening grasp, and he staggered first one step left then two steps right in an unsure moment of where he was or where he wished to be, his widening gaze of appeal capturing Banzu's fixed stare throughout his stumbler's drunken dance.

Until the indiscriminate soldier dropped to his knees, caps splashing mud, breaking eye contact and gaping down at his hands clutching two of the three protruding shafts in trembling fists. When he returned his pleading look up, the faint glimmer of dying hope glossing over his naïve young eyes, he released a tortured scream while trying though failing at pulling the arrows loose from his punctured guts, his strained face a mask of torment paling beneath the filth as hot tears of regret ran crooked trails down his cheeks.

"No . . ." His voice a bare whisper, Banzu reached out to the young man, the space between them unachievable, then lowered his futile hand. A shiver flushed cold against the rabid heat burning through his veins, not quite rocking him on his feet despite enduring the impulse to stagger for catching balance. And though he stood Powerless, action turned sluggish and slowed as therein through his battle-fevered thoughts spoke a harsh prominence blowing through the cave of his mind rife with memories not of his own making.

No true warrior holds any love for archers or arrows, boy. Poor bastard's found that out the hard way.

The soliloquy spoke with calm inflection, possessing all the time in the world for idle conversation. And with it arrived the dread suspicion of not just speaking to Banzu but through him, resembling the tone of his own inner monologue so that he questioned it for another's voice at all. And yet . . . and yet.

Arrows in your guts don't kill quick, boy. Even the hardest men scream like mewling babes while begging the gods' forgiveness and getting nothing but pain. The truest definition of Agony. Let's finish the poor bastard off.

"Yes." Banzu took one step forward then jolted stopped. "No." He shook his head, regaining wherewithal through a series of hard blinks. "No."

He banished the voice into the shadowed depths of his mind from whence it came, its absence leaving the earned understanding of another man's trials once lived, of another Soothsayer swordslinger who had witnessed such horrors before . . . and enjoyed them.

Banzu knew before returning his attentions to the oceanic battle-fray that the best that crying soldier could hope for now lived in swift death dealt by the khansmen chasing after the damning arrows' flight.

Kill him, the other's voice surged, returning from banished depths in a strong conspiratorial urging.

And Banzu swore if that voice possessed a mouth it paused and licked its lips upon a visage of feigned pity.

Do the poor bastard a favor and kill him now. A pause, an infectious chuckle, and one corner of Banzu's mouth crooked a budding smile not of his own rule. **You know you want to.**

He nodded agreement, no control to it. A ghosthand gripping the back of his neck and working muscles as if shaping clay. His left leg quivered when he took another step obedient to suggestion.

We're here for death. Kill them all!

"No!" Banzu protested a defiant yell, shutting out the tempting voice from swaying the wavering considerations of his bending will. And therein responded a maddened cackle, a mocking peal of laughter so rebellious it fissured cracks in the walls of his sanity before it fled to safer corners where it peered back at him from the shadowed depths of his breaking mind.

"No," he repeated in harsh whisper. *Gods, no, what am I doing?*

Blinking hard, regaining lost focus for the khansmen closing in on he and his remaining spearhead chargers from all angles, he gazed round through returning clarity at the paltry survivors of the fistian cavalry surrounding him in a loose circle of protection, watching him through it all, their hard stares questioning the brevity of their Soothsayer leader's apparent lapsing of sanity not out from any consideration of abandonment but through desperate want of its quick passing so they could rejoin the killing crusade with him at their commanding helm. Their faces betrayed they expected to die but also expected to take as many of the enemy with them in killing trade.

Banzu opened his mouth to shout orders—but his fistian cordon guard spun their backs to him in forced engagement to the shouting swells of crazed warriors shrinking in at them from all sides, those still mounted turning their snorting equine tanks into the surge of khansmen as they reared up then came down upon that first charging rush to stomping effect before spreading out, expanding their circle from protective to proactive while their others afoot rushed outward from behind and between the rampaging beasts, bashing and hewing through the screaming rush of khansmen frenzy.

And just like that Banzu returned to the mix of things, determination vulcanizing in eruptive flares of vengeance restored and requesting release upon every last khansman rushing his dwindling crew.

He raced forth from the broken circle's core, seeking targets, his body spending through the animal grace of feral locomotion, his red eyes fevered jewels. A guttural yell tore from his throat as he batted aside a clubbing mace, elbowed the face-painted khansman off-balance, thrust at another, then spun round at the first and slashed open arm to the bone with Venger's whistling tip after cutting through the thick handle of mace, sending the heavy spiked head thudding aside along with several detached fingers.

He snarled as he seized a flicker of Power and booted the face-painted attacker in the chest, denting armor, felt more than heard the crunch of breaking sternum, lungs puncturing beneath splintering bone, the flushing rush of fiery joy shattering orgasmic when he sent the khansman flying backwards with transferred Power-momentum to where a line of space opened up as the kicked body rammed through splitting ranks of khansmen for the length of twenty feet.

Eyes wide and wild, chest heaving not from effort but elation, he tasted the delectable draught of violence wetting his throat while the enemy continued surging forth seeking his death yet finding only their own brutal demises through limb-rending *flick-flick-flickers* of the Power he fought hard to restrain so as not to expend too much of his fueling lifeforce in cruel trade upon these minions in lieu of their Khan master.

But their numbers proved vast, ever-increasing, a deluge of screaming faces surrounding him now, he a beacon drawing their charging bids. He whirled and hacked and thrust without conscious volition, swordslinger instinct dominating, until the khansmen knot broke apart in a tumble of bodies, earning space again, a moving turmoil of figures running past, shouting. Flashing murder every instant. So much blood it existed as some other element spilling everywhere.

Banzu spun and lunged in flickers of Power, the world pulsing luminous twilight beats before his flashing eyes. He tore Venger free through thin resistance, and a faceless Bloodcloak fell, tripping up another, while cleaved helm and the top part of head it contained spun through the air. He swung at the nape of the tripped woman's neck and enjoyed the pleasing jar as Venger's stroke broke through bone with the ease of a swiping finger tearing through a spider's delicate web.

And now he held his sword two-handed, took his next enemy in the eye with Venger's driving point and tossed the dead man aside by the skull with the flick of his sword.

He sank his haunches, ducking a morning star, then arose while slicing his next charger in a Power-flicker cut from crotch through lengthwise-splitting stomach and armored chest to chin, the opened khansman's guts spilling loose in slops of organs from round exposed spine glistening white before the scream finished tearing loose from his opened throat. Banzu seized another Power-flicker and punched him in the face—and the Power-momentum of his driven fist blasted out the back of the faceless warrior's bursting skull, killing the man twice over before the gutless corpse collapsed to mound upon its spilt innards.

Strains of the sword-song reached Banzu while he made stubs of limbs with Venger's Power-hardened steel shearing through futile blocks of lesser blades then reversing stroke through flesh and bone. Venger swung lighter, dancing to the song, containing a life of its own, vibrating pulsing beats while it drank and bathed in showers of blood.

Scores of khansmen fell to the berserking Soothsayer and his blurring whirs of steel in bleeding pieces of human wreckage. A glint of the sun stole through a momentary break in the thick black churn of storm-tossed sky overhead, stabbing an unobstructed lance of light in the darkness, and flashed crimson on Venger's humming tongue, heliographing a message to the Khan through his dying loyals. For moments without time Banzu fought, enfolded in the fierce joy of killing's rapture, the heat and fury of retaliation and its continued payment blazing indiscrimination of pure hatred fueling his working limbs.

Resisting seizing the Power in more than brief flickers and go speeding for the Khan proved a laborious chore, but in truth he enjoyed cutting his way across the plains through these warriors of the false godking whom had led them here to this place of pitiless, remorseless death, their dying screams rewarding him orgasmic shatters of bliss shivering through his flowing body in ecstatic delight.

Heaven. The word tingled through his mind in a tantalizing whisper, a lover's hot breath brushing across the fine hairs of his inner ear. **Kill.**

Each part of the fight and the next played out to a secret score singing through Banzu's zealous mindscape, righteous fury returning two-fold in screams of steel against steel and his bathing in blood. A wildness infected him, and he thought whatever made him human abandoned to the inferno of vengeance fueling him forward.

Promise me . . . came and went a woman's troubled whisper pleading at the fringe of Banzu's awareness. ***You promised to—***

Kill! urged the other's voice in rebuking tone, louder and laughing in mocking scorn.

Venger's swift flash, a sickening crunch, and a shorter Bloodcloak's head spun end over end, attached to the body only by a lengthening ribbon of spouting arterial blood. Banzu booted the headless body into tripping up the charge of ten or so Bloodcloaks behind it, making of it a flailing log breaking the run from snapping leg bones. He turned to move on once thirty fistian soldiers—the last of his grounded fistian cavalry—leaped upon the mound he made for them and delivered eager repeating thrusts of steel into the piled khansmen screamers.

"Oh gods help!" A nearby yell from behind, an indiscriminate plea piercing the din of battle. "Soothsayer! Oh gods—"

Banzu spun toward the shout in a critical tug upon his waning humanity—and ducked beneath a spiked mace whiffing overhead. He shot up slicing with the full release of his stretching frame, Venger opening the offender from crotch through splitting skull in a perfect butterfly cut dividing the khansman, organs and heat spilling between the two separating halves collapsing to mud.

The shouter pierced his senses again, now a wordless iteration.

He tried locating the caller of that desperate plea turned scream begging for his assistance—and failed against the roiling sea of movement, of wild eyes and grimy faces amid clashing steel and flowing ribbons of blood.

There sounded another obscure scream for his help, followed by two more, each of different voices though fistian in origin. A fifth voice issued its wordless agony hidden among the faceless sea of battle, lost as the life that produced it. More yells for help sounded from unseen places.

But he turned away, unable to answer. And there caught sight of a nearby aizakai maiden whose coppery curls flowed back from her face in long tangles so that she resembled a screaming skull on fire. For the moment he stood gazing and impressed at the awing sight of her, whipping her arms back then throwing forward in repeat succession, as she rode upon some surging translucent breath of self-propelling wind controlled about her carried body while producing magical birth to multiple curved streaks of physical air shooting loose from her gestures in thrown scythes. Which grew in size as they sped out from her in thin spinning blades of air. These wicked razor crescents skimmed along, lowering to breast height, cutting great swathes of bloody slaughter through the close-packed enemy, each conjured blade felling a dozen or a score of khansmen while sending their sundered fragments flying among their fellows.

Banzu swallowed down the too-late warning yell bubbling up the back of his throat when the streaking flash of a spear tore the attacking aizakai of coppery flair out from the torrent of winds carrying her forward in hovering charge. The length of barbed steel impaled her through the chest, jerking her backwards and forcing her to the ground where it pinned her to place, and the winds once carrying her died away, swallowed by pain. Seconds only before khansmen swarmed upon her, hacking and chopping those flailing limbs to pieces before moving on to more spoils of war.

Banzu took two steps in pursuit then stopped. He closed his mouth and watched through the gossamer veil of his battlelust those khansmen disappear into the carnage. And he let them to it, for his true spoils awaited him across the plains at the core of the warring storm.

But he scanned about regardless, enduring an unsure moment of staying and killing . . . but no. Killing proved only one reason for his hesitation. His leaving condemned all fistians here to death in his abandonment, those who looked to him as a paragon of war. No sight of the remaining soldiers of the fistian cavalry that had borne him here . . . if any of them still lived. And of that he possessed great doubt.

The boom of explosion sounded above the battle riot close behind so that he spun round facing ground erupting in a fountain of earth spraying fanning waves of mud and tumbles of bodies on high while tearing a momentary hole in the carpet of figures both khansmen and fistian. Waves of steam and smoke billowed up from the glass-lipped fissure breathing heinous winds scorching skin raw when not burning through to white bone beneath upon faces screaming behind futile shields of hands where hung strips of cooked flesh, their bits of armor glowing red-hot and frying.

Instead of rushing forth, instead of staying to help his dying fellows, Banzu spun round and charged east, running past a tight cluster of safeguarding fistian pikemen whose tall kite shields formed a turtleshell of protection round their aizakai middleman. Surrounded by khansmen, they would not hold out long . . . only long enough.

He watched in passing as that battered metallic shell opened, allowing the nucleus of a gray-haired mage to throw out overhead metallic balls expanding from knuckle size to that of skulls released from his glowing hands. When these detonated, first arcing on high, each metallic ball burst into wicked showers of red-hot metal shards spraying out in deadly barrage, tearing men apart, maiming them, jolting them backwards in staggering screams while stripping chunks of their meat free for later feeding to war's always and inevitable aftermath of flies and maggots which had fed and would continue to feed upon all dead men until man lived no more.

Long enough passed a moment more, and that human turtleshell of shields failed, overwhelmed by sheer numbers of swarming khansmen, their axes and hammers pounding and clobbering, cracking that metallic shell open while thrusting spears and swords found chinks in which to stab.

On Banzu ran, chased by screams, abandoning his fistians fellows in need of his help, his determined sights fixed afar upon the distant figure of Hannibal Khan standing in towering loom high above the chaos. He licked the lacquer of sweat and blood from his lips and spat, saving anyone an impossible venture.

He drew in a deep nostril breath, steeling his mind of all but ahead while trying to forget those he left behind. He seized not just a flicker of the Power but the full inner grasp of it. To those round him able to spare a free eye he turned a blurring shift of murder knifing through slower khansmen while dealing swift death in passing, each step and the next leaden with betrayal as he abandoned old screams behind for new ones ahead.

Sparing no glace to his dying fellows, everything simplified when hating the Khan so that he embraced the driving potency of his animus.

Don't look back. Only ahead.

This doesn't end through khansmen slaughter.

They view Hannibal Khan as a living god.

I must become the godkiller.

CHAPTER THIRTY-NINE

Banzu accelerated across the battlefield in a blurring streak of Powered slaughter to the rhythmic cadence of **Kill . . . Kill . . . Kill** voicing prominence above the surf of a thousand voices rioting in his head, Venger's maiming hacks and rending slashes carving him a straight warpath through the tumbles of bodies and parts of bodies shorn from the murderous route of his killing spree. All the while he battled back the incessant urge to surrender and seize beyond the Power for tapping the corrupted Source, though he managed enough divided mastery over his straining willpower and restricted his Power seizings to that of shortened bursts of slow-flowing seconds at a time.

Killing bursts, he mused of these brief seizings and of himself, *a farmer scything wheat.* He craved for seizing longer stretches of the Power though wished not to exhaust that inner flex of strain before reaching his truest target farther afield upon the khansmen obstacles of harvest needing reaped between.

The parasitic leaching of his lifeforce proved a nagging ache upon his fevered spirit, his red hair already returned in inches of tufts and his blood-speckled face bearded, though the permanent cost of accelerated aging in ruthless exchange for equal trades of Power enacted a necessary tolling of his vengeful resolve.

The teasing soliloquy of his inner workings whispered fierce seductions between approving chants of killing to embrace the full splendor of the Source in a continuous surge that would speed him to his Khan target within minutes. But he refused the risk of tapping into the madness of the shared collective, fearing braving those hazardous waters allowed no sane return.

Now that he possessed the Essence of the First, the missing piece to the fractured Source, cleansing the shared collective of its thousand bloodlust-corrupted Soothsayers would only come after he found the Godstone—wherever it lay fallen.

Time for that later. After I deal with Hannibal Khan.

Raging purpose drove him forward through unopposable deathblows of Venger's blurring strokes sundering khansmen aside by the carven score in screaming waves of bloodshed, his body pure locomotion, the pelting rains washing sweat and blood replaced by more blood and sweat flowing off him in glistening ribbons, Khan's blood the panacea he desired most, the cure-all to the wretched ails clawing at his tortured soul, the magnanimous elixir to the wordless agony escaping his throat in guttural shouts piercing the din between fanning cleaves of Venger's immaculate steel, his defiant core accepting no substitute for dousing the blazing pain of his Khan-born animus and all his harbored woes.

No substitute but her, issued the apostrophe of his own interior discourse puncturing a temporary breach of another longing into the thick battle haze of his fevered mind with reflexive guilt of Melora far away in the Builder's tower instead of fighting beside him here in this chaos of slaughter.

An invisible umbilical tether of spirit tugged him somewhere west with knowing, but he shirked it aside for the stronger tether urging him east, Godstone purpose failing to Khan ambition.

He sped along undeterred, knifing through heavy sheets of thickening rain while cutting rending swath through khansmen obstacles in startlements of violence, the slowing-skipping world bursting grey and luminous through every propellant seize of Power and its supernatural velocity imposed, gaining much ground while slicing through the surprised enemy.

Until the burning stress of cumulative fatigue threatened to collapse him mid-run so that he arrested his current killing burst in a slowing stumble, having covered several miles in Powered sprint, his body craving rest as much as his inner focal flex of strain.

He came to a mud-skittering halt while releasing the Power, his turning boots splashing up the muck of the saturated plains with side-sliding feet producing a fanning wave of bloody sludge arcing on high then splattering the backs of the contingent of khansmen fighting a dwindling knot of fistian soldiers less than ten bounding strides ahead. For a time he stood motionless in all but his predator's sweeping gaze and aggressive breathing sucking cool air into his hot lungs, the heavy downpour washing out the blood soaking his shortbeard and matted hair and his sodden cling of clothes.

The closer khansmen knocked into the backs of their others, shoved by the splashing crash of muddy wave. They turned round and faced its origin while their fellows hacked and stabbed the last of the fistian knot to death.

Banzu advanced no aggression against the khansmen spreading out to surround him but for baring pinkened teeth through peeling snarl, his rage a beating pressure surmounting behind his red-eyed glare sighting targets while issuing unvoiced challenge. The khansmen cordon broke into shouting charges, a shrinking circle of glittering steel and tattooed faces, closing distance, boots squelching in the mud.

Banzu held the moment overlong—then stole into a Power-flicker whirl, eyes flaring lambent crimson, spinning in a vicious rend of circle, Venger's full extension of self slicing through sword and mace and spear for the rush of armor and flesh and bone behind the khanmen's unison charge, clearing his immediate area of attackers while buying a few restive moments before more foolish enemies rushed forth seeking swift death.

Releasing the Power, he surveyed his latest work with a proud eye. Bodies and parts of bodies lay everywhere, the ground round his feet thick of mud and lopped limbs, dismembered khansmen screamers slow in dying.

Yes! roared an approving voice, its tone more a bestial growl than anything resembling human speech. **More! Kill them all!**

No.

Yes!

No!

Banzu rebuked the voice while driving back the fevered urge it produced to surge forth into a blind killing frenzy indiscriminate of friend from foe. He turned about while catching his breath and scanned round with a hunter's surer calmness, deliberating how much closer into the eye of the battle's core he'd achieved, as well the burning fatigue of his body elevating without the Power's invigorating flushes of vitality flowing through him in nutrient feed of his lifeforce.

I'm pushing too hard and fast. The Power's drained months from me already in getting me here. I need rest, however brief. I can't fail in this. I won't!

So he took it, resting in the middle of his cleared space encircled by corpses mounded in a warning halo of dead khansmen while beyond his gory perimeter played out pockets of fighting in everywhere abundance.

Here the black churn of sky rumbled an endless thunder, each diminishing roll stealing into the rising next, vibrating the air, trembling the soggy muck. The rain shot down in thick drops of plunging arrows. The unrelenting winds blew against Banzu without clemency, punishing the loose fabric of his torn clothes by flapping and snapping bites against his hot wet skin rubbed raw by coarse fibers.

As well sang the battle-grief of uncountable men and women killing and dying so that their yells blended together in a cacophony of one long, endless scream, their weapons a relentless chorus of clangor, the discordant music of steel chiming steel, of shields resounding to blows, of hissing arrows and quarrels *thwip-thwip-thwipping* stray bites of flesh and mud or snapping plinks of armor above the clash and crash, the bellows of rage and pain.

Banzu absorbed it all while his resting flex of Power recovered, his lone figure a statue of prominence standing amid the swells and flows of aggression daring the enemy to break away from their fighting pockets to challenge him and feed their blood into the churn of mud and muck.

He watched at length the ecstasy of violence and death dominating the battle plains for miles in every perceivable direction as far as his normalized vision surveyed. He gazed out over the toiling sea of slaughter, this roiling ocean of murder, his hunter's calm expanding, enveloping his distanced awareness of his part in it all, and for the moment he wondered if this pandemonium replicated the grander chaotic scale of the Thousand Years War.

Yes, spoke the voice. **And it was absolutely wonderful.**

Banzu shuddered to the answer and all it afforded him. He closed his eyes and drew in a deep nostril breath, clearing the vocal intrusion from his mind as best he could.

I'm losing it. Or have lost it already.

He snapped his eyes open and swept his hunting gaze . . . *there,* refocusing far ahead upon the crackling flash of lightning knifing down in a white hot blaze of brilliance splitting the gloom of false night for fractions, its jagged godfinger of resplendent death torn from the sky and redirected by its ungodly commander standing on high atop his towering mobile structure. Hannibal Khan scorched asunder both earth and men alike in a great plume of smoldering bodies and boiling waves of mud erupting from the tortured ground punished by his smiting strike.

More knifing flashes of lighting pursued, charging the scintillating Lord of Storms in conductions of awesome promise then puncturing those below fighting round the base of his dominant perch in steaming sluices of charred corpses tumbling ragdoll flails through the air. The towering structure continued its slow westward advance via the considerable beasts of burden tethered at its wider base, while the Lord of Storms proved uncaring in his indiscriminant culling of those afield, a true effigy of chaos for his lightning strikes brutalized fighters of both warring sides where he commanded his stabs of jagging death in front of his mobile tower, at its sides, even behind, the structure's massive spiked wheels leaving runnels overfilled with bloody muck and the pulpy remains of crushed bodies in their miles-long wake.

Banzu beheld the false godking perched on high with a raptor's estimating gaze. Even from his distant vantage he saw the orgasmic spread of Hannibal Khan's maniacal grin, swore he heard the insane laughter singing across the battle plains above the raucous din. The Enclave-ascended warlord tyrant stood swaddled in the lusty throes of too much power's corruptive madness, locked in the psychotic thrall of his godsforged lanthium gauntlets, and possessed by the rapturous delirium all men eventually fall victim to when bestowed unequaled power with no consequential responsibility for dealing it.

Hannibal Khan did not wage war so much as indulge in every glorious bit of its gory spectacle.

So much razing power at one man's fingertips . . . and for a scrutinizing moment Banzu shuddered upon considering what holocaustic butchery such a crazed man could accomplish once he possessed the entire suit of the Dominator's Armor and not just its pervasive gauntlets.

Tens of thousands dead already. However adamant the Enclave's desires in purging Pangea through aizakai genocide to secure another Thousand Years War, they held no qualms about achieving their conquering plans of extermination through the total destruction of all whom stood in their way, even at the cost of their own insane followers.

Disgusted, Banzu banished those terrible thoughts and returned focus to the present through a rapid series of blinks. *So close now.* An anxious flutter in his chest as he licked his lips. *This is it.* The last play of his hand, the final attempt at ending this carnage of life before it absorbed all of Thurandy then spilled through Caldera Pass and infected the rest of the world in sundering plague. The time for thinking over, planning ended. *So very close. It's all or nothing now. Cut off the head of the snake and the body dies.*

You promised me. The faint whisper of a plea, its music trying to reach him from too far away. An angelic sough begging him to surrender the ails festering in his blackening heart, to abandon the flaws carving and shaping him still. And for the moment he wondered how many edges Venger truly possessed while he trembled through premonitions from the dark consideration.

But the awful anger blazing within refused abandonment, not here, not now, not with the object of his hatred so close at hand.

A single stretch of mile now, his predator's mind surmised, with not men but obstacles standing between the panacea to his pain.

Pain.

His short respite drawing closed in a seething soulflare of rage, Banzu seized the Power through fierce focal invocation and unleashed a guttural yell escaping the vengeful depths of him where lived only pain, that of his uncle's name, the volume of his voice enhanced by the Power so that it pierced the buffeting winds, the pouring rain, the din of battle. The possessive fury of retribution scorched the sensational potency of the Power flooding in to his craving essence of spirit in a torrential river of vigor, a hammering avalanche of vital force broiling his urgency for killing these misguided fools warring round him, boiling his blood into liquid fire pulsing through his swelling network of veins while the activity of war slowed to the influential sway of Power.

And with it the siphoning drain of his lifeforce in cruel trade paid in penalty, as something hot and awful relit at his core, acting as bellows to the blast furnace of his flaring animus.

His quickening heartbeat pounding behind his cage of ribs expanding to the point of creaking, his predator's lusting gaze separating lazy splashes of mud from the coppery-scented rubies of bloodspray arcing through the air in everywhere abundance, his flaring nostrils inhaling the acrid smells of sweaty flesh straining beneath oiled armor and boiled leather . . . Banzu drew in his surroundings through absorbent breath, tasting every foulness upon oversensitive buds, while luminous twilight greys flashed into prominence behind his lambent red eyes swelling with focal depths of hatred.

A hell of a thing, that, his hatred a succubus feeding upon the sustenance of his grieving soul. He welcomed it, embraced its ravaging clutch, and made love to it in the animal way it made of him, savage and sure.

"Now you die, Khan." And the bitter-sworn words escaped him as if spoken by another—and perhaps they were—while mad laughter arose in his head at the same time loosing from his throat.

You promised me, whispered an abject appeal, far and fleeting.

Small pockets of fistians appeared here and there through aizakai-induced flashes of magical brilliance *popping* into startlements of existence in the false night, knots of soldiers fighting through sacrificial bids to take down as many khansmen as possible in their dying throes, for those this close within the thick died in minutes if not seconds after their aizakai-wrought entrances burst them in amongst the surprised enemy.

And there revealed the answer as to how these fistians managed this far across the plains.

Teleportation, Banzu mused for a brief space in what shrinking part of his logical brain functioned behind the possessive pressure of rage threatening to abduct full primal control of his faculties. *Ingenious.* The teleported units made dents in the dread machine of the Khan's legion, though only that. *But still not enough.*

His restive moment ended with the surrounding scores and knots and clusters of fighting khansmen paying him due notice where he stood defiant in the small clearing he'd made of their fellows, a tangle of bisected corpses scattered round the blood and muck beneath his planted ease of stance. Round him formed an entrapping death-cirque of over fifty crazed Bloodcloaks and worship-followers setting to attack though wary of the Soothsayer standing within their midst, while behind them gathered others in a larger circle encompassing the smaller.

Through the Power's sensory enhancement Banzu listened to each of their pounding hearts distinguished from their fellows, inhaled the stink of their fear mixed with the ignorance of anger's bravery lathering their grimy skin beneath blood-caked armor and mud-sopped clothes.

Beyond the khansmen, atop the mobile tower dominating several hundred feet above the hostile sea of death and dying, Hannibal Khan perceived nothing of Banzu's presence as yet, the warlord tyrant too locked in the ecstasy of doling violence through smiting jags of lightning puncturing the fray while volleying tumbling sprouts of bodies of both sides into the air round his massive perch.

Banzu loosened his inner grasp on the Power, crinkled his nose while inhaling deep through flaring nostrils, tightened the unadulterated scorn of his lambent glare as he tightened his grip upon Venger's bastard hilt. He smiled malice. But his forbidding rictus grin did little to dissuade the gathering khansmen from charging in at him from all sides.

The moment ended with all sense of himself swallowed in action. His identity swept away before the storm of another's soliloquy of command taking dominance, the voice a repeat thunder—*Kill! Kill! Kill!*—as he bared Venger unto the cordon swarm of khansmen in quicksilver promise, his eyes afire, his expression fierce, his homicidal lusts rapacious.

* * *

The surrounding torrent of khansmen deluged in upon their targeted Soothsayer in a screaming pack of savagery. And Banzu welcomed them all, seizing the Power in a strangler's grip while spinning at the last, a twirling dancer of bladed death, Venger's Power-hardened tongue and its terminal velocity scything steel and flesh and bone while wetting the air with fantastic blooms of blood, slicing succession through its next victim and the next before the felled khansman seconds previous voiced the screeching wail of their final mistake in life.

The natural art of a genuine swordslinger taught him by swordmaster Jericho Jaicham Greenlief imposed instinctual drive through habitual lessons of practice and pain, a life spent living the sword as an extension of self. Swordforms flowed without instigative thought: always on the move, always heading somewhere with purpose, always in motion even when standing still. To flow like water, to bend though never break. And Banzu weaved Venger through keening blurs as he gripped then loosened then re-gripped Power-flickers in rapid succession while working his body through the kinetic fluidity of devastating swordform after swordform. Killing with the ease of breathing. A tiger prancing among men in this their vicious dance.

All the while the other's voice issued dark approval through his mind.

No remorse . . . no repent . . . no mercy!

And no holding back, Banzu mused in almost-answer. Except for the Source. He dared not touch that ultimate power and invite its still-tainted energies of madness upon him. Not here, not now, not so close to—

Kill them, the other urged. **Kill them all!** Maniacal laughter pursued through the vocal break. **There exists* *no mercy here. Show them what you've brought their Khan!**

Fanatical worship-followers rushed forth in recurring waves behind their felled Bloodcloaks, many of them women with skulls or scalps or both tied off round their otherwise bare waists, feathers of various birds bound as charms in their muddied tangles of hair, their exposed bodies marked with carven glyphs branded over bare breasts and down bare thighs, the poisoned raptor talons tied round their fingers and toes making of their hands and feet infectious claws doling fast though painful rakes of death.

These screeching face-painted harpies of filed spiked teeth and wild eyes showing the psychosis of their drug-induced frenzy leapt over the mounds of fresh corpses littering their paths undaunted by the feral carvings made of their fellows only seconds previous and unfaltering in their eager advance while screaming praises for their Lord of Storms.

Banzu flowed against them in violent Power-bursts, a continuous killing wind hacking and chopping rending blurs through the crazed chargers who dared presume him easy prey, making of the insignificant fools a slaughter.

The echoes of their fantastic screams enacted wild pulsing thrills through his pounding temples as the stench of their bloodletting slung from Venger's humming blade expanded his nostrils in flaring adulation with each sensational inhale. The delicious coppery tang of their spraying arcs and blooming scatters of blood fruited his saliva while he breathed the release of savory death from those dying round him by the score.

And still more foolhardy khansmen braved into his personal space of death's deliverance, earning Venger's cruel delivery of judgment while their rushing numbers dwindled.

Out from the corners of his wanton gaze Banzu glimpsed two Bloodcloaks attempting to flank him while their others in front and behind him slowed their attacks into a more calculated approach of distraction upon the one whom reduced their greater numbers by several scores in the short span of blinks.

He seized a Power flicker and spun into a whirring blur, cleaving lengthwise through a thrown spear meant for puncturing his face—the split pieces of which glided past the sides of his head and stabbed into ground and corpse behind—and spat scalding hate at the wide-eyed thrower on his right an infinitesimal second before lunging, boots skating across mud through a propellant burst of Power, Venger ripping the Bloodcloak open crossways through the middle in a fanning blur of steel.

The riven khansman divided, upper half left and lower half right, while his steaming innards spilled between. Banzu spun round, facing the erring other attempting the distraction of his turned back but too late. He chopped this second's helmed head off at the shoulders with one clean swipe of Venger's singing blade then danced aside from the delightful fountain of blood spraying from the stump of neck while the headless body continued running several steps past him before collapsing, its hands still clutching the severed sword upheld before it as if blocking Banzu's decapitating deathblow had ever existed as a real possibility.

The other's approving laughter roared in taunting appeal, serenading while demanding evermore proof of Banzu's killing worth, a mocking witness viewing out behind his eyes. And he strove to provide that proof over and again through Venger's answering blade knowing no quarter and the Power's persuasive flickers propelling it through rending arcs and slashes.

Ultra keen senses blazed with life's defining purpose of living only in the moment, of existing second by second with no thoughts of before or after, only the here and now. His body became wrath in motion, an automaton of sundering steel and fluid muscle, his mind a raging inferno driving him through avenues of butchery and massacre where echoed screams and laughter.

The heightened sound of a whistling rush pierced Banzu's hearing so that he spun in a flickering Power burst. He captured the arrow winging for his vitals in mid-flight with the blurring swipe of his hand then snapped it halved and tossed its two bits aside as useless and forgotten as the hewn bodies strewn round his dancing feet. Lusty anger arose at the thought of a simple arrow ending him. He sank his haunches in contemptuous appraisal, his raptor's gaze hunting round—*there!*

A crater of mud fanned out round his feet when he sprang up yelling, leaping in a Powered burst of stretch, propelling himself high and forward over the one-hundred foot gap of upturning khansmen heads while he switch-flipped his double-fisted grip upon Venger's leather-wound hilt mid-air. He soared down with a driving thrust, impaling the awestruck Bloodcloak bowman's face while landing upon the surprised offender feet-to-chest before ripping Venger free then, using the transfixed khansman as a springboard, he dug his heels in and sprang through the full extension of his legs in another Power flicker, back-flipping from off his backwards-leaning victim to go tumbling with rolling grace through the air while shoving that launch pad body rearwards and crashing into and knocking over an entire knot of Bloodcloaks behind it.

Banzu landed true with perfect balance, boots stamping fanning waves of mud at his sides. He scanned round his new position, teeth clenched near grinding, adrenaline's euphoric thrill saturating his sinews quivering ecstatic, his eager heart pounding in rapid patter so that he thought it might beat through his chest in open display of his arousal to this the truest combat he'd ever known, his interior monologue a roar of two voices melded.

Gods, I've never felt so alive!

More determined khansmen casualties rushed in at him.

Don't they know? Can't they see? Have they learned nothing? I am death!

He seized evermore flickers of the Power and kicked corpses away while circling about. The transferred momentum sent the rolling bodies crashing into the oncoming rushes so that their challenged legs snapped backwards, collapsing them in screaming tumbles while breaking the running fight out from them and making twisted heaps of failed warriors flailing in the mud.

Earning pause, he glared round at the wary sets of tormented stares from those still standing fixed upon him and beheld the honest fear betraying those eyes sobering from the drunkenness of savage courage. The pause stretched on, khansmen apprehension a powerful adversary of its own.

Banzu scanned past the lines of enemy reforming round him though keeping their good distance while numbers thickened at their backs, and gazed up the great heights of the mobile tower. He locked eyes for an eternal instant with Hannibal Khan, his death-dealing efforts at last demanding the Lord of Storms' attentions from on high down amongst so many of the warlord's dead and dying loyals.

Therein the roiling turmoil of Banzu's raging mind arose a fevered pitch above the thousand surf of voices, the compelling assertion of his murdered uncle demanding due reckoning within those passing fractions exchanged, while the blooming fervor for vengeance reclaimed Banzu's heart with hatred's blinding obligation.

* * *

Banzu hawked then spat his disdain at the Khan, his tunneling vision a red sheen from the mixture of khansmen blood and pelting rain running crimson streams through his hair and down his face and making of it an imbrued mask he presented up to the unworthy Lord of Storms glaring down at him from on high.

Soothsayers, a harsh inner voice said, teasing his thoughts along. **We were once revered as gods among men. And men have always striven to take that power away from us—always! Just as this man dares so now.**

A blending of thoughts, a melding of minds . . . and something within Banzu's conscious reasoning snapped to the indignant craze of rage tearing loose from his throat in a guttural shout stilling the air on all sides.

He raised Venger in aiming point at the Khan, the gesture an announcement of intent. "You," he said through clenched teeth. "And me."

He glared through the primal eyes of contemptuous dominance clearing his mind in predatory assessment, the blatant dispute of his prominence among these lesser men sickening him.

How dare this mortal man, this pretender of gods, presume to challenge me? I've faced down death too many times to count. I've survived the bloodlust curse. I murdered my uncle. I killed a god! Your khansmen are nothing. You are nothing. I will end you!

This paltry warlord daring to judge him an inferior being to be looked down upon mocked Banzu far beyond insolence. Such audacity fed the torrential anger driving the seething beast of rage roaring within the confines of his grievous cage.

"You!" he roared, seizing the Power while thrusting Venger on high, red eyes flaring luminous, voice projecting above the raucous din and torrential storm. "And me!"

I'm the last Soothsayer and gods be damned! I am the Killing Wind! I am living death! I am apex! I am alpha! I am—

Two bold Bloodcloaks rushed in from the khansmen cordon, seizing distraction through attack.

Banzu tore his gaze from the Khan and spun to the charging yells, whispering his blade up and down the first fool then carving the same twisted fate upon the second, making of them two bleeding heaps of cuts he left alive to sample the joyous songs of their thrashing screams while they writhed the mud at his feet, their wailing faces red masks of shredded skin matching the rest of their lacerated bodies.

A butcher could not have been more precise in their cutting. And the other's voice within delivered a pleasured murmur of approval.

The rest of the wary khansmen cordon balked while backing.

A tremendous thunder boomed, concussing the air.

Banzu spun round, head craned.

Hannibal Khan beheld him as target captured within his judging sights while calling forth lightning to strike down the blasphemous Soothsayer standing unchallenged within the midst of his fallen warriors.

The turbulent black sky above him swirled and churned while opening in preparation for darting another searing tongue in wrathful discharge. A white-hot finger of coruscating death tore out from the cavernous sky-throat and shot down into the upraised right arm of its human conductor. The absorbing Lord of Storms threw his left arm out to unleash through its aiming extension the smiting fury of nature's scintillating animus obeying his godsforged gauntleted command, his charged conduit body flashing a blinding white radiance, his bones temporarily visible within his plump strains of muscle, while the air spark-crackled and hissed round him and halfway down the towering structure beneath his dominating perch of a thirty-storeys-tall lightning rod.

Banzu leapt to one side, propelling himself with eyes shut tight against that too-brilliant luminescent explosion borne forth from the Khan's outstretched arm and jagging straight toward him. Having seized the Power in fraction reaction, he soared through the air, blinded, as the spearing wrath of Khan-wrought lightning ruptured a wagon-sized hole in the earth where he'd been standing only milliseconds previous, throwing up scalding debris of scorched terrain and parts of ruined khansmen.

He cleared the destructive blast just in the nick, but the uprising concussive burst beneath his propelling feet threw off his balance and his intended trajectory so that he flailed for control as he tumbled some good distance through his awkward flight.

Everything captured in that scant moment before the blinding flash and ensuing rupture—the Khan, his startled loyals gleaning their deaths while knowing no escaping course—trailed in smears of silhouetted afterimages blurring behind the shielding darkness of Banzu's clamped lids as he sailed tumbling through the electrified air . . . rising, arcing, falling . . . then crashing, jolting dazed, where he slid in the slimy mud and careened into a cluster of khansmen, bowling them over in a cacophony of screams and snapping limbs.

He pushed up onto hands and knees, spitting mud, blinking the vertigo whirl and fading white flares of phosphenes from his eyes, thankful he'd held the Power long enough for bracing him against the sliding crash. He threw a glance behind at the smoking crater of his previous position surrounded by scattered charred bodies wearing glowing bits of armor hissing against the pelting rains evincing the unlucky khansmen caught within the damning path of their Lord of Storms' smiting lightning.

Groans issued from the broken rabble of Bloodcloaks and worship-followers lying round him in twisted heaps. Some amongst the wreckage wrestled free from the entanglements of their injured fellows lying atop them, hunting reclamation of weapons while trying their fighting best at attacking him.

Get up! urged the other's voice. **Get up now! This is far from over!**

Venger. The absence of his lost sword took precedence. He flexed his hands into furious fists then beat the ground thrice for its loss, his sword having taken loose from his faulty grip sometime during their sliding crash and bowling through bodies. He straightened and scanned round, panic for Venger's recovery elevating while seconds ticked and still no sight of—*Ahh! There!*

Venger's hilt jutted from the pierced leg of one of the struck Bloodcloaks knocked farther away than those still capable of stirring to their feet closer round Banzu. The khansman belly-crawled away, using one hand for clawing and dragging while the other clutched at the sword protruding from the side of his punctured thigh.

Rip their throats out! shouted the other, hot and savage. **Bash their godsdamned skulls!**

But Banzu ignored the incessant demand, jarred by his errant leap and crashing fall back into cognizant bearing, too intent on recovering his lost sword, the blade a vital extension of self, its absence that of a missing limb demanding reclamation.

Questing on hands and knees amid heaps and twists of khansmen bodies, he made space by seizing a Power-flicker and booting the nearest fellow—a Bloodcloak belly-crawling toward him with a sword in one hand and a dagger in the other while dragging a broken leg behind—straight in the face. The khansman's head craned too sharp, his neck snapping as he collapsed amongst his striving fellows with his chin planting the mud so that his dull dead eyes stared out upon the world he took part in no more.

Seizing more Power flickers, Banzu punched at and kicked away crawling others closing ground on all sides, shattering faces with Power-hardened fists and swiveling heads upon snapping necks with Power-sped kicks of his legs, earning space, then he pushed into standing, the last khansman crawler he ended by stomping on spine and leaving an inches-deep footprint while walking over him, the impact crushing the man's innards into spraying out from his gaping mouth.

As the other's voice within elevated into a delighted cackle of mad laughter.

Banzu held predatory pause and surveyed his immediate area with a condescending upheaval of disgust. How dare these pathetic excuses of men believe themselves his equal. Such blatant debasing of his exalted station flared his pride with loathing sickness, especially so considering these lowly warriors lived no more than pathetic extensions of their Khan.

"I am Soothsayer!" He flared a Power-flicker and stomped another khansman's head, the popping squash of skull crushing steel helm pinched while brain matter sprayed. "You are nothing to me!"

Yes! Maniacal laughter roared approval. **More!**

Banzu marched toward another Bloodcloak, the woman attempting to crawl away, her fevered hands raking gobs of mud, her busted legs pitiful limp drapes dragged behind her.

"You're nothing." Banzu planted a foot atop the Bloodcloak's back, bent and grabbed round an ankle. He yanked through a flicker of Power while twisting and tore the screaming woman's leg from hip, disjoining it in a ripping of muscle fibers and tearing of ligaments. In continued momentum he spun away while loosing the dismembered limb spinning whips through the air, then beat at his chest while shouting, "You're nothing!"

Yes!

Through Powered sprint Banzu ran toward another khansman, the man sitting in the muck and staring at the broken twists of his legs. Banzu swung a blurring kick, his Power-hardened foot catching beneath chin, and punted the khansman's head off shoulders in a ripping spray of gore. Decapitated body collapsed backwards while its detached head arced spinning through the air then struck another khansman in the chest, the punching velocity of which crashed the khansman backwards and sliding in the mud.

More!

Banzu bent at the hips, gripped steel breastplate and tore it loose with the ease of Power snapping thick leather buckles then threw it aside. Another flicker of Power and he punched his hardened hand into the headless corpse's chest cavity, rupturing flesh and bone, gripped heart, and yanked it free.

Yes!

He raised the captured heart aloft while surveying the sea of terrified khansmen spectators watching back at him in gaping awe. He smiled malice and crushed the heart in the sure squeeze of his hand, pulping it, then threw it aside and shouted, "I am your only god!"

Yes! More! Yes!

Startled khansmen broke from their paralyzing fear and scrambled away, running or crawling, many hacking through their staring fellows too slow in moving aside. Others gaped up on high, their grips palsied on quavering weapons, their wide eyes silent pleas for help.

Banzu followed those imploring gazes, turning, craning his head, remembering with a fevered jolt his true purpose here amongst these paltry mortals when he glared up with greatest contempt at the effigy of his animus with focal hatred piercing the pelting sluice of rain. On high atop the towering structure the X-standing figure of Hannibal Khan gazed down not at Banzu's defiant stare but at the smoky crater of his presumed ruin in triumphant laughter.

The bastard actually thinks he got us, a melding of inner voices soliloquized.

The tempestuous sky above spark-crackled alive with more ominous energies the Khan prepared to draw into himself for another smiting strike upon the field as he turned away and loomed peering over a teleported knot of fistian soldiers—their missing aizakai coreman a good indication of the high number of losses the fistian forces suffered thus far—down beside the base of his mobile structure, these a hedgehog of fistian footmen who attacked one of the mammoth tethered beasts of burden while some few of them hacked with axes at the thick timbers of the structure itself in an attempt at slowing its ever-forward progression toward Fist as their others stabbed with long spears at the closer wooly beast.

Banzu snarled and spat. Something touched his boot. He glared at the gripping hand belonging to a tattoo-faced warrior-woman who had crawled close with a knife trapped between her teeth while dragging two broken legs and one broken arm. A testimony to her faith and courage.

Having achieved sure proximity, she spat the knife to the mud, gripped it in her only working hand with a hammer-fisted clutch, raised it for stabbing, her only pathetic attack given the miserable hindrance of the rest of her crippled body.

Banzu seized a Power-flicker and stomped. The worship-follower's head burst inside her crimping groan of steel helmet crunching squirts of gore out its pinched sides, making mashed berries of brains.

He smiled at the human ruins at his feet, and there joined his voice alongside the song of laughter teasing through his head.

Until reclamation of Venger punched into his thoughts. He turned about, scanning round, having lost track of the crawler, the khansman thigh-pierced with his sword. But another brazen swarm of Bloodcloaks and worship-followers, drawn to his area now that he stood empty-handed among them, charged in shrinking cordon.

Such was their gravest mistake.

Fools.

"Fools," Banzu repeated above the wicked laughter chiming through his mind.

He seized the Power through flaring invocation, forgetting the Khan for the others rushing in and seeking his slaughter. For a short breadth he stood motionless, baiting them under false pretense, welcoming them in to the craving fold of his awaiting death-strikes with a sinister grin.

Seconds more and he Power-flicker-flowed into unarmed feral aggression, ducking a Power-slowed swinging sword that cut only through the falling rain above his lowering head. He shot up thrusting with a stiffening Power-fueled arm while driving the palm strike not just into but *into* the Bloodcloak's face, and pulverized the khansman's skull into helmeted pulp.

He twisted while gripping breastplate and threw the fresh corpse aside into knocking down three others rushing his left, then lunged to his right per Power-flicker, boots skating the fanning mud, where he caught the shaft of a stabbing spear and, while spinning, snapped the weapon in half by way of a cutting elbow strike, then continued his spinning flicker-flow at the spearholder, puncturing the caught soldier in the guts with his own leaf-shaped spearhead before twisting the implement hard clockwise for coiling effect upon the khansman's viscera.

With a lengthened hold of Power strengthening muscles twice times the normal, Banzu lifted the impaled khansman off his kicking feet using the broken spear's shaft as a makeshift lever and tossed the screaming soldier overhead and behind though kept firm purchase on the shortened shaft of the spearhead when the body tore loose to go landing somewhere unseen behind him.

He lowered the shaft out in front and smiled at the tangle of torn intestines coiled round its leaf-shaped tip, bunched and hanging, a dark and dripping knot of steam. But he cut the smile short and dodged left in a squatting sideways lean, avoiding a whiffing mace whipping past his face by inches, the tines of it whispering a hairsbreadth from crushing his dipping shoulder. Reversing his dodging sway, he shoved both spear and intestines into the yelling attacker's throat, silencing the stupid khansman in all but choking gurgles.

Banzu shouldered the choker aside, turned and Power-booted the next oncoming khansman in the chest, the abrupt impact of breastplate denting round his punching boot arresting the other's advance while an eruptive spray of blood jetted from the khansman's gaping maw below eyeballs bulging from sockets, the caving groan of steel depressing round Banzu's driving foot to the spine while splintering ribs into squashed organs.

The jolting transfer of Power-momentum while Banzu extended the full of his kicking leg shoved the dimpled body flying backwards over twenty paces away to where it collided into more charging khansmen, their leveled spears meant for Banzu instead sprouting out the crashing corpse from back through chest and stomach while the human missile knocked the entire group of warriors over in a smash and tumble of bodies, denting armor and snapping bones and breaking the spears failing to protect them.

A glint of Venger in his peripheral so that Banzu coiled down low upon his priming haunches then sprang snapping up into a Power-leap, creating a fanning crater of mud splashing out at his sides. He sailed on high over heads upturning beneath his flight path, several stray arrows whispering past, shooting fifty feet through the air before landing stomping upon the targeted back of the khansman crawler whose innards exploded from his mouth in a fantastic spray of blood and guts and bile.

"Mine!" Banzu reclaimed Venger's leather-wound hilt into the wrapping fold of his loving right hand and shuddered orgasmic to the burning fury reconnection earned through the arousing touch of the bladed extension of himself. There he paused, acknowledging the stolen part of him restored with a wolfish grin, then removed Venger's bloodied tongue from the squashed corpse's thigh-meat with a satisfying yank.

Make them pay! urged the other's voice. **Kill them all!**

Plentifully bestrewn with spectacular gore from head to heel, Banzu offered no quarrel to the vocal compulsion rampaging through his mind. His fevered thoughts surrendered to the raging supremacy of the Power's carnal killing lusts coursing through every vibrating fiber of his raving existence. Losing himself to the blinding passion of furor, he threw his head back, hair whipping a rainbow mane of rain and blood, spread his arms out and issued rich release to a harrowing shout erupting from his lungs.

And with the Power's enhancing potency, his savage roar elevated in volume to that of the emphatic peal of some foreboding horn of alarm amplified above the din of battle so that all those nearest him startled from their activities into looking his way as, in a melded binary cry of dual dialogue he declared, *"*I'll kill you all!*"*

A sea of stricken faces stared at him in a lull of combat.

* * *

Banzu rounded in slow turn, eyeballing his next victims with hungry intent and calculating care while preparing to move in among them.

So many delicious choices. A banquet. Our feast! We'll have them all before we're through. We'll—

The inner monologue clipped short at the buzzing flight of arrows winging his way, whistling distractions he noticed too late for catching with speedy hands so that he spun instead into a Power-flicker twirl. Venger cut the hail of arrows from the air into useless bits shorn through whirling bladed grace. Banzu grinned at the foolish khansmen bowmen, smiling pure malevolence while extending one hand and affording them all a come-hither wave.

Through another Power-flicker he *sniff-sniff-sniffed* the air, nose crinkling, nostrils flaring, enjoying the stink of their fear sweating out and wafting through the heavy downpour. Fear made men desperate, and desperate men attempted desperate measures. But some men, hardened men, men used to killing . . . fear made these men more calculating, more dangerous. And more eager to die trying.

The khansmen archers abandoned their bows and joined their fellows rushing in at Banzu from all sides in shouting droves, Bloodcloaks and worship-followers charging, wailing banshees too brave or too foolish to seek out easier targets.

Banzu answered swift response in a twirling tornado of bladed butchery, ending khansman after khansman through killing bursts of slicing extermination and fanning blurs of Venger's lapping tongue. He lavished in violence and blood, lost in the amusing distraction of their futile attempts to bring him down, and though he savored each lovely musical note of their dying screams, an inner voice resurfaced above the laughter, born from the dark corners of his bitter-misted mind where lived shelved grief, issuing stark reminder of his truer purpose here.

Through playing games, no longer content with dispatching the pawns however much he reveled destroying these lesser men, they existed beneath him, unworthy of his righteous killing gift.

He ripped Venger sideways through the splitting waist of another crazed worship-follower stupid enough to run at him instead of away. While reluctant khansmen halted their charges short and backpedaled, removing to safer distance after watching so many of their fellows felled within the Soothsayer's harvesting reap. Venger's delivery severed the worship-follower's collapsing body through hips into two separating halves but for the exposed spinal cord escaping Venger's cleaving tip and keeping top and bottom pieces tethered together.

Banzu turned away while the body dropped behind him, and glared up at the mighty Khan standing on high atop the mobile tower, facing him again, attentions returned to the Soothsayer standing lone amid a small field of bodies and parts of bodies.

The Lord of Storms, swaddled in thunder, reached at the dark churn of sky, preparing to call forth more lightning for another smiting strike.

The nearest obstacle pawns swept from the gameboard, malice peeling his lips back in a savage rictus grin, Banzu raised Venger and pointed at Hannibal Khan through the pelting rains and buffeting winds in a daring pose of condemnation, his wild eyes a thinning glare up Venger's glistening length the extension of his arm and animus.

Hannibal Khan set his muscled bulk into a wide-legged stance for absorbing brace, his right fist thrown high overhead, the other outstretched and aimed down at Banzu's defiant challenge far below. The fingers of his gauntleted right hand opened then closed, a fist snatching at the heavens and clutching them into his commanding grip.

Their fervent gazes locked through the torrential downpour, neither man relenting their fixed poses of challenge, while an anxious mass hush settled over all those watching nearby, hundreds and hundreds more of khansmen and fistians alike, a foreboding silence stealing voices from lungs and the temporary fight from the observers as much as it quieted the noise from the blasting winds whipping beats of moist fabrics, the continuous din sounding beyond a distanced disturbance.

Banzu flushed with an intoxicating swell of antipathy at the threatening bite within those barbarous eyes glaring open recognition back at him.

Yes, he knows us now.

He shivered with ecstatic delight, atremble with the anticipation of stark butchery moments from playing out with the predatory best these miserable khansmen prey offered him, alpha to alpha, his body craving action though he stayed his place, defiant in the raging storm while offering the illusion of an easy target to the offender perched on high and daring to test him wrath for wrath while premonitions fond and foul oscillated behind his focal stare.

Move, the other's voice demanded, harsh and curt. **Go, now! Before he—**

"Shut up!" Banzu shouted, clipping the other short with a feral growl through clenched teeth. "I've got this." No slip of his fixed glare upon the Khan.

Your lightning flows fast, but my Power flows faster—this he mused, refusing to accept otherwise. *I'm the Killing*

Wind. I'll dodge then surge and be upon you before a second strike.

The towering structure stood three-hundred feet tall by his quick estimation. And though he had never before covered such a fantastic stretch of distance in a single Powered leap—*I can make it. I will make it. And you will scream before I am through.*

A swirling hole opened within the rippling clouds in the churning war of sky raging above the miles of killing fields below. A brilliant flash of jagging white lightning tore down, knifing the gloom and shooting into the Lord of Storms willing it forth, beckoning it, commanding it into obedient effluent charge while he absorbed its powerful electric capacity, the thick timbers of his mobile tower groaning.

Banzu's heart quickened, his mouth watering, his muscles bunching taut and reactive.

To the elevating rush of splashing mud and yelling closing from behind so that he spun round in a whirring blur at the unexpected distraction, afforded no choice but to seize a preemptive flicker of Power.

He sliced the first of his three Bloodcloak distracters into two separating halves with a lunging upstroke from crotch through head, producing a blooming crimson mist between as the dividing body-halves continued past his sides with what remained of the bisected khansman's charging momentum while Banzu rushed through the crimson mist. He lowered and spun in another flickering bid, ducking beneath a thrusting spear and a swinging sword too slow for earning his blood. He chopped through the legs of both remainder Bloodcloaks of his trio distraction below their knees in a fluid twirl, sending them crashing facedown into the mud, sliding at his sides, their kicking stumps squirting dark liquid spurts as they exchanged charging yells for pleading screams.

"Fools!" he yelled, rising, his voice a booming shout, his words a resounding echo of those raging in his head. "You're nothing to me! Nothing!"

Seething beyond sanity, bared teeth clenched to the precipice of cracking, the Power captured in his strangler's grasp, maniacal laughter roaring in his head, he spun round to the Khan.

And the scintillating brilliance of coruscating lightning jagging straight toward him.

The other's laughter clipped short with a sharp gasp.

Banzu began Power-leaping free.

But too late.

CHAPTER FORTY

So much in life is simply a matter of timing, yesss.

Sergal approached in an eager though leisure stroll the chaotic cacophony of battle—no, war, this tableau of bloodshed raging before him across the entire Azure Plains—from the east, coming in behind the Betrayer's vast legion, trailed by his necromancer Pet and his allegiant group of servitors in stalking tow. He'd enjoyed many stops over the long course of treading the Path of the Dragon in the Betrayer's destructive wake, and though incomparable to the hundreds of thousands of sworn khansmen fighting and dying upon the plains, Sergal amassed quite an impressive menagerie of devotees himself. One-hundred men rife with despair and loss, their humanity betrayed and their fealty sworn to the little girl who was not a girl while Sergal's instigative promises enticed their vengeful lusts for their lives and loved ones demolished into miserable ruins by Hannibal Khan.

Sergal stopped atop a high knoll one mile out from the outskirts of the Betrayer's eastern forces and drew lengthy pause at the surprising sight of the unexpected clusters of fighting fistians who somehow managed to achieve this far out from Fist across the battle plains. Soldiers fighting strong though dying quick amongst the Betrayer's rearmost lines of khansmen in surrounded groups of flashing steel, their pikes stabbing, their swords slashing, their axes cleaving, their maces bashing . . . then their dying screams swallowed into the obscurity of the battle din washing over them with the same crashing fervor as their outnumbering enemies. And as he stood partaking of the lovely view of frenzied killing—*miles and miles of it, yesss*—a pleased smile upturned his cold dead lips.

Here lived false night, so dark and churning the stormy sky overhead. And though the darkness proved no hindrance to the twilight highlight of Sergal's enhanced deadsight, he squinted to make out the distant figure of the Betrayer standing high atop that mobile tower so far afield and halfway across the Azure Plains.

"Sssoon," Sergal said in hissing whisper, the slip of his serpentine speech stretching his S's overlong, his projected scorn focal, reflections of cunning in his yellow eyes divided by black vertical slits. "Sssoon you shall rue your treachery against me, Betrayer, oh yesss." He fetched a tight squeeze upon the handle of his hellsteel dagger vitus in musing stare while licking thirst from his lips through the dart of his tongue. "My vengeance beginsss here at your turned back."

No matter the stretch of decades and centuries. No matter the interminable boredom of inactivity that is so much a part of stalking amongst the living. There are moments such as this that make it all worth while, yesss. These petty children of men before me with their gibbering worries so blind to the true hunter about to pierce their midst.

Blind, until I unleash the nightmare I have brought with me, releasing the true horrors of my own children of the damned, the first sacrificial slaughter of my sinistry of darken rule, oh yesss.

For now, though, the Betrayer and his mobile tower stood surrounded in a chaotic sea of fighting and dying too thick to penetrate so that Sergal removed his attentions to the immediate area before him where he sought to carve his first precious opening with the calculating designs of an assassin's wounding stroke: undetected until the blade's vicious plunge drove deep.

Some few aizakai stood amongst the unexpected fistian knots as well, free aizakai magemasters discharging dazzling blasts of magic. One to every center of the fistian clusters, their varicolored weaves of heathen-born magics blooming bright in paroxysms of attack while the protective soldiers encircling them held the enemy off. Until greater khansmen numbers overwhelmed in swarms and brought them down by cracking the turtleshells of their kite shields for the tender morsels therein. Though by whatever means these condemned clusters achieved their invasion this far across the plains into the Betrayer's colossal army Sergal couldn't quite fathom.

Until he glimpsed a brilliant flash of light so close he flinched from the intensive burst flaring then fading in his watchful eyes. The armored bodies of over fifty Bloodcloaks and worship-followers blew away from the flaring burst in tumbling outward spray. The bright light vanished, revealing another fresh knot of fistian soldiers whose bewildered faces shifted into angry recognition. They charged in all directions of attack, the lone aizakai standing hunched at their core straightening, releasing rending blasts of destructive magics between the fistian outpour when not over their helmed heads or bashing kite shields.

Teleporting, Sergal realized, enjoying the gory spectacle amid the Betrayer's surprised loyals at length, the entire field of his vision filled with the splendid sights of insignificant humans of both sides killing and dying by the thousands, their screams a elative singsong chorus to his hearing while he gazed upon the sea of chaos and bloodshed.

"Excellent." He closed his eyes, drew in a craving nostril breath, inhaled deep the pervasive aura of lingering death unexpected to greet him this far out from Fist.

A banquet of energies before me, yesss. Such feast awaiting my arrival.

An ecstatic shiver stole through him so that he shuddered while exhaling in near orgasmic delight before opening his eyes to satisfying plans knitting together. "Excellent, yesss."

So much killing, so much death, so many available resources.

He advanced one eager step—then stopped, grimacing while chastising his impatience. *No. Let them play. Let them dance and die. All the more for me to feast upon, yesss.*

Dethkore stood next to him in towering loom, silent and swaddled in living shadows of fabrics. Sergal sensed the slow absorbent feed of death's essence permeating the air in everywhere abundance, its silvery eddies and swirls enhanced aglow by his deadsight in tickles of power, a billowing fog of potency adding to the source-pool of death magic building within his necromancer Pet, swelling reserves of it to spiritual bursting.

Behind them stood the accompanying partisans accumulated along their way, one-hundred pairs of restless eyes watching the chaos ensue while thirsty tongues licked across starved lips, anxious feet shifting and hands flexing grips of thickening anticipation for the killing they traded their souls for through dark pact promises, Sergal's binding pentagram encircled by tiny hieroglyphs of ancient sovereignty carved upon their every forehead. The ravenous hunger of bridled fever coursed through his sinistry minions and into him in soulbond connection of his Pet's lanthium soulring vitus and the hellsteel dagger hitched at Sergal's hip, both objects pulsing with quickening lifebeats now that they stood upon the precipice of releasing their designated hate.

Ignoring Sera's incessant weeps soughing through their bundled mind, Sergal let anticipation's shared thrill build for minutes, hot and swelling and savage while striving for the shattering climax.

Until his threadbare patience dismantled so that he spun round and addressed the first of his two servitor groups, seventy-five in number these infectious men-no-more.

"We are here," he said while spreading his arms out in full sweeping gesture of the massive battle at play behind him, of the countless preoccupied mix of khansmen and fistians therein paying no notice to their arrival. "Go, my children, and kill. And when you die, you will arise as promised to kill again. And again. And again! Go!"

He spun away, not wanting to miss a single moment of this the beginning of his reckoning upon the failed Khan Betrayer at last. He clasped his hands behind his proud back while at his sides the first of his sworn sinistry strode past.

But they did not rush, did not yell, did not falter, for these men-no-more with everything precious in life stolen walked imbued with a determined sort of patience only those harboring nothing left to lose but an uncaring existence possessed.

His sworn devotees advanced into the fighting, pursuing routes round supply wagons while gathering stray weapons to hand, these men removed of all fear and full of possessive hate knowing no purpose but ahead. They entered the mix, hacking and slashing and stabbing not with the trained skills of soldiers but the animalistic fervor of men reduced to creatures of inhumanity.

Against so many they lasted only moments. But no matter that, for as khansmen felled Sergal's servitors in returning answer to their futile attempts at retribution, laughter erupted from his throat as both vituses at his hip and round his finger thrummed defiance while pentagrams blazed molten upon partisan foreheads.

Sergal fisted his ringed hand while his other gripped his hellsteel dagger's handle, strangling both in fevered clutches while flaring his demonic compulsion.

And now it begins, my turning of the Game, yesss, with one poisonous prick.

The slain palemen twitched with the unholy vigor of startling reanimation then arose from their felled positions, their lacerated bodies and pierced organs leaking streaming ribbons of black ichor from mortal wounds no longer mortal, their twisted and broken limbs hindering them little when they strove once more into the fighting mix of horrified khansmen as the unliving hungars made of them through blasphemous guile and ungodly diabolism.

Sergal's propitious grin grew malicious in its spreading rule for now he commanded the compulsive hold on his Pet's thrumming death magic through the unliving hungars allowing his total control over their mindless appetites knowing only the gluttony of living flesh. He willed them on in their indiscriminate killing while reforming them into their group for better cannibalistic vantage, for he sought to rend a gaping swath through the chaotic confusion and forge a pathway for his revenging bid against the ignorant Betrayer miles ahead and unaware of the infectious plague spreading at his distracted back.

The bitten victims of Sergal's savage ravagers transitioned within moments into unliving obedience, making more hungars of men filled with the insatiable appetite for the tasty manflesh of their horrified fellows, khansmen and fistians alike, their broken bodies mending with unholy rejuvenation as they fed and continued feeding without regard.

Elation flushing in ecstasies of accomplishment, Sergal smiled approval of his plans blooming to beautiful fruition, his unliving sinistry of hungars growing through the expansion of infected victims rising from his Pet's necromantic contagion and joining their hungar brothers and sisters killing and feeding in the name of their new master Sergal.

A marvelous nightmare plague flourishing in an ocean of human panic.

And though Sergal controlled his unliving servitors through the strong flexing catalyst of his demonic compulsion via his Pet's lanthium soulring vitus, he worked inward at snipping then tying off their spiritual ribbon tethers, binding their ensorcelled souls so that they acted upon their own endless hunger to rend and feed, all the while controlling their necrotic impulses with the guiding nudge of his persuasive demonic influence directing them ahead. Leaving him space to enjoy the gratuitous carnage of his multiplying army, the hilled general surveying the skirmishing of his obedient soldiers.

Splendors of minutes passed.

But I am unfinished, yesss.

Sergal turned round, faced the twenty-five others of his retained sinistry whom growled and shifted through anxious twitches of longing, the burning impatience in these altered men available in their lusty amber eyes hunting living targets among the sea of diers. "Your time," he said, "isss now."

A chorus of guttural growls elevated among the remainder of his sinistry who tore free from their restrictive clothes, ripping fabrics away with the eager ease of supernatural strength provided in trade for command over their hate-filled souls while transformation ensued through the bruising skin of their naked bodies bubbling as beneath undulating skin bones snapped and muscles shifted and grew, jaws elongating and teeth lengthening into razor fangs, tufts of hair sprouting through expanding pores into thickets of fur, the agonized screams of pain earned from the changing of these men-no-more, his shifters, turning from guttural growls into blasting predator howls.

He'd made of these men not unliving hungars but savage beasts of twisted nature unseen since the Thousand Years War, primal tools of claw and fang to join their unliving hungar brethren infecting their way through all whom they could grasp their terrible holds upon while sinking their contagious teeth.

"Your retribution is finally at hand." Sergal threw his arms up while spinning round then flung them out, pointing, yelling, "Go!"

His volley of shifters obeyed, sprinting past him in a volatile pack, pouring forth from round their laughing master and his silent necromancer Pet in a fanged and hairy torrent. Their smoked-honey eyes feral glares, their claws rending earth as they charged, running first on two legs, the process of their changing finalizing, then loping on four legs, bursting and springing forth in howling leaps. Lycanthropes, all of them save one, yapping and snarling and barking their hatred into the confusion of khansmen spread before them as banquet, making of men a feast from some primeval nightmare.

Leading the vicious lycan pack strove the once-blacksmith now vampire, Valdemar, nude and muscular and pale, his eyes glistening red rubies of thirst, his rejuvenated body strengthened with an ancient cursing Sergal assumed long lost until he chanced upon its dark remembrance while delving with strain into the knowledgeable guarded depths of his Pet's shadowed mind where lived fathoms of darkest sorceries borne from the Horror Realm and untapped in centuries.

Valdemar's pair of lengthening fangs dripped hot and craving with glistening ropes of saliva whipping loose from the corners of his snarling maw. He sped forth with sight-blinding speed, himself misting intangible one moment while blurring across hundreds of feet in seconds then returning tangible the next, where he earned screams from his victims while he sank those pearly canines deep into neck after neck and drank lifeblood from the captured throats of his struggling sufferers then tossed aside their blood-drained husks to be fed upon by the spreading plague of hungars, mutilated victims who arose with missing bites of muscles and coils of guts and strung organs depending from their torn stomachs to join their unliving brethren as mindless hungars caring only for feeding upon that which lived and screamed round them.

"Yesss," Sergal said in a pleased hiss, shuddering through elation shattering orgasmic, watching with savage delight frightened khansmen and fistians flung through the air in mangled ragdolls or smashed and clawed off their feet, their paltry bits of useless armor torn away for the tender flesh prized beneath when not bitten through by stronger lycan jaws puncturing crimps of weaker steel or scoring boiled leather, their flailing limbs wrenched from ravaged sockets of shoulders and hips while the vicious shifterkin pack ripped into the enemy as the frenzied scourge of ruthless sundering horror Sergal made of them. "Yesss!"

***

The blinding hot flash of coruscating light came first, whiting out the fevered red jewels of Banzu's Power-heightened vision into blurred obscurity. Pursued a hairsbreadth more by a deafening shock of stillness so silencing it muted all sounds save for the gothic patter of his skipping heart and the uneven rattle of breath hitching in his chest attempting a gasp from lungs jolted with paralysis.

Tremendous pain shocked through every startled nerve of his cringing body from toe to skull, though dim awareness of surviving the lightning-struck ground erupting beneath his jumping feet jarred his amplified senses raw while the scalding explosion of terra swelled upward and outward in brutal spray a fraction after he began Power-leaping away for safer ground with the intent of springing up Hannibal Khan's towering structure then upon the Lord of Storms himself. But the smiting strike reduced his plans to ruins and hurled him through the air in a wild tumble, helpless, useless, a bug shooed by a dismissing godhand.

The Khan's lightning missed Banzu by fractions, though not the eruptive flare of scalding terra it produced beneath his kicking feet, the chasing sluice rife with sharp rock shredding his boots and pants into bloody tatters while slicing up his uncoiling legs to the hips in scores of bleeding cuts and dangles of torn skin.

Noooooo!

The other's declaration raced throughout Banzu's discombobulated mind, fading in a diminishing echo possessing the stretching breadth of miles to the godsawful pain enveloping him in a physical suffering so terrible it numbed his soul, the sensational agony of it proving too great an anguish for his body to bear at once so that it shut down all physical impressions of ache but for the knowledge of its stupefying residence waiting for him—if he survived long enough to endure its wrath once feeling resurfaced through the numb ocean of his body.

The Khan's smiting strike ripped the Power from Banzu's inner grasp with the ease of a man yanking a rattle from a newborn's fragile clutch while he tumbled through the air amid the hot spray of terra and its rough cutting grit he became a shooting part of.

I should be dead . . . I should be dead a hundred times over already . . . or am I dying even now?

He clutched at his awareness of self while the straining part of his semiconscious mind clung to the acute insight of off-kilter wrongness of it all.

Drifting, spinning, while his perception of time slowed inside the jumbled stream of his dizzied thoughts, he discovered that wrongness festering inside the rage-waning core of his flustered pride where lived the harsh ache of truth.

But he strove for excuses.

I am Soothsayer.

I am alpha.

A god among men.

How can this be?

Distracted.

Not quick enough.

And found none, the discovery of blind arrogance proving only a hint of the wrongness. He struggled for more, but his mind-teeth would not sink into those honest regrets just yet, instead taking nibbles from the offered scraps of knowledge, for he hurled twirling and whirling through the air on a wayward trajectory high and arcing over the battlefield in a confusion of aimless drift carrying him hundreds of feet away from the towered Khan.

He tumbled along the buffeting winds of the Lord of Storms' tempest, blinded by the intensive flash of lightning, uncaring of all but the misery of his failure and the sundered promise to his murdered uncle, anger waning, rage receding, leaving only the hollow of despair and guilt.

His mind collapsed inward by reflex while the lingering traces of the hot and snarled nest of emotions driving him across the battlefield snuffed, making room for a queer sort of cold logic only the threat of facing one's death allowed mortal men. Amazing how the cruel combination of pain and failure disrupted his insights clear during this precious moment while he clung to the precarious precipice of his life's brink, how all excuses paled insignificant through such raw shedding of the spirit where lived humility in all its irrefutable reasons.

Oh my gods . . . I did this to myself.

And there he reflected with harrowing shame how he accepted—no, embraced the possession of his spirit while retrieving the Essence of the First, remembering his surrender to hate, his thirst for vengeance trumping all, in a replay of repressed memories flashing vivid through his mind's eye with ruthless recall.

A grievous mistake in presuming it Jericho's haunting voice driving him forward and seeking solace through him from beyond the living world, fueling him along in his culminating savage frenzy while Venger cut swath after bloody swath through countless khansmen. All while allowing the parasitic presence to thrive and fill the cracks of his broken soul with its poisoning urgency.

He recognize the presence now, not the instigative torture of his uncle but the exploitative manipulation of Simus Junes ghosting through his mindscape after replacing Jericho's sorrowed pleas for vengeance with Simus' demands of bloodlust contagion in all its perverted vainglory.

I know you now.

You know nothing!

How easy the virulent Essence of the First seeped into him while overtaking the natural wants and needs of his mind, preying upon the lusty animosity of his revenging spirit, feeding upon his fierce and furious guilt while gaining dominance of his will beneath suspicion.

The surest way to enslave someone is to allow them to believe they are free. And the infectious Essence of Simus Junes accomplished just that.

Banzu presumed his passing of Enosh's proposed testing of retrieving the Essence of the First by surviving the scarlet specter's battle in that elsewhere caveplace of his keyrings transport. Instead he became its mortal vessel, bringing the corruption of spirit back within him, where the true testing began—still played out—all the while manipulating him as he killed across the plains a paragon of slaughter.

A puppet-slave to his hate, nurturing its consumption of him through ignorant feed, taking life after life after life in his questing bid for the Khan's promised demise.

Victory through vengeance a distraction of blinding ambition, now he pierced that veil with failure's humbling shame clearing his eyes with truth.

I was so wrong. We are unfinished, you and I.

Bidden by the grievous cerebration, the mad laughter of Simus Junes arose in mocking appeal to Banzu's revelation while he—no, while *they* spun tumbles through the air.

Then all thoughts blanked for a dizzying span in a swallow of black silence and fading laughter, Banzu's limp body soaring wild through the air and Power-free.

Consciousness returned, jolting him aware amid the landing slide of his crashing descent through a tumble of pain and snapping of bones. He slowed, stopped. Lay supine and motionless in the cold wet mud, rain pelting his face as he stared up at the churning gloom of sky.

He closed his tired eyes and surrendered to private depths of reflection while questioning his existence, the quiet of his somber musing dominating his mind absent of Simus' haunting taunt commanding indiscriminate killing in psychotic rages of bloodlust, for though Banzu had cleansed the blighting trigger in himself—in the Power—with his uncle's death and his re-beginning, Malach'Ra's cursed corruptive hate-source festered strong and rapacious within the Essence of the First and the shared collective, and by proxy within himself.

But it's not my *bloodlust, and—*

Kill! shouted the hateful resurgence of Simus' voice raging again with impatient desperation. **Get up! And kill them all you worthless bastard! Kill—**

But there the vehement demands clipped short to the rousing flush of another's intruding soliloquy, a feminine tone possessing the authoritative quality of natural defiance and the soothing drive of necessity.

You promised me, she said, and not for the first time, though stronger now, her forgiving words sounding not from the fringes of Banzu's melded mind but from his imploring heart of hearts, pushing against the hateful other's beseeching vocals not by force but with sheer resplendence.

As therein Banzu waged internal war, this of opposing forces, control versus instigation.

Get up and kill!

You promised me, Ban. Her voice paused, gaining strength of breath and presence of influence. ***You said you love me. Prove it. Prove it now, then come back to me.***

Banzu produced a pitiful groan, his only available physical response, audible words no more than a jumbled mess of broken syllables soughing through his mind while unable to breach his lips. Beauty pursued the encouraging words, its materializing face framed in pale-blonde hair and smiling at him beneath appraising violet eyes.

No! Simus rallied and roared. **You're mine! Don't listen to—**

Abandon it, Ban, she continued, her voice a caressing outpour of soothing resolve. ***Let your hate go, and there will be nothing left for it to feed upon. If you die now—*** She paused, and when next she spoke there lived a touch of sorrow flecked with regret edging her tone. ***If you die now, then you'll never have me again.***

No . . . please . . . I need you.

Banzu ached through instigations of movement, but his muscles twitched round broken bones refusing obedience, the wreckage of his body complete in all but the dying.

No! Simus roared, waning and straining. **You can't! He's mine—**

He's mine! she riposted in eruptive flare that softened seconds more while shifting its vocal focus. ***If you give up here, if you give up now, then you give up me.***

Desire, the most alluring magic of all, gripped Banzu by the mourning soul and squeezed. And if his desire possessed a goddess—

"Melora." He exhaled the name on ragged breath in desperate plea, the simple yet cherished appellation a struggle surmounting his blistered lips though worth ten lifetimes the painful strain it inflicted to speak it aloud. He knew her voice as only a reflective specter of Melora herself, a mental projection of her wonderful memory imploring him from where the real Melora could not. But it proved enough to birth within him a waxing strength while the outside world rumbled on.

He lay in the mud, his shattered volition gathering its broken collection of shards, reforming him not into the entranced killer of crazed moments ago but further back, journeying beyond the hate, to the yearning man while he remembered . . . remembered all of her in their intimate times together where lived the budding glory of unvoiced love.

Desires drifting, searching for more of her kindling splendor . . . the lily scent of her pale-blonde hair, the arousing touch of her warm body pressing against his in gentle yet clinging embrace . . . then further back, recalling the steady rhythm of her soft breathing while they lay together bundled naked in their time before his re-beginning, her Spellbinder void-aura abating the infectious chillfever from his shivering body as he slowly returned to life *because* of her instead of dying as he would have *without* her.

Get up, she said, her voice an inspiration. ***Move.***

Need for her trembled a quake in his reactive heart, his desire to obey and prove her proud blooming strength otherwise impossible.

Try.

Instinct induced his swordhand into flexing . . . flexing only round gobs of mud, Venger having slipped loose from his faulty grip sometime during their tumbling flight. But no matter that. He opened his eyes, raised his head from the clinging muck, and blinked through the sparkling glaze of his blurry vision, the numbing throbs of his aches and bruises and broken bones a distant though growing pain seeping return into his wracked body.

He scanned round for something . . . someone . . . and at last his hunting gaze traced up the length of that towering mobile structure and locked upon the triumphant figure of Hannibal Khan gazing down, a wry smile upon the warlord tyrant's twisted lips.

Get up! Simus resurged in another vehement roar, refusing to be quelled, demanding to be heard in emphatic competition above figment-Melora's sweet sounds of guidance. **Get up and kill, you pathetic bastard! Kill them all!**

Banzu clenched his teeth, jolting to the pulsing flare of animus while baring an involuntary snarl, unable to resist the flushing swell of hatred suffusing through him in an emotional deluge of another's bloodlust fury seeking brazen control of their shared vessel.

His pressurizing vision pulsed with hot and throbbing reds, flares of details sharp as crushed glass in his focal glare of Khan.

I hate you.

Yes.

I'll carve your heart our and drink your blood.

That's it.

You're nothing!

Yes!

I'll—

Let it go, she said in soothing appeal. ***Just let it go—***

Never! Simus yelled in a tumultuous roar of voice. **Kill, godsdamn you—KILL!**

Assertive fury willed Banzu's body into movement, though his efforts proved a slow and painful struggle, every wincing breath a stab of broken ribs, the bones of his spine grating when he attempted sitting upright, groaning through clenched teeth. He propped on one elbow, his other arm a broken dangle, and gazed down the sickening length of his charred and shredded legs, his feet blackened twists.

He glared up at the foreboding swirl of sky-mouth opening and intent on spitting forth another searing jag of lightning into the Khan who would spend it down into a finalizing strike upon him.

He released a guttural scream while the brilliant flash of lightning tore from the churning gloom of sky and lanced down, charging its human Khan conductor with smiting capacity. A mortal so undeserving of such godly power that it sickened him to believe such an unworthy—

If you ever loved me then prove it now, she whispered, her voice pure inspiration cooling the fever of his thoughts, the rapture of her captivating siren's song a beautiful epiphany strong as the woman herself yet tender as her lover's kiss. ***You know what you have to do, Ban. Do it now. Do it for me.*** She paused in a gathering of resolve. ***Do it for us.***

How? The word trembled his lips though took no audible flight.

You know how, she said to the mindspeak of his unvoiced question.

He did know, and the knowledge of it terrified him.

But fear surrendered to the soothing touch of Melora's figment hand applying a gentle caress upon his battered face so that he reached down inside, plunging through the hot swell of churning rage of Simus' parasitic Essence, and grasped the defining hope of the real Melora awaiting him, his only value of consequence.

Spoken by the man he had yet to become, the man she believed him to be because believing mattered most, two words escaped him with newfound exhilaration. "For you."

He'd failed his uncle. He'd failed himself. But by all the gods he refused to fail her. Not while there remained an ounce of breath. Not with her out there, alone and waiting for him.

Believing in him.

"For you," he said in stronger voice, then stronger still, "For you!"

For us!

Shut up, you bitch! Simus roared in desperate tones edged with screaming. **Kill, godsdamn you!**

But the hateful appeal diminished in volume and influence as Banzu settled down, relaxing into the squishy nest of mud. He closed his eyes while embracing the soothing memory of Melora's lovely face, her beautiful smile beneath those provocative violet pools, the encouraging music of her promising voice lilting through his thoughts an invigorating summer's breeze singing upon winds of inspiration . . . as he remembered her and all the glorious feelings she afforded his lonely heart.

Do it, she said, her figment's encouraging voice scramming apprehension from his spirit. ***Do it now!***

Banzu obeyed by seizing a strong grasp on the Power through focal invocation, and allowed—no, commanded its deluging potency to flow into him as time's slowing flow overtook the outside world.

Only once, in the lonely yet relieving moments after killing his uncle, had he seized beyond the full capacity of the Power and tapped into the fractured Source. Only for sparse seconds before releasing it, so overwhelming that influx of energies, risking the true madness of the shared collective shredding his mind apart through torn memories ruptured by the tortured lives of a thousand dead men. He braced for the impending shockwave of energies threatening to shatter his psyche into an infinitesimal spray of fragments.

Try or die.

For her.

Filled with the Power, he removed the bridle of his fears to transcend the last defining line of difference and drained empty the Well of Power inside of himself, and inside of all Soothsayers through the shared collective. He drew in every last drop of magical vigor, drinking it, soaking it, absorbing it . . . then strove beyond the Power's maddening boundary and seized the full supreme magnificence of the Source.

An avalanche of energies punched into him.

Thus began the rapid supernatural restoration of his body—broken bones snapping into proper place, torn muscles and ligaments and tendons mending—as the surging influx of magical energies suffused every compliant fiber of his undulating being.

He welcomed the wonderful restorative saturation flowing through his mending mind, embraced the influx of energies rippling throughout his mutilated body, while awareness of his lifeforce fueling the blooming purpose in his blazing spirit commenced the double-edged exchange of several years' worth of physical aging in cruel accelerated trade for such necessary healing in the short span of seconds.

The world outside his mortal shell turned nonexistent while his entire life replayed through his mind's eye with all the time in the world to relive it now in his healing throes of Source.

Memories turned thick and vivid, more real than memories ought to be, and in this reflective capture of self he experienced the joyous rapture of understanding how pleasure held no true value without comparable pain, how purpose possessed no sincere meaning without neglect.

The freedom to act, the will to achieve, the courage to endure, the exquisite agony of . . . love. An emotion so powerful it transcended all boundaries. Love. The purpose to strive for something greater than living that made men whole. Love. The defining significance of someone who made a man better than he could ever achieve alone.

Melora.

I lost you once.

I won't lose you again.

* * *

A hairsbreadth of moment expanded into infinity . . . then beyond, as Banzu gasped the first full breath of his life.

He'd retrieved the Essence of the First, though now he needed to reclaim it, to tame it, and to master it before it took full possession of him and he became Banzu-no-more but Simus-once-again. If he lost his private battle here, then a bloodlust-corrupted Simus Junes would stalk the One Land of Pangea through him, as him. And if Simus took possession of the Godstone, he would reign in slaughter until no one remained, so insatiable the bloodlust curse.

I can't let that happen.

You will. The parasitic Essence of Simus writhed inside, a festering nest of maggots within its host, brazen in its feeding. **You're weak. You have no other choice. Surrender!**

I won't!

I'll find your precious bitch, and I'll kill her with your own hands.

No!

A battle of wills commenced between Banzu and Simus in an alternating struggle of emotional tides, each warring force slamming against the resistive other for sovereignty, both competing for control while seeking reclamation of rule over the single mind and body housing them in shared vessel.

Yes!

No!

Spiritual wave after wave, tidal forces of dominance and defiance smashing and crashing, pounding and slamming in rebounding contest.

Yes! Simus roared, saturated in opposing Hate.

No! Banzu thundered, imbued with imposing Love—not just a mere word or some trivial emotion but a Force. And True Love? Indomitable.

Irresistible Force impacted Immovable Object.

* * *

The keyrings flashed frigid round Banzu's fingers, and therein the jostling crash of spirits his awareness transported back to the elsewhere caveplace of his and Simus' battle, witnessing the replay of events as a spectator housed within the active vessel of his own exhausted body—while he broke into another charging attack, this one clumsiest of them all.

He said something, a garble of words leaving him in more a pitiful shout than the intimidating yell he tried to make of them. His sword whiffed through empty air as this time Simus bothered no raise of his spiritblade into another masterful parry but instead sidestepped while half-turning, avoiding Banzu's passing stumble, Banzu carried by the sluggish momentum of his swung sword, the act more a clubbing swing than any real endeavor of skill.

Panting, trembling, exhausted beyond feeble, Banzu mustered strength enough for turning round. When he did, his body betrayed him despite his weary mind's protesting screams.

He sank to his knees first right then left, almost toppled forward but for dropping his sword and palming the ground, catching his sloshing balance while steadying the vertigo whirl in his eyes. Tremulous arms threatening to unhinge at the elbows, he straightened then sagged back atop heels which spread and nestled his bottom between sore feet.

There lived plenty of fight left in him but no more energy in which to spend it. His head lolled on rubbery neck. He craned it with iron resolve, determined to look up into the eyes of the enemy who struck him down.

"Surrender is your destiny," Simus said.

Destiny. The atrocious word a pebble dropped into the pond of Banzu's life, producing ripples of events turning incidents of chance into elements of purpose drawn to him, or him to them, by his aizakai gift and his curse of birth, the events coincidental . . . until he dug deeper as was now.

"You can . . . kill me," Banzu-not-yet-Banzu said on huffing breath, fearing death less than the parasitic possession Enosh warned him about, "but you'll . . . never break me."

"Kill you?" Simus craned his head and laughed, then lowered his crimson mask and smiled. "You forget, only together are we whole. It is the *shared* collective, after all. I know all of your secrets, your desires, your pains. They lied to you, Banzu. They all lied to you. Only I speak the truth—"

Lies.

Simus paused, glanced round as if hunting for the origin of the other's voice. Then continued. "How many knives do you carry in your back? Jericho. Gwendora. Agatha. The same gods whom betrayed me." A purposeful pause. "Melora."

"Shut up!"

"Let her go. She is far from here. She tricked you. Betrayed you. Abandoned—"

"Never!" Banzu roared.

"We are meant for each other, First and Last to complete the whole again. Together we can have your revenge. And so much more. You resist, and yet I feel your willingness to join me—"

"No," Banzu said, hanging his head and shaking it. "I can't. I won't."

"You will." Simus' smile spread beneath molten eyes of malice. "There is more than one way you can serve."

"No."

"Yes."

Pain. Banzu raised his head, glared up at specter Simus closing triumphant before him. He spat at the enemy—or tried to, but instead produced such little force the gob of hot saliva caught upon his lips where it clung hanging down as a glistening little length of rope, foamy and white. *Nothing good ever comes in my life without pain.*

"Join me," Simus said, "and the world will tremble beneath our feet. Surrender, and I promise you Hannibal Khan. Yes?"

Banzu-not-quite-Banzu made to speak, to rebuke the truth of that wicked proposal.

For me.

Banzu-becoming-Banzu jolted to Melora's whisper, and startled at the flush of vigor shedding false exhaustion from his muscles. His heaving lungs filled overfull while his breathing slowed to normal in the span of a blink.

This . . . isn't real. Not physically. Only spiritually. I understand now. Oh gods, how did I not realize it before? That's why I lost. I was fighting myself. He can only hurt me if I let him. If I believe he can. There's no parasite without the host.

His plethora of bleeding cuts vanished in dissolving wisps of smoke, his bloodied ribbons of clothes no longer shorn wet tatters, the false lather of sweat evaporating from his unblemished skin. He said nothing, only smiled when he locked insightful eyes with Simus. *For her.*

"No." Simus snarled, blazing red eyes flaring then thinning while detecting something awry. "No." He drew his sword back, intent on plunging it into Banzu's chest. "No!" Then shoved forward.

"For her." Banzu-now-Banzu reached up, his arm a fanning blur, and captured the end of Simus' stabbing sword, stopping it with the ease of total resistance, earning no cut upon his gripping fingers. In stronger voice he said, "For her."

Simus' straining visage bloomed disbelief while his fevered eyes raced through avenues of surprise then angry alarm. He tried yanking his sword free for another stab.

But Banzu's grip proved too sure, too confident, too supreme. He glanced at his trapping hand glowing the same white-gold brilliance that pulsed throughout the rest of him.

"For her," he said, pressing up into a half kneeling position of rising strength, the crackling end of the harmless sword trapped within his unrelenting grip.

"No!" Simus tried stepping back, tried yanking his sword free. "No!"

"Yes." Banzu arose into standing with the sword held immobile in his clenched fist. "For her," he said in stronger appeal, his gaze unyielding, his words a declaration.

Less a threat and more an annoyance, struggle overtook Simus' twisting scarlet visage while he strained at pulling his caught sword free. "No!" he yelled in frustrated fury. "Surrender!"

"Never." Banzu smiled. And with one quick flick of his wrist he broke off the end of the sword in his trapping hand, the snapping sound of which echoed throughout the caveplace in resounding ripples of thunder.

Simus' face turned a mask of scarlet terror. He staggered backwards, dropping his broken sword in stunned retreat.

Banzu closed distance in three quick, confident strides—and Simus dropped to his knees against his victor's defiant charge.

Banzu reared his arm back, the keen spirit tip of broken sword in hand, and plunged it inches deep into Simus' chest, left of center, Banzu's luminous existence rippling through dazzling waves of white-gold energy as he shouted, "For her!"

A scintillating flash of scarlet brilliance.

Banzu slipped his grip free.

Simus threw his head back, arms whipping out at his sides, his scarlet specter Essence convulsing in thrashing spasms, his voice a tortured scream of soul-burning agony. He collapsed backwards in a splash of crimson brilliance spreading, crackling, dimming upon the floor, a twinkling shatter of strewn rubies.

"For her," Banzu whispered.

As darkness swallowed the dying light.

* * *

The Irresistible Force of Banzu's surmounting Love crashed into and smashed through the once-Immovable Object of Simus' Hate, obliterating it. The spiritual Essence of Simus rallied no more offensive to Banzu's tenacious drive, instead fleeing in screaming echoes across the battlegrounds of Banzu's clearing mindscape.

The fractured Source mended whole again, the parasitic presence of Simus scrambled into a remote recess of Banzu's mind where it hid, cowering, while the tidal cleansing of Banzu's purging flow secured Simus' weaker influence of will behind a mental source-block barricade Banzu wove into existence then set into place with his unyielding willpower of reclaimed self.

Anything but permanent, the source-block barricade would hold Simus at bay until Banzu found the Godstone and its cleansing all-power purged the bloodlust corruption from the shared collective.

Shuddering relief filled his spirit.

There sounded the faint chorus echoes of the voices of a thousand dead Soothsayers calling at him from the shared collective in agonized pleas while their sprits thrashed in futile struggle for claiming dominance over Banzu's mind as had Simus before them, each corrupted essence attempting to usurp Simus' place in frenzied bid and make of Banzu's mind their own.

But they proved weaker than Simus, and Banzu bathed in the glorious strength of renewed purpose after claiming his temporary victory within and of himself. The internal raping of a thousand angry, desperate pairs of hands scratched and clawed upon the stonewall of his willpower while attempting to sink their rabid teeth into his awareness and make it their own.

He gathered his remaining strength and, infused by the power of the still-tainted Source, he released a surging wave of Power-filled pressure which washed over them all while sweeping them up into its irresistible current, tumbling then scattering them.

Desperate cries of a thousand Soothsayers pleaded for him to end their suffering. He gathered then released wave after flowing wave upon them still, and the influx of the Source's potency—still tainted though his to command—flowed burning surfs over their bloodlust-corrupted spirits.

Then, in an unexpected turning, the still-tainted Source flowed back upon him in unruly force, pronouncing his mistake in presuming he could ever control such riotous energies for long. But he held strong upon that inner grasp while clutching his sanity, an anchor keeping him from drifting away in the stormy lunatic sea of psychosis.

He clung to and waited, until those choppy waters of madness calmed into an ocean of Power. There would raise another Source-storm, he knew, and it would ravage him worse than before. But for now . . .

He harnessed another rally of spirit and willed the shared collective behind a second source-block barricade, separate though same as Simus, where those tortured souls would lay in wait, gnashing and wailing, until he answered their desperate cries with the Godstone's cleansing grace.

For now, at least, he earned a temporary reprieve.

* * *

Glorious mayhem everywhere.

The battle plains exuded a silvery undulating carpet of death's flourishing essence, radiant swirls and billows and streams of it pronouncing to Sergal's enhanced deadsight, luminous zephyrs and eddies of abundant lifeforce subsisting throughout the war entire though unseen by the restricted mortal eyes of the khansmen and fistians contending here, together now and in enemy-of-my-enemy packs, against his growing sinistry of unliving hungars and shifterkin lycans over a thousand strong, feeding and raging amongst the frightened masses while clearing for him a grotesque pathway, its sides bestrewn with mangled corpses soon rising through infectious delivery of contagious bites rife with endemic saliva.

Sergal inhaled the wondrous flavors of death's essence as he continued toward the backside of the Betrayer's mobile tower only a few miles ahead, drawing in satisfying tastes of air stung pungent with the stink of sour sweat and the coppery tang of blood.

He trembled with knowing, edging orgasmic again and again, his leisure gait almost a drunken stupor, eyes half lidded, a lazy smile pursing his approving lips, Sera's pitiful moans a faint and soughing drift at the back of his dominant mind.

Such power . . . so much power here . . . splitting me at the seams . . . bursts of it awaiting my abuse. Powerful aizakai call this zumming, this euphoric magical spilling of seed. And this is only a mere taste of what the limitless all-power of the Godstone offers, yesss. I understand now its intoxicating allure. No wonder . . . no wonder it's so precious, so impossible to resist. I mussst have it!

Staccato flashes of Khan-wrought lightning knifed the gloom miles ahead high atop the tower then lanced down somewhere unseen though producing volcanic upheavals of bodies tumbling wayward through the air above the ocean of fighting, charred ruins of men arcing, falling, then crashing within.

Dethkore gasped.

Sergal startled stopped, his expression clearing with revelation. *Something's different.* And it struck in him a plucked and humming chord.

New awareness of a tugging thrum, from within . . . within his necromancer Pet, the failed first of the chosen Khans, that precious inner homing sense of the Godstone's presence flaring awake with active vibration.

Awakened at last by the Soothsayer's retrieval of the Essence.

"Yesss," Sergal hissed, quivering to blooming elation. He licked stray speckles of blood from his lips and swallowed, shouted, "Yesss!"

Forgetting the abundance of fighting and dying round him, he jumped up and down, clapping and laughing and shouting to the jubilant epiphany and all it afforded his shaping plans. "Yesss! Yesss! Yesss!"

He calmed his giddy celebration a moment more, demonic cunning stealing to work. No longer a possibility but an inevitability, he sensed the Godstone's presence through the acute awakening of latent awareness within his Pet, an invisible tether tugging constant request toward the thrumming beacon of all-power, straight and sure regardless any physical impediments between.

Sergal surrendered to the umbilical influence not turning him left or right or round behind but keeping him facing west. The Godstone lay somewhere by or just beyond those far frosted peaks of the Calderos Mountains, and here he endured the pain of distanced ignorance for the thrumming tether existed as a faint influence. But it would intensify with closure and proximity, of that he knew well.

He glanced up at his necromancer Pet, Dethkore swaddled in silvery eddies and swirls of lifeforce seeping into every absorbent part of him in constant nutrient feed. Though the necromancer displayed no outward signs of change upon his sullen tombstone visage, there writhed an inner sense of struggle betraying his black eyes pierced with silver pupils, ripples of effort and need to abandon his soulring servitude and strive for the Godstone.

"Soon," Sergal said, after wrestling down his own newborn fever to abandon vengeance against the Betrayer for the Godstone. He quelled his Pet's urgency to leave away with a commanding flex of his demonic compulsion, then wrestled again his own need flaring with ache, rebuking it with promise. "We will have it soon. But we are unfinished here, yesss."

More staccato flashes of Khan-wrought lighting pursued by declarations of thunder.

Sergal faced west again, smiling while fixing his avid stare, thinning it with deliberation. *There is purpose in those strikes, yesss. More than simple smiting. An order among the chaos.*

Far ahead strove two dynamic forces colliding, power impacting power. *I am meant for this, yesss. Everything isss falling into perfect place.* He stood miles apart and as yet blind to the inevitable destruction of the Soothsayer or the Betrayer, or if his apparent luck held true then the ruination of them both, as the gods' Great Game would have of them. *And I am here to destroy the pieces of the weakened victor before I claim the Godstone and reign supreme as Master.*

Sergal opened his mouth to shout adulation over his impending victory—

* * *

Perhaps a single heartbeat passed, perhaps even less, for Banzu to awaken inside to the true meaning of and in his life. He opened his eyes and sat up in the bloody muck, filled with the still-tainted Source though fractured no more, his broken bones and cuts abolished, his body renewed through years of accelerated healing stealing across the breadth of seconds.

He stared at a world of time not slowed but stopped.

Everyone and everything but him paused static in a suspension of Sourcelock.

CHAPTER FORTY-ONE

So this, Banzu mused with stupefying clarity, *is what it's really like to still the world entire.*

He gazed round in wide-eyed wonder, every detail near and far sharp as broken glass to the luminous grey fractures of his twilight eyes, time surrendered in a mute standstill of action and sound while the magnificent though still-tainted Source flowed its intoxicating exhilaration through him, awing him, the drug of its magical potency thrumming in rhythmic cadence to his beating heart.

A world-wide paralysis, a Source-born stasis, pausing all . . . all but himself.

He inhaled a sharp taste of air, exhaled overlong through a soul-shivering ecstasy pronouncing the awesome power of Source and his humbling place within it.

In an instant's flash of comprehension, everything he knew tumbled into proper place, interlocking with that which he just accomplished, the intricate puzzle of his struggles made whole so that he withdrew and viewed its full picture by delving inward through vivid recall.

The sinister parasitic Essence of Simus Junes completing the fractured Source then subdued behind a source-block barricade. As well the thousand strong of the shared collective wrangled behind a second source-block barricade.

For now, at least.

Neither consenting participants, he forced their unruly spirits into submission by proving himself their provisional master, but the bloodlust still corrupted their tortured souls, his dominance making of them unwilling slaves forced to concede him temporary control. Slaves submitting through survival while planning revolt, time and opportunity their true tools, rebellion their natural inclination, freedom of independence the truest beauty of the human spirit however much the madness of the bloodlust twisted their souls beyond human.

This is it.

He accepted this truth, okay with the knowledge. It bought him precious time, a delay to the inevitable pressure of the shared collective's gathering resistance and Simus' defiance that would strengthen behind the source-blocks in a rally of mutiny. Same as he knew once he released the Source, both hostile parties would shatter the source-blocks and tear him apart in mind and spirit while shredding his sanity with ruthless abandon the moment he dared try seizing the Source again before achieving the Godstone's cleansing grace.

This is all of it.

An almost-whisper built behind his parting lips upon a delicate breath while the inner workings of his braingears ticked and turned through mental machinations, pursuing diligent hunt for the proper words to reorient the inactive world round him. But the effort of trying to fish those words out from the dusty well of some ancient memory left him dry of speech.

No, not braingears turning but charged synapses firing throughout the clearing fog of his active wonder, imparting knowledge bleeding into his thoughts through the haunting hive mind of the shared collective and through Simus in dribbles of experience reflecting memories of the Thousand Years War when Simus had gathered then tapped the Source in similar fashion during his recurring losing battles against Malach'Ra.

Banzu realized the full red beard warming his face, and his shoulder-length hair. He withered by increments to the relinquished years of his precious limited lifeforce in cruel trade for the abundance of accelerated healing imposed by the Source.

And I'm still aging through the nutrient feed of my lifeforce so long as I hold the Source, minutes tolling through me in seconds.

A perpetual mourning soughed deep and overlong in his chamber of being, an indescribable loss of self.

Time, life's most valuable commodity, stolen from him in saving trade, stealing from him still on grander scale than ever before.

If I remain in this perpetual stasis, waiting it out, eventually I will wither with age and die, spending years of my life through days of Source-locked stillness. It's literally killing me, this slow inevitability. And yet I feel . . . gods, I feel so strong, so healthy, so . . . alive.

And mended whole again, neither scratch nor bruise upon his body, rejuvenated regardless the cost. And he knew if he cut himself it would heal instantaneous.

Even the frightening awe of his first seizing of the Power paled to the Source's true fullness of time's manipulation, daunting him through thoughts attempting to form deeper explanations which never quite connected so that he refocused his introspection outward upon the stillness of the paused world and all its quietude.

His lips mimed movement, craving appropriate words but finding none. Sitting in mud possessing no ambient temperature, he stared with Source-enhanced vision through the renewed eyes in the renewed skull of his renewed body, viewing the miraculous tableau of hundreds of fistians and thousands of khansmen captured in stasis, men and women frozen mid-leap, others mid-swing and mid-gore of axe or sword or mace or drawing of bow or throwing of spear with their faces locked in feral snarls or static blooms of terror, expressions dependent upon if they delivered the wounding stroke or received it, more others perched atop once-dancing horses now just as frozen as their riders. A vast collection of human statues within this arrested moment of absolute inaction.

Rain filled the hushed air between the immobile warriors with uncountable mid-glistening drops, these captured fractures of water and light, making of the scene the vivid unreality of some master painter's most glorious work portrayed through dramatic strokes of brush.

At the base of the Khan's mobile tower stood massive wooly beasts of burden, each impressive creature the size of a wagon loaded overfull, twenty to a side and harnessed to its thick timbers, the animals paused mid-trudge between giant iron-banded roller wheels of spiked death, several of the hulking mammoths mid-act of fending attacking fistians, the full-grown and some of them fully armored soldiers offering no more resistance than irritating playthings proving less threat to the beasts' thick and wooly hides than petulant children swept aside by long curvatures of blood-pinked tusks paused mid-sweep.

Tumbles of bodies arrested in their spaces of air, others impaled upon the lengthy tusks themselves or trampled under the stomping tonnage of mammoth feet, others still entangled in pachyderm trunks of muscle twined round and crushing cages of ribs while crimping protesting armor and squeezing spumes of viscera from scream-locked throats. Blooms of blood dappled the rain here and there, resembling thrown handfuls of rubies strewn within larger clouds of raindrop diamonds, the trillions of droplets refracting captures of light from the static flash of coruscating lightning smiting down from its lofty origin of Hannibal Khan its human conductor.

And looming on high the tower's apex stood the Lord of Storms himself, just as still as the wooly beasts of burden and his copious khansmen below, the warlord stationary in the middle of his smiting pose, the scintillating jag of godfinger lightning blasting from his outstretched arm and targeting straight for Banzu's position arrested in the all-encompassing Source-locked stasis.

The wicked bolt of searing death lanced frozen mere feet in front of Banzu's appraising Source-grey eyes, a blazing length of almost-connection stretched between them, knifing with promise and smiting intent.

Though he sensed no scalding heat from its destructive tip, for heat required the vibrational motion of molecules and here there live none. Not now. Not in time's absolute static constraint of the world.

The knowledge of this provided in a flashing instance of Source-imbued comprehension, its point of origin a fragment of understanding stolen from the shared collective though more so from an intelligence therein much more scientific-oriented than Banzu's own ignorant mind. A whisper of a thought, perhaps, the pricked bleeding of another's memories. Or more a crumb of insight dropped into his beggar's bowl—incapable of demand, he could only receive. Demanding would only come after the Godstone's cleansing grace . . . if it ever came at all before the madness of the shared collective mutinied against his sanity.

He trembled with dread premonition. If their rallying psychoses broke through the source-blocks and overwhelmed him before he achieved the Godstone's purging purity, not just the parasitic Essence of Simus Junes but the entire corrupted consciousnesses of the shared collective would possess him in a hive mind of madness, his mental faculties of self drowned beneath the crushing tide of lunacy while his physical self killed without regard through the suffusion of a thousand bloodlusts warring for dominance.

He forced that dread possibility from his mind and focused on the profound silence of the inert present. The deliberate grinding swallow of his throat resounded in his susceptive mind. He parted his lips for speech in testing bid of his voice against the haunting quietude, and the sticky peel of action produced the sound of moistened strips ripping apart to his oversensitive hearing.

No words spilled forth from bated breath, only a deep and shuddering inhale pursued by an overlong exhale possessing profound relief of his sitting a short space away from sure Khan-wrought death.

Now, though, he held all the time in the world in his figurative hands, nestled in Source-locked stasis.

Unfamiliar with such godly power, he considered the greater all-power of the Godstone awaiting him elsewhere and feared his inability to rebuke it if—no, when he claimed it with the intent to destroy it for the good of all.

Before and the Source had transported him into the past upon the track of his own lifeline. Now and he remained in the present, the Source suspending all action outside of himself. He questioned nothing of the imposed stasis, knowing the rest of the world beyond his limited scope remained as inert as the war suspended round him.

"Yes." A simple word breathed in bare whisper, it arrived subdued, deadened, almost muted even to his heightened hearing. And he knew through another bleeding drip of knowledge the word had nothing to ride on, the sound waves in the air immobilized. Then, in the same muffled tone, he added in stronger voice, "Amazing."

He raised a hand, his right hand, his main sword hand, the motion of its uprising sweeping aside paused droplets of rain through the air in a hovering scatter of glassy beads, and dug his fingers through the itchy thickness of his full red beard—*skrtich-skrtich-skritch*—the painful reminder of his accelerated healing punching his guts with sorrow for the years of his lifeforce given in trade so that he winced while lowering hand from face as a solemn suffering overtook him.

Years of me gone, just like that.

He sat in the mud for a silent length, mulling in grim wonder over how many years of his precious lifeforce the Source sapped in sacrificial exchange while shortening the total expanse of his natural life . . . was taking from him still while he maintained his grasp upon it.

Years I'll never get to spend with her.

He hung his head in a moment of self-pity, wanting to cry, and almost did until intrusive jolts not of what but of why hardened his resolve.

"For you," he whispered, smiling at the thought of Melora, of his accomplishments thus far instigated by the pure idea of her and the possibility of seeing her again. He carried passion for her within cherished memories where lived the aroma of her hair, the music of her voice, the warmth of her lips, the violet pools of her eyes. She still so far away and yet right beside him, harbored in his heart of hearts.

As well as Jericho, his uncle lost somewhere within the shared collective and still corrupted by the bloodlust.

Not just for me. I have to get the Godstone for him too. For all of them.

Awareness blossomed into his thoughts, an inner tugging pronounced within a second heartbeat pulsing faint though sure and with a rekindled sense of urgency, an inner thrum of purpose.

He twisted at the hips and glanced through the screen of suspended fighters miles wide and long, imagining the far frosty peaks of the Calderos Mountains where the inner thrum tugged upon him with umbilical influence. He could walk a straight line ending to the Godstone's fallen location by sense of feel alone. Distance weakened that knowing thrum, though it would strengthen in both pulse and rhythm with every westward step if he stood and started away.

I ignored it before. Engaging here instead of leaving like I should have. Blinded by vengeance, crazed by Simus. That's over. But . . . but I'm too in the thick of it now, and I am unfinished here. I won't get another chance like this. I can't tap the Source again without losing all of myself. I have to act while I still can.

He shelved the guiding thrum through sheer conviction of will. *The Godstone can wait a little longer. I have an uncle to avenge, a Khan to kill, and a war to end. Too many lives lost already.*

Something fierce gripped him then, an abstract force, so that he gazed up the white stretch of static lightning through ultra keen Source-sight and locked upon the twin flares of the Khan's challenging glare, cruel eyes afire within that human conductor, uncaring eyes blazing with the awful power of hate and the fierce need to spend it. Everything frightening about the man concentrated in those eyes fixed upon Banzu with bright, hard, indiscriminate hatred he too once viewed the world.

A fleeting touch of snarl twitched Banzu's lips. *At last, a worthy challenger.* But the words rang hollow so that he denied them aloud. "No. There's no more vengeance in this. In me. Only justice."

He gazed down into his upturned palms and flexed his fingers, noticing for the first real time the killer's brutality about them. And they had killed . . . so many, enacting khansmen slaughter in appalling droves. Just to reach this warlord tyrant. And for what, more killing?

Killing . . . for all the wrong reasons.

His penchant for killing shifted from a hot and unyielding desire to a cold though necessary purpose.

"I've killed enough."

And the words emptied him.

Emotional rooks bursting from his spiritual copse, all animosity fled. Sorrow filled him. Regrets claimed him. Grief wrecked him. Truth shattered him. And he knew with instinctive certainty his crossing of some threshold of spirit, never to be crossed again. Though no tears drove his cheeks, guilt flushed overwhelming.

"No more," he whispered. "It ends here. Now."

Vengeance a poisoned triumph, but justice . . .

One kill left, one last sacrifice, and then it will be done, this war, the needless killing, the destruction of uncountable lives. All that remains is to do it. To settle the score—No. To balance the scales. To end the killing.

He studied past the burnt tatters of his shredded pants down the length of his blood-smeared, mud-crusted, though unmarred legs at his pink toes and wiggled them, glad to have them restored, happy to see them there and functioning well alongside the rest of his rehabilitated though years' older body.

But then . . . he tasted it first, a wrongness in the air. Felt it second, a wrongness in himself.

—thuuuuuuump-thump.

For an infinitesimal fraction of space everything skipped into motion the slightest of increments along their predetermined paths, the noises of war sounding then swallowing through the space of a blink, as the *heartbeat-of-the-world* thumped then stilled, allowing Banzu the startling insight of time not frozen in Source-locked stasis as presumed but slowed down into such a profound lethargic pace it only seemed as if everything had stopped.

And there he shuddered through flushing panic, for along with the infinitesimal blink-shift forward in time announced by that sliver burst of noise possessing the roar of thousands, his strong inner grasp on the Source slipped loose by a minuscule fraction of control.

He captured an anxious breath deep and overlong, unsure of the transgression transpired without the imposing flex of his permissive will, his mind deliberating through brazen denial of the abrupt change in activity, and yet . . . and yet.

He recognized it despite.

The resistive slippage of time trying to right itself.

* * *

Banzu waited out the precarious moment, releasing his bated breath when no second slippage of time followed to reinforce the alarming first so that he excused it for a natural adjustment of opposing forces.

I'm treading unfamiliar waters now. Relax before you sink yourself. Of course the world's adjusting, I've stopped the whole friggin thing. Unless . . . unless I've already lost my mind and this is all some mad delusion.

He gazed round for a lengthy measure, questioning the stilled world and his possible insanity through the vivid unreality of some psychotic lie betraying his sense of self.

No. This is real. Questioning it proves as much.

And I have work to do.

Maintaining his strong inner grasp of Source, he stood, mud squishing between his toes, the tatters of his shredded pants dangling round his thighs and making of it two frayed skirts ending at his knees, the vain part of him glad the rest of his pants covered him crotch to hips, as well he maintained his sword belt and empty sheath. He considered tearing off his ruined pants to his underwear but disregarded the unimportant notion.

Forget the pants, at least I still have my legs.

He wished for the safety and comfort of his boots, but they'd burnt to cinders off his leaping feet, impossible to recover. But to replace? The experience of spending years living in the woods imposed the true value of a good pair of boots, nice dry socks a second fiddle. Deep in woodlands, men lived and died by the health of their feet. He could do nothing for socks, but he could replace his boots by filching a pair from any of those round him locked in suspension.

But what will happen if I touch them?

Unsure at best, he decided risking that possible calamity only with keen steel reclaimed and once he stood before the Khan and struck the false godking down. For now he dismissed the luxury of more comfortable feet.

He withdrew a cautious space from the blazing brilliance of the frozen diagonal jag of lightning suspended inert in the air, the mud squishing between his toes while he did so, and walked round the Source-locked bolt while keeping safe distance between, inspecting the white lance of energy with a scrutinizing eye though leaving it untouched even as his hands flexed grips of air, craving reaching test of the bolt's scintillating surface with an experimenting poke of finger.

The radiant capture of white light splendor hindered nothing of his eyes even this close to the lustrous intensity. And there, as with his previous estimation of its heat, a secret knowledge whispered through his brain across a chain of firing synapses that the lightning's photons required movement to dazzle his eyes blind.

What's a photon?

But the question faded to more immediate concerns.

He turned away from the lightning bolt and fixed shifting interest upon a stray arrow suspended in its downward flight, the missile frozen in the air just above head height. He reached up to touch it but paused his fingers two inches from contact. A foreboding shiver flushed while he rubbed the tips of his index finger and thumb together. *I need to know* . . . so that he captured bracing breath then plucked the static arrow free from whatever invisible strings held it stationary within its Source-locked flight.

He blew out his cheeks in relaxing relief that the action caused no instigative ripples of distortion upon the awing stasis of his current reality. He twisted his wrist round, turning the arrow this way and that way while inspecting it from tip to fletching, then held the arrow out the length of his arm and released his pinch in a test of his Source-stilled world.

He half expected the arrow to just *stick* back into the air the moment he released his fingers. But it surprised him by falling, earning the mud with a muted slap.

"Huh."

So I can *touch things without causing a total disruption to the rest of the frozen world. Good for me. And you,* he mused down at his bare feet. *Boots it is, then.*

He spied out a likely fitting pair on the feet of a nearby corpse lying prone in the mud, several arrows and the broken shaft of a spear jutting from its back. He started walking toward the—

—*thuuuuump-thump*. Everything jostled.

He startled and stumbled to a standstill, panic flushing his muscles tensed, his quickened heart skipping beats, the static world blink-shifting another minuscule fraction forward in time along predetermined paths. As well a second slippage of his inner grasp of Source. The first occurrence he excused for adjustment, but this second announced the dread beginnings of a pattern.

Boots forgotten, he spent an anxious moment searching, his hunter's gaze questing for his lost sword . . . somewhere . . . somewhere over *there!* Venger's familiar hilt announced its immaculate blade stabbing the mud in an almost-askance lean toward his position, requesting reclamation. He strode toward the sword in bounding strides, thick wet muck oozing sucking depressions round his eager tread, though he remained careful not to touch any of the frozen figures he wove round and stepped over in advancing bid to recover his precious weapon.

"Oh thank gods," he whispered, despite their cruel Great Game stamped upon his trampled fabric of life, when he closed to Venger in smiling relief. He bent over, reaching for the leather-wound hilt—and paused at the disturbing sight of his hand turning tremulous inches from retaking the tool of his khansmen slaughter.

"Venger," he whispered, the name of it containing a planet's worth of new gravity. He tottered on unsteady legs while the necessary evil of steel beckoned him in opposition to the hesitation gripping him by the spine. And therein bloomed a shameful appreciation. *No, not Venger, but*—"Griever."

He understood the weight and value and tribulations contained in a given name, and why his uncle had named this sword so . . . so honestly. A final lesson taught by Jericho from beyond the living realm. He drew in a steadying breath, held it overlong while flexing the trembles from his fingers, then exhaled through pursed lips. *One more kill and then it's done.*

Venger no more . . . Banzu grasped *Griever's* comforting hilt in a sure grip and pulled his uncle's former sword free from the muddy muck, thankful of the pelting rain having washed clean its steely length and recognizable hilt into better visibility, Griever's exquisite craftsmanship a shiny beacon amongst the surrounding gloom and inferior blades scattered about the frozen tableau of war. Holding Griever returned an instant's relaxation flushing reassuring ease throughout his tensed muscles, though he dared not relax in full lest his inner grasp of Source loosen then slip from him before—

—thuuump-thump. And everything jostled again a fraction through their predetermined paths in another skipping blink-shift forward through time as behind him announced though a hairsbreadth more muted the booming *thoom!* of Khan-wrought lightning striking the ground of Banzu's absence.

He faced the paused eruption of earth and bodies just beginning to swell up into the air from that smiting blast, and swallowed hard with understanding.

A third blink-shift forward through time, the still space between it and the previous a slight measure less than that between the second and first.

Oh gods, the . . . the time-blinks are recurring with less space between them while the world is trying to catch up in shrinking minutes. Friggin hell! I have to do this quick. Only minutes before another, and even less until the next.

Relax. Focus. There's still time enough. You can do this. You must.

He turned and gazed up the height of the towering structure and all its lashed timbers, fixing focal intent upon Hannibal Khan paused in the striking pose of smiting discharge. He worked his jaw, lips pressing into a frown of contempt which he tightened into a fine line of conviction.

"For you," he said, then banished thoughts of Melora to the back of his preserving mind, making space for steely determination of the present. *Less than a mile. I can make it.*

He stalked toward the base of the immobilized structure, his arbiter's gaze precise.

* * *

Banzu pursued the Khan's impending death while moving along his broken route with the careful avoidance of contact against every immobilized warrior clogging his path. He wove between or skirted round clusters and knots of fighting khansmen and dying fistians suspended mid trades of deathblows upon the battlefield presenting itself a vast statue testimonial master sculptors spent a thousand years constructing and arranging beyond perfect recreation to the grisly horrors of war.

Arranging . . . the word gave him bitter outward pause. He scanned round in quick though attentive survey. *All of these people . . . fathers and mothers, sons and daughters, so many pieces being played upon some great gaming board.* Disgusted, he hawked and spat, then eyeballed his static Khan target and continued forward.

Several times the throngs of fighting thickened so that he maneuvered through suspended mists or arcing splashes of a sufferer's bloodspray, no other choice while avoiding bumping into the contesting fighters themselves. The static crimson dapples, released from their hovers of suspension upon his brushing contact, splashed across his turning face or in his hair or beard, or soaked into the tatters of what remained of his shirt and pants with disturbing blooms of warmth.

Like it even matters, he mused of the meddlesome bloodsprays as he advanced through them while finding it harder work, squinting so as to avoid stray speckles of blood wetting into his eyes. Mud caked him from head to heel, mixed with the blood of the incalculable khansmen his fistian cavalry spearhead killed in their suicidal charge—hundreds by his sword alone—so that more added blood made small difference to him now. He just didn't want it in his eyes or mouth or up his nose.

Asides, the suspended trillions of cold raindrops filling the air in everywhere abundance splashed reactive upon contact, wetting him with every twist and turn. So much so that when he glanced down it appeared as if he pissed blood down his legs. And the mud—gobs and globs of its frozen splashes rife as raindrops.

He quested through the contending crowds of static war, carrying a peace of quiet in his mind—that shattered, staggering him, when the dizzying rush of a thousand voices shouted in unison rally, a surf of noise issued from behind the source-block barricade, so that he almost palmed the shoulder of a nearby Bloodcloak in a vertigo slosh of imbalance though straightened quick while yanking his groping hand away inches from planting contact.

He blinked the slowing whirl from his eyes, drew in deep, blew out his cheeks. And steadied on shifting feet while concentrating upon quelling the rising raucous of voices shouting through his mindscape in angry protests of revenging pain.

Bold as before though not as influential while restricted behind their punishing source-block barricade, he earned no specifics from the patchwork of their joined screams, but the emotional impact of their psychotic hate sang loud in their condemnations of primal aggression pleading, begging, edging demands that he forego the Khan and instead deliver indiscriminate slaughter upon the inactive fighters round him.

To kill—them all—for the sake of killing.

A particular voice elevated above the hive cacophony with harsh distinction, the disgusted drawl of Simus Junes.

Lambs for the slaughter. An entire field of prey meant for nothing but easy pickings, yet you pass them by like an old and toothless wolf starved of hunting, his taste of blood no more than memory. You're pathetic. We are a god among men! We—

Shut up. Banzu silenced Simus' attempted influence over him through the flexing of his Source-infused will, banishing it into the tormented collage of voices he then hushed through another flaring flex of will. *There is no we. No us.*

It unnerved him knowing Simus and the rest of the shared collective viewed out at the world through his window eyes, prisoners watching in a gathering mob crowded behind his source-block barricades, spying, festering, every one of them victims of the bloodlust, anxious for punching through the source-block and overtaking him.

Not a possibility but an eventuality if he failed to obtain the Godstone and—

—thump-thump.

Everything skipped another infinitesimal measure forward.

While Banzu startled and staggered upon the world turning a fraction beneath his feet mid-step through a fourth blink-shift forward in time.

Friggin hell!

He walked on while harnessing calm, his limited time between blink-shifts shortening, the world straining to catch up and right itself by stealing into perpetual motion again against the constraining Source-lock, his inner grasp of it slipping looser with each imposing tug of time.

The familiar lilt of a deranged cackle echoed through his mind, followed by the harsh whisper of the word **Soon** so that Banzu paused in his muddy tracks with due shiver and a striking pang of guilt.

For a fragile moment he considered lowering his guard to communicate with Jericho. But he refrained before any trial of words escaped his parting lips. He wished no travel down that dark, psychotic path of talking to his dead uncle through himself. The corrupted shared collective sought to make of him a schizophrenic serial killer, no point in catalyzing that probability through audible invite.

Still, he entertained the notion of **Soon** in wonderment of threat or the unhinged lunatic craving of a scorned madman hungry for the Khan's death awaiting them.

Banzu drew in another calming breath, this one deep with focus, and tightened his inner grasp upon the still-tainted Source while tightening his outer grip on Griever, squeezing each for increased purchase. He turned round, scanning the abrupt change in paused activity, ensuring nothing surprising occurred during that fourth blink-shifting nanosecond of unfreezing, then he spun back—and bumped into while passing by the hunched shoulder of a spear-wielding Bloodcloak poised frozen in the middle of a stabbing charge, the soldier's crimson cloak torn strips of suspended fabric.

But he gave the khansman only a perfunctory glance as he walked on, his intent upon the Khan ahead taking precedence.

Until there sounded a disturbance from behind, a voice and splashing puncturing the silence.

Banzu spun round to the unfrozen Bloodcloak sprawled facedown in the mud—and moving.

He tensed. "Oh friggin hell."

The khansman push up from the sucking muck, spitting a mouthful of filth then blasting curses before raising his head and cursing again. He clipped short his second string of profanities as he straightened then settled back bottom atop heels and gazed about in stupefied wonder at the frozen world round him.

Banzu's instincts flared for killing action while a barrage of hot screams begged him forward. He took an involuntary step toward the Bloodcloak's broad back, fingers tightening round Griever's hilt, then stopped and battled down the coercive temptation to lunge and stab the khansman in the base of his skull before the man could—

"No," Banzu said, sharp and curt, his voice a command hushing the mangled sea of requests in his head.

The Bloodcloak flinched stiff. He half twisted in the mud, and his wide eyes bloomed wider when they locked upon Banzu watching back at him with blade in hand, the only other mobile person amid their tableau of statues.

For a brittle length both men neither moved nor spoke, just stared in the delicate silence of a frozen war.

"You!" the shocked soldier shouted, startled out from mute stupor, recognition thinning his eyes to glare, his projected voice a swallow of echo. His eyes popped wide again, darting everywhere, questioning everything of his new suspended reality.

"Yes," Banzu said, his body aching for the thrusting lunge to wet Griever's tongue with this khansman's lifeblood, old habits dying hard. "Me."

The Bloodcloak spun round to better face him, splashing brown filth without care. He started rising then plopped back down, kneeling in the mud, anxious gaze noting Griever almost as much as the one with luminous grey eyes holding it.

"You're the Soothsayer." His voice a flare containing no question in his accusation. "Blasphemer of Khans!" A touch of fear betrayed his eyes, his voice, when he glanced round while shrinking back by inches. "Did you . . . did you do this?"

Gaze unyielding, Banzu's fingers fanned round Griever's leather-wound bastard hilt, sinews flexing round knuckles flashing white, while his continence wrestled down the reflexive impulse of a killing thrust by thinnest margin. "Yes."

"But how . . ." But here the Bloodcloak trailed off in a gazing stupor, his apprehensive eyes expanding into fragile blue pools of frightened wonder. "How?" he repeated in tepid whisper, fearing the question almost as much the answer.

"Doesn't matter." Banzu took a challenging step forward and angled Griever's steely length between them, inches of space from tip and breastplate. "I'm not here for you. I'm here for your Khan. And to end this godsdamned war." He jabbed the flinching Bloodcloak on the chest, Griever's tip prodding steel breastplate—*tink*. "Stay down." He tightened his eyes, his voice. "Or I'll put you down for good." In his mind he viewed Griever's rise then satisfying thrust puncturing throat, though in body he withdrew a step. "I've killed enough of you bastards already."

The Bloodcloak kneeler nodded mute response, his hung mouth aquiver while his left hand enacted a blind fumble at his side for the security of his dropped spear.

"No." Until Banzu narrowed his warning gaze and flicked Griever in cold warning. "Don't be stupid."

The khansman yanked his hunting hand away and clutched it with the other to his chest in the form of some silent prayer, his trembling lips mouthing 'Please' over and again though no sound carried from his throat.

Banzu held grim pause, the rush and surf of instigative whispers elevating in askance for him to kill this unworthy khansman then move on to the next, and the next, and the next—

"No!" he shouted while removing two steps. "Shut up!" Quelling the raging riot into hushed murmurs.

The startled Bloodcloak jerked backwards onto his back with a mud-smacking *plop*, his battered open-faced helm whipping free from his head. But he recovered quick by sitting up and palming the ground at his sides. "What?" He gaped at Banzu, blooms of terror stretching the grimy wrinkles on his face into mud- and blood-crusted pathways, his wide eyes darting about for anything in the way of help or escape yet finding neither. "What?"

Banzu stared the Bloodcloak down through scrutinizing slits, a battle contesting inside between killing and leaving . . . and a third notion of refreezing the khansman through the Source if only he knew what to do and how to do it.

He closed distance again, two challenging steps, bare feet squishing depressions.

And the Bloodcloak slapped his hands together, flinging gobs of mud, into another form of unvoiced prayer.

Banzu raised Griever and poked the limited space of air between them, sword tip jabbing above steepled fingers and between the khansman's crossing eyes. He stared overlong though said nothing, weighing and measuring those cobalt blues for a silent span, his lips twitching through impending snarl.

Behind the source-blocks arose a fevered chant: *Kill! Kill! Kill!*

He quelled it in a flare of will.

No. Just one step to walk off a cliff. I've taken it before. If I take it again, I'll plunge too far too deep and I'll never climb out.

"No," Banzu said, sharp, cold, exact, while strangling his sliver of mercy. "I'm not here for you." He turned away, turned back. "I'm giving you your life. But you so much as move from this spot and I swear to gods I'll carve your heart out and feed it to you, understand?"

The Bloodcloak nodded then shook his head then nodded again, unsure which gesture afforded him a longer life, then he stilled the motion when Banzu raised Griever's tip to his nose.

"I'll carve your godsdamned heart out," Banzu said in repeat threat, and prodded the man's nose, pricking it, the face round it scrunching, his arm a taut bar craving Griever's full thrust through face and out the back of skull. "And feed it to you."

The trembling Bloodcloak closed his eyes, whimpering.

Banzu turned away and walked away, leaving the Bloodcloak sitting in dazed confusion. But no sooner was the man behind forgotten for the Khan ahead then—

—thump-Thump.

Everything jostled along their predetermined paths through a fifth jostling blink-shift forward through time, this world-turning skip ahead longer than those previous, several seconds of passage contained inside a roaring pinch of space instigating another jarring step. And Banzu startled to the whistling rush of noise keening upon his heightened senses and edging them raw with warning.

He spun round—and almost took the thrown spear into his face if not for dodging just in the nick by unhinging at the knees while lifting his feet from the sucking muck in lieu of the slower by fractions version of ducking, thus enacting a dropping squat more than lowering. The propelled spear whizzed overhead the breadth of inches, its broad leaf-shaped tip catching through and tearing out a few wet strands of his floating hair instead of slicing open his scalp.

The spear continued past and stabbed inched deep into the back of a frozen Bloodcloak where its shaft twanged mute.

At the locking of their gazes, the once-kneeling Bloodcloak, now restored into standing during the longer blink-shift forward in time, returned a startled stare of fearful disappointment. He shook free from the paralysis of his failed throw, bent and fumbled through the thick muck for picking up the stray sword by his feet partially hidden beneath the sopping mud.

And for panicky seconds he cursed while battling against the mud-glued sword resisting his futile pulls, his wet hands slipping thrice upon the slick hilt until he achieved sure grip and, using the push of his legs, wrenched the sword free from the sucking muck, the force of its release stumbling him backwards three steps. He raised the blade, a smile cutting across his lips, a fever alight in his eyes, and broke into sprint.

Banzu eyeballed the charging Bloodcloak while ignoring the hot whispering rush of cheers elevating in his head over the inevitable prospect of killing again.

"Godsdamn you," he whispered in an almost-growl. "I gave you the chance you never would've given me." He sucked in a sharp breath through clenched teeth, huffed and yelled, "I gave you the chance!"

The Bloodcloak charged unabated, his clomping sprint splashing up thin waves of fanning mud, his battle cry the wordless holler of a crazed warrior expecting death whether he gave or received so long as it delivered.

I tried. A mocking cackle of approval arose within Banzu's mind. "Shut up!" He refocused his attentions upon the armed Bloodcloak seconds from closing while shifting his feet to bracing stance through the mud, his luminous Source-grey swordslinger's eyes targeting precise vitals in breaks of motion through acute instinct. Elaborate swordform after swordform danced through his head in a complex ballet of preclusions.

He sidestepped and stabbed while the Bloodcloak's overhead chop meant for splitting crown to chin cleaved only air and paused drops of rain.

The khansman's momentum and missed blow carried him stumbling past Banzu while Griever bit quick yet deep into exposed ribs left side of his punctured heart. Upon the sword's rapid removal—though Banzu possessed no idea how he accomplished the task but for an inner flex of inadvertent strain—the Bloodcloak's motions refroze, his startled grimace a mask capturing flourishing pain and stark understanding of his final moment in life.

Suspended static mid-run, the Bloodcloak pitched forward and slid the mud ten feet before bumping to rest against two other men locked in immobile wrestle.

Banzu considered the Bloodcloak's abrupt return to stasis instigated beyond his control with the discriminating rationale of an accident. *For all my years using the Power, and I know almost nothing of the Source.*

For a pensive moment he stared at the fallen Bloodcloak statue just another dead man amongst the litter of lives, and wondered when he released the Source and time's flow normalized if the khansman would unfreeze only to die from a punctured heart or if death already claimed him.

Doesn't matter. Dead is dead. I tried. Stupid bastard threw his own life away.

He shook his head, craned it, looked up and fixed Hannibal Khan's immobile figure perched high atop the tower with a scrutinizing stare. *And you're next.*

He continued toward the tower's base in a faster pace while walking round and avoiding contact with the plethora of others clogging his path, hoping to reach then kill the Khan and end this doomed war before another forward skip of—

—thump—Thump.

***

Another world-jostling slippage of seconds stealing past, and Banzu stumbled, cursing, as a sixth blink-shift forward through time jolted the world several turning inches beneath his ignorant feet, the stilled space of Source-locked stasis between blinking-shifts shrinking as well the slippage of time between lengthening in terrible balance.

Friggin hell! They're coming faster and faster, my control on the Source slipping and slipping. I need to do this while I still can, before the Source slips loose. I won't survive seizing it again.

It's now or never.

Screw it.

He sheathed Griever to his left hipwing and broke into sprint, uncaring of bumping into those he passed, each arrested statue converting unfrozen by his banging touch or stomping foot and returning active along their predetermined paths of motion within the otherwise suspended landscape of war, though each passing bump a forgotten mishap ignored in his rushing bid to reach the timber tower for the Khan atop it.

Confused shouts and raging bellows the sounds of muting echoes roused among the waking life behind him seconds after every bumping pass. But he ignored them all, bothering no look back, for the profound physical prowess of blurring momentum achieved through the empowering Source speeding him forward, his feet no longer puncturing the mud but gliding atop it with a feathery lightness of locomotion.

A queer and humming awareness of self flushed his every muscle, every active tendon and ligament, in exclusions of work, achieving a spatial oversensitivity turning physical control absolute. Bumped khansmen startled from stasis ricocheted at his sides and past in shouting tumbles. Pumping his arms and legs for all their worth in a curiously improved way even the Power never afforded him before, the world flashed past his peripherals in whizzing blurs while he reached top speed and prepared to leap on high and—

—Thump-Thump.

Another jarring blink-shift forward through time, Banzu's inner grasp on the still-tainted Source straining to maintain its loosening strangle, and he stumbled, slowing while pitching forward in disrupted run. He recovered lost balance with mud-slapping hands and scrambled into faster sprint, muscles priming through regaining momentum, bumping past more unfreezing khansmen rebounding away at his sides, closing toward the tower's base.

Ahead, the teleported knots of sacrificial fistians had opened several gaps through the protective hordes of Bloodcloaks and worship-followers ringing round the wooly beasts of burden pulling the wheeled structure along. Banzu targeted a particular Bloodcloak's hunched back, the static khansman kneeling over a felled fistian mid-slice of the underneath soldier's throat, and he used the convenient khansman as a springboard, planting one foot atop the motionless Bloodcloak's broad back between the shoulders then propelling through the push of his extending leg, the crush of khansman spine announcing his impact, up the steep western face of the three-hundred foot tower in strongest launching leap of Source-Powered momentum—

—Thump-Thump.

Another jarring blink-shift forward through time, and Banzu cringed mid-flight, the whole of the towering structure of lashed timbers jolting an abrupt space forward, several feet achieved in the span of a lengthened blink, his propellant leap failing at delivering him high enough to accomplish atop the apex platform as intended, its energies disrupted by the interrupting blink-shift so that he would neither make his intended landing nor even close to gripping the high top's edge for pulling up and over while joining the Khan. Instead, panic slicking his precarious grasp of Source, legs kicking and arms pinwheeling, his awesome though stunted jump arrested him short of—

—Thump-THUMP.

Another blink-shift forward and—*smack!*—pain and the taste of blood as his front struck the side of the structure several tiers below the apex. His frantic hands clawed for precious purchase while he slid down the slick timbers, scraping fingertips while banging elbows and knees upon thick wooden beams, then caught the horizontal edge of a crossways bracing timber and the jolt of his stop jarred flares of agony in his shoulders and clinging hands.

He struggled through blooms of torment while kicking his feet in wild abandon, stubbing his toes then earning another crosswise timber for standing beneath him so that he settled upon it for a few restive seconds while thanking Locha's Luck his contact returned no motion to the structure as it had the khansmen scrambling in angry confusion far below his precarious perch.

He drew in deep, blew out his cheeks, and began climbing up—

—Thump-THUMP—

—as another blink-shift of jolting momentum disrupted the paused world through brief jostling motion.

A staccato flash above, an eruptive boom below.

And now Banzu strained at keeping hold of his inner grasp on the slippery Source same as he strained to finish climbing the steep western face of the Khan's tower, the rain-slick surface of which mocked his gripping fingers and purchase-seeking feet.

He reached overhead, pushing through an anxious jump clenching his guts aflutter for the necessary reach while grabbing hold of the next higher timber where splintered a shot arrow into the thick wood two inches shy of his right hand—*thunk!*

Startled, he glanced down at the dozen or so active khansmen he'd bumped into motion, gathered below and watching up at him, one of which notched another arrow to bowstring while the armed others round the Bloodcloak archer pointed at Banzu with sword or mace or ax or spear, jabbing threats of air with their futile weapons beyond reach.

Not so a smarter khansman who struggled at wrenching free another bow from the locked hands of a static worship-follower. His cursing efforts attracted the attentions of his fellows so that several of them turned and abandoned their weapons while hunting for stray bows of their own, one woman laughing as she gathered paused arrows from the air, snatching them from hovering stasis with tugging effort.

Friggin hell! Adrenaline pumping a nervous fever, Banzu returned his gaze up and strove into faster climb. *I told you so* whispers arose in mocking appeal, scolding him for not killing the khansmen below while urging him to surrender his climbing venture and slip down into proper slaughter. But he ignored the taunting riot through concentration of climbing and sheer grit of reaching the Khan.

Another timber reached via another jumping, guts-fluttering push of his legs, another tier ascended. Almost there—

Thunk!

A second arrow bit into the thick wooden frame, spitting splinters, this one striking a hairsbreadth shy from stabbing into his left elbow and pinning his arm to the structure if not for the saving grace of his reaching limb extending his arm out from the arrow's path and up for the next and final crosswise timber just below the flat top's edge. Concentration wavering, he clenched his teeth, jumped and gripped—

—*Thump-THUMP.*

Another skipping blink-shift forward through time, and Banzu jolted, a scream tearing loose, at the flaring pain in his leg. He looked down through a hot prism of tears at the offending arrow not there stolen seconds before now sticking out the back of his punctured right calf, its tip sprouted through his split shinbone. For a cruel moment his network of nervous prickled through shivers of agony while his senses trembled with vertigo, though the shocking puncture itself tightened his muscles, securing his grip lest he fall to his death.

So close. He drew in a few panting breaths, reorienting his consciousness from the dizzying sway, and concentrated up, nothing to do about his injury but accept it. *Almost there, godsdammit.*

Hands gripping the apex platform's western edge, he clung seconds from pulling atop and claiming the precious prize awaiting him thereon. He clenched his teeth against the gnawing pain in his dangling leg and pulled, grunting with strain, while kicking swims of air, pulled himself up and over at last.

Amid static curtains of rain Hannibal Khan stood in full reveal, a glistening muscled effigy of power and promise stripped bare to the waist and suspended in smiting pose, his discharged bolt of lightning spent several blink-shifts previous, his next drawing charge of lightning seconds away and allowing Banzu safe space for moving.

Another arrow stabbed into the support beam over which Banzu hung only seconds previous, pronouncing a shot that would have bitten deep into the middle of his back and brought him down amid the cluster of unfrozen khansmen—after the lethal plummet of three-hundred feet.

He straightened from all fours then slunk back onto his bottom while sliding his right leg forward, grimacing through the throbbing pain of the motion involved, and eyeballed the offending arrow splicing his bleeding calf. He gripped the exposed parts of shaft in both hands and, grunting, snapped off the front half then yanked out the back half and tossed the two bits of broken arrow aside.

The tremendous resurgence of pain welled more hot tears in his eyes. An instant more arrived the soul-tugging drain upon his lifeforce in cruel trade as the numb-tingling sensation of the still-tainted Source's restorative flow of magical potency flushed through the wound and his split shinbone fused through accelerated healing by no will of his own while the hole of his punctured muscle sealed, fibers mending, all in the span of a blink.

"Huh." And for a dumbstruck moment he considered the true ignorance over his lack of competence with and control of the Source.

But the moment fled upon another wave of adrenaline rush, forgotten when he gazed up and locked pained eyes with the menacing glare of the stationary though imposing figure of Hannibal Khan standing before him, the warlord tyrant's right gauntleted hand inert in reaching bid high overhead at the gaping maw of swirl-caught black clouds, his other gauntleted hand outstretched in front of him with palm thrust in pushing manner though with fingers extended in a clawed grip of air and imminent projection of energies.

Pain vanished to memory in an absence of fear and worry and awareness of everything and everyone but for the here and now and nothing else as Banzu fixed his focal glare upon the origin of his harbored woes in life, this robust dealer of death twice his size though half his measure, and to his disgust a handsome man well carved from the marble of bones and well sculpted from the clay of flesh into this . . . this . . .

"Pathetic excuse for a god," he whispered upon a breath of scorn.

A chaotic frenzy of lunatic voices swelled with pressure into a roaring chorus of obscure madness issued from behind the source-block barricades in wave after crashing wave screaming for rabid release—those dead men sought only indiscriminate killing, and they cared nothing for who but how many and how soon—though a single prominent hate-filled request arose above the collage, Jericho's banshee howl dominating the noisy surf and begging for sweet release in due recognition of the Khan through the lucid veil of his nephew's window eyes, climaxing in ecstatic throes of comeuppance edging orgasmic to the shattering thrill of killing the Khan for the second time through another vessel.

Banzu closed his eyes, willing a stillness to his inner turmoil. Another kill only moments away, and the cruel gods be good that they did not slip in and steal this defining moment from either of them—

Thwish!

He jolted tensed, gasping, eyes snapping open, when a sharp breath huffed across the right side of his face, puffing through his hair, so that he winced away from the arrow shooting past his head and the ensuing pain involved, its keen steel tip having split open his ear then slashing a fine red line across his bearded cheek. A touch to the left and that arrow would have bit deep into the base of his skull. A touch to the right and it would have punctured the Khan's face instead of whizzing past it.

For a terrified moment he scorned the khansmen far below. Stray arrows made martyrs of men, and he wished no endless war carried on in brutal homage to their false godking.

I need to prove he's no god deserving worship or this'll never end. You don't kill a king in the dark, you do it in the open where everyone sees. We're surrounded by witnesses. Cut off the head of the snake and the body dies. I take his head and I'll take their faith.

He blinked hard, trying to quell the overcharged surge of Jericho's emotional rampage while the numb-tingling distraction of his split ear and cut cheek healed through the accelerated leaching drain upon his lifeforce in cruel exchange. His divided concentration waged war on two fronts, one of maintaining the source-block barricades despite the undulating pressure of the mutinous Soothsayers slamming their hate-filled wills against it, the other keeping his struggling inner grasp from slipping loose from the still-tainted Source straining to escape his strangler's grip while the Source-locked world fought at catching up.

He drew in a deep nostril breath, gathering his depleted reserves of self, all the while hoping no more arrows sped up from below to stab a lucky landing into vital parts of him or the Khan.

No emotion.

Only action.

Jericho's savage slavering pleas turned anxious lunatic laughter mocking the world and everyone in it, the contagion of his bleeding madness awful to the point that Banzu felt literally dirty inside, poisoned spiritually, the taint of the uncleansed Source leaking putrescent waters of hate through veining fractures of source-block fissures accrued by thousands of defiant pounding fists striving for release, the truth behind Jericho's psychotic ravings a wronged man caught in the ecstatic throes of vengeance seconds before the precious reckoning.

Banzu stood while allowing the fervent essence of his murdered uncle to enjoy the finite seconds of Hannibal Khan's temporal existence through his eyes before their ensuing death stroke. Malice quivered his mouth into a dark smile when he pulled Griever free—and never before did a sword weigh so little and yet so much.

He licked his lips, tasting the faint remains of a dying struggle spiced sweet with inevitability. "Finally—"

—THUMP-THUMP!

Another jostling blink-shift forward through time, and though the Khan's commanding pose changed little within those stolen passing seconds, his expression shifted from conquering confidence to blooming startlement of the armed Soothsayer in front of him and not there to him only a moment before.

As well, above him, another coruscating charge of lightning jagged down through the gaping black maw of clouds though captured inert from saturating its human Khan conductor with electrical smiting power.

Recovering balance from the tower's abrupt jostling sway beneath his feet, Banzu met the angry bloom of startlement in the Khan's cruel eyes while noting the Khan's aiming left arm had started to rise from downward angle to up between them, intent on spending that next rending bolt into Banzu's chest. He flexed his strangler's grasp of Source for all available purchase.

This is it.

While the Source contested release in violent thrashing spasms.

And a thousand raging Soothsayers punished the fracturing source-blocks with their collective fists.

Nothing matters but executing this moment.

He sidestepped left, moving out from the Khan's aiming arm of imminent blasting release.

Pain.

He raised Griever aloft in a double-fisted clutch.

Before pleasure.

He aimed down over the Khan's extended left arm, targeting the muscular forearm where godsforged lanthium gauntlet ended and thick corded brawn began.

"For you," he said of Melora. *And you,* he thought of Jericho.

A rapacious swell of screams and pressure surged behind the fracturing source-blocks, a surmounting riot of corruption beating against the failing barricades.

"For you!" Banzu yelled while swinging Griever down in a precise chopping swing—

—*THUMP-THUMP!!*

* * *

Another world-jostling blink-shift forward through time—and the scintillating brilliance of conjured lightning finished jagging into its human Khan conductor, electrifying the Lord of Storms into a blazing beacon of promising power armored in chaotic webbings of savage crackling capacity.

The hot white-light flash of energies dazzled Banzu's amplified Source-sight with blinding effluence, while the Source escaped his exhausted inner grasp. That last proved a kindness, for at the same time the source-block barricades buckled then broke, shattering into a scatter of irreparable shards to the great overstrain of indomitable pressure, allowing the deluge of corruption roaring forth in furious tides of dominance seeking total possession of Banzu's defenseless vessel.

A jarring spiritual shock, accompanied by the fading chorus of a thousand screaming voices denied their weakened prey, and the once-suspended world round Banzu returned to its perpetual flow of motion in a jolting burst of unrestricted progress.

All of this within the hairsbreadth of his swordstroke.

Shunk!

He stumbled forward, pitching against the tower's abrupt return to motion and yanked by the momentum of his chopping downswing so that he almost tumbled over the platform's southern edge but for Griever's tip stabbing down and biting inches deep into the apex platform's thick wooden planks, its hilt stopping him with its arresting punch in his guts, his elbows fanning. Behind him erupted a terrible scream while he blinked his faulty vision, all popping white stars and blurred hazes of shapes, into something resembling clarity.

He straightened from hunching, yanked Griever free then turned round and staggered through sloshing imbalance, his bare feet sliding through precarious purchase upon the slick planks. And through a dissipating haze of clearing white he watched an amalgamation of stuttering images reforming together into Hannibal Khan upholding the bleeding stump of his severed left arm and gaping at the space of his missing gauntleted appendage in pained shock.

Banzu savored the orgasmic shiver of impending victory with a wry smile in the pelting rain, his defining stroke of hope severing the necessary connection of the two gauntlets while terminating the conjured lightning a fraction before it spent through its Khan conductor and engulfed the tower's top, thus frying him alive.

Hannibal Khan stared awestruck at the spurting blood of his wound, his wide eyes expanding horrified when he transferred that startled gaze to the smiling Soothsayer standing before him in unyielding challenge with offending sword in hand, Griever's immaculate blade dripping crimson tears.

Unable to resist, Banzu winked.

Contemptuous rage overwhelmed stupefied shock. Hannibal Khan lowered his bleeding stump of arm—the disconnected godsforged gauntlet and its detached appendage within having fallen over the platform's edge to disappear somewhere down into the returning chaos of fighting far below—and flung his right hand out while lunging in a blatant attempt at seizing Banzu by the throat.

By reflex, and with ecstatic elation flourishing new energy, Banzu punted the taller Khan square in the crotch, sending the brawny warlord stumbling backwards. The dazed Khan stopped inches shy of falling over the platform's far edge and hunched forward gripping his bruised manhood. He shook his head and blew out his cheeks while wrestling down the urge to collapse to his knees and vomit.

He glanced behind at the edge nipping at his heels and the three-hundred foot plummet past it, then released a guttural yell while bursting forward into another brazen lunge for Banzu's throat to crush it within his powerful lanthium grip.

I am swordslinger. You are nothing.

Banzu twisted away, reversing through the instinctive swordform *Petals Shake the Dew,* while ducking into sidestepping promise against the roaring Khan's charge. He swung Griever roundabout in a calculated arc, spinning while bringing whirring steel up overhead, carving through rain, then down into chopping swing through flesh and bone, cleaving the Khan's extended right arm inches above elbow.

Another agonized scream knifed the air, and the armless Khan staggered past Banzu three steps before his timber-thick legs buckled and he crashed to his knees. He raised his bleeding stubs, staring abject horror at the jets of arterial blood pulsing in mocking squirts to the rhythmic beat of his thundering heart.

Banzu hawked then spat upon the Khan's turned back. In his mind he approach and slit throat from behind with a savage yanking stroke of Griever's keen edge while palming the Khan's upturned forehead and cradling the back of it against his stomach. But he rebuked the assassin's strike for he craved those eyes upon him. He rounded past the kneeling bleeder, stood in front of the false godking and waited seconds for the Khan's aporetic stare to seek him out through the pelting rain and gushing ruby jets of blood between them.

Their gazes locked in eternal instant.

Banzu repaid the Khan's indignant countenance with a smile leaving his eyes untouched in all but righteous reckoning.

Cut off the head and the body dies. "It's over, Khan. And now you die just like the rest of us."

"No!" Hannibal Khan roared, his bleeding stumps wiggling through futile raises of his missing phantom appendages offering no true shields against the impending blow.

As Banzu reared Griever back, measuring true.

Roaring, eyes ablaze, the Khan began erupting into standing. "No—"

Banzu swung, twisting at the hips through full release.

Griever's sideways fanning blur cut through the Khan's thick column of neck—*shunk!*—stifling his protest while removing head from shoulders in one fulfilling death stroke.

Eyelids aflutter above a yawning cave of mouth, the Khan's detached head rolled backwards—and Banzu sidestepped out of the way as the Khan's decapitated body pitched forward, its limp muscled bulk crashing upon the slick platform then sliding then stopping with its upper half hanging over the edge.

Banzu provided the corpse's rump a satisfying kick, spilling it over and down. He stepped to the edge and enjoyed the shrinking sight of the Khan's headless body tumbling through the air, gushing whirling trails of blood from the stumps of its arms and neck.

A deep and booming thunder rolled in final parting as the raging storm overhead dissipated, the strength of its tumultuous energies snuffed along with its conjurer's lifespark. The pelting rain softened to a drizzle then a dying mist while black churns and swirls of clouds separated and thinned through the disillusion of false night.

Banzu inhaled a haggard breath. He raked the fingers of his free hand back through his wet tangles. He struggled to maintain his feet against the powerful gravity of exhaustion's pull threatening to sink him to his knees.

For the stretch of a dozen strong heartbeats he stared defiance down over those below scrambling round their felled Lord of Storms' corpse punching the earth in a crater of sluicing mud and bodies. The pregnant pause of incredulity overtook the fighting round the mutilated Khan, spreading outward so that Bloodcloaks and worship-followers and the few remaining fistians within the mix of stunned observers ceased their brutal activities and stared up in dubious wonder at Banzu standing victorious on high above them all.

Truth, as always, proved self-evident. A growing hush of inactivity overwhelmed those crowded round the tower's base as word of the Khan's impossible demise at the hands of the Soothsayer spread out across the battle plains in ripples of revelation.

It's over. Finished. I did it. Banzu turned away with the plan of sitting down and only that. But something caught his eye. *No, not finished just yet.*

He walked to and picked up the Khan's head so close to rolling over the platform's opposite edge, gripping it by the hair. He thrust the head skyward as symbol, the building of an urgent declaration roused within the depths of him seeking release. Mustering dwindled reserves of strength, he drew in an empowering breath while perching the edge, those below bearing witness to the definitive truth of his victory over their fallen godking and their stolen faith.

"Look to me!" he yelled, his words a vehement command elevated above the calming winds of the receding storm as evermore of the stunned khansmen and fistian survivors gathering round the tower's base gazed up at him by the passing moment. He shook the head by its hair and yelled stronger still, "Look to me!"

His voice a booming shout riding outward upon the settling winds, he knew most of the hushed fighters below heard his strong command in a delivery softened by distance, but the sight of the Khan's decapitated head dangling by the hair in his fisted grip earned him true power over them.

"Hannibal Khan is dead! Your godking is no more! This war . . . *is over!*"

He whipped his arm back then threw the Khan's head out, punctuating its release with a wordless shout born from the grieving depths of him.

He staggered back in counterbalance to avoid pitching into the lethal plummet sucking at him. Exhaustion gripped him by the spine and yanked, sinking him to his knees. His tired body craved full collapse if not for the exuberance of victory maintaining him upright though teetering with the lazy sways of the mobile tower continuing its slow westward advance.

Griever's hilt released from his loosening grip in a sticky peel, his fingers too spent to care, his mind too dizzy to wonder beyond the moment, his body too fatigued for anything more than a proud smile to the quietude pervading his mind in an absence of voices.

Weariness hunched his shoulders. His hung head lolled on rubbery neck. He sagged back bottom atop heels, bones leaden, watery muscles drained of all reserves, too overworked for anything save breathing. He thought of his uncle, thought too of Melora, in raptures of unvoiced joy.

Carved, hollowed, somehow he raised his trembling hands and covered his face.

And there he wept, weeping all that mattered.

Because revenge, no matter how well repaid, soothed none of the pain involved.

CHAPTER FORTY-TWO

A parting thunder rolled throughout the clearing sky, diminishing across the war-torn plains, pronouncing definitive end to the week-long Khan-wrought storm.

Banzu lowered his hands from over his face, ignoring the dirty trails of tears smearing his cheeks, and craned his head. He appraised the beautiful periwinkle ocean above and the sun in shining apex. The rain ceased, leaving him wet with filth and blood, what little darkness hiding within the nooks and crannies of scattering clouds, these pulled pieces of lightening cotton, burned away by the sun's golden radiance achieving bright prominence over the dispersing gloom.

A cool, sharp breeze blew over him at such height atop the slain Khan's mobile tower lurching westward by the tethered beasts of burden far below and still seeking Fist through the diminishing action flourishing round it.

Corpses mashed into the churn of sodden earth beneath the wooly beasts' relentless tread, or crushed then forgotten under the tonnage of wide roller wheels spiked for clawing purchase, the towering structure a ship forged of lashed timbers and bits of shielding steel bolted at its bottom plowing through the mud and muck and bodies of its waters, those alive parting round its steady westward bid then rejoining in upward stares while the tower sought slow passage through the sea of stunned combatants.

Banzu closed his eyes and basked in the unobstructed sunshine warming his upturned face, the silence up here a song unto itself though disrupted by the distant clamor and crash of battle pervading the edge of his hearing from those too far and ignorant of the Lord of Storms' demise.

He's dead. The act of accepting the fact proved akin to swiping his hand through the gauzy mystery of a spider's delicate web—elusive beyond its clinging feel despite the action involved. And yet . . . and yet. *He's really dead.*

He opened his eyes and gazed out over the miles of combatants stretching between him and the walled city of Fist, relaxing a bit to the visual confirmation of inaction stealing outward from the tower beacon in influential ripples of surrender, though these dissipated where beyond continued death and dying, the plains too vast, the khansmen too numerous, Hannibal Khan's death only a droplet of effect in an ocean of war.

He drew in deep and expelled a withering sigh. *It's not over till it's over.*

Without looking he reclaimed Griever's leather-wound hilt in his left hand, upended the sword through tired lift then thrust its tip into the platform and used the sword as a cane aiding his standing on trembling legs. Justice delivered, he needed to claim the true prize of his victory, the slain Khan's godsforged lanthium gauntlets of power, before a foolhardy khansman collected then donned them in terrible promise of more.

More important considerations than personal stakes reigned here, a truth realized only after his revenging bid carried him across the battle plains in a savage charge of khansmen carnage while half-possessed by the parasitic Essence of Simus Junes.

My source-block barricades are gone, shattered. I seize the Source again and all of me is lost. That part of me is finished until I find the Godstone.

And he heard it now, felt it strong and clear, the influential umbilical prominence of the Godstone's thrumming tug upon the inner parts of him, the faint though urgent pattering of a second heartbeat, soft yet sure, incessant. He could point out its fallen location to the specific inch, could spin round with eyes closed and pinpoint the archaic idol of the gods' Great Game . . . and upon the thought arose a deep and loathing disgust at having been played, at being played still, so that he hawked and spat as if upon the conniving gods themselves.

How much longer must we suffer their cruel manipulations we call life?

He killed Enosh before coming here, the Builder's mortal avatar all that remained of the gods' direct influence upon the One Land of Pangea . . . but no, Banzu reflected while gazing westward across the Azure Plains, beyond the city of Fist to nowhere in particular yet at any and everywhere in pensive stare. Somewhere out there still roamed the mortal avatar of Locha the trickster god of many faces, races, sexes. Would he, or she, interfere?

I don't care. I'll end your Great Game once I destroy your Godstone.

Enosh said he would 'just know' the moment he touched the Godstone, the elusive secret of its destruction removed from the forger and locked inside the vessel itself.

But at least with the fractured Source made whole again Banzu possessed the intrinsic ability to find the godsdamned thing and—

"Oh no." He startled tensed through spiking dread of epiphany, the awakening of the Godstone's thrumming sense of presence in himself also waking within the necromaster Dethkore, Metrapheous Theaucard and Simus Junes the chosen two above all human players in the gods' Great Game of power. *Friggin hell, I completely forgot.*

He knew nothing of Dethkore's whereabouts, only the necromaster's inexplicable absence among the Khan's vast legion of Bloodcloaks and worship-followers. *Otherwise I'd be surrounded in a sea of unliving and—*

The mighty tower pitched and jostled, its lashed timbers groaning through creaking sways, over a mound of corpses. Banzu tottered through sloshing imbalance, his bare feet sliding across the slick wood planks of the apex platform awash in rain and Khan's blood, Griever his clutched anchor, jarring him out from rumination.

He yanked Griever free after the tower settled into its lazy predetermined path, approached the platform's western edge, then stabbed Griever's tip again into the thick wooden planks for leaning support, and gazed down over all those milling round the tower's base staring up at him. Thousands of khansmen speckled with fistians spreading berth for the slow passage of the tusked beasts of burden viewing the stunned onlookers as no more than obstacles needing divided or crushed from their way.

Screams erupted below, carried through distance in declarations of pain, as the cruel revelation of war's end punctuated by Hannibal Khan's death overwhelmed devout khansmen worship-followers bereft of morale who ended their lives in mourning droves by throwing aside their weapons and kneeling in sacrificial surrender, palsied hands clasped in prayer and tears streaming their cheeks, in front of the tromping feet of the wooly beasts or the crushing spiked wheels of the determined tower.

The self-sacrifices issued signal to arms through the watching Bloodcloaks rebuking suicide with stubborn preference of a soldier's good death earned through impalements of enemy steel. Instigated pockets of fighting broke out, flourishing among khansmen rallying in outraging swells over their godking's demise, while more teleported fistian knots appeared here and there to deliver slaughter in spreading pools of killing space.

Banzu raked a hand back through his hair, the other settled atop Griever's pommel, and blew out his cheeks. *The killing never ends, only . . . pauses.*

Though moments more and to his relieving surprise the local rallies quelled, khansmen surrendering to fistians no longer killing but disarming the enemy too stunned or tired or broken of spirit to continue the fight while the din of battle softened below, spent soon after starting. Onlookers of both sides gazed up at Banzu standing on high in victorious loom.

A mass hush befell those below when Hannibal Khan's decapitated corpse crushed into the muck beneath the churn of a spiked wheel. Moments more and the towering structure ceased its westward movement, jerking stopped in a groan of lashed timbers protesting momentum, the whole of it lurching forward a space then rebounding stiff, the wooly beasts of burden tethered at its base deciding they had pulled long enough.

Banzu maintained strong grip of Griever's anchoring hilt, swaying and sliding then stilling with the arresting tower.

An elevation of cheers arose from the growing knots of fistian soldiers, hardened survivors these, as well the newly teleported learning of the Lord of Storms' demise moments after their aizakai-induced arrivals across the war-torn plains among khansmen gazing round in dejected stares, leaderless warriors and religious zealots alike collapsing in weeping heaps or standing in disgruntled surrender, bloodied weapons slipping loose from demoralized hands, the misplaced faith in their slain godking shattered irreparable.

Banzu surveyed the rest of the Azure Plains through squinting grimace, beyond the masses surrounding the tower at where the fighting continued unabated, the war here terminated though the rest of it out there a persistent fever of death and dying. Hundreds of thousands decimated to tens of thousands requiring time for word of the Khan's death to spread its panacea throughout his refusing army and drain their fighting fervor with truth burning misplaced faith from devout minds while sapping courage and determination.

Unless another khansman secured then donned the godsforged lanthium gauntlets of power, rekindling the killing in reigniting spark.

That's all I need. Another power-hungry fool throwing lightning. I need the Godstone to cleanse the Source before I can use it again, but I have to find the gauntlets before—

An eruption of voices below clipped his soliloquy short, a rush of indignant outrage as arose through the tower a terrible shiver of trembling timbers vibrating up so that Banzu sank into a half squat while gripping Griever's hilt with both hands to avoid losing balance and slide then plummet over the slick platform.

He peeked down at the growing assemblage of khansmen, thousands of rallying disbelievers and deniers charging in from the outer fighting, attacking fistians in overwhelming swarms as well their surrendering fellows in startlements of violence, more of them spilling forth in shouting rushes, hacking and chopping at the structure's base when not stabbing the mammoth beasts thrashing their thick leather tethers while attempting to tear loose for rampage through the flood of khansmen laboring to deliver the tower and Banzu atop it down in ruins.

The outnumbered knots of fistians provided brief resistance to the inward flood spending round and through them, though a great many of the enemy took their leave instead of joining their obstinate fellows, fighting through the swells of khansmen and away from the tower to wherever their broken spirits carried them now that their beheaded godking lay crushed and their purposes here reduced through spoiled faith.

Gripping Griever for balancing support, Banzu attempted standing. But the groaning tower teetered and swayed, a pliable reed amid the rush of rising winds, so that he lowered into another half squat, bare wet feet sliding, then sank to one knee as the structure rocked back and forth through increasing sways of accelerating momentum. While those below continued their hacking work upon its base even as the agitated mammoths trumpeted and tore loose from their harness rigs then plowed through the growing frenzy, their long tusks gathering impalements of bodies in their bolting charges.

Banzu stole panicked glances everywhere, with plunging dread his only safe escape that of Power-leaping free in lieu of riding atop the tower's inevitable collapse and crushed within its crashing tonnage.

Friggin hell! It's always something. "Godsdammit."

Slipping and sliding through tilting angles swishing him back and forth, he strained at maintaining hold of Griever's anchoring hilt while flexing inward through exhausted tension for the Power—and startled, hissing while recoiling his inner grasp, as if having clutched fire.

"Oh gods!"

The scalding touch of pure corruption rebuked him with a thousand bloodlusting Soothsayers no longer imprisoned behind the shattered source-block barricades but free and attempting to reach into him through the Power. Seeking to claim him same as they had through the still-tainted Source. And would do so with his every attempt at seizing the Power thereafter.

The ruthless truth of consequence ravaged him with anguish.

* * *

Panic raced the currents of Banzu's pounding heart while he endured the increasing, nauseating sways of the creaking tower moments from toppling. The Power . . . he needed the Power. But the corrupted Source bled into it, infecting it, making of it a poison.

Three-hundred feet below, the clangor and clamor of fighting renewed while teleported knots of fistians clashed with the unyielding khansmen hacking and chopping at the tower's weakening base for their

Soothsayer prize atop it.

Thick timbers groaning, snapping, the moaning protests of metal shields bolted to parts of its base bending, and the rocking tower began its slow, tilting fall eastward.

Banzu scrambled into action upon the slick planks. Griever abandoned, he dove past his staked sword onto his belly and clutched the platform's western rising edge as the tower swayed its final tilt too far for returning pitch into the gradual topple of a gargantuan tree.

Fingers hooked in straining pain, his mind screamed for anything in the way of help. The world twisted sideways with a majestic lack of speed, balance shifting toward imminent doom. Panic overwhelming, he seized the barest flicker of the Power-corrupted, resisted recoiling from the fiery poison therein latching upon his inner grasp with burning claws sinking purchase inches deep into inner parts of him.

Dangling, he tucked his knees to his chest and planted the bottoms of his feet upon wet planks. He push-leaped away from the square platform in a Power-corrupted burst of extending legs and rigid fingers slipping free from wood, the tower sideways in its crashing fall.

His screaming echo of voice joined the thousand roars ripping through his roiling mindscape. He tried releasing the Power-corrupted mid plummet, but the savage snare of its refusing animus yanked him back in while he soared backwards through the air in a mad tumble of flailing limbs and whipping hair . . . the ground rising up to meet him as psychotic laughter enfolded his senses, swallowing the outside world in a torture of raking claws scarring his soul, dragging him into the festering blaze of bloodlust corruption seconds from consuming him, devouring him, possessing him.

A vacuum of silence intruded, the Power tearing loose, when his world blackened with pain, punctuated by an incredible *thoom!* possessing the quake of thunder and rife with screams.

All sense of time expanded into the dark oblivion of numb awareness.

Distanced from his nest of agony, he lay pondering the fatal fall, sure of death yet surprised to think it. His soul throbbed angry scars of hurt, shredded from the Power-corrupted torn from his inner grasp during punching impact, pain his only saving grace against succumbing to the diluvial tide of madness a hairsbreadth from possessing him.

Well past his feet the tower struck the ground, crushing thousands beneath its crashing tonnage, killing or maiming hundreds more in an explosion of splintered spears and sharp twists of metal blasting outward in all directions from its striking point, the concussive impact blowing men from feet in backwards tumbles upon gale-force winds, the few survivors trapped within the wreckage broken twists of humanity longing for quicker deaths.

Silence persisted in thousands of lungs capturing gasps of air and holding it taut in numbed shock. Then sounded moans and screams in a rising dirge of agony and regret.

A death-groan arose amidst the chaos, so close to Banzu's ear he wondered if it wasn't his own pitiful voice escaping. Until others, round and beneath him, joined in the gothic song of sufferers. Delirious with the joy at surviving such a tremendous fall, it took a moment for the true pain of his injuries to surface through his rousing awareness of self.

Beside and partways beneath him sounded the gurgling rasp of a dying khansman, blood pouring ribbons from the man's throat round a long splinter of wood punctured through his neck. Banzu glimpsed this out of his left periphery, his head cradled in the wreckage of bodies and his neck too sore for twisting, and knew but for the saving grace of mere inches that gurgling rasp would have been his instead.

Perhaps a few minutes struggled past, perhaps more—time existed as a confusing and elusive concept, something to be worked out later when ironically he had the time for doing so—before he flexed parts of himself in wincing strain, wiggles of toes and twitches of fingers, every inch of his watery muscles round broken bones producing blazes of ache. He sat up groaning, atop a huge mound of bodies—corpses, mostly, the few still alive beneath eliciting rasping moans—which had broken his fall, and his body, more than softened it. Surrendering to the nauseating vertigo whirl, he lay back and allowed the world to continue without him.

Gods . . . it hurts . . . so bad . . . I can't . . .

Consciousness faded in swirls of black . . . then returned in whirls of white when hands grabbed him in blooms of pain, pulled him free from the wreckage of crushed bodies in startlements of torture, carried him in jouncing flares of agony, then settled him down and forced him into sitting up again, every joint grinding, lids aflutter, vision blurry though clearing to detail, his mouth the taste of blood, the pressure of his protests chambered too deep in his lungs for voicing.

A woman's round face watched back at him through violet pools of cunning, inviting blooms of recognition in Banzu's stuttering consciousness framing a familiar name upon his lips that never sounded.

Spellbinder Shandra withdrew a space while eager others swarmed into her absence. She measured the wreck of Banzu from afar with a curious light in her discriminating stare and a strange half-smile tweaking her mouth at one corner plumping her chubby cheek. Her long brown hair nested strewn in frayed corkscrews of tangled roots instead of the banded ponytail he remembered, and a rather large flap of skin hung down from the left side of her injured scalp which covered half her ear, her neck and shoulder and left arm painted in blood. Spellbinder blood, the reason why she stood so far removed while the others inspected the plethora of cuts and lacerations and juts of splintered bones covering Banzu from head to heel best avoided from leaking her poisonous paralyzing blood into.

"Careful," Shandra said to the others gathered round him, two at his sides holding him sitting while several touched and poked at the tender bleeding parts of him. "Don't tear him apart now after all he's survived."

Failing speech, Banzu produced a pitiful groan—that clipped short when an arm from behind coiled round his neck and tightened, holding him to place though not so restrictive as to shut his breathing.

Shandra's half-smile fled into a tight cut of pressed lips when her meaty hands stole up behind her, gripping dachra handles in preemptive pull of her fangs. "Your eyes, Soothsayer."

Banzu struggled through a rapid series of blinks, fighting his fluttering lids to stay open while he focused on the brawny Spellbinder who approached then appraised him with closer scrutiny. She leaned forward at the hips, inches between their noses, stared overlong into the depths of his hazels, then nodded and straightened, whispered, "Thank gods for small miracles."

For a lengthy stretch no one spoke, nor did the coil of corded muscle remove from round Banzu's neck. He gasped and groaned when strong pairs of hands gripped parts of him and squeezed, holding him still.

"Do it," Shandra said, gesturing with her head while pointing at Banzu. She removed farther back and crossed her beefy arms. "Do it now."

Oh gods they're going to kill me . . . Banzu's only thought, as No and Wait died upon his lips in a withering exhale.

A short stick of a woman with a pinched face and brilliant blue eyes Banzu recognized no more than an Academy aizakai by her flowing blue robes and fistian company approached in front of him, a suspicious fear dominating her young eyes above a melancholy smile.

"Sacrifice is weighed by the pain of what is surrendered," she said, this more to herself though loud enough for Banzu to hear.

"Wha . . ." came his response.

The woman drew in a long nostril breath filling her taller, more resolute. "I accept this burden for the sake of Fist." She kissed her fingertips then touched at her shoulders then her forehead then kissed her fingertips again. "May Ahzra'il embrace me in her loving light."

She squatted and palmed her chest over her heart with her left hand while palming Banzu's in turn with her right, her touch warm, inviting. Eyes closed, her lips moved through some manner of silent incantation.

Her blonde hair arose in static charge. A brilliant flash of sparkling blue energies flared between their touching flesh in a spasm of sorcery.

The aizakai woman tensed through a piercing scream.

As Banzu gasped, plunged into the icy depths of the river of cold energy flushing into him and pouring through his swelling network of veins in hot shatters of ice, his head whipping back, eyes popping wide then snapping tight, every muscle taut and tingling. Before his lids closed he caught glimpse of the palming woman mimicking same response in her squat as the healing exhilaration of her lifeforce punched into then flooded through him, fiery icicles stabbing into knitting bones and mending flesh, not so much soothing his aches as removing them, stealing them, absorbing them.

An exchange of agony lasting seconds stretched eternal through fathoms of pain.

His handlers freeing their grips, Banzu crashed backwards to the ground, magical connection severed, his spasms decreasing into shivers, his watery muscles quivering round vibrating bones. He opened his eyes, blinking refocus, and startled into sitting up, head whipping forward then back, and gasped at sight of the little aizakai woman erupting into standing, convulsing, her grimacing face and neck and hands covered in bleeding lacerations, while a profusion of wrinkles crawled across her skin aging through decades in seconds, thinning strands of her lengthening hair falling loose while fading white.

She collapse backwards upon legs bending wrongways through sickening snaps of bones, sharp white juts protruding from bursting red seams of thigh or shin, falling into the awaiting arms of the fistian soldier behind her who caught her twisted body by the pits then lowered her to ground where she lay unmoving but for the twitching of her broken limbs, patches of her blue robes dark with blooms of blood.

Banzu gawked at her. *She . . . oh gods, she absorbed my injures.* "No." The word escaped him in shameful whisper, pursued by an unvoiced apology dying with an audible swallow of guilt.

He glanced round at the encircling guard of robed aizakai and the several hundred armed and armored fistian soldiers, half their numbers watching him while their others stood guard facing out in protective cordon.

"You did it," Shandra said, approaching him again through the chattering huddle with dividing hands parting human curtains. She offered her hand, and when he took it she pulled him into standing then punched his shoulder, twisting him, then gripped both his shoulders, strong hands squeezing, and shook him before slapping release. "You godsdamned did it!"

Banzu forced a smile leaving his eyes untouched. He gazed at Shandra in dull wonder, then gestured with a wincing nod at his malformed savior lying on the ground.

"Is she . . ." *Going to die?* But he already knew the answer, and trailed away unfinished to the obvious truth.

Shandra's smile vanished into a tight press of lips. She half turned, considered the dying aizakai. "Arlou's served her duty well," she said, turning back. "As have you."

"Arlou," Banzu whispered, cringing. "Oh gods." He stepped toward her, to thank her and apologize. "Arlou, I'm so—"

"No," Shandra said, short and sharp, stopping him by palming his chest. "Don't. There's nothing we can do for her now but the mercy of a quick death."

She turned and gestured at the soldier kneeling past Arlou's head, who had caught then lowered her down to ground. He nodded and removed the knife sheathed at his hip to slit Arlou's throat.

But she thrashed broken arms and legs while rasping in spasms, her eyes and mouth opening wide, back arching, rigid fingers clawing the mud at her sides . . . then she settled and stilled, dead before the knife could bleed the paltry remainder of life from her throat.

The fistian soldier returned his knife to sheath. He bowed his head while touching at his shoulders then forehead, whispering prayer.

All those round Banzu bowed their heads while performing the same ritual. He mimed the unfamiliar gesture.

Shandra lowered to a knee beside Banzu's dead savior, joining in whispered prayer while closing Arlou's eyelids with the slide of two fingertips. She stood and fetched a deep breath, huffed it out. Spun facing Banzu.

"We all have sacrifices to make," she said, voice a low mercy, violet eyes tightening scrutiny upon him. "Some of us more than others."

Banzu opened his mouth, closed it.

All resolute Spellbinder again, Shandra glanced round and shouted, "Spread out! We have the Soothsayer. Now let's find those godsdamned gauntlets so we can leave this hell and—"

But there she clipped short and turned when eager boots stamping splashes of mud announced a haggard fistian soldier of older years slowing his approaching rush beside her. He dropped to his knees before Banzu and bowed his helmed head while presenting Griever lying across his upturned palms in offering.

"I've recovered your blade, Soothsavior," the elder soldier said, gazing up, a proud smile adding lost youth to his wizened visage.

"Sooth . . . savior?" But before Banzu could thank the man or reach for his sword, those gathered round him not standing in encircling guard facing out lowered to one knee in the mud and bowed their heads in praise. Even Shandra granted him acknowledgement with a slight bow of head while dipping though her knee but grazed the ground before she straightened and scanned round, the violet scold of her eyes questing for spoils of war.

She found it quick, walking away to where a red-robed and red-skinned mage, Jighanese and with a dark tattoo track of tears running his left cheek from the outside corner of his eye, handed her an oversized clump of mud. She returned with the head of Hannibal Khan, her thick fingers curled within its dirty strands of hair. Smiling, she shook the head, slinging loose bits of mud, then raised it to her face and kissed its dead lips in smirking mockery before raising it out while those round her took turns spitting at it. She beckoned a younger soldier closer who held forth a leather bag, his skin Dreshian blue and the outside corners of his mouth framing little white tusks the size of pinkie fingers protruding up while squaring the cut of his jaw. Shandra spat on the dead Khan's face then slipped the head inside, and the soldier tightened the leather bag's drawstrings closed, tucked the burden up beneath an arm.

"Go," Shandra ordered of the tusk-jawed man. "Make haste to the Head Mistress. We'll be along shortly." She whipped one beefy arm out, pointing west. "Go!"

"Yes, Mistress." The soldier pounded mailed fist to dented breastplate in salute, turned and ran to the nearest horse. He climbed atop the armored warbeast then rode away westward, galloping at full career while shouting in foreign tongue.

Inside a retinue of armored cavalry a hundred strong, lancers these, surrounding the herald of the Khan's demise in protective charge to see him through the masses of khansmen.

Banzu harbored serious doubts those men would achieved across the clogged plains, but he whispered them hopeful godspeed regardless and turned away before any khansmen confirmed his doubts. He stole a glance at the bent twist of Arlou's aged corpse lying the mud. *I'm no savior.*

The soldier kneeling in front of him issued the deliberate clearing of his throat, drawing Banzu's attentions back so that he accepted Griever into his thankful grip, the killer's steel leaden with sorrow. He made to stab Griever's immaculate blade home at his left hipwing then paused, his purpose here unfinished.

He'd slain the Khan, but the Azure Plains maintained the presence of thousands of defeated Bloodcloaks and worship-followers, with thousands more rallying against the loss of their slain godking, and tens of thousands still contesting war while unaware of their leader's demise.

No, the killing is far from over. We're still right in the thick of it all. We have to find the gauntlets. One of them at least. I can't leave knowing another Khan might rise in my absence. He gazed round with a roving eye, a sickness building in his twisting guts. *Gods, where to even begin in all this mess.*

Hannibal Khan's mobile tower had collapsed, a tipsy dancer its self-destructive ballet smashing thousands beneath its toppling demolition while creating a bow-wave of mud and bodies and shrapnel blasted outwards in all directions of its destructive landing, thus clearing the immediate area of all threats for the space of a mile radius, Banzu and Shandra and their close fistian guards and mages standing at the wreckage's epicenter.

Outside the perimeter of the new clearing, dejected khansmen took their leave by the score, fighting through the mix in huddled groups for safer exit while yelling of their godking's demise and fending off scorned warriors seeking bloody vengeance for their fallen godking. Khansmen killing khansmen. The enemy, ironically, holding back the enemy.

More knots of fistian soldiers teleported in from across the battle plains, these appearing in bright sunbursts of magelight then charging forth seeking out unyielding khansmen wishing further fight while others threw their weapons aside in surrender, too numerous for capture and so allowed to leave away.

Taking prisoners of war within the chaos proved no viable option considering the paltry fistian reinforcements to the greater numbers of khansmen still plaguing the plains, hundreds of fistian blacks and blues amid surrounding thousands of Bloodcloak reds and golds. Pronounced by the ended storm and the crashing tower, word of the Khan's death spread in wildfire, though the war continued punishing the killing fields for miles, mud saturated in blood.

Banzu sighed while reflecting upon his armored fistian cavalry's suicidal spearhead charging across the plains. *A thousand brave men and women, dead, just to see me through the chaos. I cut the head from the snake, but the body is slow in dying. It writhes and writhes, refusing the inevitable.* He surmised hours if not days before the war finished its incredible tolling of lives, and he wanted no more part of it.

He glanced at Griever, grimacing disgust at the instrument of death and all the burdens its ease of killing afforded him. He wrestled down the urge to relieve its hilt from his grip and abandon it to the mud.

No. I need you still. But I've had my fill of killing, several lifetimes over.

He glanced west, hoping the cruel gods spared him no more killing on the way out instead of delivering the same heaps and droves of slaughter on his way in.

Maybe a teleporter could . . . no. If one were here they would have teleported away that soldier carrying the Khan's head.

He scanned round then settled his gaze on Shandra watching him, attempting to read his thoughts through his eyes. He wondered how she managed to accomplish the same bold advance across the battle plains . . . but for that hard scold of cold murder and ruthless aggression alight in her unyielding stare speaking volumes of unquestionable capability and fathoms of killing promises unspent. *I see you now.* A true Spellbinder warrior enduring a lifetime of rigorous training her dachra fangs while awaiting the last Soothsayer's return then denied their expected Pairing.

Gods, she must hate my guts.

And yet . . . and yet, Shandra grinned and winked before turning away.

Banzu flinched. *Gods, no, she's actually enjoying this.*

"Secure the perimeter!" she shouted while throwing a fist overhead then swirling it round-about, gesturing a circle in the air. "I want those gauntlets found. Or I'll skewer every last one of your boney asses. Go!"

Those round them not maintaining the protective cordon, soldiers and mages alike, dispersed in turning bursts of hunting movement.

Banzu sheathed Griever to his left hipwing and—

Shandra rounded on him, planted fists to hips. "Well?"

"Well what?" he asked.

She glanced at Arlou's corpse, scowling. "You've got eyes. Use them." She stepped to and gripped him by the shoulders, her strong hands crimping vises earning Banzu's wince. "Or I'll take your balls to the Head Mistress and tell her the only thing left of you is your hairy purse." She spun him round and shoved, kicking him on the rump. "Go!"

Stumbling to balance, and liking his balls right where they are, Banzu joined the others in searching through the tremendous wreckage of timbers and bodies for the Khan's godsforged lanthium gauntlets of power.

* * *

"Finally," Banzu whispered on panting breath after hefting aside another heavy piece of splintered timber—made all the heavier by the charred and dented shield-plate of thick protective steel bolted to it—revealing one godsforged lanthium gauntlet lying atop the chest of a khansman corpse, a buried treasure at last unearthed. The left and first one found of the necessary pair.

He snatched the gauntlet up, turned it over and tried shaking loose the Khan's muscled girth of hand and partial forearm contained within it to no avail, then tried gripping the forearm stub and pulling the blockage free. But his hand slipped the slick flesh, and Griever's cut had severed the forearm in a clean stroke so that he probed his fish-hooking fingers into meat and, grunting, worked flesh and bone from lanthium with a grueling tug. He tossed the appendage aside and shook loose the torn strips of skin within the gauntlet while flinging bits of gore from his fingers.

He peered inside the gauntlet's empty hollow at hundreds of tiny fine metallic thorns curiously shrinking, disappearing within the gauntlet's interior, evincing their nutrient pricks into the wearer's tissue while bonding them with permanence. He shirked off his disgust, thrust the gauntlet overhead and yelled, "I found one!"

Shouting arose behind him, several voices spread by space though joined in declaration. "Thank the gods!"

No. Don't thank them. Blame them.

He dug through more wreckage for a time, hoping the second gauntlet lay not far from the first. Minutes passed . . . then he turned round to more shouts firing behind, at Shandra not holding up the other lanthium gauntlet but shoving other fistian searchers out from her way while walking east through increasing speed.

What in friggin hell is she doing? For the moment Banzu deliberated if Shandra decided to throw herself into the fray of the Khan's fragmentizing army stewing beyond their guarded perimeter, seeking further bloodshed.

He stood half the way up the massive pile of wreckage, but the height afforded him nothing past Shandra so that he climbed the rest of the way up for better vantage and unobstructed view. Shielding his eyes from the bright sun, the gauntlet tucked under his other's folded wing, he squinted and captured what Shandra strove toward—or, rather, who.

A mile distant from his staring perch and half that beyond the fistian perimeter cordon of guards, stood a small figure outlined in a hazy dark framing to his normal, un-Powered sight. He tightened his focal squint upon the frightened girl wearing soiled and bloody rags. A little girl lost and wandering among the dying chaos.

"What in friggin hell . . ."

Behind the little girl played pale pockets of fighting shapes Banzu couldn't quite make out but for blurs of figures tangled in struggles of movement. The perplexing sight of the girl struck a mournful yet eerie discord in him. However the poor child managed survival thus far, she looked a distraught wanderer seeking safety on a field of brutal death.

Shandra's trying to save her before a khansman cuts her down. But what the frig is she even doing here?

He turned to scramble down from the pile of wreckage, to pass the found gauntlet into the hands of the closest fistian soldier or searcher, to pull Griever and sprint in Shandra's wake, to defend her while ensuring the child's safety.

No. Instead he turned back, staying his place. *I'll never make it in time.* He decided on another test of the Power-corrupted, even as several of the fistian cordon broke position and pursued after Shandra sprinting for the child.

I need to know if it's completely lost to me until I find the Godstone. The Source, yes, but the Power . . . maybe if I keep it brief. Just a flicker. A drop of its poison instead of the full swallow.

He captured a bracing breath deep in his lungs, held it overlong and seized the barest spark of Power.

And gasped, reeling, balance sloshing, skin flushing hot, mind flaring in crimson effluence, when the scalding fury of raking claws dug into him, punctuated by a thousand keening voices raging in rapacious demand for his surrender in a screaming deluge of tidal forces warring with each other while requesting consumption of their imprisoning vessel, the shared collective of the avalanching Power-corrupted seeking to crush the shreds of his soul then smother the flaming pieces beneath its crashing presence of possession so that he recoiled his reaching inner grasp a hairsbreadth from impossible escape.

He regained refocus through a rapid series of blinks while steadying the whirl of his eyes. Chest hitching through short pants of breaths, he tottered and swayed, beads of sweat dappling his brow.

But the narrow escape from his risky venture afforded him true glimpse through the sensory-enhancing Power-corrupted heightening his keener vision beyond the running void-aura blur of Shandra, a flash of vivid detail intricate as coral of the disheveled little girl's frightened mask breaking into a wide grin on her pale blood-smeared face, patches of her skin scaly and green. But more so her striking inhuman eyes, wicked yellow globes split by black vertical slits of menace.

A serpent's eyes . . . in a human child?

Paralyzing dread seeped heaviness into his bones while memories born long ago and not of his own making bubbled and surfaced with warning from the depths of his mind. *I've seen those eyes before, me but not me, hundreds of years ago and through another's stolen vantage.* He could not place them and yet could not deny the cryptic alarm they elicited.

This is wrong. She is wrong.

He opened his mouth to shout after Shandra and warn her back, his body craving movement though he remained to place in captured stare, the distance between them impossible to achieve before she reached her mark.

Fevered sprint diminishing, Shandra slowed then stopped twenty feet before the smiling girl, and stood for an awkward space, hands flexing grips of air then rising behind her, gripping dachra handles, then lowering empty. She spun round and away, running while yelling something Banzu heard nothing of from his good distance but for the fear edging her voice, her round face a blooming mask of terror.

But too late.

Out from the motions of fighting shapes behind the little girl sprang up five huge and hairy beasts, two of them leaping over her head and casting great shadows while the other three sped past her sides in snarling ferocity, glistening ropes of saliva whipping from their fanged and gaping maws, their long black claws ripping up dirt and flinging gobs of mud as more abominations joined them into loping out from the mass of khansmen fighting for their lives behind the girl, the hairy beasts snarling charges of muscle and fur, of claw and fang.

"No." The word escaped Banzu's hung mouth in barest whisper, while goosebumps pebbled his arms and up his spine. "No."

As the first two of the loping creatures covered the distance between themselves and Shandra in a nightmare of seconds. And just like that they tore her off her kicking feet, snarling and howling, lunging in upon her backside with frightening quickness.

Though Shandra pulled her dachras at the last and twisted mid tumble, slicing her steely fangs through ripples of furred muscle, stabbing into the frenzy of slavering saw-toothed jaws even as the godsforsaken creatures snapped their gleaming pink-stained fangs into her whipping arms and kicking legs, thrashing their dark-furred heads while their long razor claws worked at ripping and tearing parts of her flesh in the moment before their collective bodies struck the ground rolling.

The sheer quickness of their rending violence proved mesmerizing.

A shout died in Banzu's throat, his breath stolen by the grisly scene.

"Unholy gods!" a closer fistian mage yelled, pointing at the pitiless manbeasts bestowing slaughter upon a screaming Shandra torn to bloody shreds of fragile humanity in the cruel course of seconds. "Lycanthropes!"

Banzu flinched a brutal start, jolting to the voice from his staring stupor. He scrambled down from atop the piled wreckage. Elbowed through the mix of gasping and gawking fistians gathered there. Shoved the found gauntlet into the hands of another then broke into fevered sprint toward the sickening sight of Shandra still clinging to life and not just suffering claws and fangs but eaten alive by the ambushing lycanthrope beasts the sinister mixture of wolf and man.

But he achieved only ten bounding strides before fistian soldiers caught hold of his arms, arresting his charge, yanking him back and holding him despite his brief efforts at shaking loose from their imposing grips.

And there he stared at the feeding frenzy, mind roiling, voices at his sides shouting nothing to do for Shandra now. Several cursed those wicked beasts as well the gods themselves. Others yelled the gauntlets took precedence over any one person's life, that they needed to find them despite the sickening turn of events.

"Go!" shouted a red-robed mage in Banzu's face before shoving him backwards then turning for another look-see himself. "You've done enough, Soothsayer! We're here for the gauntlets. Find them and get them to the Head Mistress. We'll hold them off—"

But here the mage clipped short, his voice strangled by dawning despair.

A sentient presence of shadow shed from the laughing girl in a spreading pool round her feet, a shape of blackest void producing ebony tendrils whipping, growing, congealing while rising then composing into the physical form of an exceptionally tall man pale of skin and garbed in all black who stood in clear towering view beside her, his black eyes stabbed with lambent silver pupils.

Their hands moved in tandem through weaving gestures of shimmering air, the pallid girl's first followed by the pale hands of the taller man beside her in obvious traces of mimicry. The closest of the hundreds of corpses littering the grounds round them twitched through spasms and jerks of unnatural life in brazen rejections of death, khansmen and fistians both, while more of the lycanthrope beasts sprang out in snarling lopes from the gathering multitude of pale-faced soldiers rising and forming unliving shambles wailing and moaning behind them, the tormented stories of their eyes glossy and black and possessing only hunger.

In front of them, in shuddersome signal, howled one of the two lycan beasts feeding upon the remains of Shandra's dismembered corpse. Her Spellbinder blood an acidic solvent burning away patches of fur and flesh from the feasting beasts, rebuking the blasphemy of their unholy forms, its punishment neither hindered the devouring beasts nor deterred the other three who joined them in their feeding frenzy.

"Holy gods!" someone yelled at Banzu's back, a green-robed mage peeking from behind his shoulder while latched onto him, her fingers gripping his upper left arm seeking bone through muscle and strengthened by the terror rasping her voice. "Holy godsdamned gods!"

Those gripping fingers lost their strength and slipped free. A second more their owner turned and ran away screaming nonsensical words while flailing her arms overhead, uncaring of those she abandoned.

"Gods save us!" Another terrified shout, masculine though shrill, from the mage cringing squat at Banzu's right, his loosened bladder providing urine to the mud. "It's the godsdamned Eater of Souls!"

More lycanthropes gathered round Dethkore and the laughing little girl, forming a huge pack of vicious pawing beasts surrounding their master's front in a crescent moon sickle of formation. Behind them amassed an assemblage of unliving soldiers missing appendages or brandishing mortal wounds no longer mortal, their pale mouths gnawing the air smeared in fresh slicks of blood, many still chewing bits of flesh while gobs of meat and crimson drool depended from their working mouths requesting more, only more.

"The gods have abandoned us," whispered someone behind Banzu in brittle tone that elevated into desperate shout. "Soultaker's come to devour our souls! We have to . . ."

But the voice faded to padding feet racing away in diminishing splashes of mud.

A gesturing outthrust of one arm from the little girl—followed by the same mimicking gesture from Dethkore beside her—and the volatile pack of lycans sprang forth toward Banzu and his shrinking fistian group, loping and leaping in howling frenzy, black tongues lolling from their savage slathering jaws, as they clawed the ground in eager charge, their feral amber gleams of eyes possessing animal ferocity honed by human cunning.

* * *

Banzu's blood quickened to cold fever with the same punching dread unfelt since the night the unliving Trio attacked him and Melora by firelight, his first and only encounter with such dark sorcery, though a peculiar part of his mind mused sarcastic that after all he'd survived since: *At least we don't have to worry about the* living *enemy anymore.*

The truth of this revelation flourished nightmarish in front of him. The surrounding thousands of the slain Khan's despondent loyals, even those still gripped in the powerful throes of battle lust, turned away from their fistian adversaries and fled in abject terror at the daunting sight of this new enemy swarming the field in pale and hairy droves, abandoning desperate khansmen and fistians uniting against the infectious creatures seeking the indiscriminant rending and feeding of their enticing flesh.

Banzu studied past the smiling girl and her necromaster companion where more of the abominable loping beasts and the unliving palemen plague spread out amongst the frenzied soldiers, lycans attacking with claw and fang while palemen fed on felled victims to the shrieking chorus of helpless screams.

Disemboweled corpses convulsed with unholy life in their dying throes then arose with the grim spectacle of unliving vigor to stalk alongside the creatures that brought them down in rapacious feed, joining their numbers to the growing horde in spasms of death magic.

A paralysis rooted Banzu's feet against his own urgency for panicked escape, turning his legs useless in all but keeping him upright, viewing the gruesome display stunning him in immobile stare.

Nearby fistians stood locked in terrified silence, gaping at the horrific process of change amid the increasing flood. Others collapsed into frightened huddles trembling in the mud while whispering desperate prayers to Ahzra'il in quavering voices. Several turned tail and ran in whatever direction their screaming hysteria drove them so long as the course led away from the loping lycan horrors and shambling unliving . . . *hungars,* a memory of voice whispered in Banzu's mind of the reanimated palemen, the unliving shambling hungars seeking them out.

The more hardened soldiers of the remaining fistian collective mustered enough raw courage to shout orders and brandish weapons while closing defensive cordon ranks, bracing for imminent impact with the impending deluge of new enemy, their stern masks of resolve evincing death's acceptance and the intent on chopping down as many of the lycans and hungars as possible before their own inevitable doom.

A brave Academy aizakai in a flapping swirl of cerulean robes sprinted past Banzu and through a shrinking divide in the tightening fistian cordon, he perhaps applying iron control over his fear or struck delirious by it, arms outstretched with bright blue flames igniting from his thrusting palms in conjuration of a moving shieldwall of magefire three men tall and thrice that wide which blocked view of the charging lycanthropes to those behind his desperate play shouting him back.

A bold though suicidal charge, for the loping beasts, as uncaring of the blazing wall of flames as their others had been of Shandra's acidic Spellbinder blood in their callous feeding, leaped through the scorching fire in snarling defiance, their smoking bodies earning patches of burnt fur slowing them nothing when they pounced upon the offending mage and ravaged him dismembered by fang and claw within stomach-churning seconds, their tossing heads flinging broken ropes of gore from their slavering saw-toothed jaws, snuffing the summoner's flames along with his lifespark to the heartrending song of his dying screams.

Banzu stared, breath hitching tight in his chest, with dread fascination the popped and oozing ruins those damaging mageflames had inflicted upon two of the leaping lycans' eyes already reforming through accelerated healing new amber gleams of eyeballs within their putrid weeps of runny sockets while they fed, fresh dark fluffs and tufts of fur replacing burnt thatches and patches upon taut skin rippling over chorded flexes of muscle announcing raw power.

Howls pierced the din alongside human screams and hungar moans filling the air in a kind of musical headache, but above the rising dirge of horror intruded another's voice, haunted with memory, inside Banzu's mind and not of his own verbal stream of consciousness.

Silver, intoned the unknown other's deadspeak soughing with the experienced inflection of a long-dead Soothsayer whom faced down these same abominations of nature in ancient times in an ancient war . . . a war spanning almost a thousand years.

Then another's voice continued, **Only silver kissed by moonlight can truly wound these unholy beasts.**

A touch of fear broke through the notes of the other's soliloquy speech. **It burns their skin and boils their blood.**

Fear burned to ash in a flush of another joiner's anger. **Remove their heads and hearts and hack them to pieces!**

Another's voice intruded. **You have no choice now.**

Then another. **You are not alone in this. Surrender to us and kill them.**

A flare of rage punctuated by the maddened cackle of another still. **Surrender to me and I will kill them all!**

No! Banzu regained composure through a series of hard blinks while shaking thoughts loose from the collage of voices' incessant mental grips upon his defiant faculties.

The shared collective's influence . . . bleeding into me . . . they're trying to help me in their mad way, but only to save my body vessel for later possession.

Echoes of mocking laughter faded through his mind.

As he watched the horrors playing out before him, paralyzing fear waning through continued flexes of his sweaty hands stealing anxious grips of air and his nervous bare feet squishing mud through rocking balance, body craving movement and Power, doing nothing never a part of him, his battle lust flushing hot in rediscovery of the recent uncovered part of his primal nature, simple in its savagery, orgasmic in its release, impossible to deny.

The possessive Essence of Simus Junes had brought out that predatory apex arrogance then honed it keen through khansmen slaughter.

Banzu licked his lips quivering through the beginnings of a snarl, Griever's steely tooth a beckoning presence at his left hipwing so that he clutched its leather-wound hilt in the hammer-fisting squeeze of his left hand while the ball of his thumb rubbed inviting caresses upon its pommel, as the vicious pack of lycans turned their attentions from the gory ruins of the felled mage and, bursting into loping charges, glared feral amber promises at him through breaks of motion between those scattering for escape.

Until the eastern ranks of fistian soldiers once protecting the clearing's outer perimeter for the safety of the gauntlets' searchers therein rushed forth in opposing charge, intent on dealing the outnumbered lycan beasts steely death . . . though only buying their stunned others small time when the stalwart soldiers crashed into the loping frenzy of snapping fangs and ripping claws unhindered by ineffective weapons scoring temporary damage and armor punctured then torn in exposures of tender flesh beneath.

As well the swelling masses of hungars not preoccupied with feeding on screaming diers stalked forth in the lycans' wake at gesture and mimicked gesture from the pleased little girl and Dethkore beside her, many of these lurching on twisted or broken legs or stumps of missing feet, though more of their numbers freshly turned and showing only minor bite wounds sped past at full inhuman sprint.

While the hungars too mutilated to run or even shamble pursued behind their unliving brethren by clawing handfuls of mud as they dragged crippled legs connected to busted hips, or missing their lower halves entirely where viscera trailed loose in stretches of black ichor and organs no longer necessary to sustain the awful gleams of yearning rife in their wet obsidian stares, seeking to devour living flesh and renew their unliving bodies in feasting rejuvenation.

It's a nightmare. It's a godsdamned nightmare.

Banzu half turned from the brutal scene, glancing west beyond the tower's wreckage, tempted to join the others in running away into the clogging screen of bodies. But the priority of finding the Khan's gauntlets stayed him to place, gaze hunting the immediate grounds. He'd found one then lost it—though the memory of where and how and to whom turned an untouchable fantasy—so that he cursed while reflecting.

I handed it away, yes. To someone I paid no attention to. Friggin hell! But the other . . . I'll never find it now. Godsdammit! Why didn't I—

"Soothsayer!"

He snapped his focus to the little girl and the necromaster walking toward him in leisure pace, almost in casual stroll, their hands weaving gestures of shimmering air as they approached amid a growing swarm of hungars.

"Soothsayer!" the girl shouted again, her strong voice carrying the distance between them above the tortured screams and gothic moans and piercing howls upon a vocal projection of power, her yellow eyes bright stabs of cunning, her smile dark malice. "You've done my work for me! Now it's your turn to die!"

She craned her head while whipping her arms out at her sides and laughed, then struck Banzu with the burning glare of her serpentine stare while working her hands in rapid intricate gestures producing smoky traces through the shimmering air, the taller Dethkore beside her performing the same with his mimicking hands.

And Banzu realized there must exist some manner of magical connection between them, for—

Shouts behind and beside him startled him back to present. He tensed, gaze darting at the felled corpses scattered round his immediate area twitching in spasms then rising in moaning droves, the unholy conjured circle of hungars entrapping him and his fistian fellows in a cordon of living death. Their only Spellbinder defense in Shandra lay shredded and in lycan bellies, and with the Power corrupted by the bleeding psychosis of the shared collective—*I'm down to my sword and my wits.*

Banzu turned round, faced his dwindled group, despair clenching his guts. *Gods, this is all that's left of us?* A handful of soldiers and several aizakai mages, the rest of their numbers fighting outside the hungar cordon. He scanned the frightened huddle seeking guidance, flinching while their eyes darted to their fellows' dying screams.

"Gather in!" he ordered, waving them closer. "Now!"

And the paltry fistian survivors gathered in for listening, though half turned to keep their ears on him while watching the enclosing enemy shrinking distance by the second.

"Pay attention to me!" he yelled, earning head-snaps of focal stares. "I know it's bad. But we need to recoup the gauntlets. Even one will keep their power out of play. Who did I give it to? Any one here?"

Heads shook denial while several pairs of empty hands upturned. No lanthium gauntlet among them.

"Friggin hell!" He glanced over a shoulder, peering beyond the shambling cordon of hungars at the laughing girl and the necromaster closing distance, and cursed himself for not leaving away with the gauntlet seconds after finding it. *Stupid! Whoever I passed it to is probably already dead.* "We have to make a stand for as long as it takes to find one."

"How?" asked a mage, thin and pale, her long black hair dreadlocks of mud, her soiled yellow robe torn tatters.

Prompting another. "Yes, how? We're surrounded!"

"And Soultaker's here!"

"Even if we find one," said a tall mustached soldier, "we'll never make it out of here alive."

The younger soldier beside him abandoned his sword to the muck and fumbled the knife free from his belt. He raised it to his throat in palsied hand. "We should kill ourselves before Soultaker can—"

"No!" Banzu slapped him across the face then stabbed a stiff finger at it. "No. It's not over till it's over."

The older soldier beside the younger snatched the knife away and threw it then pointed at the dropped sword. "Pick it up," he said. "Now, Private. That's an order." He raised his battered mace between them, its tines covered in gore and filth. "Or I'll bust your caps and leave you in easy pickings."

"Y-Yes, s-sir." The stammering youth squatted and plucked his sword from the mud, straightened and clutched it to his chest.

"Oh gods," said another soldier, a rotund boulder of a man pacing back and forth. "I don't want to die here. Not like this. Not like one of those things. I was building a house! I never even got to—"

"Enough!" Banzu yelled. He pulled Griever free and gazed round from wary face to face. "We stand. Because we don't have a choice. It's fight or die. Are you with me?"

Heads nodded all around, many reluctant, several resolute.

"Good," he said. "Then let's do this. Whoever finds a gauntlet first, you take it and run like hell. The rest of us . . . if you go down, go down fighting." He turned away. "Now circle up!"

Banzu and his fistians formed a compact circle while facing outward, confronting the imminent stalking macabre of hungars closing in from all sides.

***

The voracious cordon of hungars converged from all sides, while loping lycans pursued from the east in a growling crescent rush of rending horror.

The quicker hungars, mottled and mire-stained, undying rage on their pale faces and an unholy light blazing in their black glares, dozens of them now with dozens more rising into reanimated life at their sides and back, a small army unto itself, surrounded Banzu and his outnumbered defenders. And behind them, shambling in through the flattened grass and over corpses yet to be resurrected or those just beginning to twitch through spasms of reanimation, pursued more hungars slowed by twisted or missing limbs, slowed but undeterred in their rapacious need to feed upon the living.

Battle ensued in a crash of chaos speeding through flashes and startlements of violence.

Bright bursts of magefire flared then snuffed at Banzu's sides as screams tore loose from throats once leaping blurs of fur and fangs sped growling past his peripherals. A dead woman's tongue writhed in his focus ahead, swollen and black and glistening, then her head swept from view on breaking neck by the crunching swing of another's mace. The dead man shambling beside her harried on, gargling dark blood while he forced Banzu backwards, tripping, falling, splashing into a sucking pool of muck.

Banzu stabbed from his downed position, twisting his blade and ripped it, carving a path through the hungar's neck, chest, and out stomach. Steamy guts flooded as the hungar pitched into the pool, splashing mud, clawing at Banzu's legs while snapping bites of air even as he tore free and drove Griever into the firmer yet spongy ground.

Fearing infection, kicking wild and hauling on his sword, he dragged himself out of the small pool. *Gods, I'm too exhausted to keep this up for long, my body too spent from my fight across the plains.* He lay on his back, panting while listening to the awful music of moans and snarls from the ferocious horde and the shouting fistians cursing them.

Living hands seized him, hauled him up onto his feet. And for the moment he watched the hungars in strange wonder, questioning if anything of the person remained when necromancy reanimated the flesh, and found he did not care.

"Soothsayer!" A masculine shout from behind. "To your left!"

Banzu spun face-to-face with more hungars groping forward in clawing reach of his face. He startled back then lunged forward, fighting the nearest off by bashing it in the face with the pommel of his sword, then another and another still, hammer-fisting hilt for lack of proper swinging area of Griever's blade so as not to accidentally injure any of his closer fistian fellows fending against the pale swarm. But the hungars proved incessant in their relentless advance, and the harm he inflicted brutalizing their bodies achieved nothing more than brief space and stalled assaults.

Outside the teeming hungar throng, lycans seduced with feral aggression and enticed by any play of movement loped away to continue their rampaging feeding frenzy elsewhere among the thousands of potential meals, unable to ignore the instinctual drive of pursuing fleeing prey.

Abandoning the safety of his fistian fellows, overwrought by pale hands grabbing at him from everywhere, Banzu fought back the reaching grips of hungars through fanning cuts of Griever slinging broken ropes of black ichor. But for every hand he lopped off, two more replaced it. He dared reach down inside, touched at the barest spark of the Power-corrupted . . .

—fiery claws ripping at his insides, attempting to drag him into their corruptive clutch forever as laughing madness rang through his mind, a thousand voices screaming claims over his essence as the diluvial tide of their possessive presence rolled forth in an avalanche of molten fire—

. . . and violently shook himself free . . .

—yanking his inner touch away from that Power-corrupted spark of potency a hairsbreadth before its molten avalanche rolled over him in irreversible consumption of his soul—

. . . so that he chopped through the next hungar just below the knees then climbed by running up and over its felled hunch and leaped for safer grounds.

But a pale hand caught his back foot by the ankle, blackened nails digging in then raking loose. Torn short from his escaping jump, he struck the ground hard and rolled in the mud, sprang up swinging, severed a head from pale shoulders then kicked the decapitated body backwards as black ichor spurted from the stump of neck, an inky fountain, what remained of his shredded clothes dangling from him in muddy tatters whipping gobs.

He glanced down at his clawed and bleeding ankle, ensuring no infectious bite, then charged forward and shouldered into another hungar. He knocked it down then, as it sat upright, lopped its head off, cleaving through skull atop lower jaw so that the black decay of its brains poured out in oozing clumps.

"Soothsayer!" someone yelled.

Another, "Oh gods no!"

Another still, "Help!"

Banzu spun round, tensing with disturbing regret, the whole of his fighter's group swarmed in his absence and torn apart in a flood of hungars and lycans. The sickening scene a mash of entrails spilling loose from torn stomachs, of jaws chewing flesh, of faces eaten when not shredded by razor claws. Tortured fistian screams drowned in a sea of howls and moans. No fight at all, really. Seconds only.

Eyes found him, pleading not for help but begging for a quicker death, brown pools widening as black talons raked the face apart into bloody shreds, exposing pinked bone then those lycan claws lost beneath a flurry of pale hands stained red.

He cursed the gods for their awful Game, their pieces not pawns but victims. He tore his gaze away from the feeding frenzy and battled through gut-wrenching dry heaves while a part of him sought the surrender of sobbing collapse, until seething anger gripped him by the stiffening spine.

When will it end? Even the khansmen dying by the score earned his sympathy. *So many lives . . . too many lives lost already.*

Alone, un-Powered, and afraid, a darker part of him craved for the re-possession of Simus Junes in reclamation of the terrible animus achieving him across the war-torn plains in a frenzy of slaughter. *No. I can't. There's no coming back from it now. Not until the Godstone . . .*

He glanced west, at the ocean of bodies occupying the miles between himself and Fist. No gauntlet, no horse to ride, no Power to accelerate him to the city in refuge. And even if he possessed the means of sure escape, a new army grew round him, one more terrible than living khansmen, a pandemic nightmare of unliving death devouring every life it swallowed.

His thoughts turned to Melora, the memory of her a brutal accusation of what she would think of his cowardly escape.

It's down to me.

Shame nestled in rage.

So be it.

I tried.

Gods know I tried.

He blanked his mind of all but the here and now, instigating the hunter's calculating calm of swordslinger focus.

Go down fighting or don't even bother. Draw them in then seize the Source and show them what true horror really is.

Simus, godsdamn you, I know you hear me. You win! You want slaughter, you got it. But go for Dethkore. Do you hear me? Go for Dethkore!

He drew in deep.

Forgive me, Melora.

Exhaled overlong.

I love you.

Swordslinger looseness flushed its prominence. He raised Griever's promising steel and pointed with it at the horde of hungars and lycans targeting their voracious sights upon him as one collective. He returned them his best mocking smile and a come-hither wave of his free hand while preparing to seize the Source and lose all of himself forever.

As a nightmare flood of hungars and lycans rushed toward him in a moaning and howling frenzy.

* * *

Banzu braced for impact both physical and spiritual—then spun jolting toward the thunder of hooves and shouts escalating behind him, startling at the hard-charging company of fistian cavalry knocking divisions and tumbles of bodies aside from the path of their plowing armored warhorses when not trampling them down.

The glorious spearhead of chargers one-hundred strong opened seconds before running over Banzu, fanning out and past his sides then converging again, fistian blacks and blues riding atop determined jounces of equine power blurring past his peripherals, surrounding him in a storm of noise, their long and menacing spines of lances bestrewn with gore and strips of flesh engaging destructive collision into the rushing horde of hungars and lycans, delaying its advance with a resounding crash, leaving only one of their others behind.

"Soothsayer!" the lone rider yelled while turning his snorting black warhorse and throwing out his hand. "More are coming. Get on quick!"

Banzu considered the gesture for all of two seconds. "No."

"No?" The older rider's face shocked through indignant surprise into tensing anger. "There's no time to argue. Get up here, godsdammit!"

"I can't." Banzu glanced over a shoulder at the fistian horsemen, their brutal charge arrested by sheer numbers, fighting a losing battle against the frenzied horde swarming them from all sides but behind, lycan claws ripping shreds of horseflesh between flurries of pale hungar hands tearing riders loose from saddle. "Find the gauntlets," he yelled above the raucous surf. "I'll hold them off as long as I can!"

He turned away from the rider—and earned a swift kick in the back of the head. He hitched through stumbling step then spun round baring his teeth.

"Are you crazy?" The rider threw his arm out, pointing at his failing fellows. "They're buying us time! And dying, for you! Get your ass up here now!"

Friggin hell. "Fine!" In one quick motion Banzu sheathed Griever and reached up, took the rider's offered hand and jumped through the aiding yank pulling him up into the saddle behind.

"Let's get the hell out of here!" The rider turned their horse about and gripped the reins for snapping into speedy exit.

But from whence the cavalry's brutal charge punctured through from the west, more eager swells of hungars closed the space, trapping Banzu and his apparent savior within the unliving swarm of chaos surrounding them in shrinking perimeter.

The veteran rider, old to fighting but new to the unholy onslaught, shrieked and kicked at pale groping hands while the finicky horse danced round, whipping and bucking and turning the wrong way, the confused animal facing them east.

Unable to pull Griever loose from his hip, Banzu did some kicking of his own, stubbing his heels and kicking his toes into pallid faces and gaping maws seeking bites of his exposed legs.

"We have to get down!" he yelled. "Before they pull us down and eat us alive!"

From over his savior's left shoulder, Banzu caught glimpse of Dethkore's pale hands rising at them in shimmering ignition of sorcery erupting in mimicked fashion to the little girl's own sweeping gestures beside him.

Oh gods. Banzu opened his mouth to issue a warning shout to the rider saddled in front of him preoccupied with kicking hungars away, but the terrible speed through which the conjured blast shot forth outpaced his voice. He snapped his teeth shut, tensing, bracing for impact, no deliverance but to endure it.

The projected shimmer of energies rippled through the air, racing round and through and past the fistian cavalry dying amid their ravaging nest of hungars and lycans.

A convulsive surge of sickness struck Banzu dizzy with vertigo in revolting flush of his stricken senses and the repugnant clench of his guts, though the shielding rider he sat behind absorbed the brunt of the nauseating miasmic blast pulsing hot with fever and plague. An equine shrill knifed the air while their horse reared up. The world spun as the bucking animal threw both riders from saddle, Banzu retching a spew of hot bile through his mad tumble before he struck the punishing ground.

Queasy, he rolled in the mud for a blank space. He sat up choking on vomit then coughing through it then gasping for precious air, his eyes hot fractured prisms of tears he swiped clear. And stared with dread as his once-rescuer sat up from his thrown position and presented him a scream-stretched face, the man's eyeballs bursting in a terrible spray of maggots also discharging from the broken jaw of a gaping mouth. Beside them danced the afflicted horse flinging maggots from its own bursting eyes and yawning mouth spewing the larvae in wriggling white scatters as it thrashed and kicked, tumbling hungars away, its tortured sounds choked off by the invading larvae wrought from the necromaster's infectious blast.

Banzu twisted from the horror while grunting through dry heaves wrenching his emptied stomach raw. Terror at suffering a second blast of Dethkore's magic flowed a cold and bitter course through his veins, helping quell the churns of sickness. He pressed up into a dizzied stagger, the world sloshing through imbalance, his immediate area clear of hungars kicked away to the mud during the warhorse's thrashing dance of pain.

A terrified scream cut short at his left so that he spun to a black tendril erupting from the ground in a spear of living shadow. It stabbed up into and through one of the remaining cavalrymen seeking to aid Banzu's rescue from the plains, the soldier on foot and minus a horse. The shadowspear drove up between the caught man's spread legs, puncturing into groin and through the rest of him, its ebony tip sprouting out the top of the man's exploding skull and knocking off his helmet in turn to go flip-spinning through the air.

Overcome by pain and the impaling of his innards, the man clawed at his face, tearing off and raking away ribbons of skin in a futile attempt at reaching the invading tendril as if to somehow yank it out from himself in those few precious seconds before his lifeforce winked out in his eyes and his limbs fell limp, though his body remained rigid and upheld by the impaling tendril alone. Until a moment more and the shadowspear removed, sucking down into the ground, and the fistian corpse collapsed atop its withdraw, a puppet with its strings cut.

Dethkore and his little girl companion stood seconds away from sending another miasmic blast of sickness Banzu's way and this time with no fortunate shielding between. The little girl smiled and laughed while working her hands through more conjuring weaves, the necromaster beside her mimicking her gestures same as always.

Panic smothered bravery while strangling hope as Banzu accepted his death. The crushing sadness of never seeing Melora again flared righteous into indignant fury while watching hungars and lycans ravage and rend the remaining fistians in a feeding frenzy of odds too overwhelming.

While round him swarmed in more hungars.

He gripped Griever's hilt in preemptive pull while bracing against the inevitable demise of his spirit as he seized the Source through focal—

He halted his seize of Source a hairsbreadth from tapping its corruption of energies when flashes of blades and stabs of lances within the thundering rush of hooves sped past his sides in a resounding crash and trample and tumble of hungars failing against the juggernaut charge of a second fistian cavalry making of themselves a protective circle round their Soothsayer center, his saviors hacking and slashing and stabbing, their armored warhorses stomping and crushing and biting.

Banzu turned round, stunned. And there hands gripped him by the shoulders. Familiar hands.

"Get on!" Jacob yelled, though he gave Banzu little choice as the veteran soldier pulled at him with surprising strength.

Yet Banzu shook free. "I can't leave yet. Dethkore—"

"Godsdammit Soothsayer, don't make me regret this! Get your ass up here now!"

"How did you—" Banzu began then clipped his question short. He climbed up into saddle, sitting behind the Head Mistress's First Sword. "Thanks."

"Don't thank me—" Jacob cut off as the protective fistian circle broke against the outer press of enemy surging in overwhelming numbers upon them and rushing between pockets of space.

Howls and screams pierced the din when a furred flurry of claws and pale hands groped bits of Jacob's warhorse's thick plated armor not simple steel but steel coated in silver and burning hot against their foul touches. Yet still the unrelenting enemy advanced.

Jacob twisted in saddle while slashing at a pair of reaching claws which flew away in a spray of blood hissing whispers after he lopped them off below the wrists, earning an ear-piercing howl while the injured lycan tumbled backwards, taking others with its muscled bulk while thrashing and biting at air, its severed flesh sizzling from the burning cut of Jacob's silver sword.

A curious surprise Banzu noticed though did not question. "But the Khan's gauntlets—"

"Are lost!" Jacob twisted and swung, earning more tortured screams through burning cuts, their mount dancing round while kicking back bodies and earning small pockets of space that closed in seconds with more hungars trampling overtop their squirming fellows.

A furred head burst forth from the smoky tangle of pale, groping hands seeking flesh. Banzu caught this out of his peripheral only, too slow in reacting but for the guttural yell tearing loose from his throat when those saw-toothed slavering jaws clamped upon his left forearm, fangs piercing flesh and crunching bone in a savage chomp which sought to drag him from saddle.

But Jacob twisted round just in the nick and stabbed down through lycan skull, puncturing left eye socket. Strong jaws released and furred head withdrew into the thickening tangle of hungars.

Jacob sheathed his sword in trade for gripping leather reins and said over a shoulder, "I'm only saving your sorry hide so the Head Mistress can make a rug of it. Hold tight! We're getting the hells out of here!"

Banzu's mind awhirl with dizzying pain from the lycan bite, he hugged round Jacbo's middle with his other arm and offered no argument against hasting escape.

A snap of reins, a buck of horse—and they burst into riding hard through the carnage of the Azure-turned-Crimson Plains, the hulking warhorse an equine battering ram sending bodies careening from its armored charge, while the survivors of the second cavalry disengaged from the frenzied horde and rode up from behind then past them into forming a protective spearhead of lancers making straight for Fist . . . leaving an ever-growing unholy army of the damned in their thundering wake.

CHAPTER FORTY-THREE

Sergal stood amid a beautiful rapture of screams and dying, a pale sea of unliving plague expanding in an ocean of war, his thrumming body a euphoric outpour of energies flourishing silver streams of effluent influence bursting from him in everywhere abundance through his absorbent necromancer Pet in filaments of control, his amplified demonic compulsion reining supreme, his sinistry of darken rule over a thousand strong and growing, though his dream of the Betrayer groveling for mercy at his feet in an agony of rending stolen by the Soothsayer usurper of his plans escaping on horseback, riding away into the screen of chaos, vanishing among the panicked humans killing their own in desperate droves while fleeing the ravenous hungar swarm peppered with rapacious lycans ripping terrified stragglers from their feet and eating them alive.

He raised a hand and fisted the air, shook it at the Soothsayer's defiant absence, his other hand pulsing agitated flexes round the handle of his vibrating souldagger vitus hitched at his left hipwing.

So close, yesss, so close. My claws closing round the victory when you snatched it away!

He bridled an indignant scream at the back of his throat, the Betrayer slain albeit in hollow victory, the Soothsayer beyond immediate pursuit.

Run, Soothsayer, and savor delaying the inevitable while you can. This is my world now, all of it, I am Master here, and hiding from me is only a false promise. Relish this moment for I am coming.

He tamed his frustrations with demonic cunning instilling its calculating coolness soothing the annoying flushes and flares of human emotions stemming from Sera's wailing presence viewing out through their shared eyes so that he whipped an internal lash of his admonishing will—*Shut up!*—and Sera's moaning despondency withdrew into the cruel oblivion of her caged misery, allowing refocus upon his vast gameboard of pawns.

"I would say these petty mortals deserve this," he mused aloud, his necromancer Pet silent beside him, "but that would imply I consider them as anything more than human chattel."

The Soothsayer gone. The Betrayer dead. Sure plans refolding through the manipulative hands of change, smothering old possibilities while breathing new potentials, Sergal's thoughts wandered, dancing upon the fringes of his bittersweet victory and all it afforded him.

Two birds with one stone, now one dead and the other fluttering with a broken wing. It should have been me, but the Betrayer is slain regardless. Irrelevant now, yesss, and the Soothsayer my only obstacle between me and the Godstone. Fly, fly away! I will still crush you, my wounded little birdie, yesss. Hope while you can. I am never far behind.

Sergal smiled in a delirium of joy, then licked his cold dead lips while scratching a little patch of scaly green skin on the underside of one forearm itchy with new growth. Other scaly patches existed elsewhere—high on his right cheekbone, the small of his back, behind one knee, at the base of his neck—in slow transmutation of his body vessel at spiritual war, but no matter that. Something in the Book of Towers would relieve his human imprisonment into a new and proper vessel soon enough. But first: "Come, my Pet. A new prize awaits us."

They strode forth into the chaotic swells of bodies, surrounded by hundreds of moaning hungars stalking in tandem to the instigative whims of their master, lycans loping here and there at the outskirts of their irrepressible advance. Sergal imposed a stronger constant draw upon his demonic compulsion over his Pet for he sought to unlock more secrets from the necromancer's darker arts through further mental probing.

He had, through great strain, learned a few new nasty tricks from the resistant deadman—glimpses and gleanings of useful knowledge contained in slivers shaven from an unwilling mind otherwise sealed—though most of the necromancer's guarded psyche, and thus his true power, remained hidden behind thick mental shields rebuking Sergal's stalwart attempts of scrutiny despite the potent energies amplifying his demonic compulsion so that he refocused upon more immediate, and more important, priorities.

I will break your mind later, Soultaker, once I hold the Godstone's limitless all-power and make of your secrets an open book, oh yesss. Your time is coming too. But for now we have work to do. We are not finished here by half.

They walked through the feeding frenzy for a time, surrounded in a gothic tide of pox, hundreds of hungars' contagious bites begetting hundreds more, thousands now, unliving moans replacing living screams, lifeforces snuffing in horrified blooms of dulling eyes then replaced by wet obsidian stares, random lycan howls of promise piercing the air in heralds of pain, Sergal tying off a plethora of spiritual weaves throughout his spreading sinistry plague infecting uncontested across the tortured plains.

Patches of prairie bluegrass not trampled into muddy ruins withered yellow-brown when captured within the suffering influence of Dethkore's miasmic death-aura radiating strong from his catalyzing core ten feet out in all directions, housing him and Sergal strolling at its center inside a discharging bubble of life-rending pestilence, this immediate area clear for even hungars shambling too close withered to the deleterious consequence of rending termination in rapid decays of pale flesh melting from crumbling bones aging brittle in the span of blinks.

But the gory spectacle soon turned a boring scene so that Sergal's lusty gaze hunted through the terrorized mix—until he stumbled over his own disobedient feet.

He stopped, swaying, grimacing, and gripped through pulsing flexes the cold handle of his hellsteel dagger vitus, an external anchor to the internal imbalance, and closed his eyes, sloshes of vertigo slow in passing. Despite the profusion of energies in everywhere abundance, his own unliving vessel required nourishment from living sustenance unprovided by the absorption of bountiful lifeforces.

How long has it been, days of chase? I . . . I can't remember. He raised his free hand and rubbed the inside corners of his eyes with pointer and thumb, massaging away the mental fog. *I need to feed again, and soon. This vessel is withering.* He snapped his eyes open. *Focus. I'm surrounded by feast. I'll feed later when there's time. Power first, pleasure thereafter.*

He relaxed his influence on Dethkore's miasmic death-aura, resting a space while it shrank inward, allowing his Pet to absorb and replenish reserves of power, fearing no decline of the available abundance of generous energies.

No sense in maintaining it before achieving Fist. There is no threat to me here, and I need all the hungars I can muster to invade the city for the Book of Towers. The Soothsayer has retreated there, I know it. Where else would he seek refuge but the heathen's den?

His smile returned, pursued by musings of his sinistry flooding through Fist's streets then ravaging the Soothsayer and the Head Mistress while eating them alive. Laughter tickled up his throat.

"Tools," he said while scanning round, everywhere he looked tools for the gathering, thousands upon thousands waiting to be utilized. "Cattle for the culling, yesss. Your legion, Betrayer, is now my legion. As it should be."

He gestured his right hand through shimmering traces of air producing glides of smoky wisps from his fingertips while flexing demonic compulsion through their soulbond, and Dethkore mimicked the same conjuring waves of fingers. A slew of khansmen corpses felled by mortal hands and lying untouched amid the feeding swarm of hungars jerked through active spasms then stole into waking motion, rising from the muck and joining their unliving brethren, lurching and lunging while seeking the delicious sustenance of living flesh.

"I'll cull you all before I'm through, yesss."

No need to speak his orders, he flared his demonic compulsion by tapping into the hungars' voracious appetites, magnifying it while tying off their spiritual weaves, then allowed them free rein.

As it should be for master and slave.

The faint though incessant thrum of the Godstone's presence, the sensation of it stronger now, amplified beyond his reasoning moments before the Betrayer's tower collapsed, tugged upon Sergal, pulling at him through the umbilical bond of his Pet's soulring vitus, urging him west, his path of carnage requiring no adjustment, only through Fist where the Godstone lay somewhere beyond and closer to the Calderos Mountains. Bloom, or perhaps Tyr.

I'll ravage both cities regardless before spilling my sinistry through the Pass upon the rest of the world.

He stared overlong at the distant tops of buildings peeking above Fist's high defensive walls encircling the entire heathen capital miles removed from his current vantage, spying out the tallest of their spires, the prominent Academy citadel, where he imagined the Head Mistress watching out at him behind a high window, mourning her failed war while clutching false hope close to her breast in futile denial of the inevitable.

I will delight while my hungars eat you from the toes up, Mistress. A slow appreciation of my gratitude while I suckle upon the shreds of your Soothsayer. Fear me well, for I am more than Khan. I am Legion! And I am coming for all of you.

Stubborn human shouts ahead drew Sergal's attentions to a cluster of soldiers breaking loose from a slew of khansmen, both parties bestrewn in splashes of black ichor gore and united in hacking through a stray clog of hungars split from the swarm and felled into pieces writhing the mud. The khansmen scattered into runs, stealing away through brief spaces of activity, leaving the paltry band of fistian survivors huddled upon this section of field, unhorsed lancers too stupid to pursue the Soothsayer's escape.

One of them, a dark-skinned woman wearing a lopsided helm and pale strips of flesh clinging to all of her corded-muscle frame, shouted while aiming her long steel spear at Dethkore and the little girl beside him.

Sergal considered them with an inviting smile. He clapped his hands then flexed his demonic compulsion while spreading his arms out wide. In front of him parted the moaning hungar swarm, shambling and lurching sideways, dividing while opening a V path. He then upturned his hands and afforded his adversaries come-hither waves, beckoning them with mockery.

The shouting knot of fistians charged, advancing into the V of space, filling it with raging terror, their eyes wide and wild, their hopes suicidal.

Laughing, Sergal ticked off seconds—then flared his demonic compulsion while clapping his hands, producing a silvery splash of shimmering energies bursting between his meeting palms then rippling outward in demands of obedience.

The spread V of hungars closed inward upon the foolhardy fistians in a crashing swallow of bodies where lived only screams and dying.

The hungars lowered, kneeling and feeding, pale hands clutching bitten organs and steamy ropes of viscera pulled from torn stomachs and cages of ribs, others fighting over juicy limbs ripped from shoulders or hips, their voracious appetites leaving little left of the fistian feast to rise through contagious bite and join their unliving brethren.

Sergal's attentions elevated past the feeding frenzy, hunting for more though startling to the scatter of fistian diggers working amid the fallen tower's incredible wreckage, not one of the Betrayer's lanthium gauntlets found but both as told by the shouting soldier upholding the newfound second lanthium gauntlet overhead for his desperate fellows to see his treasured find.

Sergal's serpentine eyes stretched wide, false breath hitching in his chest. "Yesss!"

Alarmed by the joyous outburst, the thieving fistian turned away in panicked scrambles seeking escape with his precious boon.

"No!" Sergal flared his demonic compulsion while waving his hands in frantic abandon, and Dethkore mimicked the conjuring weaves. "Mine!"

Five long thin tendrils of sentient shadows erupted from the ground round the running soldier, fountaining waves of mud in outward spray, trapping the halted escapee within a risen crown of darkness.

Sergal closed his hand into a tight fist. And the points of that shadow crown obeyed, folding inward, compacting the screamer into a mashed crunch of bones and squeezed flesh inside an undulating bud of shadow.

Sergal opened his hand, fingers wiggling, demonic will flexing, the soulring vitus round his finger burning cold with flowing energies. And the tight black bud of shadow unfurled in a blossoming of its dark flower, tendril petals unfolding outward into lashing guard of the crushed corpse mashed round the lanthium gauntlet, whipping tendrils flinging chunks and ribbons of gore while lashing in black-shadowed spite at all those daring approach of its thrashing nest of shadows.

Sergal smiled. *One down, yesss.*

A shifting of concentration, the waggle of his fingers. And the runaway possessor of the second gauntlet tripped up, fell splashing facedown into the mud when a lashing tendril shadow outstretched from the whipping crown and secured its barbed grip round the woman's right ankle. The yelling fool maintained her panicked clutch upon the gauntlet even as the obedient tendril yanked her to within the whipping crown of shadows, her other arm raking through the mud and earning no slowing purchase, her sliding body drawn along the ground so fast she broke through the legs of the others rushing to her aid.

Bodies bounced away, sharp juts of bones protruding through backwards-snapping legs.

Laughing strong, Sergal's pale little fingers working in a frenzy of dominance, Dethkore's hands a conjuring mimicry, he enjoyed the pleasing show of futile struggle as the soldiers braving too near the whipping crown of tendrils while attempting to recoup the gauntlets therein earned lashing barbed tendrils tearing away armor and clothes then ripping strips of flesh while slinging ropes of blood in rainbow arcs through the air.

Agonized screams sang sharp music above the din.

Sergal laughed and smiled while striding forth to claim his precious prize.

But a wiry-muscled woman proving herself a Spellbinder joined in the attempt at recapturing the Dominator's Gauntlets, the bleeding rent of one missing eye in her swollen face and the limp of her hobbled walk evincing the abuses she survived thus far through sheer grit. The whipping tendrils snapped and slapped at her brazen approach though dissipated into harmless shadowed wisps smoking the immediate air round her as they wither-hissed against her prevailing void-aura.

"No!" Sergal hissed, recoiling at the burning transference of pain scalding into his blackening fingers. He stopped the imposing weaves of his hands and shook them free of the heat boiling the marrow in his finger bones. He grimaced, snarling, lambent yellow eyes flaring irate then thinning with cunning.

I've not come this far just to be undone by some heathen bitch who can barely stand.

Glaring up at his necromancer Pet, Sergal flexed his demonic will while gesturing new weaves through the smoking air. Dethkore mimed the gestures without pause, his sullen tombstone visage betraying no signs of struggle against the unspoken commands imposed.

The remaining shadow tendrils of the diminishing crown slithered into the ground whipping-quick, vanishing round the blonde Spellbinder shouting orders while pointing through the hundreds of hungars surrounding Sergal and Dethkore. She moved in to retrieve the gauntlets from the bundled gore of corpses then make good her escape while her fistian fellows rushed past her.

Too bad for her she gave no notice of the shadow tendrils reappearing behind her, removed from the nullifying expanse of her void-aura, shadows erupting from the ground in the form of a giant black hand punching up while gripping a massive clump of sodden earth and bodies.

The huge shadowhand shot upwards into fantastic height, palming its earthen burden, arching on high while overturning midair and forming an earth-gripping fist that plunged, slamming down atop the Spellbinder crouched over the gauntlets and the gore of her two fellows containing them. She looked up a hairsbreadth before impact but too late, violet eyes expanding above a gaping mouth. Her body crimpled beneath the crushing tonnage of earth cutting her scream short.

"Squashed like a bug!" Sergal laughed, pleased, his soulringed fist having punched down into smacking the upturned palm of his other hand while Dethkore's hands enacted miming gesture. "A shame I didn't get to hear you beg before—"

He clipped short, swaying on his feet when another dizzy spell wrought from incessant hunger pangs sloshed his balance and blurred his focus. *No! Not now. Not yet. Not when I'm so close. But soon.* He shook loose from the sticky clings of vertigo and the growling hollow of his protesting innards craving the nutrient sustenance of living flesh and blood, regaining composure through a series of hard blinks, and refocused on the immediate.

The remaining fistians forming a blocking line to earn the Spellbinder time turned away, yelling, at the daunting sight of her abrupt demise. They abandoned their attempt to hold the hungars at bay through suicidal delay and rushed back, throwing themselves upon the mound of earth where they began frantic digging with their hands and found weapons turned desperate shovels for the buried gauntlets as well the woman crushed beneath.

Sergal spread his arms wide while flexing his demonic compulsion then threw his arms forward in shimmering ripples of air, and his hungars swarmed forth in feeding frenzy, flooding round and up the mound, making a screaming nest of the overrun fistian diggers, dragging them down, pulling them apart, eating them alive.

He craned his head and shouted, "I am Legion!"

A defiant spume of broiling mageflames rolled forth, splitting round the hissing earthen mound from behind while scorching through the charring tangles of feeding hungars and dying fistians where elevate a cacophony of screams. The divided fiery blast continued past and ignited the front lines of Sergal's surrounding hungars, making of them a flaming and thrashing chaos rife with putrid smoke hazing the air.

No. Sergal flared his demonic compulsion and willed his burning sinistry into a dividing scatter, parting the spreading inferno before him while opening a wedge of space. He fixed his focal glare upon the heathen mage rounding the smoldering mound covered in blackened bones and squirms of survivors, daring to oppose him. *Petty aizakai, you are nothing!*

He flicked his right hand in gesture while drawing strong upon the permeation of death's essence. A convex wall of shadow erupted from the ground in front of the running mage, blocking the conjured flames while fanning them out and back at their caster's sides in rebounding tongues of heat sizzling across mud.

A flick of Sergal's other wrist, fingers working through conjuring manipulations, and a second colossal shadowhand burst from the ground behind the mage, flinging tumbles of flaming bodies and smoky parts in its punching upheaval. The shadowhand severed connection from the ground and shot high into the air—Sergal's own miming fist opening into outstretched fingers wiggling—then that shadowhand burst into a cloud formed of hundreds of winged creatures flapping hovered above the mage and the few fistian survivors atop the mound still digging for the buried gauntlets despite their burned injuries.

Another flexing gesture—the twist of Sergal's wrist, his fingers stiffening then stabbing through the air—and those flapping creatures resembling the cruel mixture of crow and bat reformed their shadowed bodies into long thin spikes plunging to ground with the sped of shot arrows, stabbing into all those below in a hail of obsidian javelins.

Tortured screams escaped the receivers pincushioned in twisted poses of bleeding wrongness suffering black-shadow spikes protruding from their impaled vitals while the mageflames snuffed behind the obstructing shadowwall. Sergal gestured by way of shaking his hands, and the spikes dissipated into wispy puffs of black smoke, allowing bodies upheld to collapse in the mud as the corpses he made of them. So too did his conjured wall of shadow dissipate.

He drew in a deep, unnecessary though fulfilling breath, and smiled. *Today is proving a good day, yesss, and a delightfully creative one as well, despite the Betrayer's stolen death.*

He scanned round, gaze hunting while his mood folded into brooding over the Soothsayer and the potential of facing him here instead of Fist in some ambushing turn of surprise.

Maybe he's still . . . no, he's gone. But why was he here fighting the Khan instead of retrieving the Godstone? The bloodlust should have kept him here, too many to slaughter, and yet . . . and yet he fled.

He fixed his pensive stare beyond the ocean of bodies upon the distant Academy spire standing tallest behind the defensive stone walls encircling Fist. *Are you there yet, Soothsayer? Watching me beside your mewling Head Mistress? Cursing me? Ruing me?* Excitement flushing, he smiled and licked his lips. *Watch me now, Soothsayer. Oh yesss, watch what I do next and know there's not stopping my reclamation of your coward's gift to me.*

He swept his gaze to the mound, then past it, thinning his eyes to bitter glare upon the plethora of khansmen outside his hungar swarm considering the little girl and her escort Pet while weighing and measuring the earthen mound for the gauntlets buried beneath it with obvious toll against the value of their lives. Thousands of khansmen remained, with only one required to don the gauntlets and secure their rending power of storm.

"Traitorsss," Sergal hissed at the Bloodcloaks and worship-followers once sworn to him through the Betrayer. "All of you!"

He flexed his demonic will while working his hands through active traces of shimmering air, Dethkore beside him miming same gestures, their soulbond throbbing with crackles of instigative energies.

The ground beneath the nearest pocket of khansmen watchers considering their brandished weapons and their ability to fight through the hungars to the mound split apart in a startlement of shouts as inside their hundred-strong huddle opened a gaping maw out from which sprouted a whipping nest of black tendrils parting mud while latching barbed coils round flailing limbs or winding round torsos then pulling their thrashing victims down into the gigantic fissure, wrenching bodies through sucking yanks and twisting limbs while crimping armor and snapping bones in their strong tentacle pulls.

Screams knifed the air as scores of captured khansmen fed into the chasm swallowing them whole, while those round their dying fellows scattered in running panic, hacking and stabbing for escape. The human-eating fissure chomped closed upon its fleshy morsels to the gesture of Sergal's smacking palms, crushing bodies to pulp and paste when not burying them alive in suffocations of mud.

There arose a slew of arrows originating from beyond the closing fissure, a re-gathering of khansmen having plucked up bows and assuming such distance equated safety.

Sergal laughed and flicked his wrist, conjuring another great shadowhand punching up and rising in front of him—the effort producing another dizzy spell he cursed while shaking loose—its eruption dividing the ground while spilling thick waves of mud pooling ankle-deep round his legs. Through miming gestures the titan shadowhand slapped the descending shower of arrows from the air, bugs dispersed before the godhand swat, then Sergal curled it into a massive fist he sent hammering down, quaking the ground while crushing bodies then scattering their smashed ruins about in a litter of broken tumbles with the back-and-forth wave of his opening hand.

Such awesome power . . . it would have stolen his breath if he required any . . . *what a shame it's wasted on one so undeserving for so long.* He shot a disappointed glance up at Dethkore, the Enclave's first and failed Khan, then walked forward unopposed. He approached the smoky mound and commanded his obedient hungars to begin working at unearthing the Dominator's Gauntlets buried beneath.

A protective cordon of hungars stood guard round Sergal and his Pet, and the workers of the mound, while thousands more ran rampant and feeding among those intent on staying afield. He stood in eager praise, pulsing his demonic compulsion, while pale hands of obedience raked back and dug through the piled mud for his prizes buried beneath.

Though his thoughts soon strayed, for he'd lost sight, and contact, with his lycan brood, so that he flexed his demonic will, reaching out to them upon his spider's strings of influence, and sensed . . . nothing but the faintest touch of feral aggression, their bestial minds a strain to command from the start and now lost to savage fever within the tumult, too distracted by chasing scattering prey, their primal instincts taking dominance over the human parts of their minds.

So be it. Let them play. They'll return given time. Some of them, at least.

Mud-slinging minutes more and the hungars laboring upon the shrunken mound produced groans of agony when Spellbinder blood burned their unliving flesh, evincing the depth of their work. Sergal snapped the reins of his control, and his hungars continued digging, wailing and moaning, sizzling bits of blackening flesh melting from skeletal hands raking away sluices of mud.

Anxious seconds from commanding his hungars back to conjure physical shadows and finish the digging himself, a hungar elbow-deep in mud removed a dripping clod of gauntlet followed a moment more by another hungar unearthing its matching pair. The stump of flesh of the slain Betrayer's hand and severed forearm still filled one lanthium gauntlet.

Sergal approached his gathered find, licking his lips and gripped by new fever. He willed his necromancer Pet beside him into touching the fleshy filling and, accompanied by the strong putrescent pulse of the necromancer's miasmic death-aura, the obstruction therein withered and decayed within seconds so that the insides spilled loose to the ground in mushy black bits of desiccated matter and crumbled bone. Sergal gazed upon the lanthium prizes presented him, each gauntlet upheld atop two pairs of boney upturned hands, one dripping melting gobs of sinew, the other drips of mud.

Mine, yesss, all mine, these godhand clutches of thunder and lightning, these heralds of destruction teeming with storm and war.

He opened his mouth to voice true elation—then closed it, silent, words paling to the defining moment of his impending triumph so that he shut his eyes and shuddered through a virgin's ecstatic quiver beneath their first lover's gliding touch, apprehensive yet only wanting more, while staccatos of memories a millennia old flashed prominent through his mind's reflecting eye . . . of his demonic brethren gathering stores of lanthium ore to forge the Dominator's Armor in Volgan's secret Hellforge before the gods' Great Game commenced while Nergal played his cruel manipulations upon a grieving man edging psychosis over his brutalized wife and daughter.

A hot lash of ire spiked through the soulbond so that Sergal snapped his eyes open, jolting from reverie, the soulring vitus frosting colder round his stiffening finger so that he flexed his hand to fist then shook it. He glared at his necromancer Pet, defiance nestled in hot blazes of hatred betraying Dethkore's piercing stare yet bleeding none of the emotion upon that sullen tombstone visage, then returned his avid gaze upon the precious gauntlets awaiting reclamation.

Before meant his tortured demise if he dared attempt to wear the gauntlets himself and wield their awesome smiting power, they his former master's gift to Hannibal Khan and Nergal only their Enclave deliverer.

But that was then, oh yesss, and this is now. He licked his lips, tasting promise and power. *Now my slaver's chains are broken.* He reached forth hands palsied with thrill. *Now I have human hands to plunge and—*

No! Startling almost too late, he withdrew his reaching hands a hairsbreadth from delivery inside the tantalizing gauntlets and shuddered, teetering upon the precarious precipice of undoing himself and all of his precious plans. The Dominator's Armor infused with Malach'Ra's influential corruption, donning the gauntlets imposed their permanent bonding to the host while catalyzing their nutrient feed upon the vessel's psyche and instilling it with the fierce need to reassemble the rest of the Dominator's Armor.

Sergal removed a cautious step, not trusting himself.

No. I cannot wield them myself. Malach'Ra will lay claim over my mind while rebinding his slaver's chains. I'll lose myself, and care only for the rest of the Armor. I must have the Godstone! It sickens me to admit I'm too weak to oppose such influence.

"But you can." He smiled up at his necromancer Pet. "Put them on."

Dethkore hesitated, tensing, his arms reaching toward the gauntlets though trembling in resistive want of drawing them back. Halfway to gauntlets those pale hands stopped. His lips moved though produced no audible speech.

"Put them on," Sergal said, flexing his demonic compulsion through the soulring vitus chilling round his finger.

A rebounding stroke of defiance flared frigid through their soulbond, punctuated by Dethkore's voice. "No."

Sergal staggered through spiritual imbalance, struck by his Pet's blatant disobedience. He scowled and flared his demonic compulsion while squeezing his raised right fist between them, the soulring vitus thereon vibrating. "Put them on now!"

Pale hands resistive tremors . . . inching ever forward . . . sliding into gauntlets and finding home.

Dethkore stiffened, his head whipping back in arching rigid spasm, the sentient shadows of his swaddling fabrics writhing licks of air inches from him in everywhere abundance, his mouth open in a silent scream stretching his jaws while ominous thunder rolled deep and long throughout the blue ocean of sky to an elevating chorus of hungar moans thousands strong.

Dethkore raised his gauntleted hands, glistening ribbons of black ichor blood racing dark branches down his forearms and dripping from his elbows, evincing the hundreds of tiny lanthium thorns piercing deep into pale flesh possessing only memories of pain, the godsforged gauntlets completing their supernatural bonding while instigating the siphoning of their new unliving host.

At the same time Sergal staggered backwards, gasping to the avalanching crash of raw power surging crackling currents through the umbilical tether of their soulbond and punching fathoms of energy into the charging parts of him. He grimaced in terrifying rapture, eyes shut tight and teeth clenched, every taut sinew of his body vibrating, enduring the phantom stings of lanthium thorns sinking deep into unliving flesh, seeking penetration of bone for marrow, suffering the transfer of pain into his own hands from the hundreds of tiny siphon fangs biting into Dethkore's hands and forearms as the gauntlets awoke into wicked spark-crackling life while merging with their new bearer of power's burden.

The Dominator's Armor designed to feed upon the lifeforce of its host, draining the body's vigor while twisting the mind's sanity in parasitic splendor, Dethkore's unliving vessel provided antithesis deathforce fuel amplified by the insatiable Blackhole Abyss housed therein the chamber of his being.

And thus the connection produced an unexpected result so that Sergal, after contending with a malaise of ephemeral metaphysical trauma, awed to the daunting glory of deifying energies. Reeling, he sank to his knees, caps splashing mud, craned his head and appraised the resounding thunder pronouncing the beautiful bonding ritual complete.

"Oh . . . gods . . . yesss."

Gathering his senses while flexing the fading phantom pain from his hands, he stood on shaky legs and imposed demonic compulsion through his Pet.

Dethkore thrust his gauntleted hands out in miming gesture, fingers splayed, ebony tongues of power crackling over lanthium gauntlets.

"Yesss." Zumming in ecstasy, Sergal willed a testing discharge of current through his Pet. He flared his demonic compulsion, and a concussion of air blasted outward round them—*ka-koom!*—in a billow of tangible thunder while a wicked vein of black lightning exploded from Dethkore's outstretched hands, no reach of sky necessary for the necromaster himself provided the source-pool of energy. "Oh gods yesss!"

The awesome projection of almighty power jagged across the battlefield in a smiting lance of evisceration rending hundreds of hungars and khansmen beyond them in the space of a blink while achieving indiscriminant course of scalding black death, all light round its quarter-mile stretch of sundering path captured through brief dimming. Bodies not instantly charred into smoldering husks blasted apart into puffy clouds of gray ash twinkling with the wafting red scatters of dying embers riding upon the risen winds.

Sergal gaped through the smoky riven opening in wide-eyed, open-mouthed awe, quivering with delight, salivating at new potentials.

He blinked hard, fearing it all a dream, ensuring it for true.

"Nothing," he whispered, and paused for shuddering swallow. "Nothing can stop me now." He elevated his gaze from the decimation and fixed focal upon the distant Academy spire awaiting his arrival. "Not even you, Soothsayer. The Godstone is all but mine."

Emotions bubbling up the back of his throat, Sergal craned his head and hissed laughter.

* * *

With flexes and flares of his demonic compulsion, Sergal through Dethkore made short work of all obstacles between them and Fist.

They strode west, preceded by smiting black jags of lightning eviscerating a smoldering pathway in front of them, while at their sides and behind followed an ever-growing, ever-feeding legion of hungars. His lycans had not returned from their wayward hunting, nor did the vampiric once-blacksmith Valdemar. But no matter that. Ahead awaited Fist. Ahead awaited the Soothsayer, the Head Mistress and her Book of Towers. And beyond that the Godstone.

Outside the pursuing hungar swarm, thousands of leaderless khansmen rallied into smaller armies of their own, motley crews of semi-organized units emboldened by numbers, united by greed for power, and enticed by the battle lust to risk attaining it.

Those not seeking easy loot and plunder elsewhere among the plethora of dead sought to challenge Sergal for possession of the gauntlets despite the hungars by charging in random hacking droves. And he blasted them to ashes, slowing nothing, Dethkore's black lightning smiting through their sundered masses.

Braver khansmen bands attempted to join Sergal's marching horde then scared away, those still able, when hungars turned upon the living joiners and ate them alive, uncaring of their purpose but to feed their insatiable appetites.

And no matter that, either.

For every westward mile gained across the war-torn plains the numbers of his sinistry increased by thousand, their moaning ranks swelling to the point that he relaxed the mental chore of reanimated bonding, severing control then tying spiritual weaves of influence off, allowing new hungars outside the greater horde to wander wherever their instincts drove them unleashed while seeking living flesh.

Having reached the straining limits of control, at least until he obtained the Godstone's limitless all-power, Sergal sensed a rough count of ten-thousand obedient hungers connected to his demonic web of compulsion, with thousands more skirting the horde in looser influence.

At last.

He stopped and stared ahead, licking his lips, the taste of imminent slaughter and his impending ascension to godhood wetting his mouth.

The tall stone walls encircling Fist offered no sure resistance. Sergal flared his demonic compulsion while flinging his hands out.

And Dethkore mimicked same gesture, the air concussing round them as his crackling gauntlets projected a jagging rent of black lightning which punched a smoldering hole large enough to drive several wagons through into the thick stonework of false protection, the impact blasting smoky debris of stony shrapnel into fantastic inward spray while propelling the closer fistian masses both animal and human into screaming spins and tumbles arcing through the blood-dappled air. Bodies splattered on, ricocheted off, and smashed into nearby buildings collapsing while screaming missiles punched bloody holes through crumbling walls.

Laughing strong, Sergal whipped his arms out then, flaring his demonic compulsion, threw them forward, aiming at the gaping maw of wall and the city beyond.

Thousands upon thousands of obedient hungars flooded past his sides in a gothic tide of moans and swarmed through the hole in a pale deluge of nightmare running rampant through the city's streets while feeding upon its scattering citizens and what little remained of its military reserves rallying to fend against the overwhelming horde of feeders.

Houses collapsed beneath the sheer weight of the swarming hungars' numbers when not brought down by the mad rush of pale hands clawing and tearing through wooden beams and planks or plaster for the delectable human flesh hidden within, their sweat acting as a pungent tang laced with fear's potent intoxicant wafting the air while guiding the hungars' starving senses to the huddled human meals.

Sergal stood back watching, allowing the bottleneck of swarming hungars time to thin while making space for his entry, all the while scanning through the chaos for his next living meal to sate his own voracious hunger pangs gnawing deep inside his rotting body.

So many delicious choices. A young one, yesss, ripe with innocence. No, two.

He smiled up at his necromancer Pet. "Are you enjoying this as much as I am?"

Dethkore's perpetual scowl answered nothing.

Sergal frowned and flexed a grip on his hellsteel dagger vitus while flaring his demonic compulsion through the soulring. "Smile."

Dethkore's sullen tombstone visage tensed, the corners of his mouth twisting up in forced obedience.

Sergal laughed and fixed his gaze ahead, aching to release the life-rending erasure of his Pet's Blackhole Abyss though knowing that power lay beyond his limited control until he achieved the Godstone. He frowned again upon Sera, viewing out through their eyes, wailing at such horrors displayed before them.

"Oh shut up," he hissed. But her miserable wailing pervaded—until he lashed her quiet. *I'll deal with you soon. The Book of Towers will remedy you, and transfer me into a more suitable vessel. After I kill the Head Mistress and the Soothsayer I'll find one and—*

He startled to a glorious epiphany.

Yesss. Why kill the Soothsayer when I can possess him instead? His body, and his power, will gift me the perfect human vessel. Yesss!

Anxious, fidgety, edging triumphant, Sergal said, "I've waited long enough."

He exerted another dominating flex of his demonic compulsion while whipping his hands forward.

Dethkore threw his gauntleted hands out in mimed gesture where concussed the air and exploded another crackling projection of black lightning ripping wicked path through the clogged hungar masses blocking their route.

Sergal walked through the haze of twinkling embers, over piles of ruin and scatters of blackened bones, charred and brittle skulls crunching beneath his feet where puffed clouds of ash. He inhaled deep the delicious smells of burnt flesh flavoring the air while passing through the gaping maw into Fist, and joined the beautiful chaos.

* * *

They rode hard, galloping straight through the enormous city, the thundering hooves of their charging warhorse accompanied by Jacob's hollers opening for them a sure course through the panicked crowds filling the streets when not knocking aside those too slow for darting out from the animal's unerring path.

Houses afire and looted shops and pleading faces and overturned carts whipped by in peripheral blurs, cries of alarm rising and falling in pockets and swallows of noise, Banzu saddled behind Jacob and clinging to the veteran with his good right arm, his sense of time and place throttled by the throbbing agony of his injured left arm.

I'm a coward . . . his only recurring thought, while he drifted in a dizzied haze of escape rife with memories of the war-torn plains chasing them.

"Stay with me, Soothsayer," Jacob said, and many times, bothering no look back, instead snapping reins while digging his heels for continual speed of their charging horse. "Stay with me."

And then they raced outside the walls through the city's closing western gates, striking open country at a furious pace while weaving round or through the miles-long parade of fleeing denizens where space allowed in lieu of trampling them down.

Mothers yanked careless and crying children out from harm's way of the snorting warhorse charging by so close the wind whipped at their hair and looser clothing. Angry fathers threw walking sticks or chucked nearby stones found upon the road in the riders' thundering wake, while some of the richer folk brandished swords they possessed no true skills for using in waving threat as their servants sweated through the burden of carrying their masters' heavy packs. Shopkeepers trundling along atop their overloaded wagons barked out curses while their horses thrashed the rigging or bucked in startled whinnies.

Banzu issued brief protest that they should stop, that they were abandoning these people let alone the thousands still within the city's walls to the unliving horde of hungars, or at least slow and warn them of the coming plague of horror.

But Jacob cut him short with a curt negative then a quick over the shoulder explanation of the Head Mistress already on her way to Bloom ahead of the fistian refugees, having abandoned Fist for the Godstone reported there, and that there existed no recourse but for catching up with her soon as possible.

Banzu made to say more, but an irresistible lassitude gripped him since escaping the plains, making the simple act of staying awake a tremendous chore. Let alone the gnawing pain throbbing in his injured forearm only amplified with every jostling bounce in saddle.

"But we can't just leave them!" he yelled above the thundering rush of hooves in a last attempt at relieving his guilt. But his own lack of conviction sank him in the saddle, exhausting to the truth of the failed war, the ache of his wounded left arm, pinched in a tight squeeze between his front and Jacob's back, giving him dizzy spells so that he clutched Jacob tighter round the middle with his right arm to keep from tumbling out from saddle—and bit back a curse, hot tears stinging his eyes, for the act crushed his broken bones.

Jacob answered nothing, instead speeding their mount faster onward.

After a time, they stopped. Jacob stripped the panting warhorse of its burden of armor, abandoning the battered chanfron and peytral and flanchards and such by cutting through the thick leather cinches and tossing all aside, then allowed the overworked animal coated in foamy latherin respite. In a daze Banzu cleaned then bandaged his throbbing wound by way of strips cut from Jacob's undershirt and the only waterskin the Head Mistress's First Sword possessed on hand.

Jacob commented nothing of Banzu's lycan bite, though his scrutinizing stare betrayed suspicions while Banzu wound his gruesome injury in makeshift bandages after rinsing it clean of blood and saliva, hissing with every miserable tightening twist round his lacerated forearm protesting flares of torment. He voiced worries over running the animal lame before reaching Bloom, however Jacob reassured him the endurance of their fistian lancer mount, the animal bred for marathon speed belied by its well-muscled frame and trained since its first rider for long charges across the open miles of the Azure Plains.

Panicked people strayed from the passing caravan, recognizing the First Sword and shouting questions of the war and of the missing Head Mistress while gathering near. Others recognized Banzu and cursed his part in the misery of their disrupted lives with accusations of blame, several pelting him with rocks or sticks or spitting at him.

Until Jacob pulled his sword and shouted the growing mob back, a stern fire of warning blazing in his eyes, barking threats of martial law and his willingness to enforce it on these troubled peoples.

Though seconds more they mounted with haste and continued west at a faster pace.

On they rode, trees and hills and people and wagons blurring by.

They stopped again an hour later when the exhausted horse slowed into a huffing trot then a panting canter then a defeated walk. They exchanged the tired animal of fine fistian stock for food and water they ate and drank on the spot, and some clothes for Banzu as well two fresh mounts from a squat caravanner wearing multiple golden and jewel-encrusted rings upon every one of his fat fingers out from fear of having them stolen despite his small though respectable retinue of guards. The haughty noble of inconsequential title refused the unequal trade—until Jacob announced himself and whom he served with a firm backhand that sent the blubbering man sprawling in the dirt.

Another hour of hard riding and they passed the head of the long refugee train escaping Fist for Bloom, then left it far behind, riding strong until nightfall forced them to stop again.

Little conversation exchanged between them while they camped a touch south of the road next to a stand of birches, the haunting glow of the atrocities taking place in Fist burning in constant reminder as a soft red glow beyond the eastern horizon where new fires claimed the city.

Banzu slid out from saddle then, his watery legs unhinging at the knees soon as his sore feet touched ground, he plopped onto his bottom in sagging delivery then collapsed backwards and lay for several restive minutes, lathered in sweat, wincing in pain, his throbbing left arm draped over his chest.

Jacob led the two horses to the nearby trees, tied their leads off and removed their tack and gear. He busied himself stripping lower branches for which to make a roadside hearth. Afterwards he stood staring at the eastern horizon in silent reverie, one hand clasped behind his back with the other in fisted salute to his heart, his militant posture that of a soldier offering solemn grace for his fallen fellows.

Banzu flopped over and approached the fire in a slow, one-armed crawl on hand and knees. He sat watching Jacob's turned back for a time while raking his good hand through the itchy scruff of his unkempt beard in minor annoyance, *scritch-scritch-scritch*, his mind an oppressive fog of guilt and shame as he walked the cemetery of his recent past, fingertips brushing the tops of tombstone memories.

It's not supposed to be like this. I killed the Khan . . . and everything still turned to shit. Dethkore and that pale little girl with snake eyes. Lycans, and hungars everywhere. Gods, at least the khansmen were living, breathing, mortal people. And the gauntlets . . . oh gods the gauntlets. Left behind. Along with my courage. What have I done?

Disgusted at himself as well the heinous turn of events, he spat into the fire, feeling every bit the cowardly failure.

Jacob about-faced, approached the fire and sat opposite him, the veteran soldier's hunched back turned to the red horizon of a city falling.

Banzu glanced up, met Jacob's tortured stare, then averted his gaze to anywhere else.

Distant thundering booms punctuated the silence every few minutes, and with each faint rumble Banzu winced, knowing though thousands escaped the city, tens of thousands more remained trapped behind Fist's encircling walls of imminent doom.

He relived those enormous western gates sealing closed behind them while Jacob shouted commands of containment and quarantine when they rode through the great stone archway, viewing the scene in grim reflection every time he shut his eyes and it replayed behind his lids.

Panicked protests from the scared refugees attempting to flee and join the miles-long caravan then denied whispered through his mind in recurring echoes of regret, terrified shouts muffling behind the closing gates only a few steps short from gaining their freedom instead having it stolen. Locked up tight in a city under siege by an unspeakable nightmare plague unknown since the Thousand Years War.

Distant booms continued signaling Fist's destructive fall to the invading hordes attacking its hapless denizens, filling its streets with droves of unliving hungars and packs of ravenous lycans in a frenzy of human feasting.

Jacob barked out a gruff laugh.

Banzu snapped his gaze forward and glared, ire spiking. "Something funny?"

Jacob shook his head, dark eyes glossy remorse reflecting firelight. "No, Soothsayer. Nothing funny here. I was just thinking is all." He straightened while swiping a hand down over his face, and tugged on his goatee. "I've spent my entire life behind those walls. Protecting them. Protecting my people. Protecting my city. And now—" He huffed while shrugging and threw his hands up in relenting gesture. "Now all of it's burning at my back. Fifty-three years of my life, gone." He snapped his fingers. "Just like that."

"I'm sorry," Banzu said. "I tried. I thought if—" But he clipped short, excuses sickening him.

Jacob inhaled deep, exhaled a wilting breath. "Die with the right regrets. My father taught me that. It's all a man can ever really do against the gods." He paused, glanced behind. "At least the containment buys us time."

Banzu hung his head on hunched shoulders and whispered, "I'm sorry."

Jacob studied him a moment while shifting position, feet drawing beneath him, left hand moving to right hipwing, the other palming the ground for counterbalance or perhaps for the instigative push into abrupt standing. "How's the arm? Lycan bites are nasty business, or so the olden stories go. And they say what they don't eat eventually . . . turns." A pause, his voice gaining edge. "Turns into one of them."

Banzu raised his gaze and peered over their little hearth into those dark eyes assessing him, though more so at Jacob's sure grip upon the sword hilt at his right hipwing, and frowned.

"I'll live." He shifted his gaze past Jacob and squinted at the ruddy glow of Fist bruising the black horizon, a task better achieved if only he could seize the Power without incurring its Source-bled madness. He swallowed down accusations lathering his throat, reflections of Jacob commanding the city's gates closed for containment rife in his mind and sharpening his tongue curt. "Too bad I can't say the same for all those poor people we left behind to die."

Jacob scowled, catching Banzu's underlying drift. He began standing, began pulling his sword. "Why you son of a—" But he stopped halfway and sat down, grunting. "Don't you look at me like that. Don't you dare. I've seen more than my fair share of killing, *boy*, and there's casualties in every war." He paused, nostrils flaring huffs, hard eyes thinning. "Sometimes you have to sacrifice the few to save the many. I may be a mean old bastard, but I still have a heart." He pounded a fist to his puffing chest. "A proud fistian heart!" Then extended a stern finger at Banzu. "And it's bleeding—" With same hand he swiped stray tears from his cheeks. "It's bleeding for every godsdamned one of my people still in there and don't you forget it."

Banzu opened his mouth, closed it. He sighed, nodded. *Don't blame him. It's not his fault. He's right. What else was he supposed to do?* "I'm sorry. I didn't mean—"

"Yeah, you didn't mean and you don't know. I was busting Privates on the plains while you were still sucking milk from your mother's teat." Jacob huffed a terse breath, the scolding fire in him dying. In softer voice he added, "Just . . . just forget it. We have enough problems as it is."

Silence pervaded.

"How?" Banzu asked after a time, his mind diverting down a different track.

Jacob scrunched his face. "How what?"

"How did you know to come for me? How did you know where I was in all that mess? How did you know I was even still alive?"

Jacob smirked, short-lived. "What, you think you're the only aizakai around?" He raised his right hand and flexed it in gesture then lowered it dangling between his parted knees with the other. "I've got the farsight. Once I touch someone and print them with it I can see through their eyes. For a time, at least. Glimpses, mostly. But like all things it's faded with age. Not so keen as it used to be."

Farsight? "Oh." Banzu raised his right hand and flexed it through the memory of their parting handshake moments before he took to the battle plains in revenging bid for the Khan. *So you're not just a soldier but an aizakai. Of course. The Head Mistress wouldn't have chosen otherwise.* Jacob was her First Sword, after all, responsible for protecting her life. "I didn't know." He flexed his hand again, peering into his palm and expecting to see some sort of transferred mark though nothing marred his skin so that he closed his hand into a lowering fist. "I didn't feel anything."

Jacob shrugged. "None do. That's the beauty of it." He paused, gaze thinning. "When you first came back, I thought we'd lost you. Those godsdamned eyes of yours—" He paused again, shivered visibly. "Seeing through your eyes wasn't pleasant, I'll tell you what. But a hundred men like you and the war would've been over before it even started."

He raked a hand back through his graying raven tangles and blew out his shaven cheeks, shook his head. "All those khansmen you killed. No, slaughtered. The handshake was only meant so I could report to the Head Mistress on what was happening while we made our way to Bloom. Information is the best ally when it comes to war. But when I saw"—a pause, another visible shiver—"what I saw, I turned back without telling her."

He leaned forward, met Banzu's gaze above the fire. "I aimed to kill you after you killed the Khan. Thought it better that I try right afterwards, hoping the fight would've tired you out enough. The last thing this world needs is a turned Soothsayer running around killing everyone. Hells, you left proof enough of that back on the plains."

He sat back and raked at his goatee, twisted its pointy tip betwixt finger and thumb. "But on my way back I saw . . . no, I knew it wasn't like I'd feared. My farsight can't read minds, but I've seen enough through others' eyes to learn how to judge a man's thoughts by the way he views the world. Whatever possessed you before was gone, changed somehow. And when I watched Mistress Shandra ripped apart by those godsforsaken beasts, I knew right then that I had to try and get you out. Or die trying." He slapped the hilt at his right hipwing. "Good thing I stopped and switched out swords in the armory on my way through. If not for my farsight we'd both be dead. Or worse, one of those things."

"Possessed," Banzu said, repeating the foul word. "You don't know the half of it."

Jacob cocked an eyebrow. "Then tell me. Because when you came back with that . . . that evil in your eyes, I just about pissed my britches. And believe me I've seen plenty of bad."

Banzu drew in deep, blew out a deflating huff. "I *was* possessed. The Essence of the First? It's the spirit of Simus Junes. The keyrings took me . . . took me somewhere. That's where and why I vanished. I absorbed the Essence, brought it back with me, inside me, and it crazed my mind. It almost took all of me, but I fought it off."

"You sure about that?" Jacob stiffened, hand gripping sword hilt again, posture taut. "I'm no sage, but I'm no fool either. And I'm not taking you to the Head Mistress just to endanger her life." He stood, springy. "If this is something we have to deal with here and now—"

"I said I'm fine," Banzu said, too tired for tensing, though he waved Jacob back, unsure how much a struggle he could muster but for sticking his neck out for the slitting. "I just can't seize the Power anymore." *Or that'll be the end of Banzu Greenlief, and that sword of yours won't stop what takes my place.* "At least not until I touch the Godstone."

"Seize the Power," Jacob said, sitting, testing the words while repeating them. He cocked his head to one side while chewing on the meaning of those words before the swallow. "So you mean you can't . . ." He left the rest of his question hanging between them unfinished in all but his stare.

Banzu shook his head. "I can. But I can't. Not until I touch the Godstone." *If Enosh wasn't lying.* "My aizakai power feeds on my lifeforce while I'm using it, speeding me up and aging me faster than everyone else." With his good hand he ruffled his hair then gripped his full red beard in gesture of the obvious growth since their last meeting and their parting handshake.

Jacob eased back, blinking hard, rubbed his eyes and blinked again, only then receiving full notice of Banzu's longer hair and beard. "Gods," he whispered, shaking his head. "I'm too poor to pay attention."

"But my Power's been corrupted by the Essence of Simus," Banzu continued. "And it can only be cleansed with the Godstone." With his right hand he hitched a thumb over his right shoulder, indicating Bloom awaiting them through the indiscernible black pitch at his back long miles west. "Which I can feel, by the way. Like a second heartbeat. Growing stronger the closer we get."

"Wait a minute." Jacob scrunched his face. "You can feel it? The Godstone?"

Banzu nodded. "Through the Essence of Simus, yes." *And now so can Dethkore. Because of me.* But he put no voice behind the blaming afterthought.

"So it's true." Jacob leaned forward, appraising him once more. "That's good to hear. Confirms the reports of its falling in Bloom. Or thereabouts. The reports were vague on the exact location. Gwendora's eyes-and-ears were in a scramble just to get them to us. So she's on the right track then." He rocked back while gripping then slapping his thighs. "Oh thank gods. There's that at least."

"Thank you."

"What?"

Banzu cleared his throat, began again. "Thank you for saving me. I—"

Jacob burst into laughter.

Banzu frowned. "What?"

"Thank *me*?" Jacob shook his head. "I should be thanking you! You killed the Khan, Soothsayer, and—"

"And paved the way for an unliving army nipping at our heels." Banzu blew out his cheeks, and the effort withered him into a smaller sullen hunch. In a lower tone he added, "You should've let them kill me. I might've even taken down Dethkore with me, before those godsdamned hungars eventually overwhelmed me." Though he harbored strong doubts of actually killing the necromaster. "I deserve as much."

"That's enough of that," Jacob said, a snappy heat in his risen voice. "We still need you, Soothsayer. She still needs you." He pointed west, past Banzu, indicating the 'she' in question the Head Mistress Gwendora Pearce. "Without you there's no chance of destroying the Godstone, remember? Hells, Soothsayer, we've lost a lot of lives, but you're going to save a whole lot more."

Banzu leaned sideways while pulling Griever free from his left hipwing.

Jacob straightened stiff. "What are you doing?"

Banzu tossed then caught Griever lengthwise at the middle balance point across his upturned right palm. He stared over the blade's glimmering surface capturing flickers of firelight for the space of a dozen heartbeats, then let slip the keen length of steel off his fingers to the ground in front of his feet, grimacing disgust. He curled his empty hand into a trembling fist, wanting only to pound while cursing the instrument of death into the ground, though said nothing.

Frowning, Jacob glanced from Banzu to sword and back again. "What'd you go and do that for, Soothsayer?"

"I'm done." Banzu looked away from the sword tainted with memories too cruel to endure the burden of any longer. "I don't want it anymore." *I'm sorry.* And hoped the memory of his uncle would forgive him Griever's abandonment.

Jacob frowned. "What?"

"I've enough blood on my hands to last me ten lifetimes. You saw what I did. How easy it was. That's not me anymore. I'm done killing."

Jacob crossed his arms and assessed him a silent stretch. "Just like that, huh?"

Banzu nodded. "Just like that."

Jacob shook his head. "A man's blade is his spine, Soothsayer. I would've thought you'd know that by now. You more than most."

"I don't want to kill anyone anymore. The Khan's dead. I'm through."

Jacob expelled a mirthless chuckle. "A vow of preservation, is it? Hell of a thing for a swordslinger to swear."

Banzu shrugged.

Jacob thinned his eyes, upon Griever and Banzu both. "I'll not take it, if that's what you're asking."

Banzu peered off into the nowhere of darkness. "Then don't."

"No." Jacob grunted while rocking into standing. "We're not finished yet." He considered Banzu, considered Griever, his frown deepening into a tight scowl beneath his scolding glare. "Pick it up."

Banzu refused him with a look. "No."

"All those people back there aren't dying for nothing." Tone serrated, Jacob's visage hardened, nostrils flaring, dark eyes piercing. He took a step, gripping his sword's hilt in a dangerous fanning of fingers, the fire between them casting a flickering dance of gothic shadows up the length of him. "I said pick it up, Soothsayer. Now."

Banzu rebuked him with a testy glare, and for a time . . . silence.

Jacob trembled with bridled rage tensing all of him, his glare focal. "Godsdamn you." He took another step while pulling his sword half bared. "Pick it up! Or I swear to gods you'll wish I'd killed you on the plains."

Banzu considered the challenge—for all of three seconds. "Fine. Whatever." He snatched Griever by the hilt, leaned sideways and stabbed the sword home at his left hipwing, scowling through the motions. "And my name's not Soothsayer, it's Banzu." He looked away, glowering.

Jacob sheathed his sword though maintained his grip. "Hey," he said, curt and sharp.

"What?"

"Look at me, you miserable shit."

Banzu did, glaring. "What?"

Jacob opened his mouth then closed it, sighing through his nose, tensed posture relaxing a shave. "I've done a lot of killing myself. I've been in too many battles to count. And I've learned a thing or two about a thing or two along the way. Every man needs to test his own mettle. I get that. The gods know I've been there a few times myself." He paused and held Banzu's gaze a moment overlong. "So we'll pretend like that didn't just happen. Understand?"

Banzu held the moment overlong . . . then nodded, said nothing.

"That's right." He eyeballed Banzu an extra measure, nodding, then released his grip of hilt only after he removed then sat, their gazes never breaking. "Soothsayer—"

"Banzu."

"Okay then. Banzu. My apologies. I'm a military man. I'm used to titles is all." Jacob fixed Banzu's injured arm with a pensive stare. "You're going to have to get that looked at sooner than later. Sewn up at least. All those bandages are doing is holding it together. Gwendora didn't take any healers with her on her rush out, but there should be a few on hand in Bloom." A shrugging pause. "Maybe. If Locha's Luck turns our favor. The Baron's wife isn't exactly fond of other aizakai after what happened between her and . . . well, doesn't matter. We'll figure something out. Mabselene has Victor by the saggy balls, and he jumps at every squeeze, but he'll listen well enough to the Head Mistress."

Banzu raised the throbbing agony of his bandaged left forearm, wincing through the motion, and stared it over, glad for the change of subject despite its unsavory topic. Not the first wolf bite his arm had taken, only back then, in the timeline undone by his re-beginning, he'd earned the first and its infectious chillfever fending against a savage pack of frostwolves in truth no more than hungry dire pups. He lowered his arm, hugging it against his middle, and sighed. "Yeah. I know. I will."

A tremendous boom thundered in the eastern distance, faint though louder than the previous ones so that Jacob twisted round and threw a glance east. He twisted back smirking.

"What?" Banzu asked.

"Head Mistress left a nasty surprise behind. Sounds like they just found it."

"Surprise?"

Jacob nodded. "She slipped the Book of Towers out with Mistress Agatha soon as you pulled your little vanishing act. Just in case things turned sour. In its place is a room full of kamikaze mages. Was a room full."

A flush of panic jolted Banzu tensed. "Wait. Aggie's not with Gwen?"

Jacob shook his head. "The gods only know where she is by now. And I doubt its Bloom, or that would be one hell of a coincidence considering the reports of the Godstone didn't come in until after Mistress Agatha fled the Academy with the book for safer keeping. No, my bet is she headed west then broke north. She wouldn't cut south, that's for sure. Only a godsdamned fool would risk traveling the ghost fields of Fel Kari. She's probably holed up in some remote cave only Head Mistress knows where. Might be we won't hear from her for a good while yet."

Oh gods, Aggie. Banzu sat back, expelling a heavy sigh. *I forgot all about her.*

He stared down into his lap, fixing upon the two lanthium keyrings he still wore, Jericho's and Aggie's wedding bands, so that he raised his right hand for show. "Maybe we can trade these rings for some food and water on the way. They're lanthium. Must be worth something. Asides, they've served their purpose. I don't need them anymore."

Jacob nodded, frowning, agreeing though disapproving of trading away ancient Academy artifacts for something so minor yet necessary as food and drink. "Maybe. There's a lucky few wandering ahead of us who got out early. We're well past the train though, and we're not waiting for them to catch up." He stood, turned away to the horses then spun back. "Get some shut-eye. You've earned it. I'll wake you in a few hours. We have plenty of riding left."

Banzu sighed. "I'm exhausted, but every time I close my eyes . . ." He trailed away.

Jacob held the moment overlong before nodding understanding. "I know. But try anyways."

"And who's going to wake you?"

Jacob smirked. "I'm a military man. I rest with my eyes open."

Banzu lay back. "Must be nice."

Jacob said, "Hey."

Banzu sat up. "Yeah?"

"You did good. Real good. What you did today mattered."

Banzu nodded, forced a smile leaving his eyes untouched. "Thanks." He glanced past Jacob at the two horses tethered to the stand of birches and cropping grass. "I don't suppose you have a blanket hidden somewhere I don't know about do you?"

Jacob smirked and turned away. "Nope."

Banzu sighed. "Yeah. Didn't think so."

He lay back and curled up closer to the fire for warmth, closing his eyes while muffling his ears with his hands, trying to deafen the faint booms sounding from the east.

Nightmares intruded soon as sleep claimed him.

* * *

Hours later, still dark, the roadside hearth little more than a glowing nest of coals, Banzu awoke to Jacob's standing loom and nudging him with the toe of his boot.

He groaned while uncurling on the cold hard ground, muscles stiff protests, then groaned again while sitting up and rubbing the oblivion of too-little sleep from his blurry eyes.

And startled, staring up the length of Jacob's drawn sword the tip of which aimed inches from his flinching face.

"Grip it," Jacob said.

"What?" Banzu's right hand moved by instinct to his opposite hip for gripping Griever's hilt, but he stopped the motion halfway there at the stern shake of Jacob's head. "What for?"

"Silver is a burning bane to shifterkin. I don't know how long it's supposed to take, but there may be beast blood coursing through your veins. Best I check it now." Jacob waggled his sword. "Grip it. If it burns . . ." He trailed away, leaving the rest unsaid in all but the lines tightening round his adamant stare.

Banzu sighed, reached up.

Jacob slapped his reaching right hand away with an admonishing flick of sword then jabbed at his left. "Other hand. The bitten one."

Banzu reached out his bandage left arm, grunting painful winces earned through the extending motion, his hand tremulous. Capturing a bracing breath, he gripped the silver sword's end and felt . . . nothing but the flush of relief, the metal cold to his fevered touch.

"Nothing." He released his grip and, wincing through retraction, held up his palm in showing gesture. "See? No burns. Guess you don't have to kill me after all."

Jacob blew out his cheeks then sheathed his silver-dipped sword to his right hipwing. "I had to be sure."

Banzu nodded, grumbling curses while scratching at his itchy beard. "I know."

Jacob studied him a moment. "Here." He produced something from his back pants pocket and tossed it at Banzu's feet. "Handle that miserable rat's nest while I ready the mounts. Godsdamned thing is making *my* face itch."

Banzu picked up and unfolded the barber's razor, four inches of keen steel sharp enough to split a hair and connected to a bone handle with tiny print engraved thereon though unreadable in the dark. "Where'd you get this?"

"My lucky razor. I carry it with me wherever I go." Jacob stroked his well-manicured goatee. "That's why I always look so pretty."

He turned and tossed the rest of their firewood into the hearth, producing an updraft of twinkling embers swirling the brightening air, then walked away to the two horses hitched by the stand of birches and began dressing the animals for riding.

Banzu peered into the depths of his left palm unburned, then fixed his gaze east upon the ruddy glow of Fist still dominating the black horizon, a throbbing ruby dome churning broken columns of smoke choking out the stars above it.

With a heavy sigh he fell to task of sawing away the scruff of his itchy untamed beard.

CHAPTER FORTY-FOUR

The Calderos Mountains spanned the entire length of the western horizon, a colossal rocky spine stabbing the sky, its frosted peaks hidden deep inside the thick elevation of creeping fog and suspended clouds swallowing the upper half of the incredible range dividing eastern Bloom from western Tyr not yet burned thin by the new day.

Miles ahead the city of Bloom welcomed Banzu and Jacob in all its glorious, sparkling splendor. They rode with the blood-orange sunrise throwing warming rays upon their backs and past them, lancing bars of light highlighting the white city in a fantastic dazzle of waking illumination.

They slowed their horses from gallop through canter to trot then walk, Banzu's sore backside and tender thighs groaning appreciation for the reprieve from jouncing in saddle.

"Ahh," Jacob breathed more than said, riding at Banzu's left. "A beautiful sight to behold." *In more ways than one*, his relieved tone indicated while he stroked his goatee, twisting its pointy tip after the caressing finish.

"The Beacon City . . ." Banzu said, trailing into silence while staring ahead, gaze captured by the growing twinkles of quartzite reflecting captures of sunrise rushing past them. His knowledge of the olden title came from another's memories bleeding into his own from the shared collective, trickles of insight imparted with uncomfortable awareness of its origin.

"Aye," Jacob said, catching Banzu with a sidelong squint. "Though I haven't heard Bloom called that since I was a knee-high sprat." He stroked his goatee, slower this time, then pointed ahead at the small camp of tents and horses resting on the northern side of the road. "The Head Mistress awaits." Another stroke of his goatee, faster now, revealing itself more an anxious habit. "Best you prepare for a sour earful." He paused, frowned and nodded while amending with another nervous stroke of his goatee, "We."

Banzu nodded, only half listening, too focused on the glimmering spectacle of Bloom and the sunrise washing evermore radiant shine upon the lightening city, while inside him thrummed stronger with shrinking distance the honing presence of the Godstone through the invisible umbilical tether pulling him west.

Same as its western opposite of Tyr, the Iron City, Bloom stood carved from the side of the Calderos Mountains, the two contrasting cities connected by Caldera Pass, the only viable traveling route through the majestic mountains instead of over them, or round their long stretch north in the frozen wastes of the Thunderhell Tundra or south to the Presh Desert where lay Fel Kari south of Tyr. Though here a gigantic, exposed vein of white marble ore peppered with pretty flecks of quartzite jagged down the treacherous eastern Calderos face in a beautiful scar, the darker sides of which, honeycombed with caves and pits, lay hidden beneath the fading night's ascending shadows blanketing the riot of colors dappling green fields.

Climbing sprawls of vibrant flowers splashed the mountainside for miles beside and behind the sparkling city in a multicolored rainbow backdrop resembling a mad painter's chaotic musings in an oceanic spectacle of flowers defying all but the harshest of winters and possessing multitudes of alchemical properties within their varied pollens allowing them to bloom all year round, thus imparting the city's name. The mesmerizing sight almost helped Banzu forget the throbbing pain in his injured arm—almost.

Two days of hard riding broken only by brief periods of rest, more for the pressed horses than the riders they carried, and they'd achieved well ahead of the miles-long train of refugees fleeing Fist for Bloom. Though that train's head peeked over the eastern horizon in slow pursuit, producing a tiny pupil of people before the orange sun's rising eye behind them.

"If we're lucky," Jacob continued, "Head Mistress'll afford us a last meal before she flails us." He slapped then rubbed his trim belly. "I choose bacon, and lots of it. What for you, Soothsayer?"

Banzu said nothing to the veteran's apparent jest, for his vision shimmered and swam. He blinked hard, closed his eyes tight, swayed in saddle while shadows danced behind his lids. His heartbeat quickened with a jolt, racing while kneading knuckles at his temples. His senses flushed keen, spiking ultra-sensitive, too sharp to the point of painful so that he winced.

"Soothsayer?"

Banzu's heating blood coursed with new fever through his swelling network of veins while his bandaged lycan bite throbbed with the strange sensation of nesting larvae writhing beneath his itchy skin, catalyzing the ache for tearing loose the bandages and scratching his skin raw. A growl buried deep rumbled in the guttural depths of him, craving release.

Jacob said something, but his voice sounded a watery blur of chiming syllables.

Reeling in saddle, the Godstone's incessant honing thrum thundered at the base of Banzu's skull with headache. His breathing increased to short and rapid panting then settled when his oversensitive senses dulled normal. Lathered in sweat yet shivering, gripping the saddle horn for balance, he inhaled deep then expelled overlong, recovering.

Jacob, who had taken both horses' reins to hand and stopped the animals in the middle of the road, stared him down. "Hey. You still with me, Soothsayer?"

"Huh?" Banzu blinked through clearing vision fuzzed round all three of Jacob, the two side Jacobs retracting inwards and forming the one whole of the middle man again. "Oh. Yeah. Sorry." *Gods, what was that?*

Jacob eyeballed him a scrutinizing length, frowning. He glanced afar at the Head Mistress's camp of tents, then exchanged reins for sword hilt while turning his horse, blocking the road. He unsheathed his silver-coated blade and leveled it out between them, his arm a bar of corded muscle. "Grip it."

"I'm fine." Banzu scrubbed glistening dapples of sweat from his forehead with the back of his good forearm, his other a throbbing folded wing tucked tight against his stomach. "I'm just tired. Too long in saddle. Too little food."

Jacob tightened his eyes, his voice. "I don't care. Excuses are assholes. I said grip it. Or you'll take it in the heart."

Scowling, Banzu waved him off. "I said I'm—"

"I'll not risk her life for yours, Soothsayer. And I won't tell you again." Jacob urged his sword forward, its tip inches from pricking Banzu's chest, left of center. "Grip it. Now."

Banzu held the elder's unyielding stare in a return challenge he possessed no strength for backing up.

"You've got three seconds," Jacob said. "One. Two—"

"All right all right." Banzu huffed a terse breath while uncurling his injured arm, wincing through the motion, and snatched the end of the silver-dipped sword in a feisty grip. "See—*ow!*"

Flinching, eyes blooming wide, Jacob startled stiff in saddle.

Banzu hissed while recoiling his arm, shaking his hand, and yelped from the flaring torment of flexing muscles tensing round broken bones as his spooked horse twisted and turned beneath him, rounding him about. "Friggin hell!"

Jacob barked a curse while rearing his sword back, measuring for stabbing strike.

"No, wait!" Banzu raised his palm between them for show. "Relax! I just cut myself. See? No burns."

Jacob leaned forward into squinty inspection of Banzu's upraised palm, the hairline thin slice of crying red thereon, then leaned back and blew out his cheeks. He shook his head while sheathing his sword. And laughed.

"Holy gods, Soothsayer, don't do that to me! I about pissed my britches. And damn near killed you."

Banzu presented a lie-covering smile while swiping his bleeding palm dry on a thigh. "Sorry."

In truth and surprise the sword grabbed hot to his touch, fierce as flames though not so scalding as to brand his skin through the brief contact. *Thank gods I squeezed too hard and cut my hand before the true burn. Friggin fire slicing across my palm.* But he schooled the pain from betraying his face and otherwise instigate Jacob into taking liberties with that sword. It proved an effort not to wilt in saddle at the new revelation. *And that means . . . friggin hell. If it's not one thing it's another. Why always me?*

He wondered how much longer until the beast blood contagion questing through his veins began overruling his human nature. And hoped the Godstone's healing grace would provide a cleansing panacea to more than just the corrupted Source.

Two days since that chomp on my arm, so why now? Doesn't matter. All the more reason to see this through. I've held on this long. Just a little more. We're almost there. Won't be more than a few hours. Keep it together. Play it cool.

He flicked a gesture at the Head Mistress's camp of tents resting ten miles shy of Bloom's eastern ring of defensive walls though less than five from him and Jacob, a straight shot to both. "Time's wasting. And the Godstone's close, I can feel it gnawing at me."

Jacob perked up in saddle. "How close?"

"Very."

Jacob grunted and nodded. "Then let's get at it." He recovered his reins then turned his horse and rode away.

Banzu fetched a glance east, at the distant train of hundreds of fistian refugees surmounting the far horizon, thousands more invisibles behind them, then pursued alongside Jacob.

* * *

They approached the little makeshift camp and its slew of picketed horses. A handful of mages and soldiers scrambled out from various tents, roused alert by shouts issued from the scattered knot of armed and armored infantry standing guard through the night. Sleepy-eyed fistains gathered and startled at sight of Jacob's return then startled anew at sight of Banzu riding alongside the returning First Sword.

A few cheers arose though died short, as well several soldiers started running then arrested two or three steps out, deciding it best to stay their place.

"Brace yourself," Jacob said in low voice, as much to Banzu as himself, reining his horse to halt, leaving a hundred or so feet of space between them and the nearest watchers.

Banzu stopped his mount beside him, tensing against the weight of all those stares fixing upon him. He forced a smile, hoping to appease those cautious stares. "I'm already cringing."

Another shout bellowed while the two riders dismounted and stayed their place, side by side between their horses. A soldier disappeared within the largest tent then rushed out seconds later. He spun round and held open the azure tent's flap for the tall, dark-skinned woman exiting behind him.

Head Mistress Gwendora Pearce, garbed in blue regal riding dress trimmed with jags of black, its sides split from hips to hem unbuttoned and exposing dark leather breeches beneath, paused and stared, her kinky bush of hair tied back into a knot, her face a blank though tensed slate. She cracked it with frowning ire when she advanced through the milling fistians, more gale than woman, mages and soldiers hopping out from her warpath then closing in behind her. She stopped in front of Jacob, tall and carved from wood, her focal violet glare molten, piercing.

He opened his mouth.

She slapped him across the face—*smack!*

Banzu flinched, cringing to the phantom sting of her slap.

Gasps stole through the hush of watchers locked in stare, several soldiers wincing.

"You godsdamned fool of a man!" Gwendora fisted Jacob's shirt and shook him, then hugged her stunned First Sword in a strong embrace that arched the shorter man into a groaning backwards bend on his shifting feet. "I thought I'd lost you. Thank gods you're alive." She withdrew, the violet fire in her eyes burning strong above a soft smile that faded when she transferred her scolding glare to Banzu beside him.

Jacob opened his mouth.

But the Head Mistress already sidestepped away, left, glaring Banzu down, the kohatheen tied off at her belt gripped white-knuckled in her hand in a strangler's squeeze on the lanthium aizakai slaveband. "And you."

Banzu opened his mouth—then his head whipped right, pain flaring his left cheek, from the Head Mistress's vicious slap comparing the one she delivered Jacob to a lover's playful pat. He grunted and grimaced, firmed his lips into a tight red line, drew in a sharp nostril breath and met her glare for glare.

The tension crackled taut between them. Behind her, soldiers gripped sword hilts for pulling while shifting postures in preparation for the ordered rush. Six robed aizakai broke forth from their numbers and fanned out behind the Head Mistress, three to a side, their risen hands gesturing in preemptive traceries of sorcery.

Gwendora flinched nothing when Banzu withdrew from her a safer step and gripped Griever's hilt, wary of fending against an assault.

Jacob turned inward, facing Banzu, also gripping his sword for pulling. "Don't even think about it, Soothsayer."

Gwendora arched her eyebrows while scoffing at Banzu's defensive gesture, then flicked her dismissive wrist at his sword. "If you're going to kill me then be quick about it. Otherwise tell me why I shouldn't have you strung up by the shorthairs for what you've done." She tugged at her kohatheen. "Let alone—" But it stayed tied to her hip despite her frustrated jerks so that she fiddled it loose, muttering curses, and held it up. "Let alone lock this around your scrawny neck."

Banzu began, "Hannibal Khan is—"

"Dead," she finished for him, sharp and curt. "I know. And the gauntlets are lost to us. Both because of you."

"How?" he asked, remembering the blue-skinned Dreshian rider Shandra ordered away carrying the Khan's head in a leather bag though not seeing the jaw-tusked man present here, sure the soldier failed escaping the war-torn plains. He glanced at Jacob. "How do you know?"

"Trina's been scrying for me what's happened in Fist." Without looking, Gwendora swept her arm out behind her in gesture at the green-robed mage to her right who nodded, then she thinned her glare on Jacob. "Though hers is not nearly as focused a talent as the one that ran off. But that's neither here nor there now." She took a challenging step forward—and Banzu removed a cautious step from her towering loom. "You stubborn fool. Do you have any idea what you've done?"

Melting to the burning brunt of her admonishing glare, Banzu lowered his gaze to his fascinating feet and said nothing.

"Mistress—" Jacob began.

She ignored him as well clipped him short, too intent with reprimanding Banzu. "You were supposed to leave with me. Instead you almost ruined everything by running after the Khan."

"Mistress—" Jacob said in louder try.

She talked over him, her eyes violet stabs of focal heat, her voice a cracking whip. "And to think I trusted you! After everything we discussed. Our bargain. Your promise. You've given us an even greater enemy is what you've done. Hannibal Khan is nothing compared to that godsforsaken necromaster."

Jacob said, "Mistress—"

"You weren't out there," Banzu said. "You don't know—"

"You delivered him the Dominator's Gauntlets on a godsdamned platter you godsdamned fool!" She thrust her free hand out whipping-quick and jabbed a stern finger inches from Banzu's nose. "I never should've trusted you. I never should've listened to Aggie. I never should've removed your kohatheen—"

"Enough!" Jacob shouted.

Gwendora clipped short, grimacing, eyes flaring then thinning upon her First Sword.

Jacob rumbled his throat clear and continued in a lower, more reasonable tone. "I'm sorry, Mistress. The Khan's dead. And we're here now. That's what matters. We need to focus on what we have." A pause, an audible swallow, a glance behind. "Refugees are on their way. They'll start arriving in a day or so. I quarantined the city on our way out, but it won't hold for long. There's an unliving army approaching our backs so there's no time for bickering. He senses the Godstone. The reports are true. It's here somewhere. Somewhere close. Right, Soothsayer?"

"Is this true?" Anger receding in a flush of hope stealing the fire from her voice, Gwendora took a half-step forward, her visage fragile. "Is it?"

Banzu nodded. "I can feel its presence thrumming inside me." He raised his good arm and pointed past her, at Bloom awaiting them. "The closer I get, the stronger its pull. I can't tell how far though. Either somewhere in Bloom or just beyond it."

She considered him a moment. "The gift of retrieving the Essence of the First, I presume?"

He nodded, adding nothing of the true complications retrieving the Essence had caused him upon his return from that elsewhere caveplace of the keyrings' vanishing transport.

Gwendora smiled, relaxing a space, though her smile tightened and she tensed again when her gaze locked upon Banzu's bandaged arm. She flicked Jacob a cursory glance. "Trina viewed lycans among the hungars." She withdrew a cautious step, thinned her eyes into suspicious slits. "Are you merely injured? Or worse?"

Banzu hesitated, then decided it best just to spill it all out and be done with it. "It's broken, but . . . I was bitten by a—"

"By a warhound," Jacob cut in. "It's true, Mistress. I saw it myself. Locha's Luck the godsdamned beast sank its teeth right before I scooped him up and we rode off. Almost dragged us both out from saddle before I stabbed its eye out."

Banzu shot Jacob a sidelong glance and neither added to nor corrected the curious lie.

"A warhound." Gwendora considered them both, then fetched a suspicious glance over a shoulder at Trina who shrugged. "I see. Well." She inhaled deep and blew out a frustrated huff of cheeks. "What's done is done. You're right, Jacob. Best not to dwell. What matters now is the Godstone." She snapped her shoulders back and rolled her head from side to side, sighing. She considered the kohatheen, considered Banzu, then to his relief tied to lanthium hoop back to her belt at her left hipwing instead of attempting locking it round his neck. "We're only a few steps shy from walking off a cliff. No sense in running blind. You're here now. That's what matters."

"Mistress," Jacob said, "he needs a healer. At least some hook and gut and a splint."

She crossed her arms and regarded Banzu a lengthy moment, gaze softening to sympathy. "How bad is it?"

Banzu shrugged. "I still have my arm."

"Here." She reached out. "Let me see it."

"No." He withdrew a half step, tucking his bandaged arm to stomach while twisting away. "I'm fine."

She rolled her eyes and sighed. "Let me see it. Maybe it's not as bad as you think. Sometimes fractures only feel like they're broken. You may be only a little worse for wear."

Banzu hesitated, then stepped closer and offered his injured arm out.

She held it with tender care. "Does it hurt?"

He frowned up at her. "Of course it—"

"Good." She gripped his arm with both crimping hands and squeezed.

He yowled, flaring jolts of agony lancing up his arm and rampaging torment throughout the rest of him, watery legs unhinging at the knees so that he crashed to his caps, trembling, eyes hot fractured prisms of tears running his cheeks.

"Pain," Gwendora said, retracting her hands, "is a fantastic reminder of what happens when you don't listen to sounder minds."

"Mistress—" Jacob began.

"Don't you Mistress me," she said, jabbing a stern finger in his flinching face then shifting it to a kneeling, cringing Banzu hugging his throbbing arm. "You're lucky I don't tan both your hides." She clinched her fist and shook it at them both. "I should—I should—bah! Too much to do and too little time for doing it."

With that she spun round in an agitated huff and strode away muttering hot strings of curses at the world and every insubordinate First Sword in it, those in front of her too slow in sidestepping out from her warpath shoved backwards while she barked orders for breaking camp between threats of Soothsayer strangulation. She ducked and disappeared inside her tent while doing her irritated best at slamming its flap closed. A moment more the limp drape slapped open and out poked Gwendora's scowling face. She yelled, "Jacob! Now!" Then disappeared back within behind another failing slam of fabric.

The six mages and fifteen soldiers stared collective at Jacob though more so Banzu—for all of about three seconds.

"What are you sorry lot looking at?" Jacob asked in a commanding flare of voice. "You heard the Head Mistress. Show's over. Bust your tents and gather your gear! I want you locked and loaded on a double!"

Mages and soldiers scattered to any and everywhere, busying themselves with gathering their things while breaking camp.

"Gods that hurt." Banzu swiped tears from his eyes while Jacob helped him into standing. "What the frig is wrong with her?"

Jacob chuckled. "You disappeared, and I ran off. Can't blame her for being a little foul at us. Hells, that went a lot better than I expected. Least we still have our skins."

Banzu huffed a terse breath while glaring through the bustle at the Head Mistress's tent, part of him wanting to charge inside though the smarter part of him staying his place. "Thanks for not telling her."

"Don't thank me yet."

"Why'd you do it?"

Jacob sighed, stroked his goatee. "She has enough on her plate. No sense in piling more worries. Not when we're this close." He stared overlong at distant Bloom, then faced Banzu and poked him in the chest. "You have until the day's over to find the Godstone before I drop her your secret. I don't know how lycan bites work, but if you're lying to me, or if I see a single hair sprout out of place, I won't hesitate to kill you. Understand?"

Banzu nodded, said nothing.

"Good." Jacob slapped him on the shoulder. "Ask Trina about stitching you up. She's no healer, but she spent a year or so tending recruits in the infirmary far as I know. That'll have to do for now. Head Mistress wasn't serious about making you wait. She just wanted to prove her point."

"No," Banzu said. "I'm fine." And buried it with another lie. "I think she's right. It doesn't hurt as much as it did. It's probably only fractured. I'll worry about it after the Godstone."

Jacob shrugged. "Tough it out then. Your choice. You just remember what I said." He walked away, weaving between the bustling others breaking camp or preparing their horses for riding, and disappeared inside the Head Mistress's tent.

Banzu drew in deep, expelled overlong. He turned round and stared east, at the distant black haze of smoke rising beyond the horizon, beneath it an ever-growing miles-long train of fistian refugees slow in coming. He wondered how many hungars already swelled inside Fist's walls.

By now probably to bursting.

And worse, they have a train of fresh meat leading them straight to Bloom.

* * *

The sun burned its slow arc across the cloudless sky. The open eastern gates of Bloom welcomed the Head Mistress and her retinue of riders in to the city unpopulated despite its incredible size.

Banzu's eyebrows bent inward in suspicion while he scanned the empty streets, the unopened shops, the shuttered homes.

Where the frig is everyone?

His eyebrows rose into curious little arches when he focused far ahead through the main thoroughfare upon the distant noise of too many voices mingled together and the back of a tremendous crowd gathered in their thousands, all of them facing west while packing full the city's enormous square and beyond right up to the front steps of Castle Bloom.

Rainbow banners hung flaccid atop hundreds of tall iron poles decorating every street corner, pronouncing some hidden event having drawn the citizens from their daily rituals to gather en masse.

But for what? Fear flowered its foreboding nightshade in Banzu's active mind, the honing thrum of the Godstone growing stronger in its influential tugs upon him, urging him toward the crowd. *Oh gods, does somebody already have it? Please, no. I don't want to kill again.*

He stood his stirrups, rising inches in saddle for better viewing vantage over the crowd. No citizens walked past the front where stood an armed and armored line of bloomanese soldiers facing the crowd while keeping space between. Heavy infantry loaded down in scale armor and chain vambraces and gauntlets, kite shields, weighted longswords, spears strapped to their backs, visored and cheek-guarded helms with lobster tails, dirks and pig-stickers at their belts. And behind them another line of soldiers, these mounted atop white or spotted horses, their long and polished lances upraised and levered against their shoulders with smaller rainbow banners hanging limp inches beneath the speared points.

"The Paladins of Bloom," Banzu whispered of the legendary soldiers, recalling snippets of fantastic stories that sent his youthful mind aflutter with brave adventures Jericho sometimes regaled boy Banzu with over an evening's meal by their warming hearth, tales which claimed his dreams and he a part of them in those fading moments before the rigors of the day's hard training and a full belly delivered him into the oblivion of sleep.

Beyond the lines of paladins stood the castle, a sparkling white mountain of marble flecked with quartzite, spiked with towers topped by pointed roofs and ivory slopes, every twinkling angle and refracting bend of it glinting captures of sunlight.

"Make way for the Head Mistress," Jacob announced once they achieved the back of the crowd standing thousands thick, their retinue slowing while the people parted in an opening wedge of space for the Head Mistress of Fist and her small entourage puncturing into the dense congregation's depths.

Banzu glanced round at the plethora of lit black candles held within the dividing peoples' hands. *Mourner's candles. Thousands of them. Something's wrong. Someone of notoriety is dead or ill.*

One-half turn of an hour's slow riding, the low moaning songs of horns elevating above the muttering tones of the parting crowd, and they arrived at the opening front where stood a curvaceous woman in a tight black dress hugging every salacious curve of her, a gauzy mourner's veil draping her face, a black candle burning nestled in her upturned palms, shiny bits of wax cooled on her black-gloved hands.

Banzu stared overlong while catching parts of conversation from those bunched round him.

"Mabselene von'Bloom," the squat fistian terramancer with shaggy brown hair and brilliant green eyes whispered aside to the female mage riding at his left. He did not hide his approving smile well, nor the low whistle accompanying it. "An empath, the way I hear it. Got a touch that can curl a man's toes, heh. Heard she got expelled from the Academy a few years a'fore I joined, on account of some frisky bid'ness or another with one of the Masters. Now I see why, heh. Too bad, too, she's a butcher's lot prettier in person, and—"

"Hush up, stupid!" the stick-thin magewoman hissed, then silenced the brawny aizakai with a cutting glare and a feigned swat of her closer backhand. "Now's not the time to talk through your little prick."

Banzu dismounted at Jacob's behest and strode alongside the First Sword as they approached the Head Mistress and her flanking fistian guardsmen from behind, her cadre of six aizakai joining to stand behind them.

The lines of bloomanese soldiers parting before her, Head Mistress Gwendora Pearce strode forth from the press, her little retinue in tow, and approached the grieving noblewoman who stood perched upon the castle's lower steps though elevated above the crowd of mourners.

Two children in the beginnings of their awkward teenage years of growth, a black-haired boy with first acne peppering his chubby cheeks, and a taller and slimmer blonde girl perhaps one year older, both with cried-out eyes rimmed red, flanked the Baroness, though she sent her children up the castle steps under paladin guard when the Head Mistress approached, encroaching across the space between crowd and paladins.

"Baroness." Gwendora bowed her head. "Pray tell, what has happened here?"

"Head Mistress." Mabselene von'Bloom acknowledged a slight bow of her head and the slightest dip of her knees, then raised her veil and settled it up over her head, revealing such alabaster skin all the more pale by contrast of her black attire, her long raven hair flowing glossy past her dainty shoulders, her startling icy blues rimmed with puffy redness. "My husband—" But she stopped, her voice turning strangled, her full red lips pressing tight. She handed her mourner's candle away to a nearby paladin who shielded the flickering flame to avoid its snuffing. "The Godstone has caused us nothing but grief since its falling in the Pass. We've been holding a stalemate after Victor's failed attempt to retrieve it shortly after it fell. He passed last night, not six hours ago." She paused, her frown bordering a scowl. "If only you'd arrived sooner."

"I'm sorry for your loss, Baroness." Gwendora stepped closer, took one of Mabselene's gloved hands into hers—and the Baroness flinched, frowning, seeking to withdraw her taken hand though staying it with effort and a forced smile. "I've come to relieve your burden. Thank you for sending word. But you've named a stalemate. What has happened? Where is the Godstone?"

Mabselene withdrew her hand then and, whipping her arm out as if throwing accusation, pointed across the clogged avenues at the eastern opening of Caldera Pass where hundreds more paladins filled the space between the open gates both afoot and atop horses.

"There," she said in an almost-hiss, pretty face scrunching sour. "It fell in the middle of the Pass like a curse from the gods. Victor rode out to retrieve it, but he met with Garnihan's forces intent on doing the same. My husband arrived first, but those barbarians speared him through the lung before he could claim the Godstone. He wasn't going to touch it, Head Mistress, I swear it upon the lives of our children." She turned, waved, and a soldier approached carrying a small wooden box. "His only intent was to scoop it up then make haste for Fist and present it to you, of course."

"Of course." Gwendora nodded, the motion slight, stiff. "I'm sure your husband had the proper resolve, Baroness. My sympathies for your loss. Victor was a brave man, and a good father. This world is worse without him."

Mabselene's stark blue eyes thinned into glaring shatters of spiteful ice. "I expect you to punish those tyrian bastards for their treachery. It's the least they deserve for murdering my husband, let alone attempting to steal the—"

"I will deal appropriate judgment once I claim the Godstone," Gwendora interrupted, her firmer voice a measured calm. "I assure you, Baroness. Bloom has always been an utmost loyal friend to Fist. For now we must make haste. Tell me, please, has it remained untouched?"

Mabselene nodded. "Many have tried. All have failed. So far."

"So far?"

"It rests between a stalemate. Every attempt at retrieving it, from both sides, has been thwarted through bloodshed. But I do not know how long the deadlock will last. Our paladins grow tired. And angry. They've been standing strong for days on end."

"Then let us be quick about it." Gwendora turned, faced Banzu behind and to her right. "I don't know what we're about to walk in to, but I do know it won't be kind. Garnihan is not known for his mercy." She paused, scanned round, then in a louder voice added, "Ready yourself, Soothsayer."

"Soothsayer?" Mabselene gasped, inhaling the title more than speaking it. Her eyes blooms of startlement, she stared at Banzu while her mouth formed an O of surprise.

"Friggin hell," Banzu whispered, cringing tensed. While gasps stole throughout the crowd and people backed away, mothers hugging their children closer, husbands presenting themselves as shields in front of their wives. He shot Gwendora a sidelong glare while snagging her by the arm and tugging her closer. "Did you have to name me out like that?"

She frowned and jerked her arm free. "Yes," she said in lower voice, flaring then thinning the scold of her eyes. "Look around you. We're knee-deep in kindle, and fear will keep the fire from sparking. If these people turn into a mob there'll be no stopping them. Now tell her you serve me and only me."

Banzu scrunched his face. "What?"

She grabbed his broke arm and squeezed before release.

He snapped his teeth shut to bridle the yelp in his throat while cringing against the flare of pain threatening to buckle him at the knees. He rumbled the quaver from his voice and in raised tone said, "I serve the Head Mistress, and only the Head Mistress."

Gwendora smiled, nodded.

Mabselene withdrew a cautious step—and tripped over the higher step behind her catching her heel, almost falling but for two paladins at her sides catching her by the elbows, her lips forming words with no sound. The soldiers round her shifted while setting aside their candles for brandishing weapons in protection of their baroness.

"Is . . . is he really . . ." Mabselene surrendered to the fright stealing the rest of her fragile voice. Another tripping step backwards, another balancing catch of her elbows.

"I assure you," Gwendora said, raising her hands in soothing gesture, then turning round, her voice a pronouncement addressing the retreating crowd before completing her circuit back to the baroness, "and everyone here, we bring you no harm. We mean only peace. Now, please, Baroness, show me to the Godstone."

Mabselene von'Bloom, her stare fixed on Banzu, straightened from her holders and swiped wrinkles from her dress while gathering herself. "Of course. Yes. The Godstone." She lingered for a space while considering all of Banzu, the Head Mistress forgotten, the hint of a curious smile quirking up one corner of her mouth. "Right this way."

***

Along their way to Caldera Pass through the parting crowd of mourners thousands thick and the paladin ranks hundreds strong, and Baroness Mabselene von'Bloom informed the Head Mistress of the tragedies overtaking Bloom since the Godstone's fall.

Banzu listened with a keen ear, shrouded in suspicious and challenging gazes weighing upon him as he walked behind the Head Mistress who, while speaking with the baroness on her many troubles, relayed only vague snippets of the war against Hannibal Khan and Fist's falling to the unliving horde of hungars making its way toward Bloom.

To which the frightened baroness sent immediate orders with a squad of paladins to seal and shore the city's eastern gates. Gwendora returned the subject to the Godstone despite Mabselene's flurry of questions about the impending hungar invasion.

Banzu's mind reflexed into deliberation over all he knew of Tyr and Bloom, the brunt of it recalled from the time before his re-beginning when Melora explained the troubles between the two cities and of her mission to re-open Caldera Pass on her return journey to Fist with Jericho.

The only viable traveling route through the Calderos Mountains not over or round them, a fifteen year blood-feud existing between western Tyr and eastern Bloom, prompting Caldera Pass closed. Tyr receded from the fistian axis of peace once ruling all of Thurandy—a peace shattered by Hannibal Khan's conquering uprising in Thurandy's easternmost province of Junes—after William Henry Garnihan, rising from Tyr's brutal gladiatorial fighting pits within its famed Arena, led a revolt against the former King Millergan as well the ruling nobles grown rich and fat off the labors of its hard-working peoples. Garnihan usurped the Iron Throne and Crown through brutal force then severed all political ties of fistian influence by closing Caldera Pass.

William Henry Garnihan, the infamous Lion of Tyr, proclaimed himself the new King-General then purged the city by bloodshed with public executions and forced gladiatorial matches in the Arena, pitting noble against noble. And for it the tyrian people loved him all the more. A return to the old ways and the old gods pronounced by Garnihan's reinstatement of the Iron Challenge, a brutal law abolished soon as King Millergan's grandfather won the Iron Crown and Throne through paid political vote and the previous Head Mistress's approval.

Anyone could issue public challenge for the Iron Throne and Crown again, resulting in mortal combat in the Arena against the king-general with simple rules: a fight to the death, the winner earning the right to wear the Iron Crown and sit the Iron Throne . . . at least until the next Iron Challenger presented him or her self.

Once a proud nation of strength and worship of Tyros the elder god of war, Garnihan, as so many tyrians, believed Tyr had grown soft and weak under generations of fistian influence and noble rule. He returned Tyr to its olden ways by uniting its peoples while becoming a living hero in the bloody process.

'Strength of honor, blood of iron' became the nation's maxim once more.

The Lion of Tyr abolished fistian taxes and cut fistian laws with the efficiency of slit throats. A new peace settled over the Iron City, one of swift delivery dealt to criminals who no longer bought their freedoms or manipulated their criminalities through the deep pockets of noble bargains not afforded the poorer classes. In Tyr, all people stood again as equals.

Eye for an eye governed again. If someone stole another's property, they earned the lopping of their thieving hand. If they stole again, so too their other hand. Rapists became eunuchs. Liars and false accusers earned cut tongues. Sexual peepers one eye punctured with a scalding iron rod, or both eyes if they dared a second covet of another man's good tyrian wife or daughter.

Killing was permitted if proven justified, though murder met in turn with justice repaid by the victim's kin. And if those kin proved physically unable to doll out justice, too young or too old and feeble, Garnihan commanded a more suitable replacement punished the criminal, often volunteering himself as the one delivering swift tyrian justice with his infamous warhammer Skullcrusher, an ensorcelled weapon of old forging yet new legend said possessed of such heavy weight only the Lion of Tyr proved blessed with the strength of Tyros to wield its thunderous pound.

All of which took place within Tyr's gladiatorial Arena, where King-General Garnihan earned his nation's monies no longer by forced taxation but through willing charges of admission to the daily battles playing therein.

Some criminals received the option of choosing entry into the gladiatorial guild as combatants, their years of fighting service weighed then applied as according to their crimes. If they survived those brutal years, the tyrian populace considered them washed of their sins through bloodshed by the blessings of Tyros, and thus freed once they served out their fighting sentences.

Or, if they so chose, they could continue fighting out the rest of their lives as freemen gladiators in the Arena, and if their skills proved proficient they earned a wealthy living while becoming revered by the cheering spectators tossing their praises and monies upon the victors of gladiatorial battle, their names added to the list of honored fallen warriors by way of an honorable death once their physical prowess left them unable to survive battle.

In Garnihan's Tyr, women stood equal to men. Those whom rebuked marriage often chose to fight in the Arena for sport, a brutal few for pleasure, while earning their places among its long and legendary list of fierce warriors carved into the great circular wall surrounding the colossal Arena's fighting pit.

Banzu's active mind pieced together that which he already knew of Tyr courtesy of Melora with that which the Head Mistress and Baroness Mabselene von'Bloom discussed during their long walk to Caldera Pass, Gwendora rehashing history more than the less educated Mabselene.

They breached through the massive gates, entering the colossal maw of Caldera Pass swallowing them inside, and continued walking for miles leading them to the Godstone's fallen location still far ahead, the Pass's sheer towering walls racing to such tremendous heights when Banzu craned his head those tall mountain walls disappeared into the high fog and clouds above.

And he knew, through haunting whispers containing flecks and slivers of memories bleeding from the shared collective, that long ago, bunched centuries edging close to a millennia, the Dominator's Gauntlets had carved this incredible route through the Calderos Mountains in creation of Caldera Pass courtesy of Malach'Ra during the Thousand Years War when last his Dominator's Armor existed whole.

Neither woman ahead of Banzu spoke of it though, and he wondered if either knew the truth of lighting punching through the mountains as told him through flashing gleans of shared collective memories, himself viewing snippets of the ancient destruction through the eyes of several dead Soothsayers, their points of view rapid shifts of location sloshing his senses so that he closed his eyes for a space while blanking the untoward memories away. Echoes of ancient screams proved long in fading.

Caldera Pass ran in a straight route, roughly half a mile wide though shrinking or expanding here and there, connecting eastern Thurandy to western Ascadia from Bloom to Tyr over the course of too many miles for Banzu to bother tallying their true sum, though he surmised one-quarter of a day in casual ride from city to city and twice that time afoot.

Carven numerical glyphs marked the walls at each mile through the long rocky throat, and so far they traveled . . . well, he lost count after three to the ruins of dilapidated buildings passing at their sides and stealing his wandering attentions, these weathered remnants of shops and hostels toppled or collapsed or sagging in parts, enduring fifteen years of disuse, evincing the prosperous time when Caldera Pass stood open in free trade, as well the rusted scatter of abandoned weapons and armor and a few rotted corpses both tyrian and bloomanese strewn about the grounds lay in haunting reminder of the battle between Bloom and Tyr when Garnihan usurped the Iron Throne then closed the trade route after some unnecessary bloodshed pronouncing his new rule in defiance of Fist's political oppression.

At last they achieved behind the crowded ranks of paladins filling the Pass before them, armored tanks of bloomanese soldiers who parted at the middle to the pronouncement of their Baroness's and the Head Mistress's approach.

"There," Mabselene said while pointing once they reached the front lines where tired ranks of bloomanese bowmen held the current stalemate under watchful gaze, in front of them and just as tired a kneeling line of infantry resting in idle stare though ready to stand while lifting their heavy kite shields.

Banzu surveyed the scene leaving him as speechless as the Head Mistress beside him. Hundreds of corpses pincushioned with arrows lay strewn round the open grounds of a massive crater of shallow depression where nested at its center a small globe the size of a child's fist, the orb perfect in its unflawed roundness and possessing the silvery glimmer of liquid metal swirling beneath its reflective surface through constant though lazy motions of life containing active swims of golden hints.

Most of the felled corpses, both bloomanese and tyrian, which lay scattered round the killing grounds encircling the wide crater sported juts of arrows, though many bloomanese dead upheld soft iron spears bent useless after their lethal throws, a specialized tyrian weapon designed for bending after striking its target, deterring the enemy from yanking the malformed spear and throwing its return.

Across the shallow crater, thousands strong and facing them, stood the stalwart tyrian forces filling the Pass, the ranks of bowmen and spearwomen fronting their lines shifting through renewed tension at sight of the newcomers across the way.

"Everyone who tries for the Godstone is struck down," Mabselene said. "It has been so since the moment it fell and our forces came to face. Locha's Luck our armies advanced at the same time."

Gwendora *hmmmed* and nodded while massaging her chin and studying the lull. "We'll just have to see about that." She turned from the baroness, ordered her small retinue of fistian guardsmen and cadre of mages to hold. As well as: "Jacob? Stay here with the Baroness. Soothsayer? Come with me."

"But Mistress—" Jacob began, stepping forward while gripping his sword for pulling.

Gwendora stopped him short with an upraised palm and the curt shake of her head. "If things go awry, protect the Baroness. Banzu will escort me. We must approach alone, otherwise we risk a war I want no part of." With that she turned and walked away.

Banzu made to follow her.

Jacob delayed him by the shoulder with a firm grip. "Protect her, Soothsayer. Or I swear to gods I'll—"

"I will!" Banzu said in too loud of voice, the second heartbeat of the Godstone's thrumming pressure of presence hammering thunder in his temples at such close proximity while quickening his pulse with a fever of urgency. *Friggin hell.*

He tried shutting out the noise all his own while catching up alongside the Head Mistress who broke into a proud, elegant stride, shoulders back, chin up, her hands clasped behind the small of her back. Regal and knowing it.

Having changed into more proper attire as befitting the Head Mistress of Fist before their morning's entry into Bloom, her taut violet dress trimmed with tiny crimson weaves of fiery tongues licking round her hem and neckline and long sleeves at the wrists applied her the impression of gliding more than walking despite the ground bestrewn with various rocky debris expelled from the Godstone's punching impact, her authoritative air wafting strong while daring the tyrian bowmen and spearwomen estimating her bold approach to loose their volleys and suffer untold consequences. Her leather dachra harness caged her trim torso over her dress, and though no worry betrayed her slate expression her nervous hands rose to gripping her sheathed fangs' handles in reassuring squeeze before lowering and clasping again.

I am Spellbinder, I am Head Mistress, I am here now and I expect to be obeyed . . . her challenging posture and fluid gait declared. Though a moment more she pulled a white kerchief from up her sleeve and waved it in ivory flutters while she walked, pronouncing her peaceful intentions. Dark skin glistening with a few beads of sweat pulled surfaced upon her brow from the high sun, she skirted round strewn bodies with grace and purpose.

Banzu proved less elegant as he navigated after her by stepping round or hopping over the litter of unfortunate failed retrievers of the Godstone, hundreds of bloomanese peppered with tyrian arrows or spears, their numbers thickening closer to the shallow crater and its precious boon resting therein.

Most of the corpses here earned positions of death evincing dying crawls toward the crater, clawing the ground while leaving trails of blood in their futile wake, wounded though refusing surrender until their lifesparks snuffed. Several bodies wore plain clothes not of either legion, and he presumed them daring thieves overcome by greed's lust inducing them into risking their lives for possession of the Godstone against the obvious failures of their chances when the two armies came to face by happenstance.

". . . while I do the talking," Gwendora said, apparently finishing the orders Banzu heard none of.

"What!" His inner thrumming sense of the Godstone intensified into a wild pounding muffling his hearing the closer they strove so that he worked his jaw and popped his eardrums while focusing the noisy distraction into a softer backdrop of incessant humming. In lower voice he repeated, "What?"

Gwendora slowed while scowling him down though continued waving her white kerchief at the flustered tyrians watching them.

"Sorry," he said. "It's the Godstone. It's hammering in my ears." *And my chest. And the rest of me. Friggin hell, my bones are vibrating.* "Can you repeat—"

"Just keep your mouth shut while I do the talking."

He nodded, anxious skirls of butterflies fluttering through his belly, expecting a volley of tyrian arrows and spears thrown at a moment's turn and with no safe place for ducking. Nervous sweat dappled his brow so that he scrubbed it away with the back of his right forearm while keeping his injured other a folded wing tucked at his side.

A shrill blast of horn sounded from somewhere beyond the shifting press of tyrians raising their bows and spears, preparing to volley a hail of missiles at the two intruders daring approach.

While Banzu reached the crater's eastern rim—and stopped, jolting, the incessant pound of the Godstone's presence climaxing into a deafening thunder that seconds more swallowed mute into a gulf of silence. Though the invisible umbilical pull of it beckoning him remained, tugging at parts of him, swaying him forward so that he strained taut while rebuking the fierce need of surrendering to the suicidal impulse for rushing forward in a hail of arrows and spears.

"Oh thank gods," he whispered. "I can hear again."

"Good," Gwendora said, beside him though staring beyond the wide crater at the teeming tyrian lines on the precipice of unleashing attack yet staying their arrows and spears for word of the Head Mistress's unmistakable presence spread throughout their conversing ranks. She tossed her white kerchief to the air where it fluttered to ground. "Pay attention. Say and do nothing unless I tell you."

He rolled his eyes and huffed a terse breath. "Yeah yeah. You say jump and I jump. Good doggie."

"Banzu." She met his gaze with softening violet requests bleeding into her voice. "Please. I know you hate me, and I deserve part of your blame for Jericho's death. But this is it. What happens here matters most."

He blew out his cheeks, nodded. "I don't hate you. Just don't forget your promise. After this is done, I want Melora. No excuses. No more delays. Those hungars can kiss my ass. I want Melora first."

She frowned though schooled it away and considered him an extra beat. "Once we are finished here, I promise we will find her first and foremost."

"Then Aggie?" he asked.

The flash of her frown returned. "Never mind her. She's safe."

Under his breath he muttered, "She'd better be."

Stiffening tall, scowling, eyes flaring then thinning, Gwendora opened her mouth then closed it. She fixed her stare ahead, her refusal of rushing for let alone looking at the Godstone costing her visible effort betrayed through her tensed posture.

They waited.

Banzu inhaled the raw smell of cracked stone while squeezing reassuring flexes on Griever's hilt at his left hipwing in a sweaty grip, eyes darting from bow to spear to sword to pike, hoping the tyrian lines did not erupt into a warring tide of imminent slaughter.

Minutes passed.

Gwendora expelled a terse sigh. "Garnihan!" she shouted, the sheer walls of the Pass adding projected volume to her carried voice. "I know you're in there. The Head Mistress of Fist requests your presence for palavar. Now!"

Silence but for the shifting of soldiers. Tense minutes passed . . . then the front tyrian lines divided from behind, making space for the black warhorse bearing its bearded rider's bulk striding forth through their shuffling mix, ranks of tyrians opening before then closing behind both muscled beast and rider.

The warhorse stopped, and down from saddle slid its rider of impressive size, a man among children, his tangle of hair and beard mixing round his head and forming an unruly mane of golden splendor, with golden tufts upon wide shoulders and broad chest and forearms possessing the thickness of calves. Stripped to the waist but for the single leather strap running from his right shoulder to left hip and holding the enormous warhammer strapped to his back via iron hooks, its long handle jutting from behind his right shoulder as a grooved iron rod, his scarred torso showed not a pinch of fat anywhere to behold on the corded muscle of his bulk.

"Gods . . . the Lion of Tyr," Banzu whispered, a little too loud for his liking. The impressive physical specimen awed him, weakened him by comparison. Memories of the hulking tundarian berserker, Ma'Kurgen al'Kor, stole through his mind in knifing flashes of recall.

Though not so tall as Banzu remembered of the tundarian, Garnihan stood equally thick with muscle promising the ease of dismembering a normal man with bare hands alone, and had probably done so given the man's legendary reputation.

A sea of tyrian faces broke into smiles, though Garnihan strode lone to his side of the crater's western rim, leaving one-tenth of a mile's space between himself and the Head Mistress, Banzu beside her. He removed the thick iron warhammer fashioned to his back—one end blunted flat for smashing, its other end a long spike for piercing—then, muscles flexing and veins bulging through hints of untapped reserves of incredible strength, he settled the heavy weapon beside him with a resounding *thud* and rested his beefy left hand atop its long handle's waist-high end. He smiled a display of white teeth in a nest of golden beard.

"Ahh, Head Mistress, there you are. Sticking your nose in where it doesn't belong again." Garnihan's baritone voice carried strong along the sheer walls at their sides projecting it, enhancing its volume. "This isn't Academy business, woman. It fell in the Pass, and that makes it mine. Now tell these bloomanese bastards to withdraw before my temper grows too short for mercy."

Gwendora released a low hiss only Banzu heard, then stiffened straight, voice carrying, tone unyielding as her focal glare. "I beg to differ, Garnihan. The Godstone is not yours to claim. Otherwise I would not be here. You stole the Iron Crown, but you will not steal this."

Garnihan's scrunching face reddened, teeth baring snarl. "I have every right, woman!" He gripped his warhammer, upheld it diagonally in front of him, plump biceps bulging. "Your kind doesn't rule here any longer, aizakai. Tyr stands on its own again, and Tyros claims the Godstone through me. I've allowed your bloomy sheep time to come to their senses and stand down before the slaughter. But I've had enough of this foolishness. Back away, woman, and allow me what's mine. Or suffer the consequences."

Gwendora began, "No, Garnihan—"

He clipped her by shouting, "That's *King-General* Garnihan to you!"

A swell of approving tyrian voices rose then fell.

Gwendora snapped her mouth shut, scowling, then muttered, "This nonsense is wasted effort. I should've known better than to palavar this arrogant fool." She glanced at Banzu, then raised her voice. "Fist has fallen, King-General."

"Good!" he shouted, the boom of it projecting through the Pass.

Prompting another elevation of approving tyrian voices.

Gwendora shouted above the raucous surf. "And Dethkore lives again!"

The tyrian voices hushed throughout a sea of startling faces.

"And," Gwendora continued, "there's an unliving army approaching at our backs. This is not a negotiation. You will turn around and march your forces home and allow me the Godstone. Or else."

"Or else?" Garnihan laughed. "Or else what?"

Gwendora glanced at Banzu, a devious flare in her eyes he liked not one bit, and smiled. "Or else I'll invoke the Iron Challenge, and you will die this day as surely as I stand here before you."

Garnihan craned his head and roared mocking laughter, his soldiers behind joining in, thousands of warriors lining behind the chuckling ranks of bowmen and spearwomen banging their swords and maces against their round shields in supporting clangor. Garnihan waved the noise down behind him with a lowering hand, then fixed his hungry glare upon her once more.

"Oh please do." He licked his lips with appetite. "Hells, I'll escort you myself to the Arena. Or we can do it here. I've wanted to bash your pretty little skull in ever since you sent your first emissary through for renegotiations." A cocky tilt of his head. "How many has it been, woman? Five? Ten? I've lost count." He upheld his warhammer, presenting it while stroking its long grooved handle. "Should I count out the notches of those you've sent to their deaths before carving another one for you?"

Gwendora smiled. "Not me, you ignorant fool." She waved at Banzu beside her in flourishing gesture. "My Soothsayer will do the challenging for me."

Banzu cringed while turning on her. "What?"

A raucous of too many tyrian voices talking at once filled the Pass, echoes climbing atop echoes, shouts spilling over each other in a surf of questions and rejections of the Head Mistress's words and Banzu beside her.

"Hold on," Garnihan said, trying to achieve volume above the cacophony. "Wait a minute."

"What the frig are you doing?" Banzu asked her.

Gwendora ignored him, glorying in the noise, reveling in the reaction, smiling, enjoying it.

Garnihan's eyes tightened into a predatory glare targeting Banzu while he strangled his warhammer in a white-knuckled grip. His wide, scarred chest swelled when he drew in deep and roared, "Enough!"

A concussive silence projected through the Pass, hushing all noise but for the diminishing echo of Garnihan's shout.

He said, "Horseshit. I'll kiss that chocolate cunny of yours if that gangly sprat with the broken wing is a Soothsayer." He laughed again, prompting another chorus of mocking laughter issued from his fellow tyrians filling the western Pass.

Banzu opened his mouth to speak—then clamped it shut with a *click* of teeth when his vision swam and his heartbeat quickened into racing strain, flushing hot and pounding at his temples. He closed his eyes, balance sloshing, his senses spiking ultra keen so that the echoing laughter filling the Pass turned resounding in his head.

Oh gods, not again.

His salivating mouth filled with the sour moisture of hunger. The wound of his lycan bite throbbed anew so that he gripped it and squeezed while clenching his teeth through shocks of pain. A thunder entered the base of his skull. He winced at the crunching sensation of broken bones knitting together while panting rapid through fever—that quelled a moment more, his oversensitive senses dulling normal.

He opened his eyes to new pressure on his arm.

Gwendora stood closer and holding a gentle grip on his wounded arm, staring at him, her void-aura having soothed the beast blood malady.

"I'm not as ignorant as you think I am," she said in lowered voice. "Stay with me. I need you here."

"I'm fine." Banzu tried pulling his arm free of her hand—and winced when she maintained her refusing grip with a strong squeeze.

"I'm no fool, Banzu." She shot a glance at the distant lines of bloomanese paladins though more particular at Jacob watching back at them from among the fistians at their forefront, all well out of earshot. "Jacob is a good soldier but a terrible liar. A warhound? Really? Trina saw that lycan almost tear your arm off."

He gaped at her. "You know?"

She thinned her eyes upon him, Spellbinder scrutiny and Head Mistress cunning all bundled up into one blatant glare. "Of course I know. I just thought it best not to complicate matters." She imposed a painful squeeze of his arm before release, earning his grunting grimace. "Just do as I say, and when we're finished here we'll deal with this problem. You're a Soothsayer. Act like it."

"Gwen, I—" He sighed, began again. "I'm done with killing. I've done too much of it already." He glanced at Garnihan watching them from across the wide crater. "Besides, he's right. My arm's useless. And—" He paused, hesitated, drew in deep then expelled a frustrated huff of his cheeks. "And I can't use the Power anymore. Not until I touch the Godstone."

Confidence shattered in her eyes, her voice. She strangled out a, "What?"

"The Essence of the First, remember? Simus Junes almost possessed me on the plains. His bloodlust is still inside me, infecting the Power. I can't use it until the Godstone heals me. If I do, I'll start killing again and I won't be able to stop this time. Garnihan. You. Everyone here."

Ire flared her eyes, her voice. "Why didn't you tell me—" But she stopped her outburst there. She shot Jacob a sidelong glare that said they would share words later with plenty of yelling on her end. "Fine. Then we'll just have to improvise." She mustered tall and faced Garnihan. In a low voice meant for Banzu she added, "Now stand up straight and play your part. You're a Soothsayer. Stare him down. And lick your lips like you're thirsty for his blood."

"Uhm—"

"Just do it. He's all bluster and pride. And his fear of someone stealing the Godstone before him is the only reason why he hasn't pressed this stalemate into full-scale slaughter already. Trust me, Banzu. Presentation is half the show of threat."

He nodded and tried his best to obey her strange orders, though his stare felt more a squint, and he thought he licked his lips a little too much for any kind of intimidation.

"What will it be, Garnihan?" Gwendora asked in risen tone. "Will you surrender your position and save your life along with the lives of your men? Or should I declare the Iron Challenge and sentence them to watch as my Soothsayer cuts you down and takes your stolen crown along with the Godstone?"

She crossed her arms beneath her breasts and cocked her hips to one side in defiant stance, smiling.

"I'm waiting. And my Soothsayer is growing impatient. Why, just now he asked how many of you I would allow him to kill. It's no secret how much they enjoy slaughter." In a lower tone she added, "Grip your sword and take a step forward—now."

Banzu obeyed, stopping short when Gwendora threw her arm out and barred his way, pretending to stop him.

"Good," she whispered from the smirking corner of her mouth. "Now shove me and—"

Deep in the act, Banzu shoved her aside, hard and to the ground, then pointed while forcing his eyes wide and wild. "I want you!" he yelled at Garnihan, then shifted his aim to the startled tyrians behind while tightening his tallying gaze. "And you! And you! And you too!"

Gwendora gained her feet while grumbling curses of where Banzu's backside could put her foot.

He gripped Griever's hilt and began the threatening pull while advancing another challenging step. "I'll kill you all!"

"No!" Gwendora made a show of rushing in front of him, turning round and stopping his false charge by palming his chest. "Stop!"

Banzu stopped.

"Perfect," she whispered, then spun round smiling.

Garnihan's pinched face trembled with seething bridled fury bleeding from bulging eyes straining to break their sockets. With a guttural roar, muscles flexing through incredible twitches, he swung his long warhammer up over his head in a double-fisted grip to the full arching stretch of himself, blue crackles of energy sparking to active life and spending across the ensorcelled weapon as well down the length of its wielder's beefy arms in forking jags and fanning across his broad shoulders, down his burly back and muscled slab of chest, in licking veins of potent promise, his golden mane of hair and beard afloat in brief static charge, his spread boots depressing the cracking ground by centimeters.

He slammed Skullcrusher's blunt end down—*thoom!*—in a punching concussion of air blasting outward round a crackling splash of forking blue energies, impacting the quaking ground in front of his hunching stance, rocks rebounding the punished earth by jouncing inches, where ripped open a fissure snaking the shallow crater to half the stretch of it where the Godstone lay, Skullcrusher's thumping pound echoing throughout the Pass in diminishing thunder.

Startled at the impressive display, Banzu's nervous heart skipped several anxious flutters while transplanted tremors faded in his bones.

Beside him Gwendora stifled a gasp through sheer grit and Spellbinder pride maintaining iron resolve in her determined spine.

While the front lines of both standing forces shifted in agitated apprehension of the precarious palavar verging the fragile cusp of open war.

Silence pervaded for a dozen heartbeats.

Seething, Garnihan straightened, his bared snarl a clenched cut of white teeth in his beard, and in blustered tone said, "Take the Godstone, woman! But the Pass stays closed. And I swear by Tyros so long as there's breath in my body I'll see you pulverized for this." He raised his warhammer, advanced one challenging step, and in an incredible display of strength aimed Skullcrusher at her in extension of his corded muscle arm trembling not from effort but fury. "Your time is nigh and long in coming. By Tyros, I promise you that. And you!" He shifted his glaring aim at Banzu. "This isn't over. Far from it." He inhaled sharp through flaring nostrils then spat the snotty gob as well the word out, more condemnation than title. "Soothsayer."

Banzu reined his new healthy respect of fear for the Lion of Tyr with a hard swallow and pretended another step forward while half pulling Griever from his left hipwing—and on thankful cue Gwendora barred his way again with another outstretched arm so that he puffed his chest in mock show of bare restraint despite the apprehensive clench of his squirming guts.

"Careful, Garnihan," she said, serrated tone edging. "And remember who you threaten. We have not come to supplant your rule. But one more slip of your flippant tongue and so help me gods I'll forget the oath of peaceful palavar. More than you will die here. And Fist will reclaim Tyr as it should be."

Banzu suppressed a groan at the two contesting prides. "Stop friggin prodding him," he said in low voice through gritted teeth. "He's already given over. If he calls our bluff then we're both good as dead."

Gwendora ignored him. "Is that what you want for your people?" she asked Garnihan then paused, gestured at Banzu with the flick of her wrist while surveying the ample spread of wary tyrian watchers. "Those of you who survive him, that is. I don't know if I can stop him once he starts." She crossed her arms and fixed focal upon their King-General again. "Or if I'll even bother, considering what's at stake and all you've stolen from Fist already."

Fuming, bold eyes flaring, Skullcrusher crackling alive again in his double-fisted grip, Garnihan raised his ensorcelled warhammer overhead for another punishing hammerblow—but he restrained the mighty effort and instead returned Skullcrusher to his back. He lingered for a pause while eyeballing the Godstone between their standoff, then hawked and spat at the Head Mistress and Banzu both. He turned from the crater and shouted orders of retreat while stalking away. He climbed atop his black warhorse, sawed on the leather reins and spun the animal round while throwing a parting glare at the smiling Head Mistress though more so Banzu, then he rode away into the parting tyrian ranks who in turn about-faced and pursued him.

Banzu watched them taking leave. *Oh thank gods, it worked. It actually worked!* He inhaled deep, expelled overlong, easing relaxed though tensions slow in leaving.

Lengthy minutes passed, the thousands of tyrians flooding the Pass retreating west in a diminishing storm of noise, before Gwendora blew out relief in a deflating huff that shrank her by inches. "Well, that went better than I ever expected." She faced Banzu with a smile leaving the scold of her eyes untouched while swiping off parts of her dirtied dress. "Did you have to shove me so hard?"

He shrugged and smirked. "You said shove so I shoved."

She thinned her glare upon him. "And enjoyed every bit of it I bet." She glanced at his bandaged arm then far past him at Jacob. "Do you have any more secrets you haven't told me yet?"

He glanced at the interesting ground between his feet. *Yes.* "No."

She sighed, deep and overlong. "We have a lot to talk about after we're finished here."

With that she turned and walked down into the shallow crater, while behind them arose a chorus of cheers from the gathered bloomanese thousands approving the end to the long and grueling stalemate over the Godstone.

CHAPTER FORTY-FIVE

Gods that was close. Banzu drew in deep relief that shuddered his bones, the Head Mistress's threat of Iron Challenge proving effective at retreating Garnihan's army instead of inciting them to war within Caldera Pass. *Too close.*

He pursued Gwendora down into the shallow crater, the scorched gravel the Godstone's punching impact made of the ground crunching loose beneath his boots, surprised the Godstone rested visible at the crater's epicenter instead of buried deep considering its tremendous plummet from space after orbiting Earth's outer atmosphere for over three centuries.

They reached the crater's blackened center where rested the silvery-golden, perfectly round orb the size of a child's fist. For a long time Gwendora stood staring down, anxious hands flexing grips of air at her sides, her dark lips parted on the verge of speech that never sounded. She unfastened the silver rows of buttons running down the sides of her violet dress from hips to bottom then squatted and continued staring just as silent, focal gaze captured, breath stolen by the magnificent Godstone within ease of her reach.

Banzu squatted beside her left, every muscle taut, his mind restless with flitters of memories not his own stealing behind his pensive stare, the inner homing sense provoked by the Godstone's proximity less than the full leaning stretch of his arm away tugging at the humming inner parts of him aching to touch it, vibrating his marrow with songs of achievement. And yet . . . and yet, desire surrendered to disappointment. Insignificant but for the millions of lives it already cost. He frowned. "So that's it?"

"It's . . . everything," she whispered, mesmerized in her captured state, her breathing short and rapid, her eyes fevered violet pools of discovery, her dark skin flushed with the underlying bloom of one so close to claiming precious hope's inner heat burning so long and strong in the covetous heart of hearts.

"It's so small," he said.

"Size does not equate power," she said, her voice a thin whisper, her stare unbroken. "At long last." She hunched forward in looming lean, licking her lips, tasting her words while speaking them. "So much power . . . so much potential . . . so many possibilities. I knew . . . I dreamed . . . me." She reached forth, left hand tremulous, fingers inches from grasping contact.

Banzu snagged her by the reaching wrist, stopping her. "What in friggin hell are you doing?"

"No!" Gwendora hissed and yanked her arm free. "Don't touch me!" Eyes flaring, she shot him a sideways glare while shifting position, facing him, her crouch reframing into a preparatory pounce, hands questing up behind her back for her dachra fangs.

Tensing, Banzu rebuked the fierce challenge with a scolding glare. "Hey," he said, and snapped his fingers in front of her face. "Hey!"

She flinched, and her eyes regained focus through a rapid series of blinks that softened her face. She lowered her hands, empty of dachras, remembering herself. "I . . . I'm sorry." She closed her eyes and scrunched her face a brief space, shook her head. "I don't know what came over me."

I do. But he put no voice behind it. "I have to destroy it, remember?"

She nodded, returned her fragile stare to the Godstone. "Yes, I . . . yes, of course. I'm sorry. It's just . . . gods, it's finally here. All my life I've hoped for this moment. And now that it's here I almost can't believe it. We can—" She paused and swiped a stray tear from her dark cheek. "We can save so many lives. This is why I am Head Mistress. This is all of me." She smiled and expelled a nervous chuckle while flexing her hands through nervous grabs of air then swiped them dry on her thighs. "Gods, look at me. I feel like a terrified little girl."

"Easy," he said, forcing a smile. "I know the feeling. I felt the same before killing the Khan. Just relax. It's here. We're here." In firmer tone he added, "And I need to destroy it."

Wincing while nodding, Gwendora said nothing.

And for that I need to touch it first. And hope Enosh's words hold true that the Godstone's purging grace will cleanse the corrupted Source of the shared collective's bloodlust while healing me and imbuing me with the hidden knowledge of how to destroy it.

The shift of his gaze to the Godstone, nerves bunching taut, an audible swallow.

But what if I can't? Or worse, what if I don't want to the moment I touch it? What if it's all some mad trick played against me through Enosh's lies and the gods' Great Game?

The Godstone's apotheosis provided a limitless source-pool of energy to any aizakai who touched it for as long as they touched it. And to Banzu that meant fueling the Source in place of his lifeforce instead of draining it in ruthless exchange while aging him faster.

With it I can bend time without aging. I could undo so much. Save the thousands of lives lost upon the plains, making the hundreds I took into nothing more than memories. Hannibal Khan. Dethkore's resurrection. He jolted when beautiful epiphany grabbed his anguished heart and squeezed with revelation. *Oh gods, I could . . .*

"I could bring Jericho back," he said in such a delicate voice it dared not call itself a whisper.

Gwendora said nothing, if she even heard him at all.

Dizzy with qualm, he stared overlong at the Godstone begging for his touch while impulses of temptations fired round the edges of his mind in fathoms of promise.

I can bring him back, for me and for Aggie, then erase all the turmoil and then destroy it. Why destroy it at all? Yes, I . . . no. Use it once and I won't stop using it. And changing so many events might make everything worse. But Dethkore is coming. And the tool to defeat him is right here. If I destroy it before—

"No!" He startled out from introspection and grabbed Gwendora by the reaching wrist again, stopping her second play for plucking up the Godstone. "Don't."

She gasped and flinched, trembling to his restraining grip instead of tensing while jerking free in another rebuking flare. She broke her stare from the innocuous little orb and regarded him with fragile violets viewing more through him than at him. Eyes pleading for help where her voice failed to deliver the words.

He held her shattered stare a lengthy moment, the pain of wonderment shining therein reflecting a child denied their promised gift, while Enosh's warning that none but Banzu could resist the Godstone's tempting allure played through his mind in vicious recall.

"No," he said, denying her as well himself, and gave her captured arm a firm squeeze when it flexed resistance for another grab at the Godstone. "No."

A spasm of hurt slackened her features. She looked at the Godstone, and with her other hand she reached for it.

"No!" He jerked her onto her bottom, falling back with her while maintaining his strong clamp on her wrist.

Sitting, she shook her head while blinking hard, miming the aftermath shock of a waking slap, stare regaining focus from the fading daze of the Godstone's alluring promises seizing her in its enigmatic grip. She met Banzu's gaze through the tortured chore of her shifting eyes pulling free. "Thank you," she whispered, then twisted and shouted to those gathering closer round the crater's eastern brim behind them, "Bring me the box!"

Banzu relaxed though retained his grip of her wrist.

Gwendora drew in a deep nostril inhale and expelled overlong through pursed lips, straightening, regaining composure, all Head Mistress Gwendora Pearce again. "You can let go of me now."

He hesitated, glanced at the Godstone, then stood while pulling her up by the wrist before letting go. He advanced one step and bent at the hips, reaching for the Godstone, to claim it, to be cleansed by it, then destroy it.

"Wait!" She fisted handfuls of his shirt and yanked.

"What the—" He stumbled backwards, loose pebbles slipping beneath his stumbling feet so that he fell onto his bottom upon the slight decline. "What are you doing? I have to destroy it!"

"Not here," she said. "The gods only know what'll happen once you touch it. It could explode and kill everyone here for all we know." A pause, a wary glance at the Godstone. "We'll remove it to safer grounds and decide how best to deal with it once our minds have had time to clear for proper deliberation." A decisive nodded, agreeing with herself. "Yes, that's the best course. Jacob!" She spun round. "Where is that—*oh!*"

"I'm right here, Mistress." Jacob, having walked down to standing behind her, flinched back from her abrupt turn, between his hands the baroness Mabselene's little wooden box, his gaze holding hers in obvious resistance to glancing past her at the Godstone by tell of his taut neck muscles flexed in held strain.

"Take it back?" Banzu threw one hand in dismissive gesture at Jacob's box while waving the other at the Godstone, the pain in his injured arm flaring through the motion though dulled by adrenaline. "But it's right here! There's no sense in taking it back to Fist. Fist is gone, Gwen. We can't—"

"Not Fist." She accepted the small box from Jacob and turned away from her First Sword. "Castle Bloom." She squatted down, opened the box, upended it over the Godstone then scooped it up along with the surrounding nestle of scorched gravel and dirt by way of clamping the box's lid closed in the manner of a chomping mouth round the silvery-golden orb. She straightened tall and hugged the box, closed her eyes and shuddered, smiling, then tucked it up under her left arm in tight embrace, an undeniable glimmer in her eyes when she opened them. "If something goes wrong . . ." she began then trailed off, turning away. "Come. We haven't much time before—"

An alarm bell clanged from somewhere within the city of Bloom. Not steady. Discordant. A cacophony of panic.

The Head Mistress muttered a curse. "To the castle," she said, "and quickly."

"But—" Banzu began though clipped short.

Gwendora hurried up the shallow crater's incline, loose gravel crunching beneath while sliding round her eager boots achieving her up in graceless scramble. Once there, upon flatter and firmer ground, her small cadre of mages surrounded her, and them her retinue of fistian soldiers. They bustled away through the parting bloomanese paladins shuffling back in chimes of armor.

"On your feet, Soothsayer." Jacob extending a hand down to Banzu. "There's no time to waste. That bell's tolling for us all."

Banzu sighed, the strong umbilical tug of the Godstone changing its directive pull upon him with Gwendora's leaving, urging him after her carried prize. He glanced at the empty space of Godstone absence—*so close, I should've just grabbed the friggin thing*—then accepted Jacob's offered hand.

Pulled into standing, he noted though said nothing of Jacob's tensed expression or the First Sword's other hand gripping sword hilt and ready for pulling.

* * *

They repaired to private chambers within Castle Bloom for better seclusion, while the rest of the acropolis bustled in an uproar over the approaching horde of unliving hungars that had, as told through bloomanese scouts' returning reports, overtaken the last third of the long train of fistian refugees seeking safety in Bloom.

Baroness Mabselene von'Bloom ordered the city's eastern gates reopened to allow the first refugees safe passage inside once they arrived, though with orders to close them before any hungars drew too near regardless of those still outside and unprotected, refusing to risk contagion into the city and upon her peoples.

The hungar menace surmounted the eastern horizon by last reports, thousands strong and flooding toward Bloom in a diluvial tide of nightmare absorbing from behind the miles-long train of fistian refugees, overrunning stragglers, pulling screamers down from wagons, eating abandoned elders and children alive in a gothic swarm of feeding frenzy while spreading their unliving contagion throughout the fleeing masses.

A constant moaning pall sang in the distance, elevating with every closer mile achieved. While Bloom's paladins positioned armored ranks of riders between the city and the oncoming horde, with reserves of infantry taking defensive stations throughout the panicked city as well bowmen atop its high walls.

Rumors spread in wildfire as the first of the fistian refugees, sped by terror though slowed by brief inspections for infectious bites, rushed in to Bloom and told of the relentless flesh-eating monstrosities stalking them, while throughout the city people spoke of the Godstone claimed from Caldera Pass by the Head Mistress and her Soothsayer servitor when not wailing over the inevitable invasion of—of what?

Ignorance writhed at the core of the wide-spread panic. The dead had not stalked the living since the Thousand Years War.

The end times had come—were coming—are here! many shouted while running the streets, dragging screaming children or stumbling elders by the hand, carrying weapons or foodstuffs, seeking safety in numbers of huddled neighbors behind barred doors or in barricaded cellars. Looters plundered shops and homes, thieving riches or supplies, before escaping the city while the gates remained open and running or riding away north or south, for Caldera Pass remained closed to the west, and east . . . east stalked only death.

Bolder farmers and blacksmiths and merchants, fathers and brothers, wives and sisters, fearing the lives of their children, removed from their families once locking them away and took up unfamiliar arms of sword and mace and bow and anything else on hand alongside Bloom's paladins and military spread, intent on fighting back the approaching horde to their last breaths so long as it earned their children's safety. Mothers stayed behind and clutching knives close to breast, preparing to slit the throats of their children in desperate acts of mercy if the hungars broke through the defensive lines of paladins and swarmed into the city and over its high walls.

Within the dead Baron's private council chambers where Baroness Mabselene von'Bloom had led then left them to retreat into a guarded room somewhere in the castle she dared not reveal to anyone but her personal retinue of guards for the sake of her daughter Savitri and son Zaxler . . .

From across the room Banzu said to the Head Mistress's turned back, "We're wasting time, Gwen. I have to destroy it. Now."

His injured arm throbbed with hot pulses of fever, his skin beneath the bandages crawling, but he fought off recurring waves of dizziness through clenched teeth and sheer strength of will. As well waxing irritation at the stalling of their purpose here. *Focus, godsdammit.*

"We've only a few more hours before those hungars are at the walls." *Then inside.* He glanced at Jacob watching him. "I can't face them again. I'm too spent. And without the Power . . . we have to do this now." He began pulling Griever from his left hipwing, intent on chopping the box and the Godstone within it if necessary.

But he stopped with Griever's blade half bared when Jacob, standing beside her, half bared his own sword, both men pausing to the other's threatening motions despite the twenty feet of space between. The six aizakai gathered round their Head Mistress and also facing Banzu shifted on their feet, wary of the tension between the two swordsmen, their hands risen in preparation for throwing forth conjured weaves of sorcery.

Banzu signed and sheathed Griever.

Jacob mimed same action.

Both men maintained their grips of hilts.

This doesn't feel right. Something's changed. Something's wrong. Banzu began, "Gwen—"

"No," Gwendora said, her voice a harsh whisper of command to everyone present. She stood across the room by a table upon which rested the small wooden box and the Godstone within it, her hunched back to Banzu, her head bent, hands palming the table, her stare locked on the box as if able to view its precious cargo through the closed lid. She drew in deep, inhaling measured calm, and there entered power of authority in her voice when next she spoke, enough to fill the room despite her level tone.

"There are more Khans rising to power, Banzu." She slid her hands from the table, straightening tall, turned from the box, her effort a struggle. "I did not explain the full measure of that brutal truth before because I was afraid of distracting you. Hannibal Khan was only the first of many, the gauntlets only the first pieces to an elaborate puzzle of power. The Enclave seeks the rest of the Dominator's Armor to bring the Nameless One back into this world. It's his only sure way of returning to the mortal plane. I cannot allow that. I . . ." She paused, and pain entered her voice. "I am Head Mistress. Fist is gone. My Academy in ruins. I cannot allow them to destroy the rest of the world in another Thousand Years War we'll never survive. Dethkore is coming, and we possess the only tool to defeat him."

"What?" Banzu took one step toward her—and stopped when Jacob beside her did the same to him, staring him down, hilt-gripping fingers fanning in pulling threat. "You can't possibly mean to use it. We have to—"

"Listen!" she snapped in a flare of voice, then paused and softened her tone. "Please, Banzu, just listen. One last time. Just listen. And if I cannot change your mind then we'll destroy it." She barred her left arm across Jacob's front in an attempt at easing the tension while taking a step past her First Sword. "That I swear. Please. You've seen firsthand what's out there. Your arm is testament. Don't let these innocent people die without giving this at least a little consideration."

He opened his mouth, to rebuke her offer, then closed it. He crossed his arms, wincing through the pain of doing so, and stared at her, at her protection of aizakai ready to blast him if she so much as gestured a finger, at Jacob eyeballing him in uneasy regard . . . and for the life of him he surrendered with a nod. "Fine. I'm listening."

"Thank you." She smiled, relaxing shorter by increments. "That's all I ask."

***

Gwendora turned away and relayed orders in a low voice out of Banzu's earshot to her attending aizakai who flocked round her, in particular a raven-haired mage in black robes who, after the six aizakai left the room only he returned some minutes later carrying a kettle in one hand and two porcelain cups in the other.

The mage set the stolen kitchen wares upon the table, then cupped the kettle's sides between his hands and closed his eyes, lips moving without sound. His hands turned aglow, brightening orange with inner flushes of heat, then seconds more and steam puffed out from the heated kettle's whistling spout.

"Thank you," Gwendora said, then dismissed the mage who left, joining the fifteen retinue of fistian soldiers and the five other aizakai outside and guarding the room's only door. She unfastened the brass buckles of her boiled-leather dachra harness hugging round her torso. She shrugged out from the Spellbinder harness then beckoned Jacob closer while offering him the limp cage and the two fanged dachras sheathed within it.

She shared private conversation with her First Sword, their backs turned to Banzu in low speak, at times both peeking at him while sharing whispers.

Banzu signed—then flinched and glanced away to the door behind him when something on its other side sounded.

While Jacob dipped his hand into his back pocket and passed something off to the Head Mistress she tucked away.

Banzu returned his gaze forward and fetched another, deliberate sigh. "We're wasting time."

Gwendora scolded him with an over the shoulder look though nodded. She dismissed her First Sword, though Jacob hesitated before accepting the kohatheen tied off to the Head Mistress's belt by way of hitching the lanthium hoop overtop his sword's hilt while tossing her dachras and leather harness over the other shoulder. When he approached Banzu, he held out his hand.

"What?" Banzu asked, looking from Jacob to the Head Mistress and back again. Apprehension furrowed his brow, sharpened his tone. "What?"

"A palavar with weapons is no palavar at all," Gwendora said. Then, and with a soft smile, she spread her hands in open gesture of her disarmed self and expected the same peaceful manner from him.

"Palavar?" he asked.

She nodded.

He frowned. "We're not enemies, Gwen."

Jacob poked him in the chest with a stiff finger. "That's Head Mistress."

Banzu swatted Jacob's hand away, scowling. "There's no time for titles." He leaned in a bit, and in lower voice he asked, "What's gotten in to you?"

Jacob answered nothing, though he shifted his feet and almost—almost—averted his gaze a brief slip.

"It's okay, Jacob. He's right." She cocked Banzu an eyebrow. "All the same, we palavar."

Jacob snapped his fingers, pointed at Griever, then held out his hand, palm upturned, fingers waggling. "Fork it over. Or I take it."

Banzu tightened his challenging gaze upon the man. *You can try*. But he put no voice behind it. Instead he sighed and rolled his eyes. "Fine." He unbuckled his belt and handed it and Griever over to Jacob. "But I expect it back," he said before letting go.

Jacob glanced at Gwendora, who nodded, then he strode past Banzu and out from the room, joining his fistian fellows while closing the door, leaving Banzu and the Head Mistress alone for palavar.

"I'm sorry, Banzu," Gwendora said. "This situation has frazzled me to no end. I need this as much as you." She half turned, waved at the table and its two empty chairs. "Please, sit. And let us be civil."

Civil? What the frig is going on? But he said nothing as he walked to the table and sat, though he expelled an irritated sigh while pointing at the small kettle puffing steam atop the table next to the box. "You want to drink tea? Now?

"Yes. I do. And you are joining me."

She sat at the small square table in the chair opposite him. She removed a small leather pouch from somewhere hidden on her person and smiled, relaxing while petting it, then kissed it. "Thank gods Jacob remembered to bring this."

Banzu glanced at the box so near, at the door so far, then fixed his stare ahead. "I'm not thirsty."

She loosed a nervous chuckle. "Neither am I."

She opened her leather pouch and tore through a handful of the same lemon-peppery sweetnettle herbs she forced him into drinking before his retrieval of the Essence of Simus Junes, when they'd discussed their bargains in the fistian Academy, her preferred drink for clearing one's mind of tensions while loosening the tongue for truths.

He signed while watching her work, wanting to rebuke the nonsense as a waste of time considering the horde of hungars shrinking hours from swarming into the city. But the sweetnettle tea proved her intent of speaking with him in honest conversation, and for that he held his tongue despite his fracturing patience.

"Allow me to explain some things," she said, while tearing through her herbs. "And after I'm finished, if you still wish to destroy the Godstone here and now then I certainly won't stop you. I helped you to it, after all."

He eyeballed the small wooden box resting between them, mocking him, and huffed a terse breath. "I'll listen. But when we're through, I'm going to destroy it." He tightened his eyes, his voice. "Like I'm supposed to." *Not that I know how. Yet.*

Hands pausing, she stared at the box through half-closed lids. She smiled and nodded, whispered, "Of course, of course."

And there held her captivated stare overlong.

"Gwen?" No response. So he smacked the table. "Gwen."

She flinched, her eyes popping through refocus when they snapped up and met his gaze, her hands returning to shredding bits of herbs she piled on the table, her mouth a fading scowl. "What we have to decide is nothing simple."

Banzu stiffened when she reached for the box, preparing to slap her hand away.

But she slid the box aside and filled its absence with the two porcelain cups. She closed her eyes and rolled her neck, sighing, then drew in a deep breath and released it through pursed lips, after which she removed more herbs from her leather pouch then relaxed back in her seat while nestling her hands in her lap beneath the table's edge, arms twitching with the movements of tearing the herbs.

"I feel so . . . tired," she said. "I've spent my entire life preparing for this. Over forty years of training and struggle. My duties as Head Mistress have taken such a toll on . . ."

She went on, but Banzu paid her small mind, his focus drawn to the box and what lay inside it waiting for him to take hold, to end this nonsense with the simple touch of his hand.

If Enosh spoke true. But what if she's right? What if it explodes or something the second I touch it? Doesn't matter. I have to try.

He stared overlong, Gwendora's voice a distant carry on the fringes of his straying attentions, the festering urge to open the box and just be done with it inviting nervous twitches so that he squirmed his chair. Hot throbs pulsed through his injured left arm, though duller now, receding. He considered removing the bandages for closer inspection of his lycan bite then decided against it, hoping once he touched the Godstone it would—

"*A-hem.*" The deliberate clearing of the frowning Head Mistress's throat roused his focus returning forward. "You said you would listen."

"I am. And Enosh warned me about this."

"Enosh." She scoffed the name while rolling her eyes in dismissive gesture. "Enosh is an avatar god." She raised her hands from her lap, added more torn bits of sweetnettle herbs to her little pile upon the table, then sprinkled copious pinches of the stuff into the two porcelain cups in equal portions. "Trapped within his towers for centuries while the rest of us mortals struggle on." She upended the kettle and poured steaming hot water into the cups, producing dark muddy brown swirls therein that cleared to honey yellow, then set the kettle aside and returned her hands into the hidden nest of her lap. "Enosh knows nothing of the true suffering of Pangea. He will live on regardless whether the rest of us perish or thrive. And I intend on living for quite some time yet. Don't you?"

If I survive the Godstone and us the hungars. "Yes."

She shifted on her bottom, raised her left hand and spider-gripped round the top of one cup with her encircling fingers then slid it across the table—and hissed while grimacing, having accidentally dipped the tip of her pointer finger into the hot tea. She stuck the burned fingertip into her mouth and gave it a relieving suck.

Banzu glanced at the proffered cup and rolled his eyes, brittle patience thinning, and in no mood for drinking tea with the Godstone so close.

She muttered a curse, blew on her fingertip before nestling her hand back into her lap beneath the table then picked up her own cup with her other hand, this time careful not to burn any more fingers by nervous accident.

"What was I saying? Oh yes. I plan on living for a while yet." She sipped her tea, watching him over the brim of the upheld cup. "Don't you?"

"Of course I do." He sat forward, put both hands on the table beside his cup, though neglected picking it up, and winced at the flare of ache in his throbbing arm earned from its extension so that he withdrew it tucked back to his side. "That's why we have to destroy it. Now."

"Lycan bites are nasty business. Yours makes you a liability, you know."

He frowned. "The Godstone will heal it." He glanced at the box, considered leaning forward and throwing open its lid for touching what lay inside. "You know it will."

A concurring nod, another sip of sweetnettle tea, her steady gaze watchful over porcelain brim. "Don't you want this world to be a better place? For yourself? For all of us?" A pause, another careful sip beneath the silent measure of her violet stare. "For Melora?"

"I—" But he stopped. *Melora.* And grimaced. *She's digging there on purpose, but why?* He squirmed his creaking chair, Gwendora's words rousing mixed emotions.

Gods I miss her. And she wouldn't stand for this nonsense, not for a second. If Melora was here she'd charge straight for the Godstone regardless the consequences and . . . or would she? Gwen's her Head Mistress and Melora's obsessed with duty. Still—

"Drink," Gwendora said, gesturing with her eyes at the cup before him over her raised own. "Anger is written all over your face. Now is not the time to make rash decisions. Too many lives depend upon this. Drink, and relax."

"Relax?" He spat the word out, scowling. "There's a friggin army of hungars outside and we're sitting here drinking your stupid tea."

"Relax," she said in curt tone, eyes a thinning scrutiny. "And drink."

"Fine." He took up his cup and raised it to his lips, intent on downing the whole thing in one big swallow despite its heat just to be done with it and—

"Consider all the wonderful things I can accomplish with the Godstone," she said, black eyebrows arching.

—and with that Banzu lowered his cup to the table without so much as a sip taken, frowning. "What? How?"

She glared at his lowered cup, at him. "The Jackals of Mar roam atop the Calderos Mountains, but there are tunnels funneling through them. Hundreds of safer passageways mined by thieves and assassins long ago. Their way of delivering stolen wares and writs of execution through while bypassing Caldera Pass." A pausing smirk. "They believe them covert, but my eyes-and-ears afford me access to many secrets, Banzu. Garnihan will prove no bother as we make our escape through those tunnels and—"

"And abandon Bloom? Just like Fist? Friggin hell, Gwen, we can't do that. Not again. I won't. Running away won't save anybody."

Her disapproving frown deepened into a tight scowl she schooled away in seconds. "And I suppose you have a better idea?"

"Yes. We destroy the Godstone and—"

"And then what, hmm? Pray Dethkore and his hungars just disappear?"

"No." He looked away, resisting the urge to stand while flipping the table over and yelling. "I don't know."

"Exactly my point. I know this is hard. Believe me, I do. I'm Head Mistress. My life is making weighty decisions. But there are casualties in every war, Banzu, and Bloom is lost. These people just don't know it yet. It's a tragedy, yes." She leaned forward to better meet his eyes, elbow sliding the table. "But the mountains will contain the hungars in Thurandy so long as we hold the Pass while we rebuild what was lost with Fist's fall, and Bloom's, in Tyr. With Garnihan or against him, it doesn't matter." She leaned back, elbow sliding, chair creaking, her eyebrows knitting into a silent plea. "What matters is we have the Godstone now. And I need you."

"I can't believe this." He sighed and shook his head. *This isn't spur of the moment thinking, she's been planning this.* "You don't get it, do you? You can't use it. No one can. Not without consequence." He leaned forward, meeting those measuring violets through the waft of steam between with a discerning glare. "Or has it already enticed you into thinking otherwise?"

"I am Head Mistress of the fistan Academy!" Her voice a cracking whip, eyes flaring, she stiffened straighter.

The door opened and Jacob strode inside, dark eyes fixing on Banzu, one hand gripping the hilt of his half bared sword.

Gwendora shook her head, lowered her voice. "It's okay, Jacob. I'm okay. Please, remove. We're almost finished."

A hesitant nod, then Jacob removed once more behind the closing door.

Banzu flexed his empty hand at his left hipwing, craving Griever's return. *What the frig is his problem? He's been eyeballing me ever since the Pass.*

Gwendora worked her shoulders in pensive little shrugs, calming herself, and set down her cup. "Just think of all the wonderful things I can do with it, the peace I can bring to the world, the lives I can save. Widen your narrow scope, Banzu. We've been handed the ultimate gift. In the right hands the Godstone can heal the sick, stamp out poverty, end wars before they can even begin."

"And in the wrong hands it will cause another Thousand Years War, destroying countless lives. It's not a tool, Gwen, but a test. There's things you don't know, things Enosh told me before—" *Before I killed his mortal avatar.* But he cut those words short, began anew. "It must be destroyed before it destroys all of humanity. That's its only purpose!"

"Calm yourself." She eyed his untouched cup of tea. "And don't be ridiculous. You're the last Soothsayer, and I'm Head Mistress. Fate has decreed it that we are to cleanse the world together, you and I. But all you've given me so far is resistance in every step and defiance at every turn of my head. You're supposed to be the first Soothsavior, Banzu. Join me, please. Together our Conclave can shape this cruel world into a safer place, not just for us, for aizakai, but for everyone. War, gone. Hunger, gone. Poverty, gone. Disease, gone. I can accomplish all of that and more with the Godstone at my disposal."

My disposal. Not our but my. He studied her a moment, mulling on the taste of that lie, the premature assumption of victory that whispered of madness. "Enosh warned me not to trust anyone. He said no one can resist the temptation of the Godstone's all-power. But I never thought that included you." He grabbed his cup and downed half the tea before returning it to the table where some sloshed onto his hand. He flicked the irritating beads away. "There is no using it, Gwen. *It* uses *you.*"

Frowning, she glanced away, stare fixing upon the box, meditative in the brief silence, then she watched him, the fading gleam of hope dying in her glazed and narrowed eyes.

"Every betrayal begins with trust," she said, her disgruntled tone a low whisper.

Friggin hell, it has her in its grips. That . . . wrongness, this is it. How could I not see it before? This palavar is a pointless charade. She isn't even listening, just pretending to between excuses for using the Godstone.

He downed the rest of his tea, hoping the action would punctuate an end to their futile discussion, then lowered his cup, stamping the table with it. "Are we done here?"

The hint of a cunning smile betrayed one corner of her mouth as an ease of tension stole over her features.

"Labor pangs, Banzu. There will be pain, and bloodshed, but all for the sake of a new beginning when all of this is finished." She held considerable pause while her smile grew. "With or without you."

He scrubbed dapples of sweat from his heating brow with the back of his forearm, frowning. "What's that supposed to mean?"

She leaned forward and presented a smile more snarl than grin. "You're wrong, Banzu. And you've just proven yourself as much a stubborn fool as Jericho ever was."

He tensed through flaring anger. Seconds from standing, seconds from grabbing the box and—he winced, cramping knots twisting in his belly, his skin flushing hotter and sweating. He pounded the table with the meat of his fist, rattling the cups, then pointed at her.

"Don't you dare—" he said, then broke into a harsh coughing fit, his lungs heavy with pressure, his throat swelling tighter, his face afire with rising heat. "Don't you—"

But his throat clenched up, strangling him short and hoarse, his mind pitching and swimming through sloshes of increasing vertigo fuzzing the edges of his vision. He blinked hard and rubbed at his eyes while waves of nausea flushed through him, turning his belly queasy while trembling his limbs.

What'd you do to me? But the question sounded only in his mind for he possessed no strength of voice for speaking the accusation.

He glared at his empty cup, tried grabbing at it to squeeze it crushed. But his jellied muscles round leaden bones proved indifferent to his mental commands. Belly rumbling, skin lathered in profuse sweat, clothes a hot and sticky cling, he lurched forward to snatch his cup and throw it at the undisturbed woman sitting too relaxed across from him, her pursed lips toying with the dark mystery burnishing those violet eyes.

"What . . . have you done . . ." But the rest of his words died in his throat clenching through choking spasms.

Gwendora smiled at his horrified eyes growing wide with realized terror. From beneath her edge of the table she upheld an unfolded razor pinched between her finger and thumb, Jacob's shaver, the same one Banzu used to trim his beard Jacob must have handed off to her before his leaving during their turned discussion.

Pieces of harsh truth snapped together in Banzu's fogging mind.

Gwendora's arrogant smile grew into a sinister spread when she raised her other hand from her hidden lap, pointer finger extended, presenting the tiny slice with a single droplet of her Spellbinder blood beading upon its cut tip. The same finger she had 'accidentally' dipped into his tea while sliding him the offered cup.

Son of a . . . no!

The cold flush of panic gripped him by the spine and shook him. In his mind he erupted into standing, though in body he struggled into standing, chair sliding back, and palmed the table while fighting for balance on trembling legs, the room tilting and sloshing through the wavering field of his blurring vision, each pulse of his quickening heart and the next pitching and swaying his sense of equilibrium.

His disobedient hands fumbled at his left hipwing for a sword no longer there. A guttural growl arose in the depths of him when he attempted a murderous lunge round the table for strangling her that instead proved little more than a feeble lurch. He sank, caps striking the hard marble floor, the poisonous paralyzing agent of her blood burning wicked course through his veins in acidic fever stiffening his joints.

Garbled strangles of words escaped his parched mouth round his swelling tongue. He clawed the air in desperate reach of the Head Mistress and for it pitched forward, crashing upon the floor, front striking the hard marble flagstones.

"Oh don't be so dramatic," Gwendora said, twisting in her seat, watching down at him with a curious tilt of her head, at his arms outstretched and his fingers wriggling in futile struggle at reaching her feet, reaching in vain. "It's not enough to kill you, only to contain you for awhile."

"You bitch," he coughed out in a hoarse strangle, glaring up at her through the burning eyes of a fever-victim.

"I've been called worse." She stood, her chair scraping backwards from the fluid motion, and smiled over him, her eyes violet pools of malcontent. She bent that smile into a frown when one clawed fingertip of Banzu's closer hand made contact with the toe of her left boot so that she reared her foot back and kicked him in the face.

Pain highlighted by a thousand twinkling stars filled his watery vision while his head whipped from her kick, and the momentum rolled him to his back where he mustered enough strength to clutch at his throbbing face, his bleeding nose, his hands numb fumbles applying little actual pressure. He tried kicking his legs, but nothing below his hips responded.

"Jacob!" pierced the Head Mistress's shout. Followed by an opening door, the sound of approaching steps, an audible gasp and masculine grunt, then words exchanged.

"But you said . . ."

". . . and he refused . . ."

". . . we can't just . . ."

". . . and what's done is done."

But all logical sense of the heated conversation faded to the tumult of Banzu's sloshing senses and the ache of his face, the debilitating fever of paralysis locking his palsied limbs while the unanswered wrath for the Head Mistress's blatant betrayal blazed defiant in his heart, its thunder slowing to the Spellbinder blood reaching it.

Jacob gripped Banzu's wrists and pulled them apart with ease.

Gwendora's pleased face loomed through the wet prism of Banzu's hazy vision.

Jacob divided Banzu's arms to the floor where they stayed of their own accord, stiffened by paralysis.

Banzu produced a tortured groan, his only resistance, while watching Gwendora fiddle with her kohatheen's locking mechanism, opening it. She bent at the hips and closed the lanthium collar round his neck—*click*.

He shuddered and twitched, his paralysis restraining reactive spasms firing throughout his taut body as imposed lassitude flushed through him, bleeding its stranger sense of gravity deep into his bones while melting his watery muscles heavier to the floor.

Gwendora straightened tall, her shoulders back and chin up, all proud Head Mistress, her satisfied smile bleeding into the condemning scold of her focal glare.

"I dislike dispensing ultimatums," she said to Banzu, her tone a derisive drawl. "But you forced my hand in this." She estimated him a silent moment, lips pressing into a fine line, the scrutiny of her eyes thinning sharp. "You are either with me or against me, Banzu. And you will forget Melora. She is lost to the cause. You'll be Paired with me, or you will die."

She paused and cleared her throat while swiping wrinkles from her violet dress before continuing.

"I certainly don't intend on being trapped here when these walls are torn down," she continued. "But no matter that. I will negotiate arrangements through the Pass, one way or another. In the interim I suggest you use what little time I'm allowing you to consider your fate. Or you will die with the rest of those we leave behind. The choice is yours, Banzu. You have a few hours to deliberate. I suggest you use them well and come to your senses."

With that said, Gwendora picked up the box from the table and carried it away.

Banzu rolled his head upon the floor, struggling through the effort of his stiff neck, and glared after her from between Jacob's legs, then rolled it facing up again in mute plea.

Jacob frowned down at him, cold dark eyes betraying regrets. "I'm sorry, Soothsayer," he said, his voice rough with emotion. "I truly am. It wasn't supposed to go like this."

Banzu opened his mouth. Only ragged breath escaped his throat.

First Sword Jacob Dillingham followed after the Head Mistress. He closed the door then locked it.

Paralyzed, Banzu writhed the floor, unable to even cry, treachery blazing in his dejected heart, a defiant scream buried deep in his hitching chest.

CHAPTER FORTY-SIX

When pain bites deep in the spirit, even strong men bargain. They twist and turn, plead and beg. They offer their tormentor what 'he' wants so the hurting will stop. And when there is no tormentor to placate, just a burning agony they cannot escape, they bargain with the gods, the same cruel deities from whence that pain ultimately originates.

But Banzu bargained nothing, too busy thrashing from the inside-out while he lay kohatheen-collared and victimized by treachery, helpless against the poisonous paralyzing agencies of Gwendora's Spellbinder blood coursing its torrid journey throughout his fevered system.

The cold white-marble floor offered little comfort against the molten sluices of heat scalding through his spasming sinews incapacitating him into nothing more than a crippled agony of semi-consciousness curling by painful increments into a fetal ball of hurt. Though as the torturous minutes passed, his breaking mind divided into two separating halves of incoherent screams and indifferent thoughts, of which the second proved his numbing savior.

He fell outside of himself, the connection between mind and body severed through the acidic pain pulsing lances of torment through his veins, where lived the little boy terror ruling the fragile depths of every scared man.

It can't end like this. I need help. Oh gods . . . someone please help me!

Alone. No Jericho. No Melora. Aggie miles away and only Gwendora knew where, hiding with the precious Book of Towers.

I have no one here. Doesn't matter. Gwen has the Godstone. No, the Godstone has her.

A spasm of anger flared in brief mind-to-body reconnection reminder, twisting his clenching guts raw while shrinking his fetal curl into a smaller trembling ball of hurt compacting round his grieving core.

Shaming hindsight of Gwendora's betrayal flashed through his mind in sickening recall, her deceptive plans unfolding in cold suspicions interwoven with the hot threads of brutal treachery.

She never wanted to destroy the Godstone. She intended on helping me retrieve the Essence of the First so she could use me to find it for herself. Does Aggie know? Was she in on it this whole time? Melora too?

No. Melora would never. And Gwen wanted to destroy it. But that changed. She changed. Friggin hell, Enosh warned me. He said nobody can resist. Even Spellbinders, not immune to magic but absorbent of it, the Godstone's divine magic trumping all lesser tiers. I should've known. But I let my guard down. Too sure Gwen sought the same conclusion.

Why didn't I escape the plains when I had the chance?

I killed Hannibal Khan and he still won.

It's all my fault.

I did this to myself.

Trust swaddled in ignorance.

Gwen betrayed me but I led her right to it. Her blood won't kill me, gods it hurts but it won't kill me. It'll burn out from my system eventually. But now I've a godsdamned kohatheen locked round my neck. Might as well have snapped it on myself. And no Power. No Griever. No help.

He lay in trembling agony while sifting through reflections of Melora, the violet-eyed beauty who bent but never broke, all the loving words he wanted to say to her the moment they reunited poisoned by the blatant betrayal of her Head Mistress.

Time turned a meaningless concept . . . until and at last the burning round his bones receded, the fire in his softening muscles dying into embers then those embers cooling dark.

Body unclenching, he unfurled from his fetal curl and lay supine, possessing a perpetual lethargy from the kohatheen, paralysis slow in leaving.

Muffled noise from beyond the thick marble walls evinced distant battle at play outside, perhaps even near to the castle grounds now. *How long has it been?* Unsure, unfocused, uncaring, he lay waiting for Gwendora's return, to agree with everything she commanded if only to escape the hungar horde and see Melora again, his exhausted body melted to the floor in limp surrender.

Minutes passed.

"No," he breathed more than said upon barest whisper, voicing the defiance in his challenging heart. *I can't. I won't. Melora would never forgive me. Move, godsdammit. Move!*

Doing nothing never a part of him, he mustered enough strength to roll over onto his belly, first rocking through increasing twitches of his shoulders then jerking his floppy arm up and over and across then slapping the floor, the twist of his hips pursuing, and there he lay, turned cheek pressing the cool marble.

He attempting working sapped strength into recovering muscles by straining flexes of fingers and wiggles of toes through the faint remains of subsiding paralysis, the kohatheen's lethargic influence battling against his sluggish efforts and his unyielding will to see it through.

More minutes passed.

His hands gripped flexes of air, his feet rotating at the ankles, arms and legs twitching, the ease of his locked elbows and knees losing stiffness as well his bending neck while his sweaty pressed cheek slid back and forth by inches upon the slick marble.

Lathered in sweat, panting with effort, he surrendered the struggle in brief respite while premonitions and possibilities tumbled through his mind.

Gwen expects me to join her, or she'll leave me here to die, let the hungars tear me apart while she runs away and Bloom crumbles. Unless she orders Jacob the mercy of killing me first. No, when I refuse her she'll probably do the job herself and enjoy every second of it. She never did like me much. And the Godstone's crazed her mind.

Maybe . . . maybe I can use that against her, that determined pride blooming into defiant arrogance. There has to be some way out of this. If I die here then it's all been for nothing. I can't die knowing that.

But how am I supposed to live with myself knowing we abandoned Bloom same as Fist? Thousands will die. Thousands more hungars. Maybe I can convince her to funnel everyone into the Pass and shore the gates. Buy us time while we escape to our only refuge in Tyr?

No. Caldera Pass is closed. And Garnihan will never open the tyrian gates for safe passage. Not after what happened with the Godstone. He'll delight in watching hungars flood inside and tear everyone to pieces while hoping to claim the Godstone for himself after the slaughter. Not that he'll have any chance of that once the flood of hungars burst through the gates and ravage Tyr same as Bloom.

And Dethkore . . . oh gods, Dethkore.

A new bargain struck with Garnihan is Gwen's only conceivable escape, and she won't surrender the Godstone. It's warped her mind and twisted her mistaken intentions into delusions of grandeur. She actually believes she's doing what's best. Power's true corruption: justification through self-deception. I know well the taste of that intoxicating poison. I swallowed enough of it on the plains.

No, she has what Garnihan wants but she won't surrender the Godstone. And that leaves the tunnels honeycombing the mountains. Risking the Jackals of Mar by going over them is suicide. She'll try and sneak her way through them. And she won't risk speaking a word of it to anyone but a handful so they don't clog her escape. If she even makes it through without someone knifing her back in the dark.

He craned his head with effort, cheek sliding the floor, and eyeballed the door mocking him from across the room. Straining, he dragged himself along the floor upon forward-inching forearms, quivering legs too feeble to provide anything more than twitching half-kicks upon the smooth marble flooring. Muscles watery round leaden bones, his shimmying grunts of effort roused more feeling into his tired and tingling extremities. Halfway there he paused and pushed up onto all fours, limbs trembling on the verge of collapse, and crawled the rest of the way to the locked door. Twisting round, he sagged with his back propped against the wall beside the door at his right and awaited his executioner, be they living or unliving.

His left forearm no longer hurt so that he nested it across his lap and unwound the soiled bandage from elbow to wrist. And breath hitched in his chest at the startling reveal of his once-eviscerated flesh now knitted together through accelerated healing, leaving only a vicious webwork of pink puncture scars scored from lycan teeth sinking deep while cracking bone beneath thicker hair.

He brushed the unexpected growth in probing scrutiny.

No, not hair but . . . shorter, thicker, coarser . . . *oh gods, fur? No. Not this. Not now.*

He closed his eyes and banged the back of his head against the wall, cringing. He drew in deep, swiped his right hand down over his face, blew out his cheeks and snapped his eyes open.

If it's not one thing it's another. Always another.

He stared at his lycan bite scar while squeezing his hand, watching tendons flex taut round fused bones through no pain involved, then rewound the bandage tight from elbow to wrist, disgusted over the crooked course of his life marred so much like the white marble round him containing faint traceries of ebony swirls resembling breaths of shadows wafting in static zephyrs captured round tiny flecks of quartzite.

He hooked two fingers on the kohatheen heating his neck and tugged, grimacing, then surrendered the futile chore, hand falling to his lap.

"Friggin hell," he muttered, though it sounded more a slur over numb-tingling lips. *I'm collared like a godsdamned dog.*

Suspicions resurfaced into ruthless truths.

No, I'm not a dog but a tool. And Gwen isn't finished using me. If she kills me there'll be no stopping her. The Godstone's limitless all-power can magnify her void-aura a hundred fold while healing any wound. I'm the only one who can destroy it, me or Dethkore. He's already made his choice, and I can't even stand. I'm a toothless swordslinger without Griever.

Godsdamn you, Jacob!

And Melora . . . oh gods, Melora. I'm so sorry. I failed you. Please don't hate me. If Gwen leaves me here to die please don't believe her lies. I tried my best. I—

No. She's too smart for that. She'll pounce soon as she sees the Godstone. And she'll go down fighting. Either against Gwen or . . . or worse, torn apart beneath a swarm of hungars, screaming while they eat her alive, blaming me with every contagious sink of their teeth.

A guttural growl buried deep in his chest vibrated to the seething fury burning away the mental fog clouding his thoughts. Body craving movement, he wanted to roar while exploding into standing, to kick open the door and tear his way through the castle until he found Gwendora then rip her to pieces with his bare hands.

Give it up, Ban. You can't even stand. And she's guarded too well. Jacob has Griever. She has the Godstone. There's no way out of this but surrender and you know it.

'You are either with me or against me,' Gwendora's voice taunted in sickening recall of her parting ultimatum, so arrogant, so victorious, so sure of her mad gamble.

If only I hadn't indulged her stupid palavar and drank her stupid tea. If only I'd grabbed the Godstone in the Pass instead of believing her lie. If only . . .

He contemplated his fate as well how he'd stumbled blind into this miserable mess in the first place, while the list of regrets compiled into such a nauseating length his gullible ignorance disgusted him.

She's supposed to prevent another Thousand Years War, and now she'll usher it in beneath the false banner of world peace. Her perverse version of it, anyways. If she even survives Dethkore and his horde of hungars. No, she won't. They have sheer numbers. They'll swarm in and steal the Godstone and then there'll be no stopping them.

Unless I join her first.

He upturned his hands in makeshift scales, helping him deliberate choosing the lesser of two evils.

He flexed his left hand closed, open. *Join her and live while she enslaves the world through false peace.* He flexed his right hand closed, open. *Or refuse her and die while she does it anyways.*

He fisted both frustrated hands tight while sighing at the illusion of choice.

I trusted you, Gwen. And you betrayed me all the same. Hindsight's a cruel bitch. If only I could go back and undo everything I'd—no, Locha's Luck I'd just screw it all up worse than before. Not that I have the option with this friggin kohatheen locked round my neck and no Godstone, no Power, no nothing.

He drew in a ragged breath, expelled a withering exhale.

Gods I wish Melora was here instead of in that godsdamned tower. No. I've been away too long, and she has less patience than I do. She's probably either fought her way out through Bartholomew's bandits and is on her way to Fist, or worse already dead by them. She's fierce with her fangs, but she's only one against so many.

The rising pressure of rage beat behind his eyes and through his tensing muscles in a raw surge of returning strength so that he pounded his fists upon the floor at his sides.

No! Don't even think it. If Melora's dead . . . then none of this matters, and I have nothing left to live for but pain and regret.

"Regret." He spat the word out in bitter release. *Of that I have many. Too many. And how many more before I am through?*

The right regrets made one's life bearable, while the wrong ones ensured one's death insufferable.

He sniffed hard and swallowed, set his jaw, and shook his head while pounding the floor again, craving Melora back in his life more than the sweet release of his kohatheen.

I love you more than life itself, Mel. I never got to tell you that. And I'll never have the chance. Unless . . .

A foul blackness of grim conclusions crept through his inner workings while he considered and hated considering the possibility of her fate yet knew he must.

The Godstone mattered nothing when weighed and measured against Melora's life. If he did nothing to change the current course of events, if she wasn't dead already then she would be. Once she returned and found the corrupted woman in place of her Head Mistress, Melora would lash out in savage abandon, every inch of her the feral she-cat. But imbued with the healing power the Godstone provided its wielder, she stood no chance against Gwendora despite her mastery of dachras, only a matter of time as her body accrued mortal wounds while Gwendora's repaired.

Or would Melora react otherwise? Duty her purpose, she held it in highest regard. She might join the Head Mistress in Gwendora's misguided attempt at bringing peace to the world, believing lies while buying in to false promises.

"No," Banzu whispered, harsh and sharp, disparaging to that reality, disgusted he even entertained it. *She'll never join Gwen. And for it she'll die. I can't let that happen. I need her.*

An awful decision surmounted. Shame flushed hot and strong.

She'll view me a traitor if I accept Gwen's ultimatum.

Though he would not be the Soothsayer puppet Gwendora intended but a man trying to do the right thing in the most difficult circumstances, not that it justified his intentions.

Godsdamn you, Gwen.

And life without Melora imposed an unrelenting crush upon his heart, leaving nothing but misery.

I can't lose her again.

I won't!

Even if it means—

Conclusions clicked into decision. No course left but to deliver his answer, he raised his right fist and, without bothering a look, pounded on the door.

For her. And waited out the silence of his impending judgment. *I'll do what I have to. For her.*

* * *

Minutes passed.

The muffled noise of battle beyond the castle's thick marble walls continued, closer, evincing increased proximity.

Banzu raised his right fist out at his side and delivered another pound, thrice, upon the door.

More time lapsed.

He sat sagged and hunched against the wall, his legs stretched straight, though he occupied the wait by drawing his knees up then straightening his legs several times, glad for the movement despite the kohatheen's lethargy though unsure they would hold him standing.

More minutes passed.

He sighed, muttered, "What the frig is taking so godsdamned long?"

He pounded the door again. "Hey!" And again.

And waited as more minutes passed unanswered.

Panic clenched his guts. *Did they already leave? And leave me here to die? Oh gods.*

He twisted while raising his fist for another pound.

The door at his right unlocked and opened.

Jacob strode five steps inside and past Banzu, wearing Griever belted round his trim waist and sheathed at his left hipwing opposite his own sword. He looked round the room. "Where the hells are—"

"Right here," Banzu said.

Jacob spun round, startling, then approached Banzu's outstretched feet. For a moment overlong he just stared. Then he kicked Banzu's boots. "Kneel," he said, after gripping both swords' hilts with opposing hands.

Banzu blew out his cheeks, grunted forward while drawing his legs in. He removed from sitting and slunk onto hands and knees, sluggish, then sagged back bottom atop heels in a lethargic hunch.

Jacob cocked a curious eyebrow, expecting more of a fight or at least an argument. He pulled both swords from his waist and held them at length, blades crisscrossed at Banzu's throat above the kohatheen.

"Your answer," Jacob said, his tone cold despite the sadness betraying his eyes. "And give it quick, Soothsayer. Head Mistress plans on moving soon." A pause, the tightening of his eyes. "Don't think I won't do it." His hands squeezed the leather-wound hilts in audible creaks. "Or that I'll be happy about it."

Banzu swallowed, the crisscrossed blades' edges scraping against his juggling throat. He kept his gaze a steady bead up at the man staring him down while he spoke his final plea.

"Help me, Jacob. Please?"

Jacob shook his head, frowning. "I can't do that, Soothsayer. What Head Mistress says, goes. I'm her First Sword. You know I'm sworn to her at all costs."

"Even my life?"

Jacob answered with a reluctant nod.

"This isn't right and you know it. Please, Jacob, help me."

Jacob scowled. "I won't help you kill her—"

"Not kill," Banzu said quick. He shook his head, the slight motion earning twin fine cuts along the sides of his neck trapped between the pincer blades. "I'm done killing, remember? And I don't want to hurt her, I want to help her. We need to stop her. The Godstone has her now. You can't tell me you don't see that crazed look in her eyes, Jacob. She's not the Gwen you knew. She's not the Head Mistress you swore to protect. If we can take the Godstone from her and—"

"Stop!" Jacob removed two steps, withdrawing the swords. He uncrossed them then stabbed them into the dual leather sheaths at his hips. He studied Banzu a moment overlong, face tensed, mouth chewing through words before speaking them. He glanced at the open door, back to Banzu. "You're asking me to commit treason of the highest order."

"Did you know she would betray me?" Banzu asked, the question a struggle not to yell.

Jacob flared then thinned his eyes. He removed another step, turned round, presenting his back while staring at the far wall where rested the table and two chairs. He drew in deep, shoulders rising then falling with his slow exhale.

Silence.

He trusts me enough not to make a play for his turned back. Good. "Well, did you?"

Jacob grunted a curse, huffed and spun facing him. "Yes."

Friggin hell. "When?"

"While we were breaking camp for Bloom. After she waved me into her tent and, well, hells, all those hungars at our backs changed her mind after I told her how bad it was on the plains. And Trina's scrying didn't help the matter any."

Banzu hawked then spat at Jacob's feet in a slip of anger.

"Godsdammit Soothsayer, she's the Head Mistress of Fist! I'm sworn to obey her. That's my place. That's always been my place." Jacob slapped at his chest. "My purpose! Without her—" He paused, continued in lower tone. "Without her I'm nothing but a pastured soldier."

"And yet you left without telling her to come after me. To risk your life saving me."

Jacob crossed his arms and glared past Banzu at the empty space of open door. "Yeah. Well. That was different. And I aimed to kill you before I saw what I saw."

"What happened to Fist will happen here. Is that what you want?" Banzu straightened from sitting into kneeling and threw his arms out at his sides in indicative gesture of the muffled sounds of battle at play beyond the walls creeping closer. "Listen to what's happening out there, Jacob. People are dying. And they'll keep dying. And it won't end unless we do something. I can't stop those godsdamned things, but I can keep Dethkore from getting the Godstone. *We* can, Jacob. You and me, working together."

"Against the Head mistress," Jacob said, more accusation than statement.

"Not against her, helping her."

"She'll bring peace to the world with the Godstone," Jacob said. "That's how we help her."

Banzu suppressed a sigh. "No, she won't. She'll bring the world death in another Thousand Years War. Only this time there's no Simus Junes to stop it. Because you won't help me." He sagged back upon his heels into a weary slump. "You might as well kill me now. And yourself while you're at it. Because I'd rather have my throat slit than my face eaten off while I scream through every second of it."

Jacob frowned. "It doesn't have to be this way, Soothsayer. Swallow your pride and swear her your fealty. Help her cleanse the world. Help us bring it peace. She's right. Thurandy is lost, but the Calderos will keep those hungars at bay while we regroup in Tyr and figure the rest out. But we have to move now, and get as many as we can through before it's too late."

Banzu stared up at the veteran soldier a silent length, testing the measure of those dark eyes, sensing the elder man struggling with the multiplicity of layers of intent and design at work. He opened his mouth for more persuasion.

"Enough chatter," Jacob said, sharp and curt. He uncrossed his arms and gripped his dual sword hilts again. "We don't have time and my mind's not changing. The next word out of your mouth better be yes." Elbows fanning, he pulled both swords half bared. "Or no."

Banzu stifled the rest of his argument, no point in beating his head against the harder wall. "Fine," he said. "So be it."

He stood with effort, legs wobbly though stabilizing.

And Jacob withdrew an immediate step, half turning, right foot sliding back, body bracing, posture shifting into preemptive strike.

"You're giving me no other choice." *Just like Gwen. She's blinded by the Godstone and Jacob his duty.* "If you can't beat 'em, join 'em, right? I'll do it her way if that's what it takes. At least I can help prolong the inevitable."

"So you'll swear?"

Banzu sighed, nodded. "I'll swear."

Jacob blew out his cheeks, stance relaxing, half bared swords sliding sheathed to his hipwings. "Thank gods," he whispered.

"Let's go." Banzu turned for the door.

"Not yet."

He turned back.

Jacob produced a small length of rope from his belt. "Hold your hands out, wrists together."

Banzu sighed. "Really?"

Jacob nodded. "Really."

"Fine." Banzu obeyed.

Jacob closed distance and began tying Banzu's wrists together.

Banzu considered throwing a punch then stealing a sword, but he hesitated, unsure he possessed the strength for either let alone surviving the ensuing fight. "At least *I'll* die with the right regrets," he said.

Jacob paused his tying work, flinching at the slap of words, his gaze snapping up. He met Banzu's unyielding stare but said nothing while he finished tying Banzu's wrists together.

* * *

Banzu walked through Castle Bloom with Jacob pursuing three steps behind.

Along the way, Jacob recited the necessary words required for Banzu to swear his fealty to the Head Mistress, and Banzu repeated them several times to Jacob's satisfaction.

They strode through long corridors and up several flights of stairs. Occasional servants stole by in frantic runs, carrying bundles of clothes or foodstuffs or weapons or the overloaded mix of all three clutched in their burdened arms, giving the Head Mistress's First Sword and his Soothsayer captive passing glances only in their panicked sprints to safety, the chaos of the fighting outside a muffled raucous beyond the castle's thick marble walls. Banzu observed no soldiers along their route, and supposed them all occupied outside or elsewhere guarding huddles of hiders hoping their closed eyes provided them a child's safety from impending nightmares.

They entered a room possessing a claustrophobic tension despite its immense size, dominated with a silence separating it from the rest of the world. Wooden benches rested along the walls, some overturned and evincing hasty division, adding a tunnel's elongated depth down the room's middle. Stained-glass windows set high along the walls depicted multicolored glyphs—none of which Banzu recognized for the faint trickles of others' memories attempting to bleed into his mind from the shared collective remained blocked by his kohatheen—framed by plush drapes of flowery splendor emitting the strong aroma of burnt cinnamon from the oils rubbed into the bright sunburst fabrics.

Opposite the only door sat Head Mistress Gwendora Pearce upon a simple wooden, high-backed chair, her regal posture fashioned into the presence of a throne, arms resting atop armrests with the small wooden box nestled atop her lap, eyes closed in what looked a meditative trance, her face a blank slate, four aizakai mages flanking her position, two to a side, yet none of her fistian guardsman present. The four mages turned from her in unison at the two arrivals stopping just inside the door.

Banzu blew out his cheeks in slight relief to his fragile plans devised along the way here between his recitations, the box in Gwendora's lap still closed, no Godstone gripped in her fevered clutch. *There's still hope. Maybe I can talk her out of—no, that time has passed. She's not holding the Godstone, yet, but it's already taken her.*

Jacob closed the door, stroked his goatee, and announced their presence with the deliberate clearing of his throat.

A hint of smile betrayed the Head Mistress's tempered mask. Her eyes snapped open, and life glistened out, backed by the burning violet fire in the hearth of her contemplative mind.

She possessed an angry calm, no touch of fear in her adamant stare, nor did it flicker from Banzu, revealing cold disinterest, when a rise in the muffled noises raging outside the castle walls boxing them in penetrated the silence.

"You may approach," she said in a voice the purr of soft gravel.

Banzu obeyed, cautious though sure in his closing strides across the church room.

Jacob pursued behind, then snagged him to halt with a firm grip of arm and stood beside his left. "That's far enough, Soothsayer."

Banzu watched the Head Mistress watching him. *This is it. This is all that's left for me.* He cleared his throat and made to speak the betrayal of all that brought him here by swearing her his undying fealty.

Jacob smacked him on the back, frowning, eyeballing him sidelong. He jabbed a stern pointer at the floor. "Kneel while you swear."

Gwendora cocked an eyebrow, waiting.

Banzu lowered unto kneeling before her and her makeshift throne, eyeing her four guarding mages with their hands risen in preemptive blasts though more so the unopened box resting in Gwendora's lap less than ten bounding strides away if only he stood and rushed and grabbed and—*and died by quicker hands throwing magic before I even make it halfway. No. I'm collared. No Griever. No chance. I'm at their mercy and they know it.* He licked his lips, hating the taste of the lesser of two evils seconds from betraying over them. *It's either this or execution.*

Jacob nudged him with a knee.

Banzu nodded. He drew in a deep, preparatory breath and held it overlong, then began to recite—

"This is a glorious time," Gwendora said. "Do you not agree?"

Banzu chewed back his words and bowed his head. "I'm honored I can be a part of it, yes."

"We shall see." A mocking pause, the slight crease of her dark brow. "And why is that, Soothsayer?"

Soothsayer. Not Banzu but Soothsayer. She's speaking in titles, and wants reasons before I swear. She's testing me. Lay it on thick, Ban, just not too thick.

He maintained his gaze to the floor. "Because you're right. The Godstone is too precious a gift to destroy. In the right hands, your hands, it can heal the world. I understand that now." He glanced up. "And I'm ready to join you."

A bemused little smirk. "Elaborate."

He suppressed a sigh. "I'm the last Soothsayer. It's my new duty to protect the Head Mistress in all her endeavors. Enosh was wrong. And you've chosen to use the Godstone, so I'll protect you while you do it." He raised his gaze and met Gwendora's stare while straining to keep his from tightening into a raptor's glare. "But I have one condition. Meet it and I'll swear you all of me."

Gwendora frowned. She glanced at Jacob, back to Banzu. "What condition?"

"You know what," Banzu said.

She held brief pause, scrutinizing eyes tightening then blooming. She nodded. "Ahh, Melora, yes. I've forgotten her already. She's safe on the other side of the mountains. For now. And this isn't a negotiation. We've already had our palavar, and look where your stubbornness got you. You forced my hand in this."

"I want Melora," Banzu said, "or no deal."

Jacob pulled his sword half bared.

Gwendora sighed and rolled her eyes at Banzu while waving Jacob's sword sheathed. "Your obsession with her is annoying." She smiled at the heavy leverage wielded against him. "Very well. Swear me your fealty and I promise, on my honor, that you and Melora will be reunited."

Honor my ass. "I swear it."

Gwendora sat forward by inches, face pinching, her glare piercing violet stabs. "I'll require more than that."

Grunting, Jacob nudged him with an instigative knee and a downcast glare.

"And if you betray me," she continued, "know you are betraying Melora. I will kill her myself after killing you. Keep that in mind every time I turn you my back."

Banzu swallowed a hot string of threats by clearing his throat, and in risen tone he recited the necessary words. "I, Banzu Greenlief, pledge my undying allegiance to you, Head Mistress Gwendora Pearce, in all that you may pursue, my life for yours."

She smiled, delight in full bloom across her chocolate features. "Wonderful! Then it is done." She sat back, relaxing as much as her regal posture allowed. "We will heal this world, together and with the Godstone. I have made certain arrangements to secure us through the Pass. Fist is gone, and Bloom is lost. My new Academy will be rebuilt in Tyr, emboldened by a new army, a tyrian army, and I will reign stronger than ever."

"Mistress," Jacob said, shifting, fidgety. "What of the fistian refugees still—"

She silenced him with the scold of her shifting focus and the admonishing flick of her wrist. "Not that I need explain myself to anyone, First Sword." She gestured another wave, evincing the two missing aizakai as well the absent fistian soldiers. "But of those I sent to Tyr, Trina returned a message in your absence, sent through gleaning." She gestured at the nodding aizakai of the pair standing at her right. "Garnihan has agreed to open Caldera Pass and allow us through."

"Oh thank gods," Jacob breathed more than said, his militant posture relaxing as much as his lifetime of training would allow. "But we must hurry if we're to gather as many of the people and—"

"Us alone," Gwendora said. "Sadly, only us here will make the journey."

Tension returning, Jacob took a hesitant step forward. "But Mistress—"

"Quiet, Jacob." Her voice a cracking whip. "Your role is not to question." She swept her stern gaze back to Banzu. "I am ushering in a new age, and I'm glad that you finally see standing by my side is better than standing in my way. Now, we are finished here. Another hour and these walls will tumble on our heads. I mean to be gone well before then. You may rise, my Soothsayer."

Banzu stood, Jacob a rigid statue beside him. "Is . . . that it then?"

Gwendora laughed, cruel and sharp. "Of course not. You've sworn your allegiance, but words are wind. You'll have Melora, but you will be Paired with me and as my new First Sword soon as we're through the Pass and I deal with Garnihan."

Flinching, Jacob's mouth hung open though no voice escaped.

"Tyr," Gwendora continued, ignoring his stunned stare, "will become my new seat of power, its Arena my new Academy. And Caldera Pass will remain closed until I secure the Iron Crown and Throne under my persuasion. Ascadia is our home now, but we will return and purge Thurandy of Dethkore and his hungars while I restore peace and order once and for all."

She closed her eyes, smiling, shuddering, and drew in a long nostril breath.

"I stand upon the cusp of such greatness no Head Mistress has ever known. I will create a new and everlasting empire, one where none shall suffer, none shall starve, none shall wither or weep." She stood from her chair, clutching the small box between her hands. In a raised voice she proclaimed, "As long as they obey then they shall rejoice!"

"Mistress . . ." Jacob's voice a brittle whisper.

Banzu glanced at the veteran soldier. "So you will allow Garnihan to use the Godstone?"

Gwendora's crazed smile bent into a disapproving scowl as she clutched the box tighter against her middle, hoarding its precious content. "Of course not. Our bargain is a necessary pact of power to see us through the Pass. He will rule beneath me as my new army's general, a paper king." She gripped the box tighter still. "But the Godstone is mine and mine alone." She paused and tightened the scold of her eyes, her voice. "Or do you not approve, Soothsayer?"

Banzu bowed his head while swallowing truth for lie. "I approve of whatever it is you decide, Head Mistress—"

"Empress," she said, sharp and quick and correcting. "I am the Head Mistress now, but I will become the new Empress of all Pangea once the rebuilding begins in Tyr. Order *will* be restored." Her face softened along with her tone. "These are trying times, but I will see them ended. I've been waiting my entire life for this." She paused and stared at the box between her hands, smile blooming. "And now my time has finally come."

Banzu feigned a small smile in return, nodding, then raised his bound hands in silent question.

To which Gwendora gestured with the flick of her wrist. "Jacob, if you would, please."

Jacob blinked hard from his captured stare, nodded and stepped forth between them, turned round and faced Banzu. He pulled his folded razor from his back pocket, thumbed it open and sawed through the coarse rope tied round Banzu's joined wrists, silent, his motions mechanical.

"And the kohatheen?" Banzu asked, leaning to one side for better vantage past Jacob, the First Sword lost in blank stare, while giving his kohatheen an annoyed little tug for emphasis.

But she denied him with the shake of her head. "I'll remove it after we're through the Pass, not before."

Banzu nodded. "Of course. So we're just going to walk on through? Just like that?"

"Just like that." She nodded while fanning her fingers along the box's sides, fingernails *click-click-clicking* the wood, mimicking the motions of greedy black spider legs stretching. "I'm no fool. Garnihan has his own designs on the Godstone, but he will learn his place in my new empire." Her fevered hold increased upon the box's sides so that her knuckles flashed white as tendons flexed through gripping strain. "All will learn."

Banzu let play a dissatisfied frown.

Gwendora mimicked the gesture in return. "What?"

"It's just—" He cleared his throat, loosened his shoulders with a shrug, and began again, leaning aside while speaking past Jacob locked in distant stare. "You are more than the Head Mistress now. We shouldn't have to sneak out of here. We should walk out proud and with you carrying the Godstone in hand. Presentation is half the show, right? This is your moment. You're ushering in a new empire of peace, so let the people see it. Let the enemy fear it. Let them all witness the reigning splendor of their new Empress of Pangea coming to light. Your ascension is a moment in history that will be talked about for ages to come. If it was me, well, I'd ensure the bards and scholars have something wonderful to tell for centuries."

She estimated him a silent, calculating length . . . then smiled, a new twinkle in her eye. "You, my Soothsayer, are correct." She flicked open the box's brass latch, raised its wooden lid, and there paused, a flitter of awe dancing across her dark features. "Yes," she whispered, "I must give them something to talk about, to remember me by throughout the annals of history. I deserve no less. My ascension must be remarkable, yes."

The taller of the two aizakai standing at her right, a raven-haired fellow with sharp hawkish features, licked his lips while his hands gripped the black folds of robe at his sides in eager flexes. The spiky-haired blonde at her left took a half-step closer, stark blue eyes glistening with betrayals of focal desire, then crossed her thin arms over her small bosom as if unaware of what to do with them but for keeping them from reaching out in forbidden askance. The other two aizakai, one a burly man dressed in a green shirt and brown trousers matching his brown hair and green eyes evincing him a terramancer, the other an orange-turbaned woman with coppery skin, shifted on their feet, their lusting gazes stolen by the Godstone's reveal so close before them.

Ignoring the strong inner umbilical tugs instigated by the Godstone's close proximity requesting his rush to claim it, Banzu glanced at Jacob, who had half turned away, the First Sword not staring at the Godstone along with the others' captivated gazes but at the Head Mistress herself, his expression pained, dark eyes sorrowed.

Banzu gripped his arm, whispered, "The right regrets."

"What?" Jacob flinched and faced him, blinking hard, the bleak despair in his hushed voice so raw he averted his troubled gaze the moment their eyes met. "This isn't what she promised . . ." But he trailed away, voice dying though lips still moving.

A hungry light washed over Gwendora as she reached for the Godstone nestled within the box, the pink tip of her tongue gliding over trembling lips. She wiggled her fingers inches from the object of her utmost desires, then a frightened though satisfied gasp stole through her when she closed her fingers round the perfect orb, touching it, apparently, for the first time.

Her eyes snapped wide while turning aglow with a suffusion of energies, her charged body tautening taller, the Godstone's apotheosis filling her presence, her very being, with its almighty potency of limitless energy.

The air round her shimmered while vibrating as her magnified void-aura expanded in every direction beyond its natural capacity one-hundred fold, filling not just the entire room with magic-nullifying splendor but as well the rooms above and below and the hallways beyond.

Caught in the sweeping rush of her void-aura, the four guarding aizakai mages flanking her sides gasped in unison while staggering backwards from the invisible punch of nullifying energies.

Struck from behind, Jacob staggered forward a step.

While Banzu staggered back.

It's now or never.

But he recovered quick, the bait of his carrot tasted, then he stole forth with the offensive snare of his stick.

* * *

Adrenaline flushing, dulling his kohatheen's imposed lassitude a fading touch, Banzu snatched a grab for

Griever's hilt—startling Jacob who dropped his razor and caught Banzu by the reaching wrist, stopping him.

Banzu made to speak a final plea before dispatching Jacob by way of yanking him into a face-smashing headbutt then shoving him aside while tearing Griever loose and charging.

But Jacob's eyes silenced him, shocked him paused with their unveiling of sorrow and waking regret blooming in flinty pools of sadness. *You were right*, those self-recriminating eyes said. *And I hate you for it.*

Broken by Gwendora's appalling revelation of her new empire and all it entailed, Jacob surrendered his grip.

Banzu pulled Griever free from sheath.

"Jacob!" Gwendora yelled, her luminous eyes blazing wicked violet fire at the steel in Banzu's hands, her voice a reverberating scream. "Kill him!"

"No," Jacob said in harsh whisper, his dark eyes shattered slates of remorse. He turned and faced the Head Mistress, moving out from Banzu's way while shaking his head in denial of her order. Paling to her accusing glare, he shuffled towards the door in small backwards steps, his unfocused stare growing wide with grief above trembling lips that continued moving through dire whispers in the nest of his dark goatee. "I already . . . I cannot be a part of this . . . this treachery of our people."

"Bastard!" Gwendora thinned her glare into fiery scorn. "Kill them both!"

The four aizakai flanking her, two to a side, startled from their glassy-eyed stares upon the Godstone into instinctual obedience. All four threw their arms out while rushing forward, fingers wiggling through conjuring gestures of magical attack.

And their faces slumped in unison at the failure of their fruitless sorceries rendered null within Gwendora's Godstone-expanded void-aura.

Banzu smirked while advancing, gaze focal, his heart a quickening thunder to Griever's sweet assurance reclaimed in his hands.

Terror blossomed over the four aizakai's stricken faces as the unaffected master swordslinger sped toward them, Griever poised for delivery, though he sought nonfatal targets of incapacitation, killing his last resort so long as he reclaimed the Godstone.

Banzu lunged low into the instinctive swordform *Heron Spears the Salmon*, fighting through the forced lassitude of the kohatheen locked round his neck and leaching vigor's fullness from his working muscles. He stabbed the nearest aizakai through the thigh then twisted his blade, producing a terrible scream as the orange-turbaned woman's forward leg bent then buckled with the wrenching steel so that she collapsed to the floor in bleeding agony after he yanked free Griever's stinging tongue.

The largest of the four aizakai mages, the terramancer brute on Banzu's left, rushed him with timber arms outstretched and beefy hands seeking to crush and strangle.

I don't think so. Banzu twisted while sidestepping, swung Griever in the manner of a club, smacking the flat of his blade against the softer temple of the man's skull who stumbled past him, semiconscious, then toppled and crashed the floor.

Gwendora screamed and kicked aside the chair behind her while backing away from the fighting, double-clutching her precious Godstone tight against her full bosom, her wide eyes full of animal rage at the scene playing out, her fevered grip upon the precious Godstone unrelenting, and for it she allowed Banzu a fighter's freedom denied her aizakai guards. They might as well wear kohatheens same as him—a fact he counted on, had staked his life upon while stroking her arrogance in a betrayal all his own—for Gwendora's expanded void-aura reduced them to little more than a clumsy nuisance when compared to his superior swordslinger skills.

He leapt over the curled burden of the groaning woman bleeding on the floor and stabbed the skinny blonde aizakai behind her through the shoulder, driving the second woman backwards with the strong thrust before yanking his sword free and aided by a stiff kick against her chest, earning an arcing spurt of blood which splashed his chest instead of in his face upon Griever's prompt removal. The spiky-haired blonde stumbled, wiry-muscled arms pinwheeling at her sides, then fell and cracked the back of her head against the marble floor where she lay unmoving in all but her lids aflutter over unfocused eyes.

"No!" Gwendora yelled. She pried one straining hand loose from the Godstone, grabbed her chair then flung it forth with the whip of her arm and the twist of her hips before backing farther away. "No!"

Banzu spun away while hunching and braced for impact, the lethargy of the kohatheen allowing no sure speed for dodging the chair. Framed wood slammed against his right shoulder and broke apart. He grit his teeth and grunted through the pain. Out from his left peripheral he caught the felled terramancer pushing up from the floor onto hands and knees, a trickle of blood running from the snarling man's struck temple.

Banzu turned to hammer the rising brute down with another smacking thwack of Griever's flat, this time against the back of the man's head where thick neck met skull—but for the black-robed mage who announced his advance with a preemptive yell while launching into a brazen leap, dagger in hand, his arm poised overhead for hammer-fisting the six-inch blade into Banzu's turned back between shoulder blades where lived spine.

Banzu twisted while slicing backhanded through the downward-thrusting forearm a second before the leaping mage crashed into him where between sprayed new gouts of blood from the severed appendage. Their collision brought them to the floor in a bloody tangle where Banzu, a hot scream in his ear, lost his wet grip upon Griever's slickened hilt for wrestling the mage off him, head-butting the other in the face then throwing the lanky burden aside where the injured mage curled into a moaning ball clutching the bleeding stump of his right arm.

Banzu rolled onto hands and knees, seeking Griever's return—and craned his head at the burly terramancer standing with arms upraised over his head, Griever in his double-fisted grip and poised for downward chopping death.

"Kill him!" Gwendora yelled from across the room. "Kill him now!"

Banzu cringed.

The hefty terramancer grunted, jolting, his eyes popping wide in startlement, his body stilled in all but his eyes rolling down and fixing upon the length of silver-dipped blade protruding from his sternum. His thick arms lowered, his hands loosened, and Griever fell clattering to the floor.

Jacob withdrew his impaling sword from behind.

Gasping, the terramancer's trembling legs buckled at the knees. He collapsed, caps striking marble, his bulk rippling, then he toppled forward.

Banzu rolled free from the terramancer's crashing path just in the nick, the dead aizakai's face punching the hard marble floor with a sickening crunch and splatter of blood.

"No . . ." Jacob shook his head, gazed fixed upon his killing device. The bloodied sword stole from his grip and earned the floor in a dull clatter. Pale, his eyes wide and glistening with the remorse of a horror that could not be undone, he backed away several steps. "No . . ."

"Bastard!"

Kneeling, Banzu twisted to Gwendora's shout.

She rushed forth and scooped up the dropped dagger near the black-robed mage lying curled and clutching his bleeding stump of arm. She stepped onto then over him and whipped her arm out with the cruel finesse of expert release.

Banzu leaned back though watched the spinning blade speed past his turning face.

Six inches of fistian steel sank hilt-deep into Jacob's chest—*thunk*. His face bloomed with violent surprise. He staggered backwards, his tortured eyes locked with the burning glare of his Head Mistress. He stumbled on rubbery legs until his back achieved the far wall where he slunk down next to the door, his legs kicking out into a V on the floor.

He clutched at the dagger's handle with both hands, yanked it free with a grunt and dropped it to his lap. His lips moved through whispers producing words clipped short by the bloody cough issuing his final appeal in life while his dark eyes grew distant with death.

"No!" Gwendora yelled, surveying the gory scene before her, clutching the Godstone in both hands again while hunching over it as if to shield it away from all possible takers. "No!" She backed toward the opposite wall. "Godsdamn you, Soothsayer!"

"Is this what you wanted?" Eyes on the corpse of his savior, Banzu pushed up from the floor, retaking Griever in hand, his body a bloody canvas, his face a tensing mask of waking fury, the lassitude from the kohatheen thickening his muscles while adding weight to his bones. He wiped his bloodied hands then Griever's bloodied hilt with his shirt and faced the harpy screech of Gwendora's unintelligible scream, her face a seething rage, her eyes luminous violet fire burning with the psychosis of the Godstone's limitless all-power clutched in her fevered grip. "Is this your peace?"

He advanced one challenging step—and stopped, scanned round. *Gods what a mess.* "It's over, Gwen. I don't want to kill you. Just give me the Godstone and let's be done with this madness before more lives are lost."

The savage frenzy of her eyes darted past him to the door, the only available exit, but she said nothing.

"There's only one way out of here, Gwen, and that's through me." He leveled his sword out at her. "Please end this now. Just give me the Godstone and—"

"Never!" She raised the Godstone before her crazed face in the shimmering air, her tense fingers spread and curled round it in the unrelenting claw of her upturned left hand. "You think I'll surrender now? When I hold the Godstone and you a metal stick?" She laughed the sound of madness above the groans of her injured aizakai—those that still lived. "I'm a goddess, you fool. A goddess!"

Banzu shook his head and lowered Griever at his side, tip to floor. "It doesn't have to be this way. Please! All you have to do is let it go. Just open your hand, let it go, and step away. I'll take care of the rest."

She hissed through clenched teeth, her eyes fevered jewels, though she appraised the Godstone as if considering it and the choice of his words. She lowered it to her side and overturned her hand where it trembled as if seeking forced release of her spider's clutch . . . that did not come.

"I'm trying to save the world by making it a better place," she said, her tone level, matter-of-fact. "And you're ruining it."

She lowered her hateful glare while straightening into full towering height, drew in deep, expelled overlong through pursed lips. When she elevated her gaze, her luminous eyes possessed the calculating coolness of a predator eyeing its intended prey.

"This is all your fault." An eerie calm settled over her raging visage, smoothing her expression into a stern mask of resolve, her tense body loosening as she lowered into a preparatory crouch. "You're lucky Melora didn't kill you when she had the chance." Her right hand stole away behind her back then whipped out, dachra in its fisted grip. "I should know." Her dark smile spread, revealing murderous intent and the fierce need to see it through. "I trained her."

* * *

"Don't do this, Gwen." Banzu withdrew a cautious step from her while glancing down to avoid slipping in the splatters of slick blood greasing the marble floor. "I don't want to kill you." *I don't want to kill anyone anymore, godsdammit.* He raised his left hand palm out in warning gesture for her to: "Stop!"

She sprung forward, legs uncoiling, with the full stretch of her lithe frame. Leaping, spinning in the air, she whipped her right arm out, the fisted Godstone in her left hand a swinging counterbalance. And the dachra she loosed spun a whirring disk straight for Banzu's face.

He raised Griever in barring defense, his kohatheen's imposed lethargy adding a viscous quality to the air thinned however sparse by adrenaline, and the dachra clanged through sparks against the blocking blade's flat protection before winging aside where it clattered to the floor. Back-stepping, he made to say more.

But Gwendora continued her unrelenting approach, tossing the Godstone into the air a brief space, her left arm whipping behind her for her other dachra while her right hand snatched the Godstone in switched release, the shimmering air vanishing the span of a blink before returning through temporary loss of contact. She rushed forward in a mad sprint, closing the distance between them in seconds. Stabbing and twirling in masterful grace, her flurry of slashing and stabbing attacks drove Banzu backwards while he parried and blocked and dodged the dachra frenzy imposed against him while straining through his kohatheen's restrictive lassitude.

Gwendora flowed with the feline grace of animal fury, but her fevered clutch upon the Godstone hindered her Dance of Fangs so that Banzu caught the hint of an opening upon his next parry and drove Griever forward, stabbing his taller opponent through the stomach with a sickening plunge that jolted her with a surprised grunt.

She startled paused. Her eyes widened while her face slumped. She stared down at Griever's impaling steel thrust in her gut, its tip sprouted inches out her back. "Of course," she whispered as she stepped back, removing herself from Griever's impalement, the slick blade sliding out from the red bloom darkening the dress over her punctured stomach. And there she smiled, her mortal wound no longer mortal sealing closed the moment she backed free from Griever's keen tip, healed by the Godstone's all-power.

Banzu cringed.

A frightening twinkle dazzled in Gwendora's approving eyes. She tossed her head back and laughed the sound of madness overwhelming.

Banzu backed away two steps while throwing a glance behind. He stood no more than a few bounding strides from reaching the wall where rested Jacob's sagged corpse.

Gwendora raise her dachra to her face and sliced the fanged blade across her cheek, producing a thin red line which wet the dachra's keen edge with her Spellbinder blood, a cut sealing closed an instant more from the Godstone's healing grace suffusing her.

Banzu's spirits sank and his hopes of survival diminished in one plunging despair. "Oh gods," he whispered, realizing the full measure of her new tactic against him.

To which Gwendora shook her head and smiled, the psychotic unfocus of her stare a mocking appeal. "I am the only god here." She licked her lips. "And now you die!"

With grievous dread and no choice left, Banzu surrendered to killer instinct.

They lunged together as one, Griever meeting dachra in sparking defiance. Gwendora's savage grace of movements no longer sought only vitals to puncture but a mere cutting graze so long as it earned her bloodied dachra that defining slice of his skin to paralyze him for the imminent execution.

Banzu ducked and parried her incessant attacks while attempting to maintain distance between them by circling and dodging.

But Gwendora accepted every biting riposte of Griever's lengthy stabs and thrusts with snarling grunts, the Godstone's limitless all-power flowing through its unrelenting wielder giving no care now to the defensive balletic swordforms opposing her, every suffered slash and cut healing a hairsbreadth after taken.

You're not the first Spellbinder I've fought. Banzu detected familiar patterns to her dachraform attacks, those mimicked by Melora her student upon his re-beginning when she attacked him after his confession of killing Jericho. His experienced eyes recognized the similar patterns of movement through quick parries keeping Gwendora's savage strikes at bay so as to refrain from suffering that first vital cut where Spellbinder blood would mix with his and end their contest in the cruel span of a paralyzing coinflip.

But his muscles burned with growing fatigue magnified by the imposed lassitude of the kohatheen locked round his neck, whereas Gwendora's vitality rejuvenated by the constant drawing of the Godstone's limitless all-power.

So long as she has it, I'm fighting a losing battle. One mistake and I'm done.

He fought on, no other choice, while his mind discovered and dismantled those familiar dachraform patterns of attack fueled by her arrogant recklessness . . . until he found the only true opening presented him without earning cutting riposte and took it through the swift upswing of Griever's cutting bite.

The bloodied dachra and Gwendora's hand clutching it, lopped off at the wrist, spun into the air overhead in counter motion to her attempted downward thrust of hammer-fisting fanged steel into his face. But she swung her other hand in tandem, striking Banzu with the fisted Godstone against his temple in backhanded spin, her fingers crunching between Godstone and skull.

Banzu's head whipped aside as he staggered back, spinning round, then caught his balance and blinked his vision clear of the sparkle of stars popping round his darkened peripherals.

Gwendora screamed, not in pain but in defiance, as she watched her spinning hand and the dachra it clutched fall to the floor between them. She looked at the bloody stump of her wrist, wide eyes thinning when she upraised it and laughed, smiling as the spurting blood stopped where formed the gnarled beginnings of a new hand growing from active flesh knitting round sprouting bone healing by the all-power of the Godstone in her other clutch.

Banzu stared in a dazed stupor at the blood drying and flaking away as Gwendora's stump grew into a round lump of reforming bones and tendons webbing in freshly knitting flesh with five tiny nubs budding forth into forming the beginnings of new fingers and thumb.

"I'm a goddess!" And she watched, mesmerized, her birthing hand taking form before her approving gaze, the process slow but sure, the supernatural healing drawing the full focus of her fascinated stare. She raised the Godstone in praise of its unyielding all-power, enthralled by its divine majesty. "No one can stop me—"

Heal this! Seizing distraction, Banzu surged forward and swung, lopped her other hand off at the wrist even as she withdrew it but too late from Griever's lengthy reach. It, and the Godstone it clutched, fell to the floor. The Godstone bounced loose from limp fingers, rolled between Gwendora's spread stance and past her several feet then stopped, catching upon a crack between marble flagstones.

She screamed again, this time pain joining with her startled outrage. She looked at her blood-spurting stump, looked at her misshapen half-hand ceasing growth the moment her connection with the Godstone severed, then glared at Banzu in pleading shock.

"I'm sorry," he said. And truly he meant it.

"I hate you!" she yelled. And again, "I hate you!"

She spun round, shuffled forward, bent over while thrusting her little malformed half-hand out in reaching bid for reclamation of the Godstone.

"No!" Banzu rushed forth and, grabbing her by the hair, drove his knee up into her face, breaking her nose in a spray of blood, then yanked hard, throwing her backwards by the hair and sending her toppling to the floor where she lay sprawled on her back, semiconscious and muttering indiscernible words, her dark face webbed in glistening ribbons of blood.

He stared over her for a long stretch, breathing labored, body sagging while the full brunt of weariness gnawed at his leaden bones, their fight ended. A part of him wanted nothing more than to plunge Griever into her chest for her crazed betrayal against him as well her murderous threats against Melora if he disobeyed, but he fought the notion off with a slip of mercy. *No, this isn't her, and I've killed enough.*

He turned away to the hand on the floor and the Godstone resting nested atop the small crevice between marble flagstones close by it. He kicked the hand away, disgusted not just at it but by his rending of it, then approached the Godstone, lowered his sword to the floor and sank to one knee where he considered the small, perfectly round orb before him.

He wanted to pick it up, needed to pick it up, yearned to pick it up . . . but he hesitated, unsure if the hot urgency was him wanting it or the Godstone making him crave it so that a strange panic stole through him. Fearing the monster it might make of him same as Gwendora, he drew in a steadying breath, held it overlong. *This is it—*

A great rumble shook dust loose from the cracks of the vibrating walls muffling the noise of those fighting and dying outside, sounding so close now and just beyond the walls of the room.

He reached out, clutching hope as he intended to clutch the Godstone and be done with the cruel gods' Great Game at last.

The scrape of metal against marble sounded behind him.

Before he could snatch the Godstone up, before he could so much as begin turning his head, an awful stab punctured his kneeling leg, pain biting deep into the back of his left calf, piercing flesh and splitting shin bone. He cried out, half twisted, facing a smiling Gwendora lying in a belly-crawl behind him with her malformed hand positioned in awkward grip so that the little nubs of its fingers strained at maintaining hold round the invading dachra's hilt, runnels of blood running her face from her broken nose and smearing her bared teeth pink.

Agony arched his back, tensed his every twitching muscle. He wanted to turn, to kick her in the face, but already the poisoning paralysis of her blood burned into his wound while seeking to infect the network of his nervous system. The paralyzing pain ravaged up through his injured leg in terrible reminder of the agony suffered not long before, forcing him to the floor on his right side while the muscles of his lower half twitched in violent spasms so that he threw himself forward in reaching desperation for the Godstone.

And in his clumsy attempt he knocked it away with his bandaged forearm into rolling farther across the floor where it met the felled terramancer's corpse, bounced then rebounded and caught still atop another crack in the marble flooring, innocuous in its mocking rest. Less than one foot away from his suffering reach.

Behind him Gwendora fumbled with trying to yank the dachra from his calf for another, higher, debilitating stab. His muscles tensed and he clenched his teeth through the wrenching pain of her struggle. But her little fingers kept slipping from the hilt so that she surrendered the futile effort of trying to wrench the dachra free and instead worked her forearms into an inching crawl up the length of his twitching legs, laughing while seeking the Godstone just ahead of them.

He wanted to fight her off, wanted to shove her away, but already he lay paralyzed from the waist down, with the burning paralysis shocking up his right side in torturing ominous flow through his fevered system. He tried twisting, rolling on the floor beneath her climbing venture only to splay onto his belly as his right arm gave over to the paralysis and pinched trapped beneath his pressing weight.

The Godstone so close in front of him . . . and his fogging thoughts swam while hot paralysis veined up through his shoulder and into the right side of his neck, debilitating muscles taut. Seconds only before it neutralized all of him.

The encumbrance of Gwendora strove in higher crawl atop him, beating parts of him with her bleeding stump while raking and clawing her way up the length of him with her malformed other hand.

He threw his left arm out overhead while his foggy thoughts roiled, his tunneling vision a fractured prism blur stinging with tears of strain, his flushing blood hot with fever locking his joints. He wiggled outstretched fingers . . . wiggled them despite the joint-locking numbness creeping through his arm and gaining for that working hand to stroke it useless same as the rest of him.

Ahead, the stump of an arm rose then fell atop the back of the brawny terramancer's corpse from the opposite side. Then a joining hand, followed by a raven-haired head and jostling shoulders. The black-robed mage, eyes afire with desire in a pale face having lost too much blood, crawling forward in slow, dying bid for the Godstone's healing grace.

The Godstone lay close to Banzu's extended reach, a hairsbreadth away from his striving fingers. Seconds before full paralysis overwhelmed him. If only he could muster enough strength into achieving those few precious, necessary inches. With a struggling grunt he put every effort into lurching forward upon the floor beneath Gwendora's oppressive weight, fingers inches from the Godstone . . . reaching . . . stretching . . . a hairsbreadth from grasping his last remaining hope in life.

Progress became necessity, fortitude a will unchained. *If I die here, now, then I do it after I destroy the Godstone.* Not for himself, no, but for another. And in the toil of his reaching bid, the tips of his fingers fractions from touching salvation, his voice released, fierce with passion's heat, announcing the reason of his unyielding struggle, while Gwendora's Spellbinder venom stole through his tingling lips in fiery challenge, and the desolation of imminent failure embraced his soul.

"For . . . her."

He summoned the last ounce of his waning strength into one final reaching bid as full paralysis set in . . . reaching for the Godstone . . . fingers closing round—

BOOOOOM!!!

The white-marble wall beyond the striving black-robed mage exploded inward with a violent blast issued from without, a blazing black light flashing behind it, the explosion ripping Banzu and all things else off the floor amid the blasting spray of debris which blew all across the room in its enveloping gale.

Banzu knew only pain while he tumbled through the air then struck the far wall, bones crunching, chunks of marble and parts of bodies smashing beside and against him. He fell to the floor in a broken twist, his crumpled body covering over in the smoldering rubble falling atop him, burying him.

Darkness.

CHAPTER FORTY-SEVEN

"Where is it?" Sergal asked of the room itself while peering in through the smoldering gape of hole his Pet's lancing blast of black lightning punctured into the marble wall-no-more, his lusting yellow-eyed gaze hunting through the thick drifting haze of suspended white dust slow in settling, his voice amplified by the stillness of abrupt inaction beyond. "Where is it!"

Tortured screams long in dying echoed up the twisting lengths of the corridor above fevered grunts of fighting where the dulled chops and distant thrusts of bloomanese defenders found the relentless presses of Sergal's unliving servitors knowing neither pain nor mortal wounds an overwhelming contest. The invading throngs of hungars flooding the castle's webwork of passageways burst through barred doors hanging loose on busted hinges and spilled their swarming feeding frenzies into chambers where frightened huddles of hiders awaited their rapacious appetites in startled outcries while clutching loved ones as false shields of protection.

Sergal ignored the beautiful cacophony of human screamers at his sides and back, the city overrun with pale hordes flooding through the busted gates and swelling its streets in a moaning plague of triumphant nightmare glory. He tied off the remaining spiritual umbilical tethers to his swarming hungars, allowing them to stalk through the overrun castle at their feeding leisure while he afforded full concentration upon the greater task before him.

He'd sensed the heathen Spellbinder bitch's Godstone-enhanced magic-nullifying void-aura from without only some few minutes ago, and guided by the Godstone's inner thrumming sense through his necromancer Pet into bringing them here, after much destruction through the city straight to Castle Bloom, leading to this specific room within the immense castle. That thrumming heartbeat of awareness pounded fierce in his chest through the soulbond in reverberating thunder climaxing with pronouncement.

It's so close, yesss. My godhood is here somewhere.

Though having softened a few scant moments before the impromptu blast of wall, the decreased resistance of the Head Mistress's Spellbinder void-aura continued pushing resistance against the miasmic influence of the pestilent death-aura radiating from his necromancer Pet shrouding them in rending miasma.

But they had absorbed too much of death's intoxicating potency for the aizakai bitch to provide any lasting influence upon their vast reservoir of stolen energies. What remained of her spilled heathen blood splattered in dripping streaks across the walls and floor and speckled bits of rubble, the dismembered parts of her sundered body strewn about the debris his Pet's lightning blast made of those once therein the room.

A triumphant laugh escaped Sergal over the Head Mistress's unexpected though timely demise. He intended for her an amusement of tortures, but this . . . *yesss, this will do just fine.* Then he gasped, realizing he might need her still to obtain the Book of Towers unfound in Fist.

Though where the book lay amid the debris proved an elusive mystery he dismissed with haste when across the room shifted a heaped pile of rubble bunched against the far wall. Someone caught beneath. *Her? Obviously not. But another, yesss.*

Stare transfixed ahead, Sergal walked into the room, stepping through the smoldering destruction of his newly riven doorway, his Pet pursuing close behind, both unmindful of the sharp bits of scattered marble grit crunching beneath their advancing tread.

More of the piled rubble shifted about, chunks pushing up from beneath, falling aside, sliding away. All at once and with a heaving grunt a red-haired young man stood from within the tumbling shift, his blazing eyes twin grey suns, the bleeding cuts and scrapes on his passive face healing closed through his effort at standing, a thick ring of smoke dissipating round his bare neck below his growing red beard while ashes fell away round the youth's shoulders as he shoved aside the last blocking bits of blackened marble debris with his right hand, his fisted left hand gripping round—

"No." The word escaped Sergal in a ragged whisper, while Sera's weak though mocking laughter chimed throughout their bundled mind. Stunned by the unnerving sight, a guttural clench threatened to bow him over where he stood gaping in panicked distress. "No!" he yelled at the precious Godstone's cruel reveal clutched in the other's firm grip. "It's mine!"

The risen Soothsayer in torn and bloodied clothes did not move, did not speak, flinched nothing. He stood there staring in silent regard of the two newcomers facing him, an aura of scintillating white light exuberance suffusing the immediate air round him in crackling potentials of living sorcery radiating from his glowing skin.

Desperate terror overriding logic, Sergal broke into fevered sprint—then stopped three steps out, halting the terrible error of his irrational attempt to steal the Godstone at the sure cost of his own demise. He flexed then flared his demonic compulsion through the soulbond while throwing his hands forward, his necromancer Pet miming same response, and from Dethkore's gauntleted hands there bloomed another volatile blast of black lightning erupting into destructive sundering.

***

"No," Banzu said, his calm yet firm voice a command, accompanied by the simple wave of his empty right hand, the gesture dismissive, and the minute flexing of his empowered will.

Time stopped in a swallow of sound.

Through luminous grey eyes he viewed the inert world anew, everything bathed in a vibrant twilight glow, every miniscule detail sharp as shattered glass. A soothing warmth radiated throughout his thrumming body, pain nothing more than memory while the last of his broken bones mended whole and his torn flesh knitted through the Godstone's supernatural healing splendor, the faint remains of the poisonous paralyzing agent of Gwendora's Spellbinder blood within his network of veins burning away into nonexistence from the superior divine magic of the Godstone's limitless all-power, its paralyzing fever abolished.

And the kohatheen . . . no need for reaching up to feel its absence, incinerated to metallic dust by way of the Godstone's cleansing grace and the amplified Source, the lanthium collar infused with Spellbinder blood providing its own undoing.

He gazed down at the ancient relic of all-power clutched in his left hand, surprised he had somehow managed to grasp hold of it in that scant stretch of time while the wall blasted open and the inward force of it pushed the Godstone those necessary precious millimeters into his straining reach before throwing him with it across the room in a wild tumble along with what parts of the erupting wall not decimated into minuscule bits of dust.

The spiritual shared collective harmony of a thousand dead Soothsayers, their bloodlusts cleansed by the Godstone's purging grace upon moment of contact, sang in praising reprieve within his mind, a glorious chorus of joyous splendor so that the hint of a satisfied smile graced his lips. He stood seizing the magnified Source in unchallenged command fueled no longer by the suffering leach of his lifeforce in cruel trade but by the Godstone's limitless all-power filling his ameliorated soul with the exhilarating rush of deifying potency.

"So this," he said in a voice both competent yet curious, "is what godhood feels like."

With the Godstone in his fisted grip: *I have enough time now . . . for everything.*

The astonishing scope of this truth awed him, for the Godstone's apotheosis blessed him with immortal life and endless vitality, unbound by time's cruel aging for so long as he wielded it because of the Source.

This . . . gods, this is so much more than I ever expected. I can seize the Source forever and without cost. I can transcend time, travel it without restriction, not just my own lifeline but millennia . . . no, eons. Everything that is, was, and will ever be, mine to experience and employ.

"But," he said aloud, the single word an audible echo of his entire chain of thoughts, then left the rest unsaid, allowing the dawning expansion of his mind to finish for him.

But I never wanted this. It gifts me an immortal life, yes, but a long and lonely life as a god among desirous men possessing no true understanding of what this makes of me.

And yet . . . and yet, the Godstone's awesome all-power compelled him into deliberating the reverie of limitless potentials of manipulated history he could achieve undisputed with its wielding.

I can end wars before they begin. I can save countless lives before they're lost. I can age my enemies into dust and regress the age of loved ones within the flex of a thought. I can do and undo at my leisure. So much magnanimous power, so much destructive potential.

For a brief moment the instinctive swordslinger musings of his prior mortal self wondered on his lost sword that lay hidden somewhere beneath the strewn rubble . . . but for that he needed the keen length of Griever no longer.

Simple steel is beneath me. Time is my sword.

He stepped forth from the piled rubble shifting loose round the motions of his legs—and staggered as a diluvial flood of memories assailed him in rampant streams of lives, each trampled fabric of life imposing vivid scenes playing out from birth through death while fusing with his own webwork of cognizance, synapses firing through the network of his mind as the keen reflections of a thousand lives lived by other men interwove with his own life's patterned threads of existence, creating a vast tapestry of shared experience.

He shut his eyes tight and cringed against the assault of repressed memories unlocking, mental tumblers clicking into new order of alignment through the influence of another's turning key. The Godstone numbed all physical pain, but it did nothing to remedy mental anguish.

The emotional rush of others' feelings, hard-learned skills, natural-born talents, life-won experiences surged overwhelming so that he released a guttural scream, his brain afire with too much information overloading him at once.

And then the knifing brainpain vanished, the rampant flashes of lives gone, in their wake a suffusion of abilities learned in the span of a blink through the shared collective.

He straightened, awed with wisdom.

Oh my gods . . . I can . . . I can . . .

Paint a vivid masterpiece with the sure strokes of his accomplished hands that would steal away the observer's breath.

Smithy arms and armor unequal in their forging that would awe the most proficient of blacksmiths into kneeling before his unequaled works in sobbing adulation.

Pluck and sing heart-wrenching ballads with dancing fingers and beauteous vocals that would pull tears from the driest of eyes and the coldest of hearts.

Fire a bow from on dancing horseback and thread a needle's eye with perfect practiced precision.

All this and more gained through the shared collective's years-earned expertise now his to command.

As well his skills as a master swordslinger . . . immeasurably enhanced over a thousand fold through countless hours earned by a thousand lifetimes of training gifted him by the profound muscle-memory of a thousand Soothsayers firing through his nervous system, imbuing him with unequivocal skill no swordslinger had ever or would ever possess.

I am unrivaled.

I am unequaled.

I am—

A profound pause.

And I am alone in this.

All by myself.

As I've always felt.

"No." He struggled the defiant word out on ragged breath, fighting for focus. In stronger voice, "Melora."

I am only pieces without her.

She completes me.

I don't just need her, I require her.

He stared overlong at the Godstone so consequential and yet so puny and paltry in his hand.

Even this, all this, is meaningless without her.

He ached for her touch. To have and to hold her again. To drink of that sweet nectar, every intoxicating taste of her leaving him thirsting for another sumptuous swallow of her potent, tempestuous drink.

He held immortality in his grasp, godhood's lifeblood thrumming through his veins and bleeding from his pores. And he knew . . . *the meaning of life is to give life meaning.* For life's truest beauty dwelt within its cherished briefness. *And my meaning is her.*

Comprehension struck him with jolting epiphany. Time, life's most valuable commodity, he clutched everlasting in his fisted grip. But it provided him nothing of love, life's most precious gift.

He raised the Godstone before his face on upturned palm and appraised it for the trivial trinket.

To hoard is to hate and die, to share is to live and love.

And there he smiled, for greed and Godstone held no power over his heart. Because the heart was neither given nor stolen. The heart *surrenders.* And he had already surrendered his heart to another, stronger power.

Love.

***

Banzu loosened his shoulders with a rolling shrug, all tension gone, and scanned round the wreckage of the room at the sizzling crimson streaks of Gwendora's splattered Spellbinder blood burning away into wispy trails of smoky dissipation from the Godstone's superior all-power radiating from his Source-aura in pulsing, recurring waves of divine sorcery influence.

The Head Mistress Gwendora Pearce no more, torn apart by the rending blast of wall alongside her cadre of mage, Jacob as well or possibly buried for he saw nothing of the First Sword, and for that twist of fate Banzu grieved despite their betrayal against him.

He could not fault Gwendora her transgression when weighed against the Godstone's temptation proving too overwhelming an allure for her to resist. Bones and bits of bones stuck out from the debris, bleached of their scorched Spellbinder flesh. Dismembered parts of Gwendora, while the flesh and gore of the others amid the rubble offered brutal reminder that Banzu had not been alone only moments ago.

Nor was he now.

In no hurry, for hurry did not exist, he approached the two newcomers captured in Source-locked stasis, and the pestilent presence of the necromaster's miasmic death-aura sickening the hazy air triggered a fleeting surge of nausea he defeated with the divine suppression of the Godstone's cleansing grace. He gazed up at the pale, angular face of: "Dethkore."

The name escaped him in a bare whisper, the disturbing legends of the infamous necromaster retaining their fearsome grips upon his memories—all of them—despite that which he carried in his thrumming clutch. Even now, frozen static in Source-locked stasis, the towering Eater of Souls presented a daunting figure to behold. Especially so with Hannibal Khan's lanthium gauntlets on his outstretched hands. Risen hands caught mid-bloom with the frozen eruption of black power igniting.

A strong flexing of Banzu's indomitable willpower, and time reversed several seconds. Angry tongues of black power receded from Dethkore's gauntlets into the mystic origins of their ensorcelled lanthium birth, and time froze once more. Banzu willed this manipulation through careful whim, and only that fraction of reversal so as not to disturb the delicate balance of events and undo himself in the process.

He sidestepped left and studied down at the odd sight of the scale-patched little girl also suspended in the perpetual Source-locked stasis imposed not just on this room but upon the entire world. He peered into the hateful depths of those serpentine eyes glaring frozen rage.

I've seen those eyes before. A demon's eyes. She's possessed.

And upon her scaly right hand . . . he reached forth with perfect control, took her outstretched right hand by the dainty wrist and twisted it into better position where it stayed. He slid the necromaster's lanthium soulring vitus free from her little ringfinger, the stasis of her manipulated appendage only moving with the motions of his taking.

He withdrew two steps, waved his free hand out before him along with a flexing of his will—and a pocket of static time relaxed into normal flow round the necromaster's head, allowing the deadman thought and speech.

Banzu stared at that pale, angular face waking with awareness while the black eyes pierced by silver pupils shifting white in its sullen tombstone visage bloomed with active wonder. Then fascination when Dethkore fixed focal upon his soulring Banzu upheld pinched betwixt his right pointer and thumb.

"I . . ." Banzu blinked through unexpected reverie imposed by their face-to-face meeting at long last, and not for the first time. "I remember you. From long ago. Centuries." A pause, another blink, thoughts sifting through newfound memories earned by another of the shared collective influencing his pursuant mind. *Simus, yes.* "But I was another man, then."

"Ahh," Dethkore said, the impassiveness of his undisturbed visage unbroken despite the tortured story of his shifting eyes gaining coherence, his voice the tone of bones grinding. "And I you, Ascendant."

Banzu cocked an eyebrow at the unexpected title leaving a void in his vast reservoir of memories, and decided to probe the depths of this ancient mind before him, the knowledge of which transcended even his own shared experiences. "Ascendant?" A curious tilt of his head. "Explain."

Dethkore nodded, the motion slight upon restricted shoulders. "The old gods are leaving this world behind. As they have countless others. Ascendants shall rise to replace them, as is always the infinite cycle. You are among them, savior-slayer, as am I. Few of theirs remain, here, hidden, in this realm. And when their mortal avatars are extinguished from the Simulatrix, the new gods, the Ascendants, will rise to replace them. As it has always been. As it will always be."

Banzu nodded, gaps of knowledge filling with truth. Low, almost breathless, as if spoken by another, "Yes."

"Before then, Soothsayer, your task remains incomplete." A downward glance at Banzu's left hand, the Godstone clutched therein. "Even after the Godstone's destruction, if that is your choice. The gauntlets are but one piece to a whole. Hannibal Khan was just the first of many the Enclave seeks to manipulate into reforming the Dominator's Armor. Even now—"

"We can destroy it," Banzu said, and flinched surprise at the words leaving him of their own accord, though more so at the *We* instead of *I*.

"No." Dethkore shook his head. "The Armor must be reformed whole. Only then can Malach'Ra's influence truly be banished from this mortal plane of existence. No, Soothsayer. We could, but we mustn't."

More gaps of knowledge filling . . . and Banzu realized his true purpose beyond the Godstone's destruction through accidental glimpse of the future, flashes of it stealing through his mind's eye so that he flinched while withdrawing from the revealing glimpses. But he dared not speak it aloud, nor steal another probe into that future unveiled, for knowing the future changed the future.

"How?" Banzu asked instead, upholding the Godstone between them upon his upturned hand, the perfectly round orb perfectly balanced atop the slight depression of his palm. And the honest question surprised him, for Enosh had told him otherwise. *I'll just know, he said, and yet I don't.* "How do I destroy this judgment of humanity?"

"Malach'Ra was devious in his trickery. There is only one way to destroy the Godstone, and for that I require my soulring to conjure forth the insatiable void of the Blackhole Abyss within me." Dethkore paused and glanced aside at the little girl, straining through the motion for his Source-locked body protested his turning head. "Though I wish to exorcise the child first. Sera is possessed by the same demon who once deceived me into making me as I stand before you now. The one known as Nergal." A flash of anger tensed his pale visage, black eyes swirling with unfathomable malice. "The reaper of my former life. The true murderer of my wife and daughter. I would consume him as well."

Consume? "How can I trust you?" Banzu wrapped his fingers round the Godstone while lowering it to his side. "Why should I trust you?"

"Trust is a river which flows both ways," Dethkore said. "I do not crave power, for power I already possess. Allow me to show you, if you would but release the rest of me from stasis."

Silent, Banzu contemplated the necromaster's request for a lengthy measure.

Dethkore spoke with the rustle of dried leaves crunched underfoot. "There is no need to fear me, Soothsayer."

"I fear nothing now." *Except the breaking of my heart.*

Banzu withdrew another step and flexed his Source-infused will, allowing the pocket of time's release to expand round the necromaster and the necromaster alone, holding no fear Dethkore would move against him in brazen treachery for the Godstone's apotheosis magnified his senses a hundred fold, edging prescient reflexes, able to detect the minute vibrations of a wayward fly's buzzing wings a mile distant if he so chose to focus his attentions into such a petty course of action. A single flex of his indomitable willpower would Source-lock the necromaster again in the space of a blink. Yet still he cautioned him.

"Careful," Banzu said. "I can age you into nothing more than dust."

"You cannot kill what is already dead." Dead inside, the depths of Dethkore's remorseful tone implied.

Banzu ignored the response containing no threat or malice behind it, only scores of sadness and regret. "Show me."

Dethkore gripped his left wrist and pulled, his sullen tombstone visage straining while he ripped his left hand free from inside the godsforged lanthium gauntlet of power, tearing away chunks of his pale flesh, producing ribbons of black ichor blood streaming down his lacerated forearm and hand to wet the floor. He tossed the removed gauntlet at Banzu's feet in an echo of metal clanging marble, then grasped his right gauntleted wrist with his bony, flesh-torn left hand and, straining evermore, tore it free in the same gruesome manner then tossed the second gauntlet beside the first.

Banzu sensed the pressurized rumble of thunder bridled to his Source-lock from the gauntlets' removal though said nothing.

Dethkore closed his eyes then, the disgust on his face abolished, and there passed a short moment while the sentient shadows of black fabrics swaddling him licked and twined round his lacerated arms and hands, seeping into while mending the ruined flesh.

Once finished, Dethkore's swirling black eyes met Banzu's blazing greys once more.

"Tell me why I shouldn't age you from existence," Banzu said.

"The Godstone has cleansed your soul, Soothsayer. Please allow me to cleanse what little remains of mine. History is written by the winners, and my part of it is scribbled in lies. This is my truth. I sought not to wield the Godstone but to destroy it. Thus the reason why I took within me the Blackhole Abyss. When I learned of Malach'Ra's designs for the Godstone . . . well, he assumed he was using me, but it was I who was using him." Dethkore paused, frowning, his stare reflecting inward for a space and viewing torturous memories at play on his face, the betrayal of suffering brief, there then gone. "But I became his slave because of my soulring, unable to destroy the Godstone as I planned. You can wield it without affliction where I cannot, but only I can destroy it. Because we are its balance. Joined, we are the bane of their Great Game. And there is no other way but together. Allow me to—"

"No," Banzu said, shaking his head, his mind roiling from a discordant flex of resistant mortal desires blooming false excuses. "I can go back now. I can change things."

"And undo everything you know in the process, yes. Everything and everyone."

Melora. Banzu cringed with knowing.

"I have come to regret many things in my long life," Dethkore said. "Please do not make this another one. Help me, Soothsayer. Allow me the use of my soulring so that I may save this child. She is innocent in all of this. A pawn. As was I, until this moment of your decision. The choice is yours, Soothsayer. I cannot force you into this. No one can. Seek within and you will find your answer."

"If it takes both of us," Banzu said, reflecting upon the unliving khansmen Trio attacking him and Melora, "then why did you try to kill me? Not here, and not on the plains. Before. Why?"

"Not to kill you," Dethkore said. "To instigate you into reclaiming what you required."

"The Essence of Simus Junes," Banzu said in self-whisper.

Dethkore nodded, then clasped his pale hands behind his back and lapsed into silence, the permanent melancholy etched upon his tombstone visage adding untold depths of sadness to the ebony swirls of his watchful gaze.

Banzu estimated the necromaster a considerable moment. He closed his eyes and willed his mind's eye into peering through the smoky depths of reflection . . . where he swam through an ocean of memories each drop of which contained a single perceptible memoir of life's woven tapestries from a thousand lives lived . . . and drank, as millennia of memories assailed him.

Time became a kaleidoscope of visions, and what he saw both awed and shamed him. Past and present collided into forming a new panoramic view of awareness, turned a tableau of his existence and all the lives tethered to it.

Centuries passed before him in vivid recall.

Castles crumbling. Kingdoms falling. Battles lost and won. Families born together then torn apart. A thousand lives lived with each captured moment a perfect emotional anamnesis. Lovers, wives, children . . . ravaged by time's cruel aging. Destiny and Fate lain out before him as twin lovers embracing, and he wept inside at the understanding given.

I am limitless.

And without limits, life held no purpose but to achieve death, for without the threat of death there existed no reason to live at all. Pleasure made pain all the more bearable. And in its cruel way, death provided all meaning to life. He knew this with clarity, yet still he pursued through the streams of lives.

Hopes dared. Ambitions achieved. The joy of victory, the anguish of defeat. The merciless torment of insufferable loss. The blinding wrath of bloodlust's cruel madness as cursed Soothsayers turned upon their frightened kin in murderous rage and—

"Enough," Banzu said, scorning the magnified Source and all the harbored woes it afforded him, wincing while blinking back to present. Minute particles so fine as to make bacteria gigantic popped into and out from existence, filling the empty spaces round him, round the necromaster, round everything everywhere he looked, with literal possibilities of limitless potentials. Promises of infinite futures awaiting the action of his decision to set their forward courses into motion.

He drew in deep, exhaled slow, met those tortured pools of emotion regarding him, pained black voids of guilt pierced by white pupils of regret and containing fathoms of remorse requiring no vocal declaration of the fragile humanness they harbored.

Metrapheous Theaucard. He was a mortal man, once. A devoted husband. A loving father. Until Malach'Ra took it all away.

And he understood truly the sorrow of eternal life, its burdens unyielding, uncompromising, unforgiving. Sages claimed time healed all wounds, but they misspoke from the ignorance of mortal perspective. To love then lose that love and carry its loss without death's appeasement provided an insufferable track of miserable life stamped with the heavy tread of guilt and regret Banzu wished on no one.

He looked down at the Godstone, heartbroken by another's perpetual plight. "I don't want this. Not for myself. Not for anyone. Not even for you." He looked up at Dethkore. "What you've done," he began then paused, banishing intruding atrocities of the Thousand Years War and Dethkore's part in them from his mind, as well flitters of bitter memories torn from his own time spent slaughtering khansmen across the Azure Plains. "You've done terrible things, Metrapheous. Awful things. But we all have."

"Metrapheous," Dethkore whispered, staring more through Banzu that at him. "There's no forgiving what I've done, not here or elsewhere."

"This isn't forgiveness, it's mercy."

Dethkore's eyes regained focus. "So you do understand."

"Yes," Banzu said. "I do. And you've suffered enough. Let's finish the Game."

Dethkore nodded. "Yes." He glanced at the possessed girl Sera. "But first . . ."

They continued speaking, on many things both past and present. And in the end they struck amiable bargain.

***

Banzu endured a terrible shiver imposed the moment he shook Dethkore's cold dead hand. After releasing his grip, he flexed his hand to return stolen warmth despite the Godstone's rapid rejuvenation suffusing him.

"Stay back," Dethkore said, touching upon the instructions of their previous conversation while holding out his upturned palm, "and do not breach the event horizon. Or my Blackhole Abyss will consume you regardless the Godstone. It makes you a god, but I am much worse."

Banzu nodded and placed the lanthium soulring vitus atop the pale landscape of Dethkore's upturned palm. He stepped back into watching place while sliding the lanthium gauntlets on the floor behind him with one pushing foot in so doing.

Dethkore fisting his grip round his returned vitus and for the moment closed his eyes, human emotions at play on his sullen tombstone visage for a brief space where threatened a smile more a fine crack on that pale, angular landscape. The sentient shadows swaddling him undulated and licked tastes of his immediate air while he withdrew his hand and, in what looked a temporary struggle at the actuality of the action almost too overwhelming to endure, unfurled his fingers then plucked the soulring from his palm and, with a visible shudder, slid his left ringfinger into the lanthium ring's hollow after several hundred years of insufferable separation.

"I wanted none of this," he said in self-whisper, then turned and faced the little girl with serpentine eyes locked in stasis before him. "We wanted none of this." A contemplative pause. "Release her, Soothsayer, and I will exorcise her soul."

Banzu waved his free hand with the flexing of his Source-infused will—and time returned into forward-flowing motion.

The possessed little girl's hateful yellow eyes divided by black vertical slits popped wide in surprise then darted round at the startling change of her environment, Dethkore no longer wearing the Dominator's Gauntlets, Banzu watching back at her with Godstone in hand.

"What?" She withdrew her outstretched hands. "When?" She looked at them, in particular the bare digit of her missing soulring somehow transferred to Dethkore, cruel revelation blooming then tensing her face. "How?" She inhaled a frightened gasp, expelled a spiteful hiss. "No!"

She stole into motion, removing the hellsteel dagger from her hip, hammer-fisting its handle, while she ran past Dethkore straight for Banzu, throwing her arm overhead and poised for stabbing.

"You are not her," Dethkore said, his stern voice the sound of grinding bones. He gestured with his hands at the pale girl patched with green scales speeding past his front, his ebony eyes sucking in nearest light while his white pupils flaring silver swirled into twin spinning galaxies possessing depths of latent power unlocked within the chamber of his ancient being, silvery crackles of energies forking and veining the full towering stretch of him, their origin his soulring.

Up from the marble floor burst an encircling crown of long black shadow tendrils halting the lunging girl in her rushing tracks.

"No!" Eyes startling blooms of panic, she screamed and spun round slashing. "No!" But her hellsteel blade passed through air and shadow while scoring nothing. "No!"

"Yes," Dethkore said, pale fingers manipulations of shimmering air.

The whipping tendrils of sentient shadows latched round her thrashing limbs, twining while trapping her wrists and ankles then lifting her into the air where they held her splayed several feet above the floor. Wide eyes fevered yellow jewels, she hissed and spat and snapped bites at the air, refusing surrender.

Dethkore approached her, reached between dividing shadows, and pried loose the hellsteel dagger from her fisted grip.

"You end here, Nergal," Dethkore said, his voice edged with immortal pain and mortal promise. He leaned forward, peering into those haunted yellow eyes betraying fathoms of waking dread. "You shall rue my name as the Eater of Souls. And you will grieve with suffering as I devour every parasitic part of you from this child."

Mute with terror, her focal stare pure horror, trembling though sagging limp within her tendril containment, urine trickled down the girl's legs and speckled the floor.

Dethkore upheld the hellsteel dagger between them in his double-fisted grip, point down. Smoky black wisps curled from it while the carven beast's face and the pentacle encircling it upon its pommel glowed molten.

The girl threw her head back and screamed protests at the high ceiling while thrashing anew, but the sentient shadow tendrils holding her bound in the air by wrists and ankles increased their coiling squeezes while pulling her arms and legs taut, restricting her violent thrashes proving no defense against the necromaster's mumbling chants of exorcism. Smoky black energies crackling with silvery tongues seeped from her squirming body, bleeding from her expanding pores in dark blooms of twinkling mist achieving vaporous abandon of her unliving vessel.

Silent and watching, Banzu gripped the Godstone in a tighter clutch.

While Dethkore withdrew, allowing necessary space for the extracted energies pulled from their vessel to coalesce into that of the spectral essence of the possessive demonic spirit exorcised from the girl which gathered and glowed diaphanous between them, a throbbing nest of lambent green caged within restrictive swirls of shadows where fired crackles of forked silver tongues licking whips of air. Long translucent limbs took shape beneath scaly flesh, forming a rangy figure thrice-times larger than its former vessel hovering captured behind it.

"No!" it screamed, its eyes lambent yellow stabs of focal spite upon the whispering necromaster, its raspy projection of voice a hissing shriek rippling throughout the room, the hallways beyond, the entire castle. "No!"

The demonic spirit of Nergal surged toward the necromaster, spectral clawhands reaching—then jostled backwards when more shadow tendrils lashed forth from the misty black swirls and seized it by its ethereal wrists and ankles, wrapped round its sinuous neck, restraining its hovering presence midair.

Dethkore opened his mouth wide . . . wider . . . then wider still, his angular jaw an impossible stretch of hinges as within that gaping maw swirled blackest pitch sucking all nearest light into its vacuum while dimming the room to twilight.

Forewarned of this, Banzu tensed against the risen winds pushing at his back while pulling on his front, the marble debris round his feet rattling and bouncing the vibrating floor, the gauntlets sliding against his heels.

Scales flaking loose from face and front and clawhands, the demonic essence of Nergal released a tormented scream as larger parts and pieces of his suspended figure ripped apart and tore free in spectral dismemberment, spiraling forward in firefly particles, sundered and shredding as Dethkore's conjured Blackhole Abyss swirled chaotic while expanding into a vertical vortex vacuum within his gaping maw consuming, devouring, erasing the demon's thrashing essence piece by disintegrating piece.

His heart a quickening thunder, Banzu clutched the Godstone to his chest while bracing against the vacuum's increasing pull on him as well everything else in its vicinity. Jouncing debris slid the floor then, once captured inside the vacuum's irresistible inhale, shot up through the air and plunged while disintegrating through torn particle spirals feeding inside the endless hunger of the Blackhole Abyss.

Nergal's keening wail stretched overlong above the whipping torrent of winds, as the black shadow tendrils restraining his spectral dismemberment released their tight coils and withdrew, disappearing down into the fractured cracks between marble flagstones from whence they'd been summoned. Then even Nergal's voice devoured mute, though replaced by that of a little girl's terrified human scream, when the remains of his spectral essence shredded into a flurry of particles swallowed in a mad spiral of erasure.

Her own shadow bonds released, Sera collapsed to the floor in an unconscious heap. And slid closer by inching increments, the vacuum drawing her limp body through increasing tugs.

Banzu inched forward through the tempest in backwards lean against the strong winds seeking to yank him from the floor, wild tangles of his hair whipping beats over his ears and sides of his face, legs straining tensed to prevent sliding feet. He approached the necromaster from the left side as agreed—and stopped when Dethkore threw out his left hand between them, pale fingers outstretched.

Banzu reached forth, pinched the necromaster's offered soulring between fingertip and thumb, panic flushing when Dethkore turned his head, shifting the irresistible vortex suction of his swirling Blackhole

Abyss away from Sera's sliding body to avoid its sundering inhale.

Banzu flared his Source-infused will through the Godstone.

Time stopped in a swallow of sound, and everything stilled, frozen, captured inert in Source-locked stasis.

Banzu slid the soulring free from Dethkore's proffered hand, turned aside and blew out his cheeks while straightening, the frozen pressure of winds round him bending pliable. With the gesturing wave of his right hand accompanied by the flexing of his will through the Godstone gripped in his left, along with the keen remembrance of Enosh revealing him the necessary component of *You*, he focused upon a specific memory, most precious and cherished in his guarded heart of hearts, and conjured a similar wormhole portal through time and space.

A crimson splash of energy crackled, first a thin slice, then opened, expanding in the air at head height in creation of a round vertical window portal, its edges spiraling while the watery space between shimmered translucent into viewing clarity of the past.

Time on the other side continued unhindered. And he watched, from a hidden space across the tower's room, Melora and his younger self amid the lusty throes of their sexual ecstasies. Kissing, groping, grunting and thrusting . . . then finishing their twined carnal passion with the spilling of his seed inside her.

She removed from younger Banzu, both lovers panting in postcoital trance.

And older Banzu smirked with prescient knowledge.

An apologetic exchange of words, then Melora rushed forward and shoved younger Banzu backwards, tumbling him down into the tower's Traveling Well behind him. Seconds only and she withdrew from the eruption of divine magic triggered by younger Banzu's seizing of the Power transporting him away, and for a startled length she stood in breathless awe at feeling the influential rush of divine magic for the first time in her life before those multicolored energies splashing the rotunda's domed ceiling inhaled back within the Traveling Well.

She stared mute for a time, smiling, then gathered herself a moment more and put on her clothes. While older Banzu watched every beautiful contour of her athletic body shift and move through natural grace. He ached for breaking from his spying view and touching her again.

Instead he waited, watching her, until she caught sight of his conjured wormhole portal hovering aglow in the air past the Traveling Well then dared approach it, cautious and squinting, with creeping steps. "What the . . ."

"Stay back," Banzu said, his voice a diminishing echo projecting through the wormhole portal, though an inviting smile toyed across his lips.

Melora flinched still in her tracks, staring at him as best she could through the head-sized wormhole portal from across the tower's rotunda, from across time and space. She scrunched her face, nose crinkling, gaze thinning. "Banzu?"

"Don't come any closer." *So much to tell.* With the Godstone's divine magic amplifying his own, it would burn through the protection of her lesser void-aura if she braved too near. *Too much to tell.*

He'd made it to Fist, retrieved the Essence of the First, killed Hannibal Khan, held the Godstone and moments from destroying it.

But he put no voice behind the lengthy explanation. Despite his firm grasp on the enhanced Source, the effort proved an incredible strain of maintaining stasis *here* while time continued flowing *there* in a volatile joining of Past and Future, for even godhood possessed limits. "I'll explain later, when I see you again. For now just listen."

He flared his grasp of Source, and the wormhole portal widened in circumference by inches. He ached for straining it open larger, enough to see him through so he could go to her, but such action would achieve nothing but a broken paradox he dared not risk.

"What in all the hells is going on?" Melora asked, glancing at the traveling well. "I just pushed—wait. Is that—" Her gaze startled wide, and she gasped, at sight of the Godstone's reveal in his upraised hand. Then her shifting gaze traveled past him, widened evermore. "Dethkore!"

"Forget him. Doesn't matter." Banzu upheld the necromaster's soulring. "I need you to put this on. Understand? As soon as this portal closes, put on the ring and never take it off."

She inched forward, locked in stare not at him but beyond him.

"No!" he said in an admonishing flare of voice. "Stay back. You don't understand, you'll only get hurt. Your void-aura doesn't nullify magic, it absorbs—never mind. Later. Right now you have to trust me."

He threw the soulring through the wormhole portal, traversing linked time and space. It hit the rotunda's floor then skittered well past her, rebounded upon his rucksack, spun then settled.

"Don't leave the tower," he said. "I'll come for you soon as I'm finished here, I promise."

"But—" Melora half turned, glanced at the soulring, looked to him and threw an accusatory point. "You have the Godstone. And he's right there. Dethkore's right there!"

The feral thinning of her eyes regaining cunning focus upon the necromaster, she lowered into a crouch, legs coiling springs, every inch of her the defiant she-cat. Her arms whipped up behind her back, then out came her dachra fangs. She spun them, catching their handles into hammer-fisting grips of resolve. With no more words she broke into attacking sprint.

"The ring!" Banzu yelled, panic gripping his quickened heart.

Ignoring all but impulse, Melora stole a determined charge toward the wormhole portal and the necromaster beyond, her violet eyes intent, her body locomotion.

Banzu turned away. He whipped his arm back and threw the Godstone at Dethkore's gaping maw. In his left peripheral he saw Melora's steadfast approach, saw too the blooming startlement of pain waking across her feral features as she breached the outer limits of the portal's divine magic burning through her void-aura—then the wormhole portal snapped closed, snuffed from existence the moment the Godstone left his pitching hand, a hairsbreadth before Melora's ensuing dive took her through it.

Time resolved into its normal flow, jolting Banzu, staggering him backwards with concussive force, his inner grasp of Source slipping free. His heels caught upon the gauntlets so that he tripped, fell backwards, arms pinwheeling, and crashed onto his bottom where he watched with wide, hopeful eyes the arc of the thrown Godstone reaching the reducing expanse of its intended target.

The swirling Blackhole Abyss diminished in size, its connection severed by the removal of the soulring from its conjurer. It shrank into the space of a handspan, then smaller still into a pinprick of void, while the Godstone entered its event horizon then broke apart, torn asunder within the rending vacuum, then disintegrated into particles devoured in a shredding spiral of sparkling silver-gold energies inhaled seconds before Dethkore's distended jaws locked into natural alignment then closed in a swallow of energies.

Silence and light returned to the room.

Dethkore staggered forward three steps then stopped, bent over clutching his stomach, his pale skin blooming with spreading spots of color. His knees buckled, and he collapsed to the floor, trembling, a mortal man restored.

Banzu released his captured breath, relaxing to the proof in front of him of Melora wearing the soulring.

The little girl lying crumpled on the floor, Sera, roused awake. She sat up groaning, gazed round through startled brown eyes jeweled with silver pupils and blinked waking awareness of self, her pale skin smooth and absent of scaly green patches, her body atremble from the fading rigors of her exorcism.

Dethkore no longer, his swaddle of shadows nothing more than simple black fabrics, Metrapheous Theaucard pushed up from the floor onto all fours then straightened into kneeling, his sclera white though his black irises framed silver-jeweled pupils, his soft expression evincing a profound sorrow soothed.

"Thank you, Soothsayer." Metrapheous swept his benevolent gaze to Sera, black hair swishing his shoulders. "You're safe now, child." Then offered Banzu a sincere smile. "Remember your promise, and I will adhere to mine."

Banzu considered them both. He blew out his cheeks and nodded.

* * *

True to his word, Metrapheous offered no resistance, proving a docile captive while Banzu marched him out through Castle Bloom, leaving Griever behind and unfound somewhere buried beneath the blasted wall's rubble where lay bodies and pieces of bodies evincing the cruel aftermath of the Head Mistress's Conclave undone. Bloomanese guards gathered round their growing retinue as they made their way outside to where the ebbing chaos of the hungar invasion died.

Upon the soulring's deliverance to Melora through Banzu's wormhole portal courtesy of his memories of You, precious Reader, the hungars stalking inside the castle once under the necromaster's control collapsed, necrotic puppets with their strings cut, the severing of those sorcerous ties of compulsion catalyzed before mortality restored to the necromaster along with the rending of his dark magics imposed by his soulring's new Spellbinder ring-bearer. A plethora of pale bodies littered the grounds, rotting to putrid wastes before the surprised gazes of the victimized survivors fighting for the sanctity of their violated city, their sundered homes, their devastated families and shattered lives.

Though hundreds more hungars, those not dismembered or slain, those whose reanimated connections remained tied-off unto themselves, continued roaming throughout the city. But already hunting parties formed and chased after the pale rejections of death, hacking them to pieces while securing the streets and homes and the safety of its frightened denizens removing from their hidey holes and taking up arms in roving mobs.

Outside the ravaged city, beyond its toppled eastern gates and clawed defensive walls awash in black ichor gore, thousands more hungars roamed the wilderness seeking flesh in scatters of moaning parties, though without Sergal's compelling influence their greedy lusts proved less a hunt and more a meandering to satiate their driving hunger for living sustenance be it man or animal. Paladins intended on riding out and dispatching these roamers once Bloom restored to order.

Banzu hid Sera away in a locked and guarded room high within Castle Bloom, ensuring her safety from sharing Metrapheous' fate until he could better explain her possession through no fault of her own while hoping Metrapheous' sacrifice appeased the survivors.

Hunting parties dragged hungars from homes and piled them into the streets where they burned the masses of corpses in blazes of victory amid cheering spectators and grieving loved ones.

Crews labored quick at fixing the busted gates, securing the city from more hungars swarming inside as paladins fought them back then rushed to join the hunt for roaming lurkers behind the walls.

While Metrapheous sat within an iron-barred cage procured from a local smithy, and there he endured spiteful spits and curses from passersby, though the soldiers guarding him warded away those carrying weapons and harboring designs of vengeance for their fallen kin.

Until nightfall, in the courtyard of Castle Bloom, lit by thousands of upheld torches where the city's mourning survivors gathered en masse, drawn to the loud chimes of bells.

Banzu wove through the crowd to its forefront and stood witness to the crucifixion of Metrapheous dragged from his cage then beaten to approving cheers, his arms and legs and back clubbed broken, then his battered body lain atop lashed timbers, playing his chosen part as scapegoat, crying out when soldiers pounded thick nails into his wrists and crossed feet, pinning them to the cross, then those thick timbers raised.

For the moment a hush stole over all, breaths bated to a condemned man's final words.

Metrapheous viewed his onlookers with the guilty eyes of a malefactor accepting his due penance, for the survivors needed a target for their suffering woes, and he supplied himself as promised. He said nothing, yet those sorrowed eyes of remorse spoke volumes of regret before he closed them and craned his head skyward, tears glistening his cheeks, his upturned face bathed in moonglow, agitated flickers of torchlight dancing across the naked rest of his abused body.

Soldiers piled wood round the crucifix's base, then splashed it and Dethkore with buckets of oil before backing away.

Banzu accepted a burning torch from the soldier beside him and strode forth into the free space surrounding Metrapheous.

Banzu craned his head.

And Metrapheous lowered his pained visage on lolling neck, an honest touch of smile gracing his mouth despite the tortured story of his teary eyes.

Presentation is half the show. "Rest in peace," Banzu whispered. *Purgatory awaits your return.* He tossed his burning torch to the mound of oiled kindling then stepped back from the flaring whoosh of flames and heat.

A tortured scream arose amid the inferno consuming mortal flesh into embers and ashes. "Maria!" and "Marisha!" A mournful voice drowned beneath an elevation of cheers Banzu took no part in.

As a pale little girl watched her savior burn from afar, her unliving body unable to shed tears despite the wrenching grind of her sorrowed heart, while she clutched tight the vitus of her precious hellstell dagger in her pale little hands.

Banzu turned from the flames and gazed up at the grieving onlooker watching down over the filled courtyard from a castle window on high, at Sera, and reflected on his promise to protect her, Metrapheous' only requirement in exchange for his sacrifice.

Banzu turned back when the surrounding crowd broke into a raucous, chanting cheer, weapons and torches stabbing the air over the sea of heads.

"All hail the Soothsayer! All hail our savior! All hail the Soothsavior! All hail the Soothsavior! All hail the Soothsavior!"

Banzu took small part by smiling, though it waned while he stared overlong at the burning cross and its charring occupant. Until a light rain dappled his hair so that he tore his gaze from the hissing flames and craned his head, appraising the vast night sky and its twinkling blanket of stars.

Though those gathered nearest him proclaimed the rain as the watching gods weeping tears of solace for Bloom's fallen, another promise intruded Banzu's mind, a private vow sworn to himself so that he wondered if instead those same cruel gods wept in grieving foresight at what would soon transpire by his own condemning hands, their Great Game finished, his game of Khans only just begun.

Enclave extermination and Khan elimination. Only then will we be safe. Only then will I be finished.

Anger flared to silent rage he bunched inside for later dealing, too weary to endure the festering spite. He closed his eyes, distancing from the chants, allowing the gentle rain to patter his face while relaxing to this his blissful exhaustion of spirit.

Gods I'm tired.

So much to do.

So much unfinished.

He reflected on his uncle Jericho at last avenged, mused on Melora and of all the things both fortunate and tragic to explain when they finally reunited.

It's over.

For now.

He opened his eyes, stared ahead at the burning cross defying the rain, watching the flaming corpse nailed thereon, wondering if any other soul had ever before staggered this tortured path of destiny, and knew before him blazed the proof.

"If you want to make the gods laugh . . ." he whispered, trailing into soliloquy . . . *then tell them your plans. Well who's laughing now, you petty bastards? Who's laughing now?*

Here, nestled in the terminable silence of his introspection, Banzu contemplated the true tri-fold gods of man: Love, Hate, and the Freedom to choose.

Kinslayer.

Godslayer.

Khanslayer.

He drew in a deep nostril breath, raked a sure hand back through his hair, and blew out his cheeks.

And I've only just begun to—

He paused the sorrowing thought, correcting it with soothing musings of Melora, the pale-haired, violet-eyed heritor of his surrendered heart awaiting his return.

No, we've only just begun.

And there a private smile invited jubilant promises of more.

Together all that mattered.

~AUTHOR'S NOTE~

Book reviews matter, and I would love your honest opinion of this novel by reviewing it on Amazon.com, as well as recommending it to others.

Thank you, dear Reader, for affording me your precious time.

Veilfall is the first in a series of which I am currently hard at work. There is plenty more to come with Banzu Greenlief . . . who also thanks You, the Turner of Pages, for your essential part in his finishing the Great Game.

~Adron J. Smitley

adronjsmitley.blogspot.com

Printed in Great Britain
by Amazon

51723880R00265